MARY STEWART MARY STEWART
MARY STEWART MARY STE
STEWART MARY
MARY STEWART
MARY STEWART
WART MARY S
STEWART MA
MARY STEWART
ART MARY STE
EWART MARY
RY STEWART M
MARY STEWA
ART MARY M

MARY
STEWART

MARY STEWART

The Crystal Cave

The Hollow Hills

Wildfire at Midnight

Airs Above the Ground

Heinemann/Octopus

The Crystal Cave first published in Great Britain in 1970 by Hodder and Stoughton Limited
The Hollow Hills first published in Great Britain in 1973 by Hodder and Stoughton Limited
Wildfire at Midnight first published in Great Britain in 1956 by Hodder and Stoughton Limited
Airs Above the Ground first published in Great Britain in 1965 by Hodder and Stoughton
Limited

This edition first published
in 1978 jointly by

William Heinemann Limited   Secker and Warburg Limited
15–16 Queen Street London W1   14 Carlisle Street London W1

and
Octopus Books Limited
59 Grosvenor Street London W1

ISBN 0 905712 21 8

Jacket – Robert Estall

Printed in Great Britain by
Jarrold and Sons Ltd, Norwich

CONTENTS

The Crystal Cave

MARY STEWART

The Crystal Cave

To the Memory of
MOLLIE CRAIG
with my love

Acknowledgements

Edwin Muir's poem 'Merlin' is reprinted by permission of Faber and Faber Ltd from the *Collected Poems, 1921–58*. The poem on pages 146–7 is a free translation of verses appearing in *Barzaz Breiz;* *Chants Populaires de la Bretagne*, by the Vicomte de la Villemarqué (Paris, 1867). The Legend of Merlin is based on the translation of Geoffrey of Monmouth's *History of the Kings of Britain* which was first published in the Everyman's Library, Vol 577, by J. & M. Dent in 1912.

Merlin

O Merlin in your crystal cave
Deep in the diamond of the day,
Will there ever be a singer
Whose music will smooth away
The furrow drawn by Adam's finger
Across the meadow and the wave?
Or a runner who'll outrun
Man's long shadow driving on,
Burst through the gates of history,
And hang the apple on the tree?
Will your sorcery ever show
The sleeping bride shut in her bower,
The day wreathed in its mound of snow,
And Time locked in his tower?

Edwin Muir

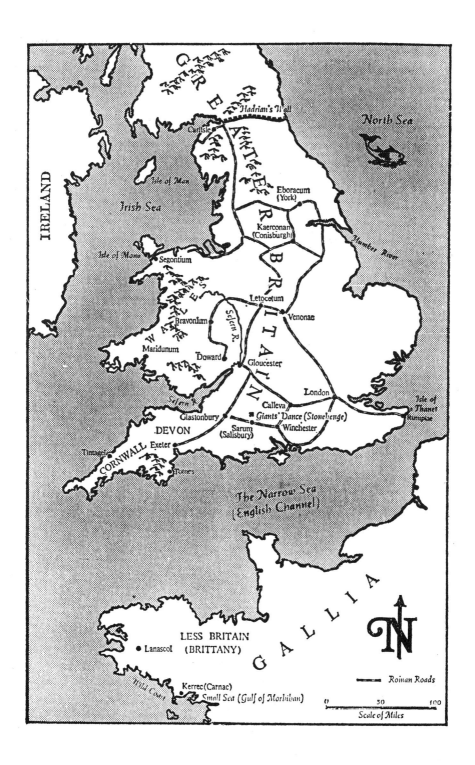

Irish Sea

Isle of Mona

Segontium (Caer'n-ar-Von)
Snowdon (Y Wyddfa)
Dinas Brenin (Dinas Emrys)

● Tomen Y Mur
● Caer Gai

Cardigan Bay   Pennal

Dyfi R.

W A L E S

Letocetum

● Bravonium

Sefern R.

Bremia ●

Gold Mines

Tywy R.   Wye R.

Doward

Maridunum
(Caer-Myrddin)

Caerleon ●

Gloucester

Milford
Haven

Sefern River

Glastonbury

Giants' Dance
(Stonehenge) ⚙ ● Amesbury
Sarum
Y (Salisbury)   Winchester

Hercules Point

Great Plain

D E V O N   Exeter ●

Tintagel   Dimilioc

The Narrow Sea

Totnes ●

━━ Roman Roads

0   20   40

CORNWALL

Scale of Miles

Prologue

The Prince of Darkness

I am an old man now, but then I was already past my prime when Arthur was crowned King. The years since then seem to me now more dim and faded than the earlier years, as if my life were a growing tree which burst to flower and leaf with him, and now has nothing more to do than yellow to the grave.

This is true of all old men, that the recent past is misted, while distant scenes of memory are clear and brightly coloured. Even the scenes of my far childhood come back to me now sharp and high coloured and edged with brightness, like the pattern of a fruit tree against a white wall, or banners in sunlight against a sky of storm.

The colours are brighter than they were, of that I am sure. The memories that come back to me here in the dark are seen with the new young eyes of childhood; they are so far gone from me, with their pain no longer present, that they unroll like pictures of something that happened, not to me, not to the bubble of bone that this memory used to inhabit, but to another Merlin as young and light and free of the air and spring winds as the bird she named me for.

With the later memories it is different; they come back, some of them, hot and shadowed, things seen in the fire. For this is where I gather them. This is one of the few trivial tricks–I cannot call it power–left to me now that I am old and stripped at last down to man. I can see still . . . not clearly or with the call of trumpets as I once did, but in the child's way of dreams and pictures in the fire. I can still make the flames burn up or die; it is one of the simplest of magics, the most easily learned, the last forgotten. What I cannot recall in dream I see in the flames, the red heart of the fire or the countless mirrors of the crystal cave.

The first memory of all is dark and fireshot. It is not my own memory, but later you will understand how I know these things. You would call it, not memory so much as a dream of the past, something in the blood, something recalled from him, it may be, while he still bore me in his body. I believe that such things can be. So it seems to me right that I should start with him who was before me, and who will be again when I am gone.

This is what happened that night. I saw it, and it is a true tale.

It was dark, and the place was cold, but he had lit a small fire of wood, which

smoked sullenly but gave a little warmth. It had been raining all day, and
from the branches near the mouth of the cave water still dripped, and a
steady trickle overflowed the lip of the well, soaking the ground below.
Several times, restless, he had left the cave, and now he walked out below
the cliff to the grove where his horse stood tethered.

With the coming of dusk the rain had stopped, but a mist had risen,
creeping knee high through the trees so that they stood like ghosts, and the
grazing horse floated like a swan. It was a grey, and more than ever ghostly
because it grazed so quietly; he had torn up a scarf and wound fragments of
cloth round the bit so that no jingle should betray him. The bit was gilded,
and the torn strips were of silk, for he was a king's son. If they had caught
him, they would have killed him. He was just eighteen.

He heard the hoofbeats coming softly up the valley. His head moved, and
his breathing quickened. His sword flicked with light as he lifted it. The
grey horse paused in its grazing and lifted its head clear of the mist. Its
nostrils flickered, but no sound came. The man smiled. The hoofbeats came
closer, and then, shoulder deep in mist, a brown pony trotted out of the
dusk. Its rider, small and slight, was wrapped in a dark cloak, muffled from
the night air. The pony pulled to a halt, threw up its head, and gave a long,
pealing whinny. The rider, with an exclamation of dismay, slipped from its
back and grabbed for the bridle to muffle the sound against her cloak. She
was a girl, very young, who looked round her anxiously until she saw the
young man, sword in hand, at the edge of the trees.

'You sound like a troop of cavalry,' he said.

'I was here before I knew it. Everything looks strange in the mist.'

'No one saw you? You came safely?'

'Safely enough. It's been impossible the last two days. They were on the
roads night and day.'

'I guessed it.' He smiled. 'Well, now you are here. Give me the bridle.' He
led the pony in under the trees, and tied it up. Then he kissed her.

After a while she pushed him away. 'I ought not to stay. I brought the
things, so even if I can't come tomorrow—' She stopped. She had seen the
saddle on his horse, the muffled bit, the packed saddle-bag. Her hands
moved sharply against his chest, and his own covered them and held her
fast. 'Ah,' she said. 'I knew. I knew even in my sleep last night. You're
going.'

'I must. Tonight.'

She was silent for a minute. Then all she said was, 'How long?'

He did not pretend to misunderstand her.

'We have an hour, two, no more.'

She said flatly: 'You will come back.' Then as he started to speak: 'No.
Not now, not any more. We have said it all, and now there is no more time. I
only meant that you will be safe, and you will come back safely. I tell you, I
know these things. I have the Sight. You will come back.'

'It hardly needs the Sight to tell me that. I must come back. And then
perhaps you will listen to me—'

'No.' She stopped him again, almost angrily. 'It doesn't matter. What
does it matter? We have only an hour, and we are wasting it. Let us go
in.'

He was already pulling out the jewelled pin that held her cloak together, as he put an arm round her and led her towards the cave.

'Yes, let us go in.'

The Dove

Chapter One

The day my uncle Camlach came home, I was just six years old.

I remember him well as I first saw him, a tall young man, fiery like my grandfather, with the blue eyes and reddish hair that I thought so beautiful in my mother. He came to Maridunum near sunset of a September evening, with a small troop of men. Being only small, I was with the women in the long, old-fashioned room where they did the weaving. My mother was sitting at the loom; I remember the cloth; it was of scarlet, with a narrow pattern of green at the edge. I sat near her on the floor, playing knuckle-bones, right hand against left. The sun slanted through the windows, making oblong pools of bright gold on the cracked mosaics of the floor; bees droned in the herbs outside, and even the click and rattle of the loom sounded sleepy. The women were talking among themselves over their spindles, but softly, heads together, and Moravik, my nurse, was frankly asleep on her stool in one of the pools of sunlight.

When the clatter, and then the shouts, came from the courtyard, the loom stopped abruptly, and with it the soft chatter from the women. Moravik came awake with a snort and a stare. My mother was sitting very straight, head lifted, listening. She had dropped her shuttle. I saw her eyes meet Moravik's.

I was halfway to the window when Moravik called to me sharply, and there was something in her voice that made me stop and go back to her without protest. She began to fuss with my clothing, pulling my tunic straight and smoothing my hair, so that I understood the visitor to be someone of importance. I felt excitement, and also surprise that apparently I was to be presented to him; I was used to being kept out of the way in those days. I stood patiently while Moravik dragged the comb through my hair, and over my head she and my mother exchanged some quick, breathless talk which, hardly heeding, I did not understand. I was listening to the tramp of horses in the yard and the shouting of men, words here and there coming clearly in a language neither Welsh nor Latin, but Celtic with some accent like the one of Less Britain, which I understood because my nurse, Moravik, was a Breton, and her language came to me as readily as my own.

I heard my grandfather's great laugh, and another voice replying. Then he must have swept the newcomer indoors with him, for the voices receded, leaving only the jingle and stamp of the horses being led to the stables.

I broke from Moravik and ran to my mother.

'Who is it?'

'My brother Camlach, the King's son.' She did not look at me, but pointed to the fallen shuttle. I picked it up and handed it to her. Slowly, and rather mechanically, she set the loom moving again.

'Is the war over, then?'

'The war has been over a long time. Your uncle has been with the High King in the south.'

'And now he has to come home because my uncle Dyved died?' Dyved had been the heir, the King's eldest son. He had died suddenly, and in great pain, of cramps in the stomach, and Elen his widow, who was childless, had gone back to her father. Naturally there had been the usual talk of poison, but nobody took it seriously; Dyved had been well liked, a tough fighter and a careful man, but generous where it suited. 'They say he'll have to marry. Will he, mother?' I was excited, important at knowing so much, thinking of the wedding feast. 'Will he marry Keridwen, now that my uncle Dyved—'

'*What?*' The shuttle stopped, and she swung round, startled. But what she saw in my face appeased her, for the anger went out of her voice, though she still frowned, and I heard Moravik clucking and fussing behind me. 'Where in the world did you get that? You hear too much, whether you understand it or not. Forget such matters, and hold your tongue.' The shuttle moved again, slowly. 'Listen to me, Merlin. When they come to see you, you will do well to keep quiet. Do you understand me?'

'Yes, mother.' I understood very well. I was well accustomed to keeping out of the King's way. 'But will they come to see me? Why me?'

She said, with a thin bitterness that made her look all at once older, almost as old as Moravik: 'Why do you think?'

The loom clacked again, fiercely. She was feeding in the green thread, and I could see that she was making a mistake, but it looked pretty, so I said nothing, watching her and staying close, till at length the curtain at the doorway was pushed aside, and the two men came in.

They seemed to fill the room, the red head and the grey within a foot of the beams. My grandfather wore blue, periwinkle colour with a gold border. Camlach was in black. Later I was to discover that he always wore black; he had jewels on his hands and at his shoulder, and beside his father he looked lightly built and young, but as sharp and whippy as a fox.

My mother stood up. She was wearing a house-robe of dark brown, the colour of peat, and against it her hair shone like corn-silk. But neither of the two men glanced at her. You would have thought there was no one in the room but I, small as I was, by the loom.

My grandfather jerked his head and said one word: 'Out,' and the women hurried in a rustling, silent group, from the chamber. Moravik stood her ground, puffed up with bravery like a partridge, but the fierce blue eyes flicked to her for a second, and she went. A sniff as she passed them was all that she dared. The eyes came back to me.

'Your sister's bastard,' said the King. 'There he is. Six years old this month, grown like a weed, and no more like any of us than a damned devil's whelp would be. Look at him! Black hair, black eyes, and as scared of cold iron as a changeling from the hollow hills. You tell me the devil himself got that one, and I'll believe you!'

My uncle said only one word, straight to her: 'Whose?'

'You think we didn't ask, you fool?' said my grandfather. 'She was whipped till the women said she'd miscarry, but never a word from her. Better if she had, perhaps–some nonsense they were talking, old wives' tales of devils coming in the dark to lie with young maids–and from the look of him they could be right.'

Camlach, six foot and golden, looked down at me. His eyes were blue, clear as my mother's, and his colour was high. The mud had dried yellow on his soft doeskin boots, and a smell of sweat and horses came from him. He had come to look at me before even taking the dirt of travel off. I remember how he stared down at me, while my mother stood silent, and my grandfather glowered under his brows, his breath coming harsh and rapid, as it always did when he had put himself in a passion.

'Come here,' said my uncle.

I took half a dozen steps forward. I did not dare go nearer. I stopped. From three paces away he seemed taller than ever. He towered over me to the ceiling beams.

'What's your name?'

'Myrddin Emrys.'

'Emrys? Child of light, belonging to the gods . . .? That hardly seems the name for a demon's whelp.'

The mildness of his tone encouraged me. 'They call me Merlinus,' I ventured. 'It's a Roman name for a falcon, the *corwalch*.'

My grandfather barked, 'Falcon!' and made a sound of contempt, shooting his arm-rings till they jingled.

'A small one,' I said defensively, then fell silent under my uncle's thoughtful look. He stroked his chin, then looked at my mother with his brows up. 'Strange choices, all of them, for a Christian household. A Roman demon, perhaps, Niniane?'

She put up her chin. 'Perhaps. How do I know? It was dark.'

I thought a flash of amusement came and went in his face, but the King swept a hand down in a violent gesture. 'You see? That's all you'll get–lies, tales of sorcery, insolence! Get back to your work, girl, and keep your bastard out of my sight! Now that your brother's home, we'll find a man who'll take the pair of you from under my feet and his! Camlach, I hope you see the sense of getting yourself a wife now, and a son or two, since this is all I'm left with!'

'Oh, I'm for it,' said Camlach easily. Their attention had lifted from me. They were going, and neither had touched me. I unclenched my hands and moved back softly, half a pace; another. 'But you've got yourself a new Queen meantime, sir, and they tell me she's pregnant?'

'No matter of that. You should be wed, and soon. I'm an old man, and these are troubled times. As for the boy–' I froze again–'forget him. Whoever sired him, if he hasn't come forward in six years, he'll not do so now. And if it had been Vortigern himself, the High King, he'd have made nothing of him. A sullen brat who skulks alone in corners. Doesn't even play with the other boys–afraid to, likely. Afraid of his own shadow.'

He turned away. Camlach's eyes met my mother's, over my head. Some message passed. Then he looked down at me again, and smiled.

I still remember how the room seemed to light up, though the sun had gone now, and its warmth with it. Soon they would be bringing the rushlights.

'Well,' said Camlach, 'it's but a fledgling falcon after all. Don't be too hard on him, sir; you've frightened better men than he is, in your time.'

'Yourself, you mean? Hah!'

'I assure you.'

The King, in the doorway, glared briefly at me under his jutting brows, then with a puff of impatient breath settled his mantle over his arm. 'Well, well, let be. God's sweet death, but I'm hungry. It's well past supper-time–but I suppose you'll want to go and soak yourself first, in your damned Roman fashion? I warn you, we've never had the furnaces on since you left . . .'

He turned with a swirl of the blue cloak and went out, still talking. Behind me I heard my mother's breath go out, and the rustle of her gown as she sat. My uncle put out a hand to me.

'Come, Merlinus, and talk to me while I bathe in your cold Welsh water. We princes must get to know one another.'

I stood rooted. I was conscious of my mother's silence, and how still she sat.

'Come,' said my uncle, gently, and smiled at me again.

I ran to him.

I went through the hypocaust that night.

This was my own private way, my secret hiding-place where I could escape from the bigger boys and play my own solitary games. My grandfather had been right when he said I 'skulked alone in corners', but this was not from fear, though the sons of his nobles followed his lead–as children do–and made me their butt in their rough war-games whenever they could catch me.

At the beginning, it is true, the tunnels of the disused heating-system were a refuge, a secret place where I could hide and be alone; but I soon found a curiously strong pleasure in exploring the great system of dark, earth-smelling chambers under the palace floors.

My grandfather's palace had been, in times past, a vast country-house belonging to some Roman notable who had owned and farmed the land for several miles each way along the river valley. The main part of the house still stood, though badly scarred by time and war, and by at least one disastrous fire which had destroyed one end of the main block and part of a wing. The old slaves' quarters were still intact round the courtyard where the cooks and house-servants worked, and the bath-house remained, though patched and plastered, and with the roof rough-thatched over the worst bits. I never remember the furnace working; the water was heated over the courtyard fires.

The entrance to my secret labyrinth was the stoke-hole in the boiler-house; this was a trap in the wall under the cracked and rusting boiler, barely the height of a grown man's knee, and hidden by docks and nettles and a huge curved metal shard fallen from the boiler itself. Once inside, you could get under the rooms of the bath-house, but this had been out of use for so long that the space under the floors was too cluttered and foul even for me. I went the other way, under the main block of the palace. Here the old hot air system had been so well built and maintained that even now the knee-high space under the floors was dry and airy, and plaster still clung to the brick pillars that held up the floors. In places, of course, a pillar had collapsed, or debris had fallen, but the traps which led from one room to another were solidly arched and safe, and I was free to crawl, unseen and unheard, even as far as the King's own chamber.

If they had ever discovered me I think I might have received a worse punishment than whipping: I must have listened, innocently, enough, to dozens of secret councils, and certainly to some very private goings-on, but that side of it never occurred to me. And it was natural enough that nobody should give a thought to the dangers of eavesdropping; in the old days the flues had been cleaned by boy-slaves, and nobody much beyond the age of ten could ever have got through some of the workings; there were one or two places where even I was hard put to it to wriggle through. I was only once in danger of discovery: one afternoon when Moravik supposed I was playing with the boys and they in turn thought I was safe under her skirts, the red-haired Dinias, my chief tormentor, gave a younger boy such a shove from the roof-tree where they were playing that the latter fell and broke a leg, and set up such a howling that Moravik, running to the scene, discovered me absent and set the palace by the ears. I heard the noise, and emerged breathless and dirty from under the boiler, just as she started a hunt through the bath-house wing. I lied my way out of it, and got off with boxed ears and a scolding, but it was a warning; I never went into the hypocaust again by daylight, only at night before Moravik came to bed, or once or twice when I was wakeful and she was already abed and snoring. Most of the palace would be abed, too, but when there was a feast, or when my grandfather had guests, I would listen to the noise of voices and the singing; and sometimes I would creep as far as my mother's chamber, to hear the sound of her voice as she talked with her women. But one night I heard her praying, aloud, as one does sometimes when alone, and in the prayer was my name, 'Emrys', and then her tears. After that I went another way, past the Queen's rooms, where almost every evening Olwen, the young Queen, sang to her harp among her ladies, until the King's tread came heavily down the corridor, and the music stopped.

But it was for none of these things that I went. What mattered to me—I see it clearly now—was to be alone in the secret dark, where a man is his own master, except for death.

Mostly I went to what I called my 'cave'. This had been part of some main chimney-shaft, and the top of it had crumbled, so that one could see the sky. It had held magic for me since the day I had looked up at midday and had seen, faint but unmistakable, a star. Now, when I went in at night I would curl up on my bed of stolen stable-straw and watch the stars wheeling slowly across, and make my own bet with heaven, which was, if the moon should show over the shaft while I was there, the next day would bring me my heart's desire.

The moon was there that night. Full and shining, she stood clear in the centre of the shaft, her light pouring down on my upturned face so white and pure that it seemed I drank it in like water. I did not move till she had gone, and the little star that dogs her.

On the way back I passed under a room that had been empty before, but which now held voices.

Camlach's room, of course. He and another man whose name I did not know, but who, from his accent, was one of those who had ridden in that day; I had found that they came from Cornwall. He had one of those thick, rumbling voices of which I caught only a word here and there as I crawled quickly through, worming my way between the pillars, concerned only not to be heard.

I was right at the end wall, and feeling along it for the arched gap to the next chamber, when my shoulder struck a broken section of flue pipe, and a loose piece of fireclay fell with a rattle.

The Cornishman's voice stopped abruptly. 'What's that?'

Then my uncle's voice, so clear down the broken flue that you would have thought he spoke in my ear.

'Nothing. A rat. It came from under the floor. I tell you, the place is falling to pieces.'

There was the sound of a chair scraping back, and footsteps going across the room, away from me. His voice receded. I thought I heard the clink and gurgle of a drink being poured. I began slowly, slowly, to edge along the wall towards the trap.

He was coming back.

. . . 'And even if she does refuse him, it will hardly matter. She won't stay here—at any rate, no longer than my father can fight the bishop off and keep her by him. I tell you, with her mind set on what she calls a higher court, I've nothing to fear, even if he came himself.'

'As long as you believe her.'

'Oh, I believe her. I've been asking here and there, and everyone says the same.' He laughed. 'Who knows, we may be thankful yet to have a voice at that heavenly court of hers before this game's played out. And she's devout enough to save the lot of us, they tell me, if she'll only put her mind to it.'

'You may need it yet,' said the Cornishman.

'I may.'

'And the boy?'

'The boy?' repeated my uncle. He paused, then the soft footsteps resumed their pacing. I strained to hear. I had to hear. Why it should have mattered I hardly knew. It did not worry me overmuch to be called bastard, or coward, or devil's whelp. But tonight there had been that full moon.

He had turned. His voice carried clearly, careless, indulgent even.

'Ah, yes, the boy. A clever child, at a guess, with more there than they give him credit for . . . and nice enough, if one speaks him fair. I shall keep him close to me. Remember that, Alun; I like the boy . . .'

He called a servant in then to replenish the wine-jug, and under cover of this, I crept away.

That was the beginning of it. For days I followed him everywhere, and he tolerated, even encouraged me, and it never occurred to me that a man of twenty-one would not always welcome a puppy of six for ever trotting at his heels. Moravik scolded, when she could get hold of me, but my mother seemed pleased and relieved, and bade her let me be.

Chapter Two

It had been a hot summer, and there was peace that year, so for the first few days of his homecoming Camlach idled, resting, or riding out with his father or the men through the harvest fields and the valleys where the apples already dropped ripe from the trees.

South Wales is a lovely country, with green hills and deep valleys, flat water-meadows yellow with flowers where cattle grow sleek, oak forests full of deer, and the high blue uplands where the cuckoo shouts in springtime, but where, come winter, the wolves run, and I have seen lightning even with the snow.

Maridunum lies where the estuary opens to the sea, on the river which is marked Tobius on the military maps, but which the Welsh call Tywy. Here the valley is flat and wide, and the Tywy runs in a deep and placid meander through bog and water-meadow between the gentle hills. The town stands on the rising ground of the north bank, where the land is drained and dry; it is served inland by the military road from Caerleon, and from the south by a good stone bridge with three spans, from which a paved street leads straight uphill past the King's house, and into the square. Apart from my grandfather's house, and the barrack buildings of the Roman-built fortress where he quartered his soldiers and which he kept in good repair, the best building in Maridunum was the Christian nunnery near the palace on the river's bank. A few holy women lived there, calling themselves the Community of St Peter, though most of the townspeople called the place Tyr Myrddin,* from the old shrine of the god which had stood time out of mind under an oak not far from St Peter's gate. Even when I was a child, I heard the town itself called Caer-Myrddin: it is not true (as they say now) that men call it after me. The fact is that I, like the town and the hill behind it with the sacred spring, was called after the god who is worshipped in high places. Since the events which I shall tell of, the name of the town has been publicly changed in my honour, but the god was there first, and if I have his hill now, it is because he shares it with me.

* *dd* is pronounced *th* as in *thus*. *Myrddin* is, roughly, *Murthin*. Caer-Myrddin is the modern Carmarthen.

My grandfather's house was set among its orchards right beside the river. If you climbed—by way of a leaning apple tree—to the top of the wall, you could sit high over the tow-path and watch the river-bridge for people riding in from the south, or for the ships that came up with the tide.

Though I was not allowed to climb the trees for apples—being forced to content myself with the windfalls—Moravik never stopped me from climbing to the top of the wall. To have me posted there as sentry meant that she got wind of new arrivals sooner than anyone else in the place. There was a little raised terrace at the orchard's end, with a curved brick wall at the back and a stone seat protected from the wind, and she would sit there by the hour, dozing over her spindle, while the sun beat into the corner so hotly that lizards would steal out to lie on the stones, and I called out my reports from the wall.

One hot afternoon, about eight days after Camlach's coming to Maridunum, I was at my post as usual. There was no coming and going on the bridge or the road up the valley, only a local grain-barge loading at the wharf, watched by a scatter of idlers, and an old man in a hooded cloak who loitered, picking up windfalls along under the wall.

I looked over my shoulder towards Moravik's corner. She was asleep, her spindle drooping on her knee, looking, with the white fluffy wool, like a burst bulrush. I threw down the bitten windfall I had been eating, and tilted my head to study the forbidden tree-top boughs where yellow globes hung clustered against the sky. There was one I thought I could reach. The fruit was round and glossy, ripening almost visibly in the hot sun. My mouth watered. I reached for a foothold and began to climb.

I was two branches away from the fruit when a shout from the direction of the bridge, followed by the quick tramp of hoofs and the jingle of metal, brought me up short. Clinging like a monkey, I made sure of my feet, then reached with one hand to push the leaves aside, peering down towards the bridge. A troop of men was riding over it, towards the town. One man rode alone in front, bare-headed, on a big brown horse.

Not Camlach, or my grandfather; and not one of the nobles, for the men wore colours I did not know. Then as they reached the nearer end of the bridge I saw that the leader was a stranger, black-haired and black-bearded, with a foreign-looking set to his clothes, and a flash of gold on his breast. His wristguards were golden, too, and a span deep. His troop, as I judged, was about fifty strong.

King Gorlan of Lanascol. Where the name sprang from, clear beyond mistake, I had no idea. Something heard from my labyrinth, perhaps? A word spoken carelessly in a child's hearing. A dream, even? The shields and spear-tips, catching the sun, flashed into my eyes. Gorlan of Lanascol. A king. Come to marry my mother and take me with him overseas. She would be a queen. And I . . .

He was already setting his horse at the hill. I began to half-slither, half-scramble, down the tree.

And if she refuses him? I recognised that voice; it was the Cornishman's. And after him my uncle's: *Even if she does, it will hardly matter . . . I've nothing to fear, so even if he came himself . . .*

The troop was riding at ease across the bridge. The jingle of arms and the hammering of hoofs rang in the still sunlight.

He had come himself. He was here.

A foot above the wall-top I missed my footing and almost fell. Luckily my grip held, and I slithered safely to the coping in a shower of leaves and lichen just as my nurse's voice called shrilly:

'Merlin? Merlin? Save us, where's the boy?'

'Here—here, Moravik—just coming down.'

I landed in the long grass. She had left her spindle and, kilting up her skirts, came running.

'What's the to-do on the river road? I heard horses, a whole troop by the noise—Saints alive, child, look at your clothes! If I didn't mend that tunic only this week, and now look at it! A tear you could put a fist through, and dirt from head to foot like a beggar's brat!'

I dodged as she reached for me. 'I fell. I'm sorry. I was climbing down to tell you. It's a troop of horse—foreigners! Moravik, it's King Gorlan from Lanascol! He has a red cloak and a black beard!'

'Gorlan of Lanascol? Why, that's barely twenty miles from where I was born! What's he here for, I wonder?'

I stared. 'Didn't you know? He's come to marry my mother.'

'Nonsense.'

'It's true!'

'Of course it's not true! Do you think I wouldn't know? You must not say these things, Merlin, it could mean trouble. Where did you get it?'

'I don't remember. Someone told me. My mother, I think.'

'That's not true and you know it.'

'Then I must have heard something.'

'Heard something, heard something. Young pigs have long ears, they say. Yours must be for ever to the ground, you hear so much! What are you smiling at?'

'Nothing.'

She set her hands on her hips. 'You've been listening to things you shouldn't. I've told you about this before. No wonder people say what they say.'

I usually gave up and edged away from dangerous ground when I had given too much away, but excitement had made me reckless. 'It's true, you'll find it's true! Does it matter where I heard it? I really can't remember now, but I know it's true! Moravik—'

'What?'

'King Gorlan's my father, my real one.'

'*What?*' This time the syllable was edged like the tooth of a saw.

'Didn't you know? Not even you?'

'No, I did not. And no more do you. And if you so much as breathe this to anyone—How do you know the name, even?' She took me by the shoulders and gave me a sharp little shake. 'How do you even know this is King Gorlan? There's been nothing said of his coming, even to me.'

'I told you. I don't remember what I heard, or where. I just heard his name somewhere, that's all, and I know he's coming to see the King about my mother. We'll go to Less Britain, Moravik, and you can come with us. You'll like that, won't you? It's your home. Perhaps we'll be near—'

Her grip tightened, and I stopped. With relief I saw one of the King's body-servants hurrying towards us through the apple trees. He came up panting.

'He's to go before the King. The boy. In the great hall. And hurry.'

'Who is it?' demanded Moravik.

'The King said to hurry. I've been looking everywhere for the boy—'

'*Who is it?*'

'King Gorlan from Brittany.'

She gave a little hiss, like a startled goose, and dropped her hands. 'What's his business with the boy?'

'How do I know?' The man was breathless—it was a hot day and he was stout—and curt with Moravik, whose status as my nurse was only a little higher with the servants than my own. 'All I know is, the Lady Niniane is sent for, and the boy, and there'll be a beating for someone, by my reckoning, if he's not there by the time the King's looking round for him. He's been in a rare taking since the outriders came in, that I can tell you.'

'All right, all right. Get back and say we'll be there in a few minutes.'

The man hurried off. She whirled on me and grabbed at my arm. 'All the sweet saints in heaven!' Moravik had the biggest collection of charms and talismans of anyone in Maridunum, and I had never known her pass a wayside shrine without paying her respects to whatever image inhabited it, but officially she was a Christian and, when in trouble, a devout one. 'Sweet cherubim! And the child has to choose this afternoon to be in rags! Hurry, now, or there'll be trouble for both of us.' She hustled me up the path towards the house, busily calling on her saints and exhorting me to hurry, determinedly refusing even to comment on the fact that I had been right about the newcomer. 'Dear, dear St Peter, why did I eat those eels for dinner and then sleep so sound? Today of all days! Here—' she pushed me in front of her into my room—'get out of those rags and into your good tunic, and we'll know soon enough what the Lord has sent for you. Hurry, child!'

The room I shared with Moravik was a small one, dark, and next to the servants' quarters. It always smelt of cooking smells from the kitchen, but I liked this, as I liked the old lichened pear tree that hung close outside the window, where the birds swung singing in the summer mornings. My bed stood right under this window. The bed was nothing but plain planks set across wooden blocks, no carving, not even a head or foot board. I had heard Moravik grumble to the other servants when she thought I wasn't listening, that it was hardly a fit place to house a king's grandson, but to me she said merely that it was convenient for her to be near the other servants; and indeed I was comfortable enough, for she saw to it that I had a clean straw mattress, and a coverlet of wool every bit as good as those on my mother's bed in the big room next to my grandfather. Moravik herself had a pallet on the floor near the door, and this was sometimes shared by the big wolfhound who fidgeted and scratched for fleas beside her feet, and sometimes by Cerdic, one of the grooms, a Saxon who had been taken in a raid long since, and had settled down to marry one of the local girls. She had died in a childbed a year later, and the child with her, but he stayed on, apparently quite content. I once asked Moravik why she allowed the dog to sleep in the room, when she grumbled so much about the smell and the fleas; I forget what she answered, but I knew without being told that he was there to give warning if anyone came into the room during the night. Cerdic, of course, was the exception; the dog accepted him with no more fuss than the beating of his tail upon the floor, and vacated the bed for him. In a way, I suppose, Cerdic fulfilled the same function as the watchdog, and others besides. Moravik never mentioned him, and neither did I. A small child is supposed to sleep very soundly, but even then, young as I was, I would wake sometimes in the middle of the night, and lie quite still, watching the stars through the window beside me, caught like sparkling silver fish in the net of the pear tree's boughs. What passed between Cerdic and Moravik meant no more to me than that he helped to guard my nights, as she my days.

My clothes were kept in a wooden chest which stood against the wall. This was very old, with panels painted with scenes of gods and goddesses, and I think originally it had come from Rome itself. Now the paint was dirty and rubbed and flaking, but still on the lid you could see, like shadows, a scene taking place in what looked like a cave; there was a bull, and a man with a knife, and someone holding a sheaf of corn, and over in the corner some figure, rubbed almost away, with rays round his head like the sun, and a stick in his hand. The chest was lined with cedarwood, and Moravik washed my clothes herself, and laid them away with sweet herbs from the garden.

She threw the lid up now, so roughly that it banged against the wall, and pulled out the better of my two good tunics, the green one with the scarlet border. She shouted for water, and one of the maids brought it, running, and was scolded for spilling it on the floor.

The fat servant came panting again to tell us that we should hurry, and got snapped at for his pains, but in a very short time I was hustled once more along the colonnade, and through the big arched doorway into the main part of the house.

The hall where the King received visitors was a long, high room with a floor of black and white stone framing a mosaic of a god with a leopard. This had been badly scarred and broken by the dragging of heavy furniture and the constant passing of booted feet. One side of the room was open to the colonnade, and here in winter a fire was kindled on the bare floor, within a loose frame of stones. The floor and pillars near it were blackened with the smoke. At the far end of the room stood the dais with my grandfather's big chair, and beside it the smaller one for the Queen.

He was sitting there now, with Camlach standing on his right, and his wife, Olwen, seated at his left. She was his third wife, and younger than my mother, a dark, silent, rather stupid girl with a skin like new milk and braids down to her knees, who could sing like a bird, and do fine needlework, but very little else. My mother, I think, both liked and despised her. At any rate, against all expectation, they got along tolerably well together, and I had heard Moravik say that life for my mother had been a great deal easier since the King's second wife, Gwynneth, had died a year ago, and within the month Olwen had taken her place in the King's bed. Even if Olwen had cuffed me and sneered at me as Gwynneth did I should have liked her for her music, but she was always kind to me in her vague, placid way, and when the King was out of the way had taught me my notes, and even let me use her harp till I could play after a fashion. I had a feeling for it, she said, but we both knew what the King would say to such folly, so her kindness was secret, even from my mother.

She did not notice me now. Nobody did, except my cousin Dinias, who stood by Olwen's chair on the dais. Dinias was a bastard of my grandfather's by a slave-woman. He was a big boy of seven, with his father's red hair and high temper; he was strong for his age and quite fearless, and had enjoyed the King's favour since the day he had, at the age of five, stolen a ride on one of his father's horses, a wild brown colt that had bolted with him through the town and only got rid of him when he rode it straight at a breast-high bank. His father had thrashed him with his own hands, and afterwards given him a dagger with a gilded hilt. Dinias claimed the title of Prince—at any rate among the rest of the children—from then on, and treated his fellow-bastard, myself, with the utmost contempt. He stared at me now as expressionless as a stone, but his left hand—the one away from his father—made a rude sign, and then chopped silently, expressively, downwards.

I had paused in the doorway, and behind me my nurse's hand twitched my tunic into place and then gave me a push between the shoulder-blades. 'Go on now. Straighten your back. He won't eat you.' As if to give the lie to this, I heard the click of charms and the start of a muttered prayer.

The room was full of people. Many of them I knew, but there were strangers there who must be the party I had seen ride in. Their leader sat near the King's right, surrounded by his own men. He was the big dark man I had seen on the bridge, full-bearded, with a fierce beak of a nose and thick limbs shrouded in a scarlet cloak. On the King's other side, but standing below the dais, was my mother, with two of her women. I loved to see her as she was now, dressed like a princess, her long robe of creamy wool hanging straight to the floor as if carved of new wood. Her hair was unbraided, and fell down her back like rain. She had a blue mantle with a copper clasp. Her face was colourless, and very still.

I was so busy with my own fears—the gesture from Dinias, the averted face and downcast eyes of my mother, the silence of the people, and the empty middle of the floor over which I must walk—that I had not even looked at my grandfather. I had taken a step forward, still unnoticed, when suddenly, with a crash like a horse kicking, he slammed both hands down on the wooden arms of his chair, and thrust himself to his feet so violently that the heavy chair went back a pace, its feet scoring the oak planks of the platform.

'By the light!' His face was mottled scarlet, and the reddish brows jutted in knots of flesh above his furious little blue eyes. He glared down at my mother, and drew a breath to speak that could be heard clear to the door where I had paused, afraid. Then the bearded man, who had risen with him, said something in some accent I didn't catch, and at the same moment Camlach touched his arm, whispering. The King paused, then said thickly, 'As you will. Later. Get them out of here.' Then clearly, to my mother: 'This is not the end of it, Niniane, I promise you. Six years. It is enough, by God! Come, my lord.'

He swept his cloak up over one arm, jerked his head to his son, and, stepping down from the dais, took the bearded man by the arm, and strode with him towards the door. After him, meek as milk, trailed his wife Olwen with her women, and after her Dinias, smiling. My mother never moved. The King went by her without a word or a look, and the crowd parted between him and the door like a stubble-field under the share.

It left me standing alone, rooted and staring, three paces in from the door. As the King bore down on me I came to myself and turned to escape into the anteroom, but not quickly enough.

He stopped abruptly, releasing Gorlan's arm, and swung round on me. The blue cloak swirled, and a corner of the cloth caught my eye and brought the tears to it. I blinked up at him. Gorlan had paused beside him. He was younger than my uncle Dyved had been. He was angry, too, but hiding it, and the anger was not for me. He looked surprised when the King stopped, and said: 'Who's this?'

'Her son, that your grace would have given a name to,' said my grandfather, and the gold flashed on his armlet as he swung his big hand up and knocked me flat to the floor as easily as a boy would flatten a fly. Then the blue cloak swept by me, and the King's booted feet, and Gorlan's after him with hardly a pause. Olwen said something in her pretty voice and stooped over me, but the King called to her, angrily, and her hand withdrew and she hurried after him with the rest.

I picked myself up from the floor and looked round for Moravik, but she was not there. She had gone straight to my mother, and had not even seen. I began to push my way towards them through the hubbub of the hall, but before I could reach my mother the women, in a tight and silent group round her, left the hall by the other door. None of them looked back.

Someone spoke to me, but I did not answer. I ran out through the colonnade, across the main court, and out again into the quiet sunlight of the orchard.

My uncle found me on Moravik's terrace.

I was lying on my belly on the hot flagstones, watching a lizard. Of all that day, this is my most vivid recollection; the lizard, flat on the hot stone within a foot of my face, its body still as green bronze but for the pulsing throat. It had small dark eyes, no brighter than slate, and the inside of its mouth was the colour of melons. It had a long, sharp tongue, which flicked out quick as a whip, and its feet made a tiny rustling noise on the stones as it ran across my finger and vanished down a crack in the flags.

I turned my head. My uncle Camlach was coming down through the orchard.

He mounted the three shallow steps to the terrace, soft-footed in his elegant laced sandals, and stood looking down. I looked away. The moss between the stones had tiny white flowers no bigger than the lizard's eyes, each one perfect as a carved cup. To this day I remember the design on them, as well as if I had carved it myself.

'Let me see,' he said.

I didn't move. He crossed to the stone bench and sat down facing me, knees apart, clasped hands between them.

'Look at me, Merlin.'

I obeyed him. He studied me in silence for a while.

'I'm always being told that you will not play rough games, that you run away from Dinias, that you will never make a soldier or even a man. Yet when the King strikes you down with a blow which would have sent one of his deerhounds yelping to kennel, you make no sound and shed no tear.'

I said nothing.

'I think perhaps you are not quite what they deem you, Merlin.'

Still nothing.

'Do you know why Gorlan came today?'

I thought it better to lie. 'No.'

'He came to ask for your mother's hand. If she had consented you would have gone with him to Brittany.'

I touched one of the moss-cups with a forefinger. It crumbled like a puff-ball and vanished. Experimentally, I touched another. Camlach said, more sharply than he usually spoke to me, 'Are you listening?'

'Yes. But if she's refused him it will hardly matter.' I looked up. 'Will it?'

'You mean you don't want to go? I would have thought . . .' He knitted the fair brows so like my grandfather's. 'You would be treated honourably, and be a prince.'

'I am a prince now. As much a prince as I can ever be.'

'What do you mean by that?'

'If she has refused him,' I said, 'he cannot be my father. I thought he was. I thought that was why he had come.'

'What made you think so?'

'I don't know. It seemed—' I stopped. I could not explain to Camlach about the flash of light in which Gorlan's name had come to me. 'I just thought he must be.'

'Only because you have been waiting for him all this time.' His voice was calm. 'Such waiting is foolish, Merlin. It's time you faced the truth. Your father is dead.'

I put my hand down on the tuft of moss, crushing it. I watched the flesh of the fingers whiten with the pressure. 'She told you that?'

'No.' He lifted his shoulders. 'But had he been still alive he would have been here long since. You must know that.'

I was silent.

'And if he is not dead,' pursued my uncle, watching me, 'and still has never come, it can surely not be a matter for great grief on anyone's part?'

'No, except that however base he may be, it might have saved my mother something. And me.' As I moved my hand, the moss slowly unfurled again, as if growing. But the tiny flowers had gone.

My uncle nodded. 'She would have been wiser, perhaps, to have accepted Gorlan, or some other prince.'

'What will happen to us?' I asked.

'Your mother wants to go into St Peter's. And you—you are quick and clever, and I am told you can read a little. You could be a priest.'

'No!'

His brows came down again over the thin-bridged nose. 'It's a good enough life. You're not warrior stock, that's certain. Why not take a life that will suit you, and where you'd be safe?'

'I don't need to be a warrior to want to stay free! To be shut up in a place like St Peter's—that's not the way—' I broke off. I had spoken hotly, but found the words failing me. I could not explain something I did not know myself. I looked up eagerly: 'I'll stay with you. If you cannot use me I—I'll run away to serve some other prince. But I would rather stay with you.'

'Well, it's early yet to speak of things like that. You're very young.' He got to his feet. 'Does your face hurt you?'

'No.'

'You should have it seen to. Come with me now.'

He put out a hand, and I went with him. He led me up through the orchard, then in through the arch that led to my grandfather's private garden.

I hung back against his hand. 'I'm not allowed in there.'

'Surely, with me? Your grandfather's with his guests, he'll not see you. Come along. I've got something better for you than your windfall apples. They've been gathering the apricots, and I saved the best aside out of the baskets as I came down.'

He trod forward, with that graceful cat's stride of his, through the bergamot and lavender, to where the apricot and peach trees stood crucified against the high wall in the sun. The place smelt drowsy with herbs and fruit, and the doves were crooning from the dove-house. At my feet a ripe apricot lay, velvet in the sun. I pushed it with my toe until it rolled over, and there in the back of it was the great rotten hole, with wasps crawling. A shadow fell over it. My uncle stood above me, with an apricot in each hand.

'I told you I'd got something better than windfalls. Here.' He handed me one. 'And if they beat you for stealing, they'll have to beat me as well.' He grinned, and bit into the fruit he held.

I stood still, with the big bright apricot cupped in the palm of my hand. The garden was very hot, and very still, and quiet except for the humming of insects. The fruit glowed like gold, and smelt of sunshine and sweet juice. Its skin felt like the fur of a golden bee. I could feel my mouth watering.

'What is it?' asked my uncle. He sounded edgy and impatient. The juice of his apricot was running down his chin. 'Don't stand there staring at it, boy! Eat it! There's nothing wrong with it, is there?'

I looked up. The blue eyes, fierce as a fox, stared down into mine. I held it out to him. 'I don't want it. It's black inside. Look, you can see right through.'

He took his breath in sharply, as if to speak. Then voices came from the other side of the wall; the gardeners, probably, bringing the empty fruit-baskets down ready for morning. My uncle, stooping, snatched the fruit from my hand and threw it from him, hard against the wall. It burst in a golden splash of flesh against the brick, and the juice ran down. A wasp, disturbed from the tree, droned past between us. Camlach flapped at it with a queer, abrupt gesture, and said to me in a voice that was suddenly all venom:

'Keep away from me after this, you devil's brat. Do you hear me? Just keep away.'

He dashed the back of his hand across his mouth, and went from me in long strides towards the house.

I stood where I was, watching the juice of the apricot trickle down the hot wall. A wasp alighted on it, crawled stickily, then suddenly fell, buzzing on its back to the ground. Its body jack-knifed, the buzz rose to a whine as it struggled, then it lay still.

I hardly saw it, because something had swelled in my throat till I thought I would choke, and the golden evening swam, brilliant, into tears. This was the first time in my life that I remember weeping.

The gardeners were coming down past the roses, with baskets on their heads. I turned and ran out of the garden.

Chapter Three

My room was empty even of the wolfhound. I climbed on my bed and leaned my elbows on the windowsill, and stayed there a long while alone, while outside in the pear tree's boughs the thrush sang, and from the courtyard beyond the shut door came the monotonous clink of the smith's hammer and the creak of the windlass as the mule plodded round the well.

Memory fails me here. I cannot remember how long it was before the clatter and the buzz of voices told me that the evening meal was being prepared. Nor can I remember how badly I was hurt, but when Cerdic, the groom, pushed the door open and I turned my head, he stopped dead and said: 'Lord have mercy upon us. What have you been doing? Playing in the bull-shed?'

'I fell down.'

'Oh, aye, you fell down. I wonder why the floor's always twice as hard for you as for anyone else? Who was it? That little sucking-boar Dinias?'

When I did not answer he came across to the bed. He was a small man, with bowed legs and a seamed brown face and a thatch of light-coloured hair. Standing on my bed as I was, my eyes were almost on a level with his.

'Tell you what,' he said. 'When you're a mite larger I'll teach you a thing or two. You don't have to be big to win a fight. I've a trick or two worth knowing, I can tell you. Got to have, when you're wren-size. I tell you, I can tumble a fellow twice my weight–and a woman too, come to that.' He laughed, turned his head to spit, remembered where he was, and cleared his throat instead. 'Not that you'll need my tricks once you're grown, a tall lad like you, nor with the girls neither. But you'd best look to that face of yours if you're not to scare them silly. Looks as if it might make a scar.' He jerked his head at Moravik's empty pallet. 'Where is she?'

'She went with my mother.'

'Then you'd best come with me. I'll fix it up.'

So it was that the cut on my cheek-bone was dressed with horse-liniment, and I shared Cerdic's supper in the stables, sitting on straw, while a brown mare nosed round me for fodder, and my own fat slug of a pony, at the full end of his rope, watched every mouthful we ate. Cerdic must have had methods of his own in the kitchens, too; the barm-cakes were fresh, there was half a chicken-leg each as well as the salt bacon, and the beer was full-flavoured and cool.

When he came back with the food I knew from his look that he had heard it all. The whole palace must be buzzing. But he said nothing, just handing me the food and sitting down beside me on the straw.

'They told you?' I asked.

He nodded, chewing, then added through a mouthful of bread and meat: 'He has a heavy hand.'

'He was angry because she refused to wed Gorlan. He wants her wed because of me, but till now she has refused to wed any man. And now, since my uncle Dyved is dead, and Camlach is the only one left, they asked Gorlan from Less Britain. I think my uncle Camlach persuaded my grandfather to ask him, because he is afraid that if she marries a prince in Wales—'

He interrupted at that, looking both startled and scared. 'Whist ye now, child! How do you know all this? I'll be bound your elders don't tattle of these high matters in front of you? If it's Moravik who talks when she shouldn't—'

'No. Not Moravik. But I know it's true.'

'How in the Thunderer's name do you know any such thing? Slaves' gossip?'

I fed the last bite of my bread to the mare. 'If you swear by heathen gods, Cerdic, it's you who'll be in trouble, with Moravik.'

'Oh, aye. That kind of trouble's easy enough to come by. Come on, who's been talking to you?'

'Nobody. I know, that's all. I–I can't explain how . . . And when she refused Gorlan my uncle Camlach was as angry as my grandfather. He's afraid my father will come back and marry her, and drive him out. He doesn't admit this to my grandfather, of course.'

'Of course.' He was staring, even forgetting to chew, so that saliva dribbled from the corner of his open mouth. He swallowed hastily. 'The gods know–God knows where you got all this, but it could be true. Well, go on.'

The brown mare was pushing at me, snuffing sweet breath at my neck. I handed her away. 'That's all. Gorlan is angry, but they'll give him something. And my mother will go in the end to St Peter's. You'll see.'

There was a short silence. Cerdic swallowed his meat and threw the bone out of the door, where a couple of the stableyard curs pounced on it and raced off in a snarling wrangle.

'Merlin—'

'Yes?'

'You'd be wise if you said no more of this to anyone. Not to anyone. Do you understand?'

I said nothing.

'These are matters that a child doesn't understand. High matters. Oh, some of it's common talk, I grant you, but this about Prince Camlach—' He dropped a hand to my knee, and gripped and shook it. 'I tell you, he's dangerous, that one. Leave it be, and stay out of sight. I'll tell no one, trust me for that. But you, you must say no more. Bad enough if you were rightwise a prince born, or even in the King's favour like that red whelp Dinias, but for you . . .' He shook the knee again. 'Do you heed me, Merlin? For your skin's sake, keep silent and stay out of their way. And tell me who told you all this.'

I thought of the dark cave in the hypocaust, and the sky remote at the top of the shaft. 'No one told me. I swear it.' When he made a sound of impatience and worry I looked straight at him and told him as much of the truth as I dared. 'I have heard things, I admit it. And sometimes people talk over your head, not noticing you're there, or not thinking you understand. But at other times–' I paused '–it's as if something spoke to me, as if I saw things . . . And sometimes the stars tell me . . . and there is music, and voices in the dark. Like dreams.'

His hand went up in a gesture of protection. I thought he was crossing himself, then saw the sign against the evil eye. He looked shamefaced at that, and dropped the hand. 'Dreams, that's what it is; you're right. You've been asleep in some corner, likely, and they've talked across you when they shouldn't, and you've heard things you shouldn't. I was forgetting you're nothing but a child. When you look with those eyes—' He broke off, and shrugged. 'But you'll promise me you'll say no more of what you've heard?'

'All right, Cerdic. I promise you. If you'll promise to tell me something in return.'

'What's that?'

'Who my father was.'

He choked over his beer, then with deliberation wiped the foam away, set down the horn, and regarded me with exasperation. 'Now how in middle-earth do you think I know that?'

'I thought Moravik might have told you.'

'Does she know?' He sounded so surprised that I knew he was telling the truth.

'When I asked her she just said there were some things it was better not to talk about.'

'She's right at that. But if you ask me, that's her way of saying she's no wiser than the next one. And if you do ask me, young Merlin, though you don't, that's another thing you'd best keep clear of. If your lady mother wanted you to know, she'd tell you. You'll find out soon enough, I doubt.'

I saw that he was making the sign again, though this time he hid the hand. I opened my mouth to ask if he believed the stories, but he picked up the drinking horn, and got to his feet.

'I've had your promise. Remember?'

'Yes.'

'I've watched you. You go your own way, and sometimes I think you're nearer to the wild things than to men. You know she called you for the falcon?'

I nodded.

'Well, here's something for you to think about. You'd best be forgetting falcons for the time being. There's plenty of them around, too many, if truth be told. Have you watched the ring-doves, Merlin?'

'The ones that drink from the fountain with the white doves, then fly away free? Of course I have. I feed them in winter, along with the doves.'

'They used to say in my country, the ring-dove has many enemies, because her flesh is sweet and her eggs are good to eat. But she lives and she prospers, because she runs away. The Lady Niniane may have called you her little falcon, but you're not a falcon yet, young Merlin. You're only a dove. Remember that. Live by keeping quiet, and by running away. Mark my words.' He nodded at me, and put a hand down to pull me to my feet. 'Does the cut still hurt?'

'It stings.'

'Then it's on the mend. The bruise is nought to worry you, it'll go soon enough.'

It did, indeed, heal cleanly, and left no mark. But I remember how it stung that night, and kept me awake, so that Cerdic and Moravik kept silent in the other corner of the room, for fear, I suppose, that it had been from some of their mutterings that I had pieced together my information.

After they slept I crept out, stepped past the grinning wolfhound, and ran along to the hypocaust.

But tonight I heard nothing to remember, except Olwen's voice, mellow as an ousel's, singing some song I had not heard before, about a wild goose, and a hunter with a golden net.

Chapter Four

After this, life settled back into its peaceful rut, and I think that my grandfather must eventually have accepted my mother's refusal to marry. Things were strained between them for a week or so, but with Camlach home, and settling down as if he had never left the place–and with a good hunting season coming up–the King forgot his rancour, and things went back to normal.

Except possibly for me. After the incident in the orchard, Camlach no longer went out of his way to favour me, nor I to follow him. But he was not unkind to me, and once or twice defended me in some petty rough and tumble with the other boys, even taking my part against Dinias, who had supplanted me in his favour.

But I no longer needed that kind of protection. That September day had taught me other lessons besides Cerdic's of the ring-dove. I dealt with Dinias myself. One night, creeping beneath his bedchamber on the way to my 'cave', I chanced to hear him and his pack-follower Brys laughing over a foray of that afternoon when the pair of them had followed Camlach's friend Alun to his tryst with one of the servant-girls, and had stayed hidden, watching and listening, to the sweet end. When Dinias waylaid me next morning I stood my ground and–quoting a sentence or so–asked if he had seen Alun yet that day. He stared, went red and then white (for Alun had a hard hand and a temper to match it) and then sidled away, making the sign behind his back. If he liked to think it was magic rather than simple blackmail, I let him. After that, if the High King himself had ridden in claiming parentage for me, none of the children would have believed him. They left me alone.

Which was just as well, for during that winter part of the floor of the bathhouse fell in, my grandfather judged the whole thing dangerous, and had it filled in and poison laid for the rats. So, like a cub smoked from its earth, I had to fend for myself above ground.

About six months after Gorlan's visit, as we were coming through a cold February into the first budding days of March, Camlach began to insist, first to my mother and then to my grandfather, that I should be taught to read and write. My mother, I think, was grateful for this evidence of his interest in me; I myself was pleased and took good care to show it, though after the incident in the orchard I could have no illusions about his motives. But it did no harm to let Camlach think that my feelings about the priesthood had undergone a change. My mother's declaration that she would never marry, coupled with her increased withdrawal among her women and her frequent visits to St Peter's to talk with the Abbess and such priests as visited the community, removed his worst fears—either that she would marry a Welsh prince who could hope to take over the kingdom in her right, or that my unknown father would come to claim her and legitimate me, and prove to be a man of rank and power who might supplant him forcibly. It did not matter to Camlach that in either event I was not much of a danger to him, and less than ever now, for he had taken a wife before Christmas, and already at the beginning of March, it seemed that she was pregnant. Even Olwen's increasingly obvious pregnancy was no threat to him, for Camlach stood high in his father's favour, and it was not likely that a brother so much younger would ever present a serious danger. There could be no question; Camlach had a good fighting record, knew how to make men like him, and had ruthlessness and commonsense. The ruthlessness showed in what he had tried to do to me in the orchard; the commonsense showed in his indifferent kindness once my mother's decision removed the threat to him. But I have noticed this about ambitious men, or men in power, that they fear even the slightest and least likely threat to it. He would never rest until he saw me priested and safely out of the palace.

Whatever his motives, I was pleased when my tutor came; he was a Greek who had been a scribe in Massilia until he drank himself into debt and ensuing slavery; now he was assigned to me, and because he was grateful for the change in status and the relief from manual work, taught me well and without the religious bias which had constricted the teaching I had picked up from my mother's priests. Demetrius was a pleasant, ineffectually clever man who had a genius for languages, and whose only recreations were dice and (when he won) drink. Occasionally, when he had won enough, I would find him happily and incapably asleep over his books. I never told anyone of these occasions, and indeed was glad of the chance to go about my own affairs; he was grateful for my silence, and in his turn, when I once or twice played truant, held his tongue and made no attempt to find out where I had been. I was quick to catch up with my studies and showed more than enough progress to satisfy my mother and Camlach, so Demetrius and I respected one another's secrets and got along tolerably well.

One day in August, almost a year after the coming of Gorlan to my grandfather's court, I left Demetrius placidly sleeping it off, and rode up alone into the hills behind the town.

I had been this way several times before. It was quicker to go up past the barrack walls and then out by the military road which led eastwards through the hills to Caerleon, but this meant riding through the town, and possibly being seen, and questions asked. The way I took was along the river bank. There was a gateway, not much used, leading straight out from our stableyard to the broad flat path where the horses went that towed the barges, and this followed the river for quite a long way, past St Peter's and then along the placid curves of the Tywy to the mill, which was as far as the barges went. I had never been beyond this point, but there was a pathway leading up past the mill-house and over the road, and then by the valley of the tributary stream that helped to serve the mill.

It was a hot, drowsy day, full of the smell of bracken. Blue dragonflies darted and glimmered over the river, and the meadowsweet was thick as curds under the humming clouds of flies.

My pony's neat hoofs tapped along the baked clay of the towpath. We met a big dapple grey bringing an empty barge down from the mill with the tide, taking it easy. The boy perched on its withers called a greeting, and the barge-man lifted a hand.

When I reached the mill there was no one in sight. Grain-sacks, newly unloaded, were piled on the narrow wharf. By them the miller's dog lay sprawled in the hot sun, hardly troubling to open an eye as I drew rein in the shade of the buildings. Above me, the long straight stretch of the military road was empty. The stream tumbled through a culvert beneath it, and I saw a trout leap and flash in the foam.

It would be hours before I could be missed. I put the pony at the bank up to the road, won the brief battle when he tried to turn for home, then kicked him to a canter along the path which led upstream into the hills.

The path twisted and turned at first, climbing the steep stream-side, then led out of the thorns and thin oaks that filled the gully, and went north in a smooth level curve along the open slope.

Here the townsfolk graze their sheep and cattle, so the grass is smooth and shorn. I passed one shepherd boy, drowsy under a hawthorn bush, with his sheep at hand; he was simple, and only stared vacantly at me as I trotted past, fingering the pile of stones with which he herded his sheep. As we passed him he picked up one of them, a smooth green pebble, and I wondered if he was going to throw it at me, but he lobbed it instead to turn some fat grazing lambs which were straying too far, then went back to his slumbers. There were black cattle further afield, down nearer the river where the grass was longer, but I could not see the herdsman. Away at the foot of the hill, tiny beside a tiny hut, I saw a girl with a flock of geese.

Presently the path began to climb again, and my pony slowed to a walk, picking his way through scattered trees. Hazel-nuts were thick in the coppices, mountain ash and brier grew from tumbles of mossed rock, and the bracken was breast high. Rabbits ran everywhere, scuttering through the fern, and a pair of jays scolded a fox from the safety of a swinging hornbeam. The ground was too hard, I supposed, to bear tracks well, but I could see no sign, either of crushed bracken or broken twigs, that any other horseman had recently been this way.

The sun was high. A little breeze swept through the hawthorns, rattling the green, hard fruit. I urged the pony on. Now among the oaks and hollies were pine trees, their stems reddish in the sunlight. The ground grew rougher as the path climbed, with bare grey stone outcropping through the thin turf, and a honeycombing of rabbit burrows. I did not know where the path led, I knew nothing but that I was alone, and free. There was nothing to tell me what sort of day this was, or what way-star was leading me up into the hill. This was in the days before the future became clear to me.

The pony hesitated, and I came to myself. There was a fork in the track, with nothing to indicate which would be the best way to go. To left, to right, it led away round the two sides of a thicket.

The pony turned decisively to the left, this being downhill. I would have let him go, but that at that moment a bird flew low across the path in front of me, left to right, and vanished beyond the trees. Sharp wings, a flash of rust and slate-blue, the fierce dark eye and curved beak of a merlin. For no reason, except that this was better than no reason, I turned the pony's head after it, and dug my heels in.

The path climbed in a shallow curve, leaving the wood on the left. This was a stand mainly of pines, thickly clustered and dark, and so heavily grown that you could only have hacked your way in through the dead stuff with an axe. I heard the clap of wings as a ring-dove fled from shelter, dropping invisibly out of the far side of the trees. It had gone to the left. This time I followed the falcon.

We were now well out of sight of the river valley and the town. The pony picked his way along one side of a shallow valley, at the foot of which ran a narrow, tumbling stream. On the far side of the stream the long slopes of turf went bare up to the scree, and above this were the rocks, blue and grey in the sunlight. The slope where I rode was scattered with hawthorn brakes throwing pools of slanted shadow, and above them again, scree, and cliff hung with ivy where choughs wheeled and called in the bright air. Apart from their busy sound, the valley held the most complete and echo-less stillness.

The pony's hoofs sounded loud on the baked earth. It was hot, and I was thirsty. Now the track ran along under a low cliff, perhaps twenty feet high, and at its foot a grove of hawthorns cast a pool of shade across the path. Somewhere, close above me, I could hear the trickle of water.

I stopped the pony and slid off. I led him into the shade of grove and made him fast, then looked about me for the source of the water.

The rock by the path was dry, and below the path was no sign of any water running down to swell the stream at the foot of the valley. But the sound of running water was steady and unmistakable. I left the path and scrambled up the grass at the side of the rock, to find myself on a small flat patch of turf, a little dry lawn scattered with rabbits' droppings, and at the back of it another face of cliff.

In the face of the rock was a cave. The rounded opening was smallish and very regular, almost like a made arch. To one side of this, the right as I stood looking, was a slope of grass-grown stones long ago fallen from above, and overgrown with oak and rowan, whose branches overhung the cave with shadow. To the other side, and only a few feet from the archway, was the spring.

I approached it. It was very small, a little shining movement of water oozing out of a crack in the face of the rock, and falling with a steady trickle into a round basin of stone. There was no outflow. Presumably the water sprang from the rock, gathered in the basin, and drained away through another crack, eventually to join the stream below. Through the clear water I could see every pebble, every grain of sand at the bottom of the basin. Hart's-tongue fern grew above it, and there was moss at the lip, and below it green, moist grass.

I knelt on the grass, and had put my mouth to the water, when I saw that there was a cup. This stood in a tiny niche among the ferns. It was a handspan high, and made of brown horn. As I lifted it down I saw above it, half hidden by the ferns, the small, carved figure of a wooden god. I recognised him. I had seen him under the oak at Tyr Myrddin. Here he was in his own hill-top place, under the open sky.

I filled the cup and drank, pouring a few drops on the ground for the god. Then I went into the cave.

Chapter Five

This was bigger than had appeared from outside. Only a couple of paces inside the archway–and my paces were very short–the cave opened out into a seemingly vast chamber whose top was lost in shadow. It was dark, but–though at first I neither noticed this nor looked for its cause–with some source of extra light that gave a vague illumination, showing the floor smooth and clear of obstacles. I made my way slowly forward, straining my eyes, with deep inside me the beginning of that surge of excitement that caves have always started in me. Some men experience this with water; some, I know, on high places; some create fire for the same pleasure: with me it has always been the depths of the forest, or the depths of the earth. Now, I know why; but then, I only knew that I was a boy who had found somewhere new, something he could perhaps make his own in a world where he owned nothing.

Next moment I stopped short, brought up by a shock which spilled the excitement through my bowels like water. Something had moved in the murk, just to my right.

I froze still, straining my eyes to see. There was no movement.

I held my breath, listening. There was no sound. I flared my nostrils, testing the air cautiously round me. There was no smell, animal or human; the cave smelt, I thought, of smoke and damp rock and the earth itself, and of a queer musty smell I couldn't identify. I knew, without putting it into words, that had there been any other creature near me the air would have felt different, less empty. There was no one there.

I tried a word, softly, in Welsh. 'Greetings.' The whisper came straight back at me in an echo so quick that I knew I was very near the wall of the cave, then it lost itself, hissing, in the roof.

There was movement there–at first, I thought, only an intensifying of the echoed whisper, then the rustling grew and grew like the rustling of a woman's dress, or a curtain stirring in the draught. Something went past my cheek, with a shrill, bloodless cry just on the edge of sound. Another followed, and after them flake after flake of shrill shadow, pouring down from the roof like leaves down a stream of wind, or fish down a fall. It was the bats, disturbed from their lodging in the top of the cave, streaming out now into the daylight valley. They would be pouring out of the low archway like a plume of smoke.

I stood quite still, wondering if it was these that had made the curious musty smell. I thought I could smell them as they passed, but it wasn't the same. I had no fear that they would touch me; in darkness or light, whatever their speed, bats will touch nothing. They are so much creatures of the air, I believe, that as the air parts in front of an obstacle the bat is swept aside with it, like a petal carried downstream. They poured past, a shrill tide of them between me and the wall. Childlike, to see what the stream would do–how it would divert itself–I took a step nearer the wall. Nothing touched me. The stream divided and poured on, the shrill air brushing both my cheeks. It was as if I did not exist. But at the same moment when I moved, the creature that I had seen moved, too. Then my outstretched hand met, not rock, but metal, and I knew what the creature was. It was my own reflection.

Hanging against the wall was a sheet of metal, burnished to a dull sheen. This, then, was the source of the diffused light within the cave; the mirror's silky surface caught, obliquely, the light from the cave's mouth, and sent it on into the darkness. I could see myself moving in it like a ghost, as I recoiled and let fall the hand which had leapt to the knife at my hip.

Behind me the flow of bats had ceased, and the cave was still. Reassured, I stayed where I was, studying myself with interest in the mirror. My mother had had one once, an antique from Egypt, but then, deeming such things to be vanity, she had locked it away. Of course I had often seen my face reflected in water, but never my body mirrored, till now. I saw a dark boy, wary, all eyes with curiosity, nerves and excitement. In that light my eyes looked quite black; my hair was black, too, thick and clean, but worse cut and groomed than my pony's; my tunic and sandals were a disgrace. I grinned, and the mirror flashed a sudden smile that changed the picture completely and at once, from a sullen young animal poised to run or fight, to something quick and gentle and approachable; something, I knew even then, that few people had ever seen.

Then it vanished, and the wary animal was back, as I leaned forward to run a hand over the metal. It was cold and smooth and freshly burnished. Whoever had hung it–and he must be the same person who used the cup of horn outside–had either been here very recently, or he still lived here, and might come back at any moment to find me.

I was not particularly frightened. I had pricked to caution when I saw the cup, but one learns very young to take care of oneself, and the times I had been brought up in were peaceful enough, at any rate in our valley; but there are always wild men and rough men and the lawless and vagabonds to be reckoned with, and any boy who likes his own company, as I did, must be prepared to defend his skin. I was wiry, and strong for my age, and I had my dagger. That I was barely seven years old never entered my head; I was Merlin, and, bastard or not, the King's grandson. I went on exploring.

The next thing I found, a pace along the wall, was a box, and on top of it shapes which my hands identified immediately as flint and iron and tinderbox, and a big, roughly made candle of what smelt like a sheep's tallow. Beside these objects lay a shape which–incredulously and inch by inch–I identified as the skull of a horned sheep. There were nails driven into the top of the box here and there, apparently holding down fragments of leather. But when I felt these, carefully, I found in the withered leather frameworks of delicate bone; they were dead bats, stretched and nailed on the wood.

This was a treasure cave indeed. No find of gold or weapons could have excited me more. Full of curiosity, I reached for the tinderbox.

Then I heard him coming back.

My first thought was that he must have seen my pony, then I realised he was coming from further up the hill. I could hear the rattling and scaling of small stones as he came down the scree above the cave. One of them splashed into the spring outside, and then it was too late. I heard him jump down on to the flat grass beside the water.

It was time for the ring-dove again; the falcon was forgotten. I ran deeper into the cave. As he swept aside the boughs that darkened the entrance, the light grew momentarily, enough to show me my way. At the back of the cave was a slope and jut of rock, and, at twice my height, a wildish ledge. A quick flash of sunlight from the mirror caught a wedge of shadow in the rock, above the ledge, big enough to hide me. Soundless in my scuffed sandals, I swarmed on to the ledge, and crammed my body into that wedge of shadow, to find it was in fact a gap in the rock, giving apparently on to another, smaller cave. I slithered in through the gap like an otter into the river-bank.

It seemed that he had heard nothing. The light was cut off again as the boughs sprang back into place behind him, and he came into the cave. It was a man's tread, measured and slow.

If I had thought about it at all, I suppose I would have assumed that the cave would be uninhabited at least until sunset, that whoever owned the place would be away hunting, or about his other business, and would return only at nightfall. There was no point in wasting candles when the sun was blazing outside. Perhaps he was here now only to bring home his kill, and he would go again and leave me the chance to get out. I hoped he would not see my pony tethered in the hawthorn brake.

Then I heard him moving, with the sure tread of someone who knows his way blindfold, towards the candle and the tinderbox.

Even now I had no room for apprehension, no room, indeed, for any but the one thought or sensation–the extreme discomfort of the cave into which I had crawled. It was apparently small, not much bigger than the large round vats they use for dyeing, and much the same shape. Floor, wall and ceiling hugged me round in a continuous curve. It was like being inside a large globe; moreover, a globe studded with nails, or with its inner surface stuck all over with small pieces of jagged stone. There seemed no inch of surface not bristling like a bed of strewn flints, and it was only my light weight, I think, that saved me from being cut, as I quested about blindly to find some clear space to lie on. I found a place smoother than the rest and curled there, as small as I could, watching the faintly-defined opening, and inching my dagger silently from its sheath into my hand.

I heard the quick hiss and chime of flint and iron, and then the flare of light, intense in the darkness, as the tinder caught hold. Then the steady, waxing glow as he lit the candle.

Or rather, it should have been the slow-growing beam of a candle flame that I saw, but instead there was a flash, a sparkle, a conflagration as if a whole pitch-soaked beacon was roaring up in flames. Light poured and flashed, crimson, golden, white, red, intolerable into my cave. I winced back from it, frightened now, heedless of pain and cut flesh as I shrank against the sharp walls. The whole globe where I lay seemed to be full of flame.

It was indeed a globe, a round chamber floored, roofed, lined with crystals. They were fine as glass, and smooth as glass, but clearer than any glass I had ever seen, brilliant as diamonds. This, in fact, to my childish mind, was what they first seemed to be. I was in a globe lined with diamonds, a million burning diamonds, each face of each gem wincing with the light, shooting it to and fro, diamond to diamond and back again, with rainbows and rivers and bursting stars and a shape like a crimson dragon clawing up the wall, while below him a girl's face swam faintly with closed eyes, and the light drove right into my body as if it would break me open.

I shut my eyes. When I opened them again I saw that the golden light had shrunk and was concentrated on one part of the wall no bigger than my head, and from this, empty of vision, rayed the broken, brilliant beams.

There was silence from the cave below. He had not stirred. I had not even heard the rustle of his clothes.

Then the light moved. The flashing disc began to slide, slowly, across the crystal wall. I was shaking. I huddled closer to the sharp stones, trying to escape it. There was nowhere to go. It advanced slowly round the curve. It touched my shoulder, my head, and I ducked, cringing. The shadow of my movement rushed across the globe, like a wind-eddy over a pool.

The light stopped, retreated, fixed glittering in its place. Then it went out. But the glow of the candle, strangely, remained; an ordinary steady yellow glow beyond the gap in the wall of my refuge.

'Come out.' The man's voice, not loud, not raised with shouted orders like my grandfather's, was clear and brief with all the mystery of command. It never occurred to me to disobey. I crept forward over the sharp crystals, and through the gap. Then I slowly pulled myself upright on the ledge, my back against the wall of the outer cave, the dagger ready in my right hand, and looked down.

Chapter Six

He stood between me and the candle, a hugely tall figure (or so it seemed to me) in a long robe of some brown homespun stuff. The candle made a nimbus of his hair, which seemed to be grey, and he was bearded. I could not see his expression, and his right hand was hidden in the folds of his robe.

I waited, poised warily.

He spoke again, in the same tone. 'Put up your dagger and come down.'

'When I see your right hand,' I said.

He showed it, palm up. It was empty. He said gravely: 'I am unarmed.'

'Then stand out of my way,' I said, and jumped. The cave was wide, and he was standing to one side of it. My leap carried me three or four paces down the cave, and I was past him and near the entrance before he could have moved more than a step. But in fact he never moved at all. As I reached the mouth of the cave and swept aside the hanging branches I heard him laughing.

The sound brought me up short. I turned.

From here, in the light which now filled the cave, I saw him clearly. He was old, with grey hair thinning on top and hanging lank over his ears, and a straight growth of grey beard, roughly trimmed. His hands were calloused and grained with dirt, but had been fine, with long fingers. Now the old man's veins crawled and knotted on them, distended like worms. But it was his face which held me; it was thin, cavernous almost as a skull, with a high domed forehead and bushy grey brows which came down jutting over eyes where I could see no trace of age at all. These were closely set, large, and of a curiously clear and swimming grey. His nose was a thin beak; his mouth, lipless now, stretched wide with his laughter over astonishingly good teeth.

'Come back. There's no need to be afraid.'

'I'm not afraid.' I dropped the boughs back into place, and not without bravado walked towards him. I stopped a few paces away. 'Why should I be afraid of you? Do you know who I am?'

He regarded me for a moment, seeming to muse. 'Let me see you. Dark hair, dark eyes, the body of a dancer and the manners of a young wolf . . . or should I say a young falcon?'

My dagger sank to my side, 'Then you do know me?'

'Shall I say I knew you would come some day, and today I knew there was someone here. What do you think brought me back so early?'

'How did you know there was someone here? Oh, of course, you saw the bats.'

'Perhaps.'

'Do they always go up like that?'

'Only for strangers. Your dagger, sir.'

I put it back in my belt. 'Nobody calls me sir. I'm a bastard. That means I belong to myself, no one else. My name's Merlin, but you knew that.'

'And mine is Galapas. Are you hungry?'

'Yes.' But I said it dubiously, thinking of the skull and the dead bats.

Disconcertingly, he understood. The grey eyes twinkled. 'Fruit and honey cakes? And sweet water from the spring? What better fare would you get, even in the King's house?'

'I wouldn't get that in the King's house at this hour of the day,' I said frankly. 'Thank you, sir, I'll be glad to eat with you.'

He smiled. 'Nobody calls me sir. And I belong to no man, either. Go out and sit down in the sun, and I'll bring the food.'

The fruit was apples, which looked and tasted exactly like the ones from my grandfather's orchard, so that I stole a sideways glance at my host, scanning him by daylight, wondering if I had ever seen him on the river bank, or anywhere in the town.

'Do you have a wife?' I asked. 'Who makes the honey cakes? They're very good.'

'No wife. I told you I belonged to no man, and to no woman either. You will see, Merlin, how all your life men, and women too, will try to put bars round you, but you will escape those bars, or bend them, or melt them at your will until, of your will, you take them round you, and sleep behind them in their shadow . . . I get the honey cakes from the shepherd's wife, she makes enough for three, and is good enough to spare some for charity.'

'Are you a hermit, then? A holy man?'

'Do I look like a holy man?'

'No.' This was true. The only people I remember being afraid of at that time were the solitary holy men who sometimes wandered, preaching and begging, into the town; queer, arrogant, noisy men, with a mad look in their eyes, and a smell about them which I associated with the heaps of offal outside the slaughter-pens. It was sometimes hard to know which god they professed to serve. Some of them, it was whispered, were druids, who were still officially outside the law, though in Wales in the country places they still practised without much interference. Many were followers of the old gods—the local deities—and since these varied in popularity according to season, their priests tended to switch allegiance from time to time where the pickings were richest. Even the Christian ones did this sometimes, but you could usually tell the real Christians, because they were the dirtiest. The Roman gods and their priests stayed solidly enshrined in their crumbling temples, but did very well on offerings likewise. The Church frowned on the lot, but could not do much about it. 'There was a god at the spring outside,' I ventured.

'Yes, Myrddin. He lends me his spring, and his hollow hill, and his heaven of woven light, and in return I give him his due. It does not do to neglect the gods of a place, whoever they may be. In the end, they are all one.'

'If you're not a hermit, then, what are you?'

'At the moment, a teacher.'

'I have a tutor. He comes from Massilia, but he's actually been to Rome. Who do you teach?'

'Until now, nobody. I'm old and tired, and I came to live here alone and study.'

'Why do you have the dead bats in there, on the box?'

'I was studying them.'

I stared at him. 'Studying bats? How can you study bats?'

'I study the way they are made, and the way they fly, and mate, and feed. The way they live. Not only bats, but beasts and fish and plants and birds, as many as I see.'

'But that's not studying!' I regarded him with wonder. 'Demetrius– that's my tutor–tells me that watching lizards and birds is dreaming, and a waste of time. Though Cerdic–that's a friend–told me to study the ring-doves.'

'Why?'

'Because they're quick, and quiet, and keep out of the way. Because they only lay two eggs, but still though everybody hunts them, men and beasts and hawks, there are still more ring-doves than anything else.'

'And they don't put them in cages.' He drank some water, regarding me. 'So you have a tutor. Then you can read?'

'Of course.'

'Can you read Greek?'

'A little.'

'Then come with me.'

He got up and went into the cave. I followed him. He lit the candle once more–he had put it out to save tallow–and by its light lifted the lid of the box. In it I saw the rolled shapes of books, more books together than I had ever imagined there were in the world. I watched as he selected one, closed the lid carefully, and unrolled the book.

'There.'

With delight, I saw what it was. A drawing, spidery but definite, of the skeleton of a bat. And alongside it, in neat, crabbed Greek letters, phrases which I immediately, forgetting even Galapas' presence, began to spell out to myself.

In a minute or two his hand came over my shoulder. 'Bring it outside.' He pulled out the nails holding one of the dried leathery bodies to the box-lid, and lifted it carefully in his palm. 'Blow out the candle. We'll look at this together.'

And so, with no more question, and no more ceremony, began my first lesson with Galapas.

It was only when the sun, low over one wing of the valley, sent a long shadow creeping up the slope, that I remembered the other life that waited for me, and how far I had to go. I jumped to my feet.

'I'll have to go! Demetrius won't say anything, but if I'm late for supper they'll ask why.'

And you don't intend to tell them?'

'No, or they'd stop me coming again.'

He smiled, making no comment. I doubt if I noticed then the calm assumptions on which the interview had been based; he had neither asked how I had come, nor why. And because I was only a child I took it for granted, too, though for politeness' sake I asked him:

'I may come again, mayn't I?'

'Of course.'

'I—it's hard to say when. I never know when I'll get away—I mean, when I'll be free.'

'Don't worry. I shall know when you are coming. And I shall be here.'

'How can you know?'

He was rolling up the book with those long, neat fingers. 'The same way I knew today.'

'Oh! I was forgetting. You mean I go into the cave and send the bats out?'

'If you like.'

I laughed with pleasure. 'I've never met anyone like you! To make smoke signals with bats! If I told them they'd never believe me, even Cerdic.'

'You won't tell even Cerdic.'

I nodded. 'That's right. Nobody at all. Now I must go. Good-bye, Galapas.'

'Good-bye.'

And so it was in the days, and in the months, that followed. Whenever I could, once and sometimes twice in the week, I rode up the valley to the cave. He certainly seemed to know when I was coming, for as often as not he was there waiting for me, with the books laid out; but when there was no sign of him I did as we had arranged and sent out the bats as a smoke signal to bring him in. As the weeks went by they got used to me, and it took two or three well-aimed stones sent up into the roof to get them out; but after a while this grew unnecessary; people at the palace grew accustomed to my absences, and ceased to question them, and it became possible to make arrangements with Galapas for meeting from day to day.

Moravik had let me go more and more my own way since Olwen's baby had been born at the end of May, and when Camlach's son arrived in September she established herself firmly in the royal nursery as its official ruler, abandoning me as suddenly as a bird deserting the nest. I saw less and less of my mother, who seemed content to spend her time with her women, so I was left pretty much to Demetrius and Cerdic between them. Demetrius had his own reasons for welcoming a day off now and again, and Cerdic was my friend. He would unsaddle the muddy and sweating pony without question, or with a wink and a lewd remark about where I had been that was meant as a joke, and was taken as such. I had my room to myself now, except for the wolfhound; he spent the nights with me for old times' sake, but whether he was any safeguard I have no idea. I suspect not; I was safe enough. The country was at peace, except for the perennial rumours of invasion from Less Britain; Camlach and his father were in accord; I was to all appearances heading willingly and at high speed for the prison of the priesthood, and so, when my lessons with Demetrius were officially done, was free to go where I wished.

I never saw anyone else in the valley. The shepherd only lived there in summer, in a poor hut below the wood. There were no other dwellings there, and beyond Galapas' cave the track was used only by sheep and deer. It led nowhere.

He was a good teacher, and I was quick, but in fact I hardly thought of my time with him as lessons. We left languages and geometry to Demetrius, and religion to my mother's priests; with Galapas to begin with it was only like listening to a storyteller. He had travelled when young to the other side of the earth, Aethiopia and Greece and Germany and all around the Middle Sea, and seen and learned strange things. He taught me practical things, too; how to gather herbs and dry them to keep, how to use them for medicines, and how to distil certain subtle drugs, even poisons. He made me study the beasts and birds, and—with the dead birds and sheep we found on the hills, and once with a dead deer—I learnt about the organs and bones of the body. He taught me how to stop bleeding, how to set a broken bone, how to cut bad flesh away and cleanse the place so that it heals cleanly; even—though this came later—how to draw flesh and sinews into place with thread while the beast is stunned with fumes. I remember that the first spell he taught me was the charming of warts; this is so easy that a woman can do it.

One day he took a book out of the box and unrolled it. 'Do you know what this is?'

I was used to diagrams and drawings, but this was a drawing of nothing I could recognise. The writing was in Latin, and I saw the words *Aethiopia* and *Fortunate Islands*, and then right out in a corner, *Brittania*. The lines seemed to be scrawled everywhere, and all over the picture were trails of mounds drawn in, like a field where moles have been at work.

'Those, are they mountains?'

'Yes.'

'Then it's a picture of the world?'

'A map.'

I had never seen a map before. At first I could not see how it worked, but in a while, as he talked, I saw how the world lay there as a bird sees it, with roads and rivers like the radials of a spider's web, or the guide lines that lead the bee into the flower. As a man finds a stream he knows, and follows it through the wild moors, so, with a map, it is possible to ride from Rome to Massilia, or London to Caerleon, without once asking the way or looking for the milestones. This art was discovered by the Greek Anaximander, though some say the Egyptians knew it first. The map that Galapas showed me was a copy from a book by Ptolemy of Alexandria. After he had explained, and we had studied the map together, he bade me get out my tablet, and make a map for myself, of my own country.

When I had done he looked at it. 'This in the centre, what is it?'

'Maridunum,' I said in surprise. 'See, there is the bridge, and the river, and this is the road through the market place, and the barrack gates are here.'

'I see that. I did not say your town, Merlin, I said your country.'

'The whole of Wales? How do I know what lies north of the hills? I've never been further than this.'

'I will show you.'

He put aside the tablet, and taking a sharp stick, began to draw in the dust, explaining as he did so. What he drew for me was a map shaped like a big triangle, not Wales only, but the whole of Britain, even the wild land beyond the Wall where the savages live. He showed me the mountains and rivers and roads and towns, London and Calleva and the places that cluster thick in the south, to the towns and fortresses at the ends of the web of roads, Segontium and Caerleon and Eboracum and the towns along the Wall itself. He spoke as if it were all one country, though I could have told him the names of the kings of a dozen places that he mentioned. I only remember this because of what came after.

Soon after this, when winter came and the stars were out early, he taught me their names and their powers, and how a man could map them as one would map the roads and townships. They made music, he said, as they moved. He himself did not know music, but when he found that Olwen had taught me, he helped me to make myself a harp. This was a rude enough affair, I suppose, and small, made of hornbeam, with the curve and forepillar of red sallow from the Tywy, and strung with hair from my pony's tail, where the harp of a prince (said Galapas) should have been strung with gold and silver wire. But I made the string-shoes out of pierced copper coins, the key and tuning-pins of polished bone, then carved a merlin on the sounding-board, and thought it a finer instrument than Olwen's. Indeed it was as true as hers, having a kind of sweet whispering note which seemed to pluck songs from the air itself. I kept it in the cave: though Dinias left me alone these days, being a warrior while I was only a sucking clerk, I would not have kept anything I treasured in the palace, unless I could lock it in my clothes-chest, and the harp was too big for that. At home for music I had the birds in the pear tree, and Olwen still sang sometimes. And when the birds were silent, and the night sky was frosted with light, I listened for the music of the stars. But I never heard it.

Then one day, when I was twelve years old, Galapas spoke of the crystal cave.

Chapter Seven

It is common knowledge that, with children, those things which are most important often go unmentioned. It is as if the child recognises, by instinct, things which are too big for him, and keeps them in his mind, feeding them with his imagination till they assume proportions distended or grotesque which can become equally the stuff of magic or of nightmare.

So it was with the crystal cave.

I had never mentioned to Galapas my first experience there. Even to myself I had hardly admitted what came sometimes with light and fire; dreams, I had told myself, memories from below memory, figments of the brain only, like the voice which had told me of Gorlan, or the sight of the poison in the apricot. And when I found that Galapas never mentioned the inner cave, and that the mirror was kept covered whenever I was there, I said nothing.

I rode up to see him one day in winter when frost made the ground glitter and ring, and my pony puffed out steam like a dragon. He went fast, tossing his head and dragging at the bit, and breaking into a canter as soon as I turned him away from the wood and along the high valley. I had at length grown out of the gentle, cream-coloured pony of my childhood, but was proud of my little Welsh grey, which I called Aster. There is a breed of Welsh mountain pony, hardy, swift, and very beautiful, with fine narrow heads and small ears, and a strong arch to the neck. They run wild in the hills, and in past times interbred with horses the Romans brought from the East. Aster had been caught and broken for my cousin Dinias, who had overridden him for a couple of years and then discarded him for a real war-horse. I found him hard to manage, with rough manners and a ruined mouth, but his paces were silken after the jogging I was used to, and once he got over his fear of me he was affectionate.

I had long since contrived a shelter for my pony when I came here in winter. The hawthorn brake grew right up against the cliff below the cave, and deep in the thickest part of it Galapas and I had carried stones to make a pen of which the back wall was the cliff itself. When we had laid dead boughs against the walls and across the top, and had carried a few armfuls of bracken, the pen was not only a warm solid shelter, but invisible to the casual eye. This need for secrecy was another of the things that had never been openly discussed; I understood without being told that Galapas in some way was helping me to run counter to Camlach's plans for me, so—even though as time went on I was left more completely to my own devices—I took every precaution to avoid discovery, finding half a dozen different ways to approach the valley, and a score of stories to account for the time I spent there.

I led Aster into the pen, took off his saddle and bridle and hung them up, then threw down fodder from a saddle-bag, barred the entrance with a stout branch, and walked briskly up to the cave.

Galapas was not there, but that he had only gone recently was attested by the fact that the brazier which stood inside the cave mouth had been banked down to a glow. I stirred it till the flames leapt, then settled near it with a book. I had not come today by arrangement, but had plenty of time, so left the bats alone, and read peacefully for a while.

I don't know what made me, that day out of all the days I had been there alone, suddenly put the book aside, and walk back past the veiled mirror to look up at the cleft through which I had fled five years ago. I told myself that I was only curious to see if it was as I had remembered it, or if the crystals, like the visions, were figments of my imagination; whatever the reason, I climbed quickly to the ledge, and dropping on my hands and knees by the gap, peered in.

The inner cave was dead and dark, no glimmer reaching it from the fire. I crawled forward cautiously, till my hands met the sharp crystals. They were all too real. Even now not admitting to myself why I hurried, with one eye on the mouth of the main cave, and an ear open for Galapas' return, I slithered down from the edge, snatched up the leather riding jerkin which I had discarded and, hurrying back, thrust it in front of me through the gap. Then I crawled after.

With the leather jerkin spread on the floor, the globe was comparatively comfortable. I lay still. The silence was complete. As my eyes grew accustomed to the darkness, I could see the faintest grey glimmer from the crystals, but of the magic that the light had brought there was no sign.

There must have been some crack open to the air, for even in that dark confine there was a slight current, a cold thread of a draught. And with it came the sound I was listening for, the footsteps of someone approaching over the frosty rock . . .

When Galapas came into the cave a few minutes later I was sitting by the fire, my jerkin rolled up beside me, poring over the book.

Half an hour before dusk we put our books aside. But still I made no move to go. The fire was blazing now, filling the cave with warmth and flickering light. We sat for a while in silence.

'Galapas, there's something I want to ask you.'

'Yes?'

'Do you remember the first day I came here?'

'Very clearly.'

'You knew I was coming. You were expecting me?'

'Did I say so?'

'You know you did. How did you know I would be here?'

'I saw you in the crystal cave.'

'Oh, that, yes. You moved the mirror so that the candlelight caught me, and you saw my shadow. But that's not what I was asking you. I meant, how did you know I was going to come up the valley that day?'

'That was the question I answered, Merlin. I knew you were coming up the valley that day, because, before you came, I saw you in the cave.'

We looked at one another in silence. The flames glowed and muttered between us, flattened by the little draught that carried the smoke out of the cave. I don't think I answered him at first, I just nodded. It was something I had known. After a while I said, merely: 'Will you show me?'

He regarded me for a moment more, then got to his feet. 'It is time. Light the candle.'

I obeyed him. The little light grew golden, reaching among the shadows cast by the flickering of the fire.

'Take the rug off the mirror.'

I pulled at it and it fell off into my arms in a huddle of wool. I dropped it on his bed beside the wall.

'Now go up on the ledge, and lie down.'

'On the ledge?'

'Yes. Lie on your belly, with your head towards the cleft, so that you can see in.'

'Don't you want me to go right in?'

'And take your jerkin to lie on?'

I was halfway up to the ledge. I whipped round, to see him smiling.

'It's no use, Galapas, you know everything.'

'Some day you will go where even with the Sight I cannot follow you. Now lie still, and watch.'

I lay down on the ledge. It was wide and flat and held me comfortably enough, prone, with my head pillowed on my bent arms, and turned towards the cleft.

Below me, Galapas said softly: 'Think of nothing. I have the reins in my hand; it is not for you yet. Watch only.'

I heard him move back across the cave towards the mirror.

The cave was bigger than I had imagined. It stretched upwards further than I could see, and the floor was worn smooth. I had even been wrong about the crystals; the glimmer that reflected the torchlight came only from puddles on the floor, and a place on one wall where a thin slither of moisture betrayed a spring somewhere above.

The torches, jammed into cracks in the cave wall, were cheap ones, of rag stuffed into cracked horns–the rejects from the workshops. They burned sullenly in the bad air. Though the place was cold, the men worked naked save for loincloths, and sweat ran over their backs as they hacked at the rock-face, steady ceaseless tapping blows that made no noise, but you could see the muscles clench and jar under the torchlit sweat. Beneath a knee-high overhang at the base of the wall, flat on their backs in a pool of seepage, two men hammered upwards with shortened, painful blows at rock within inches of their faces. On the wrist of one of them I saw the shiny pucker of an old brand.

One of the hewers at the face doubled up, coughing, then with a glance over his shoulder stifled the cough and got back to work. Light was growing in the cave, coming from a square opening like a doorway, which gave on a curved tunnel down which a fresh torch–a good one–came.

Four boys appeared, filthy with dust and naked like the others, carrying deep baskets, and behind them came a man dressed in a brown tunic smudged with damp. He had the torch in one hand and in the other a tablet which he stood studying with frowning brows while the boys ran with their baskets to the rock-face and began to shovel the fallen rock into them. After a while the foreman went forward to the face and studied it, holding his torch high. The men drew back, thankful it seemed for the respite, and one of them spoke to the foreman, pointing first at the workings, then at the seeping damp at the far side of the cave.

The boys had shovelled and scrabbled their baskets full, and dragged them back from the face. The foreman, with a shrug and a grin, took a silver coin from his pouch and, with the gambler's practised flick, tossed it. The workmen craned to see. Then the man who had spoken turned back to the face and drove the pick in.

The crack widened, and dust rushed down, blotting out the light. Then in the wake of the dust came the water.

'Drink this,' said Galapas.

'What is it?'

'One of my brews, not yours; it's quite safe. Drink it.'

'Thanks. Galapas, the cave *is* crystal still. I–dreamed it differently.'

'Never mind that now. How do you feel?'

'Odd . . . I can't explain. I feel all right, only a headache, but–empty, like a shell with the snail out of it. No, like a reed with the pith pulled out.'

'A whistle for the winds. Yes. Come down to the brazier.'

When I sat in my old place, with a cup of mulled wine in my hands, he asked: 'Where were you?'

I told him what I had seen, but when I began to ask what it meant, and what he knew, he shook his head. 'I think this has already gone past me. I do not know. All I know is that you must finish that wine quickly and go home. Do you realise how long you lay there dreaming? The moon is up.'

I started to my feet. 'Already? It must be well past supper-time. If they're looking for me—'

'They will not be looking for you. Other things are happening. Go and find out for yourself–and make sure you are part of them.'

'What do you mean?'

'Only what I say. Whatever means you have to use, go with the King. Here, don't forget this.' He thrust my jerkin into my arms.

I took it blindly, staring. 'He's leaving Maridunum?'

'Yes. Only for a while. I don't know how long.'

'He'll never take me.'

'That's for you to say. The gods only go with you, Myrddin Emrys, if you put yourself in their path. And that takes courage. Put your jerkin on before you go out, it's cold.'

I shoved a hand into the sleeve, glowering. 'You've seen all this, something that's really happening, and I–I was looking into the crystals with the fire, and here I've got a hellish headache, and all for nothing . . . Some silly dream of slaves in an old mine. Galapas, when will you teach me to see as you do?'

'For a start, I can see the wolves eating you and Aster, if you don't hurry home.'

He was laughing to himself as if he had made a great jest, as I ran out of the cave and down to saddle the pony.

Chapter Eight

It was a quarter moon, which gave just enough light to show the way. The pony danced to warm his blood, and pulled harder than ever, his ears pricked towards home, scenting his supper. I had to fight to hold him in, because the way was icy, and I was afraid of a fall, but I confess that–with Galapas' last remark echoing uncomfortably in my head–I let him go downhill through the trees a good deal too fast for safety, until we reached the mill and the level of the towpath.

There it was possible to see clearly. I dug my heels in and galloped him the rest of the way.

As soon as we came in sight of town I could see that something was up. The towpath was deserted–the town gates would have been locked long since–but the town was full of lights. Inside the walls torches seemed to be flaring everywhere, and there was shouting and the tramp of feet. I slipped from the saddle at the stableyard gate, fully prepared to find myself locked out, but even as I reached to try it the gate opened, and Cerdic, with a shaded lantern in his hand, beckoned me in.

'I heard you coming. Been listening all evening. Where've you been, lover-boy? She must have been good tonight.'

'Oh, she was. Have they been asking for me? Have they missed me?'

'Not that I know of. They've got more to think about tonight than you. Give me the bridle, we'll put him in the barn for now. There's too much coming and going in the big yard.'

'Why, what's going on? I heard the noise a mile off. Is it a war?'

'No, more's the pity, though it may end up that way. There's a message come this afternoon, the High King's coming to Segontium, and he'll lie there for a week or two. Your grandfather's riding up tomorrow, so everything's to be got ready mighty sharp.'

'I see.' I followed him into the barn, and stood watching him unsaddle, while half-absently I pulled straw from the pile and twisted a wisp for him. I handed this across the pony's withers. 'King Vortigern at Segontium? Why?'

'Counting heads, they say.' He gave a snort of laughter as he began to work the pony over.

'Calling in his allies, you mean? Then there is talk of war?'

'There'll always be talk of war, so long as yon Ambrosius sits there in Less Britain with King Budec at his back, and men remember things that's better not spoken of.'

I nodded. I could not remember precisely when I had been told, since nobody said it aloud, but everyone knew the story of how the High King had claimed the throne. He had been regent for the young King Constantius who had died suddenly, and the King's younger brothers had not waited to prove whether the rumours of murder were true or false; they had fled to their cousin Budec in Less Britain, leaving the kingdom to the Wolf and his sons. Every year or so the rumours sprang up again; that King Budec was arming the two young princes; that Ambrosius had gone to Rome; that Uther was a mercenary in the service of the Emperor of the East, or that he had married the King of Persia's daughter; that the two brothers had an army four hundred thousand strong and were going to invade and burn Greater Britain from end to end; or that they would come in peace, like archangels, and drive the Saxons out of the eastern shores without a blow. But more than twenty years had gone by, and the thing had not happened. The coming of Ambrosius was spoken of now as if it were accomplished, and already a legend, as men spoke of the coming of Brut and the Trojans four generations after the fall of Troy, or Joseph's journey to Thorny Hill near Avalon. Or like the Second Coming of Christ–though when I had once repeated this to my mother she had been so angry that I had never tried to joke again.

'Oh, yes,' I said, 'Ambrosius coming again, is he? Seriously, Cerdic, why is the High King coming to North Wales?'

'I told you. Doing the rounds, drumming up a bit of support before spring, him and that Saxon Queen of his,' and he spat on the floor.

'Why do you do that? You're a Saxon yourself.'

'That's a long time ago. I live here now. Wasn't it that flaxen bitch that made Vortigern sell out in the first place? Or at any rate you know as well as I do that since she's been in the High King's bed the Northmen have been loose over the land like a heath fire, till he can neither fight them nor buy them off. And if she's what men say she is, you can be sure none of the King's true-born sons'll live to wear the crown.' He had been speaking softly, but at this he looked over his shoulder and spat again, making the sign. 'Well, you know all this—or you would, that is, if you listened to your betters more often, instead of spending your time with books and such like, or chasing round with the People from the hollow hills.'

'Is that where you think I go?'

'It's what people say. I'm not asking questions. I don't want to know. Come up, you.' This to the pony as he moved over and started work, hissing, on the other flank. 'There's talk that the Saxons have landed again north of Rutupiae, and they're asking too much this time even for Vortigern to stomach. He'll have to fight, come spring.'

'And my grandfather with him?'

'That's what he's hoping, I'll be bound. Well, you'd best run along if you want your supper. No one'll notice you. There was all hell going on in the kitchens when I tried to get a bite an hour back.'

'Where's my grandfather?'

'How do I know?' He cocked his head at me, over the pony's rump. 'Now what's to do?'

'I want to go with them.'

'Hah!' he said, and threw the chopped feed down for the pony. It was not an encouraging sound.

I said stubbornly: 'I've a fancy to see Segontium.'

'Who hasn't? I've a fancy to see it myself. But if you're thinking of asking the King . . .' He let it hang. 'Not but what it's time you got out of the place and saw a thing or two, shake you a bit out of yourself, it's what you need, but I can't say I see it happening. You'll never go to the King?'

'Why not? All he can do is refuse.'

'All he can do—? Jupiter's balls, listen to the boy. Take my advice and get your supper and go to bed. And don't try Camlach, neither. He's had a right stand-up fight with that wife of his and he's like a stoat with the toothache.—You can't be serious?'

'The gods only go with you, Cerdic, if you put yourself in their path.'

'Well, all right, but some of them have got mighty big hoofs to walk over you with. Do you want Christian burial?'

'I don't really mind. I suppose I'll work my way up to Christian baptism fairly soon, if the Bishop has his way, but till then I've not signed on officially for anyone.'

He laughed. 'I hope they'll give me the flames when my turn comes. It's a cleaner way to go. Well, if you won't listen, you won't listen, but don't face him on an empty belly, that's all.'

'I'll promise you that,' I said, and went to forage for supper. After I had eaten, and changed into a decent tunic, I went to look for my grandfather.

To my relief Camlach was not with him. The King was in his bedchamber, sprawled at ease in his big chair before a roaring log fire, with his two hounds asleep at his feet. At first I thought the woman in the high-backed chair on the other side of the hearth was Olwen, the Queen, but then I saw it was my mother. She had been sewing, but her hands had dropped idle in her lap, and the white stuff lay still over the brown robe. She turned and smiled at me, but with a look of surprise. One of the wolfhounds beat his tail on the floor, and the other opened an eye and rolled it round and closed it again. My grandfather glowered at me from under his brows, but said kindly enough: 'Well, boy, don't stand there. Come in, come in, there's a cursed draught. Shut the door.'

I obeyed, approaching the fire.

'May I see you, sir?'

'You're seeing me. What do you want? Get a stool and sit down.'

There was one near my mother's chair. I pulled it away, to show I was not sitting in her shadow, and sat down between them.

'Well? Haven't seen you for some time, have I? Been at your books?'

'Yes, sir.' On the principle that it is better to attack than to defend, I went straight to the point. 'I . . . I had leave this afternoon, and I went out riding, so I—'

'Where to?'

'Along the river path. Nowhere special, only to improve my horsemanship, so—'

'It could do with it.'

'Yes, sir. So I missed the messenger. They tell me you ride out tomorrow, sir.'

'What's that to you?'

'Only that I would like to come with you.'

'You would like? You would like? What's this, all of a sudden?'

A dozen answers all sounding equally well jostled in my head for expression. I thought I saw my mother watching me with pity, and I knew that my grandfather waited with indifference and impatience only faintly tempered with amusement. I told the simple truth. 'Because I am more than twelve years old, and have never been out of Maridunum. Because I know that if my uncle has his way, I shall soon be shut up, in this valley or elsewhere, to study as a clerk, and before that happens—'

The terrifying brows came down. 'Are you trying to tell me you don't want to study?'

'No. It's what I want more than anything in the world. But study means more if one has seen just a little of the world–indeed, sir, it does. If you would allow me to go with you—'

'I'm going to Segontium, did they tell you that? It's not a feast-day hunting-party, it's a long ride and a hard one, and no quarter given for poor riders.'

It was like lifting a heavy weight, to keep my eyes level on that fierce blue glare. 'I've been practising, sir, and I've a good pony now.'

'Ha, yes, Dinias' breakdown. Well, that's about your measure. No, Merlin, I don't take children.'

'Then you're leaving Dinias behind?'

I heard my mother gasp, and my grandfather's head, already turned away, jerked back to me. I saw his fists clench on the chair arm, but he did not hit me. 'Dinias is a man.'

'Then do Mael and Duach go with you, sir?' They were his two pages, younger than myself, and went everywhere with him.

My mother began to speak, in a breathless rush, but my grandfather moved a hand to stop her. There was an arrested look in the fierce eyes under the scowling brows. 'Mael and Duach are some use to me. What use are you?'

I looked at him. 'Till now, of very little. But have they not told you that I speak Saxon as well as Welsh, and can read Greek, and that my Latin is better than yours?'

'Merlin—' began my mother, but I ignored her.

'I would have added Breton and Cornish, but I doubt if you will have much use for these at Segontium.'

'And can you give me one good reason,' said my grandfather drily, 'why I should speak to King Vortigern in any other language but Welsh, seeing that he comes from Guent?'

I knew from his tone that I had won. Letting my gaze fall from his was like retreating with relief from the battlefield. I drew a breath, and said, very meekly: 'No, sir.'

He gave his great bark of laughter, and thrust out a foot to roll one of the dogs over. 'Well, perhaps there's a bit of the family in you after all, in spite of your looks. At least you've got the guts to beard the old dog in his den when it suits you. All right, you can come. Who attends you?'

'Cerdic.'

'The Saxon? Tell him to get your gear ready. We leave at first light. Well, what are you waiting for?'

'To say good night to my mother.' I rose from my stool and went to kiss her. I did not often do this, and she looked surprised.

Behind me, my grandfather said abruptly: 'You're not going to war. You'll be back inside three weeks. Get out.'

'Yes, sir. Thank you. Good night.'

Outside the door I stood still for a full half minute, leaning against the wall, while my blood-beat steadied slowly, and the sickness cleared from my throat. *The gods only go with you if you put yourself in their path, and that takes courage.*

I swallowed the sickness, wiped the sweat off my palms, and ran to find Cerdic.

Chapter Nine

So it was that I first left Maridunum. At that time it seemed like the greatest adventure in the world, to ride out in the chill of dawn, when stars were still in the sky, and make one of the jostling, companionable group of men who followed Camlach and the King. To begin with most of the men were surly and half asleep, and we rode pretty well in silence, breath smoking in the icy air, and the horses' hoofs striking sparks from the slaty road. Even the jingle of harness sounded cold, and I was so numb that I could hardly feel the reins, and could think of nothing else but how to stay on the excited pony and not get myself sent home in disgrace before we had gone a mile.

And now, because the tales of childhood are tedious, and there are great affairs still to be told, I will pass as quickly as I may over our excursion to Segontium, which lasted eighteen days. It was my first sight of King Vortigern, who had at this time been High King of Britain for more than twenty years. Be sure I had heard plenty about him, truth and tales alike. He was a hard man, as one must be who had taken his throne by murder and held it with blood; but he was a strong king in a time when there was need for strength, and it was not altogether his fault that his stratagem of calling in the Saxons as mercenaries to help him had twisted in his hand like an edged sword slipping, and cut it to the bone. He had paid, and paid again, and then had fought; and now he spent a great part of every year fighting like a wolf to keep the ranging hordes contained along the Saxon Shore. Men spoke of him—with respect—as a fierce and bloodthirsty tyrant, and of his Saxon Queen, Rowena, with hatred as a witch; but though I had been fed from childhood on the tales of the kitchen slaves, I was looking forward to seeing them with more curiosity than fear.

In any event, I need not have been afraid; I saw the High King only from a distance. My grandfather's leniency had extended only to letting me go in his train; once there, I was of no more account—in fact of much less—than his pages Mael and Duach. I was left to fend for myself among the anonymous rabble of boys and servants, and, because my ways had made me no friends among my contemporaries, was left to myself. I was later to be thankful for the fact that, on the few occasions when I was in the crowd surrounding the two kings, Vortigern did not lay eyes on me, and neither my grandfather nor Camlach remembered my existence.

We lay a week at Segontium, which the Welsh call Caer-yn-ar-Von, because it lies just across the strait from Mona, the druids' isle. The town is set, like Maridunum, on the banks of an estuary, where the Seint River meets the sea. It has a splendid harbour, and a fortress placed on the rising ground above this, perhaps half a mile away. The fortress was built by the Romans to protect the harbour and the town, but had lain derelict for over a hundred years until Vortigern put part of it into repair. A little lower down the hill stood another more recent strong-point, built, I believe, by Macsen, grandfather of the murdered Constantius, against the Irish raiders.

The country here was grander than in South Wales, but to my eyes forbidding rather than beautiful. Perhaps in summer the land may be as green and gentle along the estuary, but when I saw it first, that winter, the hills rose behind the town like storm-clouds, their skirts grey with the bare and whistling forests, and their crests slate blue and hooded with snow. Behind and beyond them all towers the great cloudy top of Moel-y-Wyddfa, which now the Saxons call Snow Hill, or Snowdon. It is the highest mountain in all Britain, and is the home of gods.

Vortigern lay, ghosts or no ghosts, in Macsen's Tower. His army—he never moved in those days with less than a thousand fighting men—was quartered in the fort. Of my grandfather's party, the nobles were with the King in the tower, while his train, of which I was one, was housed well enough, if a trifle coldly, near the west gate of the fort. We were treated with honour; not only was Vortigern a distant kinsman of my grandfather's, but it seemed to be true that the High King was—in Cerdic's phrase—'drumming up support'. He was a big dark man, with a broad

fleshy face and black hair as thick and bristled as a boar's, growing grey.
There were black hairs on the back of his hands, and sprouting from his
nostrils. The Queen was not with him; Cerdic whispered to me that he had
not dared bring her where Saxons were so little welcome. When I retorted
that he was only welcome himself because he had forgotten his Saxon and
turned into good Welsh, he laughed and cuffed my ear. I suppose it was not
my fault that I was never very royal.

The pattern of our days was simple. Most of the day was spent hunting,
till at dusk we would return to fires and drink and a full meal, and then the
kings and their advisers turned to talk, and their trains to dicing, wenching,
quarrelling, and whatever other sports they might choose.

I had not been hunting before; as a sport it was foreign to my nature, and
here everyone rode out hurly burly in a crowd, which was something I
disliked. It was also dangerous: there was plenty of game in the foothills,
and there were some wild rides with necks for sale; but I saw no other
chance of seeing the country, and besides, I had to find out why Galapas had
insisted on my coming to Segontium. So I went out every day. I had a few
falls, but got nothing worse than bruises, and managed to attract no
attention, good or bad, from anyone who mattered. Nor did I find what I
was looking for; I saw nothing, and nothing happened except that my
horsemanship improved, and Aster's manners along with it.

On the eighth day of our stay we set off for home, and the High King
himself, with an escort a hundred strong, went with us to set us on our road.

The first part of the way lay along a wooded gorge where a river ran fast
and deep, and where the horses had to go singly or two abreast between the
cliffs and the water. There was no danger for so large a party, so we went at
ease, the gorge ringing with the sound of hoofs and bridle-chains and men's
voices, and the occasional croak overhead as the ravens sailed off the cliffs to
watch us. These birds do not wait, as some say, for the noise of battle; I have
seen them follow armed bands of men for miles, waiting for the clash and
the kill.

But that day we went safely, and near midday we came to the place where
the High King was to part from us and ride back. This was where the two
rivers met, and the gorge opened out into a wider valley, with forbidding
icebound crags of slate to either side, and the big river running south,
brown and swollen with melting snow. There is a ford at the watersmeet,
and leading south from this a good road which goes dry and straight over
high ground towards Tomen-y-Mur.

We halted just north of the ford. Our leaders turned aside into a sheltered
hollow which was cupped on three sides by thickly wooded slopes. Clumps
of bare alder and thick reeds showed that in summer the hollow would be
marsh-land; on that December day it was solidly frostbound, but protected
from the wind, and the sun came warmly. Here the party stopped to eat and
rest. The kings sat apart, talking, and near them the rest of the royal party. I
noticed that it included Dinias. I, as usual, finding myself not of the royal
group, not with the men-at-arms, nor yet the servants, handed Aster to
Cerdic, then went apart, climbing a short way among the trees to a wooded
dell where I could sit alone and out of sight of the others. At my back was a
rock thawed by the sun, and from the other side of this came, muffled, the

jingle of bits as horses grazed, the men's voices talking, and an occasional guffaw, then the rhythmic silences and mutterings that told me the dice had come out to pass the time till the kings completed their farewell. A kite tilted and swung above me in the cold air, the sun striking bronze from its wings. I thought of Galapas, and the bronze mirror flashing, and wondered why I had come.

King Vortigern's voice said suddenly, just behind me: 'This way. You can tell me what you think.'

I had whipped round, startled, before I realised that he, and the man he was speaking to, were on the other side of the rock that sheltered me.

'Five miles, they tell me, in either direction . . .' The High King's voice dwindled as he turned away. I heard footsteps on the frosty ground, dead leaves crackling, and the jar of nailed boots on stone. They were moving off. I stood up, taking it carefully, and peered over the rock. Vortigern and my grandfather were walking up through the wood together, deep in talk.

I remember that I hesitated. What, after all, could they have to say that could not already have been said in the privacy of Macsen's Tower? I could not believe that Galapas had sent me merely as a spy on their conference. But why else? Perhaps the god in whose way I had put myself had sent me here alone, today, for this. Reluctantly, I turned to follow them.

As I took the first step after them a hand caught my arm, not gently: 'And where do you think you're going?' demanded Cerdic under his breath.

I shook him off violently. 'Damn you, Cerdic, you nearly made me jump out of my skin! What does it matter to you where I'm going?'

'I'm here to look after you, remember?'

'Only because I brought you. No one tells you to look after me, these days. Or do they?' I looked at him sharply. 'Have you followed me before?'

He grinned. 'To tell you the truth, I never troubled. Should I have?'

But I persisted. 'Did anyone tell you to watch me today?'

'No. But didn't you see who went this way? It was Vortigern and your grandfather. If you'd any idea of wandering after them, I'd think again if I was you.'

'I wasn't going "after them",' I lied. 'I was merely taking a look round.'

'Then I'd do it elsewhere. They said special that the escort had to wait down here. I came to make sure you knew it, that's all. Very special about it, they was.'

I sat down again. 'All right, you've made sure. Now leave me again, please. You can come and tell me when we're due to move off.'

'And have you belting off the minute my back's turned?'

I felt the blood rise to my cheeks. 'Cerdic, I told you to go.'

He said doggedly: 'Look, I know you, and I know when you look like that. I don't know what's in your mind, but when you get that look in your eye there's trouble for somebody, and it's usually you. What's to do?'

I said furiously: 'The trouble's for you this time, if you don't do as I say.'

'Don't go all royal on me,' he said. 'I was only trying to save you a beating.'

'I know that. Forgive me. I had—something on my mind.'

'You can tell me, can't you? I knew there'd been something biting you this last few days. What is it?'

'Nothing that I know of,' I said truthfully. 'Nothing you can help with. Forget it. Look, did the kings say where they were going? They could have talked their fill at Segontium, surely, or on the ride here?'

'They've gone to the top of the crag. There's a place up there at the end of the ridge where you can look right up and down the valley, all ways. There used to be an old tower there, they say. They call it Dinas Brenin.'

'King's Fort? How big's the tower?'

'There's nothing there now but a tumble of stones. Why?'

'I—nothing. When do we ride home, I wonder?'

'Another hour, they said. Look, why don't you come down, and I'll cut you in on a dice game?'

I grinned. 'Thanks for nothing. Have I kept you out of your game, too? I'm sorry.'

'Don't mention it. I was losing anyway. All right, I'll leave you alone, but you wouldn't think of doing anything silly now, would you? No sense in sticking your neck out. Remember what I told you about the ring-dove?'

And at that exact moment, a ring-dove went by like an arrow, with a clap and whistle of wings that sent a flurry of frost like a wake. Close behind her, a little above, ready to strike, went a merlin.

The dove rose a fraction as she met the slope, skimming up as a gull skims a rising wave, hurtling towards a thicket near the lip of the dell. She was barely a foot from the ground, and for the falcon to strike her was dangerous, but he must have been starving, for, just as she reached the edge of the thicket, he struck.

A scream, a fierce *kwik-ik-ik* from the falcon, a flurry of crashing twigs, then nothing. A few feathers drifted lazily down, like snow.

I started forward, and ran up the bank. 'He got her!' It was obvious what had happened; both birds, locked together, had hurtled on into the thicket and crashed to the ground. From the silence, it was probable that they both now lay there, stunned.

The thicket was a steep tangle almost covering one side of the dell. I thrust the boughs aside and pushed my way through. The trail of feathers showed me my way. Then I found them. The dove lay dead, breast downwards, wings still spread out as she had struck the stones, with blood smearing bright over the iris of her neck feathers. On her lay the merlin. The steel ripping-claws were buried deep in the dove's back, the cruel beak half driven in by the crash. He was still alive. As I bent over them his wings stirred, and the bluish eyelids dropped, disclosing the fierce dark eye.

Cerdic arrived, panting, at my shoulder. 'Don't touch him. He'll tear your hands. Let me.'

I straightened. 'So much for your ring-dove, Cerdic. It's time we forgot her, isn't it? No, leave them. They'll be here when we come back.'

'Come back? Where from?'

I pointed silently to what showed ahead, directly in the path the birds had been taking. A square black gap like a door in the steep ground behind the thicket; an entrance hidden from casual sight, only to be seen if, for some reason, one pushed one's way in among the tangled branches.

'What of it?' asked Cerdic. 'That's an old mine adit, by the look of it.'

'Yes. That's what I came to see. Strike a light, and come along.'

He began to protest, but I cut him short. 'You can come or not, as you please. But give me a light. And hurry, there isn't much time.' As I began to push my way towards the adit I heard him, muttering still, dragging up handfuls of dry stuff to make a torch.

Just inside the adit there was a pile of debris and fallen stone where the timber props had rotted away, but beyond this the shaft was smooth enough, leading more or less levelly into the heart of the hill. I could walk pretty nearly upright, and Cerdic, who was small, had to stoop only slightly. The flare of the makeshift torch threw our shadows grotesquely in front of us. It showed the grooves in the floor where loads had been dragged to daylight, and on walls and roof the marks of the picks and chisels that had made the tunnel.

'Where the hell do you think you're going?' Cerdic's voice, behind me, was sharp with nerves. 'Look, let's get back. These places aren't safe. That roof could come in.'

'It won't. Keep that torch going,' I said curtly, and went on.

The tunnel bent to the right, and began to curve gently downhill. Underground one loses all sense of direction; there is not even the drift of wind on one's cheek that gives direction even on the blackest night; but I guessed that we must be winding our way deep into the heart of the hill on which had stood the old King's tower. Now and again smaller tunnels led off to left and right, but there was no danger of losing our way; we were in the main gallery, and the rock seemed reasonably good. Here and there had been falls from roof or wall, and once I was brought to a halt by a fall of rubble which almost blocked the way, but I climbed through, and the tunnel was clear beyond.

Cerdic had stopped at the barrier of rubble. He advanced the torch and peered after me. 'Hey, look, Merlin, come back, for pity's sake! This is beyond any kind of folly. I tell you, these places are dangerous, and we're getting down into the very guts of the rock. The gods alone know what lives down here. Come on back, boy.'

'Don't be a coward, Cerdic, there's plenty of room for you. Come on through. Quickly.'

'That I won't. If you don't come out this minute, I swear I'll go back and tell the King.'

'Look,' I said, 'this is important. Don't ask me why. But I swear to you there's no danger. If you're afraid, then give me that torch, and get back.'

'You know I can't do that.'

'Yes, I know. You wouldn't dare go back to tell him, would you? And if you did leave me, and anything happened, what do you suppose would happen to you?'

'They say right when they say you're a devil's spawn,' said Cerdic.

I laughed. 'You can say what you like to me when we're back in daylight, but hurry now, Cerdic, please. You're safe, I promise you. There's no harm in the air today, and you saw how the merlin showed us the door.'

He came, of course. Poor Cerdic, he could afford to do nothing else. But as he stood beside me again, with the torch held up, I saw him looking at me sideways, and his left hand was making the sign against the evil eye.

'Don't be long,' he said, 'that's all.'

Twenty paces further, round a curve, the tunnel led into the cavern.

I made a sign to him to lift the torch. I could not have spoken. This vast hollow, right in the hill's heart, this darkness hardly touched by the torch's flare, this dead stillness of air where I could hear and feel my own blood beating–this, of course, was the place. I recognised every mark of the workings, the face seamed and split by the axes, and smashed open by the water. There was the domed roof disappearing into darkness, there in a corner some rusty metal where the pump had stood. There the shining moisture on the wall, no longer a ribbon, but a curtain of gleaming damp. And there where the puddles had lain, and the seepage under the overhang, a wide, still pool. Fully a third of the floor was under water.

The air had a strange smell all its own, the breath of the water and the living rock. Somewhere above, water dripped, each tap clear like a small hammer on metal. I took the smouldering faggot from Cerdic's hand, and went to the water's edge. I held the light as high as I could, out over the water, and gazed down. There was nothing to see. The light glanced back from a surface as hard as metal. I waited. The light ran, and gleamed, and drowned in darkness. There was nothing there but my own reflection, like the ghost in Galapas' mirror.

I gave the torch back to Cerdic. He hadn't spoken. He was watching me all the time with that sidelong, white-eyed look.

I touched his arm. 'We can go back now. This thing's nearly out anyway. Come on.'

We didn't speak as we made our way back along the curving gallery, past the rubble, through the adit and out into the frosty afternoon. The sky was a pale, milky blue. The winter trees stood brittle and quiet against it, the birches white as bone. From below a horn called, urgent, in the still metallic air.

'They're going.' Cerdic drove the torch down into the frozen ground to extinguish it. I scrambled down through the thicket. The dove still lay there, cold, and stiff already. The merlin was there too; it had withdrawn from the body of its kill, and sat near it on a stone, hunched and motionless, even when I approached. I picked up the ring-dove and threw it to Cerdic. 'Shove it in your saddle-bag. I don't have to tell you to say nothing of this, do I?'

'You do not. What are you doing?'

'He's stunned. If we leave him here he'll freeze to death in an hour. I'm taking him.'

'Take care! That's a grown falcon—'

'He'll not hurt me.' I picked up the merlin; he had fluffed his feathers out against the cold, and felt soft as a young owl in my hands. I pulled my leather sleeve down over my left wrist, and he took hold of this, gripping fiercely. The eyelids were open now, and the wild dark eyes watched me. But he sat still, with shut wings. I heard Cerdic muttering to himself as he bent to retrieve my things from the place where I had taken my meal. Then he added something I had never heard from him before. 'Come on then, young master.'

The merlin stayed docile on my wrist as I fell in at the back of my grandfather's train for the ride home to Maridunum.

Chapter Ten

Nor did it attempt to leave me when we reached home. I found, on examining it, that some of its wing feathers had been damaged in that hurtling crash after the ring-dove, so I mended them as Galapas had taught me, and after that it sat in the pear tree outside my window, accepting the food I gave it, and making no attempt to fly away.

I took it with me when next I went to see Galapas.

This was on the first day of February, and the frost had broken the night before, in rain. It was a grey leaden day, with low cloud and a bitter little wind among the rain. Draughts whistled everywhere in the palace, and curtains were fast drawn across the doors, while people kept on their woollen cloaks and huddled over the braziers. It seemed to me that a grey and leaden silence hung also over the palace; I had hardly seen my grandfather since we had returned to Maridunum, but he and the nobles sat together in council for hours, and there were rumours of quarrelling and raised voices when he and Camlach were closeted together. Once when I went to my mother's room I was told she was at her prayers and could not see me. I caught a glimpse of her through the half-open door, and I could have sworn that as she knelt below the holy image she was weeping.

But in the high valley nothing had changed. Galapas took the merlin, commended my work on its wings, then set it on a sheltered ledge near the cave's entrance, and bade me come to the fire and get warm. He ladled some stew out of the simmering pot, and made me eat it before he would listen to my story. Then I told him everything, up to the quarrels in the palace and my mother's tears.

'It was the same cave, Galapas, that I'll swear! But why? There was nothing there. And nothing else happened, nothing at all. I've asked as best I could, and Cerdic has asked about among the slaves, but nobody knows what the kings discussed, or why my grandfather and Camlach have fallen out. But he did tell me one thing; I am being watched. By Camlach's people. I'd have come to see you sooner, except for that. They've gone out today, Camlach and Alun and the rest, so I said I was going to the water-meadow to train the merlin, and I came up here.'

Then as he was still silent, I repeated, worried into urgency: 'What's happening, Galapas? What does it all mean?'

'About your dream, and your finding of the cavern, I know nothing. About the trouble in the palace, I can guess. You knew that the High King had sons by his first marriage, Vortimer and Katigern and young Pascentius?'

I nodded.

'Were none of them there at Segontium?'

'No.'

'I am told that they have broken with their father,' said Galapas, 'and Vortimer is raising troops of his own. They say he would like to be High King, and that Vortigern looks like having a rebellion on his hands when he can least afford it. The Queen's much hated, you know that; Vortimer's mother was good British, and besides, the young men want a young king.'

'Camlach is for Vortimer, then?' I asked quickly, and he smiled.

'It seems so.'

I thought about it for a little. 'Well, when wolves fall out, don't they say the ravens come into their own?' As one born in September, under Mercury, the raven was mine.

'Perhaps,' said Galapas. 'You're more likely to be clapped in your cage sooner than you expected.' But he said it absently, as if his mind were elsewhere, and I went back to what concerned me most.

'Galapas, you've said you know nothing about the dream or the cavern. But this—this must have been the hand of the god.' I glanced up at the ledge where the merlin sat, broodingly patient, his eyes half shut, slits of firelight.

'It would seem so.'

I hesitated. 'Can't we find out what he—what it means?'

'Do you want to go into the crystal cave again?'

'N-no, I don't. But I think perhaps I should. Surely you can tell me that?'

He said heavily, after a few moments: 'I think you must go in, yes. But first, I must teach you something more. You must make the fire for yourself this time. Not like that—' smiling, as I reached for a branch to stir the embers. 'Put that down. You asked me before you went away to show you something real. This is all I have left to show you. I hadn't realised . . . Well, let that go. It's time. No, sit still, you have no more need of books, child. Watch now.'

Of the next thing, I shall not write. It was all the art he taught me, apart from certain tricks of healing. But as I have said, it was the first magic to come to me, and will be the last to go. I found it easy, even to make the ice-cold fire and the wild fire, and the fire that goes like a whip through the dark; which was just as well, because I was young to be taught such things, and it is an art which, if you are unfit or unprepared, can strike you blind.

It was dark outside when we had done. He got to his feet.

'I shall come back in an hour and wake you.'

He twitched his cloak down from where it hung shrouding the mirror, put it round him, and went out.

The flames sounded like a horse galloping. One long, bright tongue cracked like a whip. A log fell down with a hiss like a woman's sigh, and then a thousand twigs crackled like people talking, whispering, chattering of news . . .

It faded all into a great brilliant blaze of silence. The mirror flashed. I picked up my cloak, now comfortably dry, and climbed with it into the crystal cave. I folded it and lay down on it, with my eyes fixed on the wall of crystal arching over me. The flames came after me, rank on bright rank, filling the air, till I lay in a globe of light like the inside of a star, growing brighter and even brighter till suddenly it broke and there was darkness . . .

The galloping hoofs sparked on the gravel of the Roman road. The rider's whip cracked and cracked again, but the horse was already going full tilt, its nostrils wide and scarlet, its breath like steam in the cold air. The rider was Camlach. Far behind him, almost half a mile behind now, were the rest of the young men of his party, and still further behind them, leading his lamed and dripping horse, came the messenger who had taken the news to the King's son.

The town was alive with torches, men running to meet the galloping horse, but Camlach paid no heed to them. He drove the spiked spurs into the horse's sides, and galloped straight through the town, down the steep street, and into the outer yard of the palace. There were torches there, too. They caught the quick glint of his red hair as he swung from the horse and flung the reins into the hands of a waiting slave. The soft riding boots made no sound as he ran up the steps and along the colonnade that led to his father's room. The swift black figure was lost for a moment in shadow under the arch, then he flung the door wide and went through.

The messenger had been right. It had been a quick death. The old man lay on the carved Roman bed, and over him someone had thrown a coverlet of purple silk. They had somehow managed to prop his jaw, for the fierce grey beard jutted ceilingwards, and a little head-rest of baked clay beneath his neck held his head straight, while the body slowly froze iron-hard. There was no sign, the way he lay, that the neck was broken. Already the old face had begun to fall away, to shrink, as death pared the flesh down from the jut of the nose till it would be left simply in planes of cold candlewax. The gold coins that lay on his mouth and shut eyelids glimmered in the light of the torches at the four corners of the bed.

At the foot of the bed, between the torches, stood Niniane. She stood very still and upright, dressed in white, her hands folded quietly in front of her with a crucifix between them, her head bent. When the door opened she did not look up, but kept her eyes fixed on the purple coverlet, not in grief, but almost as if she were too far away for thought.

To her side, swiftly, came her brother, slim in his black clothes, glinting with a kind of furious grace that seemed to shock the room.

He walked right up to the bed and stood over it, staring down at his father. Then he put down a hand and laid it over the dead hands clasped on the purple silk. His hand lingered there for a moment, then drew back. He looked at Niniane. Behind her, a few paces back in the shadows, the little crowd of men, women, servants, shuffled and whispered. Among them, silent and dry-eyed, Mael and Duach stared. Dinias, too, all his attention fixed on Camlach.

Camlach spoke very softly, straight to Niniane. 'They told me it was an accident. Is this true?'

She neither moved nor spoke. He stared at her for a moment, then with a gesture of irritation, looked beyond her, and raised his voice.

'One of you, answer me. This was an accident?'

A man stepped forward, one of the King's servants, a man called Mabon.

'It's true, my lord.' He licked his lips, hesitating.

Camlach showed his teeth. 'What in the name of the devils in hell's the matter with you all?' Then he saw where they were staring, and looked down at his right hip, where, sheathless, his short stabbing dagger had been thrust through his belt. It was blood to the hilt. He made a sound of impatience and disgust and, pulling it out, flung it from him, so that it skittered across the floor and came up against the wall with a small clang that sounded loud in the silence.

'Whose blood did you think?' he asked, still with that lifted lip. 'Deer's blood, that's all. When the message came, we had just killed. I was twelve miles off, I and my men.' He stared at them, as if daring them to comment. No one moved. 'Go on, Mabon. He slipped and fell, the man told me. How did it happen?'

The man cleared his throat. 'It was a stupid thing, sir, a pure accident. Why, no one was even near him. It was in the small courtyard, the way through to the servants' rooms, where the steps are worn. One of the men had been carrying oil around to fill the lamps. He'd spilt some on the steps, and before he got back to wipe it up the King came through, in a bit of a hurry. He—he hadn't been expected there at the time. Well, my lord, he treads in the oil, and goes straight down on his back, and hits his head on the stone. That's how it happened, my lord. It was seen. There's those that can vouch for it.'

'And the man whose fault it was?'

'A slave, my lord.'

'He's been dealt with?'

'My lord, he's dead.'

While they had been talking there had been a commotion in the colonnade, as the rest of Camlach's party arrived and came hurrying along to the King's room after him. They had pressed into the room while Mabon was speaking, and now Alun, approaching the prince quietly, touched his arm.

'The news is all round the town, Camlach. There's a crowd gathering outside. A million stories going round–there'll be trouble soon. You'll have to show yourself and talk to them.'

Camlach flicked him a glance, and nodded. 'Go and see to it, will you? Bran, go with him, and Ruan. Shut the gates. Tell the people I'm coming out soon. And now, the rest of you, out.'

The room emptied. Dinias lingered in the doorway, got not even a glance, and followed the rest. The door shut.

'Well, Niniane?'

In all this time she had never looked at him. Now she raised her eyes. 'What do you want of me? It's true as Mabon tells you. What he didn't say was that the King had been fooling with a servant-girl and was drunk. But it was an accident, and he's dead . . . And you with all your friends were a good twelve miles away. So you're King now, Camlach, and there is no man can point a finger at you and say, "He wanted his father dead."'

'No woman can say that to me either, Niniane.'

'I have not said it. I'm just telling you that the quarrels here are over. The kingdom's yours–and now it's as Alun says, you had better go and speak to the people.'

'To you first. Why do you stand like that, as if you didn't care either way? As if you were scarcely with us here?'

'Perhaps because it's true. What you are, brother, and what you want, does not concern me, except to ask you one thing.'

'And that is?'

'That you let me go now. He never would, but I think you will.'

'To St Peter's?'

She bent her head. 'I told you nothing here concerned me any more. It has not concerned me for some time, and less than ever now, with all this talk about invasion, and war in the spring, and the rumours about shifts of power and the death of kings . . . Oh, don't look at me like that; I'm not a fool, and my father talked to me. But you need not be afraid of me; nothing I know or can do can ever harm your plans for yourself, brother. I tell you, there is nothing I want out of life now except to be allowed to go in peace, and live in peace, and my son too.'

'You said "one thing". That makes two.'

For the first time something came to life in her eyes; it might have been fear. She said swiftly: 'It was always the plan for him, your plan, even before it was my father's. Surely, after the day Gorlan went, you knew that even if Merlin's father could come riding in, sword in hand and with three thousand men at his back, I would not go to him? Merlin can do you no harm, Camlach. He will never be anything but a nameless bastard, and you know he is no warrior. The gods know he can do you no harm at all.'

'And even less shut up as a clerk?' Camlach's voice was silky.

'Even less, shut up as a clerk. Camlach, are you playing with me? What's in your mind?'

'This slave who spilt the oil,' he said. 'Who was he?'

That flicker in her eyes again. Then the lids dropped. 'The Saxon. Cerdic.'

He didn't move, but the emerald on his breast glittered suddenly against the black as if his heart had jumped.

She said fiercely: 'Don't pretend you guessed this! How could you guess it?'

'Not a guess, no. When I rode in the place was humming with whispers like a smashed harp.' He added, in sudden irritation: 'You stand there like a ghost with your hands on your belly as if you still had a bastard there to protect.'

Surprisingly, she smiled. 'But I have.' Then as the emerald leapt again: 'No, don't be a fool. Where would I get another bastard now? I meant that I cannot go until I know he is safe from you. And that we are both safe from what you propose to do.'

'From what I propose to do to *you*? I swear to you there is nothing—'

'I am talking about my father's kingdom. But let it go now. I told you, my only concern is that St Peter's should be left in peace . . . And it will be.'

'You saw this in the crystal?'

'It is unlawful for a Christian to dabble in soothsaying,' said Niniane, but her voice was a little over-prim, and he looked sharply at her, then, suddenly restless, took a couple of strides away into the shadows at the side of the room, then back into the light. 'Tell me,' he said abruptly. 'What of Vortimer?'

'He will die,' she said indifferently.

'We shall all die, some day. But you know I am committed to him now. Can you not tell me what will happen this coming spring?'

'I see nothing and I can tell you nothing. But whatever your plans for the kingdom, it will serve no purpose to let even the smallest whisper of murder start, and I can tell you this, you're a fool if you think that the King's death was anything but an accident. Two of the grooms saw it happen, and the girl he'd been with.'

'Did the man say anything before they killed him?'

'Cerdic? No. Only that it was an accident. He seemed concerned more for my son than for himself. It was all he said.'

'So I heard,' said Camlach.

The silence came back. They stared at one another. She said: 'You would not.'

He didn't answer. They stood there, eyes locked, while a draught crept through the room, making the torches gutter.

Then he smiled, and went. As the door slammed shut behind him a gust of air blew through the room, and tore the flames along from the torches, till shadow and light went reeling.

The flames were dying, and the crystals dim. As I climbed out of the cave and pulled my cloak after me, it tore. The embers in the brazier showed a sullen red. Outside, now, it was quite dark. I stumbled down from the ledge and ran towards the doorway.

'Galapas!' I shouted. 'Galapas!'

He was there. His tall, stooping figure detached itself from the darkness outside, and he came forward into the cave. His feet, half-bare in his old sandals, looked blue with cold.

I came to a halt a yard from him, but it was as if I had run straight into his arms, and been folded against his cloak.

'Galapas, they've killed Cerdic.'

He said nothing, but his silence was like words or hands of comfort.

I swallowed to shift the ache in my throat. 'If I hadn't come up here this afternoon . . . I gave him the slip, along with the others. But I could have trusted him, even about you. Galapas, if I'd stayed–if I'd been there–perhaps I could have done something.'

'No. You counted for nothing. You know that.'

'I'll count for less than nothing now.' I put a hand to my head; it was aching fiercely, and my eyes swam, still half-blind. He took me gently by the arm and made me sit down near the fire.

'Why do you say that? A moment, Merlin, tell me what has happened.'

'Don't you know?' I said, surprised. 'He was filling the lamps in the colonnade, and some oil spilled on the steps, and the King slipped in it and fell and broke his neck. It wasn't Cerdic's fault, Galapas. He spilt the oil, that's all, and he was going back, he was actually going back to clean it up when it happened. So they took him and killed him.'

'And now Camlach is King.'

I think I stared at him for some time, unseeing with those dream-blinded eyes, my brain for the moment incapable of holding more than the single fact.

He persisted, gently: 'And your mother? What of her?'

'What? What did you say?'

The warm shape of a goblet was put into my hand. I could smell the same drink that he had given me before when I dreamed in the cave. 'Drink that. You should have slept till I wakened you, then it wouldn't have come like this. Drink it all.'

As I drank, the sharp ache in my temples dulled to a throb, and the swimming shapes round me drew back into focus. And with them, thought.

'I'm sorry. It's all right now, I can think again, I've come back . . . I'll tell you the rest. My mother's to go into St Peter's. She tried to make Camlach promise to let me go too, but he wouldn't. I think . . .'

'Yes?'

I said slowly, thinking hard now: 'I didn't understand it all. I was thinking about Cerdic. But I believe he's going to kill me. I believe he will use my grandfather's death for this; he'll say that my slave did it . . . Oh, nobody will believe that I could take anything from Camlach, but if he does shut me up in a religious house, and then I die quietly, a little time after, then by that time the whispers will have worked, and nobody will raise a voice about it. And by that time, if my mother is just one of the holy women at St Peter's, and no longer the King's daughter, she won't have a voice to raise, either.' I cupped my hands round the goblet, looking across at him. 'Why should anyone fear me so, Galapas?'

He did not answer that, but nodded to the goblet in my hands. 'Finish it. Then, my dear, you must go.'

'Go? But if I go back, they'll kill me, or shut me up . . . Won't they?'

'If they find you, they will try.'

I said eagerly: 'If I stayed here with you—nobody knows I come here—even if they found out and came after me, you'd be in no danger! We'd see them coming up the valley for miles, or we'd know they were coming, you and I . . . They'd never find me; I could go in the crystal cave.'

He shook his head. 'The time for that isn't come. One day, but not now. You can no more be hidden now, than your merlin could go back into its egg.'

I glanced back over my shoulder at the ledge where the merlin had sat brooding, still as Athene's owl. There was no bird there. I wiped the back of a hand across my eyes, and blinked, not believing. But it was true. The firelit shadows were empty.

'Galapas, it's gone!'

'Yes.'

'Did you see it go?'

'It went by when you called me back into the cave.'

'I—which way?'

'South.'

I drank the rest of the potion, then turned the goblet up to spill the last drops for the god. Then I set it down and reached for my cloak.

'I'll see you again, won't I?'

'Yes. I promise you that.'

'Then I shall come back?'

'I promised you that already. Some day, the cave will be yours, and all that is in it.'

Past him, in from the night, came a cold stray breath of air that stirred my cloak and lifted the hairs on my nape. My flesh prickled. I got up and swung the cloak round me and fastened the pin.

'You're going, then?' He was smiling. 'You trust me so much? Where do you plan to go?'

'I don't know. Home, I suppose, to start with. I'll have time to think on the way there, if I need to. But I'm still in the god's path. I can feel the wind blowing. Why are you smiling Galapas?'

But he would not answer that. He stood up, then pulled me towards him and stooped and kissed me. His kiss was dry and light, an old man's kiss, like a dead leaf drifting down to brush the flesh. Then he pushed me towards the entrance. 'Go. I saddled your pony ready for you.'

It was raining still as I rode down the valley. The rain was cold and small, and soaking; it gathered on my cloak and dragged at my shoulders, and mixed with the tears that ran down my face.

This was the second time in my life that I wept.

Chapter Eleven

The stableyard gate was locked. This was no more than I had expected. That day I had gone out openly through the main yard with the merlin, and any other night might have chanced riding back the same way, with some story of losing my falcon and riding about till dark to look for it. But not tonight.

And tonight there would be no one waiting and listening for me, to let me in.

Though the need for haste was breathing on the back of my neck, I kept the impatient pony to a walk, and rode quietly along under the palace wall in the direction of the bridge. This, and the road leading to it, was alive with people and torches and noise, and twice in the few minutes since I had come in sight of it a horseman went galloping headlong out over the bridge, going south.

Now the wet, bare trees of the orchard overhung the towpath. There was a ditch here below the high wall, and over it the boughs hung, dripping. I slid off the pony's back and led him in under my leaning apple tree, and tethered him. Then I scrambled back into the saddle, got unsteadily to my feet, balanced for a moment, and jumped for the bough above me.

It was soaking, and one of my hands slipped, but the other held. I swung my legs up, cocked them over the bough, and after that it was only the work of moments to scramble over the wall, and down into the orchard grasses.

There to my left was the high wall which masked my grandfather's garden, to the right the dovecot and the raised terrace where Moravik used to sit with her spinning. Ahead of me was the low sprawl of the servants' quarters. To my relief hardly a light showed. All the light and uproar of the palace was concentrated beyond the wall to my left, in the main building. From even further beyond, and muted by the rain, came the tumult of the streets.

But no light showed in my window. I ran.

What I hadn't reckoned on was that they should have brought him here, to his old place. His pallet lay now, not across the door, but back in the corner, near my bed. There was no purple here, no torches; he lay just as they had flung him down. All I could see in the half-darkness was the ungainly sprawled body, with an arm flung wide and the hand splayed on the cold floor. It was too dark to see how he had died.

I stooped over him and took the hand. It was cold already, and the arm had begun to stiffen. I lifted it gently to the pallet beside his body, then ran to my bed and snatched up the fine woollen coverlet. I spread it over Cerdic, then jerked upright, listening, as a man's voice called something in the distance, and then there were footsteps at the end of the colonnade, and the answer, shouted:

'No. He's not come this way. I've been watching the door. Is the pony in yet?'

'No. No sign.' And then, in reply to another shout: 'Well, he can't have ridden far. He's often out till this time. What? Oh, very well . . .'

The footsteps went, rapidly. Silence.

There was a lamp in its stand somewhere along the colonnade. This dealt enough light through the half-open door for me to see what I was doing. I silently lifted the lid of my chest, pulled out the few clothes I had, with my best cloak, and a spare pair of sandals. I bundled these all together in a bag, together with my other possessions, my ivory comb, a couple of brooches, a cornelian clasp. These I could sell. I climbed on the bed and pitched the bag out of the window. Then I ran back to Cerdic, pulled aside the coverlet, and, kneeling, fumbled at his hip. They had left his dagger. I tugged at the clasp with fingers that were clumsier even than the darkness made them, and it came undone. I took it, belt and all, a man's dagger, twice as long as my own, and honed to a killing point. Mine I laid beside him on the pallet. He might need it where he had gone, but I doubted it; his hands had always been enough.

I was ready. I stood looking down at him for a moment longer, and saw instead, as in the flashing crystal, how they had laid my grandfather, with the torchlight and the watchers and the purple. Nothing here but darkness, a dog's death. A slave's death.

'Cerdic.' I said it half aloud, in the darkness. I wasn't weeping now. That was over. 'Cerdic, rest you now. I'll send you the way you wanted, like a king.'

I ran to the door, listened for a moment, then slipped through into the deserted colonnade. I lifted the lamp from its bracket. It was heavy, and oil spilled. Of course; he had filled it just that evening.

Back in my own room I carried the lamp over to where he lay. Now–what

I had not foreseen—I could see how he had died. They had cut his throat.

Even if I had not intended it, it would have happened. The lamp shook in my hand, and hot oil splashed on the coverlet. A burning fragment broke from the wick, fell, caught, hissed. Then I flung the lamp down on the body, and watched for five long seconds while the flame ran into the oil and burst like blazing spray.

'Go with your gods, Cerdic,' I said, and jumped for the window.

I landed on the bundle and went sprawling in the wet grass, then snatched it up and ran for the river wall.

Not to frighten the pony, I made for a place some yards beyond the apple tree, and pitched the bag over the wall into the ditch. Then back to the tree, and up it, to the high coping.

Astride of this, I glanced back. The fire had caught. My window glowed now, red with pulsing light. No alarm had yet been given, but it could only be a matter of moments before the flames were seen, or someone smelled the smoke. I scrambled over, hung by my hands for a moment, then let myself drop. As I got to my feet a shadow, towering, jumped at me and struck.

I went down with a man's heavy body on top of me, pinning me to the muddy grass. A splayed hand came hard down on my face, choking my cry off short. Just near me was a quick footstep, the rasp of drawn metal, and a man's voice saying, urgently, in Breton: 'Wait. Make him talk first.'

I lay quite still. This was easy to do, for not only had the force of the first man's attack driven the breath right out of my body, but I could feel his knife at my throat. Then as the second man spoke, my captor, with a surprised grunt, shifted his weight from me, and the knife withdrew an inch or two.

He said, in a tone between surprise and disgust: 'It's only a boy.' Then to me, harshly, in Welsh: 'Not a sound out of you, or I'll slit your throat here and now. Understood?'

I nodded. He took his hand from my mouth, and getting up, dragged me to my feet. He rammed me back against the wall, holding me there, the knife still pricking my collarbone. 'What's all this? What are you doing bolting out of the palace like a rat with the dogs after it? A thief? Come on, you little rat, before I choke you.'

He shook me as if I were indeed a rat. I managed to gasp: 'Nothing. I was doing no harm! Let me go!'

The other man said softly, out of the darkness: 'Here's what he threw over the wall. A bag full of stuff.'

'What's in it?' demanded my captor. And to me, 'Keep quiet, you.'

He had no need to warn me. I thought I could smell smoke now, and see the first flicker of light as my fire took hold of the roof beams. I flattened myself back even further into the black shadow under the wall.

The other man was examining my bundle. 'Clothes . . . sandals . . . some jewellery by the feel of it . . .'

He had moved out on to the towpath, and, with my eyes now used to the darkness, I could make him out. A little weasel of a man, with bent shoulders, and a narrow, pointed face under a straggle of hair. No one I had ever seen.

I gave a gasp of relief. 'You're not the King's men! Who are you, then?

What do you want here?'

The weaselly man stopped rooting in my bag and stared.

'That's no concern of yours,' said the big man who held me. 'We'll ask the questions. Why should you be so scared of the King's men? You know them all, eh?'

'Of course I do. I live in the palace. I'm—a slave there.'

'Marric—' it was the Weasel, sharply—'look over there, there's a fire started. They're buzzing like a wasp's nest. No point in wasting time here over a runaway slave-brat. Slit his throat and let's run for it while we can.'

'A moment,' said the big man, 'he may know something. Look now, you—'

'If you're going to slit my throat anyway,' I said, 'why should I tell you anything? *Who are you?*'

He ducked his head forward suddenly, peering at me. 'Crowing mighty fine all of a sudden, aren't you? Never mind who *we* are. A slave, eh? Running away?'

'Yes.'

'Been stealing?'

'No.'

'No? The jewellery in the bundle? And this—this isn't a slave's cloak.' He tightened his grip on the stuff at my throat till I squirmed. 'And that pony? Come on, the truth.'

'All right.' I hoped I sounded sullen and cowed enough for a slave now. 'I did take a few things. It's the prince's pony, Myrddin's . . . I—I found it straying. Truly, sir. He went out today and he's not back yet. He'll have been thrown, he's a rotten horseman. I—it was a bit of luck—they won't miss it till I'm well away.' I plucked at his clothes beseechingly. 'Please, sir, let me go. Please! What harm could I do—?'

'Marric, for pity's sake, there's no time.' The flames had taken hold now, and were leaping. There was shouting from the palace, and the Weasel pulled at my captor's arm. 'The tide's going out fast, and the gods only know if she's there at all, this weather. Listen to the noise—they'll be coming this way any minute.'

'They won't,' I said. 'They'll be too busy putting the fire out to think of anything else. It was well away when I left it.'

'When you left it?' Marric hadn't budged; he was staring down at me, and his grip was less fierce. 'Did *you* start that fire?'

'Yes.'

I had their full attention now, even Weasel's.

'Why?'

'I did it because I hate them. They killed my friend.'

'Who did?'

'Camlach and his people. The new King.'

There was a short silence. I could see Marric better now. He was a big, burly man, with a bush of black hair, and black eyes that glinted in the fire.

'And,' I added, 'if I'd stayed, they'd have killed me, too. So I burned the place and ran away. Please let me go now.'

'Why should they want to kill you? They'll want to now, of course, with the place going up like a torch—but why, before that? What had you done?'

'Nothing. But I was the old King's slave, and . . . I suppose I heard things. Slaves hear everything. Camlach thinks I might be dangerous . . . He has plans . . . I knew about them. Believe me, sir,' I said earnestly, 'I'd have served him as well as I did the old King, but then he killed my friend.'

'What friend? And why?'

'Another slave, a Saxon, his name was Cerdic. He spilled oil on the steps, and the old King fell. It was an accident, but they cut his throat.'

Marric turned his head to the other. 'Hear that, Hanno? That's true enough. I heard it in the town.' Then back to me: 'All right. Now you can tell us a bit more. You say you know Camlach's plans?'

But Hanno interrupted again, this time desperately. 'Marric, for pity's sake! If you think he's got something to tell us, bring him along. He can talk in the boat, can't he? I tell you, if we wait much longer we'll lose the tide, and she'll be gone. There's dirty weather coming by the feel of it, and it's my guess that they won't wait.' And then in Breton: 'We can as easy ditch him later as now.'

'Boat?' I said. 'You're going on the river?'

'Where else? Do you think we can go by road? Look at the bridge,' Marric jerked his head sideways. 'All right, Hanno. Get in. We'll go.'

He began to drag me across the towpath. I hung back. 'Where are you taking me?'

'That's our affair. Can you swim?'

'No.'

He laughed under his breath. It was not a reassuring sound. 'Then it won't matter to you which way we go, will it? Come along.' And he clapped his hand once more over my mouth, swung me up as if I had been no heavier than my own bundle, and strode across the path to the oily dark glimmer that was the river.

The boat was a coracle, half hidden under the hanging bank. Hanno was already casting off. Marric went down the bank with a bump and a slither, dumped me in the lurching vessel, and clambered after me. As the coracle rocked out from under the bank he let me feel the knife again against the back of my neck. 'There. Feel it? Now hold your tongue till we're clear of the bridge.'

Hanno thrust off, and guided us out with the paddle into the current. A few feet from the bank I felt the river take hold of the boat, and we gathered speed. Hanno bent to the paddle and held her straight for the southern arch of the bridge.

Held in Marric's grip, I sat facing astern. Just as the current took us to sweep us southwards I heard Aster's high, frightened whinny as he smelt the smoke, and in the light of the now roaring fire I saw him, trailing a broken rein, burst from the wall's shadow and scud like a ghost along the towpath. Fire or no fire, he would make for the gate and his stable, and they would find him. I wondered what they would think, where they would look for me. Cerdic would be gone now, and my room with the painted chest, and the coverlet fit for a prince. Would they think I had found Cerdic's body, and in my fear and shock had dropped the lamp? That my own body was there, charred to nothing, in the remains of the servants' wing? Well, whatever they thought, it didn't matter. Cerdic had gone to his gods, and I, it seemed, was going to mine.

Chapter Twelve

The black arch of the bridge swooped across the boat, and was gone. We fled downstream. The tide was almost on the turn, but the last of the ebb took us fast. The air freshened, and the boat began to rock.

The knife withdrew from my flesh. Across me Marric said: 'Well, so far so good. The brat did us a good turn with his fire. No one was watching the river to see the boat slip under the bridge. Now, boy, let's hear what you have to tell us. What's your name?'

'Myrddin Emrys.'

'And you say you were—hey, wait a minute! Did you say Myrddin? Not the bastard?'

'Yes.'

He let out a long whistling breath, and Hanno's paddle checked, to dip again hurriedly as the coracle swung and rocked across the current. 'You heard that, Hanno? It's the bastard. Then why in the name of the spirits of lower earth did you tell us you were a slave?'

'I didn't know who you were. You hadn't recognised me, so I thought if you were thieves yourselves, or Vortigern's men, you'd let me go.'

'Bag, pony, and all . . . So it was true you were running away? Well,' he added thoughtfully, 'if all tales be true, you're not much to be blamed for that. But why set the place on fire?'

'That was true, too. I told you. Camlach killed a friend of mine, Cerdic the Saxon, though he had done nothing to deserve it. I think they only killed him because he was mine and they meant to use his death against me. They put his body in my room for me to find. So I burnt the room. His people like to go to their gods like that.'

'And the devil take anyone else in the palace?'

I said indifferently: 'The servants' wing was empty. They were all at supper, or out looking for me, or serving Camlach. It's surprising—or perhaps it isn't—how quickly people can switch over. I expect they'll put the fire out before it reaches the King's apartments.'

He regarded me in silence for a minute. We were still racing with the turning tide, well out in the estuary now. Hanno gave no sign of steering to the further bank. I pulled my cloak closer round me and shivered.

'Who were you running to?' asked Marric.

'Nobody.'

'Look, boy, I want the truth, or bastard prince or not, you'll go over the side now. Hear me? You'd not last a week if you hadn't someone to go to, to take service with. Who did you have in mind? Vortigern?'

'It would be sensible, wouldn't it? Camlach's going with Vortimer.'

'He's what?' His voice sharpened. 'Are you sure?'

'Quite sure. He was playing with the idea before, and he quarrelled with the old King about it. He and his lot would have gone anyway, I think. Now of course, he can take the whole kingdom with him, and shut it against Vortigern.'

'And open it for who else?'

'I didn't hear that. Who is there? You can imagine, he wasn't being very open about it until tonight, when his father the King lay dead.'

'Hm.' He thought for a minute. 'The old King leaves another son. If the nobles don't want this alliance—'

'A baby? Aren't you being a bit simple? Camlach's had a good example in front of him; Vortimer wouldn't be where he is if his father hadn't done just what Camlach will do.'

'And that is?'

'You know as well as I do. Look, why should I say any more till I know who you are? Isn't it time you told me?'

He ignored that. He sounded thoughtful. 'You seem to know a lot about it. How old are you?'

'Twelve. I'll be thirteen in September. But I don't need to be clever to know about Camlach and Vortimer. I heard him say so himself.'

'Did you, by the Bull? And what else did you hear?'

'Quite a lot. I was always underfoot. Nobody took any notice of me. But my mother's going into retirement now at St Peter's, and I wouldn't give you a fig for my chances, so I cleared out.'

'To Vortigern?'

I said, honestly: 'I've no idea. I–I have no plans. It might have to be Vortigern in the end. What choice is there but him, and the Saxon wolves hanging at our throats for all time till they've torn Britain piecemeal and swallowed her? Who else is there?'

'Well,' said Marric, 'Ambrosius.'

I laughed. 'Oh, yes, Ambrosius. I thought you were serious. I know you're from Less Britain, I can tell by your voices, but—'

'You asked who we were. We are Ambrosius' men.'

There was a silence. I realised that the river banks had disappeared. Far off in the darkness to the north a light showed; the lighthouse. Some time back the rain had slackened and stopped. Now it was cold, with the wind off shore, and the water was choppy. The boat pitched and swung, and I felt the first qualm of sickness. I clutched my hands hard against my belly, against the cold as much as the sickness, and said sharply: 'Ambrosius' men? Then you're spies? His spies?'

'Call us loyal men.'

'Then it's true? It's true he's waiting in Less Britain?'

'Aye, it's true.'

I said, aghast: 'Then that's where you're going? You can't imagine you can get there in this horrible little boat!'

Marric laughed, and Hanno said sourly, 'We might have to, at that, if the ship's not there.'

'What ship would be there in winter?' I demanded. 'It's not sailing weather.'

'It's sailing weather if you pay enough,' said Marric drily. 'Ambrosius pays. The ship will be there.' His big hand dropped on my shoulder, not ungently. 'Never mind that, there's still things I want to know.'

I curled up, hugging my belly, trying to take big breaths of the cold clear air. 'Oh, yes, there's a lot I could tell you. But if you're going to drop me overboard anyway, I've nothing to lose, have I? I might as well keep the rest of my information to myself–or see if Ambrosius will pay for it. And there's your ship. Look; if you can't see it yet, you must be blind. Now don't talk to me any more, I feel sick.'

I heard him laugh again under his breath. 'You're a cool one, and no mistake. Aye, there's the ship, I can see her clearly enough now. Well, seeing who you are, we'll take you aboard. And I'll tell you the other reason; I liked what you said about your friend. That sounded true enough. So you can be loyal, eh? And you've no call to be loyal to Camlach, by all accounts, or to Vortigern. Could you be loyal to Ambrosius?'

'I'll know when I see him.'

His fist sent me sprawling to the bottom of the boat. 'Princeling or not, keep a civil tongue in your head when you speak of him. There's many a hundred men think of him as their King, rightwise born.'

I picked myself up, retching. A low hail came from near at hand, and in a moment we were rocking in the deeper shadow of the ship.

'If he's a man, that'll be enough,' I said.

The ship was small, compact and low in the water. She lay there, unlighted, a shadow on the dark sea. I could just see the rake of her mast swaying–sickeningly, it seemed to me–against the scudding cloud that was only a little higher than the black sky above. She was rigged like the merchantmen who traded in and out of Maridunum in the sailing weather, but I thought she looked cleaner built, and faster.

Marric answered the hail, then a rope snaked down overside, and Hanno caught it and made it fast.

'Come on, you, get moving. You can climb, can't you?'

Somehow, I got to my feet in the swinging coracle. The rope was wet, and jerked in my hands. From above an urgent voice came: 'Hurry, will you? We'll be lucky if we get back at all, with the weather that's coming up.'

'Get aloft, blast you,' said Marric, roughly, giving me a shove. It was all it needed. My hands slipped, nerveless, from the rope, and I fell back into the coracle, landing half across the side, where I hung, gasping and retching, and beyond caring what fate overtook me or even a dozen kingdoms. If I had been stabbed or thrown into the sea at that point I doubt if I would even have noticed, except to welcome death as a relief. I simply hung there over the boat's side like a lump of sodden rags, vomiting.

I have very little recollection of what happened then. There was a good deal of cursing, and I think I remember Hanno urgently recommending Marric to cut his losses and throw me overboard; but I was picked up bodily and, somehow, slung up into the waiting hands above. Then someone half carried, half dragged me below, and dropped me on a pile of bedding with a bucket to hand and the air from an open port blowing on my sweating face.

I believe the journey took four days. Rough weather there certainly was, but at least it was behind us, and we made spanking good speed. I stayed below the whole time, huddled thankfully in the blankets under the port-hole, hardly venturing to lift my head. The worst of the sickness abated after a time, but I doubt if I could have moved, and mercifully no one tried to make me.

Marric came down once. I remember it vaguely, as if it were a dream. He picked his way in over a pile of old anchor chain to where I lay, and stood, his big form stooping, peering down at me. Then he shook his head. 'And to think I thought we'd done ourselves a good turn, picking you up. We should have thrown you over the side in the first place, and saved a lot of trouble. I reckon you haven't very much more to tell us, anyway?'

I made no reply.

He gave a queer little grunt, that sounded like a laugh, and went out. I went to sleep, exhausted.

When I woke, I found that my wet cloak, sandals and tunic had been removed, and that, dry and naked, I was cocooned deep in blankets. Near my head was a water jar, its mouth stoppered with a twist of rag, and a hunk of barley bread.

I couldn't have touched either, but I got the message. I slept.

Then one day shortly before dusk, we came in sight of the Wild Coast, and dropped anchor in the calm waters of Morbihan that men call the Small Sea.

The Falcon

Chapter One

The first I knew of our coming to shore was being roused, still heavy with
that exhausted sleep, by voices talking over me.

'Well, all right, if you believe him, but do you really think even a bastard
prince would be abroad in those clothes? Everything soaking, not even a gilt
clasp to his belt, and look at his sandals. I grant you it's a good cloak, but it's
torn. More likely the first story was true, and he's a slave running away with
his master's things.'

It was, of course, Hanno's voice, and he was talking in Breton. Luckily I
had my back to them, curled up in the welter of blankets. It was easy to
pretend to be asleep. I lay still, and tried to keep my breathing even.

'No, it's the bastard all right; I've seen him in the town. I'd have
known him sooner if we'd been able to show a light.' The deeper voice
was Marric's. 'In any case it would hardly matter who he was; slave
or royal bastard, he's been privy to a lot in that palace that Ambrosius
will want to listen to. And he's a bright lad; oh, yes, he's what he says
he is. You don't learn those cool ways and that kind of talking in the
kitchens.'

'Well, but . . .' The change in Hanno's voice made my skin shift on my
bones. I kept very still.

'Well but what?'

The Weasel dropped his voice still further. 'Maybe if we made him talk to
us first . . . I mean, look at it this way. All that stuff he told us, hearing what
King Camlach meant to do and all that . . . If we'd got that information for
ourselves and got away to report it, there'd be a fat purse for us, wouldn't
there?'

Marric grunted. 'And then when he gets ashore and tells someone where
he comes from? Ambrosius would hear. He hears everything.'

'Are you trying to be simple?' The question was waspish.

It was all I could do to keep still. There was a space between my shoulder-blades where the skin tightened cold over the flesh as if it already felt the knife.

'Oh, I'm not as simple as that. I get you. But I don't see that it—'

'Nobody in Maridunum knows where he went.' Hanno's whisper was hurried and eager. 'As for the men who saw him come on board, they'll think we've taken him off with us now. In fact, that's what we'll do, take him with us now, and there are plenty of places between here and the town . . .' I heard him swallow. 'I told you before we put out, it's senseless to have spent the money on his passage—'

'If we were going to get rid of him,' said Marric bluntly, 'we'd have done better not to have paid his passage at all. Have a bit of sense, we'll get the money back now in any case, and maybe a good bit over.'

'How do you make that out?'

'Well, if the boy has got information, Ambrosius'll pay the passage, you can be sure of that. Then if it turns out he is the bastard–and I'm certain he is–there might be extra in it for us. King's sons–or grandsons–come in useful, as who should know better than Ambrosius?'

'Ambrosius must know the boy's useless as a hostage.' Hanno sounded sullen.

'Who's to tell? And if he's no use either way to Ambrosius, then we keep the boy and sell him and split the proceeds. So leave it be, I tell you. Alive, he might be worth something; dead, he's worth nothing at all, and we might find ourselves out of pocket over his passage.'

I felt Hanno's toe prodding me, not gently. 'Doesn't look worth much either way at the moment. Ever know anyone so sick? He must have a stomach like a girl. Do you even suppose he can walk?'

'We can find out,' said Marric, and shook me. 'Here, boy, get up.'

I groaned, rolled over slowly, and showed them what I hoped was a wretchedly pale face. 'What is it? Are we there?' I asked it in Welsh.

'Yes, we're there. Come on now, get to your feet, we're going ashore.'

I groaned again, more dismally than before, and clutched my belly. 'Oh, God, no, leave me alone.'

'A bucket of sea water,' suggested Hanno.

Marric straightened. 'There's hardly time.' He spoke in Breton again. 'He looks as if we'll have to carry him. No, we'll have to leave him; we've got to get straight to the Count. It's the night of the meeting, remember? He'll already know the ship's docked, and he'll be expecting to see us before he has to leave. We'd better get the report straight to him, or there'll be trouble. We'll leave the boy here for the time being. We can lock him up, and tell the watch to keep an eye on him. We can be back well before midnight.'

'You can, you mean,' said Hanno sourly. 'I've got something that won't wait.'

'Ambrosius won't wait, either, so if you want the money for that, you'd better come. They've half finished unloading already. Who's on watch?'

Hanno said something, but the creak of the heavy door as they pulled it shut behind them, and then the thudding of the bars dropping into their sockets drowned the reply. I heard the wedges go in, then lost the sound of their voices and footsteps in the noises of the off-loading operation that was shaking the ship—the creak of winches, the shouts of men above me and a few yards away on shore, the hiss and squeak of running hawsers, and the thud of loads being lifted and swung overside on to the wharf.

I threw the blankets off and sat up. With the ceasing of the dreadful motion of the ship I felt steady again—even well, with a sort of light and purged emptiness that gave me a strange feeling of well-being, a floating, slightly unreal sensation, like the power one has in dreams. I knelt up on the bedding and looked about me.

They had lanterns on the wharf to work by, and light from these fell through the small square port-hole. It showed me the wide-mouthed jar, still in place, and a new hunk of barley bread. I unstoppered the jar and tasted the water cautiously. It was musty, tasting of the rag, but good enough, and it cleared the metallic sickness from my mouth. The bread was iron-hard, but I soused it in water until I could break off a piece to chew. Then I got up, and levered myself up to look out of the port-hole.

To do this I had to reach for the sill and pull myself up by my hands, finding a hold for my toes on one of the struts that lined the bulkhead. I had guessed by the shape of my prison that the hold was in the bows, and I now saw that this was correct. The ship lay alongside a stone-built wharf where a couple of lanterns hung on posts, and by their light some twenty men—soldiers—were working to bring the bales and loaded crates off the ship. To the back of the wharf was a row of solid-looking buildings, presumably for storage, but tonight it looked as if the merchandise were bound elsewhere. Carts waited beyond the lamp posts, the hitched mules patient. The men with the carts were in uniform, and armed, and there was an officer superintending the unloading.

The ship was moored close to the wharf amidships, where the gang-plank was. Her forward hawser ran from the rail above my head to the wharf, and this had allowed the bow to swing out from the land, so that between me and the shore lay about fifteen feet of water. There were no lights at this end of the ship; the rope ran down into a comfortable pool of darkness, and beyond that was the deeper darkness of the buildings. But I would have to wait, I decided, till the unloading was finished, and the carts—and presumably the soldiers with them—moved off. There would be time later to escape, with only the watch on board, and perhaps even the lanterns gone from the wharf.

For of course I must escape. If I stayed where I was, my only hope of safety lay in Marric's goodwill, and this in its turn depended on the outcome of his interview with Ambrosius. And if for some reason Marric could not come back, and Hanno came instead . . .

Besides, I was hungry. The water and the hideous little snack of soaked bread had set the juices churning in a ferociously empty belly, and the prospect of waiting two or three hours before anyone came back for me was intolerable, even without the fear of what that return might bring. And even if the best should happen, and Ambrosius send for me, I could not be too sure of my fate at his hands once he had all the information I could give him. Despite the bluff which had saved my life from the spies, this information was scanty enough, and Marric had been right in guessing—and Ambrosius would know it—that I was useless as a hostage. My semi-royal status might impress Marric and Hanno, but neither being grandson to Vortigern's ally, nor nephew to Vortimer's, would be much of a recommendation to Ambrosius' kindness. It looked as if, royal or not, my lot would be slavery with luck, and without it, an unsung death.

And this I had no intention of waiting for. Not while the port-hole stood open, and the hawser ran, sagging only slightly, from just above me to the bollard on the wharf. The two spies, I supposed, were so little accustomed to dealing with prisoners of my size that they had not even given a thought to the port-hole. No man, not even the weaselly Hanno, could have attempted escape that way, but a slim boy could. Even if they had thought of it, they knew I could not swim, and they had not reckoned with the rope. But, eyeing it carefully as I hung there in the port-hole, I thought I could manage it. If the rats could go along it–I could see one now, a huge fat fellow, sleek with scraps, creeping down towards the shore–then so could I.

But I would have to wait. Meanwhile, it was cold, and I was naked. I dropped lightly back into the hold, and turned to hunt for my clothes.

The light from the shore was dim but sufficient. It showed me the small cage of my prison with the blankets tumbled on the pile of old sacks that had been my bed; a warped and splitting sea-chest against a bulkhead; a pile of rusty chain too heavy for me to shift; the water jar, and in the far corner–'far' meaning two paces away–the vile bucket still half-full of vomit. It showed me nothing else. It may have been a kindly impulse which had made Marric strip me of my sodden clothes, but either he had forgotten to return them, or they had been kept back to prevent me from doing this very thing.

Five seconds showed me that the chest contained nothing but some writing tablets, a bronze cup, and some leather sandal-thongs. At least, I thought, letting the lid down gently on this unpromising collection, they had left me my sandals. Not that I wasn't used to going barefoot, but not in winter, not on the roads . . . For, naked or not, I had still to escape. Marric's very precautions made me more than ever anxious to get away.

What I would do, where I would go, I had no idea, but the god had sent me safely out of Camlach's hands and across the Narrow Sea, and I trusted my fate. As far as I had a plan I intended to get near enough to Ambrosius to judge what kind of man this was, then, if I thought there was patronage there, or even only mercy, I could approach him and offer him my story and my services. It never entered my head that there might be anything absurd about asking a prince to employ a twelve-year-old. I suppose that to this extent at least, I was royal. Failing Ambrosius' service, I believe I had some hazy idea of making my way to the village north of Kerrec where Moravik came from, and asking for her people.

The sacks I had been lying on were oldish, and beginning to rot. It was easy enough to tear one of them open at the seams for my head and arms to go through. It made a dreadful garment, but it covered me after a fashion. I ripped a second one, and pulled that over my head as well, for warmth. A third would be too bulky. I fingered the blankets longingly, but they were good ones, too thick to tear, and would have been impossibly hampering on my climb out of the ship. Reluctantly, I let them lie. A couple of the leather thongs, knotted together, made a girdle. I stuffed the remaining lump of barley bread into the front of my sack, swilled my face, hands and hair with the rest of the water, then went again to the port-hole and pulled myself up to look out.

While I was dressing I had heard shouts and the tramp of feet, as if the men had been formed up ready to march. I now saw that this had indeed happened. Men and carts were moving off. The last of the carts, heavily loaded, was just creaking away past the buildings with the whip cracking over the straining mules. With them went the tramp of marching feet. I wondered what the cargo was; hardly grain at that time of year; more likely, I thought, metal or ore, to be unloaded by troops and sent to the town under guard. The sounds receded. I looked carefully round. The lanterns still hung from the posts, but as far as I could see the wharf was deserted. It was time to go, before the watch decided to come forward to check on the prisoner.

For an active boy, it was easy. I was soon sitting astride the sill of the port-hole, with my body outside and my legs gripping the bulkhead while I reached up for the rope. There was a bad moment when I found I could not reach it, and would have to stand, holding myself somehow against the hull of the ship, above the black depths between ship and wharf where the oily water lapped and sucked, rustling its drifts of refuse against the dripping walls. But I managed it, clawing up the ship's side as if I had been another of the shoregoing rats, till at last I could stretch upright and grasp the hawser. This was taut and dry, and went down at a gentle angle towards the bollard on the wharf. I gripped it with both hands, twisted to face outwards, then swung my legs free of the ship and up over the rope.

I had meant to let myself down gently, hand over hand, to land in the shadows, but what I hadn't reckoned on, being no seaman, was the waterborne lightness of a small ship. Even my slender weight, as I hitched myself down the rope, made her curtsy, sharply and disconcertingly, and then, tilting, swing her bow suddenly in towards the wharf. The hawser sagged, slackened, drooped under my weight as the strain was loosed, then went down into a loop. Where I swung, clinging like a monkey, it suddenly hung vertical. My feet lost their grip and slid away from me; my hands could not hold my weight. I went down the ship's side on that hawser like a bead on a string.

If the ship had swung more slowly I would have been crushed as she ground against the wharf-side, or drowned as I reached the bottom of the loop, but she went like a horse shying. As she jarred the edge of the wharf I was just above it, and the jerk loosened what was left of my grip and flung me clear. I missed the bollard by inches, and landed sprawling on the frost-hard ground in the shadow of a wall.

Chapter Two

There was no time to wonder whether I was hurt. I could hear the slap of bare feet on the deck above me as the watch raced along to see what had happened. I bunched, rolled, and was on my feet and running before his bobbing lantern reached the side. I heard him shout something, but I had already dodged round the corner of the buildings, and was sure he had not seen me. Even if he had, I thought I was safe enough. He would check my prison first, and even then I doubted if he would dare leave the ship. I leaned for a moment or two against the wall, hugging the rope burns on my hands, and trying to adjust my eyes to the night.

Since I had come from near-darkness in my prison, this took no more than a few seconds, and I looked quickly about me to get my bearings.

The shed that hid me was the end one of the row, and behind it–on the side away from the wharf–was the road, a straight ribbon of gravel, making for a cluster of lights some distance away. This no doubt was the town. Nearer, just where the road was swallowed by darkness, was a dim and shifting gleam, which must be the tail light of the last wagon. Nothing else moved.

It was a fairly safe guess that any wagons so guarded were bound for Ambrosius' headquarters. I had no idea whether I could get to him, or even into any town or village, but all I wanted at this stage was to find something to eat, and somewhere warm where I could hide and eat it, and wait for daylight. Once I got my bearings, no doubt the god would lead me still.

He would also have to feed me. I had originally meant to sell one of my brooches for food, but now, I thought, as I jogged in the wake of the wagons, I would have to steal something. At the very worst, I still had a hunk of barley bread. Then somewhere to hide until daylight . . . If Ambrosius was at 'a meeting', as Marric had said, it would be worse than useless to go to his headquarters and ask to see him now. Whatever my sense of my own importance, it did not stretch to privileged treatment by Ambrosius' soldiers if I turned up dressed like this in his absence. Come daylight, we should see.

It was cold. My breath puffed, grey on the black and icy air. There was no moon, but the stars were out like wolves' eyes, glaring. Frost glittered on the stones of the road, and rang under the hoofs and wheels ahead of me. Mercifully there was no wind, and my blood warmed with running, but I dared not catch up with the convoy, which went slowly, so that from time to time I had to check and hang back, while the freezing air bit through the ragged sacks and I flailed my arms against my body for warmth.

Fortunately there was plenty of cover; bushes, sometimes in crouching clusters, sometimes singly, hunched as they had frozen in the path of the prevailing wind, still reaching after it with stiff fingers. Among them great stones stood, rearing sharp against the stars. I took the first of these for a huge milestone, but then saw others, in ranks, thrusting from the turf like storm-blasted avenues of trees. Or like colonnades where gods walked—but not gods that I knew. The starlight struck the face of the stone where I had paused to wait, and something caught my eye, a shape rudely carved in the granite, and etched by the cold light like lampblack. An axe, two-headed. The standing stones stretched away from me into darkness like a march of giants. A dry thistle, broken down to the stalk, stabbed my bare leg. As I turned away I glanced at the axe again. It had vanished.

I ran back to the road, clamping my teeth against the shivering. It was the cold, of course, that made me shiver; what else? The wagons had drawn ahead again, and I ran after, keeping to the turf at the road's edge, though this in fact seemed as hard as the gravel. The frost broke and squeaked under my sandals. Behind me the silent army of stones marched dwindling into the dark, and before me now were the lights of a town and the warmth of its houses reaching out to meet me. I think it was the first time that I, Merlin, had run towards light and company, run from solitude as if it were a ring of wolves' eyes driving one nearer the fire.

It was a walled town. I should have guessed it, so near the sea. There was a high earthwork and above that a palisade, and the ditch outside the earthwork was wide and white with ice. They had smashed the ice at intervals, so that it would not bear; I could see the black stars and the crisscross map of cracks just skinning over with grey glass as the new ice formed. There was a wooden bridge across to the gate, and here the wagons halted, while the officer rode forward to speak to the guards, and the men stood like rocks while the mules stamped and blew and jingled their harness, eager for the warmth of the stable.

If I had had any idea of jumping on the back of a wagon and being carried in that way, I had had to abandon it. All the way to the town the soldiers had been strung out in a file to either side of the convoy, with the officer riding out to one side where he could scan the whole. Now, as he gave the order to advance and break step for the bridge, he wheeled his horse and made back himself to the tail of the column, to see the last cart in. I caught a glimpse of his face, middle-aged, bad tempered and catarrhal with cold. Not the man to listen patiently, or even to listen at all. I was safer outside with the stars and the marching giants.

The gate thudded shut behind the convoy, and I heard the locks drive home.

There was a path, faintly discernible, leading off eastward along the edge of the ditch. When I looked that way I saw that, some way off, so far that they must mark some kind of settlement or farm well beyond the limits of the town, more lights showed.

I turned along the path at a trot, chewing at my chunk of barley bread as I went.

The lights turned out to belong to a fair-sized house whose buildings enclosed a courtyard. The house itself, two storeys high, made one wall of the yard, which was bounded on the other three sides by single-storey buildings–baths, servants' quarters, stables, bake-house–the whole enclosure high-walled and showing only a few slit windows beyond my reach. There was an arched gateway, and beside this in an iron bracket set at the height of a man's reach, a torch spluttered, sulky with damp pitch. There were more lights inside the yard, but I could hear no movement or voices. The gate, of course, was shut fast.

Not that I would have dared go in that way, to meet some summary fate at the porter's hands. I skirted the wall, looking hopefully for a way to climb in. The third window was the bake-house; the smells were hours old, and cold, but still would have sent me swarming up the wall, save that the window was a bare slit which would not have admitted even me.

The next was a stable, and the next also . . . I could smell the horse-smells and beast-smells mingling, and the sweetness of dried grass. Then the house, with no windows at all facing outwards. The bath-house, the same. And back to the gate.

A chain clanged suddenly, and within a few feet of me, just inside the gate, a big dog gave tongue like a bell. I believe I jumped back a full pace, then flattened myself against the wall as I heard a door open somewhere close. There was a pause, while the dog growled and someone listened, then a man's voice said something curt, and the door shut. The dog grumbled to itself for a bit, snuffling at the foot of the gate, then dragged its chain back to the kennel, and I heard it settling again into its straw.

There was obviously no way in to find shelter. I stood for a while, trying to think, with my back pressed to the cold wall that still seemed warmer than the icy air. I was shaking now with the cold so violently that I felt as if my very bones were chattering. I was sure I had been right to leave the ship, and not to trust myself to the troops' mercy, but now I began to wonder if I dared knock at the gate and beg for shelter. I would get rough shrift as a beggar, I knew, but if I stayed out here I might well die of cold before morning.

Then I saw, just beyond the torchlight's reach, the low black shape of a building that must be a cattle shed or shippon, some twenty paces away and at the corner of a field surrounded by low banks crowned with thorn bushes. I could hear cattle moving there. At least there would be their warmth to share, and if I could force my chattering teeth through it, I still had a heel of barley bread.

I had taken a pace away from the wall, moving, I could have sworn, without a sound, when the dog came out of his kennel with a rush and a rattle, and set up his infernal baying again. This time the house door opened immediately, and I heard a man's step in the yard. He was coming towards the gate. I heard the rasp of metal as he drew some weapon. I was just turning to run when I heard, clear and sharp on the frosty air, what the dog had heard. The sound of hoofs, full gallop, coming this way.

Quick as a shadow, I ran across the open ground towards the shed. Beside it a gap in the bank made a gateway, which had been blocked with a dead thorn tree. I shoved through this, then crept–as quietly as I could, not to disturb the beasts–to crouch in the shed doorway, out of sight of the house gate.

The shed was only a small, roughly built shelter, with walls not much more than man-height, thatched over, and crowded with beasts. These seemed to be young bullocks for the most part, too thronged to lie down, but seemingly content enough with each other's warmth, and some dry fodder to chew over. A rough plank across the doorway made a barrier to keep them in. Outside, the field stretched empty in the starlight, grey with frost, and bounded with its low banks ridged with those hunched and crippled bushes. In the centre of the field was one of the standing stones.

Inside the gateway, I heard the man speak to silence the dog. The sound of hoofs swelled, hammering up the iron track, then suddenly the rider was on us, sweeping out of the dark and pulling his horse up with a scream of metal on stone and a flurry of gravel and frozen turf, and the thud of the beast's hoofs right up against the wood of the gate. The man inside shouted something, a question, and the rider answered him even in the act of flinging himself down from the saddle.

'Of course it is. Open up, will you?'

I heard the door grate as it was dragged open, then the two men talking, but apart from a word here and there, could not distinguish what they said. It seemed, from the movement of the light, that the porter (or whoever had come to the gate) had lifted the torch down from its socket. Moreover, the light was moving this way, and both men with it, leading the horse.

I heard the rider say, impatiently: 'Oh, yes, it'll be well enough here. If it comes to that, it will suit me to have a quick getaway. There's fodder there?'

'Aye, sir. I put the young beasts out here to make room for the horses.'

'There's a crowd, then?' The voice was young, clear, a little harsh, but that might only be cold and arrogance combined. A patrician voice, careless as the horsemanship that had all but brought the horse down on its haunches in front of the gate.

'A fair number,' said the porter. 'Mind, now, sir, it's through this gap. If you'll let me go first with the light . . .'

'I can see,' said the young man irritably, 'if you don't shove the torch right in my face. Hold up, you.' This to the horse as it pecked at a stone.

'You'd best let me go first, sir. There's a thorn bush across the gap to keep them in. If you'll stand clear a minute, I'll shift it.'

I had already melted out of the shed doorway and round the corner, where the rough wall met the field embankment. There were turfs staked here, and a pile of brushwood and dried bracken that I supposed were winter bedding. I crouched down behind the stack.

I heard the thorn tree being lifted and flung aside. 'There, sir, bring him through. There's not much room, but if you're sure you'd as soon leave him out here—'

'I said it would do. Shift the plank and get him in. Hurry, man, I'm late.'

'If you leave him with me now, sir, I'll unsaddle for you.'

'No need. He'll be well enough for an hour or two. Just loosen the girth. I suppose I'd better throw my cloak over him. Gods, it's cold . . . Get the bridle off, will you? I'm getting in out of this . . .'

I heard him stride away, spurs clinking. The plank went back into place, and then the thorn tree. As the porter hurried after him I caught something that sounded like, 'And let me in at the back, where the father won't see me.'

The big gate shut behind them. The chain rattled, but the dog stayed silent. I heard the men's steps crossing the yard, then the house door shut on them.

Chapter Three

Even if I had dared to risk the torchlight and the dog, to scramble over the bank behind me and run the twenty paces to the gate, there would have been no need. The god had done his part; he had sent me warmth and, I discovered, food.

No sooner had the gate shut than I was back inside the shippon, whispering reassurance to the horse as I reached to rob him of the cloak. He was not sweating much; he must only have galloped the mile or so from the town, and in that shed among the crowded beasts he could take no harm from cold; in any case, my need came before his, and I had to have that cloak. It was an officer's cloak, thick, soft and good. As I laid hold of it I found, to my excitement, that my lord had left me not only his cloak, but a full saddle-bag as well. I stretched up, tiptoe, and felt inside.

A leather flask, which I shook. It was almost full. Wine, certainly; that young man would never carry water. A napkin with biscuits in it, and raisins, and some strips of dried meat.

The beasts jostled, dribbling, and puffed their warm breath at me. The long cloak had slipped to trail a corner in the dirt under their hoofs. I snatched it up, clutched the flask and food to me, and slipped out under the barrier. The pile of brushwood in the corner outside was clean, but I would hardly have cared if it had been a dung-heap. I burrowed into it, wrapped myself warmly in the soft woollen folds, and steadily ate and drank my way through everything the god had sent me.

Whatever happened, I must not sleep. Unfortunately it seemed that the young man would not be here for more than an hour or two; but this with the bonus of food should be time enough to warm me so that I might bed down in comfort till daylight. I would hear movement from the house in time to slip back to the shed and throw the cloak into place. My lord would hardly be likely to notice that his marching rations had gone from his saddle-bag.

I drank some more wine. It was amazing how even the stale ends of the barley bread tasted the better for it. It was good stuff, potent and sweet, and tasting of raisins. It ran warm into my body, till the rigid joints loosened and melted and stopped their shaking, and I could curl up warm and relaxed in my dark nest, with the bracken pulled right up over me to shut out the cold.

I must have slept a little. What woke me I have no idea; there was no sound. Even the beasts in the shed were still.

It seemed darker, so that I wondered if it were almost dawn, when the stars fade. But when I parted the bracken and peered out I saw they were still there, burning white in the black sky.

The strange thing was, it was warmer. Some wind had risen, and had brought cloud with it, scudding drifts that raced high overhead, then scattered and wisped away so that shadow and starlight broke one after the other like waves across the frost-grey fields and still landscape, where the thistles and stiff winter grasses seemed to flow like water, or like a cornfield under the wind. There was no sound of the wind blowing.

Above the flying veils of cloud the stars were brilliant, studding a black dome. The warmth and my curled posture in the dark must (I thought) have made me dream of security, of Galapas and the crystal globe where I had lain curled, and watched the light. Now the brilliant arch of stars above me was like the curved roof of the cave with the light flashing off the crystals, and the passing shadows flying, chased by the fire. You could see points of red and sapphire, and one star steady, beaming gold. Then the silent wind blew another shadow across the sky with light behind it, and the thorn trees shivered, and the shadow of the standing stone.

I must be buried too deep and snug in my bed to hear the rustle of the wind through grass and thorn. Nor did I hear the young man pushing his way through the barrier that the porter had replaced across the gap in the bank. For, suddenly, with no warning, he was there, a tall figure striding across the field, as shadowy and quiet as the wind.

I shrank, like a snail into its shell. Too late now to run and replace the cloak. All I could hope was that he would assume the thief had fled, and not search too near. But he did not approach the shed. He was making straight across the field away from me. Then I saw, half in, half out of the shadow of the standing stone, the white animal grazing. His horse must have broken loose. The gods alone knew what it found to eat in that winter field, but I could see it, ghostly in the distance, the white beast grazing beside the standing stone. And it must have rubbed the girth till it snapped; its saddle, too, was gone.

At least in the time he would take to catch it, I should be able to get away . . . Or better still, drop the cloak near the shed, where he would think it had slid from the horse's back, and then get back to my warm nest till he had gone. He could only blame the porter for the animal's escape; and justly; I had not touched the bar across the doorway. I raised myself cautiously, watching my chance.

The grazing animal had lifted its head to watch the man's approach. A cloud swept across the stars, blackening the field. Light ran after the shadow across the frost. It struck the standing stone. I saw that I had been wrong; it was not the horse. Nor—my next thought—could it be one of the young beasts from the shed. This was a bull, a massive white bull, full-grown, with a royal spread of horns and a neck like a thunder-cloud. It lowered its head till the dewlap brushed the ground, and pawed once, twice.

The young man paused. I saw him now, clearly, as the shadow lifted. He was tall and strongly built, and his hair looked bleached in the starlight. He wore some sort of foreign dress—trousers cross-bound with thongs below a tunic girded low on the hips, and a high loose cap. Under this the fair hair blew round his face like rays. There was a rope in his hand, held loosely, its coils brushing the frost. His cloak flew in the wind; a short cloak, of some dark colour I could not make out.

His cloak? Then it could not be my young lord. And after all, why should that arrogant young man come with a rope to catch a bull that had strayed in the night?

Without warning, and without a sound, the white bull charged. Shadow and light rushed with it, flickering, blurring the scene. The rope whirled, snaked into a loop, settled. The man leapt to one side as the great beast tore past him and came to a sliding stop with the rope snapping taut and the frost smoking up in clouds from the side-slipping hoofs.

The bull whirled, and charged again. The man waited without moving, his feet planted slightly apart, his posture casual, almost disdainful. As the bull reached him he seemed to sway aside, lightly, like a dancer. The bull went by him so close that I saw a horn shear the swirling cloak, and the beast's shoulder passed the man's thigh like a lover seeking a caress. The man's hands moved. The rope whipped up into a ring, and another loop settled round the royal horns. The man leaned against it, and as the beast came up short once more, turning sharp in its own smoke, the man jumped.

Not away. Towards the bull, clean on to the thick neck, with knees digging into the dewlap, and fierce hands using the rope like reins.

The bull stopped dead, his feet four-square, his head thrust downwards with his whole weight and strength against the rope. There was still no sound that I could hear, no sound of hoof or crack of rope or bellow of breath. I was half out of the brushwood now, rigid and staring, heedless of anything save the fight between man and bull.

A cloud stamped the field again with darkness. I got to my feet. I believe I meant to seize the plank from the shed and rush with it across the field to give what futile help I could. But before I could move the cloud had fled, to show me the bull standing as before, the man still on its neck. But now the beast's head was coming up. The man had dropped the rope, and his two hands were on the bull's horns, dragging them back . . . back . . . up . . . Slowly, almost as if in a ritual of surrender, the bull's head lifted, the powerful neck stretched up, exposed.

There was a gleam in the man's right hand. He leaned forward, then drove the knife down and across.

Still in silence, slowly, the bull sank to its knees. Black flowed over the white hide, the white ground, the white base of the stone.

I broke from my hiding place and ran, shouting something—I have no idea what—across the field towards them.

I don't know what I meant to do. The man saw me coming, and turned his head, and I saw that nothing was needed. He was smiling, but his face in the starlight seemed curiously smooth and unhuman in its lack of expression. I could see no sign of stress or effort. His eyes were expressionless too, cold and dark, with no smile there.

I stumbled, tried to stop, caught my feet in the trailing cloak, and fell, rolling in a ridiculous and helpless bundle towards him, just as the white bull, slowly heeling over, collapsed. Something struck me on the side of the head. I heard a sharp childish sound which was myself crying out, then it was dark.

Chapter Four

Someone kicked me again, hard, in the ribs. I grunted and rolled, trying to get out of range, but the cloak hampered me. A torch, stinking with black smoke, was thrust down, almost into my face. The familiar young voice said, angrily: 'My cloak, by God! Grab hold of him, you, quick. I'm damned if I touch him, he's filthy.'

They were all around me, feet scuffling the frost, torches flaring, men's voices curious, or angry, or indifferently amused. Some were mounted, and their horses skirmished on the edge of the group, stamping and fidgeting with cold.

I crouched, blinking upwards. My head ached, and the flickering scene above me swam unreal, in snatches, as if reality and dream were breaking and dovetailing one across the other to split the senses. Fire, voices, the rocking of a ship, the white bull falling . . .

A hand tore the cloak off me. Some of the rotten sacking went with it, leaving me with a shoulder and side bare to the waist. Someone grabbed my wrist and yanked me to my feet and held me. His other hand took me roughly by the hair, and pulled my head up to face the man who stood over me. He was tall, young, with light brown hair showing reddish in the torchlight, and an elegant beard fringing his chin. His eyes were blue, and looked angry. He was cloakless in the cold. He had a whip in his left hand.

He eyed me, making a sound of disgust. 'A beggar's brat, and stinking, at that. I'll have to burn the thing, I suppose. I'll have your hide for this, you bloody little vermin. I suppose you were going to steal my horse as well?'

'No, sir. I swear it was only the cloak. I would have put it back, I promise you.'

'And the brooch as well?'

'Brooch?'

The man holding me said: 'Your brooch is still in the cloak, my lord.'

I said quickly: 'I only borrowed it, for warmth—it was so cold, so I—'

'So you just stripped my horse and left him to catch cold? Is that it?'

'I didn't think it would harm him, sir. It was warm in the shed. I would have put it back, really I would.'

'For me to wear after you, you stinking little rat? I ought to slit your throat for this.'

Someone—one of the mounted men—said: 'Oh, leave it. There's no harm done except that your cloak will have to go to the fuller tomorrow. The wretched boy's half naked, and it's cold enough to freeze a salamander. Let him go.'

'At least,' said the young officer between his teeth, 'it will warm me up to thrash him. Ah, no, you don't–hold him fast, Cadal.'

The whip whistled back. The man who held me tightened his grip as I fought to tear free, but before the whip could fall a shadow moved in front of the torchlight and a hand came lightly down, no more than a touch, on the young man's wrist.

Someone said: 'What's this?'

The men fell silent, as if at an order. The young man dropped the whip to his side, and turned.

My captor's grip had slackened as the newcomer spoke, and I twisted free. I might possibly have doubled away between the men and horses and run for it, though I suppose a mounted man could have run me down in seconds. But I made no attempt to get away. I was staring.

The newcomer was tall, taller than my cloakless young officer by half a head. He was between me and the torches, and I could not see him well against the flame. The flares swam still, blurred and dazzling; my head hurt, and the cold had sprung back at me like a toothed beast. All I saw was the tall shadowy figure watching me, dark eyes in an expressionless face.

I took a breath like a gasp. 'It was you! You saw me, didn't you? I was coming to help you, only I tripped and fell. I wasn't running away–tell him that, please, my lord. I did mean to put the cloak back before he came for it. Please tell him what happened!'

'What are you talking about? Tell him what?'

I blinked against the glare of the torches. 'About what happened just now. It was–it was you who killed the bull?'

'Who *what*?'

It had been quiet before, but now there was silence, complete except for the men's breathing as they crowded round, and the fidgeting of the horses.

The young officer said sharply: 'What bull?'

'The white bull,' I said. 'He cut its throat, and the blood splashed out like a spring. That was how I got your cloak dirty. I was trying—'

'How the hell did you know about the bull? Where were you? Who's been talking?'

'Nobody,' I said, surprised. 'I saw it all. Is it so secret? I thought I must be dreaming at first, I was sleepy after the bread and wine—'

'By the Light!' It was the young officer still, but now the others were exclaiming with him, their anger breaking round me. 'Kill him, and have done' . . . 'He's lying' . . . 'Lying to save his wretched skin' . . . 'He must have been spying . . .'

The tall man had not spoken. Nor had he taken his eyes off me. From somewhere, anger poured into me, and I said hotly, straight to him: 'I'm not a spy, or a thief! I'm tired of this! What was I to do, freeze to death to save the life of a horse?' The man behind me laid a hand on my arm, but I shook him off with a gesture that my grandfather himself might have used. 'Nor am I a beggar, my lord. I'm a free man come to take service with Ambrosius, if he'll have me. That's what I came here for, from my own country, and it was . . . it was an accident that I lost my clothes. I–I may be young, but I have certain knowledge that is valuable, and I speak five languages . . .' My voice faltered. Someone had made a stifled sound like a laugh. I set my chattering teeth and added, royally: 'I beg you merely to give me shelter now, my lord, and tell me where I may seek him out in the morning.'

This time the silence was so thick you could have cut it. I heard the young officer take breath to speak, but the other put out a hand. He must, by the way they waited for him, be their commander. 'Wait. He's not being insolent. Look at him. Hold the torch higher, Lucius. Now, what's your name?'

'Myrddin, sir.'

'Well, Myrddin, I'll listen to you, but make it plain and make it quick. I want to hear this about the bull. Start at the beginning. You saw my brother stable his horse in the shed yonder, and you took the cloak off its back for warmth. Go on from there?'

'Yes, my lord,' I said. 'I took the food from the saddle-bags, too, and the wine—'

'You were talking about *my* bread and wine?' demanded the young officer.

'Yes, sir. I'm sorry, but I'd hardly eaten for four days—'

'Never mind that,' said the commander curtly. 'Go on.'

'I hid in the brushwood stack at the corner of the shed, and I think I went to sleep. When I woke I saw the bull, over by the standing stone. He was grazing there, quite quiet. Then you came, with the rope. The bull charged, and you roped it, and then jumped on its back and pulled its head up and killed it with a knife. There was blood everywhere. I was running to help. I don't know what I could have done, but I ran, all the same. Then I tripped over the cloak, and fell. That's all.'

I stopped. A horse stamped, and a man cleared his throat. Nobody spoke. I thought that Cadal, the servant who had held me, moved a little further away.

The commander said, very quietly: 'Beside the standing stone?'

'Yes, sir.'

He turned his head. The group of men and horses was very near the stone. I could see it behind the horsemen's shoulders, thrusting up torchlit against the night sky.

'Stand aside and let him see,' said the tall man, and some of them moved.

The stone was about thirty feet away. Near its base the frosty grass showed scuffled by boots and hoofprints, but nothing more. Where I had seen the white bull fall, with the black blood gushing from its throat, there was nothing but the scuffled frost, and the shadow of the stone.

The torch-bearer had shifted the torch to throw light towards the stone. Light fell now straight on my questioner, and for the first time I saw him plainly. He was not as young as I had thought; there were lines in his face, and his brows were down, frowning. His eyes were dark, not blue like his brother's, and he was more heavily built than I had supposed. There was a flash of gold at his wrists and collar, and a heavy cloak dropped in a long line from shoulder to heel.

I said, stammering: 'It wasn't you. I'm sorry, it—I see now, I must have dreamed it. No one would come with a rope, and a short knife, alone against a bull . . . And no man could drag a bull's head up and slit its throat . . . It was one of my—it was a dream. And it wasn't you, I can see that now. I–I thought you were the man in the cap. I'm sorry.'

The men were muttering now, but no longer with threats. The young officer said, in quite a different tone from any he had used before: 'What was he like, this "man in the cap"?'

His brother said quickly: 'Never mind. Not now.' He put out a hand, took me by the chin, and lifted my face. 'You say your name is Myrddin. Where are you from?'

'From Wales, sir.'

'Ah. So you're the boy they brought from Maridunum?'

'Yes. You knew about me? Oh!' Made stupid by the cold and by bewilderment, I made the discovery I should have made long ago. My flesh shivered like a nervous pony's with cold, and a curious sensation, part excitement, part fear. 'You must be the Count. You must be Ambrosius himself.'

He did not trouble to answer. 'How old are you?'

'Twelve, sir.'

'And who are you, Myrddin, to talk of offering me service? What can you offer me, that I should not cut you down here and now, and let these gentlemen get in out of the cold?'

'Who I am makes no difference, sir. I am the grandson of the King of South Wales, but he is dead. My uncle Camlach is King now, but that's no help to me either; he wants me dead. So I'd not serve your turn even as a hostage. It's not who I am, but what I am that matters. I have something to offer you, my lord. You will see, if you let me live till morning.'

'Ah, yes, valuable information, and five languages. And dreams, too, it seems.' The words were mocking, but he was not smiling. 'The old King's grandson, you say? And Camlach not your father? Nor Dyved, either, surely? I never knew the old man had a grandson, barring Camlach's baby. From what my spies told me I took you to be his bastard.'

'He used sometimes to pass me off as his own bastard—to save my mother's shame, he said, but she never saw it as shame, and she should know. My mother was Niniane, the old King's daughter.'

'Ah.' A pause. 'Was?'

I said: 'She's still alive, but by now she's in St Peter's nunnery. You might say she joined them years ago, but she's only been allowed to leave the palace since the old King died.'

'And your father?'

'She never spoke of him, to me or any man. They say he was the Prince of Darkness.'

I expected the usual reaction to that, the crossed fingers or the quick look over the shoulder. He did neither. He laughed.

'Then no wonder you talk of helping kings to their kingdoms, and dream of gods under the stars.' He turned aside then, with a swirl of the big cloak. 'Bring him along, one of you. Uther, you may as well give him your cloak again before he dies in front of our eyes.'

'Do you think I'd touch it after him, even if he were the Prince of Darkness in person?' asked Uther.

Ambrosius laughed. 'If you ride that poor beast of yours in your usual fashion you'll be warm enough without. And if your cloak is dabbled with the blood of the bull, then it's not for you, tonight, is it?'

'Are you blaspheming?'

'I?' said Ambrosius, with a sort of cold blankness.

His brother opened his mouth, thought better of it, shrugged, and vaulted into his grey's saddle. Someone flung the cloak to me, and—as I struggled with shaking hands to wrap it round me again—seized me, bundled me up in it anyhow, and threw me up like a parcel to some rider on a wheeling horse. Ambrosius swung to the saddle of a big black.

'Come, gentlemen.'

The black stallion jumped forward, and Ambrosius' cloak flew out. The grey pounded after him. The rest of the cavalcade strung out at a hand-gallop along the track back to the town.

Chapter Five

Ambrosius' headquarters was in the town. I learned later that the town had, in fact, grown up round the camp where Ambrosius and his brother had, during the last couple of years, begun to gather and train the army that had for so long been a mythical threat to Vortigern, and now, with the help of King Budec, and troops from half the countries of Gaul, was growing into a fact. Budec was King of Less Britain, and cousin of Ambrosius and Uther. He it was who had taken the brothers in twenty years ago when they—Ambrosius then ten years old, and Uther still at his nurse's breast—were carried overseas into safety after Vortigern had murdered their elder brother the King. Budec's own castle was barely a stone's throw from the camp that Ambrosius had built, and round the two strongpoints the town had grown up, a mixed collection of houses, shops and huts, with the wall and ditch thrown round for protection. Budec was an old man now, and had made Ambrosius his heir, as well as Comes or Count of his forces. It had been supposed in the past that the brothers would be content to stay in Less Britain and rule it after Budec's death; but now that Vortigern's grip on Greater Britain was slackening, the money and the men were pouring in, and it was an open secret that Ambrosius had his eye on South and West Britain for himself, while Uther—even at twenty a brilliant soldier—would, it was hoped, hold Less Britain, and so for another generation at least provide between the two kingdoms a Romano-Celtic rampart against the barbarians from the north.

I soon found that in one respect Ambrosius was pure Roman. The first thing that happened to me after I was dumped, cloak and all, between the door-posts of his outer hall, was that I was seized, unwrapped, and—exhausted by now beyond protest or question—deposited in a bath. The heating system certainly worked here; the water was steaming hot, and thawed my frozen body in three painful and ecstatic minutes. The man who had carried me home—it was Cadal, who turned out to be one of the Count's personal servants—bathed me himself. Under Ambrosius' own orders, he told me curtly, as he scrubbed and oiled and dried me, and then stood over me as I put on a clean tunic of white wool only two sizes too big.

'Just to make sure you don't bolt again. He wants to talk to you, don't ask me why. You can't wear those sandals in this house, Dia knows where you've been with them. Leastways, it's obvious where you've been with them; cows, was it?' You can go barefoot, the floors are warm. Well, at least you're clean now. Hungry?'

'Are you trying to be funny?'

'Come along, then. Kitchen's this way. Unless, being a king's grand-bastard, or whatever it was you told him, you're too proud to eat in the kitchen?'

'Just this once,' I said, 'I'll put up with it.'

He shot me a look, scowled, and then grinned. 'You've got guts, I'll give you that. You stood up to them a fair treat. Beats me how you thought of all that stuff quick enough. Rocked 'em proper. I wouldn't have given two pins for your chances once Uther laid hands on you. You got yourself a hearing, anyway.'

'It was true.'

'Oh, sure, sure. Well, you can tell him all over again in a minute, and see you make it good, because he don't like them that wastes his time, see?'

'Tonight?'

'Certainly. You'll find that out if you live till morning; he doesn't waste much time sleeping. Nor does Prince Uther, come to that, but then he's not working, exactly. Not at his papers, that is, though they reckon he puts in a bit of uncommon hard labour in other directions. Come along.'

Yards before we reached the kitchen door the smell of hot food came out to meet me, and with it the sound of frying.

The kitchen was a big room, and it seemed, to my eye, about as grand as the dining-room at home. The floor was of smooth red tiles, there was a raised hearth at each end of the room, and along the walls the chopping-slabs with store-jars of oil and wine below them and shelves of dishes above. At one of the hearths a sleepy-eyed boy was heating the oil in a skillet; he had kindled fresh charcoal in the burners, and on one of these a pot of soup simmered, while sausages spat and crackled over a grill, and I could smell chicken frying. I noticed that–in spite of Cadal's implied disbelief in my story–I was given a platter of Samian ware so fine that it must be the same used at the Count's own table, and the wine came in a glass goblet and was poured from a glazed red jar with a carved seal and the label 'Reserve'. There was even a fine white napkin.

The cook-boy–he must have been roused from his bed to make the meal for me–hardly bothered to look who he was working for; after he had dished up the meal he scraped the burners hurriedly clean for morning, did an even sketchier job of scouring his pans, then with a glance at Cadal for permission, went yawning back to bed. Cadal served me himself, and even fetched fresh bread hot from the bake-house, where the first batch had just come out for morning. The soup was some savoury concoction of shellfish, which they eat almost daily in Less Britain. It was smoking hot and delicious, and I thought I had never eaten anything so good, until I tried the chicken, crisp-fried in oil, and the grilled sausages, brown and bursting with spiced meat and onions. I mopped the platter dry with the new bread, and shook my head when Cadal handed a dish of dried dates and cheese and honey-cakes.

'No, thank you.'

'Enough?'

'Oh, yes.' I pushed the platter away. 'That was the best meal I ever ate in my life. Thank you.'

'Well,' he said, 'hunger's the best sauce, they say. Though I'll allow the food's good here.' He brought fresh water and a towel and waited while I rinsed my hands and dried them. 'Well, I might even credit the rest of your story now.'

I looked up. 'What d'you mean?'

'You didn't learn your manners in a kitchen, that's for sure. Ready? Come along then, he said to interrupt him even if he was working.'

Ambrosius, however, was not working when we got to his room. His table—a vast affair of marble from Italy—was indeed littered with rolls and maps and writing materials, and the Count was in his big chair behind it, but he sat half sideways, chin on fist, staring into the brazier which filled the room with warmth and the faint scent of apple-wood.

He did not look up as Cadal spoke to the sentry, and with a clash of arms the latter let me by.

'The boy, sir.' This was not the voice Cadal had used to me.

'Thank you. You can go to bed, Cadal.'

'Sir.'

He went. The leather curtains fell to behind him. Ambrosius turned his head then. He looked me up and down for some minutes in silence. Then he nodded towards a stool.

'Sit down.'

I obeyed him.

'I see they found something for you to wear. Have you been fed?'

'Yes, thank you, sir.'

'And you're warm enough now? Pull the stool nearer the fire if you want to.'

He turned straight in the chair, and leaned back, his hands resting on the carved lions' heads of the arms. There was a lamp on the table between us, and in its bright steady light any resemblance between the Count Ambrosius and the strange man of my dream had vanished completely.

It is difficult now, looking back from this distance in time, to remember my first real impression of Ambrosius. He would be at that time not much more than thirty years old, but I was only twelve, and to me, of course, he already seemed venerable. But I think that in fact he did seem older than his years; this was a natural result of the life he had led, and the heavy responsibility he had borne since he was a little younger than myself. There were lines round his eyes, and two heavy furrows between his brows which spoke of decision and perhaps temper, and his mouth was hard and straight, and usually unsmiling. His brows were dark like his hair, and could bar his eyes formidably with shadow. There was the faint white line of a scar running from his left ear half over his cheekbone. His nose looked Roman, high-bridged and prominent, but his skin was tanned rather than olive, and there was something about his eyes which spoke of black Celt rather than Roman. It was a bleak face, a face (as I would find) that could cloud with frustration or anger, or even with the hard control that he exerted over these, but it was a face to trust. He was not a man one could love easily, certainly not a man to like, but a man either to hate or to worship. You either fought him, or followed him. But it had to be one or the other; once you came within reach of him, you had no peace.

All this I had to learn. I remember little now of what I thought of him, except for the deep eyes watching me past the lamp, and his hands clasped on the lions' heads. But I remember every word that was said.

He looked me up and down. 'Myrddin, son of Niniane, daughter of the King of South Wales . . . And privy, they tell me, to the secrets of the palace at Maridunum?'

'I—did I say that? I told them I lived there, and heard things sometimes.'

'My men brought you across the Narrow Sea because you said you had secrets which would be useful to me. Was that not true?'

'Sir,' I said a little desperately, 'I don't know what might be useful to you. To them I spoke the language I thought they would understand. I thought they were going to kill me. I was saving my life.'

'I see. Well, now you are here, and safely. Why did you leave your home?'

'Because once my grandfather had died, it was not safe for me there. My mother was going into a nunnery, and Camlach my uncle had already tried to kill me, and his servants killed my friend.'

'Your friend?'

'My servant. His name was Cerdic. He was a slave.'

'Ah, yes. They told me about that. They said you set fire to the palace. You were perhaps a little—drastic?'

'I suppose so. But someone had to do him honour. He was mine.'

His brows went up. 'Do you give that as a reason, or as an obligation?'

'Sir?' I puzzled it out, then said slowly: 'Both, I think.'

He looked down at his hands. He had moved them from the chair arms, and they were clasped on the table in front of him. 'Your mother, the princess.' He said it as if the thought sprang straight from what we had been saying. 'Did they harm her, too?'

'Of course not!'

He looked up at my tone. I explained quickly. 'I'm sorry, my lord, I only meant, if they'd been going to harm her, how could I have left? No, Camlach would never harm her. I told you, she'd spoken for years of wanting to go into St Peter's nunnery. I can't even remember a time when she didn't receive any Christian priest who visited Maridunum, and the Bishop himself, when he came from Caerleon, used to lodge in the palace. But my grandfather would never let her go. He and the Bishop used to quarrel over her—and over me . . . The Bishop wanted me baptised, you see, and my grandfather wouldn't hear of it. I—I think perhaps he kept it as a bribe to my mother, if she'd tell him who my father was, or perhaps if she'd consent to marry where he chose for her, but she never consented, or told him anything.' I paused, wondering if I was saying too much, but he was watching me steadily, and it seemed attentively. 'My grandfather swore she should never go into the Church,' I added, 'but as soon as he died she asked Camlach, and he allowed it. He would have shut me up, too, so I ran away.'

He nodded. 'Where did you intend to go?'

'I didn't know. It was true, what Marric said to me in the boat, that I'd have to go to someone. I'm only twelve, and because I can't be my own master, I must find a master. I didn't want Vortigern, or Vortimer, and I didn't know where else to go.'

'So you persuaded Marric and Hanno to keep you alive and bring you to me?'

'Not really,' I said honestly. 'I didn't know at first where they were going, I just said anything I could think of to save myself. I had put myself into the god's hand, and he had sent me into their path, and then the ship was there. So I made them bring me across.'

'To me?'

I nodded. The brazier flickered, and the shadows danced. A shadow moved on his cheek, as if he was smiling. 'Then why not wait till they did so? Why jump ship and risk freezing to death in an icy field?'

'Because I was afraid they didn't mean to bring me to you after all. I thought that they might have realised how—how little use I would be to you.'

'So you came ashore on your own in the middle of a winter's night, and in a strange country, and the god threw you straight at my feet. You and your god between you, Myrddin, make a pretty powerful combination. I can see I have no choice.'

'My lord?'

'Perhaps you are right, and there are ways in which you can serve me.' He looked down at the table again, picked up a pen, and turned it over in his hand, as if he examined it. 'But tell me first, why are you called Myrddin? You say your mother never told you who your father was? Never even hinted? Might she have called you after him?'

'Not by calling me Myrddin, sir. That's one of the old gods—there's a shrine just near St Peter's gate. He was the god of the hill nearby, and some say of other parts beyond South Wales. But I have another name.' I hesitated. 'I've never told anyone this before, but I'm certain it was my father's name.'

'And that is?'

'Emrys. I heard her talking to him once, at night, years ago when I was very small. I never forgot. There was something about her voice. You can tell.'

The pen became still. He looked at me under his brows. 'Talking to him? Then it was someone in the palace?'

'Oh, no, not like that. It wasn't real.'

'You mean it was a dream? A vision? Like this tonight of the bull?'

'No, sir. And I wouldn't have called that a dream, either—it was real, too, in a different way. I have those sometimes. But the time I heard my mother . . . There was an old hypocaust in the palace that had been out of use for years; they filled it in later, but when I was young—when I was little—I used to crawl in there to get away from people. I kept things there . . . the sort of things you keep when you're small, and if they find them, they throw them away.'

'I know. Go on.'

'Do you? I—well, I used to crawl through the hypocaust, and one night I was under her chamber, and heard her talking to herself, out loud, as you do when you pray sometimes. I heard her say "Emrys", but I don't remember what else.' I looked at him. 'You know how one catches one's own name, even if one can't hear much else? I thought she must be praying for me, but when I was older and remembered it, it came to me that the "Emrys" must be my father. There was something about her voice . . . and anyway, she never called me that; she called me Merlin.'

'Why?'

'After a falcon. It's a name for the *corwalch*.'

'Then I shall call you Merlin, too. You have courage, and it seems as if you have eyes that can see a long way. I might need your eyes, some day. But tonight you can start with simpler things. You shall tell me about your home. Well, what is it?'

'If I'm to serve you . . . Of course I will tell you anything I can . . . But—' I hesitated, and he took the words from me:

'But you must have my promise that when I invade Britain no harm will come to your mother? You have it. She shall be safe, and so shall any other man or woman you may ask me to spare for their kindness to you.'

I must have been staring. 'You are–very generous.'

'If I take Britain, I can afford to be. I should perhaps have made some reservations.' He smiled. 'It might be difficult if you wanted an amnesty for your uncle Camlach?'

'It won't arise,' I said. 'When you take Britain, he'll be dead.'

A silence. His lips parted to say something, but I think he changed his mind. 'I said I might use those eyes of yours some day. Now, you have my promise, so let us talk. Never mind if things don't seem important enough to tell. Let me be the judge of that.'

So I talked to him. It did not strike me as strange then that he should talk to me as if I were his equal, nor that he should spend half the night with me asking questions which in part his spies could have answered. I believe that twice, while we talked, a slave came in silently and replenished the brazier, and once I heard the clash and command of the guard changing outside the door. Ambrosius questioned, prompted, listened, sometimes writing on a tablet in front of him, sometimes staring, chin on fist, at the table-top, but more usually watching me with that steady, shadowed stare. When I hesitated, or strayed into some irrelevancy, or faltered through sheer fatigue, he would prod me back with his questions towards some unseen goal, as a muleteer goads his mule.

'This fortress on the River Seint, where your grandfather met Vortigern. How far north of Caerleon? By which road? Tell me about the road . . . How is the fortress reached from the sea?'

And: 'The tower where the High King lodged, Maximus' Tower– Macsen's, you call it . . . Tell me about this. How many men were housed there. What road there is to the harbour . . .'

Or: 'You say the King's party halted in a valley pass, south of the Snow Hill, and the kings went aside together. Your man Cerdic said they were looking at an old stronghold on the crag. Describe the place . . . The height of the crag? How far one should see from the top, to the north . . . the south . . . the east?'

Or: 'Now think of your grandfather's nobles. How many will be loyal to

Camlach? Their names? How many men? And of his allies, who? Their numbers . . . their fighting power.'

And then, suddenly: 'Now tell me this. How did you know Camlach was going to Vortimer.'

'He said so to my mother,' I told him, 'by my grandfather's bier. I heard him. There had been rumours that this would happen, and I knew he had quarrelled with my grandfather, but nobody knew anything for certain. Even my mother only suspected what he meant to do. But as soon as the King was dead, he told her.'

'He announced this straight away? Then how was it that Marric and Hanno heard nothing, apart from the rumours of the quarrel?'

Fatigue, and the long relentless questioning had made me incautious. I said, before I thought: 'He didn't announce it. He told only her. He was alone with her.'

'Except for you?' His voice changed, so that I jumped on my stool. He watched me under his brows. 'I thought you told me the hypocaust had been filled in?'

I merely sat and looked at him. I could think of nothing to say.

'It seems strange, does it not,' he said levelly, 'that he should tell your mother this in front of you, when he must have known you were his enemy? When his men had just killed your servant? And then, after he had told you of his secret plans, how did you get out of the palace and into the hands of my men, to "make" them bring you with them to me?'

'I—' I stammered. 'My lord, you cannot think that I—my lord, I told you I was no spy. I—all I have told you is true. He did say it, I swear it.'

'Be careful. It matters whether this is true. Your mother told you?'

'No.'

'Slaves' talk, then? That's all?'

I said desperately: 'I heard him myself.'

'Then where were you?'

I met his eyes. Without quite realising why, I told the simple truth. 'My lord, I was asleep in the hills, six miles off.'

There was a silence, the longest yet. I could hear the embers settling in the brazier, and some distance off, outside, a dog barking. I sat waiting for his anger.

'Merlin.'

I looked up.

'Where do you get the Sight from? Your mother?'

Against all expectation, he believed me. I said eagerly: 'Yes, but it is different. She saw only women's things, to do with love. Then she began to fear the power, and let it be.'

'Do you fear it?'

'I shall be a man.'

'And a man takes power where it is offered. Yes. Did you understand what you saw tonight?'

'The bull? No, my lord, only that it was something secret.'

'Well, you will know some day, but not now. Listen.'

Somewhere, outside, a cock crowed, shrill and silver like a trumpet. He said: 'That, at any rate, puts paid to your phantoms. It's high time you were asleep. You look half dead for lack of it.' He got to his feet. I slid softly from the stool and he stood for a moment looking down at me. 'I was ten when I sailed for Less Britain, and I was sick all the way.'

'So was I,' I said.

He laughed. 'Then you will be as exhausted as I was. When you have slept, we'll decide what to do with you.' He touched a bell, and a slave opened the door and stood aside, waiting. 'You'll sleep in my room tonight. This way.'

The bedchamber was Roman, too. I was to find that by comparison with, say, Uther's, it was austere enough, but to the eyes of a boy used to the provincial and often makeshift standards of a small outlying country, it seemed luxurious, with the big bed spread with scarlet wool blankets and a fur rug, the sheepskins on the floor, and the bronze tripod as high as a man, where the triple lamps, shaped like small dragons, mouthed tongues of flame. Thick brown curtains kept out the icy night, and it was very quiet.

As I followed Ambrosius and the slave in past the guards–there were two on the door, rigid and unmoving except for their eyes which slid, carefully empty of speculation, from Ambrosius to me–it occurred to me for the first time to wonder whether he might be, perhaps, Roman in other ways.

But he only pointed to an archway where another of the brown curtains half hid a recess with a bed in it. I suppose a slave slept there sometimes, within call.

The servant pulled the curtain aside and showed me the blankets folded across the mattress, and the good pillows stuffed with fleece, then left me and went to attend Ambrosius.

I took off my borrowed tunic and folded it carefully. The blankets were thick, new wool, and smelt of cedar-wood. Ambrosius and the slave were talking, but softly, and their voices came like echoes from the far end of a deep, quiet cave. It was bliss only to be in a real bed again, to lie, warm and fed, in a place that was beyond even the sound of the sea. And safe.

I think he said 'Good night,' but I was already submerged in sleep and could not drag myself to the surface to answer. The last thing I remember is the slave moving softly to put out the lamps.

Chapter Six

When I awoke next morning it was late. The curtains had been drawn back, letting in a grey and wintry day, and Ambrosius' bed was empty. Outside the windows I could see a small courtyard where a colonnade framed a square of garden, at the centre of which a fountain played–in silence, I thought, till I saw that the cascade was solid ice.

The tiles of the floor were warm to my bare feet. I reached for the white tunic which I had left folded on a stool by the bed, but I saw that someone had put there instead a new one of dark green, the colour of yew trees, which fitted. There was a good leather belt to go with it, and a pair of new sandals replacing my old ones. There was even a cloak, this time of a light beech-green, with a copper brooch to fasten it. There was something embossed on the brooch; a dragon, enamelled in scarlet, the same device I had seen last night on the seal-ring he wore.

It was the first time that I remember feeling as if I looked like a prince, and I found it strange that this should happen at the moment when you would have thought I had reached the bottom of my fortunes. Here in Less Britain I had nothing, not even a bastard name to protect myself with, no kin, not even a rag of property. I had hardly spoken with any man except Ambrosius, and to him I was a servant, a dependant, something to be used, and only alive by his sufferance.

Cadal brought me my breakfast, brown bread and honeycomb and dried figs. I asked where Ambrosius was.

'Out with the men, drilling. Or rather, watching the exercises. He's there everyday.'

'What do you suppose he wants me to do?'

'All he said was, you could stay around here till you were rested, and to make yourself at home. I've to send someone to the ship, so if you'll tell me what your traps were that you lost, I'll have them brought.'

'There was nothing much, I didn't have time. A couple of tunics and a pair of sandals wrapped in a blue cloak, and some little things—a brooch, and a clasp my mother gave me, things like that.' I touched the expensive folds of the tunic I wore. 'Nothing as good as this. Cadal, I hope I can serve him. Did he say what he wanted of me?'

'Not a word. You don't think he tells me his secret thoughts, do you? Now you just do as he says, make yourself at home, keep your mouth shut, and see you don't get into trouble. I don't suppose you'll be seeing much of him.'

'I didn't suppose I would,' I said. 'Where am I to live?'

'Here.'

'In this room?'

'Not likely. I meant, in the house.'

I pushed my plate aside. 'Cadal, does my lord Uther have a house of his own?'

Cadal's eyes twinkled. He was a short stocky man, with a square, reddish face, a black shag of hair, and small black eyes no bigger than olives. The gleam in them now showed me that he knew exactly what I was thinking, and moreover that everyone in the house must know exactly what had passed between me and the prince last night.

'No, he hasn't. He lives here, too. Cheek by jowl, you might say.'

'Oh.'

'Don't worry; you won't be seeing much of him, either. He's going north in a week or two. Should cool him off quickly, this weather . . . He's probably forgotten all about you by now, anyway.' He grinned and went out.

He was right; during the next couple of weeks I saw very little of Uther, then he left with troops for the north, on some expedition designed half as an exercise for his company, half as a foray in search of supplies. Cadal had guessed right about the relief this would bring me; I was not sorry to be out of Uther's range. I had the idea that he had not welcomed my presence in his brother's house, and indeed that Ambrosius' continued kindness had annoyed him quite a lot.

I had expected to see very little of the Count after that first night when I had told him all I knew, but thereafter he sent for me on most evenings when he was free, sometimes to question me and to listen to what I could tell him of home, sometimes—when he was tired—to have me play to him, or, on several occasions, to take a hand at chess. Here, to my surprise, we were about even, and I do not think he let me beat him. He was out of practice, he told me; the usual game was dice, and he was not risking that against an infant soothsayer. Chess, being a matter of mathematics rather than magic, was less susceptible to the black arts.

He kept his promise, and told me what I had seen that first night by the standing stone. I believe, had he told me to, I would even have dismissed it as a dream. As time went on, the memory had grown blurred and fainter, until I had begun to think it might have been a dream fostered by cold and hunger and some dim recollection of the faded picture on the Roman chest in my room at Maridunum, the kneeling bull and the man with a knife under an arch studded with stars. But when Ambrosius talked about it, I knew I had seen more than was in the painting. I had seen the soldiers' god, the Word, the Light, the Good Shepherd, the mediator between the one God and man. I had seen Mithras, who had come out of Asia a thousand years ago. He had been born, Ambrosius told me, in a cave at mid-winter, while shepherds watched and a star shone; he was born of earth and light, and sprang from the rock with a torch in his left hand and a knife in his right. He killed the bull to bring life and fertility to the earth with its shed blood, and then, after his last meal of bread and wine, he was called up to heaven. He was the god of strength and gentleness, of courage and self-restraint. 'The soldiers' god,' said Ambrosius again, 'and that is why we have re-established his worship here—to make, as the Roman armies did, some common meeting-ground for the chiefs and petty kings of all tongues and persuasions who fight with us. About his worship I can't tell you, because it is forbidden, but you will have gathered that on that first night I and my officers had met for a ceremony of worship, and your talk about bread and wine and bull-slaying sounded very much as if you had seen more of our ceremony than we are even allowed to speak about. You will know it all one day, perhaps. Till then, be warned, and if you are asked about your vision, remember that it was only a dream. You understand?'

I nodded, but with my mind filled, suddenly, with only one thing he had said. I thought of my mother and the Christian priests, of Galapas and the well of Myrddin, of things seen in the water and heard in the wind. 'You want me to be an initiate of Mithras?'

'A man takes power where it is offered,' he said again. 'You have told me you don't know what god has his hand over you; perhaps Mithras was the god in whose path you put yourself, and who brought you to me. We shall see. Meanwhile, he is still the god of armies, and we shall need his help . . . Now bring the harp, if you will, and sing to me.'

So he dealt with me, treating me more as a prince than I had ever been treated in my grandfather's house, where at least I had had some sort of claim to it.

Cadal was assigned to me as my own servant. I thought at first that he might resent this, as a poor substitute for serving Ambrosius, but he did not seem to mind, in fact I got the impression that he was pleased. He was soon on easy terms with me, and, since there were no other boys of my age about the place, he was my constant companion. I was also given a horse. At first they gave me one of Ambrosius' own, but after a day on that I asked shamefacedly if I might have something more my size, and was given a small stolid grey which—with my only moment of nostalgia—I called Aster.

So the first days passed. I rode out with Cadal at my side to see the country; this was still in the grip of frost, and soon the frost turned to rain so that the fields were churned mud and the ways were slippery and foul, and a cold wind whistled day and night across the flats, whipping the Small Sea to white on iron-grey, and blackening the northern sides of the standing stones with wet. I looked one day for the stone with the mark of the axe, and failed to find it. But there was another where in a certain light you could see a dagger carved, and a thick stone, standing a little apart, where under the lichen and the bird droppings stared the shape of an open eye. By daylight the stones did not breathe so cold on one's nape, but there was still something there, watching, and it was not a way my pony cared to go.

Of course I explored the town. King Budec's castle was in the centre, on a rocky outcrop which had been crowned with a high wall. A stone ramp led up to the gate, which was shut and guarded. I often saw Ambrosius, or his officers, riding up this ramp, but never went myself any nearer than the guard post at the foot of it. But I saw King Budec several times, riding out with his men. His hair and his long beard were almost white, but he sat his big brown gelding like a man thirty years younger, and I heard countless stories of his prowess at arms and how he had sworn to be avenged on Vortigern for the killing of his cousin Constantius, even though it would take a lifetime. This, in fact, it threatened to do, for it seemed an almost impossible task for so poor a country to raise the kind of army that might defeat Vortigern and the Saxons, and thereafter hold Greater Britain. But soon now, men said, soon . . .

Every day, whatever the weather, men drilled on the flat fields outside the town walls. Ambrosius had now, I learnt, a standing army of about four thousand men. As far as Budec was concerned they earned their keep a dozen times over, since not much more than thirty miles away his borders ran with those of a young king whose eye was weather-lifted for plunder, and who was held back only by rumours of Ambrosius' growing power and the formidable reputation of his men. Budec and Ambrosius fostered the idea that the army was mainly defensive, and saw to it that Vortigern learned nothing for certain: news of preparations for invasion reached him as before only in the form of rumours, and Ambrosius' spies made sure that these sounded like rumours. What Vortigern actually believed was what Budec was at pains that he should believe, that Ambrosius and Uther had accepted their fate as exiles, had settled in Less Britain as Budec's heirs, and were concerned with keeping the borders that would one day be their own.

This impression was fostered by the fact that the army was used as a foraging party for the town. Nothing was too simple or too rough for Ambrosius' men to undertake. Work which even my grandfather's rough-trained troops would have despised, these seasoned soldiers did as a matter of course. They brought in and stored wood in the town's yards. They dug and stored peat, and burned charcoal. They built and worked the smithies, making not only weapons of war, but tools for tilling and harvesting and building—spades, ploughshares, axes, scythes. They could break horses, and herd and drive cattle as well as butcher them; they built carts; they could pitch and mount guard over a camp in two hours flat, and strike it in one hour less. There was a corps of engineers who had half a square mile of workshops, and could supply anything from a padlock to a troopship. They were fitting themselves, in short, for the task of landing blindfold in a strange country and maybe living off it and moving fast across it in all weathers. 'For,' said Ambrosius once to his officers in front of me, 'it is only to fair-weather soldiers that war is a fair-weather game. I shall fight to win, and after I have won, to hold. And Britain is a big country; compared with her, this corner of Gaul is no more than a meadow. So, gentlemen, we fight through spring and summer, but we do not retire at the first October frost to rest and sharpen our swords again for spring. We fight on—in snow, if we have to, in storm and frost and the wet mud of winter. And in all that weather and through all that time, we must eat, and fifteen thousand men must eat—well.'

Shortly after this, about a month after my arrival in Less Britain, my days of freedom ended. Ambrosius found me a tutor.

Belasius was very different from Galapas and from the gentle drunkard Demetrius, who had been my official tutor at home. He was a man in his prime who was one of the Count's 'men of business' and seemed to be concerned with the estimates and accounting side of Ambrosius' affairs; he was by training a mathematician and astronomer. He was half Gallo-Roman, half Sicilian, a tallish olive-faced man with long-lidded black eyes, a melancholy expression and a cruel mouth. He had an acid tongue and a sudden, vicious temper, but he was never capricious. I soon learned that the way to dodge his sarcasms and his heavy hand was to do my work quickly and well, and since this came easily to me and I enjoyed it, we soon understood one another, and got along tolerably well.

One afternoon towards the end of March we were working in my room in Ambrosius' house. Belasius had lodgings in the town which he had been careful never to speak of, so I assumed he lived with some drab and was ashamed to risk my seeing her; he worked mainly in headquarters, but the offices near the treasury were always crowded with clerks and paymasters, so we held our daily tutorials in my room. This was not a large chamber, but to my eyes very well appointed, with a floor of red tiles locally made, carved fruitwood furniture, a bronze mirror, and a brazier and lamp that had come from Rome.

Today, the lamp was lit even in the afternoon, for the day was dark and overcast. Belasius was pleased with me; we were doing mathematics, and it had been one of the days when I could forget nothing, but walked through the problems he set me as if the field of knowledge were an open meadow with a pathway leading plain across it for all to see.

He drew the flat of his hand across the wax to erase my drawing, pushed the tablets aside, and stood up.

'You've done well today, which is just as well, because I have to leave early.'

He reached out and struck the bell. The door opened so quickly that I knew his servant must have been waiting just outside. The boy came in with his master's cloak over his arm, and shook it out quickly to hold it for him. He did not even glance my way for permission, but watched Belasius, and I could see he was afraid of him. He was about my age, or younger, with brown hair cut close to his head in a curled cap, and grey eyes too big for his face.

Belasius neither spoke nor glanced at him, but turned his shoulders to the cloak, and the boy reached up to fasten the clasp. Across his head Belasius said to me: 'I shall tell the Count of your progress. He will be pleased.'

The expression on his face was as near a smile as he ever showed. Made bold by this, I turned on my stool. 'Belasius—'

He stopped halfway to the door. 'Well?'

'You must surely know . . . Please tell me. What are his plans for me?'

'That you should work at your mathematics and your astronomy, and remember your languages.'

His tone was smooth and mechanical, but there was amusement in his eyes, so I persisted. 'To become what?'

'What do you wish to become?'

I did not answer. He nodded, just as if I had spoken. 'If he wanted you to carry a sword for him, you would be out in the square now.'

'But—to live here as I do, with you to teach me, and Cadal as my servant . . . I don't understand it. I should be serving him somehow not just learning . . . and living like this, like a prince. I know very well that I am only alive by his grace.'

He regarded me for a moment under those long lids. Then he smiled. 'It's something to remember. I believe you told him once that it was what you were, not who you were, that would matter. Believe me, he will use you, as he uses everyone. So stop wondering about it, and let it be. Now I must go.'

The boy opened the door for him to show Cadal just pausing outside, with a hand raised to knock.

'Oh, excuse me, sir. I came to see when you'd be done for the day. I've got the horses ready, Master Merlin.'

'We've finished already,' said Belasius. He paused in the doorway and looked back to me. 'Where were you planning to go?'

'North, I think, the road through the forest. The causeway's still good and the road will be dry.'

He hesitated, then said, to Cadal rather than to me: 'Then keep to the road, and be home before dark.' He nodded, and went out, with the boy at his heels.

'Before dark?' said Cadal. 'It's been dark all day, and it's raining now, besides. Look, Merlin—' when we were alone we were less formal '—why don't we just take a look along to the engineers' workshops? You always enjoy that, and Tremorinus ought to have got that ram working by now. What do you say we stay in town?'

I shook my head. 'I'm sorry, Cadal, but I must go, rain or no rain. I've got the fidgets, or something, and I must get out.'

'Well, then, a mile or two down to the port should do you. Come on, here's your cloak. It'll be pitch black in the forest; have a bit of sense.'

'The forest,' I said obstinately, turning my head while he fastened the pin. 'And don't argue with me, Cadal. If you ask me, Belasius has the right idea. *His* servant doesn't even dare to speak, let alone argue. I ought to treat you the same way—in fact I'll start straight away . . . What are you grinning at?'

'Nothing. All right, I know when to give in. The forest it is, and if we lose ourselves and never get back alive, at least I'll have died with you, and won't have to face the Count.'

'I really can't see that he'd care overmuch.'

'Oh, he wouldn't,' said Cadal, holding the door for me to go through. 'It was only a manner of speaking. I doubt if he'd even notice, myself.'

Chapter Seven

Once outside, it was not as dark as it had seemed, and it was warm, one of those heavy, dull days fraught with mists, and a small rain that lay on the heavy wool of our cloaks like frost.

About a mile to the north of the town the flattish salt-bitten turf began to give way to woodland, thin at first, with trees sticking up here and there solitary, with veils of white mist haunting their lower boughs or lying over the turf like pools which now and then broke and swirled as a deer fled through.

The road north was an old one, paved, and the men who had built it had cleared the trees and scrub back on either side for a hundred paces, but with time and neglect the open verge had grown thick with whin and heather and young trees, so that now the forest seemed to crowd round you as you rode, and the way was dark.

Near the town we had seen one or two peasants carrying home fuel on their donkeys, and once one of Ambrosius' messengers spurred past us, with a stare, and what looked like a half-salute to me. But in the forest we met no one. It was the silent time between the thin birdsong of a March day and the hunting of the owls.

When we got among the big trees the rain had stopped, and the mist was thinning. Presently we came to a crossroads where a track—unpaved this time—crossed our own at right angles. The track was one used for hauling timber out of the forest, and also by the carts of charcoal burners, and, though rough and deeply rutted, it was clear and straight, and if you kept your horse to the edge, there was a gallop.

'Let's turn down here, Cadal.'

'You know he said keep to the road.'

'Yes, I know he did, but I don't see why. The forest's perfectly safe.'

This was true. It was another thing Ambrosius had done; men were no longer afraid to ride abroad in Less Britain, within striking distance of the town. The country was constantly patrolled by his companies, alert and spoiling for something to do. Indeed, the main danger was (as I had once heard him admit) that his troops would over-train and grow stale, and look rather too hard for trouble. Meanwhile, the outlaws and disaffected men stayed away, and ordinary folk went about their business in peace. Even women could travel without much of an escort.

'Besides,' I added, 'does it matter what he said? He's not my master. He's only in charge of teaching me, nothing else. We can't possibly lose our way if we keep to the tracks, and if we don't get a canter now, it'll be too dark to press the horses when we get back to the fields. You're always complaining that I don't ride well enough. How can I, when we're always trotting along the road? Please, Cadal.'

'Look, I'm not your master either. All right, then, but not far. And watch your pony; it'll be darker under the trees. Best let me go first.'

I put a hand on his rein. 'No. I'd like to ride ahead, and would you hold back a little, please? The thing is, I—I have so little solitude, and it's been something I'm used to. This was one of the reasons I had to come out this way.' I added carefully: 'It's not that I haven't been glad of your company, but one sometimes wants time to—well, to think things out. If you'll just give me fifty paces?'

He reined back immediately. Then he cleared his throat. 'I told you I'm not your master. Go ahead. But go careful.'

I turned Aster into the ride, and kicked him to a canter. He had not been out of his stable for three days, and in spite of the distance behind us he was eager. He laid his ears back, and picked up speed down the grass verge of the ride. Luckily the mist had almost gone, but here and there it smoked across the track saddle high, and the horses plunged through it, fording it like water.

Cadal was holding well back; I could hear the thud of the mare's hoofs like a heavy echo of my pony's canter. The small rain had stopped, and the air was fresh and cool and resinous with the scent of pines. A woodcock flighted overhead with a sweet whispering call, and a soft tassel of spruce flicked a fistful of drops across my mouth and down inside the neck of my tunic. I shook my head and laughed and the pony quickened his pace, scattering a pool of mist like spray. I crouched over his neck as the track narrowed, and branches whipped at us in earnest. It was darker; the sky thickened to nightfall between the boughs, and the forest rolled by in a dark cloud, wild with scent and silent but for Aster's scudding gallop and the easy pacing of the mare.

Cadal called me to stop. As I made no immediate response, the thudding of the mare's hoofs quickened, and drew closer. Aster's ears flicked, then flattened again, and he began to race. I drew him in. It was easy, as the going was heavy, and he was sweating. He slowed and then stood and waited quietly for Cadal to come up. The brown mare stopped. The only sound in the forest now was the breathing of the horses.

'Well,' he said at length, 'did you get what you wanted?'

'Yes, only you called too soon.'

'We'll have to turn back if we're to be in time for supper. Goes well, that pony. You want to ride ahead on the way back?'

'If I may.'

'I told you there's no question, you do as you like. I know you don't get out on your own, but you're young yet, and it's up to me to see you don't come to harm, that's all.'

'What harm could I come to? I used to go everywhere alone at home.'

'This isn't home. You don't know the country yet. You could lose yourself, or fall off your pony and lie in the forest with a broken leg—'

'It's not very likely, is it? You were told to watch me, why don't you admit it?'

'To look after you.'

'It could come to the same thing. I've heard what they call you. "The watchdog."'

He grunted. 'You don't need to dress it up. "Merlin's black dog,' that's the way I heard it. Don't think I mind. I do as he says and no questions asked, but I'm sorry if it frets you.'

'It doesn't–oh, it doesn't. I didn't mean it like that . . . It's all right, it's only . . . Cadal—'

'Yes?'

'Am I a hostage, after all?'

'That I couldn't say,' said Cadal woodenly. 'Come along, then, can you get by?'

Where our horses stood the way was narrow, the centre of the ride having sunk into deep mud where water faintly reflected the night sky. Cadal reined his mare back into the thicket that edged the ride, while I forced Aster–who would not wet his feet unless compelled–past the mare. As the brown's big quarters pressed back into the tangle of oak and chestnut there was suddenly a crash just behind her, and a breaking of twigs, and some animal burst from the undergrowth almost under the mare's belly, and hurtled across the ride in front of my pony's nose.

Both animals reacted violently. The mare, with a snort of fear, plunged forward hard against the rein. At the same moment Aster shied wildly, throwing me half out of the saddle. Then the plunging mare crashed into his shoulder, and the pony staggered, whirled, lashed out, and threw me.

I missed the water by inches, landing heavily on the soft stuff at the edge of the ride, right up against a broken stump of pine which could have hurt me badly if I had been thrown on it. As it was I escaped with scratches and a minor bruise or two, and a wrenched ankle that, when I rolled over and tried to put it to the ground, stabbed me with pain momentarily so acute as to make the black woods swim.

Even before the mare had stopped circling Cadal was off her back, had flung the reins over a bough, and was stooping over me.

'Merlin–Master Merlin–are you hurt?'

I unclamped my teeth from my lip, and started gingerly with both hands to straighten my leg. 'No, only my ankle, a bit.'

'Let me see . . . No. Hold still. By the dog, Ambrosius will have my skin for this.'

'What was it?'

'A boar, I think. Too small for a deer, too big for a fox.'

'I thought it was a boar, I smelt it. My pony?'

'Halfway home by now, I expect. Of course you had to let the rein go, didn't you?'

'I'm sorry. Is it broken?'

His hands had been moving over my ankle, prodding, feeling. 'I don't think so . . . No, I'm sure it's not. You're all right otherwise? Here, come on, try if you can stand on it. The mare'll take us both, and I want to get back, if I can, before that pony of yours goes in with an empty saddle. I'll be for the lampreys, for sure, if Ambrosius sees him.'

'It wasn't your fault. Is he so unjust?'

'He'll reckon it was, and he wouldn't be far wrong. Come on now, try it.'

'No, give me a moment. And don't worry about Ambrosius, the pony hasn't gone home, he's stopped a little way up the ride. You'd better go and get him.'

He was kneeling over me, and I could see him faintly against the sky. He turned his head to peer along the ride. Beside us the mare stood quietly, except for her restless ears and the white edge to her eye. There was silence except for an owl starting up, and far away on the edge of sound another, like its echo.

'It's pitch dark twenty feet away,' said Cadal. 'I can't see a thing. Did you hear him stop?'

'Yes.' It was a lie, but this was neither the time nor the place for the truth. 'Go and get him, quickly. On foot. He hasn't gone far.'

I saw him stare down at me for a moment, then he got to his feet without a word and started off up the ride. As well as if it had been daylight, I could see his puzzled look. I was reminded, sharply, of Cerdic that day at King's Fort. I leaned back against the stump. I could feel my bruises, and my ankle ached, but for all that there came flooding through me, like a drink of warm wine, the feeling of excitement and release that came with the power. I knew now that I had had to come this way; that this was to be another of the hours when not darkness, nor distance, nor time meant anything. The owl floated silently above me, across the ride. The mare cocked her ears at it, watching without fear. There was the thin sound of bats somewhere above. I thought of the crystal cave, and Galapas' eyes when I told him of my vision. He had not been puzzled, not even surprised. It came to me to wonder, suddenly, how Belasius would look. And I knew he would not be surprised, either.

Hoofs sounded softly in the deep turf. I saw Aster first, approaching ghostly grey, then Cadal like a shadow at his head.

'He was there all right,' he said, 'and for a good reason. He's dead lame. Must have strained something.'

'Well, at least he won't get home before we do.'

'There'll be trouble over this night's work, that's for sure, whatever time we get home. Come on, then, I'll put you up on Rufa.'

With a hand from him I got cautiously to my feet. When I tried to put weight on the left foot, it still hurt me quite a lot, but I knew from the feel of it that it was nothing but a wrench and would soon be better. Cadal threw me up on the mare's back, unhooked the reins from the bough, and gave them into my hand. Then he clicked his tongue to Aster, and led him slowly ahead.

'What are you doing?' I asked. 'Surely she can carry us both?'

'There's no point. You can see how lame this one is. He'll have to be led. If I take him in front he can make the pace. The mare'll stay behind him.–You all right up there?'

'Perfectly, thanks.'

The grey pony was indeed dead lame. He walked slowly beside Cadal with drooping head, moving in front of me like a smoke-beacon in the dusk. The mare followed quietly. It would take, I reckoned, a couple of hours to get home, even without what lay ahead.

Here again was a kind of solitude, no sounds but the soft plodding of the horses' hoofs, the creak of leather, the occasional small noises of the forest round us. Cadal was invisible, nothing but a shadow beside the moving wraith of mist that was Aster. Perched on the big mare at a comfortable walk, I was alone with the darkness and the trees.

We had gone perhaps half a mile when, burning through the boughs of a huge oak to my right, I saw a white star, steady.

'Cadal, isn't there a shorter way back? I remember a track off to the south just near that oak tree. The mist's cleared right away, and the stars are out. Look, there's the Bear.'

His voice came back from the darkness. 'We'd best head for the road.' But in a pace or two he stopped the pony at the mouth of the southgoing track, and waited for the mare to come up.

'It looks good enough, doesn't it?' I asked. 'It's straight, and a lot drier than this track we're on. All we have to do is keep the Bear at our backs, and in a mile or two we should be able to smell the sea. Don't you know your way about the forest?'

'Well enough. It's true this would be shorter, if we can see our way. 'Well . . .' I heard him loosen his short stabbing sword in its sheath. 'Not that there's likely to be trouble, but best be prepared, so keep your voice down, will you, and have your knife ready. And let me tell you one thing, young Merlin, if anything should happen, then you'll ride for home and leave me to it. Got that?'

'Ambrosius' orders again?'

'You could say so.'

'All right, if it makes you feel better, I promise I'll desert you at full speed. But there'll be no trouble.'

He grunted, 'Anyone would think you knew.'

I laughed. 'Oh, I do.'

The starlight caught, momentarily, the whites of his eyes, and the quick gesture of his hand. Then he turned without speaking and led Aster into the track going south.

Chapter Eight

Though the path was wide enough to take two riders abreast, we went in single file, the brown mare adapting her long, comfortable stride to the pony's shorter and very lame step.

It was colder now; I pulled the folds of my cloak round me for warmth. The mist had vanished completely with the drop in temperature, the sky was clear, with some stars, and it was easier to see the way. Here the trees were huge; oaks mainly, the big ones massive and widely spaced, while between them saplings grew thickly and unchecked, and ivy twined with the bare strings of honeysuckle and thickets of thorn. Here and there pines showed fiercely black against the sky. I could hear the occasional patter as damp gathered and dripped from the leaves, and once the scream of some small creature dying under the claws of an owl. The air was full of the smell of damp and fungus and dead leaves and rich, rotting things.

Cadal trudged on in silence, his eyes on the path, which in places was tricky with fallen or rotting branches. Behind him, balancing on the big mare's saddle, I was still possessed by the same light, excited power. There was something ahead of us, to which I was being led, I knew, as surely as the merlin had led me to the cavern at King's Fort.

Rufa's ears pricked, and I heard her soft nostrils flicker. Her head went up. Cadal had not heard, and the grey pony, preoccupied with his lameness, gave no sign that he could smell the other horses. But even before Rufa, I had known they were there.

The path twisted and began to go gently downhill. To either side of us the trees had retreated a little, so that their branches no longer met overhead, and it was lighter. Now to each side of the path were banks, with outcrops of rock and broken ground where in summer there would be foxgloves and bracken, but where now only the dead and wiry brambles ran riot. Our horses' hoofs scraped and rang as they picked their way down the slope.

Suddenly Rufa, without checking her stride, threw up her head and let out a long whinny. Cadal, with an exclamation, stopped dead, and the mare pushed up beside him, head high, ears pricked towards the forest on our right. Cadal snatched at her bridle, pulled her head down, and shrouded her nostrils in the crook of his arm. Aster had lifted his head, too, but he made no sound.

'Horses,' I said softly. 'Can't you smell them?'

I heard Cadal mutter something that sounded like, 'Smell anything, it seems you can, you must have a nose like a bitch fox,' then, hurriedly starting to drag the mare off the track: 'It's too late to go back, they'll have heard this bloody mare. We'd best pull off into the forest.'

I stopped him. 'There's no need. There's no trouble there, I'm certain of it. Let's go on.'

'You talk fine and sure, but how can you know—?'

'I do know. In any case, if they meant us harm, we'd have known of it by now. They've heard us coming long since, and they must know it's only two horses and one of them lame.'

But he still hesitated, fingering his short-sword. The prickles of excitement fretted my skin like burrs. I had seen where the mare's ears were pointing–at a big grove of pines, fifty paces ahead, and set back above the right of the path. They were black even against the blackness of the forest. Suddenly I could wait no longer. I said impatiently: 'I'm going, anyway. You can follow or not, as you choose.' I jerked Rufa's head up and away from him, and kicked her with my good foot, so that she plunged forward past the grey pony. I headed her straight up the bank and into the grove.

The horses were there. Through a gap in the thick roof of pines a cluster of stars burned, showing them clearly. There were only two, standing motionless, with their heads held low and their nostrils muffled against the breast of a slight figure heavily cloaked and hooded against the cold. The hood fell back as he turned to stare; the oval of his face showed pale in the gloom. There was no one else there.

For one startled moment I thought that the black horse nearest me was Ambrosius' big stallion, then as it pulled its head free of the cloak I saw the white blaze on its forehead, and knew in a flash like a falling star why I had been led here.

Behind me, with a scramble and a startled curse, Cadal pulled Aster into the grove. I saw the grey gleam of his sword as he lifted it. 'Who's that?'

I said quietly, without turning: 'Put it up. It's Belasius . . . At least that's his horse. Another with it, and the boy. That's all.'

He advanced. His sword was already sliding back into its housing. 'By the dog, you're right, I'd know that white flash anywhere. Hey, Ulfin, well met. Where's your master?'

Even at six paces I heard the boy gasp with relief. 'Oh, it's you, Cadal . . . My lord Merlin . . . I heard your horse whinny–I wondered–Nobody comes this way.'

I moved the mare forward, and looked down. His face was a pale blur upturned, the eyes enormous. He was still afraid.

'It seems Belasius does,' I said. 'Why?'

'He–he tells me nothing, my lord.'

Cadal said roundly: "Don't give us that. There's not much you don't know about him, you're never more than arm's length from him, day or night, everybody knows that. Come on, out with it. Where's your master?'

'I–he won't be long.'

'We can't wait for him,' said Cadal. 'We want a horse. Go and tell him we're here, and my lord Merlin's hurt, and the pony's lame, and we've got to get home quickly . . . Well? Why don't you go? For pity's sake, what's the matter with you?'

'I can't. He said I must not. He forbade me to move from here.'

'As he forbade us to leave the road, in case we came this way?' I said. 'Yes. Now, your name's Ulfin, is it? Well, Ulfin, never mind the horse. I want to know where Belasius is.'

'I–I don't know.'

'You must at least have seen which way he went?'

'N-no, my lord.'

'By the dog,' exclaimed Cadal, 'who cares where he is, as long as we get the horse? Look, boy, have some sense, we can't wait half the night for your master, we've got to get home. If you tell him the horse was for my lord Merlin, he won't eat you alive this time, will he?' Then, as the boy stammered something: 'Well, all right, do you want us to go and find him ourselves, and get his leave?'

The boy moved then, jamming a fist to his mouth, like an idiot. 'No . . . You must not . . . You must not . . .!'

'By Mithras,' I said–it was an oath I cultivated at the time, having heard Ambrosius use it–'what's he doing? Murder?'

On the word, the shriek came.

Not a shriek of pain, but worse, the sound of a man in mortal fear. I thought the cry contained a word, as if the terror was shaped, but it was no word that I knew. The scream rose unbearably, as if it would burst him, then was chopped off sharply as if by a blow on the throat. In the dreadful silence that followed a faint echo came, in a breath from the boy Ulfin.

Cadal stood frozen as he had turned, one hand holding his sword, the other grasping Aster's bridle. I wrenched the mare's head round and lashed the reins down on her neck. She bounded forward, almost unseating me. She plunged under the pines towards the track. I lay flat on her neck as the boughs swept past us, hooked a hand in her neck-strap, and hung on like a tick. Neither Cadal nor the boy had moved or made a sound.

The mare went down the bank with a scramble and a slither, and as we reached the path I saw, so inevitably that I felt no surprise–nor indeed any thought at all–another path, narrow and overgrown, leading out of the track to the other side, just opposite the grove of pines.

I hauled on the mare's mouth, and when she jibbed, trying to head down the broader track for home, I lashed her again. She laid her ears flat and went into the path at a gallop.

The path twisted and turned, so that almost straight away our pace slackened, slowed, became a heavy canter. This was the direction from which that dreadful sound had come. It was apparent even in the starlight that someone had recently been this way. The path was so little used that winter grass and heather had almost choked it, but someone–some-thing–had been thrusting a way through. The going was so soft that even a cantering horse made very little noise.

I strained my ears for the sound of Cadal coming after me, but could not hear him. It occurred to me only then that both he and the boy must have thought that, terrified by the shriek, I had run as Cadal had bidden me, for home.

I pulled Rufa to a walk. She slowed willingly, her head up, her ears pricked forward. She was quivering; she, too, had heard the shriek. A gap in the forest showed three hundred paces ahead, so light that I thought it must mark the end of the trees. I watched carefully as we approached it, but nothing moved against the sky beyond.

Then, so softly that I had to strain my ears to make sure it was neither wind nor sea, I heard chanting.

My skin prickled. I knew now where Belasius was, and why Ulfin had been so afraid. And I knew why Belasius had said: 'Keep to the road, and be home before dark.'

I sat up straight. The heat ran over my skin in little waves, like catspaws of wind over water. My breathing came shallow and fast. For a moment I wondered if this was fear, then I knew it was still excitement. I halted the mare and slid silently from the saddle. I led her three paces into the forest, knotted the rein over a bough and left her there. My foot hurt when I put it to the ground, but the twinges were bearable, and I soon forgot them as I limped quickly towards the singing and the lighter sky.

Chapter Nine

I had been right in thinking that the sea was near. The forest ended in it, a stretch of sea so enclosed that at first I thought it was a big lake, until I smelt the salt and saw, on the narrow shingle, the dark slime of seaweeds. The forest finished abruptly, with a high bank where exposed roots showed through the clay which the tides had gnawed away year after year at the land's edge. The narrow strand was mainly of pebbles, but here and there bars of pale sand showed, and greyish, glimmering fans spreading fernlike between them, where shallow water ran seawards. The bay was very quiet, almost as if the frost of the past weeks had held it ice-bound, then, a pale line under the darkness, you could see the gap between the far headlands where the wide sea whitened. To the right–the south–the black forest climbed to a ridge, while to the north, where the land was gentler, the big trees gave shelter. A perfect harbour, you would have thought, till you saw how shallow it was, how at low tide the shapes of rock and boulder stuck black out of the water, shiny in the starlight with weed.

In the middle of the bay, so centred that at first I thought it must be man-made, was an island–what must, rather, be an island at high tide, but was now a peninsula, an oval of land joined to the shore by a rough causeway of stones, certainly man-made, which ran out like a navel cord to join it to the shingle. In the nearer of the shallow harbours made by the causeway and the shore a few small boats–coracles, I thought–lay beached like seals.

Here, low beside the bay, there was mist again, hanging here and there among the boughs like fishing nets hung out to dry. On the water's surface it floated and thinned and then wisped away to nothing, only to thicken again elsewhere, and smoke slowly across the water. It lay round the base of the island so densely that this seemed to float on cloud, and the stars that hung above reflected a grey light from the mist that showed me the island clearly.

This was egg-shaped rather than oval, narrow at the causeway end, and widening towards the far end where a small hill, as regular in shape as a beehive, stood up out of the flat ground. Round the base of this hillock stood a circle of the standing stones, a circle broken only at the point facing me, where a wide gap made a gateway from which an avenue of the stones marched double, like a colonnade, straight down to the causeway.

There was neither sound nor movement. If it had not been for the dim shapes of the beached boats I would have thought that the shriek, the chanting, were figments of a dream. I stood just inside the edge of the forest, with my left arm round a young ash tree and the weight on my right foot, watching with eyes so completely adjusted to the dark of the forest that the mist-illumined island seemed as light as day.

At the foot of the hill, directly at the end of the central avenue, a torch flared suddenly. It lit, momentarily, an opening low in the face of the hill, and clearly in front of this the torch-bearer, a figure in a white robe. I saw, then, that what I had taken to be banks of mist in the shadow of the cromlechs were groups of motionless figures also robed in white. As the torch lifted I heard the chanting begin again, very softly, and with a loose and wandering rhythm that was strange to me. Then the torch and its bearer slowly sank earthwards, and I realised that the doorway was a sunken one, and he was descending a flight of steps into the heart of the hill. The others crowded after him, groups clotting, coalescing round the doorway, then vanishing like smoke being sucked into an oven door.

The chanting still went on, but so faint and muffled that it sounded no more than the humming of bees in a winter hive. No tune came through, only the rhythm which sank to a mere throb in the air, a pulse of sound felt rather than heard, which little by little tightened and quickened till it beat fast and hard, and my blood with it . . .

Suddenly, it stopped. There was a pause of dead stillness, but a stillness so charged that I felt my throat knot and swell with tension. I found I had left the trees and stood clear on the turf above the bank, my injury forgotten, my feet planted apart, flat and squarely on the ground, as if my body were rooted through them and straining to pull life from the earth as a tree pulls sap. And like the shoot of a tree growing and thrusting, the excitement in me grew and swelled, beating through somehow from the depths of the island and along the navel cord of the causeway, bursting up through flesh and spirit so that when the cry came at length it was as if it had burst from my own body.

A different cry this time, thin and edged, which might have meant anything, triumph or surrender or pain. A death cry, this time not from the victim, but from the killer.

And after it, silence. The night was fixed and still. The island was a closed hive sealed over whatever crawled and hummed within.

Then the leader—I assumed it was he, though this time the torch was out—appeared suddenly like a ghost in the doorway and mounted the steps. The rest came behind, moving not as people move in a procession, but slowly and smoothly, in groups breaking and forming, contained in pattern like a dance, till once more they stood parted into two ranks beside the cromlechs.

Again complete silence. Then the leader raised his arms. As if at a signal, white and shining like a knife-blade, the edge of the moon showed over the hill.

The leader cried out, and this, the third cry, was unmistakably a call of triumphant greeting, and he stretched his arms high above his head as if offering up what he held between his hands.

The crowd answered him, chant and counterchant. Then as the moon lifted clear of the hill, the priest lowered his arms and turned. What he had offered to the goddess, he now offered to the worshippers. The crowd closed in.

I had been so intent on the ceremony at the centre of the island that I had not watched the shore, or realised that the mist, creeping higher, was now blurring the avenue itself. My eyes, straining through the dark, saw the white shapes of the people as part of the mist that clotted, strayed, and eddied here and there in knots of white.

Presently I became aware that this, in fact, was what was happening. The crowd was breaking apart, and the people, in twos and threes, were passing silently down the avenue, in and out of the barred shadows which the rising moon painted between the stones. They were making for the boats.

I have no idea how long it had all taken, but as I came to myself I found that I was stiff, and where I had allowed my cloak to fall away I was soaked with the mist. I shook myself like a dog, backing again into the shelter of the trees. Excitement had spilled out of me, spirit as well as body in a warm gush down my thighs, and I felt empty and ashamed. Dimly I knew that this was something different; this had not been the force I had learnt to receive and foster, nor was this spilled-out sensation the aftermath of power. That had left me light and free and keen as a cutting blade; now I felt empty as a licked pot still sticky and smelling with what it had held.

I bent, stiff-sinewed, to pull a swatch of wet and pallid grass, and cleaned myself, scrubbing my hands, and scooping mist drops off the turf to wash my face. The water smelt of leaves, and of the wet air itself, and made me think of Galapas and the holy well and the long cup of horn. I dried my hands on the inside of my cloak, drew it about me, and went back to my station by the ash tree.

The bay was dotted with the retreating coracles. The island had emptied, all but one tall white figure who came, now, straight down the centre of the avenue. The mist cloaked, revealed, and cloaked him again. He was not making for a boat; he seemed to be heading straight for the causeway, but as he reached the end of the avenue he paused in the shadow of the final stone, and vanished.

I waited, feeling little except weariness and a longing for a drink of clear water and the familiarity of my warm and quiet room. There was no magic in the air; the night was as flat as old sour wine. In a moment, sure enough, I saw him emerge into the moonlight of the causeway. He was clad now in a dark robe. All he had done was drop his white robe off. He carried it over his arm.

The last of the boats was a speck dwindling in the darkness. The solitary man came quickly across the causeway. I stepped out from under the trees and down on to the shingle to meet him.

Chapter Ten

Belasius saw me even before I was clear of the trees' shadow. He made no sign except to turn aside as he stepped off the causeway. He came up, unhurried, and stood over me, looking down.

'Ah.' It was the only greeting, said without surprise. 'I might have known. How long have you been here?'

'I hardly know. Time passed so quickly. I was interested.'

He was silent. The moonlight, bright now, fell slanting on his right cheek. I could not see the eyes veiled under the long dark lids, but there was something quiet, almost sleepy about his voice and bearing. I had felt the same after that releasing cry, there in the forest. The bolt had struck, and now the bow was unstrung.

He took no notice of my provocation, asking merely: 'What brought you here?'

'I rode down when I heard the scream.'

'Ah,' he said again, then: 'Down from where?'

'From the pine grove where you left your horse.'

'Why did you come this way? I told you to keep to the road.'

'I know, but I wanted a gallop, so we turned off into the main logging track, and I had an accident with Aster; he's wrenched a foreleg, so we had to lead him back. It was slow, and we were late, so we took a short cut.'

'I see. And where is Cadal?'

'I think he thought I'd run for home, and he must have gone after me. At any rate he didn't follow me down here.'

'That was sensible of him,' said Belasius. His voice was still quiet, sleepy almost, but cat-sleepy, velvet sheathing a bright dagger-point. 'But in spite of—what you heard—it did not in fact occur to you to run for home?'

'Of course not.'

I saw his eyes glint for a moment under the long lids. ' "Of course not?" '

'I had to know what was going on.'

'Ah. Did you know I would be here?'

'Not before I saw Ulfin and the horses, no. And not because you told me to keep to the road, either. But I—shall we say I knew something was abroad in the forest tonight, and that I had to find it?'

He regarded me for a moment longer. I had been right in thinking he would not look surprised. Then he jerked his head. 'Come, it's cold, and I want my cloak.' As I followed him up the grating shingle he added, over his shoulder: 'I take it that Ulfin is still there?'

'I should think so. You have him pretty efficiently frightened.'

'He has no need to be afraid, as long as he keeps away and sees nothing.'

'Then it's true he doesn't know?'

'Whatever he knows or doesn't know,' he said indifferently, 'he has the sense to keep silent. I have promised him that if he obeys me in these things without question, then I shall free him in time to escape.'

'Escape? From what?'

'Death when I die. It is normal to send the priests' servants with them.'

We were walking side by side up the path. I glanced at him. He was wearing a dark robe, more elegant than anything I had seen at home, even the clothes Camlach wore; his belt was of beautifully worked leather, probably Italian, and there was a big round brooch at his shoulder where the moonlight caught a design of circles and knotted snakes in gold. He looked–even under the film which tonight's proceedings had drawn over him–Romanised, urbane, intelligent. I said: 'Forgive me, Belasius, but didn't that kind of thing go out with the Egyptians? Even in Wales we would think it old-fashioned.'

'Perhaps. But then you might say the Goddess herself is old-fashioned, and likes to be worshipped in the ways she knows. And our way is almost as old as she is, older than men can remember, even in songs or stones. Long before the bulls were killed in Persia, long before they came to Crete, long before even the sky-gods came out of Africa and these stones were raised to them, the Goddess was here in the sacred grove. Now the forest is closed to us, and we worship where we can, but wherever the Goddess is, be it stone or tree or cave, there is the grove called Nemet, and there we make the offering.–I see you understand me.'

'Very well. I was taught these things in Wales. But it's a few hundred years since they made the kind of offering you made tonight.'

His voice was smooth as oil. 'He was killed for sacrilege. Did they not teach you—?' He stopped dead, and his hand dropped to his hip. His tone changed. 'That's Cadal's horse.' His head went round like a hunting dog's.

'I brought it,' I said. 'I told you my pony went lame. Cadal will have gone home. I suppose he took one of yours.'

I unhitched the mare and brought her out into the moonlight of the open path. He was settling the dagger back in its sheath. We walked on, the mare following, her nose at my shoulder. My foot had almost ceased to hurt.

I said: 'So, death for Cadal, too? This isn't just a question of sacrilege, then? Your ceremonies are so very secret? Is this a matter of a mystery, Belasius, or is what you do illegal?.

'It is both secret and illegal. We meet where we can. Tonight we had to use the island; it's safe enough–normally there's not a soul would come near it on the night of the equinox. But if word came to Budec there would be trouble. The man we killed tonight was a King's man; he's been held here for eight days now, and Budec's scouts have been searching for him. But he had to die.'

'Will they find him now?'

'Oh, yes, a long way from here, in the forest. They will think a wild boar ripped him.' Again that slanting glance. 'You could say he died easily, in the end. In the old days he would have had his navel cut out, and would have been whipped round and round the sacred tree until his guts were wrapped round it like wool on a spindle.'

'And does Ambrosius know?'

'Ambrosius is a King's man, too.'

We walked for a few paces in silence. 'Well, and what comes to me, Belasius?'

'Nothing.'

'Isn't it sacrilege to spy on your secrets?'

'You're safe enough,' he said drily. 'Ambrosius has a long arm. Why do you look like that?'

I shook my head. I could not have put it into words, even to myself. It was like suddenly having a shield put into your hand when you are naked in battle.

He said: 'You weren't afraid?'

'No.'

'By the Goddess, I think that's true. Ambrosius was right, you have courage.'

'If I have, it's hardly the kind that you need admire. I thought once that I was better than other boys because there were so many of their fears I couldn't share or understand. I had others of my own, of course, but I learned to keep them to myself. I suppose that was a kind of pride. But now I am beginning to understand why, even when danger and death lie openly waiting in the path, I can walk straight by them.'

He stopped. We were nearly at the grove. 'Tell me why.'

'Because they are not for me. I have feared for other men, but never in that way for myself. Not yet. I think what men fear is the unknown. They fear pain and death, because these may be waiting round any corner. But there are times when I know what is hidden, and waiting, or when–I told you–I see it lying straight in the pathway. And I know where pain and danger lie for me, and I know that death is not yet to come; so I am not afraid. This isn't courage.'

He said slowly: 'Yes. I knew you had the Sight.'

'It comes only sometimes, and at the god's will, not mine.' I had said too much already; he was not a man to share one's gods with. I said quickly, to turn the subject: 'Belasius, you must listen to me. None of this is Ulfin's fault. He refused to tell us anything, and would have stopped me if he could.'

'You mean that if there is any paying to be done, you're offering to do it?'

'Well, it seems only fair, and after all, I can afford to.' I laughed at him, secure behind my invisible shield. 'What's it to be? An old-fashioned religion like yours must have a few minor penalties held in reserve? Shall I die of the cramps in my sleep tonight, or get ripped by a boar next time I ride in the forest without my black dog?'

He smiled for the first time. 'You needn't think you'll escape quite freely. I've a use for you and this Sight of yours, be sure of that. Ambrosius is not the only one who uses men for what they are worth, and I intend to use you. You have told me you were led here tonight; it was the Goddess herself who led you, and to the Goddess you must go.' He dropped an arm round my shoulders. 'You are going to pay for this night's work, Merlin Emrys, in coin that will content her. The Goddess is going to hunt you down, as she does all men who spy on her mystery–but not to destroy you. Oh, no; not Actaeon, my apt little scholar, but Endymion. She will take you into her embrace. In other words, you are going to study until I can take you with me to the sanctuary, and present you there.'

I would have liked to say, 'Not if you wrapped my guts round every tree in the forest,' but I held my tongue. Take power where it is offered, he had said, and–remembering my vigil by the ash tree–there had been power there, of a kind. We should see. I moved–but courteously–from under the arm round my shoulders, and led the way up into the grove.

If Ulfin had been frightened before, he was almost speechless with terror when he saw me with his master, and realised where I had been.

'My lord . . . I thought he had gone home . . . Indeed, my lord, Cadal said—'

'Hand me my cloak,' said Belasius, 'and put this thing in the saddle-bag.'

He threw down the white robe which he had been carrying. It fell loosely, unfolding, near the tree Aster was tied to, and as it dropped near him, the pony shied and snorted. At first I thought this was just at the ghostly fall of white near his feet, but then I saw, black on the white, dimmed even as it was by the darkness of the grove, the stains and splashing, and I smelt even from where I stood, the smoke and the fresh blood.

Ulfin held the cloak up mechanically. 'My lord—' He was breathless with fear and the effort of holding the restive horse at the same time–'Cadal took the pack horse. We thought my lord Merlin had gone back to the town. Indeed, sir, I was sure myself that he had gone that way. I told him nothing. I swear—'

'There's a saddle-bag on Cadal's mare. Put it there.' Belasius pulled his cloak on and fastened it, then reached for the reins. 'Hand me up.'

The boy obeyed, trying, I could see, not only to excuse himself, but to gauge the strength of Belasius' anger. 'My lord, please believe me, I said nothing. I'll swear it by any gods there are.'

Belasius ignored him. He could be cruel, I knew; in fact, in all the time I knew him he never once spared a thought for another's anxiety or pain: more exactly, it never occurred to him that feeling could exist, even in a free man. Ulfin must have seemed at that moment less real to him than the horse he was controlling. He swung easily to the saddle, saying curtly, 'Stand back.' Then to me, 'Can you manage the mare if we gallop? I want to get back before Cadal finds you're not home, and sets the place by the ears.'

'I can try. What about Ulfin?'

'What about him? He'll walk your pony home, of course.'

He swung his horse round, and rode out between the pine boughs. Ulfin had already run to bundle up the bloodstained robe and stuff it in the brown mare's saddle-bag. He hurried now to give me his shoulder, and somehow between us I scrambled into the saddle and settled myself. The boy stood back, silent, but I had felt how he was shaking. I suppose that for a slave it was normal to be so afraid. It came to me that he was even afraid to lead my pony home alone through the forest.

I hung on the rein for a moment and leaned down. 'Ulfin, he's not angry with you; nothing will happen. I swear it. So don't be afraid.'

'Did you . . . see anything, my lord?'

'Nothing at all.' In the way that mattered this was the truth. I looked down at him soberly. 'A blaze of darkness,' I said, 'and an innocent moon. But whatever I might have seen, Ulfin, it would not have mattered. I am to be initiated. So you see why he is not angry? That is all. Here, take this.'

I slid my dagger from its sheath and flicked it to quiver point down in the pine needles.

'If it makes you easier,' I said, 'but you won't need it. You will be quite safe. Take it from me. I know. Lead my pony gently, won't you?'

I kicked the mare in the ribs and headed her after Belasius.

He was waiting for me—that is to say he was going at an easy canter, which quickened to a hand-gallop as I caught him up. The brown mare pounded behind him. I gripped the neck-strap and clung like a burr.

The track was open enough for us to see our way clearly in the moonlight. It sliced its way uphill through the forest to a crest from which, momentarily, one could see the glimmer of the town's lights. Then it plunged downhill again, and after a while we rode out of the forest on to the salt plains that fringed the sea.

Belasius neither slackened speed nor spoke. I hung on to the mare, watched the track over her shoulder, and wondered whether we would meet Cadal coming back for me with an escort, or if he would come alone.

We splashed through a stream, fetlock deep, and then the track, beaten flat along the level turf, turned right-handed in the direction of the main road. I knew where we were now; on our ride out I had noticed this track branching off just short of a bridge at the forest's edge. In a few minutes we would reach the bridge and the made road.

Belasius slackened his horse's pace and glanced over his shoulder. The mare thudded alongside, then he put up a hand and drew rein. The horses slowed to a walk.

'Listen.'

Horses. A great many horses, coming at a fast trot along the paved road. They were making for the town.

A man's voice was briefly raised. Over the bridge came a flurry of tossing torches, and we saw them, a troop riding close. The standard in the torchlight showed a scarlet dragon.

Belasius' hand came hard down on my rein, and our horses stopped.

'Ambrosius' men,' he said, at least that is what he began to say when, clear as cock-crow, my mare whinnied, and a horse from the troop answered her.

Someone barked an order. The troop checked. Another order, and horses headed our way at the gallop. I heard Belasius curse under his breath as he let go my rein.

'This is where you leave me. Hang on now, and see you guard your tongue. Even Ambrosius' arm cannot protect you from a curse.' He lashed my mare across the quarters, and she jumped forward, nearly unseating me. I was too busy to watch him go, but behind me there was a splash and a scramble as the black horse jumped the stream and was swallowed by the forest seconds before the soldiers met me and wheeled to either side to escort me back to their officer.

The grey stallion was fidgeting in the blaze of torches under the standard. One of my escorts had hold of the mare's bit, and led me forward.

He saluted. 'Only the one, sir. He's not armed.'

The officer pushed up his visor. Blue eyes widened, and Uther's too well-remembered voice said: 'It had to be you, of course. Well, Merlin the bastard, what are you doing here alone, and where have you been?'

Chapter Eleven

I didn't answer straight away. I was wondering how much to say. To any other officer I might have told a quick and easy half-truth, but Uther was likely to ride me hard, and for anyone who had been at a meeting both 'secret and illegal', Uther was not just 'any officer', he was dangerous. Not that there was any reason for me to protect Belasius, but I did not owe information—or explanation—to anyone but Ambrosius. In any case, to steer aside from Uther's anger came naturally.

So I met his eyes with what I hoped was an expression of frankness. 'My pony went lame, sir, so I left my servant to walk him home, and took my servant's horse to ride back myself.' As he opened his mouth to speak, I hoisted the invisible shield that Belasius had put into my hand. 'Usually your brother sends for me after supper, and I didn't wish to keep him waiting.'

His brows snapped down at my mention of Ambrosius, but all he said was: 'Why that way, at this hour? Why not by the road?'

'We'd gone some way into the forest when Aster hurt himself. We had turned east at the crossways into the logging track, and there was a path branching south from that which looked like a quicker way home, so we took it. The moonlight made it quite easy to see.'

'Which path was this?'

'I don't know the forest, sir. It climbed the ridge and then down to a ford about a mile downstream.'

He considered me for a moment, frowning. 'Where did you leave your servant?'

'A little way along the second path. We wanted to be quite sure that it was the right way before he let me come on alone. He'll be about climbing the ridge now, I should think.' I was praying, confusedly but sincerely, to whatever god might be listening, that Cadal was not at the moment riding back from town to find me.

Uther regarded me, sitting his fidgeting horse as if it did not exist. It was the first time I had realised how like his brother he was. And for the first time, too, I recognised something like power in him, and understood, young as I was, what Ambrosius had told me about his brilliance as a captain. He could judge men to a hairsbreadth. I knew he was looking straight through me, scenting a lie, not knowing where, or why, but wondering. And determined to find out . . .

For once he spoke quite pleasantly, without heat, even gently. 'You're lying, aren't you? Why?'

'It's quite true, my lord. If you look at my pony when he comes in—'

'Oh, yes, that was true. I've no doubt I'll find he's lame. And if I send men back up the path they'll find Cadal leading him home. But what I want to know—'

I said quickly: 'Not Cadal, my lord; Ulfin. Cadal had other duties, and Belasius sent Ulfin with me.'

'Two of a kind?' The words were contemptuous.

'My lord?'

His voice cracked suddenly with temper. 'Don't bandy words with me, you little catamite. You're lying about something, and I want to know what. I can smell a lie a mile off.' Then he looked past me, and his voice changed. 'What's that in your saddle-bag?' A jerk of his head at one of the soldiers flanking me. A corner of Belasius' robe was showing. The man thrust his hand into the bag and pulled it out. On the soiled and crumpled white the stains showed dark and unmistakable. I could smell the blood even through the bubbling resin of the torches.

Behind Uther the horses snorted and tossed their heads, scenting it, and the men looked at one another. I saw the torch-bearers eyeing me askance, and the guard beside me muttered something under his breath.

Uther said, violently: 'By all the gods below, so that was it! One of them, by Mithras! I should have known, I can smell the holy smoke on you from here! All right, bastard, you that's so mighty free with my brother's name, and so high in his favour, we'll see what he has to say to this. What have you to say for yourself now? There's not much point in denying it, is there?'

I lifted my head. Sitting the big mare, I could meet him almost eye to eye. 'Deny? I'm denying that I've broken a law, or done anything the Count wouldn't like—and those are the only two things that matter, my lord Uther. I'll explain to him.'

'By God you will! So Ulfin took you there?'

I said sharply: 'Ulfin had nothing to do with it. I had already left him. In any case, he is a slave, and does as I bid him.'

He spurred his horse suddenly, right up to the mare. He leaned forward, gripping the folds of my cloak at the neck, and tightening the grip till he half-lifted me from the saddle. His face was thrust close to mine, his armed knee hurting my leg as the horses stamped and sidled together. He spoke through his teeth. 'And you do as I bid you, hear that. Whatever you may be to my brother, you obey me, too.' He tightened the grip still further, shaking me. 'Understand, Merlin Emrys?'

I nodded. He swore as my brooch-pin scratched him, and let me go. There was a streak of blood on his hand. I saw his eyes on the brooch. He flicked his fingers to the torch-bearer, and the man pushed nearer, holding the flame high. 'He gave you that to wear? The red dragon?' Then he stopped short as his eyes came up to my face and fixed there, stared, widened. The intense blue seemed to blaze. The grey stallion sidled and he curbed it sharply, so that the foam sprang.

'Merlin Emrys . . . ' He said it again, this time to himself, so softly that I hardly caught it. Then suddenly he let out a laugh, amused and gay and hard, not like anything I had heard from him before.

'Well, Merlin Emrys, you'll still have to answer to him for where you've been tonight!' He wheeled his horse, flinging over his shoulder to the men:

'Bring him along, and see he doesn't fall off. It seems my brother treasures him.'

The grey horse jumped under the spur, and the troop surged after him. My captors, still holding the brown mare's bridle, pounded after, with me between them.

The druid's robe lay trampled and filthy in the dirt, where the troop had ridden over it. I wondered if Belasius would see it and take warning.

Then I forgot him. I still had Ambrosius to face.

Cadal was in my room. I said with relief: 'Well, thank the gods you didn't come back after me. I was picked up by Uther's lot, and he's blazing mad because he knows where I went.'

'I know,' said Cadal grimly, 'I saw it.'

'What do you mean?'

'I did ride back for you. I'd made sure you'd had the sense to run for home when you heard that . . . noise, so I went after you. When I saw no sign of you on the way I just thought you must have got a tidy turn of speed out of the mare—the ground was fair smoking under *me*, I can tell you! Then when—'

'You guessed what was happening? Where Belasius was?'

'Aye.' He turned his head as if to spit on the floor, recollected himself, and made the sign against the evil eye. 'Well, when I got back here, and no sign of you, I knew you must've gone straight down to see what was going on. High-handed little fool. Might have got yourself killed, meddling with that lot.'

'So might you. But you went back.'

'What else could I do? You should've heard what I was calling you, too. Proper little nuisance was the least of it. Well, I was about half a mile out of town when I saw them coming, and I pulled aside and waited for them to pass. You know that old posting station, the ruined one? I was there. I watched them go by, and you at the back under guard. So I guessed he knew. I followed them back to town as close as I dared, and cut home through the side streets. I've only just got in. He found out, then?'

I nodded, beginning to unfasten my cloak.

'Then there'll be the devil to pay, and no mistake,' said Cadal. 'How did he find out?'

'Belasius had put his robe in my saddle-bag, and they found it. They think it was mine.' I grinned. 'If they'd tried it for size they'd have had to think again. But that didn't occur to them. They just dropped it in the mud and rode over it.'

'About right, too.' He had gone down on one knee to unfasten my sandals. He paused, with one in his hand. 'Are you telling me Belasius saw you? Had words with you?

'Yes. I waited for him, and we walked back together to the horses. Ulfin's bringing Aster, by the way.'

He ignored that. He was staring, and I thought he had lost colour.

'Uther didn't see Belasius,' I said. 'Belasius dodged in time. He knew they'd heard one horse, so he sent me forward to meet them, otherwise I suppose they'd have come after us both. He must have forgotten I had the robe, or else chanced their not finding it. Anybody but Uther wouldn't even have looked.'

'You should never have gone near Belasius. It's worse than I thought. Here, let me do that. Your hands are cold.' He pulled the dragon brooch off and took my cloak. 'You want to watch it, you do. He's a nasty customer—they all are, come to that—and him most of all.'

'Did you know about him?'

'Not to say know. I might have guessed. It's right up his street, if you ask me. But what I meant was, they're a nasty lot to tangle with.'

'Well, he's the archdruid, or at least the head of this sect, so he'll carry some weight. Don't look so troubled, Cadal, I doubt if he'll harm me, or let anyone else harm me.'

'Did he threaten you?'

I laughed. 'Yes. With a curse.'

'They say these things stick. They say the druids can send a knife after you that'll hunt you down for days, and all you know is the whistling noise in the air behind you just before it strikes.'

'They say all sort of things. Cadal, have I another tunic that's decent? Did my best one come back from the cleaner? And I want a bath before I go to the Count.'

He eyed me sideways as he reached in the clothes-chest for another tunic. 'Uther will have gone straight to him. You know that?'

I laughed. 'Of course. I warn you, I shall tell Ambrosius the truth.'

'All of it?'

'All of it.'

'Well, I suppose that's best,' he said. 'If anyone can protect you from them—'

'It's not that. It's simply that he ought to know. He has the right. Besides, what have I to hide from him?'

He said uneasily: 'I was thinking about the curse . . . Even Ambrosius might not be able to protect you from that.'

'Oh, that to the curse.' I made a gesture not commonly seen in noblemen's houses. 'Forget it. Neither you nor I have done wrong, and I refuse to lie to Ambrosius.'

'Some day I'll see you scared, Merlin.'

'Probably.'

'Weren't you even scared of Belasius?'

'Should I be?' I was interested. 'He'll do me no harm.' I unhooked the belt of my tunic, and threw it on the bed. I regarded Cadal. 'Would you be afraid if you knew your own end, Cadal?'

'Yes, by the dog! Do you?'

'Sometimes, in snatches. Sometimes I see it. It fills me with fear.'

He stood still, looking at me, and there was fear in his face. 'What is it, then?'

'A cave. The crystal cave. Sometimes I think it is death, and at other times it is birth or a gate of vision, or a dark limbo of sleep . . . I cannot tell. But some day I shall know. Till then, I suppose I am not afraid of much else. I shall come to the cave in the end, as you—' I broke off.

'As I what?' he asked quickly. 'What'll I come to?'

I smiled. 'I was going to say "As you will come to old age."'

'That's a lie,' he said roughly. 'I saw your eyes. When you're seeing things, your eyes go queer; I've noticed it before. The black spreads and goes kind of blurred, dreaming-like–but not soft; no, your whole look goes cold, like cold iron, as if you neither saw nor cared about what's going on round you. And you talk as if you were just a voice and not a person . . . Or as if you'd gone somewhere else and left your body for something else to speak through. Like a horn being blown through to make the sound carry. Oh, I know I've only seen it a couple of times, for a moment, but it's uncanny, and it frightens me.'

'It frightens me, too, Cadal.' I had let the green tunic slide from my body to the floor. He was holding out the grey wool robe I wore for a bedgown. I reached absently for it, and sat down on the bed's edge, with it trailing over my knees. I was talking to myself rather than Cadal. 'It frightens me, too. You're right, that's how it feels, as if I were an empty shell with something working through me. I say things, see things, think things, till that moment I never knew of. But you're wrong in thinking I don't feel. It hurts me. I think this may be because I can't command whatever speaks through me . . . I mean, I can't command it yet. But I shall. I know this, too. Some day I shall command this part of me that knows and sees, this god, and that really will be power. I shall know when what I foretell is human instinct, and when it is God's shadow.'

'And when you spoke of my end, what was that?'

I looked up. Oddly enough it was less easy to lie to Cadal than it had been to Uther. 'But I haven't seen your death, Cadal, no one's but my own. I was being tactless. I was going to say "As you will come to a foreign grave somewhere . . ."' I smiled. 'I know this is worse than hell to a Breton. But I think it will happen to you . . . That is, if you stay as my servant.'

His look lightened, and he grinned. This was power, I thought, when a word of mine could frighten men like this. He said: 'Oh, I'll do that all right. Even if he hadn't asked me to, I'd stay. You've an easy way with you that makes it a pleasure to look after you.'

'Have I? I thought you found me a high-handed little fool, and a nuisance besides?'

'There you are, you see. I'd never have dared say that to anyone else your class, and all you do is laugh, and you twice royal.'

'*Twice* royal? You can hardly count my grandfather as well as my—' I stopped. What stopped me was his face. He had spoken without thought, then, on a quick gasp, had tried to catch the words back into his mouth and unspeak them.

He said nothing, just stood there with the soiled tunic in his hand. I stood up slowly, the forgotten bedgown falling to the floor. There was no need for him to speak. I knew. I could not imagine how I had not known before, the moment I stood before Ambrosius in the frosty field and he stared down in the torchlight. He had known. And a hundred others must have guessed. I remembered now the sidelong looks of the men, the mutterings of the officers, the deference of servants which I had taken for respect for Ambrosius' commands, but which I saw now was deference to Ambrosius' son.

The room was still as a cave. The brazier flickered and its light broke and scattered in the bronze mirror against the wall. I looked that way. In the firelit bronze my naked body showed slight and shadowy, an unreal thing of firelight and darkness shifting as the flames moved. But the face was lit, and in its heavily defined planes of fire and shadow I saw his face as I had seen it in his room, when he sat over the brazier waiting for me to be brought to him. Waiting for me to come so that he could ask me about Niniane.

And here again the Sight had not helped me. Men that have god's-sight, I have found, are often human-blind.

I said to Cadal: 'Everybody knows?'

He nodded. He didn't ask what I meant. 'It's rumoured. You're very like him sometimes.'

'I think Uther may have guessed. He didn't know before?'

'No. He left before the talk started to go round. That wasn't why he took against you.'

'I'm glad to hear it,' I said. 'What was it, then? Just because I got across him over that business of the standing stone?'

'Oh, that, and other things.'

'Such as?'

Cadal said, bluntly: 'He thought you were the Count's catamite. Ambrosius doesn't go for women much. He doesn't go for boys either, come to that, but one thing Uther can't understand is a man who isn't in and out of bed with someone seven nights a week. When his brother bothered such a lot with you, had you in his house and set me to look after you and all that, Uther thought that's what must be going on, and he didn't half like it.'

'I see. He did say something like that tonight, but I thought it was only because he'd lost his temper.'

'If he'd bothered to look at you, or listen to what folks were saying, he'd have known fast enough.'

'He knows now.' I spoke with sudden, complete certainty. 'He saw it, back there on the road, when he saw the dragon brooch the Count gave me. I'd never thought about it, but of course he would realise the Count would hardly put the royal cipher on his catamite. He had the torch brought up, and took a good look at me. I think he saw it then.' A thought struck me. 'And I think Belasius knows.'

'Oh, yes,' said Cadal, 'he knows. Why?'

'The way he talked . . . As if he knew he daren't touch me. That would be why he tried to scare me with the threat of a curse. He's a pretty cool hand, isn't he? He must have been thinking very hard on the way up to the grove. He daren't put me quietly out of the way for sacrilege, but he had to stop me talking somehow. Hence the curse. And also—' I stopped.

'And also what?'

'Don't sound so startled. It was only another guarantee I'd hold my tongue.'

'For the gods' sake, what?'

I shrugged, realised I was still naked, and reached for the bedgown again. 'He said he would take me with him to the sanctuary. I think he would like to make a druid of me.'

'He said that?' I was getting familiar with Cadal's sign to avert the evil eye. 'What will you do?'

'I'll go with him . . . once, at least. Don't look like that, Cadal. There isn't a cat's chance in a fire that I'll want to go more than once.' I looked at him soberly. 'But there's nothing in this world that I'm not ready to see and learn, and no god that I'm not ready to approach in his own fashion. I told you that truth was the shadow of God. If I am to use it, I must know who He is. Do you understand me?'

'How could I? What god are you talking about?'

'I think there is only one. Oh, there are gods everywhere, in the hollow hills, in the wind and the sea, in the very grass we walk on and the air we breathe, and in the blood-stained shadows where men like Belasius wait for them. But I believe there must be one who is God Himself, like the great sea, and all the rest of us, small gods and men and all, like rivers, we all come to Him in the end.–Is the bath ready?'

Twenty minutes later, in a dark blue tunic clipped at the shoulder by the dragon brooch, I went to see my father.

Chapter Twelve

The secretary was in the lobby, rather elaborately doing nothing. Beyond the curtain I heard Ambrosius' voice speaking quietly. The two guards at the door looked wooden.

Then the curtain was pulled aside and Uther came out. When he saw me he checked, hung on his heel as if to speak, then seemed to catch the secretary's interested look, and went by with a swish of the red cloak and a smell of horses. You could always tell where Uther had been; he seemed to soak up scents like a wash-cloth. He must have gone straight to his brother before he had even cleaned up after the ride home.

The secretary, whose name was Sollius, said to me: 'You may as well go straight in, sir. He'll be expecting you.'

I hardly even noticed the 'sir'. It seemed to be something I was already accustomed to. I went in.

He was standing with his back to the door, over by the table. This was strewn with tablets, and a stilus lay across one of them as if he had been interrupted while writing. On the secretary's desk near the window a half-unrolled book lay where it had been dropped.

The door shut behind me. I stopped just inside it, and the leather curtain fell close with a ruffle and a flap. He turned.

Our eyes met in silence, it seemed for interminable seconds, then he cleared his throat and said: 'Ah, Merlin,' and then, with a slight movement of the hand, 'sit down'.

I obeyed him, crossing to my usual stool near the brazier. He was silent for a moment, looking down at the table. He picked up the stilus, looked absently down at the wax, and added a word. I waited. He scowled down at what he had done, scored it out again, then threw the stilus down and said abruptly: 'Uther has been to see me.'

'Yes, sir.'

He looked up under frowning brows. 'I understand he came on you riding alone beyond the town.'

I said quickly: 'I didn't go out alone. Cadal was with me.'

'Cadal?'

'Yes, sir.'

'That's not what you told Uther.'

'No, sir.'

His look was keen now, arrested. 'Well, go on.'

'Cadal always attends me, my lord. He's—more than faithful. We went north as far as the logging track in the forest, and a short way along that my pony went lame, so Cadal gave me his mare, and we started to walk home.' I took a breath. 'We took a short cut, and came on Belasius and his servant. Belasius rode part of the way home with me, but it—it didn't suit him to meet Prince Uther, so he left me.'

'I see.' His voice gave nothing away, but I had the feeling that he saw quite a lot. His next question confirmed it. 'Did you go to the druids' island?'

'You know about it?' I said, surprised. Then as he did not answer, waiting in cold silence for me to speak, I went on: 'I told you Cadal and I took a short cut through the forest. If you know the island, you'll know the track we followed. Just where the path goes down to the sea there's a pine grove. We found Ulfin—that's Belasius' servant—there with the two horses. Cadal wanted to take Ulfin's horse and get me home quickly, but while we were talking to Ulfin we heard a cry—a scream, rather, from somewhere east of the grove. I went to see. I swear I had no idea the island was there, or what happened there. Nor had Cadal, and if he'd been mounted, as I was, he'd have stopped me. But by the time he'd taken Ulfin's horse and set off after me I was out of sight, and he thought I'd taken fright and gone home—which is what he'd told me to do—and it wasn't until he got right back here that he found I hadn't come this way. He went back for me, but by that time I'd come up with the troop.' I thrust my hands down between my knees, clutching them tightly together. 'I don't know what made me ride down to the island. At least, I do; it was the cry, so I went to see . . . But it wasn't only because of the cry. I can't explain, not yet . . .' I took a breath. 'My lord—'

'Well?'

'I ought to tell you. A man was killed there tonight, on the island. I don't know who he was, but I heard that he was a King's man who has been missing for some days. His body will be found somewhere in the forest, as if a wild beast had killed him.' I paused. There was nothing to be seen in his face. 'I thought I should tell you.'

'You went over to the island?'

'Oh, no! I doubt if I'd be alive now if I had. I found out later about the man who was killed. It was sacrilege, they said. I didn't ask about it.' I looked up at him. 'I only went down as far as the shore. I waited there in the trees, and watched it—the dance and the offering. I could hear the singing. I didn't know then that it was illegal . . . It's forbidden at home, of course, but one knows it still goes on, and I thought it might be different here. But when my lord Uther knew where I'd been he was very angry. He seems to hate the druids.'

'The druids?' His voice was absent now. He still fidgeted with the stilus on the table. 'Ah, yes. Uther has no love for them. He is one of Mithras' fanatics, and light is the enemy of darkness, I suppose. Well, what is it?' This, sharply, to Sollius, who came in with an apology, and waited just inside the door.

'Forgive me, sir,' said the secretary. 'There's a messenger from King Budec. I told him you were engaged, but he said it was important. Shall I tell him to wait?'

'Bring him in,' said Ambrosius. The man came in with a scroll. He handed it to Ambrosius, who sat down in his great chair and unrolled it. He read it, frowning. I watched him. The flickering flames from the brazier spread, lighting the planes of the face which already, it seemed, I knew as well as I knew my own. The heart of the brazier glowed, and the light spread and flashed. I felt it spreading across my eyes as they blurred and widened . . .

'Merlin Emrys? Merlin?'

The echo died to an ordinary voice. The vision fled. I was sitting on my stool in Ambrosius' room, looking down at my hands clasping my knees. Ambrosius had risen and was standing over me, between me and the fire. The secretary had gone, and we were alone.

At the repetition of my name I blinked and roused myself.

He was speaking. 'What do you see, there in the fire?'

I answered without looking up. 'A grove of whitethorn on a hillside and a girl on a brown pony, and a young man with a dragon brooch on his shoulder, and the mist knee high.'

I heard him draw a long breath, then his hand came down and took me by the chin and lifted my face. His eyes were intent and fierce.

'It's true, then, this Sight of yours. I have been so sure, and now—now, beyond all doubt, it is true. I thought it was, that first night by the standing stone, but that could have been anything—a dream, a boy's story, a lucky guess to win my interest. But this . . . I was right about you.' He took my hand from my face, and straightened. 'Did you see the girl's face?'

I nodded.

'And the man's?'

I met his eyes then. 'Yes, sir.'

He turned sharply away and stood with his back to me, head bent. Once more he picked up the stilus from the table, turning it over and over with his fingers. After a while he said: 'How long have you known?'

'Only since I rode in tonight. It was something Cadal said, then I remembered things, and how your brother stared tonight when he saw me wearing this.' I touched the dragon brooch at my neck.

He glanced, then nodded. 'Is this the first time you have had this—vision?'

'Yes. I had no idea. Now, it seems strange to me that I never even suspected—but I swear I did not.'

He stood silent, one hand spread on the table, leaning on it. I don't know what I had expected, but I had never thought to see the great Aurelius

Ambrosius at a loss for words. He took a turn across the room to the window, and back again, and spoke. 'This is a strange meeting, Merlin. So much to say, and yet so little. Do you see now why I asked so many questions? Why I tried so hard to find what had brought you here?'

'The gods at work, my lord, they brought me here,' I said. 'Why did you leave her?'

I had not meant the question to come out so abruptly, but I suppose it had been pressing on me so long that now it burst out with the force of an accusation. I began to stammer something, but he cut me short with a gesture, and answered quietly.

'I was eighteen, Merlin, with a price on my head if I set foot in my own kingdom. You know the story–how my cousin Budec took me in when my brother the King was murdered, and how he never ceased to plan for vengeance on Vortigern, though for many years it seemed impossible. But all the time he sent scouts, took in reports, went on planning. And then when I was eighteen he sent me over myself, secretly, to Gorlois of Cornwall, who was my father's friend, and who has never loved Vortigern. Gorlois sent me north with a couple of men he could trust, to watch and listen and learn the lie of the land. Some day I'll tell you where we went, and what happened, but not now. What concerns you now is this . . . We were riding south near the end of October, towards Cornwall to take ship for home, when we were set upon, and had to fight for it. They were Vortigern's men. I don't know yet whether they suspected us, or whether they were killing–as Saxons and foxes do–for wantonness and the sweet taste of blood. The latter, I think, or they would have made surer of killing me. They killed my two companions, but I was lucky; I got off with a flesh wound, and a knock on the head that struck me senseless, and they left me for dead. This was at dusk. When I moved and looked about me it was morning, and a brown pony was standing over me, with a girl on his back staring from me to the dead men and back again, with never a sound.' The first glimmer of a smile, not at me, but at the memory. 'I remember trying to speak, but I had lost a lot of blood, and the night in the open had brought on a fever. I was afraid she would take fright and gallop back to the town, and that would be the end of it. But she did not. She caught my horse and got my things from the saddle-bag, and gave me a drink, then she cleaned the wound and tied it up and then–God knows how–got me across the horse and out of that valley. There was a place she knew of, she said, nearer the town, but remote and secret; no one ever went there. It was a cave, with a spring–What is it?'

'Nothing,' I said. 'I should have known. Go on. No one lived there then?'

'No one. By the time we got there I suppose I was delirious; I remember nothing. She hid me in the cave, and my horse too, out of sight. There had been food and wine in my saddle-bag, and I had my cloak and a blanket. It was late afternoon by then, and when she rode home she heard that the two dead men had already been found, with their horses straying nearby. The troop had been riding north; it wasn't likely that anyone in the town knew there should have been three corpses found. So I was safe. Next day she rode up to the cave again, with food and medicines . . . And the next day, too.' He paused. 'And you know the end of the story.'

'When did you tell her who you were?'

'When she told me why she could not leave Maridunum and go with me. I had thought till then that she was perhaps one of the Queen's ladies—from her ways and her talk I knew she had been bred in a king's house. Perhaps she saw the same in me. But it didn't matter. Nothing mattered, except that I was a man, and she a woman. From the first day, we both knew what would happen. You will understand how it was when you are older.' Again the smile, this time touching mouth as well as eyes. 'This is one kind of knowledge I think you will have to wait for, Merlin. The Sight won't help you much in matters of love.'

'You asked her to go with you—to come back here?'

He nodded. 'Even before I knew who she was. After I knew, I was afraid for her, and pressed her harder, but she would not come with me. From the way she had spoken I knew she hated and feared the Saxons, and feared what Vortigern was doing to the kingdoms, but still she would not come. It was one thing, she said, to do what she had done, but another to go across the seas with the man who, when he came back, must be her father's enemy. We must end it, she said, as the year was ending, and then forget.'

He was silent for a minute, looking down at his hands.

I said: 'And you never knew she had borne a child?'

'No. I wondered, of course. I sent a message the next spring, but got no answer. I left it then, knowing that if she wanted me, she knew—all the world knew—where to find me. Then I heard—it must have been nearly two years later—that she was betrothed. I know now that this was not true, but then it served to make me dismiss it from my mind.' He looked at me. 'Do you understand that?'

I nodded. 'It may even have been true, though not in the way you'd understand it, my lord. She vowed herself to the Church when I should have no more need of her. The Christians call that a betrothal.'

'So?' He considered for a moment. 'Whatever it was, I sent no more messages. And when later on there was mention of a child, a bastard, it hardly crossed my mind that it could be mine. A fellow came here once, a travelling eye-doctor who had been through Wales, and I sent for him and questioned him, and he said yes, there was a bastard boy at the palace of such and such an age, red-haired, and the King's own.'

'Dinias,' I said. 'He probably never saw me. I was kept out of the way . . . And my grandfather did sometimes explain me away to strangers as his own. He had a few scattered around, here and there.'

'So I gathered. So the next rumour of a boy—possibly the King's bastard, possibly his daughter's—I hardly listened to. It was all long past, and there were pressing things to do, and always there was the same thought—if she had borne a child to me, would she not have let me know? If she had wanted me, would she not have sent word?'

He fell silent then, back in his own thoughts. Whether I understood it all then, as he talked, I do not now recollect. But later, when the pieces shook together to make the mosaic, it was clear enough. The same pride which had forbidden her to go with her lover had forbidden her, once she discovered her pregnancy, to call him back. And it helped her through the months that followed. More than that; if—by flight or any other means—she had betrayed who her lover was, nothing would have stopped her brothers from travelling to Budec's court to kill him. There must—knowing my grandfather—have been angry oaths enough about what they would do to the man who had fathered her bastard. And then time moved on, and his coming grew remote, and then impossible, as if he were indeed a myth and a memory in the night. And then the other long love stepped in to supersede him, and the priests took over, and the winter tryst was forgotten. Except for the child, so like his father; but once her duty to him was done, she could go to the solitude and peace which—all those years ago—had sent her riding along up the mountain valley, as later I was to ride out alone by the same path, and looking perhaps for the same things.

I jumped when he spoke again. 'How hard a time of it did you have, as a no-man's-child?'

'Hard enough.'

'You believe me when I say I didn't know?'

'I believe anything you tell me, my lord.'

'Do you hate me for this, very much, Merlin?'

I said slowly, looking down at my hands: 'There is one thing about being a bastard and a no-man's-child. You are free to imagine your father. You can picture for yourself the worst and the best; you can make your father for yourself, in the image of the moment. From the time I was big enough to understand what I was, I saw my father in every soldier and every prince and every priest. And I saw him, too, in every handsome slave in the kingdom of South Wales.'

He spoke very gently, above me. 'And now you see him in truth, Merlin Emrys. I asked you, do you hate me for the kind of life I gave you?'

I didn't look up. I answered, with my eyes on the flames: 'Since I was a child I have had the world to choose from for a father. Out of them all, Aurelius Ambrosius, I would have chosen you.

Silence. The flames leapt like a heartbeat.

I added, trying to make it light. 'After all, what boy would not choose the King of all Britain for his father?'

His hand came hard under my chin again, turning my head aside from the brazier and my eyes from the flames. His voice was sharp. 'What did you say?'

'What did I say?' I blinked up at him. 'I said I would have chosen you.'

His fingers dug into my flesh. 'You called me King of all Britain.'

'Did I?'

'But this is—' He stopped. His eyes seemed to be burning into me. Then he let his hand drop, and straightened. 'Let it go. If it matters, the god will speak again.' He smiled down at me. 'What matters now is what you said yourself. It isn't given to every man to hear this from his grown son. Who knows, it may be better this way, to meet as men, when we each have something to give the other. To a man whose children have been underfoot since infancy, it is not given, suddenly, to see himself stamped on a boy's face as I am stamped on yours.'

'Am I so like?'

'They say so. And I see enough of Uther in you to know why everyone said you were mine.'

'Apparently he didn't see it,' I said. 'Is he very angry about it, or is he only relieved to find I'm not your catamite after all?'

'You knew about that?' He looked amused. 'If he'd think with his brains instead of his body sometimes he'd be the better for it. As it is, we deal together very well. He does one kind of work, as I another, and if I can make the way straight, he'll make a king after me, if I have no—'

He bit off the word. In the queer little silence that followed I looked at the floor.

'Forgive me.' He spoke quietly, equal to equal. 'I spoke without thought. For so long a time I have been used to the idea that I had no son.'

I looked up. 'It's still the truth, in the sense you mean. And it's certainly the truth as Uther will see it.'

'Then if you see it the same way, my path is the smoother.'

I laughed. 'I don't see myself as a king. Half a king, perhaps, or more likely a quarter—the little bit that sees and thinks, but can't do. Perhaps Uther and I between us might make one, if you go? He's larger than life already, wouldn't you say?'

But he didn't smile. His eyes had narrowed, with an arrested look. 'This is how I have been thinking, or something like it. Did you guess?'

'No sir, how could I?' I sat up straight as it broke on me: 'Is this how you thought you might use me? Of course I realise now why you kept me here, in your house, and treated me so royally, but I've wanted to believe you had plans for me—that I could be of use to you. Belasius told me you used every man according to his capacity, and that even if I were no use as a soldier, you would still use me somehow. This is true?'

'Quite true. I knew it straight away, before I even thought you might be my son, when I saw how you faced Uther that night in the field, with the visions still in your eyes, and the power all over you like a shining skin. No, Merlin, you will never make a king, or even a prince as the world sees it, but when you are grown I believe you will be such a man that, if a king had you beside him, he could rule the world. Now do you begin to understand why I sent you to Belasius?'

'He is a very learned man,' I said cautiously.

'He is a corrupt man and a dangerous,' said Ambrosius directly, 'but he is a sophisticated and clever man who has travelled a good deal and who has skills you will not have had the chance to master in Wales. Learn from him. I don't say follow him, because there are places where you must not follow him, but learn all you can.'

I looked up, and nodded. 'You know about him.' It was a conclusion, not a question.

'I know he is a priest of the old religion. Yes.'

'You don't mind this?'

'I cannot yet afford to throw aside valuable tools because I don't like their design,' he said. 'He is useful, so I use him. You will do the same, if you are wise.'

'He wants to take me to the next meeting.'

He raised his brows but said nothing.

'Will you forbid this?' I asked.

'No. Will you go?'

'Yes.' I said slowly, and very seriously, searching for the words: 'My lord, when you are looking for . . . what I am looking for, you have to look in strange places. Men can never look at the sun, except downwards, at his reflection in things of earth. If he is reflected in a dirty puddle, he is still the sun. There is nowhere I will not look, to find him.'

He was smiling. 'You see? You need no guarding, except what Cadal can do.' He leaned back against the edge of the table, half sitting, relaxed now and easy. 'Emrys, she called you. Child of the light. Of the immortals. Divine. You knew that's what it meant?'

'Yes.'

'Didn't you know it was the same as mine?'

'My name?' I asked, stupidly.

He nodded. 'Emrys . . . Ambrosius; it's the same word. Merlinus Ambrosius—she called you after me.'

I stared at him. 'I—yes, of course. It never occurred to me.' I laughed.

'Why do you laugh?'

'Because of our names. Ambrosius prince of light . . . She told everyone that my father was the prince of darkness. I've even heard a song about it. We make songs of everything, in Wales.'

'Some day you must sing it to me.' Then he sobered suddenly. His voice deepened. 'Merlinus Ambrosius, child of the light, look at the fire now, and tell me what you see.' Then, as I looked up at him, startled, he said urgently: 'Now, tonight, before the fire dies, while you are weary and there is sleep in your face. Look at the brazier, and talk to me. What will come to Britain? What will come to me, and to Uther? Look now, work for me, my son, and tell me.'

It was no use; I was awake, and the flames were dying in the brazier, the power had gone, leaving only a room with rapidly cooling shadows, and a man and a boy talking. But because I loved him, I turned my eyes to the embers. There was utter silence, except for the hiss of ash settling, and the tick of the cooling metal.

I said: 'I see nothing but the fire dying down in the brazier, and a burning cave of coal.'

'Go on looking.'

I could feel the sweat starting on my body, the drops trickling down beside my nose, under my arms, into my groin till my thighs stuck together. My hands worked on one another, tight between my knees till the bones hurt. My temples ached. I shook my head sharply to clear it, and looked up. 'My lord, it's no use. I'm sorry, but it's no use. I don't command the god, he commands me. Some day it may be I shall see at will, or when you command me, but now it comes itself, or not at all.' I spread my hands, trying to explain. 'It's like waiting below a cover of cloud, then suddenly a wind shifts it and it breaks, and the light stabs down and catches me, sometimes full, sometimes only the flying edge of the pillars of sunlight. One day I shall be free of the whole temple. But not yet. I can see nothing.' Exhaustion dragged at me. I could hear it in my voice. 'I'm sorry, my lord. I'm no use to you. You haven't got your prophet yet.'

'No,' said Ambrosius. He put a hand down, and as I stood, drew me to him and kissed me. 'Only a son, who has had no supper and who is tired out.

Go to bed, Merlin, and sleep the rest of the night without dreaming. There is plenty of time for visions. Good night.'

I had no more visions that night, but I did have a dream. I never told Ambrosius. I saw again the cave on the hillside, and the girl Niniane coming through the mist, and the man who waited for her beside the cave. But the face of Niniane was not the face of my mother, and the man by the cave was not the young Ambrosius. He was an old man, and his face was mine.

The Wolf

Chapter One

I was five years with Ambrosius in Brittany. Looking back now, I see that much of what happened has been changed in my memory, like a smashed mosaic which is mended in later years by a man who has almost forgotten the first picture. Certain things come back to me plain, in all their colours and details; others—perhaps more important—come hazy, as if the picture had been dusted over by what has happened since, death, sorrow, changes of the heart. Places I always remember well, some of them so clearly that I feel even now as if I could walk into them and that if I had the strength to concentrate, and the power that once fitted me like my robe, I might even now rebuild them here in the dark as I rebuilt the Giants' Dance for Ambrosius, all those years ago.

Places are clear, and ideas, which came to me so new and shining then, but not always the people: sometimes now as I search my memory I wonder if here and there I have confused them one with another, Belasius with Galapas, Cadal with Cerdic, the Breton officer whose name I forget now with my grandfather's captain in Maridunum who once tried to make me into the the kind of swordsman that he thought even a bastard prince should want to be.

But as I write of Ambrosius, it is as if he were here with me now, lit against this darkness as the man with the cap was lit on that first frost-enchanted night in Brittany. Even without my robe of power I can conjure up against the darkness his eyes, steady under frowning brows, the heavy lines of his body, the face (which seems so young to me now) engraved into hardness by the devouring, goading will that had kept his eyes turned westward to his closed kingdom for the twenty-odd years it took him to grow from child to Comes and build, against all the odds of poverty and weakness, the striking force that grew with him, waiting for the time.

It is harder to write of Uther. Or rather it is hard to write of Uther as if he were in the past, part of a story that has been over these many years. Even more vividly than Ambrosius he is here with me; not here in the darkness—it is the part of me that was Myrddin that is here in the darkness. The part that was Uther is out there in the sunlight, keeping the coasts of Britain whole, following the design I made for him, the design that Galapas showed to me on a summer's day in Wales.

But there, of course, it is no longer Uther of whom I write. It is the man who was the sum of us, who was all of us—Ambrosius, who made me; Uther, who worked with me; myself, who used him, as I used every man who came to my hand, to make Arthur for Britain.

From time to time news came from Britain, and occasionally with it—through Gorlois of Cornwall—news of my home.

It seemed that after my grandfather's death, Camlach had not immediately deserted the old alliance with his kinsman Vortigern. He had to feel himself more secure before he would dare break away to support the 'young men's party', as Vortimer's faction was called. Indeed, Vortimer himself had stopped short of open rebellion, but it seemed clear that this must come eventually. King Vortigern was back between the landslide and the flood; if he was to stay King of the British he must call on his Saxon wife's countrymen for help, and the Saxon mercenaries year by year increased their demands till the country was split and bleeding under what men openly called the Saxon Terror, and—in the West especially where men were still free—rebellion only waited for a leader of leaders. And so desperate was Vortigern's situation becoming that he was forced against his better judgement to entrust the armed forces in the West more and more to Vortimer and his brothers, whose blood at least carried none of the Saxon taint.

Of my mother there was no news, except that she was safe in St Peter's. Ambrosius sent her no message. If it came to her ears that a certain Merlinus Ambrosius was with the Count of Brittany, she would know what to think, but a letter or message direct from the King's enemy would endanger her unnecessarily. She would know, said Ambrosius, soon enough.

In fact it was five years before the break came, but the time went by like a tide-race. With the possibility of an opening developing in Wales and Cornwall, Ambrosius' preparations accelerated. If the men of the West wanted a leader he had every intention that it should be, not Vortimer, but himself. He would bide his time and let Vortimer be the wedge, but he and Uther would be the hammer that drove after it into the crack. Meanwhile hope in Less Britain ran high; offers of troops and alliances poured in, the countryside shook to the tramp of horses and marching feet, and the streets of the engineers and armourers rang far into the night as men redoubled their efforts to make two weapons in the time that before it had taken to make one. Now at last the break was coming, and when it came Ambrosius must be ready, and with no chance of failure. One does not wait half a lifetime gathering the material to make a killing spear, and then loose it at random in the dark. Not only men and materials, but time and spirit and the very wind of heaven must be right for him, and the gods themselves must open the gate. And for this, he said, they had sent me to him. It was my coming just at such a time with words of victory, and full of the vision of the unconquered god, which persuaded him (and even more important, the soldiers with him) that the time was at last approaching when he could strike with the certainty of victory. So–I found to my fear–he rated me.

Be sure I had never asked him again how he intended to use me. He made it clear enough, and between pride and fear and longing I fought to learn all that I could be taught, and to open myself for the power which was all I could give him. If he had wanted a prophet ready to hand he must have been disappointed; I saw nothing of importance during this time. Knowledge, I suppose, blocked the gates of vision. But this was the time for knowledge; I studied with Belasius till I outran him, learning, as he had never done, how to apply the calculations which to him were as much an art as songs were to me; even songs, indeed, I was to use. I spent long hours in the street of the engineers, and had frequently to be dragged by a grumbling Cadal from some oily piece of practical work which unfitted me, as he said, for any company but a bath-slave's. I wrote down, too, all I could remember of Galapas' medical teaching, and added practical experience by helping the army doctors whenever I could. I had the freedom of the camp and the town, and with Ambrosius' name to back me I took to this freedom like a hungry young wolf to his first full meal. I learned all the time, from every man or woman I met. I looked, as I had promised, in the light and the dark, at the sunshine and at the stale pool. I went with Ambrosius to the shrine of Mithras below the farmstead, and with Belasius to the gatherings in the forest. I was even allowed to sit silently at meetings between the Count and his captains, though nobody pretended that I would ever be much use in the field 'unless,' said Uther once, half amused, half malicious, 'he is to stand above us like Joshua holding the sun back, to give us more time to do the real work. Though joking apart, he might do worse . . . the men seem to think of him as something halfway between a Courier of Mithras and a splinter of the True Cross–saving your presence, brother–and I'm damned certain he'd be more use stuck up on a hill like a lucky charm where they can see him, than down in the field where he wouldn't last five minutes.' He had even more to say when, at the age of sixteen, I gave up the daily sword practice which gave a man the minimum training in self-defence; but my father merely laughed and said nothing. I think he knew, though as yet I did not, that I had my own kind of protection.

So I learned from everyone; the old women who gathered plants and cobwebs and seaweeds for healing; the travelling pedlars and quack healers; the horse doctors, the soothsayers, the priests. I listened to the soldiers' talk outside the taverns, and the officers' talk in my father's house, and the boys' talk in the streets. But there was one thing about which I learned nothing: by the time I left Brittany at seventeen, I was still ignorant of women. When I thought about them–which happened often enough–I told myself that I had no time, that there was a lifetime still ahead of me for such things, and that now I had work to do which mattered more. But I suppose the plain truth is that I was afraid of them. So I lost my desires in work, and indeed, I believe now that the fear came from the god.

So I waited, and minded my own business, which–as I saw it then–was to fit myself to serve my father.

One day I was in Tremorinus' workshop. Tremorinus, the master engineer, was a pleasant man who allowed me to learn all I could from him, gave me space in the workshops, and material to experiment with. This particular day I remember how when he came into the workshop and saw me busy over a model at my corner bench, he came over to have a look at it. When he saw what I was doing he laughed.

'I'd have thought there were plenty of those around without troubling to put up any more.'

'I was interested in how they got them there.' I tilted the scale model of the standing stone back into place.

He looked surprised. I knew why. He had lived in Less Britain all his life, and the landscape there is so seamed with the stones that men do not see them any more. One walks daily through a forest of stone, and to most men it seems dead stone . . . But not to me. To me they still said something, and I had to find out what; but I did not tell Tremorinus this. I added, merely: 'I was trying to work it out to scale.'

'I can tell you something straight away: that's been tried, and it doesn't work.' He was looking at the pulley I had rigged to lift the model. 'That might do for the uprights, but only the lighter ones, and it doesn't work at all for the capstones.'

'No. I'd found that out. But I'd had an idea . . . I was going to tackle it another way.'

'You're wasting your time. Let's see you getting down to something practical, something we need and can use. Now, that idea of yours for a light mobile crane might be worth developing . . .'

A few minutes later he was called away. I dismantled the model, and sat down to my new calculations. I had not told Tremorinus about them; he had more important things to think about, and in any case he would have laughed if I had told him I had learnt from a poet how to lift the standing stones.

It had happened this way.

One day about a week before this, as I walked by the water that guarded the town walls, I heard a man singing. The voice was old and wavering, and hoarse with over-use – the voice of a professional singer who has strained it above the noise of the crowd, and through singing with the winter cold in his throat. What caught my attention was neither the voice nor the tune, which could hardly be picked out, but the sound of my own name.

Merlin, Merlin, where art thou going?

He was sitting by the bridge, with a bowl for begging. I saw that he was blind, but the remains of his voice was true, and he made no gesture with his bowl as he heard me stop near him, but sat as one sits at a harp, head bent, listening to what the strings say, with fingers stirring as if they felt the notes. He had sung, I would judge, in kings' halls.

> *Merlin, Merlin, where art thou going*
> *So early in the day with thy black dog?*
>
> *I have been searching for the egg,*
> *The red egg of the sea-serpent,*

Which lies by the shore in the hollow stone.
And I go to gather cresses in the meadow,
The green cress and the golden grasses,
The golden moss that gives sleep,
And the mistletoe high on the oak, the druids' bough
That grows deep in the woods by the running water.

Merlin, Merlin, come back from the wood and the fountain!
Leave the oak and the golden grasses
Leave the cress in the water-meadow,
And the red egg of the sea-serpent
In the foam by the hollow stone!

Merlin, Merlin, leave thy seeking!
There is no diviner but God.

Nowadays this song is as well known as the one of Mary the Maiden, or the King and the Grey Seal, but it was the first time I had heard it. When he knew who it was who had stopped to listen, he seemed pleased that I should sit beside him on the bank, and ask questions. I remember that on that first morning we talked mostly of the song, then of himself; I found he had been as a young man in Mona, the druids' isle, and knew Caer'n-ar-Von and had walked on Snowdon. It was in the druids' isle that he had lost his sight; he never told me how, but when I told him that the sea-weeds and cresses that I hunted along the shore were only plants for healing, not for magic, he smiled and sang a verse I had heard my mother sing, which, he said, would be a shield. Against what, he did not say, nor did I ask him. I put money into his bowl, which he accepted with dignity, but when I promised to find a harp for him he went silent, staring with those empty eye-sockets, and I could see he did not believe me. I brought the harp next day; my father was generous, and I had no need even to tell him what the money was for. When I put the harp into the old singer's hands he wept, then took my hands and kissed them.

After that, right up to the time I left Less Britain, I often sought him out. He had travelled widely, in lands as far apart as Ireland and Africa. He taught me songs from every country, Italy and Gaul and the white North, and old songs from the East—strange wandering tunes which had come westward, he said, from the islands of the East with the men of old who had raised the standing stones, and they spoke of lores long forgotten except in song. I do not think he himself thought of them as anything but songs of old magic, poets' tales; but the more I thought about them, the more clearly they spoke to me of men who had really lived, and work they had really done, when they raised the great stones to mark the sun and moon and build for their gods and the giant kings of old.

I said something once about this to Tremorinus, who was kindly as well as clever, and who usually managed to find time for me; but he laughed and put it aside, and I said no more. Ambrosius' technicians had more than enough to think about in those days, without helping a boy to work out a set of calculations of no practical use in the coming invasion. So I let it be.

It was in the spring of my eighteenth year that the news came finally from Britain. Through January and February, winter had closed the seaways, and it was not till early March, taking advantage of the cold still weather before the gales began, that a small trading boat put into port, and Ambrosius got news.

Stirring news it was–literally so, for within a few hours of its coming, the Count's messengers were riding north and east, to gather in his allies at last, and quickly, for the news was late.

It appeared that Vortimer had finally, some time before, broken with his father and the Saxon Queen. Tired of petitioning the High King to break with his Saxon allies and protect his own people from them, several of the British leaders–among them the men of the West–had persuaded Vortimer to take matters into his own hands at last, and had risen with him. They had declared him King, and rallied to his banner against the Saxons, whom they had succeeded in driving back south and eastwards, till they took refuge with their longships in the Isle of Thanet. Even there Vortimer pursued them, and through the last days of autumn and the beginning of winter had beleaguered them there until they pleaded only to be allowed to depart in peace, packed up their goods, and went back to Germany, leaving their women and children behind them.

But Vortimer's victorious kingship did not last long. It was not clear exactly what had happened, but the rumour was that he had died of poison treacherously administered by a familiar of the Queen. Whatever the truth of the matter, he was dead, and Vortigern his father was once more in command. Almost his first act had been (and again the blame was imputed to his wife) to send yet again for Hengist and his Saxons to return to Britain. 'With a small force,' he had said, 'nothing but a mobile peace-keeping force to help him impose order and pull together his divided kingdom.' In fact, the Saxons had promised three hundred thousand men. So rumour said, and though it was to be supposed that rumour lied, it was certain at any rate that Hengist planned to come with a considerable force.

There was also a fragment of news from Maridunum. The messenger was no spy of Ambrosius; the news we got was, as it were, only the larger rumours. These were bad enough. It seemed that my uncle Camlach, together with all his nobles–my grandfather's men, the men that I knew–had risen with Vortimer and fought beside him in the four pitched battles against the Saxons. In the second, at Episford, Camlach had been killed, along with Vortimer's brother Katigern. What concerned me more was that after Vortimer's death reprisals had been levelled at the men who had fought with him. Vortigern had annexed Camlach's kingdom to join his own lands of Guent, and, wanting hostages, had repeated his action of twenty-five years earlier; he had taken Camlach's children, one of them still an infant, and lodged them in the care of Queen Rowena. We had no means of knowing if they were still alive. Nor did we know if Olwen's son, who had met the same fate, had survived. It seemed unlikely. Of my mother there was no news.

Two days after the news came, the spring gales began, and once more the seas were locked against us and against news. But this hardly mattered; indeed, it worked both ways. If we could get no news from Britain, they could have none of us, and of the final accelerated preparations for the invasion of Western Britain. For it was certain that the time had now come. It was not only a case of marching to the relief of Wales and Cornwall, but if there were to be any men left to rally to the Red Dragon, the Red Dragon would have to fight for his crown this coming year.

'You'll go back with the first boat,' said Ambrosius to me, but without looking up from the map which was spread on the table in front of him.

I was standing over by the window. Even with the shutters closed and curtains drawn I could hear the wind, and beside me the curtains stirred in the draught. I said: 'Yes, sir,' and crossed to the table. Then I saw where his finger was pointing on the map. 'I'm to go to Maridunum?'

He nodded. 'You'll take the first westbound boat, and make your way home from wherever it docks. You are to go straight up to Galapas and get what news there is from him. I doubt if you would be recognised in the town, but take no risks. Galapas is safe. You can make him your base.'

'There was no word from Cornwall, then?'

'Nothing, except a rumour that Gorlois was with Vortigern.'

'With Vortigern?' I digested this for a moment. 'Then he didn't rise with Vortimer?'

'As far as my information goes, no.'

'He's trimming, then?'

'Perhaps. I find it hard to believe. It may mean nothing. I understand he has married a young wife, and it may only be that he kept within walls all winter to keep her warm. Or that he foresaw what would happen to Vortimer, and preferred to serve my cause by staying safe and apparently loyal to the High King. But until I know, I cannot send to him directly. He may be watched. So you are to go to Galapas, for the news from Wales. I'm told Vortigern's holed up there somewhere, while the length of Eastern Britain lies open to Hengist. I'll have to smoke the old wolf out first, then weld the West against the Saxons. But it will have to be fast. And I want Caerleon.' He looked up then. 'I'm sending your old friend with you—Marric. You can send word back by him. Let's hope you find all well. You'll want news yourself, I dare say.'

'It can wait,' I said.

He said nothing to that, but raised his brows at me, and then turned back to the map. 'Well, sit down and I'll brief you myself. Let's hope you can get away soon.'

I indicated the swaying curtains. 'I shall be sick all the way.'

He looked up from the map, and laughed. 'By Mithras, I hadn't thought of that. Do you suppose I shall be, too? A damned undignified way to go back to one's home.'

'To one's kingdom,' I said.

Chapter Two

I crossed in early April, and on the same ship as before. But the crossing could not have been more different. This was not Myrddin, the runaway, but Merlinus, a well-dressed young Roman with money in his pocket, and servants in attendance. Where Myrddin had been locked naked in the hold, Merlinus had a comfortable cabin, and marked deference paid him by the captain. Cadal, of course, was one of my servants, and the other, to my own amusement though not his, was Marric. (Hanno was dead, having overreached himself, I gathered, in a little matter of blackmail.) Naturally I carried no outward sign of my connection with Ambrosius, but nothing would part me from the brooch he had given me; I wore this clipped inside the shoulder of my tunic. It was doubtful whether anyone would have recognised in me the runaway of five years ago, and certainly the captain gave no sign, but I held myself aloof, and was careful to speak nothing but Breton.

As luck would have it, the boat was going straight to the mouth of the Tywy and would anchor at Maridunum, but it had been arranged that Cadal and I were to be put off by boat as soon as the trader arrived in the estuary.

It was, in fact, my previous journey in reverse, but in the most important respect there was no difference. I was sick all the way. The fact that this time I had a comfortable bunk and Cadal to look after me, instead of sacks and a bucket in the hold, made not the slightest difference to me. As soon as the ship nosed out of the Small Sea, and met the windy April weather of the Bay, I left my brave stance in the bows and went below and lay down.

We had what they tell me was a fair wind, and we crept into the estuary and dropped anchor just before dawn, ten days before the Ides of April.

It was a still dawn, misty and cold. It was very quiet. The tide was just on the turn, beginning its flow up the estuary, and as our boat left the ship's side the only sound was the hiss and chuckle of water along her sides, and the soft splash of the paddles. Far away, faint and metallic, I could hear cocks crowing. Somewhere beyond the mist lambs were crying, answered by the deeper bleating of sheep. The air smelt soft, clear and salty, and in some curious way of home.

We kept well out to the centre of the stream, and the mist hid us from the banks. If we spoke at all, it was in whispers; once when a dog barked from the bank we heard a man speak to it almost as clearly as if he had been in the boat with us; this was sufficient warning, and we kept our voices down.

It was a strong spring tide, and took us fast. This was as well, for we had made anchor later than we should, and the light was growing. I saw the sailors who rowed us glance anxiously upwards and then lengthen their stroke. I leaned forward, straining my eyes for a glimpse of the bank I could recognise. Cadal said in my ear: 'Glad to be back?'

'That depends on what we find. Mithras, but I'm hungry.'

'That's not surprising,' he said, with a sour chuckle. 'What are you looking for?'

'There should be a bay—white sand with a stream coming down through trees—and a ridge behind it with a crest of pines. We'll put in there.'

He nodded. The plan was that Cadal and I should be landed on the side of the estuary away from Maridunum, at a point I knew from which we could make our way unseen to join the road from the south. We would be travellers from Cornwall; I would do the talking, but Cadal's accent would pass with any but a native Cornishman. I had with me some pots of salve and a small chest of medicines, and if challenged could pass as a travelling doctor, a disguise that would serve as a pass to more or less anywhere I wanted to go.

Marric was still on board. He would go in with the trader, and disembark as usual at the wharf. He would try to find his old contacts in the town, and pick up what news he could. Cadal would go with me to the cave of Galapas, and act as connecting-file with Marric to pass over what information I got. The ship was to lie for three days in the Tywy; when she sailed Marric would take the news back with her. Whether I and Cadal would be with him would depend on what we found; neither my father nor I forgot that after Camlach's part in the rebellion Vortigern must have been through Maridunum like a fox through a hen-run, and maybe his Saxons with him. My first duty was to get news of Vortigern, and send it back; my second to find my mother and see that she was safe.

It was good to be on land again; not dry land, for the grass at the head of the ridge was long and soaking, but I felt light and excited as the boat vanished under the mist and Cadal and I left the shore and made our way inland towards the road. I don't know what I expected to find in Maridunum; I don't even know that I cared overmuch; it was not the homecoming that made my spirits lift, but the fact that at last I had a job to do for Ambrosius. If I could not yet do a prophet's work for him, at least I could do a man's work, and then a son's. I believe that all the time I was half hoping that I would be asked to die for him. I was very young.

We reached the bridge without incident. Luck was with us there, for we fell in with a horse-trader who had a couple of nags in hand which he hoped to sell in the town. I bought one of them from him, haggling just enough to prevent suspicion; he was pleased enough with the price to throw in a rather worn saddle. By the time the transaction was finished it was full light and there were one or two people about, but no one gave us more than a cursory glance, except for one fellow who, apparently recognising the horse, grinned, and said—to Cadal rather than to me: 'Were you planning to go far, mate?'

I pretended not to hear, but from the corner of my eye saw Cadal spread his hands, shrug, and turn his eyes up in my direction. The look said, all too plainly, 'I only follow where he goes, and he's crazy anyway.'

Presently the towpath was empty. Cadal came alongside, and hooked a hand through the neck-strap. 'He's right, you know. That old screw won't get you far. How far is it, anyway?'

'Probably not nearly as far as I remember. Six miles at the outside.'

'Uphill most of the way, you said?'

'I can always walk.' I smoothed a hand along the skinny neck. 'He's not as much of a wreck as he looks, you know. There's not much wrong that a few good feeds won't put right.'

'Then at least you won't have wasted your money. What are you looking at over that wall?'

'That's where I used to live.'

We were passing my grandfather's house. It looked very little changed. From the cob's back I could just see over the wall to the terrace where the quince tree grew, its brilliant flame-coloured blossoms opening to the morning sun. And there was the garden where Camlach had given me the poisoned apricot. And there the gate where I had run in tears.

The cob plodded on. Here was the orchard, the apple trees already swelling with buds, the grass springing rough and green round the little terrace where Moravik would sit and spin, while I played at her feet. And here, now, was the place I had jumped over the wall the night I ran away; here was the leaning apple tree where I had left Aster tethered. The wall was broken, and I could see in across the rough grass where I had run that night, from my room where Cerdic's body lay on its funeral pyre. I pulled the cob to a halt and craned to see further. I must have made a clean sweep that night: the buildings were all gone, my room, and along with it two sides of the outer court. The stables, I saw, were still the same; the fire had not reached them, then. The two sides of the colonnade that had been destroyed had been rebuilt in a modern style that seemed to bear no relation to the rest, big rough stones and crude building, square pillars holding up a timber roof, and square, deep windows. It was ugly, and looked comfortless; its only virtue would be that it was weatherproof. You might as well, I thought, settling back in the saddle and putting the cob in motion, live in a cave . . .

'What are you grinning at?' asked Cadal.

'Only at how Roman I've become. It's funny, my home isn't here any more. And to be honest I don't think it's in Less Britain either.'

'Where, then?'

'I don't know. Where the Count is, that's for sure. That will be this sort of place, I suppose, for some time to come.' I nodded towards the walls of the old Roman barracks behind the palace. They were in ruins, and the place was deserted. So much the better, I thought; at least it didn't look as if Ambrosius would have to fight for it. Give Uther twenty-four hours, and the place would be as good as new. And here was St Peter's, apparently untouched, showing no sign either of fire or spear. 'You know something?' I said to Cadal, as we left the shadow of the nunnery wall and headed along the path towards the mill. 'I suppose if I have anywhere I can call a home, it's the cave of Galapas.'

'Doesn't sound all that Roman to me,' said Cadal. 'Give me a good tavern any day and a decent bed and some mutton to eat, and you can keep all the caves there are.'

Even with this sorry horse, the way seemed shorter than I remembered it. Soon we had reached the mill, and turned up across the road and into the valley. Time fell away. It seemed only yesterday that I had come up this same valley in the sunshine, with the wind stirring Aster's grey mane. Not even Aster's—for there under the same thorn tree was surely the same half-wit boy watching the same sheep as on my very first ride. As we reached the fork in the path, I found myself watching for the ring-dove. But the hillside was still, except for the rabbits scuttering among the young bracken.

Whether the cob sensed the end of his journey, or whether he merely liked the feel of grass under his feet and a light weight on his back, he seemed to quicken his step. Ahead of me now I could see the shoulder of the hill beyond which lay the cave.

I drew rein by the hawthorn grove.

'Here we are. It's up there, above the cliff.' I slipped out of the saddle and handed the reins to Cadal. 'Stay here and wait for me. You can come up in an hour.' I added, on an afterthought: 'And don't be alarmed if you see what you think is smoke. It's the bats coming out of the cave.'

I had almost forgotten Cadal's sign against the evil eye. He made it now, and I laughed and left him.

Chapter Three

Before I had climbed round the little crag to the lawn in front of the cave, I knew.

Call, it foresight; there was no sign. Silence, of course, but then there usually had been silence as I approached the cave. This silence was different. It was only after some moments that I realised what it was. I could no longer hear the trickle of the spring.

I mounted to the top of the path, came out on the sward, and saw. There was no need to go into the cave to know that he was not there, and never would be again.

On the flat grass in front of the cave-mouth was a scatter of debris. I went closer to look.

It had been done not so very long ago. There had been a fire here, a fire quenched by rain before everything could properly be destroyed. There was a pile of sodden rubbish—half-charred wood, rags, parchment gone again to pulp but with the blackened edges still showing. I turned the nearest piece of scorched wood over with my foot; from the carving on it I knew what it was; the chest that had held his books. And the parchment was all that remained of the books themselves.

I suppose there was other stuff of his among the wreck of rubbish. I didn't look further. If the books had gone, I knew everything else would have gone too. And Galapas with them.

I went slowly towards the mouth of the cave. I paused by the spring. I could see why there had been no sound; someone had filled in the basin with stones and earth and more wreckage thrown out of the cave. Through it all the water welled still, sluggishly, oozing in silence over the stone lip and

down to make a muddy morass of the turf. I thought I could see the skeleton
of a bat, picked clean by the water.

Strangely enough, the torch was still on the ledge high beside the mouth
of the cave, and it was dry. There was no flint or iron, but I made fire and,
holding the torch before me, went slowly inside.

I think my flesh was shivering, as if a cold wind blew out of the cave and
went by me. I knew already what I should find.

The place was stripped. Everything had been thrown out to burn.
Everything, that is, except the bronze mirror. This, of course, would not
burn, and I suppose it had been too heavy to be looted. It had been
wrenched from the wall and stood propped against the side of the cave,
tilted at a drunken angle. Nothing else. Not even a stir and whisper from the
bats in the roof. The place echoed with emptiness.

I lifted the torch high and looked up towards the crystal cave. It was not
there.

I believe that for a couple of pulses of the torchlight I thought he had
managed to conceal the inner cave, and was in hiding. Then I saw.

The gap into the crystal cave was still there, but chance, call it what you
will, had rendered it invisible except to those who knew. The bronze mirror
had fallen so that, instead of directing light towards the gap, it directed
darkness. Its light was beamed and concentrated on a projection of rock
which cast, clear across the mouth of the crystal cave, a black wedge of
shadow. To anyone intent only on the pillage and destruction in the cave
below, the gap would be hardly visible at all.

'Galapas?' I said, trying it out on the emptiness. 'Galapas?'

There was the faintest of whispers from the crystal cave, a ghostly sweet
humming like the music I had once listened for in the night. Nothing
human; I had not expected it. But still I climbed up to the ledge, knelt down
and peered in.

The torchlight caught the crystals, and threw the shadow of my harp,
trembling, clear round the lighted globe. The harp stood, undamaged, in
the centre of the cave. Nothing else, except the whisper dying round the
glittering walls. There must be visions there, in the flash and counterflash of
light, but I knew I would not be open to them. I put a hand down to the rock
and vaulted, torch streaming, back to the floor of the cave. As I passed the
tilted mirror I caught a glimpse of a tall youth running in a swirl of flame
and smoke. His face looked pale, the eyes black and enormous. I ran out on
to the grass. I had forgotten the torch, which flamed and streamed behind
me. I ran to the edge of the cliff, and cupped a hand to my mouth to call
Cadal, but then a sound from behind me made me whip round and look
upwards.

It was a very normal sound. A pair of ravens and a carrion crow had risen
from the hill, and were scolding at me.

Slowly this time, I climbed the path that led up past the spring and out on
the hillside above the cave. The ravens went higher, barking. Two more
crows made off low across the young bracken. There was a couple still busy
on something lying among the flowering blackthorn.

I whirled the torch and flung it streaming to scatter them. Then I ran
forward.

There was no telling how long he had been dead. The bones were picked almost clean. But I knew him by the discoloured brown rags that flapped under the skeleton, and the one old broken sandal which lay flung nearby among the April daisies. One of the hands had fallen from the wrist, and the clean, brittle bones lay near my foot. I could see where the little finger had been broken, and had set again, crookedly. Already through the bare rib-cage the April grass was springing. The air blew clean and sunlit, smelling of flowering gorse.

The torch had been stubbed out in the fresh grass. I stooped and picked it up. I should not have thrown it at them, I thought. His birds had given him a seemly waygoing.

A step behind me brought me round, but it was only Cadal.

'I saw the birds go up,' he said. He was looking down at the thing under the blackthorn bushes. 'Galapas?'

I nodded.

'I saw the mess down by the cave. I guessed.'

'I hadn't realised I had been here so long.'

'Leave this to me.' He was stooping already. 'I'll get him buried. Go you and wait down where we left the horse. I can maybe find some sort of tool down yonder, or I could come back—'

'No. Let him lie in peace under the thorn. We'll build the hill over him and let it take him in. We do this together, Cadal.'

There were stones in plenty to pile over him for a barrow, and we cut sods with our daggers to turf it over. By the end of the summer the bracken and foxgloves and young grasses would have grown right over and shrouded him. So we left him.

As we went downhill again past the cave I thought of the last time I had gone this way. I had been weeping then, I remembered, for Cerdic's death, for my mother's loss and Galapas', for who knew what foreknowledge of the future? *You will see me again,* he had said, *I promise you that.* Well, I had seen him. And some day, no doubt, his other promise would come true in its own fashion.

I shivered, caught Cadal's quick look, and spoke curtly. 'I hope you had the sense to bring a flask with you. I need a drink.'

Chapter Four

Cadal had brought more than a flask with him, he had brought food—salt mutton and bread, and last season's olives in a bottle with their own oil. We sat in the lee of the wood and ate, while the cob grazed near us, and below in the distance the placid curves of the river glimmered through the April green of the fields and the young wooded hills. The mist had cleared, and it was a beautiful day.

'Well,' said Cadal at length, 'what's to do?'

'We go to see my mother. If she's still there, of course.' Then, with a savagery that broke through me so suddenly that I had hardly known it was there: 'By Mithras, I'd give a lot to know who did that up yonder!'

'Why, who could it be except Vortigern?'

'Vortimer, Pascentius, anyone. When a man's wise and gentle and good,' I added bitterly, 'it seems to me that any man's, every man's hand is against him. Galapas could have been murdered by an outlaw for food, or a herdsman for shelter, or a passing soldier for a drink of water.'

'That was no murder.'

'What, then?'

'I meant, that was done by more than one. Men in a pack are worse than lone ones. At a guess, it was Vortigern's men, on their way up from the town.'

'You're probably right. I shall find out.'

'You think you'll get to see your mother?'

'I can try.'

'Did he—have you any messages for her?' It was, I suppose, the measure of my relationship with Cadal that he dared to ask the question.

I answered him quite simply. 'If you mean did Ambrosius ask me to tell her anything, no. He left it to me. What I do tell her depends entirely on what's happened since I left. I'll talk to her first, and judge how much to tell her after that. Don't forget, I haven't seen her for a long time, and people change. I mean, their loyalties change. Look at mine. When I last saw her I was only a child, and I have only a child's memories—for all I know I misunderstood her utterly, the way she thought and the things she wanted. Her loyalties may lie elsewhere—not just the Church, but the way she feels about Ambrosius. The gods know there'd be no blame to her if she had changed. She owed Ambrosius nothing. She took good care of that.'

He said thoughtfully, his eyes on the green distance threaded by the glinting river: 'The nunnery hadn't been touched.'

'Exactly. Whatever had happened to the rest of the town, Vortigern had let St Peter's be. So you see I've to find out who is in which camp before I give any messages. What she hasn't known about for all these years, it won't hurt her to go on not knowing for as many more days. Whatever happens, with Ambrosius coming so soon, I mustn't take the risk of telling her too much.'

He began to pack away the remains of the meal while I sat, chin on hand, thinking, my eyes on the bright distance.

I added, slowly: 'It's simple enough to find out where Vortigern is now, and if Hengist's landed already, and with how many men. Marric will probably find out without too much trouble. But there were other soundings the Count wanted me to take—things they'll hardly know about in the nunnery—so now that Galapas is dead, I'll have to try elsewhere. We'll wait here till dusk, then go down to St Peter's. My mother will be able to tell me who I can still go to in safety.' I looked at him. 'Whatever king she favours, she's not likely to give me away.'

'That's true enough. Well, let's hope they'll let her see you.'

'If she knows who's asking for her, I imagine it will take more than a word from the Abbess to stop her from seeing me. Don't forget she's still a king's daughter.' I lay back on the warm grass, my hands behind my head. 'Even if

I'm not yet a king's son . . .'

But, king's son or no, there was no getting into the nunnery.

I had been right in thinking there had been no damage done here. The high walls loomed unbroken and unscarred, and the gates were new and solid, of oak hinged and bolted with iron. They were fast shut. Nor—mercifully—did any welcoming torch burn outside. The narrow street was empty and unlit in the early dusk. At our urgent summons a small square window in the gate opened, and an eye was applied to the grille.

'Travellers from Cornwall,' I said softly. 'I must have word with the Lady Niniane.'

'The Lady who?' It was the flat, toneless voice of the deaf. Wondering irritably why a deaf portress should be put at the gate, I raised my voice a little, going closer to the grille.

'The Lady Niniane. I don't know what she calls herself now, but she was sister of the late King. Is she with you still?'

'Aye, but she'll see nobody. Is it a letter you have? She can read.'

'No, I must have speech with her. Go and take word to her; tell her it's—one of her family.'

'Her family?' I thought I saw a flicker of interest in the eyes. 'They're most of them dead and gone. Do you not get news in Cornwall? Her brother the King died in battle last year, and the children have gone to Vortigern. Her own son's been dead these five years.'

'I knew that. I'm not her brother's family. And I'm as loyal as she is to the High King. Go and tell her that. And look—take this for your . . . devotions.'

A pouch passed through the grille and was grabbed in a quick monkey-snatch. 'I'll take a message for you. Give me your name. I don't say she'll see you, mind, but I'll take her your name.'

'My name's Emrys.' I hesitated. 'She knew me once. Tell her that. And hurry. We'll wait here.'

It was barely ten minutes before I heard the steps coming back. For a moment I thought it might be my mother, but it was the same old eyes that peered at me through the grille, the same clawed hand laying hold of the bars. 'She'll see you. Oh no, not now, young master. You can't come in. Nor she can't come out yet, not till prayers is over. Then she'll meet you on the river walk, she says; there's another gate in the wall there. But not to let anyone see you.'

'Very well. We'll be careful.'

I could see the whites of the eyes turning, as she tried to see me in the shadows. 'Knew you, she did, straight away. Emrys, eh? Well, don't worry that I'll say aught. These be troubled times, and the least said the better, no matter what about.'

'What time?'

'An hour after moonrise. You'll hear the bell.'

'I'll be there,' I said, but the grille was already shut.

There was a mist rising again from the river. This would help, I thought. We went quietly down the lane which skirted the nunnery walls. It led away from the streets, down towards the towpath.

'What now?' asked Cadal. 'It's two hours yet till moonrise, and by the look of the night we'll be lucky if we ever see a moon at all. You'll not risk going into the town?'

'No. But there's no sense in waiting about in this drizzle. We'll find a place out of the wet where we can hear the bell. This way.'

The stableyard gate was locked. I wasted no time on it, but led the way to the orchard wall. No lights showed in the palace. We scrambled over where the wall was broken, and walked up through the damp grass of the orchard and into my grandfather's garden. The air was heavy with the smell of damp earth and growing things, mint and sweetbriar and moss and young leaves heavy with wet. Last year's ungathered fruit squelched under our feet. Behind us the gate creaked, emptily.

The colonnades were empty, the doors shut, the shutters fastened close over the windows. The place was all darkness and echoes and the scuttle of rats. But there was no damage that I could see. I suppose that, when Vortigern took the town, he had meant to keep the house for himself, and had somehow persuaded or forced his Saxons to bypass it in their looting as—from fear of the bishops—he had forced them to bypass St Peter's. So much the better for us. We should at least have a dry and comfortable wait. My time with Tremorinus had been wasted indeed if I could not have picked every lock in the place.

I was just saying as much to Cadal when suddenly, round the corner of the house, treading softly as a cat on the mossy flagstones, came a young man walking fast. He stopped dead at the sight of us, and I saw his hand flash down to his hip. But even while Cadal's weapon hissed free of its sheath in reply the young man peered, stared, and then exclaimed: 'Myrddin, by the holy oak!'

For a moment I genuinely didn't recognise him, which was understandable, since he was not much older than myself, and had changed as much in five years. Then, unmistakably, I saw who it was; broad shoulders, thrusting jaw, hair that even in the twilight showed red. Dinias, who had been prince and king's son when I was a nameless bastard; Dinias, my 'cousin', who would not even recognise that much of a tie with me, but who had claimed the title of Prince for himself, and been allowed to get away with it.

He would hardly now be taken for a prince. Even in that fading light I could see that he was dressed, not poorly, but in clothes that a merchant might have worn, and he had only one jewel, an arm-ring of copper. His belt was of plain leather, his sword-hilt plain also, and his cloak, though of good stuff, was stained and frayed at the edge. About his whole person was that undefinable air of seediness which comes from relentless calculation from day to day or perhaps even from meal to meal.

Since in spite of the considerable changes he was still indisputably my cousin Dinias, it was to be supposed that once he had recognised me, there was little point in pretending he was wrong. I smiled and held out my hand. 'Welcome, Dinias. Yours is the first known face I've seen today.'

'What in the name of the gods are you doing here? Everyone said you were dead, but I didn't believe it.'

His big head thrust out, peering close as the quick eyes looked me up and down. 'Wherever you were, you've done all right, seemingly. How long have you been back?'

'We came today.'

'Then you've heard the news?'

'I knew Camlach was dead. I'm sorry about that . . . if you were. As you'll know, he was no friend of mine, but that was hardly political . . .' I paused, waiting. Let him make the moves. I saw from the corner of an eye that Cadal was tensed and watchful, a hand still to his hip. I moved my own hand palm downwards in a slight flattening movement, and saw him relax.

Dinias lifted a shoulder. 'Camlach? He was a fool. I told him which way the wolf would jump.' But as he spoke I saw his eyes slide sideways towards the shadows. It seemed that men watched their tongues these days in Maridunum. His eyes came back to me, suspicious, wary. 'What's your business here, anyway? Why did you come back?'

'To see my mother. I've been in Cornwall, and all we got there was rumours of fighting, and when I heard Camlach was dead, and Vortimer, I wondered what had happened at home.'

'Well, she's alive, you'll have found that out? The High King–' rather loudly '–respects the Church. I doubt if you'll get to see her, though.'

'You're probably right. I went up to the nunnery, and they wouldn't let me in. But I'll be here for a few days. I'll send a message in, and if she wants to see me, I imagine she'll find a way of doing so. But at least I know she's safe. It's a real stroke of luck, running into you like this. You'll be able to give me the rest of the news. I had no idea what I might find here, so as you see, I came in this morning quietly, alone with my servant.'

'Quietly is right. I thought you were thieves. You're lucky I didn't cut you down and ask questions afterwards.'

It was the old Dinias, the bullying note there again, an immediate response to my mild, excusing tone.

'Well, I wasn't taking any risks till I knew how the family stood. I went off to St Peter's–I waited till dusk to do that–then I came to take a look round here. Is the place empty then?'

'I'm still living here. Where else?'

The arrogance rang as hollow as the empty colonnade, and for a moment I felt tempted to ask him for hospitality and see what he would say. As if the thought had struck him at the same moment he said quickly: 'Cornwall, eh? What's the news from there? They say Ambrosius' messengers are scuttling across the Narrow Sea like waterflies.'

I laughed. 'I wouldn't know. I've been leading a sheltered life.'

'You picked the right place.' The contempt that I remembered so well was back in his voice. 'They say old Gorlois spent the winter snugged down in bed with a girl barely turned twenty, and left the rest of the kings to play their own games out in the snow. They say she'd make Helen of Troy look like a market-woman. What's she like?'

'I never saw her. He's a jealous husband.'

'Jealous of you?' He laughed, and followed it with a comment that made Cadal, behind me, suck in his breath. But the jibe had put my cousin back in humour, and off his guard. I was still the little bastard cousin, and of no account. He added: 'Well, it would suit you. You had a peaceful winter, you with your goatish old Duke, while the rest of us tramped the country after the Saxons.'

So he had fought with Camlach and Vortimer. It was what I had wanted to know. I said mildly: 'I was hardly responsible for the Duke's policy. Nor am I now.'

'Hah! It's as well for you. You knew he was in the north with Vortigern?'

'I knew he had left to join him—at Caer'n-ar-Von, was it? Are you going up there yourself?' I put the gentlest of queries into my voice, adding meekly: 'I wasn't really in a position to hear much news that mattered.'

A chill current of air eddied, loaded with damp, between the pillars. From some broken gutter above us water suddenly spilled over, to splash between us on the flagstones. I saw him gather his cloak round him. 'Why are we standing here?' He spoke with a brusque heartiness that rang as false as the arrogance. 'Come and exchange news over a flask of wine, eh?'

I hesitated, but only for a moment. It seemed obvious that Dinias had his own reasons for keeping out of the High King's eye; for one thing, if he had managed to live down his association with Camlach, he would surely be with Vortigern's army, not skulking here in this threadbare fashion in an empty palace. For another, now that he knew I was in Maridunum, I preferred to keep him under my eye than leave him now to go and talk to whom he would.

So I accepted with every appearance of flattered pleasure, only insisting that he must join me for supper, if he could tell me where a good meal was to be found, and a warm seat out of the wet . . .?

Almost before the words were out he had me by the arm and was hurrying me across the atrium and out through the street door.

'Fine, fine. There's a place over on the west side, beyond the bridge. The food's good, and they get the kind of clients that mind their own business.' He winked. 'Not that you'll be wanting to bother with a girl, eh? Though you don't look as if they'd made a clerk of you after all . . .? Well, no more for now, it doesn't do to look as though you've too much to talk about these days . . . You either fall foul of the Welsh or you fall foul of Vortigern—and the place is crawling with his spies just now. I don't know who it is they're looking for, but there's a story going about—No, take your trash away.' This to a beggar who thrust a tray of rough-cut stones and leather laces in front of us. The man moved back without a word. I saw that he was blind in one eye from a cut; a hideous scar ran right up one cheek, and had flattened the bridge of the nose. It looked as if it had been a sword cut.

I dropped a coin on the tray as we passed, and Dinias shot me a look that was far from friendly. 'Times have changed, eh? You must have struck it rich in Cornwall. Tell me, what happened that night? Did you mean to set the whole damned place on fire?'

'I'll tell you all about it over supper,' I said, and would say no more till we reached the shelter of the tavern, and got a bench in the corner with our backs to the wall.

Chapter Five

I had been right about Dinias' poverty. Even in the smoky murk of the tavern's crowded room I could see the threadbare state of his clothes, and sense the air half of resentment, half of eagerness, with which he watched while I ordered food and a jug of their best wine. While it was coming I excused myself and had a quick word aside with Cadal.

'I may get some of the facts we want from him. In any case I thought it better to stick to him—I'd rather he came under my eye for the moment. The odds are he'll be drunk enough by moonrise to be harmless, and I'll either get him bedded down safe with a girl, or if he's past it I'll see him home on my way to the nunnery. If I don't look like getting out of here by moonrise, get over yourself to the gate on the towpath to meet my mother. You know our story. Tell her I'm coming, but I fell in with my cousin Dinias and have to get rid of him first. She'll understand. Now get yourself some food.'

'Watch your step, I would, Merlin. Your cousin, did you say? Proper daisy he is, and no mistake. He doesn't like you.'

I laughed. 'You think that's news? It's mutual.'

'Oh. Well, as long as you watch it.'

'I'll do that.'

Dinias' manners were still good enough to make him wait till I had dismissed Cadal and sat down to pour the wine. He had been right about the food; the pie they brought us was stuffed full of beef and oysters in a thick, steaming gravy, and though the bread was made from barley meal it was fresh. The cheese was not, and was excellent. The tavern's other wares seemed to match the food; from time to time one got a glimpse of them as a girl peered giggling in through a curtained door, and some man put his cup down and hurried after her. From the way Dinias' eyes lingered on the curtain even while he ate, I thought I might have little difficulty in getting rid of him safely once I had the information I wanted.

I waited until he was halfway through his pie before I started asking questions. I hardly liked to wait longer for, from the way he reached for the wine-jug almost—in spite of his hunger—between every mouthful, I was afraid that if I left it too long he would not be clear-headed enough to tell me what I wanted.

Until I was quite sure how the land lay I was not prepared to venture on ground that might be tricky, but, my family being what it was, I could glean a good deal of the information Ambrosius wanted from simply asking questions about my relatives. These he answered readily enough.

To begin with, I had been presumed dead ever since the night of the fire. Cerdic's body had been destroyed, and the whole of that side of the courtyard along with it, and when my pony had found its way home and there was no sign of me, it could only be presumed that I had perished along with Cerdic and vanished the same way. My mother and Camlach had sent men out to search the countryside, but of course found no trace of me. It appeared there had been no suggestion of my having left by sea. The trading ship had not put in to Maridunum, and no one had seen the coracle.

My disappearance–not remarkably–had made very little stir. What my mother had thought about it no one knew, but she had apparently retired into the seclusion of St Peter's very soon afterwards. Camlach had lost no time in declaring himself King, and for form's sake offered Olwen his protection, but since his own wife had one son and was heavy with another, it was an open secret that Queen Olwen would soon be married off to some harmless and preferably distant chieftain . . . And so on, and so on.

So much for news of the past, which was none of it news to me or news for Ambrosius. As Dinias finished his meal and leaned back against the wall loosening his belt, relaxed by the food and wine and warmth, I thought it time to steer near more immediate questions of the present. The tavern had filled up now, and there was plenty of noise to cover what we were saying. One or two of the girls had come out from the inner rooms, and there was a good deal of laughter and some horse-play. It was quite dark now outside, and apparently wetter than ever; men came in shaking themselves like dogs and shouting for mulled drinks. The atmosphere was heavy with peat smoke and charcoal from the grills and the smells of hot food and the reek of cheap oil-lamps. I had no fear of recognition: anyone would have had to lean right over our table and peer into my face to see me properly at all.

'Shall I send for more meat?' I asked.

Dinias shook his head, belched, and grinned. 'No thanks. That was good. I'm in your debt. Now for your news. You've heard mine. Where have you been these past years?' He reached again for the jug of wine and up-ended it over his empty cup. 'Damned thing's empty. Send for more?'

I hesitated. It appeared he had a poor head for wine, and I didn't want him drunk too soon.

He mistook my hesitation. 'Come on, come on, you surely don't grudge me another jug of wine, eh? It isn't every day a rich young relative comes back from Cornwall. What took you there, eh? And what have you been doing all this time? Come on, young Myrddin, let's hear about it, shall we? But first, the wine.'

'Well, of course,' I said, and gave the order to the pot-boy. 'But don't use my name here, if you don't mind. I'm calling myself Emrys now till I see which way the wind blows.' He accepted this so readily that I realised things were even trickier in Maridunum than I had thought. It seemed it was dangerous to declare oneself at all. Most of the men in the tavern looked Welsh; there were none I recognised, which was hardly surprising, considering the company I had kept five years ago. But there was a group near the door who, from their fair hair and beards, might have been Saxon. I supposed they were Vortigern's men. We said nothing until the pot-boy had dumped a fresh flask on the table in front of us. My cousin poured it, pushed his plate aside, leaned back and looked at me enquiringly.

'Well, come on, tell me about yourself. What happened that night you left? Who did you go with? You couldn't have been more than twelve or thirteen when you went, surely?'

'I fell in with a pair of traders going south,' I told him. 'I paid my way with one of the brooches that my gr— that the old King gave me. They took me with them as far as Glastonbury. Then I had a bit of luck—fell in with a merchant who was travelling west into Cornwall with glass goods from the Island, and he took me along,' I looked down as if avoiding his eye, and twisted the cup between my fingers. 'He wanted to set up as a gentleman, and thought it would do him credit to have a boy along who could sing and play the harp, and read and write as well.'

'Hm. Very likely.' I had known what he would think of my story, and indeed, his tone held satisfaction, as if his contempt of me had been justified. So much the better. It didn't matter to me what he thought. 'Then?' he asked.

'Oh, I stayed with him for a few months, and he was pretty generous, he and his friends. I even made a fair amount on the side.'

'Harping?' he asked, with a lift of the lip.

'Harping,' I said blandly. 'Also reading and writing–I did the man's accounts for him. When he came back north he wanted me to stay with him, but I didn't want to come back. Didn't dare,' I added, disarmingly frank. 'It wasn't hard to find a place in a religious house. Oh, no, I was too young to be anything but a layman. To tell you the truth, I quite enjoyed it; it's a very peaceful life. I've been busy helping them to write out copies of a history of the fall of Troy.' His expression made me want to laugh, and I looked down at my cup again. It was good ware, Samian, with a high gloss, and the potter's mark was clear. A.M. *Ambrosius made me,* I thought suddenly, and smoothed the letters gently with my thumb as I finished for Dinias the account of the five harmless years spent by his bastard cousin. 'I worked there until the rumours started coming in from home. I didn't pay much heed to them at first–rumours were always flying. But when we knew that it was true about Camlach's death, and then Vortimer's, I began to wonder what might have happened in Maridunum. I knew I had to see my mother again.'

'You're going to stay here?'

'I doubt it. I like Cornwall, and I have a home there of a sort.'

'Then you'll become a priest?'

I shrugged. 'I hardly know yet. It's what they always meant me for, after all. Whatever the future is there, my place here is gone–if I ever had one. And I'm certainly no warrior.'

He grinned at that. 'Well, you never were, exactly, were you? And the war here isn't over; it's hardly begun, let me tell you.' He leaned across the table confidently, but the movement knocked his cup so that it rocked, and the wine washed up to the rim. He grabbed and steadied it. 'Nearly spilt that, and the wine's nearly out again. Not bad stuff, eh? What about another?'

'If you like. But you were saying—'

'Cornwall, now. I've always thought I'd like to go there. What are they saying there about Ambrosius?'

The wine was already talking. He had forgotten to be confidential; his voice was loud, and I saw one or two heads turn in our direction.

He took no notice. 'Yes, I imagine you'd hear down there, if there was any news to hear. They say that's where he'll land, eh?'

'Oh,' I said easily, 'there's talk all the time. There has been for years, you know how it is. He hasn't come yet, so your guess is as good as mine.'

'Like a bet on it?' I saw he had reached into the pouch at his waist and brought out a pair of dice, which he tossed idly from hand to hand. 'Come on, give you a game?'

'No, thanks. At any rate, not here. Look, Dinias, I'll tell you what, we'll get another flask, or two if you like, and go home and drink them there?'

'Home?' He sneered, loose-lipped. 'Where's that? An empty palace?'

He was still talking loudly, and from across the room I noticed someone watching us. Nobody I knew. Two men in dark clothes, one with a fringe of black beard, the other thin-faced and red-headed, with a long nose like a fox. Welshmen, by the look of them. They had a flask on a stool in front of them, and cups in their hands, but the flask had been at the same level now for a good half hour. I glanced at Dinias. I judged he had reached the stage now of being disposed either to friendly confidences or a loud quarrel. To insist on leaving now might be to provoke that quarrel, and if we were being watched, and if the crowd near the door were indeed Vortigern's men, it would be better to stay here and talk quietly than take my cousin out into the street, and perhaps be followed. What, after all, did a mention of Ambrosius' name matter? It would be on every man's lips, and if, as seemed likely, rumours had been flying more thickly than usual of late, everyone, Vortigern's friends and enemies alike, would be discussing them.

Dinias had dropped the dice on the table, and was pushing them here and there with a reasonably steady forefinger. At least they would give us an excuse for a heads-together session in our corner. And dice might take his attention off the wine flask.

I brought out a handful of small coins. 'Look, if you really want a game. What can you put on the table?'

As we played I was conscious that Blackbeard and the foxy man were listening. The Saxons near the door seemed harmless enough; most of them were three parts drunk already, and talking too loudly among themselves to pay attention to anyone else. But Blackbeard seemed to be interested.

I threw the dice. Five and four. Too good; I wanted Dinias to win something. I could hardly offer him money to get him behind the curtain with a girl. Meanwhile, to put Blackbeard off the scent . . .

I said, not loudly, but very clearly: 'Ambrosius, is it? Well, you know the rumours. I've heard nothing definite about him, only the usual stories that have been going the rounds these ten years. Oh, yes, men say he'll come to Cornwall, or Maridunum, or London, or Avon-mouth—you can take your pick . . . Your throw.' Blackbeard's attention had shifted. I leaned closer to watch Dinias' throw, and lowered my voice. 'And if he did come now, what would happen? You'll know this better than I. Would what's left of the West rise for him, or stand loyal to Vortigern?'

'The West would go up in flames. It's done that already, God knows. Double or quits? Flames like the night you left. God, how I laughed: Little bastard sets the place on fire and goes. Why did you? That's mine, double five. Throw you again.'

'Right. Why did I go, you mean? I told you, I was afraid of Camlach.'

'I didn't mean that. I mean why did you set the place on fire? Don't tell me it was an accident, because I don't believe you.'

'It was a funeral pyre. I lit it because they killed my servant.'

He stared, the dice for a moment still in his hands. 'You fired the King's palace for a *slave*?'

'Why not? I happened to like my servant better than I liked Camlach.'

He gave me a slightly fuddled look, and threw. A two and a four. I scooped back a couple of coins.

'Damn you,' said Dinias, 'you've no right to win, you're enough already. All right, again. Your servant, indeed! You've a mighty high tone for a bastard playing at being a scribe in a priest's cell.'

I grinned. 'You're a bastard, too, remember, dear cousin.'

'Maybe, but at least I know who my father was.'

'Keep your voice down, people are listening. All right, throw you again.'

A pause while the dice rattled. I watched them rather anxiously. So far, they had tended to fall my way. How useful it would be, I thought, if power could be brought to bear on such small things; it would take no effort, and make the way smoother. But I had begun to learn that in fact power made nothing smoother; when it came it was like having a wolf by the throat. Sometimes I had felt like that boy in the old myth who harnessed the horses of the sun and rode the world like a god until the power burned him to death. I wondered if I would ever feel the flames again.

The dice fell from my very human fingers. A two and a one. No need to have the power if you could have the luck. Dinias gave a grunt of satisfaction and gathered them up, while I slid some coins towards him. The game went on. I lost the next three throws, and the heap beside him grew respectably. He was relaxing. No one was paying us any attention; that had been imagination. It was time, perhaps, for a few more facts.

'Where's the King now?' I asked.

'Eh? Oh, aye, the King. He's been gone from here nearly a month. Moved north as soon as the weather slackened and the roads were open.'

'To Cacr'n-ar-Von, you said Segontium?'

'Did I? Oh, well, I suppose he calls that his base, but who'd want to be caught in that corner between Y Wyddfa and the sea? No, he's building himself a new stronghold, they say. Did you say you'd get another flask?'

'Here it comes. Help yourself, I've had enough. A stronghold, you said? Where?'

'What? Oh, yes. Good wine, this. I don't rightly know where he's building, somewhere in Snowdon. Told you. Dinas Brenin, they call it . . . Or would, if he could get it built.'

'What's stopping him? Is there still trouble up there? Vortimer's faction still, or something new? They're saying in Cornwall that he's got thirty thousand Saxons at his back.'

'At his back, on both sides—Saxons everywhere, our King has. But not with him. With Hengist—and Hengist and the King aren't seeing eye to eye. Oh, he's beset, is Vortigern, I can tell you!' Fortunately he was speaking quietly, his words lost in the rattle of dice and the uproar around us. I think he had half forgotten me. He scowled down at the table as he threw. 'Look at that. The bloody things are ill-wished. Like King's Fort.'

Somewhere the words touched a string of memory to a faint humming, as elusive and untraceable as a bee in the lime trees. I said casually, making my throw: 'Ill-wished? How?'

'Hah, that's better. Should be able to beat that. Oh, well, you know these Northmen—if the wind blows colder one morning they say it's a dead spirit passing by. They don't use surveyors in that army, the soothsayers do it all. I heard he'd got the walls built four times to man height, and each time by next morning they'd cracked clear across . . . How's that?'

'Not bad. I couldn't beat it, I'm afraid. Did he put guards on?'

'Of course. They saw nothing.'

'Well, why should they?' It seemed that the luck was against us both; the dice were as ill-wished for Dinias as the walls for Vortigern. In spite of myself I threw a pair of doubles. Scowling, Dinias pushed half his pile towards me. I said: 'It only sounds as if he picked a soft place. Why not move?'

'He picked the top of a crag, as pretty a place to defend as you'll find in Wales. It guards the valley north and south, and stands over the road just where the cliffs narrow both sides, and the road is squeezed right up under the crag. And damn it, there's been a tower there before. The locals have called it King's Fort time out of mind.'

King's Fort . . . Dinas Brenin . . . The humming swelled clear into a memory. Birches bone-white against a milk-blue sky. The scream of a falcon. Two kings walking together, and Cerdic's voice saying, *'Come down, and I'll cut you in on a dice game.'*

Before I even knew, I had done it, as neatly as Cerdic himself. I flicked the still turning dice with a quick finger. Dinias, up-ending the empty flask over his cup, never noticed. The dice settled. A two and a one. I said ruefully: 'You won't have much trouble beating that.'

He did beat it, but only just. He pulled the coins towards him with a grunt of triumph, then sprawled half across the table, his elbow in a pool of spilled wine. Even if I did manage, I thought, to let this drunken idiot win enough money off me, I would be lucky if I could get him even as far as the curtain leading to the brothel rooms. My throw again. As I shook the box I saw Cadal in the doorway, waiting to catch my eye. It was time to be gone. I nodded, and he withdrew. As Dinias glanced to see who I had signalled to I threw again, and flicked a settling six over with my sleeve. One and three. Dinias made a sound of satisfaction and reached for the box.

'Tell you what,' I said, 'one more throw and we'll go, win or lose, I'll buy another flask and we'll take it with us and drink it in my lodgings. We'll be more comfortable than here.' Once I got him outside, I reckoned, Cadal and I could deal with him.

'Lodgings? I could have given you lodgings. Plenty of room there, you needn't have sent your man to look for lodgings. Got to be careful these days, you know. There. A pair of fives. Beat that if you can, Merlin the bastard.' He tipped the last of the wine down his throat, swallowed, and leaned back, grinning.

'I'll give you the game.' I pushed the coins over to him, and made to stand up. As I looked round for the pot-boy to order the promised flask, Dinias slammed his hand down on the table with a crash. The dice jumped and rattled, and a cup went over, rolled, and smashed on the floor. Men stopped talking, staring.

'Oh, no, you don't! We'll play it out! Walk out just as the luck's turning again, would you? I'll not take that from you, or anyone else! Sit down and play, my bastard cousin—'

'Oh, for God's sake, Dinias—'

'All right, so I'm a bastard, too! All I can say is, better be the bastard of a king than a no-man's child who never had a father at all!'

He finished with a hiccup, and someone laughed. I laughed too, and reached for the dice. 'All right, we'll take them with us. I told you, win or lose, we'd take a flask home. We can finish the game there. It's time we drank one another into bed.'

A hand fell on my shoulder, heavily. As I twisted to see who it was, someone came on my other side and gripped my arm. I saw Dinias stare upwards, gaping. Around us the drinkers were suddenly silent.

Blackbeard tightened his grip. 'Quietly, young sir. We don't want a brawl, do we? Could we have a word with you outside?'

Chapter Six

I got to my feet. There was no clue in the staring faces round me. Nobody spoke.

'What's all this about?'

'Outside, if you please,' repeated Blackbeard. 'We don't want a—'

'I don't in the least mind having a brawl,' I said crisply. 'You'll tell me who you are before I'll go a step with you. And to start with, take your hands off me. Landlord, who are these men?'

'King's men, sir. You'd best do as they say. If you've got nothing to hide—'

'You've got nothing to fear?' I said. 'I know that one, and it's never true.' I shoved Blackbeard's hand off my shoulder and turned to face him. I saw Dinias staring with his mouth slack. This, I supposed, was not the meek-voiced cousin he knew. Well, the time for that was past. 'I don't mind these men hearing what you have to say. Tell me here. Why do you want to talk to me?'

'We were interested in what your friend here was saying.'

'Then why not talk to him.'

Blackbeard said stolidly: 'All in good time. If you'd tell me who are you, and where you come from—?'

'My name is Emrys, and I was born here in Maridunum. I went to Cornwall some years ago, when I was a child, and now had a fancy to come home and hear the news. That's all.'

'And this young man? He called you "cousin".'

'That was a form of speech. We are related, but not nearly. You probably also heard him call me "bastard".'

'Wait a minute.' The new voice came from behind me, among the crowd. An elderly man with thin grey hair, nobody I recognised, pushed his way to the front. 'I know him. He's telling the truth. Why, that's Myrddin Emrys, sure enough, that was the old King's grandson.' Then to me, 'You won't remember me, sir. I was your grandfather's steward, one of them. I tell you this—' he stretched his neck, like a hen, peering up at Blackbeard—'King's men or no King's men, you've no business to lay a hand on this young gentleman. He's told you the truth. He left Maridunum five years ago—that's right, five, it was the night the old King died—and nobody heard tell where he'd gone. But I'll take any oath you like he would never raise a hand against King Vortigern. Why, he was training to be a priest, and never took arms in his life. And if he wants a quiet drink with Prince Dinias, why, they're related, as he told you, and who else would he drink with, to get news of home?' He nodded at me, kindly. 'Yes, indeed, that's Myrddin Emrys, that's a grown man now instead of a little boy, but I'd know him anywhere. And let me tell you, sir, I'm mightily glad to see you safe. It was feared you'd died in the fire.'

Blackbeard hadn't even glanced at him. He was directly between me and the door. He never took his eyes off me. 'Myrddin Emrys. The old King's grandson.' He said it slowly. 'And a bastard? Whose son, then?'

There was no point in denying it. I had recognised the steward now. He was nodding at me, pleased with himself. I said: 'My mother was the King's daughter, Niniane.'

The black eyes narrowed. 'Is this true?'

'Quite true, quite true.' It was the steward, his goodwill to me patent in his pale stupid eyes.

Blackbeard turned to me again. I saw the next question forming on his lips. My heart was thumping, and I could feel the blood stealing up into my face. I tried to will it down.

'And your father?'

'I do not know.' Perhaps he would only think that the blood in my face was shame.

'Speak carefully, now,' said Blackbeard. 'You must know. Who got you?'

'I do not know.'

He regarded me. 'Your mother, the King's daughter. You remember her?'

'I remember her well.'

'And she never told you? You expect us to believe this?'

I said irritably: 'I don't care what you believe or what you don't believe. I'm tired of this. All my life people have asked me this question, and all my life people have disbelieved me. It's true, she never told me. I doubt if she told anyone. As far as I know, she may have been telling the truth when she said I was begotten of a devil.' I made a gesture of impatience. 'Why do you ask?'

'We heard what the other young gentleman said.' His tone and look were stolid. '"I'd rather be a bastard and have a king for a father, than a no-man's child who never had a father at all!"'

'If I take no offence why should you? You can see he's in his cups.'

'We wanted to make sure, that's all. And now we've made sure. The King wants you.'

'The King?' I must have sounded blank.

He nodded. 'Vortigern. We've been looking for you for three weeks past. You're to go to him.'

'I don't understand.' I must have looked bewildered rather than frightened. I could see my mission falling round me in ruins, but with this was a mixture of confusion and relief. If they had been looking for me for three weeks, this surely could have nothing to do with Ambrosius.

Dinias had been sitting quietly enough in his corner. I thought that most of what was said had not gone through to him, but now he leaned forward, his hands flat on the wine-splashed table. 'What does he want him for? Tell me that.'

'You've no call to worry.' Blackbeard threw it at him almost disdainfully. 'It's not you he wants. But I'll tell you what, since it was you led us to him, it's you who should get the reward.'

'Reward?' I asked. 'What talk is this?'

Dinias was suddenly stone sober. 'I said nothing. What do you mean?'

Blackbeard nodded. 'It was what you said that led us to him.'

'He was only asking questions about the family—he's been away,' said my cousin. 'You were listening. Anybody could have listened, we weren't keeping our voices down. By the gods, if we wanted to talk treason would we have talked it here?'

'Nobody mentioned treason. I'm just doing my duty. The King wants to see him, and he's to come with me.'

The old steward said, looking troubled now: 'You can't harm him. He's who he says he is, Niniane's son. You can ask her yourself.'

That brought Blackbeard round to face him quickly. 'She's still alive?'

'Oh, yes, she's that all right. She's barely a stone's throw off, at the nunnery of St Peter's, beyond the old oak at the crossways.'

'Leave her alone,' I said, really frightened now. I wondered what she might tell them. 'Don't forget who she is. Even Vortigern won't dare to touch her. Besides, you've no authority. Either over me or her.'

'You think not?'

'Well, what authority have you?'

'This.' The short sword flashed in his hand. It was sharpened to a dazzle.

I said: 'Vortigern's law, is it? Well, it's not a bad argument. I'll go with you, but it won't do you much good with my mother. Leave her alone, I tell you. She won't tell you any more than I.'

'But at least we don't have to believe her when she says she doesn't know.'

'But it's true.' It was the steward, still chattering. 'I tell you, I served in the palace all my life, and I remember it all. It used to be said she'd borne a child to the devil, to the prince of darkness.'

Hands fluttered as people made the sign. The old man said, peering up at me: 'Go with them, son, they'll not hurt Niniane's child, or her either. There'll come a time when the King will need the people of the West, as who should know better than he?'

'It seems I'll have to go with them, with the King's warrant so sharp at my throat,' I said. 'It's all right, Dinias, it wasn't your fault. Tell my servant where I am. Very well, you, take me to Vortigern, but keep your hands off me.'

I went between them to the door, the drinkers making way for us. I saw Dinias stumble to his feet and come after. As we reached the street Blackbeard turned. 'I was forgetting. Here, it's yours.'

The purse of money jingled as it hit the ground at my cousin's feet.

I didn't turn. But as I went I saw, even without looking, the expression on my cousin's face as, with a quick glance to right and left, he stooped for the purse and tucked it into his waistband.

Chapter Seven

Vortigern had changed. My impression that he had grown smaller, less impressive, was not only because I myself, instead of being a child, was now a tall youth. He had grown, as it were, into himself. It did not need the makeshift hall, the court which was less a court than a gathering of fighting chiefs and such women as they kept by them, to indicate that this was a man on the run. Or rather, a man in a corner. But a cornered wolf is more dangerous than a free one, and Vortigern was still a wolf.

And he had certainly chosen his corner well. King's Fort was as I remembered it, a crag commanding the river valley, its crest only approachable along a narrow saddleback like a bridge. This promontory jutted out from a circle of rocky hills which provided in their shelter a natural corrie where horses could graze and where beasts could be driven in and guarded. All round the valley itself the mountains towered, grey with scree and still not green with spring. All the April rain had done was to bring a long cascade spilling a thousand feet from the summit to the valley's foot. A wild, dark impressive place. If once the wolf dug himself in at the top of that crag, even Ambrosius would be hard put to it to get him out.

The journey took six days. We started at first light, by the road which leads due north out of Maridunum, a worse road than the eastbound way but quicker, even slowed down as we were by bad weather and the pace set by the women's litters. The bridge was broken at Pennal and more or less washed away, and nearly half a day was spent fording the Afon Dyfi, before the party could struggle on to Tomen-y-mur, where the road was good. On the afternoon of the sixth day we turned up the riverside track for Dinas Brenin, where the King lay.

Blackbeard had had no difficulty at all in persuading St Peter's to let my mother go with him to the King. If he had used the same tactics as with me, this was understandable enough, but I had no opportunity to ask her, or even to find out if she knew any more than I did why Vortigern wanted us. A closed litter had been provided for her, and two women from the religious house travelled with her. Since they were beside her day and night it was impossible for me to approach her for private speech, and in fact she showed no sign of wanting to see me alone. Sometimes I caught her watching me with an anxious, even perhaps a puzzled look, but when she spoke she was calm and withdrawn, with never so much as a hint that she knew anything that Vortigern himself might not overhear. Since I was not allowed to see her alone, I had judged it better to tell her the same story I had told Blackbeard; even the same (since for all I knew he had been questioned) that I had told Dinias. She would have to think what she could about it, and about my reasons for not getting in touch with her sooner. It was, of course, impossible to mention Brittany, or even friends from Brittany, without risking her guess about Ambrosius, and this I dared not do.

I found her much changed. She was pale and quiet, and had put on weight, and with it a kind of heaviness of the spirit that she had not had before. It was only after a day or two, jogging north with the escort through the hills, that it suddenly came to me what this was; she had lost what she had had of power. Whether time had taken this, or illness, or whether she had abnegated it for the power of the Christian symbol that she wore on her breast, I had no means of guessing. But it had gone.

On one score my mind was set at rest straight away. My mother was treated with courtesy, even with distinction as befitted a king's daughter. I received no such distinction, but I was given a good horse, housed well at night, and my escort were civil enough when I tried to talk to them. Beyond that, they made very little effort with me; they would give no answer to any of my questions, though it seemed to me they knew perfectly well why the King wanted me. I caught curious and furtive glances thrown at me, and once or twice a look of pity.

We were taken straight to the King. He had set up his headquarters on the flat land between the crag and the river, from where he had hoped to oversee the building of his stronghold. It was a very different camp even from the makeshift ones of Uther and Ambrosius. Most of the men were in tents and, except for high earthworks and a palisade on the side towards the road, they apparently trusted to the natural defences of the place—the river and crag on one side, the rock of Dinas Brenin on the other, and the impenetrable and empty mountains behind them.

Vortigern himself was housed royally enough. He received us in a hall whose wooden pillars were hung with curtains of bright embroidery, and whose floor of the local greenish slate was thickly strewn with fresh rushes. The high chair on the dais was regally carved and gilded. Beside him, on a chair equally ornate and only slightly smaller, sat Rowena, his Saxon Queen. The place was crowded. A few men in Courtier's dress stood near, but most of those present were armed. There was a fair sprinkling of Saxons. Behind Vortigern's chair on the dais stood a group of priests and holy men.

As we were brought in, a hush fell. All eyes turned our way. Then the King rose and, stepping down from the dais, came to meet my mother, smiling, and with both hands outstretched.

'I bid you welcome, Princess,' he said, and turned to present her with ceremonial courtesy to the Queen.

The hiss of whispers ran round the hall, and glances were exchanged. The King had made it clear by his greeting that he did not hold my mother accountable for Camlach's part in the recent rebellion. He glanced at me, briefly but I thought with keen interest, gave me a nod of greeting, then took my mother's hand on his arm and led her up on to the dais. At a nod of his head, someone hurried to set a chair for her on the step below him. He bade her be seated, and he and the Queen took their places once more. Walking forward with my guards at my back, I stood below the dais in front of the King.

Vortigern spread his hands on the arms of his chair and sat upright, smiling from my mother to me with an air of welcome and even satisfaction. The buzz of whispers had died down. There was a hush. People were staring, expectant.

But all the King said was, to my mother: 'I ask your pardon, Madam, for forcing this journey on you at such a time of year. I trust you were made comfortable enough?' He followed this up with smooth trivial courtesies while the people stared and waited, and my mother bent her head and murmured her polite replies, as upright and unconcerned as he. The two nuns who had accompanied her stood behind her, like waiting-women. She held one hand at her breast, fingering the little cross which she wore there as a talisman; the other lay among the brown folds on her lap. Even in her plain brown habit she looked royal.

Vortigern said, smiling: 'And now will you present your son?'

'My son's name is Merlin. He left Maridunum five years ago after the death of my father, your kinsman. Since then he has been in Cornwall, in a house of religion. I commend him to you.'

The King turned to me. 'Five years? You would be little more than a child then, Merlin. How old are you now?'

'I am seventeen, sir.' I met his gaze squarely. 'Why have you sent for my mother and myself? I had hardly set foot in Maridunum again, when your men took me, by force.'

'For that I am sorry. You must forgive their zeal. They only knew that the matter was urgent, and they took the quickest means to do what I wished.' He turned back to my mother. 'Do I have to assure you, Lady Niniane, that no harm will come to you? I swear it. I know that you have been in the House of St Peter now for five years, and that your brother's alliance with my sons was no concern of yours.'

'Nor of my son's, my lord,' she said calmly. 'Merlin left Maridunum on the night of my father's death, and from that day until now I have heard nothing from him. But one thing is certain, he had no part in the rebellion; why, he was only a child when he left his home–and indeed, now that I know he fled south that night, to Cornwall, I can only assume he went from very fear of my brother Camlach, who was no friend to him. I assure you, my lord King, that whatever I myself may have guessed of my brother's intentions towards you, my son knew nothing of them. I am at a loss to know why you should want him here.'

To my surprise Vortigern did not even seem interested in my sojourn in Cornwall, nor did he look at me again. He rested his chin on his fist and watched my mother from under his brows. His voice and look were alike grave and courteous, but there was something in the air that I did not like. Suddenly I realised what it was. Even while my mother and the King talked, watching one another, the priests behind the King's chair watched me. And when I stole a glance out of the corners of my eyes at the people in the hall I found that here, too, there were eyes on me. There was a stillness in the room now, and I thought, suddenly: *Now he will come to it.*

He said quietly, almost reflectively: 'You never married.'

'No.' Her lids drooped, and I knew she had become suddenly wary.

'Your son's father, then, died before you could be wed? Killed in battle, perhaps?'

'No, my lord.' Her voice was quiet, but perfectly clear. I saw her hands move and tighten a little.

'Then he still lives?'

She said nothing, but bowed her head, so that her hood fell forward and hid her face from the other people in the hall. But those on the dais could still see her. I saw the Queen staring with curiosity and contempt. She had light blue eyes, and big breasts which bulged milk-white above a tight blue bodice. Her mouth was small. Her hands were as white as her breasts, but the fingers thick and ugly, like a servant's. They were covered with rings of gold and enamel and copper.

The King's brows drew together at my mother's silence, but his voice was still pleasant. 'Tell me one thing, Lady Niniane. Did you ever tell your son the name of his father?'

'No.' The tone of her voice, full and definite, contrasted oddly with the posture of bowed head and veiled face. It was the pose of a woman who is ashamed, and I wondered if she meant to look like this to excuse her silence. I could not see her face myself, but I saw the hand that held the fold of her long skirt. I was sharply reminded of the Niniane who had defied her father, to refuse Gorlan, King of Lanascol. Across the memory came another, the memory of my father's face, looking at me across the table in the lamplight. I banished it. He was so vividly in front of me that it seemed to me a wonder that the whole hall full of men could not see him. Then it came to me, sharply and with terror, that Vortigern had seen him. Vortigern knew. This was why we were here. He had heard some rumour of my coming, and was making sure. It remained to be seen whether I would be treated as a spy, or as a hostage.

I must have made some movement in spite of myself. My mother looked up, and I saw her eyes under the hood. She no longer looked like a princess; she looked like a woman who is afraid. I smiled at her, and something came back into her face, and I saw then that her fear was only for me.

I held myself still, and waited. Let him make the moves. Time enough to counter them when he had shown me the ground to fight from.

He twisted the big ring on his finger. 'This is what your son told my messengers. And I have heard it said that no one else in the kingdom ever knew the name of his father. From what men tell me, Lady Niniane, and from what I know of you, your child would never be fathered by anyone base. Why not, then, tell him? It is a thing a man should know.'

I said angrily, forgetting my caution: 'What is it to you?'

My mother flashed me a look that silenced me. Then to Vortigern, 'Why do you ask me these questions?'

'Lady,' said the King, 'I sent for you today, and for your son, to ask you one thing only. The name of his father.'

'I repeat, why do you ask?'

He smiled. It was a mere baring of the teeth. I took a step. 'Mother, he has no right to ask you this. He will not dare—'

'Silence him,' said Vortigern.

The man beside me clapped a hand across my mouth, and held me fast. There was the hiss of metal as the other drew his sword and pressed it against my side. I stood still.

My mother cried out: 'Let him go! If you hurt him, Vortigern, king or no king, I will never tell you, even if you kill me. Do you think I held the truth from my own father and my brother and even from my son for all these years, just to tell for the asking?'

'You will tell me for your son's sake,' said Vortigern. At his nod the fellow took his hand from my mouth, and stood back. But his hand was still on my arm, and I could feel the other's sword sharp through my tunic.

My mother had thrown back her hood now, and was sitting upright in her chair, her hands gripping the arms. Pale and shaken as she was, and dressed in the humble brown robe, she made the Queen look like a servant. The silence in the hall now was deathly. Behind the King's chair the priests stood staring. I held tightly to my thoughts. If these men were priests and magicians, then no thought of Ambrosius, not even his name, must come into my mind. I felt the sweat start on my body, and my thoughts tried to reach my mother and hold her, without forming an image which these men could see. But the power had gone, and there was no help here from the god; I did not even know if I was man enough for what might happen after she told them. I dared not speak again; I was afraid that if they used force against me she would speak to save me. And once they knew, once they started to question me . . .

Something must have reached her, because she turned and looked at me again, moving her shoulders under the rough robe as if she felt a hand touch her. As her eyes met mine I knew that this was nothing to do with power. She was trying, as women will, to tell me something with her eyes. It was a message of love and reassurance, but on a human level, and I could not understand it.

She turned back to Vortigern. 'You choose a strange place for your questions, King. Do you really expect me to speak of these things here, in your open hall, and in the hearing of all comers?'

He brooded for a moment, his brows down over his eyes. There was sweat on his face, and I saw his hands twitch on the arms of the chair. The man was humming like a harp-string. The tension ran right through the hall, almost visibly. I felt my skin prickle, and a cold wolfspaw of fear walked up my spine. Behind the King one of the priests leaned forward and whispered. Then the King nodded. 'The people shall leave us. But the priests and the magicians must remain.'

Reluctantly, and with a buzz of chatter, people began to leave the hall. The priests stayed, a dozen or so men in long robes standing behind the chairs of the King and Queen. One of them, the one who had spoken to the King, a tall man who stood stroking his grey beard with a dirty ringed hand, was smiling. From his dress he was the head of them. I searched his face for signs of power, but, though the men were dressed in priests' robes, I could see nothing there but death. It was in all their eyes. More than that I could not see. The wolfspaw of cold touched my bones again. I stood in the soldier's grip without resistance.

'Loose him,' said Vortigern. 'I have no wish to harm the Lady Niniane's son. But you, Merlin, if you move or speak again before I give you leave, you will be taken from the hall.'

The sword withdrew from my side, but the man still held it ready. The guards stood back half a pace from me. I neither moved nor spoke. I had never since I was a child felt so helpless, so naked of either knowledge or power, so stripped of God. I knew, with bitter failure, that if I were in the crystal cave with fires blazing and my master's eyes on me, I should see nothing. I remembered, suddenly, that Galapas was dead. Perhaps, I thought, the power had only come from him, and perhaps it had gone with him.

The King had turned his sunken eyes back to my mother. He leaned forward, his look suddenly fierce and intent.

'And now, Madam, will you answer my question?'

'Willingly,' she said. 'Why not?'

Chapter Eight

She had spoken so calmly that I saw the King's look of surprise. She put up a hand to push the hood back from her face, and met his eyes levelly.

'Why not? I see no harm in it. I might have told you sooner, my lord, if you had asked me differently, and in a different place. There is no harm now in men knowing. I am no longer in the world, and do not have to meet the eyes of the world, or hear their tongues. And since I know now that my son, too, has retired from the world, then I know how little he will care what the world says about him. So I will tell you what you want to know. And when I tell you, you will see why I have never spoken of this before, not even to my own father or to my son himself.'

There was no sign of fear now. She was even smiling. She had not looked at me again. I tried to keep from staring at her, to school my face into blankness. I had no idea what she planned to say, but I knew that here would be no betrayal. She was playing some game of her own, and was secure in her own mind that this would avert whatever danger threatened me. I knew, for certain, that she would say nothing of Ambrosius. But still, everywhere in the hall, was death. Outside it had begun to rain, and the afternoon was wearing on towards twilight. A servant came in at the door bearing torches, but Vortigern waved him back. To do him justice, I believe he was thinking of my mother's shame, but I thought to myself: *There can be no help even there, no light, no fire . . .*

'Speak, then,' said Vortigern. 'Who fathered your son?'

'I never saw him.' She spoke quite simply. 'It was no man that I ever knew.' She paused, then said, without looking at me, her eyes still level on the King: 'My son will forgive me for what he is soon to hear, but you have forced me, and this he will understand.'

Vortigern flashed me a look. I met it stonily. I was certain of her now.

She went on: 'When I was only young, about sixteen, and thinking, as girls do, of love, it happened one Martinmas Eve, after I and my women had gone to bed. The girl who slept in my room was asleep, and the others were in the outer chamber, but I could not sleep. After a while I rose from my bed and went to the window. It was a clear night, with a moon. When I turned back to my bed-place I saw what I took to be a young man standing there, full in the middle of my bedchamber. He was handsome, and young, dressed in a tunic and long mantle, with a short sword at his side. He wore rich jewels. My first thought was that he had broken in through the outer chamber while my women slept; my second was that I was in my shift, and barefoot, with my hair loose. I thought he meant mischief, and was opening my mouth to call out and wake the women, when the youth smiled at me, with a gesture as if to tell me to be quiet, he meant me no harm. Then he stepped aside into the shadow, and when I stole after, to look, there was no one there.'

She paused. No one spoke. I remembered how she would tell me stories when I was a child. The hall was quite still, but I felt the man beside me quiver, as if he would have liked to move away. The Queen's red mouth hung open, half in wonder, half (I thought) in envy.

My mother looked at the wall above the King's head. 'I thought it had been a dream, or a girl's fancy bred of moonlight. I went to bed and told no one. But he came again. Not always at night; not always when I was alone. So I realised it was no dream, but a familiar spirit who desired something from me. I prayed, but still he came. While I was sitting with my girls, spinning, or when I walked on dry days in my father's orchard, I would feel his touch on my arm, and his voice in my ear. But at these times I did not see him, and nobody heard him but I.'

She groped for the cross on her breast and held it. The gesture looked so unforced and natural that I was surprised, until I saw that it was indeed natural, that she did not hold the cross for protection, but for forgiveness. I thought to myself, it is not the Christian God she should fear when she lies; she should be afraid of lying like this about the things of power. The King's eyes, bent on her, were fierce and, I thought, exultant. The priests were watching her as if they would eat her spirit alive.

'So all through that winter he came to me. And he came at night. I was never alone in my chamber, but he came through doors and windows and walls, and lay with me. I never saw him again, but heard his voice and felt his body. Then, in the summer, when I was heavy with child, he left me.' She paused. 'They will tell you how my father beat me and shut me up, and how when the child was born he would not give him a name fit for a Christian prince, but, because he was born in September, named him for the sky-god, the wanderer, who has no house but the woven air. But I called him Merlin always, because on the day of his birth a wild falcon flew in through the window and perched above the bed, and looked at me with my lover's eyes.'

Her glance crossed mine then, a brief flash. This, then, was true. And the Emrys, too, she had given me that in spite of them; she had kept that much of him for me after all.

She had looked away. 'I think, my lord King, that what I have told you will not altogether surprise you. You must have heard the rumours that my son was not as ordinary boys—it is not possible always to be silent, and I know there have been whispers, but now I have told you the truth, openly; and so I pray you, my lord Vortigern, to let my son and me go back in peace to our respective houses of religion.'

When she had finished there was silence. She bowed her head and pulled up her hood again to hide her face. I watched the King and the men behind him. I thought to see him angry, frowning with impatience, but to my surprise his brows smoothed out, and he smiled. He opened his mouth to answer my mother, but the Queen forestalled him. She leaned forward, licking her red lips, and spoke for the first time, to the priests.

'Maugan, is this possible?'

It was the tall man, the bearded high priest, who answered her. He spoke without hesitation, bland and surprisingly emphatic. 'Madam, it is possible. Who has not heard of these creatures of air and darkness, who batten on mortal men and women? In my studies, and in many of the books I have read, I have found stories of children being born into the world in this fashion.' He eyed me, fondling his beard, then turned to the King. 'Indeed, my lord, we have the authority of the ancients themselves. They knew well that certain spirits, haunting the air at night between the moon and the earth, cohabit at their will with mortal women, in the shape of men. It is certainly possible that this royal lady—this virtuous royal lady—was the victim of such a creature. We know—and she has said herself—that this was rumoured for many years. I myself spoke with one of her waiting-women who said that the child could surely be begotten of none but the devil, and that no man had been near her. And of the son himself, when he was a child, I heard many strange things. Indeed, King Vortigern, this lady's story is true.'

No one looked any longer at Niniane. Every eye in the place was on me. I could see in the King's face nothing that was not at once ferocious and innocent, a kind of eager satisfaction like a child's, or a wild beast's when it sees its prey loitering nearer. Puzzled, I held my tongue and waited. If the priests believed my mother, and Vortigern believed the priests, then I could not see where danger could come from. No faintest hint had turned men's thoughts towards Ambrosius. Maugan and the King seemed to hurry with eager satisfaction down the path that my mother had opened for them.

The King glanced at my guards. They had moved back from me, no doubt afraid to stand so near a demon's child. At his sign they closed in again. The man on my right still held his sword drawn, but down by his side and out of my mother's view. It was not quite steady. The man on my left surreptitiously loosened his own blade in its sheath. Both men were breathing heavily, and I could smell fear on them.

The priests were nodding sagely, and some of them, I noticed, held their hands in front of them in the sign to ward off enchantment. It seemed that they believed Maugan, they believed my mother, they saw me as the devil's child. All that had happened was that her story had confirmed their own belief, the old rumours. This, in fact, was what she had been brought here for. And now they watched me with satisfaction, but also with a kind of wary fear.

My own fear was leaving me. I thought I began to see what they wanted. Vortigern's superstition was legendary. I remembered what Dinias had told me about the stronghold that kept falling down, and the reports of the King's soothsayers that it was bewitched. It seemed possible that, because of the rumours of my birth, and possibly because of the childish powers I had shown before I left home, to which Maugan had referred, they thought I could advise or help them. If this was so, and they had brought me here because of my reputed powers, there might be some way in which I could help Ambrosius right from the enemy's camp. Perhaps after all the god had brought me here for this, perhaps he was still driving me. *Put yourself in his path* . . . Well, one could only use what was to hand. If I had no power to use, I had knowledge.

I cast my mind back to the day at King's Fort, and to the flooded mine in the core of the crag, to which the dream had led me. I would certainly be able to tell them why their foundations would not stand. It was an engineer's answer, not a magician's. But, I thought, meeting the oyster eyes of Maugan as he dry-washed those long dirty hands before him, if it was a magician's answer they wanted, they should have it. And Vortigern with them.

I lifted my head. I believe I was smiling. 'King Vortigern!'

It was like dropping a stone into a pool, the room was so still, so centred on me. I said strongly: 'My mother has told you what you asked her. No doubt you will tell me now in what way I can serve you, but first I must ask you to keep your royal promise and let her go.'

'The Lady Niniane is our honoured guest.' The King's reply seemed automatic. He glanced at the open arcade that faced the river, where the white lances of the rain hissed down across a dark grey sky. 'You are both free to go whenever you choose, but this is no time to begin the long journey back to Maridunum. You will surely wish to lie the night here, Madam, and hope for a dry day tomorrow?' He rose, and the Queen with him. 'Rooms have been prepared, and now the Queen will take you there to rest and make ready to sup with us. Our court here, and our rooms, are a poor makeshift, but such as they are, they are at your service. Tomorrow you will be escorted home.'

My mother had stood when they did. 'And my son? You still have not told us why you brought us here for this?'

'Your son can serve me. He has powers which I can use. Now, Madam, if you will go with the Queen, I will talk to your son and tell him what I want of him. Believe me, he is as free as you are. I only constrained him until you told me the truth I wished to hear. I must thank you now for confirming what I had guessed.' He put out a hand. 'I swear to you, Lady Niniane, by any god you like, that I do not hold his birth against him, now or ever.'

She regarded him for a moment, then bowed her head and, ignoring his gesture, came down to me, holding out both her hands. I crossed to her and took them in my own. They felt small and cold. I was taller than she was. She looked up at me with the eyes that I remembered; there was anxiety in them, and the dregs of anger, and some message urgently spoken in silence.

'Merlin, I would not have had you know it this way. I would have spared you this.' But this was not what her eyes were saying.

I smiled down at her, and said carefully: 'Mother, you told me nothing today that shocked me. Indeed, there's nothing you could tell me about my birth that I do not already know. Set yourself at rest.'

She caught her breath and her eyes widened, searching my face. I went on, slowly: 'Whoever my father was, it will not be held against me. You heard what the King promised. That is all we need to know.'

Whether she got this part of the message I could not guess. She was still taking in what I had said first. 'You knew? You knew?'

'I knew. You surely don't imagine that in all the years I've been away from you, and with the kind of studies I've undertaken, I never found out what parentage I had? It's some years now since my father made himself known to me. I assure you, I've spoken with him, not once but many times. I find nothing in my birth of which I need to be ashamed.'

For a moment longer she looked at me, then she nodded, and the lids drooped over her eyes. A faint colour had come up into her face. She had understood me.

She turned away, pulling her hood up again to hide her face, and put her hand on the King's arm. She went from the room, walking between him and the Queen, and her two women followed them. The priests remained, clucking and whispering and staring. I took no notice of them, but watched my mother go.

The King paused in the doorway, and I heard his voice bidding my mother good-bye. There was a crowd waiting in the outer porch. They made way for Rowena and my mother, and the half dozen women who were there followed them. I heard the swish of their dresses and the light voices of the women fade into the sound of the rain. Vortigern stood still in the doorway, watching them go. Outside the rain fell with a noise like a running river. It was darkening fast.

The King swung round on his heel and came back into the hall, with his fighting men behind him.

Chapter Nine

They crowded round me, muttering noisily, but holding back in a circle, like hounds before they close in for the kill. Death was back in the hall; I could feel it, but could not believe or understand it. I made a movement as if to follow my mother, and the swords of my guards lifted and quivered. I stood still.

I said sharply, to the King: 'What's this? You gave your word. Are you so quickly forsworn?'

'Not forsworn. I gave my word that you should serve me, that I would never hold your birth against you. This is true. It is because of what I know about you, because you are the child of no man, that I have had you brought to me today. You will serve me, Merlin, because of your birth.'

'Well?'

He mounted the steps to the throne and sat down again. His movements were slow and deliberate. All the men of the court had crowded in with him, and with them the torch-bearers. The hall filled with smoky light and the rustle and creak of leather and the clank of mail. Outside the rain hissed down.

Vortigern leaned forward, chin on fist. 'Merlin, we have learned today what in part we already suspected, that you are the child of no man, but of a devil. As such, you require mercy from no man. But because your mother is a king's daughter, and therefore something is due to you, I shall tell you why I brought you here. You know perhaps that I am building a stronghold here on the rock they call the Fortress?'

'Everyone knows it,' I said, 'and everyone knows that it will not stand, but falls down whenever it reaches man height.'

He nodded. 'And my magicians and wise men here, my advisers, have told me why. The foundations have not been properly laid.'

'Well,' I said, 'that sounds remarkably like sense to me.'

There was a tall old man to the King's right, beside the priests. His eyes were a bright angry blue under jutting white brows. He was watching me fixedly, and I thought I saw pity in his look. As I spoke, he put a hand up to his beard as if to hide a smile.

The King seemed not to have heard me. 'They tell me,' he said, 'that a king's stronghold should be built on blood.'

'They are talking, of course, in metaphors,' I said politely.

Maugan suddenly struck his staff on the floor of the dais. 'They are talking literally!' he shouted. 'The mortar should be slaked with blood! Blood should be sprinkled on the foundations. In ancient times no king built a fortress without observing this rite. The blood of a strong man, a warrior, kept the walls standing.'

There was a sharp pause. My heart had begun to beat in slow, hard strokes that made the blood tingle in my limbs. I said, coldly: 'And what has this to do with me? I am no warrior.'

'You are no man, neither,' said the King harshly. 'This is the magic, Merlin, that they have revealed to me, that I should seek out a lad who never had a father, and slake the foundations with his blood.'

I stared at him, then looked round the ring of faces. There was shifting and muttering, and few eyes met mine, but I could see it in all their faces, the death I had smelt ever since I entered the hall. I turned back to the King.

'What rubbish is this? When I left Wales, it was a country for civilised men and for poets, for artists and for scholars, for warriors and kings who killed for their country, cleanly and in daylight. Now you talk of blood and human sacrifice. Do you think to throw modern Wales back to the rites of ancient Babylon and Crete?'

'I do not speak of "human" sacrifice,' said Vortigern. 'You are the son of no man. Remember this.'

In the stillness the rain lashed into the bubbling puddles on the ground outside. Someone cleared his throat. I caught the fierce blue glance of the old warrior. I had been right; there was pity there. But even those who pitied me were not going to raise a hand against this stupidity.

It had all come clear at last, like lightning breaking. This had been nothing to do with Ambrosius, or with my mother. She was safe enough, having merely confirmed what they wanted confirmed. She would even be honoured, since she had provided what they desired. And Ambrosius had never even entered their thoughts. I was not here as his son, his spy, his messenger; all they wanted was the 'devil's child' to kill for their crude and dirty magic.

And, ironically enough, what they had got was no devil's child, not even the boy who once had thought to have power in his hands. All they had got was a human youth with no power beyond his human wits. But by the god, I thought, those might yet be enough . . . I had learned enough, power or no power, to fight them with their own weapons.

I managed to smile, looking beyond Maugan at the other priests. They were still making the sign against me, and even Maugan hugged his staff against his breast as if it had the power to protect him. 'And what makes you so sure that my father the devil will not come to my aid?'

'Those are only words, King. There's no time to listen.' Maugan spoke quickly and loudly, and the other priests pressed forward with him round the King's chair. They all spoke at once. 'Yes, kill him now. There's no time to waste. Take him up to the crag and kill him now. You shall see that the gods will be appeased and the walls stand steady. His mother will not know, and even if she does, what can she do?'

There was a general movement, like hounds closing in. I tried to think, but I was empty even of coherent thought. The air stank and darkened. I could smell blood already, and the sword blades, held openly now against me, flashed in the torchlight. I fixed my eyes on the fireshot metal, and tried to empty my mind, but all I could see was the picked skeleton of Galapas, high on the hill in the sunlight, with the wings of the birds over him . . .

I said, to the swords: 'Tell me one thing. Who killed Galapas?'

'What did he say? What did the devil's son say?' The question buzzed through the hall. A harsh voice said, loudly: 'Let him speak.' It was the old grey-bearded warrior.

'Who killed Galapas, the magician who lived on Bryn Myrddin above Maridunum?'

I had almost shouted it. My voice sounded strange, even to me. They fell silent, eyeing one another sideways, not understanding. Vortigern said: 'The old man? They said he was a spy.'

'He was a magician, and my master,' I said. 'And he taught me, Vortigern.'

'What did he teach you?'

I smiled. 'Enough. Enough to know that these men are fools and charlatans. Very well, Vortigern. Take me up to the crag and bring your knives with you, you and your soothsayers. Show me this fortress, these cracking walls, and see if I cannot tell you, better than they, why your fort will not stand. "No-man's child"!' I said it with contempt. 'These are the things they conjure up, these foolish old men, when they can think of nothing else. Does it not occur to you, King, that the son of a spirit of darkness might have a magic that outstrips the spells of these old fools? If what they say is true, and if my blood will make these stones stand, then why did they watch them fall not once, not twice, but four times, before they could tell you what to do? Let me but see the place once, and I will tell you. By the God of gods, Vortigern, if my dead blood could make your fortress stand, how much better could my living body serve you?'

'Sorcery! Sorcery! Don't listen to him! What does a lad like him know of such matters?' Maugan began to shout, and the priests to cluck and chatter. But the old warrior said gruffly and sharply: 'Let him try. There's no harm in that. Help you must have, Vortigern, be it from god or devil. Let him try, I say.' And round the hall I heard the echoes from the fighting men, who would have no cause to love the priests: 'Let him try.'

Vortigern frowned in indecision, glancing from Maugan to the warriors, then at the grey arches where the rain fell. 'Now?'

'Better now,' they said. 'There is not much time.'

'No,' I said clearly, 'there is not much time.' Silence again, all eyes on me. 'The rain is heavy, Vortigern. What kind of king is it whose fortress is knocked down by a shower of rain? You will find your walls fallen yet again. This comes of building in the dark, with blind men for counsellors. Now take me to the top of your crag, and I will tell you why your walls have fallen. And if you listen to me instead of to these priests of darkness, I will tell you how to rebuild your stronghold in the light.'

As I spoke, like the turning off of a tap, the downpour stopped. In the sudden quiet, men's mouths gaped. Even Maugan was dumb. Then like the pulling aside of a dark curtain, the sun came out.

I laughed. 'You see? Come, King, take me to the top of the crag, and I will show you in sunlight why your walls fell down. But tell them to bring the torches. We shall need them.'

Chapter Ten

Before we had fairly reached the foot of the crag I was proved right. The workmen could be seen crowded to the edge of the rock above, waiting for the King, and some of them had come down to meet him. Their foreman came panting up, a big man with rough sacking held gripped round his shoulders like a cloak, still sluicing with wet. He seemed hardly to have realised that the rain had stopped. He was pale, his eyes red-rimmed as if he had lacked sleep for nights. He stopped three paces away, eyeing the King nervously, and dashing the wet back of a hand across his face.

'Again?' said Vortigern briefly.

'Aye, my lord, and there's no one can say that it's a fault of ours, that I'll swear, any more than last time, or the times before. You saw yesterday how we were laying it this time. You saw how we cleared the whole site, to start again, and got right down to solid rock. And it is solid rock, my lord, I'll swear it. But still the wall cracks.' He licked his lips, and his glance met mine and slid away from it, so that I knew he was aware of what the King and his soothsayers planned. 'You're going up now, my lord?'

'Yes. Clear the men off the site.'

The man swallowed, turned and ran up the twisting track. I heard him shouting. A mule was brought and the King mounted. My wrist was tied roughly to the harness. Magician or no, the sacrifice was to be given no chance of escape until he had proved himself. My guards kept close to my side. The King's officers and courtiers crowded round us, talking in low voices among themselves, but the priests held back, aloof and wary. I could see that they were not much afraid of the outcome; they knew as well as I did how much their magic was the power of their gods and how much illusion working on faith. They were confident that I could do no more than they; that even if I were one of their own kind they could find a way to defeat me. All I had to put against their smooth-worn rites was, they thought, the kind of bluff they were familiar with, and the luck that had stopped the rain and brought the sun out when I spoke.

The sun gleamed on the soaked grasses of the crag's crest. Here we were high above the valley where the river wound like a bright snake between its green verges. Steam rose from the roofs of the King's camp. Round the wooden hall and buildings the small skin tents clustered like toadstools, and men were no bigger than wood-lice crawling between them. It was a magnificent place, a true eagle's eyrie. The King halted his mule in a grove of wind-bitten oaks and pointed forward under the bare boughs.

'Yesterday you could have seen the western wall from here.'

Beyond the grove was a narrow ridge, a natural hogsback or causeway, along which the workmen and their beasts had beaten a wide track. King's Fort was a craggy tower of rock, approached on one side by the causeway, and with its other three sides falling steeply away in dizzy slopes and cliffs. Its top was a plateau perhaps a hundred by a hundred paces, and would once have been rough grass with outcropping rock and a few stunted trees and bushes. Now it was a morass of churned mud round the wreck of the ill-wished tower. On three sides the walls of this had risen almost to shoulder height; on the fourth side the wall, newly split, sagged out in a chaos of piled stones, some fallen and half buried in mud, others still precariously mortared to outcrops of the living rock. Heavy poles of pine wood had been driven in here and there and canvas laid across to shelter the work from the rain. Some of the poles had fallen flat, some were obviously newly splintered by the recent crack. On those which were whole the canvas hung flapping, or had stretched and split with the wet. Everything was sodden, and pools stood everywhere.

The workmen had left the site and were crowded to one side of the plateau, near the causeway. They were silent, with fear in their faces. I could see that the fear was not of the King's anger at what had happened to the work, but at the force which they believed in and did not understand. There were guards at the entrance to the causeway. I knew that without them not one workman would have been left on the site.

The guards had crossed their spears, but when they recognised the King they drew them back. I looked up. 'Vortigern, I cannot escape from you here unless I leap off the crag, and that would sprinkle my blood just where

Maugan wants it. But neither can I see what is wrong with your foundations unless you loose me.'

He jerked his head, and one of my guards freed me. I walked forward. The mule followed, stepping delicately through the thick mud. The others came after. Maugan had pressed forward and was speaking urgently to the King. I caught words here and there: 'Trickery . . . escape . . . now or never . . . blood . . .'

The King halted, and the crowd with him. Someone said, 'Here, boy,' and I looked round to see the greybeard holding out a staff. I shook my head, then turned my back on them and walked forward alone.

Water stood everywhere, glinting in soggy pools between the tussocks, or on the curled fingers of young bracken thrusting through the pallid grass of winter. The grey rock glittered with it. As I walked slowly forward I had to narrow my eyes against the wet dazzle to see at all.

It was the western wall that had fallen. This had been built very near the edge of the crag, and though most of the collapse had been inwards, there was a pile of fallen stuff lying right out to the cliff's edge, where a new landslip showed raw and slimy with clay. There was a space in the north wall where an entrance was to be built; I picked my way through this between the piles of rubble and workmen's gear, and into the centre of the tower.

Here the floor was a thick mess of churned mud, with standing puddles struck to blinding copper by the sun. This was setting now, in the last blaze of light before dusk, and glared full in my eyes as I examined the collapsed wall, the cracks, the angle of fall, the tell-tale lie of the outcrops.

All the time I was conscious of the stir and mutter of the crowd. From time to time the sun flashed on bared weapons. Maugan's voice, high and harsh, battered at the King's silence. Soon, if I did nothing and said nothing, the crowd would listen to him.

From where he sat his mule the King could see me through the gap of the north entrance, but most of the crowd could not. I climbed—or rather, mounted, such was my dignity—the fallen blocks of the west wall, till I stood clear of the building that remained, and they could all see me. This was not only to impress the King. I had to see, from this vantage point, the wooded slopes below through which we had just climbed, trying, now that I was clear of the crowd and the jostling, to recognise the way I had taken up to the adit, all those years ago.

The voices of the crowd, growing impatient, broke in on me, and I slowly lifted both arms towards the sun in a kind of ritual gesture, such as I had seen priests use in summoning spirits. If I at least made some show as a magician it might keep them at bay, the priests in doubt and the King in hope, till I had had time to remember. I could not afford to cast falteringly through the wood like a questing dog; I had to lead them straight and fast, as the merlin had once led me.

And my luck held. As I raised my arms the sun went in and stayed in, and the dusk began to thicken.

Moreover, with the dazzle out of my eyes, I could see. I looked back along the side of the causeway to the curve of the hill where I had climbed, all those years ago, to get away from the crowd round the two kings. The slopes were thickly wooded, more thickly than I remembered. Already, in the shelter of the corrie, some early leaves were out, and the woods were dark with thorn and holly. I could not recognise the way I had gone through the winter woods. I stared into the thickening dusk, casting back in memory to the child who had gone scrambling there . . .

We had ridden in from the open valley, along that stream, under the thick trees, over the low ridge and into the corrie. The kings, with Camlach and Dinias and the rest, had sat on that southern slope, below the knot of oaks. The cooking fires had been there, the horses there. It had been noon, and as I walked away–that way–I had trodden on my shadow. I had sat down to eat in the shelter of a rock . . .

I had it now. A grey rock, cleft by a young oak. And on the other side of the rock the kings had gone by, walking up towards King's Fort. A grey rock, cleft by a young oak beside the path. And straight from it, up through the steep wood, the flight-path of the merlin.

I lowered my arms, and turned. Twilight had fallen quickly in the wake of the grey clouds. Below me the wooded slopes swam thick with dusk. Behind Vortigern the mass of cloud was edged sharply with yellow, and a single shaft of misty light fell steeply on the distant black hills. The men were in dark silhouette, their cloaks whipping in the wet breeze. The torches streamed.

Slowly I descended from my viewpoint. When I reached the centre of the tower floor I paused, full in the King's view, and stretched my hands out, palms down, as if I were feeling like a diviner for what lay below the earth. I heard the mutter go round, and the harsh sound of contempt from Maugan. Then I dropped my hands and approached them.

'Well?' The King's voice was hard and dry with challenge. He fidgeted in the saddle.

I ignored him, walking on past the mule and heading straight for the thickest part of the crowd as if it was not there. I kept my hands still by my sides, and my eyes on the ground; I saw their feet hesitate, shuffle, move aside as the crowd parted to let me through. I walked back across the causeway, trying to move smoothly and with dignity over the broken and sodden ground. The guards made no attempt to stop me. When I passed one of the torch-bearers I lifted a hand, and he fell in beside me without a word.

The track that the workmen and their beasts had beaten out of the hillside was a new one, but, as I had hoped, it followed the old deer-trod which the kings had taken. Halfway down, unmistakable, I found the rock. Young ferns were springing in the crevice among the roots of the oak, and the tree showed buds already breaking among last year's oak-galls. Without a moment's hesitation I turned off the track, and headed into the steep tangle of the woods.

It was far more thickly overgrown than I remembered, and certainly nobody had been this way in a long time, probably not since Cerdic and I had pushed our way through. But I remembered the way as clearly as if it had still been noon of that winter's day. I went fast, and even where the bushes grew more than shoulder height I tried to go smoothly, unregarding, wading through them as if they were a sea. Next day I paid for my wizard's dignity with cuts and scratches and ruined clothes, but I have no doubt that

at the time it was impressive. I remember when my cloak caught and
dragged on something how the torch-bearer jumped forward like a slave to
loosen and hold it for me.

Here was the thicket, right up against the side of the dell. More rock had
fallen from the slope above, piling between the stems of the thorn trees like
froth among the reeds of a backwater. Over it the bushes crowded, bare
elderberry, honeysuckle like trails of hair, brambles sharp and whippy, ivy
glinting in the torchlight. I stopped.

The mule slipped and clattered to a halt at my shoulder. The King's voice
said: 'What's this? What's this? Where are you taking us? I tell you, Merlin,
your time is running out. If you have nothing to show us—'

'I have plenty to show you.' I raised my voice so that all of them, pushing
behind him, could hear me. 'I will show you, King Vortigern, or any man
who has courage enough to follow me, the magic beast that lies beneath your
stronghold and eats at your foundations. Give me the torch.'

The man handed it to me. Without even turning my head to see who
followed, I plunged into the darkness of the thicket and pulled the bushes
aside from the mouth of the adit.

It was still open, safely shored and square, with the dry shaft leading level
into the heart of the hill.

I had to bend my head now to get in under the lintel. I stooped and
entered, with the torch held out in front of me.

I had remembered the cave as being huge, and had been prepared to find
that this, like other childhood's memories, was false. But it was bigger even
than I remembered. Its dark emptiness was doubled in the great mirror of
water that had spread till it covered all the floor save for a dry crescent of
rock six paces deep, just inside the mouth of the adit. Into this great, still
lake the jutting ribs of the cave walls ran like buttresses to meet the angle of
their own reflections, then on down again into darkness. Somewhere deeper
in the hill was the sound of water falling, but here nothing stirred the
burnished surface. Where, before, trickles had run and dripped like leaking
faucets, now every wall was curtained with a thin shining veil of damp
which slid down imperceptibly to swell the pool.

I advanced to the edge, holding the torch high. The small light of the
flame pushed the darkness back, a palpable darkness, deeper even than
those dark nights where the black is thick as a wild beast's pelt, and presses
on you like a stifling blanket. A thousand facets of light glittered and flashed
as the flames caught the sliding water. The air was still and cold and echoing
with sounds like birdsong in a deep wood.

I could hear them scrambling along the adit after me. I thought quickly.

I could tell them the truth, coldly. I could take the torch and clamber up
into the dark workings and point out faults which were giving way under the
weight of the building work above. But I doubted if they would listen.
Besides, as they kept saying, there was no time. The enemy was at the gates,
and what Vortigern needed now was not logic and an engineer; he wanted
magic, and something–anything–that promised quick safety, and kept his
followers loyal. He himself might believe the voice of reason, but he could
not afford to listen to it. My guess was that he would kill me first, and

attempt to shore up the workings afterwards, probably with me in them. He would lose his workmen else.

The men came pouring in at the dark mouth of the adit like bees through a hive door. More torches blazed, and the dark slunk back. The floor filled with coloured cloaks and the glint of weapons and the flash of jewels. Eyes showed liquid as they looked around them in awe. Their breath steamed on the cold air. There was a rustle and mutter as of folk in a holy place, but no one spoke aloud.

I lifted a hand to beckon the King, and he came forward and stood with me at the edge of the pool. I pointed downwards. Below the surface something—a rock, perhaps—glimmered faintly, shaped like a dragon. I began to speak slowly, as it were testing the air between us. My words fell clear and leaden, like drops of water on rock.

'This is the magic, King Vortigern, that lies beneath your tower. This is why your walls cracked as fast as they could build them. Which of your soothsayers could have showed you what I show you now?'

His two torch-bearers had moved forward with him; the others still hung back. Light grew, wavering from the walls, as they advanced. The streams of sliding water caught the light and flowed down to meet their reflections, so that fire seemed to rise through the pool like bubbles in sparkling wine to burst at the surface. Everywhere, as the torches moved, water glittered and sparked, jets and splashes of light breaking and leaping and coalescing across the still surface till the lake was liquid fire, and down the walls the lightfalls ran and glittered like crystals; like the crystal cave come alive and moving and turning round me; like the starred globe of midnight whirling and flashing.

I took my breath in painfully, and spoke again. 'If you could drain this pool, King Vortigern, to find what lay beneath it—'

I stopped. The light had changed. Nobody had moved, and the air was still, but the torchlight wavered as men's hands shook. I could no longer see the King: the flames ran between us. Shadows fled across the streams and staircases of fire, and the cave was full of eyes and wings and hammering hoofs and the scarlet rush of a great dragon stooping on his prey . . .

A voice was shouting, high and monotonous, gasping. I could not get my breath. Pain broke through me, spreading from groin and belly like blood bursting from a wound. I could see nothing. I felt my hands knotting and stretching. My head hurt, and the rock was hard and streaming wet under my cheekbone. I had fainted, and they had seized me as I lay and were killing me: this was my blood seeping from me to spread into the pool and shore up the foundations of their rotten tower. I choked on breath like bile. My hands tore in pain at the rock, and my eyes were open, but all I could see was the whirl of banners and wings and wolves' eyes and sick mouths gaping, and the tail of a comet like a brand, and stars shooting through a rain of blood.

Pain went through me again, a hot knife into the bowels. I screamed, and suddenly my hands were free. I threw them up between me and the flashing visions and I heard my own voice calling, but could not tell what I called. In front of me the visions whirled, fractured, broke open in intolerable light, then shut again into darkness and silence.

Chapter Eleven

I woke in a room splendidly lined with embroidered hangings, where sunlight spilt through the window to lay bright oblongs on a boarded floor. I moved cautiously, testing my limbs. I had not been hurt. There was not even a trace of headache. I was naked, softly and warmly bedded in furs, and my limbs moved without a hint of stiffness. I blinked wonderingly at the window, then turned my head to see Cadal standing beside the bed, relief spreading over his face like light after cloud.

'And about time,' he said.

'Cadal! Mithras, but it's good to see you! What's happened? Where is this?'

'Vortigern's best guest chamber, that's where it is. You fixed him, young Merlin, you fixed him proper.'

'Did I? I don't remember. I got the impression that they were fixing me. Do you mean they're not still planning to kill me?'

'Kill you? Stick you in a sacred cave, more like, and sacrifice virgins to you. Pity it'd be such a waste. I could use a bit of that myself.'

'I'll hand them over to you. Oh, Cadal, but it is good to see you! How did you get here?'

'I'd just got back to the nunnery gate when they came for your mother. I heard them asking for her, and saying they'd got you, and were taking the pair of you off to Vortigern at cock-light next day. I spent half the night finding Marric, and the other half trying to get a decent horse–and I might as well have saved myself the pains, I had to settle for that screw you bought. Even the pace you went, I was near a day behind you by the time you'd got to Pennal. Not that I wanted to catch up till I saw which way the land lay . . . Well, never mind, I got here in the end–at dusk yesterday–and found the place buzzing like a hive that's been trodden on.' He gave a short bark of a laugh. 'It was "Merlin this", and "Merlin that" . . . they call you "the King's prophet" already! When I said I was your servant, they couldn't shove me in here fast enough. Seems there isn't exactly a rush to look after sorcerers of your class. Can you eat something?'

'No–yes. Yes, I can. I'm hungry.' I pushed myself up against the pillows. 'Wait a minute, you say you got here *yesterday*? How long have I slept?'

'The night and the day. It's wearing on for sunset.'

'The night and the day? Then it's–Cadal, what's happened to my mother? Do you know?'

'She's gone, safe away home. Don't fret yourself about her. Get your food now, while I tell you. Here.'

He brought a tray on which was a bowl of steaming broth, and a dish of meat with bread and cheese and dried apricots. I could not touch the meat, but ate the rest while he talked.

'She doesn't know a thing about what they tried to do, or what happened. When she asked about you last night they told her you were here, "royally housed, and high in the King's favour". They told her you'd spat in the priests' eyes, in a manner of speaking, and prophesied fit to beat Solomon, and were sleeping it off, comfortable. She came to take a look at you this morning to make sure, and saw you sleeping like a baby, then she went off. I didn't get a chance to speak to her, but I saw her go. She was royally escorted, I can tell you; she'd half a troop of horse with her, and her women had litters nearly as grand as herself.'

'You say I "prophesied? Spat in the priests' eyes?"' I put a hand to my head. 'I wish I could remember . . . We were in the cave under King's Fort–they've told you about that, I suppose?' I stared at him. 'What happened, Cadal?'

'You mean to tell me you don't remember?'

I shook my head. 'All I know is, they were going to kill me to stop their rotten tower from falling down, and I put up a bluff. I thought if I could discredit their priests I might save my own skin, but all I ever hoped to do was to make a bit of time so that maybe I could get away.'

'Aye, I heard what they were going to do. Some people are dead ignorant, you'd wonder at it.' But he was watching me with the look that I remembered. 'It was a funny kind of bluff, wasn't it? How did you know where to find the tunnel?'

'Oh, that. That was easy. I've been in these parts before, as a boy. I came to this very place once, years ago, with Cerdic who was my servant then, and I was following a falcon through the wood when I found that old tunnel.'

'I see. Some people might call that luck–if they didn't know you, that is. I suppose you'd been right in?'

'Yes. When I first heard about the west wall cracking above, I thought it must be something to do with the old mine workings.' I told him then, quickly, all I could remember of what had happened in the cave. 'The lights,' I said, 'the water glittering . . . the shouting . . . It wasn't like the "seeings" I've had before–the white bull and the other things that I've sometimes seen. This was different. For one thing, it hurt far more. That must be what death is like. I suppose I did faint in the end. I don't remember being brought here at all.'

'I don't know about that. When I got in to see you, you was just asleep, very deep, but quite ordinary, it seemed to me. I make no bones about it, I took a good look at you, to see if they'd hurt you, but I couldn't find any sign of it, bar a lot of scratches and grazes they said you'd got in the woods. Your clothes looked like it, too, I can tell you . . . But from the way you were housed here, and the way they spoke of you, I didn't think they'd dare raise a finger to you–not now. Whatever it was, a faint, or a fit or a trance, more like, you've put the wind up them proper, that you have.'

'Yes, but how, exactly? Did they tell you?'

'Oh aye, they told me, the ones that could speak of it. Berric–he's the one that gave you the torch–he told me. He told me they'd all been set to cut your throat, those dirty old priests, and it seems if the King hadn't been at his wits' end, and impressed by your mother and the way the pair of you didn't seem frightened of them, he never would have waited. Oh, I heard all about it, don't worry. Berric said he'd not have given two pennies for your life back there in the hall when your mother told her story.' He shot me a look. 'All that rigmarole about the devil in the dark. Letting you in for this. What possessed her?'

'She thought it would help. I suppose she thought that the King had found out who my father was, and had had us dragged here to see if we had news of his plans. That's what I thought myself.' I spoke thoughtfully. 'And there was something else . . . When a place is full of superstition and fear, you get to feel it. I tell you, it was breathing goose-pimples all over me. She must have felt it, too. You might almost say she took the same line as I did, trying to face magic with magic. So she told the old tale about my being got by an incubus, with a few extra flourishes to carry it across.' I grinned at him. 'She did it well. I could have believed it myself if I hadn't known otherwise. But never mind, go on. I want to know what happened in the cavern. Do you mean I talked some kind of sense?'

'Well now, I didn't mean that, exactly. Couldn't make head or tail of what Berric told me. He swore he had it nearly word for word—it seems he has ambitions to be a singer or something . . . Well, what he said, you just stood there staring at the water running down the walls and then you started to talk, quite ordinary to start with, to the King, as if you were explaining how the shaft had been driven into the hill and the veins mined, but then the old priest—Maugan, isn't it?—started to shout "This is fools' talk," or something, when suddenly you lets out a yell that fair froze the balls on them—Berric's expression, not mine, he's not used to gentlemen's service—and your eyes turned up white and you put your hands up as if you was pulling the stars out of their sockets—Berric again, he ought to be a poet—and started to prophesy.'

'Yes?'

'That's what they all say. All wrapped up, it was, with eagles and wolves and lions and boars and as many other beasts as they've ever had in the arena and a few more besides, dragons and such—and going hundreds of years forward, which is safe enough, Dia knows, but Berric said it sounded, the lot of it, as true as a trumpet, and as if you'd have given odds on it with your last penny.'

'I may have to,' I said drily, 'if I said anything about Vortigern or my father.'

'Which you did,' said Cadal.

'Well, I'd better know; I'm going to have to stick by it.'

'It was all dressed up, like poets' stuff, red dragons and white dragons fighting and laying the place waste, showers of blood, all that kind of thing. But it seems you gave them chapter and verse for everything that's going to happen; the white dragon of the Saxons and the red dragon of Ambrosius fighting it out, the red dragon looking not so clever to begin with, but winning in the end. Yes. Then a bear coming out of Cornwall to sweep the field clear.'

'A bear? You mean the Boar, surely; that's Cornwall's badge. Hm. Then he may be for my father after all . . .'

'Berric said a bear. *Artos* was the word . . . he took notice, because he wondered about it himself. But you were clear about it, he says. Artos, you called him, Arthur . . . some name like that. You mean to tell me you don't remember a word of it?'

'Not a word.'

'Well look, now, I can't remember any more, but if they start coming at you about it, you could find some way of getting them to tell you everything you said. It's quite the thing, isn't it, for prophets not to know what they were talking about? Oracles and that?'

'I believe so.'

'All I mean is, if you've finished eating, and if you really feel all right, perhaps you'd better get up and dress. They're all waiting for you out there.'

'What for? For the god's sake, they don't want more advice? Are they moving the site of the tower?'

'No. They're doing what you told them to do.'

'What's that?'

'Draining the pool by a conduit. They've been working all night and day getting pumps rigged up to get the water out through the adit.'

'But why? That won't make the tower any safer. In fact it might bring the whole top of the crag in. Yes, I'm finished, take it away.' I pushed the tray into his hands, and threw back the bed-covers. 'Cadal, are you trying to tell me I said this in my—delirium?'

'Aye. You told them to drain the pool, and at the bottom they'd find the beasts that were bringing the King's fort down. Dragons, you said, red and white.'

I sat on the edge of the bed, my head in my hands. 'I remember something now . . . something I saw. Yes, that must be it . . . I did see something under the water, probably just a rock, dragon-shaped . . . And I remember starting to say something to the King about draining the pool . . . But I didn't tell them to drain it, I was saying "Even if you drained the pool, it wouldn't help you." At least, that's what I started to say.' I dropped my hands and looked up. 'You mean they're actually draining the place, thinking some water-beast is there underneath, rocking the foundations?'

'That's what you told them, Berric says.'

'Berric's a poet, he's dressing it up.'

'Maybe. But they're out there at it now, and the pumps have been working full blast for hours. The King's there, waiting for you.'

I sat silent. He threw me a doubtful look, then took the tray out, and came back with towels and a silver basin of steaming water. While I washed he busied himself over a chest at the far side of the room, lifting clothes from it and shaking out the folds, while he talked over his shoulder. 'You don't look worried. If they do drain that pool to the bottom, and there's nothing there—'

'There will be something there. Don't ask me what, I don't know, but if I said so . . . It's true, you know. The things I see this way are true. I have the Sight.'

His brows shot up. 'You think you're telling me news? Haven't you scared the toe-nails off me a score of times with what you say and the things you see that no one else can see?'

'You used to be scared of me, didn't you, Cadal?'

'In a way. But I'm not scared now, and I've no intention of being scared. Someone's got to look after the devil himself, as long as he wears clothes and needs food and drink. Now if you're done, young master, we'll see if these things fit you that the King sent for you.'

'The King sent them?'

'Aye. Looks like the sort of stuff they think a magician ought to wear.'

I went over to look. '*Not* long white robes with stars and moons on them, and a staff with curled snakes? Oh, really, Cadal—'

'Well, your own stuff's ruined, you've got to wear something. Come on, you'll look kind of fancy in these, and it seems to me you ought to try and impress them, the spot you're in.'

I laughed. 'You may be right. Let me see them. Hm, no, not the white, I'm not competing with Maugan's coven. Something dark, I think, and the black cloak. Yes, that'll do. And I'll wear the dragon brooch.'

'I hope you do right to be so sure of yourself.' Then he hesitated. 'Look, I know it's all wine and worship now, but maybe we ought to make a break for it straight away, not wait to see which way the dice fall? I could steal a couple of horses—'

'"Make a break for it?" Am I still a prisoner, then?'

'There's guards all round. Looking after you this time, not holding on to you, but by the dog, it comes to the same thing.' He glanced at the window. 'It'll be dusk before long. Look, I could spin some tale out there to keep them quiet, and maybe you could pretend to go to sleep again till dark—'

'No. I must stay. If I can get Vortigern to listen to me . . . Let me think, Cadal. You saw Marric the night we were taken. That means the news is on its way to my father, and if I'm any judge, he will move straight away. So far, lucky; the sooner the better; if he can catch Vortigern here in the West before he gets a chance to join again with Hengist . . .' I thought for a moment. 'Now, the ship was due to sail three—no, four days ago—'

'It sailed before you left Maridunum,' he said briefly.

'*What?*'

He smiled at my expression. 'Well, what did you expect? The Count's own son and his lady hauled off like that—nobody knew for sure why, but there were stories going about, and even Marric saw the sense in getting straight back to Ambrosius with *that* tale. The ship sailed with the tide the same dawn; she'd be out of the estuary before you'd hardly ridden out of town.'

I stood very still. I remember that he busied himself around me, draping the black cloak, surreptitiously pulling a fold to cover the dragon brooch that pinned it.

Then I drew a long breath. 'That's all I needed to know. Now I know what to do. "The King's prophet," did you say? They speak truer than they know. What the King's prophet must do now is to take the heart out of these Saxon-loving vermin, and drive Vortigern out of this tight corner of Wales into some place where Ambrosius can smoke him out quickly and destroy him.'

'You think you can do this?'

'I know I can.'

'Then I hope you know how to get us both out of here before they find out whose side you're on?'

'Why not? As soon as I know where Vortigern is bound for, we'll take the news to my father ourselves.' I settled the cloak to my shoulders, and grinned at him. 'So steal those horses, Cadal, and have them waiting down by the stream. There's a tree fallen clear across the water; you can't miss the place; wait there where there's cover. I'll come. But first I must go and help Vortigern uncover the dragons.'

I made for the door, but he got there ahead of me, and paused with his hand on the latch. His eyes were scared. 'You mean leave you on your own in the middle of that wolfpack?'

'I'm not on my own. Remember that; and if you can't trust me, trust what is in me. I have learnt to. I've learnt that the god comes when he will, and how he will, rending your flesh to get into you, and when he has done, tearing himself free as violently as he came. Afterwards–now–one feels light and hollow and like an angel flying . . . No, they can do nothing to me, Cadal. Don't be afraid. I have the power.'

'They killed Galapas.'

'Some day they may kill me,' I said. 'But not today. Open the door.'

Chapter Twelve

They were all gathered at the foot of the crag where the workmen's track met the marshy level of the corrie. I was still guarded, but this time–at least in appearance–it was a guard of honour. Four uniformed men, with their swords safely sheathed, escorted me to the King.

They had laid duckboards down on the marshy ground to make a platform, and set a chair for the King. Someone had rigged a windbreak of woven saplings and brushwood on three sides, roofed it, and draped the lot with worked rugs and dyed skins. Vortigern sat there, chin on fist, silent. There was no sign of his queen, or indeed of any of the women. The priests stood near him, but they kept back and did not speak. His captains flanked his chair.

The sun was setting behind the improvised pavilion in a splash of scarlet. It must have rained again that day; the grass was sodden, every blade heavy with drops. The familiar slate-grey clouds furled and unfurled slowly across the sunset. As I was led forward, they were lighting the torches. These looked small and dull against the sunset, more smoke than flame, dragged and flattened by the gusty breeze.

I waited at the foot of the platform. The King's eyes looked me up and down, but he said nothing. He was still reserving judgement. And why not, I thought. The kind of thing I seemed to have produced must be fairly familiar to him. Now he waited for proof of at least some part of my prophecy. If it was not forthcoming, this was still the time and the place to spill my blood. I wondered how the wind blew from Less Britain. The stream was a full three hundred paces off, dark under its oaks and willows.

Vortigern signed to me to take my place on the platform beside him, and I mounted it to stand at his right, on the opposite side from the priests. One or two of the officers moved aside from me; their faces were wooden, and they did not look at me, but I saw the crossed fingers, and thought: Dragon or no dragon, I can manage these. Then I felt eyes on me, and looked round. It was the greybeard. He was gazing fixedly at the brooch on my shoulder where my cloak had blown back from it. As I turned my head our eyes locked. I saw his widen, then his hand crept to his side, not to make the sign, but to loosen his sword in its scabbard. I looked away. No one spoke.

It was an uncomfortable vigil. As the sun sank lower the chilly spring wind freshened, fretting at the hangings. Where puddles lay in the reedy ground the water rippled and splashed under the wind. Cold draughts knifed up between the duckboards. I could hear a curlew whistling somewhere up in the darkening sky, then it slanted down, bubbling like a waterfall, into silence. Above us the King's banner fluttered and snapped in the wind. The shadow of the pavilion lengthened on the soaked field.

From where we waited, the only sign of activity was some coming and going in the trees. The last rays of the sun, level and red, shone full on the west face of King's Fort, lighting up the head of the crag crowned with the wrecked wall. No workmen were visible there; they must all be in the cave and the adit. Relays of boys ran across and back with reports of progress. The pumps were working well and gaining on the water; the level had sunk two spans in the last half hour . . . If my lord King would have patience, the pumps had jammed, but the engineers were working on them and meanwhile the men had rigged a windlass and were passing buckets . . . All was well again, the pumps were going now and the level was dropping sharply . . . You could see the bottom, they thought . . .

It was two full hours of chill, numb waiting, and it was almost dark, before lights came down the track and with them the crowd of workmen. They came fast but deliberately, not like frightened men, and even before they came close enough to be clearly seen, I knew what they had found. Their leaders halted a yard from the platform, and as the others came crowding up I felt my guards move closer.

There were soldiers with the workmen. Their captain stepped forward, saluting.

'The pool is empty?' asked Vortigern.

'Yes, sir.'

'And what lies beneath it?'

The officer paused. He should have been a bard. He need not have paused to gather eyes: they were all on him already.

A gust of wind, sudden and stronger than before, tore his cloak to one side with a crack like a whip, and rocked the frame of the pavilion. A bird fled overhead, tumbling along the wind. Not a merlin; not tonight. Only a rook, scudding late home.

'There is nothing beneath the pool, sir.' His voice was neutral, carefully official, but I heard a mutter go through the crowd like another surge of wind. Maugan was craning forward, his eyes bright as a vulture's, but I could see he did not dare to speak until he saw which way the King's mind was bending. Vortigern leaned forward.

'You are certain of this? You drained it to the bottom?'

'Indeed, sir.' He signed to the men beside him, and three or four of them stepped forward to tip a clutter of objects in front of the platform. A broken mattock, eaten with rust, some flint axe-heads older than any Roman working, a belt buckle, a knife with its blade eaten to nothing, a short length of chain, a metal whip-stock, some other objects impossible to identify, and a few shards of cooking pots.

The officer showed a hand, palm up. 'When I said "nothing", sir, I meant only what you might expect. These. And we got as near to the bottom as made no difference; you could see down to the rock and the mud, but we dredged the last bucket up, for good measure. The foreman will bear me out.'

The foreman stepped forward then, and I saw he had a full bucket in his hand, the water slopping over the brim.

'Sir, it's true, there's naught there. You could see for yourself if you came up, sir, right to the bottom. But better not try it, the tunnel's awash with mud now, and not fit. But I brought the last pailful out, for you to see yourself.'

With the word, he tipped the full bucket out, deluging the already sodden ground, and the water sloshed down to fill the puddle round the base of the royal standard. With the mud that had lain in the bottom came a few broken fragments of stone, and a silver coin.

The King turned then to look at me. It must be a measure of what had happened in the cavern yesterday, that the priests still kept silent, and the King was clearly waiting, not for an excuse, but an explanation.

God knows I had had plenty of time to think, all through that long, cold silent vigil, but I knew that thinking would not help me. If he was with me, he would come now. I looked down at the puddles where the last red light of sunset lay like blood. I looked up across the crag where stars could be seen already stabbing bright in the clear east. Another gust of wind was coming; I could hear it tearing the tops of the oaks where Cadal would be waiting.

'Well?' said Vortigern.

I took a step forward to the edge of the platform. I felt empty still, but somehow I would have to speak. As I moved, the gust struck the pavilion, sharp as a blow. There came a crack, a flurry of sound like hounds worrying a deer, and a cry from someone, bitten short. Above our heads the King's banner whipped streaming out, then, caught in its ropes, bellied like a sail holding the full weight of the wind. The shaft, jerked sharply to and fro in soft ground loosened further by the thrown bucketful of water, tore suddenly free of the grabbing hands, to whirl over and down. It slapped flat on the sodden field at the King's feet.

The wind fled past, and in its wake was a lull. The banner lay flat, held heavy with water. The white dragon on a green field. As we watched, it sagged slowly into a pool, and the water washed over it. Some last faint ray from the sunset bloodied the water. Someone said fearfully, 'An omen,' and another voice, loudly, 'Great Thor, the Dragon is down!' Others began to shout. The standard bearer, his face ashen, was already stooping, but I jumped off the platform in front of them all and threw up my arms.

'Can any doubt the god has spoken? Look up from the ground, and see where he speaks again!'

Across the dark east, burning white hot with a trail like a young comet, went a shooting star, the star men call the firedrake or dragon of fire.

'There it runs!' I shouted. 'There it runs! The Red Dragon of the West! I tell you, King Vortigern, waste no more time here with these ignorant fools who babble of blood sacrifice and build a wall of stone for you, a foot a day! What wall will keep out the Dragon? I, Merlin, tell you, send these priests away and gather your captains round you, and get you away from the hills of Wales to your own country. King's Fort is not for you. You have seen the Red Dragon come tonight, and the White Dragon lie beneath him. And by God, you have seen the truth! Take warning! Strike your tents now, and go to your own country, and watch your borders lest the Dragon follow you. and burn you out! You brought me here to speak, and I have spoken. I tell you, the Dragon is here!'

The King was on his feet, and men were shouting. I pulled the black cloak round me, and without hurrying turned away through the crowd of workmen and soldiers that milled round the foot of the platform. They did not try to stop me. They would as soon, I suppose, have touched a poisonous snake. Behind me, through the hubbub, I heard Maugan's voice and thought for a moment they were coming after me, but then men crowded off the platform, and began thrusting their way through the mob of workmen, on their way back to the encampment. Torches tossed. Someone dragged the sodden standard up and I saw it rocking and dripping where presumably his captains were clearing a path for the King. I drew the black cloak closer and slipped into the shadows at the edge of the crowd. Presently, unseen, I was able to step round behind the pavilion.

The oaks were three hundred paces away across the dark field. Under them the stream ran loud over smooth stones.

Cadal's voice said, low and urgent: 'This way.' A hoof sparked on stone. 'I got you a quiet one,' he said, and put a hand under my foot to throw me into the saddle.

I laughed a little. 'I could ride the firedrake itself tonight. You saw it?'

'Aye, my lord. And I saw you, and heard you, too.'

'Cadal, you swore you'd never be afraid of me. It was only a shooting star.'

'But it came when it came.'

'Yes. And now we'd better go while we can go. Timing is all that matters, Cadal.'

'You shouldn't laugh at it, master Merlin.'

'By the god,' I said, 'I'm not laughing.'

The horses pushed out from under the dripping trees and went at a swift canter across the ridge. To our right a wooded hill blocked out the west. Ahead was the narrow neck of valley between hill and river.

'Will they come after you?'

'I doubt it.'

But as we kicked the beasts to a gallop between ridge and river a horseman loomed, and our horses swerved and shied.

Cadal's beast jumped forward under the spur. Iron rasped. A voice, vaguely familiar, said clearly: 'Put up. Friend.'

The horses stamped and blew. I saw Cadal's hand on the other's rein. He sat quietly.

'Whose friend?'

'Ambrosius.'

I said: 'Wait, Cadal, it's the greybeard. Your name, sir? And your business with me?'

He cleared his throat harshly. 'Gorlois is my name, of Tintagel in Cornwall.'

I saw Cadal's movement of surprise, and heard the bits jingle. He still had hold of the other's rein, and the drawn dagger gleamed. The old warrior sat unmoving. There was no sound of following hoofs.

I said slowly: 'Then, sir, I should rather ask you what your business was with Vortigern?'

'The same as yours, Merlin Ambrosius.' I saw his teeth gleam in his beard. 'I came north to see for myself, and to send word back to him. The West has waited long enough, and the time will be ripe, come spring. But you came early. I could have saved myself the pains, it seems.'

'You came alone?'

He gave a short, hard laugh, like a dog barking. 'To Vortigern? Hardly. My men will follow. But I had to catch you. I want news.' Then, harshly: 'God's grief, man, do you doubt me? I came alone to you.'

'No, sir. Let him go, Cadal. My lord, if you want to talk to me, you'll have to do it on the move. We should go, and quickly.'

'Willingly.' We set the horses in motion. As they struck into a gallop I said over my shoulder: 'You guessed when you saw the brooch?'

'Before that. You have a look of him, Merlin Ambrosius.' I heard him laugh again, deep in his throat. 'And by God, there are times when you have a look of your devil-sire as well! Steady now, we're nearly at the ford. It'll be deep. They say wizards can't cross water?'

I laughed. 'I'm always sick at sea, but I can manage this.' The horses plunged across the ford unhindered, and took the next slope at a gallop. Then we were on the paved road, plain to see in the flying starlight, which leads straight across the high ground to the south.

We rode all night, with no pursuit. Three days later, in the early morning, Ambrosius came to land.

The Red Dragon

Chapter One

The way the chronicles tell it, you would think it took Ambrosius two months to get himself crowned King and pacify Britain. In fact, it took more than two years.

The first part was quick enough. It was not for nothing that he had spent all those years in Less Britain, he and Uther, developing an expert striking force the like of which had not been seen in any part of Europe since the disbanding nearly a hundred years ago of the force commanded by the Count of the Saxon Shore. Ambrosius had, in fact, modelled his own army on the force of the Saxon Shore, a marvellously mobile fighting instrument which could live off the country and do everything at twice the speed of the normal force. Caesar-speed, they still called it when I was young.

He landed at Totnes in Devon, with a fair wind and a quiet sea, and he had hardly set up the Red Dragon when the whole West rose for him. He was King of Cornwall and Devon before he even left the shore, and everywhere, as he moved northwards, the chiefs and kings crowded to swell his army. Eldol of Gloucester, a ferocious old man who had fought with Constantine against Vortigern, with Vortigern against Hengist, with Vortimer against both, and would fight anywhere for the sheer hell of it, met him at Glastonbury and swore faith. With him came a host of lesser leaders, not least his own brother Eldad, a bishop whose devout Christianity made the pagan wolves look like lambs by comparison, and set me wondering where he spent the dark nights of the winter solstice. But he was powerful; I had heard my mother speak of him with reverence; and once he had declared for Ambrosius, all Christian Britain came with him, urgent to drive back the pagan hordes moving steadily inland from their landing-places in the south and east. Last came Gorlois of Tintagel, straight from Vortigern's side with news of Vortigern's hasty move out of the Welsh mountains, and ready to ratify the oath of loyalty which, should Ambrosius be successful, would add the whole kingdom of Cornwall for the first time to the High Kingdom of Britain.

Ambrosius' main trouble, indeed, was not lack of support but the nature of it. The native Britons, tired of Vortigern, were fighting-mad to clear the Saxons out of their country and get their homes and their own ways back, but a great majority of them knew only guerrilla warfare, or the kind of hit-and-ride-away tactics that do well enough to harass the enemy, but will not hold him back for long if he means business. Moreover, each troop came with its own leader, and it was as much as any commander's authority was worth to suggest that they might regroup and train under strangers. Since the last trained legion had withdrawn from Britain almost a century before, we had fought (as we had done before the Romans ever came) in tribes. And it was no use suggesting that, for instance, the men of Devet might fight beside the men of North Wales even with their own leaders; throats would have been cut on both sides before the first trumpet ever sounded.

Ambrosius here, as everywhere, showed himself master. As ever he used each man for what that man's strength was worth. He sowed his own officers broadcast among the British—for co-ordination, he said, no more—and through them quietly adapted the tactics of each force to suit his central plan, with his own body of picked troops taking the main brunt of attack.

All this I heard later, or could have guessed from what I knew of him. I could have guessed, also, what would happen the moment his forces assembled and declared him King. His British allies clamoured for him to go straight after Hengist and drive the Saxons back to their own country. They were not unduly concerned with Vortigern. Indeed, such power as Vortigern had had was largely gone already, and it would have been simple enough for Ambrosius to ignore him and concentrate on the Saxons.

But he refused to give way to pressure. The old wolf must be smoked out first, he said, and the field cleared for the main work of battle. Besides, he pointed out, Hengist and his Saxons were Northmen, and particularly amenable to rumours and fear; let Ambrosius once unite the British to destroy Vortigern, and the Saxons would begin to fear him as a force really to be reckoned with. It was his guess that, given the time, they would bring together one large force to face him, which might then be broken at one blow.

They had a council about it, at the fort near Gloucester where the first bridge crosses the Sefern river. I could picture it, Ambrosius listening and weighing and judging, and answering with that grave easy way of his, allowing each man his say for pride; then taking at the end the decision he had meant to take from the beginning, but giving way here and there on the small things, so that each man thought he had made a bargain and got, if not what he wanted, then something near it, in return for a concession by his commander.

The upshot was, that they marched northwards within the week, and came on Vortigern at Doward.

Doward is in the valley of the Guoy, which the Saxons pronounce Way or Wye. This is a big river, which runs deep and placid-seeming through a gorge whose high slopes are hung with forests. Here and there the valley widens to green pastures, but the tide runs many miles up river, and these low meadows are often, in winter, awash under a roaring yellow flood, for the great Wye is not so placid as it seems, and even in summer there are deep pools where big fish lie and the currents are strong enough to overturn a coracle and drown a man.

Well north of the limit of the tidal floods, in a wide curve of the valley, stand the two hills called Doward. The one to the north is the greater, thick with forest and mined with caves inhabited, men say, by wild beasts and outlawed men. The hill called Lesser Doward is also forested, but more thinly, since it is rocky, and its steep summit, rising above the trees, makes a natural citadel so secure that it has been fortified time out of mind. Long before even the Romans came, some British king built himself a fortress on the summit which, with its commanding view, and the natural defences of crag and river, made a formidable stronghold. The hill is wide topped, and its sides steep and rough, and though siege engines could at one point be dragged up in dead ground, this ended in crags where the engines were useless. Everywhere except at this point there was a double rampart and ditch to get through before the outer wall of the fortress could be reached. The Romans themselves had marched against it once, and only managed to reduce it through treachery. This was in the time of Caractacus. Doward was the kind of place that, like Troy, must be taken from within.

This time also, it was taken from within. But not by treachery; by fire.

Everyone knows what happened there.

Vortigern's men were hardly settled after their headlong flight from Snowdon, when Ambrosius' army came up the valley of the Wye, and encamped due west of Doward Hill, at a place called Ganarew. I never heard what store of provisions Vortigern had; but the place had been kept prepared, and it was well known that there were two good springs within the fortress which had not yet been known to fail; so it might well have taken Ambrosius some time to reduce it by siege. But a siege was just what he could not afford, with Hengist gathering his forces, and the April seas opening between Britain and the Saxon shores. Besides, his British allies were restless, and would never have settled down for a prolonged siege. It had to be quick.

It was both quick and brutal. I have heard it said that Ambrosius acted out of vengeance for his long-dead brother. I do not believe this to be true. Such long-standing bitterness was not in his nature, and besides, he was a general and a good fighting commander before he was even a man. He was driven only by necessity, and in the end, by Vortigern's own brutality.

Ambrosius besieged the place in the conventional way for about three days. Where he could, he drew up siege engines and tried to break the defences. He did indeed breach the outer rampart in two places above what was still called Romans' Way, but when he found himself stopped by the inner rampart and his troops exposed to the defenders, he withdrew. When he saw how long the siege would take, and how, even in the three days, some of his British troops quietly left him and went off on their own, like hounds after the rumour of Saxon hares, he decided to make an end quickly. He sent a man to Vortigern with conditions for surrender. Vortigern, who must have seen the defection of some of the British troops, and who well understood

Ambrosius' position, laughed, and sent back the messenger without a
message, but with the man's own two hands severed, and bound in a bloody
cloth to the belt at his waist.

He stumbled into Ambrosius' tent just after sundown of the third day,
and managed to stay on his feet long enough to give the only message he was
charged with.

'They say that you may stay here, my lord, until your army melts away,
and you are left handless as I. They have food in plenty, sir, I saw it, and
water—'

Ambrosius only said: 'He ordered this himself?'

'The Queen,' said the man. 'It was the Queen.' He pitched forward on the
word at Ambrosius' feet, and from the dripping cloth at his belt the hands
fell, sprawling.

'Then we will burn out the wasps' nest, queen and all,' said Ambrosius.
'See to him.'

That night, to the apparent pleasure of the garrison, the siege engines
were withdrawn from Romans' Way and the breached places in the outer
rampart. Instead, great piles of brushwood and hewn branches were stacked
in the gaps, and the army tightened its ring round the crest of the hill, with a
circle of archers waiting, and men ready to cut down any who should escape.
In the quiet hour before daylight the order was given. From every quarter
the arrows, pointed with flaming, oil-soaked rags, showered into the
fortress. It did not take long. The place was largely built of wood, and
crowded with the wagons, provisions, beasts and their fodder. It burned
fiercely. And when it was alight the brushwood outside the walls was fired,
so that anyone leaping from the walls met another wall of fire outside. And
outside that, the iron ring of the army.

They say that throughout, Ambrosius sat his big white horse, watching,
till the flames made the horse as red as the Red Dragon above his head. And
high on the fortress tower the White Dragon, showing against a plume of
smoke, turned blood red as the flames themselves, then blackened and fell.

Chapter Two

While Ambrosius was attacking Doward I was still at Maridunum, having
parted from Gorlois on the ride south, and seen him on his way to meet my
father.

It happened this way. All through that first night we rode hard, but there
was no sign of pursuit, so at sun-up we drew off the road and rested, waiting
for Gorlois' men to come up with us. This they did during the morning,
having been able, in the near-panic at Dinas Brenin, to slip away
unobserved. They confirmed what Gorlois had already suggested to me,
that Vortigern would head, not for his own fortress of Caer-Guent, but for
Doward, on the river Wye. And he was moving, they said, by the eastbound
road through Caer Gai towards Bravonium. Once past Tomen-y-mur, there

was no danger that we would be overtaken.

So we rode on, a troop now about twenty strong, but going easily. My mother, with her escort of fighting men, was barely more than a day ahead of us, and her party, with the litters, would be much slower than we were. We had no wish to catch up with them and perhaps force a fight which might endanger the women; it was certain, said Gorlois to me, that the latter would be delivered safely to Maridunum, 'but,' he added in his sharp gruff way, 'we shall meet the escort on their way back. For come back they will; they cannot know the King is moving east. And every man less for Vortigern is another for your father. We'll get news at Bremia, and camp beyond it to wait for them.'

Bremia was nothing but a cluster of stone huts smelling of peat smoke and dung, black doorways curtained from wind and rain with hides or sacking, round which peered scared eyes of women and children. No men appeared, even when we drew rein in the midst of the place, and curs ran yapping round the horses' heels. This puzzled us, till (knowing the dialect) I called out to the eyes behind the nearest curtain, to reassure the people and ask for news.

They came out then, women, children, and one or two old men, crowding eagerly round us and ready to talk.

The first piece of news was that my mother's party had been there the previous day and night, leaving only that morning, at the Princess's insistence. She had been taken ill, they told me, and had stayed for half the day and the night in the head-man's house, where she was cared for. Her women had tried to persuade her to turn aside for a monastic settlement in the hills nearby, where she might rest, but she had refused, and had seemed better in the morning, so the party had ridden on. It had been a chill, said the head-man's wife; the lady had been feverish, and coughing a little, but she had seemed so much better next morning, and Maridunum was not more than a day's ride; they had thought it better to let her do as she desired . . .

I eyed the squalid hut from which she had come to meet me, thinking that, indeed, the danger of a few more hours in the litter might well be less than such miserable shelter in Bremia, so thanked the woman for her kindness, and asked where her man had gone. As to that, she told me, all the men had gone to join Ambrosius . . .

She mistook my look of surprise. 'Did you not know? There was a prophet at Dinas Brenin, who said the Red Dragon would come. The Princess told me herself, and could see the soldiers were afraid. And now he has landed. He is here.'

'How can you know?' I asked her. 'We met no messenger.'

She looked at me as if I were crazed, or stupid. Had I not seen the firedrake? The whole village knew this for the portent, after the prophet had spoken so. The men had armed themselves, and had gone that very day. If the soldiers came back, the women and children would take to the hills, but everyone knew that Ambrosius could move more swiftly than the wind, and they were not afraid . . .

I let her run on while I translated for Gorlois. Our eyes met with the same thought. We thanked the woman again, gave her what was due for her care of my mother, and rode after the men of Bremia.

South of the village the road divides, the main way turning south-east past the gold mine and then through the hills and deep valleys to the broad valley of the Wye whence it is easy riding to the Sefern crossing and the south-west. The other, minor, road goes straight south, a day's ride to Maridunum. I had decided that in any case I would follow my mother south and talk to her before I rejoined Ambrosius; now the news of her illness made this imperative. Gorlois would ride straight to meet Ambrosius and give him the news of Vortigern's movements.

At the fork where our ways parted we came on the villagers. They had heard us coming and taken cover—the place was all rocks and bushes—but not soon enough; the gusty wind must have hidden our approach from them till we were almost on them. The men were out of sight, but one of their miserable pack-donkeys was not, and stones were still rolling on the scree.

It was Bremia over again. We halted, and I called out into the windy silence. This time I told them who I was, and in a moment, it seemed, the roadside was bristling with men. They came crowding round our horses, showing their teeth and brandishing a peculiar assortment of weapons ranging from a bent Roman sword to a stone spearhead bound on a hay-rake. They told the same story as their women; they had heard the prophecy, and they had seen the portent; they were marching south to join Ambrosius, and every man in the West would soon be with them. Their spirit was high, and their condition pitiful; it was lucky we had a chance to help them.

'Speak to them,' said Gorlois to me. 'Tell them that if they wait another day here with us, they shall have weapons and horses. They have picked the right place for an ambush, as who should know better than they?'

So I told them that this was the Duke of Cornwall, and a great leader, and that if they would wait a day with us, we would see they got weapons and horses. 'For Vortigern's men will come back this way,' I told them. 'They are not to know that the High King is already fleeing eastwards: they will come back by this road, so we will wait for them here, and you will be wise to wait with us.'

So we waited. The escort must have stayed rather longer than need be in Maridunum, and after that cold damp ride who could blame them? But towards dusk of the second day they came back, riding at ease, thinking maybe of a night's shelter at Bremia.

We took them nicely by surprise, and fought a bloody and very unpleasant little action. One roadside skirmish is very like another. This one only differed from the usual in being better generalled and more eccentrically equipped, but we had the advantages both of numbers and of surprise, and did what we had set out to do, robbed Vortigern of twenty men for the loss of only three of our own and a few cuts. I came out of it more creditably than I would have believed possible, killing the man I had picked out before the fighting swept over and past me and another knocked me off my horse and would possibly have killed me if Cadal had not parried the stroke and killed the fellow himself. It was quickly over. We buried our own dead and left the rest for the kites, after we had stripped them of their arms. We had taken care not to harm the horses, and when next morning Gorlois said farewell and led his new troops south-east, every man had a horse, and a good weapon of some kind. Cadal and I turned south for Maridunum, and reached it by early evening.

The first person I saw as we rode down the street towards St Peter's was my cousin Dinias. We came on him suddenly at a corner, and he jumped a foot and went white. I suppose rumours had been running like wildfire through the town ever since the escort had brought my mother back without me.

'Merlin. I thought–I thought—'

'Well met, cousin I was coming to look for you.'

He said quickly: 'Look, I swear I had no idea who those men were—'

'I know that. What happened wasn't your fault. That isn't why I was looking for you.'

'—and I was drunk, you know that. But even if I had guessed who they were, how was I to know they'd take you up on a thing like that? I'd heard rumours of what they were looking for, I admit, but I swear it never entered my head—'

'I said it wasn't your fault. And I'm back here again safely, aren't I? All's well that ends well. Leave it, Dinias. That wasn't what I wanted to talk to you about.'

But he persisted. 'I took the money, didn't I? You saw.'

'And if you did? You didn't give information for money, you took it afterwards. It's different, to my mind. If Vortigern likes to throw his money away, then by all means rob him of it. Forget it, I tell you. Have you news of my mother?'

'I've just come from there. She's ill, did you know?'

'I got news on my way south,' I said. 'What's the matter with her? How bad?'

'A chill, they told me, but they say she's on the mend. I thought myself she still looked poor enough, but she was fatigued with the journey, and anxious about you. What did Vortigern want you for, in the end?'

'To kill me,' I said briefly.

He stared, then began to stutter. 'I–in God's name, Merlin, I know you and I have never been . . . that is, there've been times—' He stopped, and I heard him swallow. 'I don't sell my kinsmen, you know.'

'I told you I believed you. Forget it. It was nothing to do with you, some nonsense of his soothsayers'. But as I said, here I am safe and sound.'

'Your mother said nothing about it.'

'She didn't know. Do you think she'd have let him send her tamely home if she had known what he meant to do? The men who brought her home, they knew, you can be sure of that. So they didn't let it out to her?'

'It seems not,' said Dinias. 'But—'

'I'm glad of that. I'm hoping to get to see her soon, this time in daylight.'

'Then you're in no danger now from Vortigern?'

'I would be, I suppose,' I said, 'if the place was still full of his men, but I was told at the gate that they've cleared out to join him?'

'That's so. Some rode north, and some east to Caer-Guent. You've heard the news, then?'

'What news?'

Though there was nobody else in the street, he looked over his shoulder in the old, furtive way. I slid down out of the saddle, and threw the reins to Cadal. 'What news?' I repeated.

'Ambrosius,' he said softly. He's landed in the south-west, they say, and marching north. A ship brought the story yesterday, and Vortigern's men started moving out straight away. But—if you've just ridden in from the north, surely you'd meet them?'

'Two companies, this morning. But we saw them in good time, and got off the road. We met my mother's escort the day before, at the crossways.'

'"Met?"' He looked startled. 'But if they knew Vortigern wanted you dead—'

'They'd have known I had no business riding south, and cut me down? Exactly. So we cut them down instead. Oh, don't look at me like that—it wasn't magician's work, only soldiers'. We fell in with some Welsh who were on their way to join Ambrosius, and we ambushed Vortigern's troop and cut them up.'

'The Welsh knew already? The prophecy, was it?' I saw the whites of his eyes in the dusk. 'I'd heard about that . . . the place is buzzing with it. The troops told us. They said you'd showed them some kind of great lake under the crag—it was that place we stopped at years ago, and I'll swear there was no sign of any lake then—but there was this lake of water with dragons lying in it under the foundations of the tower. Is it true?'

'That I showed them a lake, yes.'

'But the dragons. What were they?'

I said, slowly: 'Dragons. Something conjured out of nothing for them to see, since without seeing they would not listen, let alone believe.'

There was a little silence. Then he said, with fear in his voice: 'And was it magic that showed you Ambrosius was coming?'

'Yes and no.' I smiled. 'I knew he was coming, but not when. It was the magic that told me he was actually on his way.'

He was staring again. 'You knew he was coming? Then you did have tidings in Cornwall? You might have told me.'

'Why?'

'I'd have joined him.'

I looked at him for a moment, measuring. 'You can still join him. You and your other friends who fought with Vortimer. What about Vortimer's brother, Pascentius? Do you know where he is? Is he still hot against Vortigern?'

'Yes, but they say he's gone to make peace with Hengist. He'll never join Ambrosius, he wants Britain for himself.'

'And you?' I asked. 'What do you want?'

He answered quite simply, for once without any bluster or bravado. 'Only a place I can call my own. This, if I can. It's mine now, after all. He killed the children, did you know?'

'I didn't, but you hardly surprise me. It's a habit of his, after all.' I paused. 'Look, Dinias, there's a lot to say, and I've a lot to tell you. But first I've a favour to ask of you.'

'What's that?'

'Hospitality. There's nowhere else I know of that I care to go until I've got my own place ready, and I've a fancy to stay in my grandfather's house again.'

He said, without pretence or evasion: 'It's not what it was.'

I laughed. 'Is anything? As long as there's a roof against this hellish rain, and a fire to dry our clothes, and something to eat, no matter what. What do you say we send Cadal for provisions, and eat at home? I'll tell you the whole thing over a pie and a flask of wine. But I warn you, if you so much as show me a pair of dice I'll yell for Vortigern's men myself.'

He grinned, relaxing suddenly. 'No fear of that. Come along, then. There's a couple of rooms still habitable, and we'll find you a bed.'

I was given Camlach's room. It was draughty, and full of dust, and Cadal refused to let me use the bedding until it had lain in front of a roaring fire for a full hour. Dinias had no servant, except one slut of a girl who looked after him apparently in return for the privilege of sharing his bed. Cadal set her to carrying fuel and heating water while he took a message to the nunnery for my mother, and then went to the tavern for wine and provisions.

We ate before the fire, with Cadal serving us. We talked late, but here it is sufficient to record that I told Dinias my story—or such parts of it as he would understand. There might have been some personal satisfaction in telling him the facts of my parentage, but until I was sure of him, and the countryside was known to be clear of Vortigern's men, I thought it better to say nothing. So I told him merely how I had gone to Brittany, and that I had become Ambrosius' man. Dinias had heard enough already of my 'prophecy' in the cavern at King's Fort to believe implicitly in Ambrosius' coming victory, so our talk ended with his promise to ride westwards in the morning with the news, and summon what support he could for Ambrosius from the fringes of Wales. He would, I knew, have been afraid in any case to do other than keep that promise; whatever the soldiers had said about the occasion there in King's Fort, it was enough to strike my simple cousin Dinias with the most profound awe of my powers. But even without that, I knew I could trust him in this. We talked till almost dawn, then I gave him money and said good night.

(He was gone before I woke next morning. He kept his word, and joined Ambrosius later, at York, with a few hundred men. He was honourably received, and acquitted himself well, but soon afterwards, in some minor engagement, received wounds of which he later died.)

Cadal shut the door behind him. 'At least there's a good lock and a stout bar.'

'Are you afraid of Dinias?' I asked.

'I'm afraid of everybody in this cursed town. I'll not be happy till we're quit of it and back with Ambrosius.'

'I doubt if you need worry now. Vortigern's men have gone. You heard what Dinias said.'

'Aye, and I heard what you said, too.' He had stooped to pick up the blankets from beside the fire, and paused with his arms full of bedding, looking at me. 'What did you mean, you're getting your own place here ready? You're never thinking of setting up house here?'

'Not a house, no.'

'That cave?'

I smiled at his expression. 'When Ambrosius has done with me, and the country is quiet, that is where I shall go. I told you, didn't I, that if you stayed with me you'd live far from home?'

'We were talking about dying, as far as I remember. You mean, live there?'

'I don't know,' I said. 'Perhaps not. But I think I shall need a place where I can be alone, away, aside from things happening. Thinking and planning is one side of life; doing is another. A man cannot be doing all the time.'

'Tell that to Uther.'

'I am not Uther.'

'Well, it takes both sorts, as they say.' He dumped the blankets on the bed. 'What are you smiling at?'

'Was I? Never mind. Let's get to bed, we'll have to be early at the nunnery. Did you have to bribe the old woman again?'

'Old woman nothing.' He straightened. 'It was a girl this time. A looker, too, what I could see of her with that sack of a gown and a hood over her head. Whoever puts a girl like that in a nunnery deserves—' He began to explain what they deserved, but I cut him short.

'Did you find out how my mother was?'

'They said she was better. The fever's gone, but she'll not rest quiet till she's seen you. You'll tell her everything now?'

'Yes.'

'And then?'

'We join Ambrosius.'

'Ah,' he said, and when he had dragged his mattress to lie across the door, he blew out the lamp and lay down without another word to sleep.

My bed was comfortable enough, and the room, derelict or no, was luxury itself after the journey. But I slept badly. In imagination I was out on the road with Ambrosius, heading for Doward. From what I had heard of Doward, reducing it would not be an easy job. I began to wonder if after all I had done my father a disservice in driving the High King out of his Snowdon fastness. I should have left him there, I thought, with his rotten tower, and Ambrosius would have driven him back into the sea.

It was with an effort almost of surprise that I recalled my own prophecy. What I had done at Dinas Brenin, I had not done of myself. It was not I who had decided to send Vortigern fleeing out of Wales. Out of the dark, out of the wild and whirling stars, I had been told. The Red Dragon would triumph, the White would fall. The voice that had said so, that said so now in the musty dark of Camlach's room, was not my own; it was the god's. One did not lie awake looking for reasons; one obeyed, and then slept.

Chapter Three

It was the girl Cadal had spoken of who opened the nunnery gate to us. She must have been waiting to receive us, for almost as soon as Cadal's hand was lifted to the bell-pull the gate opened and she motioned us to come in. I got a swift impression of wide eyes under the brown hood, and a supple young body shrouded in the rough gown, as she latched the heavy gate and, drawing her hood closer over her face and hair, led us quickly across the courtyard. Her feet, bare in canvas sandals, looked cold, and were splashed with mud from the puddled yard, but they were slim and well-shaped, and her hands were pretty. She did not speak, but led us across the yard and through a narrow passage between two buildings, into a larger square beyond. Here against the walls stood fruit trees, and a few flowers grew, but these were mostly weeds and wild-flowers, and the doors of the cells that opened off the courtyard were unpainted and, where they stood open, gave on bare little rooms where simplicity had become ugliness, and, too often, squalor.

Not so in my mother's cell. She was housed with adequate–if not royal–comfort. They had let her bring her own furniture, the room was limewashed and spotlessly clean, and with the change in the April weather the sun had come out and was shining straight in through the narrow window and across her bed. I remembered the furniture; it was her own bed from home, and the curtain at the window was one she had woven herself, the red cloth with the green pattern that she had been making the day my uncle Camlach came home. I remembered, too, the wolfskin on the floor; my grandfather had killed the beast with his bare hands and the haft of his broken dagger; its beady eyes and snarl had terrified me when I was small. The cross that hung on the bare wall at the foot of her bed was of dull silver, with a lovely pattern of locked but flowing lines, and studs of amethyst that caught the light.

The girl showed me the door in silence, and withdrew. Cadal sat down on a bench outside to wait.

My mother lay propped on pillows, in the shaft of sunshine. She looked pale and tired, and spoke not much above a whisper, but was, she told me, on the mend. When I questioned her about the illness, and laid a hand on her temples, she put me aside, smiling and saying she was well enough looked after. I did not insist: half of healing is in the patient's trust, and no woman ever thinks her own son is much more than a child. Besides, I could see that the fever had gone, and now that she was no longer anxious over me, she would sleep.

So I merely pulled up the room's chair, sat down and began to tell her all she wanted to know, without waiting for her questions: about my escape from Maridunum and the flight like the arrows from the god's bow straight from Britain to Ambrosius' felt, and all that had happened since. She lay back against her pillows and watched me with astonishment and some slowly growing emotion which I identified as the emotion a cage-bird might feel if you set it to hatch a merlin's egg.

When I had finished she was tired, and grey stood under her eyes so sharply drawn that I got up to go. But she looked contented, and said, as if it was the sum and finish of the story, as I suppose it was, for her:

'He has acknowledged you.'

'Yes. They call me Merlin Ambrosius.'

She was silent a little, smiling to herself. I crossed to the window and leaned my elbows on the sill, looking out. The sun was warm. Cadal nodded on his bench, half asleep. From across the yard a movement caught my eye; in a shadowed doorway the girl was standing, watching my mother's door as if waiting for me to come out. She had put back her hood, and even in the shadows I could see the gold of her hair and a young face lovely as a flower. Then she saw me watching her. For perhaps two seconds our eyes met and held. I knew then why the ancients armed the cruellest god with arrows; I felt the shock of it right through my body. Then she had gone, shrinking close-hooded back into the shadow, and behind me my mother was saying:

'And now? What now?'

I turned my back on the sunlight. 'I go to join him. But not until you are better. When I go I want to take news of you.'

She looked anxious. 'You must not stay here. Maridunum is not safe for you.'

'I think it is. Since the news came in of the landing, the place has emptied itself of Vortigern's men. We had to take to the hill-tracks on our way south; the road was alive with men riding to join him.'

'That's true, but—'

'And I shan't go about, I promise you. I was lucky last night, I ran into Dinias as soon as I set foot in town. He gave me a room at home.'

'*Dinias?*'

I laughed at her astonishment. 'Dinias feels he owes me something, never mind what, but we agreed well enough last night.' I told her what mission I had sent him on, and she nodded.

'He—' and I knew she did not mean Dinias '–will need every man who can hold a sword.' She knitted her brows. 'They say Hengist has three hundred thousand men. Will he—' and again she was not referring to Hengist '–be able to withstand Vortigern, and after him Hengist and the Saxons?'

I suppose I was still thinking of last night's vigil. I said, without pausing to consider how it would sound: 'I have said so, so it must be true.'

A movement from the bed brought my eyes down to her. She was crossing herself, her eyes at once startled and severe, and through it all afraid. 'Merlin—' but on the word a cough shook her, so that when she managed to speak again it was only a harsh whisper: 'Beware of arrogance. Even if God has given you power—'

I laid a hand on her wrist, stopping her. 'You mistake me, madam. I put it badly. I only meant that the god had said it through me, and because he had said it, it must be true. Ambrosius must win, it is in the stars.'

She nodded, and I saw the relief wash through her and slacken her, body and mind, like an exhausted child.

I said gently: 'Don't be afraid for me, mother. Whatever god uses me, I am content to be his voice and instrument. I go where he sends me. And when he has finished with me, he will take me back.'

'There is only one God,' she whispered.

I smiled at her. 'That is what I am beginning to think. Now, go to sleep. I will come back in the morning.'

I went to see my mother again next morning. This time I went alone. I had sent Cadal to find provisions in the market, Dinias' slut having vanished when he did, leaving us to fend for ourselves in the deserted palace. I was rewarded, for the girl was again on duty at the gate, and again led me to my mother's room. But when I said something to her she merely pulled the hood closer without speaking, so that again I saw no more of her than the slender hands and feet. The cobbles were dry today, and the puddles gone. She had washed her feet, and in the grip of the coarse sandals they looked as fragile as blue-veined flowers in a peasant's basket. Or so I told myself, my mind working like a singer's, where it had no right to be working at all. The arrow still thrummed where it had struck me, and my whole body seemed to thrill and tighten at the sight of her.

She showed me the door again, as if I could have forgotten it, and withdrew to wait.

My mother seemed a little better, and had rested well, she told me. We talked for a while; she had questions about the details of my story, and I filled them in for her. When I got up to go I asked, as casually as I could:

'The girl who opened the gate; she is young, surely, to be here? Who is she?'

'Her mother worked in the palace. Keridwen. Do you remember her?'

I shook my head. 'Should I?'

'No.' But when I asked her why she smiled, she would say nothing, and in face of her amusement I dared not ask any more.

On the third day it was the old deaf portress; and I spent the whole interview with my mother wondering if she had (as women will) seen straight through my carefully casual air to what lay beneath, and passed the word that the girl must be kept out of my way. But on the fourth day she was there, and this time I knew before I got three steps inside the gate that she had been hearing the stories about Dinas Brenin. She was so eager to catch a glimpse of the magician that she let the hood fall back a little, and in my turn I saw the wide eyes, grey-blue, full of a sort of awed curiosity and wonder. When I smiled at her and said something in greeting she ducked back inside the hood again, but this time she answered. Her voice was light and small, a child's voice, and she called me 'my lord' as if she meant it.

'What's your name?' I asked her.

'Keri, my lord.'

I hung back, to detain her. 'How is my mother today, Keri?'

But she would not answer, just took me straight to the inner court, and left me there.

That night I lay awake again, but no god spoke to me, not even to tell me she was not for me. The gods do not visit you to remind you what you know already.

By the last day of April my mother was so much better that when I went again to see her she was in the chair by the window, wearing a woollen robe over her shift, and sitting full in the sun. A quince tree, pinioned to the wall outside, was heavy with rosy cups where bees droned, and just beside her on the sill a pair of white doves strutted and crooned.

'You have news?' she asked, as soon as she saw my face.

'A messenger came in today. Vortigern is dead and the Queen with him. They say that Hengist is coming south with a vast force, including

Vortimer's brother Pascentius and the remnant of his army. Ambrosius is already on his way to meet them.'

She sat very straight, looking past me at the wall. There was a woman with her today, sitting on a stool on the other side of the bed; it was one of the nuns who had attended her at Dinas Brenin. I saw her make the sign of a cross on her breast, but Niniane sat still and straight looking past me at something, thinking.

'Tell me, then.'

I told her all I had heard about the affair at Doward. The woman crossed herself again, but my mother never moved. When I had finished, her eyes came back to me.

'And will you go now?'

'Yes. Will you give me a message for him?'

'When I see him again,' she said, 'it will be time enough.'

When I took leave of her she was still sitting staring past the winking amethysts on the wall to something distant in place and time.

Keri was not waiting, and I lingered for a while before I crossed the outer yard, slowly, towards the gate. Then I saw her waiting in the deep shadow of the gateway's arch, and quickened my step. I was turning over a host of things to say, all equally useless to prolong what could not be prolonged, but there was no need. She put out one of those pretty hands and touched my sleeve, beseechingly. 'My lord—'

Her hood was half back, and I saw tears in her eyes, I said sharply: 'What's the matter?' I believe that for a wild moment I thought she wept because I was going. 'Keri, what is it?'

'I have a toothache.'

I gaped at her. I must have looked as silly as if I had just been slapped across the face.

'Here,' she said, and put a hand to her cheek. The hood fell right back. 'It's been aching for days. Please my lord—'

I said hoarsely: 'I'm not a toothdrawer.'

'But if you would just touch it—'

'Or a magician,' I started to say, but she came close to me, and my voice strangled in my throat. She smelled of honeysuckle. Her hair was barley-gold and her eyes grey like bluebells before they open. Before I knew it she had taken my hand between both her own and raised it to her cheek.

I stiffened fractionally, as if to snatch it back, then controlled myself, and opened the palm gently along her cheek. The wide greybell eyes were as innocent as the sky. As she leaned towards me the neck of her gown hung forward slackly and I could see her breasts. Her skin was smooth as water, and her breath sweet against my cheek.

I withdrew the hand gently enough, and stood back. 'I can do nothing about it.' I suppose my voice was rough. She lowered her eyelids and stood humbly with folded hands. Her lashes were short and thick and golden as her hair. There was a tiny mole at the corner of her mouth.

I said: 'If it's no better by morning, have it drawn.'

'It's better already, my lord. It stopped aching as soon as you touched it.' Her voice was full of wonder, and her hand crept up to the cheek where mine had lain. The movement was like a caress, and I felt my blood jerk with a beat like pain. With a sudden movement she reached for my hand again and quickly, shyly, stooped forward and pressed her mouth to it.

Then the door swung open beside me and I was out in the empty street.

Chapter Four

It seemed, from what the messenger had told me, that Ambrosius had been right in his decision to make an end of Vortigern before turning on the Saxons. His reduction of Doward, and the savagery with which he did it, had their effect. Those of the invading Saxons who had ventured furthest inland began to withdraw northwards towards the wild debatable lands which had always provided a beachhead for invasion. They halted north of the Humber to fortify themselves where they could, and wait for him. At first Hengist believed that Ambrosius had at his command little more than the Breton invading army—and he was ignorant of the nature of that deadly weapon of war. He thought (it was reported) that very few of the island British had joined Ambrosius; in any case the Saxons had defeated the British, in their small tribal forces, so often that they despised them as easy meat. But now as reports reached the Saxon leader of the thousands who had flocked to the Red Dragon, and of the success at Doward, he decided to remain no longer fortified north of the Humber, but to march swiftly south again to meet the British at a place of his own choosing, where he might surprise Ambrosius and destroy his army.

Once again, Ambrosius moved with Caesar-speed. This was necessary, because where the Saxons had withdrawn, they had laid the country waste.

The end came in the second week of May, a week hot with sunshine that seemed to come from June, and interrupted by showers left over from April—a borrowed week, and, for the Saxons, a debt called in by fate. Hengist, with his preparations half complete, was caught by Ambrosius at Maesbeli, near Conan's Fort, or Kaerconan, that men sometimes call Conisburgh. This is a hilly place, with the fort on a crag, and a deep ravine running by. Here the Saxons had tried to prepare an ambush for Ambrosius' force, but Ambrosius' scouts got news of it from a Briton they came across lurking in a hilltop cave, where he had fled to keep his woman and two small children from the axes of the Northmen. So Ambrosius, forewarned, increased the speed of his march and caught up with Hengist before the ambush could be fully laid, thus forcing him into open battle.

Hengist's attempt to lay an ambush had turned the luck against him; Ambrosius, where he halted and deployed his army, had the advantage of the land. His main force, Bretons, Gauls, and the island British from the south and south-west, waited on a gentle hill, with a level field ahead over which they could attack unimpeded. Among these troops, medleywise, were other native British who had joined him, with their leaders. Behind this main army the ground rose gently, broken only by brakes of thorn and yellow gorse, to a long ridge which curved to the west in a series of low rocky hills, and on the east was thickly forested with oak. The men from Wales—mountainy men—were stationed mainly on the wings, the North Welsh in the oak forest and, separated from them by the full body of Ambrosius' army, the South Welsh on the hills to the west. These forces, lightly armed, highly mobile and with scores to settle, were to hold themselves in readiness as reinforcements, the swift hammer-blows which could be directed during battle at the weakest points of the enemy's defence. They could also be relied upon to catch and cut down any of Hengist's Saxons who broke and fled the field.

The Saxons, caught in their own trap, with this immense winged force in front of them, and behind them the rock of Kaerconan and the narrow defile where the ambush had been planned, fought like demons. But they were at a disadvantage: they started afraid—afraid of Ambrosius' reputation, of his recent ferocious victory at Doward, and more than both—so men told me—of my prophecy to Vortigern which had spread from mouth to mouth as quickly as the fires in Doward tower. And of course the omens worked the other way for Ambrosius. Battle was joined shortly before noon, and by sunset it was all over.

I saw it all. It was my first great battlefield, and I am not ashamed that it was almost my last. My battles were not fought with sword and spear. If it comes to that, I had already had a hand in the winning of Kaerconan before I ever reached it; and when I did reach it, was to find myself playing the very part that Uther had once, in jest, assigned to me.

I had ridden with Cadal as far as Caerleon, where we found a small body of Ambrosius' troops in possession of the fortress, and another on its way to invest and repair the fort at Maridunum. Also, their officer told me confidentially, to make sure that the Christian community—'all the community,' he added gravely with the ghost of a wink at me, 'such is the commander's piety—' remained safe. He had been detailed, moreover, to send some of his men back with me, to escort me to Ambrosius. My father had even thought to send some of my clothes. So I sent Cadal back, to his disgust, to do what he could about Galapas' cave, and await me there, then myself rode north-east with the escort.

We came up with the army just outside Kaerconan. The troops were already deployed for battle and there was no question of seeing the commander, so we withdrew, as instructed, to the western hill where the men of the South Welsh tribes eyed one another distrustfully over swords held ready for the Saxons below. The men of my escort troop eyed me in something the same manner: they had not intruded on my silence on the ride, and it was plain they held me in some awe, not only as Ambrosius' acknowledged son, but as 'Vortigern's prophet'—a title which had already stuck to me and which it took me some years to shed. When I reported with them to the officer in charge, and asked him to assign me a place in his troop, he was horrified, and begged me quite seriously to stay out of the fight, but to find some place where the men could see me, and know, as he put it, 'that the prophet was here with them'. In the end I did as he wished, and withdrew to the top of a small rocky crag hard by where, wrapping my cloak about me, I prepared to watch the battlefield spread out below like a moving map.

Ambrosius himself was in the centre; I could see the white stallion with the Red Dragon glimmering above it. Out to the right Uther's blue cloak glinted as his horse cantered along the lines. The leader of the left wing I did not immediately recognise; a grey horse, a big, heavy-built figure striding it, a standard bearing some device in white which I could not at first distinguish. Then I saw what it was. A boar. The Boar of Cornwall. Ambrosius' commander of the left was none other than the greybeard Gorlois, lord of Tintagel.

Nothing could be read of the order in which the Saxons had assembled. All my life I had heard of the ferocity of these great blond giants, and all British children were brought up from babyhood on stories of their terror. They went mad in war, men said, and could fight bleeding from a dozen wounds, with no apparent lessening of strength or ferocity. And what they had in strength and cruelty they lacked in discipline. This seemed, indeed, to be so. There was no order to be read in the vast surge of glinting metal and tossing horsehair which was perpetually on the move, like a flood waiting for the dam to break.

Even from the distance I could pick out Hengist and his brother, giants with long moustaches sweeping to their chests, and long hair flying as they spurred their shaggy, tough little horses up and down the ranks. They were shouting, and echoes of the shouts came clearly; prayers to the gods, vows, exhortations, commands, which rose towards a ferocious crescendo, till on the last wild shout of 'Kill, kill, kill!' the axeheads swung up, glinting in the May sunlight, and the pack surged forward towards the ordered lines of Ambrosius' army.

The two hosts met with a shock that sent the jackdaws squalling up from Kaerconan, and seemed to splinter the very air. It was impossible, even from my point of vantage, to see which way the fight–or rather, the several different movements of the fight–were going. At one moment it seemed as if the Saxons with their axes and winged helms were boring a way into the British host; at the next, you would see a knot of Saxons cut off in a sea of British, and then, apparently engulfed, vanish. Ambrosius' centre block met the main shock of the charge, then Uther's cavalry, with a swift flanking movement, came in from the east. The men of Cornwall under Gorlois held back at first, but as soon as the Saxons' front line began to waver, they came in like a hammer-blow from the left and smashed it apart. After that the field broke up into chaos. Everywhere men were fighting in small groups, or even singly and hand to hand. The noise, the clash and shouting, even the smell of sweat and blood mingled, seemed to come up to this high perch where I sat with my cloak about me, watching. Immediately below me I was conscious of the stirring and muttering of the Welshmen, then the sudden cheer as a troop of Saxons broke and galloped in our direction. In a moment the hilltop was empty save for me, only that the clamour seemed to have washed nearer, round the foot of the hill like the tide coming in fast. A robin lighted on a blackthorn at my elbow, and began to sing. The sound came high and sweet and uncaring through all the noise of battle. To this day, whenever I think of the battle for Kaerconan, it brings to mind a robin's song, mingled with the croaking of the ravens. For they were already circling, high overhead: men say they can hear the clash of swords ten miles off.

It was finished by sunset. Eldol, Duke of Gloucester, dragged Hengist from his horse under the very walls of Kaerconan to which he had turned to flee, and the rest of the Saxons broke and fled, some to escape, but many to be cut down in the hills, or the narrow defile at the foot of Kaerconan. At first dusk, torches were lit at the gate of the fortress, the gates were thrown open, and Ambrosius' white stallion paced across the bridge and into the stronghold, leaving the field to the ravens, the priests and the burial parties.

I did not seek him out straight away. Let him bury his dead and clear the fortress. There was work for me down there among the wounded, and besides, there was no hurry now to give him my mother's message. While I had sat there in the May sunlight between the robin's song and the crash of battle, I knew that she had sickened again, and was already dead.

Chapter Five

I made my way downhill between the clumps of gorse and the thorn trees. The Welsh troops had vanished, long since, to a man; and isolated shouts and battle cries showed where small parties were still hunting down the fugitives in forest and hill.

Below, on the plain, the fighting was over. They were carrying the wounded into Kaerconan. Torches weaved everywhere, till the plain was all light and smoke. Men shouted to one another, and the cries and groans of the wounded came up clearly, with the occasional scream of a horse, the sharp commands from the officers, and the tramp of the stretcher-bearers' feet. Here and there, in the dark corners away from the torchlight, men scurried singly or in pairs among the heaped bodies. One saw them stoop, straighten, and scurry off. Sometimes where they paused there was a cry, a sudden moan, sometimes the brief flash of metal or the quick downstroke of a shortened blow. Looters, rummaging among the dead and dying, keeping a few steps ahead of the official salvage parties. The ravens were coming down; I saw the tilt and slide of their black wings hovering above the torches, and a pair perched, waiting, on a rock not far from me. With nightfall the rats would be there, too, running up from the damp roots of the castle walls to attack the dead bodies.

The work of salvaging the living was being done as fast and efficiently as everything else the Count's army undertook. Once they were all within, the gates would be shut. I would seek him out, I decided, after the first tasks were done. He would already have been told that I was safely here, and he would guess I had gone to work with the doctors. There would be time, later, to eat, and then it would be time enough to talk to him.

On the field, as I made my way across, the stretcher parties still strove to separate friend from foe. The Saxon dead had been flung into a heap in the centre of the field; I guessed they would be burned according to custom. Beside the growing hill of bodies a platoon stood guard over the glittering pile of arms and ornaments taken from the dead men. The British dead were being laid nearer the wall, in rows for identification. There were small parties of men, each with an officer, bending over them one by one. As I picked my way through trampled mud oily and stinking with blood and slime I passed, among the armed and staring dead, the bodies of half a dozen ragged men–peasants or outlaws by the look of them. These would be looters, cut down or speared by the soldiers. One of them still twitched like a pinned moth, hastily speared to the ground by a broken Saxon weapon which had been left in his body. I hesitated, then went and bent over him. He watched me–he was beyond speech–and I could see he still hoped. If he had been cleanly speared, I would have drawn the blade out and let him go with the blood, but as it was, there was a quicker way for him. I drew my dagger, pulled my cloak aside out of the way, and carefully, so that I would be out of the jet of blood, stuck my dagger in at the side of his throat. I wiped it on the dead man's rags, and straightened to find a cold pair of eyes watching me above a levelled short-sword three paces away.

Mercifully, it was a man I knew. I saw him recognise me, then he laughed and lowered his sword.

'You're lucky. I nearly gave it to you in the back.'

'I didn't think of that.' I slid the dagger back into its sheath. 'It would have been a pity to die for stealing from that. What did you think he had worth taking?'

'You'd be surprised what you catch them taking. Anything from a corn plaster to a broken sandal strap.' He jerked his head towards the high walls of the fortress. 'He's been asking where you were.'

'I'm on my way.'

'They say you foretold this, Merlin? And Doward, too?'

'I said the Red Dragon would overcome the White,' I said. 'But I think this is not the end yet. What happened to Hengist?'

'Yonder.' He nodded again towards the citadel. 'He made for the fort when the Saxon line broke, and was captured just by the gate.'

'I saw that. He's inside, then? Still alive?'

'Yes.'

'And Octa? His son?'

'Got away. He and the cousin–Eosa, isn't it?–galloped north.'

'So it isn't the end. Has he sent after them?'

'Not yet. He says there's time enough.' He eyed me. 'Is there?'

'How would I know?' I was unhelpful. 'How long does he plan to stay here? A few days?'

'Three, he says. Time to bury the dead.'

'What will he do with Hengist?'

'What do you think?' He made a little chopping movement downwards with the edge of his hand. 'And long overdue, if you ask me. They're talking about it in there, but you could hardly call it a trial. The Count's said nothing as yet, but Uther's roaring to have him killed, and the priests want a bit of cold blood to round the day off with. Well, I'll have to get back to work, see if I can catch more civilians looting.' He added as he turned away: 'We saw you up there on the hill during the fighting. People were saying it was an omen.'

He went. A raven flapped down from behind me with a croak, and settled

on the breast of the man I had killed. I called to a torch-bearer to light me
the rest of the way, and made for the main gate of the fortress.

While I was still some way short of the bridge a blaze of tossing torches
came out, and in the middle of them, bound and held, the big blond giant
that I knew must be Hengist himself. Ambrosius' troops formed a hollow
square, and into this space his captors dragged the Saxon leader, and there
must have forced him to his knees, for the flaxen head vanished behind the
close ranks of the British. I saw Ambrosius himself then, coming out over
the bridge, followed closely on his left by Uther, and on his other side by a
man I did not know, in the robe of a Christian bishop, still splashed with
mud and blood. Others crowded behind them. The bishop was talking
earnestly in Ambrosius' ear. Ambrosius' face was a mask, the cold,
expressionless mask I knew so well. I heard him say what sounded like,
'You will see, they will be satisfied,' and then, shortly, something else that
caused the bishop at last to fall silent.

Ambrosius took his place. I saw him nod to an officer. There was a word
of command, followed by the whistle and thud of a blow. A sound—it could
hardly be called a growl—of satisfaction from the watching men. The
bishop's voice, hoarse with triumph: 'So perish all pagan enemies of the one
true God! Let his body be thrown now to the wolves and kites!' And then
Ambrosius' voice, cold and quiet: 'He will go to his own gods with his army
round him, in the manner of his people.' Then to the officer: 'Send me word
when all is ready, and I will come.'

The bishop started to shout again, but Ambrosius turned away
unheeding and, with Uther and the other captains, strode back across the
bridge and into the fortress. I followed. Spears flashed down to bar my way
then—the place was garrisoned by Ambrosius' Bretons—I was recognised,
and the spears withdrawn.

Inside the fortress was a wide square courtyard, now full of a bustling,
trampling confusion of men and horses. At the far side a shallow flight of
steps led to the door of the main hall and tower. Ambrosius' party was
mounting the steps, but I turned aside. There was no need to ask where the
wounded had been taken. On the east side of the square a long double-
storeyed building had been organised as a dressing station; the sounds
coming from this guided me. I was hailed thankfully by the doctor in
charge, a man called Gandar, who had taught me in Brittany, and who
avowedly had no use either for priests or magicians, but who very much
needed another pair of trained hands. He assigned me a couple of orderlies,
found me some instruments and box of salves and medicines, and thrust
me—literally—into a long room that was little better than a roofed shed, but
which now held some fifty wounded men. I stripped to the waist and started
work.

Somewhere around midnight the worst was done and things were
quieter. I was at the far end of my section when a slight stir near the
entrance made me look round to see Ambrosius, with Gandar and two
officers, come quietly in and walk down the row of wounded, stopping by
each man to talk or, with those worst wounded, to question the doctor in an
undertone.

I was stitching a thigh wound—it was clean, and would heal, but it was deep and jagged, and to everyone's relief the man had fainted—when the group reached me. I did not look up, and Ambrosius waited in silence until I had done and, reaching for the dressings the orderly had prepared, bandaged the wound. I finished, and got to my feet as the orderly came back with a bowl of water. I plunged my hands into this, and looked up to see Ambrosius smiling. He was still in his hacked and spattered armour, but he looked fresh and alert, and ready if necessary to start another battle. I could see the wounded men watching him as if they would draw strength just from the sight.

'My lord,' I said.

He stooped over the unconscious man. 'How is he?'

'A flesh wound. He'll recover, and live to be thankful it wasn't a few inches to the left.'

'You've done a good job, I see.' Then as I finished drying my hands and dismissed the orderly with a word of thanks, Ambrosius put out his own hand. 'And now, welcome. I believe we owe you quite a lot, Merlin. I don't mean for this; I mean for Doward, and for today as well. At any rate the men think so, and if soldiers decide something is lucky, then it is lucky. Well, I'm glad to see you safe. You have news for me, I believe.'

'Yes.' I said it without expression, because of the men with us, but I saw the smile fade from his eyes. He hesitated, then said quietly: 'Gentlemen, give us leave.' They went. He and I faced one another across the body of the unconscious man. Nearby a soldier tossed and moaned, and another cried out and bit the sound back. The place smelt vile, of blood and drying sweat and sickness.

'What is this news?'

'It concerns my mother.'

I think he already knew what I was going to tell him. He spoke slowly, measuring the words, as if each one carried with it some weight that he ought to feel. 'The men who rode here with you . . . they brought me news of her. She had been ill, but was recovered, they said, and safely back in Maridunum. Was this not true?'

'It was true when I left Maridunum. If I had known the illness was mortal, I would not have left her.'

' "Was" mortal?'

'Yes, my lord.'

He was silent, looking down, but without seeing him, at the wounded man. The latter was beginning to stir; soon he would be back with the pain and the stench and the fear of mortality. I said: 'Shall we go out into the air? I've finished here. I'll send someone back to this man.'

'Yes. And you must get your clothes. It's a cool night.' Then, still without moving: 'When did she die?'

'At sunset today.'

He looked up quickly at that, his eyes narrow and intent, then he nodded, accepting it. He turned to go out, gesturing me to walk with him. As we went he asked me: 'Do you suppose she knew?'

'I think so, yes.'

'She sent no message?'

'Not directly. She said, "When we meet again, it will be soon enough." '

She is a Christian, remember. They believe—'

'I know what they believe.'

Some commotion outside made itself heard, a voice breaking a couple of commands, feet tramping. Ambrosius paused, listening. Someone was coming our way, quickly.

'We'll talk later, Merlin. You have a lot to tell me. But first we must send Hengist's spirit to join his fathers. Come.'

They had heaped the Saxon dead high on a great stack of wood, and poured oil and pitch over them. At the top of the pyramid, on a platform roughly nailed together of planks, lay Hengist. How Ambrosius had stopped them robbing him I shall never know, but he had not been robbed. His shield lay on his breast, and a sword by his right hand. They had hidden the severed neck with a broad leather collar of the kind some soldiers use for throat guards. It was studded with gold. A cloak covered his body from throat to feet, and its scarlet folds flowed down over the rough wood.

As soon as the torches were thrust in below, the flames caught greedily. It was a still night, and the smoke poured upwards in a thick black column laced with fire. The edges of Hengist's cloak caught, blackened, curled, and then he was lost to sight in the gush of smoke and flames. The fire cracked like whips and as the logs burned and broke, men ran, sweating and blackened, to throw more in. Even from where we stood, well back, the heat was intense, and the smell of burnt pitch and roasting meat came in sickening gusts on the damp night air. Beyond the lighted ring of watching men torches moved still on the battlefield, and one could hear the steady thud of spades striking into the earth for the British dead. Beyond the brilliant pyre, beyond the dark slopes of the far hills, the May moon hung, faint through the smoke.

'What do you see?'

Ambrosius' voice made me start. I looked at him, surprised. 'See?'

'In the fire, Merlin the prophet.'

'Nothing but dead men roasting.'

'Then look and see something for me, Merlin. Where has Octa gone?'

I laughed. 'How should I know? I told you all I could see.'

But he did not smile. 'Look harder. Tell me where Octa has gone. And Eosa. Where they will dig themselves in to wait for me. And how soon.'

'I told you. I don't look for things. If it is the god's will that they should come to me, they come out of the flames, or out of the black night, and they come silently like an arrow out of ambush. I do not go to find the bowman; all I can do is stand with my breast bare and wait for the arrow to hit me.'

'Then do it now.' He spoke strongly, stubbornly. I saw he was quite serious. 'You saw for Vortigern.'

'You call it "for" him? To prophesy his death? When I did that, my lord, I did not even know what I was saying. I suppose Gorlois told you what happened—even now, I couldn't tell you myself. I neither know when it will come, nor when it will leave me.'

'Only today you knew about Niniane, and without either fire or darkness.'

'That's true. But I can't tell you how, any more than how I knew what I told Vortigern.'

'The men call you "Vortigern's prophet". You prophesied victory for us, and we had it, here and at Doward. The men believe you and have faith in you. So have I. Is it not a better title now to be "Ambrosius' prophet?" '

'My lord, you know I would take any title from you that you cared to bestow. But this comes from somewhere else. I cannot call it, but I know that if it matters it will come. And when it comes, be sure I will tell you. You know I am at your service. Now, about Octa and Eosa I know nothing. I can only guess—and guess as a man. They fight still under the White Dragon, do they?'

His eyes narrowed. 'Yes.'

'Then what Vortigern's prophet said must still hold good.'

'I can tell the men this?'

'If they need it. When do you plan to march?'

'In three days.'

'Aiming for where?'

'York.'

I turned up a hand. 'Then your guess as a commander is probably as good as my guess as a magician. Will you take me?'

He smiled. 'Will you be any use to me?'

'Probably not as a prophet. But do you need an engineer? Or an apprentice doctor? Or even a singer?'

He laughed. 'A host in yourself, I know. As long as you don't turn priest on me, Merlin. I have enough of them.'

'You needn't be afraid of that.'

The flames were dying down. The officer in charge of the proceedings approached, saluted, and asked if the men might be dismissed. Ambrosius gave him leave, then looked at me. 'Come with me to York, then. I shall have work for you there. Real work. They tell me the place is half ruined, and I'll need someone to help direct the engineers. Tremorinus is at Caerleon. Now, find Caius Valerius and tell him to look after you, and bring you to me in an hour's time.' He added over his shoulder as he turned away: 'And in the meantime if anything should come to you out of the dark like an arrow, you'll let me know?'

'Unless it really is an arrow.'

He laughed, and went.

Uther was beside me suddenly. 'Well, Merlin the bastard? They're saying you won the battle for us from the hilltop?' I noticed, with surprise, that there was no malice in his tone. His manner was relaxed, easy, almost gay, like that of a prisoner let loose. I supposed this was indeed how he felt after the long frustration of the years in Brittany. Left to himself Uther would have charged across the Narrow Sea before he was fairly into manhood, and been valiantly smashed in pieces for his pains. Now, like a hawk being flown for the first time at the quarry, he was feeling his power. I could feel it, too: it clothed him like folded wings. I said something in greeting, but he interrupted me. 'Did you see anything in the flames just now?'

'Oh, not you, too,' I said warmly. 'The commander seems to think all I have to do is to look at a torch and tell the future. I've been trying to explain it doesn't work like that.'

'You disappoint me. I was going to ask you to tell my fortune.'

'Oh, Eros, that's easy enough. In about an hour's time, as soon as you've settled your men, you'll be bedded down with a girl.'

'It's not as much of a certainty as all that. How the devil did you know I'd managed to find one? They're not very thick on the ground just here—there's only about one man in fifty managed to get one. I was lucky.'

'That's what I mean,' I said. 'Given fifty men and only one woman amongst them, then Uther has the woman. That's what I call one of the certainties of life. Where will I find Caius Valerius?'

'I'll send someone to show you. I'd come myself, only I'm keeping out of his way.'

'Why?'

'When we tossed for the girl, he lost,' said Uther cheerfully. 'He'll have plenty of time to look after you. In fact, all night. Come along.'

Chapter Six

We went into York three days before the end of May.

Ambrosius' scouts had confirmed his guess about York; there was a good road north from Kaerconan, and Octa had fled up this with Eosa his kinsman, and had taken refuge in the fortified city which the Romans called Eboracum, and the Saxons Eoforwick, or York. But the fortifications at York were in poor repair, and the inhabitants, when they heard of Ambrosius' resounding victory at Kaerconan, offered the fleeing Saxons cold comfort. For all Octa's speed, Ambrosius was barely two days behind him, and the sight of our vast army, rested, and reinforced by fresh British allies encouraged by the Red Dragon's victories, the Saxons, doubting whether they could hold the city against him, decided to beg for mercy.

I saw it myself, being right up in the van with the siege engines, under the walls. In its way it was more unpleasant even than a battle. The Saxon leader was a big man, blond like his father, and young. He appeared before Ambrosius stripped to his trews, which were of coarse stuff bound with thongs. His wrists likewise were bound, this time with a chain, and his head and body were smeared with dust, a token of humiliation he hardly needed. His eyes were angry, and I could see he had been forced into this by the cowardice—or wisdom, as you care to call it—of the group of Saxon and British notables who crowded behind him out of the city gate, begging Ambrosius for mercy on themselves and their families.

This time he gave it. He demanded only that the remnants of the Saxon army should withdraw to the north, beyond the old Wall of Hadrian, which (he said) he would count the border of his realm. The lands beyond this, so men say, are wild and sullen, and scarcely habitable, but Octa took his liberty gladly enough, and after him, eager for the same mercy, came his cousin Eosa throwing himself on Ambrosius' bounty. He received it, and the city of York opened its gates to its new king.

Ambrosius' first occupation of a town was always to follow the same pattern. First of all the establishment of order; he would never allow the British auxiliaries into the town; his own troops from Less Britain, with no local loyalties, were the ones that established and held order. The streets were cleaned, the fortifications temporarily repaired, and plans drawn up for the future work and put into the hands of a small group of skilled engineers who were to call on local labour. Then a meeting of the city's leaders, a discussion on future policy, an oath of loyalty to Ambrosius, and arrangements made for the garrisoning of the city when the army departed. Finally a religious ceremony of thanksgiving with a feast and a public holiday.

In York, the first great city invested by Ambrosius, the ceremony was held in the church, on a blazing day near the end of June, and in the presence of the whole army, and a vast crowd of people.

I had already attended a private ceremony elsewhere.

It was not to be expected that there was still a temple of Mithras in York. The worship was forbidden, and in any case would have vanished when the last legion left the Saxon Shore almost a century ago, but in the day of the legions the temple at York had been one of the finest in the country. Since there was no natural cave nearby, it had originally been built below the house of the Roman commander, in a large cellar, and because of this the Christians had not been able to desecrate and destroy it, as was their wont with the sacred places of other men. But time and damp had done their work, and the sanctuary had crumbled into disrepair. Once, under a Christian governor, there had been an attempt to turn the place into a chapel-crypt, but the next governor had been outspokenly, not to say violently, opposed to this. He was a Christian himself, but he saw no reason why the perfectly good cellar under his house should not be used for what (to him) was the real purpose of a cellar, namely, to store wine. And a wine store it had remained, till the day Uther sent a working party down to clean and repair it for the meeting, which was to be held on the god's own feast day, the sixteenth day of June. This time the meeting was secret, not from fear, but from policy, since the official thanksgiving would be Christian, and Ambrosius would be there to offer thanks in the presence of the bishops and all the people. I myself had not seen the sanctuary, having been employed during my first days in York on the restoring of the Christian church in time for the public ceremony. But on the feast of Mithras I was to present myself at the underground temple with others of my own grade. Most of these were men I did not know, or could not identify by the voice behind the mask; but Uther was recognisable, and my father would of course be there, in his office as Courier of the Sun.

The door of the temple was closed. We of the lowest grade waited our turn in the antechamber.

This was a smallish, square room, lit only by the two torches held in the hands of the statues one to either side of the temple door. Above the doorway was the old stone mask of a lion, worn and fretted, part of the wall.

To either side, as worn and chipped, and with noses and members broken and hacked away, the two stone torch-bearers still looked ancient and dignified. The anteroom was chill, in spite of the torches, and smelled of smoke. I felt the cold at work on my body; it struck up from the stone floor into my bare feet, and under the long robe of white wool I was naked. But just as the first shiver ran up my skin, the temple door opened, and in an instant all was light and colour and fire.

Even now, after all these years, and knowing all that I have learnt in a lifetime, I cannot find it in me to break the vow I made of silence and secrecy. Nor, so far as I know, has any man done so. Men say that what you are taught when young, can never be fully expunged from your mind, and I know that I, myself, have never escaped the spell of the secret god who led me to Brittany and threw me at my father's feet. Indeed, whether because of the curb on the spirit of which I have already written, or whether by intervention of the god himself, I find that my memory of his worship has gone into a blur, as if it was a dream. And a dream it may be, not of this time alone, but made up of all the other times, from the first vision of the midnight field, to this night's ceremony, which was the last.

A few things I remember. More torch-bearers of stone. The long benches to either side of the centre aisle where men reclined in their bright robes, the masks turned to us, eyes watchful. The steps at the far end, and the great apse with the arch like a cave-mouth opening on the cave within, where, under the star-studded roof, was the old relief in stone of Mithras at the bull-slaying. It must have been somehow protected from the hammers of the god-breakers, for it was still strongly carved and dramatic. There he was, in the light of the torches, the young man of the standing stone, the fellow in the cap, kneeling on the fallen bull and, with his head turned away in sorrow, striking the sword into its throat. At the foot of the steps stood the fire-altars, one to each side. Beside one of them a man robed and masked as a Lion, with a rod in his left hand. Beside the other the Heliodromos, the Courier of the Sun. And at the head of the steps, in the centre of the apse, the Father waiting to receive us.

My Raven mask had poor eyeholes, and I could only see straight forward. It would not have been seemly to look from side to side with that pointed bird-mask, so I stood listening to the voices, and wondering how many friends were here, how many men I knew. The only one I could be sure of was the Courier, tall and quiet there by the altar fire, and one of the Lions, either him by the archway, or one of the grade who watched from somewhere along the makeshift benches.

This was the frame of the ceremony, and all that I can remember, except the end. The officiating Lion was not Uther, after all. He was a shorter man, of thick build, and seemingly older than Uther, and the blow he struck me was no more than the ritual tap, without the sting that Uther usually managed to put into it. Nor was Ambrosius the Courier. As the latter handed me the token meal of bread and wine, I saw the ring on the little finger of his left hand, made of gold, enclosing a stone of red jasper with a dragon crest carved small. But when he lifted the cup to my mouth, and the scarlet robe slipped back from his arm, I saw a familiar scar white on the brown flesh, and looked up to meet the blue eyes behind the mask, alight with a spark of amusement that quickened to laughter as I started, and spilled the wine. Uther had stepped up two grades, it seemed, in the time since I had last attended the mysteries. And since there was no other Courier present, there was only one place for Ambrosius . . .

I turned from the Courier to kneel at the Father's feet. But the hands which took my own between them for the vow were the hands of an old man, and when I looked up, the eyes behind the mask were the eyes of a stranger.

Eight days later was the official ceremony of thanksgiving. Ambrosius was there, with all his officers, even Uther, 'for', said my father to me afterwards when we were alone, 'as you will find, all gods who are born of the light are brothers, and in this land, if Mithras who gives us victory is to bear the face of Christ, why, then, we worship Christ.'

We never spoke of it again.

The capitulation of York marked the end of the first stage of Ambrosius' campaign. After York we went to London in easy stages, and with no more fighting, unless you count a few skirmishes by the way. What the King had to undertake now was the enormous work of reconstruction and the consolidation of his kingdom. In every town and strongpoint he left garrisons of tried men under trusted officers, and appointed his own engineers to help organise the work of rebuilding and repairing towns, roads and fortresses. Everywhere the picture was the same; once-fine buildings ruined or damaged almost beyond repair; roads half obliterated through neglect; villages destroyed and people hiding fearfully in caves and forests; places of worship pulled down or polluted. It was as if the stupidity and lawless greed of the Saxon hordes had cast a blight over the whole land. Everything that had given light—art, song, learning, worship, the ceremonial meetings of the people, the feasts at Easter or Hallowmass or midwinter, even the arts of husbandry, all these had vanished under the dark clouds on which rode the northern gods of war and thunder. And they had been invited here by Vortigern, a British king. This, now, was all that people remembered. They forgot that Vortigern had reigned well enough for ten years, and adequately for a few more, before he found that the war-spirit he had unleashed on his country had outgrown his control. They remembered only that he had gained his throne by bloodshed and treachery and the murder of a kinsman—and that the kinsman had been the true king. So they came flocking now to Ambrosius, calling on him the blessings of their different gods, hailing him with joy as King, the first 'King of all Britain', the first shining chance for the country to be one.

Other men have told the story of Ambrosius' crowning and his first work as King of Britain; it has even been written down, so here I will only say that I was with him for the first two years as I have told, but then, in the spring of my twentieth year, I left him. I had had enough of councils and marching, and long legal discussions where Ambrosius tried to reimpose the laws that had fallen into disuse, and the everlasting meetings with elders and bishops droning like bees, days and weeks for every drop of honey. I was even tired of building and designing; this was the only work I had done for him in all the long months I served with the army. I knew at last that I must leave him, get out of the press of affairs that surrounded him; the god does not speak to those who have no time to listen. The mind must seek out what it needs to feed on, and it came to me at last that what work I had to do, I must do among the quiet of my own hills. So in spring, when we came to Winchester, I sent a message to Cadal, then sought Ambrosius out to tell him I must go.

He listened half absently; cares pressed heavily on him these days, and the years which had sat lightly on him before now seemed to weigh him down. I have noticed that this is often the way with men who set their lives towards the distant glow of one high beacon; when the hilltop is reached and there is nowhere further to climb, and all that is left is to pile more on the flame and keep the beacon burning, why, then, they sit down beside it and grow old. Where their leaping blood warmed them before, now the beacon fire must do it from without. So it was with Ambrosius. The King who sat in his great chair at Winchester and listened to me was not the young commander whom I had faced across the map-strewn table in Less Britain, or even the Courier of Mithras who had ridden to me across the frostbound field.

'I cannot hold you,' he said. 'You are not an officer of mine, you are only my son. You will go where you wish.'

'I serve you. You know that. But I know now how best I can serve you. You spoke the other day of sending a troop towards Caerleon. Who's going?'

He looked down at a paper. A year ago he would have known without looking. 'Priscus, Valens. Probably Sidonius. They go in two days' time.'

'Then I'll go with them.'

He looked at me. Suddenly it was the old Ambrosius back again. 'An arrow out of the dark?'

'You might say so. I know I must go.'

'Then go safely. And some day, come back to me.'

Someone interrupted us then. When I left him he was already going, word by word, through some laborious draft of the new statutes for the city.

Chapter Seven

The road from Winchester to Caerleon is a good one, the weather was fine and dry, so we did not halt in Sarum, but held on northwards while the light lasted, straight across the Great Plain.

A short way beyond Sarum lies the place where Ambrosius was born. I cannot even call to mind now what name it had gone by in the past, but already it was being called by his name, Amberesburg, or Amesbury. I had never been that way, and had a mind to see it, so we pressed on, and arrived just before sunset. I, together with the officers, was given comfortable lodging with the head man of the town—it was little more than a village, but very conscious now of its standing as the King's birthplace. Not far away was the spot where, many years ago, some hundred or more British nobles had been treacherously massacred by the Saxons and buried in a common grave. This place lay some way west of Amesbury, beyond the stone circle that men call the Giants' Dance, or the Dance of the Hanging Stones.

I had long heard about the Dance and had been curious to see it, so when the troop reached Amesbury, and were preparing to settle in for the night, I made my excuses to my host, and rode out westwards alone over the open plain. Here, for mile on mile, the long plain stretches without hill or valley, unbroken save for clumps of thorn trees and gorse, and here and there a solitary oak stripped by the winds. The sun sets late, and this evening as I rode my tired horse slowly westwards the sky ahead of me was still tinged with the last rays, while behind me in the east the clouds of evening piled slate-blue, and one early star came out.

I think I had been expecting the Dance to be much less impressive than the ranked armies of stones I had grown accustomed to in Brittany, something, perhaps, on the scale of the circle on the druids' island. But these stones were enormous, bigger than any I had ever seen; and their very isolation, standing as they did in the centre of that vast and empty plain, struck the heart with awe.

I rode some of the way round, slowly, staring, then dismounted and, leaving my horse to graze, walked forward between two standing stones of the outer circle. My shadow, thrown ahead of me between their shadows, was tiny, a pygmy thing. I paused involuntarily, as if the giants had linked hands to stop me.

Ambrosius had asked me if this had been 'an arrow out of the dark'. I had told him yes, and this was true, but I had yet to find out why I had been brought here. All I knew was that, now I was here, I wished myself away. I had felt something of the same thing in Brittany as I first passed among the avenues of stones; a breathing on the back of the neck as if something older than time were looking over one's shoulder; but this was not quite the same. It was as if the ground, the stones that I touched, though still warm from the spring sunlight, were breathing cold from somewhere deep below.

Half reluctantly, I walked forward. The light was going rapidly, and to pick one's way into the centre needed care. Time and storm—and perhaps the gods of war—had done their work, and many of the stones were cast down to lie haphazard, but the pattern could still be discerned. It was a circle, but like nothing I had seen in Brittany, like nothing I had even imagined. There had been, originally, an outer circle of the huge stones, and where a crescent of these still stood I saw that the uprights were crowned with a continuous lintel of stones as vast as themselves, a great linked curve of stone, standing like a giants' fence across the sky. Here and there others of the outer circle were still standing, but most had fallen, or were leaning at drunken angles, with the lintel stones beside them on the ground. Within the bigger circle was a smaller one of uprights, and some of the outer giants had fallen against these and brought them flat. Within these again, marking the centre, was a horse-shoe of enormous stones, crowned in pairs. Three of these trilithons stood intact; the fourth had fallen, and brought its neighbour down with it. Echoing this once again was an inner horse-shoe of smaller stones, nearly all standing. The centre was empty, and crossed with shadows.

The sun had gone, and with its going the western sky drained of colour, leaving one bright star in a swimming sea of green. I stood still. It was very quiet, so quiet that I could hear the sound of my horse cropping the turf, and the thin jingle of his bit as he moved. The only other sound was the whispering chatter of nesting starlings among the great trilithons overhead. The starling is a bird sacred to the druids, and I had heard that in past time the Dance had been used for worship by the druid priests. There are many stories about the Dance, how the stones were brought from Africa, and put up by giants of old, or how they were the giants themselves, caught and turned to stone by a curse as they danced in a ring. But it was not giants or curses that were breathing the cold now from the ground and from the stones; these stones had been put here by men, and their raising had been sung by poets, like the old blind man of Brittany. A lingering shred of light caught the stone near me; the huge knob of stone on one sandstone surface echoed the hole in the fallen lintel alongside it. These tenons and sockets had been fashioned by men, craftsmen such as I had watched almost daily for the last few years, in Less Britain, then in York, London, Winchester. And massive as they were, giants' building as they seemed to be, they had been raised by the hands of workmen, to the commands of engineers, and to the sound of music such as I had heard from the blind singer of Kerrec.

I walked slowly forward across the circle's centre. The faint light in the western sky threw my shadow slanting ahead of me, and etched, momentarily in fleeting light, the shape of an axe, two-headed, on one of the stones. I hesitated, then turned to look. My shadow wavered and dipped. I trod in a shallow pit and fell, measuring my length.

It was only a depression in the ground, the kind that might have been made, years past, by the falling of one of the great stones. Or by a grave . . .

There was no stone nearby of such a size, no sign of digging, no one buried here. The turf was smooth, and grazed by sheep and cattle, and under my hands as I picked myself up slowly, were the scented, frilled stars of daisies. But as I lay I had felt the cold strike up from below, in a pang as sudden as an arrow striking, and I knew that this was why I had been brought here.

I caught my horse, mounted and rode the two miles back to my father's birthplace.

We reached Caerleon four days later to find the place completely changed. Ambrosius intended to use it as one of his three main stations along with London and York, and Tremorinus himself had been working there. The walls had been rebuilt, the bridge repaired, the river dredged and its banks strengthened, and the whole of the east barrack block rebuilt. In earlier times the military settlement at Caerleon, circled by low hills and guarded by a curve of the river, had been a vast place; there was no need for even half of it now, so Tremorinus had pulled down what remained of the western barrack blocks and used the material on the spot to build the new quarters, the baths, and some brand new kitchens. The old ones had been in even worse condition than the bath-house at Maridunum, and now, 'You'll have every man in Britain asking to be posted here,' I told Tremorinus, and he looked pleased.

'We'll not be ready a moment too soon,' he said. 'The rumour's going round of fresh trouble coming. Have you heard anything?'

'Nothing. But if it's recent news I wouldn't have had it. We've been on the move for nearly a week. What kind of trouble? Not Octa again, surely?'

'No, Pascentius.' This was Vortimer's brother who had fought with him in the rebellion, and fled north after Vortimer's death. 'You knew he took ship to Germany? They say he'll come back.'

'Give him time,' I said, 'you may be sure he will. Well, you'll send me any news that comes?'

'Send you? You're not staying here?'

'No. I'm going on to Maridunum. It's my home, you know.'

'I had forgotten. Well, perhaps we'll see something of you; I'll be here myself a bit longer—we've started work on the church now.' He grinned. 'The bishop's been at me like a gadfly: it seems I should have been thinking of that before I spent so much time on the things of this earth. And there's talk, too, of putting up some kind of monument to the King's victories. A triumphal arch, some say, the old Roman style of thing. Of course they're saying here in Caerleon that we should build the church for that—the glory of God with Ambrosius thrown in. Though myself I think if any bishop should get the credit of God's glory and the King's combined it should be Gloucester—old Eldad laid about him with the best of them. Did you see him?'

'I heard him.'

He laughed. 'Well, in any case you'll stay tonight, I hope? Have supper with me.'

'Thanks. I'd like to.'

We talked late into the night, and he showed me some of his plans and designs, and seemed flatteringly anxious that I should come back from Maridunum to see the various stages of the building. I promised, and next day left Caerleon alone, parrying an equally flattering and urgent request from the camp commandant to let him give me an escort. But I refused, and in late afternoon came, alone, at last in sight of my own hills. There were rain clouds massing in the west, but in front of them, like a bright curtain, the slanting sunlight. One could see on a day like this why the green hills of Wales had been called the Black Mountains, and the valleys running through them the Valleys of Gold. Bars of sunlight lay along the trees of the golden valleys, and the hills stood slate-blue or black behind them, with their tops supporting the sky.

I took two days for the journey, going easily, and noticing by the way how the land seemed already to have got back its bloom of peace. A farmer building a wall barely looked my way as I rode by, and a young girl minding a flock of sheep smiled at me. And when I got to the mill on the Tywy, it seemed to be working normally; there were grain sacks piled in the yard, and I could hear the clack-clack-clack of the turning wheel.

I passed the bottom of the path which led up to the cave, and held on straight for the town. I believe I told myself that my first duty and concern was to visit St Peter's to ask about my mother's death, and to see where she was buried. But when I got from my horse at the nunnery gate and lifted a hand to the bell, I knew from the knocking of my heart that I had told myself a lie.

I could have spared myself the deception; it was the old portress who let me in, and who led me straight, without being asked, through the inner court and down to the green slope near the river where my mother was buried. It was a lovely place, a green plot near a wall where pear trees had been brought early into blossom by the warmth, and where, above their snow, the white doves she had loved were rounding their breasts to the sun. I could hear the ripple of the river beyond the wall, and down through the rustling trees the note of the chapel bell.

The Abbess received me kindly, but had nothing to add to the account which I had received soon after my mother's death, and had passed on to my father. I left money for prayers, and for a carved stone to be made, and when I left, it was with her silver cross with the amethysts tucked into my saddle-bag. One question I dared not ask, even when a girl who was not Keri brought wine for my refreshment. And finally, with my question unasked, I was ushered to the gate and out into the street. Here I thought for a moment that my luck had changed, for as I was untying my horse's bridle from the ring beside the gate I saw the old portress peering at me through the grille–remembering, no doubt, the gold I had given her on my first visit. But when I produced money and beckoned her close to shout my question in her ear, and even, after three repetitions, got through to her, the only answer was a shrug and the one word, 'Gone,' which–even if she had understood me–was hardly helpful. In the end I gave it up. In any case, I told myself, this was something that had to be forgotten. So I rode out of town and back over the miles to my valley with the memory of her face burnt into everything I saw, and the gold of her hair lying in every shaft of the slanting sunlight.

Cadal had rebuilt the pen which Galapas and I had made in the hawthorn brake. It had a good roof and a stout door, and could easily house a couple of big horses. One–Cadal's own, I supposed–was already there.

Cadal himself must have heard me riding up the valley, because, almost before I had dismounted, he came running down the path by the cliff, had the bridle out of my hand, and, lifting both my hands in his, kissed them.

'Why, what's this?' I asked, surprised. He need have had no fears for my safety; the messages I had sent him had been regular and reassuring. 'Didn't you get the message I was coming?'

'Yes, I got it. It's been a long time. You're looking well.'

'And you. Is all well here?'

'You'll find it so. If you must live in a place like this, there's ways and ways of making it fit. Now get away up, your supper's ready.' He bent to unbuckle the horse's girths, leaving me to go up to the cave alone.

He had had a long time in which to do it, but even so it came with a shock like a miracle. It was as it had always been, a place of green grass and sunlight. Daisies and heartsease starred the turf between the green curls of young bracken, and young rabbits whisked out of sight under the flowering blackthorn. The spring ran crystal clear, and crystal clear through the water of the well could be seen the silver gravel at the bottom. Above it, in its ferny niche, stood the carved figure of the god; Cadal must have found it when he cleared the rubbish from the well. He had even found the cup of horn. It stood where it had always stood. I drank from it, sprinkled the drops for the god, and went into the cave.

My books had come from Less Britain; the great chest was backed against the wall of the cave, where Galapas' box had been. Where his table had stood there was another, which I recognised from my grandfather's house. The bronze mirror was back in place. The cave was clean, sweet-smelling and dry. Cadal had built a hearth of stone, and logs were laid ready to light. I half expected to see Galapas sitting beside the hearth, and, on the ledge near the entrance, the falcon which had perched there on the night a small boy left the cave in tears. Deep among the shadows above the ledge at the rear was the gash of deeper shadow which hid the crystal cave.

That night, lying on the bed of bracken with the rugs pulled round me, I lay listening, after the dying of the fire, to the rustle of leaves outside the cave, and, beyond that, the trickle of the spring. They were the only sounds in the world. I closed my eyes and slept as I had not slept since I was a child.

Chapter Eight

Like a drunkard who, as long as there is no wine to be had, thinks himself cured of his craving, I had thought myself cured of the thirst for silence and solitude. But from the first morning of waking on Bryn Myrddin, I knew that this was not merely a refuge, it was my place. April lengthened into May, and the cuckoos shouted from hill to hill, the bluebells unfurled in the young bracken, and evenings were full of the sound of lambs crying, and still I had never once gone nearer the town than the crest of a hill two miles north where I gathered leaves and cresses. Cadal went down daily for supplies and for what news was current, and twice a messenger rode up the valley, once with a bundle of sketches from Tremorinus, once with news from Winchester and money from my father–no letter, but confirmation that Pascentius was indeed massing troops in Germany, and war must surely come before the end of summer.

For the rest I read, and walked on the hills, and gathered plants and made medicines. I also made music, and sang a number of songs which made Cadal look sideways at me over his tasks and shake his head. Some of them are still sung, but most are best forgotten. One of the latter was this, which I sang one night when May was in town with all her wild clouds of blossom, and greybell turned to bluebell along the brakes.

> *The land is grey and bare, the trees naked as bone,*
> *Their summer stripped from them; the willow's hair,*
> *The beauty of blue water, the golden grasses,*
> *Even the bird's whistle has been stolen,*
> *Stolen by a girl, robbed by a girl lithe as willow.*

Blithe she is as the bird on the May bough,
Sweet she is as the bell in the tower,
She dances over the bending rushes
And her steps shine on the grey grass.

I would take a gift to her, queen of maidens,
But what is left to offer from my bare valley?
Voices of wind in the reeds, and jewel of rain,
And fur of moss on the cold stone.
What is there left to offer but moss on the stone?
She closes her eyes and turns from me in sleep.

The next day I was walking in a wooded valley a mile from home looking for wild mint and bitterweed, when, as if I had called her, she came up the path through the bluebells and bracken. For all I know, I may have called her. An arrow is an arrow, whichever god looses it.

I stood still by a clump of birches, staring as if she would vanish; as if I had indeed conjured her up that moment from dream and desire, a ghost in sunlight. I could not move, though my whole body and spirit seemed to leap at once to meet her. She saw me, and laughter broke in her face, and she came to me, walking lightly. In the chequer of dancing light and shadow as the birch boughs moved she still seemed insubstantial, as if her step would hardly stir the grasses, but then she came closer and it was no vision, but Keri as I remembered her, in brown homespun and smelling of honeysuckle. But now she wore no hood; her hair was loose over her shoulders, and her feet were bare. The sun glanced through the moving leaves, making her hair sparkle like light on water. She had her hands full of bluebells.

'My lord!' The small, breathless voice was full of pleasure.

I stood still with all my dignity round me like a robe, and under it my body fretting like a horse that feels curb and spur at the same time. I wondered if she were going to kiss my hand again, and if so, what I would do. 'Keri! What are you doing here?'

'Why, gathering bluebells.' The wide innocence of her look robbed the words of pertness. She held them up, laughing at me across them. God knows what she could see in my face. No, she was not going to kiss my hand. 'Didn't you know I'd left St Peter's?'

'Yes, they told me. I thought you must have gone to some other nunnery.'

'No, never that. I hated it. It was like being in a cage. Some of them liked it, it made them feel safe, but not me. I wasn't made for such a life.'

'They tried to do the same thing to me, once,' I said.

'Did you run away, too?'

'Oh, yes. But I ran before they shut me up. Where are you living now, Keri?'

She did not seem to have heard the question. 'You weren't meant for it, either? Being in chains, I mean?'

'Not these chains.'

I could see her puzzling over this, but I was not sure what I had meant myself, so held my tongue, watching her without thought, feeling only the strong happiness of the moment.

'I was sorry about your mother,' she said.

'Thank you, Keri.'

'She died just after you'd left. I suppose they told you all about it?'

'Yes. I went to the nunnery as soon as I came back to Maridunum.'

She was silent for a moment, looking down. She pointed a bare toe in the grass, a little shy dancing movement which set the golden apples at her girdle jingling. 'I knew you had come back. Everyone's talking about it.'

'Are they?'

She nodded. 'They told me in the town that you were a prince as well as a great magician . . .' She looked up then, her voice fading to doubt, as she eyed me. I was wearing my oldest clothes, a tunic with grass stains that not even Cadal could remove, and my mantle was burred and pulled by thorns and brambles. My sandals were of canvas like a slave's; it was useless to wear leather through the long wet grass. Compared even with the plainly dressed young man she had seen before, I must look like a beggar. She asked, with the directness of innocence: 'Are you still a prince, now that your mother is gone?'

'Yes. My father is the High King.'

Her lips parted. 'Your father? The King? I didn't know. Nobody said that.'

'Not many people know. But now that my mother is dead, it doesn't matter. Yes, I am his son.'

'The son of the High King . . .' She breathed it, with awe. 'And a magician, too. I know that's true.'

'Yes. That is true.'

'You once told me you weren't.'

I smiled. 'I told you I couldn't cure your toothache.'

'But you did cure it.'

'So you said. I didn't believe you.'

'Your touch would cure anything,' she said, and came close to me.

The neck of her gown hung slack. Her throat was pale as honeysuckle. I could smell her scent and the scent of the bluebells, and the bittersweet juice of the flowers crushed between us. I put out a hand and pulled at the neck of the gown, and the drawstring snapped. Her breasts were round and full and softer than anything I had imagined. They rounded into my hands like the breasts of my mother's doves. I believe I had expected her to cry out and pull away from me, but she nestled towards me warmly, and laughed, and put her hands up behind my head and dug her fingers into my hair and bit me on the mouth. Then suddenly she let her whole weight hang against me so that, reaching to hold her, plunging clumsily into the kiss, I stumbled forward and fell to the ground with her under me and the flowers scattering round us as we fell.

It took me a long time to understand. At first it was laughter and snatched breathing and all that burns down into the imagination in the night, but still held down hard and steady because of her smallness and the soft sounds she made when I hurt her. She was slim as a reed and soft with it, and you would have thought it would make me feel like a duke of the world, but then suddenly she made a sound deep in her throat as if she was strangling, and twisted in my arms as I have seen a dying man twist in pain, and her mouth came up like something striking, and fastened on mine.

Suddenly it was I who was strangling; her arms dragged at me, her mouth sucked me down, her body drew me into that tight and final darkness, no air, no light, no breath, no whisper of waking spirit. A grave inside a grave. Fear burned down into my brain like a white hot blade laid across the eyes. I opened them and could see nothing but the spinning light and the shadow of a tree laid across me whose thorns tore like spikes. Some shape of terror clawed my face. The thorn-tree's shadow swelled and shook, the cave mouth gaped and the walls breathed, crushing me. I struggled back, out, tore myself away and rolled over apart from her, sweating with fear and shame.

'What's the matter?' Even her voice sounded blind. Her hands still moved over the space of air where I had been.

'I'm sorry, Keri. I'm sorry.'

'What do you mean? What's happened?' She turned her head in its fallen flurry of gold. Her eyes were narrow and cloudy. She reached for me. 'Oh, if that's all, come here. It's all right, I'll show you, just come here.'

'No.' I tried to put her aside gently, but I was shaking. 'No, Keri. Leave me. No.'

'What's the matter?' Her eyes opened suddenly wide. She pushed herself up on her elbow. 'Why, I do believe you've never done it before. Have you? Have you?'

I didn't speak.

She gave a laugh that seemed meant to sound gay, but came shrilly. She rolled over again and stretched out her hands. 'Well, never mind, you can learn, can't you? You're a man, after all. At least, I thought you were . . .' Then, suddenly in a fury of impatience: 'Oh, for God's sake. Hurry, can't you? I tell you, it'll be all right.'

I caught her wrists and held them. 'Keri, I'm sorry. I can't explain, but this is . . . I must not, that's all I know. No, listen, give me a minute.'

'Let me go!'

I loosed her and she pulled away and sat up. Her eyes were angry. There were flowers caught in her hair.

I said: 'This isn't because of you, Keri, don't think that. It has nothing to do with you—'

'Not good enough for you, is that it? Because my mother was a whore?'

'Was she? I didn't even know.' I felt suddenly immensely tired. I said carefully: 'I told you this was nothing to do with you. You are very beautiful, Keri, and the first moment I saw you I felt—you must know what I felt. But this is nothing to do with feeling. It is between me and—it is something to do with my—' I stopped. It was no use. Her eyes watched me, bright and blank, then she turned aside with a little flouncing movement and began to tidy her dress. Instead of "power", I finished: '—something to do with my magic.'

'Magic.' Her lip was thrust out like a hurt child's. She knotted her girdle tight with a sharp little tug, and began to gather up the fallen bluebells, repeating spitefully: 'Magic. Do you think I believe in your silly magic? Did you really think I even had the toothache, that time?'

'I don't know,' I said wearily. I got to my feet.

'Well, maybe you don't have to be a man to be a magician. You ought to have gone into that monastery after all.'

'Perhaps.' A flower was tangled in her hair and she put a hand up to pull it out. The fine floss glinted in the sun like gossamer. My eye caught the blue mark of a bruise on her wrist. 'Are you all right? Did I hurt you?'

She neither answered nor looked up, and I turned away. 'Well, good-bye, Keri.'

I had gone perhaps six steps when her voice stopped me. 'Prince—'

I turned.

'So you do answer to it?' she said. 'I'm surprised. Son of the High King, you say you are, and you don't even leave me a piece of silver to pay for my gown?'

I must have stood staring like a sleepwalker. She tossed the gold hair back over her shoulder and laughed up at me. Like a blind man fumbling, I felt in the purse at my belt and came out with a coin. It was gold. I took a step back towards her to give it to her. She leaned forward, still laughing, her hands out, cupped like a beggar's. The torn gown hung loose from the lovely throat. I flung the coin down and ran away from her, up through the wood.

Her laughter followed me till I was over the ridge and down in the next valley and had flung myself on my belly beside the stream and drowned the feel and the scent of her in the rush of the mountain water that smelled of snow.

Chapter Nine

In June Ambrosius came to Caerleon, and sent for me. I rode up alone, arriving one evening well past supper-time, when the lamps had been lit and the camp was quiet. The King was still working; I saw the spill of light from headquarters, and the glimmer on the dragon standard outside. While I was still some way off I heard the clash of a salute, and a tall figure came out whom I recognised as Uther.

He crossed the way to a door opposite the King's but with his foot on the bottom step saw me, stopped, and came back. 'Merlin. So you got here. You took your time, didn't you?'

'The summons was hasty. If I am to go abroad, there are things I have to do.'

He stood still. 'Who said you were to go abroad?'

'People talk of nothing else. It's Ireland, isn't it? They say Pascentius has made some dangerous allies over there, and that Ambrosius wants them destroyed quickly. But why me?'

'Because it's their central stronghold he wants destroyed. Have you ever heard of Killare?'

'Who hasn't? They say it's a fortress that's never been taken.'

'Then they say the truth. There's a mountain in the centre of all Ireland,

and they say that from the summit of it you can see every coast. And on top of that hill there's a fortress, not of earth and palisades, but of strong stones. That, my dear Merlin, is why you.'

'I see. You need engines.'

'We need engines. We have to attack Killare. If we can take it, you can reckon that there'll be no trouble there for a few years to come. So I take Tremorinus, and Tremorinus insists on taking you.'

'I gather the King isn't going?'

'No. Now I'll say good night; I have business to attend to, or I would ask you in to wait. He's got the camp commandant with him, but I don't imagine they'll be long.'

On this, he said a pleasant enough good night, and ran up the steps into his quarters, shouting for his servant before he was well through the door.

Almost immediately, from the King's doorway, came the clash of another salute, and the camp commandant came out. Not seeing me, he paused to speak to one of the sentries, and I stood waiting until he had done.

A movement caught my eye, a furtive stir of shadow where someone came softly down a narrow passage between the buildings opposite, where Uther was housed. The sentries, busy with the commandant, had seen nothing. I drew back out of the torchlight, watching. A slight figure, cloaked and hooded. A girl. She reached the lighted corner and paused there, looking about her. Then, with a gesture that was secret rather than afraid, she pulled the hood closer about her face. It was a gesture I recognised, as I recognised the drift of scent on the air, like honeysuckle, and from under the hood the lock of hair curling, gold in the torchlight.

I stood still. I wondered why she had followed me here, and what she hoped to gain. I do not think it was shame I felt, not now, but there was pain, and I believe there was still desire. I hesitated, then took a step forward and spoke.

'Keri?'

But she paid no attention. She slid out from the shadows and, quickly and lightly, ran up the steps to Uther's door. I heard the sentry challenge, then a murmur, and a soft laugh from the man.

When I drew level with Uther's doorway it was shut. In the light of the torch I saw the smile still on the sentry's face.

Ambrosius was still sitting at his table, his servant hovering behind him in the shadows.

He pushed his papers aside and greeted me. The servant brought wine and poured it, then withdrew and left us alone.

We talked for a while. He told me what news there was since I had left Winchester; the building that had gone forward, and his plans for the future. Then we spoke of Tremorinus' work at Caerleon, and so came to the talk of war. I asked him for the latest about Pascentius, 'for,' I said, 'we have been waiting weekly to hear that he had landed in the north and was harrying the countryside.'

'Not yet. In fact, if my plans come to anything, we may hear nothing more of Pascentius until the spring, and then we shall be more prepared. If we allow him to come now, he may well prove more dangerous than any enemy I have yet fought.'

'I've heard something about this. You mean the Irish news?'

'Yes. The news is bad from Ireland. You know they have a young king there, Gilloman? A young firedrake, they tell me, and eager for war. Well, you may have heard it, the news is that Pascentius is contracted to Gilloman's sister. You see what this could mean? Such an alliance as that might put the north and west of Britain both at risk together.'

'Is Pascentius in Ireland? We heard he was in Germany, gathering support.'

'That is so,' he said. 'I can't get accurate information about his numbers, but I'd say about twenty thousand men. Nor have I yet heard what he and Gilloman plan to do.' He lifted an eyebrow at me, amused. 'Relax, boy, I haven't called you here to ask for a prediction. You made yourself quite clear at Kaerconan; I'm content to wait, like you, on your god.'

I laughed. 'I know. You want me for what you call "real work".'

'Indeed. This is it. I am not content to wait here in Britain while Ireland and Germany gather their forces and then come together on both our coasts like a summer storm, and meet in Britain to overwhelm the north. Britain lies between them now, and she can divide them before ever they combine to attack.'

'And you'll take Ireland first?'

'Gilloman,' he said, nodding. 'He's young and inexperienced—and he is also nearer. Uther will sail for Ireland before the month's end.' There was a map in front of him. He half turned it so that I could see. 'Here. This is Gilloman's stronghold; You'll have heard of it, I don't doubt. It is a mountain fortress called Killare. I have not found a man who has seen it, but I am told it is strongly fortified, and can be defended against any assault. I am told, indeed, that it has never fallen. Now, we can't afford to have Uther sit down in front of it for months, while Pascentius comes in at the back door. Killare must be taken quickly, and it cannot—they tell me—be taken by fire.'

'Yes?' I had already noticed that there were drawings of mine on the table among the maps and plans.

He said, as if at a tangent: 'Tremorinus speaks very highly of you.'

'That's good of him.' Then, at my own tangent: 'I met Uther outside. He told me what you wanted.'

'Then will you go with him?'

'I'm at your service, of course. But sir,' I indicated the drawings, 'I have made no new designs. Everything I have designed has already been built here. And if there is so much hurry—'

'Not that, no. I'm asking for nothing new. The machines we have are good—and must serve. What we have built is ready now for shipping. I want you for more than this.' He paused. 'Killare, Merlin, is more than a stronghold, it is a holy place, the holy place of the Kings of Ireland. They tell me the crest of the hill holds a Dance of stone, a circle such as you knew in Brittany. And on Killare, men say, is the heart of Ireland and the holy place of Gilloman's kingdom. I want you, Merlin, to throw down the holy place, and take the heart out of Ireland.'

I was silent.

'I spoke of this to Tremorinus,' he said, 'and he told me I must send for you. Will you go?'

'I have said I will. Of course.'

He smiled, and thanked me, not as if he were High King and I a subject obeying his wish, but as if I were an equal giving him a favour. He talked then for a little longer about Killare, what he had heard of it, and what preparations he thought we should make, and finally leaned back, saying with a smile: 'One thing I regret. I'm going to Maridunum, and I should have liked your company, but now there is no time for that. You may charge me with any messages you care to.'

'Thank you, but I have none. Even if I had been there, I would hardly have dared to offer you the hospitality of a cave.'

'I should like to see it.'

'Anyone will tell you the way. But it's hardly fit to receive a King.'

I stopped. His face was lit with a laughter that all at once made him look twenty again. I set down my cup. 'I am a fool. I had forgotten.'

'That you were begotten there? I thought you had. I can find my way to it, never fear.'

He spoke then about his own plans. He himself would stay in Caerleon, 'for if Pascentius attacks,' he told me, 'my guess is that he will come down this way'—his finger traced a line on the map—'and I can catch him south of Carlisle. Which brings me to the next thing. There was something else I wanted to discuss with you. When you last came through Caerleon on your way to Maridunum in April, I believe you had a talk with Tremorinus?'

I waited.

'About this.' He lifted a sheaf of drawings—not mine—and handed them across. They were not of the camp, or indeed of any buildings I had seen. There was a church, a great hall, a tower. I studied them for a few minutes in silence. For some reason I felt tired, as if my heart were too heavy for me. The lamp smoked and dimmed and sent shadows dancing over the papers, I pulled myself together, and looked up at my father. 'I see. You must be talking about the memorial building?'

He smiled. 'I'm Roman enough to want a visible monument.'

I tapped the drawings. 'And British enough to want it British? Yes, I heard that, too.'

'What did Tremorinus tell you?'

'That it was thought some kind of monument to your victories should be erected, and to commemorate your kingship of a united kingdom. I agreed with Tremorinus that to build a triumphal arch here in Britain would be absurd. He did say that some churchmen wanted a big church built—the bishop of Caerleon, for instance, wanted one here. But surely, sir, this would hardly do? If you build at Caerleon you'll have London and Winchester, not to mention York, thinking it should have been there. Of them all, I suppose, Winchester would be the best. It is your capital.'

'No. I've had a thought about this myself. When I travelled up from Winchester, I came through Amesbury . . .' He leaned forward suddenly. 'What's the matter, Merlin? Are you ill?'

'No. It's a hot night, that's all. A storm coming, I think. Go on. You came through Amesbury.'

'You knew it was my birthplace? Well, it seemed to me that to put my monument in such a place could give no cause for complaint–and there is another reason why it's a good choice.' He knitted his brows. 'You're like a sheet, boy. Are you sure you're all right?'

'Perfectly. Perhaps a little tired.'

'Have you supped? It was thoughtless of me not to ask.'

'I ate on the way, thank you. I have had all I needed. Perhaps–some more wine—'

I half rose, but before I could get to my feet he was on his, and came round the table with a jug and served me himself. While I drank he stayed where he was, near me, sitting back against the table's edge. I was reminded sharply of how he had stood this way that night in Brittany when I discovered him. I remember that I held it in my mind, and in short while was able to smile at him.

'I am quite well, sir, indeed I am. Please go on. You were giving me the second reason for putting your monument at Amesbury.'

'You probably know that it is not far from there that the British dead lie buried, who were slain by Hengist's treachery. I think it fitting–and I think there is no man who will argue with this–that the monument to my victory, to the making of one kingdom under one King, should also be a memorial for these warriors.' He paused. 'And you might say there is yet a third reason, more powerful than the other two.'

I said, not looking at him, but down into the cup of wine, and speaking quietly: 'That Amesbury is already the site of the greatest monument in Britain? Possibly the greatest in the whole West?'

'Ah.' It was a syllable of deep satisfaction. 'So your mind moves this way, too? You have seen the Giants' Dance?'

'I rode out to it from Amesbury, when I was on my way home from Winchester.'

He stood up at that and walked back round the table to his chair. He sat, then leaned forward, resting his hands on the table. 'Then you know how I am thinking. You saw enough when you lived in Brittany to know what the Dance was once. And you have seen what it is now–a chaos of giant stones in a lonely place where the sun and the winds strike.' He added more slowly, watching me: 'I have talked of this to Tremorinus. He says that no power of man could raise those stones.'

I smiled. 'So you sent for me to raise them for you?'

'You know they say it was not men who raised them, but magic.'

'Then,' I said, 'no doubt they will say the same again.'

His eyes narrowed. 'You are telling me you can do it?'

'Why not?'

He was silent, merely waiting. It was a measure of his faith in me that he did not smile.

I said: 'Oh, I've heard all the tales they tell, the same tales they told in Less Britain of the standing stones. But the stones were put there by men, sir. And what men put there once, men can put there again.'

'Then if I don't possess a magician, at least I possess a competent engineer?'

'That's it.'

'How will you do it?'

'As yet, I know less than half of it. But if it was done once, it can be done again.'

'Then will you do this for me, Merlin?'

'Of course. Have I not said I am here only to serve you as best I can? I will rebuild the Giants' Dance for you, Ambrosius.'

'A strong symbol for Britain.' He spoke broodingly now, frowning down at his hands. 'I shall be buried there, Merlin, when my time comes. What Vortigern wanted to do for his stronghold in darkness, I shall do for mine in the light; I shall have the body of her King buried under the stones, the warrior under the threshold of all Britain.'

Someone must have drawn the curtains back from the door. The sentries were out of sight, the camp silent. The stone doorposts and the heavy lintel lying across them framed a blue night burning with stars. All round us the vast shadows reared, giant stones linked like pleached trees where some hands long since bone had cut the signs of the gods of air and earth and water. Someone was speaking quietly; a king's voice; Ambrosius' voice. It had been speaking for some time: vaguely, like echoes in the dark, I heard it.

'. . . and while the King lies there under the stone the Kingdom shall not fall. For as long and longer than it has stood before, the Dance shall stand again, with the light striking it from the living heaven. And I shall bring back the great stone to lay upon the grave-place, and this shall be the heart of Britain, and from this time on all the kings shall be one King and all the gods one God. And you shall live again in Britain, and for ever, for we will make between us a King whose name will stand as long as the Dance stands, and who will be more than a symbol; he will be a shield and a living sword.'

It was not the King's voice; it was my own. The King was still sitting on the other side of the map-strewn table, his hands still and flat on the papers, his eyes dark under the straight brows. Between us the lamp dimmed, flickering in a draught from under the closed door.

I stared at him, while my sight slowly cleared. 'What did I say?'

He shook his head, smiling, and reached for the wine jug.

I said irritably: 'It comes on me like a fainting fit on a pregnant girl. I'm sorry. Tell me what I said?'

'You gave me a kingdom. And you gave me immortality. What more is there? Drink now, Ambrosius' prophet.'

'Not wine. Is there water?'

'Here.' He got to his feet. 'And now you must go and sleep, and so must I. I leave early for Maridunum. You are sure you have no messages?'

'Tell Cadal he is to give you the silver cross with the amethysts.'

We faced one another in a small silence. I was almost as tall as he. He said, gently: 'So now it is good-bye.'

'How does one say good-bye to a King who has been given immortality?'

He gave me a strange look. 'Shall we meet again, then?'

'We shall meet again, Ambrosius.'

It was then I knew that what I had prophesied for him was his death.

Chapter Ten

Killare, I had been told, is a mountain in the very centre of Ireland. There are in other parts of this island mountains which, if not as great as those of our own country, could still merit the name. But the hill of Killare is no mountain. It is a gentle conical hill whose summit is, I suppose, no more than nine hundred feet high. It is not even forested, but clothed over with rough grass, with here and there a copse of thorn trees, or a few single oaks.

Even so, standing where it does, it looms like a mountain to those approaching it, for it stands alone, the only hill at the centre of a vast plain. On every hand, with barely the least undulation, the country stretches flat and green; north, south, east, west, it is the same. But it is not true that you can see the coasts from that summit; there is only the interminable view on every hand of that green gentle country, with above it a soft and cloudy sky.

Even the air is mild there. We had fair winds, and landed on a long, grey strand on a soft summer morning, with a breeze off the land smelling of bog myrtle and gorse and salt-soaked turf. The wild swans sailed the loughs with the half-grown cygnets, and the peewits screamed and tumbled over the meadows where their young nestled down between the reeds.

It was not a time, or a country, you would have thought, for war. And indeed, the war was soon over. Gilloman, the King, was young—they said not more than eighteen—and he would not listen to his advisers and wait for a good moment to meet our attack. So high was his heart that, at the first news of foreign troops landing on the sacred soil of Ireland, the young king gathered his fighting men together, and threw them against Uther's seasoned troops. They met us on a flat plain, with a hill at our backs and a river at theirs. Uther's troops stood the first wild, brave attack without giving ground even a couple of paces, then advanced steadily in their turn, and drove the Irish into the water. Luckily for them, this was a wide stream, and shallow, and, though it ran red that evening, many hundreds of Irishmen escaped. Gilloman the King was one of them, and when we got the news that he had fled west with a handful of trusted followers, Uther, guessing he would be making for Killare, sent a thousand mounted troops after him, with instructions to catch him before he reached the gates. This they just managed to do, coming up with him barely half a mile short of the fortress, at the very foot of the hill and within sight of the walls. The second battle was short, and bloodier than the first. But took place in the night, and in the confusion of the mêlée Gilloman himself escaped once more, and galloped away with a handful of men, this time nobody knew where. But the thing was done; by the time we, the main body of the army, came to the foot of Mount Killare, the British troops were already in possession, and the gates were open.

A lot of nonsense has been talked about what happened next. I myself have heard some of the songs, and even read one account which was set down in a book. Ambrosius had been misinformed. Killare was not strong-built of great stones; that is to say, the outer fortifications were as usual of earthworks and palisades behind a great ditch, and inside that was a second ditch, deep, and with spikes set. The central fortress itself was certainly stone-walled, and the stones were big ones, but nothing that a normal team, with the proper tackle, could not handle easily. Inside this fortress wall were houses of the most part built of wood, but also some strong places underground, as we have in Britain. Higher yet stood the innermost ring, a wall round the crest of the hill like a crown round the brow of a king. And inside this, at the very centre and apex of the hill, was the holy place. Here stood the Dance, the circle of stones that was said to contain the heart of Ireland. It could not compare with the Great Dance of Amesbury, being only a single circle of unlinked stones, but it was impressive enough, and still stood firm with much of the circle intact, and two capped uprights near the centre where other stones lay, seemingly without pattern, in the long grass.

I walked up alone that same evening. The hillside was alive with the bustle and roar, familiar to me from Kaerconan, of the aftermath of battle. But when I passed the wall that hedged the holy place, and came out towards the crest of the hill, it was like leaving a bustling hall for the quiet of some tower room upstairs. Sounds fell away below the walls, and as I walked up through the long summer grass, there was almost silence, and I was alone.

A round moon stood low in the sky, pale still, and smudged with shadow, and thin at one edge like a worn coin. There was a scatter of small stars, with here and there the shepherd stars herding them, and across the moon one great star alone, burning white. The shadows were long and soft on the seeding grasses.

A tall stone stood alone, leaning a little towards the east. A little further was a pit, and beyond that again a round boulder that looked black in the moonlight. There was something here. I paused. Nothing I could put a name to, but the old, black stone itself might have been some dark creature hunched there over the pit's edge. I felt the shiver run over my skin, and turned away. This, I would not disturb.

The moon climbed with me, and as I entered the circle she lifted her white disc over the cap-stones and shone clear into the centre of the ring. My footsteps crunched, dry and brittle, over a patch of ground where fires had recently been lit. I saw the white shapes of bones, and a flat stone shaped like an altar. The moonlight showed carving on one side, crude shapes twisted, of ropes or serpents. I stooped to run a finger over them. Nearby a mouse rustled and squeaked in the grass. No other sound. The thing was clean, dead, godless. I left it, moving on slowly through the moon-thrown shadows. There was another stone, domed like a beehive, or a navel-stone. And here an upright fallen, with the long grass almost hiding it. As I passed it, searching still, a ripple of breeze ran through the grasses, blurring the shadows and dimming the light like mist. I caught my foot on something, staggered, and came down to my knees at the end of a long flat stone which lay almost hidden in the grass. My hands moved over it. It was massive, oblong, uncarved, simply a great natural stone on to which now the moonlight poured. It hardly needed the cold at my hands, the hiss of the bleached grasses under the sudden run of wind, the scent of daisies, to tell me that this was the stone. All round me, like dancers drawing back from a centre, the silent stones stood black. On one side the white moon, on the other the king-star, burning white. I got slowly to my feet and stood there at the foot of the long stone, as one might stand at the foot of a bed, waiting for the man in it to die.

It was warmth that woke me, warmth and the voices of men near me. I lifted my head. I was half kneeling, half-lying with my arms and the upper part of my body laid along the stone. The morning sun was high, and pouring straight down into the centre of the Dance. Mist smoked up from the damp grass, and its white wreaths hid the lower slopes of the hill. A group of men had come in through the stones of the Dance, and were standing there muttering among themselves, watching me. As I blinked, moving my stiff limbs, the group parted and Uther came through, followed by half a dozen of his officers, among whom was Tremorinus. Two soldiers pushed between them what was obviously an Irish prisoner; his hands were tied and there was a cut on one cheek where blood had dried, but he held himself well and I thought the men who guarded him looked more afraid than he.

Uther checked when he saw me, then came across as I got stiffly to my feet. The night must have shown still in my face, for in the group of officers behind him I saw the look I had grown used to, of men both wary and amazed, and even Uther spoke a fraction too loudly.

'So your magic is as strong as theirs.'

The light was too strong for my eyes. He looked vivid and unreal, like an image seen in moving water. I tried to speak, cleared my throat, and tried again. 'I'm still alive, if that's what you mean.'

Tremorinus said gruffly: 'There's not another man in the army would have spent the night here.'

'Afraid of the black stone?'

I saw Uther's hand move in an involuntary gesture as if it sprang of itself to make the sign. He saw I had noticed, and looked angry. 'Who told you about the black stone?'

Before I could answer, the Irishman said suddenly: 'You saw it? Who are you?'

'My name is Merlin.'

He nodded slowly. He still showed no sign of fear or awe. He read my thoughts, and smiled, as if to say, 'You and I, we can look after ourselves.'

'Why do they bring you here like this?' I asked him.

'To tell them which is the king-stone.'

Uther said: 'He has told us. It's the carved altar over there.'

'Let him go,' I said. 'You have no need of him. And leave the altar alone. This is the stone.'

There was a pause. Then the Irishman laughed. 'Faith, if you bring the

King's enchanter himself, what hope has a poor poet? It was written in the stars that you would take it, and indeed, it is nothing but justice. It's not the heart of Ireland that the stone has been but the curse of it, and maybe Ireland will be all the better to see it go.'

'How so?' I asked him. Then, to Uther: 'Tell them to loose him?'

Uther nodded, and the men loosed the prisoner's hands. He rubbed his wrists, smiling at me. You would have thought we two were alone in the Dance. 'They say that in times past that stone came out of Britain, out of the mountains of the west, in sight of the Irish Sea, and that the great King of all Ireland, Fionn Mac Cumhaill was his name, carried it in his arms one night and walked through the sea with it to Ireland, and set it here.'

'And now,' I said, 'we carry it a little more painfully back to Britain.'

He laughed. 'I would have thought the great magician that's yourself would have picked it up in one hand.'

'I'm no Fionn,' I said. 'And now if you are wise, poet, you will go back to your home and your harp, and make no more wars, but make a song about the stone, and how Merlin the enchanter took the stone from the Dance of Killare and carried it lightly to the Dance of the Hanging Stones at Amesbury.'

He saluted me, laughing still, and went. And indeed he did walk safely down through the camp and away, for in later years I heard the song he made.

But now his going was hardly noticed. There was a pause while Uther frowned down at the great stone, seeming to weigh it in his mind. 'You told the King that you could do this thing. Is that true?'

'I said to the King that what men had brought here, men could take away.'

He looked at me frowningly, uncertainly, still a little angry. 'He told me what you said. I agree. It doesn't need magic and fine words, only a team of competent men with the right engines. Tremorinus!'

'Sir?'

'If we take this one, the king-stone, there will be no need to trouble overmuch with the rest. Throw them down where you can and leave them.'

'Yes, sir. If I could have Merlin—'

'Merlin's team will be working on the fortifications. Merlin, get started, will you? I give you twenty-four hours.'

This was something the men were practised at; they threw down the walls and filled in the ditches with them. The palisades and houses, quite simply, we put to the flame. The men worked well, and were in good heart. Uther was always generous to his troops, and there had been goods in plenty to be looted, arm-rings of copper and bronze and gold, brooches, and weapons well made and inlaid with copper and enamel, in a way the Irish have. The work was finished by dusk, and we withdrew from the hill to the temporary camp which had been thrown up on the plain at the foot of the slope.

It was after supper when Tremorinus came to me. I could see the torches and the fires still lit at the top of the hill, throwing what was left of the Dance into relief. His face was grimy, and he looked tired.

'All day,' he said bitterly, 'and we've raised it a couple of feet, and half an hour ago the props cracked, and it's gone back again into its bed. Why the hell did you have to suggest that stone? The Irishman's altar would have been easier.'

'The Irishman's altar would not have done.'

'Well, by the gods, it looks as if you aren't going to get this one either. Look, Merlin, I don't care what he says, I'm in charge of this job, and I'm asking you to come and take a look. Will you?'

The rest is what the legends have been made of. It would be tedious now to relate how we did it, but it was easy enough; I had had all day to think about it, having seen the stone and the hillside, and I had had the engines in my mind since Brittany. Wherever we could we took it by water–down-river from Killare to the sea, and thence to Wales and still as far as possible by river, using the two great Avons, with little more than a score of dry miles to cross between them. I was not Fionn of the Strong Arm, but I was Merlin, and the great stone travelled home as smoothly as a barge on an untroubled water, with me beside it all the way. I suppose I must have slept on that journey, but I cannot remember doing so. I went wakeful, as one is at a deathbed, and on that one voyage of all those in my life, I never felt the movement of the sea, but sat (they tell me) calm and silent, as if in my chair at home. Uther came once to speak to me–angry, I suppose, that I had done so easily what his own engineers could not do–but he went away after a moment, and did not approach me again. I remember nothing about it. I suppose I was not there. I was watching still between day and night in the great bedchamber at Winchester.

The news met us at Caerleon. Pascentius had attacked out of the north with his force of German and Saxon allies, and the King had marched to Carlisle and defeated him there. But afterwards, safely back at Winchester, he had fallen ill. About this, rumours were rife. Some said that one of Pascentius' men had come in disguise to Winchester where Ambrosius lay abed of a chill, and had given him poison to drink. Some said the man had come from Eosa. But the truth was the same; the King was very sick at Winchester.

The king-star rose again that night, looking, men said, like a fiery dragon, and trailing a cloud of lesser stars like smoke. But it did not need the omen to tell me what I had known since that night on the crest of Killare, when I had vowed to carry the great stone from Ireland, and lay it upon his grave.

So it was that we brought the stone again to Amesbury, and I raised the fallen circles of the Giants' Dance into their places for his monument. And at the next Easter-time, in the city of London, Uther Pendragon was crowned King.

The Coming of the Bear

Chapter One

Men said afterwards that the great dragon star which blazed at Ambrosius' death and from which Uther took the royal name of Pendragon, was a baleful herald for the new reign. And indeed, at the start, everything seemed to be against Uther. It was as if the falling of Ambrosius' star was the signal for his old enemies to rise again and crowd in from the darkened edges of the land to destroy his successor. Octa, Hengist's son, and Eosa his kinsman, counting themselves freed by Ambrosius' death from their promise to stay north of his borders, called together what force they could still muster for attack, and as soon as the call went out, every disaffected element rose to it. Warriors greedy for land and plunder crowded over afresh from Germany, the remnants of Pascentius' Saxons joined with Gilloman's fleeing Irish, and with whatever British thought themselves passed over by the new King. Within a few weeks of Ambrosius' death Octa, with a large army, was scouring the north like a wolf, and before the new King could come up with him had destroyed cities and fortresses clear down from the Wall of Hadrian to York. At York, Ambrosius' strong city, he found the walls in good repair, the gates shut, and men ready to defend themselves. He dragged up what siege engines he had, and settled down to wait.

He must have known that Uther would catch up with him there, but his numbers were such that he showed no fear of the British. Afterwards they reckoned he had thirty thousand men. Be that as it may, when Uther came up to raise the siege with every man he could muster, the Saxons outnumbered the British by more than two to one. It was a bloody engagement, and a disastrous one. I think myself that Ambrosius' death had shaken the kingdom; for all Uther's brilliant reputation as a soldier, he was untried as supreme commander, and it was already known that he had not his brother's calmness and judgement in the face of odds. What he lacked in wisdom, he made up in bravery, but even that would not defeat the odds that came against him that day at York. The British broke and ran, and were saved only by the coming of dusk, which at that time of the year fell early. Uther–with Gorlois of Cornwall, his second-in-command–managed to rally his remaining force near the top of the small hill called Damen. This was steep, and offered cover of a kind, cliffs and caves and thick hazel-woods, but this could only be a temporary refuge from the Saxon host which triumphantly circled the base of the hill, waiting for morning. It was a desperate position for the British, and called for desperate measures. Uther, grimly encamped in a cave, called his weary captains together while the men snatched what rest they could, and with them thrashed out a plan for outwitting the huge host waiting for them at the foot of the hill. At first nobody had much idea beyond the need to escape, but someone–I heard later that it was Gorlois–pointed out that to retreat further was merely to postpone defeat and the destruction of the new kingdom: if escape was possible, then so was attack, and this seemed feasible if the British did not wait until daylight, but used what element of surprise there was in attacking downhill out of the dark and long before the enemy expected it. Simple tactics, indeed, that the Saxons might have expected from men so desperately trapped, but Saxons are stupid fighters, and as I have said before, lacking in discipline. It was almost certain that they would expect no move till dawn, and that they slept soundly where they had lain down that night, confident of victory, and with any luck three parts drunken on the stores they had taken.

To do the Saxons justice, Octa had posted scouts, and these were wide enough awake. But Gorlois' plan worked, helped by a little mist which crept before dawn up from the low ground and surrounded the base of the hill like a veil. Through this, twice as large as life, and in numbers altogether deceiving, the British came in a silent, stabbing rush at the first moment when there was light enough to see one's way across the rocks. Those Saxon outposts who were not cut down in silence, gave the alarm, but too late. Warriors rolled over, cursing, snatching their weapons up from where they lay beside them, but the British, silent no longer, swept yelling across the half-sleeping host, and cut it to pieces. It was finished before noon, and Octa and Eosa taken prisoner. Before winter, with the north swept clear of Saxons, and the burnt long-boats smoking quietly on the northern beaches, Uther was back in London with his prisoners behind bars, making ready for his coronation the following spring.

His battle with the Saxons, his near defeat and subsequent sharp, brilliant victory, was all that the reign needed. Men forgot the bale of Ambrosius' death, and talked of the new King like a sun rising. His name was on everyone's lips, from the nobles and warriors who crowded round him for gifts and honours, to the workmen building his palaces, and the ladies of his court flaunting new dresses like a field of poppies in a colour called Pendragon Red.

I saw him only once during these first weeks. I was at Amesbury still, superintending the work of raising the Giants' Dance. Tremorinus was in the north, but I had a good team, and after their experience with the king-stone at Killare, the men were eager to tackle the massive stones of the Dance. For the raising of the uprights, once we had aligned the stones, dug the pits and sunk the guides, there was nothing that could not be done with rope and shear-legs and plumb-line. It was with the great lintels that the difficulty lay, but the miracle of the building of the Dance had been done countless years before, by the old craftsmen who had shaped those gigantic stones to fit as surely one into the other as wood dovetailed by a master carpenter. We had only to find means to lift them. It was this which had exercised me all those years, since I first saw the capped stones in Less Britain, and began my calculations. Nor had I forgotten what I had learnt from the songs. In the end I had designed a wooden crib of a kind which a modern engineer might have dismissed as primitive, but which—as the singer had been my witness—had done the task before, and would again. It was a slow business, but it worked. And I suppose it was a marvellous enough sight to see those vast blocks rising, stage by stage, and settling finally into their beds as smoothly as if they had been made of tallow. It took two hundred men to each stone as it was moved, drilled teams who worked by numbers and who kept up their rhythms, as rowers do, by music. The rhythms of the movement were of course laid down by the work, and the tunes were old tunes that I remembered from my childhood; my nurse had sung them to me, but she never sang the words that the men sometimes set to them. These tended to be lively, indecent, and intensely personal, and mostly concerning those in high places. Neither Uther nor I were spared, though the songs were never sung deliberately in my hearing. Moreover, when outsiders were present, the words were either correct or indistinguishable. I heard it said, long afterwards, that I moved the stones of the Dance with magic and with music. I suppose you might say that both are true. I have thought, since, that this must have been how the story started that Phoebus Apollo built with music the walls of Troy. But the magic and the music that moved the Giants' Dance, I shared with the blind singer of Kerrec.

Towards the middle of November the frosts were sharp, and the work was finished. The last camp fire was put out, and the last wagon-train of men and materials rolled away south back to Sarum. Cadal had gone ahead of me, into Amesbury. I lingered, holding my fidgeting horse, until the wagons had rolled out of sight over the edge of the plain and I was alone.

The sky hung over the silent plain like a pewter bowl. It was still early in the day, and the grass was white with frost. The thin winter sun painted long shadows from the linked stones. I remembered the standing stone, and the white frost, the bull and the blood and the smiling young god with the fair hair. I looked down at the stone. They had buried him, I knew, with his sword in his hand. I said to him: 'We shall come back, both of us, at the winter solstice.' Then I left him and mounted my horse, and rode towards Amesbury.

Chapter Two

News came of Uther in December; he had left London and ridden to
Winchester for Christmas. I sent a message, got no reply, and rode out once
more with Cadal to where the Giants' Dance stood frostbound and lonely in
the centre of the plain. It was the twentieth of December.

In a fold of the ground just beyond the Dance we tethered our horses and
lit a fire. I had been afraid that the night might be cloudy, but it was crisp
and clear, with the stars out in their swarms, like motes in moonlight.

'Get some sleep, if you can in this cold,' said Cadal. 'I'll wake you before
dawn. What makes you think he'll come?' Then, when I made no reply:
'Well, you're the magician, you should know. Here, just in case your magic
won't put you to sleep, you'd better put the extra cloak on. I'll wake you in
time, so don't fret yourself.'

I obeyed him, rolling myself in the double thickness of wool, and lying
near the fire with my head on my saddle. I dozed rather than slept,
conscious of the small noises of the night surrounded by the immense
stillness of that plain; the rustle and crack of the fire, the sound of Cadal
putting new wood on it, the steady tearing sound of the horses grazing at
hand, the cry of a hunting owl in the air. And then, not long before dawn,
the sound I had been expecting; the steady beat of the earth beneath my
head which meant the approach of horses.

I sat up. Cadal, blear-eyed, spoke morosely. 'You've an hour yet, I
reckon.'

'Never mind. I've slept. Put your ear to the ground, and tell me what you
hear.'

He leaned down, listened for perhaps five heartbeats, then was on his feet
and making for our horses. Men reacted quickly in those days to the sound
of horsemen in the night.

I checked him. 'It's all right. Uther. How many horses do you reckon?'

'Twenty, perhaps thirty. Are you sure?'

'Quite sure. Now get the horses saddled and stay with them. I'm going
in.'

It was the hour between night and morning when the air is still. They
were coming at a gallop. It seemed that the whole of the frozen plain beat
with the sound. The moon had gone. I waited beside the stone.

He left the troop some little way off, and rode forward with only one
companion. I did not think they had yet seen me, though they must have
seen the flicker of Cadal's dying fire in the hollow. The night had been
bright enough with starlight, so they had been riding without torches, and
their night sight was good; the two of them came on at a fast canter straight

for the outer circle of the Dance, and at first I thought they would ride straight in. But the horses pulled up short with a crunch and slither of frost, and the King swung from the saddle. I heard the jingle as he threw the reins to his companion. 'Keep him moving,' I heard him say, and then he approached, a swift striding shadow through the enormous shadows of the Dance.

'Merlin?'

'My lord?'

'You choose your times strangely. Did it have to be the middle of the night?' He sounded wide awake and no more gracious than usual. But he had come.

I said: 'You wanted to see what I have done here, and tonight is the night when I can show you. I am grateful that you came.'

'Show me what? A vision? Is this another of your dreams? I warn you—'

'No. There's nothing of that here, not now. But there is something I wanted you to see which can only been seen tonight. For that, I'm afraid we shall have to wait a little while.'

'Long? It's cold.'

'Not so long, my lord. Till dawn.'

He was standing the other side of the king-stone from me, and in the faint starlight I saw him looking down at it, with his head bent and a hand stroking his chin. 'The first time you stood beside this stone in the night, men say you saw visions. Now they tell me in Winchester that as he lay dying he spoke to you as if you were there in his bedchamber, standing at the foot of the bed. Is this true?'

'Yes.'

His head came up sharply. 'You say you knew on Killare that my brother was dying, yet you said nothing to me?'

'It would have served no purpose. You could not have returned any sooner for knowing that he lay sick. As it was, you journeyed with a quiet mind, and at Caerleon, when he died, I told you.'

'By the gods, Merlin, it was not for you to judge whether to speak or not! You are not King. You should have told me.'

'You were not King either, Uther Pendragon. I did as he bade me.'

I saw him make a quick movement, then he stilled himself.

'That is easy to say.' But from his voice I knew that he believed me, and was in awe of me and of the place. 'And now that we are here, and waiting for the dawn, and whatever it is you have to show me, I think one or two things must be made clear between us. You cannot serve me as you served my brother. You must know that. I want none of your prophecies. My brother was wrong when he said that we would work together for Britain. Our stars will not conjoin. I admit I judged you too harshly, there in Brittany and at Killare; for that I am sorry, but now it is too late. We walk different ways.'

'Yes. I know.'

I said it without any particular expression, simply agreeing, and was surprised when he laughed, softly, to himself. A hand, not unfriendly, dropped on my shoulder. 'Then we understand one another. I had not thought it would be so easy. If you knew how refreshing that is after the weeks I've had of men suing for help, men crawling for mercy, men begging for favours . . . And now the only man in the kingdom with any real claim on me will go his own way, and let me go mine?'

'Of course. Our paths will still cross, but not yet. And then we will deal together, whether we will or no.'

'We shall see. You have power, I admit it, but what use is that to me? I don't need priests.' His voice was brisk and friendly, as if he were willing away the strangeness of the night. He was rooted to earth, was Uther. Ambrosius would have understood what I was saying, but Uther was back on the human trail like a dog after blood. 'It seems you have served me well enough already, at Killare, and here with the Hanging Stones. You deserve something of me, if only for this.'

'Where I can be, I shall be at your service. If you want me, you know where to find me.'

'Not at my court?'

'No, at Maridunum. It's my home.'

'Ah, yes, the famous cave. You deserve a little more of me than that, I think.'

'There is nothing that I want,' I said.

There was a little more light now. I saw him slant a look at me. 'I have spoken to you tonight as I have spoken to no man before. Do you hold the past against me, Merlin the bastard?'

'I hold nothing against you, my lord.'

'Nothing?'

'A girl in Caerleon. You could call her nothing.'

I saw him stare, then smile. 'Which time?'

'It doesn't matter. You'll have forgotten, anyway.'

'By the dog, I misjudged you.' He spoke with the nearest to warmth I had yet heard from him. If he knew, I thought, he would have laughed.

I said: 'I tell you, it doesn't matter. It didn't then, and less than that now.'

'You still haven't told me why you dragged me here at this time. Look at the sky; it's getting on for dawn—and not a moment too soon, the horses will be getting cold.' He raised his head towards the east. 'It should be a fine day. It will be interesting to see what sort of job you've made of this. I can tell you now, Tremorinus was insisting, right up to the time I got your message, that it couldn't be done. Prophet or no prophet, you have your uses, Merlin.'

The light was growing, the dark slackening to let it through. I could see him more clearly now, standing with his head up, his hand once more stroking his chin. I said: 'It's as well you came by night, so that I knew your voice. I shouldn't have known you in daylight. You've grown a full beard.'

'More kingly, eh? There was no time to do anything else on campaign. By the time we got to the Humber . . .' He started to tell me about it, talking, for the first time since I had known him, quite easily and naturally. It may have been that now I was, of all his subjects, the only one kin to him, and blood speaks to blood, they say. He talked about the campaign in the north, the fighting, the smoking destruction the Saxons had left behind them. 'And now we spend Christmas at Winchester. I shall be crowned in London in the spring, and already—'

'Wait.' I had not meant to interrupt him quite so peremptorily, but things were pressing on me, the weight of the sky, the shooting light. There was no time to search for the words that one could use to a king. I said quickly: 'It's coming now. Stand with me at the foot of the stone.'

I moved a pace from him and stood at the foot of the long king-stone, facing the bursting east. I had no eyes for Uther. I heard him draw breath as if in anger, then he checked himself and turned with a glitter of jewels and flash of mail to stand beside me. At our feet stretched the stone.

In the east night slackened, drew back like a veil, and the sun came up. Straight as a thrown torch, or an arrow of fire, light pierced through the grey air and laid a line clear from the horizon to the king-stone at our feet. For perhaps twenty heartbeats the huge sentinel trilithon before us stood black and stark, framing the winter blaze. Then the sun lifted over the horizon so quickly that you could see the shadow of the linked circle move into its long ellipse, to blur and fade almost immediately into the wide light of a winter's dawn.

I glanced at the King. His eyes, wide and blank, were on the stone at his feet. I could not read his thoughts. Then he lifted his head and looked away from me at the outer circle where the great stones stood locked across the light. He took a slow pace away from me and turned on his heel, taking in the full circle of the Hanging Stones. I saw that the new beard was reddish and curled; he wore his hair longer, and a gold circle flashed on his helm. His eyes were blue as woodsmoke in the fresh light.

They met mine at last. 'No wonder you smile. It's very impressive.'

'That's with relief,' I said. 'The mathematics of this have kept me awake for weeks.'

'Tremorinus told me.' He gave me a slow, measuring look. 'He also told me what you had said.'

'What I had said.'

'Yes. "I will deck his grave with nothing less than the light itself."'

I said nothing.

He said slowly: 'I told you I knew nothing of prophets or priests. I am only a soldier, and I think like a soldier. But this—what you have done here—this is something I understand. Perhaps there is room for us both, after all. I told you I spend Christmas at Winchester. Will you ride back with me?'

He had asked me, not commanded me. We were speaking across the stone. It was the beginning of something, but something I had not yet been shown. I shook my head. 'In the spring, perhaps. I should like to see the crowning. Be sure that when you need me I shall be there. But now I must go home.'

'To your hole in the ground? Well, if it's what you want . . . Your wants are few enough, God knows. Is there nothing you would ask of me?' He gestured with his hand to the silent circle. 'Men will speak poorly of a King who does not reward you for this.'

'I have been rewarded.'

'At Maridunum, now. Your grandfather's house would be more suitable for you. Will you take it?'

I shook my head. 'I don't want a house. But I would take the hill.'

'Then take it. They tell me men call it Merlin's Hill already. And now it's full daylight, and the horses will be cold. If you had ever been a soldier, Merlin, you would know that there is one thing more important even than the graves of kings; not to keep the horses standing.'

He clapped me on the shoulder again, turned with a swirl of the scarlet cloak, and strode to his waiting horse. I went to find Cadal.

Chapter Three

When Easter came I still had no mind to leave Bryn Myrddin (Uther, true to his word, had given me the hill where the cave stood, and people already associated its name with me, rather than with the god, calling it Merlin's Hill) but a message came from the King, bidding me to London. This time it was a command, not a request, and so urgent that the King had sent an escort, to avoid any delay I might have incurred in waiting for company.

It was still not safe in those days to ride abroad in parties smaller than a dozen or more, and one rode armed and warily. Men who could not afford their own escort waited until a party was gathered, and merchants even joined together to pay guards to ride with them. The wilder parts of the land were still full of refugees from Octa's army, with Irishmen who had been unable to get a passage home, and a few stray Saxons trying miserably to disguise their fair skins, and unmercifully hunted down when they failed. These haunted the edges of the farms, skulking in the hills and moors and wild places, making sudden savage forays in search of food, and watching the roads for any solitary or ill-armed traveller, however shabby. Anyone with cloak or sandals was a rich man and worth despoiling.

None of this would have deterred me from riding alone with Cadal from Maridunum to London. No outlaw or thief would have faced a look from me, let alone risk a curse. Since events at Dinas Brenin, Killare and Amesbury my fame had spread, growing in song and story until I hardly recognised my own deeds. Dinas Brenin had also been renamed; it had become Dinas Emrys, in compliment to me as much as to commemorate Ambrosius' landing, and the strong-point he had successfully built there. I lived, too, as well as I ever had in my grandfather's palace or in Ambrosius' house. Offerings of food and wine were left daily below the cave, and the poor who had nothing else to bring me in return for the medicines I gave them, brought fuel, or straw for the horses' bedding, or their labour for building jobs or making simple furniture. So winter had passed in comfort and peace, until on a sharp day in early March Uther's messenger, having left the escort in the town, came riding up the valley.

It was the first dry day after more than two weeks of rain and sleety wind, and I had gone up over the hill above the cave to look for the first growing plants and simples. I paused at the edge of a clump of pines to watch the solitary horseman cantering up the hill. Cadal must have heard the hoofbeats; I saw him, small below me, come out of the cave and greet the man, then I saw him pointing his arm indicating which way I had gone. The messenger hardly paused. He turned his beast uphill, struck his spurs in, and came after me.

He pulled up a few paces away, swung stiffly out of the saddle, made the sign, and approached me.

He was a brown-haired young man of about my own age, whose face was vaguely familiar. I thought I must have seen him around Uther's train somewhere. He was splashed with mud to the eyebrows, and where he was not muddy his face was white with fatigue. He must have got a new horse in Maridunum for the last stage, for the animal was fresh, and restive with it, and I saw the young man wince as it threw its head up and dragged at the reins.

'My lord Merlin. I bring you greetings from the King, in London.'

'I am honoured,' I said formally.

'He requests your presence at the feast of his coronation. He has sent you an escort, my lord. They are in the town, resting their horses.'

'Did you say "requests"?'

'I should have said "commands", my lord. He told me I must bring you back immediately.'

'This was all the message?'

'He told me nothing more, my lord. Only that you must attend him immediately in London.'

'Then of course I shall come. Tomorrow morning, when you have rested the horses?'

'Today, my lord. Now.'

It was a pity that Uther's arrogant command was delivered in a slightly apologetic way. I regarded him. 'You have come straight to me?'

'Yes, my lord.'

'Without resting?'

'Yes.'

'How long has it taken you?'

'Four days, my lord. This is a fresh horse. I am ready to go back today.' Here the animal jerked its head again, and I saw him wince.

'Are you hurt?'

'Nothing to speak of. I took a fall yesterday and hurt my wrist. It's my right wrist, not my bridle hand.'

'No, only your dagger hand. Go down to the cave and tell my servant what you have told me, and say he is to give you food and drink. When I come down I shall see to your wrist.'

He hesitated. 'My lord, the King was urgent. This is more than an invitation to watch the crowning.'

'You will have to wait while my servant packs my things and saddles our horses. Also while I myself eat and drink. I can bind up your wrist in a few minutes. Also while I am doing it you can give me the news from London, and tell me why the King commands me so urgently to the feast. Go down now; I shall come in a short while.'

'But, sir—'

I said: 'By the time Cadal has prepared food for the three of us I shall be with you. You cannot hurry me more than that. Now go.'

He threw me a doubtful look, then went, slithering on foot down the wet hill-side and dragging the jibbing horse after him. I gathered my cloak round me against the wind, and walked past the end of the pine wood and out of sight of the cave.

I stood at the end of a rocky spur where the winds came freely down the valley and tore at my cloak. Behind me the pines roared, and under the noise the bare blackthorns by Galapas' grave rattled in the wind. An early plover screamed in the grey air. I lifted my face to the sky and thought of Uther and London, and the command that had just come. But nothing was there except the sky and the pines and the wind in the blackthorns. I looked the other way, down towards Maridunum.

From this height I could see the whole town, tiny as a toy in the distance. The valley was sullen green in the March wind. The river curled, grey under the grey sky. A wagon was crossing the bridge. There was a point of colour where a standard flew over the fortress. A boat scudded down-river, its brown sails full of the wind. The hills, still in their winter purple, held the valley cupped as one might hold in one's palms a globe of glass . . .

The wind whipped water to my eyes, and the scene blurred. The crystal globe was cold in my hands. I gazed down into it. Small and perfect in the heart of the crystal lay the town with its bridge and moving river and the tiny, scudding ship. Round it the fields curved up and over, distorting in the curved crystal till fields, sky, river, clouds held the town with its scurrying people as leaves and sepals hold a bud before it breaks to flower. It seemed that the whole countryside, the whole of Wales, the whole of Britain could be held small and shining and safe between my hands, like something set in amber. I stared down at the land globed in crystal, and knew that this was what I had been born for. The time was here, and I must take it on trust.

The crystal globe melted out of my cupped hands, and was only a fistful of plants I had gathered, cold with rain. I let them fall, and put up the back of a hand to wipe the water from my eyes. The scene below me had changed; the wagon and the boat had gone; the town was still.

I went down to the cave to find Cadal busy with his cooking pots, and the young man already struggling with the saddles of our horses.

'Let that alone,' I told him. 'Cadal, is there hot water?'

'Plenty. Here's a start and a half, orders from the King. London, is it?' Cadal sounded pleased, and I didn't blame him. 'We were due for a change, if you ask me. What is it, do you suppose? He–' jerking his head at the young man '–doesn't seem to know, or else he's not telling. Trouble, by the sound of it.'

'Maybe. We'll soon find out. Here, you'd better dry this.' I gave him my cloak, sat down by the fire, and called the young man to me. 'Let me see that arm of yours now.'

His wrist was blue with bruising, and swollen, and obviously hurt to the touch, but the bones were whole. While he washed I made a compress, then bound it on. He watched me half apprehensively, and tended to shy from my touch, and not only, I thought, with pain. Now that the mud was washed off and I could see him better, the feeling of familiarity persisted even more strongly. I eyed him over the bandages. 'I know you, don't I?'

'You wouldn't remember me, my lord. But I remember you. You were kind to me once.'

I laughed. 'Was it such a rare occasion? What's your name?'

'Ulfin.'

'Ulfin? It has a familiar sound . . . Wait a moment. Yes, I have it. Belasius' boy?'

'Yes. You do remember me?'

'Perfectly. That night in the forest, when my pony went lame, and you had to lead him home. I suppose you were around underfoot most of the time, but you were about as conspicuous as a field mouse. That's the only time I remember. Is Belasius over here for the coronation?'

'He's dead.'

Something in his tone made me cock an eye at him over the bandaged wrist. 'You hated him as much as that? No, don't answer, I guessed as much back there, young as I was. Well, I shan't ask why. The gods know I didn't love him myself, and I wasn't his slave. What happened to him?'

'He died of a fever, my lord.'

'And you managed to survive him? I seem to remember something about an old and barbarous custom—'

'Prince Uther took me into his service. I am with him now—the King.'

He spoke quickly, looking away. I knew it was all I would ever learn. 'And are you still afraid of the world, Ulfin?'

But he would not answer that. I finished tying the wrist. 'Well, it's a wild and violent place, and the times are cruel. But they will get better, and I think you will help to make them so. There, that's done. Now get yourself something to eat. Cadal, do you remember Ulfin? The boy who brought Aster home the night we ran into Uther's troops in Nemet?'

'By the dog, so it is.' Cadal looked him up and down. 'You look a sight better than you did then. What happened to the druid? Died of a curse? Come along then, and get something to eat. Yours is here, Merlin, and see you eat enough for a human being for a change, and not just what might keep one of your precious birds alive.'

'I'll try,' I said meekly, and then laughed at the expression on Ulfin's face as he looked from me to my servant and back again.

We lay that night at an inn near the crossroads where the way leads off north for the Five Hills and the gold mine. I ate alone in my room, served by Cadal. No sooner had the door shut behind the servant who carried the dishes than Cadal turned to me, obviously bursting with news.

'Well, there's a pretty carry-on in London, by all accounts.'

'One might expect it,' I said mildly. 'I heard someone say Budec was there, together with most of the kings from across the Narrow Sea, and that most of them, and half the King's own nobles, have brought their daughters along with an eye to the empty side of the throne.' I laughed. 'That should suit Uther.'

'They say he's been through half the girls in London already,' said Cadal, setting a dish down in front of me. It was Welsh mutton, with a good sauce made of onions, hot and savoury.

'They'd say anything of him.' I began to help myself. 'It could even be true.'

'Yes, but seriously, there's trouble afoot, they say. Woman trouble.'

'Oh, God, Cadal, spare me. Uther was born to woman trouble.'

'No, but I mean it. Some of the escort were talking, and it's no wonder Ulfin wouldn't. This is real trouble. Gorlois' wife.'

I looked up, startled. 'The Duchess of Cornwall? This can't be true.'

'It's not true yet. But they say it's not for want of trying.'

I drank wine. 'You can be sure it's only rumour. She's more than half as young again as her husband, and I've heard she's fair. I suppose Uther pays her some attention, the Duke being his second-in-command, and men make all they can of it, Uther being who he is. And what he is.'

Cadal leaned his fists on the table and looked down at me. He was uncommonly solemn. 'Attention, is it? They say he's never out of her lap. Sends her the best dishes at table each day, sees she's served first, even before he is, pledges her in front of everybody in the hall every time he raises his goblet. Nobody's talking of anything else from London to Winchester. I'm told they're laying bets in the kitchen.'

'I've no doubt. And does Gorlois have anything to say?'

'Tried to pass it over at first, they say, but it got so that he couldn't go on pretending he hadn't noticed. He tried to look as if he thought Uther was just doing the pair of them honour, but when it came to sitting the Lady Ygraine—that's her name—on Uther's right, and the old man six down on the other side—' He paused.

I said, uneasily: 'He must be crazed. He can't afford trouble yet—trouble of any kind, let alone this, and with Gorlois of all people. By all the gods, Cadal, it was Cornwall that helped Ambrosius into the country at all, and Cornwall who put Uther where he is now. Who won the battle of Damen Hill for him?'

'Men are saying that, too.'

'Are they indeed?' I thought for a moment, frowning. 'And the woman? What—apart from the usual dunghill stuff—do they say about her?'

'That she says little, and says less each day. I've no doubt Gorlois has plenty to say to her at night when they're alone together. Anyway, I'm told she hardly lifts her eyes in public now, in case she meets the King staring at her over his cup, or leaning across at table to look down her dress.'

'That is what I call dunghill stuff, Cadal. I meant, what is she like?'

'Well, that's just what they don't say, except that she's silent, and as beautiful as this, that and the other thing.' He straightened. 'Oh, no one says she gives him any help. And God knows there's no need for Uther to act like a starving man in sight of a dish of food; he could have his platter piled high any night he liked. There's hardly a girl in London who isn't trying to catch that eye of his.'

'I believe you. Has he quarrelled with Gorlois? Openly, I mean?'

'Not so that I heard. In fact, he's been over-cordial there, and he got away with it for the first week or so; the old man was flattered. But Merlin, it does sound like trouble; she's less than half Gorlois' age and spends her life mewed up in one of those cold Cornish castles with nothing to do but weave his war cloaks and dream over them, and you may be sure it's not of an old man with a grey beard.'

I pushed the platter aside. I remember I still felt wholly unconcerned about what Uther was doing. But Cadal's last remark came a little too near home for comfort. There had been another girl, once, who had had nothing to do but sit at home and weave and dream . . .

I said abruptly: 'All right, Cadal. I'm glad to know. I just hope we can keep clear of it ourselves. I've seen Uther mad for a woman before, but they've always been women he could get. This is suicide.'

'Crazed, you said. That's what men are saying, too,' said Cadal slowly. 'Bewitched, they call it.' He looked down at me half-sideways. 'Maybe that's why he sent young Ulfin in such a sweat to make sure you'd come to London. Maybe he wants you there, to break the spell?'

'I don't break,' I said shortly. 'I make.'

He stared for a moment, shutting his mouth on what, apparently, he had been about to say. Then he turned away to lift the jug of wine. As he poured it for me, in silence, I saw that his left hand was making the sign. We spoke no more that night.

Chapter Four

As soon as I came in front of Uther I saw that Cadal had been right. Here was real trouble.

We reached London on the very eve of the crowning. It was late, and the city gates were shut, but it seemed there had been orders about us, for we were hustled through without question, and taken straight up to the castle where the King lay. I was scarcely given time to get out of my mud-stained garments before I was led along to his bedchamber and ushered in. The servants withdrew immediately and left us alone.

Uther was ready for the night, in a long bedgown of dark brown velvet edged with fur. His high chair was drawn to a leaping fire of logs, and on a stool beside the chair stood a pair of goblets and a lidded silver flagon with steam curling gently from the spout. I could smell the spiced wine as soon as I entered the room, and my dry throat contracted longingly, but the King made no move to offer it to me. He was not sitting by the fire. He was prowling restlessly up and down the room like a caged beast, and after him, pace for pace, his wolfhound followed him.

As the door shut behind the servants he said abruptly, as he had said once before:

'You took your time.'

'Four days? You should have sent better horses.'

That stopped him in his tracks. He had not expected to be answered. But he said, mildly enough: 'They were the best in my stables.'

'Then you should get winged ones if you want better speed than we made, my lord. And tougher men. We left two of them by the way.'

But he was no longer listening. Back in his thoughts, he resumed his restless pacing, and I watched him. He had lost weight, and moved quickly and lightly, like a starving wolf. His eyes were sunken with lack of sleep, and he had mannerisms I had not seen in him before; he could not keep his hands still. He wrung them together behind him, cracking the finger-joints, or fidgeted with the edges of his robe, or with his beard.

He flung at me over his shoulder: 'I want your help.'

'So I understand.'

He turned at that. 'You know about it?'

I lifted my shoulders. 'Nobody talks of anything else but the King's desire for Gorlois' wife. I understand you have made no attempt to hide it. But it is more than a week now since you sent Ulfin to fetch me. In that time, what has happened? Are Gorlois and his wife still here?'

'Of course they are still here. They cannot go without my leave.'

'I see. Has anything yet been said between you and Gorlois?'

'No.'

'But he must know.'

'It is the same with him as with me. If once this thing comes to words, nothing can stop it. And it is the crowning tomorrow. I cannot speak with him.'

'Or with her?'

'No. No. Ah, God, Merlin, I cannot come near her. She is guarded like Danaë.'

I frowned. 'He has her guarded, then? Surely that's unusual enough to be a public admission that there's something wrong?'

'I only mean that his servants are all round her, and his men. Not only his bodyguard—many of his fighting troops are still here, that were with us in the north. I can only come near her in public, Merlin. They will have told you this.'

'Yes. Have you managed to get any message to her privately?'

'No. She guards herself. All day she is with her women, and her servants keep the doors. And he—' He paused. There was sweat on his face. 'He is with her every night.'

He flung away again with a swish of the velvet robe, and paced, soft-footed, the length of the room, into the shadows beyond the firelight. Then he turned. He threw out his hands and spoke simply, like a boy.

'Merlin, what shall I do?'

I crossed to the fire-place, picked up the jug and poured two goblets of the spiced wine. I held one out to him. 'To begin with, come and sit down. I cannot talk to a whirlwind. Here.'

He obeyed, sinking back in the big chair with the goblet between his hands. I drank my own, gratefully, and sat down on the other side of the hearth.

Uther did not drink. I think he hardly knew what he had between his hands. He stared at the fire through the thinning steam from the goblet. 'As soon as he brought her in and presented her to me, I knew. God knows that at first I thought it was no more than another passing fever, the kind I've had a thousand times before, only this time a thousand times stronger—'

'And been cured of,' I said 'in a night, a week of nights, a month. I don't know the longest time a woman has ever held you, Uther, but is a month, or even three, enough to wreck a kingdom for?'

The look he gave me, blue as a sword-flash, was a look from the old Uther I remembered. 'By Hades, why do you think I sent for you? I could have wrecked my kingdom any time in these past weeks had I been so minded. Why do you think it has not yet gone beyond folly? Oh, yes, I admit there has been folly, but I tell you this is a fever, and not the kind I have had before, and slaked before. This burns me so that I cannot sleep. How can I rule and fight and deal with men if I cannot sleep?'

'Have you taken a girl to bed?'

He stared, then he drank. 'Are you mad?'

'Forgive me, it was a stupid question. You don't sleep even then?'

'No.' He set down the goblet beside him, and knitted his hands together. 'It's no use. Nothing is any use. You must bring her to me, Merlin. You have the arts. This is why I sent for you. You are to bring her to me so that no one knows. Make her love me. Bring her here to me, while he is asleep. You can do it.'

'Make her love you? My magic? No, Uther, this is something that magic cannot do. You must know that.'

'It is something that every old wife swears she can do. And you–you have power beyond any man living. You lifted the Hanging Stones. You lifted the king-stone where Tremorinus could not.'

'My mathematics are better, that is all. For God's sake, Uther, whatever men say of that, you know how it was done. That was no magic.'

'You spoke with my brother as he died. Are you going to deny that now?'

'No.'

'Or that you swore to serve me when I needed you?'

'No.'

'I need you now. Your power, whatever it is. Dare you tell me that you are not a magician?'

'I am not the kind that can walk through walls,' I said, 'and bring bodies through locked doors.' He made a sudden movement, and I saw the feverish brightness of his eyes, not this time with anger, but, I thought, with pain. I added: 'But I have not refused to help you.'

The eyes sparked. 'You will help me?'

'Yes, I will help you. I told you when last we met that there would come a time when we must deal together. This is the time. I don't know yet what I must do, but this will be shown to me, and the outcome is with the god. But one thing I can do for you, tonight. I can make you sleep. No, be still and listen . . . If you are to be crowned tomorrow, and take Britain into your hands, tonight you will do as I say. I will make you a drink that will let you sleep, and you'll take a girl to your bed as usual. It may be better if there is someone besides your servant who will swear you were in your own chamber.'

'Why? What are you going to do?' His voice was strained.

'I shall try to talk with Ygraine.'

He sat forward, his hand tight on the arms of the chair. 'Yes. Talk to her. Perhaps you can come to her where I cannot. Tell her—'

'A moment. A little while back you told me to "make her love you". You want me to invoke any power there is to bring her to you. If you have never spoken to her of your love, or seen her except in public, how do you know she would come to you, even if the way were free? Is her mind clear to you, my lord King?'

'No. She says nothing. She smiles, with her eyes on the ground, and says nothing. But I know. I know. It is as if all the other times I played at love were only single notes. Put together, they make the song. She is the song.'

There was a silence. Behind him, on a dais in the corner of the room, was the bed, with the covers drawn back ready. Above it, leaping up the wall, was a great dragon fashioned of red gold. In the firelight it moved, stretching its claws.

He said suddenly: 'When we last talked, there in the middle of the Hanging Stones, you said you wanted nothing from me. But by all the gods, Merlin, if you help me now, if I get her, and in safety, then you can ask what you will. I swear it.'

I shook my head, and he said no more. I think he saw that I was no longer thinking of him; that other forces pressed me, crowding the firelit room. The dragon flamed and shimmered up the dark wall. In its shadow another moved, merging with it, flame into flame. Something struck at my eyes, pain like a claw. I shut them, and there was silence. When I opened them again the fire had died, and the wall was dark. I looked across at the King, motionless in his chair, watching me. I said, slowly: 'I will ask you one thing, now.'

'Yes?'

'That when I bring you to her in safety, you shall make a child.'

Whatever he had expected, it was not this. He stared, then, suddenly, laughed. 'That's with the gods surely?'

'Yes, it is with God.'

He stretched back in his chair, as if a weight had been lifted off his shoulders. 'If I come to her, Merlin, I promise you that whatever I have power to do, I shall do. And anything else you bid me. I shall even sleep tonight.'

I stood up. 'Then I shall go and make the draught and send it to you.'

'And you'll see her?'

'I shall see her. Good night.'

Ulfin was half asleep on his feet outside the door. He blinked at me as I came out.

'I'm to go in now?'

'In a minute. Come to my chamber first and I'll give you a drink for him. See he takes it. It's to give him sleep. Tomorrow will be a long day.'

There was a girl asleep in a corner, wrapped in a blue blanket on a huddle of pillows. As we passed I saw the curve of a bare shoulder and a tumble of straight brown hair. She looked very young.

I raised my brows at Ulfin, and he nodded, then jerked his head towards the shut door with a look of enquiry.

'Yes,' I said, 'but later. When you take him the drink. Leave her sleeping now. You look as if you could do with some sleep yourself, Ulfin.'

'If he sleeps tonight I might get some.' He gave a flicker of a grin at me. 'Make it strong, won't you, my lord? And see it tastes good.'

'Oh, he'll drink it, never fear.'

'I wasn't thinking of him,' said Ulfin. 'I was thinking of me.'

'Of you? Ah, I see, you mean you'll have to taste it first?'

He nodded.

'You have to try everything? His meals? Even love potions?'

'Love potions? For him?' He stared, open-mouthed. Then he laughed. 'Oh, you're joking!'

I smiled. 'I wanted to see if you could laugh. Here we are. Wait now, I won't be a minute.'

Cadal was waiting for me by the fire in my chamber. This was a comfortable room in the curve of a tower wall, and Cadal had kept a bright fire burning and a big cauldron of water steaming on the iron dogs. He had got out a woollen bedgown for me and laid it ready across the bed.

Over a chest near the window lay a pile of clothes, a shimmer of gold cloth and scarlet and fur. 'What's that?' I asked, as I sat down to let him draw off my shoes.

'The King sent a robe for tomorrow, my lord.' Cadal, with an eye on the boy who was pouring the bath, was formal. I noticed the boy's hand shaking a little, and water splashed on the floor. As soon as he had finished, obedient to a jerk of Cadal's head, he scuttled out.

'What's the matter with that boy?'

'It isn't every night you prepare a bath for a wizard.'

'For God's sake. What have you been telling him?'

'Only that you'd turn him into a bat if he didn't serve you well.'

'Fool. No, a moment, Cadal. Bring me my box. Ulfin's waiting outside. I promised to make up a draught.'

Cadal obeyed me. 'What's the matter? His arm still bad?'

'It's not for him. For the King.'

'Ah.' He made no further comment, but when the thing was done and Ulfin had gone, and I was stripping for the bath, he asked: 'It's as bad as they say?'

'Worse.' I gave him a brief version of my conversation with the King.

He heard me out, frowning. 'And what's to do now?'

'Find some way to see the lady. No, not the bedgown; not yet, alas. Get me a clean robe out–something dark.'

'Surely you can't go to her tonight? It's well past midnight.'

'I shall not go anywhere. Whoever is coming, will come to me.'

'But Gorlois will be with her—'

'No more now, Cadal. I want to think. Leave me. Good night.'

When the door had shut on him I went across to the chair beside the fire. It was not true that I wanted time to think. All I needed was silence, and the fire. Bit by bit, slowly, I emptied my mind, feeling thought spill out of me like sand from a glass, to leave me hollow and light. I waited, my hands slack on the grey robe, open, empty. It was very quiet. Somewhere, from a dark corner of the room, came the dry tick of old wood settling in the night. The fire flickered. I watched it, but absently, as any man might watch the flames for comfort on a cold night. I did not need to dream. I lay, light as a dead leaf, on the flood that ran that night to meet the sea.

Outside the door there were sounds suddenly, voices. A quick tap at the panel, and Cadal came in, shutting the door behind him. He looked guarded and a little apprehensive.

'Gorlois?' I asked.

He swallowed, then nodded.

'Well, show him in.'

'He asked if you had been to see the King. I said you'd been here barely a couple of hours, and you had had time to see nobody. Was that right?'

I smiled. 'You were guided. Let him come in now.'

Gorlois came in quickly, and I rose to greet him. There was, I thought, as big a change in him as I had seen in Uther; his big frame was bent, and for the first time one saw straight away that he was old.

He brushed aside the ceremony of my greeting. 'You're not abed yet? They told me you'd ridden in.'

'Barely in time for the crowning, but I shall see it after all. Will you sit, my lord?'

'Thanks, but no. I came for your help, Merlin, for my wife.' The quick eyes peered under the grey brows. 'Aye, no one could ever tell what you were thinking, but you've heard, haven't you?'

'There was talk,' I said carefully, 'but then there always was talk about Uther. I have not heard anyone venture a word against your wife.'

'By God, they'd better not! However, it's not that I've come about tonight. There's nothing you could do about that—though it's possible you're the only person who could talk some sense into the King. You'll not get near him now till after the crowning, but if you could get him to let us go back to Cornwall without waiting for the end of the feast . . . Would you do that for me?'

'If I can.'

'I knew I could count on you. With things the way they are in the town just now, it's hard to know who's a friend. Uther's not an easy man to gainsay. But you could do it—and what's more, you'd dare. You're your father's son, and for my old friend's sake—'

'I said I'd do it.'

'What's the matter? Are you ill?'

'It's nothing. I'm weary. We had a hard ride. I'll see the King in the morning early, before he leaves for the crowning.'

He gave a brief nod of thanks. 'That's not the only thing I came to ask you. Would you come and see my wife tonight?'

There was a pause of utter stillness, so prolonged that I thought he must notice. Then I said: 'If you wish it, yes. But why?'

'She's sick, that's why, and I'd have you come and see her, if you will. When her women told her you were here in London, she begged me to send for you. I can tell you, I was thankful when I heard you'd come. There's not many men I'd trust just now, and that's God's truth. But I'd trust you.'

Beside me a log crumbled and fell into the heart of the fire. The flames shot up, splashing his face with red, like blood.

'You'll come?' asked the old man.

'Of course.' I looked away from him. 'I'll come immediately.'

Chapter Five

Uther had not exaggerated when he said that the Lady Ygraine was well guarded. She and her lord were lodged in a court some way west of the King's quarters, and the court was crowded with Cornwall men at arms. There were armed men in the antechamber too, and in the bedchamber itself some half dozen women. As we went in the oldest of these, a greyhaired woman with an anxious look, hurried forward with relief in her face.

'Prince Merlin.' She bent her knees to me, eyeing me with awe, and led me towards the bed.

The room was warm and scented. The lamps burned sweet oil, and the fire was of apple-wood. The bed stood at the centre of the wall opposite the fire. The pillows were of grey silk, with gilt tassels, and the coverlet richly worked with flowers and strange beasts and winged creatures. The only other woman's room that I had seen was my mother's, with the plain wooden bed and the carved oak chest and the loom, and the cracked mosaics of the floor.

I walked forward and stood at the foot of the bed, looking down at Gorlois' wife.

If I had been asked then what she looked like I could not have said. Cadal had told me she was fair, and I had seen the hunger in the King's face, so I knew she was desirable; but as I stood in the airy scented room looking at the woman who lay with closed eyes against the grey silk pillows, it was no woman that I saw. Nor did I see the room or the people in it. I saw only the flashing and beating of the light as in a globed crystal.

I spoke without taking my eyes from the woman in the bed. 'One of her women stay here. The rest go. You too, please, my lord.' He went without demur, herding the women in front of him like a flock of sheep. The woman who had greeted me remained by her mistress's bed. As the door shut behind the last of them, the woman in the bed opened her eyes. For a few moments of silence we met each other eye to eye. Then I said: 'What do you want of me, Ygraine?'

She answered crisply, with no pretence: 'I have sent for you, Prince, because I want your help.'

I nodded. 'In the matter of the King.'

She said straightly: 'So you know already? When my husband brought you here, did you guess I was not ill?'

'I guessed.'

'Then you can also guess what I want from you?'

'Not quite. Tell me, could you not somehow have spoken with the King himself before now? It might have saved him something. And your husband as well.'

Her eyes widened. 'How could I talk to the King? You came through the courtyard?'

'Yes.'

'Then you saw my husband's troops and men at arms. What do you suppose would have happened had I talked to Uther? I could not answer him openly, and if I had met him in secret—even if I could—half London would have known it within the hour. Of course I could not speak to him or send him a message. The only protection was silence.'

I said slowly: 'If the message was simply that you were a true and faithful wife and that he must turn his eyes elsewhere, then the message could have been given to him at any time and by any messenger.'

She smiled. Then she bent her head.

I took in my breath. 'Ah. That's what I wished to know. You are honest, Ygraine.'

'What use to lie to you? I have heard about you. Oh, I know better than to believe all they say in the songs and stories, but you are clever and cold and wise, and they say you love no woman and are committed to no man. So you can listen, and judge.' She looked down at her hands, where they lay on the coverlet, then up at me again. 'But I do believe that you can see the future. I want you to tell me what the future is.'

'I don't tell fortunes like an old woman. Is this why you sent for me?'

'You know why I sent for you. You are the one man with whom I can seek private speech without arousing my husband's anger and suspicion—and you have the King's ear.' Though she was but a woman, and young, lying in her bed with me standing over her, it was as if she were a queen giving audience. She looked at me very straight. 'Has the King spoken to you yet?'

'He has no need to speak to me. Everyone knows what ails him.'

'And will you tell him what you have just learned from me?'

'That will depend.'

'On what?' she demanded.

I said slowly: 'On you yourself. So far you have been wise. Had you been less guarded in your ways and your speech there would have been trouble, there might even have been war. I understand that you have never allowed one moment of your time here to be solitary or unguarded; you have taken care always to be where you could be seen.'

She looked at me for a moment in silence, her brows raised. 'Of course.'

'Many women—especially desiring what you desire—would not have been able to do this, Lady Ygraine.'

'I am not "many women".' The words were like a flash. She sat up suddenly, tossing back the dark hair, and threw back the covers. The old woman snatched up a long blue robe and hurried forward. Ygraine threw it round her, over her white night-robe, and sprang from the bed, walking restlessly over towards the window.

Standing, she was tall for a woman, with a form that might have moved a sterner man than Uther. Her neck was long and slender, the head poised gracefully. The dark hair streamed unbound down her back. Her eyes were blue, not the fierce blue of Uther's, but the deep, dark blue of the Celt. Her mouth was proud. She was very lovely, and no man's toy. If Uther wanted her, I thought, he would have to make her Queen.

She had stopped just short of the window. If she had gone to it, she might have been seen from the courtyard. No, not a lady to lose her head.

She turned. 'I am the daughter of a king, and I come from a line of kings. Cannot you see how I must have been driven, even to think the way I am thinking now?' She repeated it passionately. 'Can you not see? I was married at sixteen to the Lord of Cornwall; he is a good man; I honour and respect him. Until I came to London I was half content to starve and die there in Cornwall, but he brought me here, and now it has happened. Now I know what I must have, but it is beyond me to have it, beyond the wife of Gorlois of Cornwall. So what else would you have me do? There is nothing to do but wait here and be silent, because on my silence hangs not only the honour of myself and my husband and my house, but the safety of the kingdom that Ambrosius died for, and that Uther himself has just sealed with blood and fire.'

She swung away to take two quick paces and back again. 'I am no trashy Helen for men to fight over, die over, burn down kingdoms for. I don't wait on the walls as a prize for some brawny victor. I cannot so dishonour both Gorlois and the King in the eyes of men. And I cannot go to him secretly and dishonour myself in my own eyes. I am a lovesick woman, yes. But I am also Ygraine of Cornwall.'

I said coldly: 'So you intend to wait until you can go to him in honour, as his Queen?'

'What else can I do?'

'Was this the message I had to give him?'

She was silent.

I said: 'Or did you get me here to read you the future? To tell you the length of your husband's life?'

Still she said nothing.

'Ygraine,' I said, 'the two are the same. If I give Uther the message that you love and desire him, but that you will not come to him while your husband is alive, what length of life would you prophesy for Gorlois?'

Still she did not speak. The gift of silence, too, I thought. I was standing between her and the fire. I watched the light beating round her, flowing up the white robe and the blue robe, light and shadow rippling upwards in waves like moving water or the wind over grass. A flame leapt, and my shadow sprang over her and grew, climbing with the beating light to meet her own climbing shadow and join with it, so that there across the wall behind her reared—no dragon of gold or scarlet, no firedrake with burning tail, but a great cloudy shape of air and darkness, thrown there by the flame, and sinking as the flame sank, to shrink and steady until it was only her shadow, the shadow of a woman, slender and straight, like a sword. And where I stood, there was nothing.

She moved, and the lamplight built the room again round us, warm and real and smelling of apple-wood. She was watching me with something in her face that had not been there before. At last she said, in a still voice: 'I told you there was nothing hidden from you. You do well to put it into words. I had thought all this. But I hoped that by sending for you I could absolve myself, and the King.'

'Once a dark thought is dragged into words it is in the light. You could have had your desire long since on the terms of "any woman", as the King could on the terms of any man.' I paused. The room was steady now. The words came clearly to me, from nowhere, without thought. 'I will tell you, if you like, how you may meet the King's love on your terms and on his, with no dishonour to yourself or him, or to your husband. If I could tell you this, would you go to him?'

Her eyes had widened, with a flash behind them, as I spoke. But even so she took time to think. 'Yes.' Her voice told me nothing.

'If you will obey me, I can do this for you,' I said.

'Tell me what I must do.'

'Have I your promise, then?'

'You go too fast,' she said drily. 'Do you yourself seal bargains before you see what you are committed to?'

I smiled. 'No. Very well then, listen to me. When you feigned illness to have me brought to you, what did you tell your husband and your women?'

'Only that I felt faint and sick, and was no more inclined for company. That if I was to appear beside my husband at the crowning, I must see a physician tonight, and take a healing draught.' She smiled a little wryly. 'I was preparing the way, too, not to sit beside the King at the feast.'

'So far, good. You will tell Gorlois that you are pregnant.'

'*That I am pregnant?*' For the first time she sounded shaken. She stared. 'This is possible? He is an old man, but I would have thought—'

'It is possible. But I—' She bit her lip. After a while she said calmly: 'Go on. I asked for your counsel, so I must let you give it.'

I had never before met a woman with whom I did not have to choose my words, to whom I could speak as I would speak to another man. I said: 'Your husband can have no reason to suspect you are pregnant by any man but himself. So you will tell him this, and tell him also that you fear for the child's health if you stay longer in London, under the strain of the gossip and the King's attentions. Tell him that you wish to leave as soon as the crowning is over. That you do not wish to go to the feast, to be distinguished by the King, and to be the centre of all the eyes and the gossip. You will go with Gorlois and the Cornish troops tomorrow, before the gates shut at sunset. The news will not come to Uther until the feast.'

'But . . .' She stared again . . . 'this is folly. We could have gone any time this past three weeks if we had chosen to risk the King's anger. We are bound to stay until he gives us leave to go. If we go in that manner, for whatever reason—'

I stopped her. 'Uther can do nothing on the day of the crowning. He must stay here for the days of feasting. Do you think he can give offence to Budec and Merrovius and the other kings gathered here? You will be in Cornwall before he can even move.'

'And then he will move.' She made an impatient gesture. 'And there will be war, when he should be making and mending, not breaking and burning. And he cannot win: if he is the victor in the field, he loses the loyalty of the West. Win or lose, Britain is divided, and goes back into the dark.'

Yes, she would be a queen. She was on fire for Uther as much as he for her, but she could still think. She was cleverer than Uther, clear-headed, and, I thought, stronger too.

'Oh, yes, he will move.' I lifted a hand. 'But listen to me. I will talk to the King before the crowning. He will know that the story you told Gorlois was a lie. He will know that I have told you to go to Cornwall. He will feign rage, and he will swear in public to be revenged for the insult put on him by Gorlois at the crowning . . . And he will make ready to follow you to Cornwall as soon as the feast is over—'

'But meanwhile our troops will be safely out of London without trouble. Yes, I see. I did not understand you. Go on.' She drove her hands inside the sleeves of the blue robe, and clasped her elbows, cradling her breasts. She was not so ice-calm as she looked, the Lady Ygraine. 'And then?'

'And you will be safely at home,' I said, 'with your honour and Cornwall's unbroken.'

'Safely, yes. I shall be in Tintagel, and even Uther cannot come at me there. Have you seen the stronghold, Merlin? The cliffs of that coast are high and cruel, and from them runs a thin bridge of rock, the only way to the island where the castle stands. This bridge is so narrow that men can only go one at a time, not even a horse. Even the landward end of the bridge is guarded by a fortress on the main cliff, and within the castle there is water, and food for a year. It is the strongest place in Cornwall. It cannot be taken from the land, and it cannot be approached by sea. If you wish to shut me away for ever from Uther, this is the place to send me.'

'So I have heard. This will be, then, where Gorlois will send you. If Uther follows, lady, would Gorlois be content to wait inside the stronghold with you for a year like a beast in a trap? And could his troops be taken in with him?'

She shook her head. 'If it cannot be taken, neither can it be used as a base. All one can do is sit out the siege.'

'Then you must persuade him that unless he is content to wait inside while the King's troops ravage Cornwall, he himself must be outside, where he can fight.'

She struck her hands together. 'He will do that. He could not wait and hide and let Cornwall suffer. Nor can I understand your plan, Merlin. If you are trying to save your King and your kingdom from me, then say so. I can feign sickness here, until Uther finds he has to let me go home. We could go home without insult, and without bloodshed.'

I said sharply: 'You said you would listen. Time runs short.'

She was still again. 'I am listening.'

'Gorlois will lock you in Tintagel. Where will he go himself to face Uther?'

'To Dimilioc. It is a few miles from Tintagel, up the coast. It is a good fortress, and good country to fight from. But then what? Do you think Gorlois will not fight?' She moved across to the fireside and sat down, and I saw her steady her hands deliberately, spreading the fingers on her knee. 'And do you think the King can come to me in Tintagel, whether Gorlois is there or no?'

'If you do as I have bid you, you and the King may have speech and comfort one of the other. And you will do this in peace. No—' as her head

came up sharply '—this part of it you leave with me. This is where we come
to magic. Trust me for the rest. Get yourself only to Tintagel, and wait. I
shall bring Uther to you there. And I promise you now, for the King, that he
shall not give battle to Gorlois, and that after he and you have met in love,
Cornwall shall have peace. As to how this will be, it is with God. I can only
tell you what I know. What power is in me now, is from him, and we are in
his hands to make or to destroy. But I can tell you this also, Ygraine, that I
have seen a bright fire burning, and in it a crown, and a sword standing in an
altar like a cross.'

She got to her feet quickly, and for the first time there was a kind of fear in
her eyes. She opened her mouth as if to speak, then closed her lips again and
turned back towards the window. Again she stopped short of it, but I saw
her lift her head as if longing for the air. She should have been winged. If she
had spent her youth walled in Tintagel it was no wonder she wanted to fly.

She raised her hands and pushed back the hair from her brows. She spoke
to the window, not looking at me. 'I will do this. If I tell him I am with child,
he will take me to Tintagel. It is the place where all the dukes of Cornwall
are born. And after that I have to trust you.' She turned then and looked at
me, dropping her hands. 'If once I can have speech with him . . . even just
that . . . But if you have brought bloodshed to Cornwall through me, or
death to my husband, then I shall spend the rest of my life praying to any
gods there are that you, too, Merlin, shall die betrayed by a woman.'

'I am content to face your prayers. And now I must go. Is there someone
you can send with me? I'll make a draught for you and send it back. It will
only be poppy; you can take and not fear.'

'Ralf can go, my page. You'll find him outside the door. He is Marcia's
grandson, and can be trusted as I trust her.' She nodded to the old woman,
who moved to open the door for me.

'Then any message I may have to send you,' I said, 'I shall send through
him by my man Cadal. And now good night.'

When I left her she was standing quite still in the centre of the room, with
the firelight leaping round her.

Chapter Six

We had a wild ride to Cornwall.

Easter that year had fallen as early as it ever falls, so we were barely out of
winter and into spring when, on a black wild night, we halted our horses on
the clifftop near Tintagel, and peered down into the teeth of the wind.
There were only the four of us, Uther, myself, Ulfin and Cadal. Everything,
so far, had gone smoothly and according to plan. It was getting on towards
midnight on the twenty-fourth of March.

Ygraine had obeyed me to the letter. I had not dared, that night in
London, to go straight from her quarters to Uther's chamber, in case this
should be reported to Gorlois; but in any case Uther would be asleep. I had

visited him early next morning, while he was being bathed and made ready for the crowning. He sent the servants away, except for Ulfin, and I was able to tell him exactly what he must do. He looked the better for his drugged sleep, greeted me briskly enough, and listened with eagerness in the bright, hollow eyes.

'And she will do as you say?'

'Yes. I have her word. Will you?'

'You know that I will.' He regarded me straightly. 'And now will you not tell me about the outcome?'

'I told you. A child.'

'Oh, that.' He hunched an impatient shoulder. 'You are like my brother; he thought of nothing else . . . Still working for him, are you?'

'You might say so.'

'Well, I must get one sooner or later, I suppose. No, I meant Gorlois. What will come to him? There's a risk, surely?'

'Nothing is done without risk. You must do the same as I, you must take the time on trust. But I can tell you that your name, and your kingdom, will survive the night's work.'

A short silence. He measured me with his eyes. 'From you, I suppose that is enough. I am content.'

'You do well to be. You will outlive him, Uther.'

He laughed suddenly. 'God's grief, man, I could have prophesied that myself! I can give him thirty years, and he's no stay-at-home when it comes to war. Which is one good reason why I refuse to have his blood on my hands. So, on that same account . . .'

He turned then to Ulfin and began to give his orders. It was the old Uther back again, brisk, concise, clear. A messenger was to go immediately to Caerleon, and troops to be despatched from there to North Cornwall. Uther himself would travel there straight from London as soon as he was able, riding fast with a small bodyguard to where his troops would be encamped. In this way the King could be hard on Gorlois' heels, even though Gorlois would leave today, and the King must stay feasting his peers for four more long days. Another man was to ride out immediately along our proposed route to Cornwall, and see that good horses were ready at short stages all the way.

So it came about as I had planned. I saw Ygraine at the crowning, still, composed, erect and with downcast eyes, and so pale that if I had not seen her the night before, I myself would have believed her story true. I shall never cease to wonder at women. Even with power, it is not possible to read their minds. Duchess and slut alike, they need not even study to deceive. I suppose it is the same with slaves, who live with fear, and with those animals who disguise themselves by instinct to save their lives. She sat through the long, brilliant ceremony, like wax which at any moment may melt to collapse; then afterwards I caught a glimpse of her, supported by her women, leaving the throng as the bright pomp moved slowly to the hall of feasting. About halfway through the feast, when the wine had gone round well, I saw Gorlois, unremarked, leave the hall with one or two other men who were answering the call of nature. He did not come back.

Uther, to one who knew the truth, may not have been quite so convincing as Ygraine, but between exhaustion and wine and his ferocious exaltation at what was to come, he was convincing enough. Men talked among themselves in hushed voices about his rage when he discovered Gorlois' absence, and his angry vows to take vengeance as soon as his royal guests had gone. If that anger were a little overloud and his threats too fierce against a Duke whose only fault was the protection of his own wife, the King had been intemperate enough before for men to see this as part of the same picture. And so bright now was Uther's star, so dazzling the lustre of the crowned Pendragon, that London would have forgiven him a public rape. They could less easily forgive Ygraine for having refused him.

So we came to Cornwall. The messenger had done his work well, and our ride, in hard short stages of no more than twenty miles apiece, took us two days and a night. We found our troops waiting encamped at the place selected–a few miles in from Hercules Point and just outside the Cornish border–with the news that, however she had managed it, Ygraine was fast in Tintagel with a small body of picked men, while her husband with the rest of his force had descended on Dimilioc, and sent a call round for the men of Cornwall to gather to defend their Duke. He must know of the presence of the King's troops so near his border, but no doubt he would expect them to wait for the King's coming, and could have as yet no idea that the King was already there.

We rode secretly into our camp at dusk, and went, not to the King's quarters, but to those of a captain he could trust. Cadal was there already, having gone ahead to prepare the disguises which I meant us to wear, and to await Ralf's message from Tintagel when the time was ripe.

My plan was simple enough, with the kind of simplicity that often succeeds, and it was helped by Gorlois' habit, since his marriage, of riding back nightly where he could–from Dimilioc or his other fortresses–to visit his wife. I suppose there had been too many jests about the old man's fondness, and he had formed a habit (Ralf had told me) of riding back secretly, using the private gate, a hidden postern to which access was difficult unless one knew the way. My plan was simply to disguise Uther, Ulfin and myself to pass, if we were seen, as Gorlois and his companion and servant, and ride to Tintagel by night. Ralf would arrange to be on duty himself at the postern, and would meet us and lead us up the secret path. Ygraine had by some means persuaded Gorlois–this had been the greatest danger–not to visit her himself that night, and would dismiss all her women but Marcia. Ralf and Cadal had arranged between them what clothes we should wear: the Cornwall party had ridden from London in such a hurry that some of their baggage was left behind, and it had been simple to find saddle-cloths with the blazon of Cornwall, and even one of Gorlois' familiar war cloaks with the double border of silver.

Ralf's latest message had been reassuring; the time was ripe, the night black enough to hide us and wild enough to keep most men within doors. We set off after it was full dark, and the four of us slipped out of camp unobserved. Once clear of our own lines we went at a gallop for Tintagel, and it would have been only the keen eye of suspicion which could have told that this was not the Duke of Cornwall with three companions, riding quickly home to his wife. Uther's beard had been greyed, and a bandage came down one side of his face to cover the corner of his mouth, and give some reason—should he be forced to talk—for any strangeness in his speech. The hood of his cloak, pulled down low as was natural on such a fierce night, shadowed his features. He was straighter and more powerful than Gorlois, but this was easy enough to disguise, and he wore gauntlets to hide his hands, which were not those of an old man. Ulfin passed well enough as one Jordan, a servant of Gorlois whom we had chosen as being the nearest to Ulfin's build and colouring. I myself wore the clothes of Brithael, Gorlois' friend and captain: he was an older man than I, but his voice was not unlike mine, and I could speak good Cornish. I have always been good at voices. I was to do what talking proved necessary. Cadal came with us undisguised; he was to wait with the horses outside and be our messenger if we should need one.

I rode up close to the King and set my mouth to his ear. 'The castle's barely a mile from here. We ride down to the shore now. Ralf will be there to show us in. I'll lead on?'

He nodded. Even in the ragged, flying dark I thought I saw the gleam of his eyes. I added: 'And don't look like that, or they'll never think you're Gorlois, with years of married life behind you.'

I heard him laugh, and then I wheeled my horse and led the way carefully down the rabbit-ridden slope of scrub and scree into the head of the narrow valley which leads down towards the shore.

This valley is little more than a gully carrying a small stream to the sea. At its widest the stream is not more than three paces broad, and so shallow that a horse can ford it anywhere. At the foot of the valley the water drops over a low cliff straight to a beach of slaty shingle. We rode in single file down the track, with the stream running deep down on the left, and to our right a high bank covered with bushes. Since the wind was from the south-west and the valley was deep and running almost north, we were sheltered from the gale, but at the top of the bank the bushes were screaming in the wind, and twigs and even small boughs hurtled through the air and across our path. Even without this and the steepness of the stony path and the darkness, it was not easy riding; the horses, what with the storm and some tension which must have been generated by the three of us—Cadal was as solid as a rock, but then he was not going into the castle—were wild and white-eyed with nerves. When, a quarter of a mile from the sea, we turned down to the stream and set the beasts to cross it, mine, in the lead, flattened its ears and baulked, and when I had lashed it across and into a plunging canter up the narrow track, and a man's figure detached itself from the shadows ahead beside the path, the horse stopped dead and climbed straight up into the air till I felt sure it would go crashing over backwards, and me with it.

The shadow darted forward and seized the bridle, dragging the horse down. The beast stood, sweating and shaking.

'Brithael,' I said. 'Is all well?'

I heard him exclaim, and he took a pace, pressing closer to the horse's shoulder, peering upwards in the dark. Behind me Uther's grey hoisted itself up the track and thudded to a halt. The man at my horse's shoulder said, uncertainly: 'My lord Gorlois . . . ? We did not look for you tonight. Is there news, then?'

It was Ralf's voice. I said in my own: 'So we'll pass, at least in the dark?'
I heard his breath go in. 'Yes, my lord . . . For the moment I thought it
was indeed Brithael. And then the grey horse . . . Is that the King?'

'For tonight,' I said, 'it is the Duke of Cornwall. Is all well?'

'Yes, sir.'

'Then lead the way. There is not much time.'

He gripped my horse's bridle above the bit and led him on, for which I
was grateful, as the path was dangerous, narrow and slippery and twisting
along the steep bank between the rustling bushes, not a path I would have
wished to ride even in daylight on a strange and frightened horse. The
others followed, Cadal's mount and Ulfin's plodding stolidly along, and
close behind me the grey stallion snorting at every bush and trying to break
his rider's grip, but Uther could have ridden Pegasus himself and
foundered him before his own wrists even ached.

Here my horse shied at something I could not see, stumbled, and would
have pitched me down the bank but for Ralf at its head. I swore at it, then
asked Ralf: 'How far now?'

'About two hundred paces to the shore, sir, and we leave the horses there.
We climb the promontory on foot.'

'By all the gods of storm, I'll be glad to get under cover. Did you have any
trouble?'

'None, sir.' He had to raise his voice to make me hear, but in that turmoil
there was no fear of being heard more than three paces off. 'My lady told
Felix herself—that's the porter—that she had asked the Duke to ride back as
soon as his troops were disposed at Dimilioc. Of course the word's gone
round that she's pregnant, so it's natural enough she'd want him back, even
with the King's armies so close. She told Felix the Duke would come by the
secret gate in case the King had spies posted already. He wasn't to tell the
garrison, she said, because they might be alarmed at his leaving Dimilioc
and the troops there, but the King couldn't possibly be in Cornwall for
another day at soonest . . . Felix doesn't suspect a thing. Why should he?'

'The porter is alone at the gate?'

'Yes, but there are two guards in the guard-room.'

He had told us already what lay inside the postern. This was a small gate
set low in the outer castle wall, and just inside it a long flight of steps ran up
to the right, hugging the wall. Halfway up was a wide landing, with a guard-
room to the side. Beyond that the stairs went up again, and at the top was the
private door leading through into the apartments.

'Do the guards know?' I asked.

He shook his head. 'My lord, we didn't dare. All the men left with the
Lady Ygraine were hand-picked by the Duke.'

'Are the stairs well lighted?'

'A torch. I saw to it that it will be mostly smoke.'

I looked over my shoulder to where the grey horse came ghostly behind
me though the dark. Ralf had had to raise his voice to make me hear above
the wind which screamed across the top of the valley, and I would have
thought that the King would be waiting to know what passed between us.
But he was silent, as he had been since the beginning of the ride. It seemed
he was indeed content to trust the time. Or to trust me.

I turned back to Ralf, leaning down over my horse's shoulder. 'Is there a password?'

'Yes, my lord. It is *pilgrim*. And the lady has sent a ring for the King to wear. It is one the Duke wears sometimes. Here's the end of the path, can you see? It's quite a drop to the beach.' He checked, steadying my horse, then the beast plunged down and its hoofs grated on shingle. 'We leave the horses here, my lord.'

I dismounted thankfully. As far as I could see, we were in a small cove sheltered from the wind by a mighty headland close to our left, but the seas, tearing past the end of this headland and curving round to break among the offshore rocks, were huge, and came lashing down on the shingle in torrents of white with a noise like armies clashing together in anger. Away to the right I saw another high headland, and between the two this roaring stretch of white water broken by the teeth of black rocks. The stream behind us fell seawards over its low cliff in two long cascades, which blew in the wind like ropes of hair. Beyond these swinging waterfalls, and in below the overhanging wall of the main cliff, there was shelter for the horses.

Ralf was pointing to the great headland on our left. 'The path is up there. Tell the King to come behind me and to follow closely. One foot wrong tonight, and before you could cry help you'd be out with the tide as far as the western stars.'

The grey thudded down beside us and the King swung himself out of the saddle. I heard him laugh, that same sharp, exultant sound. Even had there been no prize at the end of the night's trail, he would have been the same. Danger was drink and dreams alike to Uther.

The other two came up with us and dismounted, and Cadal took the reins. Uther came to my shoulder, looking at the cruel race of water. 'Do we swim for it now?'

'It may come to that, God knows. It looks to me as if the waves are up to the castle wall.'

He stood quite still, oblivious of the buffeting of wind and rain, with his head lifted, staring up at the headland. High against the stormy dark, a light burned.

I touched his arm. 'Listen. The situation is what we expected. There is a porter, Felix, and two men at arms in the guard-room. There should be very little light. You know the way in. It will be enough, as we go in, if you grunt your thanks to Felix and go quickly up the stair. Marcia, the old woman, will meet you at the door of Ygraine's apartments and lead you in. You can leave the rest to us. If there is any trouble, then there are three of us to three of them, and on a night like this there'll be no sound heard. I shall come an hour before dawn and send Marcia in for you. Now we shall not be able to speak again. Follow Ralf closely, the path is very dangerous. He has a ring for you and the password. Go now.'

He turned without a word and trod across the streaming shingle to where the boy waited. I found Cadal beside me, with the reins of the four horses gathered in his fist. His face, like my own, was streaming with wet, his cloak billowing round him like a storm cloud.

I said: 'You heard me. An hour before dawn.'

He, too, was looking up at the crag where high above us the castle towered. In a moment of flying light through the torn cloud I saw the castle walls, growing out of the rock. Below them fell the cliff, almost vertical, to the roaring waves. Between the promontory and the mainland, joining the castle to the mainland cliff, ran a natural ridge of rock, its sheer side polished flat as a sword blade by the sea. From the beach where we stood, there seemed to be no way out but the valley; not mainland fortress, nor causeway, nor castle rock, could be climbed. It was no wonder they left no sentries here. And the path to the secret gate could he held by one man against an army.

Cadal was saying: 'I'll get the horses in there, under the overhang, in what shelter there is. And for my sake, if not for yon lovesick gentleman's, be on time. If they as much as suspicion up yonder that there's something amiss, it's rats in a trap for the lot of us. They can shut that bloody little valley as sharp as they can block the causeway, you know that? And I wouldn't just fancy swimming out the other way, myself.'

'Nor I. Content yourself, Cadal, I know what I'm about.'

'I believe you. There's something about you tonight . . . The way you spoke just now to the King, not thinking, shorter than you'd speak to a servant. And he said never a word, but did as he was bid. Yes, I'd say you know what you're about. Which is just as well, master Merlin, because otherwise, you realise, you're risking the life of the King of Britain for a night's lust?'

I did something which I had never done before; which I do not commonly do. I put a hand out and laid it over Cadal's where it held the reins. The horses were quiet now, wet and unhappy, huddling with their rumps to the wind and their heads drooping.

I said: 'If Uther gets into the place tonight and lies with her, then before God, Cadal, it will not matter as much as the worth of a drop of that seafoam there if he is murdered in the bed. I tell you, a King will come out of this night's work whose name will be a shield and buckler to men until this fair land, from sea to sea, is smashed down into the sea that holds it, and men leave earth to live among the stars. Do you think Uther is a King, Cadal? He's but a regent for him who went before and for him who comes after, the past and future King. And tonight he is even less than that: he is a tool, and she a vessel, and I . . . I am a spirit, a word, a thing of air and darkness, and I can no more help what I am doing than a reed can help the wind of God blowing through it. You and I, Cadal, are as helpless as dead leaves in the waters of that bay.' I dropped my hand from his. 'An hour before dawn.'

'Till then, my lord.'

I left him then, and, with Ulfin following, went after Ralf and the King across the shingle to the foot of the black cliff.

Chapter Seven

I do not think that now, even in daylight, I could find the path again without a guide, let alone climb it. Ralf went first, with the King's hand on his shoulder, and in my turn I held a fold of Uther's mantle, and Ulfin of mine. Mercifully, close in as we were to the face of the castle rock, we were protected from the wind: exposed, the climb would have been impossible; we would have been plucked off the cliff like feathers. But we were not protected from the sea. The waves must have been rushing up forty feet, and the master waves, the great sevenths, came roaring up like towers and drenched us with salt fully sixty feet above the beach.

One good thing the savage boiling of the sea did for us, its whiteness cast upwards again what light came from the sky. At last we saw, above our heads, the roots of the castle walls where they sprang from the rock. Even in dry weather the walls would have been unscaleable, and tonight they were streaming with wet. I could see no door, nothing breaking the smooth streaming walls of slate. Ralf did not pause, but led us on under them towards a seaward corner of the cliff. There he halted for a moment, and I saw him move his arm in a gesture that meant 'Beware'. He went carefully round the corner and out of sight. I felt Uther stagger as he reached the corner himself and met the force of the wind. He checked for a moment and then went on, clamped tight to the cliff's face. Ulfin and I followed. For a few more hideous yards we fought our way along, faces in to the soaking, slimy cliff, then a jutting buttress gave shelter, and we were stumbling suddenly on a treacherous slope cushiony with sea-pink, and there ahead of us, recessed deep in the rock below the castle wall, and hidden from the ramparts above by the sharp overhang, was Tintagel's emergency door.

I saw Ralf give a long look upwards before he led us in under the rock. There were no sentries above. What need to post men on the seaward ramparts? He drew his dagger and rapped sharply on the door, a pattern of knocks which we, standing as we were at his shoulder, scarcely heard in the gale.

The porter must have been waiting just inside. The door opened immediately. It swung silently open for about three inches, then stuck, and I heard the rattle of a chain bolt. In the gap a hand showed, gripping a torch. Uther, beside me, dragged his hood closer, and I stepped past him to Ralf's elbow, holding my mantle tightly to my mouth and hunching my shoulders against the volleying gusts of wind and rain.

The porter's face, half of it, showed below the torch. An eye peered. Ralf, well forward into the light, said urgently: 'Quick, man. A pilgrim. It's me back, with the Duke.'

The torch moved fractionally higher. I saw the big emerald on Uther's finger catch the light, and said curtly, in Brithael's voice: 'Open up, Felix, and let us get in out of this, for pity's sake. The Duke had a fall from his horse this morning, and his bandage is soaking. There are just the four of us here. Make haste.'

The chain bolt came off and the door swung wide. Ralf put a hand to it so that, ostensibly holding it for his master, he could step into the passage between Felix and Uther as the King entered.

Uther strode in past the bowing man, shaking the wet off himself like a dog, and returning some half-heard sound in answer to the porter's greeting. Then with a brief lift of the hand which set the emerald flashing again, he turned straight for the steps which led upwards on our right, and began quickly to mount them.

Ralf grabbed the torch from the porter's hand as Ulfin and I pressed in after Uther. 'I'll light them up with this. Get the door shut and barred again. I'll come down later and give you the news, Felix, but we're all drenched as drowned dogs, and want to get to a fire. There's one in the guard-room, I suppose?'

'Aye.' The porter had already turned away to bar the door. Ralf was holding the torch so that Ulfin and I could go past in shadow.

I started quickly up the steps in Uther's wake, with Ulfin on my heels. The stairs were lit only by a smoking cresset which burned in a bracket on the wall of the wide landing above us. It had been easy.

Too easy. Suddenly, above us on the landing, the sullen light was augmented by that from a blazing torch, and a couple of men at arms stepped from a doorway, swords at the ready.

Uther, six steps above me, paused fractionally and then went on. I saw his hand, under the cloak, drop to his sword. Under my own I had my weapon loose in its sheath.

Ralf's light tread came running up the steps behind us.

'My lord Duke!'

Uther, I could guess how thankfully, stopped and turned to wait for him, his back to the guards.

'My lord Duke, let me light you–ah, they've a torch up there.' He seemed only then to notice the guards above us, with the blazing light. He ran on and up past Uther, calling lightly: 'Holà, Marcus, Sellic, give me that torch to light my lord up to the Duchess. This wretched thing's nothing but smoke.'

The man with the torch had it held high, and the pair of them were peering down the stairs at us. The boy never hesitated. He ran up, straight between the swords, and took the torch from the man's hand. Before they could reach for it, he turned swiftly to douse the first torch in the tub of sand which stood near the guard-room door. It went out into sullen smoke. The new torch blazed cleanly, but swung and wavered as he moved so that the shadows of the guards, flung gigantic and grotesque down the steps, helped to hide us. Uther, taking advantage of the swaying shadows, started again swiftly up the flight. The hand with Gorlois' ring was half up before him to return the men's salutes. The guards moved aside. But they moved one to each side of the head of the steps, and their swords were still in their hands.

Behind me, I heard the faint whisper as Ulfin's blade loosened in its sheath. Under my cloak, mine was half-drawn. There was no hope of getting past them. We would have to kill them, and pray it made no noise. I heard Ulfin's step lagging, and knew he was thinking of the porter. He might have to go back to him while we dealt with the guards.

But there was no need. Suddenly, at the head of the second flight of steps, a door opened wide, and there, full in the blaze of light, stood Ygraine. She was in white, as I had seen her before; but not this time in a night-robe. The long gown shimmered like lake water. Over one arm and shoulder, Roman fashion, she wore a mantle of soft dark blue. Her hair was dressed with jewels. She stretched out both her hands, and the blue robe and the white fell away from wrists where red gold glimmered.

'Welcome, my lord!' Her voice, high and clear, brought both guards round to face her. Uther took the last half dozen steps to the landing in two leaps, then was past them, his cloak brushing the sword blades, past Ralf's blazing torch, and starting quickly up the second flight of steps.

The guards snapped back to attention, one each side of the stair-head, their backs to the wall. Behind me I heard Ulfin gasp, but he followed me quietly enough as, calmly and without hurry, I mounted the last steps to the landing. It is something, I suppose, to have been born a prince, even a bastard one; I knew that the sentries' eyes were nailed to the wall in front of them by the Duchess's presence as surely as if they were blind. I went between the swords, and Ulfin after me.

Uther had reached the head of the stairway. He took her hands, and there in front of the lighted door, with his enemies' swords catching the torchlight below him, the King bent his head and kissed Ygraine. The scarlet cloak swung round both of them, engulfing the white. Beyond them I saw the shadow of the old woman, Marcia, holding the door.

Then the King said: 'Come,' and with the great cloak still covering them both, he led her into the firelight, and the door shut behind them.

So we took Tintagel.

Chapter Eight

We were well served that night, Ulfin and I. The chamber door had hardly shut, leaving us islanded halfway up the flight between the door and the guards below, when I heard Ralf's voice again, easy and quick above the slither of swords being sheathed:

'Gods and angels, what a night's work! And I still have to guide him back when it's done! You've a fire in the room yonder? Good. We'll have a chance to dry off while we're waiting. You can get yourselves off now and leave this trick to us. Go on, what are you waiting for? You've had your orders—and no word of this, mark you, to anyone that comes.'

One of the guards, settling his sword home, turned straight back into the guard-room, but the other hesitated, glancing up towards me. 'My lord

Brithael, is that right? We go off watch?'

I started slowly down the stairs. 'Quite right. You can go. We'll send the porter for you when we want to leave. And above all, not a word of the Duke's presence. See to it.' I turned to Ulfin, big-eyed on the stairs behind me. 'Jordan, you go up to the chamber door yonder and stand guard. No, give me your cloak. I'll take it to the fire.'

As he went thankfully, his sword at last ready in his hand, I heard Ralf crossing the guard-room below, underlining my orders with what threats I could only guess at. I went down the steps, not hurrying, to give him time to get rid of the men.

I heard the inner door shut, and went in. The guard-room, brightly lit by the torch and the blazing fire, was empty save for ourselves.

Ralf gave me a smile, gay and threadbare with nerves. 'Not again, even to please my lady, for all the gold in Cornwall!'

'There will be no need again. You have done more than well, Ralf. The King will not forget.'

He reached up to put the torch in a socket, saw my face, and said anxiously: 'What is it, sir? Are you ill?'

'No. Does that door lock?' I nodded at the shut door through which the guards had gone.

'I have locked it. If they had had any suspicion, they would not have given me the key. But they had none, how could they? I could have sworn myself just now that it was Brithael speaking there, from the stairs. It was—like magic.' The last word held a question, and he eyed me with a look I knew, but when I said nothing, he asked merely: 'What now, sir?'

'Get you down to the porter now, and keep him away from here.' I smiled. 'You'll get your turn at the fire, Ralf, when we have gone.'

He went off, light-footed as ever, down the steps. I heard him call something, and a laugh from Felix. I stripped off my drenched cloak and spread it, with Ulfin's, to the blaze. Below the cloak my clothes were dry enough. I sat for a while, holding my hands before me to the fire. It was very still in the firelit chamber, but outside the air was full of the surging din of the waters and the storm tearing at the castle walls.

My thoughts stung like sparks. I could not sit still. I stood and walked about the little chamber, restlessly. I listened to the storm outside and, going to the door, heard the murmur of voices and the click of dice as Ralf and Felix passed the time down by the gate. I looked the other way. No sound from the head of the stairs, where I could just see Ulfin, or perhaps his shadow, motionless by the chamber door . . .

Someone was coming softly down the stairs; a woman, shrouded in a mantle, carrying something. She came without a sound, and there had been neither sound nor movement from Ulfin. I stepped out on to the landing, and the light from the guard-room came after me, firelight and shadow.

It was Marcia. I saw the tears glisten on her cheeks as she bent her head over what lay in her arms. A child, wrapped warm against the winter night. She saw me and held her burden out to me. 'Take care of him,' she said, and through the shine of the tears I saw the treads of the stairway outline themselves again behind her. 'Take care of him . . .'

The whisper faded into the flutter of the torch and the sough of the storm outside. I was alone on the stairway, and above me a shut door. Ulfin had not moved.

I lowered my empty arms and went back to the fire. This was dying down, and I made it burn up again, but with small comfort to myself, for again the light stung me. Though I had seen what I wanted to see, there was death somewhere before the end, and I was afraid. My body ached, and the room was stifling. I picked up my cloak, which was almost dry, slung it round me, and crossed the landing to where in the outer wall was a small door under which the wind drove like a knife. I thrust the door open against the blast, and went outside.

At first, after the blaze of the guard-room, I could see nothing. I shut the door behind me and leaned back against the damp wall, while the night air poured over me like a river. Then things took shape around me. In front and a few paces away was a battlemented wall, waist high, the outer wall of the castle. Between this wall and where I stood was a level platform, and above me a wall rising again to a battlement, and beyond this the soaring cliff and the walls climbing it, and the shape of the fortress rising above me step by step to the peak of the promontory. At the very head of the rise, where we had seen the lighted window, the tower now showed black and lightless against the sky.

I went forward to the battlement and leaned over. Below was an apron of cliff, which would in daylight be a grassy slope covered with sea-pink and white campion and the nests of seabirds. Beyond it and below, the white rage of the bay. I looked down to the right, the way we had come. Except for the driving arcs of white foam, the bay where Cadal waited was invisible under the darkness.

It had stopped raining now, and the clouds were running higher and thinner. The wind had veered a little, slackening. It would drop towards dawn. Here and there, high and black beyond the racing clouds, the spaces of the night were filled with stars.

Then suddenly, directly overhead, the clouds parted, and there, sailing through them like a ship through running waves, the star.

It hung there among the dazzle of smaller stars, flickering at first, then pulsing, growing, bursting with light and all the colours that you see in dancing water. I watched it wax and flame and break open in light, then a racing wind would fling a web of cloud across it till it lay grey and dull and distant, lost to the eye among the other, minor stars. Then, as the swarm began their dance again it came again, gathering and swelling and dilating with light till it stood among the other stars like a torch throwing a whirl of sparks. So on through the night, as I stood alone on the ramparts and watched it; vivid and bright, then grey and sleeping, but each time waking to burn more gently, till it breathed light rather than beat, and towards morning hung glowing and quiet, with the light growing round it as the new day promised to come clear and still.

I drew breath, and wiped the sweat from my face. I straightened up from where I had leaned against the ramparts. My body was stiff, but the ache had gone. I looked up at Ygraine's darkened window where, now, they slept.

Chapter Nine

I walked slowly back across the platform towards the door. As I opened it I heard from below, clear and sharp, a knocking on the postern gate.

I took a stride through to the landing, pulling the door quietly shut behind me, just as Felix came out of the lodge below, and made for the postern. As his hand went out to the chain bolt, Ralf whipped out behind him, his arm raised high. I caught the glint in his fist of a dagger, reversed. He jumped, cat-footed, and struck with the hilt. Felix dropped where he stood. There must have been some slight sound audible to the man outside, above the roaring of the sea, for his voice came sharply: 'What is it? Felix?' And the knocking came again, harder than before.

I was already halfway down the flight. Ralf had stooped to the porter's body, but turned as he saw me coming, and interpreted my gesture correctly, for he straightened, calling out clearly:

'Who's there?'

'A pilgrim.'

It was a man's voice, urgent and breathless. I ran lightly down the rest of the flight. As I ran I was stripping my cloak off and winding it round my left arm. Ralf threw me a look from which all the gaiety and daring had gone. He had no need even to ask the next question; we both knew the answer.

'Who makes the pilgrimage?' The boy's voice was hoarse.

'Brithael. Now open up, quickly.'

'My lord Brithael! My lord—I cannot—I have no orders to admit anyone this way . . .' He was watching me as I stooped, took Felix under the armpits, and dragged him with as little noise as I could, back into the lodge and out of sight. I saw Ralf lick his lips. 'Can you not ride to the main gate, my lord? The Duchess will be asleep and I have no orders—'

'Who's that?' demanded Brithael. 'Ralf, by your voice. Where's Felix?'

'Gone up to the guard-room, sir.'

'Then get the key from him, or send him down.' The man's voice roughened, and a fist thudded against the gate. 'Do as I say, boy, or by God I'll have the skin off your back. I have a message for the Duchess, and she won't thank you for holding me here. Come now, hurry up!'

'The—the key's here, my lord. A moment.' He threw a desperate look over his shoulder as he made a business of fumbling with the lock. I left the unconscious man bundled out of sight, and was back at Ralf's shoulder, breathing into his ear:

'See if he's alone first. Then let him in.'

He nodded, and the door opened on its chain bolt. Under cover of the noise it made I had my sword out, and melted into the shadow behind the boy, where the opening door would screen me from Brithael. I stood back against the wall. Ralf put his eye to the gap, then drew back, with a nod at me, and began to slide the chain out of its socket. 'Excuse me, my lord Brithael.' He sounded abject and confused. 'I had to make sure . . . Is there trouble?'

'What else?' Brithael thrust the door open so sharply that it would have thudded into me if Ralf had not checked it. 'Never mind, you did well enough.' He strode in and stopped, towering over the boy. 'Has anyone else been to this gate tonight?'

'Why, no, sir.' Ralf sounded scared—as well he might—and therefore convincing. 'Not while I've been here, and Felix said nothing . . . Why, what's happened?'

Brithael gave a grunt, and his accoutrements jingled as he shrugged. 'There was a fellow down yonder, a horseman. He attacked us. I left Jordan to deal with him. There's been nothing here, then? No trouble at all?'

'None, my lord.'

'Then lock the gate again and let none in but Jordan. And now I must see the Duchess. I bring grave news, Ralf. The Duke is dead.'

'The Duke?' The boy began to stammer. He made no attempt to shut the gate, but left it swinging free. It hid Brithael from me still, but Ralf was just beside me, and in the dim light I saw his face go pinched and blank with shock. 'The Duke—d-dead, my lord? Murdered?'

Brithael, already moving, checked and turned. In another pace he would be clear of the door which hid me from him. I must not let him reach the steps and get above me.

'Murdered? Why, in God's name? Who would do that? That's not Uther's way. No, the Duke took the chance before the King got here, and we attacked the King's camp tonight, out of Dimilioc. But they were ready. Gorlois was killed in the first sally. I rode with Jordan to bring the news. We came straight from the field. Now lock that gate and do as I say.'

He turned away and made for the steps. There was room, now, to use a sword. I stepped out from the shadow behind the door.

'Brithael.'

The man whirled. His reactions were so quick that they cancelled out my advantage of surprise. I suppose I need not have spoken at all, but again there are certain things a prince must do. It cost me dear enough, and could have cost me my life. I should have remembered that tonight I was no prince; I was fate's creature, like Gorlois whom I had betrayed, and Brithael whom I now must kill. And I was the future's hostage. But the burden weighed heavy on me, and his sword was out almost before mine was raised, and then we stood measuring one another, eye to eye.

He recognised me then, as our eyes met. I saw the shock in his, and a quick flash of fear which vanished in a moment, the moment when my stance and my drawn sword told him that this would be his kind of fight, not mine. He may have seen in my face that I had already fought harder than he, that night.

'I should have known you were here. Jordan said it was your man down there, you damned enchanter. Ralf! Felix! Guard—ho there, guard!'

I saw he had not grasped straight away that I had been inside the gate all along. Then the silence on the stairway, and Ralf's quick move away from me to shut the gate told its own story. Fast as a wolf, too quickly for me to do anything, Brithael swept his left arm with its clenched mailed fist smashing into the side of the boy's head. Ralf dropped without a sound, his body wedging the gate wide open.

Brithael leapt back into the gateway. 'Jordan! Jordan! To me! Treachery!'

Then I was on him, blundering somehow through his guard, breast to breast, and our swords bit and slithered together with whining metal and the clash of sparks.

Rapid steps down the stairs. Ulfin's voice: 'My lord—Ralf—'

I said, in gasps: 'Ulfin . . . Tell the King . . . Gorlois is dead. We must get back . . . Hurry . . .'

I heard him go, fast up the stairs at a stumbling run. Brithael said through his teeth: 'The King? Now I see, you pandering whoremaster.'

He was a big man, a fighter in his prime, and justly angry. I was without experience, and hating what I must do, but I must do it. I was no longer a prince, or even a man fighting by the rules of men. I was a wild animal fighting to kill because it must.

With my free hand I struck him hard in the mouth and saw the surprise in his eyes as he jumped back to disengage his sword. Then he came in fast, the sword a flashing ring of iron round him. Somehow I ducked under the whistling blade, parried a blow and held it, and lashed a kick that took him full on the knee. The sword whipped down past my cheek with a hiss like a burn. I felt the hot sting of pain, and the blood running. Then as his weight went on the bruised knee, he trod crookedly, slipped on the soaked turf and fell heavily, his elbow striking a stone, and the sword flying from his hand.

Any other man would have stepped back to let him pick it up. I went down on him with all the weight I had, and my own sword shortened, stabbing for his throat.

It was light now, and growing lighter. I saw the contempt and fury in his eyes as he rolled away from the stabbing blade. It missed him, and drove deep into a spongy tuft of sea-pink. In the unguarded second as I fought to free it, his tactics shifted to match mine, and with that iron fist he struck me hard behind the ear, then, wrenching himself aside, was on his feet and plunging down the dreadful slope to where his own sword lay shining in the grass two paces from the cliff's edge.

If he reached it, he would kill me in seconds. I rolled, bunching to get to my feet, flinging myself anyhow down the slimy slope towards the sword. He caught me half on to my knees. His booted foot drove into my side, then into my back. The pain broke in me like a bubble of blood and my bones melted, throwing me flat again, but I felt my flailing foot catch the metal, and the sword jerked from its hold in the turf to skid, with how gentle a shimmer, over the edge. Seconds later, it seemed, we could hear, thin and sweet through the thunder of the waves, the whine of metal as it struck the rocks below.

But before even the sound reached us he was on me again. I had a knee under me and was dragging myself up painfully. Through the blood in my eyes I saw the blow coming, and tried to dodge, but his fist struck me in the throat, knocking me sideways with a savagery that spreadeagled me again on the wet turf with the breath gone from my body and the sight from my eyes. I felt myself roll and slip and, remembering what lay below, blindly drove my left hand into the turf to stop myself falling. My sword was still in my right hand. He jumped for me again, and with all the weight of his big body brought both feet down on my hand where it grasped the sword. The hand broke across the metal guard. I heard it go. The sword snapped upwards like a trap springing and caught him across his outstretched hand. He cursed in a gasp, without words, and recoiled momentarily. Somehow, I had the sword in my left hand. He came in again as quickly as before, and even as I tried to drag myself away, he made a quick stride forward and stamped again on my broken hand. Somebody screamed. I felt myself thrash over, mindless with pain, blind. With the last strength I had I jabbed the sword, hopelessly shortened, up at his straddled body, felt it torn from my hand, and then lay waiting, without resistance, for the last kick in my side that would send me over the cliff.

I lay there breathless, retching, choking on bile, my face to the ground and my left hand driven into the soft tufts of sea-pink, as if it clung to life for me. The beat and crash of the sea shook the cliff, and even this slight tremor seemed to grind pain through my body. It hurt at every point. My side pained as though the ribs were stove in, and the skin had been stripped from the cheek that lay pressed hard into the turf. There was blood in my mouth, and my right hand was a jelly of pain. I could hear someone, some other man a long way off, making small abject sounds of pain.

The blood in my mouth bubbled and oozed down my chin into the ground, and I knew it was I who was groaning. Merlin the son of Ambrosius, the prince, the great enchanter. I shut my mouth on the blood and began to push and claw my way to my feet.

The pain in my hand was cruel, the worst of all; I heard rather than felt the small bones grind where their ends were broken. I felt myself lurching as I got to my knees, and dared not try to stand upright so near the cliff's edge. Below me a master wave struck, thundered, fountained up into the greying light, then fell back to crash into the next rising wave. The cliff trembled. A seabird, the first of the day, sailed overhead, crying.

I crawled away from the edge and then stood up.

Brithael was lying near the postern gate, on his belly, as if he had been trying to crawl there. Behind him on the turf was a wake of blood, glossy on the grass like the track of a snail. He was dead. That last desperate stroke had caught the big vein in the groin, and the life had pumped out of him as he tried to crawl for help. Some of the blood that soaked me must be his.

I went on my knees beside him and made sure. Then I rolled him over and over till the slope took him, and he went after his sword into the sea. The blood would have to take care of itself. It was raining again, and with luck the blood would be gone before anyone saw it.

The postern gate stood open still. I reached it somehow and stood, supporting myself with a shoulder against the jamb. There was blood in my eyes, too. I wiped it away with a wet sleeve.

Ralf had gone. The porter also. The torch had burnt low in its socket and the smoky light showed the lodge and stairway empty. The castle was quiet.

At the top of the stairway the door stood partly open, and I saw light there
and heard voices. Quiet voices, urgent but unalarmed. Uther's party must
still be in control; there had been no alarm given.

I shivered in the dawn chill. Somewhere, unheeded, the cloak had
dropped from my arm. I didn't trouble to look for it. I let go of the gate and
tried standing upright without support. I could do it. I started to make my
way down the path towards the bay.

Chapter Ten

There was just light enough to see the way; light enough, too, to see the
dreadful cliff and the roaring depths below. But I think I was so occupied
with the weakness of my body, with the simple mechanics of keeping that
body upright and my good hand working and the injured hand out of
trouble, that I never once thought of the sea below or the perilous
narrowness of the strip of safe rock. I got past the first stretch quickly, and
then clawed my way, half crawling, down the next steep slide across the
tufted grasses and the rattling steps of scree. As the path took me lower, the
seas came roaring up closer beside me, till I felt the spray of the big waves
salt with the salt blood on my face. The tide was full in with morning, the
waves still high with the night's wind, shooting icy tongues up the licked
rock and bursting beside me with a hollow crash that shook the very bones
in my body, and drenched the path down which I crawled and stumbled.

I found him halfway up from the beach, lying face downwards within an
inch of the edge. One arm hung over the brink, and at the end of it the limp
hand swung to the shocks of air disturbed by the waves. The other hand
seemed to have stiffened, hooked to a piece of rock. The fingers were black
with dried blood.

The path was just wide enough. Somehow I turned him over, pulling and
shifting him as best I could till he was lying close against the cliff. I knelt
between him and the sea.

'Cadal. Cadal.'

His flesh was cold. In the near-darkness I could see that there was blood
on his face, and what looked like thick ooze from some wound up near the
hair. I put my hand to it; it was a cut, but not enough to kill. I tried to feel
the heartbeat in his wrist, but my numbed hand kept slipping on the wet
flesh and I could feel nothing. I pulled at his soaked tunic and could not get
it open, then a clasp gave way and it tore apart, laying the chest bare.

When I saw what the cloth had hidden I knew there was no need to feel
for his heart. I pulled the sodden cloth back over him, as if it could warm
him, and sat back on my heels, only then attending to the fact that men were
coming down the path from the castle.

Uther came round the cliff as easily as if he were walking across his palace
floor. His sword was ready in his hand, the long cloak gathered over his left
arm. Ulfin, looking like a ghost, came after him.

The King stood over me, and for some moments he did not speak. Then all he said was:

'Dead?'

'Yes.'

'And Jordan?'

'Dead too, I imagine, or Cadal would not have got this far to warn us.'

'And Brithael?'

'Dead.'

'Did you know all this before we came tonight?'

'No,' I said.

'Nor of Gorlois' death?'

'No.'

'If you were a prophet as you claim to be, you would have known.' His voice was thin and bitter. I looked up. His face was calm, the fever gone, but his eyes, slaty in the grey light, were bleak and weary.

I said briefly: 'I told you. I had to take the time on trust. This was the time. We succeeded.'

'And if we had waited until tomorrow, these men, aye, and your servant here as well, would still be living, and Gorlois dead and his lady a widow . . . And mine to claim without these deaths and whisperings.'

'But tomorrow you would have begotten a different child.'

'A legitimate child,' he said swiftly. 'Not a bastard such as we have made between us tonight. By the head of Mithras, do you truly think my name and hers can withstand this night's work? Even if we marry within a week, you know what men will say. That I am Gorlois' murderer. And there are men who will go on believing that she was in truth pregnant by him as she told them, and that the child is his.'

'They will not say this. There is not a man who will doubt that he is yours, Uther, and rightwise King born of all Britain.'

He made a short sound, not a laugh, but it held both amusement and contempt. 'Do you think I shall ever listen to you again? I see now what your magic is, this "power" you talk of . . . It is nothing but human trickery, an attempt at statecraft which my brother taught you to like and to play for and to believe was your mystery. It is trickery to promise men what they desire, to let them think you have the power to give it, but to keep the price secret, and then leave them to pay.'

'It is God who keeps the price secret, Uther, not I.'

'God? God? What god? I have heard you speak of so many gods. If you mean Mithras—'

'Mithras, Apollo, Arthur, Christ—call him what you will,' I said. 'What does it matter what men call the light? It is the same light, and men must live by it or die. I only know that God is the source of all the light which has lit the world, and that his purpose runs through the world and past each one of us like a great river, and we cannot check or turn it, but can only drink from it while living, and commit our bodies to it when we die.'

The blood was running from my mouth again. I put up my sleeve to wipe it away. He saw, but his face never changed. I doubt if he had even listened to what I said, or if he could have heard me for the thunder of the sea. He said merely, with that same indifference that stood like a wall between us:

'These are only words. You use even God to gain your ends. "It is God who tells me to do these things, it is God who exacts the price, it is God who sees that others should pay . . .' For what, Merlin? For your ambition? For the great prophet and magician of whom men speak with bated breath and give more worship than they would a king or his high priest? And who is it pays this debt to God for carrying out your plans? Not you. The men who play your game for you, and pay the price. Ambrosius, Vortigern. Gorlois. These other men here tonight. But you pay nothing. Never you.'

A wave crashed beside us and the spume showered the ledge, raining down on Cadal's upturned face. I leaned over and wiped it away, with some of the blood. 'No,' I said.

Uther said, above me: 'I tell you, Merlin, you shall not use me. I'll no longer be a puppet for you to pull the strings. So keep away from me. And I'll tell you this also. I'll not acknowledge the bastard I begot tonight.'

It was a king speaking, unanswerable. A still, cold figure, with behind his shoulder the star hanging clear in the grey. I said nothing.

'You hear me?'

'Yes.'

He shifted the cloak from his arm, and flung it to Ulfin, who held it for him to put on. He settled it to his shoulders, then looked down at me again. 'For what service you have rendered, you shall keep the land I gave you. Get back, then, to your Welsh mountains, and trouble me no more.'

I said wearily: 'I shall not trouble you again, Uther. You will not need me again.'

He was silent for a moment. Then he said abruptly: 'Ulfin will help you carry the body down.'

I turned away. 'There is no need. Leave me now.'

A pause, filled with the thunder of the sea. I had not meant to speak so, but I was past caring, or even knowing, what I said. I only wanted him gone. His sword-point was level with my eyes. I saw it shift and shimmer, and thought for a moment that he was angry enough to use it. Then it flashed up and was rammed home in its housings. He swung round and went on his way down the path. Ulfin edged quietly past without a word, and followed his master. Before they had reached the next corner the sea had obliterated the sound of their footsteps.

I turned to find Cadal watching me.

'*Cadal!*'

'That's a king for you.' His voice was a whisper, but it was his own, rough and amused. 'Give him something he swears he's dying for, and then, "Do you think I can withstand this night's work?" says he. A fine old night's work he's put in, for sure, and looks it.'

'Cadal—'

'You, too. You're hurt . . . your hand? Blood on your face?'

'It's nothing. Nothing that won't mend. Never mind that. But you—you—'

He moved his head slightly. 'It's no use. Let be. I'm comfortable enough.'

'No pain now?'

'No it's cold though.'

I moved closer to him, trying to shield his body with my own from the bursting spray as the waves struck the rock. I took his hand in my own good one. I could not chafe it, but pulled my tunic open and held it there against my breast. 'I'm afraid I lost my cloak,' I said. 'Jordan's dead then?'

'Yes.' He waited for a moment. 'What–happened up yonder?'

'It all went as we had planned. But Gorlois attacked out of Dimilioc and got himself killed. That's why Brithael and Jordan rode this way, to tell the Duchess.'

'I heard them coming. I knew they'd be bound to see me and the horses. I had to stop them giving the alarm while the King was still . . .' He paused for breath.

'Don't trouble,' I said. 'It's done with, and all's well.'

He took no notice. His voice was the merest whisper now, but clear and thin, and I heard every word through the raging of the sea.

'So I mounted and rode up a bit of the way to meet them . . . the other side of the water . . . then when they came level I jumped the stream and tried to stop them.' He waited for a moment. 'But Brithael . . . that's a fighter, now. Quick as a snake. Never hesitated. Sword straight into me and then rode over me. Left me for Jordan to finish.'

'His mistake.'

His cheek-muscles moved slightly. It was a smile. After a while he asked: 'Did he see the horses after all?'

'No. Ralf was at the gate when he came, and Brithael just asked if anyone had been up to the castle, because he's met a horseman below. When Ralf said no he accepted it. We let him in, and then killed him.'

'Uther.' It was an assumption, not a question. His eyes were closed.

'No. Uther was still with the Duchess. I couldn't risk Brithael taking him unarmed. He would have killed her, too.'

The eyes flared open, momentarily clear and startled. '*You?*'

'Come, Cadal, you hardly flatter me.' I gave him a grin. 'Though I'd have done you no credit, I'm afraid. It was a very dirty fight. The King wouldn't even know the rules. I invented them as I went along.'

This time it really was a smile. 'Merlin . . . little Merlin, that couldn't even sit a horse . . . You kill me.'

The tide must be on the turn. The next wave that thundered up sent only the finest spray which fell on my shoulders like mist. I said: 'I have killed you, Cadal.'

'The gods . . .' he said, and drew a great, sighing breath. I knew what that meant. He was running out of time. As the light grew I could see how much of his blood had soaked into the soaking path. 'I heard what the King said. Could it not have happened without . . . all this?'

'No, Cadal.'

His eyes shut for a moment, then opened again. 'Well,' was all he said, but in the syllable was all the acquiescent faith of the past eight years. His eyes were showing white now below the pupil, and his jaw was slack. I put my good arm under him and raised him a little. I spoke quickly and clearly:

'It will happen, Cadal, as my father wished and as God willed through me. You heard what Uther said about the child. That alters nothing. Because of this night's work Ygraine will bear the child, and because of this night's work she will send him away as soon as he is born, out of the King's sight. She will send him to me, and I shall take him out of the King's reach, and keep him and teach him all that Galapas taught me, and Ambrosius, and you, even Belasius. He will be the sum of all our lives, and when he is grown he will come back and be crowned King at Winchester.'

'You know this? You promise me that you know this?' The words were scarcely recognisable. His breath was coming now in bubbling gasps. His eyes were small and white and blind.

I lifted him and held him strongly against me. I said, gently and very clearly: 'I know this. I, Merlin, prince and prophet, promise you this, Cadal.'

His head fell sideways against me, too heavy for him now as the muscles went out of control. His eyes had gone. He made some small muttering sound and then, suddenly and clearly, he said, 'Make the sign for me,' and died.

I gave him to the sea, with Brithael who had killed him. The tide would take him, Ralf had said, and carry him away as far as the western stars.

Apart from the slow clop of hoofs, and the jingle of metal, there was no sound in the valley. The storm had died. There was no wind, and when I had ridden beyond the first bend of the stream, I lost even the sound of the sea. Down beside me, along the stream, mist hung still, like a veil. Above, the sky was clear, growing pale towards sunrise. Still in the sky, high now and steady, hung the star.

But while I watched it the pale sky grew brighter round it, flooding it with gold and soft fire, and then with a bursting wave of brilliant light, as up over the land where the herald star had hung, rose the young sun.

The Legend of Merlin

Vortigern, King of Britain, wishing to build a fortress in Snowdon, called together masons from many countries, bidding them build a strong tower. But what the stone-masons built each day, collapsed each night and was swallowed up by the soil. So Vortigern held council with his wizards, who told him that he must search for a lad who never had a father, and when he had found him should slay him and sprinkle his blood over the foundations, to make the tower hold firm. Vortigern sent messengers into all the provinces to look for such a lad, and eventually they came to the city that was afterwards called Carmarthen. There they saw some lads playing before the gate, and being tired, sat down to watch the game. At last, towards evening, a sudden quarrel sprang up between a couple of youths whose names were Merlin and Dinabutius. During the quarrel Dinabutius was heard to say to Merlin: 'What a fool must thou be to think thou art a match for me! Here am I, born of the blood royal, but no one knows what thou art, for never a father hadst thou!' When the messengers heard this they asked the bystanders who Merlin might be, and were told that none knew his father, but that his mother was daughter of the King of South Wales, and that she lived along with the nuns in St Peter's Church in that same city.

The messengers took Merlin and his mother to King Vortigern. The King received the mother with all the attention due to her birth, and asked her who was the father of the lad. She replied that she did not know. 'Once,' she said, 'when I and my damsels were in our chambers, one appeared to me in the shape of a handsome youth who, embracing me and kissing me, stayed with me some time, but afterwards did as suddenly vanish away. He returned many times to speak to me when I was sitting alone, but never again did I catch sight of him. After he had haunted me in this way for a long time, he lay with me for some while in the shape of a man, and left me heavy with child.' The King, amazed at her words, asked Maugantius the soothsayer whether such a thing might be. Maugantius assured him that such things were well known, and that Merlin must have been begotten by one of the 'spirits there be betwixt the moon and the earth, which we do call incubus daemons.'

Merlin, who had listened to all this, then demanded that he should be allowed to confront the wizards. 'Bid thy wizards come before me, and I will convict them of having devised a lie.' The King, struck by the youth's boldness and apparent lack of fear, did as he asked and sent for the wizards. To whom Merlin spoke as follows: 'Since ye know not what it is that doth hinder the foundation being laid of this tower, ye have given counsel that the mortar thereof should be slaked with my blood, so that the tower should stand forthwith. Now tell me, what is it that lieth hid beneath the foundation, for somewhat is there that doth not allow it to stand?' But the wizards, afraid of showing ignorance, held their peace. Then said Merlin (whose other name is Ambrosius): 'My lord the King, call thy workmen and bid them dig below the tower, and a pool shalt thou find beneath it that doth forbid thy walls to stand.' This was done, and the pool uncovered. Merlin then commanded that the pool should be drained by conduits; two stones, he said, would be found at the bottom, where two dragons, red and white, were lying asleep. When the pool was duly drained, and the stones uncovered, the dragons woke and began to fight ferociously, until the red had defeated and killed the white. The King, amazed, asked Merlin the meaning of the sight, and Merlin, raising his eyes to heaven, prophesied the coming of Ambrosius and the death of Vortigern. Next morning, early, Aurelius Ambrosius landed at Totnes in Devon.

After Ambrosius had conquered Vortigern and the Saxons and had been crowned King he brought together master craftsmen from every quarter and asked them to contrive some new kind of building that should stand for ever as a memorial. None of them were able to help him, until Tremorinus, Archbishop of Caerleon, suggested that the King should send for Merlin, Vortigern's prophet, the cleverest man in the kingdom, 'whether in foretelling that which shall be, or in devising engines of artifice.' Ambrosius forthwith sent out messengers, who found Merlin in the country of Gwent, at the fountain of Galapas where he customarily dwelt. The King received him with honour, and first asked him to foretell the future, but Merlin replied: 'Mysteries of such kind be in no wise to be revealed save only in sore need. For if I were to utter them lightly or to make laughter, the spirit that teaches me would be dumb and would forsake me in the hour of need.' The King then asked him about the monument, but when Merlin advised him to send for the 'Dance of the Giants that is in Killare, a mountain in Ireland,' Ambrosius laughed, saying it was impossible to move stones that everyone knew had been set there by giants. Eventually, however, the King was persuaded to send his brother Uther, with fifteen thousand men, to conquer Gilloman, King of Ireland, and bring back the Dance. Uther's army won the day, but when they tried to dismantle the giant circle of Killare and bring down the stones, they could not shift them. When at length they confessed defeat, Merlin put together his own engines, and by means of these laid the stones down easily, and carried them to the ships, and presently brought them to the site near Amesbury where they were to be set up. There Merlin again assembled his engines, and set up the Dance of Killare at Stonehenge exactly as it had stood in Ireland. Shortly after this a great star appeared in the likeness of a dragon, and Merlin, knowing that it betokened Ambrosius' death, wept bitterly, and prophesied that Uther would be King under the sign of the Dragon, and that a son would be born to him 'of surpassing mighty dominion, whose power shall extend over all the realms that lie beneath the ray (of the star).'

The following Easter, at the coronation feast, King Uther fell in love with Ygraine, wife of Gorlois, Duke of Cornwall. He lavished attention on her, to the scandal of the court; she made no response, but her husband, in fury, retired from the court without leave, taking his wife and men at arms back to Cornwall. Uther, in anger, commanded him to return, but Gorlois refused to obey. Then the King, enraged beyond measure, gathered an army and marched into Cornwall, burning the cities and castles. Gorlois had not enough troops to withstand him, so he placed his wife in the castle of Tintagel, the safest refuge, and himself prepared to defend the castle of Dimilioc. Uther immediately laid siege to Dimilioc, holding Gorlois and his troops trapped there, while he cast about for some way of breaking into the castle of Tintagel to ravish Ygraine. After some days he asked advice from one of his familiars called Ulfin. 'Do thou therefore give me counsel in what wise I may fulfil my desire,' said the King, 'for, and I do not, of mine inward sorrow shall I die.' Ulfin, telling him what he knew already—that Tintagel was impregnable—suggested that he send for Merlin. Merlin, moved by the King's apparent suffering, promised to help. By his magic arts he changed Uther into the likeness of Gorlois, Ulfin into Jordan, Gorlois' friend, and himself into Brithael, one of Gorlois' captains. The three of them rode to Tintagel, and were admitted by the porter. Ygraine, taking Uther to be her husband the Duke, welcomed him, and took him to her bed. So Uther lay with Ygraine that night, 'and she had no thought to deny him in aught he might desire'. That night, Arthur was conceived.

But in the meantime fighting had broken out at Dimilioc, and Gorlois, venturing out to give battle, was killed. Messengers came to Tintagel to tell Ygraine of her husband's death. When they found 'Gorlois', apparently still alive, closeted with Ygraine, they were speechless, but the King then confessed the deception, and a few days later married Ygraine.

Uther Pendragon was to reign fifteen more years. During those years he saw nothing of his son Arthur, who on the night of his birth was carried down to the postern gate of Tintagel and delivered into the hands of Merlin, who cared for the child in secret until the time came for Arthur to inherit the throne of Britain. Throughout Arthur's long reign Merlin advised and helped him. When Merlin was an old man he fell dotingly in love with a young girl, Vivian, who persuaded him, as the price of her love, to teach her all his magic arts. When he had done so she cast a spell on him which left him bound and sleeping; some say in a cave near a grove of whitethorn trees, some say in a tower of crystal, some say hidden only by the glory of the air around him. He will wake when King Arthur wakes, and come back in the hour of his country's need.

Author's Note

No novelist dealing with Dark Age Britain dares venture into the light without some pen-service to the Place-Name Problem. It is customary to explain one's usage, and I am at once less and more guilty of inconsistency than most. In a period of history when Celt, Saxon, Roman, Gaul and who knows who else shuttled to and fro across a turbulent and divided Britain, every place must have had at least three names, and anybody's guess is good as to what was common usage at any given time. Indeed, the 'given time' of King Arthur's birth is somewhere around A.D. 470, and the end of the fifth century is as dark a period of Britain's history as we have. To add to the confusion, I have taken as the source of my story a semi-mythological, romantic account written in Oxford by a twelfth century Welshman,* who gives the names of places and people what one might call a post-Norman slant with an overtone of clerical Latin. Hence in my narrative the reader will find Winchester as well as Rutupiae and Dinas Emrys, and the men of Cornwall, South Wales and Brittany instead of Dumnonii, Demetae and Armoricans.

My first principle in usage has been, simply, to make the story clear. I wanted if possible to avoid the irritating expedient of the glossary, where the reader has to interrupt himself to look up the place-names, or decide to read straight on and lose himself mentally. And non-British readers suffer further; they look up Calleva in the glossary, find it is Silchester, and are none the wiser until they consult a map. Either way the story suffers. So wherever there was a choice of names I have tried to use the one that will most immediately put the reader in the picture: for this I have sometimes employed the device of having the narrator give the current crop of names, even slipping in the modern one where it does not sound too out of place. For example: 'Maesbeli, near Conan's Fort, or Kaerconan, that men sometimes call Conisburgh.' Elsewhere I have been more arbitrary. Clearly, in a narrative whose English must be supposed in the reader's imagination to be Latin or the Celtic of South Wales, it would be pedantic to write of Londinium when it is so obviously London; and I have used the modern names of places like Glastonbury and Winchester and Tintagel, because these names, though mediaeval in origin, are so hallowed by

* Or (possibly) Breton.

association that they fit contexts where it would obviously be impossible to intrude the modern images of (say) Manchester or Newcastle. These 'rules' are not, of course, intended as a criticism of any other writer's practice; one employs the form the work demands; and since this is an imaginative exercise which nobody will treat as authentic history, I have allowed myself to be governed by the rules of poetry: what communicates simply and vividly, and sounds best, is best.

The same rule of ear applies to the language used throughout. The narrator, telling his story in fifth century Welsh, would use in his tale as many easy colloquialisms as I have used in mine; the servants Cerdic and Cadal would talk some kind of dialect, while, for instance, some sort of 'high language' might well be expected from kings, or from prophets in moments of prophecy. Some anachronisms I have deliberately allowed where they were the most descriptive words, and some mild slang for the sake of liveliness. In short, I have played it everywhere by ear, on the principle that what sounds right is acceptable in the context of a work of pure imagination.

For that is all *The Crystal Cave* claims to be. It is not a work of scholarship, and can obviously make no claim to be serious history. Serious historians will not, I imagine, have got this far anyway, since they will have discovered that the main source of my storyline is Geoffrey of Monmouth's *History of the Kings of Britain.*

Geoffrey's name is, to serious historians, mud. From his Oxford study in the twelfth century he produced a long, racy hotch-potch of 'history' from the Trojan War (where Brutus 'the King of the Britons' fought) to the seventh century A.D., arranging his facts to suit his story, and when he got short on facts (which was on every page), inventing them out of the whole cloth. Historically speaking, the *Historia Regum Brittaniae* is appalling, but as a story it is tremendous stuff, and has been a source and inspiration for the great cycle of tales called the Matter of Britain, from Malory's *Morte d'Arthur* to Tennyson's *Idylls of the King*, from *Parsifal* to *Camelot.*

The central character of the *Historia* is Arthur, King of the first united Britain. Geoffrey's Arthur is the hero of legend, but it is certain that Arthur was a real person, and I believe the same applies to Merlin, though the 'Merlin' that we know is a composite of at least four people; prince, prophet, poet and engineer. He appears first in legend as a youth. My imaginary account of his childhood is coloured by a phrase in the *Historia*: 'the well of Galapas,★ where he wont to haunt', and by a reference to 'my master Blaise'–who becomes in my story Belasius. The Merlin legend is as strong in Brittany as in Britain.

One or two brief notes to finish with.

I gave Merlin's mother the name Niniane because this is the name of the girl (Vivian/Niniane/Nimue) who according to legend seduced the enchanter in his dotage and so robbed him of his powers, leaving him shut in his cave to sleep till the end of time. No other women are associated with him. There is so strong a connection in legend (and indeed in history) between celibacy or virginity, and power, that I have thought it reasonable to insist on Merlin's virginity.

★ So *fontes galebes* is sometimes translated.

Mithraism had been (literally) underground for years. I have postulated a local revival for the purpose of my story, and the reasons given by Ambrosius seem likely. From what we know of the real Ambrosius, he was Roman enough to follow the 'soldiers' god'.*

About the ancient druids so little is known that (according to the eminent scholar I consulted) they can be considered 'fair game'. The same applies to the megaliths of Carnac (Kerrec) in Brittany, and to the Giants' Dance of Stonehenge near Amesbury. Stonehenge was erected around 1500 B.C., so I only allowed Merlin to bring one stone from Killare. At Stonehenge it is true that one stone–the largest–is different from the rest. It comes originally, according to the geologists, from near Milford Haven, in Wales. It is also true that a grave lies within the circle; it is off centre, so I have used the midwinter sunrise rather than the midsummer one towards which the Dance is oriented.

All the places I describe are authentic, with no significant exceptions but the cave of Galapas–and if Merlin is indeed sleeping there 'with all his fires and travelling glories around him', one would expect it to be invisible. But the well is there on Bryn Myrddin, and there is a burial mound on the crest of the hill.

It would seem that the name 'merlin' was not recorded for the falcon *columbarius* until mediaeval times, and the word is possibly French; but its derivation is uncertain, and this was sufficient excuse for a writer whose imagination had already woven a series of images from the name before the book was even begun.

Where Merlin refers to the potter's mark A.M., the A. would be the potter's initial or trade mark; the M stands for *Manu*, literally 'by the hand of'.

The relationship between Merlin and Ambrosius has (I believe) no basis in legend. A ninth century historian, Nennius, from whom Geoffrey took some of his material, called his prophet 'Ambrosius'. Nennius told the story of the dragons in the pool, and the young seer's first recorded prophecy. Geoffrey, borrowing the story, calmly equates the two prophets: 'Then saith Merlin, that is also called Ambrosius . . .' This throwaway piece of 'nerve', as Professor Gwyn Jones calls it,† gave me the idea of identifying the 'prince of darkness' who fathered Merlin–gave me, indeed, the main plot of *The Crystal Cave*.

My greatest debt is obviously to Geoffrey of Monmouth, master of romance. Among other creditors too numerous to name and impossible to repay, I should like especially to thank Mr Francis Jones, County Archivist, Carmarthen; Mr and Mrs Morris of Bryn Myrddin, Carmarthen; Mr G. B. Lancashire of The Chase Hotel, Ross-on-Wye; Brigadier R. Waller, of Wyaston Leys, Monmouthshire, on whose land lie Lesser Doward and the Romans' Way; Professor Hermann Brück, Astronomer Royal for Scotland, and Mrs Brück, Professor Stuart Piggott of the Department of Archaeology at Edinburgh University; Miss Elizabeth Manners, Headmistress of

* Bede, the seventh century historian, calls him 'Ambrosius, a Roman'. (*Ecclesiastical History of the English Nation.*)
† Introduction to the Everyman ed. of *History of the Kings of Britain*.

Felixstowe College; and Mr Robin Denniston, of Hodder & Stoughton Ltd, London.

M.S.

February 1968–February 1970

The
Hollow Hills

MARY
STEWART

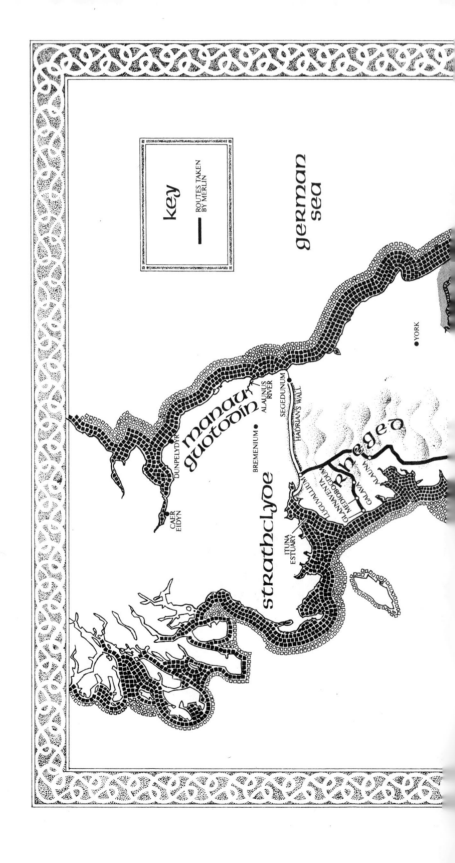

key

— ROUTES TAKEN
   BY MERLIN

german
sea

manau
guotooin

strathclyoe

Rheged

DUNPELYDR

CAER
EIDYN

BREMENIUM

ALAUNUS
RIVER

SEGEDUNUM

HADRIAN'S WALL

ITUNA
ESTUARY

LIGUVALLIUM

GLANNAVENTA

MEDIOBOGDUM

GALAVA

ALAUNA

YORK

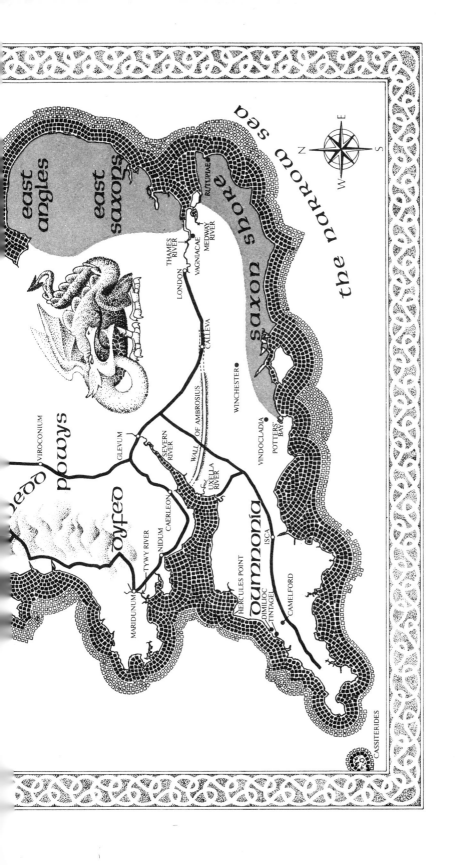

The Hollow Hills

To the memory of my father

The Waiting

Chapter One

There was a lark singing somewhere high above. Light fell dazzling against my closed eyelids, and with it the song like a distant dance of water. I opened my eyes. Above me arched the sky, with its invisible singer lost somewhere in the light and floating blue of a spring day. Everywhere was a sweet, nutty smell which made me think of gold, and candle flames, and young lovers. Something, smelling not so sweet, stirred beside me, and a rough young voice said: 'Sir?'

I turned my head. I was lying on turf, in a hollow among furze bushes. These were full of blossom, golden, sweet-smelling flames called out by the spring sun. Beside me a boy knelt. He was perhaps twelve years old, dirty with a matted shag of hair and clad in some coarse brown cloth; his cloak, made of skins roughly stitched together, showed rents in a dozen places. He had a stick in one hand. Even without the way he smelt I could have guessed his calling, for all around us his herd of goats grazed among the furze bushes, cropping the young green prickles.

At my movement he got quickly to his feet and backed off a little, peering, half wary and half hopeful, through the filthy tangle of hair. So he had not robbed me yet. I eyed the heavy stick in his hand, vaguely wondering through the mists of pain whether I could help myself even against this youngster. But it seemed that his hopes were only for a reward. He was pointing at something out of sight beyond the bushes. 'I caught your horse for you. He's tied over there. I thought you were dead.'

I raised myself to an elbow. Round me the day seemed to swing and dazzle. The furze blossom smoked like incense in the sun. Pain seeped back slowly, and with it, on the same tide, memory.

'Are you hurt bad?'

'Nothing to matter, except my hand. Give me time, I'll be all right. You caught my horse, you say? Did you see me fall?'

'Aye. I was over yonder.' He pointed again. Beyond the mounds of yellow blossom the land rose, smooth and bare, to a rounded upland broken by grey rock seamed with winter thorn. Behind the shoulder of the land the sky had that look of limitless and empty distance which spoke of the sea. 'I saw you come riding up the valley from the shore, going slow. I could see you was ill, or maybe sleeping on the horse. Then he put his foot wrong–a hole, likely–and you came off. You've not been lying long. I'd just got down to you.'

He stopped, his mouth dropping open. I saw shock in his face. As he spoke I had been pushing myself up till I was able to sit, propped by my left arm, and carefully lift my injured right hand into my lap. It was a swollen, crusted mass of dried blood, through which fresh red was running. I had, I guessed, fallen on it when my horse had stumbled. The faint had been merciful enough. The pain was growing now, wave on wave grinding, with the steady beat and drag of the tide over shingle, but the faintness had gone, and my head, though still aching from the blow, was clear.

'Mother of mercy!' The boy was looking sick. 'You never did that falling from your horse?'

'No. It was a fight.'

'You've no sword.'

'I lost it. No matter. I have my dagger, and a hand for it. No, don't be afraid. The fighting's done. No one will hurt you. Now, if you'll help me on to my horse, I'll be on my way'.

He gave me an arm as I got to my feet. We were standing at the edge of a high green upland studded with furze, with here and there stark, solitary trees thrust into strange shapes by the steady salt wind. Beyond the thicket where I had lain the ground fell away in a sharp slope scored by the tracks of sheep and goats. It made one side of a narrow, winding valley, at the foot of which a stream raced, tumbling, down its rocky bed. I could not see what lay at the foot of the valley, but about a mile away, beyond the horizon of winter grass, was the sea. From the height of the land where I stood one could guess at the great cliffs which fell away to the shore, and away beyond the land's farthest edge, small in the distance, I could see the jut of towers.

The castle of Tintagel, stronghold of the Dukes of Cornwall. The impregnable fortress rock, which could only be taken by guile, or by treachery from within. Last night, I had used both.

I felt a shiver run over my flesh. Last night, in the wild dark of the storm, this had been a place of gods and destiny, of power driving towards some distant end of which I had been given, from time to time, a glimpse. And I, Merlin, son of Ambrosius, whom men feared as prophet and visionary, had been in that night's work no more than the god's instrument.

It was for this that I had been given the gift of Sight, and the power that men saw as magic. From this remote and sealocked fortress would come the King who alone could clear Britain of her enemies, and give her time to find herself; who alone, in the wake of Ambrosius the last of the Romans, would hold back the fresh tides of the Saxon Terror, and, for a breathing space at least, keep Britain whole. This I had seen in the stars, and heard in the wind: it was I, my gods had told me, who would bring this to pass; this I had been born for. Now, if I could still trust my gods, the promised child was begotten; but because of him–because of me–four men had died. In that night lashed by storm and brooded over by the dragon-star, death had seemed commonplace, and gods waiting, visible, at every corner. But now, in the still morning after the storm, what was there to see? A young man with an injured hand, a King with his lust satisfied, and a woman with her penance beginning. And for all of us, time to remember the dead.

The boy brought my horse up to me. He was watching me curiously, the wariness back in his face.

'How long have you been here with your goats?' I asked him.

'A sunrise and a sunrise.'

'Did you see or hear anything last night?'

Wariness became, suddenly, fear. His eyelids dropped and he stared at the ground. His face was closed, blank, stupid. 'I have forgotten, lord.'

I leaned against my horse's shoulder, regarding him. Times without number I had met this stupidity, that flat, expressionless mumble; it is the only armour available to the poor. I said gently: 'Whatever happened last night, it is something I want you to remember, not to forget. No one will harm you. Tell me what you saw.'

He looked at me for perhaps ten more seconds of silence. I could not guess what he was thinking. What he was seeing can hardly have been reassuring; a tall young man with a smashed and bloody hand, cloakless, his clothes stained and torn, his face (I have no doubt) grey with fatigue and pain and the bitter dregs of last night's triumph. All the same the boy nodded suddenly, and began to speak.

'Last night in the black dark I heard horses go by me. Four, I think. But I saw no one. Then, in the early dawn, two more following them, spurring hard. I thought they were all making for the castle, but from where I was, up there by the rocks, I never saw torches at the guard-house on the cliff top, or on the bridge going across to the main gate. They must have gone down the valley there. After it was light I saw two horsemen coming back that way, from the shore below the castle rock.' He hesitated. 'And then you, my lord.'

I said slowly, holding him with my eyes: 'Listen now, and I will tell you who the horsemen were. Last night, in the dark, King Uther Pendragon rode this way, with myself and two others. He rode to Tintagel, but he did not go by the gate-house and to the bridge. He rode down the valley, to the shore, and then climbed the secret path up the rock and entered the castle by the postern gate. Why do you shake your head? Don't you believe me?'

'Lord, everyone knows the King had quarrelled with the Duke. No one could get in, least of all the King. Even if he did find the postern door, there's none would dare open it to him.'

'They opened last night. It was the Duchess Ygraine herself who received the King into Tintagel.'

'But—'

'Wait,' I said. 'I will tell you how it happened. The King had been changed by magic arts into a likeness of the Duke, and his companions into likenesses of the Duke's friends. The people who let them into the castle thought they were admitting Duke Gorlois himself, with Brithael and Jordan.'

Under its dirt the boy's face was pale. I knew that for him, as for most of the people of this wild and haunted country, my talk of magic and enchantment would come as easily as stories of the loves of kings and violence in high places. He said, stammering: 'The King—the King was in the castle last night with the Duchess?'

'Yes. And the child that will be born will be the King's child.'

A long pause. He licked his lips. 'But—but—when the Duke finds out . . .'

'He won't find out,' I said. 'He's dead.'

One filthy hand went to his mouth, the fist rammed against his teeth. Above it his eyes, showing white, went from my injured hand to the bloodstains on my clothing, then to my empty scabbard. He looked as if he would have liked to run away, but did not dare even do that. He said breathlessly: 'You killed him? You killed our Duke?'

'Indeed no. Neither I nor the King wished him dead. He was killed in battle. Last night, not knowing that the King had already ridden secretly for Tintagel, your Duke sallied out from his fortress of Dimilioc to attack the King's army, and was killed.'

He hardly seemed to be listening. He was stammering: 'But the two I saw this morning . . . It was the Duke himself, riding up from Tintagel. I saw him. Do you think I don't know him? It was the Duke himself, with Jordan, his man.'

'No. It was the King with his servant Ulfin. I told you the King took the Duke's likeness. The magic deceived you, too.'

He began to back away from me. 'How do you know these things? You—you said you were with them. This magic—who are you?'

'I am Merlin, the King's nephew. They call me Merlin the enchanter.'

Still backing, he had come up against a wall of furze. As he looked this way and that, trying which way to run, I put out a hand.

'Don't be afraid. I'll not hurt you. Here, take this. Come, take it, no sensible man should fear gold. Call it a reward for catching my horse. Now, if you'll help me on to his back, I'll be on my way.'

He made a half movement forward, ready to snatch and run, but then he checked, and his head went round, quick as a wild thing's. I saw the goats had already stopped grazing and were looking eastwards, ears pricked. Then I heard the sound of horses.

I gathered my own beast's reins in my good hand, then looked round for the boy to help me. But he was already running, whacking the bushes to chase the goats in front of him. I called to him, and, as he glanced over his shoulder, flung the gold. He snatched it up and then was gone, racing up the slope with his goats scampering round him.

Pain struck at me again, grinding the bones of my hand together. The cracked ribs stabbed and burned my side. I felt the sweat start on my body, and round me the spring day wavered and broke again in mist. The noise of approaching hoofs seemed to hammer with the pain along my bones. I leaned against my horse's saddle, and waited.

It was the King riding again for Tintagel, this time for the main gate, and by daylight, with a company of his men. They came at a fast canter along the grassy track from Dimilioc, four abreast, riding at ease. Above Uther's head the Dragon standard showed red on gold in the sunlight. The King was himself again; the grey of his disguise had been washed from his hair and beard, and the royal circlet glinted on his helmet. His cloak of kingly scarlet was spread behind him over his bay's glossy flanks. His face looked still, calm and set; a bleak enough look, and weary, but with over all a kind of contentment. He was riding to Tintagel, and Tintagel was his at last, with all that lay within the walls. For him, it was an end.

I leaned against my horse's shoulder, and watched them come level with me.

It was impossible for Uther not to see me, but he never glanced my way. I saw, from the troop behind him, the curious glances as I was recognised. No man was there but must have some inkling now of what had happened last night in Tintagel, and of the part I had played in bringing the King to his heart's desire. It was possible that the simpler souls among the King's companions might have expected the King to be grateful; to reward me; at the very least to recognise and acknowledge me. But I, who had dealt all my life with kings, knew that where there is blame as well as gratitude, blame must be allotted first, lest it should cling to the King himself. King Uther could only see that, by what he called the failure of my foreknowledge, the Duke of Cornwall had died even while he, the King, was lying with the Duchess. He did not see the Duke's death for what it was, the grim irony behind the smiling mask that gods show when they want men to do their will. Uther, who had small truck with gods, saw only that by waiting even one day he might have had his way with honour and in the sight of men. His anger with me was genuine enough, but even if it were not, I knew that he must find someone to blame: whatever he felt about the Duke's death—and he could hardly fail to see it as a miraculously open gate to his marriage with Ygraine—he must in public be seen to show remorse. And I was the public sacrifice to that remorse.

One of the officers—it was Caius Valerius, who rode at the King's shoulder—leaned forward and said something, but Uther might never have heard. I saw Valerius look doubtfully back at me, then with a half shrug, and a half salute to me, he rode on. Unsurprised, I watched them go.

The sound of hoofs dwindled sharply down the track towards the sea. Above my head, between one wing-beat and the next, the lark's song shut off, and he dropped from the bright silence to his rest in the grass.

Not far from me a boulder jutted from the turf. I led the horse that way, and somehow, from the boulder's top, scrambled into the saddle. I turned the beast's head east by north for Dimilioc, where the King's army lay.

Chapter Two

Gaps in memory can be merciful. I have no recollection of reaching the camp, but when hours later, I swam up out of the mists of fatigue and pain I was within doors, and in bed.

I awoke to dusk, and some faint and swimming light that may have been firelight and candle flame; it was a light hazed with colour and drowned with shadows, threaded by the scent of woodsmoke and, it seemed distantly, the trickle and splash of water. But even this warm and gentle consciousness was too much for my struggling senses, and soon I shut my eyes and let myself drown again. I believe that for a while I thought I was back in the edges of the Otherworld, where vision stirs and voices speak out of the dark, and truth comes with the light and the fire. But then the aching of my bruised muscles and the fierce pain in my hand told me that the daylight world still held me, and the voices that murmured across me in the dusk were as human as I.

'Well, that's that, for the moment. The ribs are the worst of it, apart from the hand, and they'll mend soon enough; they're only cracked.'

I had a vague feeling that I knew the voice. At any rate I knew what he was; the touch on the fresh bandages was deft and firm, the touch of a professional. I tried to open my eyes again, but the lids were leaden, gummed together and sticky with sweat and dried blood. Warmth came over me in drowsy waves, weighting my limbs. There was a sweet, heavy smell; they must have given me poppy, I thought, or stunned me with smoke before they dressed the hand. I gave up, and let myself drift back from the shore. Over the dark water the voices echoed softly.

'Stop staring at him and bring the bowl nearer. He's safe enough in this state, never fear.' It was the doctor again.

'Well, but one's heard such stories.' They were speaking Latin, but the accents were different. The second voice was foreign; not Germanic, nor yet from anywhere on the Middle Sea. I have always been quick at languages, and even as a child spoke several dialects of Celtic, along with Saxon and a working knowledge of Greek. But this accent I could not place. Asia Minor, perhaps? Arabia?

Those deft fingers gently turned my head on the pillow, and parted my hair to sponge the bruises. 'Have you never seen him before?'

'Never. I hadn't imagined him so young.'

'Not so young. He must be two and twenty.'

'But to have done so much. They say his father the High King Ambrosius never took a step, in the last year or two, without talking it over with him. They say he sees the future in a candle flame and can win a battle from a hilltop a mile away.'

'They would say anything, of him.' The doctor's voice was prosaic and calm. Brittany, I thought, I must have known him in Brittany. The smooth Latin had some overtone I remembered, without knowing how. 'But certainly Ambrosius valued his advice.'

'Is it true he rebuilt the Giants' Dance near Amesbury that they call the Hanging Stones?'

'That's true enough. When he was a lad with his father's army in Brittany he studied to be an engineer. I remember him talking to Tremorinus—that was the army's chief engineer—about lifting the Hanging Stones. But that wasn't all he studied. Even as a youth he knew more about medicine than most men I've met who practise it for a livelihood. I can't think of any man I'd rather have by me in a field hospital. God knows why he chooses to shut himself away in that godforsaken corner of Wales now—at least, one can guess why. He and King Uther never got on. They say Uther was jealous of the attention his brother the King paid Merlin. At any rate, after Ambrosius' death, Merlin went nowhere and saw no one, till this business of Uther and Gorlois' Duchess. And it seems as if that's brought him trouble enough . . . Bring the bowl nearer, while I clean his face. No, here. That's right.'

'That's a sword cut, by the look of it?'

'A glancing scratch from the point, I'd say. It looks worse than it is, with all the blood. He was lucky there. Another inch and it would have caught his eye. There. It's clean enough; it won't leave a scar.'

'He looks like death, Gandar. Will he recover?'

'Of course. How not?' Even through the lulling of the nepenthe, I recognised the quick professional reassurance as genuine. 'Apart from the ribs and the hand, it's only cuts and bruising, and I would guess a sharp reaction from whatever has been driving him the last few days. All he needs is sleep. Hand me that ointment there, please. In the green jar.'

The salve was cool on my cut cheek. It smelt of valerian. Nard, in the green jar . . . I made it at home. Valerian, balm, oil of spikenard . . . The smell of it took me dreaming out among the mosses at the river's edge, where water ran sparkling, and I gathered the cool cress and the balsam and the golden moss . . .

No, it was water pouring at the other side of the room. He had finished, and had gone to wash his hands. The voices came from further off.

'Ambrosius' bastard, eh?' The foreigner was still curious. 'Who was his mother, then?'

'She was a king's daughter, Southern Welsh, from Maridunum in Dyfed. They say he got the Sight from her. But not his looks; he's a mirror of the late King, more than Uther ever was. Same colouring, black eyes, and that black hair. I remember the first time I saw him, back in Brittany when he was a boy; he looked like something from the hollow hills. Talked like it, too, sometimes; that is, when he talked at all. Don't let his quiet ways fool you; it's more than just book-learning and luck and a knack of timing; there's power there, and it's real.'

'So the stories are true?'

'The stories are true,' said Gandar flatly. 'There. He'll do now. No need to stay with him. Get some sleep. I'll do the rounds myself, and come and take a look at him again before I go to bed. Good night.'

The voices faded. Others came and went in the darkness, but these were voices without blood, belonging to the air. Perhaps I should have waited and waked to listen, but I lacked the courage. I reached for sleep and drew it round me like a blanket, muffling pain and thought together in the merciful dark.

When I opened my eyes again it was to darkness lit by calm candle-light. I was in a small chamber with a barrel roof of stone and rough-hewn walls where the once bright paint had darkened and flaked away with damp and neglect. But the room was clean. The floor of Cornish slate had been well scrubbed, and the blankets that covered me were fresh-smelling and thick, and richly worked in bright patterns.

The door opened quietly, and a man came in. At first, against the stronger light beyond the doorway, I could only see him as a man of middle height, broad shouldered and thickly built, dressed in a long plain robe, with a round cap on his head. Then he came forward into the candle-light, and I saw that it was Gandar, the chief physician who travelled with the King's armies. He stood over me, smiling.

'And about time.'

'Gandar! It's good to see you. How long have I slept?'

'Since dusk yesterday, and now it's past midnight. It was what you needed. You looked like death when they brought you in. But I must say it made my job a lot easier to have you unconscious.'

I glanced down at the hand which lay, neatly bandaged, on the coverlet in front of me. My body was stiff and sore inside its strapping, but the fierce pain had died to a dull aching. My mouth was swollen, and tasted still of blood mingled with the sick-sweet remnants of the drug, but my headache had gone, and the cut on my face had stopped hurting.

'I'm thankful you were here to do it,' I said. I shifted the hand a little to ease it, but it was no use. 'Will it mend?'

'With the help of youth and good flesh, yes. There were three bones broken, but I think it's clean.' He looked at me curiously. 'How did you come by it? It looked as if a horse had trodden on you and then kicked your ribs in. But the cut on your face, that was a sword, surely?'

'Yes. I was in a fight.'

His brows went up. 'If that was a fight, then it wasn't fought by any rules I ever heard of. Tell me—wait, though, not yet. I'm on fire to know what happened—we all are—but you must eat first.' He went to the door and called, and presently a servant came in with a bowl of broth and some bread. I could not manage the bread at first, but then sopped a little of it in the broth, and ate that. Gander pulled a stool up beside the bed, and waited in silence till I had finished. At length I pushed the bowl aside, and he took it from me and set it on the floor.

'Now do you feel well enough to talk? The rumours are flying about like stinging gnats. You knew that Gorlois was dead?'

'Yes.' I looked about me. 'I'm in Dimilioc itself, I take it? The fortress surrendered, then, after the Duke was killed?'

'They opened the gates as soon as the King got back from Tintagel. He's already had the news of the skirmish, and the Duke's death. It seems that the Duke's men, Brithael and Jordan, rode to Tintagel as soon as the Duke fell, to take the Duchess the news. But you'd know that; you were there.' He stopped short as he saw the implications. 'So that was it! Brithael and Jordan—they ran into you and Uther?'

'Not into Uther, no. They never saw him; he was still with the Duchess. I was outside with my servant Cadal—you remember Cadal?—guarding the doors. Cadal killed Jordan, and I killed Brithael.' I smiled, wryly, with my stiff mouth. 'Yes, you may well stare. He was well beyond my weight, as you can see. Do you wonder I fought foul?'

'And Cadal?'

'Dead. Do you think otherwise that Brithael would have got to me?'

'I see.' His gaze told again, briefly, the tally of my hurts. When he spoke, his voice was dry. 'Four men. With you, five. It's to be hoped the King counts it worth the price.'

'He does,' I said. 'Or he will soon.'

'Oh, aye, everyone knows that. Give him time only to tell the world that he is guiltless of Gorlois' death, and to get him buried with honour, so that he can marry the Duchess. He's gone back to Tintagel already, did you know? He must have passed you on the road.'

'He did,' I said drily. 'Within a yard or two.'

'But didn't he see you? Or surely—he must have known you were hurt?' Then my tone got through to him. 'You mean he saw you, like that, and left you to ride here alone?' I could see that he was shocked, rather than surprised. Gandar and I were old acquaintances, and I had no need to tell him what my relationship had been with Uther, even though he was my father's brother. From the very beginning, Uther had resented his brother's love for his bastard son, and had half feared, half despised my powers of vision and prophecy. He said hotly: 'But when it was done in his service—'

'Not his, no. What I did, I did because of a promise I made to Ambrosius. It was a trust he left with me, for his kingdom.' I left it at that. One did not speak to Gandar of gods and visions. He dealt, like Uther, with things of the flesh. 'Tell me.' I said, 'those rumours you were talking of. What are they? What do people think happened at Tintagel?'

He gave a half-glance over his shoulder. The door was shut, but he lowered his voice. 'The story goes that Uther had already been in Tintagel, with the Princess Ygraine, and that it was you who took him there and put him in the way of entering. They say you changed the King by enchantment into a likeness of the Duke, and got him past the guards and into the Duchess's bedchamber. They say more than that; they say she took him to her bed, poor lady, thinking he was her husband. And that when Brithael and Jordan took her the news of Gorlois' death, there was "Gorlois" sitting large as life beside her at breakfast. By the Snake, Merlin, why do you laugh?'

'Two days and nights,' I said, 'and the story has grown already. Well, I suppose that is what men will believe, and go on believing. And perhaps it is better than the truth.'

'What is the truth, then?'

'That there was no enchantment about our entry into Tintagel, only disguise, and human treachery.'

I told him the story then, exactly as it had happened, with the tale I had given the goat-herd. 'So you see, Gandar, I sowed that seed myself. The nobles and the King's advisers must know the truth, but the common folk will find the tale of magic, and a blameless Duchess, better to believe—and, God knows, easier—than the truth.'

He was silent for a while. 'So the Duchess knew.'

'Or we would not have got in,' I said. 'It shall not be said, Gandar, that this was a rape. No, the Duchess knew.'

He was silent again, for rather longer. Then he said, heavily: 'Treachery is a hard word.'

'It is a true one. The Duke was my father's friend, and he trusted me. It would never have occurred to him that I would help Uther against him. He knew how little I cared for Uther's lusts. He could not guess that my gods demanded that I should help him satisfy this one. Even though I could not help myself, it was still treachery, and we shall suffer for it, all of us.'

'Not the King.' He said it positively. 'I know him. I doubt if the King will feel more than a passing guilt. You are the one who is suffering for it, Merlin, just as you are the one who calls it by its name.'

'To you,' I said. 'To other men this will remain a story of enchantment, like the dragons which fought at my bidding under Dinas Emrys, and the Giants' Dance which floated on air and water to Amesbury. But you have seen how Merlin the King's enchanter fared that night.' I paused, and shifted my hand on the coverlet, but shook my head at the question in his face. 'No, no, let be. It's better already. Gandar, one other truth about that night must be known. There will be a child. Take it as hope, or take it as prophecy, you will see that, come Christmas, a boy will be born. Has he said when he will marry her?'

'As soon as it's decent. Decent!' He repeated the word on a short bark of laughter, then cleared his throat. 'The Duke's body is here, but in a day or two they'll carry him to Tintagel to bury him. Then, after the eight days' mourning, Uther is to marry the Duchess.'

I thought for a moment. 'Gorlois had a son by his first wife. Cador, he was called. He must be about fifteen. Have you heard what is to become of him?'

'He's here. He was in the fight, beside his father. No one knows what has passed between him and the King, but the King gave an amnesty to all the troops that fought against him in the action at Dimilioc, and he has said, besides, that Cador will be confirmed Duke of Cornwall.'

'Yes,' I said. 'And Ygraine's son and Uther's will be King.'

'With Cornwall his bitter enemy?'

'If he is,' I said wearily, 'who is to blame him? The payment may well be too long and too heavy, even for treachery.'

'Well,' said Gandar, suddenly brisk, gathering his robe about him, 'that's with time. And now, young man, you'd better get some more rest. Would you like a draught?'

'Thank you, no.'

'How does the hand feel?'

'Better. There's no poison there; I know the feel of it. I'll give you no more trouble, Gandar, so stop treating me like a sick man. I'm well enough, now that I've slept. Get yourself to bed, and forget about me. Good night.'

When he had gone I lay listening to the sound of the sea, and trying to gather, from the god-filled dark, the courage I would need for my visit to the dead.

Courage or no, another day passed before I found the strength to leave my chamber. Then I went at dusk to the great hall where they had put the old Duke's body. Tomorrow he would be taken to Tintagel for burial among his fathers. Now he lay alone, except for the guards, in the echoing hall where he had feasted his peers and given orders for his last battle.

The place was cold, silent but for the sounds of wind and sea. The wind had changed and now blew from the north-west, bringing with it the chill and promise of rain. There was neither glazing nor horn in the windows, and the draught stirred the torches in their iron brackets, sending them sideways, dim and smoking, to blacken the walls. It was a stark, comfortless place, bare of paint, or tiling, or carved wood; one remembered that Dimilioc was simply the fortress of a fighting man; it was doubtful if Ygraine had ever been here. The ashes in the hearth were days old, the half-burnt logs dewed with damp.

The Duke's body lay on a high bier in the centre of the hall, covered with his war cloak. The scarlet with the double border of silver and the white badge of the Boar was as I had seen it at my father's side in battle. I had seen it, too, on Uther as I led him disguised into Gorlois' castle and his bed. Now the heavy folds hung to the ground, and beneath them the body had shrunk and flattened, no more than a husk of the tall old man I remembered. They had left his face uncovered. The flesh had sunk, grey as twice-used tallow, till the face was a moulded skull, showing only the ghost of a likeness to the Gorlois I had known. The coins on his eyes had already sunk into the flesh. His hair was hidden by his war helm, but the familiar grey beard jutted over the badge of the Boar on his chest.

I wondered, as I went forward soft-footed over the stone floor, by which god Gorlois had lived, and to which god he had gone in dying. There was nothing here to show. Christians, like other men, put coins on the eyes. I remembered other death-beds, and the press of spirits waiting round them; there was nothing here. But he had been dead three days, and perhaps his spirit had already gone through that bare and windy gap in the wall. Perhaps it had already gone too far for me to reach it and make my peace.

I stood at the foot of his bier, the man I had betrayed, the friend of my father Ambrosius the High King. I remembered the night he had come to ask me for my help for his young wife, and how he had said to me: 'There are not many men I'd trust just now, but I trust you. You're your father's son.' And how I had said nothing, but watched the firelight stain his face red like blood, and waited my chance to lead the King to his wife's bed.

It is one thing to have the gift of seeing the spirits and hearing the gods who move about us as we come and go; but it is a gift of darkness as well as light. The shapes of death come as clear as those of life. One cannot be visited by the future without being haunted by the past; one cannot taste comfort and glory without the bitter sting and fury of one's own past deeds. Whatever I had thought to encounter near the dead body of the Duke of Cornwall, it would hold no comfort and no peace for me. A man like Uther Pendragon, who killed in open battle and open air, would think no more of this than a dead man dead. But I who in obeying the gods had trusted them even as the Duke had trusted me, had known that I would have to pay, and in full. So I had come, but without hope.

There was light here from the torches, light and fire. I was Merlin; I should be able to reach him; I had talked with the dead before. I stood still, watching the flaring torches, and waited.

Slowly, all through the fortress, I could hear the sounds dwindling and sinking to silence as men finally went to rest. The sea soughed and beat below the window, the wind plucked at the wall, and ferns growing there in the crevices rustled and tapped. A rat scuttled and squeaked somewhere. The resin bubbled in the torches. Sweet and foul, through the sharp smoke,

I smelled the smell of death. The torchlight winked blank and flat from the coins on the dead eyes.

The time crawled by. My eyes ached with the flame, and the pain from my hand, like a biting fetter, kept me penned in my body. My spirit was pared down to nothing, blind as the dead. Whispers I caught, fragments of thought from the still and sleepy guards, meaningless as the sound of their breathing, and the creak of leather or chime of metal as they stirred involuntarily from time to time. But beyond these, nothing. What power I had been given on that night at Tintagel had drained from me with the strength that had killed Brithael. It had gone from me and was working, I thought, in a woman's body; in Ygraine, lying even now beside the King in that grim and battered near-isle of Tintagel, ten miles to the south. I could do nothing here. The air, solid as stone, would not let me through.

One of the guards, the one nearest me, moved restlessly, and the butt of his grounded spear scraped on the stone. The sound jarred the silence. I glanced his way involuntarily, and saw him watching me.

He was young, rigid as his own spear, his fists white on the shaft. The fierce blue eyes watched me unwinkingly under thick brows. With a shock that went through me like the spear striking I recognised them. Gorlois' eyes. It was Gorlois' son, Cador of Cornwall, who stood between me and the dead, watching me steadily, with hatred.

In the morning they took Gorlois's body south. As soon as he was buried, Gandar had told me, Uther planned to ride back to Dimilioc to rejoin his troops until such time as he could marry the Duchess. I had no intention of waiting for his return. I called for provisions and my horse and, in spite of Gandar's protestations that I was not yet fit for the journey, set out alone for my valley above Maridunum and the cave in the hill which the King had promised should remain, in spite of everything, my own.

Chapter Three

No one had been inside the cave during my absence. This was hardly to be wondered at, since the people held me in much awe as an enchanter, and moreover it was commonly known that the King himself had granted me the hill Bryn Myrddin. Once I left the main road at the water-mill, and rode up the steep tributary valley to the cave which had become my home, I saw no one, not even the shepherd who commonly watched his flocks grazing the stony slopes.

In the lower reaches of the valley the woods were thick; oaks still rustled their withered leaves, chestnut and sycamore crowded close, fighting for the light, and hollies showed black and glinting between the beeches. Then the trees thinned, and the path climbed along the side of the valley, with the stream running deep down on the left, and to the right slopes of grass, broken by scree, rising sharply to the crags that crowned the hill. The grass was still bleached with winter, but among the rusty drifts of last year's bracken the bluebell leaves showed glossy green, and blackthorn was budding. Somewhere, lambs were crying. That, and the mewing of a buzzard high over the crags, and the rustle of the dead bracken where my tired horse trod, were all the sounds in the valley. I was home, to the solace of simplicity and quiet.

The people had not forgotten me, and word must have gone round that I was expected. When I dismounted in the thorn grove below the cliff and stabled my horse in the shed there I found that bracken had been freshly strewn for bedding, and a netful of fodder hung from a hook beside the door; and when I climbed to the little apron of lawn which lay in front of my cave I found cheese and new bread wrapped in a clean cloth, and a goatskin full of the local thin, sour wine, which had been left for me beside the spring.

This was a small spring, a trickle of pure water welling out of a ferny crack in the rock to one side of the entrance to the cave. The water ran down, sometimes in a steady flow, sometimes no more than a sliding glimmer over the mosses, to drip into a rounded basin of stone. Above the spring the little statue of the god Myrddin, he of the winged spaces of the air, stared from between the ferns. Beneath his cracked wooden feet the water bubbled and dripped into the stone basin, lipping over into the grass below. Deep in the clear water metal glinted; I knew that the wine and bread, like the thrown coins, had been left as much as an offering to the god as to me; in the minds of the simple folk I had already become part of the legend of the hill, their god made flesh who came and went as quietly as the air, and brought with him the gifts of healing.

I lifted down the cup of horn which stood above the spring, filled it from the goatskin, then poured wine for the god, and drank the rest myself. The god would know whether there was more in the gesture than ritual homage. I myself was tired beyond thought, and had no prayer to offer; the drink was for courage, nothing more.

To the other side of the cave entrance, opposite the spring, was a tumble of grass-grown stones, where saplings of oak and mountain ash had seeded themselves, and grew in a thick tangle against the rocky face. In summer their boughs cast a wide pool of shade, but now, though overhanging it, they did nothing to conceal the entrance to the cave. This was a smallish arch, regular and rounded, as if made by hand. I pushed the hanging boughs aside and went in.

Just inside the entrance the remnants of a fire still lay in white ash on the hearth, and twigs and damp leaves had drifted over it. The place smelt already of disuse. It seemed strange that it was barely a month since I had ridden out at the King's urgent summons to help him in the matter of Ygraine of Cornwall. Beside the cold hearth stood the unwashed dishes from the last, hasty meal my servant had prepared before we set out.

Well, I would have to be my own servant now. I put the goatskin of wine and the bundle of bread and cheese on the table, then turned to re-make the fire. Flint and tinder lay to hand where they had always lain, but I knelt down by the cold faggots and stretched out my hands for the magic. This was the first magic I had been taught, and the simplest, the bringing of fire out of the air. It had been taught me in this very cave, where as a child I had learned all I knew of natural lore from Galapas, the old hermit of the hill. Here, too, in the cave of crystal which lay deeper in the hill, I had seen my first visions, and found myself as a seer. 'Some day,' Galapas had said, 'you will go where even with the Sight I cannot follow you.' It had been true. I had left him and gone where my god had driven me; where none but I, Merlin, could have gone. But now the god's will was done, and he had forsaken me. Back there in Dimilioc, beside Gorlois' bier, I had found myself to be an empty husk; blind and deaf as men are blind and deaf; the great power gone. Now, weary though I was, I knew I would not rest until I saw if, here in my magic's birthplace, the first and smallest of my powers was left to me.

I was soon answered, but it was an answer I would not accept. The westering sun was dropping red past the boughs at the cave mouth, and the logs were still unkindled, when finally I gave up, with the sweat running scalding on my body under my gown, and my hands, outstretched for the magic, trembling like those of an old man. I sat by the cold hearth and ate my supper of bread and cheese and watered wine in the chill of the spring dusk, before I could gather even strength enough to reach for the flint and tinder and try with them.

Even this, a task that every wife does daily and without thought, took me an age, and set my maimed hand bleeding. But in the end fire came. A tiny spark flew in among the tinder and started a slow, creeping flame. I lit the torch from it, and then, carrying the flame high, went to the back of the cave. There was something I still must do.

The main cavern, high-roofed, went a long way back. I stood with the torch held high, looking up. At the back of the cave was a slope of rock leading up to a wide ledge, which in its turn climbed into the dark, high shadows. Invisible among these shadows was the hidden cleft beyond which lay the inner cave, the globed cavity lined with crystals where, with light and fire, I had seen my first visions. If the lost power lay anywhere, it lay there. Slowly, stiff with fatigue, I climbed the ledge, then knelt to peer through the low entrance to the inner cave. The flames from my torch caught the crystals, and light ran round the globe. My harp still stood where I had left it, in the centre of the crystal-studded floor. Its shadow shot towering up the shimmering walls, and flame sparked from the copper of the string-shoes, but no stir of the air set it whispering, and its own arching shadows quenched the light. I knelt there for a long time, eyes wide and staring, while round me light and shadow shivered and beat. But my eyes ached, empty of vision, and the harp stayed silent.

At length I withdrew, and made my way down into the main cave. I remember that I picked my way slowly, carefully, like a man who has never been that way before. I thrust the torch under the dry wood I had piled for a fire, till the logs caught, crackling; then went out and found my saddle-bags, and lugged them back into the human comfort of the firelight, and began to unpack them.

My hand took a long time to heal. For the first few days it pained me constantly, throbbing so that I was afraid it was infected. During the day this did not matter so much, for there were tasks to do; all that my servant had done for me for so long that I hardly knew how to set about it; cleaning, preparing food, tending my horse. Spring came slowly to South Wales that year, and there was no grazing yet on the hill, so I had to cut and carry fodder for him, and walk further than I cared to in search of the healing plants I needed. Luckily food for myself was always forthcoming; gifts were left almost daily at the foot of the small cliff below the lawn. It may have been that the country folk had not yet heard that I was out of favour with the King, or it may simply have been that what I had done for them in the way of healing outweighed Uther's displeasure. I was Merlin, son of Ambrosius; or, as the Welsh say it, Myrddin Emrys, the enchanter of Myrddin's Hill; and in another way, I suppose, the priest of the old god of the hollow hill, Myrddin himself. What gifts they would have brought for him they brought now for me, and in his name I accepted them.

But if the days were full enough, the nights were bad. I seemed always wakeful, less perhaps from the pain of my hand than from the pain of my memories: where Gorlois' death chamber had been empty, my own cave was full of ghosts. Not the spirits of the loved dead whom I would have welcomed; but the spirits of those I had killed went past me in the dark with thin sounds like the cry of bats. At least, this is what I told myself. I believe now that I was often touched with fever: the cave still housed the bats that Galapas and I had studied, and it must have been these I heard, passing to and from the cave mouth during the night. But in my memory of this time they are the voices of dead men, restless in the dark.

April went by, wet and chill, with winds that searched you to the bone. This was the bad time, empty except for pain, and idle except for the barest efforts to live. I believe I ate very little; water and fruit and black bread was my staple diet. My clothes, never sumptuous became threadbare with no one to care for them, and then ragged. A stranger seeing me walking the hill paths would have taken me for a beggar. Days passed when I did little but huddle over the smoking fire. My chest of books was unopened, my harp was left where it stood. Even had my hand been whole, I could have made no music. As for magic, I dared not put myself to the test again.

But gradually, like Ygraine waiting in her cold castle to the south, I slid into a sort of calm acceptance. As the weeks went by my hand healed, cleanly enough. I was left with two stiff fingers, and a scar along the outer edge of the palm, but the stiffness passed with time, and the scar never troubled me. And as time went by the other wounds healed, too. I grew used to loneliness, as I had been accustomed to solitude, and the nightmares ceased. Then as May drew on the winds changed, grew warm, and grass and flowers came springing. The grey clouds packed away, and the valley was full of sunlight. I sat for hours in the sun at the mouth of the cave, reading, or preparing the plants I had gathered, or from time to time watching–but no more than idly–for the approach of a rider which could mean a message. (Even so, I thought, must my old teacher Galapas have sat here many a time in the sunlight, looking down the valley where, one day, a small boy would come riding.) And I built up again my stock of plants and herbs, wandering further and further from the cave as my strength came back to me. I never went into the town, but now and again when poor folk came for medicines

or for healing, they brought snatches of news. The King had married
Ygraine with as much pomp and ceremony as such a hasty union would
permit, and he had seemed merry enough since the wedding, though
quicker to anger than he used to be, and would have sudden morose fits,
when folk learnt to avoid him. As for the Queen, she was silent, acceding in
everything to the King's wishes, but rumour had it that her looks were
heavy, as if she mourned in secret . . .

Here my informant shot a quick sidelong look at me, and I saw his fingers
move to make the sign against enchantment. I let him go on, asking no more
questions. The news would come to me in its own time.

It came almost three months after my return to Bryn Myrddin.

One day in June, when a hot morning sun was just lifting the mist from
the grass, I went up the hill to find my horse, which I had tethered out to
graze on the grassland above the cave. The air was still, and the sky was full
of singing larks. Over the green mound where Galapas lay buried the
blackthorns showed green leaves budding through fading snowbanks of
flowers, and bluebells were thick among the fern.

I doubt if I actually needed to tether my horse. I usually carried with me
the remnants of the bread my benefactors left for me, so when he saw me
coming he would advance to the end of his tether and stand waiting,
expectant.

But not today. He was standing at the far stretch of his rope, on the edge
of the hill, head up and ears pricked, apparently watching something away
down the valley. I walked over to him, and, while he nuzzled in my hand for
the bread, looked where he had been looking.

From this height I could see the town of Maridunum, small in the
distance, clinging to the north bank of the placid Tywy as it wound its way
down the wide green valley towards the sea. The town, with its arched stone
bridge and harbour, lies just where the river widens towards the estuary.
There was the usual huddle of masts beyond the bridge, and nearer, on the
towpath that threaded its way along the silver curves of the river, a slow
grey horse towed a grain barge up to the mill. The mill itself, lying where
the stream from my own valley met the river, was hidden in woodland; out
of these trees ran the old military road which my father had repaired,
straight as a die through five open miles, to the barracks near Maridunum's
eastern gate.

On this road, perhaps a mile and a half beyond the water-mill, there was a
cloud of dust where horsemen skirmished. They were fighting; I saw the
flash of metal. Then the group resolved itself, clearer through the dust.
There were four mounted men, and they were fighting three to one. The
lone man seemed to be trying to escape, the others to surround him and cut
him down. At length he burst free in what looked like a desperate bid for
escape. His horse, pulled round hard, struck one of the others on the
shoulder, and its rider fell, dislodged by the heavy blow. Then the single
man, crouched and spurring hard, turned his horse off the road and across
the grass, making desperately for the cover afforded by the edge of the
woodland. But he did not reach it. The other two spurred after him; there
was a short, wild gallop, then they had caught him up, one to each side, and

as I watched he was dragged from his horse and beaten to his knees. He tried to crawl away, but he had no chance. The two horsemen circled, their weapons flashing, and the third man apparently uninjured, had remounted and was galloping to join them. Then suddenly he checked his horse, so sharply that it reared. I saw him fling up an arm. He must have shouted a warning, for the other two, abruptly abandoning their victim wheeled their beasts, and the three of them galloped off, full stretch, with the loose horse pelting behind them, to be lost to sight eastwards beyond the trees.

Next moment I saw what had startled them. Another group of horsemen was approaching from the direction of the town. They must have seen the retreating trio, but it soon appeared that they had seen nothing of the attack, for they came on at a canter, riding at ease. I watched them as they drew level with the place where the fallen man—injured or dead—must be lying. They passed it without slackening pace. Then they, too, were lost to sight below the woodland.

My horse, finding no more bread, nipped me, then jerked his head away sharply, ears flattened. I caught him by the halter, pulled up the tether, peg and all, and turned his head downhill.

'I stood on this spot once before,' I told him, 'while a King's messenger came riding to see me and bid me go and help the King to his desire. I had power that day; I dreamed I held the whole world cupped in my hands, shining and small. Well, maybe I've nothing today but the hill I stand on, but that might be a Queen's messenger lying down yonder, with a message still in his pouch. Message or not, he'll need help if he's still alive. And you and I, my friend, have had our fill of idleness. It's time to be doing again.'

In a little less than twice the time it would have taken my servant to do the job, I had the horse bridled, and was on my way down the valley. Reaching the mill road, I turned my horse's head to the right, and drove my heels in.

The place where I had seen the horseman fall was near the edge of the woods, where the bushes were thick, a place of bracken and undergrowth and scattered trees. The smell of horses still hung in the air, with the tang of trampled bracken and sweet briar and, foul through it all, the smell of vomit. I dismounted and tethered my horse, then pushed my way forward through the thick growth.

He lay on his face, half hunched as he had crawled and collapsed, one hand still trapped under his body, the other outflung and gripping a tuft of bracken. A youth, lightly built but well grown, fifteen, perhaps, or a little more. His clothes, torn and grimed and bloodstained by the fight and his crawl through the thorns, had been good, and there was a glint of silver on one wrist, and a silver brooch at his shoulder. So they had not managed to rob him, if robbery had been the motive for the attack. His pouch was still at his belt, and fastened.

He made no move as I approached him, so I thought him insensible, or dead. But when I knelt beside him I saw the slight movement as his hand clenched more tightly on the stems of bracken, and I realised that he was exhausted or hurt beyond all caring. If I were one of his murderers come to finish him off, he would lie there and let me.

I spoke gently. 'Be easy, I shan't hurt you. Lie still a moment. Don't try to move.'

There was no response. I laid careful hands on him, feeling for wounds
and broken bones. He flinched from my touch, but made no sound. I
satisfied myself soon that no bones were broken. There was a bloodied
swelling near the back of his head, and one shoulder was already blackened
with bruising, but the worst that I could see was a patch of crushed and
bleeding flesh on the hip, which looked—and indeed later proved—to be
where a horse's hoof had struck him.

'Come,' I said at length, 'turn over, and drink this.'

He moved then, though wincing from the touch of my arm round his
shoulder, and turned slowly round. I wiped the dirt and sickness from his
mouth and held my flask to his lips; he gulped greedily, coughed, and then,
losing strength again, leaned heavily against me, his head drooping against
my chest. When I put the flask back to his mouth he turned his head away. I
could feel him using all his strength not to cry out against the pain. I
stoppered the flask and put it away.

'I have a horse here. You must try and sit him somehow, and I'll get you
home, where I can see to your hurts.' Then, when he made no response:
'Come now. Let's get you out of this before they decide to come back and
finish what they started.'

He moved then, abruptly, as if these were the first words that had got
through to him. I saw his hand grope down to the pouch at his belt, discover
it was still there, and then fall limply away. The weight against my chest
sagged suddenly. He had fainted.

So much the better, I thought, as I laid him down gently and went to
bring up my horse. He would be spared the painful jolting of the ride, and
by the gods' mercy I might have him in bed with his hurts bandaged before
he woke. Then in the very act of stooping to lift him again I paused. His face
was dirty, grime mingled with bloodstains from scratches and a cut above
the ear. Under the mask of dirt and blood the skin was drained and grey.
Brown hair, shut eyes, a slack mouth. But I recognised him. It was Ralf,
Ygraine's page, who had let us into Tintagel that night, and who with Ulfin
and myself had guarded the Duchess's chamber until the King had had his
desire.

I stooped and lifted the Queen's messenger, and heaved his mercifully
unconscious body across my waiting horse.

Chapter Four

Ralf did not regain his senses during the journey up to the cave, and only
after I had washed and bound his wounds and put him into bed did he open
his eyes. He stared at me for a few moments, but without recognition.

'Don't you know me?' I said. 'Merlinus Ambrosius. You brought your
message safely enough. See.' I held up the wallet, still sealed. But his eyes,
cloudy and unfocused, slid past it, and he turned his head against the pillow,
wincing as he felt the pain from the bruising on the back of his neck. 'Very

well,' I told him, 'sleep now. You're in safe hands.'

I waited beside him till he drifted back into sleep, then took the wallet and its contents out to my seat in the sunlight. The seal was, as I had expected, the Queen's, and the superscription was mine. I broke the seal and read the letter.

It was not from the Queen herself, but from Marcia, Ralf's grandmother and the Queen's closest confidante. The letter was brief enough, but held all I wanted to know. The Queen was indeed pregnant, and the child would be born in December. The Queen herself–said Marcia–seemed happy to be bearing the King's child, but, where she spoke of me at all, spoke with bitterness, throwing on me the responsibility for her husband Gorlois' death. 'She says little, but it is my belief that she mourns in secret, and that even in her great love for the King there will always be the shadow of guilt. Pray God her feelings for the child may not be tainted with it. As for the King, it is seen that he is angry, though he is as ever kind and loving to my lady, and there is no man who doubts but that the child is his. Alas, I could find it in me to fear for the child at the King's hands, if it were not unthinkable that he should so grieve the Queen. Wherefore, Prince Merlin, I beg by this letter to commend to you as your servant my grandson Ralf. For him, too, I fear at the King's hands; and I believe that, if you will take him, service abroad with a true prince is better than here with a King who counts his service as betrayal. There is no safety for him in Cornwall. So pray you, lord, let Ralf serve you now, and after you, the child. For I think I understand what you were speaking of when you said to my lady, "I have seen a bright fire burning, and in it a crown, and a sword standing in an altar like a cross."'

Ralf slept until dusk. I had lit the fire and made broth, and when I took it to the back of the cave where he lay I saw his eyes open, watching me. There was recognition in them now, and a wariness that I could not quite understand.

'How do you feel now?'

'Well enough, my lord. I–this is your cave? How did I come here? How did you find me?'

'I'd gone up the hill above here, and from there I saw you being attacked. The men were frightened off, and ran away, leaving you. I went down to get you, and carried you up here on my horse. So you recognise me now?'

'You've let your beard grow, but I'd have known you, my lord. Did I speak to you before? I don't remember anything. I think they hit me on the head.'

'They did. How is it now?'

'A headache. But not bad. It's my side'–wincing–'that hurts most.'

'One of the horses struck you. But there's no real damage done; you'll be well enough in a few days. Do you know who they were?'

'No.' He knitted his brows, thinking, but I could see the effort hurt him, so I stopped him.

'Well, we can talk later. Eat now.'

'My lord, the message—'

'I have it safely. Later.'

When I went back to him he had finished the broth and bread, and looked more like himself. He would not take more food, but I made him drink a little wine, and watched the colour come back into his face. Then I drew up a chair, and sat down beside the bed.

'Better?'

'Yes.' He spoke without looking at me. He looked down at his hands, nervously plucking at the covers in front of him. He swallowed. 'I–I haven't thanked you yet, my lord.'

'For what? Picking you up and bringing you here? It was the only way to get your news.'

He glanced up at that, and for a startled second I realised that he thought it was no more than the truth. I saw then what there was in that look he had given me; he was afraid of me. I thought back to that night in Tintagel, the gay youth who had dealt so bravely for the King, and so truly with me. But for the moment I let it go. I said:

'You brought me the news I wanted. I've read your grandmother's letter. You know what she tells me in it about the Queen?'

'Yes.'

'And about yourself?'

'Yes.' he shut his mouth on the syllable, and looked away, sullen, like someone unfairly trapped and held for questioning, who is determined not to answer. It seemed that, whatever Marcia's motives for sending him to me, he himself was far from willing to offer me service. From which I guessed that she had told him nothing about her hopes for the future.

'All right, we'll leave that for the moment. But it seems that somebody wants to harm you, whoever it may be. If those men this morning weren't just roadside cut-throats, it would help to know who they were, and who paid them. Have you no idea who they might have been?'

'No,' still mumbling.

'It's of some interest to me,' I said mildly. 'They might conceivably want to kill me, too.'

That startled him out of his resentment. 'Why?'

'If you were attacked out of revenge for the part you played at Tintagel, then presumably they will attack me as well. If you were attacked for the message you carried to me, I want to know why. If they were plain thieves, which seems the most likely, then they may still be hereabouts, and I must get a message to the troopers down at the barracks.'

'Oh. Yes, I see.' He looked disconcerted and slightly ashamed. 'But it's true, my lord; I don't know who they were. I–it was of interest to me, too. I've been trying to think, all this time, but I've no idea. There's no clue that I can remember. They didn't wear badges; at least I don't think so . . .' His brows drew together, painfully. 'I'd have noticed badges, surely, if they'd had them?'

'How were they dressed?'

'I–I hardly noticed. Leather tunics, I think, and chain-mail caps. No shields, but swords and daggers.'

'And they were well mounted. I saw that. Did you hear their speech?'

'Not that I remember. They hardly spoke, a shout or two, that was all. British speech, but I couldn't tell where from. I'm not good at accents.'

'There was nothing you can think of that might have marked them for the King's men?'

This was probing too near the wound. He went scarlet, but said levelly enough: 'Nothing. But is it likely?'

'I wouldn't have thought so,' I said. 'But kings are queer cattle, and queerest of all when they have bad consciences. Well, then, Cornishmen?'

The flush had ebbed, leaving him if possible more sickly pale than before. His eyes were sullen and unhappy. This was the wound itself; this was a thought he had lived with. 'Duke's men, you mean?'

'They told me before I left Dimilioc that the King was to confirm young Cador as Duke of Cornwall. That's one man, Ralf, who will have no love for you. He won't stop to consider that you were the Duchess's man, and were serving her as you were bidden. He is full of hatred, and it might extend to vengeance. One could hardly blame him if it did.'

He looked faintly surprised, then in some odd way set at ease by this dispassionate handling. After a bit he said, with an attempt at the same tone: 'They might have been Cador's men, I suppose. There was nothing to show it, one way or the other. Maybe I'll remember something.' He paused. 'But surely, if Cador intended to kill me, he could have cut me down in Cornwall. Why come all the way here? To follow me to you? He must hate you as much.'

'More,' I said. 'But if he had intended to kill me, he knew where to find me; the whole world knows that. And he'd have come before this.'

He eyed me doubtfully. Then he appeared to find an explanation for my apparent lack of fear. 'I suppose no one would dare come after you here, for fear of your magic?'

'It would be nice to think so,' I agreed. There was no point in telling him how thin my defences were. 'Now, that's enough for the moment. Rest again, and you'll find you feel better tomorrow. Will you sleep, do you think? Are you in pain?'

'No,' he said, not truthfully. Pain was a weakness he would not admit to me. I stooped and felt for the heart-beat in his wrist. It was strong and even. I let the wrist drop, and nodded at him. 'You'll live. Call me in the night if you want me. Good night.'

Ralf did not in fact remember anything more next morning that would give a clue to the identity of his attackers, and I forbore for a few days from questioning him further about the contents of Marcia's letter. Then one evening, when I judged he was better, I called him to me. It had been a damp day, and the evening had brought a chill with it, so I had lit a fire and sat with my supper beside it.

'Ralf, bring your bowl and eat beside me where it's warm. I want to talk to you.'

He came obediently. He had somehow managed to mend and tidy his clothes, and now, with the cuts and bruises fading, and with colour back in his face, he was almost himself again, except for a limp where the wound on his hip had not yet mended; and except, still, for his silence, and the sullen shadow of wariness in his face. He limped across and sat where I pointed.

'You said you knew what else was in your grandmother's letter to me besides news of the Queen?' I asked him.

'Yes.'

'Then you know she sent you to take service with me, because she feared the King's displeasure. Did the King himself give you any reason to fear him?'

A slight shake of the head. He would not meet my eyes. 'Not to fear him, no. But when the alarm came of a Saxon landing on the south coast, and I asked to ride with his men, he would not take me.' His voice was sullen and furious. 'Even though he took every other Cornishman who had fought against him at Dimilioc. But myself, who had helped him, he dismissed.'

I looked thoughtfully at the bent head, the hot averted cheek. This, of course, was the reason for his attitude to me, the wary resentment and anger. He could only see, understandably enough, that through his service to me and the King he had lost his place near the Queen; worse, he had incurred his Duke's anger, had been disgraced as a Cornish subject and banished from his home to a kind of service he disdained.

I said: 'Your grandmother tells me little except that she feels you had better seek a career for yourself outside Cornwall. Leave that for a moment; you can't seek anything much until your leg is healed. But tell me, did the King ever say anything to you directly about the night of Gorlois' death?'

A pause, so long that I thought he would not answer. Then he said: 'Yes. He told me that I had served him well, and he—he thanked me. He asked me if I wanted a reward. I said no, the service was reward enough. He didn't like that. I think he wanted to give me money, and requite me, and forget it. He said then that I could no longer serve him or the Queen. That in serving him I had betrayed my master the Duke, and that a man who had betrayed one master could betray another.'

'Well?' I said. 'Is that all?'

'*All?*' His head jerked up at that. He looked startled and contemptuous. '*All?* An insult like that? And it was a lie, you know it was! I was my lady's man, not Duke Gorlois'! I did not betray the Duke!'

'Oh, yes, it was an insult. You can't expect the King to be level-headed yet, when he himself feels as guilty as Judas. He's got to put the betrayal on someone's shoulders, so it's yours and mine. But I doubt if you're in actual danger from him. Even a doting grandmother could hardly call that a threat.'

'Who was talking about threats?' said Ralf hotly. 'I didn't come away because I was afraid! Someone had to bring the message, and you saw how safe that was!'

It was hardly the tone a servant uses. I hid my amusement, and said peaceably: 'Don't ruffle your feathers at me, young cockerel. No one doubts your courage. I'm sure the King does not. Now, tell me about this Saxon landing. Where? What happened? I've had no news from the south for over a month now.'

In a little while he answered me civilly enough. 'It was in May. They landed south of Vindocladia. There's a deep bay there, they call it Potter's Bay. I forget its real name. Well, it's outside federated territory, in Dumnonia, and that was against all the agreements the Federates made. You would know that.'

I nodded. It is hard to remember now, looking back down the years to the time I write of, Uther's time, that today men hardly remember even the name of Federate. The first of the Federated Saxons were the followers of Hengist and Horsa, who had been called in by King Vortigern as mercenary help to establish him on his stolen throne. When the fighting was done, and the rightful princes Ambrosius and Uther had fled to Brittany, the usurper Vortigern would have dismissed his Saxon mercenaries; but they refused to withdraw, demanding territory where they could settle, and promising, as federated settlers, to fight as Vortigern's allies. So, partly because he dared not refuse them, partly because he foresaw that he might need them again, Vortigern gave them the coastal stretches in the south, from Rutupiae to Vindocladia—the stretch that was called the Saxon Shore. In the days of the Romans it had been so called because the main Saxon landings had been there: by Uther's time the name had taken on a direr and truer significance. On a clear day you could see the Saxon smoke from London Wall.

It had been from this secure base, and from similar enclaves in the north-east, that the new attacks had come when my father was King. He had killed Hengist and his brother, and had driven the invaders back, some northwards into the wild lands beyond Hadrian's Wall and others behind their old boundaries where once again—but this time forcibly—they had been bound by treaty. But a treaty with a Saxon is like writing in water: Ambrosius, not trusting to the prescribed boundaries, had thrown up a wall to protect the rich lands which marched with the Saxon Shore. Until his death the treaty—or the Wall—had held them, nor had they openly joined in the attacks led by Hengist's son Octa and Eosa his kinsman in the early days of Uther's reign; but they were uneasy neighbours: they provided a beach-head for any wandering longships, and the Saxon Shore grew crowded and still more crowded, till even Ambrosius' Wall looked frail protection. And everywhere along the eastern shores raiders came in from the German Sea, some to burn and rape and sail again, others to burn and rape and stay, buying or extorting new territory from the local kings.

Such an attack, now, Ralf was describing to me.

'Well, of course the Federates broke the agreement. A new war-band—thirty ships it was—landed in Potters' Bay, well west of the boundary, and the Federates welcomed them and came out in force to help them. They established a beach-head near the river's mouth and started to push up towards Vindocladia. I think if they had once got to Badon Hill—what is it?'

He broke off, staring at me. There was amazement in his face, and a touch of fear.

'Nothing,' I said. 'I thought I heard something outside, but it's only the wind.'

He said slowly: 'You looked for a moment the way you did that night at Tintagel, when you said the air was full of magic. Your eyes went strange, all black and blurred, as if you were seeing something, out there beyond the fire.' He hesitated: 'Was it prophecy?'

'No. I saw nothing. All I heard was a sound like horses galloping. It was only the wild geese going over in the wind. If it was prophecy, it will come again. Go on. You were speaking of Badon Hill.'

'Well, the Saxons can't have known that King Uther was in Cornwall,

326 The Hollow Hills

with all the force he'd brought down to fight Duke Gorlois. He gathered his army and called on the Dumnonians to help him, and marched to drive the Saxons back.' He paused, compressing his lips, then finished briefly: 'Cador went with him.'

'Did he indeed?' I was thoughtful. 'You didn't happen to hear what had passed between them?'

'Only that Cador had been heard to say that since he couldn't defend his part of Dumnonia alone he didn't mind fighting alongside the Devil himself, as long as the Saxons could be cleared from the coast.'

'He sounds a sensible young man.'

Ralf, hot on his grievance, was not listening. 'You see, he didn't exactly make peace with Uther—'

'Yes. One gathers that.'

'—but he did march with him! And I could not! I went to him, and to my lady, and begged to go, but he wouldn't take me!'

'Well,' I said, reasonably. 'How could he?'

That stopped him. He stared at me, ready to be angry again. 'What do you mean? If *you* think me a traitor—'

'You're the same age as Cador, aren't you? Then try to show as much commonsense. Think. If Cador was to go into battle beside the King, then the King, for your sake, could hardly take you. Uther may suffer a few pangs of conscience when he lays eyes on you, but Cador must see you as one of the causes of his father's death. Do you think he would bear you near him, however much he may need the King and his legions? Now do you see why you were left at home, and then sent north to me?'

He was silent. I said, gently: 'What's done is done, Ralf. Only a child expects life to be just; it's a man's part to stand by the consequences of his deeds. As we both shall, believe me. So put all this behind you, and take what the gods send. Your life is not over because you have had to leave the court, or even because you have had to leave Cornwall.'

There was a longer silence. Then he picked up his empty bowl and mine and got to his feet. 'Yes, I see. Well, since for the moment I can't do much else, I'll stay and serve you. But not because I am afraid of the King, or because my grandmother wants to get me out of Duke Cador's way. It's because I choose. And indeed'–he swallowed–'I reckon I owe it to you.' His tone was neither grateful nor conciliatory. He stood there like a soldier, stiffly, the bowls clutched to his ribs.

'Then start paying your debt and wash the supper dishes,' I said equably, and picked up a book.

He hung on his heel a moment, but I neither spoke nor looked up. He went then, without another word, to draw water from the spring outside.

Chapter Five

Bruises on the young heal quickly, and Ralf was soon active again, and insistent that he no longer needed doctoring. The wound on his hip, however, gave some trouble, and left him limping for a week or two.

In 'choosing' to stay with me, he had made the best of a bad job, since for the time being he was tied to the cave by his injury and by the loss of his horse, but he served me well, mastering what resentment he might yet feel towards me and his new position. He was silent still, but this suited me, and I went quietly about my affairs, while Ralf gradually fell into my ways, and we got along tolerably well together. Whatever he thought of my quarters in the cave, and the menial tasks which between us we had to do, he made it clear that he was a page serving a prince.

Somehow, through the days that followed, I found myself relieved, bit by bit, of burdensome work which I had begun to take for granted; I had leisure again to study, to replenish my store of medicines, even to make music. It was strange at first, and then in some way comforting, to lie wakeful in the night and hear the boy's untroubled breathing from the other side of the cave; after a while, I found I was sleeping better; as the nightmares receded, strength and calmness came back; and if power still withheld itself, I no longer despaired of its return.

As for Ralf, though I could see that he still fretted against his exile–to which, of course, he could see no clear end–he was never less than courteous, and as time went on seemed to accept his banishment with a better grace, and either lost or hid his unhappiness in a kind of contentment.

So the weeks went by, and the valley fields yellowed towards harvest, and the message came at last from Tintagel. One evening in August, towards dusk, a messenger came spurring up the valley. Ralf was not with me. I had sent him that afternoon across the hill to the hut where the shepherd, Abba, lived all summer; I had been treating Abba's son, Ban, who was simple, for a poisoned foot; this was almost healed, but still needed salves.

I went out to meet the messenger. He had dismounted below the cliff, and now clambered on to the flat alp in front of the cave. He was a young man, spruce and lively, and his horse was fresh. I guessed from this that his message was not urgent; he had taken his time, and come at his ease. I saw him take in my ragged robe and threadbare mantle in one swift, summing glance, but he doffed his cap and went on one knee. I wondered if the salute was for the enchanter, or for the King's son.

'My lord Merlin.'

'You are welcome,' I said. 'From Tintagel?'

'Yes, sir. From the Queen.' A quick upward glance. 'I came privily, without the King's knowledge.'

'So I had imagined, or you would have borne her badge. Get up, man. The grass is damp. Have you had supper?'

He looked surprised. It was not thus, I reckoned, that most princes received their messengers. 'Why, no, sir, but I bespoke it at the inn.'

'Then I won't keep you from it. I've no doubt it will be better than you'd get here. Well then, your business? You've brought a letter from the Queen?'

'No letter, sir, just the message that the Queen desires to see you.'

'Now?' I asked sharply. 'Is there anything wrong with her, or with the child she bears?'

'Nothing. The doctors and the women say that all is well. But'—he dropped his eyes—'it seems she has that on her mind which makes her want to talk with you. As soon as possible, she said.'

'I see.' Then, with my voice as carefully neutral as his: 'Where is the King?'

'The King plans to leave Tintagel in the second week of September.'

'Ah. So any time after that it will be "possible" for me to see the Queen.'

This was rather more frank than he cared for. He flashed me a glance, then looked at the ground again. 'The Queen will be pleased to receive you then. She has bidden me make arrangements for you. You will understand that it will not do for you to be received openly in the castle of Tintagel.' Then, in a burst of candour: 'You must know, my lord, there is no man's hand in Cornwall but will be against you. It would be better if you came disguised.'

'As for that,' I said, fingering my beard, 'you will see that I'm half disguised already. Don't worry, man, I understand; I'll be discreet. But you'll have to tell me more. She gave no reason for this summons?'

'None, my lord.'

'And you heard nothing—no gossip from among the women, things like that?'

He shook his head, then, at the look in my face, added quickly: 'My lord, she was urgent. She did not say so, but it must concern the child, what else?'

'Then I will come.' I thought he looked shocked. As he lowered his eyes, I said, sharply: 'Well, what did you expect? I am not the Queen's man. No, nor the King's either, so there's no need to look scared.'

'Whose, then?'

'My own, and God's. But you can go back to the Queen and tell her I will come. What arrangements have you made for me?'

He hurried, relieved, on to his own ground. 'There is a small inn at a ford of the River Camel, in the valley about five miles from Tintagel. It is kept by a man called Caw. He is a Cornishman, but his wife Maeve was one of the Queen's women, and he will keep his counsel. You can stay there without fear; they will expect you. You may send messages to Tintagel, if you will, by one of Maeve's sons—it would not be wise to go near the castle until the Queen sends for you. Now for the journey. The weather should still be fine in mid-September, and the seas are usually calm enough, so—'

'If you are about to advise me that it is easier to go by sea, you're wasting your breath,' I said. 'Has no one ever told you that enchanters can't cross water? At least, not with any comfort. I should be seasick did I so much as cross the Severn River in the ferry. No, I go by road.'

'But the main road takes you past the barracks at Caerleon. You might be recognised. And then the bridge at Glevum is guarded by King's troops.'

'Very well. I'll take the river crossing, but make it a short one.' I knew that he was right. To go by the main road through Caerleon and then by the Glevum Bridge would, even without the prospect of discovery by Uther's troops, put several days on my journey. 'I'll avoid the military road. There's a good track along the coast through Nidum; I'll go that way, if you can bespeak me a boat at the mouth of the Ely river?'

'Very well, my lord.' And so it was arranged. I would cross from the Ely to the mouth of the Uxella in the country of the Dumnonii, and from there I would find my way south-west by the tracks, avoiding the roads where I might fall in with Uther's troops or Cador's men.

'Do you know the way?' he asked me. 'For the last part, of course, Ralf can guide you.'

'Ralf will not be with me. But I can find it. I've been through that country before, and I have a tongue in my head.'

'I can arrange for horses—'

'Better not,' I said. 'We agreed, did we not, that I would be better disguised? I'll use a disguise that has served me before. I'll be a travelling eye doctor, and a humble fellow like that doesn't expect to post with fresh horses all the way. Have no fear, I shall be safe, and, when the Queen wants me, I shall be there.'

He was satisfied, and stayed for a while longer answering my questions and giving me what news there was. The King's brief punitive expedition against the coastal raiders had been successful, and the newcomers had been pushed back behind the agreed boundaries of the Federated West Saxons. For the moment things were quiet in the south. From the north had come rumours of tougher fighting where Anglian raiders, from Germany, had crossed the coast near the Alaunus river in the country of the Votadini. This is the country that we of Dyfed call Manau Guotodin, and it is from here that the great King Cunedda came, invited a century ago by the Emperor Maximus, to drive the Irish from Northern Wales and settle there as allies to the Imperial Eagles. These were, I suppose, the first of the Federates; they drove the Irish out, and afterwards remained in Northern Wales, which they called Gwynedd. A descendant of Cunedda held it still; Maelgon, a stark king and a good warrior, as a man would have to be to keep that country in the wake of the great Magnus Maximus.

Another descendant of Cunedda still held the Votadini country; a young king, Lot, as fierce and as a good a fighter as Maelgon; his fortress lay near the coast south of Caer Eidyn, in the centre of his kingdom of Lothian. It was he who had faced and beaten off the latest attack of the Angles. He had been given his command by Ambrosius, in the hope that with him the kings of the north—Gwalawg of Elmet, Urien of Gore, the chiefs of Strathclyde, King Coel of Rheged—would form a strong wall in the north and east. But Lot, it was said, was ambitious and quarrelsome; and Strathclyde had sired nine sons already and (while they fought like young bull seals each for his square of territory) was cheerfully siring more. Urien of Gore had married Lot's sister and would stand firm, but was, it was said, too close in Lot's shadow. The strongest of them was still (as in my father's time) Coel of Rheged, who held with a light hand all the smaller chiefs and earls of his kingdom, and brought them together faithfully against the smaller threat to the sovereignty of the High Kingdom.

Now, the Queen's messenger told me, the King of Rheged, with Ector of Galava and Ban of Benoic had joined with Lot and Urien to clear the north of trouble, and for the time being they had succeeded. On the whole the news was cheering. The harvest had been good everywhere, so hunger would not drive any more Saxons across before winter closed the seaways. We should have peace for a time; enough time for Uther to settle any unrest caused by the quarrel with Cornwall and his new marriage, to ratify such alliances as Ambrosius had made, and to strengthen and extend his system of defences.

At length the messenger took his leave. I wrote no letters, but sent news of Ralf to his grandmother, and a message of compliance to the Queen, with thanks for the gift of money she had sent me by the messenger's hand to provide for my journey. Then the young man rode off cheerfully down the valley towards the good company and the better supper that awaited him at the inn. It remained now for me to tell Ralf.

This was more difficult even than I expected. His face lit when I told him about the messenger, and he looked eagerly about for the man, seeming very disappointed when he found that he had already gone. Messages from his grandmother he received almost impatiently, but plied me with questions about the fighting south of Vindocladia, listening with such eagerness to all I could tell him of that and the larger news that it was obvious that his forced inaction in Maridunum fretted him far more than he had shown. When I came to the Queen's summons he showed more animation than I had seen in him since he had come to me.

'How long before we set out?'

'I did not say "we" would set out. I shall go alone.'

'*Alone?*' You would have thought I had struck him. The blood sprang under the thin skin and he stood staring with his mouth open. Eventually he said, sounding stifled: 'You can't mean that. You can't.'

'I'm not being arbitrary, believe me. I'd like to take you, but you must see it isn't possible.'

'Why not? You know everything here will be perfectly safe; in any case, you've left it before. And you can't travel alone. How would you go on?'

'My dear Ralf. I've done it before.'

'Maybe you have, but you can't deny I've served you well since I've been here, so why not take me? You can't go to Tintagel–back to where things are happening–and leave me here! I warn you—' He took a breath, eyes blazing, all his careful courtesy collapsing in ruins–'I warn you, my lord, if you go without me, I shan't be here when you come back!'

I waited till his gaze fell, then said mildly: 'Have some sense, boy. Surely you see why I can't take you? The situation hasn't changed so much since you had to leave Cornwall. You know what would happen if any of Cador's men recognised you, and everyone knows you round about Tintagel. You'd be seen, and the word would go round.'

'I know that. Do you still think I'm afraid of Cador? Or of the King?'

'No. But it's foolish to run into danger when one doesn't need to. And the messenger certainly seemed to think there was still danger.'

'Then what about you? Won't you be in danger, too?'

'Possibly. I shall have to go disguised, as it is. Why do you think I've been letting my beard grow all this while?'

'I didn't know. I never thought about it. Do you mean you've been expecting the Queen to send for you?'

'I didn't expect this summons, I admit,' I said. 'But I knew that, come Christmas, when the child is born, I must be there.'

He stared. 'Why?'

I regarded him for a moment. He was standing near the mouth of the cave, against the sunset, just as he had come in from his trip across the hill to the shepherd's hut. He was still clutching the osier basket which had held the salves. It held a small bundle now, wrapped in a clean linen cloth. The shepherd's wife, who lived across in the next valley, sent bread up weekly to her man; some of this Abba regularly sent on to me. I could see the boy's fists clenched bone-white on the handle of the basket. He was tense, as angry and fretting as a fighting dog held back in the slips. There was something more here, I was sure, than home-sickness, or disappointment at missing an adventure.

'Put that basket down, for goodness' sake,' I said, 'and come in. That's better. Now, sit down. It's time that you and I talked. When I accepted your service, I did not do so because I wanted someone to scour the cooking pots and carry gifts from Abba's wife on baking day. Even if I am content with my life here on Bryn Myrddin, I'm not such a fool as to think it contents you—or would do so for long. We are waiting, Ralf, no more. We have fled from danger, both of us, and healed our hurts, and now there is nothing to do but wait.'

'For the Queen's childbed? Why?'

'Because as soon as he is born, the Queen's son will be given to me to care for.'

He was silent for a full minute before he said, sounding puzzled: 'Does my grandmother know this?'

'I think she suspects that the child's future lies with me. When I last spoke with the King, on that night at Tintagel, he told me he would not acknowledge the child who would be born. I think this is why the Queen has sent for me.'

'But . . . not to acknowledge his eldest son? You mean he will send him away? Will the Queen agree? A baby—surely they would never send it to *you*? How could you keep it? And how can you even know it will be a boy?'

'Because I had a vision, Ralf, that night in Tintagel. After you had let us in through the postern gate, while the King was with Ygraine, and Ulfin kept guard outside the chamber, you diced with the porter in the lodge by the postern. Do you remember?'

'How could I ever forget? I thought that night would never end.'

I did not tell him that it had not ended yet. I smiled. 'I think I felt the same, while I waited alone in the guard-room. It was then that I saw—was shown—for certain why God had required me to do as I had done, shown for sure that my prophecies had been true. I heard a sound on the stairs, and went out of the guard-room on to the landing. I saw Marcia, your grandmother, coming down the steps towards me from the Queen's room, carrying a child. And though it was only March, I felt the chill of midwinter, and then I saw the stairs and the shadows clear through her body, and knew it was a vision. She put the child into my arms and said, "Take care of him." She was weeping. Then she vanished, and the child too, and the winter's chill went with her. But this was a true picture, Ralf. At Christmas I shall be there, waiting, and Marcia will hand the Queen's son into my care.'

He was silent for a long time. He seemed awed by the vision. But then he said, practically: 'And I? Where do I come into this? Is this why my grandmother told me to stay with you and serve you?'

'Yes. She saw no future for you near the King. So she made sure you would be near his son.'

'A baby?' His voice was blank. He sounded horrified, and far from flattered. 'You mean that if the King won't acknowledge the child, you'll have to keep it? I don't understand—oh, I can see why my grandmother concerns herself, and even why you do; but not why she dragged me into it! What sort of future does she think there is in looking after a king's bastard that won't be acknowledged?'

'Not a king's bastard,' I said. 'A king.'

There was silence, but for the fluttering of the fire. I had not spoken with power, but with the full certainty of knowledge. He stared, open-mouthed, and shaken.

'Ralf,' I said, 'you came to me in anger, and you stayed from duty, and you have served me as well and as faithfully as you knew how. You were no part of my vision, and I don't know if your coming here, or the wounds that held you here with me, were part of God's plan; I have had no message from my gods since Gorlois died. But I do know now, after these last weeks, that there is no one I would sooner choose to help me. Not with the kind of service you have given till now: when this winter comes it isn't a servant I shall need; I shall need a fighting man who is loyal, not to me or to the Queen, but to the next High King.'

He was pale, and stammering. 'I had no idea. I thought . . . I thought . . .'

'That you were suffering a kind of exile? In a way, we both were. I told you it was a waiting time.' I looked down at my hands. It was dark now outside the cave; the sun had gone, and dusk drew in. 'Nor do I know clearly what lies ahead, except danger and loss and treachery, and in the end some glory.'

He sat quiet, without moving, till I roused myself from my thoughts and smiled at him. 'So now, perhaps, you will accept that I don't doubt your courage?'

'Yes. I'm sorry I spoke as I did. I didn't understand.' He hesitated, chewing his lip, then came to a decision. 'My lord, you really don't know why the Queen sends for you now?'

'No.'

He leaned forward, hands on knees. 'But because you know that your vision of the birth was a true one, you know that you will go safely this time to Cornwall, and return?'

'You could say so.'

'Then if your magic is always true, might it not be because I go with you to protect you that you make the journey safely?'

I laughed. 'I suppose it's a good quality in a fighting man, never to admit defeat. But can't you see, taking you would only be taking two risks instead of one. Because my bones tell me I shall be safe, it doesn't mean that you will.'

'If you can be disguised, so can I. If you even say that we must go as beggars and sleep in the ditches . . . whatever the danger . . .' He swallowed, sounding all at once very young. 'What is it to you if I run a risk? *You* are to be safe, you told me so. So taking me can't endanger you, and that's all that matters. Won't you let me take my own risks? Please?'

His voice trailed away. Silence again, and the fire flickering. Time was, I thought, not without bitterness, when I would only have had to watch the flames to find the answer there. Would he be safe? Or would I carry the burden of yet another death? But all that the firelight showed me was a youth who needed to find manhood. Uther had denied it to him; I could not let my conscience do the same.

At length I said heavily: 'I told you once that men must stand by their own deeds. I suppose that means I have no right to stop you. Very well, you may come . . . No, don't thank me. You'll dislike me thoroughly enough before we're done. It will be a damned uncomfortable journey, and before we set out, you'll have work to do that won't suit you.'

'I'm used to that,' he said, and straightened, laughing. He was shining, excited, the gaiety that I remembered back in his face. 'But you don't mean you're going to teach me magic?'

'I do not. But I shall have to teach you a little medicine, whether you like it or not. I shall be a travelling eye doctor; it's a good passport anywhere, and one can pay one's way easily without spending the Queen's gold abroad where questions might be asked. So you will have to be my assistant, and that means learning to mix the salves properly.'

'Well, if I must, but God help the patients! You know I can't tell one herb from the other.'

'Never fear, I wouldn't let you touch them. You can leave me to select the plants. You'll just prepare them.'

'And if any of Cador's men show signs of recognising us, just try some of my salves on them,' he said buoyantly. 'Talk about magic, it'll be easy. The eye doctor's skilled assistant will simply strike them blind.'

Chapter Six

We came to the inn at Camelford two days before the middle of September.

The Camel valley is winding, with steep sides clothed with trees. For the last part of the way we followed the track along the water side. The trees were closely crowded, and the path where we rode was so thickly padded with moss and small, dark green ferns that our horses' hoofs made no sound. Beside us the river wrangled its way down through granite boulders that glittered in the sun. Around and above us the dense hangers of oak and beech were turning yellow, and acorns crunched among the dead leaves where the horses trod. Nuts ripened in the thickets; the willows trailed amber leaves in the tugging shallows; and wherever the bright sun splashed through the boughs it shimmered on the spiders' webs of autumn furred and glittered, sagging deep with dew.

Our journey had been uneventful. Once south of the Severn and beyond hourly danger of recognition we had ridden at ease, and in pleasant stages. The weather, as so often in September, was warm and bright, but with a crisp feel to the air that made riding a pleasure. Ralf had been in high spirits all the way, in spite of poor clothes, an undistinguished horse (bought with some of the Queen's gold) and the work he had had to do for me making the washes and ointments with which I largely paid our way. We were only questioned once, by a troop of King's men who came on us just short of Hercules Point. Uther kept the old Roman camp there garrisoned as a strongpoint, and by the purest mischance we fell foul of a scouting party which was making its way home by the moorland track we followed. We were taken to the camp and questioned, though it seemed this was merely a matter of form as, after a cursory look at our baggage, my story was accepted. We were sent on our way with our flasks refilled with the ration wine, the richer for a copper coin given me by a man off duty who followed us out of camp and begged a pot of salve from me.

I found the men's vigilance interesting, and would have liked to know more of the state of affairs in the north, but that would have to wait. To have asked questions here would have attracted attention I did not want. No doubt I would find out what I wished to know from the Queen herself.

'Did you see anyone you knew?' I asked Ralf, as we headed over the moors at a brisk canter away from the gate of the camp.

'None. Did you?'

'I'd met the officer before, a few years ago. His name is Priscus. But he gave no sign of recognising me.'

'I wouldn't have known you myself,' said Ralf. 'And it isn't just the beard. It's the way you walk, your voice, everything. It's like that night at Tintagel, when you were disguised as the Duke's captain. I'd known him all my life, and I'd have sworn you were he. It's no wonder folks are talking about magic. I thought it was magic myself.'

'This is easier,' I said. 'If you carry a trade or a skill with you men think about that, instead of looking at you too closely.'

Indeed, I had troubled very little with disguise. I had bought a new riding cloak, brown, with a hood which could be pulled about my face, and I spoke Celtic with the accent of Brittany. This is a tongue close to the Cornish one, and would be understood where we were going. This, with the beard, and my humble tradesman's bearing, should keep any but my intimates from knowing me. Nothing would part me from the brooch my father had given me, with its royal cipher of the Red Dragon on gold, but I wore it clipped inside the breast of my tunic, and had threatened Ralf with every fate in the Nine Books of Magic if he called me 'my lord' even in private.

We reached Camelford towards evening. The inn was a small squat building of daubed stone built where the coast road ran down into the ford. It stood at the top of the bank, just clear of flood level. Ralf and I, approaching by the country track along the river, came on it from the rear. It seemed a pleasant place, and clean. Someone had given the stones a wash of red ochre, the colour of the rich earth thereabouts, and fat poultry picked about among the ricks at the edge of a swept yard. A chained dog dozed in the shade of a mulberry tree heavy with fruit. There was a tidy stack of firewood against the byre, and the midden was fully twenty feet from the back door.

As luck would have it, the innkeeper's wife was out at the back with a maidservant, taking in bedding which had been spread over the bushes in the sun. As we approached the dog flew out, barking, at the length of his chain. The woman straightened, shading her eyes against the light, and staring.

She was a young woman, broadly built and lively looking, with a fresh, high colour and prominent light-blue eyes. Her bad teeth and plump figure gave away a rash passion for sweetmeats, and the lively blue eyes spoke even more clearly of other pleasures. They ran now over Ralf, who rode ahead of me, appraised him as likely, but young for it; then, more hopefully, over me, to dismiss me finally as less likely, and probably too poor to pay my shot anyway. Then, as her gaze returned to Ralf, I saw her recognise him. She stiffened, looking quickly back at me. Her mouth fell open, and I thought for an anxious moment that she was going to curtsy, but then she had command of herself. A word sent the maid packing indoors with an armful of bedding, a shrill bidding to the dog drove him back, ears down and growling, into the mulberry shade, then she was greeting us, smiling widely, eyes curious and excited.

'You'll be the eye doctor, likely?'

We drew our horses to a halt in the dust of the yard. 'Indeed, mistress. My name is Emrys, and this is my servant Ban.'

'We've been expecting you. Your beds is bespoke.' Then under her breath as she came close to my horse's shoulder: 'You be very welcome, my lord, and Ralf, too. I declare he do look a handspan taller than when I seen him last. Will you be pleased to come in?'

I dismounted and handed the reins to Ralf. 'Thank you. It's good to be here, we're both weary. Ralf will look after the horses himself. Now before we go in, Maeve, give me the news from Tintagel. Is all well with the Queen?'

'Yes, indeed, sir, praise be to all the saints and fairies. You need have no worries there, surely.'

'And the King? He's still at Tintagel?'

'Aye, my lord, but the word goes that he'll ride out any day now. You'll not have long to bide. You're as safe here as anywhere in Cornwall. We'll have good enough warning of troops moving, and you can hear them on this road a mile off. And never worry about Caw—that's my husband; he's a Duke's man, sure enough, but he'll do nothing to harm my lady, and besides, he always does as I tell him. Leastways, not always. There's some things he don't do near often enough for my liking.' This with a burst of cheery laughter. I saw Ralf grinning as he led the horses away, then Maeve, talking loudly about beds and supper-time, and the sore eyes of her youngest which could do with looking at, led me through the back door of the inn.

When I saw her husband later that evening I knew that I need have no fears for his discretion. He was a dry stick of a man, and silent as an oyster. He came in as we were sitting down to supper, stared at Ralf, nodded at me, then went about his business of serving wine without a word spoken. His wife treated him—and all comers—with the same rough, frank kindliness, and saw to it without fuss that we were well served and comfortably housed. It was as good a house of its kind as I have ever been in, and the food was excellent.

Understandably, the inn was always busy, but there was little danger of our being recognised. My character as a travelling healer was not only my pass to people's incurious acceptance, it gave Ralf and me the excuse to be abroad in the countryside. Each day early we would take food and wine with us, and make our way up by one of the deep, densely wooded glens that fed the Camel valley, to the windy upland that lay between Camelford and the sea. Ralf knew all the ways. We would separate, more often than not, and each choose some hidden point of vantage from which he could watch the two roads which Uther and his men might take out of Tintagel. He might turn north-east along the coast for Dimilioc and the camp near Hercules Point, or—if he was making straight for Winchester or the trouble centres along the Saxon Shore—he would follow the valley tracks through Camelford and from there climb south-east to the military road which ran along the spine of Dumnonia. Here on the wind-swept heights the forest thins, and there are great tracts of broken moorland treacherous with bog and watched over by strange stony hills. The old Roman road, crumbling fast in that wild country, but still serviceable, runs straight through Isca, into the kinder lands behind Ambrosius' Wall. It was my guess that this latter was the way that Uther would take, and I wanted to see who rode with him. Ralf and I gave it out that I was searching for plants for my medicines, and indeed I came back each evening to my meeting-place with him with a pouch full of roots and berries which did not grow at home, and which I was glad to have. Luckily the weather continued fine, and no one wondered to see us ride abroad. They were too glad to have a doctor staying there who, each evening, would treat any who came to him, and ask no more than they could afford to pay.

So the days went by, serene and still, while we waited for the King to move, and the Queen to send word.

It was a week before he rode out. He went the way I had expected, and I was there watching.

There is a place where the track from Tintagel to Camelford runs straight for some quarter of a mile along the foot of a steeply wooded bank. For the most part the wood is too steep and thickly grown to penetrate, but there were places at the wood's edge open to the sun, stony banks deep in ferns and drifting thistledown, where brambles and bracken grew in thickets over the rocks. The blackthorn bushes were high, and glinting with fruit. Some of the little sloe-plums were still greenish, but most were ready, black bloomed over pale blue with ripeness. There is an extract one can make of the fruit which is sovereign for a flux of the bowels: one of Maeve's children had been suffering in this way, and I had promised a draught that night. It would need no more than a handful, but the fruit was ripe to perfection, and so tempting that I went on gathering. If the berries are crushed and added in a certain way to juniper-wine they make a good drink, rich, astringent, and powerful. I had told Maeve of it, and she wanted to try it.

My bag was almost full when I heard, like a soft thunder in the distance, horses coming steadily along the track below me. I withdrew quickly into the edge of the wood, and watched from hiding. Soon the head of the column came in sight; then the long train of dust, filled with the beat of trotting hoofs, the clash of mail, the coloured glint of pennants, rolled past along the foot of the slope. A thousand, perhaps more. I stood stone-still in the shadow of the trees, and watched them go by.

A horse's length to the front the King rode, and behind him, on his left hand, his standard-bearer carried the Red Dragon. Other colours showed through the dust, but there was no wind to move the banners, and though I strained my eyes the length of the column I could not swear to most that I saw. Nor did I glimpse the one I was watching for, though it might well have been there. I waited till the last horseman disappeared at a smart trot round a bend in the road, then I made my way to the place where I had arranged to meet Ralf.

He met me halfway, panting. 'Did you see them?'

'Yes. Where were you? I sent you to watch the other road.'

'I was watching. There was nothing stirring there, nothing at all. I was on my way back here when I heard them, so I ran. I almost missed them—only saw the tail end. It was the King, wasn't it?'

'It was. Ralf, could you pick out the devices? Did you see any that you knew?'

'I saw Brychan, and Cynfelin, but no others from Dyfnaint that I recognised. The men from Garlot were there, and Cernyw, too, I think, and others I thought I knew, but there was too much dust to make sure. They were round that bend before I could get a good sight of them.'

'Was Cador there?'

'My lord, I'm sorry, I didn't see.'

'No matter. If the others were there from Cornwall, you may be sure he would be. No doubt they'll know at the inn. And had you forgotten that you were not to call me "my lord", even when we were alone?'

'I'm sorry . . . Emrys.' It was a measure of our new, easier relationship that he should add, with a suspicious meekness: 'And had you forgotten that my name is Ban?' Then, laughing as he dodged my cuff at his head: 'Do you have to call me after the halfwit?'

'It's the first name that came into my head. It's a king's name too, the King of Benoic, so you can take your choice which was your sponsor.'

'Benoic? Where's that?'

'In the north. Come now, we'll get back to the inn. I doubt if the Queen will send before tomorrow, but I've a draught to make tonight, and it's a decoction that takes time. Here, carry these.'

I was right; the messenger came next morning. Ralf had gone out down the road to watch for him, and the two of them came back together, with the news that I was to ride to Tintagel immediately for my audience with the Queen.

I had not confessed it to Ralf, nor even hardly admitted it to myself, but I was apprehensive about the coming interview with Ygraine. On that night at Tintagel when the child was conceived I had been certain, in every way a seer can be certain, that the boy who was to be born would be given to me to foster, and that I should be the guardian of a great King. Uther himself, in his bitterness and anger over Gorlois' death, had sworn to reject the 'bastard' he had begotten, and from Marcia's letter I knew he was still of the same mind. But in the six long months since that March night I had had no direct message from Ygraine, and no means of knowing whether she would obey her husband, or whether as the time drew near she would find it impossible to face separation from her child. I had gone over in my mind a hundred times all the arguments I might bring to bear, remembering half incredulously the sureness with which I had spoken to her before, and to the King. Indeed my god had been with me then. And in truth, and how bitterly, was he gone from me now. There were even times when, lying wakeful in the night, I saw my sure visions in the past as chances, illusions, dreams fed by desire. I remembered the King's bitter words to me: '*I see now what your magic is, this "power" you talk of. It is nothing but human trickery, an attempt at statecraft which my brother taught you to like and to play for, and to believe was your mystery. You use even God to gain your ends. "It is God who tells me to do these things, it is God who exacts the price, it is God who sees that others should pay . . ." For what, Merlin? For your ambition? And who is it pays this debt to God for carrying out your plans? Not you. The men who play your game for you, and pay the price. But you pay nothing.*' When I listened to such words as these, heard clearly in the nights when nothing else spoke to me, I wondered if I had read my vision of the future aright, or if everything I had done and dreamed of had been a mockery. Then, thinking of those who had paid with death for my dream, I would wonder if that death had not been kinder than this desert of self-doubt where I lay fixed, waiting in vain for even the smallest of my gods to speak to me. Oh, yes, I paid. Every night of those nine long months I paid.

But now it was day, and I would soon find out what the Queen wanted with me. I remember how restlessly I fidgeted around while Ralf saddled my horse and made ready. Maeve was with the maids in the kitchen, washing the sloes for the wine-making. A pan of them was on the stove, coming to the simmer. It seemed a strange memory to take with me on my visit to the Queen, the smell of sloe wine. Suddenly I found the pungent sweetness intolerable, and made, choking, for the air outside. But then one of the girls came running to ask something about the mixing, and in answering her I forgot my sickness, and then all at once Ralf was at my elbow to summon me, and the three of us—Ralf, the messenger, and I—were heading for Tintagel at a hand-gallop through the soft, blowing September noon.

Chapter Seven

It was only a few months since I had last seen Ygraine, but she seemed very much changed. At first I thought this was only the pregnancy; her once slim body was greatly swollen and, though her face was full of the bloom of health, she had that pinched and shadowy look that women get around the eyes and mouth. But the change was deeper than this; it was in the expression of her eyes, in her gestures, the way she sat. Where before she had seemed young and burning, a wild bird beating her wings against the wires of the cage, now she seemed to brood, wings clipped, gravid, a creature of the ground.

She received me in her own chamber, a long room above the curtain wall, with a deep circular recess where the turret stood at the north-west corner. There were windows in the long wall facing south-west, and through these the sunlight fell freely, but the queen was sitting by one of the narrow turret windows, through which came the breeze of the soft September afternoon, and the eternal noise of the sea on the rocks below. So much was still here, then, of the Ygraine I remembered. It was like her, I thought, to choose the wind and the sea sounds, rather than the sunlight. But even here, in spite of the light and air, one got the feeling of a cage: this was the room in which the young wife of Gorlois the old Duke had passed those pent years before the fateful trip to London where she had met the King. Now, after that brief flight, she was penned again, by her love for the King, and by the weight of his child. I never loved a woman, except one, but I have pitied them. Now, looking at the Queen, young, beautiful, and with her heart's desire, I pitied her even as I feared her for what she might say to me.

She was alone. I had been led by a chamberlain through the outer room where the women span and weaved and gossiped. Bright eyes looked at me in momentary curiosity, and the chattering was stilled, only to begin again as soon as I had passed. There was no recognition in their faces, only perhaps here and there some disappointment at the sight of so ordinary and humble a fellow. No diversion here. To them I was a messenger, to be received by the Queen in the King's absence; that was all.

The chamberlain rapped on the door of the inner chamber and then withdrew. Marcia, Ralf's grandmother, opened the door. She was a grey-haired woman with Ralf's eyes in a lined and anxious face, but in spite of her age she bore herself as straight as a girl. Though she was expecting me, I saw her eyes rest on me for a moment without recognition, then with a flicker of surprise. Even Ygraine looked startled for a moment, then she smiled and held out her hand.

'Prince Merlin. Welcome.' Marcia curtsied to the air somewhere between me and the Queen, and withdrew. I went forward to kneel and kiss the Queen's hand.

'Madam.'

She raised me kindly. 'It was good of you to come so quickly for such a strange summons. I hope the journey was easy?'

'Very easy. We are well lodged with Maeve and Caw, and so far no one has recognised me, or even Ralf. Your secret is safe.'

'I must thank you for taking so much care of it. I promise you I'd not have known you until you spoke.'

I fingered my chin, smiling. 'As you see, I've been preparing for some time.'

'No magic, this time?'

'As much as there was before,' I said.

She looked at me straightly then, the beautiful dark blue eyes meeting mine in the way I remembered, and I saw that this was still the old Ygraine, direct as a man, and with the same high pride. The heavy stillness was just an overlay, the milky calm that seems to come on women in pregnancy. Beneath the stillness, the placidity, was the old fire. She spread her hands out. 'Looking at me now, do you still tell me that when you spoke to me that night in London, and promised me the King's love, there was no magic there?'

'Not in the ruse that brought the King to you, Madam. In what happened after, perhaps.'

'"Perhaps?"' There was a quick lift to her voice that warned me. Ygraine might be a Queen, with mettle as high as a man's, but she was a woman nearing her seventh month. My fears were my own, and must stay my own. I hesitated, searching for words, but she went on quickly, burningly, as if to convince herself across my silence: 'When you first spoke with me and told me you could bring the King to me, there was magic there, I know there was. I felt it, and I saw it in your face. You told me that your power came from God, and that in obeying you I was God's creature, even as you were. You said that because of the magic that would bring Uther to me, the kingdom should have peace. You spoke of crowns and altars . . . And, now, see, I am Queen, with God's blessing, and I am heavy with the King's child. Dare you tell me now that you deceived me?'

'I did not deceive you, Madam. That was a time full of visions, and a passion of dreams and desires. We are quit of those now, and we are sober, and it is daylight. But magic is here, growing in you, and this time it is fact, not vision. He will be born at Christmas, they tell me.'

'"He?" You sound very sure.'

'I am sure.'

I saw her press her lips together as if at a sudden spasm of pain, then she looked away from me, down at her hands which lay folded across her belly. When she spoke, she spoke calmly, straight to her hands, or to what they covered. 'Marcia told me of the messages she sent to you in the summer. But you must have known, without her telling you, the way my lord the King thinks of this matter.'

I waited, but she seemed to expect an answer. 'He told me himself,' I said. 'If he's still of the same mind now as he was then, he won't acknowledge the child as his heir.'

'He is still of the same mind.' Her eyes came swiftly up to mine again. 'Don't misunderstand me, he has not the faintest doubt of me, nor ever had. He knows that I was his from the first moment I saw him, and that from that moment, on one excuse or another, I never lay with the Duke. No, he does not doubt me; he knows the child is his. And for all his high speech'–there was the glimmer of a smile, and suddenly her voice was indulgent, the voice of a woman speaking of her child or of a loved husband–'and for all his rough denials, he knows your power and fears it. You told him a child would come out of that night, and he would trust your word, even if he could not trust mine. But none of this alters the way he feels about it. He blames himself–and you, and even the child–for the Duke's death.'

'I know.'

'If he had waited, he says, Gorlois would still have died that night, and I would have been Queen, and the child conceived in wedlock, so that no one could question his parentage, or call him bastard.'

'And you, Ygraine?'

She was silent for a long time. She turned that lovely head of hers and gazed out of the window, where the sea birds swung and tilted, crying, on the wind. I saw, I am not sure how, that her calm was that of a soldier who has won one battle, and rests before the next. I felt my nerves tighten. I did not hold Ygraine lightly, should the battle be with me.

She said, very quietly: 'What the King says may well be true. I don't know. But what's done is done, and it is the child who must concern me now. This is why I sent for you.' A pause. I waited. She faced me again. 'Prince Merlin, I fear for the child.'

'At the King's hands?' I asked.

This was too straight, even for Ygraine. Her eyes were cold, and her voice. 'This is insolence, and folly, too. You forget yourself, my lord.'

'I?' I spoke as coldly. 'It is you who forget, Madam. If my mother had been wed to Ambrosius when he begot me, Uther would not now be King, nor would I have helped him to your bed to beget the child you carry. There should be no talk of insolence or folly from you to me. I know, who better, what chance there is in Britain for a prince conceived out of wedlock and unacknowledged by his sire.'

She had flushed as red as she was pale before. Her eyes dropped from mine, their anger dying. She spoke simply, like a girl. 'You are right, I had forgotten. I ask your pardon. I'd forgotten, too, what it was like to talk freely. There is no one here besides Marcia and my lord, and I cannot talk to Uther about the child.'

I had been standing all this while; now I turned aside to bring up a chair, and set it near her in the turret embrasure. I sat down. Things had changed between us, suddenly, as when a wind changes. I knew then that the battle was not with me, but with herself, her own woman's weakness. She was watching me now as a woman in pain watches her doctor. I said gently: 'Well, I am here. And I am listening. What did you send for me to tell me?'

She drew in her breath. When she spoke her voice was calm, but no more than a whisper. 'That if this child is a boy, the King will not allow me to rear him. If it's a girl I may keep her, but a boy so begotten cannot be acknowledged as a prince and legitimate heir, so he must not remain here, even as a bastard.' Visibly, she steadied herself. 'I told you, Uther does not doubt me. But because of what happened that night, my husband's death, and all the talk of magic, he swears that men may still believe that the Duke and not himself begot this child. There will be other sons, he says, whose begetting no man will question, and among them he will find the heir to the High Kingdom.'

'Ygraine,' I said, 'I know what a heavy thing it is–however it happens–for a woman to lose her child. Perhaps there is no grief heavier. But I think the King is right. The boy should not remain here to be reared as a bastard in times so wild and uncertain. If there should be other heirs, declared and acknowledged by the King, they might count him a danger to themselves, and certainly they would be a danger for him. I know what I'm talking about; this is what happened in my own childhood. And I, as a royal bastard, found fortune as this prince may never find it; I had my father's protection.'

A pause. She nodded without speaking, her eyes once again on the hands that lay in her lap.

'And if the child is to be sent away,' I said, 'it's better that he should be taken straight from the birth chamber, before you have had time even to hold him. Believe me'–I spoke quickly, though she had not moved–'this is true. I'm speaking now as a doctor.'

She moistened her lips. 'Marcia says the same.'

I waited a moment, but she said no more. I started to speak, found my voice came hoarsely, and cleared my throat. In spite of myself, my hands tightened on the arms of my chair. But my voice was calm and steady as I came to the core of the interview. 'Has the King told you where the child is to be fostered?'

'No. I told you it wasn't easy to talk to him about it. But when we last spoke of it he said he would take counsel; and he spoke of Brittany.'

'*Brittany?*' For all my care, the word came out with a cutting edge. I fought to recover my calm. My hands had clenched on the chair, and I relaxed them and held them still. So, my doubts were real. Oddly enough, the knowledge hardened me. If I must fight the King as well as Ygraine–yes, and my delphic gods as well–then I would do so. As long as I could see the ground to fight from . . . 'So Uther will send him to King Budec?'

'It seems so.' She seemed to have noticed nothing strange in my manner. 'He sent a messenger a month ago. That was just before I sent to ask you to come. Budec is the obvious choice, after all.'

This was true. King Budec of Less Britain was a cousin of the King's. It was he who, some thirty years ago, had taken my father and the young Uther under his protection when the usurper Vortigern murdered their elder brother King Constans, and in his capital of Kerrec they had assembled and trained the army which had won the High Kingdom back from Vortigern. But I shook my head. 'Too obvious. If anyone should look for the boy to harm him, they'll guess where to go. Budec can't protect him all the time. Besides—'

'Budec cannot care for my child as he should be cared for!' The words came forcibly, stopping me short, but the interruption was not uncivil. It came almost like a cry. It was plain that she had not heard a word I had said. She was fighting herself, choosing words. 'He is old, and besides, Brittany is a long way off, and less secure even than this Saxon-ridden land. Prince Merlin, I–Marcia and I–we think that you—' The hands suddenly twisted together in her lap. Her voice changed. 'There is no one else we can trust. And Uther–whatever Uther says, he knows that his kingdom, or any part of it, would be safe in your hands. You are Ambrosius' son, and the child's closest kinsman. Everyone knows your power, and fears it–the child would be safe with you to protect him. It's you who must take him, Merlin!' She was begging me now. 'Take him safe, somewhere away from this cruel coast, and rear him for me. Teach him as you were taught, and rear him as a king's son should be reared, and then when he is grown, bring him back and let him take his place as you did, at the next King's side.'

She faltered. I must have been staring at her like a fool. She fell quiet, twisting her hands. There was a long silence, filled with the scent of the salt wind and the crying of the gulls. I had not been aware of rising, but I found myself standing at the window with my back to the Queen, staring out at the sky. Below the turret wall the gulls wheeled and mewed in the wind, and far below, at the foot of the black cliff, the sea dashed and whitened. But I saw and heard nothing. My hands were pressed down hard on the stone of the sill, and when at length I lifted them and straightened they showed a mottled bar of bloodless flesh where the stone had bitten in. I began to chafe them, only now feeling the small hurt as I turned back to meet the Queen's eyes. She too had hold of herself again, but I saw strain in her face, and a hand plucked at her gown.

I said flatly: 'Do you think you can persuade the King to give him to me?'

'No. I don't think so. I don't know.' She swallowed. 'Of course I can talk to him, but—'

'Then why send for me to ask me this, if you have no power to sway the King?'

She was white, and her lips worked together, but she kept her head up and faced me. 'I thought that if you agreed, my lord, you could–you would—'

'I can do nothing with Uther now. You should know that.' Then, in sudden, bitter comprehension: 'Or did you send for me as you did last time, hoping for magic to order, as if I were an old spell-wife, or a country druid? I would have thought, Madam—' I stopped. I had seen the flinching in her eyes, and the drawn pallor round her mouth, and I remembered what she carried in her. My anger died. I turned up a hand, speaking gently: 'Very well. If it can be done, Ygraine, I will do it, even if I have to talk to Uther myself to remind him of his promise.'

'His promise? What did he promise you, and when?'

'When he first sent for me, and told me of his love for you, he swore to obey me in anything, if only he could have his way.' I smiled at her. 'It was meant as a bribe rather than a promise, but no matter, we'll hold him to it as a royal oath.'

She began to thank me, but I stopped her. 'No, no, keep your thanks. I may not succeed with the King; you know how little he loves me. You were wise to send secretly, and you'll be wiser not to let him know we talked of this together.'

'He shan't know from me.'

I nodded. 'Now, for the child's sake and your own, you must put your fears aside. Leave this to me. Even if we can't move the King, I promise you that wherever the child is fostered, I shall make it my business to watch over him. He will be kept safely and reared as a king's son should be reared. Will that content you?'

'If it has to, yes.'

She drew a long breath then, and moved at last, rising from her chair and, still gracefully in spite of her bulk, pacing down the long room to one of the far windows. I made no move to follow her. She stood there for a while with her back to me, in silence. When at length she turned, she was smiling. She lifted a hand to beckon me and I went to her.

'Will you tell me one thing, Merlin?'

'If I can.'

'That night when we spoke in London, before you brought the King to me here. You talked of a crown, and a sword standing in an altar like a cross. I have wondered so much about it, thinking . . . Tell me now, truly. Was it my crown you saw? Or did you mean that this child–this boy who has cost so much–that he will be King?'

I should have said to her: 'Ygraine, I do not know. If my vision was true, if I was a true prophet, then he will be King. But the Sight has left me, and nothing speaks to me in the night or in the fire, and I am barren. I can only do as you do, and take the time on trust. But there is no going back. God will not waste all the deaths.'

But she was watching me with the eyes of a woman in pain, so I said to her: 'He will be King.'

She bent her head, and stood silent for a few moments, watching the sunlight on the floor, not as if thinking, but as if listening to what stirred within her. Then she looked up at me again.

'And the sword in the altar?'

I shook my head. 'Madam, I don't know. It has not come yet. If I am to know, I will be shown.'

She put out a hand. 'One more thing . . .' From something in her voice, I knew that this mattered most to her. Not knowing what was coming, I braced myself to lie. She said: 'If I must lose this child . . . Shall I have others, Merlin?'

'That is three things you have asked me, Ygraine.'

'You won't answer?'

I had spoken only to gain time, but at the flash of fear and doubt in her eyes I was glad to tell her the truth. 'I would answer you, Madam, but I do not know.'

'How is that?' she asked sharply.

I lifted my shoulders. 'That again I cannot answer. Further than this boy you carry, I have not seen. But it seems probable, since he is to be King, that you will have no other sons. Girls, maybe, to bring you comfort.'

'I shall pray for it,' she said simply, and led the way back to the embrasure. She gestured me to sit. 'Will you not take a cup of wine with me now, before you leave? I've received you poorly, I'm afraid, after asking such a journey of you, but I was in torment until I had talked with you. Won't you sit down with me now for a little while, and tell me what the news is with you?'

So I stayed a short while longer and, after I had given her my meagre news, I asked where Uther was bound with his troops. She told me that he was heading, not for his capital at Winchester as I had supposed, but northwards to Viroconium, where he had called a council of leaders and petty kings from the north and north-east. Viroconium is the old Roman town which lies on the border of Wales, with the mountains of Gwynedd between it and the threat of the Irish Shore. It was still at this time a market centre, and the roads were well maintained. Once out of the Dumnonian peninsula, Uther could make good speed north by the Glevum bridge. He might even, if the weather stayed fair and the country quiet, be back for the Queen's lying-in. For the moment, Ygraine told me, the Saxon Shore was quiet; after Uther's victory at Vindocladia the invaders had retired on the hospitality of the federated tribes. There was no clear news from the north, but the King (she told me) feared some kind of concerted action there in the spring between the Picts of Strathclyde and the invading Angles: the meeting of the kings at Viroconium had been called in an attempt to thrash out some kind of united plan of defence.

'And Duke Cador?' I asked her. 'Does he stay here in Cornwall, or go on to Vindocladia to watch the Saxon Shore?'

Her answer surprised me. 'He is going north with the King, to the council.'

'Is he indeed? Then I'd better guard myself.' At her quick look I nodded. 'Yes, I shall go straight to the King. Time grows short, and it's luck for me that he's travelling north. He's bound to take his troops by the Glevum bridge, so Ralf and I can cross by the ferry and get there before him. If I intercept him north of the Severn, there's nothing to show him that I ever left Wales.'

Soon after that I took my leave. When I left her she was standing by the window again. Her head was held high, and the breeze was ruffling her dark hair. I knew then that when the time came the child would not be taken from a weeping and regretful woman, but from a Queen, who was content to let him go to his destiny.

Not so with Marcia. She was waiting for me in the anteroom, bursting with questions, regrets, and anger against the King which she barely smothered into discretion. I reassured her as best I could, swore several times on every god in every shrine and hollow hill in Britain that I would do my utmost to get possession of the child and keep him safe, but when she started to ask me for spells for protection in childbed, and to talk of wet-nurses, I left her talking, and made for the door.

Forgetting herself in her agitation, she followed me and grabbed my sleeve. 'And did I tell you? The King says she must have his own physician, a man he can trust to put the right stories about afterwards, and say nothing about where the poor mite goes for fostering. As if it wasn't more important that my lady should be properly looked after! Give any doctor enough gold, and he'd swear his own mother's life away, everybody knows that.'

'Certainly,' I said gravely. 'But I know Gandar well, and there's no one better. The Queen will be in good hands.'

'But an army doctor! What can he know about childbirth?'

I laughed. 'He served with my father's army in Brittany for a long time. Where there are fighting men, there are also their women. My father had a standing army in Brittany of fifteen thousand men, encamped. Believe me, Gandar has had plenty of experience.'

With that she had to be content. She was talking again about wet-nurses when I left her.

She came to the inn that night, cloaked and hooded, and riding straight as a man. Maeve led her to the room her family shared, drove out everyone—including Caw—who was still awake, then took Ralf in to talk to his grandmother. I was in bed before she left.

Next morning Ralf and I set out for Bryn Myrddin, with a flask or two of sloe wine to cheer us on our way. To my surprise, Ralf seemed every bit as cheerful as he had been on the way south: I wondered if, after the brief spell back in the scene of his childhood, service with me had begun to look like freedom. He had heard all the news from his grandmother; he told it me as we rode; most of it was what I had learned already from the Queen, with some court gossip added which was entertaining but hardly informative, except for the talk which was inevitably going round about Uther's rejection of the child.

Ralf, to my secret amusement, seemed as anxious now as Marcia for me to get custody of the baby.

'If the King refuses, what will we do?'

'Go to Brittany to talk to King Budec.'

'Do you think he'll let you stay with the prince?'

'Budec is my kinsman too, remember.'

'Well, but would he risk offending King Uther? Would he keep it secret from him?'

'That I can't tell you,' I said. 'If it had been Hoel, now—Budec's son—that would be different. He and Uther always fought like dogs after the same bitch.'

I did not add that the description was in fact more accurate than was decent. Ralf merely nodded, chewing (we had stopped on a sunny hillside to eat), and reached for a flask. 'Have some of this?' He was offering me the sloe wine.

'God of green grapes, boy, no! It won't be ready to drink for a year. Wait till next harvest's ripe, and open it then.'

But he insisted, and unstoppered the flask. It certainly smelled odd and, he admitted, tasted worse. When I suggested, not unkindly, that Maeve had probably made a mistake and given him the medicine for the flux, he spat the mouthful out on the grass, then asked me a little stiffly what I was laughing at.

'Not at you. Here, let me taste the stuff . . . Well, there's nothing in it that there shouldn't be; but I must have been thinking of something else when they asked me about the mixing. No, I was laughing at myself. All these months–these years, even, hammering at heaven's door to get what? A baby and a wet-nurse. If you insist on staying with me, Ralf, the next few years will certainly bring new experiences for both of us.'

He merely nodded; he was busy pursuing present anxieties.

'If we have to go to Brittany, you mean we might have to stay disguised like this? For *years*?' He flicked with a contemptuous finger at the coarse stuff of his cloak.

'That will depend. Not quite like this, I hope. Hold step till you reach your bridges, Ralf.'

His face showed me that this was not how enchanters were expected to talk. They built their own bridges, or flew across without them. 'Depend on the King, you mean? Must you seek him out? My grandmother says, if it's put about that the baby's stillborn, it could be handed to you secretly, and the King never know.'

'You forget. Men must know if a prince is born. How else, when Uther dies, can they be brought to accept him?'

'Then what are you going to do, my lord?'

I shook my head, not answering. He took my silence for refusal to tell him, and accepted it, with no more questions. For my part, I had perforce to take my own advice about crossing bridges; I was waiting to see a way over. With the Queen won, the harder half of the game was played; now I must plan how best to deal with the King–whether to seek his consent openly, or go first to Budec. But as we sat finishing our meal I was not thinking overmuch about Brittany, or the King, or even the child; I was content to rest in the sun and let the time go over. What had just happened at Tintagel had happened without my contriving. Something was moving; there was a kind of breathing brightness in the air, the wind of God brushing by, invisible in sunlight. Even for men who cannot see or hear them, the gods are still there, and I was not less than a man. I had not the arrogance–or the hardihood–to test my power again, but I put on hope, as a naked man welcomes rags in a winter storm.

Chapter Eight

The weather held, so we went easily, taking care not to tread too closely on the heels of Uther's force; if we were caught west of the Uxella marshes–or indeed south of the Severn at all–it would be only too obvious where we had been. Uther usually moved fast, and there was nothing to delay him here in settled country, so we followed cautiously, waiting until his army should be clear of the southern end of the Severn ferry. If we were lucky with the ferry, and, once we were across the Severn, made good speed northwards, we should be able (having apparently just come innocently for the purpose from Maridunum) to fall in with the troops on their way up the Welsh border, and try to have speech with the King.

On the way south we had avoided the main road, but had used the pack tracks which run near the coast, winding in and out of the valleys. Now, since we dared not fall too far behind Uther, we kept as closely as we dared to the straight route along the ridges, but avoiding the paved road where the posting stations might be left guarded in the army's wake.

We were even more careful than we had been formerly. After we had left the shelter of Maeve's roof we sought out no more inns. Indeed, the ways we went boasted of no inns even had we looked for them; we lodged where we could—in wood-cutters' cabins, sheep shelters, even once or twice in the lee of a stack of bracken cut for bedding—and blessed the mild weather. It was wild country through which we went. There are high ridged stretches of moorland, where heather grows among the granite tors, and the land is good to feed nothing except the sheep and the wild deer; but just below the rocky spine of the land the forest begins. On the uplands the trees grow sparsely, raked by the wind, already in early autumn half scoured of leaves. But lower, in every dip and valley, the forest is dense, of trees crowded and hugely grown, impassable with undergrowth as toughly woven as a fisherman's net. Here and there, unnoticed until you stumble across them, are crags and bouldered screes of rock thickly clothed with thorn and creeper, invisible and deadly as a wolf trap. Even more dangerous are the stretches of bog, some black and slimy, some innocent and green as a meadow, where a man on horseback can sink from sight as easily and almost as quickly as a spoon sinking into a bowl of gruel. There are secret ways through these places, known to the beasts and the forest dwellers, but mostly men shun them. At night the soft ground flickers with marsh-lights and strange dancing flames which, men say, are the souls of the wandering dead.

Ralf had known the ways in his own country, but once we struck the low-lying marshy forests through which the Uxella and its tributaries flow towards the Severn we had to go more cautiously, relying on information from the people of the forest, charcoal-burners and woodmen, and once or twice a solitary hermit or holy man who offered us a night's shelter in some cave or woodland shrine. Ralf seemed to enjoy the rough travel and rougher lodging, and even the danger that seemed to lie about us in forest and track, and the threat of the army so few miles ahead. Both of us grew daily more unkempt and more like the roles we had assumed. It might be said that our disguise was more necessary here even than in Tintagel; woe betide the King's messenger or merchant who rides off the guarded road in these parts, but the poor are received kindly, vagrants or holy men with nothing to steal, and Ralf and I, as poor travelling healers, met welcome everywhere. There was nowhere we could not buy food and shelter with a copper penny and a pot of medicine. The marsh folk always need medicine, living as they do at the edge of the fetid bogland, with agues and swollen joints and the fear of fever. They build their huts right at the borders of the scummed pools, just clear of the deep black mud at the edge, or even set them on stilts right over the stagnant water. The huts crack and rot and fall to pieces every year, and have to be patched each spring, but in spring and autumn the flocks of travelling birds fly down to drink, in summer the waters are full of fish and the forest of game, and in winter the folk break the ice and lie in wait for the deer to come and drink. And always the place is loud with frogs; I have eaten these many times in Brittany, and it is true that they make a good meal. So the folk of the marshes cling to their stinking cabins, and eat well and drink the standing water, and die of the fever and the flux; nor do they fear the walking fires which haunt the marsh at night, for these are the souls of men they knew.

We were still twelve miles short of the ferry, and it was growing dusk, when the first hint of trouble came. The oak forests had given way to a lighter woodland of birch and alder, the trees crowding so closely to the sides of the track that we had to lie low on the horses' necks to avoid the whipping branches. Though there had been no rain the ground was very soft, and now and again our horses' hoofs splashed deep in the black mire. Soon, somewhere near us, I smelt the marsh, and before long through the thinning trees we could see the dull glimmer of the bog pools reflecting the last light from the sky. My horse stumbled, floundering, and Ralf, who was riding ahead of me, checked and put a quick hand to my rein. Then he pointed ahead.

Ahead of us, a different light pricked the dusk; the steady, dull yellow of candle or rushlight. The hut of a marsh dweller. We rode towards it.

The dwelling was not set over the water, but the ground was very wet, and was no doubt flooded in bad weather, for the hut was raised on piles, and approached by a narrow causeway of logs sawn short and jammed together across a ten-foot moat of mud.

A dog barked. I could see a man, a shadow against the dully lit interior of the hut, peering out at us. I hailed him. The marsh dwellers speak a tongue of their own, but they understand the Celtic of the Dumnonii.

'My name is Emrys. I'm a travelling doctor, and this is my servant. We're making for the ferry at Uxella. We came by the forest because the King's army is on the road. We're looking for shelter, and can pay for it.'

If there was one thing the poor folk of these parts understood, it was the need for a man to keep out of the way of troops on the march. In a few moments a bargain was struck, the dog was hauled back into the hut and tied up, and I was picking my way gingerly across the slippery logs, leaving Ralf to tend the horses and tether them on the driest piece of ground he could find.

Our host's name was Nidd; he was a short, agile-looking fellow with black hair and a black bristle of beard. His shoulders and arms looked immensely strong, but he limped badly from a leg which had been broken, then set by guesswork and left to knit crooked. His wife, who was probably little more than thirty, was white-haired and bent double on herself with rheumatism; she looked and moved like an old woman, and her face was drawn into tight lines round a toothless mouth. The hut was cramped and foul-smelling, and I would rather have slept in the open, but the evening had turned chilly, and neither Ralf nor I wished to spend a night out in the sodden forest. So when we had had our fill of black bread and broth we accepted the space of floor offered to us, and prepared to lie down wrapped in our cloaks, and take what rest we could. I had mixed a potion for the woman, and she was already asleep, huddled against the other wall under a pile of skins, but Nidd made no move to join her. He went instead to the doorway, peering again into the night, as if expecting someone. Ralf's eyes met mine, and his brows lifted;

his hand moved towards his dagger. I shook my head. I had heard the light, quick footsteps on the causeway. The dog made no sound, but his tail beat the floor. The curtain of rough-tanned deerhide was pushed aside from the doorway, and a boy came running in, his mouth one huge grin in a filthy face. He stopped short when he saw Ralf and me, but his father said something in patois and the boy, still eyeing us curiously, dumped the bundle of faggots he carried on the table and undid the thong that held it together. Then, with a swift wary look at me, he pulled from the middle of the faggots a dead fowl, a few strips of salted pork, a bundle which he shook out to reveal a pair of good leather trews, and a well-sharpened knife of the kind issued to the soldiers of the King's armies.

I approached the table, holding out my hand. The man stood watchful, but made no move, and after a moment the boy dropped the knife into my palm. I weighed it in my hand, considering. Then I laughed and dropped it point down, to the table. It stuck there beside the fowl, quivering.

'You've had good hunting tonight, haven't you? That's easier than waiting for the wild duck to fly in at dawn. So, the King's army lies nearby? How near?'

The boy merely stared, too shy to answer, but with the help of his father I got the information bit by bit.

It was not reassuring. The army had made camp barely five miles away. The boy had lurked in a tree at the forest's edge, watching his chance to steal food, and had overheard scraps of talk among the men who had gone in among the trees to relieve themselves. It seemed, if the boy had rightly understood what he had heard, that though the main body of the army would no doubt head on its way in the morning, a troop was to be detached and sent directly to Caerleon, with a message for the commander there. They would obviously go by the quickest way, the river crossing. They would certainly commandeer whatever boats were available.

I looked at Ralf. He was already fastening his cloak. I nodded, and turned to Nidd.

'We must go, I'm afraid. We must get to the ferry before the King's troops, and no doubt they'll ride at first light. We'll have to leave now. Can the boy guide us?'

The boy would do anything, it seemed, for the copper penny I gave him, and he knew all the ways through the marsh. We thanked our host, left the fee and medicines we had promised, and were soon on our way, with the boy—whose name was Ger—at my horse's head.

There were stars, and a quarter moon, but hazed over with fitful cloud. I could barely see the path, but the boy never hesitated. He seemed able to see even in the dark under the trees. The beasts trod softly enough on the forest floor, but the boy made no sound at all.

It was difficult to tell, what with the dark, the bad going, and the winding track, what kind of distance we were covering. It seemed a long time before the trees dwindled and thinned, and the way stretched clearer ahead of us. As the moon grew stronger, the clouds diffusing her pale light, I could see more clearly. We were still in the marsh; water gleamed on either hand, islanded with blackness. Underfoot mud pulled and sucked at the horses' hoofs. Rushes swished and rustled shoulder high. There was a noise of frogs everywhere, and now and again a splash as something took to the water. Once, with a clap and a call and a flash of white, a feeding bird shot off not a yard in front of my horse's hoofs, and, had it not been for the boy's hand on the reins, I must have been unseated and thrown into the water. After that my horse picked his way nervously, starting even at the faint sucking sounds from the pools where the marshlights flickered and bubbles popped under the wisps of vapour which hung and floated over the water. Here and there, sticking up black out of the bog, was the stripped skeleton of a tree.

It was strange, dead-looking landscape, and smelling of death. From Ralf's silence, I knew that he was afraid. But our guide, at my horse's head, plodded on through the wandering mists and the wisps of fire that were the souls of his fathers. The only sign he gave was when, at a fork in the track, we passed a hollow tree, a thick trunk twice the height of a man, with a gaping hole in the bark, and inside this a greenish glow that, with the help of the moonlight, faintly lit a crouching shape of eyes, mouth, and crudely carved breasts. The old goddess of the crossways, the Nameless One, who sits staring from her hollowed log like the owl who is her creature; and in front of her, decaying with the greenish glow that folk call enchanter's light, an offering of fish, laid in an oyster shell. I heard Ralf's breath go in, and his hand flickered in a defensive gesture. The boy Ger, without even looking aside, muttered the word under his breath, and held straight on.

Half an hour later, from the head of a rise of solid ground, we saw the wide, moonlit stretch of the estuary, and smelt salt on the clean and moving air.

Down by the shore where the ferry plied there was a red glimmer of light, the flame of the cresset on the wharf. The road to it, clear in the moonlight, crossed the ridge not far from us and ran straight downhill to the shore. We drew rein, but when I turned to thank the boy I found that he had already vanished, melting back into the darkness as silently as one of the wandering marsh-lights fading. We headed our weary horses down towards the distant glimmer.

When we reached the ferry we found that our luck had deserted us as swiftly and as decisively as our guide. The cresset burned on its post at the strip of shingle where the ferry beached, but the ferry was not there. Straining my ears, I thought I heard, above the ripple of water, the splashing of oars some way out on the estuary. I gave a hail, but got no reply.

'It looks as if he expects to come back to this side soon,' said Ralf, who had been exploring. 'There's a fire in the hut, and he's left the door open.'

'Then we'll wait inside,' I said. 'It's not likely the King's troops will set out before cock-crow. I can't imagine his message to Caerleon is as urgent as that, or he'd have sent a rider posting last night. See to the horses, then come in and get some rest.'

The ferryman's hut was empty, but the remains of a fire still glowed in the ring of stones that served for a hearth. There was a pile of dry kindling beside it, and before long a comforting tongue of flame licked up through the wood and set the turf glowing. Ralf was soon dozing in the warmth, while I sat watching the flames and listening for the return of the ferry.

But the sound that roused me was not the sound of a keel grating on

shingle; it was the soft and distant thudding of a troop of horse coming at the
canter.

Before my hand could reach Ralf's shoulder to shake him awake, he was
on his feet.

'Quick, my lord, if we ride fast along the shingle—the tide's not full yet—'

'No. They'd hear us, and in any case the horses are too tired. How far
away would you say they were?'

He was at the door in two strides, his head slanted, listening. 'Half a mile.
Less. They'll be here in a few minutes. What are you going to do? We can't
hide. They'll see the horses, and the country's open as a map in the sand.'

This was true. The road down which the horsemen were coming ran
straight up from the shore to the head of the ridge. To right and left of it lay
the marshlands, glinting with water, and white with mist. Behind us the
estuary stretched glimmering, throwing back the moonlight.

'What you can't run from, you must face,' I said. 'No, not like that'—as
the boy's hand went to his sword—'not against King's men, and we wouldn't
stand a chance anyway. There's a better way. Get the bags, will you?'

I was already stripping off my stained and ragged tunic. He threw me a
doubtful look, but ran to obey. 'You won't get away with that doctor
disguise again.'

'I don't intend to try. When fate forces your hand, Ralf, go with it. It
looks as if I may get to see the King sooner than I'd hoped to.'

'Here? But you—he—the Queen—'

'The Queen's secret will be safe. I've been thinking how to deal with this
if it happened. We'll let them think we've just come south from Maridunum, hoping to see the King.'

'But the ferryman? If they check with him?'

'It could be awkward, but we'll have to chance it. Why should they, after
all? Even if they do, I can deal with it. Men will believe anything of the
King's enchanter, Ralf, even that he could cross the estuary on a cloud, or
ford it knee high at floodtide.'

While we were talking he had unstrapped one of the saddlebags and
pulled out of it the decent dark robe and stitched doeskin boots I had worn
for my interview with the Queen, while I bent over the bucket of water by
the door and swilled the weariness of the journey and the stench of the
marshlander's hut off my face and hands. *When fate forces you*, I had said to
Ralf. I felt my blood running fast and light with the hope that this stroke—ill
luck we had thought it —might be the first cold, dangerous touch of the god's
hand.

When the troop rode up, halting with a clatter and slither of shingle in
front of the ferryman's hut, I was standing waiting for them in the open
doorway, with the firelight behind me, and the bright moonlight catching
the royal dragon at my shoulder.

Behind me in the shadows I heard Ralf mutter thankfully: 'Not
Cornwall's men. They won't know me.'

'But they'll know me.' I said. 'That's Ynyr's badge. They're Welshmen
from Guent.'

The officer was a tall man, with a thin hawk face and a white scar twisting
the corner of his mouth. I did not remember him, but he stared, saluted, and

said: 'By the Raven himself! How came you here, sir?'

'I must have words with the King. How far away is his camp?'

As I spoke, a kind of ripple of movement went among the troop, horses fidgeting and one suddenly rearing as if curbed too nervously. The officer snapped something over his shoulder, then turned back to me. I heard him swallow before he answered me.

'Some eight miles off, sir.'

There was something more here, I thought, than surprise at finding me in this deserted place, and the awe that I was accustomed to meeting among common men. I felt Ralf move up close behind me to my shoulder. A half glance showed me the sparkle in his eyes; show Ralf danger, and he came alive.

The officer said abruptly: 'Well, my lord, this has saved us something. We were on the way to Caerleon. We had the King's orders to find you and bring you to him.'

I caught the sharp intake of Ralf's breath. I thought fast, through a sudden quickening of the heart. This explained the soldiers' reaction; they thought the King's enchanter must have had magical foreknowledge of the King's will. On a plainer level, it settled the matter of the ferryman; if this troop was an escort for me, they would not now need to cross the ferry. Ralf could buy the man's silence when I had gone with the troops. I would not risk taking the boy back within reach of Uther's displeasure.

There was no harm in driving the point home. I said pleasantly: 'So I have saved you the trip to Bryn Myrddin. I'm glad. Where did the King plan to receive me? At Viroconium? I didn't think he meant to lie at Caerleon.'

'Nor does he,' said the man. I could hear the effort of control, but his voice was hoarse, and he cleared his throat. 'You—you knew the King was travelling north to Viroconium?'

'How not?' I asked him. From the edge of my eye I saw the nods and head-turning among the men, that also asked *How not?* 'But I had a mind to talk to him sooner than that. Did he charge you with a letter for me?'

'No, sir. Instructions to take you to him, that was all.' He leaned forward in the saddle. 'I think it was on account of the message he got last evening from Cornwall. Ill news, I think, though he told no one what it was. He seemed angry. Then he gave the order to fetch you.'

He waited, looking down at me as if I would be sure to know the contents of the message.

I was only too afraid that I did. Someone had recognised us, or made a guess, and sent to tell the King. The messenger could easily have passed us on the road. So; whatever was to happen between Uther and myself, I had to get Ralf out of danger first. And although I was not afraid for the Queen at Uther's hands, there were others, Maeve, Caw, Marcia, the child him-self . . . The skin on my nape stung and roused like a dog's that smells danger. I took a long, steadying breath and looked about me. 'You have a spare horse? My beast is weary, and must be led. My servant will rest here, and go back at first light with the ferry, to make ready for me at home. The King will no doubt see me escorted there when my business with him is done.'

The officer's voice, apologetic but definite, cut across Ralf's furious whisper of dissent. 'If it please you, sir, you will both come. Those were my orders. We have horses. Shall we ride?'

At the lift of his hand the men were already moving forward to close us round. There was nothing to be done. He had his orders, and I would risk more by arguing than by obeying. Besides, every minute's delay might bring the ferry back. I had heard nothing, but the fellow must have seen the soldiers' torches and might even now be heading back for custom.

A trooper came up with the spare horses, and took our own beasts in hand. We mounted. The officer barked an order, and the troop wheeled and fell in behind us.

We were barely two hundred paces from the shore when I heard, clear behind me, the sound of a boat's bottom grating on shingle. No one else paid any attention. The officer was busy telling me about the council to be held in the north, and behind me I could hear Ralf's voice, gay and amused, promising the troopers 'a skin of sloe wine, the best stuff you ever tasted. A recipe of my master's. It's what they give you with the rations now in Caerleon, so you'll see what you've missed. That's what comes of sending messages for a wizard, who knows everything that's happened before it's even happened at all . . .'

The King was abed when we arrived at the camp, and we were lodged—and guarded—in a tent not far from his. We said nothing to each other that could not be overheard. And, danger or no danger, it was the most comfortable lodging we had had since we left the inn at Camelford. Ralf was soon asleep, but I lay wakeful, watching the empty dark, listening to the little wind which had sprung up throwing handfuls of rain against the walls of the tent, and telling myself: 'It must happen. It must happen. The god sent me the vision. The child was given to me.' But the dark stayed empty, and the wind swept the tent walls and withdrew into silence, and nothing came.

I turned my head on its uneasy pillow, and saw dimly the shine of Ralf's eyes, watching me. But he turned over without speaking, and soon his breathing slackened again into sleep.

Chapter Nine

The King received me alone, soon after dawn.

He was armed and ready for the road, but bareheaded. His helmet with its gold circlet lay on a stool beside his chair, and his sword and shield stood propped against the box which held the travelling altar of Mithras that he always carried with him. The tent was hung with skins and worked curtains, but it was chilly, and draughts crept everywhere. Outside were the sounds of the army breaking camp. I could hear the snap and flutter of the Dragon standard by the entrance.

He greeted me briefly. His face still wore the bleak expression I remembered, empty of friendliness, but I could see neither anger nor enmity there. His look was cool and summing, his voice brisk.

'You and your Sight have saved me a little trouble, Merlin.'

I bent my head. If he asked no questions I need answer none. I came to the point. 'What do you want with me?'

'Last time we spoke together I was harsh with you. I have since thought that this was perhaps unworthy of a king to whom you had just done a service.'

'You were bitter at the Duke's death.'

'As to that, he fought against his King. Whatever the circumstances, he raised a sword to me, and he died. It's done, and it is past. We, you and I, are left with the future. This is what concerns me now.'

'The child,' I said, assenting.

The blue eyes narrowed. 'Who sent you the news? Or is this still the Sight?'

'Ralf brought the news. When he left your court, he came to me. He serves me now.'

He considered that for a moment, his brows drawing together, then smoothing as he found no harm in it. I watched him. He was a tall man, with reddish hair and beard, and a fair high-coloured skin that made him look younger than his years. It was just over a year, I thought, since my father had died and Uther had lifted the Pendragon standard. Kingship had steadied him; I could see discipline in his face as well as the lines drawn there by passion and temper, and kingship along with his victories clothed him like a cloak.

He moved a hand, dismissively, and I knew that Ralf need fear him no longer. 'I said the past was past, but there is one thing I must ask you. On that night in Tintagel when this child was begotten, I bade you keep away from me and trouble me no more. Do you remember?'

'I remember.'

'And you replied that you would not trouble me again, that I should not need your service again. Was this foresight, or only anger?'

I said quietly: 'When I spoke, I spoke the words that came to me. I thought they were foresight. All the words I spoke and the things I did throughout that night I took as if they came straight from the gods. Why do you ask? Have you sent for me now to command service of me?'

'To ask it, rather.'

'As a prophet?'

'No. As a kinsman.'

'Then I'll tell you, as a kinsman, that it was not prophecy that night, nor was it anger, sir, but only grief. I was grieving for my servant's death, and for the deaths of Gorlois and his companions. But now, as you say, the past is past. If I can serve you, you have only to command me.'

But, I thought, as I waited for him to speak, if it was no prophecy, then none of that night was God's and He never spoke to me. No, I had told the truth when I said that Uther would have no need of my service; it had not been Uther whom I served that night; it was not Uther I would serve now. I remembered the words of the other King, my father: '*You and I between us, Merlin, we will make such a king as the world has never known.*' It was the dead King, and the one still unborn, who commanded me.

If there had been any hesitation in my manner, Uther had not noticed it. He nodded, then set his elbow on his knee and his chin on his fist and thought for a while, frowning.

'There is one other thing I said that night. I told you that I would not acknowledge the child begotten then. I spoke in anger, but now I speak coldly, after taking thought and counsel, and I tell you, Merlin, that I'm still of the same mind.'

He seemed to expect an answer, but I was silent. He went on, half irritably: 'Don't misunderstand me, I don't doubt the Queen. I believe her when she tells me that she never lay with Gorlois after he brought her to London. The child is mine, yes, but he cannot be my heir, nor can he be reared in my house. If the child is a girl, then none of this matters, but if it is a boy it would be folly to rear him as heir to the High Kingdom, when men will only have to count on their fingers to say that Gorlois begot him of his wife, Ygraine, half a month before the High King married her.' He looked at me. 'You must know this as well as I do, Merlin. You have lived in kings' houses. There will always be those who doubt his birth, so there will always be those who would try to pull him off the throne in favour of men with a "better claim", and God knows there will always be claims in plenty. And the best claims will be those of my other sons. So, even brought up as my bastard at my court, the child is dangerous. He may try to come at the kingship by the deaths of my other children. By the Light, this is not unknown. I will not have my house a battleground. I must beget myself another son, an undoubted heir, conceived in wedlock to the satisfaction of all men, and reared at my side when the kingdom is settled and the Saxon wars are over. Do you accept this?'

'You are the King, Uther, and the child's father.'

It was hardly an answer, but he nodded as if I had agreed. 'There is more. This child is not only dangerous, he'll be a victim of danger. If men can say that he was not mine, that he must have been begotten by Gorlois on Ygraine his wife, then it follows that he is the true son of the Duke of Cornwall, with a claim on the younger son's portion of the lands which Cador holds, now that I've confirmed him as Duke in his father's place. You see? King's son or Duke's son, Cador is bound to be the child's enemy, and there are some who'd follow him quickly enough.'

'Is Cador loyal to you?'

'I trust him.' He gave a short laugh. 'So far. He's young, but hard-headed. He wants Cornwall, and he won't risk anything that could lose it—yet. But later, who knows? And when I am gone . . .' He let it hang. 'No, Cador is not my enemy, but there are others who are.'

'Who?'

'God knows, but what king was ever without them? Even Ambrosius . . . they're still saying he died of poison. I know you told me this was not true, but even so I have Ulfin taste my food. Ever since I took Octa and Eosa prisoner, they've been the storm centre for every disaffected leader who thinks he can see his way to a crown like Vortigern's—backed with Saxon forces, and paid for with British lives and lands. But what else can I do? Let them go, to raise the Federates against me? Or kill them, and give their sons in Germany a grievance to be wiped out in blood? No. Octa and his cousin are my hostages. Without them, Colgrim and Badulf would have been here long since, and the Saxon Shore would have burst its bounds and be lapping at Ambrosius' Wall. As it is, I'm buying time. You can't tell me anything, Merlin? Have you heard anything, or seen?'

He was not asking for prophecy; Uther looked askance and white-eyed at things of the Otherworld, like a dog that sees the wind. I shook my head.

'Of your enemies? Nothing, except that when Ralf came to me after leaving your court, he was set upon, and nearly killed. The men had no badge. They may have thought he was your messenger, or perhaps the Queen's. Troops from the barracks hunted the woods, but found no trace of them. More than that, I've heard nothing. But be sure that if I ever learn anything I will tell you.'

He gave a brief nod, then went on, slowly, choosing his words. His manner was abrupt, almost reluctant. For myself, my mind was spinning, and I had to fight to hold myself calm and steady. We were coming now on to the battleground, but it must be a very different battle from the one I had planned for. 'You and I,' he had said. He would hardly have sent for me unless I was to have some concern in the child's future.

He was going over the same ground that Ygraine and I had covered. '. . . so you see why, if the child is a boy, he cannot stay with me, yet if I send him away, he is beyond my power to protect. But protection he must have. Bastard or no, he is my child and the Queen's, and if we have no other sons he must one day be declared my heir to the High Kingdom.' He turned up a hand. 'You see where this leaves me. I must consign him to a guardian who will keep him in safety for the first few years of his life . . . at least until this torn kingdom is settled and safe, and in the hands of strong and loyal allies, and my own declared heirs.'

He waited again for my agreement. I nodded, then said, carefully neutral: 'Have you chosen this guardian?'

'Yes. Budec.'

So the Queen had been right, and the decision was made. But still he had sent for me. I held myself still, and said, so flatly that it sounded indifferent: 'It was the obvious choice.'

He shifted in his chair, and cleared his throat. I saw with some surprise that he was uneasy, nervous even. He even looked half pleased at my commendation of his choice. The knowledge steadied me. I realised that I had been so single-minded–so wrapped in what I had believed was my and the child's driving fate–that I had seen Uther falsely as the enemy. He was not so concerned: the plain fact was that Uther was a war-leader harassed perpetually by the strife in and around his borders, working desperately against time to patch a dam here, a sea-wall there, against the piling flood-water; and to him this affair of the child, though it might prove one day vitally important, was now little but a rub in the way of major issues, something he wanted out of the way and delegated. He had spoken without emotion, and indeed had set the thing out fairly enough. It was possible that he had sent for me, genuinely, to ask my advice, as his brother had been used to do. In which case . . . I wetted dry lips, and schooled myself to listen quietly, an adviser with a man beset by trouble.

He was speaking again, something about a letter. The message which had come yesterday. He pointed to the stool beside him where the parchment lay, crumpled as if he had thrown it down in anger. 'Did you know about this?'

I picked the letter up and smoothed it out. It was brief, a message from Brittany, that had been sent to the King at Tintagel and brought here after him. King Budec had fallen sick of a fever, it said, during the summer. He had seemed on the way to recovery, then, towards the end of August, he had quite suddenly died. The letter finished with protestations of formal friendship from the new king, Hoel, Uther's 'devoted cousin and ally . . .'

I looked up. Uther had sat back in his chair, shifting a fold of the scarlet mantle over his arm. Everything seemed quite still. Outside, the wind had dropped. The sounds of the camp came from far away, faintly. Uther's chin was sunk on his chest, and he was watching me with a mixture of worry and impatience.

I was noncommittal. 'This is heavy news. Budec was a good man and a good friend.'

'Heavy enough, even if it had not destroyed my plans. I was preparing to send messages even when this letter came. Now I can't see my way clear. Have they told you that I go to a council of kings at Viroconium?'

'Audagus told me.' Audagus was the officer who had escorted us from the ferry.

He threw out a hand. 'Then you see how much I want to turn aside to deal with this. But it must be dealt with now. This is why I sent for you.'

I flicked the seal with a forefinger. 'You won't send the child to Hoel, then? He swears himself your devoted cousin and ally.'

'He may be my devoted cousin and ally, but he's also a—' Uther used a phrase that became a soldier rather than a king in council. 'I never liked him, nor he me. Oh, Mithras knows he would never mean harm to a son of mine, but he's not the man his father was, and he might not be able to protect the boy from his ill-wishers. No, I'll not send him to Hoel. But what other court can I send him to? Reckon it for yourself.' He told over a few names, all powerful men, all of them kings whose lands lay in the southern part of the country, behind the Wall of Ambrosius. 'Well? Do you see my problem? If he goes to one of the nobles or petty kings in safe country he could still be in danger from an ambitious man; or worse, become a tool of treachery and rebellion.'

'So?'

'So I come to you. You are the only man who can steer me between these clashing rocks. On the one hand, the child must be sworn and acknowledged my own, in case there is no other heir. On the other, he must be taken away out of danger for himself and the kingdom, and brought up in ignorance of his birth until the time comes when I send for him.' He turned over a hand on his knee and asked me as simply as he had asked me once before: 'Can you help me?'

I answered him as simply. The bewilderment, the confused whirl of thought, settled suddenly into a pattern, like coloured leaves blown down into a tapestry on the grass when the spinning wind drops still. 'Of course. You need wreck no part of your kingdom on either of these rocks. Listen, and I will tell you how. You told me you had "taken counsel". Other men, then, know of your plans to send the boy to Budec?'

'Yes.'

'Have you spoken to anyone of this letter, and your doubts of Hoel?'

'No.'

'Good. You will give it out that your plan stays as formerly, and that the boy will go to Hoel's court at Kerrec. You will write to Hoel requesting this. Have someone make all arrangements to send the boy with his nurse and attendants as soon as the weather allows. See that it is given out that I will accompany him there myself.'

He was frowning, intent, and I could see protest in his face, but he made none. He said merely: 'And?'

'Next,' I said, 'I must be at Tintagel for the birth. Who is her physician?'

'Gandar.' He seemed about to say something more, then changed his mind and waited.

'Good. I'm not suggesting I should attend her.' I smiled. 'In view of what I shall suggest, that might lead to some rather dangerous rumours. Now, will you be there yourself for the lying-in?'

'I shall try, but it's doubtful.'

'Then I shall be there to attest the child's birth, as well as Gandar and the Queen's women, and whoever you can appoint. If it is a boy, the news will be sent to you by beacon, and you will declare him your son by the Queen, and, in default of a son begotten in wedlock, your heir until another prince shall be born.'

He took some time over that, frowning, and obviously reluctant to commit himself. But it was only the conclusion of what he had himself said to me. Finally he nodded, and spoke a little heavily: 'Very well. It is true. Bastard or not, he is my heir until I get another. Go on.'

'Meantime the Queen will keep her chamber, and once he has been seen and sworn to, the child will be taken back to the Queen's apartments and kept there, seen only by Gandar and the women. Gandar can arrange this. I myself will leave openly, by the main gate and the bridge. Then after dark I shall go down secretly to the postern gate on the cliff, to receive the child.'

'And take him where?'

'To Brittany. No, wait. Not to Hoel, nor by the ship which everyone will be watching. Leave that part of it to me. I shall take him to someone I know in Brittany, on the edge of Hoel's kingdom. He will be safe, and well cared for. You have my word for it, Uther.'

He brushed that aside as if there had been no need for me to say it. He was already looking lighter, glad to be relieved of a care that must, among the weighty cares of the kingdom, seem trivial, and—with the child still only a weight in a woman's womb—unreal. 'I'll have to know where you take him.'

'To my own nurse, who reared me and the other royal children, bastard and true alike, in the nurseries at Maridunum. Her name is Moravik, and she's a Breton. After the sack by Vortigern she went home to her people. She has married, since. While the child is sucking, I can think of no better place. He won't be looked for in such a humble home. He will be guarded, but better than that, he will be hidden and unknown.'

'And Hoel?'

'He will know. He must. Leave Hoel to me.'

Outside a trumpet sounded. The sun was growing stronger, and the tent was warm. He stirred, and flexed his shoulders, as a man does when he lays off his armour. 'And when men find that the child is not on the royal ship, but has vanished? What do we tell them?'

'That for fear of the Saxons in the Narrow Sea the prince was sent, not by the royal ship, but privily, with Merlin, to Brittany.'

'And when it is found he is not at Hoel's court?'

'Gandar and Marcia will swear to it that I took the child safely. What will be said I can't tell you, but there's no one who will doubt me, or that the child is safe as long as he's under my protection. And what my protection means you know. I imagine that men will talk of enchantments and vanishings, and wait for the child to reappear when my spells are lifted.'

He said prosaically: 'They're more likely to say the ship foundered and the child is dead.'

'I shall be there to deny it.'

'You mean you won't stay with the boy?'

'I must not, not yet. I'm known.'

'Then who will be with him? You said he would be guarded.'

For the first time I hesitated fractionally. Then I met his eyes. 'Ralf.'

He looked startled, then angry, then I saw him thinking back past his anger. He said slowly: 'Yes. I was wrong there, too. He will be true.'

'There is no one truer.'

'Very well, I am content. Make what arrangements you please. It's in your hands. You of all men in Britain will know how to protect him.' His hands came down on to the arms of his chair. 'So, that is settled. Before we march today I shall send a message to the Queen telling her what I have decided.'

I thought it wise to ask: 'Will she accept it? It's no easy thing for a woman to bear, even a queen.'

'She knows my decision, and she will do as I say. There's one thing, though, where she'll have her way; she wants the child baptised a Christian.'

I glanced at the Mithras altar against the tent wall. 'And you?'

'He lifted his shoulders. 'What does it matter? He will never be King. And if he were, then he would pay service where he had to, in the sight of the people.' A hard, straight look. 'As my brother did.'

If it was a challenge, I declined it, saying merely: 'And the name?'

'Arthur.'

The name was strange to me, but it came like an echo of something I had heard long before. Perhaps there had been Roman blood in Ygraine's family . . . The Artorii; that would be it. But that was not where I had heard the name . . .

'I'll see to it,' I said. 'And now, with your permission, I'll send the Queen a letter, too. She'll lie the easier for being assured of my loyalty.'

He nodded, then stood up and reached for his helmet. He was smiling, a cold ghost of the old malicious smile with which he had baited me when I was a child. 'It's strange, isn't it, Merlin the bastard, that I should talk so easily of trusting the body of my own ill-begotten son to the one man in the kingdom whose claim to the throne is better than his? Are you not flattered?'

'Not in the least. You'd be a fool if you didn't know by now that I have no ambitions towards your crown.'

'Then don't teach my bastard any, will you?' He turned his head, shouting for a servant, then back to me. 'And none of your damned magic, either.'

'If he's your son,' I said drily, 'he won't take very kindly to magic. I shall teach him nothing except what he has the need and the right to know. You have my word on it.'

On that we parted. Uther would never like me, nor I him, but there was a kind of cold mutual respect between us, born of our shared blood and the different love and service we had given to Ambrosius. I should have known that he and I were linked in this as closely as the two sides of the same counter, and that we would move together whether we willed it or not. The gods sit over the board, but it is men who move under their hands for the mating and the kill.

I should have known; but I had been so used to God's voice in the fire and stars that I had forgotten to listen for it in the counsels of men.

Ralf was waiting, alone in the guarded tent. When I told him the result of my talk with the King, he was silent a long time. Then he said: 'So it will all happen, just as you said it would. Did you expect it to come like this? When they brought us here last night, I thought you were afraid.'

'I was, but not in the way you mean.'

I expected him to ask how, but, oddly, he seemed to understand. His cheek flushed and he busied himself over some detail of packing. 'My lord, I have to tell you . . .' His voice was stifled. 'I have been very wrong about you. At first I—because you are not a man of war, I thought—'

'You thought I was a coward? I know.'

He looked up sharply. 'You knew? You didn't mind?' This, obviously, was almost as bad as cowardice.

I smiled. 'When I was a child among budding warriors, I grew used to it. Besides, I have never been sure myself how much courage I have.'

He stared at that, then burst out: 'But you are afraid of nothing! All the things that have happened—this journey—you'd have thought we were riding out on a summer morning, instead of going by paths filled with wild beasts and outlaws. And when the King's men took us—even if he is your uncle, that's not to say you'd never be in danger from him. Everyone knows the King's unchancy to cross. But you just looked cold as ice, as if you expected him to do what you wanted, just as everyone does! You, afraid? You're not afraid of anything that's real.'

'That's what I mean,' I said. 'I'm not sure how much courage is needed to face human enemies—what you'd call "real"—knowing they won't kill you. But foreknowledge has its own terrors, Ralf. Death may not lie just at the next corner, but when one knows exactly when it will come, and how . . . It's not a comfortable thought.'

'You mean you do know?'

'Yes. At least, I think it's my death that I see. At any rate it is darkness, and a shut tomb.'

He shivered. 'Yes, I see. I'd rather fight in daylight, even thinking I might die perhaps tomorrow. At least it's always "perhaps tomorrow", never "now". Will you wear the doeskin boots for riding, my lord, or change them now?'

'Change them. Thank you.' I sat down on a stool, and stretched out a foot for him. He knelt to pull off my boots. 'Ralf, there is something else I must tell you. I told the King you were with me, and that you would go to Brittany to guard the child.'

He looked up at that, struck still. 'You told him *that*? What did he say?'

'That you were a true man. He agreed, and approved you.'

He sat back on his heels, my boots in his hands, gaping at me.

'He has had time to think, Ralf, as a king should think. He has also had time—as kings do—to still his conscience. He sees Gorlois now as a rebel, and the past as done with. If you wish to go back into his service he will receive you kindly, and give you a place among his fighting men.'

He did not answer, but stooped forward again and busied himself fastening my boots. Then he got to his feet and pulled back the flap of the tent, calling to a man to bring up the horses. 'And hurry. My lord and I ride now for the ferry.'

'You see?' I said. 'Your own decision this time, freely given. And yet who can say it is not as much a part of the pattern as the "chance" of Budec's death?' I got to my feet, stretching, and laughed. 'By all the living gods, I'm glad that things are moving now. And gladder for the moment of one thing more than any other.'

'That you're to get the child so easily?'

'Oh, that, of course. No, I really meant that now at last I can shave off this damnable beard.'

Chapter Ten

By the time Ralf and I reached Maridunum my plans, so far as could be at this stage, were made. I sent him by the next ship to Brittany, with letters of condolence to Hoel, and with messages to supplement the King's. One letter, which Ralf carried openly, merely repeated the King's request that Hoel should give shelter to the baby during his infancy; the other, which Ralf was to deliver secretly, assured Hoel that he would not be burdened with the charge of the child, nor would we come by the royal ship or at the time ostensibly fixed, I begged his assistance for Ralf in all the arrangements for the secret journey at Christmas that I planned. Hoel, easy-going and lazy by nature, and less than fond of his cousin Uther, would be so relieved, I knew, that he would help Ralf and myself in every way known to him.

With Ralf gone, I myself set out for the north. It was obvious that I would not be able to leave the baby too long in Brittany; the refuge with Moravik would serve for a while, till men's interest died down, but after that it might be dangerous. Brittany was the place (as I had said to the Queen) where Uther's enemies would look for the child; the fact that the child was not—had never been—at his publicly declared refuge at Hoel's court might make them believe that the talk of Brittany had been nothing but a false trail. I would make certain that no real trail would lead them to Moravik's obscure village. But this was only safe as long as the boy was an infant. As soon as he grew and began to go about, some query or rumour might start. I knew how easily this could happen, and for the child of a poor house to be so cared for and guarded as must happen here, it would be very easy for some question to start a rumour, and a rumour to grow too quickly into a guess at the truth.

More than this, once the child was weaned from women and the nursery, he would have to be trained, if not as a young prince, then as a young noble and a warrior. It was obvious that Bryn Myrddin, on no count, could be his home: he must have the comfort and safety of a noble house around him. In the end I had thought of a man who had been a friend of my father's, and whom I had known well. His name was Ector, styled Count of Galava, one of the nobles who fought under King Coel of Rheged, Uther's most considerable ally in the north.

Rheged is a big kingdom, stretching from the mountainous spine of Britain right to the western coast, and from the Wall of Hadrian in the north clear down to the plain of Deva. Galava, which Ector held under Coel, lies about thirty miles in from the sea, in the north-west corner of the kingdom. Here there is a wild and mountainous tract of country, all hills and water and wild forest; in fact, one of the names it goes by is the Wild Forest. Ector's castle lies on the flat land at the end of one of the long lakes that fill these valleys. There was in past time a Roman fortress there, one of a chain on the military road running from Glannaventa on the coast to join the main way from Luguvallium to York. Between Galava and the port of Glannaventa lie steep hills and wild passes, easily defended, and inland is the well-guarded country of Rheged itself.

When Uther had talked of fostering the child in some safe castle he had thought only of the rich, long-settled lands inside Ambrosius' Wall, but even without his fears of the nobles' loyalty, I would have counted that country dangerous; these were the very lands that the Saxons, immured along the Shore, coveted most dearly. It was these lands which, I guessed, they would fight for first and most bitterly. In the north, in the heart of Rheged, where no one would look for him and where the Wild Forest itself would guard him, the boy could grow up as safely as God would allow, and as freely as a deer.

Ector had married a few years back. His wife was called Drusilla, of a Romano-British family from York. Her father, Faustus, had been one of the city magistrates who had defended the city against Hengist's son Octa, and had been one of those urgent to advise the Saxon leader to yield himself to Ambrosius. Ector himself was fighting at the time in my father's army. It was in York that he had met Drusilla, and had married her. They were both Christians, and this was possibly why their paths and Uther's had not often crossed. But I, along with my father, had been to Faustus' house in York, and Ambrosius had there taken part in many long discussions about the settlement of the northern provinces.

The castle at Galava was well protected, being built on the site of the old Roman fort, with the lake before it, and a deep river on the one hand, and the wild mountains near. It could be approached only from the open water, or by one of the easily watched and defended valley passes. But it did not have the air of a fortress. Trees grew near it, now rich with autumn, and there were boats out and men fishing where the river flowed deep and still through its sedgy flatlands. The green meadows at the water's head were full of cattle, and there was a village crowded under the castle walls as there had been in the Roman Peace. Two full miles beyond the castle walls lay a monastery, and so secluded were the valleys that right up on the heights above the tree-line where the land stretched bare of all but short grass and stones, one saw the strange little blue-fleeced sheep that breed in Rheged, with some shepherd boy cheerfully braving the wolves and fierce hill foxes with the protection of a stick and a single dog.

I travelled alone, and quietly. Though the hated beard had gone, and with it the heavy disguise, I managed the journey unnoticed and unrecognised, and came to Galava towards late afternoon on a bright, crisp October day.

The great gates were wide open, giving on a paved yard where men and boys were unloading a wagon of straw. The oxen stood patiently, chewing their cud; near them a lad was watering a pair of sweating horses. Dogs barked and skirmished, and hens pecked busily among the fallen straw. There were trees in the yard, and to either side of the steps up to the main door someone had planted beds of marigolds, which blazed orange and yellow in the late sunshine. It looked like a prosperous farm rather than a fortress, but through an open door I could see the rows of freshly burnished weapons, and from behind one of the high walls came shouted orders and the clash of men drilling.

I had barely paused between the posts of the archway when the porter was barring my way and asking my business. I handed him my Dragon brooch, wrapped in a small pouch, and bade him take it to his master. He came hurrying back to the gate within minutes, and the chamberlain, puffing in his wake, showed me straight to Count Ector.

Ector was not much changed. He was a man of medium height, growing now into middle age; if my father had lived they would have been of an age now, I reckoned, which made him something over forty. He had a brown beard going grey, and brown skin with the blood springing healthily beneath it. His wife was more than ten years younger; she was tall, a statuesque woman still in her twenties, reserved and a little shy, but with smoky-blue eyes that belied her cool manner and distant speech. Ector had the air of a contented man.

He received me alone, in a small chamber where spears and bows stood stacked against the walls, and the hearth was four deep in deer-hounds. The fire was heaped as high as a funeral pyre with pine logs blazing, and small wonder, for the narrow windows were unglazed and open to the brisk October air, and the wind whined like another hound in the bowstrings that were stacked there.

He gripped my arms with a bearlike welcome, beaming. 'Merlinus Ambrosius! Here's a pleasure indeed! What is it, two years? Three? There's been water under the bridge, aye, and stars fallen, since we last met, eh? Well, you're welcome, welcome. I can't think of any man I'd rather see under my roof! You've been making a name for yourself, haven't you? The tales I've heard tell . . . Well, well, but you can tell me the truth of it yourself. God's sweet death, boy, you get more like him by the day! Thinner, though, thinner. You look as if you've seen no red meat for a year. Come, sit down by the fire now, and let me send for supper before we talk.'

The supper was enormous and excellent, and would have served me ten times over. Ector ate enough for three, and pressed me to finish the rest. While we ate we exchanged news. He had heard of the Queen's pregnancy, and spoke of it, but for the moment I let it go, and asked him instead what had happened at Viroconium. Ector had attended the King's council there, and was but newly returned home.

'Success?' he asked, in reply to my question. 'It's hard to say. It was well attended. Coel of Rheged, of course, and all from these lands'–he named half a dozen neighbours–'except Riocatus of Verterae, who sent to say he was sick.'

'I gather you didn't believe it?'

'When I believe anything that jackal says,' said Ector forcibly, 'I'm a spit-licker too. But the wolves were there, all of them, so the scavengers hardly matter.'

'Strathclyde?'

'Oh, aye, Caw was there. You know the Picts in the western half of his land have been giving trouble–when haven't they given trouble, come to that? But for all Caw's Pictish himself, he'll co-operate with any plan that'll help him keep control of that wild territory of his, so he was well disposed to the idea of the council. He'll help, I'm sure of it. Whether he can control that pack of sons he's sired is another matter. Did you know that one of them, Heuil, a wild young blackguard scarcely old enough (you'd have thought) to lift a spear, took one of Morien's girls by force last spring when she was on her way to the monastery her father had promised her to since birth? He lifted his spear to *her* easily enough; by the time her father got the news she was over the border with him, and in no condition for any monastery, however broad-minded.' He chuckled. 'Morien cried rape, of course, but everyone was laughing, so he made the best of it. Strathclyde had to pay, naturally, and he and Morien sat on opposite benches at Viroconium, and Heuil wasn't there at all. Ah, well, but they agreed to sink their differences. King Uther managed it well enough, so what between Rheged and Strathclyde, there's half the northern frontier solid for the King.'

'And the other half?' I asked. 'What about Lot?'

'Lot?' Ector snorted. 'That braggart! He'd swear allegiance to the Devil and Hecate combined if it would give him a few more acres for himself. He cares no more for Britain than that hound by the hearthstone. Less. He and his wild brood of brothers sitting on that cold rock of theirs. They'll fight when it pays them, and that's all.' He fell silent, scowling at the fire, poking with a foot at the hound nearest to him; it yawned with pleasure, and flattened its ears. 'But he talks well, and maybe I'm black-guarding him. Times are changing, and even barbarians like Lot ought to be able to see that unless we band together with a strong oath, and keep it, it'll be the Flood Year all over again.'

He was not referring to an actual flood, but to the year of the great invasion a century ago, when the Picts and Saxons, joined with the Scots from Ireland, poured across Hadrian's Wall with axe and fire. Maximus commanded then, in Segontium. He drove them back and broke them, and won for Britain a time of peace; and for himself an empire and a legend.

I said: 'Lothian is a key to the defence that Uther's planning, even more than Rheged or Strathclyde. I'd heard tell—I don't know if it's true—that there are Angles settled on the Alaunus, and that the strength of the Anglian Federates south of York along the Abus has doubled since my father's death?'

'It's true.' He spoke heavily. 'And south of Lothian there's only Urien on the coast, and he's another carrion crow, picking at Lot's leavings. Nay, that may be another one I'm doing an injustice to. He's married to Lot's sister, when all's done, so he'd be bound to cry the same way. Talking of which—'

'Talking of what?' I asked, as he paused.

'Marriage.' He scowled, then he began to grin. 'If it wasn't so plaguy dangerous, it would be funny. You knew Uther had a bastard girl, I forget her name, she must be seven or eight years old?'

'Morgause. Yes, I remember her. She was born in Brittany.'

Morgause was a sideslip of Uther's by a girl in Brittany who had followed him to Britain hoping, I suppose, for marriage, since she was of good family, and the only woman, so far as anyone knew then for certain, who had borne him a child. (It had always been a matter of amazement, and a good deal of private and public conjecture among Uther's troops, how he managed to avoid leaving a train of bastards in his wake like seedlings following the sower down a furrow. But this girl was, to public knowledge, the only one. And I believe to Uther's knowledge too. He was a fair man and a generous one, and no girl had suffered any loss worse than maidenhead through him.) He acknowledged the child, kept both child and mother at one of his houses, and after the mother's marriage to a lord of his household, had taken the girl into his own. I had seen her once or twice in Brittany, a thin pale-haired girl with big eyes and a mouth folded small.

'What about Morgause?' I asked.

'Uther was casting out feelers for marrying her to Lot, come the time she'll be ready for bedding.'

I cocked an eyebrow at him. 'And what did Lot think about that?'

'Eh, you'd have laughed to watch him. Black as a wolverine at the suggestion that Uther's byblow was good enough, but careful to keep his talk sweet in case there's no other daughter born in the right bed now the King's wedded. Bastards—and their mates—have inherited kingdoms before now. Saving your presence, of course.'

'Of course. Lot casts his eyes as high as that, then?'

He gave a short nod. 'High as the High Kingdom itself, you can take my word for it.'

I digested that, frowning. I had never met Lot; he was at this time

scarcely older than myself—somewhere in his early twenties—and though he
had fought under my father, his path and mine had not crossed. 'So Uther
wants to tie Lothian to him, and Lot wants to be tied? Whether it's for his
own ambition or not, it means surely that Lot will fight for the High King
when the time comes? And Lothian is our main bulwark against the Angles
and the other invaders from the north.'

'Oh, aye, he'll fight,' said Ector. 'Unless the Angles offer him a better
bribe than Uther does.'

'Do you mean that?' I was alarmed. Ector, for all his bluff ways, was a
shrewd observer, and few men knew more about the changing shifts of
power along our shores.

'Maybe I was putting it a trifle high. But for my money Lot's unscrupled
and ambitious, and that's a combination that spells danger to any overlord
who can't placate him.'

'How is he with Rheged?' I was thinking of the child to be lodged here
perhaps at Galava, with Lot east by north across the Pennines.

'Oh, friends, friends. As good friends as two big hounds each with his
own full platter of meat. No, it's not yet a matter for concern, and may never
be. So forget it, and drink up.' He drank deeply himself, then set down his
cup and wiped his mouth. Then he fixed me with a sharp and curious eye.
'Well? You'd better get to it, boy. You didn't come all this way for a good
supper and a prattle with an old farmer. Tell me how I can serve
Ambrosius' son?'

'It is Ambrosius' nephew you will be serving,' I said, and then told him
the rest. He heard me out in silence. For all his warmth and heartiness, there
was nothing impulsive or over-quick about Ector. He had been a cold-
brained and calculating officer; a valuable man in any circumstance, from a
pitched fight to a long and careful siege. After a sharp glance of surprise and
a lift of the brows when I spoke of the King's decision and my guardianship
of the child, he listened without moving and without taking his eyes off me.

When I had finished, he stirred. 'Well . . . I'll say one thing to start with,
Merlin; I'm glad and proud you should have come to me. You know how I
felt about your father. And to tell you the truth, boy'—He cleared his throat,
hesitated, then looked away into the fire as he spoke—'it always sorrowed my
heart that you yourself were a bastard. And that's between these four walls,
I don't have to tell you. Not that Uther's made a bad shot at being High
King—'

'A far better shot than I'd ever have made,' I said, smiling. 'My father
used to say that Uther and I, between us, shared out some of the qualities of
a good king. It was a dear dream of his that some day, between us, we might
fashion one. And this is the one.' Then, as his head went up, 'Oh, I know, a
baby not yet born. But all the first part has happened as I knew it must
happen; a child begotten by Uther and given to me to raise. I know this is
the one. I believe he will be such a king as this poor country has never had
before, and may never see again.'

'Your stars tell you this?'

'It has been written there, certainly, and who writes among the stars but
God?'

'Well, God grant it is so. There's coming a time, Merlin, maybe not next year, or for five years, or even for ten, but it is coming—when Flood Year will come again, and pray God that this time there's a king here to raise the sword of Maximus against it.' He turned his head sharply. 'What's that? That sound?'

'Only the wind in the bowstrings.'

'I thought it was a harp sounding. Strange. What is it, boy? Why do you look so?'

'Nothing.'

He looked at me doubtfully for a moment longer, then grunted and fell silent, and behind us the long humming stretched out, a cold music, something from the air itself. I remembered how, as a child, I had lain watching the stars and listening for the music which (I had been told) they made as they moved. This must, I thought, be how it sounded.

A servant came in then with logs to replenish the fire, and the sound died. When he had gone, and the door had shut behind him, Ector spoke again in quite a different tone. 'Well, I'll do it, of course, and proud to. You're right; in the next few years I can't see that Uther will have much time for him, and for that matter he'd be hard put to it to keep the child safe. Tintagel might have done, but as you say, there's Cador there . . . Does the King know that you've come to me?'

'No. Nor will I tell him, yet.'

'Indeed?' He thought it over for a moment, frowning a little. 'Do you think he'll be content with that?'

'Possibly. I don't know. He didn't press me too hard about Brittany. I think that just now he wants as little to do with it as need be. The other thing is'—I smiled a little wryly—'the King and I have a truce declared, but I wouldn't bank on its staying that way; and out of sight, out of mind. If I'm to have anything to do with the child's teaching, then it had better be at a fair distance from the High King.'

'Aye, I've heard that, too. It's never a wise thing to help kings to their heart's desire. Will the boy be a Christian?'

'The Queen wants it, so he'll be baptised in Brittany if I can arrange it. He's to be called Arthur.'

'You'll stand for him?'

I laughed. 'I believe the fact that I was never baptised myself puts me out of the running.'

His teeth showed. 'I forgot you were a pagan. Well, I'm glad to hear about the boy. There'd have been a peck of trouble else.'

'Your wife, you mean? She's so devout?'

'Poor lass,' he said, 'she's had nothing else since our second died. There'll be no more, they say. In fact it will be God's mercy if we take this boy into our house; my son Cei's a headstrong little ruffian for all he's only three, and the women spoil him. It will be good to have a second child. What did you say his name was to be? Arthur? You'll leave this with me to talk over with Drusilla? Though there's no question, she'll be as glad as I am to have him. And I can tell you that she's close-mouthed enough, for all she's a woman. He'll be safe with us.'

'I was sure of it. It doesn't need the stars to tell me that.' But when I began to thank him, he cut me short.

'Well, then, that's settled. We can talk over the details later. I'll speak with Drusilla tonight. You'll stay a while, of course?'

'Thank you, but I can't—no longer than it takes to rest myself and my horse. I have to be at Tintagel again in December, and before that I must be home when Ralf gets back from Brittany. There's a lot to be arranged.'

'A pity. But you'll be back. I'll look forward to it.' He grinned, stirring the hounds again. 'I'll enjoy seeing you installed as tutor to the household, or whatever you think will give you some claim on the boy. And I own I should like to see Cei licked into shape. Maybe he'll mind his manners with you, if he thinks he can be turned into a toad for disobeying you.'

'Bats are my speciality,' I said, smiling. 'You are very good, and I'll never be out of your debt. But I'll find a place of my own.'

'Look, boy, Ambrosius' son doesn't wander the countryside looking for a home while I have four walls and a fireplace to offer him. Why not here?'

'Because I might be recognised, and where Merlin is for the next few years, men will look for Arthur near him. No, I must stay unknown. A household as big as this is too risky, and, with all my thanks to you, four walls are not always the best shelter for such as me.'

'Ah, yes. A cave, isn't it? Well, there are a few hereabouts, they tell me, if you can turn the wolves out first. Well, you know your own business. But tell me, what of the Queen? You didn't say where she stood in this? What woman would let her first child be taken from the bed where she bore him, and never try to see him again or make herself known to him?'

'The Queen herself sent for me secretly, and asked me to take him. She has suffered, I know, but it's the King's will, and she knows that it's more than a whim born of anger; she sees the dangers as well as he. And she is a queen before she is a woman.' I added, carefully: 'I think that the Queen is not a woman for a family, any more than Uther is a family man. They are man and woman for each other, and outside their bed they are King and Queen. It may be that in the future Ygraine will wonder, and ask questions; but that is with the future. For the moment she is content to let him go.'

After this we talked on, late into the night, arranging as far as we could the details of the time ahead. Arthur would be left in Brittany until he was three or four years old, then at a safe time of the year Ralf would bring him across from Brittany to Ector's home.

'And you?' asked Ector. 'Where will you be?'

'Not in Brittany, for the same reason that I can't live here. I shall vanish, Ector. It's a talent that magicians have. And when I do appear again, it will be somewhere that draws men's eyes away from Brittany and Galava.' When he questioned me further, I laughed, and refused to enlighten him.

'Truth to tell, my plans are not yet fixed. Now, I've kept you out of your bed for long enough. Your wife will be wondering what sort of mystery man you have been closeted with all these hours. I'll make my apologies when I present me in the morning.'

'And I'll make my own now,' he said, getting to his feet. 'But that's one apology I enjoy making. You miss a lot, you know, Merlin—but then you can't know.'

'I know,' I said.

'You do? Then you must think it's worth it, life without women?'

'For me, yes.'

'Well, then, come this way to your cold bed,' he said, and held the door for me.

Chapter Eleven

The boy was born on the eve of Christmas, an hour before midnight.

Just before the birth I and the two nobles appointed as witnesses were called into the Queen's chamber, where Gandar attended with Marcia and other women of the Queen's household. One of these was a girl called Branwen who had lately been brought to bed of a dead child; she was to be the child's wet-nurse. When all was done, the baby washed and swaddled, and the Queen sleeping, I took my leave and rode out of the castle and along the track towards Dimilioc. As soon as the lights of the gate-house were out of view I turned my horse aside down the steep path into the valley which runs from the high fields above the headland down to the shore.

The castle at Tintagel is built on a promontory of rock, or near-island, a crag jutting up out of the fearsome seas, which is joined to the cliffs of the mainland only by a narrow causeway. To either side of this causeway the cliffs drop away sheer to small bays of rock and shingle tucked in under the cliff. From one of these a path, narrow and precarious, and passable only on a receding tide, leads up the face of the cliff to a small gate let into the roots of the castle walls. This is the postern, the secret entrance to the castle. Inside is a narrow stairway of stone leading up to the private door of the royal apartments.

Halfway up the steep stairway was a broad landing, and a guardroom. Here I was to wait, until the child was judged fit to be taken abroad into the winter's cold. There were no guards; months past, the King had had the postern sealed, and the guardroom's other door, giving on to the main part of the castle, had been built up. For tonight the postern gate had been opened, but no porter manned it; only Ulfin, the King's man, and Valerius, his friend and trusted officer, waited there to let me in. Valerius took me up to the guardroom, while Ulfin went down the path into the bay to take my horse. Ralf was not with me. He had gone to ensure that the Breton ship was waiting as it had promised, and he was also to bring horses and to keep watch each night in the bay below the secret path.

I waited for two days and nights. There was a pallet in the guardroom, and Ulfin himself had kindled a fire to banish the disused chill of the place, and from time to time brought food and fuel, and the news from above stairs. He would have waited on me if I had let him; he was grateful still for some kindness I had shown him in the past, and I think the King's disfavour had distressed him. But I sent him back to his post at the Queen's door, and spent the waiting time alone.

At the other side of the landing, in the outer wall of the castle and opposite the guardroom door, was another door leading out on to a narrow, level platform skirted waist-high by a battlement. It was not overlooked by any of the castle windows, and below it, between the castle wall and the sea, was an apron of grass sloping down to the edge of the sheer cliffs. In summer the place was alive with nesting sea-birds, but now, in mid-winter, it was barren and crisp with frost. From below, incessantly, came the suck and hush and thud of the winter sea.

Each day, at dawn and sunset, I walked out to this platform to see if the weather had changed. But for three days there was no change. The air was cold, and below me the grass, grey with rime, was barely distinguishable in the thick mist that held the whole place shrouded, from the invisible sea below the invisible cliffs, to the pale blur where the winter sun fought to clear the sky. Below the blanket of mist the sea was quiet, as quiet as it ever is on that raging coast. And every midnight, before I slept, I went out into the icy dark and looked upwards for the stars. But there was only the blank pall of the mist.

Then on the third night, the wind came. A small wind from the west, that crept across the battlements and in under the doors and set the flames fluttering blue round the birch logs. I stood up, listening. I had a hand to the latch of the door when I heard a sound, in the quiet, from the head of the stairway. The door to the Queen's apartments had opened and shut again, gently. I opened the door and looked upwards.

Someone was coming softly down the stairs; a woman, shrouded in a mantle, carrying something. I stepped out on to the landing, and the light from the guardroom came after me, firelight and shadow.

It was Marcia. I saw the tears glisten on her cheeks as she bent her head over what lay in her arms. A child, wrapped warm against the winter night. She saw me and held her burden out to me. 'Take care of him,' she said. 'Take care of him, as God loves him and you.'

I took the child from her. Inside the woollen wrappings I caught the glint of cloth of gold. 'And the token?' I asked. She handed me a ring. It was one I had often seen on Uther's hand, made of gold, enclosing a stone of red jasper with a dragon crest carved small. I slipped it on my own finger, and saw her instinctive movement of protest, stilled as she remembered who I was.

I smiled. 'For safe keeping only. I shall put it away for him.'

'My lord prince . . .' She bent her head. Then she threw a quick glance over her shoulder to where the girl Branwen, hooded and cloaked, was coming down the stairway, with Ulfin behind her carrying a pack with her effects. Marcia turned back to me swiftly and laid a hand on my arm. 'You will tell me where you are taking him?' It was a plea, whispered.

I shook my head. 'I'm sorry. It's better that no one should know.'

She was silent, her lips working. Then she straightened herself. 'Very well. But you promise me that he will be safe? I'm not asking you as a man, or even as a prince. I'm asking you from your power. He will be safe?'

So Ygraine had said nothing, even to Marcia. Marcia's guess at the future was still only a guess. But in the days to come both these women would feel the bitter need for each other's confidence. It would be cruel to leave the Queen isolated with her knowledge and her hopes. It is not true that women cannot keep secrets. Where they love, they can be trusted to death and beyond, against all sense and reason. It is their weakness, and their great strength.

I met Marcia's eyes full for a moment. 'He will be King,' I said. 'The Queen knows it. But for the child's sake, you will tell no one else.'

She bent her head again, without replying. Ulfin and Branwen were beside us. Marcia leaned forward gently and drew back a fold of the shawl from the child's face. The baby was sleeping. The eyelids, curiously full, lay over the shut eyes like pale shells. There was a thick down of hair on his head. Marcia stooped and kissed him lightly on the head. He slept on, undisturbed. She pulled the fold of wool back to shelter him, then with gentle expert hands settled the bundle closer into my arms. 'So. Hold his head so. You will be careful going down the path?'

'I will be careful.'

She opened her mouth to speak again, then shook her head quickly, and I saw a tear slide from her cheek to fall on the child's shawl. Then she turned abruptly away, and started back up the stairs.

I carried the baby down the secret path. Valerius went ahead, with his sword drawn and ready, and behind me, with Ulfin's arm to help her, came Branwen. As we reached the bottom and stepped on the grating pebbles, Ralf's shadow detached itself from the immense darkness of the cliffs, and we heard his quick, relieved greeting, and the tread of hoofs on the shingle.

He had brought a mule for the girl, tough and sure-footed. He settled her in the saddle, then I handed the baby up to her, and she folded him close in the warmth of her cloak. Ralf vaulted to the back of his own horse and took the mule's rein in hand. I was to lead the pack-mule. This time I planned to travel as an itinerant singer—a harper is free of kings' courts where a drug-pedlar is not—and my harp was strapped to the mules saddle. Ulfin gave me the lead-rein, then held my gelding for me; it was fresh, and anxious to be moving and warm itself. I said my thanks and farewells, then he and Valerius started back up the cliff path. They would seal the postern again behind them.

I turned my horse's head into the wind. Ralf and the girl had already put their mounts to the bank. I saw the dim shapes pause above me, waiting, and the pale oval of Ralf's face as he turned back to watch me. Then his arm went out, pointing.

'Look!'

I turned.

The mist was lifting, drawing back from a sparkling sky. Faintly, high over the castle promontory, grew a hazy moon of light. Then the last cloud blew clear, billowing before the west wind like a sail blowing towards Brittany, and in its wake, blazing through the sparkle of the lesser stars, grew the great star that had lit the night of Ambrosius' death, and now burned steady in the east for the birth of the Christmas King.

We set spurs to our horses and rode for the ship.

Chapter Twelve

The wind stayed fair for Brittany, and we came in sight of the Wild Coast at dawn on the fifth day. Here the sea is never quiet; the cliffs, high and dangerous, towered black with the early light behind them and the teeth of the sea gnawing white at the base; but once round Vindanis Point the seas flattened and ran calmer, and I was even able to leave my cabin in time to watch our arrival at the wharf south of Kerrec which my father and King Budec had built years back when the invasion force was being assembled here.

The morning was still, with a touch of frost and a thin mist pearling the fields. The country hereabouts is flat, field and moorland stretching inland where the wind scours the grass with salt, and for miles nothing grows but pine and windbitten thorn. Thin streams wind between steep mud-banks down to the bays and inlets that bite everywhere into the coast, and at low tide the flats teem with shellfish and are loud with the cries of wading birds. For all its dour seeming it is a rich country, and had provided a haven not only for Ambrosius and Uther when Vortigern murdered their brother the King, but for hundreds of other exiles who fled from Vortigern and the threat of the Saxon Terror. Even then, they found parts of the country already peopled by the Celts of Britain. When the Emperor Maximus, a century before, had marched on Rome, those British troops who survived his defeat had straggled back to the refuge of this friendly land. Some had gone home, but a great many had remained to marry and settle; my kinsman, King Hoel, came of one such family. The British had indeed settled in such numbers that men called the peninsula Britain also, dubbing it Less Britain, as their homeland was known as Greater Britain. The language spoken here was still recognisably the same as that of home, and men worshipped the same gods, but the memories of older gods still visibly held the land, and the place was strange. I saw Branwen gazing out over the ship's rail with wide eyes and wondering face, and even Ralf, who had travelled here before as my messenger, had a look of awe as we drew nearer the wharf and saw, beyond the huts and the piles of casks and bales, the first ranks of the standing stones.

These line the fields of Less Britain, rank on rank, like old grey warriors waiting, or armies of the dead. They have stood there, men say, since time began. No one knows why, or how they came there. But I had long known that they were raised, not by giants or gods or even enchanters, but by human engineers whose skill lives on only in song. These skills I learnt, when as a boy I lived in Brittany, and men called it magic. For all I know they may be right. One thing is certain, though men's hands lifted the stones, and are long since dust under their roots, the gods they served still walk there. When I have gone between the stones at night, I have felt eyes on my back.

But now the sun was up, gilding the granite surfaces, and throwing the shadows of the stones slanting blue across the frost. The wharf-side was already busy; carts stood ready for loading, and men and boys ran about the business of tying up and unloading the ship. We were the only passengers, but no one cast more than a glance at the travellers in their decent, sober clothes; the musician with the harp in his baggage, his wife and baby beside him, and his servant in attendance. Ralf had lifted the baby from Branwen's arms, and was supporting her as she trod gingerly down the gangplank. She was silent and pale, and leaned heavily on him. I saw, as he bent over her, how–suddenly, it seemed–he had grown from boy to man. He would be turned sixteen now, and though Branwen was perhaps a year older than he, Ralf might well be taken for her husband, rather than I. He looked brisk and bright, sleek as a springtime cockerel in his neat new clothes. He was the only one of our party, I thought sourly, feeling the wharf tilt and sway under me as if it had still been the heaving deck, who had weathered the passage well.

The escort he had arranged was waiting for us. Not the escort of troops which King Hoel had wanted to provide, but simply a mule litter for Branwen and the child, with a muleteer and one other man, who had brought horses for Ralf and myself. This man came forward now to greet me. From his bearing I judged him to be an officer, but he was not in uniform, and there was nothing to show that the escort came from the King. Nor apparently had the officer been told anything about us, beyond the fact that we were to be led into town and housed there until the King should send for us.

He greeted me civilly, but without the courtesies of rank. 'You are welcome, sir. The King sends his greetings, and I am here to escort you into town. I trust you had a good voyage?'

'They tell me so,' I said, 'but neither I nor the lady are inclined to believe them.'

He grinned. 'I thought she looked a little green. I know how she feels. I'm not a great one for the sea, myself. And you, sir? Can you ride as far as the town? It's little more than a mile.'

'I can try,' I said. We exchanged courtesies while Ralf helped Branwen into the litter and drew the curtains against the morning chill. As she settled herself into the warmth the baby woke and began to cry. He had very good lungs, had Arthur. I suppose I must have winced. I saw a gleam of amusement in the officer's face, and said drily:

'Are you married?'

'Yes, indeed.'

'I used to think sometimes what I might be missing. Now I begin to know.'

He laughed at that. 'One can always escape. It's the best reason I know for being a soldier. Will you mount, sir?'

He and I rode side by side on the way into the town. Kerrec was a sizeable settlement, half civil, half military, walled and moated, clustered round a central hill where the King's stronghold lay. Near the ramp which led up to the castle gate was the house where my father had lived during his years of exile, while he and King Budec assembled and trained the army which had invaded Britain to claim it back for him, her rightful King.

And now, perhaps, her next and greater King was here at my side, still yelling lustily, muffled in a litter, and being carried over the wooden bridge that spanned the moat, and in through the gate of the town.

My companion was silent beside me. Behind us the others rode at ease; they chatted among themselves, the sound of their voices and the sharp clop of the horses' hoofs on the cobbles and the jingling of bits sounding loud in the still and misty daybreak. The town was just waking. Cocks crowed from yards and middens; here and there doors were opened and women, shawled against the cold, could be seen moving with pails or armfuls of kindling to start the day's work.

I was glad of my companion's silence as I looked about me. Even in the five years since I had left it the place seemed to have changed completely. I suppose one cannot pull a standing army out of a town where it had been built and trained for years, and not leave an echoing shell. The army, indeed, had been mainly quartered outside the walls, and the camps had long since been dismantled and gone back to grassland. But in the town, though King Budec's own troops remained, the orderly bustle and the air of purpose and expectancy which had characterised the place in my father's time, had gone. In the street of the engineers, where I had served my apprenticeship with Tremorinus, there were a few workshops open and already clanging in the early dawn, but the air of high purpose had gone with the crowd and the clamour, and something almost like desolation had taken its place. I was glad that the way to our lodging did not pass my father's house.

We were lodged with a decent couple, who made us welcome; Branwen and the baby were carried straight off to some women's fastness, while I was shown to a good room where a fire blazed and breakfast was spread waiting beside it. A servant carried the baggage in, and would have stayed to wait on me, but Ralf dismissed him and served the meal himself. I bade him eat with me, and he did so, cheerful and brisk as if the last week or so had been spent holidaying, and when we had done asked if I wanted to go out to explore the town. I gave him leave, but said that I would stay within doors. I am a strong man, and do not readily tire, but it takes more than a mile on dry land and a good breakfast to dispel the grinding sickness and exhaustion of a winter voyage. So I bade Ralf merely see to it that Branwen and the child were comfortable, and, after he had gone, composed myself to rest and wait for the King's summons.

It came at lamplighting, and Ralf with it, wide-eyed, with a robe over his arm of soft combed wool dyed a rich dark blue, with a border worked in gold and silver thread.

'The King sent this for you. Will you wear it?'

'Certainly. It would be an insult to do anything else.'

'But it's a prince's robe. People will wonder who you are.'

'Not a prince's, no. A singer's robe of honour. This is a civilised country, Ralf, like my own. It's not only princes and soldiers who are held in high esteem. When will King Hoel receive me?'

'In an hour's time, he says. He will receive you alone, before you sing in the hall. What are you laughing at?'

'King Hoel being cunning from necessity. There's only one catch about going as a singer to Hoel's court; he happens to be tone deaf. But even a tone deaf king will receive a travelling singer, to get the news. So he receives me alone. Then if the barons in his hall want to hear me, he doesn't have to sit through it.'

'He sent that harp along, though.' Ralf nodded to the instrument which stood shrouded near the lamp.

'He sent it, yes, but it was never his; it's my own.' He looked at me in surprise. I had spoken more curtly than I had meant to. All day the silent harp had stood there, untouched, but speaking for me of memories, of most, indeed, that I had ever had of happiness. As a boy here in Kerrec, in my father's house, I had played it almost nightly. I added: 'It was one I used here, years ago. Hoel's father must have kept it for me. I don't suppose it's been touched since I last played it. I'd better try it before I go. Uncover it, will you?'

A scratch at the door then heralded a slave with an ewer of steaming water. While I washed, and combed my hair, then let the slave help me into the sumptuous blue robe, Ralf uncovered the harp and set it ready.

It was bigger than the one I had brought with me. That was a knee harp, easy to transport; this was a standing harp, with a greater range and a tone which would reach the corners of a King's hall. I tuned it carefully, then ran my fingers over the strings.

To remember love after long sleep; to turn again to poetry after a year in the market place, or to youth after resignation to drowsy and stiffening age; to remember what once you thought life could hold, after telling over with muddied and calculating fingers what it has offered; this is music, made after long silence. The soul flexes its wings, and, clumsy as any fledgling, tries the air again. I felt my way, groping back through the chords, for the passion that slept there in the harp, exploring, testing as a man tests in the dark ground which once he knew in daylight. Whispers, small jags of sound, bunches of notes dragged sharply. The wires thrilled, catching the firelight, and the long running chords lapsed into the song.

> *There was a hunter at the moon's dark*
> *Who sought to lay a net of gold in the marshes.*
> *A net of gold, a net heavy as gold.*
> *And the tide came in and drowned the net,*
> *Held it invisible, deep, and the hunter waited,*
> *Crouching by the water in the moon's dark.*
>
> *They came, the birds flighting the dark,*
> *Hundred on hundred, a king's army.*
> *They landed on the water, a fleet of ships,*
> *Of king's ships, proud with silver, silver masted,*
> *Swift ships, fierce in battle,*
> *Crowding the water in the moon's dark.*

The net was heavy beneath them, hidden, waiting to catch them.
But he lay still, the young hunter, with idle hands.
Hunter, draw in your net. Your children will eat tonight,
And your wife will praise you, the cunning hunter.

He drew in his net, the young hunter, drew it tight and fast.
It was heavy, and he drew it to shore, among the reeds.
It was heavy as gold, but nothing was there but water.
There was nothing in it but water, heavy as gold,
And one grey feather,
From the wing of a wild goose.

They had gone, the ships, the armies, into the moon's dark.

And the hunter's children were hungry, and his wife lamented.
But he slept dreaming, holding the wild goose feather.

King Hoel was a big, thick-bodied man in his middle thirties. During the time I had spent in Kerrec–from my twelfth to my seventeenth year–I had seen very little of him. He had been a lusty and dedicated fighting man, while I was only a youth, and busy with my studies in hospital and workshop. But later he had fought with my father's troops in Greater Britain, and there we had come to know and to like one another. He was a man of big appetites and, as such men often are, good-natured and tending to laziness. Since I had last seen him he had put on flesh, and his face had the flush of good living, but I had no doubt he would be as stalwart as ever in the field.

I started by speaking of his father King Budec and the changes that had come, and we talked for a while of past times.

'Ah, yes, those were good years.' He stared, chin on fist, into the fire. He had received me in his private chamber, and after we had been served with wine, had dismissed the servants. His deer-hounds lay stretched on the skins at his feet, dreaming still of the chase they had had that day. His hunting spears, freshly cleaned, stood against the wall behind his chair, their blades catching the firelight. The King stretched his massive shoulders, and spoke wistfully. 'I wonder, when will such years come again?'

'You are talking of the fighting years?'

'I am talking of Ambrosius' years, Merlin.'

'They will come again, with your help now.' He looked puzzled, then startled, and uneasy. I had spoken prosaically enough, but he had caught the implications. Like Uther, he was a man who liked everything normal, open, and ordinary. 'You mean the child? The bastard? After all we've heard about it, he'll be the one to succeed Uther?'

'Yes. I promise you.'

He fidgeted with his cup, and his eyes slid away from mine. 'Ah, yes. Well, we shall keep him safely. But tell me, why the secrecy? I had a letter from Uther asking me openly enough to care for the boy. Ralf couldn't tell me much more than was in the letters he brought. I'll help, of course, every way I can, but I don't want to quarrel with Uther. His letter to me made it pretty clear that this boy's only his heir in default of a better claim.'

'That's true. Don't be afraid, I don't want a quarrel, either, between you and Uther. One doesn't throw a precious morsel down between two fighting-dogs and expect it to survive. Until there is a boy with what Uther calls a better claim, he's as anxious as I am to keep this one safe. He knows what I'm doing, up to a point.'

'Ah.' He cocked an eye at me, intrigued. I had been right about him. He might be well disposed towards Britain, but he was not above doing a quietly back-handed turn to Britain's King. 'Up to what point?'

'The time when the baby is weaned, and grown enough to need men's company and to be taught men's art. Four years, perhaps, or less. After that I shall take him back from you, and he must go home to Britain. If Uther asks where he is, he will have to be told, but until he does—well, there's no need to seek him out, is there? Myself, I doubt if Uther will question you at all. I think he would forget this child if he could. In any case, if there is blame, it is mine. He put the boy in my charge, to rear as I thought fit.'

'But will it be safe to take him back? If Uther's sending him here now because of enemies at home, are you sure it will be better then?'

'It's a risk that will have to be taken. I want to be near the child as he grows. It should be in Britain, and therefore it must be in secret. There are bad times coming, Hoel, for us all. I cannot yet see what will happen, beyond these facts; that this boy—this bastard if you like—will have enemies, even more than Uther has. You call him bastard; so will other men with ambition. His secret enemies will be more deadly even than the Saxons. So he must be hidden until the time comes for him to take the crown, and then he must take it with no cast of doubt, and be raised King in the sight of all Britain.'

'"He must be?" You have seen things, then?' But before I could answer he shied quickly away from the strange ground, and cleared his throat. 'Well, I'll keep him safe for you, as well as I may. Just tell me what you want. You know your own business, always did. I'll trust you to keep me right with Uther.' He gave his great laugh. 'I remember how Ambrosius used to say that your judgment in matters of policy, even when you were a youngling, was worth ten of any bedroom emperor's.' My father, naturally, had said no such thing; and in any case would hardly have said it to Hoel, who had a fair reputation himself as a lover, but I took it as it was intended, and thanked him. He went on: 'Well, tell me what you want. I confess I'm puzzled . . . These enemies you talk of; won't they guess he's in Brittany? You say Uther made no secret of his plans, and when the time comes for the royal ship to sail and it's seen that you and the child aren't on it, won't they simply think he was sent over earlier, and search first for him here in Brittany?'

'Probably. But by that time he'll be disposed of in the place I've arranged for him, and that's not the kind of place where Uther's nobles would think of looking. And I myself will be gone.'

'What place is that? Am I to know?'

'Of course. It's a small village near your boundary, north, towards Lanascol.'

'What?' He was startled, and showed it. One of the hounds stirred and opened an eye. 'North? At the edge of Gorlan's land? Gorlan is no friend to the Dragon'.

'Nor to me,' I said. 'He's a proud man, and there is an old score between his house and my mother's. But he has no quarrel with you?'

'No, indeed,' said Hoel fervently, with the respect of one fighting man for another.

'So I believed. So Gorlan isn't likely to make forays into the edge of your territory. What's more, who would dream that I would hide the child so near him? That with all Brittany to choose from, I'd leave him within bowshot of Uther's enemy? No, he'll be safe. When I leave him, I'll do so with a quiet mind. But that's not to say I'm not deeply in your debt.' I smiled at him. 'Even the stars need help at times.'

'I'm glad to hear it,' said Hoel gruffly. 'We mere kings like to think we have our parts to play. But you and your stars might make it a bit easier for us, perhaps? Surely, in all that great forest north of here, there must be safer places than the very edge of my lands?'

'Possibly, but it happens that I have a safe house there. The one person in both the Britains who'll know exactly what to do with the child for the next four years, and will care for him as she would for her own.'

'She?'

'Yes. My own nurse, Moravik. She's a Breton born, and after Maridunum was sacked in Camlach's war she left South Wales and went home. Her father owned a tavern north of here at a place called Coll. Since he'd grown too old for work, a fellow called Brand kept it for him. Brand's wife was dead, and soon after Moravik returned home she and Brand married, just to keep things right in the sight of God . . . and, knowing Moravik, I'm not just talking about the inn's title deeds . . . They keep the place still. You must have passed it, though I doubt if you'd ever stop there—it stands where two streams join and a bridge crosses them. Brand's a retired soldier of your own, and a good man—and in any case will do as Moravik bids him.' I smiled. 'I never knew a man who didn't, except perhaps my grandfather.'

'Ye—es.' He still sounded doubtful. 'I know the village, a handful of huts by the bridge, that's all . . . As you say, hardly a likely place to hunt a High King's heir. But an inn? Isn't that in itself a risk? With men—Gorlans too, since it's a time of truce—coming and going from the road?'

'So, no one will question your messengers or mine. My man Ralf will stay there to guard the boy, and he'll need to stay abreast of news, and get messages to you from time to time, and to me.'

'Yes. Yes, I see. And when you take the child there, what's your story?'

'No one will think twice about a travelling harper plying his trade on a journey. And Moravik has put a story round that will explain the sudden appearance of Ralf and the baby and his nurse. The story, if anyone questions it, will be that the girl, Branwen, is Moravik's niece, who bore a child to her master over in Britain. Her mistress cast her from the house, and she had no other place to go, but the man gave her money for the passage to her aunt's house in Brittany, and paid the travelling singer and his man to escort her. And the singer's man, meanwhile, will decide to leave his master and stay with the girl.'

'And the singer himself? How long will he stay there?'

'Only as long as a travelling singer might, then I'll move on and be forgotten. By the time anyone even thinks to look further for Uther's child, how can they find him? No one knows the girl, and the baby is only a baby. Every house in the country has one or more to show.'

He nodded, chewing it over this way and that, and asked a few more questions. Finally he admitted: 'It will serve, I suppose. What do you want me to do?'

'You have watchers in the kingdoms that march with yours?'

He laughed shortly. 'Spies? Who hasn't?'

'Then you'll hear quickly enough if there's any hint of trouble from Gorlan or anyone else. And if you can arrange for some quick and secret contact with Ralf, should it be necessary—?'

'Easy. Trust me. Anything I can do, short of war with Gorlan . . .' He gave his deep chuckle again. 'Eh, Merlin, it's good to see you. How long can you stay?'

'I'll take the boy north tomorrow, and with your permission will go unescorted. I'll come back as soon as I see all is safe. But I'll not come here again. You might be expected to receive a travelling singer once, but not actually to encourage him.'

'No, by God!'

I grinned. 'If this weather holds, Hoel, could the ship stay for me for a few days?'

'For as long as you like. Where do you plan to go?'

'Massilia first, then overland to Rome. After that, eastwards.'

He looked surprised. 'You? Well, here's a start! I'd always thought of you being as fixed as your own misty hills. What put that into your head?'

'I don't know. Where do ideas come from? I have to lose myself for a few years, till the child needs me, and this seemed to be the way. Besides, there was something I heard.' I did not tell him that it had only been the wind in the bowstrings. 'I've had a mind lately to see some of the lands I learnt about as a boy.'

We talked on then for a while. I promised to send letters back with news from the eastern capitals, and, as far as I could, I gave him points of call to which he would send his own tidings and Ralf's about Arthur.

The fire died down and he roared for a servant. When the man had been and gone—

'You'll have to go and sing in the hall soon,' said Hoel. 'So if we've got all clear, we'll leave it at that, shall we?' He leaned back in his chair. One of the hounds got to its feet and pushed against his knee, asking for a caress. Over the sleek head the King's eye gleamed with amusement. 'Well now, you've still to give me the news from Britain. And the first thing you can do is to tell me the inside story of what happened nine months ago.'

'If you in your turn will tell me what the public story is.'

He laughed. 'Oh, the usual stories that follow you as closely as your cloak flapping in the wind. Enchantments, flying dragons, men carried through the air and through walls, invisibly. I'm surprised, Merlin, that you take the trouble to come by ship like an ordinary man, when your stomach serves you so ill. Come now, the story.'

It was very late when I got back to our lodging. Ralf was waiting, half asleep in the chair by the fire in my room. He jumped up when he saw me, and took the harp from me.

'Is all well?'

'Yes. We go north in the morning. No, thank you, no wine. I drank with the King, and they made me drink again in the hall.'

'Let me take your cloak. You look tired. Did you have to sing to them?'

'Certainly.' I held out a handful of silver and gold pieces, and a jewelled pin. 'It's nice to think, isn't it, that one can earn one's keep so handsomely? The jewel was from the King, a bribe to stop me singing, otherwise they'd have had me there yet. I told you this was a cultured country. Yes, cover the big harp. I'll take the other with me tomorrow.' Then as he obeyed me: 'What of Branwen and the baby?'

'Went to bed three hours since. She's lying with the women. They seem very pleased to have a baby to look after.' He finished on a note of surprise which made me laugh.

'Did he stop crying?'

'Not for an hour or two. They didn't seem to mind that, either.'

'Well, no doubt he'll start again at cock-crow, when we rouse them. Now go to bed and sleep while you can. We start at first light.'

Chapter Thirteen

There is a road leading almost due north out of the town of Kerrec, the old Roman road which runs straight as a spear-cast across the bare, salty grassland. A mile out of town, beyond the ruined posting station, you can see the forest ahead of you like a slow tidal wave approaching to swallow the salt flats. This is a vast stretch of woodland, deep and wild. The road spears straight into it, aiming for the big river that cuts the country from east to west. When the Romans held Gallia there was a fort and settlement beyond the river, and the road was built to serve it; but now the river marks the boundary of Hoel's kingdom, and the fort is one of Gorlan's strongholds. The writ of neither King runs far into the forest, which stretches for countless hilly miles, covering the rugged centre of the Breton peninsula. What traffic there is, keeps to the road; the wild land is served only by the tracks of charcoal-burners and wood-cutters and men who move secretly outside the law. At the time of which I write the place was called the Perilous Forest, and was reputed to be magic-bound and haunted. Once leave the road and plunge into the tracks that twist through the tangled trees, and you could travel for days and hardly see the sun.

When my father had held command in Brittany under King Budec, his troops had kept order even in the forest, as far as the river where King Budec's land ended and King Gorlan's began. They had cut the trees well back to either side of the road, and opened up some of the subsidiary tracks, but this had been neglected, and now the saplings and the bushes had

crowded in. The paved surface of the road had long since been broken by
winter, and here and there it crumbled off into patches of iron-hard mud
that in soft weather would be a morass.

We set out on a grey, cold day, with the wind tasting faintly of salt. But
though the wind blew damp from the sea it brought no rain with it, and the
going was fair enough. The huge trees stood on either hand like pillars of
metal, holding a weight of low, grey sky. We rode in silence, and after a few
miles the thickly encroaching growth of the underwood forced us, even on
this road, to ride in single file. I was in the lead, with Branwen behind me,
and Ralf in the rear leading the pack-mule. I had been conscious for the first
hour or so of Ralf's tension, the way his head turned from side to side as he
watched and listened; but we saw and heard nothing except the quiet winter
life of the forest; a fox, a pair of roe deer, and once a shadowy shape that
might have been a wolf slipping away among the trees. Nothing else, no
sound of horses, no sign of men.

Branwen showed no hint of fear. When I glanced back I saw her always
serene, sitting the neat-footed mule stolidly, with an unmoved calm that
held no trace of uneasiness. I have said little about Branwen, because I have
to confess that I remember very little about her. Thinking back now over
the span of years, I see only a brown head bent over the baby she carried, a
rounded cheek and downcast eyes and a shy voice. She was a quiet girl
who—though she talked easily enough to Ralf—rarely addressed me of her
own will, being painfully in awe of me both as prince and enchanter. She
seemed to have no inkling of any risk or danger in our journey, nor did she
seem stirred—as most girls would have been—by the excitement of travelling
abroad to a new country. Her imperturbable calm was not due to confidence
in myself or Ralf; I came to see that she was meek and biddable to the point
of stupidity, and her devotion to the baby was such as to blind her to all else.
She was the kind of woman whose only life is in the bearing and rearing of
children, and without Arthur she would, I am sure, have suffered bitterly
over the loss of her own baby. As it was, she seemed to have forgotten this,
and spent the hours in a kind of dreamy contentment that was exactly what
Arthur needed to make the discomforts of the journey tolerable.

Towards noon we were deep in the forest. The branches laced thick
overhead, and in summer would have shut out the sky like a pitched shield,
but above the bare boughs of winter we could see a pale and shrouded point
of light where the sun struggled to be through. I watched for a sheltered
place where we could leave the road without showing too many traces, and
presently, just as the baby woke and began to fret, saw a break in the
undergrowth and turned my horse aside.

There was a path, narrow and winding, but in the sparse growth of winter
it was passable. It led into the forest for a hundred paces or so before it
divided, one path leading on deeper among the trees, the other—no more
than a deer-trod—winding steeply up to skirt the base of a rocky spur. We
followed the deer-trod. This picked its way through fallen boulders tufted
with dead and rusty fern, then led upwards round a stand of pines, and
faded into the bleached grass of a tiny clearing above the rock. Here, in a
hollow, the sun came with a faint warmth. We dismounted, and I spread a
saddle-cloth in the most sheltered spot for the girl, while Ralf tethered the

horses below the pines and threw down feed from the hay nets. Then we sat ourselves down to eat. I sat at the lip of the hollow, with my back against a tree, a post from which I could see the main path running below the rock. Ralf stayed with Branwen. It had been a long time since we had broken our fast, and we were all hungry. The baby, indeed, had begun to yell lustily as the mule scrambled up the steep path. Now he found his cries stifled against the girl's nipple, and fell silent, sucking busily.

The forest was very quiet. Most wild creatures lie still at noon. The only thing moving was a carrion crow, which flapped heavily down on to a pine above us, and began to caw. The horses finished their feed and dozed, hip-shotten, heads low. The baby still fed, but more slowly, drowsing into a milky sleep. I leaned back against the stem of the tree. I could hear Branwen murmuring to Ralf. He said something, and I heard her laugh, then through the murmur of the two young voices I caught another, distant, sound. Horses, at the trot.

At my word the boy and girl fell abruptly silent. Ralf was on his feet in the blink of an eye, and kneeling beside me to watch the path below. I signed Branwen to stay where she was. I need not have troubled; she had turned a wondering look on us, then the baby hiccupped, and she held him to her shoulder, patting him, all her attention on him again. Ralf and I knelt at the edge of the clearing, watching the path below.

The horses—there were two of them by the sound of it—could not be wood-cutters' beasts nor the slow train of the charcoal-burners. Trotting horses, in the Perilous Forest, meant only one thing, trouble. And travellers who carried, as we did, gold for the baby's keep, were quarry for any outlaws and disaffected men. Hampered as we were by Branwen and Arthur, both fighting and flight were impossible. Nor was it easy, with the baby, to keep silent and let danger pass by so closely. I had made it clear to Ralf that whatever happened he was to stay with the girl and, at the least hint of danger, leave it to me to devise some way of drawing the danger away. Ralf had protested, mutinied, then finally seen the sense of it and sworn to obey.

So now when I whispered, 'Only two, I think. If they don't come up this way they'll not see us. Get to the horses. And for God's sake tell the girl to keep the baby quiet,' he merely nodded, melting back from my side. He stooped to whisper to Branwen, and I saw her nod placidly, shifting the child to her other breast. Ralf slipped like a shadow among the pines where the horses stood. I waited, watching the path.

The riders were approaching. There was no other sound except the crow, still cawing high in the pine tree. Then I saw them. Two horses, trotting single file; poor beasts, heavy bred and none too well fed by the look of them, careless how they put their feet, and having to be hauled up by their cursing riders at every hole or root across the path. It was a fair enough guess that the men were outlaws. They were as unkempt as their beasts, and looked half savage, and dangerous. They were dressed in what looked like old uniforms, and on the arm of one of them was a dirty badge, half torn away. It looked like Gorlan's. The fellow in the rear rode carelessly, lolling in the saddle as if half drunken, but the man in front pricked at the alert, as such men learn to do, his head moving from side to side like that of a

questing dog. He held a bow at the ready. Through the rotten leather of the
sheath at his thigh I saw the long knife, burnished to a killing point.

They were almost below me. They were passing. There had been no
sound from the baby, nor from our horses, hidden among the pines. Only
the carrion crow, balancing high in the sunshine, scolded noisily.

I saw the fellow with the bow lift his head. He said something over his
shoulder, in a thick accent I could not catch. He grinned, showing a row of
rotten teeth, then lifted his bow, notched it, and sent an arrow whizzing into
the pine. It hit. The crow shot upwards off the bough with a yell, then fell,
transfixed. It landed within two paces of Branwen and the child, flapped for
a second or two, then lay still.

As I dodged back and ran for the pines I heard both men laughing. Now
the marksman would come to retrieve his arrow. Already I could hear him
forcing his beast through the under-brush. I picked up the arrow, crow and
all, and flung it out over the edge of the hollow. It landed down among the
boulders. From the path the man could not have seen where the bird fell; it
was a chance that he might believe it had fluttered there, and would ride no
further. I saw Branwen's eyes, startled and wondering, as I ran past her. But
she did not stir, and the baby slept at her breast. I gave her a sign which was
meant to convey reassurance, approval, and warning all in one, and ran for
my horse.

Ralf was holding the beasts quiet, heads together, muffling eyes and
nostrils with his cloak. I paused beside him, listening. The outlaws were
coming on. They must not have seen the crow; they came on without
pausing, making for the pines.

I seized my sorrel's bridle from Ralf, and turned it to mount. The horse
circled, treading the dry stalks and snapping twigs. I heard the sudden
clatter and tramp as the outlaws dragged their beasts to a standstill. One of
them said, 'Listen!' in Breton, and there was the rasp of metal as weapons
came hissing out. I was in my saddle. My own sword was out. I pulled the
sorrel's head round, and had opened my mouth to shout when I heard
another cry from the path, then the same voice yelling 'Look! Look there!'
and my horse reared sharply back on its haunches as something broke out of
the bushes beside me and went by so close that it almost brushed my leg.

It was a hind, white against the winter forest. She scudded through the
pines like a ghost, bounded along the top of the hollow where we had lain,
stood poised for a moment in view at the edge, then vanished down the
steep, boulder-strewn slope, straight into the path of the two outlaws. I
heard shouts of triumph from below, the crack of a whip, the sudden thud
and flurry of hoofs as the men wrenched their horses back to the path and
lashed them to a gallop. They were giving hunting calls. I jumped from the
saddle, threw the sorrel's reins to Ralf, and ran back to my place above the
rock. I reached it in time to see the two of them going back full tilt the way
they had come. Ahead of them, dimly seen for a moment, like a scud of mist
through the bare trees, fled the white hind. Then the laughter, the hunting
cries, the hammer of hard-driven horses, echoed plunging back through the
forest, and was gone.

Chapter Fourteen

The river which marks the boundary of Hoel's kingdom flows right through the heart of the forest. In places it cuts a deep gorge between overhanging banks of trees, and everywhere in the central part of the forest the land is seamed by small, wild valleys where tributary streams wind or tumble into the main. But there is a place, almost in the centre of the forest, where the river valley is wider and more gentle, forming a green basin where men have tilled the fields, and over the years have cut back the forest to make grazing land round the small settlement called Coll, which in Breton means the Hidden Place. Here there had been, in past times, a Roman transit camp on the road from Kerrec to Lanascol. All that remained of this now was the squared outline where the original ditch had been dug beside the tributary. Here lay the village. On two sides of it the stream made a natural defence or moat; for the rest, the Roman ditch had been cleared and widened, and filled with water. Inside this were steep defensive earthworks, crowned with palisades. The bridge had been a stone one in Roman times; the piles still stood and were spanned now with planking. Though the village lay near Gorlan's border, it was accessible from it only through the narrow pass cut by the river, and there the road had crumbled almost back to the original rocky path that wolves and wild men had used before the Romans ever came. Coll was well named.

Brand's tavern lay just inside the gate. The main street of the village was little more than a dirty alley floored unevenly with cobbles. The inn stood a little way back from this, on the right. It was a low building, roughly built of stone, with mortar slapped haphazardly into the gaps. The outbuildings round the yard were no more than wattle huts, daubed with mud. The roof was newly thatched, with good close work of reeds held down by a net of rope weighted with heavy stones. The door was open, as the door of an inn should be, with a heavy curtain of skins hung across the opening to keep the weather out. Through the chimney hole at one end rose a sluggish column of smoke that smelt of peat.

We arrived at dusk when the gates were closing. Everywhere mingled with the peat smoke came the smells of supper cooking. There were few people about; the children had been called in long since, and the men were home at their supper. Only a few hungry-looking dogs skulked here and there; an old woman hurried past with a shawl held over her face and a fowl squawking under her other arm; a man led a yoke of weary oxen along the street. I could hear the clink of a smith's anvil not far away, and smell the sharp fume of burnt hoofs.

Ralf eyed the inn dubiously. 'It looked better in October, on a sunny day.

It's not much of a place, is it?'

'All the better,' I said. 'No one will come looking in a place like this for the son of the King of Britain. Go in now and play your part, while I hold the horses.'

He pushed aside the curtain and went in. I helped Branwen dismount, and settled her on one of the benches beside the door. The baby woke, and began to whimper, but almost immediately Ralf came out again, followed by a big, burly man and a boy. The man must be Brand himself; he had been a fighting man and still bore himself like one, and I saw the puckered seam of an old wound across the back of one hand.

He hesitated, uncertain how to greet me. I said quickly: 'You'll be the innkeeper? I'm Emrys the singer, who was to bring your wife's niece along with us, with the baby. You're expecting us, I believe?'

He cleared his throat. 'Indeed, indeed. You're most welcome. My wife's been looking for you this week past.' He saw the boy staring, and added sharply: 'What are you waiting for? Take the horses round the back.'

The boy darted to obey. Brand, ducking his head at me and indicating the door of the inn with a gesture that was half invitation, half salute, said: 'Come in, come in. Supper's cooking.' Then, doubtfully, 'It's mighty rough company we get here, but maybe—'

'I'm used to rough company,' I said tranquilly, and preceded him through the door.

This was not a time of year for much coming and going on the roads, so the place was not crowded. There were some half dozen men, dimly seen in a room lit by one tallow candle and the light from the peat fire. The talk hushed as we went in, and I saw the looks at the harp I carried, and the whisper that went round. Nobody spared a glance for the girl carrying the baby. Brand said, a shade too quickly: 'On through there. That far door, behind the fire.' Then the door shut behind us, and there in the back room stood Moravik, fists on her hips, waiting to greet us.

Like everyone else whom one has not seen since childhood, she had shrunk. When I had last seen her I had been a boy of twelve, and tall for my age. Even then she had seemed much bigger than I was, a creature of bulk and commanding voice, surrounded by the aura of authority and infallible decisions left over from the nursery. Now she came no higher than my collarbone, but she still had the bulk and the voice, and–I was to find–the authority. Though I had turned out to be the favoured son of the High King of all Britain, I was still, obviously, the wayward small boy from her first nursery.

Her first words were characteristic. 'And a fine time of night to come, with the gates just shutting! You could have been out in that forest all night, and a precious lot there'd have been left of you by morning, what with the wolves, and worse, that lives out there. And damp, too, I shouldn't wonder–sweet saints and stars preserve us, look at your cloak! Get it off this minute, and come to the fire. There's a good supper cooking, special for you. I remember all the things you like, and I never thought to see you sitting at my table again, young Merlin, not after that night when the place burned down round you, and there was nothing to be found of you in the morning but a few burned bones in your room.' Then suddenly she came forward with a rush and had hold of me. There were tears on her face. 'Eh, Merlin, little Merlin, but it's good to see you again.'

'And you, Moravik.' I embraced her. 'I swear you must have got younger every year since you left Maridunum. And now you're putting me in your debt again, you and your good man here. I'll not forget it, and neither will the King. Now, this is Ralf, my companion, and this'–drawing the girl forward–'is Branwen, with the child.'

'Eh, the baby! The good Goddess save us all! What with seeing you, Merlin, I'd forgotten all about him! Come near the fire, girl, don't stand there in the draught. Come to the fire, and let me see him . . . Eh, the lamb, the bonny lamb . . .'

Brand touched my arm, grinning. 'And now, what with seeing *him*, she'll forget everything else, my lord. It's lucky she got the supper ready for you before she got a sight of the baby. Sit you down here. I'll serve you myself.'

Moravik had made a rich mutton stew, satisfying and very hot. The mutton of the Breton salt flats is as good even as anything we get in Wales. There were dumplings with the stew, and good new bread hot from the oven. Brand brought a jug of red wine, very much better than anything we can make at home. He waited on us while Moravik busied herself with Branwen and the baby, whose whimpering had broken now into lusty crying, only to be stilled by Branwen's breast. The fire blazed and crackled, the room was warm and smelt of good food and wine, the firelight traced the shape of the girl's cheek, and the baby's head. I became conscious of someone watching me, and turned my head to see Ralf's eye on my face. He opened his mouth as if to speak, but at that moment some clamour from the outer room made Brand set the wine-jug down on the table, excuse himself quickly to me, and hurry out. He left the door slightly ajar. Beyond it I could hear voices raised in what sounded like persuasion or argument. Brand answered, quietly, but the clamour persisted.

He came back into the room, looking worried, and shut the door behind him. 'My lord, there's those outside who saw you come in, and saw you'd a harp with you. Now, well, it's only natural, my lord, they want a song. I tried to argue them out of it, said you were tired, and had come a long way, but they insisted. Said they'd pay for your supper, between them, if the song was a good one.'

'Well,' I said, 'why not let them?'

His mouth dropped open. 'But–sing to them? You?'

'Don't you hear anything in Brittany?' I asked him. 'I really am a singer. And it wouldn't be the first time I've earned my fee.'

From her place near Branwen beside the fire, Moravik looked up quickly. 'Here's a new start! Potions and such I knew about, learned from that old hermit above the mill, and even magic—' crossing herself. 'But music? Who taught you?'

'Queen Olwen taught me the notes,' I said, adding, to Brand, 'That was my grandfather's wife, a Welsh girl who sang like a laverock. Then later when I was here in Brittany with Ambrosius I learned from a master. You may have heard of him, perhaps? An old blind singer, who had travelled and made music in every country in the world.'

Brand nodded as if he knew the man I spoke of, but Moravik looked doubtfully at me, tut-tutting, and shaking her head. I suppose no one who has reared a boy from babyhood, and not seen him since his twelfth year, ever thinks he can be a master at anything. I grinned at them. 'Why, I played in front of King Hoel, back there in Kerrec. Not that he's anything of a judge, but Ralf has heard me, too. Ask him, if you think I can't earn my supper.'

Brand said doubtfully: 'But you'll not want to be singing to the likes of them, my lord?'

'Why not? A travelling minstrel sings where he's hired to sing. And that's what I am, while I'm in Less Britain.' I got to my feet. 'Ralf, bring me the harp. Finish the wine yourself, and then get to bed. Don't wait for me.'

I went out into the tavern's public room. This had filled up now; there were about twenty men there, crowded in the smoky warmth. When I went in there were shouts of, 'The singer, the singer!' and 'A tale, a tale!'

'Make room for me then, good people,' I said. A stool was vacated for me near the fire, and someone poured me a cup of wine. I sat down and began to tune the harp. They fell still, watching me.

They were simple folk, and such folk like tales of marvels. When I asked them what they would have, they asked for this tale and that of gods and battles and enchantments, so in the end—my mind, I think, on the child sleeping in the next room—I gave them the story of Macsen's Dream. This is as much a tale of magic as any of the rest, though its hero is the Roman commander Magnus Maximus, who was real enough. The Celts call him Macsen Wledig, and the legend of Macsen's Dream was born in the singing valleys of Dyfed and Powys where every man claims Prince Macsen as his own, and the stories have gone from mouth to mouth until, if Maximus himself appeared to tell them the truth, no one would believe him. It's a long story, the Dream, and every singer has his own version of it. This is the one I sang that night:

Macsen, Emperor of Rome, went hunting, and being tired in the heat of the day lay down to sleep on the banks of the great river that flows towards Rome, and he dreamed a dream.

He dreamed that he journeyed along the river towards its source, and came to the highest mountain in the world; and from there followed another fair flowing river through the rich fields and broad woodlands till he reached the mouth of the river; and there at its mouth was a city of turrets and castles crowded round a fair harbour. And in that harbour lay a ship of gold and silver with no man on board, but with all sails set and shivering to the wind out of the east. He crossed a gang-plank made of the white bone of a whale, and the ship sailed.

And soon, after a sunset and a sunset, he came to the fairest island of all the world, and leaving the ship, he traversed the island from sea to sea. And there on the western shore he saw an island at hand across a narrow strait. And on the near shore where he stood was a fair castle, with an open gate. Then Macsen entered the castle and found himself in a great hall with golden pillars, and walls dazzling with gold and silver and precious stones. In that hall two youths sat playing chess on a silver board, and near them an old man in an ivory chair carved chessmen for them out of crystal. But Macsen had no eyes for all this splendour. More beautiful than silver and ivory and precious stones was a maiden, who sat still as a queen in her golden chair. The moment the Emperor saw her he loved her, and, raising her, he embraced her and begged her to be his wife. But in the very moment of the embrace he woke, and found himself in the valley outside Rome, with his companions watching him.

Then Macsen leapt to his feet and told his dream; and messengers were sent the length and breadth of the world, to find the land he had traversed, and the castle with the beautiful maiden. And after many months, and a score of false journeys, one man found them, and came home to tell his master. The island, most beautiful in all the world, was Britain, and the castle by the western sea was Caer Seint, by Segontium, and the island across the shining strait was Mona, isle of druids. So Macsen journeyed to Britain, and found everything just as he had dreamed it, and requested the hand of the maiden from her father and her brothers, and made her his Empress. Her name was Elen, and she bore Macsen two sons and a daughter, and in her honour he built three castles, in Segontium, Caerleon, and Maridunum, which was called Caer Myrddin in honour of the gods of high places.

Then, because Macsen stayed in Britain and forgot Rome, they made a new emperor in Rome, who set his standard on the walls and defied Macsen. So Macsen raised an army of the Britons, and, with Elen and her brothers at his side, set out for Rome; and he conquered Rome. Thereafter he stayed in Rome, and Britain saw him no more, but Elen's two brothers took the British forces back to their homes, and to this day the seed of Macsen Wledig reigns in Britain.

When I had done, and the last note had hummed away to nothing in the smoky stillness there was a roar of applause, cups thumping on the tables, and rough voices calling for more music, and more wine. Another cupful was pressed on me, and while I drank and rested before singing again, the men went back to talking among themselves, but softly, lest they disturb the singer's thoughts.

It was as well they could not guess at them; I was wondering what they would do if they knew that the last and latest scion of Maximus lay sleeping on the other side of the wall. For this part of the legend, at least, was true, that my father's family was descended straight from Maximus' marriage with the Welsh princess Elen. The rest of the legend, like all such tales, was a kind of dreaming distortion of the truth, as if an artist, reassembling a broken mosaic from a few worn and random fragments, rebuilt the picture in his own shimmering new colours, with here and there the pieces of the old, true picture showing plain.

The facts were these. Maximus, a Spaniard by birth, had commanded the armies in Britain under his general Theodosius at a time when Saxons and Picts were raiding the coasts constantly, and the Roman province of Britain looked like crumbling to its fall. Between them the commanders repaired the Wall of Hadrian, and held it, and Maximus himself rebuilt and garrisoned the great fortress at Segontium in Wales, and made it his headquarters. This is the place that is called Caer Seint by the British; it is the 'fair castle' of the Dream, and here it must have been that Maximus met his Welsh Elen, and married her.

Then in the year that Ector had called the Flood Year it was Maximus (though his enemies denied him the credit) who after months of bitter fighting drove the Saxons back and constructed the provinces of Strathclyde and Manau Guotodin, buffer states, in whose shelter the people of Britain–his people–might live in peace. Already 'Prince Macsen' to the folk of Wales, he was declared Emperor by his troops, and so might have remained, but for the events everyone knows of which took him abroad to avenge his old general's murder, and thereafter to march on Rome itself.

He never came back; here again the Dream is true; but not because he conquered Rome and stayed to rule it. He was defeated there, and later executed, and though some of the British forces who had gone with him came home and pledged themselves to his widow and his sons, the brief peace was over. With Maximus dead the Flood came again, and this time there was no sword to stop it.

Small wonder, in the dark years that followed, that the short stretch of Maximus' victorious peace should appear to men like a lost age as golden as any the poets sing. Small wonder that the legend of 'Macsen the Protector' had grown and grown until his power compassed the earth, and in their dark times men spoke of him as of a god-sent saviour . . .

My thoughts went back to the baby sleeping in the straw. I lifted my harp again, and when they hushed for me, sang them another song:

> *There was a boy born,*
> *A winter king.*
> *Before the black month*
> *He was born,*
> *And fled in the dark month*
> *To find shelter*
> *With the poor.*

> *He shall come*
> *With the spring*
> *In the green month*
> *And the golden month*
> *And bright*
> *Shall be the burning*
> *Of his star.*

'And did you earn your supper?' asked Moravik.

'Plenty to drink, and three copper coins.' I laid them on the table and put the leather bag containing the King's gold beside them. 'That's for your care of the child. I'll send more when it's needed. You'll not regret this, you and Brand. You've nursed kings before, Moravik, but never such a king as this one will be.'

'What do I care for kings? That's nought but a bonny bairn, that should never have been set to such a journey in this weather. He should be home in his own nursery, and you can tell your King Uther that from me! Gold, indeed!' But the leather bag had vanished into some fastness of her skirt, and the coins with it.

'He's come to no harm on the journey?' I asked quickly.

'None that I can see. That's a good, strong boy, and like to flourish as well as any of my children. He's abed now, and those two young things with him, poor children, so keep your voice down and let them sleep.'

Branwen and the child lay on a pallet in the far corner of the room, away from the fire. Their bed was underneath the flight of rough wooden steps which led up to a platform, like a small loft such as they used for hay in kings' stables. Indeed there was hay stacked there, and our beasts had been led in from the yard at the back, and were tethered now under the loft. A donkey, which I suppose was Brand's own, stood near them in the straw.

'Brand brought yours in,' said Moravik. 'There isn't much room, but he daren't leave them outside in the byre. That sorrel of yours with the white blaze, someone might know it for King Hoel's own, and there'd be questions asked that weren't too easy to answer. I've put you up above, and the boy. It's maybe not what you're used to, but it's soft, and it's clean.'

'It'll be fine. But don't send me to bed yet, please, Moravik. May I stay up and talk to you?'

'Hm. Send you to bed, indeed! Aye, you always did look meek and talk soft, and you doing exactly as you wanted all the time . . .' She sat down by the fire, spreading her skirts, and nodded to a stool. 'Well, now, sit down and let me look at you. Mercy me, and here's a change! Who'd ever have thought it, back there in Maridunum, with hardly a decent rag to your name, that you'd turn out a son of the High King himself, and a doctor and a singer . . . and the sweet saints only know what else besides!'

'A magician, you mean?'

'Well, that never surprised me, the way I heard you'd been running off to the old man at Bryn Myrddin.' She crossed herself, and her hand closed on an amulet at her neck. I had seen it glinting in the firelight; it was hardly a Christian symbol. So Moravik still hedged herself around with every talisman she could find. In this she was like most of the folk bred in the Perilous Forest, with its tales of old hauntings, and things seen in the twilight and heard in the wind. She nodded at me. 'Aye, you always were a queer lad, with your solitary ways, and the things you'd say. Always knew too much, you did. I thought it was with listening at doors, but it seems I was wrong. "The King's prophet", they tell me you're called now. And the doings I've heard about, if the half of them's to be believed, which I doubt they're not . . . Well, now, tell me. Tell me everything.'

The fire had burnt low, almost to ash. There was silence from the next room now; the drinkers had either gone home or settled to sleep. Brand had climbed the ladder an hour since, and snored softly beside Ralf. In the corner beside the dozing beasts, Branwen and the child slept, unmoving.

'And now here's this new start,' said Moravik softly. 'This baby here, you tell me he's the son of the High King, Uther himself, that won't own to him. Why do you have to take it on yourself to look after him? I'd have thought there's others he might ask, that could do it easier.'

'I can't answer for King Uther,' I said, 'but for myself, you might say the child was a trust left to me by my father, and by the gods.'

'The gods?' she asked sharply. 'What talk is this for a good Christian man?'

'You forget, I was never baptised.'

'Not even yet? Aye, I remember the old King would have none of it. Well, that's no concern of mine now, only of your own. But this child, is he christened?'

'No. There's been no time. If you want to, then have him christened.'

'"If you want to?" What way is that to talk? What "gods" were you talking of just now?'

'I hardly know. They—he—will make himself known in his own good time. Meanwhile have the boy christened, Moravik. When he leaves Brittany he's to be reared in a Christian household.'

She was satisfied. 'As soon as may be. I'll see him right with the dear Lord and his saints, trust me for that. And I've hung the vervain charm over his crib, and seen the nine prayers said. The girl says his name's Arthur. What sort of name is that?'

'You would say Artos,' I told her. This is a name meaning 'Bear' in Celtic. 'But don't call him by that name here. Give him some other name that you can use, and forget the other.'

'Emrys, then? Ah, I thought that would make you smile. I'd always hoped that one day there'd be a child I could call after you.'

'No, after my father Ambrosius, as I was called.' I tried the names over to myself, in Latin and then in the Celtic tongue. '*Artorius Ambrosius, last of the Romans . . . Artos Emrys, first of the British . . .*' Then aloud to Moravik, smiling: 'Yes, call him so. Once, long ago, I foretold it, the coming of the Bear, a king called Arthur, who would knit past and future. I had forgotten, till now, where I had heard the name before. Christen him so.'

She was silent for a few minutes. I saw her quick eyes searching my face. 'In trust to you, you said. A king such as there hasn't been before. He will be King, then? You swear he will be King?' Then suddenly: 'Why do you look like that, Merlin? I saw you look the same way a while back when the girl put the child to her breast. What is it?'

'I don't know . . .' I spoke slowly, my eyes on the last glimmer of fire where the burned logs hollowed round a red cave. 'Moravik, I have done what I have done because God—whichever god he is—drove me to do it. Out of the dark he told me that the child which Uther begot of Ygraine that night at Tintagel would be King of all Britain, would be great, would drive the Saxons out of our shores and knit our poor country into a strong whole. I did nothing of my own will, but just for this, that Britain might not go down into the dark. It came to me whole, out of the silence and the fire, and as a certainty. Then for a time I saw nothing and heard nothing, and wondered if, in my love for my father's land, I had been led astray, and had seen vision where there was nothing but hope and desire. But now, see, there it lies, just as the god told me.' I looked at her. 'I don't know if I can make you understand, Moravik. Visions and prophecies, gods and stars and voices speaking in the night . . . things seen cloudy in the flames and in the stars, but real as pain in the blood, and piercing the brain like ice. But now . . .' I paused again, '. . . now it is no longer a god's voice or a vision, it is a small human child with lusty lungs, a baby like any other baby, who cries, and sucks milk, and soaks his swaddling clothes. One's visions do not take account of this.'

'It's men who have visions,' said Moravik. 'It's women who bear the children to fulfil them. That's the difference. And as for that one there,' she nodded towards the corner, 'we shall see what we shall see. If he lives—and why should he not live, he's strong enough?—if he lives he has a good chance to be King. All we can do now is see that he makes a man. I'll do my part as you've done yours. The rest is with the good God.'

I smiled at her. Her sturdy commonsense seemed to have lifted a great weight from me. 'You're right. I was a fool ever to doubt. What will come, will come.'

'Then sleep on that.'

'Yes. I'll go to bed now. You have a good man there, Moravik. I'm glad of it.'

'Between us, boy, we'll keep your little King safely.'

'I'm sure of that,' I said, and after we had talked a little longer I climbed the ladder to bed.

That night I dreamed. I was standing in a field I knew near Hoel's town of Kerrec. It was a place of ancient holiness, where once a god had walked and I had seen him. In my dream I knew that I had come in the hope of seeing him again.

But the night was empty. All that moved was the wind. The sky arched high, bright with indifferent stars. Across its black dome, soft through the glitter of the fiercer stars, lay the long track of light they call the Galaxy. There was no cloud. About me stretched the field, just as I remembered it, bitten by the wind and sown by the sea's salt, with bare thorn trees hunched along the banks, and, solitary in the centre, a single giant stone. I walked towards it. In the scattered light of the stars I cast no shadow, nor was there a shadow by the stone. Only the grey wind blurring the grass, and behind the stone the faint drifting of the stars that is not movement, but the heavens breathing.

Still the night was empty. My thoughts arrowed up into the shell of silence, and fell back spent. I was trying, with every grain of skill and power which I had fought and suffered for, to recall the god whose hand had been over me then, and whose light had led me. I prayed aloud, but heard no sound. I called on my magic, my gift of eyes and mind that men called the Sight, but nothing came. The night was empty, and I was failing. Even my human vision was failing, night and starlight melting into a blur, like something seen through running water . . .

The sky itself was moving. The earth held still, but heaven itself was moving. The Galaxy gathered and narrowed into a shaft of light, then froze still as a stream in the bite of winter. A shaft of ice—no, a blade, it lay across the sky like a king's sword, with the great jewels blazing in the hilt. Emerald I saw, topaz, sapphires, which in the tongue of swords mean power and joy and justice and clean death.

For a long time the sword lay there, still, like a weapon newly burnished, waiting for the hand which will lift and wield it. Then, of itself, it moved. Not as a weapon is lifted in battle, or in ceremony, or sport. But as a blade slides home to its housing it slid, how gently, down towards the standing stone, dropping into it as a sword slips resting into its scabbard.

Then there was nothing but the empty field and the whistling wind, and a grey stone standing.

I woke to the darkness of the inn room, and a single star, small and bright, showing through a gap above the rafters. Below me the beasts breathed sweet breath, while all around were the snores and stirrings of the sleepers. The place smelt warmly of horses and peat smoke and hay and mutton stew.

I lay unmoving, flat on my back, watching the little star. I hardly thought about the dream. Vaguely, I remembered that there had been talk of a sword, and now this dream . . . But I let it pass me. It would come. I would be shown. God was back with me; time had not lied. And in an hour or two it would be morning.

The Search

Chapter One

The gods, all of them, must be accustomed to blasphemy. It is a blasphemy even to question their purposes, and to wonder, as I had done, who they were or if they even existed, is blasphemy itself. Now I knew my god was back with me, that his purpose was working, and though I still saw nothing clearly, I knew that his hand would be over me when the time was right, and I would be guided, driven, shown–it did not matter which, nor in what form he came. He would show me that, too. But not yet. Today was my own. The dreams of the night had vanished with the stars that made them. This morning the wind was only the wind, and the sunlight nothing but light.

I do not think I even looked back. I had no fear for Ralf or the child. The Sight may be an uncomfortable thing to possess, but foreknowledge of catastrophe relieves the possessor of the small frets of day to day. A man who has seen his own old age and bitter end does not fear what may come to him at twenty-two. I had no doubts about my own safety, or the boy's whose sword I had seen–twice now–drawn and shining. So I was free to dread nothing worse than the next sea voyage, which took me, suffering but alive, to the port of Massilia on the Inland Sea, and landed me there on a bright February day which, in Britain, we would have called summer.

Once there, it did not matter who saw me and reported meeting me. If it should be noised abroad that Prince Merlin had been seen in Southern Gaul, or Italy, then perhaps Uther's enemies would watch for me for a while, hoping for a lead to the vanished prince. Eventually they would give up and search elsewhere, but by that time the trail would be cold. In Kerrec the visit of the inconspicuous singer would be forgotten, and Ralf, quietly anonymous in the forest tavern, would be able to come and go without fear between Coll and the castle at Kerrec, with news of the child's progress for Hoel to transmit to me. So, once landed in Massilia, and recovered from my voyage, I set about making open preparations for my journey eastwards.

With no need this time for disguise, I travelled in comfort, if not in princely style. Appearances had never troubled me; a man makes his own; but I had friends to visit, and if I could not do them honour, at least I must not shame them. So I hired a body-servant and bought horses and baggage mules and a slave to look after them, and set off for my first destination, which was Rome.

The road out of Massilia is a straight, sun-beaten ribbon of white dust running along the shore where the villages built by Caesar's veterans crouch among their carefully tended olive groves and vines. We set out at sunrise, with our horses' shadows long behind us. The road was still dewed, and the air smelled of dung and peppery cypress and the smoke of the early fires. . Cockerels crowed and curs ran out yapping at our horses' heels. Behind me the two servants talked, low voiced, so as not to intrude on me. They seemed decent men; the freeman, Gaius, had seen service before, and came to me well recommended. The other, Stilicho, was the son of a Sicilian horse-dealer who had cheated himself into debt and sold his son to pay it. Stilicho was a thin, lively youth with a cheerful eye and unquenchable spirits. Gaius was solemn and efficient, and more conscious of my dignity than I had ever been myself. When he discovered my royal status he took on an aura of pomp which amused me, and impressed Stilicho into silence for almost twenty minutes. I believe that thereafter it was continually used as a threat or a bribe for service. Certainly, whatever means the two of them employed, I was to find my journey almost a miracle of smoothness and comfort.

Now, as my horse pricked his ears at the morning sun, I felt my mood lift to meet the growing brilliance. It was as if the griefs and doubts of the last year streamed back from me like my horse's shadow. As I set off eastwards with my little train I was for the first time in my life free; free of the world in front of me, and free of the obligations at my back. Until this moment I had lived always towards some goal; I had sought for and then served my father, and after his death had waited in grief until, with Arthur, my servitude might start again. Now the first part of my work was done; the boy was safe and, as my gods and my stars could be trusted, he would remain so. I was still young, and facing the sun, and, call it solitude or call it freedom, I had a new world in front of me and a span of time ahead when at last I could travel the lands of which as a boy I had been taught so much, and which I had longed to see.

So in time I came to Rome, and walked on the green hills between the cypresses, and talked with a man who had known my father when he was the age I was now. I lodged in his house, and wondered how I had ever thought my father's house in Kerrec a palace, or seen London as a great city, or even a city at all. Then from Rome to Corinth, and overland through the valleys of the Argolid where goats grazed the baked summer hills, and people lived, wilder than they, among the ruins of cities built by giants. Here at last I saw stones greater even than those in the Giants' Dance, lifted and set just as the songs had told me, and as I travelled further east I saw lands yet emptier with giant stones standing in desert sunlight, and men who lived as simply as roving wolf-packs, but who made songs as easily as birds, and as marvellously as the stars moving in their courses. Indeed, they know more about the movements of the stars than any other men; I suppose their world is made up of the empty spaces of the desert and the sky. I spent eight months with a man near Sardis, in Maeonia, who could calculate to a hair's breadth, and with whose help I could have lifted the Giants' Dance in half the time had it been twice as great. Another six months I spent on the coast of Mysia, near Pergamum, in a great hospital where sick men flock for treatment, rich and poor alike. I found much that was new to me there in the art of healing; in Pergamum they use music with the drugs to heal a man's mind through dreams, and his body after it. Truly the god must have guided me when he sent me to learn music as a child. And all the time, on all my journeys. I learnt smatterings of strange tongues, and heard new songs and new music, and saw strange gods worshipped, some in holy places, and some in manners we would call unclean. It is never wise to turn aside from knowing, however the knowing comes.

Through all this time I rested, steady and secure, in the knowledge that, back there in the Perilous Forest in Brittany, the child grew and thrived in safety.

Messages from Ralf came occasionally, sent by King Hoel to await me at certain prearranged ports of call. This way I learned that, as soon as might be, Ygraine was pregnant again. She was delivered in due time of a daughter, who was called Morgian. By the time I read them, the letters were of course long out of date, but as far as the boy Arthur was concerned I had my own more immediate source of reassurance. I watched, in the way I have, in the fire.

It was in a brazier lit against the chill of a Roman evening that I first watched Ralf make the journey through the forest to Hoel's court. He travelled alone and unremarked, and when he set out again in the misty dark to make for home he was not followed. In the depths of the forest I lost him, but later the smoke blew aside to show me his horse safely stabled, and Branwen smiling in the sunlit yard with the baby in her arms. Several times after that I watched Ralf's journey, but always smoke or darkness seemed to gather and lie like mist along the river, so that I could not see the tavern, or follow him through the door. It was as if, even from me, the place was guarded. I had heard it said that the Perilous Forest of Brittany was spell-bound land; I can affirm that this is true. I doubt if any magic less potent than mine could have spied through the wall of mist that hid the inn. Glimpses I had, no more than that, from time to time. Once, fleetingly, I saw the baby playing among a litter of puppies in the yard while the bitch licked his face and Brand looked on, grinning, till Moravik burst scolding out of her kitchen to snatch the child up, wipe his face with her apron, and vanish with him indoors. Another time I saw him perched aloft on Ralf's horse while it was drinking at the trough, and yet again astride the saddle in front of Ralf, hanging on to the mane with both hands while the beast trotted down to the river's edge. I never saw him closely, or even clearly, but I saw enough to know that he thrived and grew strong.

Then, when he was four years old, the time came when Ralf was to take him from the Forest's protection and seek Count Ector's.

The night his ship set sail from the Small Sea of Morbihan I was lying under a black Syrian sky where the stars seem to burn twice as big and ardent as the stars at home. The fire I watched was a shepherd's, lit against the wolves and mountain lions, and he had given me its hospitality when my servants and I were benighted crossing the heights above Berytus. The fire was stacked high with wind-dried wood, and blazed fiercely against the night. Somewhere beyond it I could hear Stilicho talking, then the rough mutter of the shepherd, and laughter shushed by Gaius' grave tones, till the roar and crackling of the fire drowned them. Then the pictures came, fragmentary at first, but as clear and vivid as the visions I had had as a boy in the crystal cave. I watched the whole journey, scene by scene, in one night's vision, as you can dream a lifetime between night and morning . . .

This was my first clear sight of Ralf since I had parted from him in Brittany. I hardly knew him. He was a tall young man now, with the look of a fighter, and an air of decision and responsibility that gave him weight and sat well on him. I had left it to Hoel's and his discretion whether or not an armed escort would be needed to convoy his 'wife and child' to the ship: in the event they played safe, though it was obvious that the secret was still our own. Hoel had contrived that a wagon-load of goods should be despatched through the Forest under the escort of half a dozen troopers; when it set off back towards Kerrec and the wharf where the ship lay, what more natural than that the young man and his family should travel back to Kerrec with the return load—I never saw what was in those corded bales—using its protection for themselves? Branwen rode in the wagon, and so, in the end, did Arthur. It looked to me as if he had already outgrown women's care; he would have spent all his time with the troopers, and it took Ralf's authority to make him ride concealed in the wagon with Branwen, rather than on the saddlebow at the head of the troop. After the little party had reached the ship and embarked safely, four of the troop took ship along with Ralf, apparently convoying those precious bales to their destination. So the ship set sail. Light glittered on the firelit sea, and the little ship had red sails which spread against a breezy sky of sunset, till they dwindled and vanished small in the blowing fire.

It was in a blaze of sunrise, perhaps lit only by the Syrian flames, that the ship docked at Glannaventa. I saw the ropes made fast and the party cross the gangplank to be met by Ector himself, brown and smiling, with a full-armed body of men. They bore no badge. They had brought a wagon for the cargo, but as soon as they were clear of the town the wagon was left to follow, while out of it came a litter for Branwen and Arthur, and then the party rode as fast as might be for Galava, up the military road through the mountains which lie between Ector's castle and the sea. The road climbs through two steep passes with between them a low-lying valley sodden with marsh, which is flooded right through till late spring. The road is bad, broken by storm and torrents and winter frosts, and in places where the hillsides had slipped in flood time the road has vanished, and all that remains of it are the ghosts of the old tracks that were there before the Romans came. Wild country and a wild road, but straight going on a May day for a body of well-armed men. I watched them trotting along, the litter swinging between its sturdy mules, through flame-lit dawn and fire-lit day, till suddenly with evening the mist rolled down dark from the head of the pass, and I saw in it the glitter of swords that spelled danger.

Ector's party was clattering downhill from the second summit, slowing to a walk at a steep place where crags crowded the edge of the road. From here it was only a short descent to the broad river valley and the good flat road to the waterhead where the castle stands. In the distance, still lit by evening, where the big trees and the blossoming orchards and the gentle green of the farmlands. But up in the pass among the grey crags and the rolling mist it was dark, and the horses slipped and stumbled on a steep scree where a torrent drove across the way and the road had collapsed into the water's bed. The rush of water must have blanketed all other sound from them. No one saw, dim behind the mist, the other men waiting, mounted and armed.

Count Ector was at the head of the troop, and in the middle of it, surrounded, the litter lurched and swung between its mules with Ralf riding close beside it. They were approaching the ambush; were beside it. I saw Ector's head turn sharply, then he checked his horse so suddenly that it tried to rear and instead plunged, slipping on the scree as Ector's sword flashed out and his arm went up. The troopers, surrounding the litter as best they might on the rushing slope, stood to fight. At the moment of clashing, shouting attack I saw what none of the troop appeared yet to have seen, other shadows riding down out of the mist beyond the crags.

I believe I shouted. I made no sound, but I saw Ralf's head go up like a hound's at his master's whistle. He yelled, wheeling his horse. Men wheeled with him, and met the new attack with a crash and flurry that sent sparks up from the swords like a smith's hammer from the anvil.

I strained my eyes through the visionary firelight to see who the attackers were. But I could not see. The wrestling, clashing darkness, the sparkling swords, the shouting, the wheeling horses—then the attackers vanished into the mist as suddenly as they had come, leaving one of their number dead on the scree, and carrying another bleeding across a saddle.

There was nothing to be gained by pursuing them across mountains thick with the misty twilight. One of the troopers picked up the fallen man and flung him across a horse. I saw Ector point, and the trooper searched the body, looking, apparently, for identification, but finding none. Then the guard formed again round the litter, and rode on. I saw Ralf, surreptitious, winding a rag round his left arm where a blade had hacked in past the shield. A moment later I saw him, laughing, stoop in the saddle to say through the curtains of the litter: 'Well, but you're not grown yet. Give it a year or two, and I promise you we'll find you a sword to suit your size.' Then he reached to pull the leather curtains of the litter close. When I strained my sight to see Arthur, smoke blew grey across the scene and the shepherd called something to his dog, and I was back on the scented hillside with the moon coming out above the ruins of the temple where nothing remains now of the Goddess but her night-owls brooding.

So the years passed, and I used my freedom in travels which I have told of in other places; there is no room for them here. For me they were rich years, and lightly borne, and the god's hand lay gently on me, so that I saw all I asked to see: but in all the time there was no message, no moving star, nothing to call me home.

Then one day, when Arthur was six years old, the message came to me near Pergamum, where I was teaching and working in the hospital.

It was early spring, and all day rain had been falling like whips on the streaming rock, darkening the white limestone and tearing ruts in the pathway which leads down to the hospital cells by the sea. I had no fire to bring me the vision, but in that place the gods stand waiting by every pillar, and the air is heavy with dreams. This was only a dream, the same as other men's, and came in a moment of exhausted sleep.

A man had been carried in late in the night, with a leg badly gashed and the life starting to pump out of the great vein. I and the other doctor on duty had worked over him for more than three hours, and afterwards I had gone out into the sea to wash off the blood which had gushed thick and then hardened on me. It was possible that the patient would live; he was young, and slept now with the blood staunched and the wound safely stitched. I stripped off my soaked loin-cloth—that climate allows one to work near naked on the bloodier jobs—swam till I was clean, then stretched on the still warm sand to rest. The rain had stopped with evening, and the night was calm and warm and full of stars.

It was no vision I had, but a kind of dream of wakefulness. I lay (as I thought) open-eyed, watching, and watched by, the bright swarm. Among that fierce host of stars was one distant one, cloudy, its light faint among the others like a lamp in a swirl of snow. Then it swam closer, closer still, till its clouded air blotted out the brighter stars, and I saw mountains and shore, and rivers running like the veins of a leaf through the valleys of my own country. Now the snow swirled thicker, hiding the valleys, and behind the snow was the growl of thunder, and the shouting of armies, and the sea rose till the shore dissolved, and salt ran up the rivers and the green fields bleached to grey, and blackened to desert with their veins showing like dead men's bones.

I woke knowing that I must go back. It was not yet, the flood, but it was coming. By the next snow-time, or the next, we would hear the thunder, and I must be there, between the King and his son.

Chapter Two

I had planned to go home by Constantinopolis, and letters had already gone ahead of me. Now I would have preferred to take a quicker way, but the only ship I could get was one plying north close inshore towards Chalcedon, which lies just across the straight from Constantinopolis. Arrived here, delayed by freakish winds and uncertain weather, luck still seemed against me; I had just missed a westbound ship, they told me, and there was no other due to leave for a week or more. From Chalcedon the trade is mostly small coastbound craft; the bigger shipping uses the great harbour of Constantinopolis. So I took the ferry over, not averse, in spite of the need I felt for haste, to seeing the city of which I had heard so much.

I had expected the New Rome to surpass the old Rome in magnificence, but found Constantine's city a place of sharper contrasts, with squalor crowding close behind the splendour, and that air of excitement and risk which is breathed in a young city looking forward to prosperity, still building, spreading, assimilating, and avid to grow rich.

Not that the foundation was new; it had been capital of Byzantium since Byzas had settled his folk there a thousand years before; but it was almost a century and a half now since the Emperor Constantine had moved the heart of the empire eastwards, and started to build and fortify the old Byzantium and call it after himself.

Constantinopolis is a city marvellously situated on a tongue of land which holds a natural harbour they call the Golden Horn; and rightly; I had never imagined such a traffic of richly laden ships as I saw in the brief crossing from Chalcedon. There are palaces and rich houses, and government buildings with corridors like a maze and the countless officials employed by the government coming and going like bees in a hive. Everywhere there are gardens, with pavilions and pools, and fountains constantly gushing; the city has an abundance of sweet water. To the landward side Constantine's Wall defends the city, and from its Golden Gate the great thoroughfare of the Mesé runs, magnificently arcaded through most of its length, through three fora decorated with columns, to end at the great triumphal arch of Constantine. The Emperor's immense church dedicated to the Holy Wisdom sits high over the walls that edge the sea. It was a magnificent city, and a splendid capital, but it had not the air of Rome as my father had spoken of it, or as we had thought of it in Britain; this was still the East, and the city looked to the East. Even the dress, though men wore the Roman tunic and mantle, had the look of Asia, and, though Latin was spoken everywhere, I heard Greek and Syrian and Armenian in the markets, and once beyond the arcades of the Mesé you might have supposed yourself in Antioch.

It is a place not easy to picture, if one has never been beyond Britain's shores. Above everything it was exciting, with an air full of promise. It was a city looking forward, where Rome and Athens and even Antioch had seemed to be looking back; and London, with its crumbling temples and patched-up towers and men always watching with their hands to their swords, seemed as remote and near as savage as the ice-lands of the northmen.

My host in Constantinopolis was a connection of my father's, distant, but not too distant to let him greet me as cousin. He was descended from one Adean, brother-in-law of Maximus, who had been one of Maximus's officers and had followed him on the final expedition to Rome. Adean had been wounded outside Rome and left for dead, but rescued and nursed back to health by a Christian family. Later he had married the daughter of the house, turned Christian, and though he never took service with the Eastern Emperor (being content with the pardon granted him through his father-in-law's intercession) his son entered the service of Theodosius II, made a fortune at it, and was rewarded with a royally connected wife and a splendid house near the Golden Horn.

His great-grandson bore the same name, but pronounced it with the accent of Byzantium; Ahdjan. He was still discernibly of Celtic descent, but looked, you might say, like a Welshman gone bloodless by being drawn too high towards the sun. He was tall and thin, with the oval face and pale skin, and the black eyes set straight, that you see in all their portraits. His mouth was thin-lipped, bloodless too; the court servant's mouth, close-lipped with keeping secrets. But he was not without humour, and could talk wisely and entertainingly, a rarity in a country where men—and women—argue perpetually about matters of the spirit in terms of the more than stupid flesh. I had not been in Constantinopolis half a day before I found myself remembering something I had read in a book of Galapas': 'If you ask someone how many obols a certain thing costs, he replies by dogmatising on the born and unborn. If you ask the price of bread, they answer you, the Father is greater than the Son, and the Son is subordinate to Him. If you ask is my bath ready, they answer you, the Son has been made out of nothing.'

Ahdjan received me very kindly, in a splendid room with mosaics on the walls and a floor of golden marble. In Britain, where it is cold, we put the pictures on the floor and hang thick coverings over walls and doors; but they do things differently in the East. This room glittered with colour; they use a lot of gold in their mosaics, and with the faintly uneven surface of the tesserae this has the effect of glimmering movement, as if the wall-pictures were tapestries of silk. The figures are alive, and full of colour, some of them very beautiful. I remembered the cracked mosaic at home in Maridunum, which as a child I had thought the most wonderful picture in the world; it had been of Dionysos, with grapes and dolphins, but none of the pictures was whole, and the god's eyes had been badly mended, and showed a cast. To this day I see Dionysos with a squint. One side of Ahdjan's room opened to a terrace where a fountain played in a wide marble pool, and cypress and laurel grew in pots along the balustrade. Below this the garden lay, scented in the sun, with rose and iris and jasmine (though it was hardly into April) competing with the scent of a hundred shrubs, and everywhere the dark fingers of cypress, gilded with tiny cones, pointing straight at the brilliant sky. Below the terraces sparkled the waters of the Horn, as thickly populated with ships as a farm pond at home is with water-beetles.

There was a letter waiting for me, from Ector. After Ahdjan and I had exchanged greetings, I asked his leave, then unrolled and read it.

Ector's scribe wrote well, though in long periods which I knew were a gloss on what that forthright gentleman had actually said. But the news, sorted out from the poetry and the perorations, bore out what I already knew or suspected. In more than guarded phrases he conveyed to me that Arthur (for the scribe's sake he wrote of 'the family, Drusilla and both the boys') was safe. But for how long 'the place' might be safe, said Ector, he could not guess, and went on to give me the news as his informers reported it.

The danger of invasion, always there but for the last few years sporadic, had begun to grow into something more formidable. Octa and Eosa, the Saxon leaders defeated by Uther in the first year of his reign, and kept prisoner since then in London, were still safely held; but lately pressure had been brought to bear—not only by the Federates, but by some British leaders who were afraid of the growing discontent along the Saxon Shore—on King Uther to free the Saxon princes on terms of treaty. Since he had refused this, there had been two armed attempts to release them from prison. These had been punished with brutal severity, and now other factions were pressing Uther to kill the Saxon leaders out of hand; a course he was apparently afraid to take for fear of the Federates. These, firmly ensconced along the Shore, and crowding too close for comfort even to London, were again showing threatening signs of inviting reinforcements from abroad, and pressing up into the rich country near Ambrosius' Wall. Meanwhile there were worse rumours: a messenger had been caught, and under torture had confessed, that he carried tokens of friendship from the Angles on the Abus in the east, to the Pictish kings of the wild land west of Strathclyde. But nothing more, added Ector, than tokens; and he personally did not think that trouble could yet come from the north. Between Strathclyde and the Abus, the kingdoms of Rheged and Lothian still stood firm.

I skimmed through the rest, then rolled up the letter. 'I must go straight home,' I told Ahdjan.

'So soon? I was afraid of it.' He signed to a servant, who lifted a silver flagon from a bowl of snow, and poured the wine into glass goblets. Where the snow had come from I did not know; they have it carried by night from the hilltops, and stored underground in straw. 'I'm sorry to lose you, but when I saw the letter, I was afraid it might be bad news.'

'Not bad yet, but there will be bad to come.' I told him what I could of the situation, and he listened gravely. They understand these things in Constantinopolis. Since Alaric the Goth took Rome, men's ears are tuned to listen for the thunder in the north. I went on: 'Uther is a strong king and a good general, but even he cannot be everywhere, and this division of power makes men uncertain and afraid. It's time the succession was made sure.' I tapped the letter. 'Ector tells me the Queen is with child again.'

'So I had heard. If this is a boy he'll be declared the heir, won't he? Hardly a time for a baby to inherit a kingdom, unless he had a Stilicho to look after his interests.' He was referring to the general who had protected the empire of the young Emperor Honorius. 'Has Uther anyone among his generals who could be left as regent if he were killed?'

'For all I know they'd be as likely to kill as to protect.'

'Well, Uther had better live, then, or allow the son he's already got to be his legitimate heir. He must be–what? Seven? Eight? Why cannot Uther do the sensible thing and declare him again, with you to become regent if the King should be killed during the boy's minority?' He looked at me sideways over his glass. 'Come, Merlin, don't raise your brows at me like that. The whole world knows you took the child from Tintagel and have him hidden somewhere.'

'Does the world say where?'

'Oh, yes. The world spawns solutions the way that pool yonder spawns frogs. The general opinion is that the child is safe in the island of Hy-Brasil, nursed by the white paps of nine queens, no less. It's no wonder he flourishes. Or else that he is with you, but invisible. Disguised perhaps as a pack-mule?'

I laughed. 'How would I dare? What would that make Uther?'

'You'd dare anything, I think. I was hoping you'd dare tell me where the boy is, and all about him . . . No?'

I shook my head, smiling. 'Forgive me, but not yet.'

He moved a hand gracefully. They understand secrets, too, in Constantinopolis. 'Well, at least you can tell me if he's safe and well?'

'I assure you of it.'

'And will succeed, with you as regent?'

I laughed, shook my head, and drained my wine. He signalled to the slave, who was standing out of hearing, and the man hurried to refill my glass. Ahdjan waved him away. 'I've had a letter, too, from Hoel. He tells me that King Uther has sent men in search of you, and that he doesn't speak of you with kindness, though everyone knows how much he owes you. There are rumours, too, that even the King himself does not know where his son is hidden, and has spies out searching. Some say the boy is dead. There are also those who say that you keep the young prince close for your own ambitious ends.'

'Yes,' I agreed equably, 'there would be some who say that.'

'You see?' He threw out a hand. 'I try to goad you into speaking, and you are not even angry. Where another man would protest, would even fear to go back, you say nothing, and—I'm afraid—decide to take ship straight for home.'

'I know the future, Ahdjan, that's the difference.'

'Well, I don't know the future, and it's obvious you won't tell me, but I can make my own guess at the truth. What men are saying is just that truth twisted: you keep the boy close because you know he must one day be King. You can tell me this, though. What will you do when you get back? Bring him out of hiding?'

'By the time I get back the Queen's child should be born,' I said. 'What I do must depend on that. I shall see Uther, of course, and talk to him. But the main thing, as I see it, is to let the people of Britain know—friend and enemy alike—that Prince Arthur is alive and thriving, and will be ready to show himself beside his father when the time comes.'

'And that's not yet?'

'I think not. When I reach home I hope I shall see more clearly. With your leave, Ahdjan, I'll take the first ship.'

'As you will, of course. I shall be sorry to lose your company.'

'I regret it, too. It's been a happy chance that brought me after all to Constantinopolis. I might have missed seeing you, but I was delayed by bad weather and lost the ship I should have got at Chalcedon.'

He said something civil, then looked startled as he saw the implications. 'Delayed? You mean you were on your way home already? Before you saw the letter? You knew?'

'No details. Only that it was time I was home.'

'By the Three!' For a moment I had seen the Celt looking out of his eyes, though it was the Christian god that he swore by; they only have one other oath in Constantinopolis, and that is 'By the One', and they fight to the death over them. Then he laughed. 'By the Three! I wish I'd had you beside me last week in the Hippodrome! I lost a cool thousand on the Greens—a sure thing, you'd have sworn, and they ran like three-legged cows. Well, it seems that whatever prince has you to guide him, he's lucky. If *he* had had you, I might have had an empire today, instead of a respectable government post—and lucky to get that without being a eunuch besides.'

He nodded as he spoke at the great mosaic on the main wall of the room behind us. I had noticed it already, and wondered vaguely at the Byzantine strain of melancholy which decorates a room with such scenes instead of the livelier designs one sees in Greece and Italy. I had already observed, in the entrance hall, a crucifix done life-size with mourning figures and Christian devices all round it. This, too, was an execution, but a noble one, on the battlefield. The sky was dark, done with chips of slate and lapis hammered into clouds like iron, with among them the staring heads of gods. The horizon showed a line of towers and temples with a crimson sun setting behind. It seemed meant to be Rome. The wide plain in front of the walls was the scene of the battle's end: to the left the defeated host, men and horses dead or dying on a field scattered with broken weapons: to the right the victors, clustered behind the crowned leader, and bathed in a shaft of light descending from a Christ poised in blessing above the other gods. At the victor's feet the other leader knelt, his neck bared to the executioner's blade. He was lifting both arms towards his conqueror, not for mercy, but in formal surrender of the sword which lay across his hands. Below him, in the corner of the picture, was written *Max.* On the right, below the victor, were stamped the words *Theod. Imp.*

'By the One!' I said, and saw Ahdjan smile; but he could not have known what had brought me so quickly to my feet. He rose gracefully and followed me to the wall, obviously pleased at my interest.

'Yes, Maximus' defeat by the Emperor. Good, isn't it?' He smoothed a hand over the silken tesserae. 'The man who did it can't have known much of the ironies of war. In spite of all this, you might say it came out even enough in the end. That hang-dog fellow on the left behind Maximus is Hoel's ancestor, the one who took the remnants of the British contingent home. This holy-looking gentleman shedding blood all over the Emperor's feet is my great-great-grandfather, to whose conscience and good business sense I owe both my fortune and the saving of my soul.'

I hardly listened. I was staring at the sword in Maximus' hand. I had seen it before. Glowing on the wall behind Ygraine. Flashing home to its scabbard in Brittany. Now here, the third time, imaged in Maximus' hand outside the walls of Rome.

Ahdjan was watching me curiously. 'What is it?'

'The sword. So it was his sword.'

'What was? Have you seen it, then?'

'No. Only in a dream. Twice, I've seen it in dreams. Now here for the third time, in a picture . . .' I spoke half to myself, musing. Sunlight, striking up off the pool on the terrace, sent light rippling across the wall, so that the sword shimmered in Macsen's hands, and the jewels in its hilt showed green and yellow and vivid blue. I said, softly: 'So that is why I missed the ship at Chalcedon.'

'What do you mean?'

'Forgive me, I hardly know. I was thinking of a dream. Tell me, Ahdjan, this picture . . . Are those the walls of Rome? Maximus wasn't murdered at Rome, surely?'

'Murdered?' Ahdjan, speaking primly, looked amused. 'The word on our side of the family is "executed". No, it wasn't at Rome. I think the artist was being symbolic. It happened at Aquileia. You may not know it; it's a small place near the mouth of the Turrus river, at the northern end of the Adriatic.'

'Do ships call there?'

His eyes widened. 'You mean to go?'

'I would like to see the place where Macsen died. I would like to know what became of his sword.'

'You won't find that at Aquileia,' he said. 'Kynan took it.'

'*Who?*'

He nodded at the picture. 'The man on the left. Hoel's ancestor, who took the British back home to Brittany. Hoel could have told you.' He laughed at my expression. 'Did you come all this way for that piece of information?'

'It seems so,' I said, 'though until this moment I didn't know it. Are you telling me that Hoel has that sword? It's in Brittany?'

'No. It was lost long since. Some of the men who went home to Greater Britain took his things with them; I suppose they would have taken his sword to give his son.'

'And?'

'That's all I know. It's a long time ago, and all it is now is a family tale, and the half of it's probably not true. Does it matter so much?'

'Matter?' I said. 'I hardly know. But I've learnt to look close at most things that come my way.'

He was watching me with a puzzled look, and I thought he would question me further, but after a short hesitation he said merely: 'I suppose so. Will you walk out now into the garden? It's cooler. You looked as if your head hurt you.'

'That? It was nothing. Someone playing a lyre on the terrace down there. It isn't in tune.'

'My daughter. Shall we go down and stop her?'

On the way down he told me of a ship due to leave the Horn in two days' time. He knew the master, and could bespeak me a passage. It was a fast ship, and would dock at Ostia, whence I would certainly find a vessel plying westwards.

'What about your servants?'

'Gaius is a good man. You could do worse than employ him yourself. I freed Stilicho. He's yours if he'll stay, and he's a wizard with horses. It would be cruelty for me to take him to Britain; his blood's as thin as an Arabian gazelle's.'

But when the morning came Stilicho was there at the quayside, stubborn as the mules he had handled with such skill, his belongings in a stitched sack, and a cloak of sheepskin sweltering round him in the Byzantine sun. I argued with him, traducing even the British climate, and my simple way of living which he might find tolerable in a country where the sun shines, but would be hardship itself in that land of icy winds and wet. But, seeing finally that he would have his way even if he paid his own passage with the money I had given him as a parting gift, I gave way.

To tell the truth I was touched, and glad to have his company on the long voyage home. Though he had had none of Gaius' training as a body-servant, he was quick and intelligent, and had already shown skill in helping me with plants and medicines. He would be useful, and besides, after all these years away life at Bryn Myrddin looked a little lonelier than it had used to, and I knew well that Ralf would never come back to me.

Chapter Three

It was late summer when I reached Britain. Fresh news met me on the quay, in the person of one of the King's chamberlains, who greeted me with passionate relief, and such a total absence of surprise that I told him: 'You should be in my business.'

He laughed. He was Lucan, whom I had known well when my father was King, and he and I were on terms. 'Soothsaying? Hardly. This is the fifth ship I've met. I own I expected you, but I never thought to see you so soon. We heard you went east a long while back, and we sent messengers, hoping to reach you. Did they find you?'

'No. But I was already on my way.'

He nodded, as if I had confirmed his thoughts. He had been too close to my father, Ambrosius, to question the power that guided me. 'You knew the King was sick, then?'

'Not that, no. Only that the times were dangerous, and I should get home. Uther ill? That's grave news. What's the sickness?'

'A wound gone bad. You knew he's been seeing to the rebuilding of the Saxon Shore defences, and training the troops there himself? Well, an alarm was raised about longships up the Thames—they'd been seen level with Vagniacae—too near London for comfort. A small foray, nothing serious, but he was first into it as usual, and got a cut, and the wound didn't heal. This was two months since, and he's still in pain, and losing flesh.'

'Two months? Hasn't his own physician been attending him?'

'Indeed yes. Gandar's been there from the beginning.'

'And he could do nothing?'

'Well,' said Lucan, 'according to him the King was mending, and he says—along with the other doctors who've been consulted—that there's nothing to fear. But I've watched them conferring in corners, and Gandar looks worried.' He glanced at me sideways. 'There's a kind of uneasiness—you might even call it apprehension—infecting the whole court, and it's going to be hard to keep it contained there. I don't have to tell you, it's a bad time for the country to doubt if their leader's going to be fit to lead them. In fact, rumours have started already. You know the King can't have the bellyache without a scare of poison; and now they whisper about spells and hauntings. And not without reason; the King looks, sometimes, like a man who walks with ghosts. It was time you came home.'

We were already moving along the road from the port. The horses had been there ready saddled at the quayside, and an escort waiting; this more for ceremony than for safety; the road to London is well-travelled and guarded. It occurred to me that perhaps the armed men who rode with us were there, not to see that I came to the King unharmed, but that I came there at all.

I said as much, drily, to Lucan. 'It seems the King wants to make sure of me.'

He looked amused, but only said with his courtier's smoothness: 'Perhaps he was afraid that you might not care to attend him. Shall we say that a physician who fails to cure a king does not always add to his reputation.'

'Does not always survive, you mean. I trust poor Gandar's still alive?'

'So far.' He paused, then said neutrally: 'Not that I'm much of a judge, but I'd have said it's not the King's body that lacks a cure, but his mind.'

'So it's my magic that's wanted?' He was silent. I added: 'Or his son?'

His eyelids drooped. 'There are rumours about him, too.'

'I'm sure there are.' My voice was as bland as his. 'One piece of news I did hear on my travels, that the Queen was pregnant again. I reckon she should have been brought to bed a month ago. What is the child?'

'It was a son, stillborn. They say that it was this sent the King out of his mind, and fevered his wound again. And now there are rumours that the eldest son is dead, too. In fact some say he died in infancy, that there is no son.' He paused. His gaze was fixed on his horse's ears, but there was the faintest of queries in his voice.

'Not true, Lucan,' I said. 'He's alive, a fine boy, and growing fast. Don't be afraid, he'll be there when he's needed.'

'Ah.' It was a long exhalation of relief. 'Then it's true he's with you! This is the news that will heal the kingdom, if not the King. You'll bring the boy to London now?'

'First I must see the King. After that, who knows?'

A courtier knows when a subject has been turned, and Lucan asked no more questions, but began to talk of more general news. He told me in more detail what I had already learned from Ector's letters; Ector had certainly not exaggerated the situation. I took care not to ask too many questions about the possible danger in the north, but Lucan spoke of it himself, of the manning of strongpoints north of Rheged along the old line of Hadrian's Wall, and then of Lot's contribution to the defence of the north-east. 'He's making hard going of it. Not because the raids are bad—the place has been quiet lately—but perhaps because of that very fact. The small kings don't trust Lot; they say he's a hard man and niggardly with spoils, and cares little for any interests except his own. When they see there's no fighting to be done yet, and nothing to win, they desert him wholesale and take their men home to till the fields.' He made a sound of contempt, as near to a snort as a courtier ever gets. 'Fools, not to see that whether they like their commander or not, they'll have no fields to till, nor families to till them for, unless they fight.'

'But Lot's whole interest lies in his alliances, especially to the southward. I suppose that that with Rheged is safe enough? Why do his allies distrust him? Do they suspect him of lining his own nest at their expense? Or perhaps of something worse?'

'That I can't tell you.' His voice was wooden.

'Is there no one else Uther can appoint as commander in the north?'

'Not unless he goes himself. He can't demote Lot. His daughter is promised to him.'

I said, startled: 'His daughter? Do you mean that Lot accepted Morgause after all?'

'Not Morgause, no,' said Lucan. 'I doubt that marriage wasn't tempting enough for Lothian, for all the girl's turned out such a beauty. Lot's an ambitious man, he'd not dangle after a bastard when there was a true-born princess to be had. I meant the Queen's daughter; Morgian.'

'*Morgian?* But she can hardly be five years old!'

'Nevertheless, she's promised, and you know that's binding between kings.'

'If I don't, who should?' I said drily, and Lucan knew what I was thinking of: my own mother who had borne me to Ambrosius with no bond but a promise made in secret; and my father who had let the promise bind him as securely as a ceremonial oath.

We came in sight of London Wall, and the traffic of the morning market thronged about us. Lucan had given me plenty to think about, and I was glad when the escort closed up, and he was silent, and left me to my thoughts.

I had expected to find Uther attended, and about some at least of his affairs, but he was still keeping his own chamber, and alone.

As I was led through the antechambers towards his room I saw nobles, officers, and servants all waiting, and there was an apprehensive quiet about the crowded rooms which told its own tale. Men conferred in small groups, low-voiced and worried, the servants looked nervous and edgy, and in the outer corridors, where merchants and petitioners waited, there was the patient despondency of men who have already passed the point of hope.

Heads turned as I went through, and I heard the whisper run ahead of me like wind through a waste land, and a Christian bishop, forgetting himself, said audibly: 'God be praised! Now we'll see the spell lifted.' One or two men whom I knew started forward with warm greetings, and a spate of questions ready, but I smiled and shook my head and went through with no more than a quick word. And since with kings one can never quite rule out the thought of malice or murder, I checked the faces that I knew: somewhere in this crowd of armed and jewelled lords there might be one who would not welcome my return to the King's side; someone who watched for Uther to fail before his son was grown; someone who was Arthur's enemy, and therefore mine.

Some of them I knew well, but even these, as I greeted them, I studied. The leaders from Wales, Ynyr of Guent, Mador and Gwilim from my own country of Dyfed. Not Maelgon himself from Gwynedd, but one of his sons, Cunedda. Beside them, with a handful of their countrymen, Brychan and Cynfelin from Dyfnaint, and Nentres of Garlot, whom I had watched ride out with Uther from Tintagel. Then the men from the north; Ban of Benoic, a big, handsome man so dark that he might have been, like Ambrosius and myself, a descendant of the Spaniard Maximus. Beside Ban stood his cousin from Brittany, whose name I could not recall. Then Cadwy and Bors, two of the petty kings from Rheged, neighbours of Ector's; and another neighbour, Arrak, one of the numerous sons of Caw of Strathclyde. These I marked carefully, recalling what I knew of them. Nothing of importance yet, but I would remember, and watch. Rheged himself I did not see, nor Lot; it was to be assumed that their affairs in the north were more pressing even than the King's illness. But Urien, Lot's brother-in-law, was here, a thin, red-haired man with the light blue eyes and high colour of temper; and Tudwal of Dinpelydr, who ran with him; and his blood-brother Aguisel, of whose private doings in his cold fortress near Bremenium I had heard strange tales.

There were others I did not know, and these I scanned briefly as I passed them. I could find out later who they were, from Lucan, or from Caius Valerius, who stood over near the King's door. Beside Valerius was a young man I thought I should recognise; a strongly built, sunburned man of twenty or so, with a face that I found faintly familiar. I could not place him. He watched me from his stance near Uther's doorway, but he neither spoke nor made any sign of greeting. I said under my breath to Lucan: 'The youth near the door, by Valerius. Who is he?'   .

'Cador of Cornwall.'

I knew it now, the face I had last seen watching by Gorlois' body in the midnight hall of Dimilioc. And with the same look; the chill blue eyes, the frowning bar of brows, the warrior's face grown with the years more than ever like his father's and every whit as formidable.

Perhaps I needed to look no further. Of all those present he had most reason to hate me. And he was here, though Lucan had told me he was commander of the Irish Shore. In Rheged's absence, and Lot's, I supposed that he was the nearest there to Uther, except only myself.

I had to pass within a yard of him to get to the door of the King's room. I held his eyes deliberately, and he returned my look, but neither saluted nor bent his head. The blue eyes were cold and impassive. Well, I thought, as I greeted Valerius beside him, we should see. No doubt I could find out from Uther why he was here. And how much, if the King failed to recover, the young Duke stood to gain.

Lucan had gone in to tell the King of my arrival. Now he came out again and beckoned me forward. On his heels came Gandar. I would have paused to speak with him, but he shook his head quickly.

'No. He wants you to go straight in. By the Snake, Merlin, I'm glad to see you! But have a care . . . There, he's calling. A word with you later?'

'Of course. I'll be grateful.'

There was another, peremptory call from inside the room. Gandar's eyes, heavy with worry, met mine again briefly as he stood aside to let me pass. The servant shut the door behind us and left me with the King.

Chapter Four

He was up, and dressed in a house robe open at the front, with beneath it a tunic girded by a jewelled belt with a long dagger thrust through. His sword, the King's sword Falar, lay across its hangers below the gilded dragon that climbed the wall behind the bed. Though it was still summer there had been through the night a chill breeze from the north, and I was glad—my blood thin, I suppose, from my travels—to see a brazier glowing red on the empty hearth, with chairs set near.

He came quickly across the room to greet me, and I saw that he limped. As I answered his greeting I studied his face for signs of the sickness or distraction that I had been led to expect. He was thinner than before, with new lines to his face which made him look nearer fifty than forty (which was his age), and I saw that drawn look under the eyes which is one of the signs of long-gnawing pain or sleeplessness. But apart from the slight limp he moved easily enough, and with all the restless energy I remembered. And his voice was the same as ever, strong and quick with arrogant decision.

'There's wine there. We will serve ourselves. I want to talk to you alone. Sit down.'

I obeyed him, pouring the wine and handing him a goblet. He took it, but set it down without drinking, and seated himself across from me, pulling the robe about his knees with an abrupt, almost angry gesture. I noticed that he did not look at me, but at the brazier, at the floor, at the goblet, anywhere not to meet my eyes. He spoke with the same abruptness, wasting no time on civilities about my journey. 'They will have told you that I have been ill.'

'I understood you still were,' I said. 'I'm glad to see you on your feet and so active. Lucan told me about the skirmish at Vagniacae; I understand it's about two months now since you were wounded?'

'Yes. It was nothing much, a spear glancing, not deep. But it festered, and took a long time to heal.'

'It's healed now?'

'Yes.'

'Does it still pain you?'

'No.'

He almost snapped the word, pushing himself suddenly back in his chair to sit upright with his hands clenched on the arms, and his eyes on mine at last. It was the hard blue gaze I remembered, showing nothing but anger and dislike. But now I recognised both look and manner for what they were, those of a man driven against his will to ask help where he had sworn never again to ask it. I waited.

'How is the boy?'

If the sudden question surprised me, I concealed it. Though I had told Hoel and Ector that the King need only be told of the child's whereabouts if he demanded to know, it had seemed wise to send reports from time to time—couched in phrases that no one but the King would understand—of the boy's health and progress. Since Arthur had been at Galava the reports had gone to Hoel, and thence to Uther; nothing was to pass directly between Galava and the King. Hoel had written to me that, in all the years, Uther had made no direct enquiry about the boy. It was to be inferred that now he had no idea of his son's whereabouts.

I said: 'You should have had a report since the last one I saw. Has it not come?'

'Not yet. I wrote myself a month ago to ask Hoel where the boy was. He has not replied.'

'Perhaps his answer went to Tintagel, or to Winchester.'

'Perhaps. Or perhaps he is not prepared to answer my question?'

I raised my brows. 'Why not? It was always understood, surely, that the secrecy should not extend to you. Has he refused to answer you before?'

He said coldly, disconcerted and covering it: 'I did not ask. There has been no need before.'

This told me something beyond what I already knew. The King had only felt the need to locate Arthur since the Queen's last miscarriage. I had been right in thinking that, if she had given him other sons, he would have preferred to forget the 'bastard' in Brittany. It also told me something I did not like: if he felt a need for Arthur now, this summons might be to tell me that my guardianship was ended before it had really begun.

To give myself time, I ignored what he had just said. 'Then depend upon it, Hoel's answer is on its way. In any case it doesn't matter, since I am here to answer you instead.'

His look was still stony, allowing no guesses. 'They tell me you have been abroad all these years. Did you take him with you?'

'No. I thought it better to keep away from him till the time came when I could be of use to him. I made sure of his safety, then after I had left Brittany I kept close touch.' I smiled slightly. 'Oh, nothing that your spies could have seen . . . or any other man's. You know I have ways of my own. I took no risks. If you yourself have no inkling now of his whereabouts, you may be sure that no one else has.'

I saw from the brief flicker in his eyes before the lids veiled them that I had guessed rightly: messages, and constant reports of my movements had been sent back to him. No doubt, wherever he could, he had had me watched. It was no more than I expected. Kings live by information. Uther's enemies had probably watched me, too, and perhaps the King's own informants might have picked up some kind of lead to them. But when I asked him about this, he shook his head. He was silent for a while, following some private track of his own. He had not looked at me again. He reached for the goblet at his elbow, but not to drink; he fidgeted with it, turning it round and round where it stood. 'He'll be seven years old now.'

'Eight this coming Christmas, and strong for his age and well doing. You need have no fears for him, Uther.'

'You think not?' Another flash, of bitterness stronger than any anger. In spite of my outward calmness I felt a violent moment of apprehension: if, contrary to appearances, the King's sickness was in fact mortal, what chance would the boy have at the head of this kingdom now, with half the petty kings (I saw Cador's face again) at his throat? And how was even I to know, through the light and the smoke, what the god's smile portended?

'You think not?' said the King again. I saw his finger-bones whiten where he held the goblet, and wondered that the thin silver did not crush. 'When we last spoke together, Merlin, I asked a service of you, and I have no doubt it has been faithfully performed. I believe that service has almost reached its end. No, listen to me!' This though I had not spoken, nor even taken breath to speak. He talked like a man in a corner, attacking before he is even in danger. 'I don't have to remind you what I said to you before, nor do I have to ask if you obeyed me. Wherever you have kept the boy, however you have trained him, I take it he is ignorant of his birth and standing, but that he is fit to come to me and stand before all men as a prince and my heir.'

The blood ran fizzing-hot and thin under my skin in a flush I could feel. 'Are you trying to tell me that you think the time has come?'

I had forgotten to school my voice. The silver goblet went back on the table with a rap. The angry blue eyes came back to me. 'A king does not "try to tell" his servants what they must do, Merlin.'

I dropped my eyes with an effort and slowly, deliberately unclenched the apprehension that gripped me, the way one levers open the jaws of a fighting dog. I felt his angry stare on me, and heard the breath whistle through his pinched nostrils. Make Uther really angry, and it might take me years to fight my way back to the boy's side. I was aware in the silence that he shifted in his chair as if in sudden discomfort. In a breath or two I was able to look up and say: 'Then supposing you tell me, King, whether you sent for me to discuss your health, or your son. Either way, I am still your servant.'

He stared at me in rigid silence, then his brow slowly cleared, and his mouth relaxed into something like amusement. 'Whatever you are, Merlin, you are hardly that. And you were right; I am trying to tell you something, something which concerns both my health and my son. By the Scorpion, why can I not find the words? I have sent for you not to demand my son of you, but to tell you that, if your healing skill fails me now, he must needs be King.'

'You told me just now that you were healed.'

'I said the wound was healed. The poison has gone, and the pain, but it has left a sickness behind it of a kind that Gandar cannot cure. He told me to look to you.'

I remembered what Lucan had told me about the King who walked with ghosts, and I thought of some of the things I had seen at Pergamum. 'You don't look to me like a man who is mortally ill, Uther. Are you speaking of a sickness of the mind?'

He didn't answer that, but when he spoke, it was not in the voice of a man changing the subject. 'Since you were abroad, I have had two more children by the Queen. Did you know that?'

'I heard about the girl Morgian, but I didn't know about this last stillbirth until today. I'm sorry.'

'And did this famous Sight of yours tell you that there would be no more?' Suddenly, he slammed the goblet down again on the table beside his chair. I saw that the silver had indeed dented under his fingers' pressure. He got to his feet with the violence of a thrown spear. I could see then that what I had taken for energy was a kind of drawn and dangerous tightness, nerves and sinews twanging like bowstrings. The hollows under his cheekbones showed sharp as if something had eaten him empty from within. 'How can anyone be a King who is less than a man?' He flung this question at me, and then strode across the room to the window, where he leaned his head against the stone, looking out at the morning.

Now at last I understood what he had been trying to tell me. He had sent for me once before, to this very room, to tell me how his love for Ygraine, Gorlois' wife, was eating him alive. Then, as now, he had resented having to call upon my skill: then, as now, he had shown this same feverish and tightly drawn force, like a bowstring ready to snap. And the cause had been the same. Ambrosius had once said to me, 'If he would think with his brains instead of his body sometimes he'd be the better for it.' Until this matter of Ygraine, Uther's violent sexual needs had served his ends—not only of pleasure and bodily ease, but because his men, soldiers like himself, admired the prowess which, if not boasted of, was at any rate unconcealed. To them it was a matter for envy, amusement, and admiration. And to Uther himself it was more than bodily satisfaction; it was an affirmation of self, a pride which was part of his own picture of himself as a leader.

He still neither moved nor spoke. I said: 'If you find it hard to talk to me, would you rather I consulted with your other doctors first?'

'They don't know. Only Gandar.'

'Then with Gandar?'

But in the end he told me himself, pacing up and down the room with that quick, limping stride. I had risen when he did, but he motioned me back impatiently, so I stayed where I was, turned away from him, leaning back in my chair beside the brazier, knowing that he walked up and down the room only because he would not face me as he talked. He told me about the raid as Vagniacae and the defending party he had led, and the sharp skirmish on the shingle. The spear thrust had taken him in the groin, not a deep wound but a jagged one, and the blade had not been clean. He had had the cut bound up, and, because it did not trouble him overmuch, had disregarded it; on a new alarm about a Saxon landing in the Medway, he had followed this up immediately, taking no rest until the menace was over. Riding had been uncomfortable, but not very painful, and there had been no warning until it was too late that the wound had begun to fester. In the end even Uther had to admit that he could no longer sit his horse, and he had been carried in a litter back to London. Gandar, who had been with the troops, had been sent for, and under his care, slowly, the poison had dried up, and the festering scars healed. The King still limped slightly where the muscles had knitted awry, but there was no pain, and everything had seemed to be set for full recovery. The Queen had been all this time at Tintagel for her lying-in, and as soon as he was better himself, Uther made ready to go to her. Apparently quite recovered, he had ridden to Winchester, where he had halted his party to hold a council. Then, that night, there had been a girl—

Uther stopped talking abruptly, and took another turn of the room, which sent him back to the window. I wondered if he imagined I had thought him faithful to the Queen, but it had never occurred to me. Where Uther was, there had always been a girl.

'Yes?' I said.

And then at last the truth came out. There had been a girl and Uther had taken her to bed, as he had taken so many others in passing but urgent lust. And he found himself impotent.

'Oh, yes'—as I began to speak—'it has happened before, even to me. It happens to us all at times, but this should not have been one of the times. I wanted her, and she was skilful, but I tell you there was nothing—nothing . . . I thought that perhaps I was weary from the journey, or that the discomfort of the saddle—it was no more than discomfort—had fretted me overmuch, so I waited there in Winchester, to rest. I lay with the girl again, with her and with others. But it was no use, not with any of them.' He swung away from the window then and came back to where I sat. 'And then a messenger came from Tintagel to say that the Queen had been brought to bed early, of a stillborn prince.' He was looking down at me, almost with hatred. 'That bastard you hold for me. You've always been sure, haven't you, that he would be King after me? It seems you were right, you and your damned Sight. I'll get no other children now.'

There was no point in commiseration, and he would not have wanted it from me. I said merely: 'Gandar's skill in surgery is as great as mine. You can have no reason to doubt it. I will look at you if you wish, but I should like to talk to Gandar first.'

'He has not your way with drugs. There is no man living who knows more about medicine. I want you to make me some drug that will bring life back to my loins. You can do this, surely? Every old woman swears she can concoct love potions—'

'You've tried them?'

'How could I try them without telling every man in my army—yes, and every woman in London—that their King is impotent? And can you hear the songs and stories if they knew this about me?'

'You are a good King, Uther. People don't mock that. And soldiers don't mock the men who lead them to victory.'

'How long can I do that, the way I am? I tell you I am sick in more than body. This thing eats at me . . . I cannot live as half a man. And as for my soldiers—how would you like to ride a gelding into battle?'

'They'd follow you even if you rode in a litter, like a woman. If you were yourself, you would know that. Tell me, does the Queen know?'

'I went on from Winchester to Tintagel. I thought that, with her . . . but . . .'

'I see.' I was matter of fact. The King had told me enough, and he was suffering. 'Well, if there is a drug that will help you, be sure I shall find it. I learnt more of these things in the East. It may be that this is only a matter of time and treatment. We have seen this happen too often to think of it as the end. You may yet get another son to supplant the "bastard" I hold for you.'

He said harshly: 'You don't believe that.'

'No. I believe what the stars tell me, if I have read them rightly. But you can trust me to help you as best I can: whatever happens, it's with the gods.

Sometimes their ways seem cruel; who knows this better than you and I? But there is something else I have seen in the stars, Uther; whoever succeeds you, it will not be yet. You'll fight and win your own battles for a few years to come.'

From his face, I knew then that he had feared worse things than his impotence. I saw, from the lightening of his look, that the cure of mind and body might well have begun. He came back to his chair, sat, and picking up the goblet, drained it, and set it down.

'Well,' he said, and smiled for the first time, 'now I shall be the first to believe the people who say that the King's prophet never lies. I shall be glad to take your word on this . . . Come, fill the cups again, Merlin, and we'll talk. You have a lot to tell me: I can listen now.'

So we talked for a while longer. When I began to tell him what I knew of Arthur, he listened calmly and with deep attention; I realised from the way he spoke that for some time now he must, whether consciously or not, have been pinning his hopes on his eldest born. I told him where the boy was now, and to my relief he raised no objections; indeed, after a few questions and a pause for thought he nodded approvingly.

'Ector is a good man. I might have thought of him myself, but as you know I was telling over the kings' courts, and never spared a thought for such as he. Yes, it will do . . . Galava is a good place, and safe . . . And by the Light Himself, if the treaties I have made in the north hold good, I shall see that it remains so. And what you tell me about the boy's status there, and training . . . It will do well. If blood and training tell, he'll be a good fighter and a man whom men can trust and follow. We must see that Ector gets the best master-at-arms in the country.'

I must have made a slight movement of protest, because he smiled again. 'Oh, never fear, I can be secret too. After all, if he is to have the most illustrious teacher in the land, then the King must try to match him. How do you propose to get yourself up there to Galava, Merlin, without having half Britain follow you looking for magic and medicines?'

I answered with something vague. My public coming to London had served its purpose; already the buzz would have gone out that Prince Arthur was alive and thriving. As to my next disappearance, I did not yet know how or when it must be done; I could hardly think beyond the fact that the King had accepted all my plans, and that there was no question of Arthur's being removed from my care. I suspected that, as before, it was a decision taken with relief; once I had gone to my secret post at Galava, the King would forget me more readily than ever would the good folk at Maridunum.

He was speaking of it now. Unless the need came sooner, he said, he would send for the boy when he was grown—fourteen or so, and ready to lead a troop—and present him publicly, ratifying the young prince as his heir.

'Providing still that I have no other,' he added, with a flash of the old hard look, and dismissed me to go and talk with Gandar.

Chapter Five

Gandar was waiting for me in the room which had been allotted to me. While I had been talking with the King my baggage had been brought from the ship, and unpacked by my servant Stilicho. I showed Gandar the drugs I had brought with me, and after we had talked the King's case over, suggested that he send an assistant to study their use and preparation with me over the next few days, before I left London. If he had no one whom he could sufficiently trust to tend the King and be silent about it, I would lend him Stilicho.

At his look of surprise, I explained. As I have said, Stilicho had discovered a fair talent for preparing the dried plants and roots I had brought with me from Pergamum. He could not read, of course, but I put signs on the jars and boxes, and to begin with allowed him to handle only the harmless ones. But he proved reliable, and oddly painstaking for so lively a boy. I have learned since that men of his race have this facility with plants and drugs, and that the little kings of that country dare not eat even an unblemished apple without a taster. I was pleased to have found a servant who could be of use to me in this way, and had taught him a good deal. I would have been sorry to leave him behind in London, so was relieved when Gandar replied that he had an assistant he could trust, who should be sent to me as soon as I was ready.

I started work immediately. At my request Stilicho had been given a small chamber to himself, with a charcoal stove, and a table, and the various bowls and implements he needed. The room adjoined my own, with no door between, but I had had a double thickness of curtain hung across the doorway. Stilicho had by no means come to terms with the British summer, and kept his room at eruption point with heat.

It was about three days before I found a formula which promised some help for the King, and sent a message to Gandar. He, gasping before he had fairly got through the curtains, came himself, but instead of the assistant I expected he brought a girl with him, a young maiden whom I recognised after a moment as Morgause, the King's bastard daughter. She could be no more than thirteen or fourteen, but she was tall for her age, and it was true that she was beautiful. At that age many girls only show promise of beauty; Morgause had the thing itself, and even I, who am no judge of women, could see that this might be a beauty to send men mad. Her body was slight with a child's slenderness, but her breasts were full and pointed and her throat round as a lily stem. Her hair was rosy gold, streaming long and unbound over the golden-green robe. The large eyes that I remembered were gold-green too, liquid and clear as a stream running over mosses, and the small mouth lifted into a smile over kitten's teeth as she dropped a deep reverence to me.

'Prince Merlin.' It was a demure child's voice, little more than a whisper. I saw Stilicho glance round from his work, then stand staring.

I gave her my hand. 'They told me you had grown into a beauty, Morgause. Some man will be fortunate. You're not contracted yet? Then all the men in London have been slow.'

The smile deepened, folding itself into dimples at the corner of her mouth. She did not speak. Stilicho, catching my glance, bent over his work again, but not, I thought, with quite the concentration it required.

'Phew,' said Gandar, fanning himself. I could see the sweat already beading his broad face. 'Do you have to work in a tepidarium?'

'My servant comes from a more blessed corner of the earth than this. They breed salamanders in Sicily.'

'More blessed, you call it? I'd die in an hour.'

'I'll have him bring the things out into my chamber.' I offered.

'No need, for me. I'll not stay. I only came to present you my assistant, who will care for the King. Aye, you may well look surprised. You'll hardly believe me, but this child here is skilled already with drugs. Seems she had a nurse in Brittany, one of their wise women, who taught her the gathering and drying and preparing, and since she came over here she's been eager to learn more. But an army medical unit didn't seem quite the place for her.'

'You surprise me,' I said drily. The girl Morgause had moved near the table where Stilicho was working, and bent her graceful little head towards him. A tress of the rose-gold hair brushed his hand. He labelled two jars at random, both wrongly, before he recovered himself and reached for a knife to melt the seals again.

'So,' said Gandar, 'when she heard the King needed drugs, she asked to look after them. She's practised enough, no fear of that, and the King has consented. For all she's young, she knows how to keep her counsel, and who better to care for him and keep his secrets than his own daughter?'

It was a good idea, and I said so. Gandar himself, though nominally the King's chief physician, had charge of the army medical teams. Until this recent wounding the King had hardly needed his personal care, and in any action or threat of it Gandar's place would be with the army. In Uther's present predicament his own daughter, so fortunately skilled, would answer very well.

'She's more than welcome to learn all she can here.' I turned to the girl. 'Morgause, I've distilled a drug which I think will help the King. I've copied out the formula for you here—can you make it out? Good. Stilicho has the ingredients, if he'll take time to label them correctly . . . Now, I'll leave him to show you how to compound the medicine. If you give him half an hour to get his apparatus out of this steam bath—'

'No need, for me,' she said in a demure echo of Gandar. 'I like the heat.'

'Then I'll leave you,' said Gandar with relief. 'Merlin, will you come and sup with me tonight, or are you with the King?'

I followed him out into the cool airiness of my own room. From beyond the curtain came the murmur, hesitant with shyness, of the servant's voice, and an occasional soft question from the girl.

'It'll be all right, you'll see,' said Gandar. 'No need to look so doubtful.'

'Was I? Not about the medicine, at any rate, and I'll take your word for the girl's skill.'

'In any case, you'll surely stay a little while, and see how she does?'

'Certainly. I don't want to be too long in London, but I can give it a few days. You'll be here yourself?'

'Yes. But there's been such a marked change in him even in this last three days since you came, that I can't see he'll need me in attendance much longer.'

'Let's hope it continues,' I said. 'To tell you the truth, I'm not much troubled . . . Certainly not for his general health. And as for the impotence–if he gets ease and sleep, his mind may stop tormenting his body, and the condition may right itself. This seems to be happening already. You know how these things go.'

'Oh, aye, he'll mend—' he glanced towards the curtained door and dropped his voice—'as far as need be. And as to whether we can get the stallion back to the stand again, I can't see that it matters, now that we know there's a prince safe, and growing, and likely for the crown. We'll get him out of his distemper, and if by God's grace and the drugs you brought he lives to fight . . . and stays king of the pack—'

'He'll do that.'

'Well . . .' he said, and let it go. I may say here that the King did in fact mend rapidly. The limp disappeared, he slept well and put on flesh, and I learned some time later from one of his chamberers that, although the King was never again the Bull of Mithras that his soldiers had laughed over and admired, and though he fathered no more children, he took certain satisfactions in his bed, and the unpredictable violences of his temper declined. As a soldier he was soon, again, the single-minded warrior who had inspired his troops and led them to victory.

When Gandar had gone, I went back into the boy's room to find Morgause slowly conning over the paper I had given her, while Stilicho showed her, one by one, the simples for distillation, the powders for sleeping draughts, the oils for massage of the pulled muscles. Neither of them saw me come in, so I watched for a few minutes in silence. I could see that Morgause missed nothing, and that, though the boy still watched her sideways and tended to shy from her beauty like a colt from fire, she seemed as oblivious of his sex as a princess should be of a slave.

The heat of the room was making my head ache. I crossed quickly to the table. Stilicho's monologue stopped short, and the girl looked up and smiled.

I said: 'You understand it all? Good. I'll leave you now with Stilicho. If there's anything you want to know that he can't tell you, send for me.'

I turned then to give instructions to the boy, but to my surprise Morgause made a quick movement towards me, laying a hand on my sleeve.

'Prince—'

'Morgause?'

'Must you really go? I–I thought you would teach me, you yourself. I want so much to learn from you.'

'Stilicho can teach you all you need to know about the drugs the King will

want. If you wish, I will show you how to help him over the pain of the
tightened muscles, but I should have thought his bath-slave would do that
better.'

'Oh, yes, I know. I wasn't thinking of things like that: it's easy enough to
learn what is needed for the King's care. It was—I had hoped for more.
When I asked Gandar to bring me to you, I had thought—I had hoped—'

The sentence died and she drooped her head. The rose-gold hair fell in a
gleaming curtain to hide her face. Through it, as through rain, I saw her
eyes watching me, thoughtful, meek, childlike.

'You had hoped—?'

I doubt if even Stilicho, four paces away, heard the whisper. '—that you
might teach me a little of your art, my lord Prince.' Her eyes appealed to me,
half hopeful and half afraid, like a bitch expecting to be whipped.

I smiled at her, but I knew my manner was stiff and my voice over-formal.
I can face an armed enemy more easily than a young girl pleading like this,
with a pretty hand on my sleeve, and her scent sweet on the hot air like fruit
in a sunny orchard. Strawberries, was it, or apricots . . .? I said quickly:
'Morgause, I've no art to teach you that you cannot learn as easily from
books. You read, don't you? Yes, of course you do, you read the formula
Then learn from Hippocrates and Galen. Let them be your masters; they
were mine.'

'Prince Merlin, in the arts I speak of you have no master.'

The heat of the room was overpowering. My head hurt me. I must have
been frowning, because she came close with a gentle dipping movement,
like a bird nestling, and said rapidly, pleadingly: 'Don't be angry with me.
I've waited so long, and I was so sure that the chance had come. My lord, all
my life I have heard people speak of you. My nurse in Brittany—she told me
how she used to see you walking through the woods and by the seashore,
gathering the cresses and roots and the white berries of the thunder-bough,
and how sometimes you went with no more sound than a ghost, and no
shadow even on a sunny day.'

'She was telling stories to frighten you. I am a man like other men.'

'Do other men talk of the stars as if they were friends in a familiar room?
Or move the standing stones? Or follow the druids into Nemet and not die
under the knife?'

'I did not die under the druids' knife because the archdruid was afraid of
my father,' I said bluntly. 'And when I was in Brittany I was hardly a man,
and certainly not a magician. I was a boy then, learning my trades as you are
learning yours. I was barely seventeen when I left there.'

She seemed hardly to have heard. I noticed how still she was, the long
eyes shadowed under the curtained hair, the narrow white hands folded
below her breast against the green gown. She said: 'But you are a man now,
my lord, and can you deny that you have worked magic here in Britain?
Since I have been here with my father the King, I have heard you spoken of
as the greatest enchanter in the world. I have seen the Hanging Stones,
which you lifted and set in their place, and I have heard how you foretold
Pendragon's victories and brought the star to Tintagel, and made the
King's son vanish away to the isle of Hy-Brasil—'

'So you heard that here, too, did you?' I tried for a lighter tone. 'You'd better stop, Morgause, you're scaring my servant, and I don't want him running off, he's too useful.'

'Don't laugh at me, my lord. Do you deny that you have the arts?'

'No, I don't deny it. But I couldn't teach you the things you want to know. Certain kinds of magic you can learn from any adept, but the arts which are mine are not mine to give away. I could not teach them to you, even if you were old enough to understand them.'

'I could understand them now. I already have magic–such magic as young maids can learn, no more. I want to follow you and learn from you. My lord Merlin, teach me how to find power like yours.'

'I've told you it isn't possible. You will have to take my word for that. You are too young. I'm sorry, child. I think that for power like mine you will always be too young. I doubt if any woman could go where I go and see what I see. It is not an easy art. The god I serve is a hard master.'

'What god? I only know men.'

'Then learn from men. What I have of power, I cannot teach you. I have told you it is not my gift.'

She watched me without comprehension. She was too young to understand. The light from the stove glimmered on the lovely hair, the wide, clever brows, the full breasts, the small, childish hands. I remembered that Uther had offered her to Lot, and that Lot had rejected her in favour of the young half-sister. I wondered if Morgause knew; and, compassionately, what would become of her.

I said gently: 'It's true, Morgause. He only lends his power for his own ends. When they are achieved, who knows? If he wants you, he will take you, but don't walk into the flames, child. Content yourself with such magic as young maids can use.'

She began to speak, but we were interrupted. Stilicho had been heating something in a bowl over the burner, and was no doubt so busy straining to hear what was being said that he let the bowl tilt, and some of the liquid spilled on to the flames. There was a hiss and a spitting, and a cloud of herb-smelling steam billowed thick between me and the girl, obscuring her. Through it I saw her hands, those still hands, moving quickly to fan the pungent mist away from her eyes. My own were watering. Vision blurred and glittered. The pain in my head blinded me. The movement of the small white hands through the steam was weaving a pattern like a spell. The bats went past me in a cloud. Somewhere near me the strings of my harp whimpered. The room shrank round me, chilled to a globe of crystal, a tomb . . .

'I'm sorry, master. Master, are you ill? Master?'

I shook myself awake. My vision cleared. The steam had thinned, and the last of it was wisping away through the window. The girl's hands were still again, folded as before; she had shaken her hair back, and was watching me curiously. Stilicho had lifted the bowl from the burner, and peered at me across it, anxious and scared.

'Master, it's one you mix yourself. You said there was no harm in it . . .'

'No harm at all. But another time, watch what you're doing.' I looked down at the girl. 'I'm sorry, did I frighten you? It's nothing, a headache. I get them sometimes. Sudden, and soon gone. Now I must go. I leave

London at the end of the week. If you need my help before then, send to me and I shall be glad to come.' I smiled, and reached out a hand to touch her hair. 'No, don't look so downcast, child. It's a hard gift to have, and not for young maids.'

She curtsied to me again as I went out, the small lovely face hidden once more behind the curtaining hair.

Chapter Six

I think this was the only time in my life that I saw Bryn Myrddin not as the home I was eager to reach, but as a mere halting place on a journey. And once I had arrived in Maridunum, instead of welcoming the familiar quiet of the valley, the company of my books, the time to think and to work with my music and my medicines, I found myself fretting to be away, all my being straining northwards to where the boy lived who was to be my life from this time on.

All I knew of him, apart from the cryptic reassurances which had come to me through Hoel and Ector, was that he was healthy and strong, though smaller for his age than Cei, Ector's own son, had been. Cei was eleven years old now, to Arthur's eight, and as familiar to my visions as the young prince. I had watched Arthur's scuffling with the older boy, riding a horse that to my coward's eyes looked far too big for him, playing at swordsmanship with staves, and then with swords. I suppose these must have been blunted, but all I saw was the dangerous flash of the metal, and here, though Cei had the strength and the longer reach, I could see that Arthur was quick as a sword himself. I watched the pair of them fishing, climbing, racing through the edge of the Wild Forest in a vain bid to escape Ralf who (with the help of Ector's two most trusted men) rode guard on Arthur at all times, day or night. All this I watched in the fire, in the smoke or the stars, and once where there were none of these and the message was straining to be through, in the side of a precious crystal goblet which Ahdjan was displaying to me in his palace by the Golden Horn. He must have wondered at my sudden inattention, but probably put it down to indigestion after one of his lavish meals, which to an Eastern host is rather a compliment than otherwise.

I could not even be sure that I should recognise Arthur when I saw him, nor could I tell what kind of boy he had grown to be. Daring I could see, and gaiety, and stubborn strength, but of his real nature I could be no judge; visions may fill the mind's eye, but it takes blood to engage the heart. I had not even heard him speak. Nor had I as yet any clear idea how to enter his life when I did reach the north country, but every night of my journey from London to Bryn Myrddin I walked outside under the stars, searching for what they had to tell me, and always the Bear hung there straight ahead of me, glittering, speaking of the dark North and cool skies and the smell of pines and mountain water.

Stilicho's reaction when he saw the cave where I lived was not what I expected. When I had left home to go on my travels, since I was to be away for so long, I had hired help to look after the place for me. I had left money with the miller on the Tywy, asking him to send one of his servants up from time to time; it was apparent that this had been done, for the place was clean, dry and well provisioned. There was even fresh bedding for the horses, and we had barely dismounted before the girl from the mill came panting after us up the track with goats' milk and fresh bread and five or six newly caught trout. I thanked her, and then, because I would not let Stilicho clean the fish at the holy well, asked her to show him where the runaway water trickled down below the cliff. While I checked my sealed jars and bottles, making sure that the lock on my chest was untouched and that the books and instruments within were undamaged, I could hear the two young voices outside still clacking as busily as the mill wheel, with a good deal of laughter as each tried to make the other understand the foreign tongue.

When at length the girl went and the boy came in with the fish neatly gutted and split ready for roasting, he seemed happily prepared to find the place as convenient and comfortable as any of the houses we had stayed in on my travels. At first I put this down in some amusement to the compensation he had just discovered, but I found later that he had in fact been born and reared in just such a cave in his own country, where people of the lower sort are so poor that the owners of a well-placed and dry cavern count themselves lucky, and often have to fight like foxes to keep their den to themselves. Stilicho's father, who had sold him with rather less thought than one would give to an unwanted puppy, had been well able to spare him out of a family of thirteen; his room in the cave had been more valuable than his presence. As a slave, his quarters had been in the stables, or more usually out in the yard, and even since he had been in my service I was aware that I had lodged in places where the grooms were worse housed than the horses. The chamber he had occupied in London was the first he had ever had to himself. To him my cave on Bryn Myrddin was spacious and even luxurious, and now it promised further pleasures which did not often come the way of a young slave in the sharp competition of the servants' quarters.

So he settled in cheerfully, and word soon got round that the enchanter was back in his hill, and the folk came for drugs, and paid as they had always done with food and comforts. The miller's girl, who name was Mai, seized every opportunity to come up the valley with food from the mill, and sometimes with the people's offerings which she brought for them. Stilicho, in his turn, made a practice of calling at the mill every time he went down to the town for me. And before very long it appeared that Mai had made him welcome in every way known to her. One night when I could not sleep I went out on to the lawn beside the holy well to look at the stars, and heard, in the night's quiet, the horses moving and stamping restlessly in their shed below the cliff. It was a night bright with stars and a white scythe of a moon, so I did not need a torch, but called softly to Stilicho to follow me and trod quickly down to the thorn grove to find out what was disturbing the beasts. It was only when I saw, through the half-opened door, the two young bodies coupling in the straw, that I realised Stilicho was there before me. I withdrew without being seen, and went back to my own bed to think.

A few days later when I talked to the boy, and told him that I planned to
go north soon, but wanted no one to know of it, so would leave him behind
to cover my retreat, he was enthusiastic, and fervent in protestations of
faithfulness and secrecy. I was sure I could trust him; another gift he had
besides his facility with drugs, he was a marvellous liar. I am told that this,
too, is a gift of his people. My only fear was that he might lie too well, like
his horse-trading father, and cheat himself and me into trouble. But it was a
risk I had to take, and I judged him too loyal to me, and too happy in his life
at Bryn Myrddin, to put it at risk. When he asked (trying not to sound too
eager) when I would be gone, I could only tell him that I was waiting for a
time, and a sign. As always, he accepted what I said, simply and without
question. He would as soon have questioned a priestess mouthing in her
shrine—they hold the Old Religion in Sicily—or Hephaistos himself when he
breathed flame from the mountains. I had found that he believed every tale
the people told of me, and would have shown no surprise if I had vanished
in a puff of smoke or conjured gold from thin air. I suspected that, like
Gaius, he made the most of his status as my servant; certainly Mai was
terrified of me, and could not be persuaded to set foot beyond the thorn
grove. Which was just as well for the plans I had in mind.

It was no magic sign that I was waiting for. If I had been certain it was
safe, I would have set off for the north soon after I had reached home from
London. But I knew that I would be watched. Uther would almost certainly
continue to have me spied upon. There was no danger in this—not, that is,
from the King; but if one man can buy a spy's loyalty, so can another, and
there must be many others who, even only for curiosity, would be
watching me. So I curbed my impatience, stayed where I was, and went
about my business, waiting for the watchers to show themselves.

One day I sent Stilicho down with the horses to the forge at the edge of
the town. Both animals had been shod for the journey from London, and
though normally the shoes would have been removed before winter, I
wanted my own mare left shod in preparation for my journey. Her girth
buckles, too, were in need of repair, so Stilicho had ridden down, and was to
do some errands in the town while the smith looked after the animals.

It was a day of frost, dry and still, but with the kind of thick sky that cuts
the rays from the sun and lets it hang red and cold and low. I went over the
hilltop to the hut of Abba the shepherd. His son Ban, the simpleton, had cut
his hand a few days ago on a stake, and the wound had festered. I had cut the
swelling and bound it with salve, but I knew that Ban could be trusted no
more than a bandaged dog, and would worry the thing off if it hurt him.

I need not have troubled; the bandage was still in place, and the wound
healing fast and neatly. Ban—I have noticed this with simple folk—mended
like a child or a wild animal. Which was just as well, since he was one of
those men who can hardly pass a week without injuring themselves in some
way. After I had tended the hand I stayed. The hut was in a sheltered part of
the valley, and Abba's sheep were all in fold. As sometimes happens, there
were early lambs due, though it was only December. I stayed to help Abba
with a hard lambing where the simpleton's hand would not have served
him. By the time the twin lambs were curled, dry and sleeping, on Ban's
knee near the fire, with the ewe watching nearby, the short winter's day had

drawn to a red dusk. I took my leave, and walked home over the hilltop. The way took me across my own valley higher up, and it was dark when I reached the pine wood above the cave. The sky had cleared, the night was still and brightly starred, with a blurred moon throwing blue shadows on the frost. And shadows I saw, moving. I stopped dead, and stood to watch.

Four men on the flat lawn outside my cave. From the thorn thicket below the cliff came the movement and clink of their tethered horses. I could hear the mutter of the men's voices as they huddled together, conferring. Two of them had swords in their hands.

Every moment the moonlight strengthened and fresh stars showered out into the frosty sky. Far away at the foot of the valley I heard the bark of a dog. Then, faintly, the clip of hoofs coming at a gentle pace. The intruders below me heard it, too. One of them gave a low command, and the group turned and made at speed for the path which would take them down to the grove.

They had barely reached the head of the path when I spoke from directly above them. 'Gentlemen?'

You would have thought I had fallen straight from heaven in a chariot of flame. I suppose it was alarming enough, to be addressed out of the dark by a man they thought they had just heard riding up the valley some half mile away. Besides, any man who sets out to spy on a magician starts more than half terrified, and ready to believe any marvel. One of them cried out in fear, and I heard a stifled oath from the leader. In the starlight their faces, upturned, looked grey as the frost.

I said: 'I am Merlin. What do you want with me?'

There was a silence, in which the hoof-beats came nearer, quickening as the horses scented home and supper. I caught a movement below me as if they were half minded to turn and run. Then the leader cleared his throat. 'We come from the King.'

'Then put up your foolish swords. I will come down.'

When I reached them I saw they had obeyed me, but their hands hovered not far from their weapons, and they huddled close together.

'Which of you is the leader?'

The biggest of them stepped forward. He was civil, but with truculence behind it. He had not relished that moment of fear. 'We were waiting for you, Prince. We bring messages from the King.'

'With swords drawn? Well, you are only four to one, after all.'

'Against enchantment,' said the man, nettled.

I smiled. 'You should have known that my enchantment would never work against King's men. You could have been sure of your welcome.' I paused. Their feet shuffled in the frost. One of them muttered something, half curse, half invocation, in his own dialect. I said: 'Well, this is hardly the place to talk. My home is open to all comers, as you see. Why did you not kindle the fire and light the lamps and wait for me in comfort?'

More shuffling. They exchanged glances. No one answered. Clearly where we stood the scuffled frost showed their tracks up to the cave mouth. So, they had been inside. 'Well,' I said, 'be welcome now.'

I crossed to the holy well where the wooden image of the god stood, barely visible in its dark niche. I lifted down the cup, poured for him and drank. I invited the leader with a gesture. He hesitated, then shook his head. 'I am a Christian. What god is that?'

'Myrddin,' I said, 'the god of high places. This was his hill before it was mine. He lends it to me, but he watches it still.'

I saw the movement I had been waiting for among the men. Hands were behind backs as they made the sign against enchantment. One of them, then another, came forward to take the cup, drink, and spill for the god. I nodded at them. 'It does not do to forget that the old gods still watch from the air and wait in the hollow hills. How else did I know you were here?'

'You knew?'

'How not? Come in.' I turned in the cave mouth, holding back the boughs that half screened the entrance. None of them moved, except the leader, and he took one step only, then hesitated. 'What's the matter?' I asked him. 'The cave is empty, isn't it? Or isn't it? Did you find something amiss when you went in, that you are afraid to tell me?'

'There was nothing amiss,' said the leader. 'We didn't go in—that is—' He cleared his throat, and tried again. 'Yes, we went inside, only a pace over the threshold, but—' He stopped. There was muttering, and more glances, and I heard. 'Go on, tell him, Crinas.'

Crinas started again. 'The truth is, sir—'

His story was a long time coming, with many hesitations and promptings, but I got it in the end, still waiting in the cave mouth with the troopers standing round in a half circle, like wary cattle.

It seemed they had come to Maridunum a day or so before, waiting their chance to ride up to the cave unobserved. They had had orders not to approach me openly, for fear that other watchers (whose presence the King suspected) might waylay them and take from them any message I might put into their hands.

'Yes?'

The man cleared his throat. This morning, he said, they had seen my mare tethered outside the smithy, saddled and shod. When they asked the smith where I was he told them nothing, leaving them to assume that I was somewhere in the town, with business to pursue that would keep me until the mare was ready. They had imagined that whoever else was watching me would be staying near me in the town, so had seized the chance and ridden up to the cave.

Another pause. They could see nothing in that darkness, but I could feel they were straining to guess my reactions to their story. I said nothing, and the man swallowed, and ploughed on.

The next part of the story had, at least, the ring of truth. During their wait in Maridunum they had asked, among other idle-sounding questions, the way to the cave. Be sure they had been told, with nothing spared about the holiness of the place, and the power and awesomeness of its owner. The people of the valley were very proud of their enchanter, and my deeds would lose nothing in the telling. So the men had ridden up the valley half afraid already.

They had found, as they expected, a deserted cave. The frost outside held the lawn blank and printless. All that had met them was the silence of the winter hills, broken only by the trickle of the spring. They had lit a torch and peered in through the entrance; the cave was orderly but empty, and the ashes were cold . . .

'Well?' I asked, as Crinas stopped.

'We knew you were not there, sir, but there was a feeling about the place . . . When we called out there was no reply, but then we heard something rustling in the dark. It seemed to come from the inner cave, where the bed is with the lamp beside it—'

'Did you go in?'

'No, sir.'

'Or touch anything?'

'No, sir,' he said quickly. 'We—we did not dare.'

'It's just as well,' I said. 'And then?'

'We looked all about us, but there was no one. But all the time, that sound. We began to be afraid. There had been stories . . . One of the men said you might be there watching, invisible. I told him not to be a fool, but indeed there was a feeling . . .'

'Of eyes in one's back? Of course there was. Go on.'

He swallowed 'We shouted again And then—they came down out of the roof. The bats, like a cloud.'

We were interrupted then. Stilicho had reached the grove and seen the troopers' horses tied there. I heard the shed door slam shut on our horses, then the boy came racing up the twisting pathway and across the flat grass, dagger in hand.

He was shouting something. Moonlight caught the blade of the long knife, held low and level, ready to stab. Metal rasped as the men whirled to defend themselves. I took two swift strides forward, pushing them aside, and bore down hard on the boy's knife hand, bringing him up short.

'No need. They're King's men. Put up.' Then, as the others put their weapons back: 'Were you followed, Stilicho?'

He shook his head. He was trembling. A slave is not trained to arms like a free man's son. Indeed, it was only since we had come to Bryn Myrddin that I had let him carry a knife at all. I let him go, and turned back to Crinas. 'You were telling me about the bats. It sounds to me as if you had let the stories trouble you overmuch, Crinas. If you disturbed the bats, they might certainly alarm you for a moment, but they are only bats.'

'But that was not all, my lord. The bats came down, yes, out of the roof, somewhere in the dark, and went past us into the air. It was like a plume of smoke, and the air stank. But after they had gone by us we heard another sound. It was music.'

Stilicho, standing close to me, stared from them to me, wide-eyed in the dusk. I saw they were making the sign again.

'Music all around us,' said the man. 'Soft, like whispering, running round and round the wall of the cave in an echo. I'm not ashamed, my lord, we came out of that cave, and we did not dare go in again. We waited for you outside.'

'With swords drawn against enchantment. I see. Well, there is no need to wait longer in the cold. Will you not come in now? I assure you that you will not be harmed, so long as you do not raise a hand against me or my servant. Stilicho, go in and kindle the fire. Now, gentlemen? No, don't try to go.

Remember you have not yet given me the King's message.'

Finally, between threats and reassurance, they came in, treading very softly indeed, and not speaking above a whisper. The leader consented to sit with me, but none of the others would come in as far, preferring to sit between the fire and the mouth of the cave. Stilicho hurried to warm wine with spices, and hand it round.

Now that they were in the light I could see that they were not dressed in the uniform of the King's regular troops; there was neither badge nor blazon to be seen; they might be taken for the armed troops of any petty leader. They certainly carried themselves like soldiers, and though they paid Crinas no obvious deference, it was apparent that there was some difference of rank between them.

I surveyed them. The leader sat stolidly, but the others fidgeted under my gaze, and I saw one of them, a thin, smallish man with black hair and a pale face, still surreptitiously making the sign.

At length I spoke: 'You have come, you tell me, with messages from the King. Did he charge you with a letter?'

Crinas answered me. He was a big man, reddish fair, with light eyes. Some Saxon blood, perhaps: though there are red Celts as fair as this. 'No, sir. Only to convey his greetings, and ask after his son's welfare.'

'Why?'

He repeated my question in apparent surprise. 'Why, my lord?'

'Yes, why? I have been gone from the court four months. In that time the King has had reports. Why should he send you now, and to me? He knows the child is not here. It seems obvious'—I lingered on the word, looking from one to the other of the armed men—'that he could not be safe here. The King also knew that I would wait at Bryn Myrddin for a while before I left to join Prince Arthur. I expect to be spied on, but I find it hard to believe that he sent you with such a message.'

The three beyond the fire looked at one another. A broad fellow with a red, pimpled face shifted his sword belt forward nervously, his hand playing unthinkingly with the hilt. I saw Stilicho's eyes on him; then he moved round with the wine jug to stand near-by.

Crinas held my eyes for a moment in silence, then nodded. 'Well, sir, all right. You've smoked us out. I didn't hope to get away with a thin tale like that, not with you. It was all I could think of at a jump, when you surprised us like that.'

'Very well. You are spies. I still want to know why?'

He lifted his broad shoulders. 'You know, sir, who better, what kings are. It wasn't for us to question when we were told to come here and look the place over without letting you see us.'

Behind him the others nodded, agreeing anxiously. 'And we did no harm, my lord. We never came into the cave. That much was true.'

'No, and you told me why not.'

He turned up a hand. 'Well, sir, I don't say but you do right to be angry. I'm sorry. This isn't our normal business, as you'll guess, but orders are orders.'

'What were you ordered to find out?'

'Nothing special, just ask around, and take a look at the place, and find out when you were going.' A quick look sideways, to see how I was taking it. 'It was my understanding that there was a lot you hadn't told the King, and he wanted to find out. Did you know he had you followed from the minute you left London?'

Another grain of truth. 'I guessed it,' I said.

'Well, there you are.' He managed to say it as if it explained everything. 'It's a way kings have, trusting nobody and wanting to know everything. It's my belief—if you'll excuse me for saying it, my lord—'

'Go on.'

'I think the King didn't believe what you told him about where you were keeping the young prince. Maybe he thought you'd shift him, and keep him hidden, like before. So he sent us on the quiet, hoping we'd find some clue.'

'Perhaps. Wanting knowledge is a disease of kings. And speaking of that, is there any worsening of the King's health which might have made him suddenly anxious for news?'

I saw, as clearly as if he had said it, that he wished he had thought of this himself. He hesitated, then decided that where it could be told, the truth was safer. 'As to that, my lord, we've no information, and I've not seen him myself lately. But they say the sickness has passed, and he's back in the field.'

This tallied with what I had been told. I said nothing for a while, but watched them thoughtfully. Crinas drank, with an assumption of ease, but his eyes on me were wary. At length I said: 'Well, you have done as you were bidden, and found out what the King wanted. I am still here, and the child is not. The King must trust me for the rest. As for when I am going, I will tell him in my own good time.'

Crinas cleared his throat. 'That's an answer we'd sooner not take, sir.' His voice came over-loud, like a braggart's, but he was not bluffing. The others shared his fear, but without his measure of courage; though this was no comfort to me; I knew that frightened men are dangerous. One of the troopers—the small fellow with black eyes shifting in a face pale with nerves—leaned forward and plucked at his leader's sleeve. I caught the mutter of, 'Better go. Don't forget who he is . . . Quite enough now . . . Make him angry.'

I said crisply: 'I am not angry. You are doing your duty, and it is not your fault if the King trusts no one, but must have each story ratified twice over. You may tell him this—' I paused as if for thought, and saw them craning '—that his son is where I told him, safe and thriving, and that I am only waiting for good weather to make the voyage.'

'*Voyage?*' Crinas asked sharply.

I lifted my brows. 'Come now. I thought all the world knew where Arthur was. In any case, the King will understand.'

One of the men said hoarsely: 'Yes, we know, but it was only a whisper. Then it's true about the island?'

'Quite true.'

'Hy-Brasil?' asked Crinas. 'That's a myth, my lord, saving your presence.'

'Did I give it a name? I am not responsible for the whispers. The place has many names, and enough stories are told about it to fill the Nine Books of

Magic . . . And every man who sees it sees something different. When I took Arthur there—'

I paused to drink, as a singer wets his throat before touching the chords. The three in front of me were all attention now. I did not look at Crinas, but spoke past him, giving my voice the tale-teller's extra pitch and resonance.

'You all know that the child was handed to me three nights after he was born. I took him to a safe place, then when the time was right and the world quiet, I carried him westward, to a coast I know. There, below the cliffs, is a bay of sand where the rocks stand up like the fangs of wolves, and no boat or swimmer can live when the tide is breaking round them. To right and left of the bay the sea has driven arches through the cliff. The rocks are purple and rose-coloured and pale as turquoise in the sun, and on a summer's evening when the tide is low and the sun is sinking, men see on the horizon land that comes and goes with the light. It is the Summer Isle, which (they say) floats and sinks at the will of heaven, the Island of Glass through which the clouds and stars can be seen, but which for those who dwell there is full of trees and grass and springs of sweet water . . .'

The pale-faced man was straining forward, open-mouthed, and I saw the shoulders of another shift under his woollen cloak as if with cold. Stilicho's eyes were like shield-bosses.

'. . . It is the Isle of Maidens, where kings are carried at their endings. And there will come a day—'

'My lord! I have seen it myself!' That the pale man should interrupt a prophet apparently on the point of prophecy showed a nerve scraped raw. 'I have seen it myself! When I was a boy I saw it! Clear, as clear as the Cassiterides on a fair day after rain. But it seemed an empty land.'

'It is not empty. And it is not only there when men like you can see it. It can be found even in winter, for those who know how to find it. But there are not many who can travel to it and then return.'

Crinas had listened without moving, his face expressionless. 'Then he's on Cornish land?'

'You know it too?'

There was no hint of mockery in my voice, but he said with a snap: 'I do not,' and set down his empty cup and made ready to rise. I saw his hand go to his sword-belt. 'Is this the message we have to take back to the King?'

At a movement of his head the others rose with him. Stilicho set the wine jug down with a clatter, but I shook my head at him and laughed. 'It would go hard with you, I think, if that were all? And hard with me, to have fresh spies set on me. For all our sakes, I'll set his mind at rest. Will you bear a letter back to London for me?'

Crinas stood still a moment, his eyes fast on mine. Then he relaxed, his thumb hooking harmlessly in his belt. When I heard his breath of relief I knew how near he had been to questioning me further in the only way he knew. 'Willingly, sir.'

'Then wait a while longer. Sit down again. Fill their cups, Stilicho.'

The letter to Uther was brief. I began by asking after his health, then wrote that, according to my private sources of information, the prince was well. As soon as the spring came, I told him, I intended to travel and see the boy myself. Meantime I would watch him in my own way, and send the

King all the news there was.

After I had sealed the message I took it back into the outer cave. The men had been talking quietly among themselves in undertones, while Stilicho hovered with the wine jug. They broke off as I came in, and got to their feet. I handed the letter to Crinas.

'Anything else I have to say is in that letter. He will be satisfied.' I added: 'Even if your mission did not work out precisely to orders, you have nothing to fear from the King. Leave me now, and the god of going watch you on your way.'

They went at last, perhaps not so grateful as they might have been for my parting invocation. As they hurried out across the frost I saw the quick sidelong glances into the shadows, and the hunching of cloaks close round their shoulders as if the night were breathing on their backs. As they passed the holy well every one of them made a sign, and I do not think that the last–Crinas'–was the sign of the Cross.

Chapter Seven

The sound of their horses' hoofs dwindled down the valley track. Stilicho came racing back from the cliff above the grove.

'They've all gone.' His eyes were wide, dilated not only with the frosty dark. 'My lord, I thought they were going to kill you.'

'It was possible. They were brave men, and they were frightened. It's a risky combination, especially as one of them was a Christian.'

He was on to that as quickly as a house dog on to a rat. 'Meaning he didn't believe you?'

'Meaning just that. He was sure he didn't believe me, but he wouldn't have staked anything on its being a lie. Now find me some food, Stilicho, will you? It doesn't matter what, but hurry, and put together what you can for a journey. I'll see to my clothes myself. Is the mare ready?'

'Why, yes, lord, but–you're going tonight?'

'As soon as I can. This is the chance I have been waiting for. They've shown themselves, and by the time they find that the trail I gave them is false I shall be gone–vanished to the island beyond the west . . . Now, you know what to do; we've talked of it many times.'

This was true. We had planned that, when I went, Stilicho would remain at Bryn Myrddin, fetching and carrying supplies as usual, keeping up for as long as he could the illusion that I was still at home. I had built up a store of medicines, and for some time now had let him compound the simpler ones himself and dispense them to the poor folk who came up the valley, so they would not suffer by my absence, and it would be a little time before anyone would raise a question. We might not gain much time in this way, but I should gain enough. Once I was across the nearer hills and had reached the valley tracks in the forest, I would be hard indeed to follow.

So now Stilicho merely nodded, and ran to do as I bade him. In a very short time food was ready, and while I ate he packed together what I would need for the journey. I could see he was bursting with questions, so I let him talk. I could talk to him haltingly in his own tongue, but mainly he got along with his fluent but heavily accented Latin. Since we had left Constantinopolis most of his natural lively spirits had flowed in my direction; he had to talk to someone, and it would have been cruelty to insist on the silent respect which Gaius had tried to instil. Besides, this is not my way. So, as he hurried about his tasks, the questions came eagerly.

'My lord, if that man Crinas didn't really believe in the Isle of Glass, and he had to have the information about the prince, why did he go away?'

'To read my letter. He thinks the truth will be in that.'

His eyes widened. 'But he'll never dare open a letter to the King! Did you write the truth in it?'

I raised my brows at him. 'The truth? Don't you believe in the Isle of Glass, either?'

'Oh, yes. Everyone knows about that.' He was solemn. 'Even in Sicily we knew of the invisible island beyond the west. But that's not where you're going now, *I'd* stake anything on that!'

'Why so sure?'

He gave me a limpid look. 'You, lord? Across the Western Sea? In winter? I'll believe anything, but not that! If you could use magic instead of a ship, we'd have journeyed more easily in the Middle Sea. Do you remember the storm off Pylos?'

I laughed. 'With no magic but mandragora . . . Too well, I remember it. No, Stilicho, I gave nothing away in the letter. That letter will never get to the King. They weren't King's men.'

'Not King's men?' He paused, open-mouthed, to stare, then remembered himself and stooped again over the saddle-bag he was packing. 'How do you know? Did you know them?'

'No. But Uther doesn't use troops to spy; how could he hope to keep them secret? These are troops, sent—as Crinas told me—to ask questions in the market and the taverns in Maridunum, and then to search this place while we were out of it, and find, if not the prince, some clue to him. They weren't even spies. What spy would dare go back to his master and say he had been discovered, but had been given a letter to carry for his victim, with the information in it? I tried to make it easy for them, and it's possible they think they deceived me, but in any case they had to take the chance and get their hands on the letter. I give Crinas best, he's a quick thinker. When I caught them at it, he did well enough. It wasn't his fault that the other man gave him away.'

'What do you mean, lord?'

'The small man with the pale face. I heard him say something in his own tongue. I doubt if Crinas heard it. He was speaking in Cornish. So later I spoke of the Isle of Glass, and described the bay, and he knew of that, too, and the Cassiterides. They are islands off the Cornish coast, ones in which even Crinas must believe.'

'Cornish?' asked the boy, trying the word.

'From Cornwall, in the south-west.'

'Queen's men, then?' Stilicho had not spent all his time in London in the stillroom with Morgause. He listened almost as much as he talked, and had regaled me continually since we left Uther's court with what 'they' were saying about every subject under the sun. 'They said she was still in the south-west after the lying-in.'

'That's true. And she might use Cornishmen for secret work, but I think not. Neither the King nor the Queen keep Cornish troops close to them these days.'

'There are Cornish troops at Caerleon. I heard it in the town.'

I looked up sharply. 'Are there indeed? Under whom?'

'I didn't hear. I could find out.' He was looking at me eagerly, but I shook my head.

'No. The less you know about it, the better. Leave it now. They'll stop watching me for the length of time it takes to read that letter, and by the time they find someone who can read Greek—'

'Greek?'

'The King has a Greek secretary,' I said blandly. 'I didn't see why I should make it easy. And I doubt if they know I suspect them. They'll be in no hurry. Besides, I put something in the letter to make them think I would stay here until spring.'

'Will they come back?'

'I doubt it. What are they to do? Come back to tell me they read the King's letter, and are not King's men? As long as they think I'm here, they will be afraid to do that, in case I report to the King. They dare not kill me, and they dare not let me find out who they are. They will keep away. As it is, the next time you go into Maridunum, see that a message is sent to the garrison commander to watch for these Cornishmen, and tell him to report what has happened to the King. I will send a message to the King myself. We may as well use his spies to guard us from the others . . . There, I've finished. You've packed the food? Fill the flask now, will you? Meanwhile, if anyone does come up here, what is your story?'

'That you have been out daily on the hillside, and that you went last towards Abba's valley, and that I think you must be staying to help him with the sheep.' He looked up doubtfully. 'They won't believe me.'

'Why not? You're an accomplished liar. Be careful, you're spilling that wine.'

'A prince help with the sheep? It's not very likely.'

'I've done stranger things.' I said. 'They'll believe you. In any case, it's true. Where do you think I got the bloodstains on my old cloak today?'

'Killing someone, I thought.'

He was quite serious. I laughed. 'That doesn't happen often, and usually by mistake.'

He shook his head in unbelief, and stoppered the wine. 'If those men had drawn swords on you, my lord, would you have stopped them with magic?'

'I hardly needed magic, with your dagger so ready. I haven't thanked you yet for your courage. Stilicho. It was well done.'

He looked surprised. 'You're my master.'

'I bought you for money, and gave you back the freedom you were born with. What sort of a debt is that?'

He merely looked without understanding, and presently said: 'There, all's ready, lord. You will want your thick boots, and the sheepskin cloak. Shall I get Strawberry ready while you dress?'

'In a moment,' I said. 'Come here. Look at me. I have promised you that you will be safe here. This is true; I have seen no danger coming, not for you. But once I am clear away, if you are afraid, go down to the mill and stay there.'

'Yes, lord.'

'Don't you believe me?'

'Yes.'

'Then why are you afraid?'

He hesitated, swallowing. Then he said: 'The music they spoke of, lord. What was it? Was it really from the gods?'

'In a way. My harp speaks sometimes, of itself, when the air moves. I think that's what they heard and, because they were guilty, they were afraid.'

He glanced over to the corner where the big harp stood. I had had it sent across from Britanny, and since I had come home had used it constantly, restoring the other to its place. 'That one? How could it, lord, muffled like that against the air?'

'No, not that one. That harp stays dumb until I touch it. I meant the little one I travelled with. I made it myself, here in this cave with Galapas the magician to help me.'

He wetted his lips. You could see that this was hardly a reassurance. 'I've not seen it since we got home. Where do you keep it?'

'I was going to show you anyway, before I left. Come, boy, there's no need for you to fear it. You've carried it yourself a thousand times. Now, get me a torch, and come and see.'

I led him to the back of the main chamber. I had never shown him the crystal cave, and, because I kept my chest of books and my table across the rough rock-slope that led to the ledge, he had never climbed that way and found it. Now I motioned him to help me shift the table, and holding the torch high mounted to the shadowy ledge where the crystal cave lay hidden. I knelt down at the entrance and beckoned him forward beside me.

The torch in my hand threw firelight, glimmering through moving smoke, round the globed walls of crystal. Here as a boy I had seen my first visions in the leap and flash of moving flame. Here I had seen myself begotten, the old King dead, the tower of Vortigern built on water, the dragon of Ambrosius leaping to victory. Now the globe was empty but for the harp which stood there, with its shadow thrown clear round the sparkling walls.

I glanced down at the boy's face. Awe was stirring in it, even at the empty globe and the empty shadows.

'Listen,' I said. I said it loudly, and as my voice stirred the still air the harp whispered, and the music ran humming round and round the crystal walls.

'I was going to show you the cave,' I said. 'If ever you want to hide, hide here. I did myself, as a boy. Be sure the gods will watch over you, and you will be safe. Where safer, than right in God's hand, in his hollow hill? Now, go and see to Strawberry. I'll bring the harp down myself. It's time I was gone.'

When morning came I was fifteen miles away, riding north through the oak forest which lies along the valley of the Cothi. There is no road there, only tracks, but I knew them well, and I knew the glass-blowers' hut deep in the wood. At this time of the year it would be empty.

I and my mare shared its shelter half that December day. I watered her at the stream, and threw fodder that I had brought into a corner of the hut. I myself was not hungry. There was something else for me to feed on; that deep excited feeling of lightness and power which I recognised. The time had been right, and something lay ahead of me. I was on my way.

I drank a mouthful of wine, wrapped myself warmly in Abba's sheepskins, and fell asleep as soundly and thoughtlessly as a child.

I dreamed again of the sword, and I knew, even through the dream, that this came straight from the god. Ordinary dreams are never so clear; they are jumbles of desires and fears, things seen and heard, and felt though unknown. This came clear, like a memory.

I saw the sword close for the first time, not vast and dazzling like the sword of stars over Brittany, or dim and fiery as it had shimmered against the dark wall in Ygraine's chamber. It was just a sword, beautiful in the way of a weapon, with the jewels on the hilt set in gold scrollwork, and the blade glimmering and eager, as if it would fight of itself. Weapons are named for this; some are eager fighters, some dogged, some unwilling; but all are alive.

This sword was alive; it was drawn, gripped in the hand of an armed man. He was standing by a fire, a camp fire lit apparently in the middle of a darkened plain, and he was the only person to be seen in all that plain. A long way behind him I saw, dim against the dark, the outline of walls and a tower. I thought of the mosaic I had seen in Ahdjan's house, but it was not Rome this time. The outline of the tower was familiar, but I could not remember where I had seen it, nor even be sure that I had not seen it only in dreams.

He was a tall man, cloaked, and the dark cloak fell in a long heavy line from shoulder to heel. The helmet hid his face. His head was bent, and he held the sword naked across his hands. He was turning it over and over, as if weighing its balance, or studying the runes on the blade. The firelight flashed and darkened, flashed and darkened, as the blade turned. I caught one word, KING, and then again KING, and saw the jewels sparkling as the sword turned. I saw then that the man had a circle of red gold on his helmet, and that his cloak was purple. Then as he moved the firelight lit the ring on his finger. It was a gold ring carved with a dragon.

I said: 'Father? Sir?' but, as sometimes happens in dreams, I could make no sound. But he looked up. There were no eyes under the peak of the helmet. Nothing. The hands that had held the sword were the hands of a skeleton. The ring shone on bone.

He held the sword out to me, flat across the skeleton hands. A voice that was not my father's said: 'Take it.' It was not a ghost's voice, or the voice of bidding that comes with vision: I have heard these, and there is no blood in them; it is as if the wind breathed through an empty horn. This was a man's voice, deep and abrupt and accustomed to command, with a rough edge to it such as comes from anger, or sometimes from drunkenness; or sometimes, as now, from fatigue.

I tried to move, but I could not, any more than I could speak. I have never feared a spirit, but I feared this man. From the blank of shadow below the helmet came the voice again, grim, and with a faint amusement, that crept along my skin like the brush of a wolf's pelt felt in the dark. My breath stopped and my skin shivered. He said, and now I clearly heard the weariness in the voice: 'You need not fear me. Nor should you fear the sword. I am not your father, but you are my seed. Take it, Merlinus Ambrosius. You will find no rest until you do.'

I approached him. The fire had dwindled, and it was almost dark. I put my hands out for the sword, and he reached to lay it across them. I held still, though my flesh shrank from touching his bony fingers; but they were not there to touch. As the sword left his grip it fell, through his hands and through mine, and between us to the ground. I knelt, groping in the darkness, but my hand met nothing. I could feel his breath above me, warm as a living man's, and his cloak brushed my cheek. I heard him say: 'Find it. There is no one else who can find it.' Then his eyes were open and it was full noon, and the strawberry mare was nuzzling at me where I lay, with her mane brushing my face.

Chapter Eight

December is certainly no time for travelling, especially for one whose business does not allow him to use the roads. The winter woods are open and clear of undergrowth, but there are many places in the remoter valleys where there is no clear going save along the stream-side, and that is tortuous and rough, and the banks are apt to be dangerously broken—or even washed right away—with floods and bad weather. Snow, at least, I was spared, but on the second day out of Bryn Myrddin the weather worsened to a cold wind with flurries of sleet, and there was ice in all the ways.

Going was slow. On the third day, towards dusk, I heard wolves howling somewhere up near the snow-line. I had kept to the valleys, travelling in deep forest still, but now and again where the forest thinned I had caught glimpses of the hilltops and they were white with fresh snow. And there was more to come; the air had the smell of snow, and the soft cold bite on one's cheek. The snow would drive the wolves down lower. Indeed, as dark drew in and the trees crowded closer I thought I saw a shadow slipping away between the trunks, and there were sounds in the underbrush which might have been made by harmless creatures such as deer or fox; but I noticed that Strawberry was uneasy; her ears flattened repeatedly, and the skin on her shoulders twitched as if flies were settling there.

I rode with my chin on my shoulder and my sword loose in its sheath. '*Mevysen*'—I spoke to my Welsh mare in her own language—'when we find this great sword that Macsen Wledig is keeping for me, you and I will no doubt be invincible. And find it we must, it seems. But just at the moment I'm as scared of those wolves as you are, so we'll go on till we find some place that's defensible with this poor weapon and my poorer skill, and we'll sit the night out together, you and I.'

The defensible place was a ruinous shell of a building deep in the forest. Literally a shell; it was all that remained of a smallish erection the shape of a kiln, or a beehive. Half of it had fallen away, leaving the standing part like an egg broken endways, the curving half-dome backed against the wind and offering some sort of protection from the intermittent sleet. Most of the fallen masonry had been removed–probably stolen for building stone–but there was still a ragged rampart of broken stuff behind which it was possible to take shelter, and conceal myself and the mare.

I dismounted, and led her in. She picked her way between the mossed stones, shook her wet neck, and was soon settled quietly enough with her nosebag, under the dry curve of the dome. I set a heavy rock on the end of her rope, then pulled the dead fronds of some fern from a dry corner under the wall, dried her damp hide with it, and covered her. She seemed to have lost her fears, and munched steadily. I made myself as comfortable as I could with one saddle-bag for a dry seat, and what remained to me of food and wine. I would have dearly liked to light a fire, as much against the wolves as for comfort, but there might be other enemies than wolves looking for me by now, so, with my sword ready to hand, I huddled into my sheepskins and ate my cold rations and fell at last into a waking doze which was the nearest to sleep that danger and discomfort would allow.

And dreamed again. No dream, this time, of kings or swords or stars moving, but a dream half-waking, broken and uneasy, of the small gods of small places; gods of hills and woods and streams and crossways; the gods who still haunt their broken shrines, waiting in the dusk beyond the lights of the busy Christian churches, and the dogged rituals of the greater gods of Rome. In the cities and the crowded places men have forgotten them, but in the forests and the wild hill country the folk still leave offerings of food and drink, and pray to the local guardians of the place who have dwelt there time out of mind. The Romans gave them Roman names, and let them be; but the Christians refuse to believe in them, and their priests berate the poorer folk for clinging to the old ways–and no doubt for wasting offerings which would do better at some hermit's cell than at some ancient holy place in the forest. But still the simple folk creep out to leave their offerings, and when these vanish by morning, who is to say that a god has not taken them?

This, I thought, dreaming, must be such a place. I was in the same forest, and the apse of stone where I sat was the same, even to the rampart of mossed boulders in front of me. It was dark, and my ears were filled with the roaring of the upper boughs where the night wind poured across the forest. I heard nothing approaching, but beside me the mare stirred and breathed gustily into the fodder-bag, and lifted her head, and I looked up to see eyes watching me from the darkness beyond the rampart.

Held by sleep, I could not move. In equal silence, and very swiftly, others came. I could discern them only as shadows against the cold darkness; not wolves, but shadows like men; small figures appearing one by one, like ghosts, and with no more sound, until they ringed me in, eight of them, standing shoulder to shoulder across the entrance to my shelter. They stood there, not moving or speaking, eight small shadows, as much part of the forest and the night as the gloom cast by the trees. I could see nothing except–when high over the bare trees a cloud swept momentarily clear of the winter stars–the gleam of watching eyes.

No movement, no word. But suddenly, without any conscious change. I knew I was awake. And they were still there.

I did not reach for my sword. Eight to one is not a kind of odds that makes sense, and besides, there are other ways to try first. But even those I never got a chance to use. As I moved, taking breath to speak, one of them said something, a word that was blown away in the wind, and the next thing I knew I was thrown back forcibly against the wall behind me, while rough hands forced a gag into my mouth, and my hands were pulled behind my back and the wrists bound tightly together. They half-lifted, half-dragged me out of the walled shelter, and flung me down outside with my back against the bruising stones that formed the rampart. One of them produced flint and iron, and after a long struggle managed to set light to the twist of rag stuck in a cracked ox horn which did duty as a torch; the thing burned sullenly with a feeble and stinking light, but with its help they set to work to hunt through the saddle-bags, and examine the mare herself with careful curiosity. Then they brought the torch to where I sat with two of them standing over me and, thrusting the reeking rag almost into my face, examined me much as they had done the mare.

It seemed clear from the fact that I was still alive that they were not simple robbers; indeed, they took nothing from the saddle-bags, and though they disarmed me of sword and dagger, they did not search me further. I began to fear, as they looked me over closely with nods and grunted comments of satisfaction, that they had actually been looking for me. But in that case, I thought, if they had wanted to know my destination, or had been paid to find it out, they would have done better to stay invisible, and follow me. No doubt I would have led them in the end to Count Ector's doorstep.

Their comments told me nothing about their business with me, but they did tell me something as important; these men spoke in a tongue I had never heard before, but all the same I knew it; the Old Tongue of the Britons, which my master Galapas had taught me.

The Old Tongue has still something the same form as our own British language, but the people who speak it have for so long lived away from other men that their speech has altered, adding its own words and changing its accent until now it takes study and a good ear to follow it at all. I could hear the familiar inflections, and here and there a word recognisable as the Welsh of Gwynedd, but the accent had changed, slurred and strange through five hundred years of isolation, with words surviving that had long fallen out of use in other dialects, and sounds added like the echoes of the hills themselves, and of the gods and wild creatures that dwell there.

It told me who these men must be. They were the descendants of those tribesmen who had, long since, fled to the remoter hills, leaving the cities and the cultivable lands to the Romans, and after them to Cunedda's Federates from Guotodin, and had roosted, like homeless birds, in the high tracts of the forest where living was scarce and no better men would dispute it with them. Here and there they had fortified a hilltop and held it, but in most cases any hill that could be so fortified was desirable to conquerors, so was eventually stormed or starved out and taken. So, hilltop by hilltop, the remnants of the unconquered had retreated, till there was left to them only the crags and caves and the bare land which the snow locked in winter. There they lived, seen by none except by chance, or when they wished it. It was they, I guessed, who crept down by night to take the offerings from the country shrines. My waking dream had been true enough. These, perhaps, were all who could be seen by living eyes, of the dwellers in the hollow hills.

They were talking frccly—as freely as such folk ever do—not knowing I could understand them. I kept my eyelids lowered, and listened.

'I tell you, it must be. Who else would be travelling in the forest on a night like this? And with a strawberry mare?'

'That's right. Alone, they said, with a red roan mare.'

'Maybe he killed the other, and stole the mare. He's hiding, that's certain. Why else lie out here in winter without a fire, and the wolves coming down this low?'

'It's not the wolves he's afraid of. Depend on it, this is the man they were wanting.'

'And paying for.'

'They said he was dangerous. He didn't look it to me.'

'He had a sword drawn ready.'

'But he never picked it up.'

'We were too quick for him.'

'He had seen us. He had time. You shouldn't have taken him like that, Cwyll. They didn't say take him. They said find him and follow him.'

'Well, it's too late now. We've taken him. What do we do? Kill him?'

'Llyd will know.'

'Yes. Llyd will know.'

They did not speak as I have reported it, but in snatches one across the other, brief phrases bandied to and fro in that strange, sparse language. Presently they left me where I lay between my two guards, and withdrew a short distance. To wait, I supposed, for Llyd.

Some twenty minutes later he came, with two companions; three more shadows suddenly no longer part of the forest's blackness. The others crowded round him, talking and pointing, and presently he seized the torch—which was now little more than a singed rag smelling of pitch—and strode towards me. The others crowded after.

They stood in a half circle round me as they had stood before. Llyd held the torch high, and it showed me my captors, not clearly, but enough to know them again. They were small men, dark-haired, with surly lined faces beaten by weather and hard living to a texture like gnarled wood. They were dressed in roughly tanned skins, and breeches of thick, coarse-woven cloth dyed the browns and greens and murreys that you can make with the mountain plants. They were variously armed, with clubs, knives, stone axes chipped to a sheen, and—the one who had given the orders until Llyd came—with my sword.

Llyd said: 'They have gone north. There is no one in the forest to hear or see. Take the gag out.'

'What's the use?' It was the fellow holding my sword who spoke. 'He doesn't know the Old Tongue. Look at him. He does not understand. When we spoke just now of killing him he did not look afraid.'

'What does that tell us except that he is brave, which we know already? A man attacked and tied as he is might well be expecting death, but there is no fear in his eyes. Do as I say. I know enough to ask him his name and where he is bound for. Take out the gag. And you, Pwul, and Areth, see if you can find dry stuff to burn. Let us have good light to see him by.'

One of the two beside me reached for the knot, and got the gag loosened. It had cut my mouth at the corner, and was foul with blood and spittle, but he thrust it into his pouch. Theirs was a degree of poverty that wasted nothing. I wondered how much 'they' had offered to pay for me. If Crinas and his followers had tracked me this far and set the hill-dwellers to watch me and discover where I was bound, Cwyll's hasty action had spoiled that plan. But it had also spoiled mine. Even if they decided now to let me go, so that they could follow me in secret, my journey was fruitless. Forewarned though I was, I could never elude these watchers. They see everything that moves in the forest, and they can send messages as quickly as the bees. I had known all along that the forest would be full of watchers, but normally they stay out of sight and mind their own concerns. Now I saw that my only hope of reaching Galava unbetrayed was to enlist them. I waited to hear what their leader had to say.

He spoke slowly, in bad Welsh. 'Who are you?'

'A traveller. I go north to the house of an old friend.'

'In winter?'

'It was necessary.'

'Where . . .' He searched for the words '. . . where do you come from?'

'Maridunum.'

This, it appeared, tallied with what 'they' had told them. He nodded. 'Are you a messenger?'

'No. Your men have seen what I carry.'

One of them said quickly, in the Old Tongue: 'He carries gold. We saw it. Gold in his belt, and some stitched in the mare's girth.'

The leader regarded me. I could not read his face; it was about as transparent as oak bark. He said over his shoulder, without taking his eyes off me: 'Did you search him?' He was speaking his own language.

'No. We saw what was in his pouch when we took his weapons.'

'Search him now.'

They obeyed him, not gently. Then they stood back and showed him what they had found, crowding to look by the light of the meagre torch. 'The gold: look how much. A brooch with the Dragon of the King's house. Not a badge, feel the weight, it is gold. A brand with the Raven of Mithras. And he rides from Maridunum towards the north, and secretly.' Cwyll pulled my cloak again across the exposed brand and stood up. 'It must be the man the soldiers told us about. He is lying. He is the messenger. We should let him go and follow him.'

But Llyd spoke slowly, staring down at me. 'A messenger carrying a harp, and the sign of the Dragon, and the brand of the Raven? And he rides alone out of Maridunum? No. There is only one man it can be; the magician from Bryn Myrddin.'

'Him?' This was the man who held my sword. It went slack, suddenly, in his grasp, and I saw him swallow and take a fresh grip. 'Him, the magician? He is too young. Besides, I have heard of that magician. They say he is a giant, with eyes that freeze you to the marrow. Let him go, Llyd, and we will follow him, as the soldiers asked us.'

Cwyll said, uncomfortably: 'Yes, let him go. Kings are nothing to us, but a magician is unchancy to harm.'

The others crowded close, curious and uneasy.

'A magician? They said nothing about that, or we would never have touched him.'

'He's no magician, see how he's dressed. Besides, if he knew magic, he could have stopped us.'

'He was asleep. Even enchanters have to sleep.'

'He was awake. He saw us. He did nothing.'

'We gagged him first.'

'He is not gagged now, and see, he says nothing.'

'Yes, let him go, Llyd, and we will get the money the soldiers offered. They said they would pay us well.'

More mutters, and nods of assent. Then one man said, thoughtfully: 'He has more on him than they offered us.'

Llyd had not spoken for some time, but now he broke angrily across the talk. 'Are we thieves? Or hirelings to give information for gold? I told you before, I will not blindly do as the soldiers asked us, for all their money. Who are they that we, the Old Ones, should do their work? We will do our own. There are things here that I should like to know. The soldiers told us nothing. Perhaps this man will. I think there are great matters afoot. Look at him; that is no man's messenger. That is a man who counts among men. We will untie him, and talk. Light the fire, Areth.'

While he had been talking the two he had bidden had brought together a pile of boughs and fallen stuff, and built a pyre ready for lighting. But there could have been no dry twig in the forest that night. Though the sleet showers had stopped some while back, all was dripping wet, and the ground felt spongy as if it must be soaked right to the earth's centre.

Llyd made a sign to the two who guarded me. 'Untie his hands. And one of you, bring food and drink.'

One of them hurried off, but the other hesitated, fingering his knife. Others crowded round, arguing. Llyd's authority, it seemed, was not that of a king, but of an accepted leader whose companions have the right to query and advise. I caught fragments of what they were saying, and then Llyd clearly: 'There are things we must know. Knowledge is the only power we have. If he will not tell us of his own will, then we shall have to make him . . .'

Areth had managed to get the damp stuff smouldering, but it gave neither heat nor light, only an intermittent gusting of smoke, acrid and dirty, which blew into all quarters as the wind wandered, making the eyes smart and choking the breath.

It was time, I thought, that I made an end. I had learned enough. I said, clearly, in the Old Tongue: 'Stand back from the fire, Areth.'

There was a sudden complete silence. I did not look at them. I fixed my eyes on the smoking logs. I blotted out the bite of my bound wrists, the pain of my bruises, the discomfort of my soaked clothes. And, as easily as a breath taken and then released on the night air, the power ran through me, cool and free. Something dropped through the dark, like a fire arrow, or a shooting star. With a flash, a shower of white sparks that looked like burning sleet, the logs caught, blazing. Fire poured down through the sleet, caught, gulped, billowed up again gold and red and gloriously hot. The sleet hissed in on to the fire, and, as if it had been oil, the fire fed on it, roaring. The noise of it filled the forest and echoed like horses galloping.

I took my eyes from it at last, and looked about me. There was no one there. They had vanished as if they had indeed been spirits of the hills. I was alone in the forest, lying against the tumbled rocks, with the steam rising already from my drying clothes, and the bonds biting painfully into my wrists.

Something touched me from behind. The blade of a stone knife. It slid between the flesh of my wrists and the ropes, sawing at my bonds. They gave way. Stiffly, I flexed my shoulders and began to chafe the bruised wrists. There was a thin cut, bleeding, where the knife had caught me. I neither spoke nor looked behind me, but sat still, chafing my wrists and hands.

From somewhere behind me a voice spoke. It was Llyd's. He spoke in the Old Tongue.

'You are Myrddin called Emrys or Ambrosius, son of Ambrosius the son of Constantius who sprang from the seed of Macsen Wledig?'

'I am Myrddin Emrys.'

'My men took you in error. They did not know.'

'They know now. What will you do with me?'

'Set you on your journey when you choose to go.'

'And meanwhile question me, and force me to tell you of the grave matters that concern me?'

'You know we can force you to do nothing. Nor would we. You will tell us what you wish, and go when you wish. But we can watch for you while you sleep, and we have food and drink. You are welcome to what we have to offer.'

'Then I accept it. Thank you. Now, you have my name. I have heard yours, but you must give it to me yourself.'

'I am Llyd. My ancestor was Llyd of the forests. There is no man here who is not descended from a god.'

'Then there is no man here who need fear a man descended from a king. I shall be glad to share your supper and talk with you. Come out now, and share the warmth of my fire.'

The food was part of a cold roast hare, with a loaf of black bread. They had venison, fresh killed, the result of tonight's foray; this they kept for the tribe, but thrust the pluck into the fire to roast, and along with it the carcass of a black hen and some flat uncooked cakes that looked, and smelt, as if they had been mixed with blood. It was an easy guess where these and the hare had been picked up; one sees such things at every crossways stone in that part of the country. It is no blasphemy in these people to take the wayside sacrifices: as Llyd had said to me they consider themselves descended from the gods and entitled to the offerings; and indeed, I see no harm in it. I accepted the bread, and a piece of venison heart, and a horn of the strong sweet drink they make themselves from herbs and wild honey.

The ten men sat round the fire, while Llyd and I, a little apart from them, talked.

'These soldiers,' I said, 'who wanted me followed. What sort of men were they?'

'Five men, soldiers fully armed, but with no blazon.'

'Five? One of them red-haired, big, in a brown jerkin and a blue cloak? And another on a pied horse?' This was the only horse recognisable to Stilicho, who had glimpsed its white patches in the murk of the grove. They must have had a fifth man, left on watch at the foot of the valley. 'What did they say to you?'

But Llyd was shaking his head. 'There was no man such as you describe, nor any such horse. The leader was a fair man, thin as a hay-fork, with a beard. They asked us only to watch for a man on a strawberry roan mare, who rode alone, on business that they had no knowledge of. But they said their master would pay well to know where he went.'

He threw the bone he had been gnawing over his shoulder, wiped his mouth, and met my eyes straightly. 'I said I would not ask your business, but tell me this much, Myrddin Emrys. Why is the son of the High King Ambrosius and the kin of Uther Pendragon hiding alone in the forest while Urien's men hunt him, wishing him ill?'

'*Urien's men?*'

There was deep satisfaction in his voice. 'Ah. Some things your magic will not tell you. But in these valleys, no one moves but we know of it. No one comes here but he is marked and followed until we know his business. We know Urien of Gore. These men were his, and spoke with the tongue of his country.'

'Then you can tell me about Urien,' I said. 'I know of him; a small king of a small country, brother by marriage to Lot of Lothian. There is no reason that I know why he should hunt me. I am on King's business, and Urien has no quarrel with me or with the King. He and his brother of Lothian are allies of Rheged and of the King. Has Urien, then, become the creature of some other man? Duke Cador?'

'No. Only of King Lot.'

I was silent. The fire roared and above us the forest stirred and ruffled. The wind was dying. I was thinking savagely. That Crinas and his gang were Cador's I had no doubt: now it seemed that there had been other spies from the north, watching and waiting, and that somehow they had stumbled across my trail. Urien, Lot's jackal. And Cador. Two of Uther's most powerful allies, his right hand and his left: and the moment the King began to fail they had spies out looking for the prince . . . The pattern broke and re-formed as a reflection in a pool re-forms after a rock has been thrown into it; but not the same pattern; the rock is there in the centre, changing everything. King Lot, the betrothed of Morgian the High King's daughter. King Lot.

I said at length: 'I heard you say these men had ridden on north. Were they going straight to report to Urien, or still trying to find and follow me?'

'To follow you. They said they would cast further north to find some trace of you. If they find none they will seek us out at a place we arranged with them.'

'And will you meet them there?'

He spat sideways, not troubling to answer.

I smiled. 'I shall go on tomorrow. Will you guide me to a path that the troopers will not know?'

'Willingly, but to do that I must know where you are making for.'

'I am following a dream I had,' I told him. He nodded. These folk of the hills find this reasonable. They work by instinct like animals, and they read the skies and wait for portents. I thought for a minute, then asked him: 'You spoke of Macsen Wledig. When he left these islands to go to Rome, did any of your people go with him?'

'Yes. My own great-grandfather led them under Macsen.'

'And came back?'

'Indeed.'

'I told you I had had a dream. I dreamed that a dead King spoke to me, and told me that before I could raise the living one I had a quest to fulfil. Did you ever hear what became of Macsen's sword?'

He threw up a hand in a sign I had never seen before. But I recognised what it was, a strong sign against strong magic. He muttered to himself, some rune in words I did not know, then, hoarsely, to me: 'So. It has come. Arawn be praised, and Bilis, and Myrddin of the heights. I knew these were great matters. I felt it on my skin as a man feels the rain falling. So this is what you seek, Myrddin Emrys?'

'This is what I seek. I have been East, and was told there that the sword, with the best of the Emperor's treasure, came back to the West. I think I have been led here. Can you help me further?'

He shook his head slowly. 'No. Of that matter I knew nothing. But there are those in the forest who can help you. The word was handed down. That is all I can tell you.'

'Your great-grandfather said nothing?'

'I did not say that. I will tell you what he said.' He dropped into the singsong voice that the tale-tellers use. I knew he would give me the exact words; these people hand words down from generation to generation, as changeless and as precisely worked as the chasing on a cup. 'The sword was laid down by a dead Emperor, and shall be lifted by a living one. It was brought home by water and by land, with blood and with fire, and by land and water shall it go home, and lie hidden in the floating stone until by fire it shall be raised again. It shall not be lifted except by a man rightwise born of the seed of Britain.'

The chanting stopped. The others round the fire had stopped their talking to listen; I saw eyes glint white, and hands move in the ancient sign. Llyd cleared his throat, spat again, and said gruffly: 'That's all. I told you it would be no help.'

'If I am to find the sword,' I said, 'help will come, no fear of that. And now I know I am getting nearer to it. Where the song is, the sword cannot be far away. And after I have found it . . . I think I know where I am going.'

'Where else should Myrddin Emrys be going, secretly and on a winter journey, except to the Prince's side?'

I nodded. 'He is beyond your territory, Llyd, but not beyond the eyes of your people. Do you know where he is?'

'No. But we will.'

'I'm content that you should. Watch me if you wish, and when you see where I am going, watch him for me. This is a king, Llyd, who will deal as justly with the Old Ones of the hills as ever he does with the kings and bishops who meet in Winchester.'

'We will watch him for you.'

'Then I shall go north, as I was going before, and wait for guidance. Now, with your permission, I should like to sleep.'

'You will be safe,' said Llyd. 'At first light we will see you on your way.'

Chapter Nine

The way they showed me was a path no better and no worse than I had followed hitherto, but it was easier to follow by the secret signs they told me of, and it was shorter even than keeping to the road. There were sudden twists and ascents to narrow passes which, without the signs, I would not have suspected of holding a way through. I would ride up some narrow, tree-filled gorge with an apparently solid wall of mountain straight ahead, and the sound of a torrent swelling and echoing between the rocks; but always, when I reached it, there was the pass, narrow and often dangerous, but clear, leading through some (till now) invisible cleft into the steep descent beyond. So for two days more I journeyed, seeing no one, resting little, and keeping myself and the mare alive on what the Old Ones had given me.

On the morning of the third day the mare cast a shoe. As luck would have it we were in easy ground, a ridge of smooth sheep-turf between valley and valley, deserted at this season, but smooth going. I dismounted, and led Strawberry along the ridge, scanning the valleys below me for signs of a road, or the smoke of a settlement. I knew roughly where I was now; though mist and snowstorms veiled the higher crests, I had seen, when they lifted, the white top of the great Snow Hill which holds up the winter sky. I had ridden this way before by the road, and recognised the shape of some of the nearer hills. I was sure that I had not far to travel to find a road, and a smith.

I had considered trying, myself, to remove Strawberry's other three shoes, but the going had been hard as iron, and if I had not kept her shod, she would have been lame long since. Besides, we were running out of food, and there was none to find in the winter ways. I must take the risk of being seen and recognised.

It was a still clear day of frost. At about noon I saw the smoke of a village, and a few minutes later the gleam of water in the valley below it. I turned the mare's head downhill. We went gently down under the shelter of sparsely set oaks, whose boughs still held a rustle of dead leaves. Soon I could see, below ahead of us through the bare trunks, the grey glitter of the river sliding between its banks.

Just above it I halted the mare at the edge of the oak wood. No movement, no sound, except the noisy river which drowned even the distant sound of barking dogs that marked the village.

I was certain that I was now not far from the course of the road. My best hope for a forge was where road and river met. Such places are generally near a ford or a bridge. Keeping just within the edge of the oak wood, I led Strawberry gently on towards the north.

So we journeyed for another hour or so, when suddenly the valley took a turn to the north-west, and there ahead of me, joining it from a neighbouring valley, ran the open belt of green that spoke of a road. And I could hear, clear on the winter's stillness, the metallic clang of a hammer.

There was no sign of the settlement, but where the road met the river the woods were very thick, and I knew that any village in these parts would be built on some hillock or rising ground from which men might defend themselves. The smith, in his solitary forge down by the water, need have no such fears. Such men are too useful, and have nothing worth the taking, and besides, there is still about them some of the old awe that hangs over the places where roads and waters meet.

The smith himself might indeed have been another of the Old Ones. He was a small man, bent by his trade, but immensely broad of shoulder, with arms knotted with muscle and covered with a pelt as thick as a bear's. His hands, broad and cracked, were almost as black as his hair.

He looked up from his work as my shadow fell across the doorway. I greeted him, then tied the mare to a ring by the door and sat down to wait, glad of the heat of the fire which was being blown to a blaze by a boy in a leather apron. The smith answered my greeting, with a sharp stare from under his brows, then without pausing in the rhythm of his work, went back to his hammering. He was making a share. With a hiss of steam and the gradual dulling of the strokes, the share slowly greyed and cooled to its cutting edge. The smith muttered something to the boy at the bellows, who let the air run out, then, picking up the water bucket, left the forge. The smith, setting down his hammer, straightened and stretched. He hooked a wine skin down from the wall and drank, then wiped his mouth. The expert eyes ran over the mare. 'Did you bring the shoe?' I had half expected him to speak the Old Tongue, but it was plain Welsh. 'Otherwise it'll take more time than you like to spare, I dare say. Or will I just take the other three off?'

I grinned. 'And pay me for them?'

'I'd do it for nothing,' said the smith, showing a black-toothed grin.

I handed him the cast shoe. 'Put this back on and there's a penny in it for you.'

He took the thing and examined it, turning it slowly in those horny hands. Then he nodded, and picked up the mare's foot.

'Going far?'

Part of a smith's payment was, of course, whatever news his customers could give him. I had expected this, and had a story ready. He rasped and listened, while the mare stood quietly between us, head down and ears slack. After a while the boy came back with a full bucket and tipped water into the tub. He had taken a long time, and he breathed as if he had been hurrying. If I thought about it at all, I imagined that he had seized, boy-like, the opportunity to spend as long over the errand as he could, and had had to hurry back. The smith made no comment, other than to grunt at him to get back to his bellows, and soon the fire roared up, and the shoe began to glow to red heat.

I suppose I should have been more alert, though to be here at all was a risk I had had to take. And there had been a chance that the troopers asking for the rider with the strawberry mare had not passed this way. But it seemed that they had.

What with the roar of the furnace and the clanging hammer I heard nothing of any approach, just saw, suddenly, the shadows between me and the doorway, then the four men standing there. They were all armed, and they all held their weapons ready, as if they were fully prepared to use them. Two of them held spears, none the less deadly for being home-made, one had a woodsman's hacking-knife, its blade honed to a bright edge that would go through living oak, and the fourth held, with some expertness, a Roman short sword.

The last one was the spokesman. He greeted me civilly enough, while the smith held his hammering, and the boy stared.

'Who are you, and where are you bound for?'

I answered him in his own dialect, and without moving from where I sat. 'My name is Emrys, and I am travelling north. I have had to come out of my way because, as you see, my mare has cast a shoe.'

'Where are you from?'

'From the south, where we do not send armed men against a stranger who passes through our village. What are you afraid of, coming four to one?'

He growled something, and the two with the spears grounded them, shuffling their feet. But the swordsman stood firm.

'You speak our language too well to be a stranger. I think you are the man we have been told to look for. Who are you?'

'No stranger to you, Brychan,' I said calmly. 'Did you get that sword at Kaerconon, or did we take it when we cut Vortigern's troop to pieces at the crossroads by Bremia?'

'Kaerconan?' The sword-point wavered and fell. 'You fought there, for Ambrosius?'

'I was there, yes.'

'And at Bremia? With Duke Gorlois?' The point dropped completely. 'Wait, you said your name was Emrys? Not Myrddin Emrys, the prophet that won the battle for us, and then doctored our hurts? Ambrosius' son?'

'The same.'

The men of my race do not easily bend the knee, but as he slid his sword back into his belt and showed his blackened teeth in a wide grin of pleasure, the effect was the same. 'By all the gods, so it is! I didn't know you, sir. Put your weapons up, you fools, can't you see he's a prince, and no meat of ours?'

'Small blame to them if they can't see any such thing,' I said, laughing. 'I'm neither prince nor prophet now, Brychan, *braud*. I'm travelling secretly, and I need help . . . and silence.'

'You shall have anything we can give you, my lord.' He had caught my involuntary glance towards the smith and the staring boy, and added quickly: 'There's no man here will say a word, look you. No, nor boy neither.'

The boy nodded, swallowing. The smith said gruffly: 'If I'd known who you were—'

'You'd not have sent your boy scampering to take the news to the village?' I said. 'No matter. If you are a King's man as Brychan is, I can trust you.'

'We are all King's men here,' said Brychan harshly, 'but if you were Uther's worst enemy, instead of his brother's son and the winner of his battles, I would help you, and so would my kinsmen and every man in these parts. Who was it saved this arm of mine after Kaerconan? It's thanks to you that I was able to carry this sword against you today.' He clapped the hilt of his belt. I remembered the arm; one of the Saxon axes had driven deep into the flesh, hacking a collop of muscle and laying the bone bare. I had stitched the arm and treated it; whether it was the virtue of the medicine, or Brychan's faith in anything 'the King's prophet' might do, the arm had healed. A great part of its strength was gone for ever, but it served him. 'And as for the rest of us,' he finished, 'we're all your men, my lord. You're safe here, and your secrets with you. We all know where the future of these lands lies, and that's in your hands, Myrddin Emrys. If we'd known you were the "traveller" those soldiers were seeking, we'd have held them here till you came—aye, and killed them if you'd so much as nodded your head.' He gave a fierce look round him, and the others nodded, muttering their agreement. Even the smith grunted some sort of assent, and brought his hammer clanging down as if it was an axe on an enemy's neck.

I said something to them, of thanks and acknowledgment. I was thinking that I had been out of the country too long; for too long had been talking with statesmen and lords and princes. I had begun to think as they were thinking. It was not only the nobles and the fighting kings who would help Arthur to the high throne and maintain him there; it was the folk of Britain, rooted in the land, feeding it and drawing life from it like its own trees, who would lift him there and fight for him. It was the faith of the people, from the high lands to the low, that would make him High King of all the realms and islands in a full sense which my father had dreamed of but had been unable to achieve in the short time allowed him. It had been the dream, too, of Maximus, the would-be emperor who had seen Britain as the foremost in a yoke of nations pulling the same way against the cold wind from the north. I looked at Brychan with his disabled arm, at his kinsmen, poor men of a poor village they would die to defend, at the smith and his ragged boy, and thought of the Old Ones keeping faith in their cold caves with the past and the future, and thought: this time it will be different. Macsen and Ambrosius tried it with force of arms, and laid the paving stones. Now, God and the people willing, Arthur will build the palace. And then, suddenly: that it was time I left courts and castles and went back into the hills. It was from the hills that help would come.

Brychan was speaking again. 'Will you not come to the village with us now, my lord? Leave the smith here to finish your mare, and come yourself up to my house, and rest and eat and give us your news. We are sharp set, all of us, to know why troopers should come seeking you, with money in their hands, and as urgent about it as if there was a kingdom at stake.'

'There is. But not for the High King.'

'Ah,' he said. 'They would have had us believe they were King's troops, but I thought they were not. Whose, then?'

'They serve Urien of Gore.'

The men exchanged glances. Brychan's look was bright with intelligence. 'Urien, eh? And why should Urien pay for news of you? Or maybe it was news of Prince Arthur he'd be paying for?'

'The two are the same,' I said, nodding. 'Or soon will be. He wants to know where I am going.'

'So he can follow you to the boy's hiding-place. Yes. But how would that profit Urien of Gore? He's a small man, and not likely to get bigger. Or—wait, I have it, of course. It would profit his kinsman, Lot of Lothian?'

'I think so. I've been told that Urien is Lot's creature. You may be sure he is working for him.'

Brychan nodded, and said slowly: 'And King Lot is promised to a lady that's likely to be Queen if Arthur dies . . . So he's paying troops to find where the boy is kept? My lord, that adds up to something I don't like the smell of.'

'Nor I. We may be wrong, Brychan, but my bones tell me we are right. And there may be others besides Lot and Urien. Were these men the only ones? You had no Cornishmen pass this way?'

'No, my lord. Rest easy, if any others come this way, they'll get no help.' He gave a short bark of laughter. 'I'd trust your bones sooner than most men's pledged word. We'll see no danger follows you to the little prince . . . If any pursuit of you comes through Gwynedd we'll see that it bogs down as surely as a stag's scent fails when he takes to water. Trust us, my lord. We're your men, as we were your father's. We know nothing of this prince you hold in your hand for us, but if he's yours, and you tell us to follow him and serve him, then, Myrddin Emrys, we'll be his men as long as we can hold swords. That's a promise, and it's for you that we make it.'

'Then I'll accept it for him, and give you my thanks.' I got to my feet. 'Brychan, it would be better if I did not come to the village with you, but there is something you could do for me now, if you will. I need food for the next few days, and wine for my flask, and fodder for the mare. I have money. Could you get these for me?'

'Nothing easier, and you can put away your money. Did you take money of me when you mended my arm? Give us an hour, and we'll get all you want, and no word said. The boy can come with us—folk are used to seeing him bring goods down to the forge. He'll bring what you need.'

I thanked him again, and we talked for a little longer, while I gave him what news there was from the south; then they took their leave. It is a matter of fact that, then or at any time, none of them, down to the boy, said a word to any man about my visit.

The boy had not yet returned from the village when the smith finished his job. I paid him his fee and commended him on his work. He took this as no more than his due, and, though he must have heard all that had passed between Brychan and me, showed no awe of me. Indeed, I have never seen why any man skilled in his trade, and surrounded by the articles of his craft, should be in awe of princes. Their task differs, that is all.

'Which way do you ride,' he asked me. Then, as I hesitated: 'I told you not to fear me. If that magpie Brychan and his brothers can be silent, then so can I. I serve the road and all men on it, and I'm no more a King's man than any smith who is bound to serve the road, but I spoke to Ambrosius once. And my grandfather's grandfather, why, he shod the horses of the Emperor Maximus himself.' He mistook the reason for the look on my face. 'Aye, you may well stare. That's a long time ago. But even then, my granda told me, this anvil had been worked by father and son and father and son further back than the oldest man in the village could remember. Why, it's said hereabouts that the first smith who set up his iron here had been taught his trade by Weland Smith himself. So who else would the Emperor come to? Look.'

He pointed at the door, which was set wide open, back against the wall. It was made of oak, adzed smooth as beaten silver, and age and weather had so bleached and polished it that its surface was bone pale, meshed and rippled like grey water. From a hook nearby hung a bag of iron nails, and then a rack of branding irons. All over the silky wood of the door were the scars of brands where the generations of smiths had tried them as they were fashioned.

An A caught my eye, but the brand was new, still charred and black. Beneath it and overlaid by it was some sign that looked like a bird flying; then an arrow, and an eye, and one or two cruder signs scrawled in with red hot metal by idle jesters waiting for the smith to finish the job. But to one side, clear of them all, faded so that they were only dark silver on light, were the letters M.I. Just below these was a deeper scar on the door, a half moon indented, with the marks of nails. It was at this that the smith was pointing. 'They say that's where the Emperor's stallion kicked out, but I don't believe it. When I and mine handle a horse, be he the wildest entire straight off the hills, he doesn't kick. But that, there, above it, that's true enough. That brand was made here, for the horses Macsen Wledig took east with him, the time he killed the King of Rome.'

'Smith,' I said, 'that is the only part of your legend that is false. The King of Rome killed Maximus, and took his sword. But the men of Wales brought it back here to Britain. Was the sword made here, too?'

He was a long time replying, and I felt my heart quicken as I waited. But at last he said, reluctantly: 'If it was, I have never heard it.' It was obvious that it had cost him a struggle not to add the sword to the forge's credit, but he had told me the truth.

'I was told,' I said, 'that somewhere in the forest is a man who knows where the Emperor's sword is hidden. Have you heard of this, or do you know where I can find it?'

'No, how should I? They say there is a holy man a long way north of here who knows everything. But he lives north of the Deva, in another country.'

'That is the way I was riding,' I said. 'I shall seek him out.'

'Then if you don't want to meet yon soldiers, don't go by the road. Six miles north of here there's a crossroads, where the road for Segontium heads west. Keep by the river from here, and it'll take you clear across the corner till the west-bound road crosses it.'

'But I'm not going to Segontium. If I bear too far to the west—'

'You leave the river where it meets the road again. Straight across from the ford the track runs up into the forest, through a shaw of hollies, and after that it's plain enough to see. It'll carry you on northwards, and never a glimpse of a road you'll see till you reach the Deva. If you ask the ferryman there about the holy man in the Wild Forest, he'll tell you the way. You go by the river. It's a good track, and impossible to miss.'

I have found that people never say this unless, in fact, the way is very easy to miss. However, I said nothing and, the boy arriving at that moment with the provisions, helped him stow them. As we did so he whispered: 'I heard what he said, lord. Don't listen to him. It's a bad track to follow, and the river's high. Stay with the road.'

I thanked him and gave him a coin for his pains. He went back to his bellows, and I turned to take my leave of the smith, who had vanished into some dark and cluttered recess at the back of the smithy. I could hear the clattering of metal, and his whistling between his broken teeth. I called out above it. 'I'm on my way now. My thanks.' Then my breath caught in my throat. Suddenly, back in the dark clatter behind the chimney, the newly leaping flame had lit the outline of a face.

A stone face; a familiar face once seen at every crossways. One of the first Old Ones, the god of going, the other Myrddin whose name was Mercury, or Hermes, lord of the high roads and bearer of the sacred snake. As one born in September, he was mine. He lay back now, the old Herm who had once stood out in the open watching the passers-by, head propped against the wall, the moss and lichen on him long since dried to powdered grey. Clearly under the blurred and fretted lines of carving I recognised the flat face rimmed with beard, the blank eyes as oval and bulging as grapes, the hands clasped across the belly, the once protruding genitals smashed and mutilated.

'If I had known you were there, Old One,' I said, 'I would have poured the wine for you.'

The smith had reappeared at my elbow. 'He gets his rations, never fear. There's none who serves the road would dare neglect him.'

'Why did you bring him in?'

'He never stood here. He was at the ford I told you of, where the old track that they call Elen's Causeway crossed the river Seint. When the Romans built their new road to Segontium they put their post station right in front of him. So he was brought here, I never heard how.'

I said slowly: 'At the ford you told me of? Then I think I must go that way after all.' I nodded to the smith, then raised a hand in salute to the god. 'Go with me now,' I said to him, 'and help me find this way—which it is impossible to miss.'

He went with me for the first part of the way; indeed, so long as the track clung to the river's bank it could hardly be missed. But towards late afternoon, when the dim winter sun hung low to its setting, a mist began to gather and hang near the water, thickening with dust into a damp and blinding fog. It might have been possible to follow the sound of water, though under the mist this was misleading, sometimes loud and near at hand, at others muted and deceivingly distant; but where the river took a bend, the track cut straight across, and twice, following this, I found myself astray and picking a way through the deep forest with no sign or sound of the river. In the end, a stray for the third time, I dropped the reins on Strawberry's neck, and let her pick her own way, reflecting that, ironically, had I risked the road I would have been safe enough. I would have heard the troopers approaching, and have been safe from their eyes had I withdrawn only a few yards into the fog-bound forest.

There must be a moon above the low-lying mist. This drifted like lighted cloud, not solid, but rivers of vapour with dark between, banks of pale stuff clinging round the trees like snow. Through it, hiding and showing, the gaunt trees laced their black boughs overhead. Underfoot the forest floor was thick as velvet and as quiet to walk on.

Strawberry plodded steadily on, without hesitation, following some path unseen to me, or some instinct of her own. Now and again she pricked her ears, but at something I could neither hear nor see, and once she checked and flung up her head sideways, coming as near as she ever did to shying, but before I could pick up the reins again, she slacked her ears, dropped her head, and quickened her pace along the invisible line of her choosing. I let her alone. Whatever was drifting past us in the misty silence, it would do us no harm. If this was the way—and I was sure now that it was—we were protected.

An hour after full dark, the mare carried me softly out of the trees, across a hundred paces or so of flat ground, and came to a halt in front of a looming square of blackness that could only be a building. There was a water trough outside. She lowered her head, blew, and began to drink.

I dismounted and pushed open the door of the building. It was the posting station the smith had told me of, empty now and half derelict, but apparently still in use by travellers such as myself. In one corner a pile of half charred logs showed where a fire had been lit recently, and in another stood a bed made from some tolerably clean planks laid across stones to raise it from the draught. It was rough comfort, but better than some we had had. I fell asleep within the hour to the sound of Strawberry's munching, and slept deeply and dreamlessly till morning.

When I woke, it was in the dusk of dawn, the sun not yet up. The mare dozed in her corner, slack-hipped. I went out to the trough for water to wash with.

The mist had gone, and with it the milder air. The ground was grey with frost. I looked about me.

The posting station stood a few paces back from the road which ran straight as a spear from east to west through the forest. Along this line the woodland had been cleared when the Romans made the road, the trees felled and the undergrowth hacked down a hundred paces back to either side from the gravelled way. Now saplings had grown up again and the low growth was thick and tangled, but still, near where I stood, I thought I could see under it the line of the old track that had been there before the Romans came. The river, smooth here and quiet-running, slid over the ruins of the causeway that took the road through it, hock deep. Beyond this, at the further edge of the cleared land, I could see, black against the grey winter oaks, the shaw of holly which marked my road to the north.

Satisfied, I cracked the wafer of ice on the water of the trough and washed. As I did so, behind me, the sun came up between the trees in the red of a cold dawn. Shadows grew and sharpened, barring the stiff grass. The frost sparkled. Light grew, like the smith's furnace under the bellows. When I turned, the sun, low and dazzling, blazed into my eyes, blinding me. The winter trees stood black and unbodied against a sky like a forest fire. The river ran molten.

There was something between me and the river, a tall shape, massive and yet insubstantial against the blaze, standing knee deep in the underbush at the edge of the road. Something familiar, but familiar in another setting, of darkness, and strange places, and outland gods. A standing stone.

For a sharp moment I wondered if I was still asleep, and this was my dream again. I put up an arm against the light and narrowed my eyes under it, peering.

The sun came clear of the treetops. The shadow of the forest moved back. The stone stood clear against the sparkling frost.

It was not after all a standing stone. Nothing strange at all, or out of place. It was an ordinary milestone, perhaps two cubits taller than was normal, but bearing only the usual inscription to an emperor, and below this the message: A. SEGONTIO. M. P. XXII.

When I approached it I saw the reason for its height; instead of being sunk in the turf it had been mounted on a squared plinth of stone. A different stone. The plinth where the Herm had stood? I stooped to push the frosted grass aside. The red sunlight struck the stone, showing a mark on the plinth that might have been an arrow. Then I saw what it was; the remains of some ancient writing, the ogam letters blurred and worn till they showed like the fletching on a shaft, and a barbed head pointing westward.

Well, I thought, why not? The signs were simple, but messages do not always come from the gods beyond the stars. My god had spoken to me before in ways as small as this, and I had told myself only yesterday to look low as well as high for the things of power. And here they were—a cast horseshoe, a word from a wayside smith, and some scratches on a stone—conspiring to turn me aside from my northern journey and take me westwards to Segontium. I thought again, why not? Who knew but that the sword might really have been made down at the forge yonder, and chilled in the Seint river, and that after his death they had carried it home to his wife's country, where she lodged still with his infant son? Somewhere in Segontium, the Caer Seint of Macsen Wledig, the King's Sword of Britain might lie, waiting to be lifted in fire.

Chapter Ten

The inn I stayed at in Segontium was a comfortable one, at the edge of the town, but not serving the main highway. A few travellers lodged there, but the place mostly served food and drink to the local men who attended the market, or who were on their way with goods down to the port.

The place had seen better days, having been built to serve the soldiers at the vast barracks above the town. It must have stood there, at the least, for a couple of hundred years; originally it had been well built of stone, with one handsome room, almost a hall, where a vast fireplace stood, and oaken beams as solid as iron held up the roof. The remains of the benches and the stout tables were still there, stained and burned, and here and there hacked where the daggers of drunken legionaries had carved their names, along with other things less respectable. It was a marvel that anything remained: some of the stone had been pillaged, and once at least the inn had been burned by raiders from Ireland, so that now the stone oblong of the hall was all that remained, and the blackened beams held up a roof of thatch instead of tiles. The kitchen was no more than a lean-to of daubed wattle behind the great fireplace.

But there was a big fire of logs blazing, and a smell of good ale, with bread baking in the oven outside; and a shed with decent bedding and fodder for the mare. I saw her warm and groomed and fed before I went into the inn myself to bespeak a bed-place and a meal.

At that time of year the port was all but closed to traffic; few travellers were on the road, and men did not stay out late drinking, but got themselves home to their beds soon after dusk. No one looked curiously at me, or ventured a question. The inn was quiet early, and I went to bed and slept soundly.

In the morning it was fine, with one of those glittering sharp days that December sometimes throws down like bright gold among the lead of winter's coinage. I breakfasted early, looked in at the mare, then left her resting and went out on foot.

I turned east, away from the town and the port, along the river's bank where, on rising ground about half a mile above the town, stood the remains of Segontium Roman fortress. Macsen's Tower stands just outside it, a little way down the hill. Here the High King Vortigern had lodged his men when my grandfather the King of South Wales had ridden up from Maridunum with his train to talk with him. I, a boy of twelve, had been with them, and on that journey had discovered for the first time that the dreams of the crystal cave were true. Here, in this wild and quiet corner of the world, I had first felt power, and found myself as a seer.

That had been a winter journey, too. As I walked up the weedy road towards the gateway set between its crumbling towers, I tried to conjure again the colours of cloaks and banners and bright weapons where now, in the blue shadows of morning, lay only the unprinted frost.

The vast complex of buildings was deserted. Here and there on the naked and fallen masonry the black marks of fire told their story. Elsewhere you could see where men had taken the great stones, stripping the very paving from the streets and carrying it off for their own building. There were dry thistles in the window spaces, and young trees rooted on the walls. A well-shaft gaped, choked with rubble. The cisterns brimmed with rain water, which slopped out through the grooves on the edge where men had sharpened their swords. No, there was nothing to see. The place was empty, even of ghosts. The winter sun shone down on a wide and crumbling waste land. The silence was complete.

I remember that as I walked through the shells of the buildings I was thinking, not of the past, not even of my present quest, but practically, as Ambrosius' engineer, of the future. I was weighing up the place as Tremorinus the chief engineer and I had been used to do; shifting this, repairing that, making the towers good, abandoning the north-easterly blocks to make good the west and south . . . Yes, if Arthur should ever need Segontium . . .

I had come to the top of the rise, the centre of the fort where the Commandant's house–Maximus' house–had stood. It was as derelict as the rest. The great door still hung on rotting hinges, but the lintel was broken and sagging, and the place was dangerous. I went cautiously inside. In the main chamber there was daylight spilling through gaps in the roof, and piles of rubble half hid the walls where paint still showed, flaked and dark with damp. In the dimness I could see the remains of a table–too massive to take away, and not worth chopping for kindling–and behind it the shredded remnants of leather hangings on the wall. A general had sat here once, planning to conquer Rome, as formerly Rome had conquered Britain. He had failed, and died, but in failing he had sown the seeds of an idea which after him another king had picked up. 'It will be one country, a kingdom in its own right,' my father had said, 'not merely a province of Rome. Rome is going, but for a while at least, we can stand.' And through this came the memory of another voice, the voice of the prophet who sometimes spoke through me. 'And the kingdoms shall be one Kingdom, and the gods one God.'

It would be time to listen to those ghostly voices when a general sat there once again. I turned back into the bright morning stillness. Where, in this waste land, was the end of my quest?

From here you could see the sea, with the small crowded houses of the port, and across from this the druids' isle that is called Mona, or Von, so that the people call the place Caer-y-n'ar Von. To the other side, behind me, reared the Snow Hill, Y Wyddfa, where if a man could climb and live among the snows, he would meet the gods walking. Against its distant whiteness showed, dark and ruined, the remains of Macsen's Tower. And suddenly, from this new angle, I saw it afresh. The tower of my dream; the tower in the picture on Ahdjan's wall . . . I left the Commandant's house and walked quickly out of the fortress gate towards it.

It stood in a wilderness of tumbled stones, but I knew that near it, dug into the side of the little valley beyond the gate, and running in almost beneath the tower itself, was the temple of Mithras; and on the thought I found that my feet had led me, with no will of my own, down the path which led to the Mithraeum door.

There were steps here, cracked and slippery. Halfway down the flight one tread thrust upwards vertically, half blocking the stairway, and at the foot was a pile of mud and shards, fouled by rats and prowling dogs. The place stank of damp and dirt and some ancient noisomeness that might have been spilled blood. On the ruined wall above the steps some roosting birds had whitened the stones; the dung was greening over now with slime. A jackdaw's perch, perhaps? A raven of Mithras? A merlin? I trod cautiously forward over the slimy flags, and paused in the temple doorway.

It was dark, but some sunlight had followed me in, and there was enough light from a hole broken in the roof somewhere, so that I could see dimly. The temple was as filthy and forlorn as the stairway that led to it. Only the strength of the vaulted roof had saved the place from falling in under the weight of the hillside above. The furnishings had gone long since, the braziers, benches, carvings; this, like the scoured ruin overhead, was a shell empty of its tenant. The four lesser altars had been broken and defaced, but the central altar stood there still, fixed and massive, with its carved dedication MITHRAE INVICTO, but above the altar, in the apse, axe and hammer and fire had obliterated the story of the bull and the conquering god. All that remained of the picture of the bull-slaying was an ear of wheat, down in one corner, its carving still sharp and new and miraculously unspoiled. The air, sour with the smell of some fungus, caught at the lungs.

It seemed fitting to say a prayer to the god departed. As I spoke aloud, something in the echo of my voice came, not like an echo, but an answer. I had been wrong. The place was not yet empty. It had been holy, and was stripped of its holiness; but something was still held down to that cold altar. The sour smell was not the smell of fungus. It was unlit incense, and cold ashes, and unsaid prayers.

I had been his servant once. There was no one here but I. Slowly, I walked forward into the centre of the temple, and held out my open hands.

Light, and colour, and fire. White robes and chanting. Fires licking upwards like light blowing. The bellow of a dying bull and the smell of blood. Outside somewhere the sun blazing and a city rejoicing to welcome its new king, and the sound of laughter and marching feet. Round me incense pouring heavy and sweet, and a voice that said through it, calm and small: 'Throw down my altar. It is time to throw it down.'

I came to myself coughing, with the air round me swirling thick with dust, and the sound of a crash still echoing round and round the vaulted chamber. The air trembled and rang. At my feet lay the altar, hurled over on its back into the curve of the apse.

I stared, dazed still and with swimming sight, at the hole it had torn in the floor where it had stood. My head sang with the echo; the hands I held stiffly before me were filthy, and one of them showed a bleeding gash. The altar was heavy, of massive stone, and in my right mind I would never have laid hands to it; but here it lay at my feet, with the echo of its fall dying in the roof, followed by the whisper of settling masonry as the crumbled pavement began to slide down into the hole where the altar had stood.

Something showed in the depths of the hole; a hard straight edge and a corner too sharp for stone. A box. I kneeled down and reached for it.

It was of metal, and very heavy, but the lid lifted easily. Whoever had buried it had trusted the god's protection rather than a lock. Inside, my hands met canvas cloth, long rotten, which tore; then inside that again, wrappings of oiled leather. Something long and slender and supple; here at last it was. Gently, I took the wrappings off the sword and held it naked across my hands.

A hundred years since they had put it here, those men who had made their way back from Rome. It shone in my hands, as bright and dangerous and beautiful as on the day it had been made. It was no wonder, I thought, that already in that hundred years it had become a thing of legend. It was easy to believe that the old smith, Weland himself, who was old before the Romans came, might have made this last artefact before he faded with the other small gods of wood and stream and river, into the misty hills, leaving the crowded valleys to the bright gods of the Middle Sea. I could feel the power from the sword running into my palms, as if I held them in water where lightning struck. *Whoso takes this sword from under this stone is rightwise King born of all Britain . . .* The words were clear as if spoken, bright as if carved on the metal. I, Merlin, only son of Ambrosius the King, had taken the sword from the stone. I, who had never given an order in battle, nor led so much as a troop; who could not handle a war stallion, but rode a gelding or a quiet mare. I, who had never even lain with a woman. I, who was no man, but only eyes and a voice. A spirit, I had said once, a word. No more.

The sword was not for me. It would wait.

I wrapped the beautiful thing up again in the filthy wrappings, and knelt to replace it. I saw that the box was deeper than I had thought; there were other objects there. The rotten canvas had fallen away to show the shape, gleaming in the dimness, of a wide-mouthed dish, a krater such as I had seen on my travels in countries east of Rome. It seemed to be of red gold, studded with emeralds. Beside it, still half muffled in wrappings, gleamed the bright edge of a lance-head. The rim of a platter showed, crusted with sapphire and amethyst.

I leaned forward to lay the sword back in its place. But before I could do it, without any warning, the heavy lid of the box fell shut with a crash. The noise set the echoes drumming again, and brought down with it a cascade of stone and plaster from the apse and the crumbling walls above. It happened so quickly that in the single movement of my own sharp recoil the box, hole and all had vanished from view under the rubble.

I was left kneeling there in the choking cloud of dust, with the shrouded sword held fast in my filthy and bleeding hands. From the apse, the last of the carving had vanished. It was only a curved wall, showing blank, like the wall of a cave.

Chapter Eleven

The ferryman at the Deva knew the holy man of whom the smith had spoken. It seemed he lived in the hills above Ector's fortress, at the edge of the great tract of mountain land they call the Wild Forest. Though I no longer felt myself to need the hermit's guidance, it would do no harm to talk to him, and his cell–a chapel, the ferryman called it–lay on my way, and might give me lodging until I considered how best to present myself at Count Ector's gates.

Whether or not the possession of the sword had in fact carried power with it, I travelled fast and easily, and with no more alarms. A week after leaving Segontium we–the mare and I–cantered easily along the green margin of a wide, calm lake, making for a light which showed pale in the early dusk, high as a star among the trees on the other shore.

It was a long way round the lake, and it was full dark when at last I trotted the tired mare up the forest track into a clearing and saw, against the soft and living darkness of the forest, the solid wedge of the chapel roof.

It was a smallish oblong building set back against the trees at the far side of a large clearing. All round the open space the pines stood in a dark and towering wall, but above was a roof of stars, and beyond the pines, on every side, the glimmer of the snow-clad heights that cupped this corrie high in the hills. To one side of the clearing, in a basin of mossy rock, stood a still, dark pool; one of those springs that well up silently from below, for ever renewing itself without sound. The air was piercingly cold, and smelt of pines.

There were mossed and broken steps leading up to the chapel door. This was open, and inside the building the light burned steadily. I dismounted and led the mare forward. She pecked against a stone, her hoof rapping sharply. You would have thought that anyone living in this solitary place would have come out to investigate, but there was no sound, no movement. The forest hung still. Only, far overhead, the stars seemed to move and breathe as they do in the winter air. I slipped the mare's bridle off over her ears, and left her to drink at the well. Gathering my cloak round me, I trod up the mossy steps, and entered the chapel.

It was small, oblong in shape, with a highish barrel roof; a strange building to find in the wild heart of the forest, where at most one might have expected a rough-built hut, or at least a cave, or dwelling contrived among the stones. But this had been built as a shrine, a holy place for some god to dwell in. The floor was of stone flags, clean and unbroken. In the centre, opposite the door, stood the altar, with a thick curtain of some worked stuff hung behind it. The altar itself was covered with a clean, coarse cloth, on which stood the lighted lamp, a simple, country-made thing which nevertheless gave a strong and steady light. It had recently been filled with oil, and the wick was trimmed and unsmoking. To one side of the altar, on the step, was a stone bowl of the kind I had seen used for sacrifice; it had been scoured white, and held sweet water. To the other side stood a lidded pot of some dark metal, pierced, such as the Christians use to burn incense. The air of the chapel still held, faintly, the sweet gummy smell. Three bronze lamps, triple-branched, stood unlit against a wall.

The rest of the chapel was bare. Whoever kept it, whoever had lighted the lamp and burnt the incense slept elsewhere.

I called aloud: 'Is anyone there?' and waited for the echoes to run up into the roof and die. No answer.

My dagger was in my hand; it had sprung there without conscious thought on my part. I had met this kind of situation before, and it had only meant one thing; but that had been in Vortigern's time, the time of the Wolf. Such a man as this hermit, living alone in a solitary place, trusted to the place itself, its god and its holiness, to protect him. It should have been enough, and in my father's time had certainly been so. But things had changed, even in the few years since his death. Uther was no Vortigern, but it seemed sometimes that we were sliding back to the time of the Wolf. The times were wild and violent, and filled with alarms of war; but more than this, faiths and loyalties were changing faster than men's minds could grow to apprehend them. There were men about who would kill even at the altar's horns. But I had not thought there were any such in Rheged, when I chose it for Arthur's sanctuary.

Struck by an idea, I stepped carefully past the altar and drew back the edge of the curtain. My guess had been right; there was a space behind the curtain, a semicircular recess which was apparently used as storage room; dimly the lamplight showed a clutter of stools and oil jars and sacred vessels. At the back of the recess a narrow doorway had been cut in the wall.

I went through. It was here, obviously, that the keeper of the place lived. There was a small square chamber built on the end of the chapel, with a low window deeply recessed, and another door giving, presumably, straight on the forest. I felt my way across in the dimness and pushed the door open. Outside the starlight showed me the rampart of pine trees crowding close, and to one side a lean-to-shed, and with its overhanging roof sheltering a stack of fuel. Nothing else.

Leaving the door wide, I surveyed what I could see of the room. There was a wooden bed with skins and blankets piled on it, a stool, and a small table with a cup and platter where the remains of a meal lay half-eaten. I picked up the cup; it was half full of thin wine. On the table a candle had burned down into a mess of tallow. The smell of the dead candle still hung there, mixed with the smell of the wine and the dead embers on the hearth. I put a finger to the tallow; it was still soft.

I went back into the chapel. I stood by the altar, and shouted again. There were two windows, one to either side, high in the wall; they were unglazed, open on the forest. If he was not too far away, he would surely hear me. But again there was no reply.

Then, huge and silent as a ghost, a great white owl swept in through one window and sailed across the lamplit space. I caught a glimpse of the cruel beak, the soft wings, the great eyes, blind and wise, then it was gone with no more sound than a spirit makes. It was only the *dillyan wen*, the white owl which haunts every tower and ruin in the country, but my flesh crept on my bones. From outside came the long, sad, terrible cry of the owl, and after it, like an echo, the sound of a man moaning.

Without his moaning I would not have found him till daylight. He was robed and hooded in black, and he lay face down under the dark trees at the edge of the clearing, beyond the spring. A jug fallen from his hand showed what his errand had been. I stooped and gently turned him over.

He was an old man, thin and frail, with bones that felt as brittle as a bird's. When I had made sure that none was broken, I picked him up in my arms and carried him back indoors. His eyes were half open, but he was still unconscious; in the lamplight I could see how one side of his face was dragged down as if a statuary had run his hand down suddenly over the clay, blurring the outline. I put him into his bed, wrapped warm. There was kindling left by the hearth, and what looked like a winter-stone ready among the ashes. I brought more fuel, then made fire and, when the stone was warm, drew it out, wrapped it in cloth, and put it to the old man's feet. For the moment there was nothing more that could be done for him, so after I had seen to the mare I made a meal for myself, then settled by the dying fire to watch through the rest of the night.

For four days I tended him, while none came near except the forest creatures and the wild deer, and at night the white owl haunting the place as if it waited to convoy his spirit home.

I did not think he could recover; his face was fallen in and grey, and I had seen the same blue tinge round the mouths of dying men. From time to time he seemed to come half to the surface, to know I was beside him. At such time he was restless always, fretting, I understood, about the care of the shrine. When I tried to talk to him and reassure him, he seemed not to understand, so in the end I drew back the curtains that parted the room from the shrine, so that he might see the lamp still burning in its place on the altar.

It was a strange time for me, by day tending the chapel and its keeper, and by night snatching sleep while I watched the sick man and waited for his restless muttering to make sense. There was a small store of meal and wine in the place, and with the dried meat and raisins left in my pack, I had sufficient food. The old man could scarcely swallow; I kept him alive on warm wine mixed with water, and a cordial I made for him from the medicines I carried. Each morning I was amazed that he had lived through the night. So I stayed, tending the place by day, and by night spending long hours beside him watching, or else in the chapel where the smell of incense slowly faded and the sweet air of the pines floated in and set the flame of the lamp aslant in its well of oil.

Now when I look back on that time it is like an island in moving waters. Or like a dreaming night which gives rest and impetus between the hard days. I ought to have been impatient to get on with my journey, to meet Arthur and to talk with Ralf again and arrange with Count Ector how best, without betraying either of us, I might enter the fabric of Arthur's life. But I troubled myself with none of these things. The shrouding forest, the still and glowing shrine, the sword lying where I had hidden it under the thatch of the shed, these held me there, serene and waiting. One never knows when the gods will call or come, but there are times when their servants feel them near, and this was such a time.

On the fifth night, as I carried in wood to build the fire, the hermit spoke to me from the bed. He was watching me from his pillows, and though he had not the strength to lift his head, his eyes were level and clear.

'Who are you?'

I set down the wood and went over to the bedside. 'My name is Emrys. I was passing through the forest, and came on the shrine. I found you by the well, and brought you back to your bed.'

'I . . . remember. I went to get water . . .' I could see the effort that the memory cost him, but intelligence was back in his eyes, and his speech, though blurred, was clear enough.

'You were taken ill,' I told him. 'Don't trouble yourself now. I'll get you something to drink, then you must rest again. I have a brew here which will strengthen you. I am a doctor; don't be afraid of it.'

He drank, and after a while his colour seemed better, and his breathing easier. When I asked if he was in pain, his lips said, 'No,' without sound, and he lay quietly for a while, watching the lamp beyond the doorway. I made the fire up and propped him higher on his pillows to ease his breathing, then sat down and waited with him. The night was still; from close outside came the hooting of the white owl. I thought: *You will not have long to wait, my friend.*

Towards midnight the old man turned his head easily on the pillows and asked me suddenly: 'Are you a Christian?'

'I serve God.'

'Will you keep the shrine for me when I am gone?'

'The shrine shall be kept. Trust me for it.'

He nodded, as if satisfied, and lay quiet for a time. But I thought something still troubled him; I could see it working behind his eyes. I heated more wine and mixed the cordial and held it to his lips. He thanked me with courtesy, but as if he was thinking of something else, and his eyes went back to the lighted doorway of the shrine.

I said: 'If you wish, I will ride down and bring you a Christian priest. But you will have to tell me the way.'

He shook his head, and closed his eyes again. After a while he said, thinly: 'Can you hear them?'

'I can hear nothing but the owl.'

'Not that, no. The others.'

'What others?'

'They crowd at the doors. Sometimes on a night of mid-summer you can hear them crying like young birds, or like flocks on the far hills.' He moved his head on the pillow. 'Did I do wrong, I wonder, to shut them out?'

I understood him then. I thought of the bowl of sacrifice, the well outside, the unlit lamps in the sacred nine of an older religion than any. And I think some part of my mind was with the white shadow that floated through the forest boughs outside. The place, if my blood told me aright, had been holy time out of mind. I asked him gently: 'Whose was the shrine, Father?'

'It was called the place of the trees. After that the place of the stone. Then for a while it had another name . . . but now down in the village they call it the chapel in the green.'

'What was the other name?'

He hesitated, then said: 'The place of the sword.'

I felt the nape of my neck prickle, as if the sword itself had touched me. 'Why, Father? Do you know?'

He was silent for a moment, and his eyes watched me, considering. Then he gave the ghost of a nod, as if he had reached some conclusion that satisfied him. 'Go into the shrine and draw the cloth from the altar.'

I obeyed him, lifting the lamp down to the step in front of the altar, and taking off the cloth that had draped it to the ground. It had been possible to see even through the covering cloth that the altar was not a table such as the Christians commonly use, but as high as a man's waist, and of the Roman shape. Now I saw that this was indeed so. It was the twin of the one in Segontium, a Mithras altar with a squared front and the edge scrolled to frame the carving. And carving there had been, though it was there no longer. I could make out the words MITHRAE and INVICTO across the top, but on the panel below where other words had been, a sword had been cut clear through them, its hilt, like a cross, marking the centre of the altar. The remains of the other letters had been gouged away, and the sword blade carved in high relief among them. It was rough carving, but clear, and as familiar to my eyes as that hilt was already familiar to my hand. I realised then, staring at it, that the sword in the stone was the only cross the chapel held. And above it, only the dedication to Mithras Unconquered remained. The rest of the altar was bare.

I went back to the old man's bedside. His eyes waited, with a question in them. I asked him: 'What does Macsen's sword do here, carved like a cross in the altar?'

His eyes closed, then opened again, lightly. He fetched a long, light breath. 'So. It is you. You have been sent. It was time. Sit down again, while I tell you.' As I obeyed him, he said, strongly enough, but in a voice stretched thin as wire: 'There is just time to tell you. Yes, it is Macsen's sword, him the Romans called Maximus, who was Emperor here in Britain before the Saxons ever came, and who married a British princess. The sword was forged south of here, they say, from iron found in Snow Hill within sight of the sea, and tempered with water that runs from that hill into the sea. It is a sword for the High King of Britain, and was made to defend Britain against her enemies.'

'So when he took it to Rome, it availed him nothing?'

'It is a marvel it did not break in his hand. But after he was murdered they brought the sword home to Britain, and it is ready for the King's hand that can find it, and finding, raise.'

'And you know where they hid it?'

'I never knew that, but when I was a boy and came here to serve the gods, the priest of the shrine told me that they had taken it back to the country where it was made, to Segontium. He told me the story, as it happened in this very place, years before his time. It was . . . it was after the Emperor Macsen had died at Aquileia by the Inland Sea, and those of the British who were left came home. They came through Brittany, and landed here on the west, and took the road home through the hills, and they came by here. Some of them were servants of Mithras, and when they saw this place was holy, they waited here for the summer midnight, and prayed. But most were Christians, and one was a priest, so when the others had done they asked him to say a mass. But there was neither cross nor cup, only the altar as you see it. So they talked together, and went to where their horses were standing, and took from the bundles tied there treasure beyond counting. And among the treasure was the sword, and a great krater, a grail of the Greek fashion, wide and deep. They stood the sword over against the altar for a cross, and they drank from the grail, and it was said afterwards that no man was there that day but found his spirit satisfied. They left gold for the shrine, but the sword and the grail they would not leave. One of them took a chisel and a hammer and made the altar as you see it. Then they rode away with the treasure, and did not come this way again.'

'It's a strange story. I never heard it before.'

'No man has heard it. The keeper of the shrine swore by the old gods and the new that he would say nothing save to the priest who came after. And I, in my turn, was told.' He paused. 'It is said that one day the sword itself will come back to the shrine, to stand here for a cross. So in my time I have struggled to keep the shrine clean of all but what you see. I took the lights away, and the offering bowls, and threw the crooked knife into the lake. The grass has grown now over the stone. I drove out the owl that nested in the roof, and I took the silver and copper coins from the well and gave them to the poor.' Another long pause, so long that I thought he had gone. But then his eyes opened again. 'Did I do right?'

'How can I tell? You did what you thought was right. No one can do more than that.'

'What will you do?' he asked.

'The same.'

'And you will tell no man what I have told you, save him who should know?'

'I promise.'

He lay quietly, with trouble still in his face, and his eyes intent on something distant and long ago. Then, imperceptibly but as definitely as a man stepping into a cold stream to cross it, he made a decision. 'Is the cloth still off the altar?'

'Yes.'

'Then light the nine lamps and fill the bowl with wine and oil, and open the doors to the forest, and carry me where I can see the sword again.'

I knew that if I lifted him, he would die in my hands. His breath laboured harshly in the thin chest, and the frail body shook with it. He turned his head on the pillows, feebly now.

'Make haste.' When I hesitated, I saw fear touch his face. 'I tell you I must see it. Do as I say.'

I thought of the shrine scoured and swept of all its ancient sanctities; and then of the sword itself, hidden with the King's gold in the roof-beams of the stable outside. But it was too late even for that. 'I cannot lift you, Father,' I said, 'but lie still, I will bring the altar here to you.'

'How can you—?' he began, then stopped with wonder growing in his face, and whispered: 'Then bring it quickly, and let me go.'

I knelt beside the bed, facing away from him, looking at the red heart of the fire. The logs had fallen from their blaze into a glowing cave, crystals glimmering in a globe of fire. Beside me the difficult breathing came and went like the painful beat of my own blood. The beat surged in my temples, hurting me. Deep in my belly the pain grew and burned. The sweat ran scalding down my face, and my bones shook in their sheath of flesh as, grain by grain and inch by shining inch, I built that altar-stone for him against the dark, blank wall. It rose slowly, solid, and blotted out the fire. The surface of the stone was lucent against the dark, and ripples of light touched it and wavered across it, as if it floated on sunlit water. Then, lamp by lamp, I lit the nine flames so that they floated with the stone like riding-lights. The wine brimmed in the bowl, and the censer smoked. INVICTO, I wrote, and groped, sweating, for the name of the god. But all that came was the single word INVICTO, and then the sword stood forward out of the stone like a blade from a splitting sheath, and the blade was white iron with runes running down it in the wavering water-light, below the flashing hilt and the message in the stone TO HIM UNCONQUERED . . .

It was morning, and the first birds were stirring. Inside, the place was very quiet. He was dead, gone as lightly as the vision I had made for him out of shadows. It was I who, stiff and aching, moved like a ghost to cover the altar and tend the lamp.

The Sword

Chapter One

When I had promised the dying man to see that the chapel was cared for, I had not thought of doing this myself. There was a monastery in one of the little valleys not far from Count Ector's castle, and it should not be hard to find someone from there who would live here and care for the place. This did not mean I must hand over the sword's secret to him; it was mine now, and the end of its story was in my hands.

But as the days passed, I thought better of my decision to approach the brothers. To begin with, I was forced to inaction, and given time to think.

I buried the old man's body, and just in time, as the next day the snow came, falling thick, soft, and silent, to shroud the forest deep, and island the chapel and block the tracks. To tell the truth I was glad to stay; there was enough food and fuel, and both the mare and I needed the rest.

For two weeks or more the snow lay; I lost track of days, but Christmas came and went, and the start of the year. Arthur was nine years old.

So perforce I kept the shrine. I supposed that whoever came as keeper would, like the old man, fight to keep the place clear for his own God, but in the meantime I was content to let what god would take the place. I would open it again to any who would see it. So I put away the altar cloth and cleaned the three bronze lamps and set them about the altar and lighted the nine flames. About the stone and the spring I could do nothing until the snow melted. Nor could I find the curving knife, and for this I was thankful; that Goddess is not one to whom I would willingly open a door. I kept the sweet holy water in her bowl of sacrifice, and at morning and evening burned a pinch of incense. The white owl came and went at will. By night I shut the chapel door to keep out the cold and the wind, but it was never locked, and all day it stood open, with the lights shining out over the snow.

Some time after the turn of the year the snow melted, and the tracks through the forest showed black and deep in mire. Still I made no move. I had had time to think, and I saw that I must surely have been led up to the

chapel by the same hand that had guided me to Segontium. Where better
could I stay to be near Arthur without attracting attention? The chapel
provided the perfect hiding-place. I knew well enough that the place would
be held in awe, and its guardian with it. The 'holy man of the forest' would
be accepted without question. Word would go round that there was a new
and younger holy man, but, country memories being long, folk would recall
how each hermit as he died had been succeeded by his helper, and before
long I would simply be 'the hermit of the Wild Forest' in my turn and in my
own right. And with the chapel as my home and my cure, I could visit the
village for supplies, talk to the people, and in this way get news, at the same
time ensuring that Count Ector would hear of my installation in the Wild
Forest.

About a week after the thaw started, before I would risk taking
Strawberry down through the knee-deep mud of the tracks, I had visitors.
Two of the forest people; a small, thick-set dark man dressed in badly cured
deerskins, which stank, and a girl, his daughter, wrapped in coarse woollen
cloth. They had the same swarthy looks and black eyes as the hill men of
Gwynedd, but under its weather-beaten brown the girl's face was pinched
and grey. She was suffering, but dumbly like an animal; she neither moved
nor made a sound when her father unwrapped the rags from her wrist and
forearm swollen and black with poison.

'I have promised her that you will heal her,' he said simply.

I made no comment then, but took her hand, speaking gently in the Old
Tongue. She hung back, afraid, until I explained to the man—whose name
was Mab—that I must heat water and cleanse my knife in the fire; then she
let him lead her inside. I cut the swelling, and cleaned and bound the arm. It
took a long time, and the girl made no sound throughout, but under the dirt
her pallor grew, so when I had done and had wrapped clean bandages round
the arm I heated wine for both of them, and brought out the last of my dried
raisins, and meal cakes to go with them. These last I had made myself,
trying my hand at them as I had so often watched my servant do at home. At
first my cakes had been barely eatable, even when sopped in wine, but lately
I had got the trick of it, and it gave me pleasure to see Mab and the girl eat
eagerly, and then reach for more. So from magic and the voices of gods to
the making of meal cakes; this, perhaps the lowest of my skills, was not the
one in which I took least pride.

'Now,' I said to Mab, 'it seems that you knew I was here?'

'Word went through the forest. No, do not look like that, Myrddin
Emrys. We tell no one. But we follow all who move in the forest, and we
know all that passes.'

'Yes. Your power. I was told so. I may need its help, while I stay here
keeping the chapel.'

'It's yours. You have lighted the lamps again.'

'Then give me the news.'

He drank, and wiped his mouth. 'The winter has been quiet. The coasts
are bound with storms. There was fighting in the south, but it is over and
the borders are whole. Cissa has taken ship to Germany. Aelle stays, with
his sons. In the north there is nothing. Gwarthegydd has quarrelled with his
father Caw, but when did that breed ever rest quiet? He had fled to Ireland,

but that is nothing. They say also that Riagath is with Niall in Ireland. Niall has feasted with Gilloman, and there is peace between them.'

It was a bare recital of facts, told through with neither expression nor real understanding, as if learnt by rote. But I could piece it together. The Saxons, Ireland, the Picts of the north; threats on all sides, but no more than threats: not yet.

'And the King?' I asked.

'Is himself, but not the man he was. Where he was brave, now he is angry. His followers fear him.'

'And the King's son?' I waited for the answer. How much did these folk really see?

The black eyes were unreadable. 'They say he is on the Isle of Glass, but then what do you do here in the Wild Forest, Myrddin Emrys?'

'I tend the shrine. You are welcome to it. All are welcome.'

He was silent for a while. The girl crouched beside the fire, watching me, her fear apparently gone. She had finished eating, but I had seen her slip a couple of the meal cakes into the folds of her clothes, and smiled to myself.

I said to Mab: 'If I should need to send a message, would your people take it?'

'Willingly.'

'Even to the King?'

'We would contrive that it should reach him.'

'As for the King's son,' I said. 'You say that you and your people see all that passes in the forest. If my magic should reach out to the King's son in his hiding place, and call him to me through the forest, will he be safe?'

He made the strange sign that I had seen Llyd's men make, and nodded. 'He will be safe. We will watch him for you. Did you not promise Llyd that he would be our king as well as the king of those in the cities of the south?'

'He is everyone's King,' I said.

The girl's arm must have healed cleanly, for he did not bring her back. Two days later a freshly snared pheasant appeared at the back door, with a skin of the honey mead. In my turn I cleared the drifted snow from the stone, and put a cup in the place made for it above the spring. I never saw anyone near either, but there were signs I recognised, and when I left part of a new batch of meal cakes at the back door they would vanish overnight, and some offering appear in their place—a piece of venison, perhaps, or the leg of a hare.

As soon as the forest tracks were clear I saddled Strawberry and rode down towards Galava. The way led down the banks of the stream, and along the northern shore of a lake. This was a smaller lake than the great stretch of water at whose head Galava lay; it was little more than a mile long, and perhaps a third of a mile wide, with the forest crowding down on every hand right to the water. About midway along, but nearer the southern shore, was an island, not large, but thickly grown with trees, a piece of the surrounding forest broken off and thrown down into the quiet water. It was a rocky island, its trees crowding steeply up towards the high crags which reared at the centre. These were of grey stone, outlined still with the last of the snow, and looking for all the world like the towers of a castle. On that day of leaden stillness there was about them a kind of burnished brightness. The island swam above its own reflection, the mirrored towers seeming to sink, fathoms deep, into the still centre of the lake.

From the other end of this lake the stream flowed out again, this time as a young river, swollen with snow water, cutting its way deep and fast through beds of pallid rushes and black marshland seamed with willow and alder, towards Galava. In a mile or so the valley widened, and the marsh gave way to the cultivated land and the walls of small farms, and the cottages of the settlement crowding close under the protection of the castle walls. Beyond Ector's towers, jutting grey and uncompromising through the black winter trees, was the great lake which stretched as far as the eye could see, to merge with the sullen sky.

The first place I came to was a farm set a short way back from the river-side. It was not the kind of farm we have in the south and south-west, built on the Roman plan, but a place such as I had become used to seeing here in the north. There was a cluster of circular buildings, the farmhouse and the sheds for the beasts, all within a big irregular ring protected by a palisade of wood and stone. As I passed the gate a dog hurtled to the end of his chain, barking. A man, the owner by his dress, appeared in the doorway of a barn and stood staring. He had a billhook in his hand. I reined in and called a greeting. He came forward with a look of curiosity, but with the wariness that one saw everywhere in the country nowadays when a stranger approached.

'Where are you bound, stranger? For the Count's castle of Galava?'

'No. Only to the nearest place where I may buy food—meat and meal and perhaps some wine. I've come from the chapel up there in the forest. You know it?'

'Who doesn't? How does the old man up there, old Prosper? We've not seen him since before the snow.'

'He died at Christmas.'

He crossed himself. 'You were with him?'

'Yes. I keep the chapel now.' I gave no details. If he liked to assume I had been there for some time, helping the chapel's keeper, that was all to the good. 'My name is Myrddin,' I told him. I had decided to use my own name, rather than the 'Emrys'. Myrddin was a common enough name in the west, and would not necessarily be connected with the vanished Merlin; on the other hand if Arthur was still known as 'Emrys', it might provoke questions if a stranger of that name suddenly appeared in the district, and began to spend time in the boy's company.

'Myrddin, eh? Where are you from?'

'I kept a hill shrine for a time in Dyfed.'

'I see.' His eyes summed me, found me harmless, and he nodded. 'Well, each to his task. No doubt your prayers serve us in their way as much as the Count's sword when it's needed. Does he know of the change up yonder?'

'I've seen no one since I came. The snow fell just after Prosper died. What sort of man is this Count Ector?'

'A good lord and a good man. And his lady as good as he. You'll not lack while they hold the forest.'

'Has he sons?'

'Two, and likely boys both. You'll see them, I dare say, when the weather loosens. They ride in the forest most days. No doubt the Count will send for you when he comes home; he's away now, and the elder son with him. They expect him back at the turn of spring.' He turned his head and called, and a woman appeared in the doorway of the house. 'Catra, here's the new man from the chapel. Old Prosper died at mid-winter: you were right he wouldn't last the new year in. Have you bread to spare from the baking, and a skin of wine? Good sir, you'll take a bite with us till the fresh batch comes from the oven?'

I accepted, and they made me welcome, and found me all I needed, bread and meal and a skin of wine, sheeps' tallow to make candles, oil for the lamps and chopped feed for the mare. I paid for them, and Fedor—he told me his name—helped me pack my saddle-bags. I asked no more questions, but listened to all he told me of local news, and then, well content, rode back to the shrine. The news would get to Ector, and the name; he would be the one person who would immediately connect the new hermit of the Wild Forest with the Myrddin who had vanished with the winter from his cold hilltop in Wales.

I rode down again at the beginning of February, this time to the village itself, where I found that the folk knew all about my coming and, as I had guessed, accepted me already as part of the place. Had I tried to find a niche in village or castle I would still, I knew, have been 'the foreigner' and 'the stranger' and a subject of ceaseless gossip, but holy men were a class apart, and often wanderers, and the good folk took them as they came. I had been relieved to find that they never came up to the chapel; there was too much of its ancient awesomeness still hanging about the place. They were most of them Christians, and turned for their comfort to the community of brothers near-by, but old beliefs die hard, and I was regarded with more respect, I believe, than the abbot himself.

The same image of ancient holiness clung, I had found, about the island in the lake. I had asked one of the hill men about it. It was known, he told me, as Caer Bannog, which means the Castle in the Mountains, and was said to be haunted by Bilis the dwarf king of the Otherworld. It was reputed to appear and disappear at will, sometimes floating invisible, as if made of glass. No one would go near it, and though people fished on the lake in summer and animals were grazed on the flat grassland at the western end where the river flowed into the valley, no one ventured near the island. Once a fisherman, caught in a sudden storm, had had his boat driven on to the island, and had passed a night there. When he came home next day he was mad, and talked of a year spent in a great castle made of gold and glass, where strange and terrible creatures guarded a hoard of treasure beyond man's counting. No one was tempted to go and look for the treasure, for the fisherman was dead, raving, within the week. So no man set foot now on the island, and though (they said) you could see the castle clearly sometimes of a fine sunset evening, when a boat rowed nearer it vanished clear away, and it was well known that if you set foot on the shore, the island would sink beneath you.

Such stories are not always to be dismissed as shepherd's tales. I had thought about it often, this other 'isle of glass' that I found now almost on my doorstep, and wondered if its reputation would make it a safe hiding-place for Macsen's sword. It would be some years yet before the boy Arthur could take and lift the sword of Britain, and meanwhile it was neither safe nor fitting that it should be hidden in the roof of a beasts' shed out there in the forest. It was a marvel, I had sometimes thought, that it did not set light to the thatch. If it was indeed the King's sword of Britain, and Arthur was to be the King who would lift it, it must lie in a place as holy and as haunted as the shrine where I myself had found it. And when the day came the boy must be led to it himself, even as I had been led. I was the god's instrument, but I was not the god's hand.

So I had wondered about the island. And then, one day, I was sure.

I went down to the village again in March for my monthly supplies. When I rode back along the lake-side the sun was setting, and a light mist wreathed along the water's surface. It made the island seem a long way off, and floating, so that one might well imagine it ghostly, and ready to sink under a random foot. The sun, sinking in splendour, caught the crags, and sent them flaming up from the dark hangers of trees behind. In this light the strange formations of the rock looked like high embattled towers, the crest of a sunlit castle standing above the trees. I looked, thinking of the legends, then looked again, and reined Strawberry in sharply and sat staring. There, across the flat sheen of the lake, above the floating mist, was the tower of my dream again. Macsen's Tower, whole once more and built out of the sunset. The tower of the sword.

I took the sword across next day. The mist was thicker than ever, and hid me from anyone who might have been there to see.

The island lay less than two hundred paces from the south shore of the lake. I would have swum the mare across, but found that she could go through breast high. The lake was still as glass, and as silent. We forged across with no more splashing than the wild deer make, and saw no living thing but a pair of diver ducks, and a heron beating slowly past in the mist.

I left the mare grazing, and carried the sword up through the trees till I reached the foot of the towered crags. I think I knew what I would find. Bushes and young trees grew thickly along the scree at the foot of the cliffs, but the boughs were barely budding, and through them I could see an opening, giving on a narrow passageway which led steeply downwards into the cliffs. I had brought a torch with me. I lit it, then went quickly down the steep passage, and found myself in a deep inner cavern where no light came.

In front of my feet lay a sheet of water, black and still, flooring half the cavern. Beyond the pool, against the back of the cavern, stood a low block of stone; I could not tell if it was a natural ledge, or if men's hands had squared it, but it stood there like an altar, and to one side of it a bowl had been hollowed in the stone. This was full of water, which in the smoky torchlight looked red as blood. Here and there from the roof water welled slowly, dripping down. Where it struck the surface of the pool the water broke with the sound of a plucked harp-string, its echo rippling away with the widening rings of torchlight. But where it dropped dull on stone it had not, as you might expect, worn the rock into hollows, but had built pillars, and above these from the dripping rocks hung solid stone icicles that had grown to meet the pillars below. The place was a temple, pillared in pale marble and floored with glass. Even I, who was here by right, and hedged with power, felt my scalp tingle.

By land and water shall it go home, and lie hidden in the floating stone until by fire it shall be raised again. So had the Old Ones said, and they would have recognised this place as I did; as the dead fisherman did who came back from the Otherworld raving of the halls of the dark King. Here, in Bilis' ante-chamber, the sword would be safe till the youth came who had the right to lift it.

I waded forward through the pool. The floor sloped and the water deepened. Now I could see how the dark passageway ran on, back and down behind the stone table, until the roof met the water's surface and the passage vanished below the level of the lake. Ripples ringed and lapsed against the rock, and the echoes ran round the walls and broke between the pillars. The water was ice cold. I laid the sword, still wrapped as I had found it, on the stone table. I went back across the pool. The place sang with echoes. I stood still, while they sank to a humming murmur and then died. My very breathing sounded all at once too loud, an intrusion. I left the sword to its silent waiting, and went quickly back up towards daylight. the shadows parted and let me through.

Chapter Two

April came, when Ector was expected home. For the first week of the month it rained and blew, weather like winter, so that the forest roared like the sea and the draughts through the shrine kept the nine lights plunging sidelong and smoking. The white owl watched from the place where she sat her eggs in the roof.

Then I woke in the night to silence. The wind had dropped, the pines were still. I rose and threw my cloak about me and went out. Outside the moon was high, and there in the north the Bear wheeled so low and brilliant that one felt one could reach up and touch it, were it not that its touch would burn. My blood ran light and free; my body felt rinsed and new clean as the forest. For the rest of the night I slept no more than a lover does, and at first light rose and broke my fast and went to saddle Strawberry.

The sun rose brilliant in a clear sky, and its early light poured into the glade. Yesterday's rain lay thick and glittering on the grasses and the new young curls of fern: it dripped and steamed from the pines so that their scent pierced the air. Beyond their bloomed crests the encircling hills smoked white towards the sky.

I let the mare out of the shed, and was carrying the saddle over to her when suddenly she lifted her head from her grazing, and put her ears up. Seconds later I heard what she had heard, the beat of hoofs, coming at a fast gallop, far too fast for safety on a twisting path seamed with roots and overhung by branches. I set the saddle down, and waited.

A neat black horse, galloped hard on a tight rein, burst out of the forest, came to a sliding stop three paces from me, and the boy who had been lying along its back like a leech slid, all in the same movement, to the ground. The horse was sweating hard, and the bit dripped foam. Red showed inside the blown nostrils. The neat-footed gallop and the collected stop had been a matter of hard control, then. Nine years old? At his age I had been riding a fat pony which had to be kicked to a trot.

He gathered the reins competently in one hand and held the horse still when it tried to thrust past him to the water. He did it absently; his attention was all on me.

'Are you the new holy man?'

'Yes.'

'Prosper was a friend of mine.'

'I'm sorry.'

'You don't look much like a hermit. Are you really keeping the chapel now?'

'Yes.'

He chewed his lip thoughtfully, regarding me. It was a look of approval, a weighing-up. Under it, as under no other I had encountered, I could feel my muscles clench themselves to hold nerves and heart-beats steady. I waited. I knew that, as ever, my face gave nothing away. What he must be seeing was merely a harmless-looking man, unarmed, saddling an un-distinguished horse for his routine ride down the valley for supplies.

He came apparently to a decision. 'You won't tell anyone you saw me?'

'Why, who's looking for you?'

His lips parted, surprised. I got the impression that I had been supposed to say: 'Very well, sir.' Then he turned his head sharply, and I heard it, too. Hoofs coming, soft on the mossy ground. Fast, but not as fast as the hard-ridden black.

'You haven't seen me, remember?' I saw his hand start towards his pouch, then stop halfway. He grinned, and the sudden flash startled me: till that moment he had been so like Uther, but that sudden lighting of the face was Ambrosius', and the dark eyes were Ambrosius', too. Or mine.

'I'm sorry.' He said it politely, but very fast. 'I do assure you I'm not doing anything wrong. At least, not very. I'll let him catch me soon. But he won't let me ride the way I like to.' He grabbed the saddle, ready to mount.

'If you ride like that on these tracks,' I said, 'I don't blame him. Do you need to go? Get inside there while I throw him off the scent, and I'll put your horse somewhere to cool off.'

'I knew you weren't a holy man,' he said, in the tone of someone conveying a compliment, and throwing me the reins, he vanished through the back doorway.

I led the black horse across to the shed, and shut the door on him. I stood there for a moment or two, breathing deeply as a man does when he comes out of rough water, steadying myself. Ten years, waiting for this. I had broken Tintagel's defences for Uther, and killed Brithael its captain, with a steadier pulse than I had now. Well, he was here, and we should see. I went to the edge of the clearing to meet Ralf.

He was alone, and furious. His big chestnut came up the track at a slamming canter, with Ralf crouched low on its neck. There was a thin scarlet mark on one cheek where a branch had whipped his face.

The sun was full on the clearing, and he must have been dazzled. I thought for a moment he was going to ride right over me. Then he saw me, and reined his horse hard to its haunches.

'Hey, you! Did a boy ride through here a few minutes ago?'

'Yes.' I spoke softly, and put my hand up to the rein. 'But hold a moment—'

'Out of the way, fool!' The chestnut, feeling the spurs go home, reared violently, tearing the rein from my hand. On the same breath Ralf said, thunderstruck: 'My lord!' and hauled the horse sideways. The striking hoofs missed me by inches. Ralf came out of the saddle as lightly as the boy Arthur, and reached for my hand to kiss it.

I drew it back quickly. 'No. And get off your knee, man. He's here, so watch what you do.'

'Sweet Christ, my lord, I nearly ran you down! The sun in my eyes–I couldn't see who it was!'

'So I imagined. A rather rough welcome, though, for the new hermit, Ralf? Are those the usual manners of the north?'

'My lord–my lord, I'm sorry. I was angry . . .' Then, honestly; 'Only because he fooled me. And even when I sighted the young devil I couldn't come up with him. So I . . .' Then what I had said got through to him. His voice trailed off, and he stood back, taking me in from head to foot as if he could hardly believe his eyes. 'The new hermit? *You?* You mean *you* are the 'Myrddin' of the shrine? . . . Of course! How stupid of me, I never connected him with you . . . And I'm sure no one else has–I haven't heard so much as a hint that it might be Merlin himself—'

'I hope you never will. All I am now is the keeper of the shrine, and so I shall remain, as long as it's necessary.'

'Does Count Ector know?'

'Not yet. When is he due home?'

'Next week.'

'Tell him then.'

He nodded, and then laughed, the surprise giving way to excitement, and what looked like pleasure. 'By the Rood, it's good to see you again, my lord! Are you well? How have you fared? How did you come here? And now–what will happen now?'

The questions came pouring out. I put up a hand, smiling. 'Look,' I said quickly, 'we'll talk later. We'll arrange a time. But now, will you go and lose yourself for an hour or so, and let me make the boy's acquaintance on my own?'

'Of course. Will two hours do? You'll get a lot of credit for that–I'm not usually thrown off his track so easily.' He glanced round the glade, but with his eyes only, not moving his head. The place was still in the morning sun, and silent but for the cock thrush singing. 'Where is he? In the chapel? Then in case he's watching us, you'd better do some misdirecting.'

'With pleasure.' I turned and pointed up one of the tracks which led out of the glade. 'Will that one do? I don't know where it goes, but it might suffice to lose you.'

'If it doesn't kill me,' he said resignedly. 'Of course it had to be that one, didn't it? In the normal way I'd just call that a bad guess, but seeing it's you—'

'It was only a random choice, I assure you. I'm sorry. Is it so dangerous?'

'Well, if I'm supposed to be looking for Arthur there, it's guaranteed to keep me out of the way for quite some time.' He gathered the reins, miming hasty agreement for the benefit of the unseen watcher. 'No, seriously, my lord—'

'Myrddin. No lord of yours now, nor of any man's.'

'Myrddin, then. No, it's a rough track but it's rideable—just. What's more, it's just the way that devil's cub would have chosen to take . . . I told you, nothing you can do can ever be quite random.' He laughed. 'Yes, it's good to have you back. I feel as if the world has been lifted off my shoulders. These last few years have been pretty full ones, believe me!'

'I believe you.' He mounted, saluting, and I stepped back. He went across the glade at a canter, and then the sound of hoofs dwindled up the ferny track and was gone.

The boy was sitting on the table's edge, eating bread and honey. The honey was running off his chin. He slid to his feet when he saw me, wiped the honey off with the back of his hand, licked the hand and swallowed.

'Do you mind very much? There seemed to be plenty, and I was starving.'

'Help yourself. There are dried figs in that bowl on the shelf.'

'Not just now, thank you. I've had enough. I'd better water Star now, I think. I heard Ralf go.'

As we led the horse across to the spring, he told me: 'I call him Star for that white star on his forehead. Why did you smile then?'

'Only because when I was younger than you I had a pony called Aster; that means Star in Greek. And like you, I escaped from home one day and rode up into the hills and came across a hermit living alone—it was a cave he lived in, not a chapel, but it was just as lonely—and he gave me honey cakes and fruit.'

'You mean you ran away?'

'Not really. Only for the day. I just wanted to get away alone. One has to, sometimes.'

'Then you did understand? Is that why you sent Ralf away, and didn't tell him I was here? Most people would have told him straight away. They seem to think I need looking after,' said Arthur in a tone of grievance. The horse lifted a streaming muzzle and blew the drops from its nostrils and turned from the water. We began to walk back across the clearing. He looked up. 'I haven't thanked you yet. I'm much obliged to you. Ralf won't get into trouble, you know. I never tell when I give them the slip. My guardian would be angry, and it's not their fault. Ralf will come back this way, and I'll go with him then. And don't worry yourself, either; I won't let him harm you. It's always me he blames, anyway.' That sudden grin again. 'It's always my fault, as a matter of fact. Cei is older than me, but I get all the ideas.'

We had reached the shed. He made as if to hand me the reins, then, as he had gone before, stopped in mid-gesture, led the horse in himself and tied him up. I watched from the doorway.

'What's your name?' I asked.

'Emrys. What's yours?'

'Myrddin. And, oddly enough, Emrys. But then that's a common name where I come from. Who is your guardian?'

'Count Ector. He's Lord of Galava.' He turned from his task, his cheeks flushed. I could see he was waiting for the next question, the inevitable question, but I did not ask it. I had spent twelve years myself having to tell every man who spoke to me that I was the bastard of an unknown father: I did not intend to force this boy through the same confession. Though there were differences. If I was any judge, he had better defences already than I had had at twice his age. And as the well-guarded foster-son of the Count of Galava, he did not have to live, as I had, with bastard shame. But then, I thought again, watching him, the differences between this child and myself went deeper: I had been content with very little, not guessing my power; this boy would never be content with less than all.

'And how old are you?' I asked him. 'Ten?'

He looked pleased. 'As a matter of fact I've just had my ninth birthday.'

'And can ride already better than I do now.'

'Well, you're only a—' He bit it off, and went scarlet.

'I only started work as a hermit at Christmas,' I said mildly. 'I've really ridden around the place quite a lot.'

'What doing?'

'Travelling. Even fighting, when I had to.'

'Fighting? Where?'

As we talked I had led him round to the front entrance of the chapel, and up the steps. These were mossed with age, and steep, and I was surprised at the child's lightness of foot as he trod up them beside me. He was a tall boy, sturdily built, with bones that gave promise of strength. There was another kind of promise, too, Uther's sort; he would be a handsome man. But the first impression one got of Arthur was of a controlled swiftness of movement almost like a dancer's or a skilled swordsman's. There was something in it of Uther's restlessness, but it was not the same; this sprang from some deep inner core of harmony. An athlete would have talked of co-ordination, an archer of a straight eye, sculptor of a steady hand. Already, in this boy, they came together in the impression of a blazing but controlled vitality.

'What battles were you in? You would be young even when the Great Wars were being fought? My guardian says that I will have to wait until I am fourteen before I go to war. It's not fair, because Cei is three years older, and I can beat him three times out of four. Well, twice, perhaps . . . Oh!'

As we went in through the chapel doorway the bright sunlight behind us had thrown our shadows forward, so that at first the altar had been hidden. Now, as we moved, the light reached it, the strong light of early morning, by some freak falling straight on the carved sword so that the blade seemed to lift clear and shining from its shadow on the stone.

Before I could say a word he had darted forward and reached for the hilt. I saw his hand meet the stone, and the shock of it go through his flesh. He stood like that for seconds, as if tranced, then dropped the hand to his side and stepped back, still facing the altar.

He spoke without looking at me. 'That was the queerest thing. I thought
it was real. I thought, "There is the most beautiful and deadly sword in the
world, and it is for me." And all the time it wasn't real.'

'Oh, it's real,' I said. Through the dazzling swirl of sunmotes I saw the
boy, hazed with brightness, turn to stare at me. Behind him the altar
shimmered white with the ice-cold fire. 'It's real enough. Some day it will
lie on this very altar, in the sight of all men. And he who then dares to touch
and lift it from here it lies, shall . . .'

'Shall what? What shall he do, Myrddin?'

I blinked, shook the sun from my eyes, and steadied myself. It is one
thing to watch what is happening elsewhere on middle-earth; it is quite
another to see what has not yet come out of the heavens. This last, which
men call prophecy, and which they honour me for, is like being struck
through the entrails by that whip of God that we call lightning. But even as
my flesh winced from it I welcomed it as a woman welcomes the final pang
of childbirth. In this flash of vision I had seen it as it would happen in this
very place; the sword, the fire, the young King. So my own quest through
the Middle Sea, the painful journey to Segontium, the shouldering of
Prosper's tasks, the hiding of the sword in Caer Bannog–now I knew for
certain that I had read the god's will aright. From now, it was only waiting.

'What shall I do?' the voice demanded, insistent.

I do not think the boy was conscious of the change in the question. He was
fixed, serious, burning. The end of the lash had caught him, too. But it was
not yet time. Slowly, fighting the other words away. I gave him all he could
understand.

I said: 'A man hands on his sword to his son. You will have to find your
own. But when the time comes, it will be there for you to take, in the sight of
all men.'

The Otherworld drew back then, and let me through, back into the clear
April morning. I wiped the sweat away from my face and took a breath of
sweet air. It felt like a first breath. I pushed back the damp hair and gave my
head a shake. 'They crowd me,' I said irritably.

'Who do?'

'Oh,' I said, 'those who keep wake here.' His eyes watched me, at stretch,
ready for wonders. He came slowly down the altar steps. The stone table
behind him was only a table, with a sword rudely carved. I smiled at him. 'I
have a gift, Emrys, which can be useful and very powerful, but which is at
times inconvenient, and always damnably uncomfortable.'

'You mean you can see things that aren't there?'

'Sometimes.'

'Then you're a magician? Or a prophet?'

'A little of both, shall we say. But that is my secret, Emrys. I kept yours.'

'I shan't tell anyone.' That was all, no promises, no oaths, but I knew he
would keep it. 'You were telling the future then? What did it mean?'

'One cannot always be sure. Even I am not always sure. But one thing for
certain; some day, when you are ready, you will find your own sword, and it
will be the most beautiful and deadly sword in the world. But now, just for
the moment, would you find me a drink of water? There's a cup beside the
spring.'

He brought it, running. I thanked him and drank, then handed it back.
'Now, what about those dried figs? Are you still hungry?'

'I'm always hungry.'

'Then next time you come, bring your rations with you. You might pick a
bad day.'

'I'll bring you food if you want it. Are you very poor? You don't look it.'
He considered me again, head aslant. 'At least, perhaps you do, but you
don't speak as if you were. If there's anything you'd like, I'll try and get it
for you.'

'Don't trouble yourself. I have all I need, now,' I said.

Chapter Three

Ralf came back duly, with questions in his eyes, but none on his lips except
those he might ask a stranger.

He came too soon for me. There were nine years to get through, and
judgments to make. And too soon, I could see, for the boy, though he
received Ralf with courtesy, and then stood silent under the lash of the
eloquent young man's tongue. I gathered from Arthur's expression that if it
had not been for my presence he might have been thrashed by more than
words. I understood that he lived under hard discipline: that kings must be
brought up harder than other men he must have known, but not that the
rule applied to him. I wondered what rule applied to Cei, and what Arthur
thought the discrimination meant. He took it well, and when it was finished
and I offered Ralf the appeasement of wine, went meekly enough to serve it.

When at length he was sent to lead the horses out, I said quickly to Ralf:
'Tell Count Ector I would rather not come down to the castle. He'll
understand that. The risks are too great. He'll know where we can meet in
safety, so I'll leave it to him to suggest a place. Would he normally come up
here, or might that make people wonder?'

'He never came before, when Prosper was here.'

'Then I'll come down whenever he sends a message. Now Ralf, there's
not much time, but tell me this. You've no reason to suppose that anyone
has suspected who the boy is? There's been no one watching about the
place, nothing suspicious at all?'

'Nothing.'

I said slowly: 'Something I saw, when you first brought him over from
Brittany. On the journey across by the pass, your party was attacked. Who
were they? Did you see?'

He stared. 'You mean up there by the rocks between here and
Mediobogdum? I remember it well. But how did you know that?'

'I saw it in the fire. I watched constantly then. What is it, Ralf? Why do
you look so?'

'It was a queer thing,' he said slowly. 'I've never forgotten it. That night,
when they attacked us, I thought I heard you call my name. A warning,

clear as a trumpet, or a dog barking. And now you say you were watching.' He shifted his shoulders as if at a sudden draught, then grinned. 'I'd forgotten about you, my lord. I'll have to get used to it again, I suppose. Do you still watch us? It could be an awkward thought, at times.'

I laughed. 'Not really. If there was danger it would come through me, I think. Otherwise it seems I can leave it to you. But come, tell me, did you ever find who it was attacked you that night?'

'No. They wore no blazon. We killed two of them, and there was nothing on them to show whose men they were. Count Ector thought they must be outlaws or robbers. I think so, too. At any rate there's been nothing since then, nothing at all.'

'I thought not. And now there must be nothing to connect Myrddin the hermit with Merlin the enchanter. What has been said about the new holy man of the chapel in the green?'

'Only that Prosper had died and that God had sent a new man at the appointed time, as he has always done. That the new man is young, and quiet-seeming, but not as quiet as he seems.'

'And just what do they mean by that?'

'Just what they say. You don't always bear yourself just like a humble hermit, sir.'

'Don't I? I can't think why not; it's what I normally am. I must guard myself.'

'I believe you mean that.' He was smiling, as if amused. 'I shouldn't worry, they just think you must be holier than most. It's always been a haunted place, this, and more so now, it seems. There are stories of a spirit in the shape of a huge white bird that flies in men's faces if they venture too far up the track, and—oh, all the usual tales you always get about hauntings, silly country stories, things one can't believe. But two weeks back—did you know that a troop of men was riding this way from somewhere near Alauna, and a tree fell across the way, with no wind blowing, and no warning?'

'I hadn't heard that. Was anyone hurt?'

'No. There's another path; they used that.'

'I see.'

He was watching me curiously. 'Your gods, my lord?'

'You might call them that. I hadn't realised I was to be so closely guarded.'

'So you knew something like this might happen?'

'Not until you told me. But I know who did it, and why.'

He frowned, thinking. 'But if it was done deliberately . . . If I am to bring Emrys this way again—'

'Emrys will be safe. And he is your safe conduct, too, Ralf. Don't fear them.'

I saw his brows twitch at the word 'fear', then he nodded. I thought he seemed anxious, even tense. He asked me: 'How long do you suppose you will be here?'

'It's hard to judge. You must know it depends on the High King's health. If Uther recovers fully, it may be that the boy will stay here until he is fourteen, and ready to go to his father. Why, Ralf? Can you not resign yourself to obscurity for a few more years? Or do you find it too taxing riding guard on that young gentleman?'

'No–that is, yes. But–it isn't that . . .' He stammered, flushing.

I said, amused: 'Then who is she?'

I did not quite understand his scowling look until, after a pause, he asked: 'How much else did you see, when you watched Arthur in the fire?'

'My dear Ralf!' It was not just the moment to tell him that the stars tend only to mirror the fate of kings and the will of gods. I said mildly: 'The Sight doesn't as a rule take me beyond bedchamber doors. I guessed. Your face is about as concealing as a gauze curtain. And you must remember to call him Emrys even when you are angry.'

'I'm sorry. I didn't mean–Not that there was anything you couldn't have watched–I mean, I've never even been in her bedchamber . . . I mean, she's–oh, hell and damnation, I should have known you'd know all about it. I didn't mean to be insolent. I'd forgotten you never take anything the way other men do. I never know where I am with you. You've been away too long . . . There are the horses now. He seems to have saddled yours as well. I thought you said you weren't coming down today after all?'

'I hadn't intended to. It must be Emrys' idea.'

It was. As soon as he saw us in the doorway, Arthur called out: 'I brought your horse, too, sir. Will you not ride down part of the way with us?'

'If we go at my pace, not yours.'

'We'll walk the whole way if you like.'

'Oh, I won't subject you to that. But we'll let Ralf lead the way, shall we?'

The first part of the descent was steep. Ralf went in front and Arthur behind him, and the black horse must have been very sure-footed indeed, for Arthur rode with his chin on his shoulder the whole way, talking to me. To anyone who did not know, it might have seemed that it was the boy who had nine years to make up; I hardly had to question him; all the detail, small and great, of his life came tumbling out, till I knew as much about Count Ector's household and the boy's place in it as he knew himself–and more besides.

We came at length down from the edge of the pines into a wood of oak and chestnut where the going was easier, and after half a mile or so struck into the easy track along the lake. Caer Bannog floated, sunlit, above its secret. The valley widened ahead of us, and presently, cloudy along its green curve, showed the line of willows that marked the river.

Where the river left the lake I checked my horse. As I took my leave of them the boy asked quickly: 'May I come back soon?'

'Come whenever you like–whenever you can. But you must promise me one thing.'

He looked wary, which meant that what he promised he would keep. 'What's that?'

'Don't come without Ralf, or whoever escorts you, don't break away next time. This is not called the Wild Forest for nothing.'

'Oh, I know it's supposed to be haunted, but I'm not afraid of what lives in the hills, not now that I've seen—' He checked, and changed direction without a tremor '—not with you there. And if it's wolves, I have my dagger, and wolves don't attack by day. Besides, there are no wolves that could catch Star.'

'I was thinking of a different kind of wild beast.'

'Bears? Boars?'

'No, men.'

'Oh.' The syllable was a shrug. It was bravery, of course; there were outlaws here as well as anywhere, and he must have heard stories, but it was innocence as well. Such had been Count Ector's care of him. The most vulnerable and sought-for head in the kingdoms, and danger was still only a story to him.

'All right,' he said, 'I promise.' I was satisfied. The guardians from the hollow hills might watch him for me, but guarding him was another thing. That took Ector's kind of power, and mine.

'My greetings to Count Ector,' I told Ralf, and saw that he had understood my thoughts. We parted then. I stood watching them ride off along the turf by the river, the black horse fighting to be away and snatching at the bit, Ralf's big chestnut simmering alongside, while the boy talked excitedly, gesturing. At length he must have got his way, for suddenly Ralf's heels moved, and the chestnut leapt forward into a gallop. The black, set alight a fraction later, tore after it. As the two flying figures vanished round the shaw of birch trees, the smaller turned in the saddle, and waved. It had begun.

He was back next day, trotting decorously into the clearing with Ralf half a length in the rear. Arthur carried a gift of eggs and honey cakes and the information that Count Ector was still away, but the Countess seemed to think contact with the holy man might do good where it was most needed, and was glad to let him come meanwhile. The Count would arrange to see me as soon as he got back.

Arthur gave me the message, not Ralf, and obviously saw nothing in it but the strict precautions of a guardian who he must have long ago decided was over-zealous to an uncomfortable degree.

Four of the eggs were broken. 'Only Emrys,' said Ralf, 'could possibly have imagined he could carry eggs on that wild colt of his.'

'You must admit he did very well only to break four.'

'Oh, aye, only Emrys could have done it. I've never had a quieter ride since I last escorted you.'

He went off then on some excuse. Arthur washed the eggs out of his horse's mane and then settled down to help me eat the honey cakes, and ply me with questions about the world that lay outside the Wild Forest.

A few days later Ector returned to Galava, and arranged through Ralf to meet me.

Word would have gone round by now that the boy Emrys had ridden up two or three times to the chapel in the green, and people might well expect Count Ector or his lady to send for the new incumbent to look him over. It was arranged that Ector and I were to meet as if by chance at Fedor's farm. Fedor himself and his wife could be trusted, I was told, with anything; the other folk there would only see the hermit calling for supplies as usual, and the Count riding by and taking the opportunity to speak with him.

We were shown into a smallish, smoke-filled room, and our host brought wine and then left us.

Ector had hardly altered, save to add a little grey to his hair and beard. When, after the first greetings were over, I told him so, he laughed. 'That's hardly surprising. You tip a gilded cuckoo's egg into my quiet nest and think to find me carefree? No, no, man, I was only jesting. Neither Drusilla nor I would have been without the boy. Whatever comes of it in the end, these have been good years, and if we've done a good job, we had the finest stuff in the world to work on.'

He plunged then into an account of his stewardship. Five years is a long time, and there was a great deal to say. I spoke hardly at all, but listened readily. Some of what he told me I knew already, from the fire, or from the boy's own talk. But if I was familiar enough with the tenor of Arthur's life here in Galava, and could judge its results for myself, what came chiefly out of Ector's talk of him was the deep affection which he and his wife felt for their charge. Not only these two, but the rest of the household who had no idea who Arthur was held him, apparently, in the same affection. My impressions of him had been right; there was courage and quick wit and a burning desire to excel. Not enough cool sense and caution, perhaps–faults like his father's–'But who the devil wants a young boy to be cautious? That much he'll learn the first time he's hurt, or, worse, when he finds a man that can't be trusted,' said Ector gruffly, obviously torn between pride in the boy and in his own successful guardianship.

When I began to talk of this, and to thank him for what he had done, he cut me off abruptly.

'Well, now, you've got yourself settled nicely in here, from all I hear about it. That was a fine chance, wasn't it, that led you up to the Green Chapel in time to take old Prosper's place?'

'Chance?' I said.

'Oh, aye, I'd forgotten who I was talking to. It's a long time since we had an enchanter in these parts. Well, to a jogging mortal like me it would have come as chance. Whatever it was, it's the best thing; you couldn't have taken a place in the castle, as it happens; we've got a man here who knows you well; Marcellus, him that married Valerius' sister. He's my master-at-arms. Maybe I shouldn't have taken him on, knowing you'd be likely to come back, but he's one of the best officers in the country, and God knows we're going to need all we have, here in the north. He's the best swordsman in the country, too. For the boy's sake, I couldn't miss the chance.' He shot me a sharp look from under his brows. 'What are you laughing at? Wasn't that chance, either?'

'No,' I said, 'It was Uther.' I told him of the talk I had had with the King on the subject of Arthur's training. 'How like Uther to send a man who knew me. But then he never did have room for more than one thought at a time . . . Well, I'll keep away. Can you find a good reason for letting the boy ride up to see me?'

He nodded. 'I've given it about that I know of you, and you're a learned man and have travelled widely, and there are things you can teach the boys that they'd not learn from Abbot Martin or the fathers. I'll let it be known that they may ride up your way whenever they wish.'

'"They?" Hasn't Cei outgrown a tutor, even an unorthodox one?'

'Oh, he wouldn't come for the learning.' His father's voice held a kind of rueful pride. 'He's like me, is Cei, not a thought in his head but what you might call the arts of the field. Not that even so he'll be the kind of swordsman Arthur's shaping for, but he's dogged and takes all the pains in the world. He'll not come twice if there's book learning to be discussed, but you know what boys are, what one has the other wants, and I couldn't keep him away if I tried, after all Arthur's been saying. He's talked of nothing else since I got home, even told Drusilla it was his holy duty to ride up there every day to see you got sufficient food. Yes, you may well laugh. Did you set a spell on him?'

'Not that I'm aware of. I'd like to see Cei again. He was a fine boy.'

'It's not easy for him,' said Ector, 'knowing the younger one is near as good as he is already, for all the three years' difference, and is likely to surpass him when they both come to man. And when they were younger it was always "Remember to let Emrys have as much as you—he's the foster-son, and a guest". It might have been easier if there'd been others. Drusilla's had the hardest time of it, not liking to favour one or the other, but having to let Cei see all the way that he was the real son, without letting Arthur feel he was on the outside. Cei's done well enough by the other boy, even if he does tend to jealousy, but there'll be nothing to fear in the future, I assure you. Show him where he can be loyal, and no one will shift him. Like his father; a slow dog, but where he grips, he holds.' He talked on a little longer, and I listened, remembering my own very different upbringing as the bastard and outsider at another court. Where I had been quiet and showed no talents that could rouse jealousy in boy or man, Arthur by his very nature must shine out among the other boys in the castle like a young dragon hatching in a clutch of pond newts.

At last Ector sighed, drank, and set down his cup. 'But there, those are nursery tales now, and long past. Cei stays by me now, among the men, and there's Bedwyr to keep Arthur company. When I said "they" I wasn't thinking of Cei. We've another boy with us now. I brought him back with me from York. Bedwyr, his name is, son of Ban of Benoic. Know him?'

'I've met him.'

'He asked me to take Bedwyr for a year or two. He'd heard Marcellus was here with me, and wanted Bedwyr to learn from him. He's about the same age as Arthur, so I wasn't sorry when Ban made the suggestion. You'll like Bedwyr. A quiet boy; not a great brain, so Abbot Martin tells me, but a good lad, and seems to like Emrys. Even Cei thinks twice before he tangles with the pair of them. Well, that's that, isn't it? It's just to be hoped Abbot Martin doesn't try to spoke the wheel.'

'Is it likely?'

'Well, the boy was baptised a Christian. It's thought that Prosper served God in the later years, but it's well known that the Green Chapel has housed other gods than the true Christ in its time. What do you do now, up there in the forest?'

'I believe in giving due honour to whatever god confronts you,' I said. 'That's commonsense in these days, as well as courtesy. Sometimes I think the gods themselves have not yet got it clear. The chapel is open to the air and the forest, and they come in who will.'

'And Arthur?'

'In a Christian household, Arthur will owe duty to Christ's God. What he does on the field of battle may be another matter. I don't know yet which god will give the boy his sword–though I doubt if Christ was much of a swordsman. But we shall see. May I pour you more wine?'

'What? Oh, thank you.' Ector blinked, wetted his lips, and changed the subject. 'Ralf was saying you'd asked about that ambush at Mediobogdum five years back. They were robbers, no more. Why do you ask? Have you reason to think that someone's interested now?'

'I had some small trouble on the way north,' I said. 'Ralf tells me there has been nothing here.'

'Nothing. I've been twice myself to Winchester and once to London, and there's never a soul so much as questioned me, which they'd have been quick to do if anyone had thought the boy might be anywhere in the north.'

'Lot has never approached you or shown interest?'

Another quick look. 'Him, eh? Well, nothing would surprise me there. Some of the trouble we've been having in these parts might easily have been avoided if that same gentleman had minded his kingdom's business instead of paying court to a throne.'

'So they say that, do they? It's the King's place he's after, not just a place at the King's side?'

'Whatever he's after, they're handfast now, he and Morgian: they'll be married as soon as the girl is twelve years old. There's no way out of that union now, even if Uther wanted to end it.'

'And you don't like it?'

'No one does, up in this part of the country. They say that Lot's stretching his borders all the time, and not always with the sword. There's talk of meetings. If he gets too much power by the time the High King fails, we might well find ourselves back in the time of the Wolf. The Saxons coming every spring and burning and raping as far as the Pennine Way, aye, and the Irish coming down to join them, and more of our men taking to the high hills and what cold comfort they can find there.'

'How recently did you see the King?'

'Three weeks past. When he lay at York he sent for me, and asked privately about the boy.'

'How did he look?'

'Well enough, but the cutting edge was gone. You understand me?'

'Very well. Was Cador of Cornwall with him?'

'No. He was still at Caerleon then. I have heard since—'

'At Caerleon?' I asked sharply. 'Cador himself was there?'

'Yes,' said Ector, surprised. 'He'd be there just before you left home. Did you not know?'

'I should have known,' I said. 'He sent a party of armed men to search my home on Bryn Myrddin, and to watch my movements. I gave them the slip, I think, but what I didn't reckon on was being watched by two parties at the same time. Urien of Gore had men there in Maridunum, too, and they traced me north into Gwynedd.' I told him about Crinas, and Urien's party, and he listened, frowning. I asked him: 'You haven't heard reports of any such up here? They'd ask no questions openly, but wait and watch, and listen.'

'No. If there were strangers, it would have been reported. You must have shaken them off. Be easy, Cador's men will never come this way. He's in Segontium now, did you know?'

'When I was there I heard he was expected. Do you know if he plans to make his headquarters at Segontium, now Uther's put him in charge of the Irish Shore defences? Has there been talk of re-investing it?'

'There was talk, yes, but I doubt if it will ever come to anything. That's a task that'll take more time and money than Uther is likely to spare, or to have, just yet. If I can make a guess, Cador will garrison Segontium and the frontier fortresses, and base himself inland where he can keep his forces moving to the point of attack. Perhaps at Deva. Rheged himself is in Luguvallium. We do what we can.'

'And Urien? I trust he's fixed on the east, where he belongs?'

'Well dug in on his rock,' said Ector, with grim satisfaction. 'And one thing's for sure. Until Lot marries Morgian with every bishop in the realm in attendance, and proof positive of consummation, he won't stir a hand to bring Uther down, or let Urien do so, either. Nor will he find Arthur. If they haven't had a sniff of the boy in nine years, they'll never pick the scent up now. So be easy. By the time Morgian is twelve, and ready for bedding, Arthur will be fourteeen, and coming to the time when the King has promised to bring him before the kingdom. It will be time then to deal with Lot and Urien, and if the time comes before then, why, it is with God.'

On that we parted, and I rode back alone to the shrine.

Chapter Four

After this Arthur, sometimes with the other two boys, but usually just with Bedwyr, rode up to the chapel to see me two or three times a week. Cei was a big fair-haired boy, with a look of his father, and his manner to Arthur was a compound of patronage and hectoring affection which must have been galling at times to the younger boy. But Arthur seemed fond of his foster-brother, and eager to share with him the pleasure (for so he seemed to find it) of his visits to me. Cei enjoyed the tales I had to tell of foreign lands and the histories of fighting and conquests and battle, but he grew quickly tired of discussing the way the people lived and governed their countries, and the talk of their legends and beliefs, which Arthur loved. As time went by Cei stayed more often at home, going (the other two told me) on sport or business with his father; hunting sometimes, or on patrol, or accompanying Count Ector on his occasional visits to his neighbours. After the first year, I rarely saw Cei at all.

Bedwyr was quite different, a quiet boy of Arthur's own age, gentle and dreamy as a poet, and a natural follower. He and Arthur were like two sides of the same apple. Bedwyr trailed, doglike in devotion, after the other boy; he made no attempt to hide his love for Arthur, but there was nothing soft about him, for all his gentle ways and poet's eyes. He was a plain boy, with his nose flattened in some fight, and badly set, and the scar of some nursery burn on his cheek. But he had character and kindness, and Arthur loved him. As the son of Ban, a petty king, Bedwyr was the superior even of Cei, and as far as any of the boys knew, right out of Arthur's star. But this never occurred to either Bedwyr or Arthur; the one offered devotion, the other accepted it.

One day I said to them: 'Do you know the story of Bisclavaret, the man who became a wolf?' Bedwyr, without troubling to answer, brought the harp out from under its shroud, and put it gently by me. Arthur, prone on the bed with chin on fist and eyes brilliant in the firelight–it was a chill afternoon of late spring–said impatiently: 'Oh, let be. Never mind the music. The story.' Then Bedwyr curled beside him on the blankets, and I tuned the strings and started.

It is an eerie tale, and Arthur took it with sparkling face, but Bedwyr gew quieter than ever, all eyes. It was growing dark when they went home, with a husky servant that day for escort. Arthur, alone with me next day, told me how Bedwyr had woken in the night with the nightmare. 'But do you know, Myrddin, when we were on the way home yesterday, when he must have been full of the story, we saw something slink off beyond the trees and we thought it was a wolf, and Bedwyr made me ride between him and Leo. I know he was frightened, but he said it was his right to protect me, and I suppose it was, since he is a king's son, and I—'

He stopped. It was as near as he had ever got to the boggy ground. I said nothing, but waited.

'—and I was his friend.'

I talked to him then about the nature of courage, and the moment passed, I remember what he said afterwards of Bedwyr. I was to remember it many times in later years, when, on even less certain ground, the trust between him and Bedwyr held true.

He said now, seriously, as if at nine years old he knew: 'He is the bravest companion, and the truest friend in all the world.'

Ector and Drusilla had, of course, taken care to see that Arthur knew all that was good to know about his father and the Queen. He knew, too, as much as everyone in the country knew about the young heir who waited–in Brittany, in the Isle of Glass, in Merlin's tower–to succeed to the kingdom. He told me once, himself, the story that was current about the 'rape at Tintagel'. The legend had lost nothing in the telling. By now, it seemed, men believed that Merlin had spirited the King's party, horses and all, invisibly within the walls of the stronghold, and out again in the broad light of next morning.

'And they say,' finished Arthur, 'that a dragon curled on the turrets all night, and in the morning Merlin flew off on him, in a trail of fire.'

'Do they? It's the first I heard of that.'

'Don't you know the story?' asked Bedwyr.

'I know a song,' I said, 'which is closer to the truth than anything you've heard up here. I got it from a man who'd once been in Cornwall.'

Ralf was there that day, listening silently, amused. I raised my brows at him and he shook his head slightly. I had not thought he would have let Arthur know he came from Tintagel, and indeed I doubt if anyone now would have guessed. He spoke as nearly as might be with the accent of the north.

So I told the boys the story, the truth as I knew it—and who knew better?—without the extra trimmings of fantasy that time and ignorance had added to it. God knows it was magical enough without; God's will and human love driving forward together in the black night under the light of the great star, and the seed sown which would make a king.

'So God had his way, and the King through him, and men—as men always do—made mistakes and died for them. And in the morning the enchanter rode away alone, to nurse his broken hand.'

'No dragon?' this from Bedwyr.

'No dragon,' I said.

'I prefer the dragon,' said Bedwyr firmly. 'I shall go on believing the dragon. Riding away alone, that's a let-down. A real enchanter wouldn't do that, would he, Ralf?'

'Of course not,' said Ralf, getting to his feet. 'But we must. Look, it's dusk already.'

He was ignored. 'I'll tell you what I don't understand,' said Bedwyr, 'and that's a king who would risk setting the whole kingdom at blaze for a woman. Keeping faith with your peers is surely more important than having any woman. I'd never risk losing anything that really mattered, just for that.'

'Nor would I,' said Arthur slowly. He had been thinking hard about it, I could see. 'But I think I understand it, all the same. You have to reckon with love.'

'But not to risk friendship for it,' said Bedwyr quickly.

'Of course not,' said Arthur, I could see that he was thinking in general terms, where Bedwyr meant one friendship, one love.

Ralf began to speak again, but at that moment something, a shadow, swept silently across the lamplight. The boys hardly glanced up, it was only the white owl, sailing silently in through the open window to its perch in the beams. But its shadow went across my skin like a hand of ice, and I shivered.

Arthur looked up quickly. 'What is it, Myrddin? It's only the owl. You look as if you'd seen a ghost.'

'It was nothing,' I said. 'I don't know.'

I did not know, either, then, but I know now. We had been speaking Latin, as we usually did, but the word he had used for the shadow across the light was the Celtic one, *guenhwyvar*.

Be sure I told them too, about their own country, and about the times recently past, of Ambrosius and the war he had fought against Vortigern, and how he had knit the kingdoms together into one, and made himself High King, and brought to the length and breadth of the land justice, with a sword at its back, so that for a short span of years men could go peacefully about their affairs anywhere in the country, and not be molested; or if they were, could seek, and get, the King's justice equally for high or low. Others had given them the stories as history; but I had been there, and closer to affairs than most, being at the High King's side and, in some cases, the architect of what had happened. This, of course, they would not be allowed to guess; I told them merely that I had been with Ambrosius in Brittany, and thereafter at the battle of Kaerconan, and through the next years of the rebuilding. They never asked how or why I was there, and I think this was out of delicacy, in case I should be forced to confess how I had served in some humble capacity as assistant to the engineers, or even as a scribe. But I still remember the questions Arthur poured out about the way the Count of Britain–as Ambrosius then styled himself–had assembled, trained, and equipped his army, how he had shipped it across the Narrow Sea to the land of the Dumnonii where he had set up his standard as High King before he swept northwards to burn Vortigern out of Doward, and finally to smash the vast army of the Saxons at Kaerconan. Every detail of organisation, training, and strategy I had to recall for him as best I could, and every skirmish of which I could tell them anything was fought over and over again by the two boys, poring over maps drawn in the dust.

'They say there will be war again soon,' said Arthur, 'and I am too young to go.' He mourned over it, openly, like a dog which is bidden to stay at home on a hunting morning. It was three months before his tenth birthday.

It was not all talk of war and high matters, of course. There were days when the boys played like young puppies, running and wrestling, racing their horses along the river side, swimming naked in the lake and scaring every fish within miles, or taking bows with Ralf up to the hills to look for hares or pigeons. Sometimes I went with them, but hunting was not a sport I cared for. It was different when it occurred to me to rummage out the old hermit's fishing rod and take it to try the waters of the lake. We would pass the time happily there. Arthur fishing with more fury than success, myself watching him, and talking. Bedwyr did not care for fishing, and on these occasions went with Ralf, but Arthur, even on the days when wind or weather made fishing useless, seemed to prefer to stay with me rather than go with Ralf or even Bedwyr to look for sport in the forest.

Looking back, I do not remember now that I ever paused to question this. The boy was my whole life, my love for him so much a part of every day that I was content to take the time as it came, accepting straight from the gods the fact that the boy seemed to like above all else to be with me. I told myself merely that he needed to escape from the crowded household, from the patronage of an elder brother preparing now for a position which he himself could never hope for, and also a chance to be with Bedwyr in a world of imagination and brave deeds where he felt himself to belong. I would not allow myself to ascribe it to love, and if I had guessed the nature of the love, could have offered no comfort then.

Bedwyr stayed at Galava for more than a year, leaving for home in the autumn before Arthur's eleventh birthday. He was to return the following summer. After he had gone Arthur moped visibly for a week, was unwontedly quiet for another, then recovered his spirits with a bound, and rode up to see me, in defiance of the weather, rather more often than before.

I have no idea what reasons Ector gave for letting him come so often. Probably he needed no reason: as a rule the boy rode out daily except in the foulest weather, and if nothing was volunteered as to where he went, nothing would be asked. It became known, as it was bound to, that he came often to the Green Chapel where the wise man lived, but if people thought about it at all, they commended the boy's sense in seeking out a man known for his learning, and let it be.

I never attempted to teach Arthur in the way that Galapas, my master, had taught me. He was not interested in reading or figuring, and I made no attempt to press them on him; as King, he would employ other men in these arts. What formal learning he needed, he received from Abbot Martin or others of the community. I detected in him something of my own ear for languages, and found that, besides the Celtic of the district where he lived, he had retained a smattering of Breton from his babyhood, and Ector, mindful of the future, had been at pains to correct his northern accent into something which the British of all parts would understand. I decided to teach him the Old Tongue, but was amazed to find that he already knew enough of it to follow a sentence spoken slowly. When I asked where he had learnt it he looked surprise and said: 'From the hill people, of course. They are the only ones who speak it now.'

'And you have spoken with them?'

'Oh, yes. When I was little once I was out with one of the soldiers and he was thrown and hurt himself, and two of the hill people came to help me. They seemed to know who I was.'

'Did they indeed?'

'Yes. After that I saw them quite often, here and there, and I learnt to speak with them a little. But I'd like to learn more.'

Of my other skills, music and medicine, and all the knowledge I had so gladly amassed about the beasts and birds and wild things, I taught him nothing. He would have no need of them. He cared only about beasts to hunt them, and there, already, he knew almost as much as I about the ways of wild deer and wolf and boar. Nor did I share with him much of my knowledge about engines; here again it would be other men who would make and assemble them; he needed only to learn their uses, and most of this he was taught along with the arts of war he learnt from Ector's soldiers. But as Galapas had done with me, I taught him how to make maps and read them, and showed him the map of the sky.

One day he said to me: 'Why do you look at me sometimes as if I reminded you of someone else?'

'Do I?'

'You know you do. Who is it?'

'Myself, a little.'

His head came up from the map we were studying. 'What do you mean?'

'I told you, when I was your age I used to ride up into the hills to see my friend Galapas. I was remembering the first time he taught me to read a map. He made me work a great deal harder than ever I make you.'

'I see.' He said no more, but I thought he was downcast. I wondered why he should imagine I could tell him anything about his parentage; then it occurred to me that he might expect me to 'see' such things at will. But he never asked me.

Chapter Five

There was no war that year, or the next. In the spring after Arthur's twelfth birthday Octa and Eosa at last broke from prison, and fled south to take refuge behind the boundaries of the Federated Saxons. The whisper went that they had been helped by lords who professed themselves loyal to Uther. Lot could not be blamed directly, nor Cador; no one knew who were the traitors, but rumours were rife, and helped to swell the feeling of unease throughout the country. It seemed as if Ambrosius' forceful uniting of the kingdoms were to go for nothing: each petty king, taking Lot's example, carved and kept his own boundaries. And Uther, no longer the flashing warrior men had admired and feared, depended too much on the strength of his allies, and turned a blind eye to the power they were amassing.

The rest of that year passed quietly enough, but for the usual tale of forays both from north and south of the wild debatable land to either side of Hadrian's Wall, and summer landings on the east coast which were not (it was said) wholeheartedly repelled by the defenders there. Storms in the Irish Sea kept the west peaceful, and Cador, I was told, had made a beginning on the fortifications at Segontium. King Uther, heedless of the advisers who told him that when trouble came it would come first from the north, stayed between London and Winchester, throwing his energies into keeping the Saxon Shore patrolled and Ambrosius' Wall fortified, with his main force ready to move and strike wherever the invaders broke the boundaries. Indeed there seemed little to turn him yet towards the north: the talk of a great alliance of invaders was still only talk, and the small raids continued along the southern coast throughout the year, keeping the King down there to combat them. The Queen left Cornwall at this time, and moved to Winchester with all her train. Whenever the King could, he joined her there. It was observed, of course, that he no longer frequented other women as he had been used to do, but no rumour of impotence had gone around: it seemed as if the girls who had known of it had seen it simply as a passing phase of his illness, and said nothing. When it was seen now that he spent all his time with the Queen, the story went round that he had taken vows of fidelity. So, though the girls might mourn their lover, those citizens rejoiced who had been wont to lock their daughters away when word went round that the King was coming, and praised him for adding goodness to his powers as a fighting man.

These latter he certainly seemed to have recovered, though there were stories of the uncertain temper he showed, and of sudden ferocities in the treatment of defeated enemies. But on the whole this was welcomed as a sign of strength at a time when strength was needed.

I myself seemed to have managed to drop safely out of sight. If people wondered from time to time where I had gone, some said that I had crossed the Narrow Sea again and resumed my travels, others, that I had retired once more into a new solitude to continue my studies. I heard from Ralf and Ector—and sometimes, innocently, from Arthur—that there were rumours of me from all parts of the country. It was said that when the King first fell sick, Merlin had appeared immediately in a golden ship with a scarlet sail and ridden to the palace to heal him, and afterwards vanished into the air. He had been seen next at Bryn Myrddin, though none had seen him ride there. (This in spite of the fact that I had changed horses at the usual places, and stayed every night in a public tavern.) And since then, the talk went, Merlin the enchanter had been wont to appear and vanish here and there all over the country. He had healed a sick woman near Aquae Sulis, and a week later had been seen in the Caledonian Forest, four hundred miles away. The host of tales grew, coined by idle folk anxious for the importance that such 'news' would give them. Sometimes, as had happened before, wandering healers or would-be prophets would style themselves 'another Merlin', or even use my very name: this inspired trust in the healers, and if the patient recovered, did no harm. If the patient died, folk tended to say simply, 'It cannot have been Merlin after all; *his* magic would have succeeded.' And since the false Merlins would by that time have completely vanished, my reputation would survive the imposture. So I kept my secret, and lost nothing. Certainly no wandering suspicion lighted on the quiet keeper of the Green Chapel.

I had contrived from time to time to send messages of reassurance to the King. My chief fear was that he would grow impatient, and either send for the boy too soon, or by some hasty inadvertence betray Ector or myself to the people who watched him. But he remained silent. Ector, speaking of it to me, wondered if the King still thought the danger of treachery too great to have the boy by him in London, or if he still hoped against bitter hope that some day he would get another son.

Myself I think it was neither. He was beset, was Uther, with treachery and trouble and the lack of the fine health that he was used to: and besides, the Queen started to ail that winter. He had neither time nor mind to give to the young stranger who was waiting to take what he himself found it harder and harder to hold.

As for the Queen, there had been many times during the years when I had wondered at her silence. Ralf had, through means of his own, kept secretly in touch with his grandmother who served Ygraine, and through her had assured the Queen of her son's well-being. But from all accounts Ygraine, though she loved her daughter Morgian, and would have loved her son as dearly, was able to watch—indifferently enough, it seemed—her children used as tools of royal policy. Morgian and Arthur were, to her, pledges only of her love for the King, and having given them birth she turned back to her husband's side. Arthur she had barely seen, and was content to know that one day he would emerge from his fastness safe and strong, in the King's time of need. Morgian, to whom she had given all the mother-love of which she was capable, was to be sent (without a backword glance, said Marcia in a letter to Ralf) to the marriage bed which would join the cold northern kingdom and its grim lord to Uther's side in the coming struggle. When I had tried to show Arthur something of the all-consuming sexual love which had obsessed Uther and Ygraine, I had spoken only half the truth. She was Uther's first, then she was queen; and though she was the bearer of princes, she cared no more than the hawk does when its fledglings fly. As things stood, for her sake, it was better so; and, I thought, for Arthur too. All he needed now, he had from Ector and his gentle wife.

I kept no contact with Bryn Myrddin, but in some round-about way Ector got news for me. Stilicho had married Mai, the miller's girl, and the child was a boy. I sent my felicitations and a gift of money, and a threat of various dire enchantments should he let either of his new family touch the books and the instruments that remained at the cave. Then I forgot about them.

Ralf married, too, during my second summer in the Wild Forest. His reason was not the same as Stilicho's; he had wooed the girl long enough, and only found his happiness in her bed after a Christian wedding. Even if I had not known the girl was virtuous, and that Ralf had been fretting after her like a curbed colt for a year or more, I could have guessed it from his relaxed and glowing strength as the weeks went by. She was a beautiful girl, gay and good, and with her maidenhead gave him all her worship. As for Ralf, he was a normal young man and had looked here and there, as young men will, but after his marriage I never knew him to look aside again, though he was handsome, and in later years was not unnaturally high in the King's favour and found many who tried to use him as a stepping stone to power as much as to pleasure. But he was never to be used.

I believe that there were those in Galava who wondered why such an able young gentleman was kept riding guard on Ector's foster-son when even young Cei joined his father and the troops whenever there was an alarm, but Ralf had a high temper, and a fine self-assurance these days, and had, besides, the Count's orders to quote. It might have been hard if his wife had taunted him, but she was soon with child, and too thankful to have him tied at home near her ever to question it. Ralf himself fretted a little, I knew, but he confessed to me once when we were alone that if he could only see Arthur acknowledged and get in his rightful place beside the High King, he would count it a good life's work.

'You told me the gods were driving us that night at Tintagel,' he said. 'I am no familiar of the gods, as you are, but I can think of no youth I have known who is worthier to take up the High King's sword when he had to lay it down.'

All reports bore this out. When I went down to the village for supplies, or to the tavern for gossip, I heard plenty about Ector's foster-son 'Emrys'. Even then his was a personality that gathers legend as a drip-stone gathers lime.

I heard a man say once, in the crowded tavern room: 'I tell you this, if you told me he was one of the Dragon's breed, a bastard of the High King that's gone, I'd believe you.'

There were nods, and someone said: 'Well, why not? He could be a bastard of Uther's, couldn't he? It's always surprised me that there aren't more of those around. He was one for the women, sure enough, before his sickness put the fear of hell on him.'

Someone else said: 'If there were more, you can be sure he'd have acknowledged them.'

'Aye, indeed,' said the fellow who had spoken first. 'That's true. He never showed any more shame than the farm bull, and why should he? They say that the girl he got in Brittany—Morgause, was it?—is high in his favour at court, and goes everywhere with him. Those are all the children we know of, the two girls, and the prince that's being reared at some foreign court.'

Then the talk passed, as it often did these days, to the succession, and the young Prince Arthur growing up somewhere in the foreign kingdom to which Merlin the enchanter had secretly spirited him away.

Though how long he might be kept hidden I could not guess. Watching him come riding up the forest track, or diving and wrestling with Bedwyr in the summer waters of the lake, or drinking in the wonders I showed him as the earth absorbs rain, it was a marvel to me that everyone did not see, as I could, the kingship shining from him as it had shone in that moment's flashing vision from the sword in the altar stone.

Chapter Six

Then came the year that, even now, is called the Black Year. It was the year after Arthur's thirteenth birthday. The Saxon leader Octa died at Rutupiae, of some infection caught in the long imprisonment; but his cousin Eosa went to Germany, and there met Octa's son Colgrim, and it was not hard to guess at their counsels. The King of Ireland crossed the sea, but not to the Irish Shore, where Cador waited for him at Deva, and Maelgon of Gwynedd behind the scrambled-up fortifications of Segontium: his sails were watched from Rheged's shore as he made landfall in Strathclyde and was received kindly by the Pictish kings there. These latter had had a treaty with Britain since Macsen's time, renewed with Ambrosius: but what answers they would make now to Ireland's proposals no man could guess.

Other troubles hit nearer home and more immediately. It was a year of starvation. The spring was long and cold and wet, the fields everywhere flooded, long past the time when corn should have been sown and growing. Cattle disease was everywhere in the south, and in Galava even the hardy blue-fleeced hill sheep died, their feet rotted away so that they could not move on the fells to feed themselves. Late frost blasted the fruit buds, and even as the green corn grew, it turned brown and rotted in the stagnant fields. Strange tales came north. A druid had run mad and attacked Uther for leading the country away from the Old Religion; and a Christian bishop stood up in church and railed against him for being a pagan. There was a story of an attempt on the King's life, and of the hideous way in which the King had punished the men responsible.

So spring and summer wore through, in disaster, and by the beginning of autumn the country lay like a waste land. People died of starvation. Folk talked of a curse laid on the country; but whether God was angry because the country shrines still claimed their sacrifices, or whether the old gods of hill and woodland exacted vengeance for neglect, no one was sure. All that was certain was that there was a blight on the land, and the King ailed. There was a meeting of nobles in London demanding that Uther should name his heir. But it seemed—Ector told me this—as if he still feared, not knowing friend from foe; all he would say was that his son lived and thrived, and would be presented to the nobles at the next Easter feast. Meanwhile his daughter Morgian passed her twelfth birthday, and would be taken north for her wedding at Christmas.

With the autumn the weather changed, and a mild, dry season set in. It was too late to help the crops or the dying cattle, but grateful to men starved of the sun, and the bright weather came in time to ripen some of the fruit the spring storms and the summer rot had left on the trees. In the Wild Forest the mists curled through the pines in the early morning, and the September dews glittered everywhere on the cobwebs. Ector left Galava to meet with Rheged and his allies at Luguvallium. The King of Ireland had sailed for home and there was still peace in Strathclyde, but the defence line along the Ituna Estuary from Alauna to Luguvallium was to be manned, and there was talk of Ector as its commander. Cei went with his father. Arthur, scarce three months from his fourteenth birthday, tall enough for sixteen, and already (according to Ralf) a notable swordsman, fretted visibly, and grew daily more silent. He spent all his days now in the forest, often with me (though not so much as formerly), but most of the time, Ralf told me, hunting or taking breakneck rides through the rough country.

'If only the King would make some move,' said Ralf to me. 'The boy will kill himself else. It's as if he knew that there was something in the future for him, something unguessed-at, but that gives him no peace. I'm afraid he'll break his neck before it happens. That new horse of his—Canrith, he calls it—I wouldn't care to get astride it myself, and that's the truth. I can't think what possessed Ector to give it to him; a guilt gift perhaps.'

I thought he was right. The white stallion had been left for Arthur when Ector took Cei up to Luguvallium with him. Bedwyr had gone, too, though he was no older than Arthur. Ector was hard put to it to explain to Arthur why he could not go. But until Uther spoke, we could no nothing.

The full moon came, the September moon that they call the harvester. It shone out in a dry mild night over the rotting fields, doing no good that anyone could see except light the outlaws who crept out of their fastnesses to pillage the outlying farms, or the troops who were constantly on the move these days to one or the other point of threat.

I could not sleep. My head ached, and phantoms crowded close, as they do when they bring vision; but nothing came forward into light or shape; nothing spoke. It was like suffering the threat of thunder, as close as the blankets that wrapped me, but without the lightning to break it, or the cleansing rain to bring a clear sky. When day broke at last, grey and misty, I rose, took bread, and a handful of olives from the crock, and went down through the forest to the lake, to wash the aching of the night away.

It was a quiet morning, so still that you could not tell where the mist ended and the surface of the lake began. The water met the flattened shingle of the beach without movement and without sound. Behind me the forest stood wrapped in the mist, its scents still sleeping. It seemed a kind of desecration to break the hush and plunge into that virgin water, but the fresh chill of it washed away the clinging strands of the night, and when I came out and was dry again and dressed, I ate my breakfast with pleasure, then settled down with my fishing rod to wait for the morning rise, and hope for a breeze at sun-up to ruffle the glassy water.

The sun came up at last, pale through the mist, but brought no breeze with it. The tops of the trees swam up out of the greyness, and at the far side of the lake the dark forest lifted, cloudy, towards the smoking hilltops. The water was bloomed with mist, like a pearl.

No ring or ripple broke the glassy water, no sign of a breeze to come. I had just decided that I might as well go, when I heard something coming fast through the forest at my back. Not a horseman; too light for that, and coming too fast through the brake.

I stayed as I was, half-turned, waiting. A prickling ran up the skin of my back, and I remembered the night's sleepless pain. The tingling ran into my fingers; I found I was clutching the rod until it hurt the flesh. All night, then, this had been coming. All night this had been waiting to happen. All night? If I was not mistaken, I had been waiting for this for fourteen years.

Fifty paces along the lake-side from where I sat, a stag broke cover. He saw me immediately, and stopped short, head high, poised to break the other way. He was white. In contrast the wide branches on his brow looked like polished bronze, and his eyes showed red as garnet. But he was real; there were stains of sweat on the white hide, and the thick hair of belly and neck was tagged with damp. A trail of yellow loosestrife had caught round his neck, and hung there like a collar. He looked back over his shoulder, then, stiff-legged, leapt from the bank into the water, and in two more bounds was shoulder-deep and swimming straight out into the lake.

The polished water broke and arrowed back. The splash was echoed by a crashing deep in the forest. Another beast coming, headlong.

I had been wrong in thinking that nothing could come through the forest as fast as a fleeing deer. Arthur's white hound, Cabal, broke from the trees exactly where the stag had broken, and hurled himself into the water. Seconds later Arthur himself, on the stallion Canrith, burst out after it.

He checked his horse on the shore, bringing it up rearing, fetlock deep. He had his bow strung ready in his hand. He pulled the stallion sideways and raised the bow, sighting from the back of the plunging horse. But deer swim low; only the stag's head showed above water, a wedge spearing away fast, its antlers flat behind it on the surface like boughs trailing. The hound, swimming strongly, was in line with it. Arthur lowered the bow, and turned the stallion back to breast the bank. In the moment before his spurs struck he saw me. He shouted something, and came cantering along the shingle.

His face was blazing with excitement. 'Did you see him? Snow-white, and a head like an emperor! I never saw the like in my life! I'm going round. Cabal was closing, he'll hold him till I get there. Sorry I spoiled your fishing.'

'Emrys—'

He checked impatiently. 'What?'

'Look. He's making for the island.'

He swung to look where I pointed. The stag had vanished into the mist, and the hound with him. There was no sign of them but for the fading ripples flattening towards the shore.

'The island, is it? Are you sure?'

'Certain.'

'All the devils of hell,' he said angrily. 'What a cursed piece of luck! I thought I had him when Cabal sprang him so close.' He hung on the rein, hesitating, staring out over the clouded lake while the stallion fretted, sidling. I suppose he was as much in awe of the place as anyone brought up in that valley. Then he set his mouth, curbing Canrith sharply. 'I'm going to the island. I can say goodbye to the stag, I suppose—that was too good to be true—but I'm damned if I lose Cabal. Bedwyr gave him to me, and I've no mind to lose him to Bilis or anyone else, either in this world or the other.' He put two fingers to his mouth and whistled shrilly. 'Cabal! Cabal! Here, sir, here!'

'It's no good, you'll hardly turn him now.'

'No.' He took a breath. 'Well, there's nothing for it, it'll have to be the island. If your magic will reach that far, Myrddin, send it with me now.'

'It's with you always, you know that. You're not going to swim him across, are you?'

'He'll go,' said Arthur, a little breathlessly, as he forced the reluctant stallion towards the water. 'It's too far to go round. If that beast takes to the crags, and Cabal follows it—'

'Why not take the boat? It's quicker, and that way you can bring Cabal back.'

'Yes, but the wretched thing'll need baling. It always does.'

'I baled it this morning. It's quite ready.'

'Did you? That's the first bit of luck today! You were going out, then? Will you come with me?'

'No. I'll stay here. Come now, Emrys, go and find your hound.'

For a moment boy and horse were quite still. Arthur stared down at me, something showing in his face that was half speculation, half awe, but which was quickly swallowed up in the larger impatience. He slid off the stallion's back and pushed the reins into my hand. Then he unstrung his bow and slung it across his shoulder and ran to the boat. This was a primitive flat-bottomed affair which usually lay beached in a reedy inlet a short way along the shore. He launched it with one flying shove, and jumped in. I stood on the shingle, holding the horse, watching him. He poled it out through the shallows, then had the oars out, and began to row.

I pulled the rolled cloth from behind the horse's saddle, slung it over the animal's steaming back, then tethered him where he could graze, and went back to my seat at the edge of the lake.

The sun was well up now, and gaining power. A kingfisher flashed by. Gauze-winged flies danced over the water. There was a smell of wild mint, and a dabchick crept out from a tangle of water forget-me-not. A dragonfly, tiny, with a scarlet body, clung pulsing to a reed. Under the sun the mist moved gently, smoking off the glassy water, shifting and restless like the phantoms of the night, like the smoke of the enchanted fire . . .

The shore, the scarlet dragonfly, the white horse grazing, the cloudy forest at my back, faded, became phantoms themselves. I watched, my eyes wide and fixed on that silent and sightless cloud of pearl.

He was rowing hard, chin on shoulder as he neared the island. It loomed first as a swimming shape of shadow, growing to a shore-line hung over with the low boughs of trees. Behind the trees, misty and unreal, the shapes of rocks soared like a great castle brooding on its crag. Where the strand met the water lay a line of gleaming silver, drawn sharp between the island and its image. The cloudy trees and the high towers of the crags floated weightless on the water, phantoms themselves in the phantom mist.

The boat forged ahead. Arthur glanced over his shoulder, calling the hound's name.

'Cabal! Cabal!'

The call echoed loudly across the water, swam up the high crags, and died. There was no sign of either hound or stag. He bent to his oars again, sending the light boat leaping through the water.

Its bottom grated on shingle. He jumped out. He pulled it up and trod up through the narrow verge of grass. The light was stronger now as the sun rose higher, reflecting from white mist and white water. Over the shore the boughs of birch and rowan reached low, still heavy with moisture. The rowan berries were red as flame, and glossy. The turf was powdered with daisies and speedwell and small yellow pimpernel. Late foxgloves crowded down the banks, their spires thrusting through the trails of blackberry. Meadowsweet, rusting over with autumn, filled the air with its thick, heavy scent.

The boy thrust the hanging boughs aside, plunged through the bramble trails, and stood squarely on the flowery turf, narrowing his eyes at the crags above him. He called again, and again the sound echoed emptily, and died. The mist was lifting faster now, rolling upwards towards the tops, showing the lower reaches of rock bathed in a clear but swimming light. Suddenly he stiffened, gazing upwards. Midway up the crags, along what looked no more than a seam in the rock, the white stag cantered easily, light as a drift of the mist that wreathed away to air below it.

Arthur ran forward up the slope. His footsteps on the thick turf made no sound. He brushed waist high through brakes of yellowing fern, sending the bright drops scattering, and came out at the foot of the cliff.

He paused again, looking about him. He seemed held by the same awe that had touched him earlier. He looked, not afraid, but as a man looks who knows that by a movement he may start something of which he cannot see the end. He craned his neck, searching the towering crags above him. There was no sign of the white stag, but the rocks looked more than ever like a castle crowned with the sun.

He took a breath, shaking his head as if he came out of water, then he spoke again, but quietly. 'Cabal? Cabal?'

From somewhere very near him, bursting the awed silence, came the baying of the hound. There was something in it of excitement, something of fear. It came from the cliff. The boy looked round him, sharply. Then, behind the green curtain of the trees, he saw the cave. As he started forward

Cabal bayed again, not in fear or pain, but like a beast questing.

With no more hesitation, Arthur plunged into the darkness of the cave.

He could never say afterwards how he found his way. I think he must have picked up the torch and flint I had left there, and lit it, but he remembers nothing of that. Perhaps what he does remember is the truth: there seemed, he said, to be everywhere some faintly diffused and swimming light, as if reflected from the burnished surface of the pool deep in the pillared cave.

There, beyond the shining pool, the sword lay on its table. From the rock above a trickle of water had run and dripped, the lime in it hardening through the years until the oiled leather of the wrappings, though proof enough to keep the metal bright, had hardened under the dripping till it felt like stone. In this the thing had rested, the crust of lime forming to hide all but its shape, the long slenderness of the weapon and the hilt formed like a cross.

It still looked like a sword, but a stone one, some random accident of dripping limestone. Perhaps he remembered the other hilt he had grasped in the Green Chapel, or perhaps for a moment he, too, saw the future break open in front of him. With an action too quick for thought, and too instinctive to prevent, he laid his hand to the hilt.

He spoke to me, as if I stood beside him. Indeed, I suppose I was as near to him, and as real, as the white hound that crouched, whining, at the pool's edge.

'I pulled at it, and it came clear of the stone. It is the most beautiful sword in the world. I shall call it Caliburn.'

The mist had gone from the forest now, sucked up by the sun. But it still lay over the island; this was invisible, floating on its sea of pearl.

I did not know how much time had passed. The sun was hot, beating down on the lake cupped in its hills. My eyes ached from the glare of water. I blinked them, moved, and stretched my stiff limbs.

There was a movement behind me; a sudden trampling, as if the white stallion had got loose. I turned quickly.

Thirty paces away, softly as a cloud, Cador of Cornwall rode out of the wood on a grey horse, with a troop at his back.

Chapter Seven

I believe that the thought uppermost in my mind was anger that I had not been warned. I was not only thinking of Arthur's guardians among the hill people; but even for me, Merlin, there had been no hint of danger in the sky, and the vision which had blanketed the troop's approach from my eyes and hearing had held nothing but light and promise leaping at last towards fulfilment. The only mitigation of my anger was that Arthur had not been found with me, and the only faint hope of safety lay in maintaining my character as hermit and trusting that Cador would not recognise me, and would ride on before the boy returned from the island.

All this went through my mind in the space it took Cador to raise a hand to halt the men behind him, and for me to pick up the discarded fishing rod and get to my feet. With some lie already forming on my lips I turned humbly to face Cador as he rode forward, to halt his grey ten paces off. Then all hope of remaining unrecognised vanished as behind him among the troop I saw Ralf with a gag in his mouth, and a trooper on either side of him.

I straightened. Cador bent his head, saluting me as low as he would have done the King. 'Well met, Prince Merlin.'

'Is it well met?' I was savagely angry. 'Why have you taken my servant? He's none of yours now. Loose him.'

He made a sign, and the troopers released Ralf's arms. He tore the gag from his mouth.

'Are you hurt?' I asked him.

'No.' He was angry too, and bitter. 'I'm sorry, sir. They fell on me as I was riding up through the forest. When they recognised me, they thought you might be near. They gagged me so that I could not give warning. They wanted to take you unawares.'

'Don't blame yourself. It was no fault of yours.' I had myself under control now, groping all the while for the shreds of the vision which had fled. Where was Arthur now? Still on the island, with Cabal and the wonderful sword? Or already on his way back through the mist? But I could see nothing except what was here, in plain daylight, and I knew that the spell was broken and I could not reach him.

I turned on Cador. 'You go about your business strangely, Duke! Why did you lay hands on Ralf! You could have found me any time you cared to ride this way. The forest is free to everyone, and the Green Chapel is open day and night. I would not have run from you.'

'So you are the hermit of the chapel in the green?'

'I am he.'

'And Ralf serves you?'

'He serves me.'

He signed to his men to stay where they were, and himself rode forward, nearer where I stood. The white stallion screamed and plunged as the grey horse passed it. Cador drew to a halt beside me, and looked down, his brows raised. 'And that horse? Is it yours? A strange choice for a hermit?'

I said acidly: 'You know it is not mine. If you caught Ralf in the forest, then no doubt you saw one of Count Ector's sons as well. They were riding together. The boy came here to fish. I don't know how long he'll be; he often stays away half the day.' I turned decisively away from the water. 'Ralf, wait here for him. And you, my lord Duke, since you were so urgent to see me that you mishandled my servant, will you come with me now to the chapel, and say what you have to say in privacy? And you can tell me, too, what—besides this private hunt of yours—brings you and the men of Cornwall so far north?'

'War brings me; war, and the King's command. I doubt if even here you have been too isolated to know of Colgrim's threats? But you might say it was a happy chance that made me ride this way.' He smiled, and added, pleasantly: 'And this was hardly a private hunt. Did you not know, Prince Merlin, that men have been searching the length and breadth of the land to find you?'

'I was aware of it. I did not choose to be found. Now, Duke, will you come with me? Leave Ralf to wait here for the boy—'

'Count Ector's son, eh?' He had made no move to follow me away from the water's edge. He sat his big horse easily, still smiling. His manner was confident and assured. 'And you really expect me to ride with you and leave Ralf to wait for this—son of Count Ector? No doubt to spirit him away for another span of years? Believe me, prince—'

From the water, sharply, came Cabal's bark, the warning of a hound alert to danger. Then a word from Arthur, silencing the hound. The sound of oars as the boat jumped forward, suddenly driven hard through the water.

Cador swung his horse to face the sound, and in spite of myself I moved with him. My look must have been grim, for two of his officers spurred forward.

'Keep them back,' I said sharply, and he flashed me a look and then lifted a hand. The men stopped short, a spear-cast off. I spoke quietly, for Cador alone:

'If you don't want Ector at your throat, with all Rheged behind him—yes, and Colgrim sweeping in to pick the fragments apart—let Ralf and the boy go now. Anything you have to say can be said to me. I shall not try to escape you. But for my life, Duke Cador, the King himself will answer.'

He hesitated, glancing from the misty lake to where his troopers stood. They had pricked to the alert. I did not think they had recognised me, or realised what quarry their Duke was hunting today; but they had seen his interest in the sounds from behind the mist, and though they stayed where they were near the edge of the wood, the spears stirred and rattled like a reed-bed in the wind.

'As to that—' began Cador, but he was interrupted.

The boat ran out of the mist's edge and cut through the shallows. Seconds before it grounded, Cabal, with a growl in his throat, flung himself over the thwart and made for the shore. One of the officers swung his horse round and drew his sword. Cador heard it, and shouted something. The man hesitated, and the hound, leaping up the bank, silent now, went in a rush for Cador himself. The grey horse reared back. The hound missed his grab, caught the edge of the saddle-cloth. It tore, and a piece came away in his jaws.

Behind me, Arthur yelled at the hound and ran the boat hard ashore. Ralf jumped forward, intending, I could see, to grab Cabal, but the troopers nearest him spurred forward and crossed their spears with a clash, holding him back. Cabal tossed the torn cloth over his shoulder and turned snarling to attack the men who held Ralf. One of them hefted his spear ready, and swords flashed out. Cador barked an order. The swords went up. The Duke lifted, not his sword, but his whip, and spurred the big grey round as the hound gathered himself to spring.

I took a stride forward under the whip, gripped the hound's collar, and threw my weight against his. I could scarcely hold him. Arthur's voice came fiercely, '*Cabal! Back!*' and even as the hound's pull slackened the boy jumped from the boat and in two strides was between me and Cador with the new sword naked and shining in his hand.

'You,' he panted, 'sir–whoever you are . . .' The sword's point slanted up at the Duke's breastbone. 'Keep back! If you touch him. I swear I'll kill you, even if you had a thousand men at your back.'

Cador slowly lowered the whip. I let Cabal go, and he sank to the ground behind Arthur, growling. Arthur stood squarely in front of me, angry and undoubtedly dangerous. But the Duke did not even seem to notice the sword or its threat. His eyes were on the boy's face. They flicked to mine, momentarily, then back to the boy.

All this had passed in a few breathless seconds. The Duke's men were still moving forward, the officers ranging to his side. As someone shouted an order, I shot a hand out and caught Arthur's arm and swung him round to face me, with his back to the Cornishmen.

'Emrys! What folly is this? There is no danger here, except from your hound. You should control him better. Take him now, and get yourself straight back to Galava with Ralf.'

I had never spoken to him so in all the years he had known me. He stood still, his mouth slackening with surprise, like someone who has been struck for nothing. While he still stared dumbly I added, curtly: 'This gentleman and I are acquainted. Why should you think he means me harm?'

'I–I thought—' he stammered. 'I thought–they had Ralf–and swords drawn on you—'

'You thought wrongly. I'm grateful to you, but as you see, I need no help. Put up your sword now, and go.'

His eyes searched my face again, briefly, then he looked down at the sword he held. The sunlight blazed from it and the jewelled hilt sparkled. His hand looked young and tense on the hilt. I remembered the feel and fit of that hilt, and the life that ran back from the blade, clear into the sinews and the leaping blood. He had braved the very halls of the Otherworld for this, and had brought the bright thing back from darkness into the light that owned it, to find his first danger waiting, and himself–with the wonderful sword–its equal. And I had spoken to him like this.

I gave his arm a little shake, and released it. 'Go. No one will stop you.'

He rubbed it where I had gripped him, not stirring. His colour was just beginning to come back, and with it a smoulder of anger. He looked so like Uther that I said, brutal with apprehension: 'Go now and leave us, do you hear? I shall have time for you tomorrow.'

'Emrys?' It was Cador, smoothly. Before I could stop him the boy had turned, and I saw that it was too late for pretence. Cador was looking from Arthur's face to mine, and there was excitement in his eyes.

'That is my name,' said Arthur. He sounded sullen, narrowing his eyes up at the Duke against the sun. Then he seemed to notice the badge on the other's shoulder. 'Cornwall? What are you doing so far north of your command, and with what authority do you lead your troops across our land?'

'Across your land? Count Ector's?'

'I'm his foster-son. But perhaps,' said Arthur, silky with cold courtesy, 'you have already passed Galava and spoken with his lady?'

He knew, of course, that Cador had not; he had not long ridden out of Galava himself. But Cador had given him the chance to recover the pride that I had damaged. He stood very straight, his back firmly turned to me, his eyes level on the Duke's.

Cador said: 'So you are a ward of Count Ector's? Who is your father, then, Emrys?'

Arthur did not jib at this question now. He said coolly: 'That, sir, I am not at liberty to tell you. But my breeding is not something of which I need to be ashamed.'

This set Cador at pause. There was a curious expression on his face. He knew, of course. How could he not have known, the moment the boy flew out of the mist to my defence? From before that moment, it had been beyond repair. But there was still a chance that the others might not guess; Cador's big grey stood between Arthur and the troop, and even while the thought crossed my mind he turned and made a sign, and the officers and men moved back, once again beyond earshot.

I was calm now, knowing what I must do. The first thing was to salvage Arthur's pride, and whatever love I had not already destroyed by destroying this hour for him. I touched him gently on the shoulder. 'Emrys, will you give us leave now? The Duke of Cornwall will not harm me, and he and I must talk together. Will you ride up to the chapel now with Ralf, and wait for me there?'

I expected Cador to intervene, but he sat without stirring. He was not watching the boy's face now, but the sword, still bare and flashing in Arthur's hand. Then he seemed to come to himself with a start. He signed to his men again, and Ralf, released, brought Canrith forward for Arthur, and mounted his own horse. He looked worried and questioning, wondering, probably, whether to take what I said at face value, or whether he must try to escape with Arthur into the forest.

I nodded to him. 'Up to the shrine, Ralf. Wait for me there, if you will. Have no fear for me; I shall come later.'

Arthur still hesitated, his hand on Canrith's bridle. Cador said: 'It's true, Emrys, I mean him no harm. Don't be afraid to leave him. I know better than to tangle with enchanters. He'll come to you safely, never fear.'

The boy threw me a strange look. He still looked doubtful, almost dazed. I said gently, not caring now who heard me: 'Emrys—'

'Yes?'

'I have to thank you. It is true that I thought there was danger. I was afraid.'

The sullen look lifted. He did not smile, but the anger died from his face, and life came back into it, as vividly as the bright sword leaping from its dull sheath. I knew then that nothing I had done had even smudged the edges of his love for me. He said, with little to be heard in his tone except exasperation: 'How long will it be before you realise that I would give my life itself to keep you from hurt?'

He glanced down again at the sword in his hand, almost as if he wondered how it had got there. Then he looked up, straight at Cador.

'If you harm him in any way, the kingdoms will not be wide enough to hold us both. I swear it.'

'Sir,' said Cador, speaking, warrior to warrior, with grave courtesy, 'that I well believe. I swear to you that I shall not harm him or anyone, save only the King's enemies.'

The boy held his eyes for a moment longer, then nodded. He swallowed, and the tension went out of him. Then he leapt astride his horse, saluted Cador formally, and, without another word, rode off along the lake-side track. Cabal ran with him, and Ralf followed. I saw the boy glance back as he reached the bend in the track that would carry him out of my sight. Then they were gone, and I was alone with Cador and the men of Cornwall.

Chapter Eight

'Well, Duke?' I said.

He did not answer immediately, but sat biting his lip, staring down at the saddle-bow. Then, without turning, he signalled one of his officers who came forward and took his bridle as he dismounted. 'Take the men down the shore a hundred paces. Water the horses, and wait for me there.'

The man went, and the troop wheeled and clattered out of sight beyond a jut of woodland. Cador gathered his cloak over his arm and looked about him.

'Shall we talk here?'

We sat down where a flat rock overhung the water. He drew his dagger, for no worse purpose than to draw patterns in the wild thyme. When he had done a circle, and fitted a triangle inside it, he spoke to the ground. 'He's a fine boy.'

'He is.'

'And like his sire.'

I said nothing.

The dagger drove into the ground and stayed there. His head came up. 'Merlin, why should you think I am his enemy?'

'Are you not his enemy?'

'No, by all the gods! I shall tell no one where he is unless you give me leave. There, you see? You look amazed. You thought of me as his enemy, and yours. Why?'

'If any man has reason for enmity, Cador, you have. It was through my action and Uther's that your father was killed.'

'That is not quite true. You planned to betray my father's bed but not my father himself. It was his own rashness, or bravery if you like, that caused his death. I believe that you did not forsee it. Besides, if I am to hate you because of that night, how much more should I hate Uther Pendragon?'

'And do you not?'

'God's death, man, have you not heard that I ride beside him and serve him as his chief captain?'

'I had heard it. And I wondered why. You must know how I have doubted you.'

He laughed, a harsh laugh, like his father's rough bark. 'You made it clear. I don't blame you. No, I don't hate Uther Pendragon; neither, I confess, do I love him. But when I was a boy I saw enough of divided kingdoms; Cornwall is mine, but she cannot stand alone. There is only one future for Cornwall now, and this is the same future as Britain's. I am linked to Uther, whether I like it or not. I will not bring division again, to see the people suffer. So I am Uther's man . . . or, which is nearer the truth, the High King's.'

I watched the kingfisher, reassured now that the troop had gone, dive in a jewelled splash below us. He came up with a fish, shook his feathers, and flashed away. I said: 'Did you send men to spy on me in Maridunum, years back, before I came north?'

His lips thinned. 'Those. Yes, they were mine . . . and fine work they made of it! You guessed straight away, didn't you?'

'It was an obvious conclusion. They were Cornish, and your troops were at Caerleon. I learned later that you yourself had been there. Am I to be blamed if I thought you were trying to find Arthur?'

'Not at all. That is exactly what I was trying to do. But not to harm him.' He frowned down again at the dagger. 'Remember those years, Prince Merlin, and think how it was with me then. The King ailing, and for all one could see, pledging more and more power to Lot and his friends. He offered Morgause in marriage before ever Morgian was born, did you know that? And even now, I doubt if he really sees where Lot's ambition is leading him . . . I tried to tell him myself, but from me it came like an echo of the same ambition. I feared what would happen to the kingdoms should Uther die–or should Uther's son die. And though I didn't doubt your power to protect that son in your own way, there's a place for my way as well.' The dagger thudded back into the turf. 'So I wanted to find him, and watch him. As, for a different reason, I have been watching Lot.'

'I see. You never thought of approaching me yourself and telling me this?'

He looked sideways at me, the corners of his mouth lifting. 'If I had, would you have believed me?'

'It's probable. I am not easy to deceive.'

'And told me where the boy was?'

I smiled. 'That. No.'

He hunched a shoulder. 'Well, there's your answer. I sent my foolish spies, and found nothing. I even lost you. But I never meant you harm, I swear it. And though I may once have been your enemy, I was never Arthur's. Will you believe that now?'

I looked around me at the tranquil day, the sunlit trees, the light mist lifting from the lake. 'I should have known it long ago. All day I have been wondering why I had had no warning of danger.'

'If I were Arthur's enemy,' he said, smiling, 'I would know better than to try and snatch him from under Merlin's arm and eye. So if there had been danger in the air today, you would have known it?'

I drew a breath. I felt light again as the summer air around me. 'I am sure of it. It worried me, that I had let you come so close today, and never felt the cold on my skin. Nor do I feel it now. Duke Cador, I should ask your forgiveness, if you will give it me.'

'Willingly.' He began to clean the tip of his dagger in the grass. But if I am not his enemy, Merlin, there are those who are. I don't have to tell you about the dangers of this Christmas marriage; not only for Arthur's claim to the throne, but the dangers for the kingdom itself.'

I nodded. 'Division, strife, the dark end to a dark year. Yes. Is there anything more you can tell me about King Lot, that all men do not already know?'

'Nothing definite, not more than before. I am hardly in Lot's private counsels. But I can tell you this; if Uther delays much longer over proclaiming his son, the nobles may decide to choose his successor among themselves. And the choice is there, ready, in Lot who is a tried and known warrior, who has fought at the King's hand, and is—will be soon—the King's son-in-law.'

'Successor?' I said. 'Or supplanter?'

'Not openly, no. Morgian would not see Lot stepping across her father's body to the kingdom. But once he is married to her, and is the King's apparent heir until Arthur is produced, then Arthur himself, when he does appear, will have to show both a stronger claim and a stronger backing.'

'He has both.'

'The claim, yes. But the backing? Lot has more men at his back than I.' I said nothing, but after a bit he nodded. 'Yes. I see. If he is backed by you, yourself in person . . . You can enforce his claim?'

'I can try. I shall have help. Yours, too, I hope?'

'You have it.'

'You shame me, Cador.'

'Hardly that,' he said. 'You were right. It was true that I hated you. I was young then, but I have come to see things differently; perhaps more clearly. For my own sake, if for nothing else, I cannot stand by and see Uther so bound to Lot, and Lot succeeding in his ambition. Arthur's is the one strong claim which can't be denied, and his is the one hand which can hold the kingdoms together—if any hand can do it now. Oh, yes, I would support him.'

I was reflecting that even at fifteen Cador had been a realist; now, his tough-minded commonsense was like a gust of cold air through a musty council-chamber. 'Does Lot know this?' I asked him.

'I have made it clear, I think. Lot knows I would oppose him, and so would the northern lords of Rheged, and the kings of Wales. But there are others I am not sure of, and many who will be swayed either way if their lands are threatened. The times are dangerous, Merlin. You knew Eosa went to Germany, and was consorting with Colgrim and Badulf? Yes? Well, news came a short while ago that longships had been massing across the German Sea from Segedunum and that the Picts have opened their harbours to them.'

'I had not heard that. Then there'll be fighting before winter?'

He nodded. 'Before the month is out. That's why I am here. Maelgon stays on the Irish Shore, but the danger is not on the west; not yet. The attack will come from east and north.'

'Ah.' I smiled. 'Then certain things will be made clear very soon, I think.'

He had been watching me intently. Now his mouth relaxed, and he nodded again. 'You see it? Of course you do. Yes, one good thing may come out of this clash–Lot must declare himself. If, as rumour has it, he has been making advances to the Saxons, then he will have to declare for Colgrim. If he wants Morgian, and the High Kingdom along with her, he'll have to fight for Uther.' He laughed with genuine amusement. 'It's Octa's death that has brought Colgrim raging straight across the German Sea, and forced Lot's hand. If he'd waited for the spring, Lot would have had Morgian, and could have received Colgrim too, and used the Saxons to set himself up as High King, like Vortigern before him. As it is, we shall see.'

'Where is the King?' I asked.

'On his way north. He should be at Luguvallium within the week.'

'He'll lead the field himself?'

'He intends to, though as you know he's a sick man. It seems that Colgrim may have forced Uther's hand, too. I think he will send for Arthur now. I think he will have to.'

'Whether he sends or not,' I said, 'Arthur will be there.' I saw the excitement spring to Cador's face again, and asked him: 'Will you give him escort, Duke?'

'Willingly, by God! You'll come with him?'

I said: 'After this, where he is, I am.'

'And you'll be needed,' he said meaningly. 'Pray God Uther has not left it too late. Even with proof of Arthur's parentage, and the King's own sword fast in his hand, it won't be easy to persuade the nobles to declare for an untried boy . . . And Lot's faction will fight back every foot of the way. Better to take them by surprise, like this. The boy will need all you can throw into the scale for him.'

I smiled. 'He can throw in quite a lot himself. He's to be reckoned with, Cador, make no mistake. He's no kingmaker's toy.'

He grinned. 'You don't need to tell me that. Did you know he was more like you than ever like the King?'

I spoke with my eyes on the glittering surface of the lake. 'I think it is my sword, not Uther's, which will carry him to the kingship.'

He sat up sharply. 'Yes. That sword. Where in middle-earth did he find that sword?'

'On Caer Bannog.'

His eyes widened. 'He went *there*? Then, by God, he's welcome to it and all it brings him! I'd not have dared! What took him there?'

'He went to save the hound. It had been given him by his friend. You might call it chance that took him there.'

'Oh, aye. The same kind of chance that brought me along the lake-side today, to find a poor hermit, and a boy called Ambrosius, who holds a sword which might well befit a king?'

'Or an emperor,' I said. 'It's the sword of Macsen Wledig.'

'*So?*' He drew in his breath. I saw the same look in his eyes as there had been in the Cornish troopers' when I spoke of the enchanted island. 'This was the claim you were speaking of? You found that sword for him? You cast your net wide, Merlin.'

'I cast no net, I go with the time.'

'Yes. I see.' He drew another long breath, and looked about him as if he saw the day for the first time, with all its sunlight and moving breezes and the island floating on the water. 'And now for you, and for him and all of us, the time is come?'

'I think so. He found the sword where I had laid it, and you came, hard on its finding. All the year the King has been urged to make proclamation and he has done nothing. So instead, we will do it. You lie tonight at Galava?'

'Yes.' He sat up, pushing the dagger home in its sheath with a rap. 'You'll join us there? We ride at sun-up.'

'I shall be there tonight,' I said, 'and Arthur with me. Today he stays with me in the forest. We have things to say to one another.'

He looked at me curiously. 'He knows nothing yet?'

'Nothing,' I said. 'I promised the King.'

'Then until the King speaks publicly, I'll see he learns nothing. Some of my men may suspect, but they are all loyal. You needn't fear them.'

I got to my feet, and he followed suit. He raised a hand to his watching officer in the distance. I heard the words of command, and the sounds of the troop mounting. They rode towards us along the lake-side.

'You have a horse?' asked Cador. 'Or shall I leave one with you now?'

'Thank you, no. I have one. I'll walk back to the chapel when I'm ready. There's something I have to do first.'

He looked again at the sunlit forest, the still lake, the dreaming hills, as if power or magic must be ready to fall on me from their light. 'Something still to do? Here?'

'Indeed.' I picked up the fishing rod. 'I still have to catch my dinner, and for two now, instead of one. And see, this day of days has even produced a breeze for me. If Arthur can lift the sword of Maximus from the lake, surely I shall be granted at least two decent fish?'

Chapter Nine

Ralf met me at the edge of the clearing, but we could not have much talk because Arthur was near-by, sitting in the sun on the chapel steps, with Cabal at his feet.

I told Ralf quickly what he must do. He was to ride down now to the castle and tell Drusilla what had happened, that Arthur was safe with me, and that we would join Duke Cador on the ride north tomorrow. A message was to go ahead to Count Ector, and one to the King. Meanwhile Ralf was to ask the Countess to arrange with Abbot Martin to have the shrine tended during my absence.

'And are you going to tell him now?' asked Ralf.

'No. It's for Uther to tell him.'

'Don't you think he may guess already, after what happened down yonder? He's been silent ever since, but with a look to him as if he'd been given more than a sword. What is that sword, Merlin?'

'It's said that Weland Smith himself made it, long ago. What is sure is that the Emperor Maximus used it, and that his men brought it home for the King of Britain.'

'*That* one? And he tells me he found it on Caer Bannog . . . I begin to see . . . And now you take him to the King. Are you trying to force Uther's hand? Do you think the King will accept him?'

'I am sure of it. Uther must claim him now. I think we may find that he has sent for him already. You'd better go, Ralf. There'll be time to talk later. You'll ride with us, of course.'

'You think I'd let you leave me behind?' He spoke gaily, but I could see that he was torn between relief and regret; on the one hand the knowledge that the long watch was over, on the other, that Arthur would now be taken from his care and committed to mine and the King's. But there was happiness, too, that he would soon be back in the press of affairs in an open position of trust, and able to wield his sword against the kingdom's enemies. He saluted me, smiling, then turned and rode off down the track towards Galava.

The hoof-beats faded down through the forest. Sunlight poured into the clearing. The last of the water-drops had vanished from the pines, and the smell of resin filled the air. A thrush was singing somewhere. Late harebells were thick among the grass, and small blue butterflies moved over the white flowers of the blackberry. There was a hive of wild bees under the roof of the chapel; their humming filled the air, the sound of summer's end.

Through a man's life there are milestones, things he remembers even into the hour of his death. God knows that I have had more than a man's share of rich memories; the lives and deaths of kings, the coming and going of gods, the founding and destroying of kingdoms. But it is not always these great events that stick in the mind: here, now, in this final darkness, it is the small times that come back to me most vividly, the quiet human moments which I should like to live again, rather than the flaming times of power. I can still see, how clearly, the golden sunlight of that quiet afternoon. There is the sound of the spring, and the falling liquid of the thrush's song, the humming of the wild bees, the sudden flurry of the white hound scratching for fleas, and the sizzling sound of cooking where Arthur knelt over the wood fire, turning the trout on a spit of hazel, his face solemn, exalted, calm, lighted from within by whatever it is that sets such men alight. It was his beginning, and he knew it.

He did not ask me much, though a thousand questions must have been knocking at his lips. I think he knew, without knowing how, that we were on the threshold of events too great for talk. There are some things that one hesitates to bring down into words. Words change an idea by definitions too precise, meanings too hung about with the references of every day.

We ate in silence. I was wondering how to tell him, without breaking my promise to Uther, that I proposed to take him with me to the King. I thought that Ralf was wrong; the boy did not begin to guess the truth; but he must be wondering about the events of the day, not only the sword, but what there was between myself and Cador, and why Ralf had been so handled. But he said nothing, not even asking why Ralf had gone away and left him here alone with me. He seemed content with the moment. The angry little skirmish down by the lake might never have been.

We ate in the open air, and when we had finished Arthur, without a word, removed the dishes and brought water in a bowl for me to wash with. Then he settled beside me on the chapel steps, lacing the fingers of his hands round one knee. The thrush still sang. Blue and shadowed, and misty with presence, the hills brooded, chin on knees, round the valley. I felt myself crowded already by the forces that waited there.

'The sword,' he said. 'You knew it was there, of course.'

'Yes, I knew.'

'He said . . . He called you an enchanter?' There was the faintest of queries in his voice. He wasn't looking at me. He sat on the step below me, head bent, looking down at the fingers laced round his knee.

'You knew that. You have seen me use magic.'

'Yes. The first time I came here, when you showed me the sword in the stone altar, and I thought it was real . . .' He stopped abruptly, and his head came up. His voice was sharp with discovery. 'It *was* real! This is the one, isn't it? The one the stone sword was carved from? Isn't it? Isn't it?'

'Yes.'

'What sword is it, Myrddin?'

'Do you remember my telling you—you and Bedwyr—the story of Macsen Wledig?'

'Yes, I remember it well. You said that was the sword carved in the altar here.' Again that note of discovery. 'This is the same? His very sword?'

'Yes.'

'How did it come there, on the island?'

I said: 'I put it there, years back. I brought it from the place where it had been hidden.'

He turned fully then, and looked at me. A long look. 'You mean you found it? It's your sword?'

'I didn't say that.'

'You found it by magic? Where?'

'I can't tell you that, Emrys. Some day you may need to search for the place yourself.'

'Why should I?'

'I don't know. But a man's first need is a sword, to use against life, and conquer it. Once it is conquered, and he is older, he needs other food, for the spirit . . .'

After a bit I heard him say, softly: 'What are you seeing, Myrddin?'

'I was seeing a settled and shining land, with corn growing rich in the valleys, and farmers working their fields in peace as they did in the time of the Romans. I was seeing a sword growing idle and discontented, and the days of peace stretching into bickering and division, and the need of a quest for the idle swords and the unfed spirits. Perhaps it was for this that the god took the grail and the spear back from me and hid them in the ground, so that one day you might set out to find the rest of Macsen's treasure. No, not you, but Bedwyr . . . It is his spirit, not yours, which will hunger and thirst, and slake itself in the wrong fountains.'

As if from far away, I heard my own voice die, and silence come back. The thrush had flown, the bees seemed quiet. The boy was on his feet now, and staring.

He said, with all the force of simplicity: 'Who are you?'

'My name is Myrddin Emrys, but I am known as Merlin the enchanter.'

'*Merlin?* But then–but that means you are–you were—' He stopped, and swallowed.

'Merlinus Ambrosius, son of Ambrosius the High King? Yes.'

He stood silent for a long time. I could see him thinking back, remembering, assessing. Not guessing about himself–he had been too deeply rooted, and for too long, in the person of Ector's bastard foster-son. And, like everyone else in the kingdom, he assumed that the prince was being royally reared in some court beyond the sea.

He spoke at length quietly, but with such a kind of inward force and joy that one wondered how he could contain it. What he said surprised me. 'Then the sword was yours. You found it, not I. I was only sent to bring it to you. It is yours. I will get it for you now.'

'No, wait, Emrys—'

But he had already gone. He brought the sword, running, and held it out to me.

'Here. It's yours.' He sounded breathless. 'I ought to have guessed who you were . . . Not away in Brittany with the prince, as some people have it, but here, in your own country, waiting till the time came to help the High King. You are the seed of Ambrosius. Only you could have found it, and I found it only because you sent me there. It is for you. Take it.'

'No. Not for me. Not for a bastard seed.'

'Does that make a difference? Does it?'

'Yes,' I said gently.

He was silent. The sword sank to his side and was quenched in his shadow. I mistook his silence, and I remember that at the time I was relieved merely that he said no more.

I got to my feet. 'Bring it now into the chapel. We'll leave it there, where it belongs, on the god's altar. Whichever god is sovereign in this place will watch it for us. It must wait here till the time comes for it to be claimed in the sight of men, by the legitimate heir to the kingdom.'

'So. That's why you sent me for it? To bring it for him?'

'Yes. In due time it will be his.'

A little to my surprise he smiled, apparently satisfied. He nodded calmly. We took the sword together into the chapel. He laid it on the altar, above its carved replica. They were the same. His hand left the hilt, lingeringly, and he stepped back to my side.

'And now,' I said, 'I have something to tell you. The Duke of Cornwall brought news—'

I got no further. The sound of hoofs, approaching rapidly through the forest, brought Cabal up, roach-backed and growling. Arthur whipped round. His voice was sharp.

'Listen! Is that Cornwall's troop back again? Something must be wrong . . . Are you sure they mean you well?'

I put a hand to his arm and he stopped, then, at the look on my face, asked: 'What is it, then? Were you expecting this?'

'No. Yes. I hardly know. Wait, Emrys. Yes, this had to come. I thought it must. The day is not over yet.'

'What do you mean?'

I shook my head. 'Come with me and meet them.'

It was not Cornwall's troops that came clattering into the clearing. The Dragon glittered, red on gold. King's men. The officer halted his troop and rode forward. I saw his eye take in the wide clearing, the overgrown shrine, my own plain robes; it touched the boy at my side, no more than a touch, then came back to my face, and he saluted, bowing low.

The greeting was formal, in the King's name. It was followed by the news I had already had from Cador; that the King was marching north with his army, and would lie at Luguvallium, there to face the threat from Colgrim's forces. The man went on to tell me, looking troubled, that of late the King's sickness seemed to have taken hold of him again, and there were days when he had not the strength to ride but proposed, if need be, to take the field in a litter. 'And this is the message I was charged to give you, my lord. The High King, remembering the strength and help you gave to the army of his brother Aurelius Ambrosius, asks that you will come now out of your fastness, and go to him where he waits to meet his enemies.' The message came, obviously, by rote. He finished: 'My lord, I am to tell you that this is the summons you have been waiting for.'

I bent my head. 'I was expecting it. I had already sent to tell the King I was coming, and Emrys of Galava with me. You are to escort us? Then no doubt you will have the goodness to wait a while until we are ready. Emrys—' I turned to Arthur, standing in a white trance of excitement at my side '—come with me.'

He followed me back into the chapel. As soon as we were out of sight of the troop he caught at my arm. 'You're taking me? You're really taking me? And if it comes to a battle—'

'Then you shall fight in it.'

'But my father, Count Ector . . . He may forbid it.'

'You will not fight beside Count Ector. These are King's troops and you go with me. You will fight with the King.'

He said joyously: 'I knew this was a day of marvels! I thought at first that the white stag had led me to the sword, that it was for me. But now I see that it was just a sign that today I should ride to my first battle . . . What are you doing?'

'Watch now,' I said. 'I told you I would leave the sword in the god's protection. It has lain long enough in the darkness. Let us leave it now in the light.'

I stretched out my hands. From the air the pale fire came, running down the blade, so that runes—quivering and illegible—shimmered there. Then the fire spread, engulfing it, till, like a brand too brightly flaring, the flames died, and when they had gone, there stood the altar, pale stone, with nothing against it but the stone sword.

Arthur had not seen me use this kind of power before, and he watched open-mouthed as the flames broke out of the air and caught at the stone. He drew back, awed and a little frightened, and the only colour in his face was the wan light cast by the flames.

When it was done he stood very still, licking dry lips. I smiled at him. 'Come, be comfortable. You have seen me use magic before.'

'Yes. But seeing this–this kind of thing . . . All this time, when Bedwyr and I were with you, you never let us know what sort of man you were . . . This power; I had no idea. You told us nothing of it.'

'There was nothing to tell. There was no need for me to use it, and it wasn't something you could learn from me. You will have different skills, you and Bedwyr. You won't need this one. Besides, if you do, I shall be there to give it to you.'

'Will you? Always? I wish I could believe that.'

'It is true.'

'How can you know?'

'I know,' I said.

He stared at me for a moment longer, and in his face I could see a whole world of uncertainty and bewilderment and desire. It was a boy's look, immature and lost, and it was gone in a moment, replaced by his normal armour of bright courage. He smiled then, and the sparkle was back. 'You may regret that, you know! Bedwyr's the only person who can stand me for long.'

I laughed. 'I'll do my best. Now, if you will, tell them to bring our horses out.'

When I was ready I went out to join the waiting men. Arthur was not mounted and fretting to be off, as I had expected; he was holding my horse for me, like a groom. I saw his eyes widen a little when he saw me; I had put on my best clothes, and my black mantle was lined with scarlet and pinned on the shoulder by the Dragon brooch of the royal house. He saw that I was amused, and had guessed his thought, and smiled a little in return as he swung himself up on his white stallion. I took care that he should not see what I was thinking then; that the youth with the plain mantle and the bright, proud look did not need a brooch to declare himself Pendragon, and royal. But he drew the stallion soberly in behind my mild roan mare, and the men were watching me.

So we left the chapel of the Wild Forest in the care of whichever god owned it, and rode down towards Galava.

The King

Chapter One

The danger from the Saxons had been more immediate even than Cador had supposed. Colgrim had moved fast. By the time Arthur and I with our escort approached Luguvallium we found, just south-east of the town, the King's forces and Cador's moving into position with the men of Rheged, to face an enemy already massing in great numbers for the attack.

The British leaders were closeted with the King in his tent. This had been pitched on the summit of a small hill which lay behind the field of battle. There had in times past been some kind of a fortress there, and a few ruined walls still stood, with the remains of a tower, and lower down on the slopes were the tumbled stones and weedy garths of an abandoned village. The place was a riot of blackberry and nettle, with huge old apple trees still standing among the fallen stones, golden with ripening fruit. Here, below the hill, the baggage trains were rumbling into place; the trees and the half-ruined walls would provide shelter for the emergency dressing station. Soon the apparent chaos would resolve itself; the King's armies still fought with a pattern of the Roman discipline enforced by Ambrosius. Looking at the huge spreading host of the enemy, the field of spears and axes and the horse-hair tossing in the breeze like the foam of an advancing sea, I thought that we would need every last scruple of strength and courage that we could muster. And I wondered about the King.

Uther's tent had been pitched on a little level lawn, before the ruined tower. As our troop rode towards it through the noise and bustle of the battalions assembling into fighting order, I saw men turn to stare, and even above the shouts of command and the clash of arms could hear the word go round. 'It's Merlin. Merlin. Merlin the prophet is here. Merlin is with us.' Men turned, stared, shouted, and elation seemed to spread like a buzz through the field. A fellow with the device of Dyfed shouted as I passed, in my own tongue: 'Are you with us then, Myrddin Emrys, *braud*, and have you seen the shooting star for us today?'

I called back, clearly, so that it could be heard: 'Today it is a rising star. Watch for it, and the victory.'

As I dismounted with Arthur and Ralf at the foot of the hill, and walked up to Uther's tent, I heard the word spread through the field with a rush like the wind racing over ripe corn.

It was a bright September day, full of sunlight. Outside the King's tent the Dragon blew, scarlet on yellow. I went straight in, with Arthur on my heels. The boy had armed himself at Galava, and looked at every point a young warrior. I had expected him to appear with Ector's blazon, but he carried no device, and his cloak and tunic were of plain white wool. 'It's my colour,' he had said, when he saw me looking. 'The white horse, the white hound, and I shall carry a white shield. Since I have no name, I shall write on it myself. My device will be my own, when I get it.' I had said nothing, but I thought now, as the boy trod forward beside me across the King's tent, that if he had deliberately courted all men's eyes on the field of battle, he could not have done better. The unmarked white, and his air of eager and shining youth, stood out among the tossing brilliance of colour on that bright morning, as surely as if the trumpets had already proclaimed him prince. And as Uther greeted us. I could see the same thought in the eager and hungry gaze he fixed on the boy's face.

Myself, I was shocked at Uther's appearance. It bore out the reports I had had of him, of a man visibly failing, 'as if a canker gnawed at his guts, not with pain but with daily wasting'. He was thin and his colour was bad, and I noticed that from time to time his hand went to his chest, as if he found it hard to draw breath. He was splendidly dressed, with gold and jewels glinting on his armour; the stuff of his great cloak was gold, too, with scarlet dragons entwined. He held himself upright, kingly in the great chair. There was grey now in the reddish hair and beard, but his eyes were vivid and alive as ever, burning in their deep sockets. The thinness of his face made it look more hawk-like, and if possible more kingly than before. The flashing gold and jewels and the great cloak hid the thinness of his body. Only the wrists and bony hands showed where the long wasting sickness had gnawed the flesh away.

Arthur waited behind me with Ralf as I went forward. Count Ector was there, near the King, along with Coel of Rheged, and Cador, and a dozen other of Uther's leaders whom I knew. I saw Ector eyeing Arthur with a kind of wonder. I did not see Lot anywhere.

Uther greeted me with a courtesy only thinly overlaying the eagerness below. It is possible that he had intended there and then to present his son to the commanders, but there was no time. Trumpets were sounding outside. Uther hesitated, looking indecisive, then he made a sign to Ector who stepped forward and formally presented Arthur to the King as his foster-son, Emrys of Galava. Arthur, with this new quiet and self-contained maturity, knelt to kiss the King's hand. I saw Uther's hand close on his, and I thought he would speak then, but at that moment the trumpets shrilled again, nearer, and the door of the tent was pulled open. Arthur stood back. Uther—the effort was apparent—tore his eyes from the boy's face and gave the word. The commanders saluted hurriedly and dispersed to mount and gallop away to their stations. The ground shook to the trampling of horses, and the air to the shouting and the clash of metal. Four men ran in with poles, and I saw then that Uther's chair was a kind of litter, a big carrying-chair, in which he could be borne on to the battlefield. Someone ran to him with his sword and put it into his hand, whispering as he did so, and the four fellows bent to the poles, waiting for the King's word.

I stood back. If any memory came to me of the young, tough commander who had fought so ably at his brother's side through all the early years of war, it touched me now with no feeling of pity or regret, as the King turned his head and smiled, the same fierce, eager smile that I knew. The years had dropped away from him. If it had not been for the litter, I could have sworn that he was a whole man. There was even colour in his cheeks, and his whole person glittered.

'My servant here tells me you have foretold us victory already?' He laughed, a young man's laugh, full and ringing. 'Then you have indeed brought us today all that we could desire. Boy!'

Arthur, at the tent door speaking to Ector, stopped and looked back. The King beckoned. 'Here. Stay by me.'

Arthur flashed an enquiring look at his foster-father, then at me. I nodded. As the boy moved to obey the King I saw Ector make a sign to Ralf, and the latter moved quietly with Arthur to the left of the King's litter. Ector hung on his heel a moment in the tent doorway, but Uther was saying something to his son, and Arthur was bent to listen. The Count hitched his cloak over his shoulder, nodded abruptly to me, and went out. The trumpets sounded again, and then the sunshine and the shouting were all about us as the King's chair was carried out towards the waiting troops.

I did not follow it down the hillside, but stayed where I was, on the high ground beside the tent, while below me on the wide field the armies formed. I saw the King's chair set down, and the King himself stand to speak to the men. From this distance I could hear nothing of what was said, but when he turned and pointed to where I stood high in the sight of the whole army, I heard the shout of 'Merlin!' again, and the cheers. There was an answering shout from the enemy, a yell of derision and defiance, and then the clamour of trumpets and the thunder of the horses drowned everything, and shook the day.

Beside the tower wall stood an ancient apple tree, its bark now gnarled and thick with lichen like verdigris, but its boughs heavy with yellow fruit. In front of it was a tumble of stone with a plinth where perhaps there had once been an altar or a statue. I stepped up on to this, with my back to the laden apple tree, and watched the course of the fighting.

There was still no sign of Lot's banner. I beckoned a fellow running past–he was a medical orderly on his way to the dressing station lower down the hill–and asked him: 'Lot of Lothian? Are his troops not come?'

'There's no sign of them yet, sir. I don't know why. Maybe they're to be held back as reserves on the right?'

I glanced where he was pointing. To the right of the field was the winding glimmer of a stream, flanked for some fifty paces to either hand by broken and sedgy ground. Beyond this the field rose through alder and willow and scrubby oak to thicker woodland. Between the trees the slope was rough and broken, but not too steep for horses, and the woods could well hide half an army. I thought I could see the glint of spear-heads through the thick of the trees. Lot, coming from the north-east, would have had early news of the Saxon advance, and would hardly have come late for the battle. He must be there, waiting and watching. But not, I was sure, by order as a reserve placed there by the King. The dilemma that Cador and I had spoken of might well be resolved today for Lot: if Uther looked like winning the victory, then Lot could throw his army in and share the time of triumph and its aftermath of reward and power; but if Colgrim should bear away the day, then Lot would have the chance of fixing his interest with the Saxon conquerors—in time, moreover, to deny his marriage with Morgian and take whatever power the new Saxon rule would offer him. I might well, I thought sourly, be doing the man an injustice, but my bones told me I was not. I wished there had been time to learn before the battle what Uther's dispositions had been. If Lot was anywhere at hand he would not miss this battle, of all battles, with the chances it held for him. I wondered how soon he would see me, or hear that I had come. And once he knew, he would have no doubt at all of the identity of the white-cloaked youth on the white horse, who fought so close on the King's left hand.

It was evident that the High King's presence, even in a litter, had cheered and fortified the British. Though, borne as he was in his chair, he could not lead the charge, he was there with the Dragon above him, right in the centre of the field, and, though the press of his followers round him would hardly let an enemy get within striking distance, the fighting was fiercest round the Dragon, and from time to time I saw the flutter of the golden cloak and the flash of the King's own sword. Out on the right rode the King of Rheged, flanked by Caw and at least three of his sons. Ector too was on the right, fighting with dogged ferocity, while Cador on the left showed all the dash and dazzle of the Celt on his day of luck. Arthur I knew to be endowed by nature with the qualities of both, but today he would doubtless be more than content with his position guarding the King's left side. Ralf, in his turn, held himself back to guard Arthur's. I watched the chestnut horse swerve and turn and rear, never more than a pace away from the white stallion's flank.

This way and that the battle went. Here a banner would go down, swamped apparently under the savage tide of attack, then somehow there would be a recovery, and the British would press forward under the swinging axes, and push back the yelling waves of Saxons. From time to time a solitary horseman—a messenger, it could be assumed—spurred off eastwards across the boggy land by the stream, and up into the trees. And now it was certain that Lot's force was there, hidden and waiting in the wood. And, as surely as if I had read his mind, I knew that he was waiting there by no orders from the King. Whatever calls for help those messengers brought to him, he would delay his coming until he saw how the day went. So, for two fierce hours, lengthening through midday to three, the British forces fought, deprived of what should have been their fresh fighting right. The King of Rheged fell wounded, and was carried back: his forces held their positions, but it could be seen that they were wavering. And still the men of Lothian held back. Soon, if they did not come in, it might be too late.

All at once, it seemed that it was. There was a shout from the centre, a shout of anger and despair. There, in the thick of the press round the King's chair, I saw the Dragon standard waver, rock violently, then slope to its fall. Suddenly, for all the distance, it was as if I was there, close by the King's chair, seeing it all clearly. A body of Saxons, huge fair giants, some of them red with unfelt wounds, had rushed the group that surrounded the King, breaking it, it seemed, with sheer weight and ferocity. Some were cut down, some were forced back by desperate fighting, but two got through. They smashed their way forward, axes whirling, on the King's left. One axe struck the shaft of the standard, which splintered, rocked, and began to fall. The man who had carried it went down with the blood spouting from his severed wrist, and disappeared under the mashing hoofs. With scarcely a pause the axe whirled through its bright arc towards the King. Uther was on his feet, his sword up to meet the axeman, but Ralf's sword whirled and bit, and the Saxon fell clear across the King's chair, his blood gushing out over the golden cloak. The King was pinned back under the fallen man's weight. The other Saxon rushed forward yelling. Ralf, cursing, fought to thrust his horse between the helpless King and the new attacker, but the Saxon, towering above the British, brushed their weapons aside as a mad bull brushes the long grass, and charged forward. It seemed nothing could stop him reaching the King. I saw Arthur drive his horse forward, just as the rocking standard fell, striking the white stallion across the chest. The stallion reared, screaming. Arthur, holding the horse with his knees, seized the falling standard, and shouting flung it clear across the King's chair into a soldier's ready grip, then swung the screaming, striking horse right into the path of the giant Saxon. The great axe whirled into its flashing circle, and came down. The stallion swerved and leapt, and the blow missed, but glancing spent from the boy's sword, knocked it spinning from his hand. The stallion climbed high again, striking out with those killing forefeet, and the axeman's face vanished in a pash of bright blood. The white horse plunged back to the side of the King's chair and Arthur's hand went down to his dagger. Then quiet, but clear as a shout, the King called, 'Here!' and flung his own sword, hilt first, into the air. Arthur's hand shot out and caught it by the hilt. I saw it catch the light. The white horse reared again. The standard was up, and streaming in the wind, scarlet on gold. There was a great shout, spreading out from the centre of the field where the white stallion, treading blood, leapt forward under the Dragon banner. Shouting, the men surged with him. I saw the standardbearer hesitate fractionally, looking back at the King, but the King waved him forward, then lay back, smiling, in his chair.

And now, too late for whatever spectacular intervention Lot had intended, the Lothian troops swept down out of the woodland and swelled the ranks of the attacking British. But the day was already won. There was no man there on the field who had not seen what happened. There, white on a white horse, the King's fighting spirit had leapt, it seemed, out of his failing body, and run ahead, like the spark on the tip of a fighting spear, straight to the heart of the Saxon forces.

Soon, as the Saxons, breaking from stand to fighting stand, were pressed gradually backwards towards the marshes that fringed the field, and the British followed them with steadily growing ferocity and triumph, men started to run in behind the fighting troops to bring out the hurt and the dying. Uther's chair, which should have been borne back at the same time, was forging forward steadily in Arthur's wake. But the main press of the fighting was no longer round it; that was well forward of the field where, under the Dragon, everyone could see the white stallion and the white cloak and the flashing blade of the King's sword.

My post as a visible presence on the hill was no longer either heeded or necessary. I went down to where the emergency dressing station had been set up below the fallen tangles of the apple orchard. Already the tents were filling, and the orderlies were hard at work. I sent a boy running for my box of instruments and, taking off my cloak, slung it over the low boughs of an apple tree to make a shelter from the sun's rays; and as the next stretcher went by me I called to the bearers to set the wounded man down in the improvised shade.

One of the bearers was a lean and greying veteran whom I recognised. He had worked as orderly for me at Kaerconan. I said: 'A moment, Paulus, don't hurry away. There are plenty to do the carrying; I'd rather have you help here.'

He looked pleased that I had recognised him. 'I thought you might need me, sir. I've got my kit with me.' He knelt on the other side of the unconscious man, and together we began to slit the leather tunic away where it was torn open by a bloody gash.

'How is it with the King?' I asked him

'Hard to say, sir. I thought he'd gone, and a lot else gone with him, but he's there now with Gandar, and sitting peaceful as a babe, and smiling. As well he might.'

'Indeed . . . That's far enough, I think. Let me look . . .' It was an axe wound, and the leather and metal of the man's tunic had been driven deep into the hacked flesh and splintered bone. I said: 'I doubt if there's much we can do here, but we'll try. God's on our side today, and he may well be on this poor fellow's, too. Hold this, will you? . . . As you were saying, well he might. The luck won't change now.'

'Luck, is it? Luck on a white horse, you might say. A fair treat it was to see that youngster, the way he pushed through just at the right moment. It needed something like that, with the King falling back as if he was dead, and the Dragon going down. We were looking for King Lot then, but no sign of him. Believe me, sir, another half minute and we'd have been going the other way. Battle's like that; it makes you wonder sometimes, to think what hangs on a few seconds and a bit of luck. A piece of nice timing like that, and the right person to do it—that's all it takes, and you've won or lost a kingdom.'

We worked for a while in silence then, quickly, because the man was beginning to stir under my hands, and I had to finish before he woke to cruel life. When I had done all I could, and we were bandaging, Paulus said, ruminatively: 'Funny thing.'

'What?'

'Remember Kaerconan, sir?'

'Will I ever forget it?'

'Well, that youngster had a look of *him*—Ambrosius, I mean, that was

Count of Britain then. White horse and all, and the Dragon flying over it. Men were saying so . . . And the name's the same, sir, isn't it? Emrys? Connection of yours, perhaps?'

'Perhaps.'

'Ah, well,' said Paulus, and asked no more questions. He did not need to say more; I knew already that rumours must have been flying round the camp from the moment that Arthur and I had ridden in with the escort. Let them run. Uther had shown his hand. And between the boy's bravery, and the luck of the battle and his own misjudgment, Lot would have a hard struggle of it now to change the King's mind, or to persuade the other nobles that Uther's son was no fit leader.

The man between us woke then and began to scream, and there was no more time for talking.

Chapter Two

By nightfall the field was cleared of the fallen. The King had withdrawn when it was seen that the tide of victory was sure, and not to be stemmed by any late action of the Saxons. The battle over, the main forces of the British fell back on the township two miles to the north-west, leaving Cador, with Caw of Strathclyde, to hold the field. Lot had not stayed to test his position with the other leaders, but had withdrawn into the town as soon as the fighting was done, and had gone like Ajax to his quarters, since where no man had seen him. Already stories were going round about his fury at the King's action in favouring the strange youth on the battlefield, and his black silence when he heard that Emrys was bidden with me to the victory feast, where no doubt he would be further honoured. There were rumours, too, about the reason for the belated entrance into battle of Lot's troops. No one went so far as to speak of treachery, but it was said openly that, had he delayed much longer, and had not Arthur performed his small miracle, Lothian's inaction might have cost Uther the victory. Men wondered too, aloud, whether Lot would emerge from his sullen silence to share in the feast which was decreed for the following night. But I knew that he could not keep away. He dared not. Though he had said nothing, he must certainly know who 'Emrys' was, and if he was ever to discredit him and seize the power he had schemed for, he would have to do it now.

After the emergency cases had been dealt with at the orchard dressing station, the medical units had also moved back to the town, where a hospital had been set up. I went with them, and dealt with a steady stream of cases all afternoon and evening. Our losses had not been heavy as such things commonly go, but still the burial parties would be hard at work all night, watched by the wolves and the gathering ravens. From the marshes came the distant flicker of flames, where the Saxon dead were burning.

I finished work in the hospital at about midnight, and was in an outer room, watching while Paulus packed my instruments away, when I heard someone coming quickly across the court outside, and was aware of a stir near the door behind me.

Call me an old fool if you like, remembering back through the years to what never happened, and you may be more than half right; but it was not only love which made me recognise his coming before I even turned my head. A current of fresh sweet air blew with him, cutting through the fumes of drugs and the stench of sickness and fear. The very lamps burned brighter.

'Merlin?' He spoke softly, as one does in a sickroom, but the excitement of the day was still in his voice. I looked at him smiling, then more sharply.

'Are you hurt? You young fool, why didn't you come to me sooner? Let me see.'

He drew back the arm in its stiffened sleeve. 'Can't you tell black Saxon blood when you see it? I never had a scratch. Oh, Merlin, what a day! And what a King! To go out in the field crippled and in a chair—that's real courage, far more than it takes to ride into a fight with a good horse and a good sword. I'll swear *I* never even had to think . . . it was so easy . . . Merlin, it was splendid! It's what I was born for—I know it now! And did you see what happened? What the King did? His sword? I'll swear it pulled me forward of its own will, not mine . . . And then the shouting and the way the soldiers moved forward, like the sea. I never even had to use a spur on Canrith . . . Everything moved so fast, and yet so slowly and clearly, every moment seemed to last for ever. I never knew one could be blazing hot and ice-cold all at the same moment, did you?'

He did not wait for answers, but talked on, fast and sparkling, his eyes alight still with the thrill of battle and the overwhelming experience of the day. I hardly listened, but I watched him, and watched the faces of the orderlies and servants, and of those men who were still awake and near enough to hear us. I saw it begin: even so, after battle, Ambrosius' very presence had given the wounded strength, and the dying comfort, Whatever it was he had about him, Arthur had the same; I was to see it often in the future; it seemed that he shed brightness and strength round him where he went, and still had it ever renewed in himself. As he grew older, I knew it would be renewed more hardly and at a cost, but now he was very young, with the flower of manhood still to come. After this, I thought, who could maintain that youth made him unfit for kingship? Not Lot, stiffened in his ambition, grimly scheming for a dead king's throne. It was Arthur's very youth which had whistled up today the best that men had in them, as a huntsman calls up the following pack, or an enchanter whistles up the wind.

He recognised, in one of the beds, a man who had fought near him, and went softly down the hospital room to speak to him, and then to others. Two of them, at least, I heard him call by name.

Give him the sword, my dream had said, *and his own nature will do the rest. Kings are not created out of dreams and prophecies: before ever you began to work for him, he was what you see now. All you have done is to guard him while he grew. You, Merlin, are a smith like Weland of the black forge; you made the sword and gave it a cutting edge, but it carves its own way.*

'I saw you up there beside the apple tree,' said Arthur gaily. He had followed me out of the hospital room, and I had stopped in the anteroom to give instructions to a night orderly. 'The men were saying it was an omen. That when you were there, above us on the hill, the fight was as good as won. And it's true, because through it all, even when I wasn't thinking, I could feel you watching me. Quite close beside me, too. It was like a shield at one's back. I even thought I heard—'

He stopped in mid-sentence. I saw his eyes widen and fix on something beyond me. I looked to see what had gagged him.

Morgause would be two and twenty now, and she was even lovelier than when I had last seen her. She wore grey, a long plain gown of dove-colour which should have made her look like a nun, but somehow did not. She wore no jewels, and needed none. Her skin was pale as marble, and the long eyes that I remembered were gold-green under the tawny lashes. Her hair, as befitted a woman still unwed, fell loose and shining over her shoulders, and was bound back from her brow with a broad band of white.

'Morgause!' I said, startled. 'You should not be here!' Then I remembered her skills, and saw behind her two women and a page carrying boxes and linen cloths. She must have been working, as I had, among the wounded; or probably she still attended the King, and had been with him. I added, quickly: 'No, I see; forgive me, and forgive my lack of greeting. Your skill is welcome here. Tell me, how is the King?'

'He has recovered, my lord, and is resting. He seems well enough, and his spirits are good. It seems it was a notable fight. I wish I might have seen it.' She glanced past me then at Arthur, an interested, summing look. It was obvious that she recognised him as the youth who had won everyone's praise that day, but it seemed that the King had not yet told her who he was. There was no hint of such a knowledge in her face or voice as she made him a reverence. 'Sir.'

The colour was up in Arthur's face, bright as a banner. He stammered some kind of greeting, suddenly sounding no more than an awkward boy, he whose boyhood had never been awkward.

She took it coolly, then turned her eyes back to me, dismissing him as a woman of twenty dismisses a child. I thought: No, she does not know yet.

She said, in that light, sweet voice: 'My lord Merlin, I came with a message to you from the King. Later, when you have rested, he would like to speak with you.'

I said doubtfully: 'It's very late. Would he not be better to sleep?'

'I think he would sleep better if he spoke with you first. He was impatient to see you as soon as he came back from the field, but he needed to rest, so I gave him a draught, and he slept then. He's awake now. Can you come within the hour?'

'Very well.'

She curtsied again with lowered eyes, and went, as quickly as she had come.

Chapter Three

I supped alone with Arthur. I had been allotted a room whose window overlooked a strip of garden on the river bank; the garden was a terrace enclosed by gates and high walls. Arthur's room adjoined mine, and both were approached through an anteroom where guards stood armed. Uther was taking no chances.

My room was large and well appointed, and a servant waited there with food and wine. We spoke little while we ate. I was tired and hungry, and Arthur showed his usual appetite, but after his flow of exalted spirits he had fallen strangely quiet, probably, I thought, out of deference to me. For my part I could think of little else but the coming interview with Uther, and of what the morrow might bring; at that moment I could bring nothing to them myself but a sort of weariness of the spirit, which I told myself was no more than reaction from a long journey and a hard day. But I thought it was more than that, and felt like a man who comes out of a sunlit plain into boggy ground, where mist hangs heavy.

Ulfin, Uther's body-servant, came to take me to the King. From the way his look lingered on Arthur I could see he knew the truth, but he said nothing of it as he led me through the corridors to the King's chamber. Indeed he seemed to have little room in his mind for anything but anxiety about the King's health. When I was ushered into Uther's presence, I could see why. Even since the morning, the change was startling. He was in bed, propped in furred bedgown against pillows, and, shorn of the kingly trappings of armour and scarlet and gold tissue, anyone could see how mortally wasted his body was. Now I could see his death clearly in his face. It would not be tonight, nor should it be tomorrow, but it must come soon; and this, I told myself, must be the cause of the formless dread that was weighing on me. But, though weak and weary, the King seemed pleased to see me, and eager to talk, so I pushed my foreboding aside. Even with tonight and tomorrow, Uther and I and whatever was working for us should have time to see our soaring star riding high and safe to his bright zenith.

He talked first of the battle, and of the day's events. It was evident that all his doubts were set aside, and that (though he would not admit it) he was regretting the lost years since Arthur had come near manhood. He plied me with questions, and, though afraid of taxing him too much, I could see that he would rest better when he knew all I had to tell him. So, as clearly and quickly as I could, I told him the story of the past years, all the detail of the boy's life in the Wild Forest that could not be put into the reports I had sent him. I told him, too, what suspicions and certainties I had had about Arthur's enemies; when I spoke about Lot he made no sign, but he heard me out without interruption. Of the sword of Maximus I said nothing. The King had himself today publicly put his own sword into his son's hand; he could not have declared more openly that the boy was his favoured heir. Macsen's sword, when there was need for it, would be given by the god. Between the two gifts was still a dark gap of fate through which I could not see; there was no need to trouble the King with it.

When I had done he lay back on his pillows awhile in silence, his eyes on a far corner of the room, deep in thought. Then he spoke.

'You were right, Merlin. Even where it was hard to understand, and where not understanding I condemned you, you were right. The god had us all in his hand. And doubtless it was the god himself who put it in my mind to deny my son and leave him in your care, to be brought in safety and secrecy to such manhood as this. At least it has been granted me to see what manner of man I begot on that wild night at Tintagel, and what kind of king will come after me. I should have trusted you better, bastard, as my brother did. I don't need to tell you that I am dying, do I? Gandar hums and haws and begs the question, but you'll admit the truth, King's prophet?'

The question was peremptory, requiring an answer. When I said, 'Yes,' he smiled briefly, with a look almost of satisfaction. I found myself liking Uther better now than I ever had before, seeing him bring this kind of bleak courage to his coming death. This was what Arthur had recognised in him today, the kingly quality to which he had come late, but not too late. It could be that now, almost in the moment of fulfilment of the past years, he and I found ourselves united in the person of the boy.

He nodded. The strain of the day and night was beginning to show, but his look was friendly and his manner still crisp. 'Well, we've cleared the past. The future is with him, and with you. But I'm not dead yet, and I'm still High King. The present is with me. I sent for you to tell you that I shall proclaim Arthur my heir tomorrow at the victory feast. There'll never be a better moment. After what happened today no one can argue his fitness; he has already proved himself in public, more, in the sight of the army. Even if I wished to, I doubt if I could keep his secret any longer, rumour has run through the camp like a fire through straw. He knows nothing yet?'

'It seems not. I would have thought he would begin to guess, but it seems not. You'll tell him yourself tomorrow?'

'Yes. I'll send for him in the morning. For the rest of the time, Merlin, stay by him and keep him close.'

He spoke then about his plans for the morrow. He would talk with Arthur, and then in the evening, when everyone had recovered from the fighting, and erased the scars of battle, Arthur would be brought with glory and acclaim in front of the nobles at the victory feast. As for Lot—he came to it flatly and without excuse—there was doubt as to what Lot would do, but he had lost too much public credit over his delay in the battle, and even as the betrothed of the King's daughter he would hardly dare (Uther insisted) stand up in public against the High King's own choice. He said nothing about the darker possibility, that Lot might even have thrown his weight on to the Saxons' side of the balance; he saw the delay only as a bid for credit—that Lot's intervention should seem to carry the British to victory. I listened, and said nothing. Whatever the truth of that, the trouble would soon be other men's, and not the King's.

He spoke then of Morgian, his daughter. The marriage, firmly contracted as it was, must go through; it could hardly be broken now without offering a mortal and dangerous insult to Lot and the northern kings who hunted with him. And as things had fallen out, it would be safer so; Lot would by the same token not dare to refuse the marriage, and by accepting it would bind himself publicly to Arthur; and Arthur already (months before the marriage) proclaimed, accepted, and established. Uther had almost said 'and crowned', but let the sentence drift. He was looking tired now, and I made a move to leave him, but one of the thin hands lifted, and I waited. He did not speak for a few moments, but lay back with closed eyes. Somewhere a draught crept through the room, and the candles guttered. The shadows wavered, throwing dark across his face. Then the light steadied, and I could see his eyes, still bright in their deep sockets, watching me.

I heard his voice, thin with effort now, asking me something. Not asking, no. Uther the High King was begging me to stay beside Arthur, to finish the work I had begun, to watch him, advise him, guard him . . .

His voice faded, but the eyes watched me, intent, and I knew what they were saying. '*Tell me the future, Merlin, prophet of kings. Prophesy for me.*'

'I shall be with him,' I said, 'and the rest of it I have said before. He will bear a king's sword, and with that sword he will do all and more than men hope for. Under him the countries will be one, and there shall be peace, and light before darkness. And when there is peace I myself will go back into my solitude, but I will be there, waiting, always, to be called up as quickly as a man might whistle for the wind.'

I was not speaking with vision: this was something which has never come to me when asked for, and besides, visions did not live easily in the same room as Uther. But to comfort him I spoke from remembered prophecies, and from a knowledge of men and times, which sometimes comes to the same thing. It satisfied him, which was all that was needed.

'That is all I wanted to know,' he said. 'That you will stay near him, and serve him at all times . . . Perhaps, if I had listened to my brother, and kept you near me . . . You have promised, Merlin. There is no man who has more power, not even the High King.'

He said it without rancour, in the tone of one making a plain statement. His voice was tired suddenly, the voice of a sick man.

I got to my feet. 'I'll leave you now, Uther. You had better sleep. What is the draught Morgause gives you?'

'I don't know. Some poppy-smelling thing; she puts it in warm wine.'

'Does she sleep here, near you?'

'No. Along the corridor, in the first of the women's rooms. But don't disturb her now. There's some of the drug still in that jar yonder.'

I crossed the room, picked up the jar, and sniffed it. The potion, whatever it was, was already mixed in wine; the smell was sweet and heavy; poppy there was and other things I recognised, but it was not quite familiar. I dipped a finger in and put it to my lips. 'Has anyone touched it since she mixed it?'

'Eh?' He had been drifting away, not in sleep, but as sick men do. 'Touched it? No one that I have seen, but there's no one will try to poison me. It's well known that all my food is tasted. Call the boy in, if you wish.'

'No need,' I said. 'Let him sleep.' I poured some into a cup, but when I lifted it to my mouth he said with sudden vigour: 'Don't be a fool! Let be!'

'I thought you said it would not be poisoned.'

'No matter of that, we'll not take the chance.'

'Do you not trust Morgause?'

'Morgause?' He knitted his brows, as if at an irrelevancy. 'Of course, why not? When she has cared for me all these years, refusing to wed, even when . . . But no matter of that. Her fate is "in the smoke", she says, and she is content to wait for it. She riddles like you, sometimes, and I've scant patience with riddles, as you may remember. No, how could I doubt my daughter? But tonight of all nights we must be wary, and of all men, except my son, I can least spare you.' He smiled then, momentarily the Uther that I remembered, hard and gay, and slightly malicious. 'At least, not until he is proclaimed, and then no doubt you and I will well spare one another.'

I smiled. 'Meantime I'll taste your wine. Calm yourself, I can smell nothing hurtful, and I assure you that my death is not yet.'

I did not add, 'So let me make sure that you live to proclaim your son tomorrow.' This strange shadow that brooded still behind my shoulder, it could not be my own death, nor (I knew) was it Arthur's, but it might, against all probability, be the King's. I took a sip, letting the wine rest for a moment on my tongue, then swallowed. The King lay back on his pillows and watched me, tranquil once more. I sipped again, then crossed the room to sit down by the great bed, and, more idly now, we talked: of the past seamed with memories; of the future, shadows still across glory. We understood one another tolerably well at last, Uther and I. When it was patent that the wine was harmless I poured a draught for him, watched him drink it, then called his servant Ulfin, and left him to sleep.

Chapter Four

All was so far well. Even if Uther died tonight—and nothing in his look or in my bones told me that he would—all was surely still set fair. I, with Cador's backing and Ector's support, could proclaim Arthur to the nobles as well as the King could, and prestige with power behind it had every chance of forcing the thing through. The King's gesture in flinging his sword to the boy in battle would be, to many of the soldiers, proof enough of Arthur's right to succeed him, and the warriors who had followed him so gladly today would follow him still. It was surely only the dissidents of the north-east who would not rejoice to see the days of uncertainty finished, and the succession pass clear and undoubted into Arthur's hands.

Then why, I thought, as I trod quietly along the corridors towards my own chamber, was my heart so heavy in me; what was this foreboding black enough for a death? Why, if this was a heavy matter that my blood prophesied, could I not see it? What shadow hung, clawed and waiting, over the day's bright success?

A moment later, as I nodded to the guard outside my antechamber, and went quietly through into the room itself, I saw the edge of the shadow. Beyond the doorway connecting Arthur's room to my own I could see his bed. It was empty.

I went quickly back to the antechamber, and had stooped to shake the sleeping servant awake, when my nostrils caught a familiar smell, the drug that had been in the King's wine. I dropped the man's shoulder and left him snoring, and in three swift strides was back in the corridor. Before I had said a word, the guard flattened himself back against the wall, as if afraid of what he saw in my face.

But I spoke softly: 'Where is he?'

'My lord, he's safe. There's no reason for alarm . . . We had our orders, there was no harm could come to him. The other guard saw him right to the door, and stayed there—'

'*Where is he?*'

'In the women's rooms, my lord. When the girl came to him—'

'Girl?' I asked sharply.

'Indeed, my lord. She came here. We stopped her, of course, wouldn't let her in, but then he came out to the door himself . . .' Reassured now by my silence, the man was relaxing. 'Indeed, my lord, all's well. It was one of the Lady Morgause's women, the black-haired one, you may have noticed her, plump as a robin, and the prettiest, as was proper for my young lord this night—'

I had noticed her; small and rounded, with a high colour and black eyes bright as a bird's. A pretty creature, very young, and healthy as a summer's day. But I bit my lip. 'How long ago?'

'Two hours, as near as might be.' A grin touched his mouth. 'Time enough. My lord, where's the harm? Even if we'd tried, how could we have stopped him? We didn't let her in; we'd had our orders, and he knew it; but when he said he'd go with her, what could we do? After all, it's a fair end to a man's first battle day.'

I said something to him, and went back into my room. The fellow was right enough, the guards had done their duty as they saw it, and this was one situation in which no guard would have interfered. And where indeed was the harm? The boy had seized one half of his manhood today out under the sun; it was inevitable that the rest should come to him tonight. As his sword had quenched its lust in blood, so the boy would burn alive till he quenched his own excitement in a girl's body. Anybody, I thought bitterly, but a god-bound prophet, would have foreseen this. Any normal guardian would let this night take its normal course. But I was Merlin, and the room was full of shadows, and I was afraid.

I stood there alone, with the shadows pressing round me, controlling myself to coldness, facing the fear. The blackness came from my mind; very well, was it human merely, was it black jealousy, that Arthur at fourteen should take so easily a pleasure that at twenty I had burned for even as he, and had fumbled, failing? Or was it a fear worse than jealousy, the fear of losing or even sharing a love so dear and lately found; or was I fearful only for him, knowing what a girl could do to rob a man of power? And as this thought struck me I knew I was acquitted; the shadows were not from this. I had known, that day at twenty, when I fled from the girl's angry and derisive laughter, that for me there had been a cold choice between manhood and power, and I had chosen power. But Arthur's power would be different, that of full and fierce manhood, that of a king. He had shown me often that however much he might love and learn from me, he was Uther's son in the flesh; he wanted all that manhood could give. It was right that he should lie with his first girl tonight. I ought to smile, like the sentry, and go to bed myself and sleep, leaving him to his pleasure.

But the cold in my entrails and the sweat on my face was not there for nothing. I stood still, while the lamp flared and dimmed and flared again, and thought.

Morgause, I thought, one of Morgause's girls. And she'd drugged my servant, who might have come to tell me that Arthur had gone two hours since to her chamber . . . And Morgause is Morgian's half-sister, and might be in Lot's pay, with the promise of some rich future should Lot become King. True, she had made no attempt on the King, but she knew he always used a taster, and it would have served no purpose to be rid of him until Lot was married to Morgian and able to declare himself legitimately heir to the High Kingdom. But now Uther was dying, and Arthur had appeared, with a claim which would eclipse Lot's. If Morgause was indeed an enemy, and wanted Arthur put out of the way before tomorrow's feast, then the boy might even now be drugged, captive in Lot's hands, or dying . . .

This was folly. It was not for death that the god had given him the sword and shown him to me as High King. There was no reason for Morgause to wish him ill. As his half-sister she might expect more from Arthur as King than from Lot, her sister's husband. Arthur's death, I thought coldly, would not profit her. But death was here, in a form and with a smell I did not know. A smell like treachery, something remembered dimly from my childhood, when my uncle planned to betray his father's kingdom, and to murder me. It was not a matter of reason, but of knowing. Danger was here, and I had to find it.

I could not walk through the house, asking where Arthur was. If he was happily bedded with a girl, this was something he would never forgive me. I would have to find him by other means, and since I was Merlin, the means were here. Standing rigid there in the dim chamber, with my hands held stiff-fisted at my sides, I stared at the lamp . . .

I know that I never moved from the place or left my chamber, but in my memory now it seems as if I went out, silent and invisible as a ghost, across the antechamber, past the guard, and along the dim corridor towards Morgause's door. The other sentry was there; he was full awake, and watching, but he never saw me.

There was no sound from within. I went in.

In the outer room the air was heavy and warm, and smelt of scents and lotions such as women use. There were two beds there, and sleepers in them. In the threshold of the inner chamber Morgause's page was curled on the floor, sleeping.

Two beds, each with its sleeper. One was an old woman, grey-haired, mouth open, snoring slightly. The other slept silently, and over her pillow the long black hair lay heavy, braided for the night. The little dark girl slept alone.

I knew it now, the horror that oppressed me; the one thing that, looking for larger issues of death and treachery and loss, I had never thought of. I have said men with god's sight are often human-blind: when I exchanged my manhood for power it seemed I had made myself blind to the ways of women. If I had been simple man instead of wizard I would have seen the way eye answered eye back there at the hospital, have recognised Arthur's silence later, and known the woman's long assessing look for what it was.

Some magic she must have had, to blind me so. It may be that now, knowing I could do nothing, she let the magic lapse and thin; or let it waver as she sank towards sleep. Or it may be only that my power outstripped hers, and she had no shield against me. God knows I did not want to look, but I was nailed there by my own power, and because there is no power without knowledge, and no knowledge without suffering, the walls and door of Morgause's sleeping chamber dissolved in front of me, and I could see.

Time enough, the guard had said. They had indeed had time enough. The woman lay, naked and wide-legged, across the covers of the bed. The boy, brown against her whiteness, lay sprawled over her in the heavy abandonment of pleasure. His head was between her breasts, half turned from me; he was not asleep, but the next thing to it, his face close and quiet, his blind mouth searching her flesh as a puppy nuzzled for its mother's nipple. Her face I saw clearly. She held his head cradled, and about her body was the same heavy langour, but her face showed none of the tenderness that the gesture seemed to express. And none of the pleasure. It held a secret exultation as fierce as I have ever seen on a warrior's face in battle; the gilt-green eyes were wide and fixed on something invisible beyond the dark; and the small mouth smiled, a smile somewhere between triumph and contempt.

Chapter Five

He came back to his room just before daylight. The first bird had whistled, and a few moments later the sudden jargoning of the early chorus almost drowned the clink of arms at the outer door, and his soft word to the guard. He came in, his eyes full of sleep, and stopped short just inside the door when he saw me sitting in the high-backed chair beside the window.

'Merlin! Up at this hour? Couldn't you sleep?'

'I haven't yet been to bed.'

He came suddenly wide awake, sharpened and alert. 'What is it? What's wrong? Is it the King?'

At least, I thought, he doesn't jump to the conclusion that I stayed awake to question his night's doings. And one thing he must never know; that I followed him through that door.

I said: 'No, not the King. But you and I must talk before the day comes.'

'Oh, the gods, not now, if you love me,' he said, half laughing, and yawned. 'Merlin, I've got to sleep. Did you guess where I'd gone, or did the guard tell you?'

As he came forward into the room I could smell her scent on him. I felt sickened, and I suppose I was shaken. I said curtly: 'Yes, now. Wash yourself, and wake up. I have to talk to you.'

I had put out all the lamps but one, and this was burning low, only half competing with the leaden light of dawn. I saw his face go rigid. 'By what right—?' He checked himself, and I saw the quick control come down over his anger. 'Very well. I suppose you do have the right to question me, but I don't like the time you choose.'

It was something altogether different from the injured boyish anger he had shown before, how short a time ago, beside the lake. So far they had already taken him between them, the sword and the woman. I said: 'I have no right to question you, and I've no intention of doing so. Calm yourself, and listen. It's true I want to talk to you—among other things—about what happened tonight, but not for the reasons you seem to impute to me. Who do you think I am, Abbot Martin? I don't dispute your right to take your pleasure as and where you wish.' He was still hostile, between anger and pride. To relax him and pass the moment over I added mildly: 'Perhaps it wasn't wise to venture through this house at night where there are men who hate you for what you did yesterday. But how can I blame you for going? You showed yourself a man in battle, why not then in your bed?' I smiled. 'Though I've never lain with a woman myself, I've known what it is to want one. For the pleasure you had, I'm glad.'

I stopped. His face had been pale with anger; now even in that lack of light I could see the anger drain away, and with it the last vestiges of colour. It was as if blood and breath had stopped together. His eyes looked black. He narrowed them at me as if he could not see me properly, or as if he were seeing me for the first time, and could not get me in focus. It was a discomforting look, and I am not easily discomforted.

'You have never lain with a woman?'

Somehow, to the matters boiling in my mind, the question came as sheer irrelevancy. I said, surprised: 'I said no. I believe it's a matter of common knowledge. I also believe it's a fact that some men hold in contempt. But those—'

'Are you a eunuch, then?'

The question was cruel; his manner, harsh and abrupt, made it seem meant so. I had to wait a moment before I answered.

'No. I was going to add, that those who hold chastity in contempt, are not men whose contempt would disturb me. Have I yours, then?'

'What?' He had obviously not heard a word of what I had been saying. He jerked himself free of whatever strong emotion was riding him, and made for his room like a man who is choking, and in need of air. As he went he said, muffled: 'I'll go and wash.'

The door shut behind him. I stood up quickly and set my hands on the window sill, leaning out into the chill September dawn. A cock was crowing; from further off others answered it. I found that I was shaking; I,

Merlin, who had watched while kings and priests and princes plotted my death openly in front of my eyes; who had talked with the dead; who could make storm and fire and call the wind. Well, I had called this wind; I must face it. But I had counted on his love for me to get us both through what I had to tell him. I had not reckoned on losing his respect—and for such a reason—at this moment.

I told myself that he was young; that he was Uther's son, fresh from his first woman, and in the flush of his new sexual pride. I told myself that I had been a fool to see love given back where I gave it, when what the boy was rendering to me was no more than I had given my own tutor Galapas, affection tinged with awe. I told myself these and other things, and by the time he came back I was seated again, calm and waiting, with two goblets of wine poured ready on a table at my hand. He took one without a word, then sat across the room from me, on the edge of my bed. He had washed even his hair; it was still damp, and clung to his brow. He had changed his bedgown for day dress, and in the short tunic, without mantle or weapon, looked like a boy again, the Arthur of the summer and the Wild Forest.

I had been casting round carefully for what to say, but now could find nothing. It was Arthur who broke the silence, not looking at me, turning the goblet round and round in his hands, watching the swirl of wine as if his life depended on it.

He said, flatly, and as if it explained everything, as I suppose it did:

'I thought you were my father.'

It was like facing an opponent's sword, only to find that the sword and the enemy are in fact illusions, but in the same moment to feel that the very ground on which one has made one's stand is a shaking bog. I fought to rearrange my thoughts.

Respect and love, yes, I had had these from him, but they could have been given to me for the man I was; in fact, only in such a way does a boy give them to his father. But other things became suddenly plain; above all the deference which he would have given to no other man but Ector, his obedience, his assumption of my ready welcome, and more than all—I saw it like the sudden rift of daffodil sky which opened in the grey beyond the window—the shining anticipation with which he had come with me to Luguvallium. I remembered my own ceaseless childhood search for my father, and how I had looked for and seen him everywhere, in every man who looked my mother's way. Arthur had had only his foster-parents' story of noble bastardy, and a vague promise of recognition 'when you are grown enough to bear arms'. As children do—as I had done—he had said little, but waited and wondered, ceaselessly. Then into this perpetual search and expectation I had come, with some mystery about me, and I suppose the air that Ralf had spoken of, of a man used to deference and moved by some strong purpose. The boy may have seen his own likeness to me; more likely others, Bedwyr even, had commented on it. So he had waited, reaching his own conclusions, prepared to give love, accept authority, and trust me for the future. Then came the sword, a gift, it seemed, from me; father to son. And the discovery that had followed hard on it, that I was Ambrosius' son, and the Merlin of the thousand legends told at every fireside. Bastard or no, suddenly he had found himself, and he was royal.

So he had followed me to the King at Luguvallium, seeing himself as Ambrosius' grandson and great-nephew to Uther Pendragon. From this knowledge had come that flashing confidence in battle. He must have thought this was why Uther had flung him the sword, because in default of the absent prince, he, bastard or not, was the next in blood. So he had led the charge, and afterwards accepted the duties and the favours due to a prince.

It also explained why he had never seemed to suspect that he might be the 'lost' prince. The stares and whispers and the deference he received he had put down to recognition as my son. He accepted, as most men did, the fact that the High King's heir was abroad at a foreign court, and thought nothing more about it. And once he imagined he had found his place, why should he think again? He was mine, and he was royal, and through me he had a place at the centre of the kingdom. Now all at once, cruelly enough, as he must see it, he found himself not only deprived of ambition and the place he had dreamed of, but even of a place as a man's acknowledged son. I, who had lived my youth as a bastard and a no-man's child, knew how that canker can eat: Ector had tried to spare Arthur this by telling him that he would one day be acknowledged nobly; it had never struck me that he would count in love and confidence on the acknowledgment coming from me.

'Even my name, you see.' The dull apology of his tone was worse than the cruelty that shock had brought him from him before.

At least, if I could heal nothing else, I could heal his pride. The cost would be counted presently, but he had to know now. I had many times thought how, if it were left to me, I would tell him. Now I spoke straight, the simple truth. 'We bear the same name because we are in fact kin to one another. You are not my son, but we are cousins. You, like me, are a grandson of Constantius and a descendant of Maximus the Emperor. Your true name is Arthur, and you are the legitimate son of the High King and Ygraine his Queen.'

I thought the silence this time would never break. At my first word his eyes had come up from watching the swirling wine, and fastened on me. His brows were knitted like those of a deaf man straining to hear. The red washed through his face like blood staining a white cloth, and his lips parted. Then he set the goblet down very carefully, and standing up came to the window near me, and, just as I had done earlier, set his hands on the sill and leaned out into the air.

A bird flew into the bough beside him and began to sing. The sky faded to heron's-egg green, then slowly cooled to hyacinth where thin flakes of cloud floated. Still he stood there, and I waited, without movement or speech.

At length, without turning, he spoke to the bough with its singing bird. 'Why this way? Fourteen years. Why not where I belonged?'

So at last I told him the whole story. I began with the vision Ambrosius had shared with me, of the kingdoms united under one king, Dumnonia to Lothian, Dyfed to Rutupiae; Romano-Briton and Celt and loyal *foederatus* fighting as one to keep Britain clear of the black flood that was drowning the rest of the Empire; a version, humbler and more workable, of Maximus' imperial dream, adapted and handed down by my grandfather to my father, and lodged in me by my master's teaching and by the god who had marked me for his service. I told him about Ambrosius' death without other issue, and the ravelled clue the god had thrust into my hand, bidding me follow it. About the sudden passion of the new King Uther for Ygraine, wife of Cornwall's Duke, and about my own connivance at their union, shown by the god that this was the union which would bring its next king to Britain. About Gorlois' death and Uther's remorse, mingled as it was with relief at a death he had more than half wished, but wanted publicly to disclaim and disown: then the consequent banishment of myself and Ralf, and Uther's own threats to disown the child so begotten. Then finally, how pride and commonsense between them prevailed, and the child had been handed to me to look after through the dangerous first years of Uther's reign; and how since then the King's illness and the growing power of his enemies had forced him to leave his son in hiding. About some things I said nothing: I did not tell Arthur what I had seen waiting for him, of greatness or pain or glory; and I said no word about Uther's impotence. Nor did I speak of the King's desperate wish for another son to supplant the 'bastard' of Tintagel; these were Uther's secrets, and he would not have long now to keep them.

Arthur listened in silence, without interruption. Indeed, at first without movement, so that one might have thought his whole attention was on the slowly brightening sky outside the window, and the song of the blackbird on the bough. But after a while he turned and–though I was not looking at him–I felt his eyes on me at last. When I came to the Coronation feast, and the King's demand for me to bring him to Ygraine's bed, he moved again, going softly across to his former place on the bed. My tale of that wild night when he was begotten was told plainly, exactly as it had happened. But he listened as if it had been the same half-enchanted tale I had told him in the Wild Forest with Bedwyr beside him, himself curled half-sitting, half-lying on my bed, chin on fist, his dark eyes, calm now and shining, on my face.

As I came towards an end it was to be seen that the tale fitted in with all that I had taught him in the past, so that now I was just handing him the last links in the golden lineage and saying, in effect: 'All that I have ever taught or told you is summed up in you, yourself.'

I stopped at length, and took a draught of wine. He uncurled swiftly from the bed and, bringing the jug, poured more into my goblet. When I thanked him, he stooped and kissed me.

'You,' he said quietly, 'you, from the very beginning. I wasn't so far wrong after all, was I? I'm as much yours as the King's–more; and Ector's, too . . . Then Ralf, I'm glad to know about Ralf. I see . . . Oh, yes, now I begin to see a lot of things.' He paced about the room, talking in snatches, half to himself, as restless as Uther. 'So much–it's too much to take in. I'll have to have time . . . I'm glad it was you who told me. Did the King mean to tell me himself?'

'Yes. He would have talked to you earlier, if there had been time. I hope there will still be time.'

'What do you mean?'

'He's dying, Arthur. Are you ready to be King?'

He stood there, the wine-jug still in his hand, hollow-eyed with lack of sleep, thoughts crowding in on him too fast for expression. '*Today?*'

'I think so. I don't know. Soon.'

'Will you be with me?'

'Of course. I told you so.'

It was only then, as he set down the jug, smiling, and turned to put out the lamp, that the other thing struck him. I saw the moment when his breath stopped, then was let out again cautiously, the way a man tries his breathing after a mortal stroke.

He had his back to me, reaching up to quench the lamp. I saw that his hand was quite steady. But the other hand, which he tried to hide from me, was making the sign against evil. Then, being Arthur, he did not stay turned away, but faced me.

'I have something to tell *you* now.'

'Yes?'

The words came like something being dragged up from a depth. 'The woman I was with tonight was Morgause.' Then, as I did not speak, sharply: 'You knew?'

'Only when it was too late to stop you. But I should have known. Before I ever went to see the King, I knew that something was wrong. Oh, no, nothing of what it was, only that the shadows pressed on me.'

'If I had stayed in my room, as you told me . . .'

'Arthur. The thing has happened. It's no use saying "if this" and "if that"; can't you see that you're innocent? You obeyed your nature, it's something young men will do. But I, I am to blame. You could curse me, if you wished, for all this secrecy. If I had told you sooner about your birth—'

'You told me to stay here. Even if you didn't know what ill was in the wind, you knew that if I obeyed you I would be safe. If I had obeyed you, I'd be more than safe, I would still be—' He bit off some word I did not quite hear, then finished '—clean of this thing. Blame *you*? The blame is mine, and God knows it and will judge between us.'

'God will judge us all.'

He took three restless strides across the room and back again. 'Of all women, my sister, my father's daughter . . .' The words came hard, like a morsel one gags on. I could see the horror clinging to him, like a slug to a green plant. His left hand still made the sign against evil: it is a pagan sign; the sin has been a heavy one before the gods since time began. He halted suddenly, squarely in front of me, even at this moment able to think beyond himself. 'And Morgause herself? When she knows what you have just told me, what will she think, knowing the sin we've committed between us? What will she do? If she falls into despair—'

'She will not fall into despair.'

'How can you know? You said you didn't know women. I believe that for women these matters are heavier.' Horror struck at him again as he thought why. 'Merlin, if there should be a child?'

I think there has been no moment in my life when I have had to exert more self-command. He was staring wildly at me; if I had let my thoughts show in my face, God only knows what he might have done. As he spoke the last sentence it was as if the formless shadows which had clawed and brooded over me all night suddenly took form and weight. They were there, clinging round my shoulders, vultures, heavy-feathered and stinking of carrion. I, who had schemed for Arthur's conception, had waited blind and idle while his death also was conceived.

'I shall have to tell her.' His voice was edged, desperate. 'Straight away. Even before the High King declares me. There may be those who guess, and she may hear . . .'

He talked on, a little wildly, but I was too busy with my own thoughts to listen. I thought: if I tell him that she knew already, that she is corrupt and that her power, such as it is, is corrupt; if I tell him that she used him deliberately to gather more power to herself; if I tell him these things now, while he is shaken out of his wits by all that has happened in this last day and night, he will take his sword and kill her. And when she dies the seed will die that is to grow corrupt as she is, and eat at his glory as this slug of horror eats at his youth. But if he kills them now he will never use a sword again in God's service, and their corruption will have claimed him before his work is ever begun.

I said calmly: 'Arthur. Be still now, and listen. I told you, what is done is done, and men must learn to stand by their deeds. Now hear me. One day soon you will be High King, and as you know, I am the King's Prophet. So listen to the first prophecy I shall make for you. What you did, you did in innocence. You alone of Uther's seed are clean. Has no one ever told you the gods are jealous? They insure against too much glory. Every man carries the seed of his own death, and you will not be more than a man. You will have everything; you cannot have more; and there must come a term to every life. All that has happened tonight is that you yourself have set that term. What more could a man want, that he determines his own death? Every life has a death, and every light a shadow. Be content to stand in the light, and let the shadow fall where it will.'

He grew quieter as he listened, and at length asked me, calmly enough: 'Merlin, what must I do?'

'Leave this to me. For yourself, put it behind you, forget about the night, and think of the morning. Listen, there are the trumpets. Go now, and get some sleep before the day begins.'

So, imperceptibly, was the first link forged in the new chain that bound us. He slept, to be ready for the great doings of the morrow, and I sat watchful, thinking, while the light grew and the day came.

Chapter Six

Ulfin, the King's chamberer, came at length to bid Arthur to the King's presence. I woke the boy, and later saw him go, silent and self-contained, showing a sort of impossible calm like smooth ice over a whirlpool. I think that, being young, he had already begun to put behind him the shadow of the night; the burden was mine now. This was a pattern which was common in the years to come.

As soon as he was gone, ushered out with a ceremony wherein I could see Ulfin remembering that night so long ago, of the boy's conception, and which Arthur himself accepted as if he had known it all his life, I called a servant and bade him bring the Lady Morgause to me.

The man looked surprised, then doubtful; it was to be surmised that the lady was used to do her own summoning. I had neither time nor patience this morning for such things. I said briefly: 'Do as I say,' and the fellow went, scuttling.

She kept me waiting, of course, but she came. This morning she wore red, the colour of cherries, and over the shoulders of the gown her hair looked rosy fair, larch buds in spring, the colour of apricots. Her scent was heavy and sweet, apricots and honeysuckle mixed, and I felt my stomach twist at the memory. But there was no other resemblance to the girl I had loved—had tried to love—so long ago; in Morgause's long-lidded green eyes there was not even the pretence of innocence. She came in smiling that close-lipped smile, with the prick of a charming dimple at the corner of her mouth, and, making me a reverence, crossed the room gracefully to seat herself in the high-backed chair. She disposed her robe prettily about her, dismissed her women with a nod, then lifted her chin and looked at me enquiringly. Her hands lay still and folded against the soft swell of her belly, and in her the gesture was not demure, but possessive.

Somewhere, coldly, a memory stirred. My mother, standing with her hands held so, facing a man who would have murdered me. 'I have a bastard to protect.' I believe that Morgause read my thoughts. The dimple deepened prettily, and the gold-fringed lids drooped.

I did not sit, but remained standing across the window from her. I said, more harshly than I had intended: 'You must know why I sent for you.'

'And you must know, Prince Merlin, that I am not used to being sent for.'

'Let us not waste time. You came, and it's just as well. I wish to speak with you while Arthur is still with the King.'

She opened her eyes wide at me. 'Arthur?'

'Don't make those innocent eyes at me, girl. You knew his name when you took him to your bed last night.'

'Can the poor boy not even keep his bed secrets from you?' The light pretty voice was contemptuous, meant to sting. 'Did he come running to your whistle to tell you about it, along with everything else? I'm surprised you let him off the chain long enough to take his pleasure last night. I wish you joy of him, Merlin the kingmaker. What sort of king is a half-trained puppy going to make?'

'The sort who is not ruled from his bed,' I said. 'You have had your night, and that was too much. The reckoning comes now.'

Her hands moved slightly in her lap. 'You can do me no harm.'

'No, I shall do you no harm.' The flicker in her eyes showed that she had noticed the change of phrase. 'But I am also here,' I said, 'to see that you do Arthur no harm. You will leave Luguvallium today, and you will not come back to the court.'

'I leave court? What nonsense is this? You know that I look after the King; he depends on me for his medicines, I am his nurse. I and his chamberer look after him in all things. You cannot imagine that the King will ever agree to let me go.'

'After today,' I said, 'the King will never want to see you again.'

She stared. Her colour was high. This, I could see, mattered to her. 'How can you say that? Even you, Merlin, cannot stop me from seeing my father, and I assure you he will not want to let me go. You surely don't mean to tell him what has happened? He's a sick man, a shock might kill him.'

'I shall not tell him.'

'Then what will you say to him? Why should he agree to having me sent away?'

'That is not what I said, Morgause.'

'You said that after today the King would never want to see me again.'

'I was not speaking of your father.'

'I don't see—' She took a sharp breath, and the green-gilt eyes widened. 'But you said . . . the King?' Her breath shortened. 'You were speaking of that boy?'

'Of your brother, yes. Where is your skill? Uther is marked for death.'

Her hands were working together in her lap. 'I know. But . . . you say it comes today?'

I echoed my own question. 'Where is your magic? It comes today. So you had better leave, had you not? Once Uther is gone, who will protect you here?'

She thought for a moment. The lovely green-gilt eyes were narrow and sly, not lovely at all. 'Against what? Against Arthur? You're so sure you can make them accept him as King? Even if you do, are you trying to tell me that I will need protection against him?'

'You know as well as I do that he will be King. You have skill enough for that, and—in spite of what you said to anger me—skill enough to know what kind of a king. You may not need protection against him, Morgause, but it is certain that you will need it against me.' Our eyes locked. I nodded, 'Yes. Where he is, I am. Be warned, and go while you can. I can protect him from the kind of magic you wove last night.'

She was calm again, seeming to draw into herself. The small mouth tightened in its secret smile. Yes, she had power of a kind. 'Are you so sure you are proof against women's magic? It will snare you in the end, Prince Merlin.'

'I know it,' I said calmly. 'Do you think I have not seen my end. And all our ends, Morgause. I have seen power for you, and for the thing you carry, but no joy. No joy, now or ever.'

Outside the window, against the wall, was an apricot tree. The sun warmed the fruit, globe on golden globe, scented and heavy. Warmth reflected from the stone wall, and wasps hummed among the glossy leaves, sleepy with scent. So, once before, in a sweet-smelling orchard, I had met hatred and murder, eye to eye.

She sat very still, her hands locked against her belly. Her eyes held mine, seeming to drink at them. The scent of honeysuckle thickened, visibly, drifting in green-gold haze across the lighted window, mingling with the sunshine and the smell of apricots . . .

'Stop it!' I said contemptuously. 'Do you really think that your girl's magic can touch me? No more now than it could before. And what are you trying to do? This is hardly a matter of magic. Arthur knows now who he is, and he knows what he did last night with you. Do you think he will bear you near him? Do you think that he will watch daily, monthly, while a child grows in your belly? He is not a cold nor a patient man. And he has a conscience. He believes that you sinned in innocence, as he did. If he thought otherwise, he might act.'

'Kill me, you mean?'

'Do you not deserve killing?'

'He sinned, if you call it sin, as much as I.'

'He did not know he was sinning, and you did. No, don't waste your breath on me. Why pretend? Even without your magic, you must know that half the court has whispered it since he and I rode in together yesterday. You knew he was Uther's son.'

For the first time there was a shade of fear in her face. She said obstinately: 'I did not know. You cannot prove I knew. Why should I do such a thing?'

I folded my arms and leaned a shoulder back against the wall. 'I will tell you why. First, because you are Uther's daughter, and like him a seeker after casual lusts. Because you have the Pendragon blood in you that makes you desire power, so you take it as it mostly offers itself to women, in a man's bed. You knew your father the King was dying, and fear that there would be no place of power for you as half-sister of the young King whose Queen would later dispossess you. I think you would not have hesitated to kill Arthur, but that you would have less standing, even, at Lot's court, with your own sister as Queen. Whoever became High King would have no need of you, as Uther has. You would be married to some small king and taken to some corner of the land where you would pass your time bearing his children and weaving his war cloaks, with nothing in your hands but the petty power of a family, and what women's magic you have learned and can practise in your little kingdom. That is why you did what you did, Morgause. Because, no matter what it was, you wanted a claim on the young King, even if it was to be a claim of horror and of hatred. What you did last night you did coldly, in a bid for power.'

'Who are you to talk to me so? You took power where you could find it.'

'Not where I could find it; where it was given. What you have got you took, against all laws of God and men. If you had acted unknowingly, in simple lust, there would be no more to say. I told you, so far he thinks you have no blame. This morning, when he knew what he had done, his first thought was for your distress.' I saw the flash of triumph in her eyes, and finished, gently: 'But you are not dealing with him, you are dealing with me. And I say that you shall go.'

She got swiftly to her feet. 'Why did you not tell him then, and let him kill me? Would you not have wanted that?'

'To add another and worse sin? You talk like a fool.'

'I shall go to the King.'

'To what purpose? He will spare no thought for you today.'

'I am always by him. He will need his drugs.'

'I am here now, and Gandar. He will not need you.'

'He'll see me if I say I've come to say farewell! I tell you, I will go to him!'

'Then go,' I said. 'I'll not stop you. If you were thinking of telling him the truth, think again. If the shock kills him, Arthur will be High King all the sooner.'

'He would not be accepted! They wouldn't accept him! Do you think Lot will stand by and listen to you? What if I tell *them* what Arthur did last night?'

'Then Lot would become High King,' I said equably. 'And how long would he let you live, bearing Arthur's child? Yes, you'd better think about it, hadn't you? Either way, there is nothing you can do, except go while you can. Once your sister is married at Christmas, get Lot to find you a husband. That way, you may be safe.'

Suddenly, at this, she was angry, the anger of a spitting cat in a corner. 'You condemn me, you! You were a bastard, too . . . all my life I have watched Morgian get everything. Morgian! That child to be a Queen, while I . . . Why, she even learns magic, but she has no more idea how to use it for her own ends than a kitten has! She'd do better in a nunnery than on a Queen's throne, and I–I . . .' She stopped on a little gasp, and caught her underlip in her teeth. I thought she changed what she had been about to say . . . 'I, who have something of the power which has made you great, Merlin my cousin, do you think I will be content to be nothing?' Her voice went flat, the voice of a wise-woman speaking a curse which will stick. 'And that is what you will be, who are no man's friend, and no woman's lover. You are nothing, Merlin, you are nothing, and in the end you will only be a shadow and a name.'

I smiled at her. 'Do you think you can frighten me? I see further than you, I believe. I am nothing, yes; I am air and darkness, a word, a promise. I watch in the crystal and I wait in the hollow hills. But out there in the light I have a young king and a bright sword to do my work for me, and build what will stand when my name is only a word for forgotten songs and outworn wisdom, and when your name, Morgause, is only a hissing in the dark.' I turned my head then, and called a servant. 'Now enough of this, there is no more to say between us. Go and make yourself ready, and get you from court.'

The man had come in, and was waiting inside the door glancing, I thought apprehensively, from one to the other of us. From his look, he was a black Celt from the mountains of the west; it is a race that still worships the old gods, so it is possible he could feel, if only partly, some of the stinging presences still haunting the room.

But for me, now, the girl was only a girl, tilting a pretty, troubled face to mine, so that the rose-gold hair streamed from her pale forehead down the cherry gown. To the servant waiting beside the door, it should have seemed an ordinary leave-taking, but for those stinging shadows. She never glanced his way, or guessed what he might see.

When she spoke her voice was composed, calm and low. 'I shall go to my sister. She lies at York till the wedding.'

'I shall see to it that an escort is ready. No doubt the wedding will still be at Christmas, according to plan. King Lot should join you soon, and give you a place at your sister's court.'

There was a brief flash at that, discreetly veiled. I might have tried a guess at what she planned there–that she hoped, even at this late date, to take her sister's place at Lot's side—but I was weary of her. I said: 'I'll bid you farewell, then, and a safe journey.'

She made a reverence, saying, very low: 'We shall meet again, cousin.'

I said formally, 'I shall look forward to it.' She went then, slight, erect, hands folded close again, and the servant shut the door behind her.

I stood by the window, collecting my thoughts. I felt weary, and my eyes were gritty from lack of sleep, but my mind was clear and light, already free of the girl's presence. The fresh air of morning blew in to disperse the evil lingering in the room, till, with the last fading scent of honeysuckle, it was gone. When the servant came back I rinsed face and hands in cold water, then, bidding him follow me, went back to the hospital dormitory. The air was cleaner there, and the eyes of dying men easier to bear than the presence of the woman who was with child of Mordred, Arthur's nephew and bastard son.

Chapter Seven

King Lot, brooding on the edge of affairs, had not been idle. Certain busy gentlemen, friends of his, were seen to be hurrying here and there, protesting to anyone who would listen that it would be more appropriate for Uther to declare his heir from one of his great palaces in London or Winchester. This haste, they said, was unseemly; the thing should be done by custom, with due notice and ceremony, and backed by the blessing of the Church. But they whispered in vain. The ordinary people of Luguvallium, and the soldiers who at present outnumbered them, thought otherwise. It was obvious now that Uther was near his end, and it seemed not only necessary, but right, that he should declare his successor straight away, near the field where Arthur had in a fashion declared himself. And if there was no bishop present, what of it? This was a victory feast and was held, so to speak, still in the field.

The house where the King held court in Luguvallium was packed to the doors, and well beyond them. Outside, in the town and around it, where the troops held their own celebration, the air was blue with the smoke of fires, and thick with the smell of roasting meat. Officers on their way to the King's feast had to work quite hard to turn a blind eye to the drunkenness in camp and street, and a deaf ear to the squeals and giggles coming from quarters where women were not commonly allowed to be.

I hardly saw Arthur all day. He was closeted with the King until afternoon, and in the end only left to allow his father to rest before the feast. I spent most of the day in the hospital. It was peaceful there, compared with the crush near the royal apartments. All day, it seemed, the corridors outside my rooms and Arthur's were besieged; by men who wanted favours from the new prince, or just his notice; by men who wanted to talk with me, or to court my favour by gifts; or simply by the curious. I let it be known that Arthur was with the King, and would speak with no one before the time of the feast. To the guards I gave private orders that if Lot should seek me out, I was to be called. But he made no approach. Nor, according to the servants I questioned, was he to be seen in the town.

But I took no chances, and early that morning sent to Caius Valerius, a King's officer and an old acquaintance of mine, for extra guards for my rooms and Arthur's to reinforce the duty sentries outside the main door, in the antechamber, and even at the windows. And before I went to the hospital I made my way to the King's rooms, to have a word with Ulfin.

It may perhaps seem strange that a prophet who had seen Arthur's crowning so plain and clear and ringed with light should take such pains to guard him from his enemies. But those who have had to do with the gods know that when those gods make promises they hide them in light, and a smile on a god's lips is not always a sign that you may take his favour for granted. Men have a duty to make sure. The gods like the taste of salt; the sweat of human effort is the savour of their sacrifices.

The guards on duty at the King's door lifted their spears without a challenge and let me straight through into the outer chamber. Here pages and servants waited, while in the second chamber sat the women who helped to nurse the King. Ulfin was, as ever, beside the door of the King's room. He rose when he saw me, and we talked for a little while, of the King's health, of Arthur, of the events of yesterday, and the prospects for tonight; then—we were talking softly, apart from the women—I asked him:

'You knew Morgause had left the court?'

'I heard so, yes. Nobody knows why.'

'Her sister Morgian is waiting in York for the wedding,' I said, 'and anxious for her company.'

'Oh, yes, we heard that.' It was to be inferred from the woodenness of his expression that nobody had believed it.

'Did she come to see the King?' I asked.

'Three times.' Ulfin smiled. It was apparent that Morgause was no favourite of his. 'And each time she was turned away because the prince was still with him.'

A favoured daughter for twenty years, and forgotten in as many hours for a true-born son. '*You were a bastard, too,*' she had reminded me. Years ago, I remembered, I had wondered what would become of her. She had had position and authority of a sort here with Uther, and might well have been fond of him. She had (the King had hinted yesterday) refused marriage to stay near him. Perhaps I had been too harsh with her, driven by the horror of foreknowledge and my own single-minded love for the boy. I hesitated, then asked him: 'Did she seem much distressed?'

'Distressed?' said Ulfin crisply. 'No, she looked angry. She's bad to cross, is that lady. Always been so, from a child. One of her maids was crying, too; I think she'd been whipped.' He nodded towards one of the pages, a fair boy, very young, kicking his heels at a window. 'He was the one sent to turn her away the last time, and she laid his cheek open with her nails.'

'Then tell him to take care it does not fester,' I said, and such was my tone that Ulfin looked sharply at me, cocking a brow. I nodded. 'Yes, it was I who sent her away. Nor did she go willingly. You'll know why, one day. Meanwhile, I take it that you look in now and again upon the King? The interview isn't tiring him overmuch?'

'On the contrary, he's better than I've seen him for some time. You'd think the boy was a well to drink at; the King never takes his eyes from him, and gains strength by the hour. They'll take their midday meal together.'

'Ah. Then it will be tasted? That's what I came to ask.'

'Of course. You can be easy, my lord. The prince will be safe.'

'The King must take some rest before the feast.'

He nodded. 'I've persuaded him to sleep this afternoon after he has eaten.'

'Then will you also—which will be more difficult—persuade the prince that he should do the same? Or, if not rest, then at least go straight to his rooms, and stay in them till the hour of feasting?'

Ulfin looked dubious. 'Will he consent to that?'

'If you tell him that the order—but you'd better call it a request—came from me.'

'I'll do that, my lord.'

'I shall be in the hospital. You'll send for me, of course, if the King needs me. But in any case you must send to tell me the moment the prince leaves him.'

It was about the middle of the afternoon when the fair-haired page brought the message. The King was resting, he told me, and the prince had gone to his rooms. When Ulfin had given the prince my message the latter had scowled, impatient, and had said sharply (this part of the message came demurely, verbatim) that he was damned if he'd skulk indoors for the rest of the day. But when Ulfin had said the message came from Prince Merlin the prince had stopped short, shrugged, and then gone to his rooms without further word.

'Then I shall go, too,' I said. 'But first, child, let me see that scratched cheek.' When I had put salve on it, and sent him scampering back to Ulfin, I made my way through corridors more thronged than ever to my rooms.

Arthur was by the window. He turned when he heard me.

'Bedwyr is here, did you know? I saw him, but could not get near. I sent a message that we'd ride out this afternoon. Now you say I may not.'

'I'm sorry. There will be other times to talk to Bedwyr, better than this.'

'Heaven and earth, they couldn't be worse! This place stifles me. What do they want with me, that pack in the corridors outside?'

'What most men want of their prince and future King. You will have to get used to it.'

'So it seems. There's even a guard here, outside the window.'

'I know. I put him there.' Then, answering his look: 'You have enemies, Arthur. Have I not made it clear?'

'Shall I always have to be hemmed in like this, surrounded? One might as well be a prisoner.'

'Once you are undoubted King you can make your own dispositions. But until then, you must be guarded. Remember that here we are only in an emergency camp: once in the King's capital, or in one of his strong castles, you'll have your own household, chosen by yourself. You'll be able to see all you want of Bedwyr, or Cei, or anyone else you may appoint. It will be freedom of a sort, as much as you can ever have now. Neither you nor I can go back to the Wild Forest again, Emrys. That's over.'

'It was better there,' he said, then gave me a gentle look, and smiled. 'Merlin.'

'What is it?'

He started to say something, changed his mind, shook his head instead and said abruptly: 'At this feast tonight. You'll be near me?'

'Be sure of it.'

'The King has told me how he will present me to the nobles. Do you know what will happen then? These enemies you speak of—'

'Will try to prevent the assembly from accepting you as Uther's heir.'

He considered for a moment, briefly. 'May they carry arms in the hall?'

'No. They'll try some other way.'

'Do you know how?'

I said: 'They can hardly deny your birth to the King's face, and with me there and Count Ector they can't quarrel with your identity. They can only try to discredit you; shake the faith of the waverers, and try to swing the army's vote. It's your enemies' misfortune that this has come on a battlefield where the army outnumbers the council of nobles three to one—and after yesterday the army will take some convincing that you are not fit to lead them. It's my guess that there will be something staged, something that will take men by surprise and shake their belief in you, even in Uther.'

'And in you, Merlin?'

I smiled. 'It's the same thing. I'm sorry, I can't see further yet than that. I can see death and darkness, but not for you.'

'For the King?' he asked sharply.

I did not answer. He was silent for a moment, watching me, then, as if I had answered, he nodded, and asked:

'Who are these enemies?'

'They are led by the King of Lothian.'

'Ah,' he said, and I could see he had not let his senses be stifled through the brief hours of that crowded day. He had seen and heard, watched and listened. 'And Urien who runs with him, and Tudwal of Dinpelydr, and—whose is the green badge with the wolverine?'

'Aguisel's. Did the King say anything to you about these men?'

He shook his head. 'We talked mostly of the past. Of course he has heard all about me from you and Ector over these past years, and'—he laughed—'I doubt if any son ever knew more about his father and his father's father than I, with all you have told me; but telling is not the same. There was a lot of knowing to make up.'

He talked on for a little about the interview with the King, speaking of the missed years without regret, and with the cool commonsense that I had come to see was part of his character. That much, I thought, was not from Uther; I had seen it in Ambrosius, and in myself, in what men called coldness. Arthur had been able to stand back from the events of his youth; he had thought the thing through, and with the clear sight that would make him a king he had set feeling aside and come to the truth. Even when he went on to speak of his mother it was evident that he saw the matter much as Ygraine had done, and with the same hard expediency of outlook. 'If I had known that my mother was still alive, and had been so willingly parted from

me, it might have come hard to me, as a child. But you and Ector spared me
that by telling me she was dead, and now I see it as you say she saw it; that to
be a prince one must be ruled always by necessity. She did not give me up
for nothing.' He smiled, but his voice was still serious. 'It was true as I told
you. I was better in the Wild Forest thinking myself motherless, and your
bastard, than waiting yearly in my father's castle for the Queen to bear
another child to supplant me.'

In all those years I had never seen it so. I had been blinded by my larger
purposes, thinking all the time of his safety, of the kingdom's future, of the
gods' will. Until the boy Emrys had burst into my life that morning in the
Wild Forest he had hardly been a person to me, only a symbol, another life
(as it were) for my father, a tool for me. After I came to know and love him I
had seen only the deprivations we had subjected him to, with his high
temper and leaping ambition to be first and best, and his quick generosity
and affection. It was no use telling myself that without me he might never
have come near his heritage at all; I had lived with guilt for all that he had
been robbed of.

No question but that he had felt the deprivation, the bite of dispossession.
But even here, even now in the moment of finding himself, he could see
clearly what that princely childhood would have meant. I knew he was
right. Even apart from the daily dangers, he would have had a hard time of it
beside Uther, and the high qualities, wasting with time and hope deferred,
might have turned sour. But the admission, to absolve me, had to come from
him. Now it lifted my guilt from me as cool air lifts a marsh mist.

He was still speaking of his father. 'I like him,' he said. 'He has been a
good king as far as it was in him. Standing apart from him as I have done, I
have been able to listen to men talking, and to judge. But as a father—as to
how we would have dealt together, that's another matter. There is time still,
to know my mother. She will need comfort soon, I think.'

He referred only once, briefly, to Morgause.

'They say she has left the town?'

'She went this morning while you were with the King.'

'You spoke with her? How did she take it?'

'Without distress,' I said, with perfect truth. 'You needn't fear for her.'

'Did you send her away?'

'I advised her to go. As I advise you to put it out of your mind. For the
moment, at any rate, there is nothing to be done. Except—I suggest—sleep.
Today has been hard, and will be harder for both of us before it's done. So if
you can forget the crowds outside and the guard beyond the window, I
suggest we both sleep till sundown.'

He yawned suddenly, widely, like a young cat, then laughed. 'Have you
put a spell on me to make sure of it? Suddenly I feel I could sleep for a
week . . . All right, I'll do as you say, but may I send a message to Bedwyr?'

He did not speak of Morgause again, and I think that soon, in the final
preparations for the evening's feast, he forgot her. Certainly the haunted
look of the morning had left him, and it seemed to me that no shadow
touched him now; doubt and apprehension would have wisped off his
charged and shining youth like water-drops from white hot metal. Even if
he had guessed, as I did, what the future held—that it was greater than he

could have imagined, and in the end more terrible—I doubt if it would have dimmed his brightness. When one is fourteen, death at forty seems still to be several lifetimes away.

An hour after sundown, they came for us to lead us to the hall of feasting.

Chapter Eight

The hall was packed to the doors. If the place had seemed crowded before, by the time the trumpets sounded for the feast there was barely breathing-room in the corridors; it seemed as if even those sturdy Roman-built walls must bulge and crumble under the press of excited humanity. For rumour had run like a forest fire through the countryside that this was no ordinary victory feast, and even from parts of the province twenty or thirty miles off people were pouring into Luguvallium to be there for the great occasion.

It would have been impossible to sift and select the followers of those privileged nobles who were allowed into the main hall where the King would sit. At a feast of this kind men expected to leave their weapons outside, and this was enforced, till the antechamber, stacked as it was with thickets of spears and swords, looked like a grove of the Wild Forest. More than this the guards could not do, save run an eye over each man's person as he entered the hall, to see that he carried only the knife or dagger he needed for his food.

By the time the company was assembled the sky outside was paling to dusk, and torches were lit. Soon, with the smoky torchlight and the mild evening, the food and wine and talk and laughter, the place was uncomfortably warm, and I watched the King anxiously. He seemed in good enough spirits, but his colour was too high and his skin had a glazed, transparent look that I have seen before in men who are pushed to the limits of their strength. But he was perfectly in command of himself, talking cheerfully and courteously to Arthur on his right, and to the others about him, though at times he would fall into silence and seem to be drifting, forgetfully, into some place far away from which he would recall himself with a jerk. At one point he asked me—I was seated on his left—if I knew why Morgause had not come to see him that day. He asked without concern, without even much interest; it was obvious that he had not taken in the fact that she had left the court. I told him that she had wanted to go to her sister at York, and that since the King had been unable to see her I myself had given her permission, and sent her with an escort. I added quickly that the King need have no fears for his health, since I was here and would attend him personally. He nodded and thanked me, but as if my offer of help was something no longer needed: 'I have had the best doctors I could have had this day; victory, and this boy beside me.' He laid a hand on Arthur's arm, and laughed. 'You heard what the Saxon dogs were calling me? The half-dead King. I heard them shouting it when I was carried forward in my chair . . . And so in truth I think I was, but now I have both victory and life.'

He had spoken clearly, and men leaned forward to listen, and afterwards murmured approval, while the King went back to picking at his food. Ulfin and I had both warned him that he must eat and drink sparingly, but there had been no need for such advice; he had little appetite, and Ulfin saw to it that his wine was well watered. And Arthur's, too. He sat beside his father, his back straight as a spear, and the tension and excitement of the occasion had taken some of the colour from his cheeks. For once he hardly seemed to notice what he was eating. He spoke little, and then only when he was addressed, answering briefly and obviously only for courtesy. Most of the time he sat silent, his eyes on the throng in the hall below the royal dais. I, who knew him, could see what he was doing; he was telling over face by face, blazon by blazon, the toll of the men who were there, and noting where they sat. Noting also how they looked. This face was hostile, that friendly, this undecided and ready to be swayed by promises of power or gain, that foolish or merely curious. I could read them myself, as clearly as if they were red and white pieces ready on the board to play, but for a youth not yet turned fifteen, and on such a highly charged occasion, it was a marvel that he could collect himself to watch them so. Years afterwards he was still able to tally exactly the forces which assembled for and against him that first night of his power. Only twice did that cool look linger and soften; on Ector, not far from where we sat, solid, dependable Ector, beaming a little moist-eyed across his wine as he watched his foster-son jewelled and resplendent in white and silver at the High King's side. (I thought that Cei's glance beside him was less than enthusiastic, but Cei had, at best, low brows and a narrow face that gave even his enthusiasms a grudging look.) Down the hall, beside his father King Ban of Benoic, was Bedwyr, his plain face flushed and his soul, as they say, in his eyes. The two boys' eyes met and met again during the feasting. Here, already, the next strong thread was being woven of the new kingdom's pattern.

The feast wore on. I watched Uther carefully, wondering if he could last until the proclamation was made and the thing done, or if he would lack the strength to see it through. In which case I would have to choose the moment to intervene, or the work would have to be done with fighting. But his strength held. At last he looked round and raised a hand, and the trumpets rang out for silence. The clamour hushed, and all eyes turned to the high table. This had been deliberately raised, for it was beyond the King's strength to stand. Even so, upright in his great chair, with the blaze of lights and banners behind him, he looked alert and splendid, commanding silence.

He laid his hands along the carved arms of his chair, and began to speak. He was smiling.

'My lords, you all know why we are met here tonight. Colgrim has been put to flight, and his brother Badulf, and already reports have been coming back that the enemy is fled in disorder back towards the coast, beyond the wild lands to the north.' He went on to speak of the previous day's victory, as decisive, he said, as his brother's victory at Kaerconan had been, and as potent an augury for the future. 'The power of our enemies, which has been massing and threatening for so many years, is broken and driven back for a time. We have a breathing space. But more important than this, my lords, we have seen how this breathing space was won; we have seen what unity can do, and what we might suffer from the lack of it. Singly, what could we do, the kings of the north, the kings of the south and west? But together, held and fighting together, with one leader and one plan, we can thrust the sword of Macsen again into the heart of the enemy.'

He had spoken, of course, figuratively, but I caught Arthur's half-start of recollection, and the flash of a glance across at me, before he went back to his steady scrutiny of the hall.

The King had paused. Ulfin, behind him, moved forward with a goblet of wine, but the King motioned it aside, and began to speak again. His voice was stronger, with the ring almost of his old vigour. 'For this is a lesson which the last years have taught us. There must be one leader, one strong High King to whom all the kingdoms pay undoubted homage. Without this, we are back where we were before the Romans came. We are divided and lost as Gaul and Germany have been divided and lost; we splinter into small peoples, fighting each other as wolves do for food and space, and never turning against the common enemy; we become a submerged province of Rome, sliding with her to her downfall, instead of a new kingdom emerging as a unit with its own people, its own gods. With the right king, faithfully followed, I believe that this will come. Who knows, the Dragon of Britain may be lifted, if not as high as the Eagles of Rome, then with a pride and a vision that will be even further seen.'

The silence was absolute. It could have been Ambrosius speaking. Or Maximus himself, I thought. So do the gods speak when they are waited for.

This time the pause was longer. The King had contrived that it should seem like an orator's, a pause to gather eyes, but I saw how his hands whitened on the chair-arms, how carefully he used the pause to gather strength. I thought I was the only one who noticed; hardly an eye was on Uther, they all watched the boy at his right. All, that is, except the King of Lothian; he was watching the High King, with a kind of eagerness in his face. Ulfin, as the King paused, was beside him again with the goblet; catching my eye he touched it to his own lips, tasted, then gave it to the King, who drank. There was no way of disguising the tremor in the hand which raised the goblet to his mouth, but before he could betray his weakness further, Ulfin had gently taken the thing from his hand, and set it down. All this, I saw, Lot had followed, still with that same concentrated eagerness. He must recognise how sick Uther was, and minute by minute he must be hoping for the High King's strength to fail him. Either Morgause had told him, or he had guessed what I knew for certain, that Uther would not live long enough physically to establish Arthur on the throne, and that in the free-for-all which might develop round the person of so young a ruler, Arthur's enemies would find their chance.

When Uther began to speak again his voice had lost much of its vigour, but the silence was so complete that he hardly needed to raise it. Even those men who had drunk too much were solemnly intent as the King began to speak again about the battle, about those who had distinguished themselves, and the men who had fallen; finally, about the part Arthur had played in saving the day, and then about Arthur himself.

'You have all known, for these many years, that my son by Ygraine my Queen was being nurtured and trained for the kingship in lands away from these, and in hands stronger than, alas, my own have been since my malady overtook me. You have known that when the time came, and he was grown, he would be declared by name, Arthur, as my heir, and your new King. Now be it known to all men where their lawful prince has spent the years of his youth; first under the protection of my cousin Hoel of Brittany, then in the house of my faithful servant and fellow-soldier, Count Ector of Galava. And all the time he has been guarded and taught by my kinsman Merlin called Ambrosius, to whose hands he was committed at his birth, and whose fitness for the guardianship no man can question. Nor will you question the reasons which prompted me to send the prince away until such time as he might publicly be shown to you. It is a practice common enough among the great, to rear their children in other courts, where they may stay unspoiled by arrogance, uncorrupted by flattery, and safe from the contriving of treachery and ambition.' He waited for a moment to regain his breath. He was looking down at the table as he spoke, and met no one's eyes, but here and there a man shifted in his seat or glanced at another; and Arthur's cool gaze took note of it.

The King went on: 'And those of you who had wondered what sort of shifts might be used to train a prince, other than sending him as a boy into battle, and into council alongside his father, have seen yesterday how he received the King's sword easily from the King's hand, and led the troops to victory as surely as if he had been High King himself and a seasoned warrior.'

Uther's breath was short now, and his colour bad. I saw Lot's eyes intent, and Ulfin's worried look. Cador was frowning. I thought briefly back, with thankfulness, to the talk I had had with him beside the lake. Cador and Lot: had Cador been less his father's son, how easy it would have been for the two of them to tear the land north and south, parcel it out between them like a pair of fighting dogs, while the landless pup whined starving.

'And so,' said the High King, and in the silence his gasping breath was horribly apparent, 'I present to you all my true born and only son, Arthur called Pendragon, who will be High King after my death, and who will carry my sword in battle from this time on.'

He reached his hand to Arthur, and the boy stood up, straight and unsmiling, while the shouting and the cheering went roaring up into the smoky roof. The noise must have been heard clear through the town. When men paused to draw breath the echoes of the acclamation could be heard running out through the streets as a fire runs through stubble on a dry day. There was approval in the shouting, there was obvious relief that at last the issue was clear, and there was joy. I saw Arthur, cool as a cloud, assessing which lay where. But from where I sat I could also see the pulse leaping below the rigid jawline. He stood as a swordsman stands, at rest after one victory, but alert for the next challenge.

It came. Clear above the shouting and the thumping of drinking-vessels on the boards came Lot's voice, harsh and carrying.

'I challenge the choice, King Uther!'

It was like throwing a boulder down into the path of a fast-flowing stream. The noise checked; men stared, muttered, shifted, and looked about them. Then all at once it could be seen that the stream divided. There was cheering still for Arthur and the King's choice, but here and there were shouts of 'Lothian! Lothian!' and through it all Lot said strongly: 'An untried boy? A boy who has seen one battle? I tell you, Colgrim will be back all too soon, and are we to have a boy to lead us? If you must hand on your sword, King Uther, hand it to a tried and seasoned leader, to be held in trust for this young boy when he is grown!' He finished the challenge with a crash of his fist on the table, and round him the clamour broke out again: 'Lothian! Lothian!' and then further off down the hall, confusedly, other challenges being shouted down by 'Pendragon!' and 'Cornwall!' and even 'Arthur!' It was to be seen then, as the clamour mounted, that only the fact that men were unarmed prevented worse things than insults being hurled from side to side of the hall. The servants had backed to the walls, and chamberlains bustled here and there, white-faced and placatory. The King, ashen, threw up a hand, but the gesture went almost unnoticed. Arthur neither moved nor spoke, but he had gone rather pale.

'My lords! My lords!' Uther was shaking, but with rage; and rage, as I knew, was as dangerous to him as a spear thrust. I saw that Lot knew it, too. I laid a hand on Uther's arm. 'All will be well,' I told him softly. 'Sit back now and let them shout it out. Look, Ector is speaking.'

'My lord King!' Ector's voice was brisk, friendly, matter-of-fact, cooling the atmosphere in the hall. He spoke as if addressing the King alone. The effect was noticeable; the hall grew quiet as men strained to hear him. 'My lord King, the King of Lothian has challenged your choice. He has a right to speak, as all your subjects have a right to speak before you, but not to challenge, not even to question, what you have said tonight.' Raising his voice a little he turned to the listening hall. 'My lords, this is not a matter of choice or election; a king's heir is begotten, not chosen by him, and where chance has provided such a begetting at this, what question is there? Look at him now, this prince who has been presented to you. He has been in my household for ten years, and I, my lords, knowing him as I do, tell you that here is a prince to be followed—not later, not "when he is further grown", but now. Even if I could not stand before you here to attest his birth, you have only to look at him and to think back to yesterday's field, to know that here, with all fortune and God's blessing, we have our true and rightful King. This is not open to challenge, even to question. Look at him, my lords, and remember yesterday! Who more fit to unite the kings from all the corners of Britain? Who more fit to wield his father's sword?'

There were shouts of 'True! True!' and, 'What doubt can there be? He is Pendragon, and therefore our King!' and a hubbub of voices that was louder and more confused even than before. Briefly, I remembered my father's councils, their power and order; then I saw again how Uther shook, ashen in his great chair. The times were different; this was the way he had had to do it; he could not enforce it other than by public acclaim.

Before he could speak, Lot was smoothly on his feet again. He was no longer shouting; he spoke weightily, with an air of reason, and a courteous inclination towards Ector. 'It was not the prince's begetting that I challenged, it was the fitness of a young and untried youth to lead us. We know that the battle yesterday was only the preliminary, the first move in a longer and more deadly fight even than Ambrosius faced, a struggle such as we have not seen since the days of Maximus. We need better leadership than is shown by a day's luck in a skirmish. We need, not a sick king's deputy, but a man vested with all the authority and God-given blessing of an anointed ruler. If this young prince is indeed fit to carry his father's sword, would his father be content to yield it to him now, before us all?'

Silence again, for three heart-beats. Every man there knew what it meant for the King formally to hand over the royal sword; it was abdication. Only I, of all the men in the hall except perhaps Ulfin, knew that it mattered nothing whether or not Uther abdicated now; Arthur would be King before night. But Uther did not know, and whether, even knowing his weakness, Uther was great enough to renounce publicly the power which had been the breath of life to him, was not known even to me. He was sitting quite straight, apparently impassive, and only one as near to him as I could see how the palsy from time to time shook his body, so that the light shivered in the circlet of red gold that bound his brow, and shook in the jewels on his fingers. I rose quietly from my chair and went to stand close beside him, at his left hand. Arthur, frowning, glanced questioningly at me. I shook my head at him.

The King licked his lips, hesitating. Lot's change of tone had puzzled him, as, it could be seen, it had puzzled others in the hall. But it had also relieved the waverers, those who were scared by the idea of rebellion, but found relief from their fear of the future in his air of reason and his deference to the High King. There were murmurs of approval and agreement. Lot spread his hands wide, as if including with him everyone in the body of the hall, and said, with that air of speaking reasonably for all of them: 'My lords, if we could but see the King give his chosen heir the royal sword with his own hands, what could we do but acknowledge him? Afterwards, it will be time enough to discuss how best to face the coming wars.'

Arthur's head turned slightly, like a hound's that catches an unfamiliar scent. Ector too looked round at the other man, surprised perhaps and distrustful of the apparent capitulation. Cador, silent at the other side of the room, stared at Lot as though he would drag his soul out from his eyes. Uther bent his head slightly, a gesture of abnegation which became him like nothing I had seen in him before.

'I am willing.'

A chamberlain went running. Uther leaned back in the great chair, shaking his head as Ulfin proffered wine again. I·dropped a hand unobtrusively to the wrist beside me; his pulse was all anyhow, a grasshopper pulse in a wrist gone suddenly frail and stringy, which before had been narrow with nerve and sinew. His lips were dry, and his tongue came out to moisten them. He said softly: 'There's some trick here, but I can't see it. Can you?'

'Not yet.'

'He has no real following. Not even among the army, after yesterday. But now . . . you may have to deal with it. They don't want facts, or even promises. You know them, what they want is a sign. Can you not give them one?'

'I don't know. Not yet. The gods come when they come.'

Arthur had caught the whisper. He was as tight as a strung bow. Then he looked across the hall, and I saw his mouth relax slightly. I followed his look. It was Bedwyr, scarlet with fury, held down forcibly in his seat by his father's heavy hand. Otherwise I think that he would have been at Lot's throat with his bare hands.

The chamberlain came running, with Uther's battle sword laid, scabbarded, across his palms. The rubies in the hilt glinted balefully. The scabbard was of silver gilded, crusted with fine goldwork and gems. There was no man there but had seen the sword a hundred times at Uther's side. The man laid it flat on the table in front of the King. Uther's thin hand went out to the hilt, the fingers curving round it without thinking, fitting to the guard, a caress rather than a grip, the hold of the good fighting man. Arthur watched him, and I could see the flicker of puzzlement between his brows. He was thinking of the sword in the stone up there in the Wild Forest, wondering no doubt where that came into this formal scene of abdication.

But I, as the fire from the great rubies burned against my eyes, knew at last what the gods were doing. It was clear from the beginning, fire and dragon-star and the sword in the stone. And the message did not come through the smoke from the doubly-smiling god, it was clear as the flame in the ruby. Uther's sword would fail, as Uther himself had failed. But the other would not. It had come by water and by land and lay waiting now for this, to bring Arthur his kingdom, and keep and hold it, and afterwards go from men's sight for ever.

The King laid firm hold of the hilt, and drew his sword. 'I, Uther Pendragon, do by this token give to Arthur my son—'

There was a great gasp, then a hubbub of noise. Men cried out fearfully, 'A sign! A sign!' and someone shouted, 'Death! It means death!' and the whispers that had been stilled by victory, waking again: 'What hope for us, a wasted land, and a maimed king, and a boy without a sword?'

As the sword came clear of the scabbard Uther lurched to his feet. He held it crookedly, half-lifted, staring down at it with ashen face and his mouth half open, struck still like a man out of his wits. The sword was broken. A handspan from the point the metal had snapped jaggedly, and the break shone raw and bright in the torchlight.

The King made some sound; it was as if he tried to speak, but the words choked in his throat. The sword sank with a clatter to the board. As his legs failed under him, Ulfin and I took him gently by the arms and eased him back into his chair. Arthur moved, fast as a mountain cat, to bend over him. 'Sir? Sir?'

Then he straightened slowly, his eyes on me. There was no need for me to tell him what every man in the hall could see. Uther was dead.

Chapter Nine

Uther dead did more than Uther dying could have done to control the panic that had swept the hall. Every man there was held, silent and still, on his feet, watching the High King as we lowered him gently against the back of the chair. In the stillness the flames in the torches rustled like silk, and the goblet Ulfin had dropped rolled ringing in a half circle and back again. I leaned forward over the dead King and closed his eyes.

Then Lot's voice, collected and forceful: 'A sign indeed! A dead king and a broken sword! Do you still say, Ector, that God has appointed this boy to lead us against the Saxon invader? A maimed land indeed, with nothing between us and the Terror but a boy with a broken sword!'

Confusion again. Men shouting, turning to one another, staring about them in fear and amazement. Part of my mind noted, coldly, that Lot had not been surprised. Arthur, eyes blazing in a face paler than ever with shock, straightened from his father's body and whipped round to face the shouting in the hall, but I said swiftly: 'No. Wait,' and he obeyed me. But his hand had dropped to his dagger and gripped there, whitening. I doubt if he knew it, or, knowing, could have stopped himself. The turmoil of astonishment and fear jarred from wall to wall like waves in the wind.

Through the commotion came Ector's voice again, harsh and shaken, but sturdily matter-of-fact as before, brushing aside the strands of super-stitious fear like a broom clearing cobwebs. 'My lords! Is this seemly? Our High King is dead, here before our eyes. Dare we oppose his plain will when his eyes are hardly closed? We all saw what caused his death, the sight of the royal sword, which yesterday was whole, broken in its sheath. Are we to let this—accident'—he dropped the word heavily into the hush—'frighten us like children from doing what it is plain that we should do? If you look for a sign, there it is.' He pointed at Arthur, standing straight as a pine beside the dead King's chair. 'As one king falls, another is ready in his place. God sent him today for this. We must acknowledge him.'

A pause, full of murmuring, while men looked at one another. There were nods, and shouts of agreement, but here and there still looks of doubt, and voices calling out, 'But the sword? The broken sword?'

Ector said sturdily: 'King Lot here called it a sign, this broken sword. A sign of what? I say, my lords, of treachery! This sword did not break in the High King's hand, nor in his son's.'

'That's true,' said another voice forcibly. Bedwyr's father, the King of Benoic, was on his feet. 'We all saw it, whole in the battle. And by God, we saw it used!'

'But since then?' The questions came from every quarter of the hall.

'Afterwards? Would the King have sent for it had he known it to be broken?' Then from some speaker at the end of the hall, invisible in the press: 'But would the High King have consented to hand it to the boy, if it had still been whole?' And another voice, which I thought was Urien's: 'He knew he was dying. He gave up the maimed land with the broken sword. It is for the strongest now to take up the kingship.'

Ector, darkly flushed, broke in again: 'I spoke the truth when I talked of treachery! In good time did the High King present his heir to us, or Britain would indeed be maimed, torn apart by disloyal dogs such as you, Urien of Gore!'

Urien shouted with anger, and his hand went to his dagger. Lot spoke to him, sharply, under cover of the tumult, and he subsided. Lot was smiling, his eyes narrow and watchful. His voice came smoothly: 'We all know what interest Count Ector has in proclaiming his ward High King.'

There was a sudden, still pause. I saw Ector glance round him, as if he would have conjured a weapon out of the air. Arthur's hand clenched tighter on his dagger's hilt. Then suddenly there was a stir from the right of the hall, where Cador stood forward among his men. The white Boar of Cornwall stretched and hunched itself on his sleeve as he moved. He looked round for quiet, and got it. Lot turned his head quickly; it was evident that he did not know what to expect. Ector controlled himself and subsided, rumbling. All around I saw the frightened men, the waverers, the time-servers, looking at Cador as men look for a lead in danger.

Cador's voice was clear and totally lacking in emotion. 'What Ector says is true. I myself saw the High King's sword after the battle, when his son handed it back to him. It was whole and unmarked, save with the blood of the enemy.'

'Then how is it broken? Is it treachery? Who broke it?'

'Who indeed?' said Cador. 'Not the gods, for sure, whatever King Lot may think. The gods do not break the swords of the kings they favour with victory. They give them, and give them whole.'

'Then if Arthur is our King,' cried someone, 'what sword have they given him?'

Cador looked up the hall: it was to be seen that he was expecting me to speak. But I said nothing. I had drawn back to stand behind Arthur in the shadow of the King's great chair. It was my place, and it was time they saw me take it. There was a kind of waiting pause, as heads turned to where I stood, a black shadow behind the boy's white and silver. Men shuffled and murmured. There were those here who had known my power, and there was no man present who doubted it. Not even Lot: the whites of his eyes showed as he looked askance. But when I still did not speak, there were smiles. I could see the tension in Arthur's shoulders, and I spoke to him in silence with my will. *'Not yet, Arthur, not yet. Wait.'*

He was silent. He had picked up the broken sword, and was gently fitting it back into its scabbard. As it went, it gave one sharp flash and then was quenched.

'You see?' said Cador to the hall. 'Uther's sword is gone, and so is he. But Arthur has a sword, his own, and greater than this royal one that men have broken. The gods gave it to him. I saw it in his hand myself.'

'When?' they asked. 'Where? What gods? What sword was this?'

Cador waited, smiling, for the buzz of questions to die. He stood easily, a big man with that air of his of relaxed but ready power. Lot was biting his lip, and frowning. There was sweat thick on his forehead, and his eyes shifted round the hall, reckoning the tally of those who still supported him. From his look, he had still hoped that Cador might range himself against Arthur.

Cador had not looked at him. 'I saw him once with Merlin,' he told the company, 'up in the Wild Forest, and he carried a sword more splendid than any I have seen before, jewelled like an Emperor's, and with a blade of light so bright that it burned the eyes.'

Lot cleared his throat. 'An illusion. It was done by magic. You said Merlin was there. We all know what that means. If Merlin is Arthur's master—'

A man interrupted, smallish, with black hair and a high colour. I recognised Gwyl from the western coast, on whose hills the druids meet still. 'And if it was magic, what then? Look you, a king who has magic in his hand is a king to follow.'

This brought a yell of approval. Fists hammered on the tables. Many of the men in the hall were mountain Celts, and this was talk they understood. 'That is true, that is true! Strength is good, but of what use is it without luck? And our new King, though he is young, has both. It was true what Uther said, good training and good counsel. What better counsel could he have, than Merlin to stand beside him?'

'Good training indeed,' shouted a boy's voice, 'that doesn't hang back in battle till it's almost too late!' It was Bedwyr, forgetting himself. His father quenched him with a cuff to the side of the head, but the blow fell lightly, and the admonitory hand slid over to ruffle the boy's hair. There were smiles. The heat was cooling. The ferment brought about by the stroke of superstitious fear had passed, and men were calming, ready now to listen and to think. One or two who had seemed to favour Lot and his faction were seen to withdraw a little from him. Then someone called out: 'Why doesn't Merlin speak? Merlin knows what we should do. Let him tell us!' Then the shouting began: 'Merlin! Merlin! Let Merlin speak!'

I let them shout for a few minutes. Then when they were ready to tear the hall stone from stone to hear me, I spoke. I neither moved nor raised my voice, standing there between the dead King and the living one, but they hushed, listening.

'I have two things to tell you,' I said. 'First, that the King of Lothian was wrong. I am not Arthur's master. I am his servant. And the second is what the Duke of Cornwall has already told you; that between us and the Saxon Terror is a king, young and whole, with a sword given straight into his hand by God.'

Lot could see the moment slipping from him. He looked around him, shouting: 'A fine sword indeed, that appears in his hand as an illusion, and vanishes from it in battle!'

'Don't be a fool,' said Ector gruffly. 'That was one I lent him that was cut from him in the fight. My second best, too, so I'm not repining.'

Someone laughed. There were smiles, and when Lot spoke again there was defeat under the sick rage in his voice. 'Then where did he get this sword of marvels, and where is it now?'

I said: 'He went alone to Caer Bannog and lifted it from its place below the lake.'

Silence. There was no one here who did not know what that meant. I saw hands moving to make the sign against enchantment.

Cador stirred. 'It is true. I myself saw Arthur come back from Caer Bannog with the thing in his hand, wrapped in an old scabbard as if it had lain in hiding for a hundred years.'

'Which it had,' I said into the silence. 'Listen, my lords, and I will tell you what sword this is. It is the sword which Macsen Wledig took to Rome, and which was brought back to Britain by his people and hidden until it should please the gods to lead a King's son to find it. Must I remind you of the prophecy? It was not my prophecy, it was made before I was born; that the sword should come by water and by land, treasured in darkness and locked in stone, until he should come who is rightwise king born of all Britain, and lift it from its hiding place. And there it has lain, my lords, safe in Caer Bannog, in Bilis' castle, until by magic signs sent from the gods did Arthur find it, and lifted it easily into his hand.'

'Show us!' they cried. 'Show us!'

'I shall show you. The sword lies now on the altar in the chapel of the Wild Forest where I laid it. It shall lie there till Arthur lifts it in the sight of you all.'

Lot was beginning to be afraid; they were against him now, and by his actions he had confirmed himself as Arthur's enemy. But so far I had spoken quietly, without power, and he still saw a chance. The obstinacy which had driven him, and the stupidity of his own hope of power sustained him now. 'I have seen that sword, the sword in the altar of the Green Chapel. Many of you have seen it! It is Macsen's sword, yes, but it is made of stone!'

I moved then. I lifted my arms high. From somewhere, a breeze ran in through the open windows and stirred the coloured hangings so that behind Arthur the scarlet Dragon clawed up the golden banner, and sent my shadow towering like the Dragon's shadow, with arms raised like wings. The power was here. I heard it in my voice.

'And from the stone has he lifted it, and will lift it again, in the sight of you all. And from this day on, the chapel shall be called the Chapel Perilous, for if any man who is not the rightful King shall so much as touch the sword, it shall burn like levin in his hand.'

Someone in the crowd said strongly: 'If he has indeed got the sword of Macsen, he got it by God's gift, and if he has Merlin beside him, then by any god he follows, I follow him!'

'And I,' said Cador.

'And I! And I!' came the shouts from the hall. 'Let us all see this magic sword and this perilous altar!'

Every man was on his feet. The shouting rose and echoed in the roof. 'Arthur! Arthur!'

I dropped my arms. '*Now, Arthur, it is now.*'

He had not once looked at me, but he heard my thought, and I felt the power going out of me towards him. I could see it growing round him as he stood there, and every man in the hall could see it too. He raised a hand, and they waited for him. His voice came clear and firm: no boy's voice, but that of a man who has fought his first decisive battles, there in the field, and here in the hall.

'My lords. You saw how fate sent me to my father without a sword, as was fitting. Now treachery has broken the weapon he would have given me, and treachery has tried to take with it my birthright that is proven in front of you all, and was attested by my father the High King in open hall. But as Merlin has told you, God had already put another, greater weapon into my hand, and I shall indeed take it up in front of you all, as soon as I may come, with all this company, to the Perilous Chapel.'

He paused. It is not easy to speak after the gods have spoken. He finished simply, cool water after the flames. The torches had died to red and my shadow had dwindled from the wall. The Dragon banner hung still.

'My lords, we shall ride there in the morning. But now it is seemly that we should attend the High King, and see his body laid in kingly fashion, and guards set, before it can be taken to its resting-place. Then those who will may take up their swords and spears, and ride with me.'

He finished. Cador came striding up the hall and with him Ector, and Gwyl, and Bedwyr's father King Ban, and a score of others. I stepped quietly back leaving Arthur standing there alone, with the King's guard behind him. I made a sign, and servants stooped to lift and carry the chair where, all this time, the dead King had sat stiffening, with no man looking his way save only Ulfin, who was weeping.

Chapter Ten

As soon as I left the hall I sent a servant running with a message that a swift horse was to be made ready for me. Another fetched my sword and cloak, and very soon, without attracting much notice, I was able to slip quietly through the thronged corridors and out to the courtyard.

The horse was there, ready. I thought I recognised it, then saw from its housings that it was Ralf's big chestnut. Ralf himself waited at its head, his face strained and anxious. Beyond the high walls of the courtyard the town hummed like a tumbled skep of bees, and lights were everywhere.

'What's this?' I asked him. 'Didn't they get my message right? I go alone.'

'So they said. The horse is for you. He's faster than your own, and sure on his feet, and he knows the forest tracks. And if you do meet trouble—' He left the sentence unfinished, but I understood him. The horse was trained to battle, and would fight for me like an extra arm.

'Thank you.' I took the reins from him, and mounted. 'They're expecting me at the gate?'

'Yes. Merlin'—He still kept a hand on the reins—'let me come with you. You shouldn't ride alone. You've a bad enemy there who'll stop at nothing.'

'I know that. You'll serve me better by staying here and seeing that no one rides after me. Are the gates shut?'

'Yes, I saw to it. No rider but you leaves this place now until Arthur and the others ride out. But they tell me that there were two men slipped out before the company left the hall.'

I frowned. 'Lot's?'

'No one seems clear on that. They said they were messengers taking the news of the King's death south.'

'No messenger was sent,' I said curtly. I had ordered this myself. The news of the High King's death, with the fear and uncertainty it would engender, must not be carried beyond the walls until there could go with it news of a new King and a new crowning.

Ralf nodded. 'I know. These two got through just before the order came. It could just be someone hoping for a purse—one of the chamberlains, perhaps, sending word south as soon as it happened. But it could just as soon be Lot's men, you know it could. What could he be planning? To break Macsen's sword, as he broke Uther's?'

'You think he could?'

'N—no. But if he can do nothing, then why are you riding up there now? Why not wait and ride up with the prince?'

'Because it's true that Lot will stop at nothing now to destroy Arthur's claim. He's worse than ambitious now, he's frightened. He'll do anything to discredit me, and shake men's faith in the sword as God's gift. So I must go. God does not defend himself. Why are we here, if not to fight for him?'

'You mean—? I see. They could desecrate the shrine, or destroy the altar . . . If they could even prevent your being there to receive the King . . . And they'll kill the servant you left to tend the shrine. Is that it?'

'Yes.'

He took the chestnut by the bit, so roughly that it jibbed, snorting. 'Then do you think that Lot would hesitate to murder you?'

'No. But I don't think he'll succeed. Now let me go, Ralf. I shall be safe enough.'

'Ah.' There was relief in his voice. 'You mean there are no more deaths in the stars tonight?'

'There is death for someone. It's not for me, but I'll take no one with me, to put more at risk. Which is why you are not coming, Ralf.'

'Oh, God, if that's all—'

I laid the reins on the chestnut's neck and it gathered itself, sidling. 'We had this fight once before, Ralf, and I gave way. But not tonight. I can't force you to obey me; you are not mine now. But you are Arthur's, and your duty is to stay with him and bring him safely to the chapel. Now let me go. Which gate?'

There was a stretched pause, then he stepped back. 'The south. God go with you, my dear lord.'

He turned his head and called an order to the guard. The courtyard gate swung open, and crashed shut again behind my galloping horse.

There was half a moon, shadow-edged, thin silver. It lit the familiar track along the valley. The willows along the river's edge stood humped above blue shadows. The river ran fast, full with rain. The sky sparkled with stars, and brighter than any of them burned the Bear. Then moon, stars and river were blotted from sight as the chestnut, feeling my heels, stretched his great stride and carried me at his sure gallop into the blackness of the Wild Forest.

For the first part of the way the track went straight and smooth, and here and there through breaks in the leafage the pale moon sifted down, throwing a faint grey light to the forest floor. Roots, ribbing the pathway, rapped under the horse's hoofs. I lay low on his neck to avoid the sweeping branches. Presently the track began to climb, gently at first, then steep and twisting as the forest ran up into the foot-hills. Here and there the way bent sharply to avoid crags which thrust up among the crowded trees. Somewhere deep down on the left was the noise of a mountain stream, fed like the river with the autumn rains. Save for the horse's thudding gallop there was no sound. The trees hung still. No breeze could penetrate so far into the thick darkness. Nothing else stirred. If deer, or wolf, or fox was abroad that night, I never saw them.

The way grew steeper. The chestnut, sure-footed, breasted the rough track with heaving ribs and stride at last slackening to a heavy canter. Not far now. A gap in the boughs above let starlight through, and I could see ahead where a twist of the path took it round like a tunnel into yet thicker blackness. An owl cried, away to the left. From the right, another answered. The sounds burst in my brain like a cry as the chestnut took the bend, and I hauled at his mouth, throwing my whole weight back on the rein. A better horseman could have stopped him in time. But not I, and I had left it just too late.

He pulled to a plunging, trampling stop, but travelling as he was his hoofs ploughed up the muddy track, and he hurtled half-sideways towards the tree which lay fallen full across the way. A pine, dry and long-dead, with its branches thrusting out pointed and rigid as the spikes of a cavalry trap. Too high and too dense to jump, even had it lain in the open moonlight and not just at the darkest bend in the track. The place was well chosen. To one side of the track there was a steep and rocky drop forty feet to the rush of the stream; to the other a thicket of thorn and holly, too dense for a horseman to thrust through. There was no space even to swerve. Had we gone round the corner at a gallop, the horse would have been speared on the boughs, and I myself flung headlong against their crippling spikes.

If the enemy lay hidden, expecting me to gallop hard on to the spikes, there might be a few seconds in which we could get back from the ambush and off the track into deep forest. I turned the chestnut sharply and lashed the reins down. He came round fast, rearing, scoring his side along the wall of thorns and driving the sharp end of some branch deep into my thigh. Then suddenly, as if spurred, he snorted and hurled himself forward. Under us the path broke open with a crashing of boughs. A black pit gaped. The horse lurched, pitched half down, then went over in a thrashing of hoofs. I was flung clear over his shoulder into the space between the pit and the fallen tree. I lay for a moment half-stunned, while the horse, with a heave and a scramble, floundered out of the shallow pit and stood trembling, while two men, daggers in hand, broke out of the forest and came running.

I had been flung into the deepest of the dark shadow, and I suppose I was lying so still that for the moment I was invisible. The noise the stream made drowned most other sounds, and they may have thought I had been flung straight down into the gully. One of them ran to the edge, peering downwards, while the other pushed past the horse and came warily forward to the edge of the pit.

They had not had time to dig this deep enough, only deep enough to lame the horse and to throw me. Now in the black darkness it acted as a kind of protection, preventing them both from jumping me at once. The one near me called out to his fellow, but the rush of water below us drowned the words. Then he took a cautious step forward past the pit towards me. I saw the faint glimmer of the weapon in his hand.

I rolled, got him by the ankle, and heaved. He yelled, pitching forward half into the hole, then twisted free, slashed sideways with his dagger, and rolled away quickly to his feet. The other threw a knife. It struck the tree behind me and fell somewhere. One weapon the less. But now they knew where I was. They drew back beyond the pit, one to each side of the track. In the hand of one man I saw the glint of a sword, but could see nothing of the other. There was no sound but the rush of water.

At least the narrowness of the path, while it made for a good ambush, had effectively stopped them bringing up their own horses. Mine was dead lame. Their beasts must be tethered somewhere behind them in the trees. It was impossible to scramble through the fallen pine behind me; they would have caught and speared me there in seconds. Nor could I get through the wall of thorn. All that was left was the gully; if I could get down there unseen, somehow get past them and back into the forest, perhaps even find their horses . . .

I moved cautiously sideways, towards the rim of the gully. I had my free hand out, feeling my way. There were bushes, and here and there saplings or young trees, rooted in the rocks. My hand met smooth bark, gripped it, tested it. I moved warily crabwise, over the edge. My eyes were still on that glimmer of metal, the sword behind the pit. The man was still there. My groping foot slid down a sharp and muddy step, the rim of the gully. A bramble snatched at it.

So did a man's hand. He had used my own trick. He had slid quietly down the bank, flattened himself there, and waited. Now he flung his whole weight, sharply, on my foot and, caught off balance, I fell. His knife just missed me, biting deep into the bank bare inches from my face as I pitched down past him.

He had meant to send me crashing down the rocky bank, to be broken and stunned on the rocks below, where they could follow and finish me together. If he had been content with this, he might have succeeded. But his lunge with the knife shook his own balance, and besides, as he grabbed at me, instead of resisting I went with him, stamping hard downwards at the grabbing hand. My boot went into something soft; he grunted with pain, then yelled something as my weight broke his grip, and, loosing whatever hold he had, he went hurtling with me down the steep side of the gully.

I had been falling the faster of the two, and I landed first, halfway down, hard up against the stem of a young pine. My attacker rolled after me in a crash of broken bushes and a shower of stones. As he hurtled against me in a flying tangle of limbs I braced myself to meet him. I flung myself over him, clamping my body hard over his, clasping his arms with both of mine and pinning him with my weight. I heard him cry out with pain. One leg was doubled under him. He lashed out with the other, and I felt a spur rake my leg through the soft leather of my boot. He fought furiously, thrashing and twisting under me like a landed fish. At any moment he would dislodge me from my purchase against the pine, and we would fall together to the gully. I struggled to hold him, and to get my dagger hand free.

The other murderer had heard us fall. He shouted something from the brink above, then I could hear him letting himself down the slope towards us. He came cautiously, but fast. Too fast. I shifted my grip on the man beneath me, forcing my full weight down to hold his arms pinned. I heard something crack; it sounded like a dead twig, but the fellow screamed. I managed to drag my right hand from under him. My fist was clamped round the dagger and the hilt had bitten into the flesh. I lifted it. Some stray glimmer of moonlight touched his eyes, a foot from mine; I could smell the fear and pain and hatred. He gave a wild heave that nearly unseated me, wrenching his head sideways from the coming blow. I reversed the dagger and struck with all the strength of the shortened blow at the exposed neck, just behind the ear.

The blow did not reach him. Something–a rock, a heavy billet of wood, hurled down from above–struck me hard on the point of the shoulder. My arm jerked out, useless, paralysed. The dagger spun away into the blackness. The other murderer crashed down the last few feet through the bushes and rocks above me. I heard his drawn sword scrape a stone. The moon marked it as it whipped upwards to strike. I tried to wrench myself clear of my opponent, but he clung close, teeth and all, grappling like a hound, holding me there for that hacking sword to finish me.

It finished him. His companion jumped, and slashed downwards at the place where, a second before, my exposed back had been, plain in the moonlight. But I was already half free, and falling, my clothes tearing from my opponent's grasp, and my fist bloody from his teeth. It was his back that met the sword. It drove in. I heard the metal grate on bone, then the scream covered the sound, and I was free of him and half-sliding, half-falling, towards the noise of the water.

A bush checked me, tore at me, let me through. A bough whipped me across the throat. A net of brambles ripped what was left of my clothing to ribbons. Then my hurtling body hit a boulder, checked, lay breathless and half-stunned against it for the two long moments it took to let me hear the second murderer coming after me. Then with no warning but a sudden gentle shift of earth the boulder went from me and I fell down the last sheer drop straight to the slab of rock over which the icy water slid, racing, towards the edge of a deep pool.

If I had fallen into the pool itself I might not have been hurt. If I had struck one of the great boulders where the water dashed and wrangled, I would probably have been killed. But I fell into a shallow, a long flat stretch of rock across which the water slid no more than a span deep, before plunging on and down into the next of the forest pools. I landed on my side, half-stunned and winded. The icy rush filled my mouth, nose, eyes, weighing down my heavy clothes, dragging at my bruised limbs. I was sliding with it along the greasy rock. My hands clawed for a hold, slipped, missed, scraped with bending nails.

Beside me with a thud and splash that shook the very rock, the second murderer landed, slipped, regained his foothold in the rushing water, and for the second time swung the sword high. It caught the moonlight. There were stars behind it. A sword lying clear across the night sky, in a blaze of stars. I took my hands from the rock, and the stream rolled me over to face the sword. The water blinded me. The noise of the cascade shook my bones apart. There was a flash like a shooting star, and the sword came down.

It was like a dream that repeated itself. Once before I had sat near a fire in the forest, with the small dark hill men waiting round me in a half circle, their eyes gleaming at the edge of the firelight like the eyes of forest creatures.

But this fire they had lit themselves. In front of it my torn clothes steamed, drying. Myself they had wrapped in their own cloaks; sheepskins, smelling too reminiscently of their first owners, but warm and dry. My bruises ached, and here and there a sharper pain told me where some stroke, unfelt in the scrimmage, had gone home. But my bones were whole.

I had not been unconscious long. Beyond the circle of firelight lay the two dead men, and near them a sharpened stake and a heavy club from which the blood had not yet been wiped. One of the men was still cleaning his long knife in the ground.

Mab brought me a bowl of hot wine, with something pungent overlying the taste of the grapes. I drank, sneezed, and pushed myself up straight.

'Did you find their horses?'

He nodded. 'Over yonder. Your own is lame.'

'Yes. Tend him for me, will you? When I get up to the shrine I'll send the servant down this way. He can lead the lame one home. Bring me one of the others now, and get me my clothes.'

'They're still wet. It's barely ten minutes since we got you out of the pool.'

'No matter,' I said, 'I must go. Mab, above here on the track there's a fallen tree, and a pit beside it. Will you ask your people to clear the path before morning?'

'They are there already. Listen.'

I heard it then, beyond the rush of the stream and the crackling of the fire. Axe and mattock thudding, above us in the forest. Mab met my eyes. 'Will the new King ride this way, then?'

'He may,' I smiled. 'How soon did you hear?'

'One of our people came from the town to tell us.' He showed a gap of broken teeth. 'Not by the gates you locked, master . . . But we knew before that. Did you not see the shooting star? It went across the heavens from end to end, crested like a dragon and riding a trail of smoke. So we knew you would come. But we were beyond the Wolves' Road when the firedrake ran, and we were almost too late. I am sorry.'

'You came in time,' I said. 'I'm in your debt for my life. I shan't forget it.'

'I was in yours,' he said. 'Why did you ride alone? You should have known there was danger.'

'I knew there was death, but I wanted no more deaths on my hands. Pain is another thing, and is soon over.' I got to my feet, stiffly. 'If I'm ever to move again, Mab, I must move now. My clothes?'

The clothes were wet still, a mass of mud and rents. But apart from the sheepskins there was nothing else; the hill people are small, and nothing of theirs would have fitted me. I shrugged myself into what was left of my court clothing, and took the bridle of a stolid brown horse from one of the men. The wound in my thigh was bleeding again, and from the feel of it there were splinters there. I got them to sling one of the sheepskins over the saddle, and climbed gingerly on.

'Shall we come with you?' they asked me.

I shook my head. 'No. Stay and see the road cleared. In the morning, if you wish, come to the shrine. There will be a place there for you all.'

The moonlit space at the forest's centre was as still as a painted picture, and as unreal as a midnight dream. Moonlight edged the chapel roof and silvered the furred tops of the surrounding pines. The doorway showed an oblong of gold, where the nine lamps shone steadily round the altar.

As I rode softly round to the back the door opened there, and the servant peered fearfully out. All was well, he told me; no one had been by. But his eyes stretched wide when he saw the state I was in, and he was obviously glad when I handed the bridle to him and told him to leave me. Then I went in thankfully to the firelight to tend my hurts and change my clothing.

Slowly the silence seeped back. A brush of soft wind over the tree-tops swept the last sound of retreating hoofs away; it crept in through the chapel, thinning the lamp flames and drawing thin lines of smoke which smelled like sweet gums burning. Outside in the clearing the moon and stars poured their rare light down. The god was here. I knelt before the altar, emptying myself of mind and will, till through me I felt the full tide of God's will flowing, and bearing me with it.

The night lay silver and quiet, waiting for the torches and the trumpets.

Chapter Eleven

They came at last. Lights and clamour and the trampling of horses flowed nearer through the forest, till the clearing was filled with flaring torchlight and excited voices. I heard them through the waking sleep of vision, dim, echoing, remote, like bells heard from the bottom of the sea.

The leaders had come forward. They paused in the doorway. Voices hushed, feet shuffled. All they would see was the swept and empty chapel, deserted but for one man standing facing them across the stone altar. Round the altar the nine lamps still dealt their steady glow, showing the carved stone sword and the legend MITHRAE INVICTO, and lying across the top of the altar the sword itself, unsheathed, bare on the bare stone.

'Put out the torches,' I told them. 'There will be no need of them.'

They obeyed me, then at my signal pressed forward into the chapel.

The place was small, the throng of men great. But the awe of the occasion prevailed; orders were given, but subdued; soft commands which might have come from priests in ritual rather than warriors recently in battle. There were no rites to follow, but somehow men kept their places; kings and nobles and kings' guards within the chapel, the press of lesser men outside in the silent clearing and overflowing into the gloom of the forest itself. There, they still had lights; the clearing was ringed with light and sound where the horses waited and men stood with torches ready; but forward under the open sky men came lightless and weaponless, as beseemed them in the presence of God and their King. And still, this one night of all the great nights, there was no priest present; the only intermediary was myself, who had been used by the driving god for thirty years, and brought at least to this place.

At length all were assembled, according to order and precedence. It was as if they had divided by arrangement, or more likely by instinct. Outside, crowding the steps, waited the little men from the hills; they do not willingly come under a roof. Inside the chapel, to my right, stood Lot, King of Lothian, with his group of friends and followers: to the left Cador, and those who went with him. There were a hundred others, perhaps more, crowded into the small and echoing space, but these two, the white Boar of Cornwall, and the red Leopard of Lothian, seemed to face one another balefully from either side of the altar, with Ector four-square and watchful at the door between them. Then Ector, with Cei behind him, brought Arthur forward, and after that I saw no one but the boy.

The chapel swam with colour and the glint of jewels and gold. The air smelled cold and fragrant, of pines and water and scented smoke. The rustle and murmuring of the throng filled the air and sounded like the rustle of flames licking through a pile of fuel, taking hold . . .

Flames from the nine lamps, flaring and then dying; flames licking up the stone of the altar; flames running along the blade of the sword until it glowed white hot. I stretched my hands out over it, palms flat. The fire licked my robe, blazing white from sleeve and finger, but where it touched, it did not even singe. It was the ice-cold fire, the fire called by a word out of the dark, with the searing heat at its heart, where the sword lay. The sword lay in its flames as a jewel lies embedded in white wool. *Whoso taketh this sword* . . . The runes danced along the metal: the emeralds burned. The chapel was a dark globe with a centre of fire. The blaze from the altar threw my shadow upwards, gigantic, into the vaulted roof. I heard my own voice, ringing hollow from the vault like a voice in a dream.

'Take up the sword, he who dares.'

Movement, and men's voices, full of dread. Then Cador: 'That is the sword. I would know it anywhere. I saw it in his hand, full of light. It is his, God witness it. I would not touch it if Merlin himself bade me.'

There were cries of, 'Nor I, nor I,' and then, 'Let the King take it up, let the High King show us Macsen's sword.'

Then finally, alone, Lot's voice, gruffly: 'Yes. Let him take it. I have seen, by God's death, I have seen. If it is his indeed, then God is with him, and it is not for me.'

Arthur came slowly forward. Behind him the place was dim, the crowd shrunk back into darkness, the shuffle and murmur of their presence no more than the breeze in the forest trees outside. Here between us, the white light blazed and the blade shivered. The darkness flashed and sparkled, a crystal cave of vision, crowded and whirling with bright images. A white stag, collared with gold. A shooting star, dragon-shaped, and trailing fire. A king, restless and desirous, with a dragon of red gold shimmering on the wall behind him. A woman, white-robed and queenly, and behind her in the shadows a sword standing in an altar like a cross. A circle of vast linked stones standing on a windy plain with a king's grave at its centre. A child, handed into my arms on a winter night. A grail, shrouded in mouldering cloth, hidden in a dark vault. A young king, crowned.

He looked at me through the pulse and flash of vision. For him, they were flames only, flames which might burn, or not; that was for me. He waited, not doubtful, nor blindly trusting; waiting only.

'Come,' I said gently. 'It is yours.'

He put his hand through the white blaze of fire and the hilt slid cool into the grip for which, a hundred and a hundred years before, it had been made.

Lot was the first to kneel. I suppose he had most need. Arthur raised him, speaking without either rancour or cordiality; the words of a sovereign lord who is able to see past a present wrong to a coming good.

'I could not find it in me, Lot of Lothian, to quarrel with any man this day, least of all my sister's lord. You shall see that your doubts of me were groundless, and you and your sons after you will help me guard and hold Britain as she should be held.'

To Cador he said simply: 'Until I get myself another heir, Cador of Cornwall, you are he.'

To Ector he spoke long and quietly, so that no man could hear save they two, and when he raised him, kissed him.

Thereafter for a long span of time he stood by the altar, as men knelt before him and swore loyalty on the hilt of the sword. To each one he spoke, directly as a boy, and grandly as a king. Between his hands, held like a cross, Caliburn shone with his own light only, but the altar with its nine dead lamps was dark.

As each man took his oath and pledged himself, he withdrew, and the chapel slowly emptied. As it grew quieter, the encircling forest filled with life and expectation and noise, where they crowded, clamorously excited now, waiting for their sworn King. They were bringing up the horses out of the wood, and the clearing filled with torchlight and trampling and the jingling of accoutrements.

Last of all Mab and the men of the hills withdrew, and save for the bodyguard ranged back against the shadowed wall, the King and I were alone.

Stiffly, for pain still locked my bones, I came round the altar till I stood before him. He was almost as tall as I. The eyes that looked back at me might have been my own.

I knelt in front of him and put out my hands for his. But he cried out at that, and pulled me to my feet, and kissed me.

'You do not kneel to me. Not you.'

'You are High King, and I am your servant.'

'What of it? The sword was yours, and we two know it. It doesn't matter what you call yourself, my servant, cousin, father, what you will—you are Merlin, and I'm nothing without you beside me.' He laughed then, naturally, the grandeur of the occasion fitting him as easily as the hilt had fitted his hand. 'What became of your state robe? Only you could have worn that dreadful old thing on such an occasion. I shall give you a robe of gold tissue, embroidered with stars, as befits your position. Will you wear it for me?'

'Not even for you.'

He smiled. 'Then come as you are. You'll ride down with me now, won't you?'

'Later. When you have time to look round for me, you will find that I am beside you. Listen, they are ready to take you to your place. It's time to go.'

I went with him to the door. The torches still tossed flaring, though the moon had set long since and the last of the stars had died into a morning sky. Golden and tranquil, the light grew.

They had brought the white stallion up to the steps. When Arthur made to mount they would not let him, but Cador and Lot and half a dozen petty kings lifted him between them to the saddle, and at last men's hopes and joy rang up into the pines in a great shout. So they raised to be king Arthur the young.

I carried the nine lamps out of the chapel. Come daylight, I would take them where they now belonged, up to the caves of the hollow hills, where their gods had gone. Of the nine, all had been overturned, the oil spilled unburned along the floor. With them lay the stone bowl, shattered, and a pile of dust and crumbled fragments where the cold fire had struck. When I swept these away with the oil that had soaked into them, it could be seen that the carving had gone from the front of the altar. These were the fragments that I held, caked with oil. All that was left of the carving on the altar's face was the hilt of the sword, and a word.

I swept and cleaned the place and made it fair again. I moved slowly, like an old man. I still remember how my body ached, and how at length, when I knelt again, my sight blurred and darkened as if still blind with vision, or with tears.

The tears showed me the altar now, bare of the nine-fold light that had pleasured the old, small gods; bare of the soldier's sword and the name of the soldiers' god. All it held now was the hilt of the carved sword standing in the stone like a cross, and the letters still deep and distinct above it: TO HIM UNCONQUERED.

The Legend

When Aurelius Ambrosius was High King of Britain, Merlin, also called Ambrosius, brought the Giants' Dance out of Ireland and set it up near Amesbury, at Stonehenge. Shortly after this a great star appeared in the likeness of a dragon, and Merlin, knowing that it betokened Ambrosius' death, wept bitterly, and prophesied that Uther would be King under the sign of the dragon, and that a son would be born to him 'of surpassing mighty dominion, whose power shall extend over all the realms that lie beneath the ray (of the star)'.

The following Easter, at the Coronation feast, King Uther fell in love with Ygraine, wife of Gorlois, Duke of Cornwall. He lavished attention on her, to the scandal of the court; she made no response, but her husband, in fury, retired from the court without leave, taking his wife and men-at-arms back to Cornwall. Uther, in anger, commanded him to return, but Gorlois refused to obey. Then the King, enraged beyond measure, gathered an army and marched into Cornwall, burning the cities and castles. Gorlois had not enough troops to withstand him, so he placed his wife in the castle of Tintagel, the safest refuge, and himself prepared to defend the castle of Dimilioc. Uther immediately laid siege to Dimilioc, holding Gorlois and his troops trapped there, while he cast about for some way of breaking into the castle of Tintagel to ravish Ygraine. After some days he asked advice from one of his familiars called Ulfin, who suggested that he send for Merlin. Merlin, moved by the King's apparent suffering, promised to help. By his magic arts he changed Uther into the likeness of Gorlois, Ulfin into Jordan, Gorlois' friend, and himself into Brithael, one of Gorlois' captains. The three of them rode to Tintagel, and were admitted by the porter. Ygraine, taking Uther to be her husband the Duke, welcomed him, and took him to her bed. So Uther lay with Ygraine that night, 'and she had no thought to deny him in aught he might desire.'

But in the meantime fighting had broken out at Dimilioc, and in the battle Ygraine's husband, the Duke, was killed. Messengers came to Tintagel to tell Ygraine of her husband's death. When they found 'Gorlois', apparently still alive, closeted with Ygraine, they were speechless, but the King then confessed the deception, and a few days later married Ygraine. Some say that Ygraine's sister Morgause was married on the same day to Lot of Lothian, and the other sister Morgan le Fay was put to school in a nunnery, where she learnt necromancy, and thereafter was wedded to King Urien of Gore. But others aver that Morgan was Arthur's own sister, born after him of the marriage of King Uther and Ygraine his Queen, and that Morgause was also his sister, but not by the same mother.

Uther Pendragon was to reign for fifteen more years, and during those years he saw nothing of his son Arthur. Before the child was born Merlin sought out the King and spoke with him. 'Sir, ye must purvey you for the nourishing of your child.' 'As thou wilt,' said the King, 'be it.' So on the night of his birth the child Arthur was carried down to the postern gate of Tintagel and delivered into the hands of Merlin, who took him to the castle of Sir Ector, a faithful knight. There Merlin had the child christened, and named Arthur, and Sir Ector's wife took him as her foster-son.

All through Uther's reign the country was sorely troubled by the Saxons and the Scots from Ireland. The two Saxon leaders whom the King had imprisoned managed to escape from London and fled thence to Germany, where they gathered a great army which struck terror throughout the kingdom. Uther himself was stricken with a grievous malady, and appointed Lot of Lothian, who was betrothed to his daughter Morgause, as his chief captain. But as often as Lot put the enemy to flight, they came back in even greater strength, and the country was laid waste. Finally Uther, though sorely ill, gathered his barons together and told them that he himself must lead the armies, so a litter was made for him, and he was carried in it at the head of his army against the enemy. When the Saxon leaders learnt that the British King had taken the field against them in a litter, they disdained him, saying that he was half-dead already, and it would not become them to fight him. But Uther, with a return of his old strength, laughed and called out: 'They call me the half-dead king, and so indeed I was. But I would rather conquer them in this wise, than be conquered by them and live in shame.' So the army of the Britons defeated the Saxons. But the King's malady increased, and the woes of the kingdom. Finally, when the King lay close to death, Merlin approached him in the sight of all the lords and bade him acknowledge his son Arthur as the new King. Which he did, and afterwards died, and was buried by the side of his brother Aurelius Ambrosius within the Giants' Dance.

After his death the lords of Britain came together to find their new King. No one knew where Arthur was kept, or where Merlin was to be found, but they thought the King would be recognised by a sign. So Merlin had a great sword fashioned, and fixed it by his magic art into a great stone shaped like an altar, with an anvil of steel in it, and floated the stone on water to a great church in London, and set it up there in the churchyard. There were gold letters on the sword which said: 'Whoso pulleth out this sword of this stone and anvil, is rightwise king born of all England.' So a great feast was made, and at the feast all the lords came to try who could pull the sword from the stone. Among them came Sir Ector, and Kay his son, with Arthur, who had neither sword not blazon, following as a squire. When they came to the jousting Sir Kay, who had forgotten his sword, sent Arthur back to look for it. But when Arthur returned to the house where they were lodging, everyone was gone and the doors were locked, so in impatience he rode to the churchyard, and drew the sword from the stone, and took it to Sir Kay.

Then of course the sword was recognised, but even when Arthur showed that he alone of all men could pull it from the stone, there were those who cried out against him, saying it was great shame to them and to the realm to accept as king a boy of no high blood born, and that fresh trial must be made at Candlemas. So at Candlemas all the greatest in the land came together, and then again at Pentecost, but none of them could pull the sword from the stone, save only Arthur. But still some of the lords were angry and would not accept him, until in the end the common people cried out: 'We will have Arthur unto our king, we will put him no more in delay, for we all see that it is God's will that he shall be our king, and who that holdeth against it, we will slay him.' So Arthur was accepted by the people, high and low, and all men rich and poor kneeled to him and begged his mercy because they had delayed him so long, and he forgave them. Then Merlin told them all who Arthur was, and that he was no bastard, but begotten truly by King Uther upon Ygraine, three hours after the death of her husband the Duke. So they raised to be king, Arthur the young.

Author's Note

Like its predecessor *The Crystal Cave* this novel is a work of the imagination, though firmly based in both history and legend. Not perhaps equally in both: so little is known about Britain in the fifth century A.D. (the beginning of the 'Dark Ages') that one is almost as dependent on tradition and conjecture as on fact. I for one like to think that where tradition is so persistent—and as immortal and self-perpetuating as the stories of the Arthurian Legend—there must be a grain of fact behind even the strangest of the tales which have gathered round the meagre central facts of Arthur's existence. It is exciting to interpret these sometimes weird and nonsensical legends into a story which has some sort of coherence as human experience and imaginative truth.

I have tried with *The Hollow Hills* to write a story which stands on its own, without reference to its forerunner *The Crystal Cave*, or even to whatever explanatory notes follow here. Indeed, I only add these notes for the benefit of those readers whose interest may go beyond the novel itself, but who are not familiar enough with the ramifications of the Arthurian Legend to follow the thinking behind some parts of my story. It may give them pleasure to trace for themselves the seeds of certain ideas and the origins of certain references.

In *The Crystal Cave* I based my story mainly on the 'history' related by Geoffrey of Monmouth[*] which is the basis of the later and mainly mediaeval tales of 'Arthur and his Court', but I set the action against the fifth-century Romano-British background which is the real setting for all that we know of the Arthurian Fact.[†] We have no fixed dates, but I have followed some authorities who postulate A.D. 470 or thereabouts as the date of Arthur's birth. The story of *The Hollow Hills* covers the hidden years between that date and the raising of the young Arthur to be war-leader (*dux bellorum*) or, as legend has had it for more than a thousand years, King of Britain. What I would like to trace here are the threads I have woven to make this story of a

[*] *History of the Kings of Britain*. Translated by Sebastian Evans and revised by Charles W. Dunn (Everyman's Library, 1912).
[†] See *Roman Britain and the English Settlements*. R. G. Collingwood and J. N. L. Myres (Oxford, 1937).
Celtic Britain. Nora K. Chadwick, Vol. 34 in the series *Ancient Peoples and Places*, ed. Glyn Daniel (Thames and Hudson, 1963).

period of Arthur's life which tradition barely touches, and history touches not at all.

That Arthur existed seems certain. We cannot say even that much for certain about Merlin. 'Merlin the magician', as we know him, is a composite figure built almost entirely out of song and legend; but here again one feels that for such a legend to persist through the centuries, some man of power must have existed, with gifts that seemed miraculous to his own times. He first appears in legend as a youth, even then possessed of strange powers. On this story as related by Geoffrey of Monmouth I have built an imaginary character who seemed to me to grow out of and epitomise the time of confusion and seeking that we call the Dark Ages. Geoffrey Ashe, in his brilliant book *From Caesar to Arthur** describes this 'multiplicity of vision':

> When Christianity prevailed and Celtic paganism crumbled into mythology, a great deal of this sort of thing was carried over. Water and islands retained their magic. Lake-spirits flitted to and fro, heroes travelled in strange boats. The haunted hills became fairy-hills, belonging to vivid fairy folk hardly to be paralleled among other nations. Where barrows existed they often fitted this role. Unseen realms intersected the visible, and there were secret means of communication and access. The fairies and the heroes, the ex-gods and the demi-gods, jostled the spirits of the dead in kaleidoscopic confusion . . . Everything grew ambiguous. Thus, long after the triumph of Christianity, there continued to be fairy-hills; but even those which were not barrows might be regarded as havens for disembodied souls . . . There were saints of whom miracles were reported; but similar miracles, not long since, might have been the business of fully identifiable gods. There were glass castles where a hero might lie an age entranced; there were blissful fairylands to be reached by water or by cave-passageways . . . Journeys and enchantments, combats and imprisonments–theme by theme the Celtic imagination articulated itself in story. Yet any given episode might be taken as fact or imagination or religious allegory or all three at once.

Merlin, the narrator of *The Hollow Hills*, the 'enchanter' and healer gifted with the Sight, is able to move in and out of the different worlds at will. And as Merlin's legend is linked with the caves of glass, the invisible towers, the hollow hills where he now sleeps for all time, so I have seen him as the link between the worlds; the instrument by which as he says, 'all the kings become one King, and all the gods one God'. For this he abnegates his own will and his desire for normal manhood. The hollow hills are the physical point of entry between this world and the Otherworld, and Merlin is their human counterpart, the meeting point for the interlocking worlds of men, gods, beasts, and twilight spirits.

One meeting of the real and the fantasy worlds can be seen in the figure of Maximus. Magnus Maximus, the soldier with the dream of empire, was a fact; he commanded at Segontium until the time when he crossed to Gaul in his vain bid for power. 'Macsen Wledig' is a legend, one of the Celtic 'seeking' stories later to flower into the Quest of the Holy Grail. In this novel I have linked the facts of Arthur's great precursor and his imperial

---

* Published by Collins, 1960. See also *The Quest for Arthur's Britain,* ed. Geoffrey Ashe (Pall Mall Press, 1968).

dream to the sword episodes of the Arthurian Legend, and lent them the shape of a Quest story.

The tale of the 'Sword of Maximus' is my invention. It follows the archetypal 'seeking and finding' pattern of which the Quest of the Grail, which later attached itself to the Arthurian Legend, is only one example. The stories of the Holy Grail, identifying it with the Cup from the Last Supper, are twelfth-century tales modelled in their main elements on some early Celtic 'quest' stories; in fact they have elements even older. These Grail stories show certain points in common, changing in detail, but fairly constant in form and idea. There is usually an unknown youth, the *bel inconnu*, who is brought up in the wilds, ignorant of his name or parentage. He leaves his home and rides out in search of his identity. He comes across a Waste Land, ruled by a maimed (impotent) king; there is a castle, usually on an island, on which the youth comes by chance. He reaches it in a boat belonging to a royal fisherman, the Fisher King of the Grail Legends. The Fisher King is sometimes identified with the impotent king of the West Land. The castle on the island is owned by a king of the Otherworld, and there the youth finds the object of his quest, sometimes a cup or a lance, sometimes a sword, broken or whole. At the quest's end he wakes by the side of the water with his horse tethered near him, and the island once again invisible. On his return from the Otherworld, fertility and peace are restored to the Waste Land. Some tales figure a white stag collared with gold, who leads the youth to his destination.

For further reference see *Arthurian Literature in the Middle Ages*; A Collaborative History edited by R. S. Loomis (Oxford University Press, 1959); and *The Evolution of the Grail Legend* by D. D. R. Owens (University of St Andrews Publications, 1968).

SOME OTHER BRIEF NOTES

Segontium. Geoffrey of Monmouth in the *Vita Merlini* tell us of cups made by Weland the Smith in Caer Seint (Segontium), which were given to Merlin. There is also another story of a sword made by Weland which was given to Merlin by a Welsh king. There is a brief reference in *The Anglo-Saxon Chronicle* for the year A.D. 418. 'In this year the Romans collected all the treasures which were in Britain and hid some in the earth so that no one afterwards could find them, and some they took with them into Gaul.'

Galava. The main body of legend places King Arthur in the Celtic countries of the west, Cornwall, Wales, Brittany. In this I have followed the legends. But there is evidence which supports another strong tradition of Arthur in the north of England and in Scotland. So this story moves north. I have placed the traditional 'Sir Ector of the Forest Sauvage' (who reared the young Arthur) at Galava, the modern Ambleside in the Lake District. I have often wondered if 'the fountain of Galabes* where he (Merlin) wont to haunt' could be identified with the Roman Galava or Galaba. (In *The Crystal Cave* I gave it a different interpretation. The mediaeval romancers make 'Galapas' a giant—a version of the old guardian of the spring or

* fontes galabes.

waterway.) The fostering of Arthur on Ector, and the lodging at Galava of Bedwyr, are feasible; we find in Procopius that, as in later times, boys of good family were sent away to be educated. As for the 'chapel in the green', once I had invented a shrine in the Wild Forest I could not resist calling it the Green Chapel, after the mediaeval Arthurian poem of *Sir Gawaine and the Green Knight*, which has its setting somewhere in the Lake District.

Ambrosius' Wall. This is the Wansdyke, or Woden's Dyke, so called by the Saxons, who saw it as the work of the gods. It ran from Newbury to the Severn, and parts of it are still traceable. It was probably built some time between A.D. 450 and 475, so I have ascribed it to Ambrosius.

Caer Bannog. This name, old Celtic for 'the castle of the peaks' is my own interpretation of the various names–Carbonek, Corbenic, Caer Benoic, etc.–given to the castle where the youth finds the Grail.
There is a Celtic legend in which Arthur carries off a cauldron (magic vessel or grail) and a wonderful sword from Nuadda or Llyd, King of the Otherworld.

Cei and Bedwyr. They are Arthur's companions in legend. Cei was Ector's son and became Arthur's seneschal. Bedwyr's name was later mediaevalised to Bedivere, but in his relationship with Arthur he seems to be the original of Lancelot. Hence the reference to the *guenhwyvar* (white shadow: Guinevere) which falls between the boys on page 486.

Cador of Cornwall. When Arthur died without issue, we are told that he left his kingdom to Cador's son.

Morgause. On the subject of Arthur's unwitting incest with his sister, there is a rich confusion of legend. The most usual story is that he lay with his half-sister Morgause, wife (or mistress) of Lot, and begot Mordred who was eventually his downfall. His own sister Morgan, or Morgian, became 'Morgan le Fay', the enchantress. Morgause is said to have borne four sons to Lot, who later were to become Arthur's devoted followers. This seemed unlikely if Arthur had lain with her when she was Lot's wife, so I have taken my own way through the confusion of the stories, with the suggestion that after leaving the court Morgause will lose no time in taking her sister's place as Lot's queen. I believe there was in the fifth century a nunnery near Caer Eidyn (Edinburgh) in Lothian to which Morgian could have retired. This could be the 'house of witches' or 'wise women' of legend, and it is tempting to suppose that Morgian and her nuns came from there to take Arthur away and nurse him after his last battle against Mordred at Camlann.

Coel, King of Rheged, is the original of the Old King Cole of the nursery rhymes. We are told that Hueil, one of the nineteen sons of Caw of Strathclyde, was much disliked by Arthur. Another of the sons, Gildas the monk, seems to have returned this dislike. It is he who, in A.D. 540, wrote *The Loss and Conquest of Britain*, without once mentioning Arthur by name, though he refers to the Battle of Badon Hill, the last of Arthur's twelve great battles, in which he broke the Saxon power. From the tone of Gildas' book it is to be inferred that, if Arthur was a Christian at all, his Christianity went no further than lip-service. At any rate he was no friend to the monks.

Caliburn is the most pronounceable of the names for Arthur's sword, which was later romanticised as Excalibur. White was Arthur's colour; his white hound, Cabal, has a place in legend. Canrith means 'white phantom'.

It will be seen from these necessarily sketchy notes that any given episode of my story may—to quote Geoffrey Ashe again—'be taken as fact or imagination or religious allegory or all three at once'. In this, if in nothing else, it is wholly true to its time.

M.S.

November 1970–November 1972

Wildfire
at Midnight

MARY
STEWART

Wildfire at Midnight

For FHS

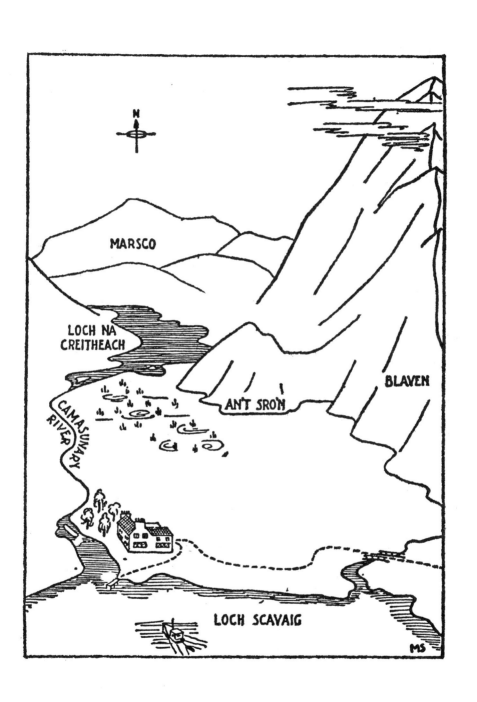

Chapter One

The Misty Island

In the first place, I suppose, it was my parents' fault for giving me a silly name like Gianetta. It is a pretty enough name in itself, but it conjures up pictures of delectable and slightly overblown ladies in Titian's less respectable canvases, and, though I admit I have the sort of colouring that might have interested that Venetian master, I happen to be the rather inhibited product of an English country rectory. And if there is anything further removed than that from the *bagnio* Venuses of Titian's middle period, I don't know what it is.

To do my parents justice, I must confess straight away that the *bagnio* touch was there in the family—nicely in the past, of course, but known nevertheless to be there. And my mother is just sufficiently vague, artistic, and sentimental to see nothing against calling a red-haired daughter after the Vixen Venus, the lovely red-headed Gianetta Fox, who was once the rage of London, and a Beauty in the days when beauties had a capital B, and were moreover apt to regard beauty and capital as one and the same thing. She was a nobody, the lovely Gianetta; her mother, I believe, was half Italian, and if she knew who her father was, she never admitted to him. She simply appeared, Venus rising from the scum of Victorian Whitechapel, and hit London for six in the spring of 1858. She was just seventeen. By the time she was twenty she had been painted by every painter who mattered (Landseer was the only abstainer), in every conceivable allegorical pose, and had also, it was said, been the mistress of every one of them in turn—I should be inclined here, too, to give Landseer the benefit of the doubt. And in 1861 she reaped the due reward of her peculiar virtues and married a baronet. He managed to keep her long enough to beget two children of her before she left him—for a very 'modern' painter of the French school who specialized in nudes. She left her son and daughter behind in Sir Charles's scandalized care; the former was to be my maternal grandfather.

So my nice, vague, artistic mother, who spends her time in our Cotswold rectory making dear little pots and bowls and baking them in a kiln at the bottom of the garden, called me after my disreputable (and famous) great-grandmother, without a thought about the possible consequences to me when I hit London in my turn, in 1945.

I was nineteen, had left school a short eight months before, and now, fresh from a West End training course for mannequins, was ingenuously setting out on a glamorous career with a fashion-house, modelling clothes. I had a share in a bed-sitting-room, a small banking-account (gift from Father), two hand-thrown pots and an ash-tray (gift from Mother), and an engagement diary (gift from my brother Lucius). I was on top of the world.

I was still on top of the world when the Morelli Gallery acquired the Zollner canvas called *My Lady Greensleeves*, and Marco Morelli–*the* Marco Morelli–decided to make a splash with it. You remember the fuss, perhaps? Morelli's idea was, I think, to stage a sort of come-back of art after the austerities and deprivations of the war. He could hardly have chosen a more appropriate picture to do it with. *My Lady Greensleeves* has all the rioting *bravura* of Zollner's 1860 period: the gorgeous lady who languishes, life-size, in the centre of the canvas is the focus of a complicated shimmer of jewels and feathers and embroidered silk–I doubt if any material has ever been more miraculously painted than the coruscating damask of the big green sleeves. As an antidote to austerity it was certainly telling. And even Zollner's peacock riot of colour could not defeat his model's triumphant vitality, or drain the fire from that flaming hair. It was Gianetta Fox's last full-dress appearance in canvas, and she had all the air of making the most of it.

So had Morelli, and his cousin Hugo Montefior, the dress-designer, who happened to be my employer. And there really was nothing against the idea that Montefior should re-create the dress with the lovely green sleeves, and that I should wear it at the showing, and that there should be a Sensation in the right circles, thereby doing the cousins a lot of good. And, possibly, me too, though this honestly didn't occur to me when Hugo put his idea in front of me. I was merely flattered, excited, and terribly nervous.

So I wore the Greensleeves gown at the show, and Morelli got his Sensation, and I was so scared of the fashionable crowd that when I spoke at all, it was in a tight, flat little voice that must have sounded the last word in bored brittle sophistication. I must have looked and sounded, in fact, like a pale copy of that arrogant worldling behind me in Zollner's canvas, for that is what Nicholas Drury undoubtedly took me for, when at length he elbowed his way through the crowds and introduced himself. I had heard of him, of course, and this in no way increased my self-confidence: he had at that time–he was twenty-nine–three terrifyingly good novels to his credit, as well as a reputation for a scarifying tongue. I, for one, was so thoroughly scarified that I froze into complete stupidity, and under his sardonic look stammered some meaningless schoolgirl rubbish that, God help us both, he took for coquetry. We were married three months later.

I have no wish to dwell on the three years that followed. I was wildly, madly, dumbly in love with him, of course, a silly little star-dazzled adolescent, plunged into a life completely strange and rather terrifying. And Nicholas, it became very quickly apparent, wasn't on his own ground either. What he had meant to marry was a modern Gianetta Fox, a composed young sophisticate who could hold her own in the fast-moving society to which he was accustomed; what he'd actually got was only Gianetta Brooke, not long out of school, whose poise was a technique very recently acquired in Montefior's salons and the Mayfair mannequin factory.

Not that this initial miscasting was the cause of our little tragedy; love is a great builder of bridges, and it did seem at first as though what was between us could have spanned any gap. And Nicholas tried as hard as I: looking back now I can see that; if I did achieve sophistication, and a little wisdom, Nicholas struggled to rediscover tenderness. But it was too late; already, when we met, it was too late. The times were out of joint for us, the gap too wide—not the ten-years' gap between our ages, rather, the thousand-year-long stretch of a world war that to me was only an adolescent memory hardly denting the surface of my life, but to Nicholas was a still-recurring nightmare agony leaving scars on the mind which were then only precariously skinning over. How was I, untouched nineteen, to apprehend the sort of stresses that drove Nicholas? And how was he to guess that, deep down under my precarious self-confidence, lurked the destroying germs of insecurity and fear?

Whatever the causes, the break came soon enough. In two years the marriage was as good as over. When Nicholas travelled, as he often did, in search of materials for his books, he more and more frequently found reasons for not taking me with him, and when at length I found he was not travelling alone, I felt no surprise, but I was hurt and humiliated, and so—I have red hair, after all—blazingly outspoken.

If I had wanted to keep Nicholas, I should have done better to have held my tongue. I was no match for him on a battlefield where love had become a weakness and pride the only defence against a cynicism both brutal and unanswerable. He won very easily, and he cannot have known how cruelly. . . .

We were divorced in 1949. For the sake of my mother, who is so High Church as to be verging (according to Father), on Popish Practices, I kept Nicholas' name, and I still wore my wedding ring. I even, after a time, went back to London and to Hugo Montefior, who was angelically kind to me, worked me to death, and never once mentioned Nicholas. Nor did anyone else, except Mother, who occasionally asked after him in her letters, and even, on two occasions, wondered if we were thinking of starting a family. . . . After a year or so I even managed to find this amusing, except when I was run-down and tired, and then the gentle timelessness of Mother and Tench Abbas Rectory became more than I could bear.

So in mid-May 1953, when London had been packed to suffocation for weeks with the Coronation crowds already massing for the great day, and Hugo Montefior one morning took a long look at my face, took another, and promptly told me to go away for a fortnight, I rang up Tench Abbas, and got Mother.

'A holiday?' said Mother. 'The beginning of June? How lovely, darling. Are you coming down here, or will Nicholas find it too dull?'

'Mother, I—'

'Of course we haven't got television,' said Mother proudly, 'but we can listen to the *whole thing* on the wireless. . . .'

I spared a glance for Montefior's salon windows, which have a grandstand view of Regent Street. 'That would be lovely,' I said 'But Mother dearest, would you mind if I went somewhere else for a bit first? Somewhere away from everything . . . you know, just hills and water birds, and things. I'd thought of the Lake District.'

'Not far enough,' said Mother promptly. 'Skye.'

Knowing Mother, I thought for one wild moment that she was recommending Heaven as suitably remote. But then she added: 'Your father was talking about it at the Dunhills' garden-party the other day. It rained *all* the time, you know, and so we had to be indoors–you know it *always* rains for the Dunhills' garden-party, darling?–well, it did so *remind* Maisie Dunhill. They were there a fortnight once, and it rained *every day*.'

'Oh,' I said, as light dawned. 'Skye.'

'And,' said Mother, clinching it, 'there's *no television*.'

'It sounds a very nice place,' I said, without irony. 'Did Mrs D. give you an address?'

'There are the pips,' said Mother distractedly. 'We *can't* have had three minutes, and they *know* how it puts me off. What was–oh, yes, the Dunhills . . . do you know, darling, they've bought a new car, a *huge* thing, called a Jackal or a Jaeger or something, and—'

'Jaguar, Mother. But you were going to give me the address of the hotel where the Dunhills stayed.'

'Oh yes, that was it. But you know Colonel Dunhill *never* drives at more than thirty-five miles an hour, and your father says–what, dear?'

I heard Father's voice speaking indistinguishably somewhere beyond her. Then she said: 'Your father has it, dear, written down. I don't quite know how . . . well, here it is. The Camas Fhionnaridh Hotel—'

'The *what* hotel, Mother?'

'Camas–I'll spell it.' She did. 'I really don't think–I don't remember–but this *must* be the one. What did you say, dear?' This to Father again, as she turned away from the receiver, leaving me listening in some apprehension for the pips, which always reduce Mother from her normal pleasant abstraction to a state of gibbering incoherence. 'Your father says it's Gaelic and pronounced Camasunary,' said Mother, 'and it's at the back of *beyond*, so you go there, darling, and have a lovely time with the birds and the–the water, or whatever you said you wanted.'

I sat clutching the receiver, perched there above the roar of Regent Street. Before my mind's eye rose, cool and remote, a vision of rain-washed mountains.

'D'you know,' I said slowly, 'I think I will.'

'Then that's settled,' said Mother comfortably. 'It sounds the very thing, darling. So *handy* having that address. It's as if it were *meant*.'

I am glad to think that Mother will never appreciate the full irony of that remark.

So it came about that, in the late afternoon of Saturday, May 30th, 1953, I found myself setting out on the last stage of my journey to Camas Fhionnaridh in the Isle of Skye. Mother, I found, had been right enough about the back of beyond: the last stage had to be undertaken by boat, there being only a rough cart-road overland from Strathhaird to Camas Fhionnaridh, which the solitary local bus would not tackle. This same bus had brought me as far as Elgol, on the east side of Loch Scavaig, and had more or less dumped me and my cases on the shore. And presently a boatman, rather more ceremoniously, dumped me into his boat, and set out with me, my cases, and one other passenger, across the shining sea-loch towards the distant bay of Camasunary.

Nothing could have been more peaceful. The sea-loch itself was one huge bay, an inlet of the Atlantic, cradled in the crescent of the mountains. The fishing-village of Elgol, backed by its own heather-hills, was within one tip of the crescent; from the other soared sheer from the sea a jagged wall of mountains, purple against the sunset sky. The Cuillin, the giants of the Isle of Mist.

And, locked in the great arms of the mountains, the water lay quiet as a burnished shield, reflecting in deeper blue and deeper gold the pageantry of hill and sky. One thin gleaming line, bright as a rapier, quivered between the world of reality and the water-world below. Our boat edged its way, with drowsily purring engine, along the near shore of the loch. Water lipped softly under the bows and whispered along her sides. The tide was at half-ebb, its gentle washes dwindling, one after one, among the sea-tangle at its edge. The sea-weeds, black and rose-red and olive-green, rocked as the salt swell took them, and the smell of the sea drifted up, sharp and exciting. The shore slid past; scree and heather, overhung with summer clouds of birch, flowed by us, and our wake arrowed the silk-smooth water into ripples of copper and indigo.

And now ahead of us, in the centre of the mountain-crescent, I could see the dip of a bay, where a green valley cut through the hills to the sea's edge. Higher up this valley, as I knew, was a loch, where the hills crowded in and cradled the water into a deep and narrow basin. Out of this the river flowed, I could see the gleam of it, and just discernible at that distance, a white building set among a mist of birch-trees where the glittering shallows fanned out to meet the sea. The boat throbbed steadily closer. Now I could see the smoke from the hotel chimneys, a faint pencilling against the darker blue of the hills. Then the glitter of water vanished as the sun slipped lower, and the enormous shadow of the Cuillin strode across the little valley. One arrogant wing of rock, thrusting itself across the sun, flung a diagonal of shadow over half the bay.

'Garsven,' said the other passenger, at my elbow. I jumped. Such had been my absorption in the scene, so great the sense of solitude imposed by these awful hills, that I had forgotten I was not alone.

'I beg your pardon?'

He smiled. I saw now that he was a pleasant-looking man of perhaps thirty, with hair of an unusual dark gold colour, and very blue eyes. He was tall and lightly built, but he looked strong and wiry, and his face was tanned as if he spent most of his time in the open. He was wearing an ancient ulster over what had, once, been very good tweeds.

'This must be your first visit,' he said.

'It is. It's a little—overpowering, wouldn't you say?'

He laughed. 'Decidedly. I know the district like the back of my hand, but they still take my breath away, every time.'

'They?'

'The Cuillin.' He gave the word what I imagined must be its local pronunciation. His gaze had moved beyond me, and I turned to follow it. 'Garsven,' he said again. 'That's the one at the end that sweeps straight up out of the sea at that impossible angle.' His hand came over my shoulder, pointing. 'And that's Sgurr nan Eag; then the big one blotting out the sun—that's the Pointed Peak, Sgurr Biorach.'

'You mean Sgurr Alasdair,' put in the boatman unexpectedly from behind

us. He was a sturdy Skye man with a dark square face and the soft voice of
the Islands. He steered the boat nonchalantly, and now and then spat to
leeward. 'Sgurr Alasdair,' he said again.

The fair man grinned, and said something in Gaelic which brought an
answering grin to the boatman's face. Then he said to me: 'Murdo's right,
of course. It's Alasdair on the maps—it was re-christened after some
mountaineer or other; but I like the old names best. Sgurr Biorach it is, and
that next to it is Sgurr Dearg, the Red Peak.' His pointing finger swung
towards the last towering pinnacle, black against the sunset. 'Sgurr nan
Gillean.' He dropped his hand and gave me the sort of smile that holds the
hint of an apology—the Britisher's regret for having displayed an emotion.
He said lightly: 'And you couldn't have had your first sight of them under
better conditions. Sunset and evening star—all the works, in fact, in glorious
Technicolor.'

'You must be a mountaineer,' I said.

'A climber? Yes, of a sort.'

'He's a good man on the hill, is Mr Grant,' said Murdo.

Grant took out his cigarettes, offered them to me and Murdo, then spun a
spent match into the water. He said to me: 'Have you come for long?'

'A week or ten days. It depends on the weather. If it stays like this, it'll be
heaven.'

'It won't,' he said confidently. 'What d'you say, Murdo?'

The boatman cast a dubious eye at the south-west, where the Atlantic
merged its long and glimmering reaches into a deep blue sky. He jerked a
thumb in that direction, and spoke briefly and to the point. 'Rain,' he said.

'Oh dear.' I was dismayed. This golden prospect seemed, now that I was
here, to be infinitely more desirable than the rain-washed hills of my
dreams.

'Never mind,' said Mr Grant cheerfully, 'it'll improve the fishing.' I must
have looked blank, because he added: 'You do fish, of course?'

'Oh no.' To my own surprise I sounded apologetic. 'But I—I could learn.'

His interest quickened. 'You climb, then?'

'No.' I felt suddenly very urban and tripperish. 'Actually I came for a—a
rest, and quiet. That's all.'

His eye fell on my cases. 'London?' He grinned. 'Well, you've certainly
come to the right place if you want to get out of the crowds. You'll have no
neighbours except the Black Cuillin, and the nearest of them is—' He
stopped abruptly.

'Nearest?' I glanced at the hotel, much closer now, islanded in its green
valley, dwarfed and overborne by one great solitary mountain to the east.
'That mountain? Is that one of them too? You didn't speak of it before.
What's it called?'

He hesitated perceptibly. 'That's Blaven.'

The boatman took his cigarette from his mouth, and spat into the water.
'Blah-ven,' he repeated, in his soft Highland voice. 'Mmph—mm. . . .'

'The Blue Mountain . . .' said Grant in a voice that was almost abstracted.
Then he pitched his cigarette into the water, and said abruptly: 'Was
London so very crowded?'

'Oh yes. It's been steadily filling up with people and excitement for months. Now it's like a great pot slowly simmering to boiling-point.'

Murdo turned the boat's nose neatly towards the river mouth. 'London, is it?' His voice held a naïve note of wonder. 'Did ye not want to stay and see the Coronation, mistress?'

'In a way, I did. But I—I've been a bit overworked, so I thought a holiday was a better idea after all.'

'What made you come here?' asked Grant. His eyes were still on the Blue Mountain.

'To Skye? Oh, I don't know—everybody wants to visit Skye at some time or other, don't they? And I wanted quiet and a complete change. I shall go for long walks in the hills.'

'Alone?' There was something in Murdo's expression that made me stare at him.

'Why, yes,' I said in surprise.

I saw his eyes meet Grant's for a moment, then slide away to watch the approaching jetty. I laughed. 'I shan't get lost,' I said. 'The walks won't be long enough for that—don't forget I'm a city-bird. I don't suppose I'll get further than the loch, or the lower slopes of—Blaven, was it? Nothing much can happen to me there!' I turned to Mr Grant. 'Does Murdo think I'll go astray in the mist, or run off with a water-kelpie?' Then I stopped. His eyes meeting mine, held some indefinable expression, the merest shadow, no more, but I hesitated, aware of some obscure uneasiness.

The blue eyes dropped. 'I imagine Murdo means—'

But Murdo cut out the engine, and the sudden silence interrupted as effectively as an explosion. 'London . . .' said Murdo meditatively into the bowels of his engine. 'That's a long way now! A long way, indeed, to come. . . .' The guileless wonder was back in his voice, but I got the embarrassing impression that he was talking entirely at random. And, moreover, that his air of Highland simplicity was a trifle overdone; he had, I judged, a reasonably sophisticated eye. 'A very fine city, so they say. Westminster Abbey, Piccadilly Circus, the Zoo. I have seen pictures—'

'Murdo,' I said suspiciously, as we bumped gently alongside a jetty, and made fast. 'When did *you* last see London?'

He met my eye with a limpid gaze as he handed me out of the boat. 'Eight years ago, mistress,' he said in his soft voice, 'on my way back frae Burma and points East. . . .'

The man called Grant had picked up my cases and had started walking up the path to the hotel. As I followed him I was conscious of Murdo staring after us for a long moment, before he turned back to his boat. That simple Skyeman act had been—what? Some kind of smoke-screen? But what had there been to hide? Why had he been so anxious to change the conversation?

The path skirted the hotel to the front door, which faced the valley. As I followed my guide round the corner of the building my eye was once again, irresistibly, drawn to the great valley like a hawk.

Blaven? The Blue Mountain?

I turned my back on it and went into the hotel.

Chapter Two

Back of Beyond

It was an hour later. I had washed, brushed the railway smoke out of my hair, and changed. I sat in the hotel lounge, enjoying a moment of solitude before the other guests assembled for dinner. I was sipping an excellent sherry, my feet were in front of a pleasant fire, and on three sides of the lounge the tremendous mountain scenery was mine for the gazing. I felt good.

The door of the hotel porch swung and clashed, and presently, through the glass of the lounge doors, I saw two women come into the hall and cross it towards the stairs. One I judged to be about my own age; she was shortish, dark, thickset, with her hair cropped straight and mannishly, and the climber's uniform of slacks, boots, and heavy jersey exaggerated her masculine appearance. The other was a girl of about twenty, very young-looking, with bright red cheeks and straight black hair. She did not, I thought, look particularly happy, and her shoulders strained forward under her rucksack as if she were tired. The pair of them stumped up the first flight of the stairs and round the corner.

In a minute or so they were followed by an elderly couple, both tall, thin, and a little stooping, with gentle well-bred faces and deplorable hats. They solemnly carried an empty fishing-creel between them up the stairs, and on their heels another woman trudged, hands thrust deep into the pockets of an ulster. I couldn't see her face, but her hunched shoulders and lifeless step told their own story of depression or weariness.

I yawned and stretched a toe to the blaze, and drank some more sherry. Idly I turned the pages of an old Society weekly which lay at my elbow. The usual flashlighted faces, cruelly caught at Hunt suppers and charity balls, gaped from the glossy pages . . . beautiful horses, plain women, well-dressed men . . . the *London Telephone Directory*, I thought, would be far more interesting. I flicked the pages. There was the usual photograph of me, this time poised against an Adam mantelpiece, in one of Hugo Montefior's most inspired evening gowns . . . I remembered it well, a lovely frock. Here was the theatre page—Alec Guinness in an improbable beard, Vivien Leigh making every other woman within reach look plain, Marcia Maling giving the camera the famous three-cornered smile, staring at vacancy with those amazing eyes. . . .

The lounge door swung open and whooshed shut with a breathless little noise. Marcia Maling came in, sat down opposite me, and rang for a drink.

I blinked at her. There was no mistake. That smooth honey-gold hair, the wide lovely eyes, the patrician little nose, and the by-no-means patrician mouth—this was certainly the star of that string of romantic successes that had filled one of London's biggest theatres from the first years of the war, and was still packing it to-day.

The drink came. Marcia Maling took it, tasted it, met my eyes across it, and smiled, perfunctorily. Then the smile slid into a stare.

'Forgive me'–it was the familiar husky voice–'but haven't we met? I know you, surely?'

I smiled. 'It's very brave of you to say so, Miss Maling. I imagine you usually have to dodge people who claim they've met you. But no, we've never met.'

'I've seen you before, I'm sure.'

I flicked the pages of the magazine with a finger-nail.

'Probably. I model clothes.'

Recognition dawned. 'So you do! Then *that*'s where! You model for Montefior, don't you?'

'More often than not–though I do a bit of free-lancing too. My name's Drury. Gianetta Drury. I know yours, of course. And of course I saw your show, *and* the one before, *and* the one before that—'

'Back to the dawn of time, my dear. I know. But how nice of you. You must have been in pigtails when we did *Wild Belles*.'

I laughed. 'I cut them off early. I had a living to earn.'

'And how.' Marcia drank gin, considering me. 'But I remember where I saw you now. It wasn't in a photograph: it was at Leducq's winter show last year. I bought that divine cocktail frock—'

'The topaz velvet. I remember it. It was a heavenly dress.'

She made a face over her glass. 'I suppose so. But a mistake for all that. You know as well as I do that it wasn't built for a blonde.'

'You weren't a blonde when you bought it,' I said, fairly, before I thought. 'Sorry,' I added hastily, 'I—'

But she laughed, a lovely joyous gurgle of sound. 'Neither I was. I'd forgotten. I'd gone auburn for *Mitzi*. It didn't suit me, and *Mitzi* was a flop anyway.' She stretched her exquisite legs in front of her and gave me the famous three-cornered smile. 'I'm so glad you've come. I've only been here three days and I'm homesick already for town. This is the first time since I left that I've been able to think about civilized things like clothes, and I do so adore them, don't you?'

'Of course. But as they're my job—'

'I know,' she said. 'But nobody here talks about *anything* but fishing or climbing, and I think they're too utterly dreary.'

'Then what on earth are you doing here?' The question was involuntary, and too abrupt for politeness, but she answered without resentment.

'My dear. Resting.'

'Oh, I see.' I tried not to sound non-committal, but Marcia Maling lifted an eyebrow at me and laughed again.

'No,' she said, 'I mean it; really resting–not just out of a job. The show came off a week ago. Adrian said I positively *must vegetate*, and I had just read a divine book on Skye, so here I am.'

'And doesn't Skye come up to the book?'

'In a way. The hills are quite terribly pretty and all that, and I saw some deer yesterday with the cutest baby, but the trouble is you can't really get around. Do you like walking–*rough* walking?'

'I do, rather.'

'Well, I don't. And Fergus just simply refuses to take the car over some of these roads.'

'Fergus? You're here with your husband, then?' I tried vainly to remember who was Marcia Maling's current man.

'My *dear*! I'm not married *at all*, just now. Isn't it heaven, for a change?' She gave a delicious little chuckle over her pink gin, and I found myself smiling back. Her charm was a tangible thing, something radiant and richly alive, investing her silliest clichés and her out-dated extravagances of speech with a heart-warming quality that was as real as the blazing fire between us. 'No. Fergus is my chauffeur.'

'Marcia!' The name was out before I realized it; the fact that I used it was, in a way, a tribute to that charm. 'You haven't brought a *car and chauffeur* here? Is that what you call vegetating?'

'Well, I hate walking,' she said reasonably, 'and anyway, we're not staying here all the time. I'm on a sort of tour of the Highlands and Islands. Let's have another drink. No, really, it's on me. She reached out and pressed the bell. 'In a way, we came here because of Fergus. He was born here. Not that he cares much for the auld lang syne and all that, but it seemed as good a place as any to come to.'

I stared at her. I couldn't help it. 'You're very–considerate,' I said. Your employees—'

She looked at me. This time the famous smile was definitely the one from that very naughty show *Yes, My Darling*. 'Aren't I just? But Fergus–oh, a dry sherry, isn't it? And another pink gin.' She gave the order and turned back to me. 'D'you know, if I talked like this to anyone else in the hotel they'd freeze like–like stuffed trout.'

'Who else is in the hotel?'

'Well, let's see. . . . There's Colonel and Mrs Cowdray-Simpson. They're dim, but rather sweet. They fish all the time, day and night, and have never, to my certain knowledge, caught anything at all.'

'I think I saw them come in. Elderly, with an empty creel?'

'That's them all right. Then, still talking of fish, there's Mr and Mrs Corrigan and Mr Braine.'

'Not Alastair Braine, by any odd chance?'

'I believe that is his name.' Her glance was speculative. 'A friend of yours?'

'I've met him. He's in advertising.'

'Well, he's with this Corrigan couple. And,' added Marcia meditatively, 'if ever I could find it in me to pity a woman who's married to a man as good-looking as Hartley Corrigan, I'd pity that one.'

'Why?' I asked, amused. Marcia Maling's views on marriage, delivered personally, ought to be worth listening to.

'Fish,' she said, simply.

'Fish? Oh, I get it. You mean *fish*?'

'Exactly. He and Alastair Braine, they're just like the Cowdray-Simpsons. Morning, noon, and night. *Fish*. And she does nothing–*nothing*–to fight it, though she's obviously having an utterly foul time, and has been for weeks. She moons miserably about alone with her hands in her pockets.'

I remembered the depressed-looking woman who had trudged upstairs in the wake of the Cowdray-Simpsons. 'I think I've seen her. She didn't look too happy, I agree. But I doubt,' I said thoughtfully, 'if there's a woman living who could compete with fish, once they've really got hold of a man.'

Marcia Maling wriggled her lovely body deeper into her chair, and said: 'No?'

'All right,' I said. 'You, possibly. Or Rita Hayworth. But no lesser woman.'

'But she doesn't even *try*!' said Marcia indignantly. 'And he—oh well, who else?'

'I saw two women—' I began.

'Oh yes, the—what's the word?—*schwärmerinen*,' said Marcia, in her lovely, carrying voice. 'They—'

'Marcia, *no*! You really mustn't!'

But the crusading spirit seemed to be unexpectedly strong in Miss Maling. Her fine eyes flashed. 'That child!' she exclaimed. 'Nineteen if she's a day, and dragged everywhere by that impossible female with the moustache! My dear, she bullies her, positively!'

'If she didn't like the female,' I said reasonably, 'why would she come with her?'

'I told you. They're—'

'*No*, Marcia. It's slander, or something. Do remember this is a Scottish fishing-hotel, not a theatre cocktail-party.'

'I suppose you're right.' She sighed. 'Actually, they come from the same school, or something. The little one's just started teaching there, and the other one takes P.K. or R.T. or something. I heard her actually *admitting* it.'

'Admitting what?' I asked, startled.

'Teaching this R.T. or whatever it is. What is it?'

'Muscular Christianity, I should think.'

'Well, there you are,' said Marcia gloomily.

'Who else is there? I met a man in the boat coming over from Elgol—'

'That would be Roderick Grant. He practically *lives* here, I believe. Tallish, nice-looking, with rather gorgeous hair?'

'That's the one. Blue eyes.'

'And how,' said Marcia, with feeling. 'He's *definitely* interesting, that is, if it wasn't for—' She broke off and drank some gin.

Conscious of a steadily mounting curiosity to see Fergus, I said merely: 'I gathered that this Roderick Grant was a fisherman too.'

'What? Oh, yes, they all are,' said Marcia bitterly. 'But I must say, he's only spasmodic about it. Most of the time he walks, or something. He's never in the hotel.'

'He's a climber,' I said, amused.

'Probably. There's another climber chap called Beagle.'

'Ronald Beagle?'

'I believe so. Another friend of yours?'

'No. I've never met him, but I've heard of him. He's a famous climber.'

She showed a spark of interest. 'Really? Yes, now you mention it, he does

sit every night poring over maps and things, or glued to the radio listening
to this Everest climb they're making.'

'That's who it is, then. He wrote a book once on Nanga Parbat.'

'Oh?' said Marcia without interest. 'Well, he goes round with another
man, a queer little type called Hubert Hay. I don't think they came
together, but I gather Hay's quite a writer as well. He's little and round and
quite, quite sorbo.'

'Sorbo?'

'Yes. Unsquashable.'

'I see. But what an odd word. Sorbo . . . is it Italian?'

She gave a charming little choke of laughter. 'My God, but that dates me,
doesn't it? I'll have to watch myself. No, darling, it's not Italian. Some way
back, in the thirties, when you were in your pram, they sold unsquashable
rubber balls for children. Sorbo Bouncers, they were called.'

'And you used to play with them?'

'Darling,' said Marcia again. 'But how sweet of you. . . . Anyway, the little
man's definitely sorbo in nature *and* appearance, and wears fancy
waistcoats. There's another man whose name I don't know, who got here
last night. I've a feeling he writes, too.'

'Good heavens.'

'I know. Just a galaxy of talent, haven't we? Though probably none of
them are any good; Sorbo is definitely not. But this chap looks as though he
might be—all dark and damn-your-eyes,' said Marcia poetically, then
gloomed at her gin. 'Only—he fishes, too.'

'It sounds a very intriguing collection of people,' I said.

'Doesn't it?' she said without conviction. 'Oh, and there's an aged, aged
lady who I *think* is Cowdray-Simpson's mother and who knits *all the time*,
my dear, in the most ghastly colours. And three youths with bare knees who
camp near the river and come in for meals and go about with hammers and
sickles and things—'

'Geology students, I'll bet,' I said. 'And I rather doubt the sickles.
There's only one thing for it, you know; you'll have to take up fishing for
yourself. I'm going to. I'm told it's soothing to the nerves.'

She shot me a look of horror mingled with respect. 'My God! How
marvellous of you! But'—then her gaze fell on my left hand, and she nodded.
'I might have known. You're married. I suppose he makes you. Now, if that
wretched Mrs Corrigan—'

'I'm not married,' I said.

She caught herself. 'Oh, sorry, I—'

'Divorced.'

'O–oh!' She relaxed and sent me a vivid smile. 'You too? My dear, so'm
I.'

'I know.'

'*Three times*, honey. Too utterly exhausting, I may tell you. Aren't they
stinkers?'

'I beg your pardon?'

'Men, darling. Stinkers.'

'Oh, I see.'

'Don't tell me yours wasn't a stinker too?'

'He was,' I said. 'Definitely.'

'I knew it,' said Marcia. I thought I had never seen two pink gins go further. 'What was his name?'

'Nicholas.'

'The beast,' she said generously. The old crusading instinct was rising again, I could see. 'Have another drink, Jeanette darling, and tell me *all* about it.'

'This one's on me, I said firmly, and pressed the bell. 'And my name is Gianetta. Gee-ann-etta. Of Italian origin, like sorbo.'

'It's pretty,' said she, diverted. 'How come you've an Italian name?'

'Oh, it's old history. . . .' I ordered the drinks, glad to steer the conversation in a new direction. . . . 'My great-grandmother was called Gianetta. She's the kind of ancestress one wants to keep in the family cupboard, tightly locked away, only my great-grandmamma never let herself be locked away anywhere, for a moment.'

'What did she do?' asked Marcia, intrigued.

'Oh, she took the usual road to ruin. Artists' model, artists' mistress, then married a baronet, and—'

'So did I once,' said Marcia cheerfully. 'I left him, though. Did she?'

'Of course. She bolted with a very advanced young artist to Paris, where she made a handsome fortune—don't ask me how—then died in a nunnery at the happy old age of eighty-seven.'

'Those were the days.' Marcia's voice was more than a little wistful. 'Not the nunnery bit, but the rest. . . . What a thoroughly worthy great-grandmother to have—especially the bit about the fortune and the title.'

I laughed. 'They didn't survive. Mother was the only grandchild, and Gianetta left all her money to the convent—as fire-insurance, I suppose.' I put down my empty glass 'So—unlike my great-grandmamma—I wear clothes for a living.'

Through the glass door I could see the Cowdray-Simpsons coming down the stairs. A maid bustled across the hall towards the dining-room. Outside, behind the steep crest of Sgurr na Stri, the red of the sky was deepening to copper, its brightness throwing the jagged rock into towering relief. I saw three young men—the campers, no doubt—coming along from the river; they skirted the windows of the lounge, and a moment later I heard the porch door swing open and shut.

Somewhere a clock struck seven.

'I'm hungry,' I said 'Thank heaven it's dinner-time.'

I got out of my chair, and moved to the window that faced east. Away in front of the hotel stretched the breadth of the valley-floor, almost a mile of flat sheep-bitten turf, unbroken save by little peaty streams that here and there meandered seawards. The road, narrow and rutted, curved away across it, following the shore-line, then lifted its grey length up through the heather and out of sight. To the right the sea murmured, pewter-dark now and unillumined in the shadow of the mountains. Far to the left, at Blaven's foot a glimmer of water recalled the copper sky.

A late grouse shouted 'Comeback!' and fell silent. A gull on the shore stretched its wings once, then settled them again upon its back. The sea seemed still. It was a prospect wild and dreary enough; no sound but a bird's call and a sheep's lament, no movement but the shake of a gull's wing, and the stride of a late-comer walking unhurriedly across the grass.

Then the walker trod on the gravel of the road. The scrunch of his boot on the rough surface startled the stillness. A feeding snipe flashed up beside him, and fled up the glen in a zigzag of lightning flight. I saw the silver gleam of his underwings once, twice, against the towering menace of Blaven, then I lost him.

'Blaven . . .' I said thoughtfully. 'I wonder—'

Behind me, Marcia's voice was sharp and brittle. 'Not any more of that, please. D'you mind?'

I looked back at her in surprise. She was gulping the last of her third gin, and across it she met my eyes queerly. Disconcerted, and a little shaken, as one always is by rudeness, I stared back at her. I had shifted the talk rather arbitrarily, I knew, to Gianetta and her misdeeds, but then I hadn't wanted to talk about Nicholas. And she had seemed interested enough. If I had been boring her—but she had not appeared to be bored. On the contrary.

She gave an apologetic little grin. 'I can't help it,' she said. 'But don't let's. Please.'

'As you wish,' I said, a little stiffly. 'I'm sorry.' I turned back to the window.

The mountain met me, huge and menacing. And I looked at it in sudden enlightenment. *Blaven.* It had been my mention of Blaven, not of Gianetta, that had made Marcia retreat into her gin-glass like a snail into its shell. Roderick Grant, and Murdo, and now Marcia Maling . . . or was I being over-imaginative? I stared out at the gathering dusk, where the late-comer was just covering the last twenty yards to the hotel door. Then my look narrowed on him. I stiffened, and looked again. . . .

'Oh my God,' I said sharply, and went back into the room like a pea from a catapult.

I stopped on the hearthrug, just in front of a goggle-eyed Marcia Maling, and drew a long, long breath.

'Oh my *dear* God,' I said again.

'What's up? Is it because I—'

'It's not you at all,' I said wearily. 'It's the man who's just arriving at the front door of this hotel.'

'Man?' She was bewildered.

'Yes. I presume he is your nameless, dark, damn-your-eyes writer . . . except that he doesn't happen to be nameless to me. His name is Nicholas Drury.'

Her mouth opened. '*No!* You mean—'

I nodded. 'Just that. My husband.'

'The—the stinker?'

I smiled mirthlessly. 'Quite so. As you say. This holiday,' I added without any conviction whatsoever, 'is going to be *fun.*'

Chapter Three

Camasunary I

Yes, there it was, as large as life, the arrogant black signature in the visitors' book: *Nicholas Drury, London. May 29th, 1953.* I looked down at it for a moment, biting my lip, then my eye was caught by another entry in the same hand, high up on the preceding page: *Nicholas Drury, London. April 28th, 1953.* He had been here already this summer, then. I frowned down at the book, wondering what on earth he could be doing in Skye. He must, of course, be collecting material for some book; he would hardly have chosen a place like this for a holiday. This Highland fastness, all trout and misty heather and men in shabby tweeds, accorded ill with what I remembered of Nicholas. I picked up the pen, conscious that my hands were not quite steady. All the carefully acquired poise in the world was not going to make it any more possible for me to meet Nicholas Drury again with the casual camaraderie which was, no doubt, fashionable among the divorcés of his London circle.

I dipped the pen in the inkstand, hesitated, and finally wrote: *Gianetta Brooke, Tench Abbas Rectory, Warwickshire.* Then I tugged my wedding-ring rather painfully off my finger and dropped it into my bag. I would have to tell Major Persimmon, the hotel proprietor, why Mrs Drury had suddenly become Miss Brooke: there were, it seemed to me, altogether too many embarrassments contingent on there being a Mr and Mrs Drury in the same hotel. Marcia Maling had already promised to say nothing. And Nicholas was not to know that I had not become Miss Brooke again four years ago. He would probably be as annoyed and uncomfortable as I, when we met, and would surely try and pass off the awkward encounter as easily as possible. So, at any rate, I assured myself, as I blotted and shut the book, though, remembering my handsome and incalculable husband as I did, I felt that there was very little dependence to be placed on the good behaviour of Nicholas Drury.

Then I jumped like a nervous cat as a man's voice said behind me: 'Janet Drury, as I live!'

I turned quickly, to see a man coming down the stairs towards me.

'Alastair! How nice to see you again! Where've you been all these years?'

Alastair Braine took both my hands and beamed down at me. He was a big, rugged-looking man, with powerful shoulders, perpetually untidy brown hair, and a disarming grin that hid an exceptionally shrewd mind. He looked anything but what he was—one of the coming men in the ruthless world of advertising.

'America mostly, with a dash of Brazil and Pakistan. You knew I was working for the Pergamon people?'

'Yes, I remember. Have you been back long?'

'About six weeks. They gave me a couple of months' leave, so I've come up here with some friends for a spot of fishing.'

'It's lovely seeing you again,' I said, 'and I must say your tan does you credit, Alastair!'

He grinned down at me. 'It's a pity I can't return the compliment, Janet, my pet. Not'–he caught himself up hastily–'that it's not lovely to see you, too, but you look a bit Londonish, if I may say so. What's happened to the schoolgirl complexion? Nick been beating you?'

I stared at him, but he appeared to notice nothing odd in my expression. He said, cheerfully: 'He never told me you were joining him here, the scurvy devil.'

'Oh Lord,' I said. 'Alastair, don't tell me you didn't know? We got a divorce.'

He looked startled, even shocked. '*Divorce?* When?'

'Over four years ago now. D'you mean to tell me you hadn't heard?'

He shook his head. 'Not a word. Of course, I've been abroad all the time, and I'm the world's lousiest letter-writer, and Nick's the next worst, so you can see—' He broke off and whistled a little phrase between his teeth. 'Ah, well. Sorry, Janet. I–well, perhaps I'm not so very surprised, after all . . . you don't mind my saying that?'

'Don't give it a thought.' My voice was light and brittle, and would do credit, I thought, to any of Nicholas' casual London lovelies. 'It was just one of those things that couldn't ever have worked. It was nobody's fault; he just thought I was another kind of person altogether. You see, in my job you tend to look–well, tough and sort of well-varnished, even when you're not.'

'And you're not.'

'Well, I wasn't then,' I said. 'I've a better veneer now.'

'Three years of my great friend Nicholas,' said Alastair, 'would sophisticate a Vestal Virgin. Bad luck, Janet. But, if I may ask, what are you doing here?'

'Having a holiday like you, and dodging the Coronation crowds. I need hardly say I had no idea Nicholas was going to be here. I was a bit run down, and wanted somewhere restful, and I heard of the hotel through some friends of the family.'

'Somewhere restful.' He gave a little bark of laughter. 'Oh my ears and whiskers! And you have to run slap into Nick!'

'Not yet,' I told him grimly. 'That's a pleasure in store for us both.'

'Lord, Lord,' said Alastair ruefully, then began to grin again. 'Don't look so scared, my child. Nick won't eat you. It's he should be nervous, not you. Look, Janet, will you let me dine at your table to-night? I'm with a couple who could probably do with having to have a little of one another's society.'

'I'd love you to,' I said gratefully. 'But how on earth is it that Nicholas didn't tell you about us?'

'I've really seen very little of him. He's apparently in Skye collecting stuff on folk-lore and such-like for a book, and he's been moving from one place to another, with this as a main base. He's out most of the time. I did ask after you, of course, and he just said: "She's fine. She's still with Hugo, you know. They've a show due soon." I thought nothing of it.'

'When was this?'

'Oh, when I first got here and found he was staying. May the tenth, or thereabouts.'

'We *were* getting a show ready then, as it happens. But how on earth did he know?'

'Search me,' said Alastair cheerily, and then turned to greet the couple who were crossing the hall towards us. The woman was slight, dark, and almost nondescript save for a pair of really beautiful brown eyes, long-lidded and flecked with gold. Her dress was indifferently cut, and was a depressing shade of green. Her hair had no lustre, and her mouth drooped petulantly. The man with her was a startling contrast. He, too, was dark, but his thinness gave the impression of a great wiry strength and vitality. His eyes were blue, dark Irish blue, and he was extraordinarily handsome, though there were lines round the sensitive mouth that spoke of a temper too often given rein.

I said quickly: 'The name's Brooke, Alastair, not Drury. Do remember. I thought it might be awkward—'

'I couldn't agree more. Ah'—as they came up–'Hart, Alma, this is Gianetta Brooke, Janet, Mr and Mrs Corrigan.'

We murmured politely. I saw Mrs Corrigan eyeing my frock; her husband's blue eyes flicked over me once, with a kind of casual interest, then they sought the lounge door, as if he were waiting for someone else.

'I'm going to desert you at dinner, Alma, if you'll forgive me.' Alastair made his excuses. 'Miss Brooke and I are old friends, and we've a lot to talk about.'

Mrs Corrigan looked vaguely resentful, and I wondered for a moment if she were going to invite me to join their table, until I realized that she was hesitating between two evils, the hazard of having another woman near her husband, and the loss of the society of her husband's friend. She had, in fact, the air of one for whom life has for a long time been an affair of perpetual small calculations such as this. I felt sorry for her. Through Alastair's pleasant flow of conversational nothings, I shot a glance at Hartley Corrigan, just in time to see the look on his face as the lounge door opened behind me, and Marcia Maling drifted towards us on a cloud of Chanel No. 5. My pity for Alma Corrigan became, suddenly, acute. She seemed to have no defences. She simply stood there, dowdy, dumb, and patently resentful, while Marcia, including us all in her gay, 'How were the fish, my dears?' enveloped the whole group in the warm exuberance of her personality. The whole group, yes—but somehow, I thought, as I watched her, and listened to some absurd fish-story she was parodying—somehow she had cut out Hartley Corrigan from the herd, and penned him as neatly as if she were champion bitch at the sheep-trials, and he was a marked wether. And as for the tall Irishman, it was plain that, for all he was conscious of the rest of us, the two of them might as well have been alone.

I found I did not want to meet Alma Corrigan's eyes, and looked away. I was wishing the gong would go. The hall was full of people now; all the members of Marcia's list seemed to be assembled. There were the Cowdray-Simpsons, being attentive to an ancient white-haired lady with a hearing-aid; there, in a corner, were the two oddly assorted teachers, silent and a little glum; my friend of the boat, Roderick Grant, was consulting a barometer in earnest confabulation with a stocky individual who must be Ronald Beagle; and, deep in a newspaper, sat the unmistakable Hubert Hay, dapper and rotund in the yellowest of Regency waistcoats.

Then Nicholas came quickly round the corner of the stairs, and started down the last flight into the hall.

He saw me straight away. He paused almost imperceptibly, then descended the last few stairs, and came straight across the hall.

'Alastair,' I said, under my breath, furious to find that my throat felt tight and dry.

Alastair turned, saw Nicholas, and took the plunge as smoothly as an Olympic swimmer.

'Hi, Nick!' he said. 'Look who's here. . . . Do you remember Janet Brooke?'

He stressed the surname ever so slightly. Nicholas' black brows lifted the fraction of an inch, and something flickered behind his eyes. Then he said: 'Of course. Hello, Gianetta. How are you?'

It came back to me sharply, irrelevantly, that Nicholas was the only person who had never shortened my name. I met his eyes with an effort, and said, calmly enough: 'I'm fine, thank you. And you?'

'Oh, very fit. You're here on holiday, I take it?'

'Just a short break. Hugo sent me away. . . .'' It was over, the awkward moment, the dreaded moment, sliding past in a ripple of commonplaces, the easy mechanical politeness that are so much more than empty convention; they are the greaves and cuirasses that arm the naked nerve. And now we could turn from one another in relief, as we were gathered into the group of which Marcia Maling was still the radiant point. She had been talking to Hartley Corrigan, but I could see her watching Nicholas from under her lashes, and now she said, turning to me: 'Another old friend, darling?'

I had forgotten for the moment that she was an actress, and stared at her in surprise, so beautifully artless had the question been. Then I saw the amusement at the back of her eyes, and said coolly: 'Yes, another old friend. My London life is catching me up even here, it seems. Nicholas, let me introduce you to Miss Marcia Maling—*the* Marcia Maling, of course. Marcia, this is Nicholas Drury.'

'*The* Nicholas Drury?' Marcia cooed it in her deepest, furriest voice, as she turned the charm full on to him with something of the effect that, we are told, a cosmic ray-gun has when turned on to an earthly body. But Nicholas showed no sign of immediate disintegration. He merely looked ever so slightly wary as he murmured something conventional. He had seen that amused look of Marcia's, too, I knew. He had always been as quick as a cat. Then Hartley Corrigan came in with some remark to Marcia, and, in less time than it takes to write it, the whole party was talking about fish. The men were, at any rate; Marcia was watching Hartley Corrigan, Alma Corrigan watched Marcia, and I found myself studying Nicholas.

He had changed, in four years. He would be thirty-six now, I thought, and he looked older. His kind of dark, saturnine good looks did not alter much, but he was thinner, and, though he seemed fit enough, there was tension in the way he held his shoulders, and some sort of strain about his eyes, as if the skin over his cheek-bones was drawn too tightly back into the scalp. I found myself wondering what was on his mind. It couldn't just be the strain of starting a new book, though some stages, I knew, were hell. No, knowing him as I did, I knew that it must be something else, some other obscure stress that I couldn't guess at, but which was unmistakably there. Well, at any rate, I thought, this time I couldn't possibly be the cause of his mood; and neither, this time, did I have to worry about it.

I was just busily congratulating myself that I didn't have to care any more, when the gong sounded, and we all went in to dinner.

Chapter Four

Debatable Land

It became more than ever obvious, after dinner, that the awkwardness of my own situation was by no means the only tension in the oddly assorted gathering at the Camasunary Hotel. I had not been over-imaginative. That there were emotional undercurrents here seemed more than ever apparent, but I don't think I realized, at first, quite how strong they were. I certainly never imagined they might be dangerous.

By the time I got back into the lounge after dinner, the groups of pele had broken and re-formed, and, as is the way in small country hotels, conversation had become general. I saw with a little twinge of wry amusement that Marcia Maling had deserted the Corrigans and was sitting beside Nicholas. It was, I supposed, a change for the better. She could no more help being pulled into the orbit of the nearest interesting man than she could help breathing, but I wished she would leave Hartley Corrigan alone. She had much better spend her time on Nicholas; he could look after himself.

Alastair found a chair for me in a corner, than excused himself and went off to see about weighing and despatching the salmon he had caught that day. I saw Corrigan get up, without a word to his wife, and follow him from the room. Alma Corrigan sat without looking up, stirring and stirring at her coffee.

'Will you have coffee? Black or white?'

I looked up to meet the bright gaze of the younger of the two teachers, who was standing in front of me with a cup in either hand. She had changed into a frock the colour of dry sherry, with a cairngorm brooch in the lapel. It was a sophisticated colour, and should not have suited her, but somehow it did; it was as if a charming child had dressed up in her elder sister's clothes. She looked younger than ever, and touchingly vulnerable.

I said: 'Black please. Thank you very much. But why should you wait on me?'

She handed me a cup. 'Oh, nobody serves the coffee. They bring it all in on a huge tray, and we each get our own. You've just come, haven't you?'

'Just before dinner.' I indicated the chair at my elbow. 'Won't you sit down? I've been deserted for a fish.'

She hesitated, and I saw her shoot a glance across the room to where her companion was apparently deep in a glossy magazine. Then she sat down, but only on the edge of the chair, remaining poised, as it were, for instant flight.

'The fish certainly have it all their own way,' she admitted. 'I'm Roberta Symes, by the way.'

'And I'm Gianetta Brooke. I take it you don't fish?'

'No. We're walking, Marion and I–that's Marion Bradford, over there; we're together. At least, we're climbing, sort of.'

'What d'you mean by sort of?' I asked, amused. The Skye hills had not struck me as being the kind you could sort of climb.

'Well, Marion's a climber, and I'm not. That's really what I mean. So we go scrambling, which is a kind of half-way solution.' She looked at me ingenuously. 'But I'm *dying* to learn. I'd like to be as good as Mr Beagle, and climb on every single Cuillin in turn, including the Inaccessible Pinnacle!'

'A thoroughly unworthy ambition,' said a voice above us. Roderick Grant had come across, and was standing over us, coffee-cup in hand.

Roberta's eyes widened. 'Unworthy? That from *you*! Why, Mr Grant?'

He turned and, with a sweep of one arm, indicated the prospect from the lounge windows.

'Look at them,' he said. 'Look at them. Thirty million years ago they thrust their way up from God knows where, to be blasted by wind and ice and storm, and chiselled into the mountain-shapes you walk over to-day. They've been there countless ages, the same rocks, standing over the same ocean, worn by the same winds. And you, who've lived out a puny little twenty or thereabouts, talk of scaling them as if they were—'

'Teeth?' said Roberta, and giggled. 'I know what you mean though. They do make one feel a bit impermanent, don't they? But then it's all the more of a challenge, don't you feel? Mere man, or worse still mere woman, conquering the–the giants of time, climbing up—'

'Everest!' Colonel Cowdray-Simpson's exclamation came so pat that I jumped, and Roberta giggled again. *The Times* rustled down an inch or two, and the Colonel peered over it at Nicholas, who was nearest the radio. 'Turn on the wireless, will you, Drury? Let's hear how they're getting on.'

Nicholas obeyed. The news was nearly over: we had, luckily, missed the conferences, the strikes, the newest atomic developments, the latest rumours from the U.S.S.R., and had come in just in time for a fuss about the seating in Westminster Abbey, a description of the arches in the Mall, and a hint of the general excitement in a London seething already towards its Coronation boiling-point three days hence. And nothing yet, apparently, about Everest. . . .

Nicholas switched off.

'But I think they're going to make it,' he said.

'It's too thrilling, isn't it?' said Marcia comfortably.

'It's certainly a magnificent effort,' said Colonel Cowdray-Simpson.

'They deserve their luck. What d'ye say, Beagle? What are the chances with the weather?'

'Fair enough.' Beagle looked faintly uncomfortable at being thus appealed to in public. I remembered, with a quickening of interest, that this unassuming little man had been involved in an earlier attempt on Everest. But he seemed unwilling to pursue the subject. He groped in his jacket pocket and produced his pipe, turning the conversation abruptly. 'I'd say they had a chance of better weather there than we have here, at any rate. I don't like the look of the sky. There's rain there.'

'All the better for the fishing,' said Mrs Cowdray-Simpson placidly, but Roberta moaned.

'Oh *no*! And I wanted to start *really* climbing to-morrow.'

'Quite determined to conquer the Cuillin, then?' said Roderick Grant.

'Quite!'

'Where d'you intend to start?'

'I don't know. I'm leaving that to Marion.'

'Garsven's not hard,' said someone–I think it was Alma Corrigan. 'There's a way up from the Coruisk end—'

Marion Bradford interrupted: 'The best first climbs are Bruach na Frithe and Sgurr na Banachdich, but they're too far away. Garsven is within reach, but of course it's just plain dull.' Her flat voice and uncompromising manner fell hardly short, I considered, of being just plain rude. Alma Corrigan sat back in her chair with a little tightening of the lips. Roberta flushed slightly and leaned forward.

'Oh, but Marion, I'm sure Mrs Corrigan's right. It doesn't look hard, and there must be a wonderful view—'

'There's a wonderful view from every single one of the Cuillins,' said Marion dampingly.

'You've climbed them all?' asked Roderick gently.

'If you mean do I know what I'm talking about, the answer is yes,' said Marion Bradford.

There was a little pause, in which everyone looked faintly uncomfortable, and I wondered what on earth made people behave like that without provocation. Colonel and Mrs Cowdray-Simpson returned to *The Times* crossword, and Roderick Grant lit a cigarette, looking all at once impossibly remote and well-bred. Nicholas was looking bored, which meant, I knew, that he was irritated, and Marcia Maling winked across at me and then said something to him which made his mouth twitch. Roberta merely sat silent, fiery red and unhappy. As an exercise in Lifemanship, it had been superb.

Then Hubert Hay spoke for the first time, completely ignoring both Marion Bradford's rudeness and the hiatus in the conversation. I remembered Marcia's definition of him as sorbo, and felt amused.

'If I were you,' he said cheerily to Roberta, 'I'd try the Bad Step. Wait till high tide, and then you won't break your neck if you fall. You'll only drown. Much less uncomfortable, they say.'

He had a curiously light, high little voice, and this, together with his odd appearance, produced a species of comic relief. Roberta laughed. 'I can swim.'

'In climbing boots and a rucksack?'

'Oh well, perhaps not!'

'What on earth's the Bad Step?' I asked.

Hubert Hay pointed towards the west windows. 'You see that hill beyond the river's mouth, between us and the Cuillin?'

'Yes.'

'That's Sgurr na Stri. It's a high tongue of land between here and the bay at the foot of Garsven. You can take a short cut across it, if you want a scramble. But if you follow the coast round to Loch Coruisk and the Cuillin, you have to cross the Bad Step.'

'It sounds terrible. Is it a sort of Lovers' Leap?'

'Oh no. It's only a slab of gabbro tilted at a filthy angle—about sixty degrees—'

'Not as much,' said Roderick Grant.

'No? Maybe you're right. Anyway, it hangs over the sea, and you have to cross it by a crack in the rock, where your nails can get a good grip.'

'Your *nails*?' said Marcia, horror-stricken. 'My God! D'you mean you have to *crawl* across?'

Nicholas grinned. 'No, lady. He's talking about your boots.'

'It sounds just my style,' announced Roberta buoyantly. 'After all, who minds drowning? Let's go round there, Marion, and come back over Sgurr na Stri.'

'I've made up my mind where we're going,' said Marion, in that flat, hard voice which carried so disastrously. 'We're going up Blaven.'

There was a sudden silence. I looked up sharply. I had been right, then, in thinking that some queer reaction took place every time that name was mentioned. This time it was unmistakable. And I was not imagining the note of defiance in Marion Bradford's voice. She knew that her announcement would fall on the room in just that kind of silence.

Ronald Beagle spoke then, diffidently. 'Is that quite—er, wise, Miss Bradford? It's not exactly a beginner's scramble, is it?'

'It's easy enough up the ridge from this end,' she said shortly.

'Oh, quite. But if the weather's bad—'

'A spot of rain won't hurt us. And if mist threatens we won't go. I've got that much sense.'

He said no more, and silence held the room again for a moment. I saw Nicholas move, restlessly, and I wondered if he felt, as I did, a discomfort in the atmosphere sharper than even Marion Bradford's rudeness could warrant.

Apparently Marion herself sensed something of it, for she suddenly stabbed out her cigarette viciously into an ash-tray and got up.

'In any case,' she said, in that tight, aggressive voice of hers, 'it's time *someone* broke the hoodoo on that blasted mountain, isn't it? Are you coming, Roberta?'

She stalked out of the room. Roberta gave me an uncomfortable little smile, and got up to follow her. For an instant I felt like advising her to stay, then decided that, whatever the cross-currents of emotion that were wrecking the comfort of the party, I had better not add to them. I merely smiled at her, and she went out after her friend.

There was the inevitable awkward pause, in which everyone madly wanted to discuss Marion Bradford, but, naturally, couldn't. Then Marcia, who, as I was rapidly discovering, had no inhibitions at all, said:

'Well, really! I must say—'

Colonel Cowdray-Simpson cleared his throat rather hastily, and said, across her, to Ronald Beagle: 'And where do you propose to go to-morrow, Beagle?'

'Weather permitting, sir, I'm going up Sgurr nan Gillean. But I'm afraid. . . .'

I got to my feet. I had had enough of this, and I felt cramped and stale after my journey. And if Murdo and Beagle were right, and it was going to rain in the morning, I might as well go out now for an hour. As I turned to put my coffee-cup on the tray, I saw, to my dismay, that Nicholas had risen too, and was coming across the room in my direction. It looked very much as if he were going to speak to me, or follow me out, and I felt, just then, that a *tête-à-tête* with Nicholas would be the final straw. I turned quickly towards the nearest woman, who happened to be Alma Corrigan.

'I'm going out for a short walk,' I said, 'and I don't know my way about yet at all. I wonder if you'd care to join me?'

She looked surprised, and, I thought, a little pleased. Then the old resentful look shut down on her face again, and she shook her head.

'I'd have liked to very much.' She was politely final. 'But, if you'll forgive me, I'm a bit tired. We've been out all day, you know.'

Since she had already told me, before dinner, that she had spent the day sitting on a boulder while the men fished the Strath na Creitheach, this was a very efficient rebuff.

'Of course,' I said, feeling a fool. 'Some other time, perhaps.' I turned away to find Roderick Grant at my elbow.

'If I might—' He was looking diffidently down at me. 'There's a very pleasant walk up to the loch, if you'll let me be your guide. But perhaps you prefer to go alone?'

'By no means,' I assured him. Nicholas had stopped when Roderick Grant spoke, and I knew that he was frowning. I smiled back at Mr Grant. 'Thanks very much: I'll be glad of your company.'

Nicholas had not moved. I had to pass him on my way to the door. Our glances met; his eyes, hard and expressionless, held mine for a full three seconds, then he gave a twisted little smile and deliberately turned back to Marcia Maling.

I went to get my coat.

Chapter Five

Loch na Creitheach

At half-past nine on a summer's evening in the Hebrides, the twilight has scarcely begun. There is, perhaps, with the slackening of the day's brilliance, a sombre note overlying the clear colours of sand and grass and rock, but this is no more than the drawing of the first thin blue veil. Indeed, night itself is only a faint dusting-over of the day, a wash of silver through the still-warm gold of the afternoon.

The evening was very still, and, though the rain-threatening clouds were slowly packing higher behind us, in the south-west, the rest of the sky was clear and luminous. Above the ridge of Sgurr na Stri, above and beyond the jagged peaks of the Cuillin, the sun's warmth still lingered in the flushed air. Across this swimming lake of brightness one long bar of cloud lay sullenly, one thin line of purple shadow, struck from below to molten brilliance by the rays of a now invisible sun.

We turned northwards up the valley, and our steps on the short sheep-turf made no sound in the stillness. The flat pasture of the estuary stretched up the glen for, perhaps, half a mile, then the ground rose, steep and broken, to make the lower spurs and hillocks that were Blaven's foothills. One of these, the biggest, lay straight ahead of us, a tough little heather-clad hill which blocked the centre of the glen and held the southern shore of the loch. To the left of it curved the river: on the east a ridge of rock and heather joined it to the skirts of Blaven.

'Isn't there a path along the river?' I asked.

'Oh yes, but if you want to climb An't Sròn—that hill in front—for a view of the loch, we'd better keep to the Blaven side of the glen. There's a bog further on, near the river, which isn't too pleasant.'

'Dangerous, you mean, or merely wet?'

'Both. I don't know whether it would actually open and swallow you up, but the ground shakes in a beastly fashion, and you start to sink if you stand still. The deer avoid it.'

'Then,' I said with a shiver, 'by all means let us avoid it too. It seems I ought to be very grateful to you for coming with me!'

He laughed. 'It's actually pure selfishness on my part. If one loves a place very much one likes to show it off. I wasn't going to miss a fresh opportunity for taking credit to myself for this scenery. It must be one of the loveliest corners of the world.'

'This particular corner, do you mean, or Skye and the Islands in general?'

'This bit of Skye.' His hands were thrust deep into his pockets, but his eyes lifted briefly to the distant peaks, and to the great blue heights of Blaven dwarfing the glen where we walked. 'Those.'

'Is this your home, Mr Grant?'

He shook his head. 'No. I was born among mountains, but very different ones. My father was minister of a tiny parish away up in the Cairngorms, a little lost village at the back of the north wind. Auchlechtie, at the foot of Bheinn a' Bhuird. D'you know it?'

'I'm afraid not.'

He grinned. 'I've never yet met anyone who did. . . . Well, that's where I learned my mountain-worship! I'd no mother; my father was a remote kind of man, who had very little time for me; it was miles to school, so as often as not I just ran wild in the hills.'

'You must have been a very lonely little boy.'

'Perhaps I was. I don't remember. I don't think I felt lonely.' He grinned again. 'That is, until an uncle died, and left us a lot of money, and my father made me put shoes on and go to a public school to learn manners.'

'That was bad luck.'

'I hated it, of course. Particularly the shoes.'

'And now you spend your time climbing?'

'Pretty well. I travel a bit—but I always seem to end up here, at any rate in May and June. They're the best months in the West, although'—he flung a quick glance over his shoulder—'I think our friend Beagle was right about the weather. We'll have rain to-morrow, for certain, and once the Cuillin get a good grip on a rain-storm, they're very reluctant to let it go.'

'Oh dear,' I said, 'and I was wanting to walk. I begin to see why people take up fishing here; it must be sheer self-defence.'

'Very possibly. Watch your step, now. It's tricky going in this light.'

We had reached the foot of the little hill called An't Sròn, and began to climb the rough heathery slope. A cock grouse rose with a clap from somewhere near at hand, and planed down towards the river, chakking indignantly. The light had faded perceptibly. Like an enormous storm-cloud above the valley Blaven loomed, and behind his massive edge hung, now, the ghost of a white moon past the full.

Roderick Grant paused for a moment in his stride, and looked thought-fully up at the wicked ridges shouldering the sky.

'I wonder if those two fool women will really go up there to-morrow?'

'Is it a bad climb?'

'Not if you know which way to go. Straight up the south ridge it's only a scramble. But there are nasty places even there.'

'Miss Bradford said she knew her way about,' I said.

A smile touched his mouth. 'She did, didn't she? Well, we can't do much about it.'

'I suppose not.' We were more than half-way up the little hill. The going was getting steeper and rougher. 'Mr Grant,' I said, a little breathlessly.

'Yes?'

I hesitated, then said flatly: 'What did Miss Bradford mean about a hoodoo on Blaven? What's wrong with it?'

He stopped and glanced down at me. He looked surprised, almost blank. 'Wrong with it?' He repeated the phrase half-mechanically.

'Yes. Why does everyone shy off it like that? I'm sure they do. I can't be mistaken. And if it comes to that, what's wrong with the people in the hotel?

Because there's *something*, and if you haven't noticed it—'

'*You don't know?*'

'Of course I don't know!' I said, almost irritably. 'I've only just arrived. But even to me the set-up seems uncomfortably like the opening of a bad problem-play.'

'You're not far astray at that,' said Roderick Grant. 'Only we're half-way through the play, and it looks as if the problem isn't going to be solved at all.' He paused, and looked gravely down at me in the gathering dusk. 'It's a nasty problem, too,' he said, 'the nastiest of all, in fact. There's been murder done.'

I took a jerky little breath. '*Murder?*'

He nodded. His blue eyes, in that light, were dark under lowered brows. 'Two and a half weeks ago it happened, on the thirteenth of May. It was a local girl, and she was murdered on Blaven.'

'I—see.' Half-unbelievingly I lifted my eyes to the great mass ahead. Then I shivered and moved forward. 'Let's get to the top of this hill,' I said, 'and then, if you don't mind, I think you'd better tell me about it.'

We sat on a slab of rock, and lit cigarettes. Away below us, cradled in its purple hollow, Loch na Creitheach gleamed with a hard bright light like polished silver. Two duck flew across it, not a foot above their own reflections.

'Who was the girl?' I asked. 'And who did it?'

He answered the latter question first. 'We still don't know who did it. That's what I meant when I said it was a nasty problem. The police—' He frowned down at the cigarette in his fingers, then said: 'I'd better start at the beginning, hadn't I?'

'Please do.'

'The girl's name was Heather Macrae. Her father's a crofter, who does some ghillying for the hotel folks in summer-time; you'll probably meet him. His croft's three or four miles up the Strath na Creitheach, the river that flows into the far end of this loch. . . . Well, it seems Heather Macrae was "keeping company" with a lad from the village, one Jamesy Farlane, and so, when she took to staying out a bit later in the long spring evenings, her folk didn't worry about it. They thought they knew who she was with.'

'And it wasn't Jamesy after all?'

'Jamesy says not. He says it very loud and clear. But then, of course,' said Roderick Grant, 'he would.'

'And if it wasn't Jamesy, who could it have been?'

'Jamesy says he and Heather had a quarrel—yes, he admits it quite openly. He says she'd begun to avoid him, and when finally he tackled her with it, she flared up and said she was going with a better chap than he was. A gentleman, Jamesy says she told him.' He glanced at me. 'A gentleman from the hotel.'

'Oh *no!*' I said.

'I'm afraid so.'

'But—that doesn't mean the man from the hotel was necessarily—'

'The murderer? I suppose not, but there's a strong probability—if, that is, he existed at all. We only have Jamesy Farlane's word for that. What we do know is that Heather Macrae went out on the evening of May the thirteenth to meet a man. She told her parents that she "had a date".'

'And–on Blaven, you said?'

His voice was sombre. 'This bit isn't nice, but I'd better tell you. At about midnight that night, some men who were out late on Loch Scavaig–I suspect they were poaching sea-trout–saw what looked like a great blaze of fire half-way up Blaven. They were mystified, but of course not alarmed. It's bare rock, so they weren't afraid of its spreading. They went on with their job, whatever it was, and kept an eye on the fire. One of them had a look through night-glasses, and said it was a column of flame, like a big bonfire, but that its base was out of sight behind a rocky bluff.'

He paused. 'Well, they got more and more puzzled. Who on earth would light a bonfire away up there, and what on earth could he be burning there anyway? Whether they were being wise after the event, or not, I don't know, but one of them, Rhodri MacDowell, says that gradually, watching that leaping column of fire where no fire ought to be, they grew first of all uneasy, then alarmed, then downright frightened. And when the chap with the glasses reported seeing a dark figure moving in front of the flames, they decided to investigate.'

He frowned down at the shining loch. 'By the time they got to it, of course, the fire was out, and it was only the remains of the smoke licking up the rock face that guided them. They found a widish ledge–easy enough to get to–with the remains of charred driftwood and birch and heather blackened and scattered, deliberately it seemed, all over the rock. Lying in the middle of the blackened patch was Heather's body, flat on its back.' He drew sharply on his cigarette, and his voice was flat and colourless. 'She was not very much burned. She had been dead when he put her there. Ashes had been scattered over her, and her throat was cut.'

'Oh dear God,' I said.

'She was,' said Roderick, in that flat, impersonal voice, 'fully clothed, and she was lying quietly, with her hands crossed on her breast. The oddest thing was, though, that she was bare-footed, and all her jewellery had been taken off.'

'Jewellery?' I said, astounded. 'But good heavens—'

'Oh no, not stolen,' he said quickly. 'She hadn't anything worth stealing, poor child, let alone worth getting herself murdered for. It was all there, in a little pile in the corner of the ledge; her shoes, a leather belt, and all the ornaments she'd been wearing–a ring, a cheap bracelet and brooch, earrings–even a couple of hair-clips. Odd, don't you think?'

But I wasn't thinking about its oddness. I said savagely: 'The poor kid had certainly put on all her finery for him, hadn't she?'

He shot me a look. 'It's quite particularly unpleasant, isn't it?'

'It certainly is.' I looked up and along the towering curve of Blaven's south ridge. 'And the police: do they favour Jamesy, or the gentleman from the hotel?'

He shrugged, and ground his cigarette out on the rock. 'God knows. They've been coming and going ever since that day, putting us all through it–very quietly and unobtrusively, but nevertheless thoroughly. But you see why nerves are a little bit on edge?'

'I see,' I said grimly. 'I must say it seems a little strange that Major Persimmon didn't warn new guests of what was going on. They might even have preferred not to come.'

'Quite,' said Roderick Grant. 'But his line is, obviously, that Jamesy's talking nonsense to protect himself, and that it's nothing to do with the hotel. The heavy questioning is all over, and the police are in any case being very quiet about it all. You can hardly expect Bill–Major Persimmon–to ruin his season, and possibly his hotel, can you?'

'I suppose not.' I squashed out my cigarette, and rose. He got up too, and stood looking down at me.

'I hope this hasn't upset you too much,' he said, a little awkwardly.

'If it has,' I said, 'it can hardly matter, can it? It's that poor child, going up to her death on the mountain, all decked out in her best. . . .' I bit my lip, and kicked at a tuft of heather, then raised my head and looked straight at him. 'Just tell me,' I said, 'precisely which "gentlemen" were in this hotel on May the thirteenth?'

The blue eyes met mine levelly. 'All those,' he said expressionlessly, 'who are here now, with the exception of Miss Maling's chauffeur.'

'And which of you,' I said doggedly, feeling unhappy and absurd at the same time, 'has an alibi?'

'None of us that I know of.' Nothing in his voice betrayed any awareness of the change of pronoun which all at once gave the story a horrible immediacy. 'Two of those boys camping by the river swear they were together; the third, no. Colonel Cowdray-Simpson and Bill Persimmon are vouched for by their wives, but that counts for very little, of course. Corrigan and Braine were out fishing on Loch an Athain.'

'At *midnight*?'

'Quite a lot of people do, it's never really dark at this time of the year.'

'Then they were together?'

'No. They separated to different beats some time after eleven, and went back to the hotel in their own time. Mrs Corrigan says her husband got in well before midnight.'

There was an odd note in his voice, and I took him up sharply. 'You don't believe her?'

'I didn't say that. I only think it was pretty good going to get back to Camasunary by midnight. Loch an Athain's another mile beyond the end of Creitheach, and the going's heavy.'

'Did he let himself into the hotel?'

'It's open all night.'

'How nice,' I said. 'And Mr Hay?'

'In bed. A very difficult alibi to break.'

'Or prove.'

'As you say. Mine happens to be the same.'

'I–I'm sorry,' I said, feeling suddenly helpless. 'This is–fantastic, isn't it? I can't *believe* . . . and anyway, I've no earthly business to be questioning you as if you were Suspect Number One. I really am sorry.'

He grinned. 'That's all right. And it is your business, after all, if you're going to stay here. You've got to judge whom, if anyone, you feel safe with.'

I put a hand to my cheek. 'Oh Lord,' I said, 'I suppose so. I–I hadn't thought of that.'

He spoke quickly, with contrition. 'And I'm a fool to have mentioned it before we got back to lights and company. . . . Come along.' He took my arm and turned quickly, helping me over the boulder-strewn turf. 'We'll get back to the hotel. After all, for all you know, I *might* be Suspect Number One. This way; there's a path along the top of the ridge. We'll follow it along the hill a bit before we go down.'

I went with him, disconcerted to find that my heart was pumping violently. The night had grown perceptibly darker; we had our backs to the lucent west, and before us the ghost-moon swam in a deepening sky, where the mass of Blaven stooped like Faustus' mountain, ready to fall on us.

And its menacing shape was repeated, oddly, in a shadow that loomed in front of us, right in our path . . . a tall pile of something, heaped on the heather as if to mark the crest of the hill. Roderick Grant guided me past it without a look, but I glanced back at it uncertainly.

'What's that? A cairn?'

He flicked a casual look over his shoulder. 'That? No. It's a bonfire.'

I stopped dead, and his hand fell from my arm. He turned in surprise. I noticed all at once how still the glen was, how still and lonely. The lights of the hotel seemed a very long way off.

I said: 'A–a bonfire?' and my voice came out in a sort of croak.

He was staring at me. 'Yes. What's up?' Then his voice changed. 'Oh my God, I've done it again, haven't I? I never thought–I didn't mean to scare you. I'm a fool. . . .' He took two strides back towards me, and his hands were on my shoulders. 'Miss–Janet'–I doubt if either of us really noticed his use of my name–'don't be frightened. It's only the local Coronation celebration: they've been collecting stuff for the bonfire for weeks? It's nothing more sinister than that!' He shook me gently. 'And I promise you I'm not a murderer either!'

'I never thought you were,' I said shakily. 'It's I who'm the fool. I'm sorry.'

His hands dropped to his sides, and I saw him smiling down in the dusk. 'Then let's get back to the hotel, shall we?' he said.

We turned towards the lights of Camasunary.

After all, it was not so very late. The hotel was bright and warm and safe, and one or two people were still about. Through the lounge door I could see Hartley Corrigan and Alastair sitting over a last drink, and, nearby, Ronald Beagle placidly reading.

And the idea that any of the men that I had met could be guilty of a crime at once so revolting and so bizarre, was fantastic enough to border on lunacy. It was on a slightly shamefaced note that I said good night to Roderick Grant, and went up to my room.

The head of the staircase opened on the central point of the main upper corridor, which was like a large E, its three branches all ending in windows facing east, over the front of the hotel. My room lay in the far south-eastern corner, at the end of the lower arm of the E. The bathroom next to me was, I found, occupied, so, wrapping my white velvet housecoat round me, I set out in search of another, which I found eventually at the far end of the main corridor. I took a long time over my bath, and by the time I had finished the hotel seemed to have settled into silence for the night. I let myself softly out of the bathroom, and padded back along the now darkened corridor.

I went softly across the head of the stairs, and was almost past before I realized that someone was standing, still and quiet, at the end of the passage opposite, silhouetted against the dim window. Almost with a start, I glanced over my shoulder.

It was two people. They had not seen me, and for a very good reason. They were in one another's arms, kissing passionately.

The woman was Marcia Maling. I recognized the fall of her pale hair even before her scent reached my nostrils. I remember vaguely thinking 'Fergus?'–and then I recognized, too, the set of the man's shoulders, and the shape of his head.

Not Fergus. Nicholas.

Hurriedly I looked away, and went softly down the main corridor towards my room.

Somewhere behind me, on the other side of the passage, I heard a door shut softly.

Chapter Six

Camasunary II

It was precisely one-forty-eight a.m. when I decided that I was not going to be able to sleep, and sat up in bed, groping for the light-switch. The tiny illuminated face of my travelling-clock stared uncompromisingly back at me from the bedside table. One-forty-eight a.m. I scowled at it, and pressed the switch. Nothing happened. Then I remembered that the hotel made its own electricity, and that this was turned off at midnight. There had been a candle-stick, I recollected . . . my hand groped and found it. I struck a match and lit the candle.

I scowled at the clock again, then slipped out of bed. I was jaded and depressed, and I knew that I had already reached the stage when my failure to sleep was so actively irritating that sleep had become an impossibility. What was worse, I knew I was in for one of the blinding nervous headaches that had devastated me all too often in the last three or four years. I could feel the warning now, like a tiny electric wire thrilling behind my eyes, pain, with the elusive threat of worse pain to come.

I sat on the edge of the bed, pressing my hands hard against my eyes, trying to will the pain away, while still in my wincing brain whirled and jostled the images that, conspiring to keep sleep at bay, had switched the agonizing current along my nerves. . . . Fire at midnight . . . fire on Blaven . . . and *a gentleman from the hotel*. Corrigan? Roderick? Alastair? Nicholas?

I shivered, then flinched and stood up. I wasn't even going to try and ride this one out; I was going to dope myself out of it, and quickly. The life-saving tablets were in my handbag. I padded across the room to get it, groping vaguely among the grotesque shadows that distorted the corners of the room. But it wasn't on the dressing-table. It wasn't on the mantelpiece. Or on the floor near the hand-basin. Or by the bed. Or–it was by now a search of despair–under the bed. It wasn't anywhere in the room.

I sat down on the bed again, and made myself acknowledge the truth. I hadn't taken my handbag on that walk with Roderick Grant. I had left it in the lounge. I could see it in my mind's eye, standing there on the floor beside my chair, holding that precious pill-box, as remote from me as if it had been on a raft in the middle of the Red Sea. Because nothing, I told myself firmly, wincing from a fresh jag of pain, *nothing* was going to get me out of my room that night. If anyone was to perform the classic folly of taking a midnight stroll among the murderous gentlemen with whom the hotel was probably packed, it was not going to be me.

On this eminently sensible note I got back into bed, blew out the candle, and settled down to ride it out.

Seventeen minutes later I sat up, lit the candle again, got out of bed, and grabbed my housecoat. I had reached, in seventeen minutes of erratically increasing pain, an even more sensible decision–and how much this was a product of reason and how much of desperation I can now judge more accurately than I could then. It was quite a simple decision, and very satisfactory. I had decided that Jamesy Farlane had murdered Heather Macrae. And since Jamesy Farlane didn't live in the hotel, I could go and get my tablets in perfect safety.

Perfect safety, I told myself firmly, thrusting my feet into my slippers and knotting the girdle of my housecoat tightly round me–as long as I was *very* quick, and *very* quiet, and was prepared to scream like blazes if I saw or heard the least little thing. . . .

Without pausing to examine the logic of this corollary to my decision, I seized my candle, unlocked my door, and set off.

And at once I saw that this was not to be, after all, the classic walk through the murder-haunted house, for, although the corridor lights were of course unlit, the glimmer from the eastern windows was quite sufficient to show me my way, and to lay bare the quiet and reassuring emptiness of the passages, flanked by their closed doors. I went softly along the main corridor, shielding my candle, until I reached the stair-head.

The staircase sank down into shadow, and I hesitated for a moment, glancing involuntarily over my shoulder towards the window where I had seen Marcia and Nicholas. No one was there, this time; the window showed an empty oblong framing the pale night. I could see, quite distinct against the nebulous near-light of the sky, the massive outline of Blaven's shoulder. The moon had gone.

Then I heard the whispering. I must have been listening to it, half-unconsciously, during the few seconds I had been standing there, for when at length my conscious mind registered, with a jerk, the fact that two people were whispering behind the door to my right, I knew immediately that the sound had been going on all along.

It should have reassured me to know that someone else was still awake; it certainly shouldn't have disturbed and frightened me, but that is just what it did. There was, of course, no reason why someone else in the hotel should not be sleepless too. If Colonel Cowdray-Simpson and his wife, or the Corrigans, were wakeful, and consequently talkative, at this ungodly hour, they would certainly keep their voices down to avoid disturbing the other guests. But there was something about the quality of the whispering that was oddly disquieting. It was as if the soft, almost breathless ripple of sound in the darkness held some sort of desperation, some human urgency, whether of anger or passion or fear, which communicated itself to me through the closed panels, and made the hairs prickle along my forearms as if a draught of chilly wind had crept through a crack in the door.

I turned to go, and a board creaked as my weight shifted.

The whispering stopped. It stopped as abruptly as an engine shuts off steam. Silence dropped like a blanket, so that in a matter of seconds the memory of the sound seemed illusory, while the silence itself surged with millions of whisperings, all equally unreal. But the sense of desperation was still there, even in the silence. It was as if the stillness were a held breath, that might burst at any moment in a scream.

I moved away quickly–and tripped over a pair of shoes which had been standing in the corridor waiting to be cleaned in the morning. The carpet was thick, but the small sound, in that hush, was like thunder. I heard a muffled exclamation from behind the door, then, staccato, sibilant, the splutter of a question. A deeper voice said something in reply.

There was only one pair of shoes: a woman's. I hastily retrieved the one I had kicked over, and put it back beside its fellow. They were hand-made Laforgues, exquisite, absurd things with four-inch heels. Marcia Maling's.

There was silence now behind the door. I almost ran down the stairs, plunging, heedless of the streaming candle-flame, into the darker depths of the hall. I felt angry and ashamed and sick, as if I myself had been caught out in some questionable action. God knew, I thought bitterly, as I crossed the hall and pushed open the glass door of the lounge, it was none of my business, but all the same. . . . She had, after all, only met Nicholas to-night. And where was Fergus in all this? Surely I hadn't misread the hints she had dropped about Fergus? And where, too, did Hartley Corrigan come in, I wondered, remembering the look in his eyes, and, even more significantly, the look in his wife's face.

And here I paid for my speed and my heedlessness as the swing door rushed shut behind me and tore the flame from my candle into a long streamer of sharp-smelling smoke. Shadows surged up towards me, pouncing from the corners of the dim lounge, and I halted in my tracks and put a hand back to the door, already half in retreat towards the safety of my room. But the lounge was untenanted save by those shadows; in the glow of the banked peat fire I could see it all now clearly enough. I threw one haunted glance back at the hall beyond the glass door, then I went very quietly across the lounge towards where I knew my handbag ought to lie.

Marcia and Nicholas . . . the coupled names thrust themselves back into my mind. The odd thing about it, I thought, was that one couldn't dislike Marcia Maling–though I might feel differently about it if, like Mrs

Corrigan, I had a man to lose. It was to be supposed—I skirted a coffee-table with some care—it was to be supposed that she couldn't help it. There was a long and ugly name for her kind of woman, but, remembering her vivid, generous beauty as she sat opposite me in this very room, I could not find it in me to dislike her. She was impossible, she was wanton, but she was amusing, and very lovely, and, I thought, kind. Perhaps she was even being kind to me, in a queer way, by attracting Nicholas' attention to herself when she guessed I wished to escape it—though this, I felt, was perhaps giving a little too much credit to Miss Maling's disinterested crusading spirit.

I grinned wryly to myself as I stooped and groped beside the chair for my precious handbag. My fingers met nothing. I felt anxiously along the empty floor, sweeping my hands round in little questing circles that grew wider and more urgent with failure . . . and then I saw the faint glint of the bag's metal clasp, not on the floor, but on a level with my eye as I stooped. Someone must have picked it up and put it on the book-shelf beside the chair. I grabbed it, yanked out with it some magazines and a couple of books, and flew back across the lounge with my long skirts billowing behind me.

I was actually at the glass door, and shoving it open with my shoulder, when I heard the outer door of the hotel porch open, very quietly. I stood stock still, clutching books and bag and dead candle to a suddenly thudding heart.

Someone came softly into the porch. I heard the scrape of a nailed boot on the flags, and faint sounds as he moved about among the climbing and fishing gear that always cluttered the place. I waited. Roderick Grant had told me the hotel stayed open all night: this was surely—*surely*—nothing more sinister than some late fisherman, putting his things away. That was all.

But all the same, I was not going to cross the hall and climb the stairs in full view of him whoever he was. So I waited, trying to still my sickening heart-beats, backing away from the glass door as I remembered my white housecoat.

Then the outer door opened and shut again, just as softly as before, and, clear in the still night, I heard his boots crunch once, twice, on the gravel road. I hesitated only for a moment, then I shouldered aside the glass door and flew across the hall to the outer porch, peering after him through the window.

The valley was mist-dimmed, and full of vague shadows, but I saw him. He had stepped off the gravel on to the grass and was walking quickly away, head bent, along the verge of the road towards Strathaird. A man, slim, tallish, who walked with a long, swinging stride. I saw him pause once, and turn, looking back over his shoulder, but his face was no more than a dim blur. Then he vanished into the shadows.

I turned back from the window in the not-quite-darkness, gazing round the little porch. My eyes had adjusted themselves now: I could see the table, with its weighing-machine and the white enamel trays for fish; the wicker chairs holding rucksacks, boots, fishing-nets; pale ovals of climbing-rope depending from pegs; coats and mackintoshes, scarves and caps, fishing-rods and walking-sticks. . . .

Behind me the door opened without a sound, and a man came quietly in out of the night.

I didn't scream, after all. Perhaps I couldn't. I merely dropped everything with a crash that seemed to shake the hotel, and then stood, dumb and paralysed, with my mouth open.

The porch door swung to with a bang behind him. He jerked out a startled oath, and then, with a click, a torch-beam shot out and raked me, blindingly.

He said: 'Janet!' And then laughed. 'My God, but you startled me! What on earth are you doing down here at this hour?'

I blinked into the light, which went off.

'Alastair?'

'The same.' He swung his haversack from his shoulder, and began to take off his Burberry. 'What was that you dropped? It sounded like an atom-bomb.'

'Books mostly,' I said. 'I couldn't sleep.'

'Oh.' He laughed again, and pitched his coat over a chair. 'You looked like a ghost standing there in that white thing. I was unmanned; but positively. I nearly screamed.'

'So did I.' I stooped to pick up my things. 'I'd better go back to bed.'

He had a foot up on one of the chairs. 'If you'd stay half a minute more and hold the torch for me, Janet, I could get these blasted bootlaces undone. They're wet.'

I took the torch. 'Is it raining?'

'In fits and starts.'

'You've been fishing, I suppose?'

'Yes. Up the Strath.'

'Any luck?'

'Pretty fair. I got two or three good trout; and Hart took a beauty; one and a half pounds.'

'Hart? Oh—Hartley Corrigan.'

'Mm. Don't wave the light about, my girl.'

'Sorry. Is Mr Corrigan not back yet, then?'

'Lord, yes. He came back a couple of hours since, but I'd just had some good rises, so I stayed. Strictly illegal, of course, so don't tell on me, will you?'

'Illegal?'

'It's the Sabbath, my dear, had you forgotten? I should have stopped at midnight, like Hart.' He pulled his second boot off, and straightened up.

'His fish aren't in the tray,' I said.

'What?' His eyes followed the torch-beam to the table. 'Neither they are . . . that's odd.'

'Alastair.'

He turned his head sharply at the note in my voice.

'Well?'

I said, baldly: 'Someone came into this porch five minutes ago, messed around for a bit, and then went out again.'

'What? Oh—' he laughed. 'Don't sound so worried! That would be Jamesy.'

'*Jamesy?*'

'Jamesy Farlane; he was out with us. He's a better walker than I am, and he was in a hurry. He lives some way over towards Strathaird.'

'I see,' I said. I swallowed hard.

'Did you think he was a burglar? You don't need to worry about such urban horrors here, Janet. Nobody locks their doors in the Islands. There aren't such things as thieves.'

'No,' I said. I put the torch down on the table, and turned to go. 'Only murderers.'

I heard the sharp intake of his breath.

'Who told you?'

'Roderick Grant.'

'I see. Worried?'

'Naturally.'

He said: 'I shouldn't be. Whatever it was all about, it can't touch you.'

'I wasn't worried about myself.'

'Who, then?' He sounded wary.

I said, with an edge to my voice: 'Heather Macrae, of course. The girl—and her people. What had she done that a filthy grotesque thing like that should catch up with her? What was it all about? There's something more than queer about it, Alastair. I can't explain just how I feel about it, but it—it's somehow particularly nasty.'

He said, inadequately: 'Murder's never pretty.'

'But it can be plain,' I said, 'and this isn't just plain, wicked murder. She wasn't just hit or stabbed or choked in a fit of human passion. She was deliberately done to death, and then—arranged. It was cold-blooded, calculating, and—and *evil*. Yes, evil. Here, too, of all places, where you'd think that sort of perverted ugliness had no existence. It's haunting me, Alastair.'

He said, a little lamely: 'The police are still on it, and they won't let up, you know.'

I said: 'Who do you think did it?'

'Janet—'

'You must have thought about it. Who? Jamesy Farlane?'

'I—look, Janet, I wouldn't talk too much about it—'

I said: 'You mean, in case it's someone in the hotel?'

He said, uncomfortably: 'Well—'

'*Do* you think it's someone in the hotel?'

'I don't know. I—don't—know. If it frightens you, my dear, why don't you go somewhere else? Broadford, or Portree, or—'

'I'm staying here,' I said. 'I want to be here when they do nose out this devil, whoever he is. *Whoever* he is.'

He was silent.

I said: 'Good night, Alastair,' and went back upstairs to my room.

I never took the tablets, after all. My dead-of-night walk among the murderers must have been the kind of shock-therapy that my headache needed, for when I got back to my room I realized that the pain had completely gone.

I got into bed and surveyed the rest of my booty.

I had got, I discovered, two copies of *The Autocar*; the books were *The Bride of Lammermoor*, and the abridged edition of Frazer's *Golden Bough*.

The Bride of Lammermoor put me to sleep in something under ten minutes.

Chapter Seven

Sgurr na Stri

Next morning, sure enough, it was raining, with a small, persistent, wetting rain. The sheep grazing in the glen near the hotel looked damp and miserable, and all but the nearest landmarks were invisible. Even Sgurr na Stri, just beyond the river, was dim in its shroud of grey.

When I came down, a little late, to breakfast, the place was quiet, though this was the Sabbath quiet rather than a depression due to the weather. I could see Alastair Braine and the Corrigans sitting over newspapers in the lounge, while Mrs Cowdray-Simpson and the old lady had already brought their knitting into play. There were, however, signs that even a wet Sunday in the Highlands could not damp some enthusiasms; Colonel Cowdray-Simpson, at the grille of the manager's office, was conducting a solemn discussion on flies with Major Persimmon and a big countryman in respectable black; Marion Bradford and Roberta were in the porch, staring out at the wet landscape; and near them Roderick Grant bent, absorbed, over a landing-net that he was mending with a piece of string.

He looked up, saw me, and grinned. 'Hullo. It's too bad it's Sunday, isn't it? Wouldn't you have loved a nice day's fishing in the rain?'

'No, thank you,' I said with decision. 'I suppose this is what you fishing maniacs call ideal weather?'

'Oh, excellent.' He cocked an eye at the sullen prospect. 'Though it mightn't prove too dismal even for laymen. This is the sort of day that can clear up in a flash. Miss Symes might get her climb after all.'

'Do you think so?' Roberta turned eagerly.

'It's possible. But'—he shot a wary half-glance at Marion Bradford's back, still uncompromisingly turned—'be careful if you do go, and don't get up too high. The mist can drop again just as quickly as it can rise.'

He had spoken quietly, but Marion Bradford heard. She turned and sent him a smouldering look.

'More good advice?' she asked in that tense, over-defiant voice that made anything she said sound like an insult.

Roberta said quickly: 'It's good of Mr Grant to bother, Marion. He knows I know nothing about it.'

.

Marion Bradford looked as if she would like to retort, but she merely pressed her lips together and turned back to stare out of the window. Roderick smiled at Roberta and turned his attention to his landing-net. Then Ronald Beagle came out into the porch, with a rucksack on his back.

'Why,' said Roberta, 'Mr Beagle's going. Are you really going up Sgurr nan Gillean in this, Mr Beagle?'

'I think it'll clear,' said Beagle. 'I'm going over there anyway, and if it clears in an hour or so, as I think it will, I'll be ready.' He waves vaguely to all of us, and went out into the rain.

'Well,' I said to Roberta, 'both the oracles have spoken, so I hope you do get your climb.'

'Are you going out too?'

'My dear, I haven't even had my breakfast yet! And if I don't hurry I doubt if I'll get any!'

But as I was half-way across the hall towards the dining-room I was stopped by Major Persimmon's voice calling me from the office grille. I went over. The tall, thickset countryman was still there, bending over a tray of casts, his big fingers moving them delicately.

Bill Persimmon leaned forward across the counter.

'I believe you said you wanted to hire a rod, Mrs—er, Miss Brooke, and fish a bit?'

'Yes, I do, but I'm not quite sure when. I think I might wait a day or so, and have a look round first.'

'Just as you like, of course, only—' He glanced at the other man. 'If you'd really like to be shown some fishing, you might care to fix it up in advance with Dougal Macrae here. He'd be glad to go with you, I know.'

The big man looked up. He had a square, brown face, deeply lined, and smallish blue eyes that looked as if, normally, they were good tempered. Just now, they held no expression at all.

He said, in the wonderfully soft voice of the Island men: 'I should be glad to show the lady how to take a fish.'

'That's very good of you,' I said. 'Perhaps—shall we say Wednesday?'

'Wednesday iss a free day.' Dougal Macrae nodded his big head. 'Yess, indeed.'

'Thank you very much,' I said.

'Where shall I put you down for?' asked Major Persimmon.

Dougal Macrae said: 'The Camasunary river, please; the upper beat. If we cannot take a fish out of there it will be a bad day indeed.'

He straightened up, and picked up a well-brushed and formidable bowler hat from the office counter. 'And now I must be on my way, or I shall be late at the kirk. Good day to you, mistress. Good day, Major Persimmon.'

And he went out into the grey morning. I found myself looking after him. It had been only the most trivial of conversations, but it was my first acquaintance with the beautifully simple courtesy of the Highlander, the natural but almost royally formal bearing of the crofter who has lived all his life in the Islands. I was very much impressed with this quiet man. Dougal Macrae. Heather Macrae's father. . . .

I nodded to Major Persimmon, and went to get my belated breakfast.

I had been (rather foolishly, I suppose) dreading my next meeting with

Marcia, so I was glad that she was not in the dining-room. Indeed, before I had poured out my first cup of coffee, I saw a big cream-coloured car come slowly past the window, and slide to a halt outside the porch door. Almost immediately Marcia, looking enchanting and very urban in royal blue, hurried out of the hotel and was ushered into the front of the car by a handsome boy in uniform, who tucked rugs round her with solicitous care. Still in expensive and effortless silence, the car moved off.

I drank coffee, wishing I had a morning paper, so that I could pretend I hadn't noticed Nicholas who, apart from Hubert Hay, was the only other occupant of the dining-room.

But it was after all the latter who in a short while rose and came over to my table.

He walked with an odd, tittupping little step that made me think again of Marcia's bouncy rubber balls, or of a self-confident robin. This latter impression was heightened by the rounded expanse of scarlet pullover which enlivened his already gay green tweeds. His face was round, too, with a small pernickety mouth, and pale eyes set in a multitude of radiating wrinkles. He had neat little hands, and wore a big gold ring set with a black stone.

He smiled at me, showing a flash of gold in his mouth.

'Miss–er–Brooke? My name is Hay.'

'How do you do?' I murmured politely.

'I hope you don't mind me coming over to speak, Miss Brooke, but the fact is'–he hesitated, and looked at me a little shyly–'the fact is, I wanted to ask a favour.'

'Of course.' I wondered what on earth was coming next.

'You see,' he went on, still with that bashful expression that sat comically upon his round face, 'you see, I'm footloose.'

'You're *what?*' I said, startled.

'Footloose.'

'That's what I thought you said. But—'

'It's my nom de ploom,' he said. 'I'm a writer.' The scarlet pullover broadened perceptibly. 'Footloose.'

'Oh, I see! A writer–but how very clever of you, Mr Hay. Er, novels, is it?'

'Travel books, Miss Brooke, travel books. I bring beauty to you at the fireside–that's what we put on the covers, you know. "To you in your armchair I bring the glories of the English countryside." And,' he added fairly, 'the Scotch. That's why I'm here.'

'I see. Collecting material?'

'Takin' walks,' said Hubert Hay simply. 'I go walks, and write about them, with maps. Then I mark them A, B, or C, according as to how difficult they are, and give them one, two, or three stars according as to if they're pretty.'

'How–very original,' I said lamely, conscious of Nicholas sitting well within hearing. 'It must take a lot of time.'

'It's dead easy,' said Hubert Hay frankly, 'that is, if you can write like I can. I've always had the knack, somehow. And it pays all right.'

'I shall look out for your books,' I promised, and he beamed down at me.

'I'll send you one, I will indeed. The last one was called *Sauntering in Somerset*. You'd like it. And they're not *books* really, in a manner of speaking–they're paper-backs. I think the best I ever did was *Wandering through Wales*. I'll send you that too.'

'Thank you very much.'

I noticed then that he was holding an old *Tatler* and a *Country Life* in his hand. He put the two magazines down on the table and tapped them with a forefinger.

'I saw your photo in these,' he said. 'It *is* you, isn't it?'

'Yes.'

He leafed through *Country Life* until he found the picture. It was me, all right, a David Gallien photograph in tweeds, with a brace of lovely Irish setters stealing the picture. Hubert Hay looked at me, all at once shy again.

'I take photos for my books,' he said hesitantly.

I waited, feeling rather helpless. Out of the corner of my eye I saw Nicholas stand up, and begin leisurely to feel in his pockets for tobacco. Hubert Hay said, with a rush: 'When these geology chaps take a picture of a rock, they put a hammer in to show you the scale. I thought if I took a picture of the Coolins I'd like to–to put a lady in, so that you could tell how big the hills were, and how far away.'

Nicholas was grinning. I sensed rather than saw it. Hubert Hay looked at me across David Gallien's beautifully composed advertisement, and said, wistfully: 'And you do photograph nice, you do really.'

Nicholas said casually: 'You'd better find out what she charges. I believe it comes pretty high.'

Hubert Hay looked at him, and then back at me, in a kind of naïve bewilderment. 'I–shouldn't I have—?'

He looked so confused, so uncharacteristically ready to be deflated, that I forgot my own embarrassment, and Hugo Montefior's probable apoplexy. I looked furiously at Nicholas. 'Mr Drury was joking,' I said swiftly. 'Of course you may take a picture of me if you want to, Mr Hay. I'd love to be in your book. When shall we do it?'

He flushed with pleasure, and the scarlet pullover expanded again to its original robin-roundness. 'That's very kind of you, I'm sure, very kind indeed. I'm honoured, I am really. If it clears up, how about this afternoon, on Sgurr na Stri, with the Coolins behind?'

'Fine,' I said firmly.

'Bill Persimmon has a spaniel.' Nicholas' voice was bland.

'Has he?' Hubert Hay took that one happily at its face value. 'Maybe that's a good idea, too. I'll go and ask him if we can borrow it.'

He trotted gaily off. Nicholas stood looking down at me, still with that expression of sardonic amusement that I hated. 'What's Hugo going to say when he sees you starring in *Staggering through Skye*, or whatever this masterpiece is going to be called?'

'He won't see it,' I said tartly, as I rose. 'The only travelling Hugo's interested in is Air France to Paris and back.'

I started after Hubert Hay, but Nicholas moved, barring my way to the door.

'I want to talk to you, Gianetta.'

I regarded him coldly. 'I can't think that we have much to say to one another.'

'I still want to talk to you.'

'What about?'

'About us.'

I raised my eyebrows. 'There isn't any "us", Nicholas. Remember? We're not bracketed together any more. There's a separate you and a separate me, and nothing to join us together. Not even a name.'

His mouth tightened. 'I'm very well aware of that.'

I said, before I realized what I was saying: 'Was that you with Marcia Maling last night?'

His eyes flickered, and then went blank. He said: 'Yes.'

I walked past him out of the room.

The oracles had been right. By eleven o'clock the rain had cleared, and the clouds began to lift with startling rapidity. I saw Marion Bradford and Roberta set off up the valley about half an hour later, and, not long afterwards, Nicholas went out along the track towards Strathaird.

Shortly before noon, the sun struggled out, and, in a moment, it seemed, the sky was clear and blue, and the mist was melting from the mountain-tops like snow. Sedge and heather glittered with a mass of jewels, and the frail gossamers sagged between the heather-tips weighted with a Titania's ransom of diamonds.

Hubert Hay and I set out with Bill Persimmon's spaniel soon after lunch. We went down through the little birch-grove to the stepping-stones which spanned the Camasunary river. The birches were old and lichened, but they moved lightly in the wind, censing the bright air with rain-drops, an intermittent sun-shower that we had to dodge as we took a short cut through the grove towards the river, picking our way over the wet bilberry-leaves and mosses and the scattered chunks of fungus that had fallen from the trees.

We crossed the river by the stepping-stones, and, after an hour or so of steep but not-too-difficult walking, reached the crest of Sgurr na Stri. Hubert Hay, for all his rotundity, was light on his feet, and proved, a little to my surprise, to be an entertaining companion. His knowledge and love of the countryside was not as superficial as our conversation had led me to expect; he talked knowingly of birds and deer and hill-foxes, and knew, it appeared, a good deal about plants. He babbled on as he chose his 'picture' and set his camera, and though he talked incessantly in clichés, I could sense that his satisfaction in what he called 'the great outdoors' was deep and genuine. His resemblance to a cocky little robin became every minute more remarkable, but the quality that Marcia had called 'sorbo' was, I discovered, due to an irrepressible gaiety, a delighted curiosity about everything, rather than to self-satisfaction. He was, in fact, a rather attractive little man.

We took three photographs. From the top of Sgurr na Stri you can see the whole range of the Black Cuillin, the forbidding arc that sweeps from Garsven in the south to Sgurr nan Gillean in the north, with Loch Coruisk, black as an inkwell, cupped in the roots of the mountains. I posed with the spaniel, an aristocratic but witless beast, against mountain, sky, and loch in turn, while Hubert Hay fussed with his camera and darted from one point to another with little cries of polite satisfaction.

When at length he had finished we sat down together on a rock, and lit cigarettes. He seemed to have something on his mind, and smoked jerkily for a bit. Then he said:

'Miss Brooke, do you–d'you mind me saying something to you?'

'Of course not. What is it?'

'You're here alone, aren't you?'

'Yes.'

His round face was worried as he looked at me earnestly. 'Don't go out by yourself with anyone, Miss Brooke. You're all right with me here to-day, of course, but you weren't to know that.' His rather absurd voice was somehow scarifying in its vehemence. '*But don't go with anyone else.* It's not safe.'

I said nothing for a moment. I realized that I had, actually, since breakfast that morning, forgotten the sort of danger that was walking these hills.

'You don't mind me saying?' asked Hubert Hay anxiously.

'Of course not. You're perfectly right. I promise you I'll be careful.' There was a certain irony about the admonition, repeating as it did Roderick Grant's warning of the night before. Could I, then, eliminate two of the suspects among the 'gentlemen from the hotel', or were these warnings some subtle kind of double bluff? If I went on going for walks with the 'gentlemen', no doubt I should find out soon enough. I shivered a little, and pulled the dog's ears. 'It's not a very pleasant thought, is it?'

His face flushed dark red. 'It's damnable! I–I beg your pardon, I'm sure. But that's the only word I can think of. Miss Brooke'–he turned to me with a queer, almost violent gesture–'that girl, Heather Macrae–she was only eighteen!'

I said nothing.

'It was her birthday.' His funny high little voice held a note almost of savagery. 'Her eighteenth birthday.' He took a pull at his cigarette, and then spoke more calmly: 'I feel it a bit, Miss Brooke. You see, I knew her.'

'You knew her? Well?'

'Oh dear no. Only to speak to, as you might say. I'd stopped at the croft a couple of times, when I was out walking, and she'd made me a pot of tea. She was a pretty girl, gay and a bit cheeky, and kind of full of life. There wasn't a bit of badness in her. Nothing to ask for–what she got.'

'*You* didn't get any hint as to who she was going with?' It was a silly question, of course, as the police would have gone over the ground with meticulous thoroughness, but he answered without impatience: 'No, none at all.'

But his voice had altered subtly, so that I glanced at him. 'You got *something*?'

'A very little hint,' he said carefully. 'I told her that I was writing a book, of course, and she was interested: people usually are. . . . She said that quite a lot of folks came around the crofts, one way and another, asking questions about local customs and superstitions and the like. I asked her if she had any special superstitions–just joking-like–and she said no, of course not, she was a modern girl. Then I said wasn't there any magic still going on in the Islands like there used to be, and'–he turned pale round eyes on me–'she shut up like an oyster, and pretty near hustled me out of the kitchen.'

'*Magic?*' I said. 'But that's absurd!'

He nodded. 'I know. But, you know, I can't help having a feeling about this murder. It must have been all *planned*, you see. The stuff he'd used for the bonfire must have been taken up there, bit by bit, quite deliberately. There was heather and peat and branches of birchwood, and a big chunk of oak hardly charred, and a lot of that dry fungus–agaric–that you get on birch-trees.'

I made an exclamation, but he hadn't heard me. 'Then, when he is ready, he gets the girl up there. . . . Just think a minute, if you'll excuse me bringing it up again . . . the fire, and the shoes and things in a neat pile, all tidy, and the girl laid out with her throat cut and her hands crossed, and ashes on her face. . . . Why, it's like a–a *sacrifice!*'

The last word came out with a jerk. I was on my feet, staring down at him, with my spine prickling.

'But that's *crazy!*'

The pale, troubled eyes glanced up. 'That's just it, isn't it? Whoever did it must be just plain crazy. And he looks and acts just as sane as you or me . . . except sometimes.' He got to his feet and regarded me solemnly. 'So I wouldn't go for walks with anybody, if I was you.'

'I won't,' I said fervently. 'In fact, I'm beginning to think that I might go back to London, after all.'

'It wouldn't be a bad idea, at that,' said he, picking up his camera, and turning to follow me down the hill.

Chapter Eight

Camasunary III

I was still wondering if it wouldn't, after all, be wisest to ditch my plans and leave the hotel, when something happened that made me decide, at any rate for the time being, that I must stay.

It was in the lounge, after dinner, that the first stirrings of a new uneasiness began to make themselves plain. Alastair Braine, carrying coffee-cups, paused in the middle of the room and said, on a slight note of surprise: 'Hullo, aren't the climbers back yet?'

'They weren't at dinner,' said Alma Corrigan.

Colonel Cowdray-Simpson said: 'Good God, neither they were. I hope there's nothing amiss.'

'That fool woman!' said Mrs Cowdray-Simpson, roundly. 'She shouldn't have gone up on a day like this.'

Alastair said reassuringly: 'I shouldn't worry. They've probably only gone a little further than they meant to, and after all, it's still light.'

Nicholas looked up from a letter he was writing. 'The weather was clearing nicely when they went, and there's been no mist on Blaven this afternoon. They'll be all right.'

'If only,' said Marcia Maling, 'if only that *awful* woman hasn't gone and done something silly, just to impress! That *poor* child Roberta—'

Roderick Grant said quietly: 'Miss Bradford is actually a very accomplished climber. She wouldn't take any risks with a beginner. And Drury is quite right about the weather. After all, Ronald Beagle went up Sgurr nan Gillean, and he certainly wouldn't have gone if it hadn't been all right.'

'He's not back either,' said Hubert Hay.

There was a little silence. I sensed discomfort and uneasiness growing.

'Neither he is,' said Alma Corrigan, rather stupidly. 'Well, I suppose—'

'Where's your husband?' asked Mrs Cowdray-Simpson.

The question sounded abrupt, but there was nothing in it to make Alma Corrigan flush scarlet, as she did. 'He–he went out walking.'

She was so obviously embarrassed that everybody else began to feel embarrassed too, without knowing the reason. Alastair said quickly: 'We all went out after lunch to walk up to the ridge for the view over Loch Slapin. I brought Mrs Corrigan back but Hart went further.'

'Oh, you went that way? Did you see the women, then, on Blaven?' asked Colonel Cowdray-Simpson.

'Not a sign. We saw someone–I believe it was Drury–in the distance, but not another living soul.'

'I wasn't on Blaven,' said Nicholas, 'so I didn't see them either.'

Roderick Grant put down his coffee-cup and got to his feet. 'It's only eight-thirty, and I don't personally think we need to worry yet, but they certainly should have got back by this. I think I'll have a word with Bill. They may have told him if they were going to be late.'

He went quickly into the hall, where I could see him leaning over the office counter, in earnest conversation with Major Persimmon.

'Sensible chap,' said Colonel Cowdray-Simpson. 'No point in starting a fuss.'

But Marcia was not to be stopped so easily. 'This is *too* ghastly, isn't it? What d'you suppose *could* have happened to them?'

'Plenty of things can happen in the Cuillin,' said Alma Corrigan, rather tartly, 'and altogether too many things have been happening lately.'

'*That* affair?' said Alastair. 'That can hardly have any connection—'

'I'm not talking about the murder,' said Alma brutally, I heard Marcia give a little gasp. 'I'm talking about climbing accidents.' She looked round the circle of faces, her fine eyes serious and a little frightened. 'Do you realize how many people have been killed by the Cuillin, this year alone?'

Her use of the preposition gave the sentence an oddly macabre twist, and I saw Marcia glance over her shoulder to where the great hills towered against the massed clouds of evening. 'Is it–a lot?' She sounded a little awe-stricken.

'Four,' said Alma Corrigan, and added, almost absently, 'so far. . . .'

I felt the little cold caress of fear along the back of my neck, and was grateful for the Colonel's brisk interposition. 'Well,' he said, practically, 'if people will go wandering out in these mountains with only the haziest ideas about how to climb them, they must expect accidents. In almost every case these mishaps are brought about by ignorance or carelessness, and I'm sure we can acquit both Beagle and Miss Bradford on both those grounds. We're making an unnecessary fuss, and I think we'd better stop talking about it and frightening ourselves.'

He turned to Alastair with some remark about to-morrow's sport, and in a few minutes tension seemed to be relieved, and people were chatting generally.

I turned to Marcia Maling. 'Where did you go to-day?'

'To Portree, my dear'—her face lit up with the familiar warm *gamine* charm—'along the most *ghastly* roads, with poor dear Fergus snarling like a tom-cat all the way because he'd just washed the car!'

'I thought there was an excellent road from Broadford?'

'Oh, there is. But it goes *snaking* about with the most *ghastly* hairpin bends and cliffs and things—'

'But, Marcia, the views—'

The views were dismissed with a wave of her cigarette. 'It was divine, of course,' she said quickly, 'only it was raining. And then Portree on a Sunday is the utter *end*. But I got some marvellous tweed there on Friday; I'll show it to you to-night. It's a sort of misty purple, and quite gorgeous.'

But here Roderick came back into the lounge, and there was a lull in the conversation as eyes turned towards him.

'Bill Persimmon says there's no earthly reason to worry,' he said reassuringly, but, as he crossed the room towards me, I thought I saw uneasiness in the glance he cast at the sky outside.

Someone switched on the radio, and the lugubrious weather-report insinuated itself into the conversation. Colonel Cowdray-Simpson moved nearer to listen.

'Waiting for news of Everest,' said Roderick to me with a grin. 'That, with the notable absence of fish in the rivers, seems to be the Colonel's main preoccupation.'

'He's rather sweet,' I said. 'I'd hate him to be disappointed, but, you know, I have the oddest feeling about Everest . . . I believe I'd be almost sorry to see it climbed.'

'Sorry?' He looked at me curiously. 'Why on earth?'

I laughed. 'Not really, I suppose. But I'd always imagined it as the last inviolate spot that arrogant man hadn't smeared himself over, sort of remote and white and unattainable. Immaculate, that's the word I want. I somehow think it would be a pity to see man's footmarks in the snow.'

'I didn't know you were a poet, Gianetta,' said Nicholas' voice above me, lazily mocking. He had come over to the window just behind my chair.

I felt myself flushing, and Roderick looked a little annoyed.

'Why should you? I didn't know you knew Miss Brooke.'

His voice was curt. Nicholas eyed him for a moment.

'Why should you?' he echoed, unpleasantly, and turned away to the window. 'And here, if I'm not mistaken, is our friend Beagle at last.'

'Alone?' asked Mrs Cowdray-Simpson.

'Yes . . . that's odd.'

'What's odd?' asked Alastair, joining him.

'He's coming down the glen from Loch na Creitheach. I thought he went up Sgurr nan Gillean,' said Nicholas thoughtfully. 'Wouldn't it have been easier for him to come down the west side of the glen and over the stepping-stones?'

'There's nothing in it,' said Alastair. 'That's a shorter way, certainly, but the going's terrible, while there's a path down the Blaven side of Creitheach.'

Roderick said: 'He may have seen the two women, if he's come along the glen. It's still light enough to see someone on the south ridge.'

But Beagle, when he came in, denied that he had seen anyone. And the worried look that came over his face when he heard that the two girls were still out, brought back with a rush the apprehensions that we had been trying to dismiss. He went to change and eat a late meal, and we all sat, talking in fits and starts, and trying not to look out of the window too often, for another half-hour of steadily mounting anxiety.

By half-past nine it was pretty dark. Rain-clouds had massed in great indigo banks right across the sky, shutting out any speck of residual light that might linger in the west. Wisps of wet mist scudded underneath the high cloud, and the fingers of the gusty wind clawed at the windows, flinging rain in spasmodic handfuls against the glass. By now everybody, I think, was convinced that something had happened to the two women, and it was almost a relief when, at nine-thirty exactly, Bill Persimmon came into the lounge and said, without preamble:

'I think we'd better go out and look for them. Mr Corrigan has just come in with Dougal, and they say there's still no sign of them coming down the glen.'

The men were on their feet.

'You're sure they went up Blaven?'

Persimmon said: 'Certain. They—'

'They might have changed their minds,' said Nicholas.

Bill Persimmon looked at him, queerly, I thought. He said, slowly: 'They went to Blaven, all right. They were seen on it.'

'Seen?' said Roderick. 'When? Whereabouts?'

'At the Sputan Dhu,' said Persimmon dryly.

Ronald Beagle started forward. 'At the—but my God, man, that's no place for a beginner! The Black Spout! That's a devilish tricky climb. Are you sure, Persimmon?'

We all stared at Bill Persimmon, while our imagined fears gradually assumed a horrible reality.

'Who saw them?' asked Nicholas quickly.

Bill looked at him again. 'Dougal Macrae. He saw them making for the gully at about four o'clock. All three of them.'

My throat was suddenly dry. I heard myself say in a strange voice: 'All *three* of them?'

He nodded, and his eyes went round the group of faces where a new sort of fear was beginning to dawn. He said: 'Dougal says there were three. And . . . everybody else is back. Odd, isn't it?'

'Perhaps they had a guide,' said Nicholas.

'They set out without one,' said Roderick.

Bill Persimmon backed to the swing door, thrusting it open with his shoulder. 'We'll discuss it after we've found them and brought them in,' he said. 'The ladies would be well advised to stay indoors. Will the men be ready in five minutes? Come along to the kitchen then, and my wife'll have sandwiches and coffee ready.'

I got up. 'Can't we help there?'

'That would be very good of you, ma'am. I expect she'd be glad of a hand.'

Then he pushed through the door with the other men after him.

When, at length, they had all gone out into the gusty dark, I went slowly back to the lounge. I was thinking, not very coherently, about Dougal Macrae's story. Three climbers? *Three?*

There could be no possible connection, of course—but I found myself wondering what Jamesy Farlane looked like.

Alma Corrigan had gone to bed, and Mrs Cowdray-Simpson was upstairs with her mother-in-law. Marcia and I were alone again in the lounge. The curtains had been drawn to shut out the storm, but the rain was hurtling against the windows in fistfuls, and the wind sounded vicious. Behind its spasmodic bursts of violence droned the steady sound of the sea.

Marcia shivered, and stretched her legs to the fire. Her eyes looked big and scared.

'Isn't this too utterly ghastly?' she said, and through the outworn extravagance of the phrase I could hear the strain plucking at her throat.

'I'm afraid it does look as if something had happened,' I said. 'Look, I brought us both a drink, Marcia.'

'Oh, you angel.' She took the glass and drank a generous mouthful. 'My God, I needed that!' She leaned forward in her chair. The big eyes seemed bigger than ever. 'Janet, do you believe there *is* a hoodoo on that mountain?'

I gave a laugh that was probably not very convincing. 'No, of course not. They just went climbing in too hard a place and got stuck. It's always happening. They'll turn up all right.'

'But—the other climber?'

'Whoever it was,' I said robustly, 'it certainly wasn't a ghost.'

She gave a little sigh. 'Well, the quicker they're found the sooner to sleep. I hope to heaven nothing's happened to that Roberta child. She's rather sweet—pathetic, in a way. I wonder—'

'It was the other one I found pathetic,' I said, and then realized with a shock that I had spoken in the past tense.

But Marcia had not noticed. 'That ghastly Bradford woman? But my dear, she's *impossible!* Not that I'd want anything to happen to her, but really—'

'She must be a very unhappy woman,' I said, 'to be like that. She must know she's making everybody dislike her, and yet some devil inside her drives her perpetually to antagonize everyone she meets.'

'Frustrated,' said Marcia cruelly, '*and* how. She's in love with Roderick Grant.'

I set down my glass with a click, and spoke almost angrily. 'Marcia! That's absurd!'

She giggled. She looked like a very pretty cat. 'It is not. Haven't you seen the way she looks at him?'

I said sharply: 'Don't talk nonsense. She was abominably rude to him, both last night and this morning. I heard her.'

'Uh-huh,' said Marcia, on a rising note of mockery. 'All the same, you watch the way she looks at him. It's just about as noticeable as the way he *doesn't* look at her—just looks down his nose in that charming well-bred way he has, and then jumps at the chance of taking *you* for a walk! If I were you, darling, I'd keep out of her range.'

'Oh, nonsense,' I said again, feeling horribly uncomfortable. I got up. 'I think I'll go to bed.'

Marcia uncurled herself, and drained her glass. 'I'll come too. I'm certainly not going to sit down here alone. I imagine we'll hear them coming back, and'll find out what's happened then.'

She linked her arm in mine as we went up the stairs, and grinned at me. 'Annoyed with me?'

'Of course not. Why should I be?'

'Honey, on account of I say things I oughtn't. And that reminds me—I'm afraid I gave you away to-night. I didn't mean to.'

'Gave me away? What d'you mean?'

'I let out to Roderick Grant that you and Nicky had been divorced. I forget how it came up—it was during the shemozzle to-night, when you were in the kitchen. I'm sorry, truly I am.'

'It's all right.' Nicky, I thought. Nicky. I'll bet she spells it Nikki. . . .

'I hope it doesn't matter,' said Marcia.

I laughed. 'Why should it? I don't suppose he'll tell anyone else.'

'Oh, well. . . .' We had reached the stair-head. '*That's* all right, then. Come and see my tweed before you go to bed.'

I followed her to her room. The window at the end of the passage showed, to-night, only a square of roaring grey against which our reflections glimmered, distorted and pale. Marcia pushed her door open and went in, groping for the light-switch.

'Just a sec., I'll see—' The light went on.

I heard her gasp. She was standing as if frozen, her back to me, her hands up to her throat.

Then she screamed, a high, tearing scream.

For a paralysed, horrified moment I couldn't move. My body turned to ice and I stood there, without breath.

Then she screamed again, and whirled round to face me, one hand flung out in a gesture of terror, the other clutching her throat.

I moved then. I jumped forward and seized the hand. I said: 'Marcia, for God's sake, what is it?'

Her breath came roughly, in gasps. '*The murderer. Oh my God, the murderer*. . . .'

'Marcia, there's no one here.'

She was shaking violently. She grabbed my arm and held it tightly. She pointed to the bed, her lips shaking so much that she couldn't speak coherently.

I stared down at the bed, while the slow gooseflesh pricked up my spine.

Lying on the coverlet was a doll, the kind of frivolous doll in a flounced skirt that the Marcias of this world love to have sprawling about on divans and sofas among the satin cushions. I had seen dozens of them—flaxen-headed, blue-eyed, pink and white and silken.

But this one was different.

It was lying flat on its back on the bed, with its legs straight out and its hands crossed on its breast. The contents of an ash-tray had been scattered over it, and a great red gash gleamed across its neck, cutting its throat from ear to ear.

Chapter Nine

Sputan Dhu

They found no trace, that night, of either Marion Bradford or Roberta.

The night had been black and wild, and, after several fruitless and exhausting hours of climbing and shouting in the blustering darkness, the searchers had struggled home in the early hours of daylight, to snatch food and a little sleep before setting out, haggard-eyed and weary, for a further search. Bill Persimmon had telephoned for the local rescue team, and, at about nine the next morning, a force some twenty strong set out once again for what must now certainly be reckoned the scene of an accident.

This time, I went with them. Even if I couldn't rock-climb, I would at least provide another pair of eyes, and I could help to cover some of the vast areas of scree and rough heather bordering the Black Spout.

The morning—I remembered with vague surprise that it was the eve of Coronation Day—had broken grey and forbidding. The wind still lurched among the cairns and heather-braes with inconsequent violence, and the frequent showers of rain were arrow-sharp and heavy. We were all muffled to the eyes, and trudged our way up the sodden glen with heads bent to meet the vicious stabbing of the rain.

It was a little better as we came under the shelter of the hill where Roderick and I had talked two nights ago, but, as we struggled on to the crest of it, the wind met us again in force. The rain-drops drove like nails before it, and I turned my back to it for a moment's respite. The storm-gust leaped past me, wrenching at my coat, and fled down the valley towards the sea.

The hotel looked far away and small and lonely, with, behind it, the sea-loch whitening under the racing feet of the wind. I saw a car move slowly away from the porch, and creep along the storm-lashed track to Strathaird. It was a big car, cream, with a black convertible top.

'Marcia Maling's car,' said a voice at my elbow. It was Alma Corrigan, looking business-like in Burberry and scarlet scarf and enormous nailed boots. She looked also, I noticed, decidedly attractive, now that the wind had whipped red into her cheeks and a sparkle into her fine eyes. She added, with a touch of contempt, as we turned to make our way along the top of the spur: 'I suppose it would be too much to expect her to come along as well but she needn't have taken the chauffeur away with her. Every man we can get—'

'She's leaving,' I said.

She checked in her stride. 'Leaving? You mean going home?'

'Yes. She's going back to London. She told me so last night.'

'But I thought she planned to stay a week at least! I suppose this affair, on top of the other business—'

'I suppose so,' I said, non-committally. I was certainly not going to tell anyone the reason for Marcia's sudden decision. Mrs Persimmon knew, and Mrs Cowdray-Simpson, but if Marcia's hysterics had not disturbed Alma Corrigan the night before, so much the better. And I was more than ever certain that I, myself, was going home to-morrow. But since I had not, like Marcia, been, so to speak, warned away, I felt I could hardly go without finding out what had happened to Marion and Roberta.

'Well!' said Mrs Corrigan, on an odd note which was three parts relief and one of something else I could not identify; 'I can't pretend I'm broken-hearted to see her go. She's only been here five days, and'–she broke off and sent me a sidelong glance up from under her long lashes–'you'd understand how I feel, if you were a married woman, Miss Brooke.'

'No doubt.' I added gently: 'She couldn't help it, you know. . . . She's been spoiled, I suppose, and she *is* such a lovely creature.'

'You're more charitable than I am,' said Alma Corrigan, a little grimly. 'But then, you haven't so much to lose.'

I didn't pretend to misunderstand her. 'She had to have men's admiration,' I said, 'all the time, no matter who got hurt in the process. I–forgive me, but I'd put it behind you, if I were you. Can't you begin to pretend it never happened?'

She laughed a little, hardly. 'It's easy to see you don't know much about dealing with men.'

I didn't speak for a moment. I wondered irritably why married women so often adopted that tone, almost, of superior satisfaction in the things they had to suffer. Then I told myself that she was probably right. I had after all failed utterly to deal with the man I had married, so who was I to give her advice? I thought wryly that nobody ever wanted advice anyway: all that most people sought was a ratification of their own views.

We were passing the Coronation bonfire, and I changed the subject. 'I suppose they'll hardly light that bonfire now: I mean, celebrations won't exactly be in keeping, if anything's happened to these two girls.'

She said morosely: 'The sticks'll be wet, anyway,' and added, with the determined gloom of a mouse returning to its accustomed treadmill: 'But how can Hart just expect to go on the way he has? He's been following her round like a lap-dog, making a fool of me, ever since she came. Oh, you haven't seen much of it: she switched to that Drury man last night, but *really*–I mean, *everybody* must have noticed. It's all very well saying she can't help it, but what about Hart? Why should Hart be allowed to get away with that sort of thing? I've a damned good mind to—'

I said abruptly: 'Do you want to keep your husband or don't you?'

'I–of course I want to keep him! What a silly question!'

'Then leave him alone,' I said. 'Don't you know yet that there's no room for pride in marriage? You have to choose between the two. If you can't keep quiet, then you must make up your mind to lose him. If you want *him*, then swallow your pride and shut up. It'll heal over; everything does, given time enough and a bit of peace.'

She opened her mouth, probably to ask me what I knew about it anyway. 'We're getting left behind,' I said, almost roughly. 'Let's hurry.'

I broke away from her and forged ahead up the rapidly steepening path.

We had climbed to a good height already, and I was thankful to notice, as we began to thread our way up the deer-tracks on the westerly flanks of Blaven itself, that the force of the wind was lessening. The gusts were less frequent and less violent, and, by the time we had reached the base of the first scree-slopes, the rain had stopped, shut off as suddenly as if by the turning of a tap.

The party was strung out now in single file, forging at a steeply climbing angle along the mountain-side. Most of the men carried packs; several had coils of rope. The going got harder: the deer-paths narrowed and steepened. These were foot-wide depressions–no more–in the knee-deep heather, and they were treacherous with the rain. Occasionally we found ourselves having to skirt great outcrops of rock, clinging precariously to roots and tufts of heather, with our feet slithering, slipping on the narrow ledge of mud which was all that remained of the path.

Above us towered the enormous cliffs of the south ridge, gleaming-black with rain, rearing steeply out of the precipitous scree like a roach-backed monster from the waves. The scree itself was terrifying enough. It fell away from the foot of the upper cliffs, hundreds of feet of fallen stone, slippery and overgrown and treacherous with hidden holes and loose rocks, which looked as if a false step might bring half the mountain-side down in one murderous avalanche.

The place where Dougal Macrae had seen the climbers was about half-way along Blaven's western face. There the crest of the mountain stands up above the scree in an enormous hog's-back of serrated peaks, two thousand feet and more of grim and naked rock, shouldering up the scudding sky. I stopped and looked up. Streams of wind-torn mist raced and broke round the buttresses of the dreadful rock; against its silver precipices the driven clouds wrecked themselves in swirls of smoke; and, black and terrible, above the movement of the storm, behind the racing riot of grey cloud, loomed and vanished and loomed again the great devil's pinnacles that broke the sky and split the winds into streaming rack. Blaven flew its storms like a banner.

And from some high black corrie among the peaks spilled the tiny trickle of water that was to form the gully of the Sputan Dhu. I could just see it, away up on some remote and fearful face of rock–a thin white line, no more, traced across the grey, a slender, steady line that seemed not to move at all save when the force of the wind took it and made it waver a little, like gossamer in the breeze. And the slowly falling gossamer-line of white water had cut, century by century, deep into the living rock, slashing a dark fissure for itself down the side of the mountain. Through this it slid, and rushed, and slid again, now hidden, now leaping clear, but all the time growing and loudening and gathering force until it reached the lowest pitch of the mountain and sank clamorously out of sight in the cleft that split the upper edge of the precipice above the scree.

And then at last it sprang free of the mountain. From the base of the cleft, some hundred feet up the face, it leaped as from a gutter-spout, a narrow jet of roaring water that jumped clear of the rock to plunge the last hundred feet in one sheer white leap of foam. And then it vanished into the loud depths of the gully it had bitten through the scree.

Up the edge of this gully the rescue party slowly picked its way. At intervals, someone shouted, but the only answer was the bark of a startled raven, which wheeled out from the cliff above, calling hoarsely among the mocking echoes.

I clawed my way over the wet rocks, my shoes slipping on slimy tufts of grass and thrift, my breath coming in uneven gasps, my face damp and burning with exertion in spite of the intermittent buffets of the chill wet wind. The men forged steadily ahead, their careless-seeming slouch covering the ground at a remarkable speed. I clambered and gasped in their wake, lifting my eyes occasionally to the menace of those black cliffs ahead that rode, implacably grim and remote, above the flying tails of the storm. Down to our left, at the bottom of the gully, the water brawled and bellowed and swirled in its devil's pot-holes. Here was a veritable demon's cleft; a black fissure, seventy feet deep, bisecting the scree-slope. Its walls were sheer, black and dripping, its floor a mass of boulders and wrestling water.

Suddenly, and for the first time clearly, I realized that somewhere here, in this wilderness of cruel rock and weltering water, two young women were probably lying dead. Or, at best, alive and maimed and unable, above the intermittent roar of wind and water, to make themselves heard.

I found myself repeating, breathlessly, stupidly, in a whisper: 'Roberta . . . Roberta. . . .'

The man directly in front of me was Alastair. He turned and gave me a quick, reassuring smile, and reached out a big hand to steady me up the slope.

'Don't go too near the edge, Janet . . . that's better. We'll soon get them now, if Dougal was right. These rescue chaps know every inch of the place, you know.'

'But . . . Alastair'–exertion had made me only half articulate–'they can't be alive still. They must have–must be—'

'If they managed to creep into shelter, they could quite easily be alive, providing they weren't seriously hurt by a fall. It wasn't cold last night.'

'Do you believe there were three of them?'

'Dougal Macrae isn't exactly given to flights of fancy,' said Alastair.

'Are any of the local men missing?'

'I'm told not.'

'Then, if there *were* three people, the third climber must be someone from the hotel. And nobody's missing from there either.'

'Exactly so,' said Alastair, in a blank non-committal sort of voice.

'And if nobody from the hotel reported the accident, then it means—'

'Exactly so,' said Alastair again. He paused and took my arm. Then with his free arm he pointed upwards, and a little to the right of where we were standing.

'That's where the bonfire was, that night,' he said. Then he dropped my arm and addressed himself to the climb again.

I followed, numbly. Murder? Again? Who on earth would want to murder Marion and Roberta? It was absurd. But then what reason could there have been for the murder of Heather Macrae–and such a murder? But again (I told myself) between the two incidents there could be no possible similarity. The disappearance of two climbers was, if not normal, at any rate not tainted with the fantastic, almost ritual air of the other death. Or was it? When we found the bodies . . .

I pushed the wet hair back from my face with an unsteady hand, and looked up.

The men ahead had stopped climbing, and were gathered on the edge of the gully at the point where the waterfall leaped its final hundred feet or so from the upper cliff. Someone was pointing downwards. Ropes were being uncoiled.

I hauled myself up the last step of rock and paused. Then I walked slowly forward to join them.

I was afraid, horribly afraid. I felt that no power on earth would make me look down over that edge of rock to see Roberta staring up at me with sightless eyes, with her throat cut like that of Marcia's silken doll, and the bright blood splashed into pink by the rain, crawling between the clumps of blossoming thrift.

But it appeared that no sign of either Roberta or Marion had yet been seen, though anxious eyes scanned the depths of the black gully. Dougal Macrae pointed out to the rest of the men the place where he had seen the climbers–he had not, it is true, seen them actually on the cliff, but they were making for it at an angle which suggested that they intended either to climb on the face of the Spout itself or to cross above the fall by the upper rocks.

Roderick Grant turned his head and saw me, and came over, tugging a battered carton of cigarettes from some inner pocket. He handed me one, and we lit up–no easy process this, as the force of the gusty wind had not appreciably diminished.

'What are they going to do?' I asked anxiously.

'If Dougal's right, and they were starting to climb across the Spout, then the first move is to do the same climb. There may be some traces in the rocks above the gully, or the climbers may be able to see down below the fall.'

'Did you get this far last night?'

'Yes, but of course it was no use in the dark. All we could do was shout.'

I looked down into the cleft, where the white water leaped and wrangled. The sides of the gully gleamed and dripped, the hanging tufts of fern and heather tossing in the currents of wind that roared up the cleft like air in a wind-tunnel. With each gust the water of the fall was blown back, and flattened in its own spray against the rock. The echo was uncanny.

I shivered, and then looked up again at the grim pitch above us. 'Is it a very bad place to climb?'

He was grave. 'It's pretty bad for anyone, and for a beginner it's—well, it's sheer lunacy.'

'Can the men get down into the gully if they—if they have to?' I asked fearfully.

'Oh yes. Beagle says he'll go, and Rhodri MacDowell is going with him. He's a local chap and a pretty good climber.'

I peered down again into the echoing depths. 'Doesn't the gully flatten out further down the mountain? I mean, couldn't they start down there, and work their way up the bottom of it?'

'This is quicker. It would take hours to work up from below. The stream goes down in leaps, you see—anything from seven to twenty feet at a time. It's much simpler to go straight down here.'

Operations were beginning at the foot of the cliff. Three of the men, of whom Beagle was one, were roping themselves together, preparatory to making the climb across the Spout. The rest of the group had split up, and small parties of men seemed to be casting back along the hillside, among the smaller clefts and fissures in the scree.

'What do we do?' I asked Roderick.

'I should wait here. If they do find them, injured, you might be able to help.' He smiled at me reassuringly. 'The odds aren't quite as bad as they look, Janet. It won't be long before we have them safely back at the hotel.'

Then he was gone, and I was left with Alma Corrigan and the little group of men who remained to watch the climb across the gully.

Chapter Ten

The Echoing Tomb

I don't pretend to know anything about the art of rock-climbing. The three men who were climbing out across the face of the Sputan Dhu were all, it appeared, experts at the job; and indeed, they moved so easily and smoothly on the rock that it was hard to believe the traverse was as dangerous as Roderick had made out.

I had gone further up the scree to a point near the start of the climb, and sat, watching and nervously smoking, while the three climbers moved steadily, turn and turn about, across the wet cliff. The route they followed took them at a steep angle up the rock-face, at one point straddling the narrow cleft above the spout of water. Even to my ignorant eyes it was obvious that the wet rock and gusty wind must add considerably to the risks of the climb, but the climbers appeared unaffected by the conditions. Ronald Beagle was first on the rope, leading with a smooth precision that was beautiful to watch. The other two, Rhodri MacDowell and a lad called Iain, were members of the local rescue team. All three—it seemed to me—took the climb very slowly, with long pauses between each man's move, when, I imagine, they were looking for traces of the other climbers. They gave no sign, however, of having found any, but moved on, unhurriedly, up and across the dreadful gap.

Dougal Macrae said, just behind me: 'That's a bonny climber.'

Ronald Beagle was half-way up what looked like a perpendicular slab of gleaming rock—a hideously exposed pitch, as the slab was set clear above the gully. He climbed rhythmically and easily, making for the next stance, which was an in-tilted ledge some fifteen feet above him.

'I think he's wonderful,' I said warmly. 'I don't know anything about climbing, but it looks uncommonly tricky to me.'

'It's a fery nasty place,' said Dougal. 'And that bit that Mr Beagle is on now—that is the worst.'

'It looks like it.'

'He must be right out over the gully. Ah, he's up. He's belaying now.'

Beagle had swung himself easily on to the ledge, and was busy looping himself in some way to a jut of rock beside him. Then he turned and called down something to the men below. I couldn't hear what it was, but he must have been telling them to wait, for neither of them moved from their stances. Beagle turned to face outwards and, crouching in the support of the belayed rope, he bent to peer down into the gully.

I cried out involuntarily: 'But they can't be down there, Mr Macrae! It's impossible!'

He looked sombrely down over his pipe. 'If they fell from yon piece of rock that's where they'll be.'

'That's what I mean.' I fumbled with chilled fingers for another cigarette. 'They'd never have crossed that piece of rock. That girl, Roberta Symes—she'd never have tackled a climb like that. She'd never climbed before!'

His brows drew down. 'D'ye say so?'

'That's what she told us. And Miss Bradford was apparently a good climber; she'd never have let Roberta try this route—surely she wouldn't!'

'No. You'd think not.' He raised troubled eyes again to the dangerous pitch. 'No. But it was for this place they were making when I saw them. It did look indeed as if they were planning to cross the Sputan Dhu—ah, they've moved again.'

Rhodri MacDowell, the middle man, was now on Beagle's ledge, while Beagle himself was out of sight round an overhang which beetled over the far side of the gully. Iain, who was last on the rope, was moving up.

I dragged on my cigarette with a nervous movement, and shifted on the wet stone. 'I—I wonder if they've seen anything—down there?' The words, tremulous and reluctant, were snatched into nothing by the wet wind.

'We'll hope ye're right, and that they'd never let the lassie try the place. It may be—'

'They?' I turned on him quickly. 'It was you who said there were three climbers, wasn't it? I suppose you couldn't have made a mistake, could you? You're really sure about it?'

'Oh aye.' The soft voice was decisive. 'There were three, sure enough.'

'And the third one—was it a man or a woman?'

'I don't know. At that distance I could not tell very much about them, and nowadays all the ladies wear trousers on the hill, it seems. There was not anything I could be picking out, except that the middle one had a red jacket on.'

'That would be Miss Symes,' I said, and remembered with a pang how the scarlet windcheater had suited Roberta's bright Dutch-doll face and black hair.

'It would make it easy enough to find her now, you'd think,' said Dougal.

'I—I suppose so.' The second climber had disappeared now. The rope gleamed in a pale pencilled line across the overhang to where Iain was working his way up to the ledge. He gained it presently, and belayed. I heard him call something and soon Ronald Beagle reappeared some way beyond him, making for what looked like the end of the climb, a wildish ledge above the scree at the far side of the gully, from which the descent was only an easy scramble.

In a very few minutes more all three climbers had foregathered on the ledge, and seemed to be holding some sort of a conference. The people on our side of the gully, Alma Corrigan, Dougal Macrae, myself, and the handful of men who had not gone to search the scree-slopes, watched in stony silence, frozen into a dismal set-piece of foreboding. I sat there with my forgotten cigarette burning one-sidedly between wet fingers, stupidly straining eyes and ears to interpret the distant sounds and gestures of the men's conversation.

Dougal said suddenly: 'I think they must have seen something in the gully.'

'No,' I said, and then again, foolishly, as if I could somehow push the truth further away from me, 'no.'

'Rhodri MacDowell is pointing. I thought he had seen something when he was on the cliff.'

I blinked against the wet wind, and saw that one of the men was, indeed, gesturing back towards the gully. The three of them had disengaged themselves from the rope, and now began to make a rapid way down the scree towards the far side of the gully. There was about them a purposeful air that gave Dougal's guess the dismal ring of truth.

Then Alma Corrigan turned abruptly from the little group near by, and strode across to us.

'They're down there,' she announced baldly.

I just stared at her, unable to speak, but I got stiffly to my feet. Behind her the hotel proprietor, Bill Persimmon, said quickly: 'We don't know for certain, but it does seem as if they've seen something.'

'Ye'll be going down the gully then,' said Dougal Macrae.

'I suppose so.' Bill Persimmon turned back to watch the climbers' approach.

Behind us we heard the rasp and slither of boots on wet heather. Nicholas came down the slope, with Roderick not far in the rear. Nicholas' eyes, narrowed against the wind, were intent on Beagle as he approached the opposite side of the gully.

'It's time someone else took a turn,' he said abruptly. 'If they've been seen in the gully, I'll go down. What about you, Bill?'

'I think,' began Major Persimmon, 'that perhaps we ought—'

'Did they see anything down there?' Roderick's voice cut anxiously across his. 'We came back because it looked as if–we thought—' He saw my face, and stopped; then he came over quickly to stand beside me, giving me a little smile of reassurance.

But I shook my head at it. 'I'm afraid they did,' I said under my breath. 'Dougal says one of the men saw something.'

'Yes. Rhodri. We saw him pointing. I'm very much afraid—' He stopped again, and bit his underlip. 'Why don't you go back to the hotel, Janet?'

'Good Lord,' I said, almost savagely, 'don't worry about *me. I'm* all right.'

And now the three climbers were at the edge of the gully. Beagle's voice came gustily across the fitful noises of wind and water.

'. . . Below the pool . . . couldn't really see . . . might be . . . a leg . . . going down now. . . .'

I sat down again, rather suddenly, on my stone. I think I was surprised that, now it had happened, I felt no horror, only numbness. The small things–the sluggish misery of wet shoes, the chilly drizzle, my handkerchief sodden in my coat pocket–each petty detail of discomfort seemed in turn to nag at my attention, to fix it, dazedly, upon myself. I suppose it is one kind of automatic defence; it may be a variety of shock; at any rate I just sat there, dumbly working my fingers into my damp gloves, while all round me preparations were made for the final horror of discovery.

Beagle and Rhodri MacDowell went down after all. To me, watching them with that same detached, almost childish interest, it seemed an amazing operation. They were so incredibly quick. Beagle was still shouting his informations across the gully when Rhodri and the lad Iain had thrown the rope over a little pylon of rock that jutted up beside them. The ends of the doubled rope snaked down into the depths, touched bottom, and hung there. Rhodri said something to Iain, heaved the rope somehow between his legs and over his shoulder, and then simply walked backwards over the cliff. He backed down it rapidly, leaning out, as it were, against the rope that acted as a sliding cradle. It looked simple–and crazy. I must have made some kind of exclamation, because, beside me, Roderick gave a little laugh.

'It's called abseiling. . . .' He himself was busy with a rope. 'Quite a normal method of descent, and much the quickest. . . . No, Bill, I'll go. We'll shout up fast enough if we want reinforcements.'

Rhodri had vanished. The boy Iain stayed by the spike of rock that anchored the rope, and Beagle was already on his way down. Nicholas turned back from the edge.

'I'm coming down,' he said briefly.

Roderick, bending to anchor his own rope, shot him a swift upward look and hesitated. 'You? I didn't know you climbed?'

'No?' said Nicholas, not very pleasantly. Roderick's eyes flickered, but he merely said, mildly enough: 'I'd better go first, perhaps.'

And as quickly as Rhodri–and rather more smoothly–he was gone. Nicholas watched him down, with his back squarely turned to me where I sat huddled on my wet stone. Then, at a shout from below, he, too, laid hold of the ropes, and carefully lowered himself over the edge.

The little group of waiting men had moved forward to the brink of the gully, and once more there was about them, peering down into the echoing depths, that air of foreboding that gradually freezes through dread to certainty. I got up and moved to join them.

And almost at once a shout came from below–a wordless sound whose message was nevertheless hideously clear. I started forward, and felt Dougal Macrae's big hand close on my arm.

'Steady now!'

'He's found them!' I cried.

'Aye, I think so.'

Major Persimmon was kneeling at the gully's edge; there were further exchanges of shouting, which the wind swept into nothingness: then the group of men broke from its immobility into rapid and practised activity, two more of the local rescue team preparing to descend, while the main party made off at some speed down the scree.

'Where are they going?'

'For the stretchers,' said Dougal.

I suppose hope dies hard. My passionate hope, and my ignorance, between them, made me blind to his tone, and to the expressions of the other men. I pulled myself eagerly out of his grip, starting forward to the edge of the gully.

'Stretcher? They're alive? Can they possibly be still alive?'

Then I saw what was at the bottom of the gully. Beagle and Nicholas were carrying it between them, slowly making their awkward way across the slabs that funnelled the rush of water. And there was no possible mis-apprehension about the burden that they were hauling from the fringes of the cascade. . . . I had forgotten that a dead body would be stiff, locked like some grotesque woodcarving in the last pathetic posture of death. Navy trousers, blue jacket smeared and soaked almost to black, filthy yellow mittens on horror-splayed fingers . . . Marion Bradford. But it was no longer Marion Bradford; it was a hideous wooden doll that the men held between them, a doll whose head dangled loosely from a lolling neck. . . .

I went very quietly back to my stone, and sat down, staring at my feet.

Even when the stretchers came, I did not move. There was nothing I could do, but I somehow shrank from going back to the hotel now, alone–and Alma Corrigan showed no disposition to leave the place. So I stayed where I was, smoking too hard and looking away from the gully, along the grey flank of the mountain, while from behind me came the sounds of the rescue that was a rescue no longer. The creak and scrape of rope; a soft rush of Gaelic; grunts of effort; a call from Roderick, strained and distant; Beagle's voice, lifted in a sharp shout; Major Persimmon's, near by, saying '*What? My God!*' then another splutter of Gaelic close beside me–this time so excited that I stirred uneasily and then looked round.

It was Dougal who had exclaimed. He and Major Persimmon were on their knees side by side, peering down into the gully. I heard Persimmon say again: '*My God!*' and then the two men got slowly to their feet, eyeing one another.

'He's right, Dougal.'

Dougal said nothing. His face was like granite.

'What is it? What are they yelling about down there?' Alma Corrigan's voice rose sharply.

Bill Persimmon said: 'She fell from the slab all right. The rope is still on her body. And it's been cut.'

Her face was sallow under the bright scarf. 'What–what d'you mean?'

He lifted a shoulder, and said wearily: 'Just what I say. Someone cut the rope, and she fell.'

Alma Corrigan said, in a dry little whisper: '*Murder*. . . .'

I said, 'And Roberta Symes?'

His gaze flicked me absently as he turned back to the cliff's edge. 'They haven't found her yet.'

And they did not find her, though they searched that dreadful gully from end to end, and though for the rest of the day they toiled once more up and down the endless scree.

Chapter Eleven

An't Sròn

The search went on all day. Towards late afternoon the wind dropped, only wakening from time to time in fitful gusts. The rain held off, but great slate-coloured clouds hung low, blotting out the Cuillin and crowding sullenly over the crest of Blaven. Marsco, away to the north, was invisible, and, a long way below us, Loch na Creitheach lay dull and pewter-grey.

They finally got Marion Bradford's body down to the mouth of the gully at about four o'clock. From high up on the scree, I watched the sombre little procession bumping its difficult way over the wet heather, with the sad clouds sagging overhead. It reached the lower spur of An't Sròn and wound drearily along its crest, past the pathetic irony of the celebration bonfire, and out of sight over the end of the hill.

Dispiritedly I turned back to the grey scree, fishing for another cigarette. The Coronation bonfire . . . and to-morrow, in London, the bells would be ringing and the bands playing, while here–there would be no celebration here, to-morrow. The lonely bubbling call of the curlew, the infinitely sad pipe of the golden plover, the distant drone of the sea, these were the sounds that would hold Camasunary glen to-morrow, as they did now. And if Roberta were still missing. . . .

I heard the scrape of boot on rock above me, and looked up to see Roderick Grant edging his way down one of the innumerable ledges that ran up to the cliff above the Sputan Dhu. His head was bare, and the fair hair was dark with the rain. He looked indescribably weary and depressed, and one of his hands was bleeding. I remembered what Marcia had told me, and wondered suddenly if he had known of Marion Bradford's *penchant* for him, and was feeling now some odd sort of self-reproach.

His expression lightened a little when he saw me, then the mask of strain dropped over it again. His eyes looked slate-blue in the uncertain light.

'You should have gone back to the hotel,' he said abruptly. 'You look done in.'

'I suppose so,' I said wearily. My hands were wet and cold, and I was fumbling ineptly with matches. He took me gently by the shoulders and pushed me down to a seat on a boulder. I sat thankfully, while he flicked his lighter into flame and lit my cigarette, then he pulled open his haversack and produced a package.

'What have you had to eat?'

'Oh, sandwiches. I forget.'

'Because it was far too long ago,' he said. 'Here—I got a double chukker. Help me eat these. Did you have some coffee?'

'Yes.'

He held out a flat silver flask. 'Have a drop of this; it'll do the trick.'

It did. It was neat Scotch, and it kicked me back to consciousness in five seconds flat. I sat up on my rock, took another sandwich, and felt fine.

He was eyeing me. 'That's better. But all the same, I think you'd better go back to the hotel.'

I shook my head. 'I can't. Not yet. I'd never be able to settle down and wait, not now. We've got to find Roberta. Another night on the hill—'

His voice was gentle. 'I doubt if another night will make much difference to Roberta, Janet.'

'She *must* be alive,' I said stubbornly. 'If she'd fallen into the gully with Marion Bradford, she'd have been found. Dougal Macrae said she could have been stopped higher up, by a ledge or something. There must be places near the top of the gully—'

'I've raked the whole of the upper gully twice over,' he said wearily. 'Drury and I and Corrigan have been there all day. There's no sign of her.'

'She must be somewhere.' My voice sounded dogged and stupid. 'She must have been hurt, or she'd have answered you; and if she was hurt, she can't have gone far. Unless—'

I felt my muscles tightening nervously as, perhaps for the first time, the possible significance of that severed rope-end fully presented itself. I turned scared eyes to him.

'Roderick'—I used his name without thinking—'you were down in the gully. You saw Marion's climbing-rope. That cut can only mean one thing, can't it?'

He dragged hard on his cigarette, and expelled a cloud of smoke like a great sigh. 'Yes. Murder—again. . . .'

I said slowly: 'And Dougal swears there *was* a third climber, but whether it was a man or woman he can't say.'

He made a slight impatient gesture. 'If he's to be believed.'

'Oh, I think he is. If anyone in this world's dependable, I'd say it was Dougal Macrae. If there wasn't a third climber, then we've got to believe that it was Roberta who cut the rope, and that's fantastic.'

'But is it?'

My eyes widened. 'You can't believe that *Roberta*—'

'She was a beginner. If Marion fell, and was pulling her loose from her hold, she might panic, and—'

'I don't believe it! And what's more, neither do you!'

He gave a wry little smile. 'No.'

'So there *was* a third climber,' I said, 'and he cut the rope, so he's a murderer. He was there when Marion fell. And Roberta—whether she fell or not—can't be found. It doesn't add up to anything very pretty, does it?'

'You think the *murderer* removed Roberta?'

'What else can we think? We can't find her. If she was dead, he could safely have left her. If she was only injured, he'd have to silence her. He may have killed her and hidden her, hoping that the delay in finding the bodies would help him in some way or other.' I fetched a sigh. 'I don't know. I'm just in a dreary sort of whirl, praying she's all right and—oh God, yes, knowing all the time she can't be. . . .'

I got to my feet.

'Let's get on with this,' I said.

The dark drew down, and all along the mountain-slopes, indefatigably, the searchers toiled. Beagle and Rhodri MacDowell, who had been down with the stretcher, returned bringing food, soup, coffee, and torches from the hotel. We ate and drank, standing round in the gathering darkness. There was not much said; the men's faces were drawn and strained, their movements heavy. What little conversation there was related simply to accounts of areas searched and suggestions for further reconnaissance.

I found myself beside Ronald Beagle, who, despite the exacting role he had played in the rescue, was showing very little sign of strain. He was draining his mug of hot coffee as Alastair came up, seeming to loom over the smaller man in the darkness.

'That gully below the Sputan Dhu,' he said abruptly. 'What's the bottom like?'

Beagle glanced up at him. There was mild surprise in his voice. 'Pretty rough. All devil's pot-holes and fallen boulders. The stream drops down a series of cascades to the foot of the scree. Why? I assure you we couldn't have missed her.'

'Any caves or fissures in the sides of the gully?'

'Plenty.' Ronald Beagle bent to put his coffee-mug in the hotel's basket. 'But there were four of us, and I assure you—'

'Can you assure me,' said Alastair evenly, 'that at least two of you searched each of these fissures?'

There was silence for a moment; I saw the rapid glow and fade, glow and fade, of Alastair's cigarette. Then another cigarette glowed beside it. Roderick's voice spoke from behind it.

'Why? What are you suggesting?'

'I'm suggesting that one of us here is a murderer,' said Alastair brutally.

Hartley Corrigan's voice broke in. 'That's a filthy thing to say! It's tantamount to accusing Beagle or Grant or Drury—'

'He's quite right, you know,' said Beagle mildly. 'It could quite easily be one of us. But why should it be in the murderer's interest to conceal the second body, once the first was found? It would certainly be to his interest to be the first to find her if she were still alive, so that he could silence her.'

He looked up at Alastair again. 'But he didn't. I imagine every crevice in that gully was searched, solo and chorus, by every one of us.'

'And that's a fact.' Rhodri MacDowell spoke unexpectedly out of the darkness.

'Okay, okay,' said Alastair. He looked at Beagle: 'You know how it is. . . .'

'I know. It's quite all right.'

The group was moving now, breaking and reforming its knots of shadow-shapes, as men gathered once more into their parties for the search. I found Nicholas beside me.

He said shortly, his voice rough with fatigue: 'This is absurd, Gianetta. Get back to the hotel at once.'

I was too tired to resent his tone. 'I can't give up yet,' I said dully. 'I couldn't stand sitting about waiting, listening with the Cowdray-Simpsons for the Everest news, and just wondering and wondering what was happening on the hill.'

'There's no sense in your staying here,' said Ronald Beagle. 'You want to get back and rest, and find some way of taking your mind off this business. And talking of Everest—' He gave a jerk to his haversack, and raised his voice. I saw his teeth gleam in an unexpected grin. 'I forgot to tell you,' he said to the dim groups scattered round him, 'that the news came through on the A.F.N. a short while ago. They've done it. By God they have. They've climbed Everest.'

There was a buzz of excitement, and for a moment the grim nature of the quest on which we were engaged was forgotten, as a host of eager questions was flung at him. He answered with his usual calm, but soon moved off, alone, and immediately afterwards the group broke up, and the parties vanished in various directions in the darkness to resume their search. I heard their voices as they moved away, animatedly discussing Beagle's announcement: he had, it seemed to me, deliberately kept back his news and then used it to galvanize the weary searchers into fresh activity. My respect for him increased.

Beside me, Nicholas spoke again, angrily: 'Now look here, Gianetta—'

Roderick broke across it: 'Leave her alone.'

'What the hell do you mean?'

Torches were flashing near by, and in their fitful flickering I could see Roderick's face. It was quite white, and blazing with a kind of nervous fury. His eyes were on Nicholas, and in that light they looked black and dangerous.

'What I said. What Janet does is nothing to do with you, and I rather fancy she prefers you to leave her alone.'

It was a nasty, snarling little scene, and it had all blown up so quickly that I stood, gaping, between the pair of them, for a good fifteen seconds before I realized what was happening. This was Marcia's doing, blast her.

'Stop it, you two,' I said sharply. 'What I do is my own affair and nobody else's.' I took hold of Roderick's arm, and gave it a little shake. 'But he's right, Roderick. I'm no use here, and I'm going back now. So both of you leave me alone.' I pulled my woollen gloves out of a pocket and began to drag them on over cold hands. 'We're all tired and edgy, so for heaven's sake don't let's have a scene. I'm going to pack these thermos flasks and things, and take them straight down to the hotel, and then I'm going to bed.'

I knelt down and began to pack mugs into the basket. I hadn't even glanced at Nicholas. He didn't say a word, but I saw him pitch his cigarette savagely down the hillside, then he turned in silence and plunged off into the darkness after Ronald Beagle. Above me, Roderick said, hesitatingly:

'Have you got a torch?'

'Yes,' I said. 'Don't worry about me, I know my way. Go and help the others.' I looked up then at him uncertainly: 'And—Roderick.'

'Yes?' His voice was still tight and grim.

'Find her, won't you?'

'I'll try.' Then he, too, was gone. I packed all the débris I could find by the light of my torch, and then I sat down for a few minutes and lit another cigarette. I had just finished smoking one, but my nerves were still jumping, and the last little scene, with all its curious overtones, had upset me more than I wanted to admit.

It was quite dark now. Behind me the hill flashed with scattered torchlight, and I could hear, distorted by the gusts of wind, the occasional shouts of the searchers. In the intervals of the wind I heard the scrape of boots on rock, and, twice, away to my left, a sharp bark that I took to be the cry of a hill-fox.

I got up at last, ground out my cigarette with my heel, lifted the basket, and began to pick my way down the mountainside. I gave the gully a very wide berth, and scrambled slowly and carefully, with the aid of my torch, down through the tumbled boulders of the scree. Half-way down, I knew, I would come upon the deer-track that led, roughly but safely, to the lower spur of An't Sròn. Away below, a flock of oyster-catchers flew up the glen from the shore, wrangling noisily among themselves. I could hear their cheery vulgar chirking echoing along the water of the loch, then falling silent. The wind blew strongly on my face, with its clear tang of sea and grass and peat. I let myself carefully down on to a muddy ledge and found that I was on the deer-track.

Going was easier now, but I still went slowly and cautiously, hampered by basket and torch, which left me no hand free in case I slipped. It must have been well over an hour after I started my journey back, before I found myself, with relief, walking on the heather of the ridge that joined Blaven with An't Sròn.

I had been so afraid of stumbling, or of losing the deer-track, that I had come down the hillside with my eyes glued to the little circle of ground that my torch lit at my feet. But as I reached the level heather of the ridge, I became conscious of a new element in the tangy wind that blew against my face. Even when I identified this as the smell of smoke, I still walked forward unalarmed, unrealizing.

Until I lifted my eyes and saw it, a pale climbing column of smoke, no more than a hundred yards ahead.

The bonfire. Someone had lit the bonfire. The smoke from the damp wood towered and billowed, ghostly against the black night, but there was a flickering glare at the heart of the smoke, and I heard the crackle as a flame leapt.

I suppose I stood there, looking at it, for a full half-minute, while my slow brain registered the fact that somebody, who had not heard about the accident, had lit the celebration bonfire. Then another branch crackled, the smoke billowed up redly, and across in front of the glow moved the black figure of a man.

It was as if a shutter in my brain had clicked, and, in place of this, an older picture had flashed in front of me. A column of flame, with a man's shadow dancing grotesquely in front of it. A blackened pyre, with the body of a murdered girl lying across it like a careful sacrifice. . . .

Roberta!

It was for this that the murderer had kept Roberta.

I dropped the basket with a crash, and ran like a mad thing towards the smoking pyre. I don't know what I hoped to do. I was acting purely by instinct. I hurled myself forward, shouting as I ran, and I had the heavy torch gripped in my hand like a hammer.

There was an answering shout from the hill behind–close behind–but I hardly heeded it. I ran on, desperately, silent now but for my sobbing, tearing breath. The fire was taking hold. The smoke belched sideways in the wind, and whirled over me in a choking cloud.

I was there. The smoke swirled round me, billowing up into the black sky. The flames snaked up with the crack of little whips, and the criss-cross of burning boughs stood out in front of them like bars.

I came to a slithering, choking halt at the very foot of the pyre, and tried to shield my eyes as I gazed upwards.

I saw the smoke fanning out under something that was laid across the top of the pile. I saw the glass of a wrist-watch gleam red in the flame. I saw a boot dangling, the nails in the sole shining like points of fire.

I flung myself at the burning pile and clawed upwards at the arm and leg.

Then a shadow loomed behind me out of the smoke. A man's strong hands seized me and dragged me back. I whirled and struck out with the torch. He swore, and then he had me in a crippling grip. I struggled wildly, and I think I screamed. His grip crushed me. Then he tripped, and I was flung down into the wet heather, with my attacker's heavy body bearing me down.

Dimly, I heard shouting, the thud of feet, a voice saying hoarsely: '*Gianetta!*' Then someone dragged my assailant off me. I heard Alastair's voice say, in stupefaction: '*Jamesy Farlane!* What goes on, in the name of God?' as he took the young man in a vicious grip. It was Dougal Macrae who hauled me on to my feet. I was shivering and, I think, crying. He said: 'Are ye all right, mistress?'

I clung to him, and whispered through shaking lips: 'On the fire–Roberta–*hurry*.'

He put an arm round me. His big body was trembling too, and as I realized why, my pity for him gave me the strength to pull myself together. I said, more calmly: 'Is she dead?'

Another voice spoke. I looked up hazily. There was a man standing a little way from the bonfire. It was Hartley Corrigan, and he was looking down at the thing that lay at his feet.

His voice was without expression. He said: 'It's not Roberta Symes. It's Beagle. And someone has cut his throat.'

Chapter Twelve

Camasunary IV

I slept late next morning, after a night of nightmares, and woke to a bright world. Mist still haunted the mountain-tops, lying like snowdrifts in crevice and corrie, but the wind had dropped, and the sun was out. Blaven looked blue, and the sea sparkled.

But it was with no corresponding lift of the spirits that, at length, I went downstairs, to be met by the news that Roberta had not yet been found, and that the police had arrived. I could not eat anything, but drank coffee and stared out of the window of the empty dining-room, until Bill Persimmon, looking tired and grave, came and told me that the police would like a word with me.

As luck would have it, the officer in charge of the Macrae murder had come over from Elgol that morning, to pursue some further enquiries relating to the earlier case. So, hotter upon the heels of the new development than any murderer could have expected, came the quiet-eyed Inspector Mackenzie from Inverness, and with him an enormous red-headed young sergeant called Hector Munro. A doctor, hastily summoned in the small hours by telephone, had already examined the bodies of Marion and Beagle, and a constable had been despatched to the site of the new bonfire, to guard whatever clues might be there for the Inspector to pick up, when he should have finished his preliminary questions at the hotel.

This information was relayed to me hastily by Bill Persimmon, as he led me to a little sitting-room beside the residents' lounge, where the Inspector had his temporary headquarters.

Absurdly enough, I was nervous, and was in no way reassured when the Inspector turned out to be a kind-looking middle-aged man with greying hair and deeply-set grey eyes, their corners crinkled as if he laughed a good deal. He got up when I entered, and we shook hands formally. I sat down in the chair he indicated, so that we faced each other across a small table. At his elbow the enormous red-headed sergeant, solemnly waiting with a note-book, dwarfed the table, his own spindly chair, and, indeed, the whole room.

'Well now, Miss Brooke . . .' the Inspector glanced down at a pile of papers in front of him, as if he were vague about my identity, and had to reassure himself: 'I understand that you only arrived here on Saturday afternoon?'

'Yes, Inspector.'

'And, before you came here, had you heard anything about the murder of Heather Macrae?'

I was surprised, and showed it. 'Why—no.'

'Not even read about it in the papers?'

'Not that I recollect.'

'Ah . . .' he was still looking down at the table, talking casually. 'And who told you about it?'

I said carefully, wondering what he was getting at: 'I gathered, from hints that various people let drop, that something awful had happened, so I asked Mr Grant about it, and he told me.'

'That would be Mr Roderick Grant?' He flicked over a couple of papers, and the sergeant made a note.

'Yes. And then Mr Hay talked of it again next day.' I added politely, to the sergeant: 'Mr Hubert Hay. Footloose.'

'Quite so.' The Inspector's eyes crinkled momentarily at the corners. 'Well, we'll let that go for the moment. I understand that it was you who found Mr Beagle's body on the bonfire last night?'

'Yes. At least, I was first on the scene. I don't know who pulled him off the bonfire.'

The Inspector looked straight at me for the first time, and I saw that his eyes were quite impersonal, remote even, and very cold. The effect, in his homely pleasant face, was disconcerting and a little frightening. He said: 'When was it that you first noticed that the fire had been lit?'

'Not until I was quite close to it—do you know the hill, Inspector Mackenzie?'

'I've been on it a good bit in the past three weeks.'

'Of course. How stupid of me.'

He smiled suddenly. 'And Hecky and I have a map. Now, Miss Brooke, just tell me in your own words what happened on your way down from the hill.'

So I told him. He listened quietly, his grey eyes placidly enquiring. At his elbow the red-headed sergeant—equally placid—made notes in a competent shorthand.

'. . . And then I saw a shadow, like a man, near the bonfire '

'Only one?'

'Yes.'

'I take it that you didn't recognize him?'

'No.'

'Was he carrying or hauling a body then?'

'Oh no. He was just moving about on the fringe of the smoke—it was billowing here and there, you know, in the wind. I remembered the—the other murder, and I thought it was Roberta being murdered this time—'

'Roberta?'

'Roberta Symes, the girl who's missing. Inspector, oughtn't we all to be out looking—'

He said quietly: 'There are men out now on the hill. Go on.'

'That's all there is. I just ran towards the bonfire. I don't know what I imagined I could do. I saw there was something—a body—on top of it, and then just as I tried to get to the body before the fire did, the murderer attacked me.'

'In actual fact,' said the Inspector calmly, 'it was James Farlane who attacked you.'

I stared at him. 'I know that. Surely—?'

He interrupted me. 'Now. Let's get this picture right. You realize no doubt that Mr Beagle cannot have been killed very long before you found him. You met or passed nobody at all on your way down to An't Sròn?'

'No one.'

'Did you hear anything? Any footsteps, or—?'

'Nothing. I could hear the men shouting occasionally away above on the scree, but nothing else. When I saw the bonfire and screamed, someone shouted quite close behind me, but I hadn't heard him till then. The wind was strongish, you see, and—'

'Quite so.' Once more he appeared to contemplate the table in front of him. 'You last saw Mr Beagle alive when the group broke up for the final search last night?'

'I— Are you allowed to ask leading questions, Inspector?'

He grinned. 'I've already heard the answer to this one a dozen times. I'm saving time. Did you?'

'Yes.'

'Did you see which way he went?'

'Downhill.'

'Alone?'

'Yes.'

'Sure?'

I regarded him levelly. 'Quite.'

'I see. Now let's get back to the bonfire, shall we? You ran towards it, and screamed. Did you recognize the shout that answered you–from close behind you, I think you said?'

'No, I didn't. But I assumed it was Alastair–Mr Braine–because it was he who pulled Jamesy Farlane off me. He must have got there pretty quickly. Dougal Macrae was there too.'

'Mr Alastair Braine, then, was first on the scene–and very prompt.' His voice was contemplative and pleasant. I felt my muscles tightening. 'Who else was there?'

'Mr Corrigan. He was standing by the bonfire. He–he must have pulled the body off.' I swallowed, and added quickly: 'He and Alastair probably came down together.'

'No,' said the Inspector gently to the table top. 'Both gentlemen tell me they arrived independently. . . .' His grey eyes lifted to mine, suddenly hard and bright. 'Who else was there?'

'Why–nobody.'

'Jamesy Farlane and Dougal Macrae; Mr Braine and Mr Corrigan, all there within seconds of your scream. Who else?'

I looked at him. 'That was all: I saw nobody else.'

The grey eyes regarded me, then dropped. 'Just so,' said the Inspector vaguely, but I had the most uncomfortable impression of some conclusion reached in the last five minutes which was anything but vague. He shuffled a few papers in a desultory way, and said, without looking at me: 'You booked your room a week ago?'

'I–yes.'

'After the murder of Heather Macrae.'

'I suppose so. I didn't know—'

'Quite. Sergeant Munro has your statement to that effect. . . . You booked your room, Miss Brooke, in the name of Drury, Mrs Nicholas Drury.'

It was absurd that he should be treating me as if I were a hostile witness, absurd that I should sit there with jumping nerves and tight-clasped hands just because his manner was no longer friendly.

I said, sounding both guilty and defiant: 'That is my name.'

'Then why did you change it to Brooke as soon as you got here? And why have you and your husband been at some pains to ignore one another's presence?'

'He's—not my husband.' I found myself hurrying to explain. 'We were divorced four years ago. I didn't know he was here. When I saw him the first evening I was horribly embarrassed, and I changed to my maiden name to avoid questions.'

'I—see.' Then, suddenly, he smiled. 'I'm sorry if I've distressed you, Miss Brooke. And you've been very helpful—very helpful indeed.'

But this, oddly enough, was far from reassuring me. I said sharply: 'But why does all this matter? Surely it's all settled? You've got the murderer, and—'

His brows shot up. 'Got the murderer?'

'Jamesy Farlane!' I cried. 'Jamesy Farlane! Who else could it be? He was at the bonfire, and he attacked me there. What more do you want?'

'A bit more,' said Inspector Mackenzie, with a little smile. 'Farlane's story is that he was going back from the hotel after bringing the stretcher in. He was at the foot of An't Sròn when he saw the bonfire go up. He went up the hill as fast as he could, and was nearly at the top when he heard you scream, and then you came running and, he says, flung yourself at the bonfire. He thought you were going to be burned, and he jumped in and hauled you off. You hit at him, and in the ensuing struggle you both fell down the heather-slope. . . . Is that right, Hecky?'

'That's right, sir.' Hector Munro nodded his red head.

'You see?' said Inspector Mackenzie to me.

'It might even be true,' I said.

He grinned. 'So it might. Especially as Dougal Macrae was with him at the time. . . .'

There was a sharp little silence. Then he rose and began to gather up his papers. I stood up.

'If I may,' he said, 'I'll see you again later, but just at present I'd better get up on to An't Sròn.' He held the door for me with punctilious courtesy. 'You'll be about all day, I take it?'

'I'll be up on the hill myself,' I said, and was unable to keep the asperity out of my voice. 'There's still somebody missing, you know.'

'I hadn't forgotten,' he said gravely, and shut the door behind me.

Chapter Thirteen

The Black Spout

Two nights and a day—it was a very long time to be out on the mountain-side. I think that, by now, we had all given up all prospect of finding Roberta alive. I had, to begin with, built a lot of hope upon the fact that there had been no trace of her within range of Marion Bradford's dead body. A direct fall in the same place must have killed her. The fact that she was nowhere near appeared to indicate some not-too-serious injury which had allowed her to crawl away into shelter. But, of course, if she were still conscious, she must have heard the search-parties. And two nights and a day, even in summer weather, was a very long time. . . .

I had by now abandoned my grisly theory that the murderer—the third climber—had taken Roberta away, alive or dead, for reasons of his own. If the murderer of the bonfires and the murderer of the cut climbing-rope were one and the same—which was so probable as to be a certainty—then, surely, he would hardly have killed poor Beagle for his second bonfire if he had had Roberta's body handy.

That he had any real motive for killing Ronald Beagle I could not believe. It seemed more than ever certain that we were dealing with a maniac. There was a causeless crazy flavour about the killings that was nauseating: Hubert Hay's word 'sacrifice' occurred to me again, with shuddering force.

But where these two apparently ritual killings fitted with the deaths of Marion and Roberta I had no idea. At least, I thought, trudging once again up the deer-track behind Hubert Hay, there was something we could *do*. The finding of Roberta, or Roberta's body, might help the police a little in their hunt for what was patently a madman.

The sun was still brilliant in the blue heaven. Yesterday, under the heavy grey sky, it had been easy to see the mountain-side as the background to tragedy, but to-day, with the sunlight tracing its gold-foil arabesques on the young bracken, and drawing the hot-coconut smell from the gorse, Blaven was no longer the sinister mountain that it had been yesterday. It was alive with the summer. The mountain-linnets were playing over scrubs of bright furze, chirping and trilling, and everywhere in the corners of the grey rock glowed the vivid rose-purple of the early bell-heather.

The search-parties seemed at last to have abandoned the Black Spout, and were scattered about the mountain, still searching the screes and slopes of deep heather. One of the parties, Hubert Hay told me, had climbed higher up the cliffs above the Sputan Dhu, and was out of sight in the upper reaches of the mountain. I realized, as I scanned once again the acre upon acre of steep rocky scree, split by its gullies and fissures, how people could lie for a week, a month, out in the mountains, and their bodies not be found.

And there were still, Hubert Hay told me, climbers lost years ago, of whom no trace had yet come to light.

As we reached the point where, yesterday, I had met Roderick climbing down from the Black Spout, we heard a shout, and saw, away to our right, a small party of men, one of whom—it looked like Hartley Corrigan—waved his arm and called something.

'Do you suppose they've found her?' I asked breathlessly.

'It doesn't look like it,' returned Hubert Hay. 'They may have decided on some new plan of search. I'll go along and have a word with them.'

He began to make his way towards the other party, and I, left alone, stood for a while gazing up at the rocks above me. I was, I noticed, almost directly below the spot where Heather Macrae had been found. For a moment I dallied with the macabre fancy that there, up on that blackened ledge, we would find Roberta lying. Then I shook the thought away like the rags of last night's bad dream, and turned my eyes instead to the more accessible route which led towards the climb over the Black Spout.

I knew that the area had been searched already: searched, moreover, by a team of men who knew far more about the hill than I. But there is something in all of us which refuses to be satisfied with another report, however reliable, that someone else has looked for something and failed to find it. We cannot rest until we have looked for ourselves. And it was surely possible, I told myself, that some corner or hole or crevice of this awful country might have been overlooked.

I began doggedly to scramble up towards the tumble of rocks and heather at the side of the Sputan Dhu.

It was terrible going. The rock was dry to-day, and there was no wind, but each boulder represented a major scramble, and between the rocks were treacherous holes, thinly hidden by grass and heather. I was soon sweating freely, and my head was swimming from too much peering under slabs and down the chutes of small scree that tunnelled below the larger rocks. I struggled on, without realizing how high I had climbed, until exhaustion made me pause and straighten up to look back down the way I had come.

And almost at once something caught my eye—a tiny point of light among the heather, a sparkle as of an infinitesimal amber star. I saw the gleam of metal, and stooped to look more closely.

It was a brooch of a kind very common in souvenir shops in Scotland, a circle of silvery metal set with a cairngorm. I stooped for it, suddenly excited. Roberta—surely Roberta had been wearing this on that first evening at the hotel? I wiped the dirt off it, then lit a cigarette and sat down with the brooch in my hand, considering it. It meant no more, of course, than that Roberta had been this way—and that I already knew from Dougal Macrae's testimony. But for me that winking amber star had somehow the excitement of discovery about it that set me scanning the empty slopes about me with renewed hope.

I was out of sight of the party, and could no longer hear their voices. The only sounds that held the summer air were the rush of the waterfall and the sudden rich burst of song from an ouzel I had disturbed from his perch. I frowned up at the steep pitch of rock above the gully, trying to picture what might have happened there two days ago.

Looking back now I can realize that this was perhaps one of the queerest moments in the whole affair. If I had not been so abysmally ignorant—and so stupid—over the business of that climb across the Sputan Dhu, if I had worked on the evidence plainly available (as the others were even now working), I, too, would have abandoned the gully and searched elsewhere, and the story would have had a very different ending. But I sat there in the sun, smoking and piecing together my own bits of evidence, and deciding that, come what may, I had to finish seeing for myself if Roberta was on this side of the Sputan Dhu. So I stubbed out my cigarette and got up to resume my search.

I have no idea how long I took. I clambered and slithered and peered, pushing aside mats of heather and woodrush, and crawling into the most unlikely places. At first I called occasionally, my breathless '*Roberta!*' ringing queerly back from the cliffs above. Soon I was too exhausted to call but climbed and searched in a grim, hard-breathing silence, brought, minute by minute, to acknowledge that Roderick had been right when he said that he had searched every inch of the place. Roberta was not there.

At length, when I was all but giving up, my foot slipped when I was investigating a ledge. This was wide enough, and I suppose I was in no actual danger, but the brink of the ledge overhung the gully itself, and I was so badly frightened that I had to sit down, my back pressed against the wall of the rock, to collect my wits and my courage.

The sun poured down, slashing the rock with purple shadows. The towering cliffs shut out all sound but the rush of the lonely water. I might have been hundreds of miles from anywhere. The stillness was thick, frightening, uncanny. I sat still, listening to my own heart-beats.

It was then that I heard the moan.

From somewhere to my left it came, to the left and behind me.

I was on my feet in a flash, fatigue and fright alike forgotten.

'*Roberta!*' My voice was shrill and breathless. I waited.

It came again, a tiny animal whimpering. It seemed to come from some-where along the ledge, somewhere back from it, inside the very rock . . . I turned my back resolutely to the gully and my face to the cliff, and went as quickly as I dared towards the sound.

I came to a jutting rock, a corner, and peered round it, with my heart thudding in my throat. Beyond the buttress, the ledge ran along the gully side, rising gradually and dwindling to a mere crack in the cliff. I could see the whole of it from where I stood. There was nothing there. Nothing.

I called again: 'Roberta!'

I waited. There was no sound. The sun beat upon the empty rock.

'*Roberta!*'

There it was again, the tiny moaning.

I squeezed cautiously past the corner, and along the ledge. This was wide enough at first even for me, who am not used to mountains, but when I found it growing narrower, and taking a nasty outward slant at the same time, I stopped, bewildered and, once more, afraid. There was certainly nothing on the ledge. And, just as certainly, this ledge had already been searched. I had seen the imprint of boots which led as far as the corner. I was imagining things.

In that moment I heard the little whimper of pain again, but this time back to my left.

I looked back the way I had come, almost giddy now with bewilderment and excitement, my heart thudding, and my legs and wrists none too steady. Then I saw the answer to the riddle. I had pressed past the jutting buttress of rock at the corner, without seeing that behind it, and running sharply back into the face of the cliff, was a narrow fissure. Most of the opening was masked by a hanging mat of weeds and heather, but there was a little space below this, through which someone might have crawled. . . .

I tore at the heather-mat with desperate hands. It was tough, but chunks of it came away, and I flung it down the gully. Pebbles and peat spattered down on to the ledge. I yanked at a great trail of green and threw it down, so that the sunlight streamed past me into what was, in effect a small dry cave.

She was there, all right. She was lying in a little curled huddle, her back against the wall of the cave. One leg stuck out at an ugly angle, and her hands were torn and covered with dirt and dried blood.

But she was alive. I flew across the cave to kneel beside her. Her eyes were shut, and the bright face that I remembered was a frightening grey-white, with a film of sweat over it like cellophane. The flesh was pulled back from the bones, so that her nose jutted out as sharp as a snipe's beak.

I thrust a shaking hand inside the brave red jacket and tried to find her heart. . . .

A man's shadow fell across the floor of the cave.

Chapter Fourteen

Edge of Nowhere

Roderick's voice said: 'My God, you've found her!'

I turned with a great sob of relief, 'Oh, Roderick—oh, thank heaven someone's come! She's alive, and—'

'*Alive?*' His voice was incredulous. He took a stride across the cave, towering over us both. '*Alive?*'

'Yes. Yes, she is! I heard her moaning—that's how I found her.'

He was down on his knees beside me now, his hands moving over Roberta. His face was grim.

'Yes, she's alive, but only just, Janet. I'm very much afraid—' He broke off, while his hands gently explored her head. She whimpered and moved a little. I said: 'I'll stay with her, Roderick. You go and get the others. You'll go faster than me!'

He hardly seemed to hear me: he was still intent on Roberta. He looked remote, absorbed. When he spoke, it was with suddenly impersonal authority: 'Janet, I left my haversack at the end of the ledge. You'll find my brandy-flask in the pocket. Get it, will you?'

I went quickly. The sunshine met me in a dazzle of light and warmth as I stepped through the cave door. Behind me, Roberta whimpered again, and said something in the blurred little voice of delirium. I caught the word *'Marion. . . .'*

It halted me in mid-stride, as the implications—the terrifying implications—of our discovery of Roberta came fully to me for the first time. I swung round. Roderick turned his head, and my frightened eyes met his. And beneath their still impersonal coolness I saw the same thought that was driving my heart in sickening jerks against my ribs.

'Roderick. . . .' I almost whispered it. 'Roderick, she—she knows who did it.'

There was a grim twist to his mouth. 'I realize that,' he said. 'And by God she's going to stay alive till she tells us. Get that brandy, please.'

'We ought to wrap her up first. Have my coat. . . . We've got to get her warm somehow until we can call the others.' I began to take off my coat. He followed suit rapidly, and I knelt down to wrap the now-quiescent Roberta as warmly as I could in the two garments.

He added, still with that grim note to his voice: 'And I'm not going for help either, to leave you here with this amount of potential dynamite; nor are you going to wander this hill alone any more, my dear. You fetch that brandy while I have a look at her leg, and then you'd better get along above the end of the ledge and just yell bloody murder till somebody comes. And if you don't like the look of whoever comes, just yell bloody murder for me.' He smiled suddenly. 'And I'll be there. Now hurry.'

'All right,' I said. But as I tucked Roberta's cold hands gently inside my coat and made to rise, she began to stir once more, restlessly. The grey lips parted again in a whimper, and I saw that her eyelids were flickering.

'She's coming to,' I whispered. My heart began to thump violently. Roderick's hand gripped my shoulder.

Then Roberta's eyes opened wide; they were dark and pain-filled, but sensible. For a moment she stared at me, as if bewildered, then her gaze moved beyond me.

Someone else was coming along the ledge.

Roberta's hands moved feebly under mine, like frightened animals. Her eyes dilated in an unmistakable look of pure terror. Then she fainted again.

I looked around. Framed in the narrow doorway of the cave was Hartley Corrigan, with Nicholas just behind him. And I could hear Alastair's voice as he followed the others along the ledge.

Alma Corrigan was waiting at the end of the ledge, and was now summoned with a shout. With the coming of the others my responsibility had lightened, and I had time to feel the slackening of nervous tension that comes with reaction. All at once exhaustion seemed to sweep over me like a drowning wave, and it was with feelings of unmixed thankfulness that I found myself elbowed aside by Mrs Corrigan as she proceeded, with Roderick, to take charge of Roberta. I heard her giving rapid orders for first-aid, while Roderick curtly deputed Nicholas to go and summon the other searchers and commandeer a stretcher.

The cave was now uncommonly crowded, but, remembering that look of terror in Roberta's eyes, I stayed where I was. I did go out on to the ledge, but there I remained, leaning against the rock in the sunlight, watching the others inside. If any of those people was the murderer who had sent Roberta to her death, it hardly seemed likely that he could finish his work here and now before she could speak and identify him—but I was taking no risks. I leaned there against the warm rock, and watched the others in the cave ministering to Roberta.

Presently I heard a shout from Nicholas, away up near the main cliff. This was answered by a more distant call. And after that, it did not seem so very long before the stretcher-party arrived, and I could at last abandon my post and leave the ledge to them.

Dougal Macrae was with them, and the boy Iain, and Hubert Hay, who was certainly not the third climber, as he had been with me on Sgurr na Stri when Marion fell to her death. Roberta would be safe enough now, that is, if the murderer's work had not been already done too well, and she were to die of exposure.

But at least she had been found. The long strain was over. I sat among the heather, waiting for the stretcher to be brought off the ledge, and lifted my face to the sun, shutting my eyes and feeling, for the first time for two days, a sense of relaxation. The warm, sweet heather-smelling afternoon insisted, with every lark-note, every linnet-call, on the normality of the day and place. Even when, with mutterings, and cautious scrapings of boot on stone, the stretcher was manoeuvred along the ledge and balanced on to the scree, even then I still felt strangely light-hearted, as though the worst were over.

I had forgotten that Roberta had only to open her mouth and speak, and that a man—a man I knew—would hang by the neck until he was dead and then be buried in quicklime in a prison yard.

Inspector Mackenzie, with the enormous Hecky and Neill, the young local constable, was on An't Sròn when the stretcher was brought down. Hecky stayed where he was, and continued what was apparently a minute examination of the ground round the bonfire, but Inspector Mackenzie, after one glance at Roberta, summoned young Neill from his job, and with him accompanied the stretcher back to the hotel.

As soon as he was told that I had found Roberta, he dropped back from the main party with me, and began to question me. I told him, as exactly as I could, what had passed. He listened quietly, and as soon as I had finished, he took me through it all again, putting a question here and there, until I must have repeated every action and every word from the moment I heard the first moan, to the arrival of the stretcher-party. As I told my story, trudging wearily beside him down the valley, I found that the precarious tranquillity that had lit my little hour upon the hillside had already vanished, a snow-on-the-desert passing that left me picking my old lonely way through the grey wastes of uncertainty and desolation. And that little cold wind of terror fumbled and plucked again, ice-fingered, at my sleeve, so that I stumbled once or twice in my narrative. But I recounted, honestly and flatly enough, all that I remembered, and left him to draw what conclusions he would.

Then he surprised me. He looked sideways at me and said abruptly: 'I'm putting young Neill on to guard yon lassie, and we'll send for a nurse straight away. But we'll not get one before to-morrow at soonest, as the doctor told me this morning that the district nurse is tied up just now with a tricky case. So someone's got to look after Miss Symes till the nurse comes. Do you know anything about nursing?'

'A little, I suppose, but—'

'That's fine. Will you do it? Stay with her to-night and watch her for me?'

'Why, of course,' I said. 'But surely someone else–I mean isn't there anyone more competent, more practised, perhaps, than I am? Mrs Corrigan seems to know her stuff, and I imagine Mrs Persimmon—'

'No doubt,' he said drily. 'But has it not struck you, ma'am, that you're the only woman in the hotel who wasn't here at the time of the first murder?'

'I–I suppose I am. But, Inspector, you can't suspect a *woman*, surely? I mean—'

'Maybe not,' he said, 'but Mrs Corrigan and Mrs Persimmon have husbands. And I want *no one* into that room who might be in any way–er–involved.' He shot me a queer look. 'No one, on any excuse whatever. You follow me?'

'If you mean Nicholas,' I said tartly, 'I'm hardly "involved" with him; and I assure you he's not likely to be admitted.'

His mouth relaxed a little. 'Now, now, lassie,' he said, almost indulgently, 'I wasn't meaning any such thing. Then I take it you'll do it?'

'Of course.' I looked at him curiously. 'Do you mean to tell me that I'm the only person here you don't suspect?'

'Let's say,' he said cautiously, 'that I don't suspect you of wanting to kill Roberta Symes.'

And with that, we reached the hotel. Since Marion Bradford's body was in the room which she had shared with Roberta, and this had been locked by the police, I suggested that Roberta should be given the other bed in my room. The offer was approved by the Inspector, and accepted gratefully by the Persimmons, who were already harassed beyond belief. I left her being tucked up by Mrs Persimmon and Mrs Cowdray-Simpson, with Neill and the Inspector in attendance, and went along to have a bath.

When eventually I got back to my room I found that a bright fire had been kindled on the hearth, and that a kettle was already singing on the bars. All the apparatus for making hot drinks was there, and a half-bottle of brandy gleamed on the bedside table.

The Inspector had gone, but Mrs Persimmon was still busy over something by the hearth, and Neill rose from the chair by the fire and grinned shyly at me. He was a tall, overgrown lad of perhaps twenty, with graceful coltish movements, and the black hair and blue eyes of the true Celt. He said: 'The doctor will be here soon, Mistress Brooke. Inspector Mackenzie told me to tell you. He says will you stay here with me till then?'

'Of course. Do we do anything for her meanwhile?'

Mrs Persimmon rose to her feet. 'We've packed her in hot-water bottles,' she said. 'She's as warm as we can get her, so all we can do now is wait for the doctor.' She bent in a harassed way over Roberta's bed, twitching the blankets unnecessarily into place. She was a small woman, with a round face that normally was good-humoured, and wispy, untidy brown hair. Her eyes were of the true glass-grey that you so seldom see, clear and lovely, but just now they were puckered and clouded with worry. 'If she comes round enough to swallow, you could give her a little sweet tea—and I'll go down now and make some really good clear broth. But that's all we can do for the moment.'

'Except,' said Neill softly, 'to watch her.'

We both looked at him. I said uncertainly: 'It all sounds very—very frightening, Neill. Does he really expect the murderer to try and get her in here?'

He spread out calloused, beautifully shaped hands. 'If she talks, we can hang him,' he said simply.

I went over to the bed and looked at her. She was lying very quietly now, and though I fancied that her skin had lost some of its icy glaze, it still had a tight-stretched pallor that was frightening. Her face was pinched and small; her body, too, was still and small in its packed blankets. Not dangerous; not 'potential dynamite'; not worth the ghastly risk of silencing her. . . . It seemed impossible that those dry lips should ever speak again.

But even as I turned from the bedside she stirred and moaned and her eyelids fluttered. The dark head shifted restlessly on the pillow.

'Here,' said Mrs Persimmon from the hearth. 'Here's the tea.'

With anxious concentration we fed a few drops of the weak sweet stuff between her lips, and saw with delight the faint ripple of the throat-muscles as she swallowed. I began spoonful by spoonful, to pour the life-giving glucose into her, watching anxiously for any sign of change in that effigy of a face.

'I'll go and see about the broth,' said Mrs Persimmon at length, and went out.

The telephone rang. I jumped violently, spilling tea on the bedclothes. Neill lifted the receiver, listened and then said to me: 'The Inspector's on his way up, ma'am. The doctor's here.'

'Thank heaven for that!' I said fervently.

'Yes indeed.'

A minute later we admitted Inspector Mackenzie and the doctor, and thankfully watched the competent way in which the latter examined Roberta. At length he pulled the bedclothes back over her, and looked across the bed at the Inspector.

'I can't find anything wrong except the leg,' he said brusquely. 'Bruises and lacerations, yes; they'll heal, given time. But we'll have to deal with the leg now. I'll need Mary Persimmon to help me, and someone else.'

He glanced at me from under enquiring brows, but the Inspector intervened. 'No, Miss Brooke's done enough for to-day, and besides, she has to be night nurse. Tell Mrs Persimmon to bring one of the maids up with her, and I'll stay here myself. There's a telephone, doctor, if you want to give your orders.'

'What? Oh, ah, yes.' The doctor lifted the receiver, and began to dictate a list of his requirements.

Inspector Mackenzie turned to me. 'I've asked the cook to give you something to eat as soon as possible,' he said. 'It'll be ready in the kitchen in ten minutes or so. You go on down, lassie. I'll call you when we want you back.'

I gave another look at the small figure in the bed, and then made my way downstairs to the lounge.

Chapter Fifteen

Camasunary V

Roderick was in the hall. He must have been waiting for me, because, as soon as I appeared, he strode towards the foot of the stairs, looking anxious.

'Is she all right? What does the doctor say?'

'He didn't say very much,' I replied. 'He's found no actual damage beyond the broken leg, but I imagine it's the two nights in the cave that will kill her if anything does.'

'What does he think of her chances?'

'He didn't say. I suppose she has as good a chance as anyone could have after what she's been through. She's young and very strong, and she did find herself a dry corner out of the wind and rain.'

'She's still unconscious, of course?'

'Oh yes.'

'She'll pull through it,' he said confidently. 'Once they get the leg set—I suppose they're doing that now?'

'Yes. Mrs Persimmon's helping. They sent me down, I'm glad to say.'

'And I'm glad they did. You look washed out, Janet.'

I smiled. 'Thank you for nothing.'

'Sorry, but it's true.' He was still looking worried. 'You won't have to go back and sit with her, will you?'

'I think the Inspector wants me to stay in the room to-night.'

'But that's absurd!' he said angrily. 'You've done more than enough for one day! Why can't Mrs Corrigan stay with her?'

'She's done quite as much as I have.'

'Well, Mrs Cowdray-Simpson, then?'

I said, carefully: 'Inspector Mackenzie has allowed me to understand that he doesn't include me in his list of suspects.'

'He doesn't—?' He broke off, and his blue eyes narrowed. 'Surely he doesn't suspect *any* of the women?'

'I rather think he suspects everybody,' I said, uncomfortably. 'At any rate, I'm not married to a suspect either, you see.'

He opened his mouth as if to speak, and then shut it again in a hard line. His eyes slid away from mine and he studied the pattern of the carpet.

I swallowed, and said hastily: 'I'll be all right, Roderick. All I have to do is give her a drink every now and again, and I can get some sleep between times. In fact it's terribly snug in there, with a fire, and a kettle to make tea, and all the works!'

'Does the Inspector—?' He paused, and shot a quick glance round the hall, then lowered his voice. 'Does the Inspector think there's still any danger to Roberta from–him?'

The last syllable fell queerly, whispered in the empty hall. I found myself lowering my voice in reply.

'I think so. But he's taking precautions. Roberta'll be safe enough, and, by the same token, so will I.' I smiled at him again. 'So don't worry!'

'Very well, then, I won't. As a matter of fact,' his voice was suddenly grave, and a little abstracted, 'as a matter of fact, I think you're probably the only person in the hotel who isn't—'

'Suspected of murder?'

'No. Who isn't in danger from the murderer. . . .'

He looked at me then, with a strange hesitant look that seemed to be mingled of both pity and dread, and something else that I found it hard to read. I felt my heart jump and twist painfully inside my ribs, and I could not meet his look. I turned sharply away towards the lounge door, saying in a tight, flat little voice: 'I'll go and ring for a drink. . . .'

There seemed to be a crowd of people in the lounge, all gathered into small groups near the blazing fire. The air was a hiss of whispered conversations, which ceased abruptly as I came in. Heads swivelled, eyes stared, and then a fusillade of questions met me.

'How is she?' came simultaneously from Mrs Cowdray-Simpson, her husband, Hubert Hay, and Alastair. Alma Corrigan's quick '*Has she said anything yet?*' cut across it like a knife.

I crossed to the fire and held my hands to the blaze. 'The doctor's with her now, setting the leg. Apart from that, the damage appears to be superficial, and the doctor said nothing to me about her chances of recovery from the exposure.' I looked at Alma Corrigan, who was twisting an empty whisky-glass round and round in her fingers. She looked, I thought, frightened. I said: 'I don't think she's said anything yet.'

As I turned to ring for a drink, I saw that Hartley Corrigan had moved up near his wife, and had sat down on the arm of her chair. It made a nice change, anyway, I thought, and wondered, a trifle sardonically, where Marcia was at this moment. One thing was certain, she was well out of whatever was going on here, though just now I would have welcomed the company of one other person in the same equivocal position as myself. There was nothing overt in the manner of anyone in the room to suggest that they knew or resented the fact that I alone was free from police suspicion, but still I felt isolated among them, uncomfortably a sheep in the middle of the goats. And there had been something oddly protective about that gesture of Hartley Corrigan's.

Mrs Cowdray-Simpson looked up again from the inevitable knitting. 'I presume–I hope–the police will take adequate precautions to protect that girl from this beast that's loose among us?'

The phrase sounded curiously shocking, and the speaker seemed to realize this, for the pale eyes behind her spectacles moved round the group, and she said, almost defensively: 'There's a murderer in the room; you can't get away from that fact.'

'Not necessarily,' said Alastair, rather drily. 'We're not all here. Grant,

Drury, Persimmon, not to mention Jamesy Farlane . . . they lengthen the odds a little, Mrs Cowdray-Simpson.' He gave a hard little laugh that held no trace of amusement.

'What odds do I lengthen a little?' This was from Roderick, pushing through the swing doors with a glass in either hand.

'We're just beginning to take seriously the fact that someone in this hotel is a murderer,' said Alastair.

Roderick gave me a glass, and his eyes met mine in a quick look. He said, a little coldly: 'Is anything to be gained by discussing it here? I imagine the police have it pretty well in hand. They can usually be trusted to do their own job.'

'If they only look after that girl Roberta, and pull her round,' said Mrs Cowdray-Simpson, 'she'll do the job for them.'

'There'll be a constable watching her all night,' I said.

'Young Neill Graham? Is that quite—adequate?'

I hesitated, and then said: 'I'm staying with her too.' I added, lamely: 'She's in my room.'

'Oh. . . .' Once again I felt the imperceptible withdrawal of the group, leaving me, as it were, marooned alone on the hearthrug, isolated by my innocence.

'Won't you be frightened?' This from Alma Corrigan. Was there, or was I imagining it, a trace of malice in her tone?

'I don't think so.' I took a drink, and gave the group a quick look over the rim of my glass. 'Where's Mr Drury?'

'I think he went out to the garage.' It was Hubert Hay who answered. 'He's lost a book, and he thinks he left it in his car.'

'Why?' asked Alma Corrigan, and this time I certainly heard the venom in her voice. 'Has the Inspector asked for a report on our movements?'

I felt myself go scarlet, but I held on to my temper, and said, very evenly: 'I am not, as you imply, Mrs Corrigan, appointed by the police to spy on you all. I happen to be in the lucky position of not being a suspect, simply because I wasn't here when the first murder was committed, and, since the odds are that we only have one murderer and not two, I can't be guilty. So the Inspector can leave me with Roberta until the nurse comes.'

'It's monstrous to suggest—' began Roderick, hotly to Alma Corrigan, but I cut across him.

'It's all right, Roderick. And the suggestion isn't so very monstrous after all. I'm certainly co-operating with the police—I hope we all are. And if that includes giving the Inspector an account of anyone's movements at any time, I'll do my utmost to describe them for him.'

'Well!' said Alma Corrigan. 'I must say—' Her husband dropped a hand on her arm, and she broke off. I said to her, coldly: 'I should hardly need to point out that this isn't a case of the police *versus* a bunch of suspects. It's a case of the murderer *versus* every single other person here.'

'Good for you!' said Hubert Hay unexpectedly.

Colonel Cowdray-Simpson cleared his throat. His face looked all at once remote and austere, with a curious withdrawn intelligence that his gentleness had hidden before; it was a look both forbidding and compassionate, the look of a judge rather than of a soldier. I found myself wondering if he were a magistrate. 'It is more than that, my dear young lady,' he said to me. 'Each case of murder is a case of the murderer *versus* every civilized human being. Once a man has put his hand to murder he is automatically outcast. I would go further than that. I would assert that once the very idea of extreme physical violence has occurred to a man as an acceptable solution to any problem, then he is in danger of forfeiting his claim to consideration as a civilized being.'

'That's a strong statement, sir,' said Roderick.

'I happen to feel strongly about it,' retorted the Colonel.

'Do you apply the same principle to nations as to individuals? You are a military man?'

'I do.'

'To acts of war?'

'To acts of aggression. It seems to me a denial of the intellectual progress of centuries, for a nation to consider violence as a tool of policy.'

'All the same,' said Alma Corrigan mulishly, 'it's absurd that we should all be treated as suspects. The police *must* have some idea who did it.'

'If they haven't now,' said Hubert Hay, 'they certainly will have as soon as Roberta Symes opens her mouth.'

There was a nasty little silence.

I set down my glass with a *click* on the glass-topped table. 'Well,' I said, 'for the sake of everybody here who isn't a murderer, I promise you that Roberta will be kept safe until she *does* open her mouth.'

Then I walked out of the room.

It didn't take much, I thought, to skin the veneer of politeness and sophistication off people who were in some kind of danger. There had been some strong undercurrents there in the lounge to-night, and I had a feeling that, if one had been able to trace them out, one would be a fair way to solving the mystery. On the face of it, I thought (as I crossed the hall and started down the dark passage towards the kitchens and back premises), I would be inclined to absolve the Colonel. He had delivered himself so convincingly of his principles; but then (I added a despairing rider), that, surely, might be just what a murderer would do? And, heaven knew, our murderer was clever. He was an actor who could hide the instincts of a werwolf under an impeccably civilized exterior. Nobody in the lounge to-night, hearing his own condemnation, the statement of his utter isolation from the rest of us, had so much as batted an eyelid. But then, of course, the murderer might not have been in the lounge. . . . There were other possibilities, as Alastair had pointed out.

I turned a corner of the passage and ran straight into Nicholas.

Literally ran into him, I mean. He caught me by the arms and steadied me, peering down in the dimness of the passage.

'Why,' he said softly, 'it's our little copper's nark. The Inspector's not down this way, darling.'

I did lose my temper then. I blazed at him, pulling against the pressure of his hands. 'Let me go, damn you! *Let me go!* Don't you dare to speak to me like that! You've no right—'

'So you keep telling me. Where are you going?'

'That's none of your damned business!'

'It's anybody's business in this murderous locality to stop you from wandering about in the dark alone.'

'I'm going to the kitchen to get some food,' I said waspishly, 'and I'm in a hurry.'

He did not move. 'Where's the boy friend?'

'What d'you mean?'

'Your *preux chevalier* with the golden hair. Why isn't he playing bodyguard?'

'You always did have a filthy tongue, Nicholas,' I said bitterly.

'I did, didn't I?' He grinned sardonically. 'You could say it's a valuable stock-in-trade as a writer, though perhaps as a husband—'

'Exactly. Now let me go.'

'Just a moment. I'm quite serious, as it happens, Gianetta. It seems to me you're altogether too fond of wandering about the place alone–or with somebody you don't know. If you had a grain of sense you'd know this chap meant business. Aren't you scared?'

'I wasn't,' I said tartly, 'until three minutes ago.'

I don't know what made me say it. The instant the words were out I regretted them, but it was too late. He dropped his hands from my arms and stood looking down at me in the semi-darkness. I thought he must hear the thudding of my heart.

'O–ho . . .' he said at length, and then, very softly: 'Sits the wind in that quarter?'

I was silent. I wanted to run from him, towards the lights and warmth of the kitchen, but I was held there, nailed to the passage-wall by the hammer-blows of my own heart.

Nicholas said: 'So you're afraid I'll kill you, Gianetta *mia*? . . . Do you really think I'd do that, Gianetta? Cut that pretty throat, Gianetta . . . and all for what? Auld lang syne?'

'Do you need a reason?' My voice was a whisper that sounded strange to me. This could not be happening; this fantastic conversation could not be taking place. . . . 'Do you need a reason?' I whispered.

He did not reply. He stood looking at me in silence, his face, in that uncertain light, quite inscrutable. At length he said, in quite a different tone: 'What's your proof?'

I almost jumped. 'I haven't any.'

'If you had, would you hand me over–for auld lang syne?'

Fantasy . . . thickening round us like the spinning of a spider's web. He might have been asking if I wanted more house-keeping money. I put a hand to my head. 'I–don't know, Nicholas.'

'You–don't–know.' His tone brought the blood to my face.

'Nicholas,' I said desperately, 'try to understand—'

'You were my wife.'

'I know, but—'

'You always used to say that you didn't believe in divorce.'

'I know,' I said again, a little drearily. It was auld lang syne all right. Every quarrel we had ever had, had ended with my being forced on to the defensive. I heard the familiar note of excuse creeping into my voice again now, feebly, infuriatingly: 'But it wasn't my fault we got divorced.'

'Even so, according to what you used to say, you should think of yourself as still bound to me . . . or do you—*now?*'

'Now? I don't follow.'

'No? I was harking back to the blond boy friend.'

'Damn you, Nicholas!'

He gave a hard little laugh. 'You've got a nasty problem, haven't you, Gianetta. Moral loyalty *versus* civic duty . . . or does the situation simplify itself now into the old love *versus* the new? It would save you a lot of trouble if you could hand me over this minute, wouldn't it?'

The outrage that swept over me was as real, as physical, as shock. I went cold. My voice dropped to a flat icy calm. 'If you had been in the lounge just now, you'd have heard Colonel Cowdray-Simpson expressing what happen to be my views. He said that by an act of violence, like murder, a man cuts himself off from his fellows, and forfeits his—his human rights. If I were still your wife'—I put my hands against the wall behind me, feeling for its solid bracing comfort—'if I were still—legally—your wife, I shouldn't help to incriminate you, even if I could, because, as your wife, I should be identified with you in all you did . . . but I would leave you. I couldn't stay with you, knowing you were—'

'Cain?'

'I—yes.'

There was an odd note in his voice. 'And as it is?'

'As it is—' I stopped, and to my horror my voice caught on a little sob. 'As it is,' I said raggedly. 'I don't know, God damn you. Now let me by.'

He moved without a word, and I ran past him, and down the passage to the kitchen.

Chapter Sixteen

Trust Country

In the kitchen there was light, and warmth, and the good smell of food. The cook was busy over the Aga, and one of the girls who waited at table was bustling about with stacks of plates.

I hesitated inside the doorway, conscious suddenly of my shaking hands and the tears in my eyes, but Cook looked up, gave me a flushed, fat smile, and pointed to a place set at one end of the big scrubbed table.

'If it's nae odds, mistress,' she said in a brisk Lowland voice, 'ye can hae yer denner in here. Ye'll get it hetter and quicker. Yon Inspector telt me ye'd want it the noo.'

'It's very good of you. I hope it's not too much of a nuisance.'

'Nae trouble at all,' said Cook comfortably, not moving from the range. 'Effie, gie the lady some soup.'

Effie was thin and dark, with enormous eyes that devoured me with curiosity. She brought me a plate of steaming soup, putting it down in front of me warily, almost as if I might bite. Then she backed off a step or two, gripping the front of her apron.

'Noo, Effie!' This sharply, from Cook. 'Gang awa' intae the dining-room wi' the breed!'

Effie went, casting a longing, lingering look behind. As the kitchen door swung to behind her, Cook put down her ladle, and said, in a hoarse, impressive whisper: 'Sic a cairry-on, mistress, wi' a' them murrders! It's fair awesome. It garrs yer bluid rin cauld!'

I agreed mechanically. The hot soup was wonderfully comforting, and the bright warmth of the kitchen rapidly helped to dispel the effect of that fantastic little interview in the passage. Cook leaned her plump red fists on the opposite end of the table and regarded me with a sort of professional pleasure.

'Noo, they're grand broth, aren't they?'

'They're–it's excellent, Cook.'

'They're pittin' a bit reid intae yer cheeks. Ye looked fair weshed oot and shilpit-like when ye cam' in, I'll say. They were sayin' it was you found her?'

'Yes, I was lucky.'

'It was her that was lucky, the puir lassie, to be livin' the day.' She nodded heavily. 'Mony's the yin that hasnae been sae lucky–and I canna mind a waur simmer.'

'Well,' I said, 'it isn't every year you get–murder.'

'No. Goad be thankit. But I wasna' meanin' that.' She whipped away my empty soup plate and substituted a lamb chop flanked with peas and roast potatoes. 'It was the accidents on the hill I was meanin'.'

'Oh?' I remembered something somebody else had said. 'Has this year really been worse than usual?'

'Aye, that it has, miss. Thae twa lassies'–she jerked her head vaguely towards the ceiling–'they're the third casualties we've had this season, no' coontin' murrders.'

'Who were the others?'

'Weel, there was a pair frae London–the daft craturs went into the Cuillins wi' neither map nor compass. They were no' fun' till a week after, lyin' at the fit o' a pressy-piece.'

'How dreadful! Had the mist come down on them?'

'The day they went up it was as clear as–as consommay,' said Cook. 'Naebody kens what happened.'

'It's a big price to pay for a bit of carelessness,' I said.

'Aye, it's that. But them hills are no' to be taen lightly . . . aye, and that puir man lyin' upstairs, he's mony a time said the verra same, and a grand climber he was an' a'. Aipple tairt.'

'I beg your pardon? Oh, I see. Thank you, Cook. This is very good.'

'It's no' sae bad,' said Cook complacently, watching me sample her rich, flyaway pastry. 'Then there was twa o' them students, frae the College at Oxford-and-Cambridge. They baith tummled doon frae a muckle rock–gey near the same bit.'

'Dead?'

'Aye, deid as a stane. The rope snappit.'

I put my spoon and fork down carefully, side by side, on my empty plate, and stared at them for a moment. But I wasn't seeing them. I was seeing, in a queer fugitive vision, two pairs of climbers climbing in the Cuillin . . . but in each case, another climber moved with them; the third climber, in whose presence ropes snapped, and bodies hurtled to their death. . . .

'A cup o' coffee noo?' suggested Cook.

'I'd love one,' I said, 'but I think I'd better take it upstairs to drink. The doctor must have finished up there, and Mrs Persimmon'll want to come down.'

'Hoo was the lassie when ye left her?' She set a large blue cup on the table, and began to pour coffee.

'Not too good. But I've a feeling she's going to be all right.'

'Thank guidness. I've gien ye the big cup. Ye'd better tak' it quick, while it's warm. Sugar?'

'Please. Thank you very much, Cook. That was excellent. I feel a whole lot better.'

'Aye, an' ye look it,' said Cook. 'Mind ye keep the door lockit the nicht, ma lassie.'

'I certainly will,' I said fervently, and got up as she turned to her stove.

There was no one in the passage. I went quickly along it, round the corner with my heart beating a little jerkily, then out into the open hall. Nicholas was there, leaning over the reception desk talking in an undertone to Bill Persimmon. He saw me, but beyond a slight twitch of his black brows he gave no sign. I ignored him, and almost ran up the stairs, balancing my cup of coffee carefully.

I met Mrs Persimmon and a maid on the landing.

'Oh, there you are, Miss Brooke!' Mrs Persimmon still sounded harassed, which was hardly surprising. 'Did you get some dinner?'

'Yes, thank you, I've done very well.'

'Oh, good, good. Well, the police are expecting you now, I think. . . .'

'How's Miss Symes?'

'I hardly know. Still unconscious, and the doctor won't say very much. Oh dear, oh dear. . . .' And she plunged downstairs, followed by the maid laden with crumpled linen. I heard her still lamenting faintly as I went along to my room and knocked on the door.

The Inspector opened it.

'Ah, Miss Brooke. Come away in.'

He shut the door carefully behind me. The doctor had gone. Roberta, in her blankets, looked very white and still, so white that I exclaimed anxiously: 'Inspector Mackenzie, is she all right?'

He nodded. 'The doctor thinks so. He says she'll pull through.'

'That's wonderful.'

His eyes was on Roberta's quiet, shuttered face. 'Aye,' he said, his voice expressionless. Then he turned to me. 'And you? Did you get some food?'

'Yes. Cook fed me in the kitchen.'

'Good. How do you feel now?'

I smiled. 'Ready for anything— But I hope you're going to tell me what to do, before I'm left alone with the patient.'

'The doctor left instructions, and I wrote them down for you.' He indicated a paper on the bedside table. 'But it's mostly a case of keeping the hot-bottles filled and the room warm. You can give her a little broth, or tea with a dash of brandy in, whenever she'll take it. The doctor had a confinement due, so he had to go, but if you get at all worried, you can get hold of me, and I'll ring up the Broadford hospital for advice.'

'D'you mean I'm to send Neill for you?'

'No. Use the telephone. I'm using Miss Maling's room. I'll probably be up most of the night, but when I do go upstairs, I'll switch it through to there. Don't hesitate to ring up if you're in the least nervous or worried. We'll be about all night.'

'I won't.'

'Good. Well, now,' he turned to Neill, who had appeared in the doorway, 'Neill, you know what to do. Make yourself comfortable. Sergeant Munro'll relieve you at two o'clock, and I'll be along myself now and again to see everything's all right. I doubt if any of us'll get much sleep to-night. . . .' He crossed to the window and stood looking out. 'There's a mist coming up. A pity; it's never a help on this kind of job. I think. . . .' He reached a hand up and snecked the window shut. 'That disposes of *that*; d'you mind being a trifle stuffy?'

'Under the circumstances, not at all.'

'That's all right, then. Well, I'll leave you. I'm afraid you've a long night ahead of you, but I think it's a safe night. And—oh, yes, Major Persimmon is to keep the dynamo running all night, so the lights will be on. All right, Neill?'

'Yes, sir.'

He turned to me. 'Are you a light sleeper, lassie?'

'I think so.'

'There's no need for you to stay awake all night, you know. She'll sleep, and if she wants you, Neill will wake you. Get some rest yourself between whiles. Right?'

'Right.'

'Well, good night, lassie.'

'Inspector Mackenzie—'

He was already at the door. He turned with his hand on the knob. 'Yes?'

'There are some things—I have a few things you ought to know.'

'Important?'

'I—I'm not sure.'

'Anything that'll enable me to arrest our murderer here and now?'

'Oh no. No.'

His eyes considered me, queerly. 'You've located him, haven't you?'

'*No!*' The single syllable came violently, surprising me as much as the Inspector.

He looked at me for a moment. 'Then I dare say it'll keep till morning, ma'am,' he said.

He went out. I went quickly across the room and turned the key. The whirr and click of the wards was reassuring, and the *chock* as the bolt slid home punctuated our security with sharp finality.

Chapter Seventeen

Forests of the Night

The long evening dragged through and the night came. I nodded over the fire with *The Bride of Lammermoor*, fighting off the feeling of desperate tiredness that threatened to overwhelm me. Neill sat in the shadows beside Roberta's bed, his long body still and relaxed in the wicker chair, his back to me and the rest of the room. Roberta stirred once or twice, but her breathing seemed every moment more natural, and her colour improved, so that it was with a reasonably quiet mind that I eventually put down my book and decided to try and get some sleep.

I crossed the room softly towards my bed. 'Good night, Neill.'

'Good night, miss,' he answered, without turning his head, and, absurdly enough, I felt a wave of relief pass over me at the quiet reply. It was as if one of the still shadows of the room had offered reassurance; and it brought home to me the unwelcome realization that, in spite of all precautions, in spite of Neill's very presence, I was really very nervous indeed. I chided myself sharply as I wound up my little bedside clock and slid my feet out of my slippers. The room was locked, door and window, and Neill, solid dependable Neill, was here with me; and there, at arm's length, on the other end of the telephone, was Inspector Mackenzie.

I turned back the eiderdown and crept underneath it, wrapping the full skirt of my housecoat round me. My whole body ached with weariness, but I had no fear that I should sleep too soundly to hear Roberta moving. There were other fears that would keep me too near the edge of consciousness for that. . . .

I was quite right. I dozed and waked, and dozed again—little uneasy snatches of sleep that might have been of a minute's or of an hour's duration. Twice, Roberta stirred and whimpered and had me up on my elbow in a flash; but each time she subsided once more into sleep. Once, some time soon after midnight, she seemed to rouse more fully, so I got up and heated broth, and Neill and I managed to make her swallow half a dozen spoonfuls before she turned her head away with a tiny petulant movement, and subsided again into sleep. Another time I remember boiling more water for bottles, and I recollect, dimly, the quiet change-over of watchers, as Hector Munro relieved Neill at two o'clock; and I remember twice, as in a recurrent dream, the Inspector's voice outside the locked door, asking how we did. Some time during the dead hours Hecky made a cup of tea—strong, this time—and I drank it curled up warmly under my eiderdown before I got up yet again to fill hot-water bottles. . . .

I did my job efficiently enough, I know, but I must have moved through that firelit fantasy in a state suspended between wakefulness and dream, so that, looking back now, I can hardly tell where the reality ended and the nightmare began. Indeed, my memory now is of a night of continuous nightmare, where the ordinariness of the tasks which engaged me could not hold at bay the shadows haunting, uneasily, the corners of the firelit room. The ticking of my little clock, the workaday hum of the singing kettle–these homely sounds became, to me lying dozing through the small, crawling hours, distorted into the very stuff of nightmare–manifestations as eerie and terror-filled as the shadows that gibbered across the fire-flickering ceiling above my head. Shadows and fire . . . shadows across the glare . . . shadows coalescing even as I watched into the image of a murderer gesticulating before the flames, dancing crazily round a pyre that grew and swelled and dilated into a gigantic smoking shape, a red-hot Paracutin of a bonfire, a veritable hell's mountain. . . . And now it was Blaven itself that loomed over me, lit with flames. And a solitary, faceless climber straddled that devil's gully, pulling after him a length of cut rope. Somewhere, a knife gleamed, and I heard the soft stutter of two voices in counterpoint, wavering through the sound of falling water. . . . *You were my wife. . . . You've located him, haven't you? . . . you've got a nasty problem, haven't you? . . . you've located him, haven't you . . . haven't you? . . .*

My own 'No!' woke me finally, with such a jerk that I wondered if I had spoken aloud, and strained my ears for the vibration of my own voice among the shadows. Or was it Hecky who had spoken? Or Roberta? I pushed myself up on to my elbow and looked across at her. She was moving, making fretful little noises of pain, but it was not this that made my heart jump and my body stiffen in its little nest under the eiderdown. Hecky wasn't there.

Even as I reacted to this in a manner that betrayed the lamentable state of my nerves, I turned my head and saw him, like the spectre of my dream, in front of the fire. But this fire threw no terrifying shadow back into the room, and for the worst of reasons. It was almost out.

A glance at my clock told me that it was a quarter-past four. I had not been asleep long, and Hecky had presumably not been to sleep at all, but in spite of us the peat fire, inexpertly stacked, had dwindled and died into an inert-looking mass of black sods.

Now a peat fire is a tricky thing for an amateur to manage. Once it is going well, it is wonderfully hot, a red glowing mass like the heart of a blast furnace. Mrs Persimmon had banked this one expertly, and Neill, too, had known what to do with it, but Hecky was a townsman and a Lowlander, while I was the most helpless of amateurs. Between us we must have handled it very clumsily, for it had burned itself almost out, and as Hecky stirred it the peat crumbled, and fell away into fragments that rapidly began to blacken.

I swung myself off the bed, thrust my feet into my slippers, and went softly across to the fireplace.

'Won't it go at all, Sergeant?'

'It will not.'

'Isn't there any more peat?'

'Och, yes, there's plenty. It's the putting it on that's tricky. Have you the way of it at all, miss?'

'Far from it, but we've got to try.' There was a small pile of fresh peats on the hearth. I knelt down beside Hecky and together we stacked them over the embers and tried to blow them to a flame. But to no avail; the red ash waned and darkened, and the peats steamed sullenly, black and unresponsive. The room felt cold.

'It's no good,' I said. 'It's going out.'

We looked at one another in some dismay, then I stood up, biting my lip. I had to put fresh bottles in Roberta's bed. I had to be ready to make her another drink. I had to get the room warm against the chill hours of daybreak.

'I'm sorry,' said Hecky.

'It's my fault as much as yours. In fact, neither of us is to blame if we can't manage the dashed thing. What we should have done is to ask Mrs Persimmon for some wood to help us keep it going. I'm afraid it didn't occur to me.'

He stood up, dusting his hands lightly together. 'Will I go and get some wood, then?'

'There should be some somewhere,' I said. 'The lounge fire was made up with logs, I remember. Perhaps—'

'I ken fine where it is. We've been all over this place at one time and another, you'll mind. It's oot the back.'

I said, doubtfully: 'Should you go, d'you think?'

'You've got to get this fire going, have ye no?'

'Yes. Yes, I have.'

'Well, then, I reckon I'd better go. And if you don't open the door till I get back, there'll be no harm done.'

'I–I suppose not. How am I going to be sure it's you when you come back?'

'I'll knock–this way.' He moved nearer. His hand went out to the mantelpiece beside me. A finger fluttered. I heard a tiny tapping, the sort that might be made by a grasshopper's feet landing a little raggedly on a leaf: *tap–taptap–taptaptap–tap.* . . . Nobody else but I, with my ear some nine inches away, could possibly have heard it.

'Right,' I said. 'Don't be long, for goodness' sake. And–oh, Sergeant—'

'Yes, miss?'

'If there's a kettle hot on the Aga, you might bring it up. It'll save time.'

'O.K., miss.'

'You–you'll be all right?'

He grinned down at me. 'Don't worry about me, now. I'd give a year's pay to meet that chap, whoever he is, down by the woodshed! I'll no' be more than five minutes, miss, and if I see Inspector Mackenzie prowling around, I'll send him along.'

He let himself out, and I locked and bolted the door again behind him. I heard him go softly down the passage. Silence.

My heart was beating uncomfortably hard, and once again I had to take myself sharply to task. I turned resolutely from the door, and went over to have a look at Roberta. She seemed to have relaxed a little, and her breathing was less shallow, but her eyelids twitched from time to time, as if the light troubled her. I took my green silk scarf out of a drawer and dropped it over her bedside light, then went back to nurse my little core of red fire till Hecky should come back.

He was surprisingly quick. I had ripped some pages from the *Autocar*, and, with these, and some small crumblings of peat, was getting a nice little lick of flame, when I heard the soft tap at the door.

I was half-way across the room before I realized that the sound had not been the grasshopper-tapping that Hecky and I had arranged.

It came again, a tiny sound: '*Tap-tap-tap.*'

I was standing three feet from the door, with my hands, in rigid fists, pressed down against the front of my thighs. My heart began to jerk in slow, sickening thuds. I stood, turned to marble, with my eyes on the door, while the seconds ticked madly by on the little bedside clock.

Ever so gently, the door-handle turned. Ever so softly, the door rattled as somebody pressed against it.

If I screamed, I thought, people would wake up, and they would catch him there . . . the murderer, trying to get at Roberta.

But if I screamed, it might penetrate that still slumber of Roberta's, and I had no idea of the possible effect of such a shock. It was not a risk that I felt I had any right to take.

Then I was at the door.

'Hullo?' I was surprised that my voice sounded so normal. 'Is that you, Sergeant?'

Of course it wasn't; but if he said it was. . . .

'No.' The vigorous whisper was certainly not Hecky's. 'It's Inspector Mackenzie. I came to take a look at her. Open up, will you, lassie?'

Even as I accepted the statement with a quick uprush of relief, I surprised myself again, I heard my voice saying calmly: 'Just a minute, Inspector. I'll get a dressing-gown on.'

In three strides I was at the telephone, and had lifted the receiver. My little clock chittered the seconds crazily away beside me . . . two, four, seven seconds, seven dragging light-years before I heard the *click* of the other receiver being lifted, and Inspector Mackenzie's voice, soft, but alert, saying sharply: 'Mackenzie here. What is it?'

I cupped a hand round the mouthpiece and whispered into it: 'Come quickly! *Quickly! He's at the door!*'

The line went dead. My knees gave way under me, and I sat down slowly on my bed, with the receiver still clutched in my hand. My head turned, stiff as a doll's head, to watch the door.

There was no sound, no rattle, no movement of the handle. The door stood blind, bland in its smooth white paint, telling nothing.

There was a swift stealthy rush of feet up the corridor. A voice.

'Inspector? Is anything the matter?'

'Where the devil have you been, Hector Munro?'

'To get wood. I'm sorry, sir. Is something wrong?'

Doors opened. I heard Hartley Corrigan's voice, raw-edged with nerves. 'What the devil's going on here?' Then his wife's scared whisper: 'Has something–happened?'

'Nothing, madam. Please go back to bed.' The Inspector's voice sank to a reassuring mumble, and, since I could now hear three or four voices murmuring in the corridor, I opened my door.

The Corrigans were just withdrawing into their room, which was opposite my own. The only other people who seemed to have been disturbed were Colonel Cowdray-Simpson and Hubert Hay, whose rooms were just round the corner from our passage, in the main corridor. As I opened the door, Hecky, standing rather shamefacedly before the Inspector, with a bundle of wood under one arm and a still steaming kettle in his hand, turned and saw me, and came hurrying down the passage in some relief.

Inspector Mackenzie whipped round after him. His voice was still low, but clear and urgent.

'Hecky! Don't touch that door! Miss Brooke, stand away from the door, please.'

'Look here, Inspector'–this was Colonel Cowdray-Simpson, still surprisingly authoritative in a deplorable old dressing-gown, and without his teeth–'what's wrong?'

'Please accept my assurance that there's nothing wrong, sir. You can reassure Mrs Cowdray-Simpson. And you, Mr Hay; I promise you that if I want help I'll ask for it, but just at the moment—'

'O.K. I'm off.' And Hubert Hay, resplendent in Paisley silk, disappeared reluctantly.

The Inspector came swiftly down to where I was still standing. 'Now, what's all this?'

It was so much the conventional policeman's opening that I felt an absurd desire to laugh. I said, shakily: 'He–he was at the door. The murderer. He said–he said—'

He took my arm and drew me gently into the room towards my bed.

'You sit down there. Don't try to talk.' He shot a rapid glance at Roberta, and was apparently satisfied. 'Hecky, get that fire going. . . . No, on second thoughts, let me do it; you go to my room and get my bag and give that door a going-over.' He looked at me. 'You said he was at the door. I suppose he touched it?'

'Yes. He pushed it, and turned the knob.'

He gave a small grunt of satisfaction. 'The knob, Hecky. No, man, leave it standing open, then no ghosts can wipe it clean before you come back. Aah!'

This was an exclamation of satisfaction as the dry sticks caught alight, and the flames roared up the chimney in a crackling blaze.

'I suppose there wasn't a sign of anybody when you came?' I said.

'No.' He was expertly stacking peat.

'He must have heard me telephoning you. I'm sorry.'

'On the contrary, you did very well.'

'Well, I'm sorry I made Hecky go downstairs, then. It was my fault for letting the fire down, but I had to get it going again.'

He pushed the kettle down among the now-blazing peats, and stood up: 'It might have been a lucky stroke,' he said, 'if we *had* seen the murderer. Now, supposing you tell me what happened.'

I told him about it, while Hecky busied himself over the surface of the door, and Roberta lay quietly in her blankets in the little green glow of the bedside lamp.

He listened in silence, his eyes on my face, 'Hum,' he said at length. 'He must either have heard Hecky go, or have seen him go out across the yard. It doesn't get us much forrarder, except for one thing.'

'What's that?'

'It proves that Miss Symes can convict him. He was our third climber, all right; he cut that rope.'

I said flatly: 'Inspector do you know who this murderer is?'

'Have you finished, Hecky?'

'Aye, sir. Juist aboot it.'

'Inspector, please—'

'Any luck, Hecky?'

Hecky straightened up. His face was rueful. 'No, sir. It's been wiped.'

'*What?*' The Inspector was across the room in three strides, and was examining the door. His mouth was thin and hard. 'Damn!' he said explosively, then added: 'All right, Hecky. Shut the door and get back to your chair.' He came back into the room looking angry. 'Bang goes my proof,' he said bitterly.

'Proof?' I said. 'Then you *do* know who it is?'

'Know? Hardly that, perhaps. Call it a pretty sure guess. . . . But a guess is no good to a policeman, and we've no proof at all—not a shred; and if yon lassie on the bed doesn't open her mouth soon, I'm afraid of what may happen. Look at to-night, for instance; look at the kind of chance he takes—and might very well get away with, God help us, because nobody in their right senses would expect him to take a risk like that.'

'He'll tempt his luck once too often,' I said.

'*Luck!*' His voice seemed to explode on the word. 'He murders Heather Macrae with a twenty-foot blaze of fire on the open side of Blaven. He kills Miss Bradford in full sight of Camasunary glen in the middle of the afternoon. He cuts Beagle's throat within yards—*yards*—of witnesses. And now this!' He looked at me, and added, quietly: 'I've been on this corridor all night. I only went downstairs to the office twenty minutes ago. And then—only then—your fire goes out, and he sees Hecky Munro going off and leaving you alone.'

'I—I'm sorry,' I said feebly.

He smiled at that. 'Don't say that, lassie. I told you it wasn't your fault. You've been quite a useful recruit to the Force, indeed you have. . . . That kettle's boiling. Shall I do those for you?'

'I can manage, thanks.' I began to fill Roberta's bottles.

He was standing by her feet, staring down at her face as if he would draw her secret from behind the pale barrier of her brow. His own forehead was creased, his hair tousled, his chin grey with unshaven stubble. His fists were thrust deep into his pockets, and his shoulders were rounded. He looked like any worried middle-aged man wakened out of sleep by the baby's wailing. Then he turned his head, and the quiet intelligent eyes gave the picture the lie. 'Do you mind finishing your watch now?'

'No.'

'Don't send Hecky away any more.'

'I certainly won't!'

'I shan't be on the end of the telephone. I have—a few things to do. But don't worry. And who knows, it may all be over sooner than you think. We'll get him. Oh yes, we'll get him. . . .' And his eyes were no longer kind, but cold and frightening.

Chapter Eighteen

Borderland

When, once again, I had locked and bolted the door behind him, I busied myself over Roberta. It was a full twenty minutes before I had finished my tasks, and, when I had done, all desire for sleep had gone.

I drew a curtain aside and looked out of the window. It was still misty. I could see the faint grey of the first morning light filtering hazily through the veil like light through a pearl. It looked dank and chilly, and I was glad to be able to turn back to the firelit room.

Hecky had made more tea, and I took a cup back to bed with me, wishing yet again that I had something reasonable to read. At this hour of the morning, my heart failed me at the thought of *The Bride of Lammermoor*, and I had torn up most of the *Autocars* to light the fire. There remained *The Golden Bough*—an odd thing, surely, to find in a remote hotel in Scotland? It was a pleasant title, I thought, but I had a vague feeling that it was as heavy going, in its own way, as *The Bride of Lammermoor*. Something to do with primitive religions . . . hardly a bedside book, and hardly, I thought, picking it up incuriously, the sort of book with which to while away even the wettest day in Skye. Except, of course, Sunday, when there was no fishing.

But someone had been reading it. There was a bookmark, an old envelope, thrust between the pages, and, of its own accord, the heavy book fell open at the place thus marked. It opened in the ready and accustomed manner of a book much handled at that particular page.

I looked at it, mildly curious.

The Beltane Fires, I read. *In the Central Highlands of Scotland bonfires, known as the Beltane fires, were formerly kindled with great ceremony on the first of May, and traces of human sacrifice at them were particularly clear and unequivocal. . . .*

I sat up, staring unbelievingly at the page, my brain whirling. It was as if the words had exploded into the silence of the room, and I glanced across at Hecky Munro's broad back, hardly able to believe that he could be unconscious of their impact. My eye skipped down the cold, precise print; from it, as if they had been scrawled in luminous paint, words and phrases leapt out at me. . . . *Their sacrifices were therefore offered in the open air, frequently upon the tops of hills . . . a pile of wood or other fuel . . . in the islands of Skye, Mull and Tiree . . . they applied a species of agaric which grows on old birch-trees and is very combustible. . . .*

There flashed between me and the printed page a vivid memory: the birch-grove, silver gilt and summer-lace, with broken pieces of fungus still littering the wet ground between the smooth-skinned trees. And the brown fans of agaric pushing, palms-up, from some of the sleek boles. *Very combustible*. . . .

I read on, the cool detached prose bringing to my racing mind picture after picture: *in the Hebrides, in Wales, in Ireland*–in the queer Celtic corners of the land those fires were lit, and rites were performed that echoed grotesquely, though innocently, the grim and bloody rites of an older day. May-day fires, Midsummer fires, Hallowe'en fires–for countless years these had purified the ground, protected the cattle from plague, burned the witches. . . .

Burned the witches. Another memory swam up, sickeningly; a young girl lying in the embers with her throat cut; Hubert Hay's voice talking of magic and folk-lore and writers who questioned Heather Macrae about old superstitions.

I found that my hands were wet with perspiration, and the print was see-sawing in front of my eyes. It was absurd. *Absurd*. No modern young woman of eighteen, even if she did live in a lonely corner of the earth, was going to be sacrificed as a witch. *That* part of it was nonsense, anyway. But why had she been killed, then, and in that unmistakably ritual manner? Hardly in order to protect the crops. Even Jamesy Farlane, born and bred in the mountains, could no longer believe—

I jerked myself out of my thoughts, and read on. I read how, when the sacrificial fire was built, it was lighted, not from 'tame' fire, but from new fire, 'needfire', the living wildfire struck afresh from dry oak, and fed with wild agaric. I read how those who struck the living fire 'would turn their pockets inside out, and see that every piece of money and all metals were off their persons'. I read how, in some localities, the one who made the wildfire must be young and chaste. . . .

The print swam away from me finally then in a wild and drowning dance of words. I put my hands to my face and thought, in a slow painful enlightenment, of Heather Macrae, who was young and chaste, and who divested herself of her pathetic little gew-gaws to make the needfire for her murderer. She must have thought the whole affair crazy, I mused bitterly, but she thought it was fun, it was 'different', it was the sort of romantic craziness that a clever bookish gentleman from London might indulge in.

My thoughts skidded away from that same clever gentleman from London, as I tried, vainly, to fit the other killings into the same framework of primitive ritual. Where, in the plans of this primeval throwback of a murderer, did Beagle's murder fit? Or Marion Bradford's cut rope? Or the students from Oxford and Cambridge? Or Marcia Maling's doll?

It became more than ever certain, on the evidence of this book, that the only kind of logic that could knot together crimes so various, must be the cracked logic of madness. And that the book was evidence there was no doubt. There were too many parallels between its calm statements and the crazy ritual murder on Blaven hill. Nor could it be mere coincidence that the book itself was here, in this hotel. There was the probability that it was the murderer's own: a man whose studies had made him sufficiently familiar with such rites and customs–a man of unstable mind–might, when that mind finally overturned, wallow in just such a botched travesty of ritual as Heather's murder now showed itself to be. Or it was possible—

I was, I found, still clutching in my damp fist the crumpled envelope that had marked the page. My hand shook a little as I smoothed it out.

I sat looking at it for a very long time.

The envelope was in my father's handwriting. It had no stamp, but it bore, in his clear, beautiful hand, a name and address:

Nicholas Drury, Esq.,
at The Camas Fhionnaridh Hotel,
Isle of Skye,
Inverness-shire.

Chapter Nineteen

Abhainn Camas Fhionnaridh

The morning brought misty sunshine and the nurse. The latter was a youngish, square-built woman, who looked kind and immensely capable. With relief I abandoned Roberta to her and went down to breakfast.

As I went into the dining-room, heads turned, and Mrs Cowdray-Simpson asked quickly: 'The girl—how is she?'

I smiled. 'All right so far, thank you. The nurse is with her now, and says she's getting on well.'

'I'm so glad! I was so afraid that all that disturbance in the night—'

'It was nothing,' I said. 'I let the fire out, and the Inspector heard Sergeant Munro prowling down the stairs to get wood for me.'

Nobody else spoke to me while I ate my breakfast, for which I was grateful. I found myself being careful not to catch anybody's eye. I had just poured my second cup of coffee when Effie, round-eyed, appeared at my elbow.

'If you please, miss, the Inspector says—when you're ready, he says, but not to be interrupting yourself—'

Her voice was high-pitched and possessed remarkable carrying-power. It was into a dead and listening silence that I replied: 'I'll go and see the Inspector at once. Thank you, Effie.'

I picked up *The Golden Bough*, which I had wrapped in yet another piece of *The Autocar*, took my cup of coffee in the other hand, and walked out of the dining-room, still in that uncomfortable silence. My face was flaming. Last night's quarantine seemed still to be isolating me, Nicholas' mocking phrase to be whispering me out of the room. In each look that followed me I could sense the same resentment: in one pair of eyes there might also be fear. My cheeks were still flying scarlet banners when I got to the Inspector's temporary office.

He greeted me cheerfully, with a shrewd glance at my face which provoked me into saying, tartly: 'I could do without the distinction of not being a suspect, Inspector Mackenzie!'

He was unperturbed. 'Is that so? Don't they like it?'

'Of course they don't! I feel—cut off . . . and the funny thing is that it's *I* who feel guilty. I wish it was all over!'

'I'm with you there.' He stretched out a hand. 'Is that for me?'

I handed him *The Golden Bough*. In some curious way I felt that, by doing so, I had committed myself to something, had started down a path from which there was no turning back. I sat down. 'I've marked the place,' I said.

I bent my head over my coffee-cup, stirring it unnecessarily, concentrating on the brown swirl of the liquid against the blue sides of the cup. I heard the Inspector make an odd little sound, then he said sharply: 'Where did you find this?'

I told him.

'And when did you see this marked section?'

'Last night.' I told him about that, too. But not about the crumpled envelope. It was in my pocket. I could not go quite so far down the path. Not yet.

'It was you who marked these passages?'

'Yes.'

'Do you know whose book this is?'

The envelope burned in my pocket. 'No.'

There was a pause. I looked up to find his eyes watching me. He said: 'You had other things to tell me, I believe. You told me so, before you found this book. Now, Miss Brooke'—he was being very formal this morning—'what is it that you think I ought to know?'

'The first thing,' I said, 'concerns the cut climbing-rope that killed Marion Bradford.'

'Yes?'

I began to tell him about my trip downstairs in the darkness on my first night in the hotel, and how both Jamesy Farlane and Alastair Braine had been in the hotel porch.

'And Mr Corrigan had been fishing with them,' I said slowly. 'Alastair said he'd already come back—but yesterday his wife said he didn't get in that night till three o'clock. It was about half-past two when I spoke to Alastair.'

The Inspector was writing rapidly. He looked up when I fell silent. 'What you're trying to tell me is that each one of these three men had the opportunity to damage the girls' climbing-rope the night before the climb.'

'Yes,' I said, miserably.

'Then where does Dougal Macrae's third climber come in?'

'He might be innocent,' I said, 'and just be frightened! When he saw them fall—'

'Aye, aye, lassie,' said the Inspector drily, and, again, gave me that long considering look. 'And had you anything else to tell me?'

So I told him about the episode of Marcia's doll, feeling, with every word, more and more like the despicable little informer Nicholas had called me.

Finally I sat back, and looked unhappily across the table at him. 'But perhaps you knew?'

He nodded. 'Mrs Persimmon told me about that. But you can forget it; it's not a mystery any longer, and it never was a piece of this mystery in any case. I think I may tell you that it was part of a little private feud between Mrs Corrigan and Miss Maling.'

'Oh? You mean *Alma Corrigan* did it?'

'Yes. She told me this morning. She did it to frighten Miss Maling away from the hotel for–er, reasons of her own.'

'I–see.' I was remembering Alma Corrigan's face as she watched Marcia's car driving away across the glen. 'Well, it appears to have worked.'

His mouth relaxed a little. 'Quite so.' Then he looked down at his notes. 'Well, I'm much obliged to you for telling me these things. I think you were right to do so. Is there anything else?'

'No,' I said, but I was not well enough guarded yet, and his eyes lifted quickly to my face. They had sharpened with interest.

He said flatly: 'You're lying to me, aren't you? There is something else.'

'No.' But I said it too loudly.

He looked at me very gravely for a few long seconds. Then he laid the pencil carefully down on his papers, and put his hands, palm downwards, flat on the desk. 'Lassie'–his tone was no longer official; it was very kind–'I think you told me a lie last night, didn't you?'

'I? A lie? What—'

'When you said you hadn't guessed who the murderer was.'

I bit my lip and sat rigid, my eyes on the floor.

He said: 'Do you really think a woman of Marion Bradford's experience wouldn't have noticed if the rope was damaged when she put it on? Do you really think that rope was cut in the hotel porch that night?'

'I–it might have been.'

'It might. But do you think it was.'

'N-no.'

He paused. 'I'll tell you how we think this murder was done,' he said at length. 'You realized, of course, that Roberta Symes never climbed across the Sputan Dhu at all?' He added, as I stared at him: 'There was no rope on her body, was there?'

I said slowly. 'No. No, there wasn't. Of course . . . if she'd been middle man on the rope the murderer *couldn't* have cut it between her and Marion. D'you know, I never worked that out? How stupid of me!'

'It's just as well you didn't, or you'd have left the Sputan Dhu to look for her elsewhere.'

'What did happen, then?'

'We think he offered to do the climb with Marion Bradford, Roberta watching. When he got Miss Bradford to the one pitch that's out of sight of the other side–there's an overhang—'

'I know. I noticed it. He could have cut the rope then without being seen.'

He nodded. 'He pulled her off and cut the rope. Roberta would see an "accident", see her fall. Then she would hear him shout that he was coming back. He could get back quite easily alone by going higher above the gully. She would wait for him in who knows what agony of mind, there by the gully's edge. And in her turn, when he came there, he would throw her down.'

I said nothing. I couldn't speak, couldn't think. I believe I shut my eyes. I know I was trembling.

'Lassie,' he said, very gently, 'if a man's a murderer, and a murderer like this one, crazy and—yes, vicious and crazy, he's not fit to defend, you know.'

I said chokily: 'Loyalty—'

'Doesn't enter into it. He's an outlaw. Your loyalty is to the rest of us, the sane ordinary people who want him locked up so that they can be safe.'

'Well, why don't you arrest him, if you're so sure?'

'I told you. I can't possibly move without proof. I'm waiting for some information to come from London. Or—there's Roberta.'

'Why did you leave me with her, if you're so sure I'd shield the murderer?' I cried.

'Because I'm a good enough judge of people to know that, when it comes to the point, you'll be on the right side, whatever your—loyalties.'

'My instinct, you mean,' I said bitterly. 'If you'd been in the lounge last night, you'd have heard me talking very fine and large about my principles, but now—' I got up. 'Has no one ever told you that people mean more to women than principles? I'm a woman, Inspector Mackenzie.'

He had risen, and his eyes met mine levelly. 'So was Heather Macrae.'

I blazed at him at that. 'I don't know why you're treating me to a sermon on loyalty, Inspector Mackenzie! Even if I *did* guess who your murderer was it's only a guess! How am I supposed to be able to help you catch him? I've told you everything—'

'No.' His voice was soft, but it brought me up short. 'I still don't believe you.' He surveyed me grimly. 'And if this fact—whatever it is—that you are keeping back, is one that will give me the proof I want, then I must warn you—'

'Proof? I haven't any proof! I swear I haven't! And if I had—oh God, I must have time to think,' I said shakily, and almost ran out of the room.

There may have been people in the hall: I never saw them. I went blindly across it, making without coherent thought for the glass porch, and the fresh air and freedom of the glen. But when I pushed my way through the swing doors into the porch I came face to face with Dougal Macrae coming in. He greeted me gravely.

'Good morning, mistress. It's a grand morning for it, forbye a bit of mist coming up frae the bay. Are you wanting to go right away?'

'Go?' I looked at him blankly.

'It was to-day I was taking you fishing, Mistress Brooke. Had you forgotten?'

'Fishing? Oh—' I began to laugh, rather weakly, and then apologized. 'I'm sorry; but it seems odd to be thinking of fishing after—after all this.'

'To be sure it does. But ye canna juist be sitting round to wait for what's going to happen, mistress. Ye'll be better out in the clear air fishing the Abhainn Camas Fhionnaridh and taking your mind off things. Fine I know it.'

'Yes, I suppose you do. . . . All right, Mr Macrae, I'll come. Give me five minutes.'

Three-quarters of an hour later, as I stood on the heather where the Camasunary River flows out of Loch na Creitheach, I knew that Dougal had been right.

The mist that, earlier that morning, had blanketed the glen, had now lifted and rolled back, to lie in long vapour-veils on the lower slopes of Blaven and Sgurr na Stri. Just beside us, An't Sròn was all but invisible in its shroud, and from its feet the loch stretched northwards, pale-glimmering, to merge with the mist above it in a shifting opalescent haze. Marsco had vanished; the Cuillin had withdrawn behind the same invisible cloak, but directly above our heads the sky was blue and clear, and the sun shone warmly down. The river, sliding out of the loch in a great slithering fan of silver, narrowed where we stood into a deeper channel, wrangling and glittering among boulders that broke it into foam or shouldered it up in glossy curves for all the world like the backs of leaping salmon. Close under the banks, in the little backwaters, piles of froth bobbed and swayed on water brown as beer. The smell of drying heather and peaty water, strong and fresh, was laced with the pungent odour of bog-myrtle.

Dougal was a good instructor. He soon showed me how to assemble my hired rod, how to fix the reel and tie the fly, and then, with infinite patience, he began to teach me how to cast. Neither of us spoke a word about anything but the matter in hand, and very few, even, about that. It was not long before I found, to my own surprise, that the difficult art I was attempting had, indeed, a powerful fascination, before which the past faded, the future receded, and the whole of experience narrowed down to this stretch of glancing, glimmering water, and the fly I was trying to cast across it. The timeless scene and the eternal voice of the water created between them a powerful hypnosis under whose influence the hotel with its inmates and its problems seemed far away and relatively unimportant.

And even if my own problem did not recede with the others, it did—so passionately did I refuse to face it—relax a little of its claw-hold on my mind.

Dougal had put up his own rod, but did not at first use it. He sat on the bank smoking and watching me, occasionally getting up to demonstrate a cast. Of course I never caught anything; I did not get even the suspicion of a bite. But so powerfully had the peace and timelessness of the place worked upon me that when at length Dougal began to unwrap sandwiches for lunch I was able to think and speak with tolerable composure.

We ate at first in silence, while the water ran bubbling-brown past our feet, and a dipper flew zit-zitting up and down the centre of the river. A fish leaped in a flashing silver arc.

'That's just where I was fishing,' I said humbly. 'I must have been casting over him all the time, and never caught him.'

'You might yet; I've known stranger things happen,' said Dougal. It could hardly be called an encouraging answer, but I supposed that, from a Highlander, it might even be accounted praise. He looked up at the sky. 'It's a bit over-bright for the fish, in fact. If the mist came down a little, and took some of the glare off, it might be better.'

'It seems a pity to wish the sun away.'

'You'll not notice, once you're fishing again.'

We finished our lunch in silence, then Dougal got out his ancient pipe, while I fished in my pocket for cigarettes. As my fingers closed over the remains of yesterday's rather battered packet of Players, they encountered something else, something metallic and unfamiliar.

I gave an exclamation as I remembered what it was. Dougal turned an enquiring eye in my direction, through a small fog of pipe-smoke.

'I ought to have given this to the Inspector, I suppose,' I said, withdrawing my hand from my pocket with the cairngorm brooch. 'It's Roberta's, and—'

'*Where did ye get that?*' The big Scotsman's voice was harsh. His pipe fell unheeded into the heather, and his hand shot out and grabbed the brooch from my palm. He turned it over and over in a hand that shook.

'Why—up on the hill, yesterday,' I said, uncertainly. 'On the scree near the Sputan Dhu. I—I thought Miss Symes must have dropped it there.'

'It was Heather's.' Dougal's voice was unsteady too.

'*Heather's?*' Confusedly I tried to remember where I had picked it up . . . yes, it had been lying on the scree below the ledge where she had been found. Could it have dropped or been kicked off that little pile of metal in the corner? . . . I turned to look back at Blaven, only to find that the mist was, indeed, rolling down the slopes behind us like a tide of smoking lava. Blaven was already invisible, and a great wall of mist bore steadily across the glen behind us, obliterating the afternoon.

'I gave it to her for her birthday,' said Dougal, his voice unnaturally loud and harsh. 'She was wearing it when she went out that night. . . .' He stared at it for a moment longer, then thrust it back at me. 'You'd best take it, mistress. Give it to the Inspector and tell him where you found it. God knows it won't help him, but—' He broke off, and turned with bent head to hunt for his pipe. By the time he had got it alight again his face was once more impassive, and his hands steady. He glanced round at the silently advancing mist.

'This'll be better for the fish,' he said, and relapsed into silence.

The sun had gone, and with it, the peace of the place had vanished too. The finding of that pathetic brooch had brought back, only too vividly, the horrors which had beset this lovely glen. My own miserable doubts and fears began again to press in on me as the grey mist was pressing. The other side of the river was invisible now. We seemed, Dougal and I, to be in the centre of a world of rolling grey cloud, islanded between the loud river and the lake, whose still and sombre glimmer dwindled, by degrees, into a grey haze of nothing.

I shivered. 'Don't you think we ought to go back, Mr Macrae? I think I ought to give the brooch to the Inspector straight away.'

He got up. 'It's as you wish, mistress. Shall I take down the rods, then?'

I hesitated. Perhaps it was only the eeriness of the mist-wrapped glen, but, suddenly, violently, I wanted to be gone. I could escape this thing no longer; I must face my problem now, and take whatever uneasy peace was left to me.

'I think we will go back,' I said at length. 'I know I ought to go and see the Inspector, and it isn't right to put it off any more. And I—I don't like the mist.'

'We can't lose our way along the river bank even in this. Don't worry your head about the mist. Just bide still a minute while I get my rod, then we'll get away back.'

He turned down-river, and before he had gone ten yards, was swallowed in the mist. I stubbed out my cigarette on the now-chilly stone, and watched the grey swirl where he had disappeared. The obliterating cloud pressed closer, on heather, on rock, on the chuckling water.

The dipper warned me first. It burst from under the fog, fleeing upstream with a rattle of alarm-notes that made my nerves jump and tingle.

Then through the blank wall of the mist there tore a cry. A curse. A thudding, gasping noise, and the sickening sound of a blow. And a sharp yell from Dougal.

'*Lassie! Run!*'

Then the horrible sound of harsh breath choking, rasping in a crushed throat; another thud; and silence.

Chapter Twenty

The Blasted Heath

Of course I screamed. The sound was like a bright knife of panic, slashing at the mist. But the grey swirls deadened it; then they were all round me, clawing and fingering at me, as I stumbled forward towards where Dougal's voice had been.

I am not brave. I was horribly frightened, with a chill and nauseating terror. But I don't think anybody normal would unhesitatingly run *away* if they heard a friend being attacked near by.

So I leaped forward, only to falter and trip before I had gone five yards, so blinding now was the mist that shrouded the moor. Even the edge of the river was invisible, and a hasty step could result in a broken ankle, or, at best, a plunge into the rock-ridden swirl of waters. I put out my hands, foolishly, gropingly, as if they could pull aside the pale blanket of the mist. I plunged another four yards into it, then I stepped on nothing, and went hurtling down a bank to land on my knees in deep heather.

It was only then that I noticed how complete was the silence. The sounds of the struggle had ceased. Even the river, cut off from me by the bank, ran muted under the mist. I crouched there, shaken and terrified, clutching the wet heather-stems, and straining with wide, blind eyes into the blankness around me. I found I was turning my head from side to side with a blind weaving motion, like a new-born beast scenting the air. The mist pressed close, the bewildering, sense-blotting nothingness of the mist, so that I no longer knew which way the river ran, or where I had heard the men fighting, or—where the murderer might, now, be supposed to be.

Then I heard him breathing.

There was a soft step; another. Water-drops spattered off the heather; the stiff sedge rustled, and was still. Silence.

He had been ahead of me, to the right. Of that I was certain, but how near . . .?

The breathing surely came from behind me now. My head jerked round on neck-muscles as tight and dry as rope. I could feel my eyes straining wider, my mouth slackening in panic. My hands tightened on the heather-stems till I thought he must hear the bones cracking.

And now the breathing had stopped. Somewhere, the river poured its unheeding waters along under the peat-banks. Behind me? Before? To the right? I found I could no longer trust my senses, and, on the heels of that betrayal, panic came.

All at once the mist was full of noises: the rustle of heather was the murderer's breathing, the thud of my own frightened heart his footstep; the surging of blood in my temples blended with the rush of the invisible river, eddying, wavering, distorted by the dizzying mist into the very stuff of terror. . . .

There was salt on my tongue; blood. My lips throbbed painfully where I had bitten it, but the pain had checked the panic. I flattened myself in the long heather, closed my eyes, and listened.

He was there: there had been no illusion about that. He was fairly close, moving towards me, but a little way to one side, between me and the river. I could hear the water now, quite clearly, some few yards away on the right. I went lower in the heather, flat in my form like a hunted animal, glad now of the bewildering mist which was the friend of the hunted more than of the hunter. I had only to keep still; perhaps, when he had passed me, I could break cover and run, and. . . .

He was level with me now, between me and the river. His breathing was shallow, rapid, excited. He stopped.

Then, further away, down along the river-bank, I heard something else. Footsteps, heavy, uncertain footsteps that thudded on heather and then scraped on rock. Dougal Macrae's voice called, thickly: 'Lassie . . . lassie, are ye there?'

A great sob of thankfulness tore at my throat, but I choked it back, wondering wildly what to do. If I answered . . . the murderer was within six yards of me, I knew. I heard his harsh indrawn breath; sensed the tensing of his muscles as he realized that he had failed to eliminate Dougal. If I called to Dougal, was there anything to save my throat from that bright butcher's knife not twenty feet away? A knife which could despatch me in a matter of seconds, and then turn its dripping point to wait for Dougal to answer my call. . . .

But I must call. . . . Not for help, but for warning. I must cry out, and tell Dougal that he is here, the killer is here, just beside me. *Somehow I must cry out*, and then run, run into the lovely blinding mist, away from the knife and the excited hands of the butcher coming behind me.

And Dougal was coming. He plunged towards us, as bold and heavy as an angry bull. I was on my knees, and my mouth was gaping to shout a warning, when suddenly the murderer turned, and was running up-river like a stag. I could hear him bounding, sure as a deer, through the long heather. And Dougal heard him too. He let out a yell that was a curse, and flung himself after the escaping man. I saw him looming through the fog: I caught the gleam of a blade in his lifted fist, and I saw in his face such a white blaze of anger as to make him unrecognizable. He looked like some avenging giant out of an old myth.

I gasped out something as he plunged past me, but he paid no heed. He brushed by me as if I were not there, and blundered on into the mist after the killer. Even as I cried, in panic: '*Dougal!*' he vanished up-river into the fog. He must have glimpsed or heard his quarry, because my cry was drowned in a harsh eerie yell that startled the sullen heather with its pagan echoes, and sent a flock of oyster-catchers screaming up into the mist like witches.

'*A mhurtair! A mhich an diabhil! Aie!* You bloody murthering bastard! *Aie!*'

One of the birds rocketed over my head with the screech of a damned soul, the mist streaming from its wings in swaths like grey grass under the scythe.

It vanished, and the mist swept down in its wake, and the sound of the men's running was blotted out once more by the muffled silence.

I turned and ran blindly in the opposite direction.

I do not know how long that stumbling terrified flight through the heather lasted. I had succumbed finally to pure panic—mindless, senseless, sobbing panic. I was no longer frightened of the killer: reason had stayed with me just long enough to show me that he was no longer concerned with me. Attacking an unsuspecting man out of the mist was one thing: facing an armed Highlander, fighting-mad on his own ground, was quite another. No, the murderer had to lose Dougal very effectively in the fog before he dared turn back to me—and then he had to find me.

But panic has nothing to do with reason. Reason, now, had slipped her cogs, and my brain was spinning sickeningly, uselessly, out of control. I ran and jumped and slithered, and the salt tears slid down my face with the wet mist-drops, and flicked into my open mouth on to my tongue. The white mist met me like a blank wall; my hands were out like a blind man's; the skin of my face and my palms was wincing as I thrust myself wildly against the intangible barrier. And as I ran I chattered crazily to myself: '*No—oh no—oh no. . . .*'

What brought me up, all standing, with the panic knocked out of me as at the slash of a whip, was the fact that the ground over which I blundered was shaking beneath my feet.

Half-dazedly I peered at the tufted mosses over which I had been running. Tentatively I took another step. The ground shivered, and I backed quickly, only to feel the surface of the moor rocking like the bottom-boards of a punt.

I stood very still.

There was a small dreadful sound beneath my feet, as if the ground had sucked in a bubbling breath.

Chapter Twenty-one

Slough of Despond

My lapse from reason had cost me dearly enough. I was well out in the bog of which Roderick had once spoken, and how far out, I had, I found, no idea. Nor could I tell at all accurately from what direction I had been running when I made this last frightening discovery.

Fear flickered its bats'-wings at me afresh, but I shook my head sharply, as if by doing so I could drive it away. I stood exactly where I was, trying to ignore the ominous trembling of the earth, and listened for the sound of the river.

But it was of no use. The more I strained my ears, the more confused were the sounds that eddied and swung round me in the mist. I heard, faintly, the muted murmur of flowing water, but it seemed to come from every quarter at once, reflected off the banks of fog, and, over it, all the time, whispered and clucked the invisible life of the bog—small lippings, suckings, a million tiny bubbles popping, uneasy breaths. . . .

My feet were sinking. With an almost physical effort, I gathered the last rags of my self-control round me, then stepped quietly towards a tussock of heather a couple of yards away. The feel of its tough, resistant stems under my feet did much to steady my nerves, but my body was shaking uncontrollably now, and my teeth were chattering. I stood islanded on my little tump of heather, peering vainly along the ground in every direction and being met, in every direction, by the same few feet of boggy green, swimming and shifting under the treacherous mist.

But I knew that I must move, must leave my little tuft of safety and go in some direction—any direction. I told myself that the bog was unlikely to be really dangerous, but here, again, reason was no real help. I think it was the fact of being blinded that brought panic pressing so persistently close. If I could have seen even four yards in front of me, seen where my feet were going five steps ahead, it would not have been so bad. But I should be moving blindly over this hideous shivering bog, ignorant of the real gravity of the danger; and moving, possibly, further out into a worse place. . . .

I clenched my hands into icy knots, turned in what I imagined to be the direction of the river, and walked slowly forward.

The sheer effort of self-control needed to make me move slowly was so enormous that, mercifully, I could not think about anything else. I wanted to run: dear God, how I wanted to run! But I made myself go slowly, testing each step. Once I trod unwarily on a patch of lighter green, and went up to the knee into black mud. And by the time I had skirted the light patch, stepping warily from one moss hag to the next, I had completely lost all sense of direction again, so that, when a ghostly skeleton-shape floated out of the mist beside me, my whole body jerked like a marionette's with fear. It was only the pale ghost of a young birch, a bone-bare branch that lay rotting on the bog: touchwood, crumbling to decay; but in that misty morass it looked solid, and where it lay the tufted reeds were tall and dark and promised safety.

And I drew a breath of hope. The shape that showed so insubstantial through the fog was one I had seen before. Surely Roderick and I had passed quite near a fallen birch on that first evening's walk? It had lain on our left, not many yards away, between us and the river. I had only to remember which way it had lain in relation to our path, and I could make without delay for the safe ground.

I trod towards it warily, trying to see it again in my mind's eye as I had noticed it the first night. It was quite possibly not the same tree, but in the mind-annihilating swirl of mist even this frail compass was as sure as the pillar of fire in the wilderness. I stood by it, anchored by its deceptive solidity, and tried to remember, steadying myself quite deliberately with hope.

It had been lying, roughly, north and south. Of that I felt sure. And surely I must still be to the river side of it? In which case the safe ground was beyond it, about thirty yards beyond. If I could once reach that, I would, sooner or later, find a sheep-track that would lead me down the glen, to within sound of the sea. Or I might find some trickle of running water, that would lead me safely to the river and the hotel.

A black shape shot out of the mist at my back, and skimmed, whirring, into invisibility. A grouse. I swore at it under my breath, and quieted my hammering pulses once again. Then I stepped carefully over the birch-tree and took what I thought were my bearings, straining my eyes once more against the mist.

It was only then that I became fully conscious of something that had been tugging at the skirts of my senses for a little time. The ground was shaking. I was standing perfectly still, but the ground was shaking.

So complete had been my absorption in my new fear that I had actually forgotten that, somewhere out in the blind world, there was a murderer looking for me with a knife. . . . And here he was, moving steadily across the quaking bog.

I dropped to my face behind the skeleton of the birch. The rushes were thick and tall. Beneath me the ground shivered and breathed. I lay frozen, this time not even frightened, simply frozen, icy, numb. I doubt if even the knife, ripping down through the mist, would have had the power to move me.

'Gianetta. . . .' It was a tiny whisper, no more than a harsh breath. It could have been the breathing of the bog, the exhaling of the marsh gas in its million tiny bubbles.

'Gianetta. . . .' It was nearer now. 'Gianetta. . . .' The mist was rustling with my name. It floated in little dry whispers like falling leaves, swirling lightly down to rest on the shivering ground.

He was moving slowly: under my body I could feel the measured vibrations of his tread. His hands would be out in front of him, groping for me: his whispering probed the silence, reaching out to trap me.

I recognized it, of course. Oh yes, I knew him now, beyond all doubt. I knew now that my unhappy guessing had been right enough; knew now why the Inspector had pitied me; and why Alastair, four nights ago, had given me that look of unexpressed compassion.

'*Gianetta*. . . .' There it was again, that name—the name that no one else ever called me . . . the name I had heard shouted through the darkness beside Ronald Beagle's funeral pyre. . . . His voice floated down through the mist, a little fainter now, as if he had turned his head away. '*Gianetta*, where are you? In God's name, *where are you?*'

Roderick had guessed, too, of course. I wondered, pressing my body closer to the wet ground, why he had been so sure that I, alone of all people at Camasunary, would be unharmed.

'Are you there, Gianetta? *Don't be afraid. . . .*'

I don't think I was afraid, now that I knew for certain it was Nicholas. It wasn't that I believed, with Roderick, that, because of the past, Nicholas would never hurt me. It was just that, as that terrible whispering brought my suspicions to life and made them into truth, I didn't care any more. Not about anything.

'Gianetta . . . Gianetta . . . Gianetta. . . .' The syllables pattered down through the mist in a fantastic muttered counterpoint. I put my cold cheek down on the soggy grasses, and cried silently, while the fog wavered and whispered with my name, and its ghostly grey fingers pressed me into the marsh.

And then he was gone. The groping voice had faded, echoed, and faded again. The quaking of the bog had ceased. A bird had slipped silently and unalarmed across the grass. He was gone.

I got up stiffly, and, myself moving like a weary ghost, trudged uncaring, heedless, mindless, across the bog, away from the last mocking echo of his voice.

And almost at once I was on firm ground, among stones and long heather. I quickened my pace instinctively. The ground was rising steadily away from the bog, and presently I found the mist was wavering and dwindling round me. I plunged up the slope at an increasing rate as my range of vision extended. The fog thinned, shrank, and ebbed away behind me.

As suddenly as a swimmer diving up through the foam of a wave to meet the air, I burst out of the last swirl of mist into the vivid sunshine.

Chapter Twenty-two

Cloud Cuckoo-land

The relief was so colossal, the change so unbelievable, that I could only stand, blinking, in the clear light of the afternoon sun. My eyes, blinded with mist, and still dazzled with crying, took several seconds to get used to the flood of light. Then I saw where I was. I had clambered a little way up the lower slope of Blaven, at a point where a great dyke of rock bisected the scree, a wall laid uphill like an enormous buttress against the upper cliffs.

The foot of this buttress was lipped by the fog, which held the lower ground still invisible under its pale tide. The glen itself, the loch, the long Atlantic bay, all lay hidden, drowned under the mist which stretched like a still white lake from Blaven to Sgurr na Stri, from Garsven to Marsco. And out of it, on every hand, the mountains rose, blue and purple and golden-green in the sunlight, swimming above the vaporous sea like fabulous islands. Below, blind terror might grope still in the choking grey, here above, where I stood, was a new and golden world. I might have been alone in the dawn of time, watching the first mountains rear themselves out of the clouds of chaos. . . .

But I was not alone.

Hardly had my eyes adjusted themselves to the brilliant spaciousness of my new world above the clouds, when I became aware of someone about fifty yards away. He had not seen me, but was standing near the foot of the great rock buttress, gazing past it, away from me, towards the open horizon of the south-west. It was Roderick Grant. I could see the dark-gold gleam of his hair in the sunlight.

I called 'Roderick!' and was amazed at the harsh croak that my stiff throat produced.

He did not move. My knees were shaking, and it was with difficult, uncertain steps that I made my way towards him over the rough ground.

I said his name again: 'Roderick!'

He heard then. He swung round. He said: 'Yes?' and then '*Janet!*' His voice sounded raw with shock, but at that I could hardly feel surprised. God knows what I looked like, death-white and shaking, wet and filthy, with the ghosts of terror and despair still looking out of my eyes.

He took two swift strides to meet me, and caught hold of my hands, or I would have fallen. He thrust me down on to a flat rock with my back against the warm stone of the buttress. I shut my eyes, and the sunlight beat against the lids in swirls of red and gold and violet. I could feel its heat washing over me in great reviving waves, and I relaxed in it, drawing my breath more smoothly. Then at length I opened my eyes and looked up at Roderick.

He was standing in front of me, watching me, and in those blue eyes I saw, again, that dreadful look of compassion. I knew what it meant, now, and I could not meet it. I looked away from him, and busied myself pulling off my sodden shoes and unfastening my coat, which slid off my shoulders to lie in a wet huddle on the rock. My blouse was hardly damp, and the grateful heat poured through it on to my shoulders.

He spoke then: 'You don't–know?'

I nodded.

He said slowly, an odd note in his voice: 'I told you that you would not be hurt. I shouldn't have said it. It was—'

'It hardly matters,' I said, wearily. 'Though why you thought, after what Nicholas put me through when we got divorced, that he'd have any scruples about me now, I don't know.' My left hand was flat on the hot rock. The line where my wedding-ring had been showed clear and white on the third finger. I said, still with the weight of dreariness pressing on me: 'It was wrong of me to try and protect him, suspecting what he was. I see that now. One shouldn't really put people before principles. Not when the people are–outlaws.'

My voice dwindled and stopped. He had turned away from me, and his eyes were on the distant peaks of the Cuillin, where they swam above the vaporous lake.

'Why did you do it?'

I blinked stupidly. 'Why did I do what?'

'Protect–him.' There was a curious light tone to his voice that might have been relief.

I hesitated, then said flatly: 'Because I'm his wife.'

He turned his head sharply. 'Divorced.'

'Oh yes. But–but that made no difference to some things. I mean, one has loyalties—'

He said harshly: 'Loyalties? Why call it loyalty when you mean love?'

I said nothing.

'Don't you?'

'I suppose so.'

He was silent. Then he said abruptly: 'What happened down there? How did you find out?'

'He was looking for me in the mist. He called me. I knew his voice.'

'He *called* you! But surely—'

'I was with Dougal Macrae, fishing, when the mist came down. Dougal had gone to get his rod. I heard a struggle, and Dougal must have been knocked out, then he–Nicholas–started looking for me. Only, Dougal recovered and went after him. They both chased off into the mist, and I ran away, but I got lost. And then–and then—'

'Yes?'

'I heard him coming across the bog, calling for me. Not calling, really, only whispering. I suppose he'd given Dougal the slip, and had doubled back to look for me. And he daren't call loudly in case Dougal heard him.'

'He must know that you've guessed who–what–he is.'

I shivered a little. 'Yes.'

He was peering down at the thick pall that covered the valley. 'So Drury is down there. In that?'

'Yes.'

'How far away?'

'I don't know. I suppose it was only a few minutes ago that—'

He swung round on me, so suddenly that I was startled.

'Come on,' he said, abruptly, almost roughly. 'We've got to get out of this. Get your shoes.'

He had hold of my wrist, and pulled me to my feet.

'Down into that?' I said, doubtfully. 'Shouldn't we wait till it clears a little? He's—'

'Down? Of course not. We're going up.'

'What on earth d'you mean?'

He laughed, almost gaily. '*I will lift up mine eyes unto the hills. . . .*' He seized my coat where it lay on the rock, and shook out its damp folds. Something tinkled sharply on to a boulder, and rolled aside with a glint. 'Don't ask questions, Janet. Do as I say. What's that?'

'Oh!' I cried, stooping after it. 'It's Heather's brooch!'

'Heather's brooch?' His tone was casual, so casual that I looked at him in surprise.

'Yes. I found it yesterday under that dreadful ledge. I thought it was Roberta's, but Dougal said—'

Once again my voice dwindled and died in my throat. I stood up, the brooch in my hand, and looked up into his eyes.

I said: 'The first night I was here, you told me about Heather's murder. You told me about the little pile of jewellery that was found on the ledge. A bracelet, you said, and a brooch, and–oh, other things. But the brooch *wasn't* on the ledge when she was found. And since she had only been given it that day, for her birthday, you couldn't have known about it, *unless you saw her wearing it yourself. Unless you, yourself, put it on to that little pile on the ledge beside the bonfire.*'

High up, somewhere, a lark was singing. Round us, serene above the mist, the mountains swam. Roderick Grant smiled down at me, his blue eyes very bright.

'Yes,' he said gently. 'Of course. But what a pity you remembered, isn't it?'

Chapter Twenty-three

Blaven

So we faced each other, the murderer and I, marooned together on our island Ararat above the flood of cloud: alone together, above the silent world, on the mountain where already he had sent three people to their deaths.

He was smiling still, and I saw in his face again the look of compassion that, now, I understood. He liked me, and he was going to kill me. He was sorry, but he was going to kill me.

But, just for a moment, even this knowledge was crowded out by the one glorious surge of elation that swept through me. The whole of that silent, cloud-top world was drenched with the light of the sun and the song of the lark–and the knowledge that I had been criminally, stupidly, cruelly wrong about Nicholas. I think that for two full minutes I stared into Roderick Grant's mad blue eyes and thought, not: 'I am here alone with a maniac killer,' but: 'it was not Nicholas, *it was not Nicholas*. . . .'

Roderick said regretfully: 'I'm so sorry, Janet. I really am, you know. I knew when I heard you talking to Dougal by the river, that sooner or later you'd remember. I didn't really mean to, but of course I'll have to kill you now.'

I found to my surprise that my voice was quite calm. I said: 'It won't help you if you do, Roderick. The Inspector knows.'

He frowned. 'I don't believe you.'

'He told me so. He said he was just waiting for information from London to confirm what he knew. And of course there's Roberta.'

His face darkened: 'Yes. Roberta.'

The vivid eyes hooded themselves as he brooded over his failure with Roberta. I wondered if he had killed Dougal, or if Dougal, with Nicholas, were still hunting through the mist below us . . . the lovely, safe mist, not many yards below us—

'Don't try and run away,' said Roderick. 'I'd only have to bring you back again. And don't scream, Janet, because then I'd have to throttle you, and'–he smiled gently at me–'I always cut their throats, if I can. It's the best way.'

I backed against the cliff of the buttress. It was warm and solid, and there were tiny tufts of saxifrage in the cleft under my fingers. Real. Normal. I forced my stiff lips to smile back at Roderick. At all costs, I must try and keep him talking. Keep him in this mad gentle mood. I must speak smoothly and calmly: if I should panic again, my fear might be the spark that would touch off the crazy train of his murderer's mind.

So I smiled. 'Why did you do it at all, Roderick? Why did you kill Heather Macrae?'

He looked to me in surprise. 'They wanted it.'

'They?'

'The mountains.' He made an oddly beautiful gesture. 'All these years, these ages, they've waited, dreaming like this, above the clouds, watching over the green life of the valleys. Once, long ago, men paid them worship, lit fires for them, gave them the yearly sacrifice of life, but now'–his voice had an absent, brooding tone–'now they have to take for themselves what they can. A life a year, that's what they need . . . blood and fire, and the May-Day sacrifices that men paid them when the world was young and simple, and men knew the gods that lived on the mountains.'

He looked at me. It was uncanny and horrible, to look at someone's familiar face, to listen to someone's familiar voice, and to see a complete stranger looking out of his eyes.

'She helped me carry the wood and the peat; together we collected the nine woods and the wild agaric and the oak to make the wildfire. She made the fire for me, and then I cut her throat and—'

I had to stop him. I said abruptly: 'But why did you kill Marion Bradford?'

His face darkened with anger. 'Those two women! You heard the little one–Roberta–that night. You heard her talking sacrilege, you heard how she chattered of conquering–*conquering*–these.' Again the flowing gesture that embraced the dreaming peaks. 'And the other one–Miss Bradford–she was the same.' He laughed suddenly, and sounded all at once perfectly normal and charming. 'It was quite easy. The elder one, that dreadful, stupid woman, she was a little in love with me, I think. She was pleased and flattered when I met them on the mountain and offered to show her the climb across the Sputan Dhu.'

'I suppose you thought they were both dead when you left them.'

'They should have been,' he said. 'Wasn't it bad luck?'

'Very,' I said drily. My eyes went past him, scanning the fringes of the mist. No one. Nothing.

He was frowning at a sprig of heather that he had pulled. 'That ledge where you found Roberta,' he said. 'I'd been along the damned thing three times already, but I never went further than the corner when I saw the ledge was empty. I wanted to find her first, of course.'

'Of course.' The lark had stopped singing. There was no sound in the blue-and-gold day but the grotesque exchange of our pleasant, polite voices, talking about murder.

'But *you* found her.' The cock of his eyebrow was almost whimsical. 'And you nearly–oh so nearly–gave me the chance I wanted, Janet.'

I forgot about being calm and quiet. I cried out: 'When you sent me to get the flask! You were going to kill her then!'

He nodded. 'I was going to kill her then. A little pressure on the throat, and—' This time the gesture was horrible. 'But you came back, Janet.'

I licked my lips. 'When she opened her eyes,' I said hoarsely, 'it was *you* she saw. *You*, standing behind me.'

'Of course.' He laughed. 'You thought it was Drury, didn't you? Just as you thought it was Drury who killed Ronald Beagle—'

'Why did you do that?'

He hesitated, and into the blue eyes came a look of naïve surprise. 'D'you know, I don't quite know, Janet. I'd hated him for a long time, of course, because I knew that to his mind, *they* were just so many peaks to be climbed, so many names to be recorded. And then he came among us that night, on the mountain, talking so glibly of Everest–Everest conquered, those untouchable snows defiled and trampled, where I had thought no man could ever put his sacrilegious feet. . . . *You* said that, Janet; you remember? You spoke like that about it once, and, because of that, I thought that I could never hurt you. . . . But Beagle–I followed him down the hill. I caught him from behind and killed him. . . .' His eyes met mine ingenuously. 'I think,' he said, 'I must have been a little mad.'

I said nothing. I was watching the edge of the mist, where it frothed along the empty mountain-side.

'And now,' said Roderick, feeling in his coat pocket 'where's my knife?' He patted his coat carefully, as a man does when he is wondering where he

has put his pipe. The sun gleamed on his dark-gold hair. 'It doesn't seem
to be—oh yes, I remember now. I was sharpening it. I put it down somewhere. . . .' He smiled at me, then he turned and scanned the heather
anxiously. 'Can you see it, Janet, my dear?'

Little bubbles of hysteria rose in my throat. My fingers dug and scraped
at the rock behind me. I stiffened myself with a jerk and flung out an arm,
pointing at the ground beyond him.

'There, Roderick! There it is!'

He swung round, peering.

I couldn't get past him, down into the mist. I had to go up.

I went up the end of that buttress like a cat, like a lizard, finding holds
where no holds were, gripping the rough rock with stockinged feet and
fingers which seemed endowed with miraculous, prehensile strength.

I heard him shout '*Janet!*' and the sound acted like the crack of a whip on
a bolting horse. I went up ten feet of rock in one incredible, swarming
scramble, to haul myself, spreadeagled, on to the flat crest of the buttress.

The enormous wing of rock soared in front of me up to the high crags. Its
top was, perhaps, eight feet wide, and strode upwards at a dizzy angle, in
giant steps and serrations, like an enormous ruined staircase. I had landed,
somehow, on the lowest tread, and I flung myself frantically at the face of
the next step, just as the ring of boots on rock told me that he had started
after me.

How I got up what seemed to be twenty feet of perpendicular rock, I do
not know. But my mad impetus still drove me, holding me against the cliff,
clamping my hands instinctively into crannies, bracing my feet against juts
of safe rock, propelling me upwards as thoughtlessly and as safely as if I
were a fly walking up a wall.

With a heave and a jerk I dragged myself on to the wider ledge that
marked the second step. And, inexorably, the next perpendicular barred my
way, this time gashed from summit to foot by a vertical crack, or chimney. I
flew at this, only to be brought up short as I saw that the rock on which I
stood was a stack, a chunk split off the main buttress, and between me and
the next upright there yawned a gap which dropped sheer away to the level
of the scree.

The gap was perhaps four feet wide, no more. And at the other side, on
one wall of the chimney, was a smallish, triangular ledge, above which a
deep crevice held a slash of shadow.

There was my handhold, there the ledge for my feet, if I could only get
across that dreadful gap. . . . But I was nearly foundered, and I knew it. My
breath was coming in painful gasps; I had knocked one of my feet; my hands
were bleeding.

I hesitated there, on the blink of the split in the rock. Then I heard the
rattle of pebbles behind me—close behind. I turned, a terrified thing at bay,
my eyes desperately searching for another way off the top of the stack. To
left, to right, a sheer drop of thirty feet to the scree. Before me, the chasm. A
hand swung up over the edge of the platform where I stood. A dark-gold
head rose after it. Mad blue eyes, rinsed of all humanity, stared into mine.

I turned and leaped the gap without a second's thought. I landed on the
little ledge. My knee bumped rock, but I hardly felt it as my hands, clawing

wildly, found a safe anchorage in the crevice above. Then my knee was in the crevice. With a heave and a wriggle I pulled my body up to it, and was in the chimney, which was narrow enough to let me wedge myself against one side of it while I sought for holds in the other. I swarmed up it like a chimney-boy whose master had lit a fire beneath him.

Then my hand slid into a deep grip; I braced myself and with one last heave, one final convulsion, dragged myself out of the chimney and on to a deep ledge sheltered by an overhang.

And this time I was cornered. I knew it. Even if I could have climbed the overhang that bulged above me, the impulse had given out; nature had swung back on me. I was finished. And the place where I now found myself was no more than a ledge of rock, some four feet by ten, piled with small boulders and blazing with bell-heather.

I crouched among the scented flowers and peered down.

Roderick was standing twenty feet below me at the edge of the gap, his convulsed face lifted to mine. His breathing was ragged and horrible. I saw the sweat gleaming on his flushed cheekbones, and on the knuckles of the hand in which he held the knife. . . .

I screamed then. The sound splintered against the rocks into a million jarring, tearing echoes that ripped the silence of the afternoon into tatters. The raven swept out from high above me with a frightened bark.

Something flashed past my cheek with the whistle of a whip-lash. The wind of it seared my face. Roderick's knife struck the cliff behind me, and shattered into a hundred little tinkling notes that were whirled into the bellow of the echo as I screamed again.

The empty rock flung my terror back at me, hollow, reverberating. The raven swung up, yelling, into the empty blue air. Away to the west, in the greater emptiness, the Cuillin dreamed on indifferently. I crouched in my eyrie high above the sea of cloud, an insignificant insect clinging to a crack in a wall.

Roderick swore harshly below me, and his now empty hands lifted, the fingers crooked like claws.

'I'm coming up,' he said on a savage breathless note, and I saw his knees flex for a leap across the gap.

My fingers scrabbled at the heather, caught up a big jagged rock, and held it poised on the brink of the ledge.

'Keep off!' My voice was a croak. 'Stay where you are, or I'll smash your head in!'

He glanced up again, and I saw him recoil half a pace. Then he laughed, and with the laugh the whole situation split up, and re-formed into a yet crazier pattern, for the laughter was genuine and full of amusement. From the face he lifted to me, all the savagery had been wiped clean; it held the familiar gaiety and charm, and—yes, affection.

He said ruefully: 'I broke my knife, Janet. Let me come up.'

I held on to the rags of my own sanity. '*No!* Stay where you are or I'll throw this down on you!'

He shook the hair out of his eyes. 'You wouldn't do a thing like that, Janet darling,' he said, and leaped the gap like a deer.

Then he was standing on the little triangular ledge below me, one hand

locked in the crevice. I saw his muscles tense as he prepared to heave
himself up the chimney after me.

His head was back: his blue eyes held mine.

'You couldn't do a thing like that, could you?' he said.

And, God help me, I couldn't. My fingers clutched the jagged boulder. I
lifted it, ready to heave it down . . . but something held me–the imagined
impact of rock on flesh, the smashing of bone and eyes and hair into a
splintered nothing . . . I couldn't do it. I turned sick and dizzy, and the rock
slipped from my hands back on to the ledge among the flowers.

'No,' I said, and I put both my hands as if to ward off the sight of the
violence I could not do. 'No–I can't. . . .'

He laughed again, and I saw the knuckles of his left hand whiten for the
upward pull. Then something smashed into the rock not six inches from his
head. The report of the gun slammed against the echoing mountain with a
roar like an express bursting from a tunnel.

'Don't worry, Gianetta, I can,' said Nicholas grimly, and fired again.

Chapter Twenty-four

The Eyrie

Only then did I become aware that, a little way to the north, the edge of the
mist was broken and swirling at last, as men thrust out of it and began to
race along the hillside, the Inspector, Hecky, Neill, and Jamesy Farlane, all
making at the double for the foot of the stack.

Nicholas, well ahead of them, had already reached the base of the
buttress. The slam of his second shot tore the echoes apart, and now the
rock by Roderick's hand splintered into fragments. I heard the whine of a
ricocheting bullet, and I saw Roderick flinch and, momentarily, freeze
against the rock.

The other men, running at a dangerous pace along the scree, had almost
come up with Nicholas. I heard the Inspector shout something.

Roderick half-turned on his little ledge, braced himself for an instant,
then flung himself, back across the gap between the ledge and the stack. The
nails of his boots ripped screaming along the rocky platform, then they
gripped. In the same moment I heard the scrape and clink of boots as the
pursuers, spreading out, started to climb the north face of the buttress.

Roderick paused for an instant, balanced, as it were, in mid-flight on the
top of the stack. The sun glinted on his hair as he glanced quickly this way,
that way. . . . Then he leaped for the south side of the stack, swung himself
over, and disappeared from view.

Someone yelled. Hecky was half up a lower step of the buttress, and had
seen him. I saw him cling and point, shouting, before he addressed himself
even more desperately to the cliff.

But Roderick had a good start, and he climbed like a chamois. In less time than it takes to tell, I saw him dart out on to the scree south of the buttress, and turn downhill. He was making for the mist, with that swift leaping stride of his, and I heard the Inspector curse as he, too, started to run downhill.

But Nicholas had moved faster. He must have heard Roderick jump down on to the scree, for only a few seconds after the latter began his dash for the shelter of the mist, Nicholas had turned and started down for the north side of the buttress.

From my dizzy eyrie, I could see them both. To that incredible day, the race provided as fantastic a climax as could well be imagined. There was the great dyke, swooping down the side of the mountain, to lose itself in the sea of fog; and there, on either side of it, ran hunter and hunted, law and out-law, slithering, leaping, glissading down the breakneck scree in a last mad duel of speed.

Once, Roderick slipped, and fell to one knee, saving himself with his hands. Nicholas gained four long strides before he was up again and hurtling downhill, unhurt, to gain the shelter of the mist. Not far to go now . . . thirty yards, twenty . . . the buttress had dwindled between them to a ridge, a low wall . . . then Roderick saw Nicholas, and swerved, heading for safety at an angle away from him.

I saw Nicholas thrust out a foot, and brake to a slithering ski-turn in a flurry of loose shale. Something gleamed in his hand.

The Inspector's yell came from somewhere out of sight below me. '*Don't use that gun!*'

The gun flashed down into the heather as Nicholas put a hand to the low dyke and vaulted it. Roderick gave one quick glance over his shoulder, and in three great bounds reached the margin of the mist. It swirled and broke around his bolting form, then swallowed him into invisibility.

Twenty seconds later the same patch swayed and broke as Nicholas thrust into it, and vanished.

Then, all around me, the cliffs and the clear blue air swung and swayed, dissolving like the mist itself. The scent of the heather enveloped me, sickening-sweet as the fumes of ether, and the sunlight whirled into a million spinning flecks of light, a vortex into which, helpless, I was being sucked. An eddy, a whirlpool . . . and I was in it. I was as light as a cork, as light as a feather, as insubstantial as blown dust. . . .

Then out of the spinning chaos came Inspector Mackenzie's voice, calm, matter-of-fact, and quite near at hand.

He said: 'Wake up, lassie, it's time we got you down from there.'

I found that my hands were pressed to my eyes. I took them away, and the boiling light slowly cleared. The world swung back into place, and I looked down.

Inspector Mackenzie was on top of the stack, standing where Roderick had stood, and Jamesy Farlane was with him. 'How in the world did you get up there, anyway?'

'I don't remember,' I said truthfully. I sat there on my cushion of heather and looked down at the two men, feeling suddenly absurd. 'I–I can't get down, Inspector.'

He was brisk. 'Well, lassie, you'll have to be fetched. Stay where you are.' The pair of them became busy with ropes, and then Jamesy approached my cliff. He got across the gap with ludicrous ease, and paused there, examining the chimney.

The Inspector, I saw, was looking back over his shoulder.

'Nicholas—' I said hoarsely, but he cut me short.

'Hoots awa' wi' ye'—it was the one conventionally Scottish expression that I ever heard him use—don't worry about that. Hecky and Neill both went after him, as you'd have seen if you hadn't been so busy fainting. Your man's safe enough, my dear.'

And, even as he finished speaking, I saw Nicholas come slowly up out of the mist. He moved stiffly, like a very tired man, but he seemed to be unhurt. He raised his head and looked up towards us, then quickened his pace, lifting a hand in some sort of gesture which I could not interpret, but which seemed to satisfy the Inspector, for he grunted, and gave a little nod as he turned back to watch Jamesy's progress.

I cannot pretend that I was anything but an appalling nuisance to poor Jamesy, when at last he appeared beside me on the ledge with a rope, and attempted to show me how to descend from my eyrie. In fact, I can't now remember how this descent was eventually accomplished. I remember his tying the rope around me, and passing it round his own body, and round a spoke of rock; I also remember a calming flood of instructions being poured over my head as I started my climb, but whether I obeyed them or not I have no idea. I suspect not; in fact, I think that for the main part of the descent he had to lower me, helplessly swinging, on the end of the rope. And since I could not possibly have jumped the gap to the stack, Jamesy lowered me straight down the other thirty feet or so into the bottom of the cleft itself. I remember the sudden chill that struck me as I passed from the sunlit chimney into the shadow of the narrow gully.

Then my feet touched the scree, and, at the same moment, someone took hold of me, and held me hard.

I said: 'Oh, Nicholas—' and everything slid away from me again into a spinning, sunshot oblivion.

Chapter Twenty-five

Delectable Mountain

When Nicholas dived into the pool of mist after Roderick, he was not much more than twenty yards behind him, and, though the mist was still thick enough to be blinding, he could hear the noise of his flight quite distinctly. It is probable that Roderick still believed Nicholas to have a gun, while he himself, having lost his knife, was unarmed; he may, too, have heard Neill and Hecky thudding down the hillside in Nicholas' wake; or he may, simply, have given way at last to panic and, once running, have been unable to stop: at any rate, he made no attempt to attack his pursuer, but fled ahead of him through the fog, until at length they reached the level turf of the glen.

Here going was easier, but soon Nicholas realized he was rapidly overhauling his quarry. Roderick, it will be remembered, had already had to exert himself considerably that afternoon, and now he flagged quickly; the panic impulse gave out and robbed him of momentum. Nicholas was closing in, fifteen yards, ten, seven . . . as the gap closed, panic supervened again, and Roderick turned and sprang at his pursuer out of the fog.

It was a sharp, nasty little struggle, no holds barred. It was also not quite equal, for whereas Nicholas had only, so to speak, a mandate to stop the murderer getting away, the murderer wanted quite simply to kill his pursuer if possible. How it would have ended is hard to guess, but Neill and Hecky, guided by the sounds of the struggle, arrived in a very short time, and Roderick, fighting literally like a madman, was overpowered. And when Dougal Macrae, still breathing fire and slaughter, suddenly materialized out of the fog as well, the thing was over. Roderick, unresisting now, was taken by the three men back to the hotel, where he would be held until transport arrived. Nicholas, breathing hard, and dabbing at a cut on his cheek, watched the mist close round them, then he turned and made his way back up the hillside into the sun. . . .

So much I had learned, sitting beside Nicholas on the heather at the foot of the buttress, with my back against its warm flank. I had been fortified with whisky and a cigarette, and was content, for the moment, to rest there in the sun before attempting the tramp back to the hotel.

The Inspector, it appeared, was to set off immediately with his prisoner for Inverness. He paused before us as he turned to go.

'Are you sure you're all right, lassie?'

'Quite, thank you,' I said, and smiled at him through the smoke of my cigarette.

He glanced from me to Nicholas, and back again. 'It seems I was wrong,' he said drily.

'What d'you mean?'

'In thinking you were withholding evidence that mattered.'

I felt myself flushing. 'What did you imagine I knew that I hadn't told you?'

'I thought you'd recognized the man you saw in front of the bonfire.'

'Oh. No, I hadn't. I hadn't, really.'

'I believe you. . . .' But his glance was speculative, and I felt the flush deepen. 'Even so, I could almost have sworn you were lying just then about something.'

'I was,' I said, 'but not about that. It was something I heard, not something I saw.'

His gaze flicked to Nicholas once more, and he smiled. 'Ah,' he said. 'Just so. Well, I'll be away. I'm glad to be leaving you in such good hands. Take care of her, sir; she's had a rough time.'

'I will,' said Nicholas.

'One thing'—Inspector Mackenzie regarded him with some severity—

'you have, of course, got a licence for your gun?'

'Gun?' said Nicholas blankly. 'What gun?'

The Inspector nodded. 'I thought as much,' he said drily. 'Well, see you get one.'

And, with another nod, he turned and was presently swallowed up in the mist.

And we were alone on the mountain-side, islanded in the pool of mist, where, on every hand in the golden distance, the mountain-tops drifted, drowsing in their own halcyon dreams. Sweet and pungent, the honey-smell of rock-rose and heather thickened round us in the heat, and, once more, the lark launched himself into the upper sky, on a wake of bubble-silver song.

I drew a little sigh, and settled my shoulders gratefully against the warm rock.

'It's all over,' I said. 'I can hardly believe it, but it's all over.'

'My God, but you had me worried!' said Nicholas. 'I knew Grant had gone out, but the Inspector had put Neill on to watch him, and then when the mist dropped like that, all in a moment, and Neill came back and said he'd lost his man. . . .' He glanced briefly down at me. 'I knew where you and Dougal were fishing, so I made up-river as fast as I could. The police turned straight out after Grant. Then I heard a yell from Dougal, and you screamed, and I ran like blazes. I found your fishing-rods, but you'd gone, so I started hunting you. I went across the bog—'

'I know. I heard you. I was hiding quite near.'

'Silly little devil.'

'Well, I was scared; I thought you were the murderer—and you didn't help by whispering my name in that blood-curdling way.'

He laughed ruefully. 'I'm sorry. But I knew Grant might be nearer you than I was, and if you'd called out from too far away he might have reached you first. No, I wanted to get you safe under my wing, and then—'

'So you *knew* it was Roderick.'

He glanced down sideways at me. 'Then, yes. I'd been wondering about him for quite some time, and so had Inspector Mackenzie, but there was no proof.'

'What was the information he was waiting for from London? Or—no, you'd better start at the beginning, Nicholas. Tell me—'

'That *is* the beginning. The information that came to-day is really the beginning of the story. It concerns Roderick Grant's family. Did you know his father was a minister?'

'He told me a little bit about it. I felt rather sorry for him, a lonely little boy all by himself at the back of the north wind—that was what he called his home.'

'It's not a bad description either. I've been through Auchlechtie: it's a tiny hamlet of a dozen cottages in a valley near Bheinn a' Bhùird. The manse, where the Grants lived, was four miles even from the village, up beside the ruins of the old church and its primitive graveyard. The new church had been built down in the village itself, but the minister's house had no one for neighbour except that little square of turf, walled off from the heather, and filled with crumbling headstones and mounds covered with ivy and brambles and old, split yews deformed by the wind.'

'And he told me he lived alone with his father.'

'So he did. His mother died when he was born and his grandmother, his father's mother, brought him up till he was nine. Then she died—in an asylum.'

'Oh, Nicholas, how dreadful. So his father—his father's family—'

'Exactly. His father had always been the stern, unbending, austere kind of godly Presbyterian that used to be common in fiction and, possibly, even in fact. In him the—the taint showed itself at first only in an increasing remoteness and austerity, a passionate absorption in his studies of the past which, gradually, took complete possession of him, and became more real than real life round him—if you can apply the term "real life" to that tiny hamlet, four miles down the empty glen. The history of the long-dead bones, in that long-dead graveyard, became, year by year, the only thing that meant anything to him. And the little boy only mattered as being someone to whom he could pour out his half-learned, half-crank theories about the ancient customs and legends of the Highlands.'

'Roderick told me that he learned to worship the mountains,' I said. 'I never guessed he meant it literally.'

'But he did, quite literally. He must have spent a large part of his childhood listening to his father's stories and theories, imbibing his mad, garbled versions of the old folk-customs of the North, the sort of half-connected, inaccurate rubbish you said he was telling you to-day. He must have built, bit by bit in his crazed mind, a new sort of mythology for himself, of which the so-called "ritual" murder of Heather Macrae was a concrete example; a jumble of facts from books and from his father's researches, half-remembered, distorted bits of folk-lore that shook together like glass in a kaleidoscope and made a picture of violence that seemed, to a madman's brain, to be quite logical.'

'I know. I found some of the bits in *The Golden Bough*.'

'Oh yes, my *Golden Bough*! The Inspector told me you had it. I was looking all over the place for it last night. I thought I'd left it in my car.'

'I'd taken it to read, quite by accident.' I told him about it. He glanced down at me with an enigmatic expression.

'So you handed it to the Inspector. If you'd known it was mine—'

'But I did. There was an envelope in it addressed to you in Daddy's writing. I have it in my pocket.'

'Have you indeed?' I could feel his eyes on me still, but I would not meet them. 'Why didn't you give that to the Inspector, if you knew the book was mine?'

'I—I don't know.'

The lark was descending now, in lovely little curves of sound. 'How did Daddy know you were here, anyway?'

'What?' He sounded oddly disconcerted. 'Oh, I wrote to him and asked him to lend me his copy of the book. There was no one in my flat, so I couldn't send for my own copy. You see, Grant had made one or two remarks that had made me wonder about him—queer little mis-statements and inaccuracies that sounded like half-remembered quotations from Frazer and the older books that were Frazer's sources. And when I saw how some of Frazer's details checked with poor Heather Macrae's May-Day sacrifice—'

'May-Day?'

'May the thirteenth *is* May-Day, according to the old calendar. Ancient lore again, you see. Oh, everything fitted, even though it did so in a queer mad way; so, of course, I showed the book to Inspector Mackenzie.'

'You did what?' I exclaimed. 'When was this?'

'Last week.'

'Then he *knew* the book was yours!'

'Of course.'

'Then why—' A memory flashed back at me, of the Inspector's kind, compassionate gaze. 'Did he ever suspect *you*, Nicholas?'

'He may have done, to begin with, and of course, even after I turned up the evidence of *The Golden Bough* he may have kept me under suspicion, along with Hubert Hay, since we two, as well as Grant, have made some sort of study of local folk-lore. But Hay had an alibi—with you—for Marion's murder, while I, if you discount the intolerable possibilities of bluff and double-bluff, had indicated my innocence by giving evidence to the police. Which left Grant.'

'Then why,' I said again, 'was the Inspector so—so kind, and so *sorry* for me this morning? He talked about loyalties, and—'

'And you thought he was warning you that I was guilty? Why should you assume that your loyalty should be directed towards me, Gianetta?'

Abruptly, between one wing-beat and the next, the lark's song ceased. He shut his wings and dropped like a flake of shadow into the heather. I said, stupidly: D'you mean he thought it was *Roderick* I saw by the bonfire?'

'Of course. He thought you were falling for Roderick Grant. That was my fault, I'm afraid: I'd told him so—on very little evidence except that Grant, in his own way, was quite patently interested in you.'

I was stupefied. 'You told the Inspector that I was in love with Roderick Grant?'

'I did, more or less. Sorry, Gianetta. Sheer dog-in-the-manger-stuff. Jealousy exaggerates, you know.'

I let that one pass. After a moment he went on: 'The Inspector could only take my word for it, and when you seemed to be protecting Grant he thought you suspected him yourself, but hesitated to give him away.'

'But that's absurd! Of course I was never in love with him! I liked him, yes. I thought he was very charming—but *in love!*' I spoke hotly, indignantly. 'It's fantastic nonsense!'

'Why?' The question was bland as cream.

'*Why?* Because—' I stopped short, and bit my lip. I felt the colour flooding my cheeks, and shot a quick glance at him. His eyes, narrowed against the smoke from his cigarette, were fixed dreamily, almost in-attentively, on the long glimmering verge of the mist where it lay along the far sea's edge. But there was a smile touching the corner of his mouth. I said hurriedly: 'But when did the Inspector finally fix on Roderick? Surely the others at the hotel were suspect too?'

'Of course. Any of the other men—Braine, Corrigan, Persimmon, Beagle, could have had an unconfessed interest in folk-lore, but Marion's murder, remember, narrowed the field down sharply, since it demanded that the murderer also be an efficient climber. And soon afterwards the only climber of the group—poor Beagle—was murdered too.'

'Which leaves us with Roderick again.'

'As you say. When the Inspector came over yesterday morning he found Roderick, so to speak, leading the field and hardly anyone else running, but still without a thing that could be pinned on him. Then you found Roberta, and he might have got his proof, but he didn't dare wait much longer for her to open her mouth. He put another hurried call through to London for any information about Grant that they could rake up. He was going to risk pulling him in on suspicion if he got anything from them that could justify him. But nothing came through till this morning.'

'The fact that his grandmother had died insane? Was that enough?'

'It wasn't all,' said Nicholas soberly. 'His father died in a mental home two years ago.'

'Oh God,' I said.

'Quite enough,' said Nicholas grimly, 'to warrant his being detained—got somehow out of circulation till Roberta could talk. But it was too late. That damned fog came down like a curtain, and Grant gave Neill the slip, and went out looking for you.' His arm, somehow, was round my shoulders. 'Bloody little fool,' he said angrily, his mouth against my hair.

'I'd have been all right with Dougal if the mist hadn't come down,' I said defensively. 'Nicholas, tell me something.'

'Yes?'

'Dougal—he had a knife. I saw it. Did he—down there when you caught Roderick—he didn't—hurt him?'

His arm tightened, as if in protection. 'No,' he said soberly. 'He came up spitting fire and brimstone and revenge, poor devil, but he shut up as soon as he saw Grant.'

'Why?'

'Grant collapsed. When I caught him first, he fought like a wildcat, but when Dougal got there as well, and he saw it was hopeless, he just seemed to deflate. To break. He went suddenly quite helpless and gentle, and—I can't describe it, quite. It was rather beastly. He seemed to change character all in an instant.'

'He did it with me.'

'Did he? Then you'll know just how unspeakable it was. I'd just hit him on the jaw, and then there he was smiling at me like a nice child, and wiping the blood away.'

'Don't think about it, Nicholas. He wouldn't remember you'd just hit him.'

'I suppose not. He just smiled at all of us. That was when Dougal put his knife away and took him by the arm and said "Come on, laddie. Ye'd best be getting back oot of the fog. . . ." He went quite happily with the three of them.' He dragged at his cigarette. 'After they'd gone a little way off, into the fog, I heard him singing.'

'Singing?' I stared at him.

'Well, crooning a tune, half to himself.' His eyes met mine. '"*I to the hills will lift mine eyes, From whence doth come mine aid. . . .*"' He looked away.

'Poor devil. Poor crazy devil. . . .'

I said swiftly: 'They'll never hang him, Nicholas.'

'No.'

He ground out his cigarette on a stone, and pitched it away as if with it he could extinguish and discard the memory of that nasty little scene. Then he turned his head again, and his voice changed abruptly.

'You saw me with Marcia Maling, didn't you?'

'Yes.'

'I heard you go past us when she–when we were kissing outside her room.'

'You heard me? But I hardly made a sound.'

He smiled crookedly. 'My dear girl, my instincts work overtime where you're concerned. Even in the dark, and when I'm kissing another woman.'

'Perhaps even more when you're kissing another woman,' I said drily, and got a wry look from him.

'I suppose I deserve that one. But this time, I promise you, I was more kissed against than kissing.'

'All night?' I said

His brows shot up. 'What the devil d'you mean?'

I told him how I had heard a man's voice in her room later that night. 'So of course I assumed it was you. And when I asked you next morning—'

'I–see. I thought you were just referring to the kiss you'd seen. No, Gianetta, I did not spend the night with her. I merely got–how shall I put it?–momentarily waylaid, through no intention of my own.'

'I'm sure you struggled madly.'

He grinned, and said nothing.

'I suppose the man in her room was Hartley Corrigan? Oh yes, I *see*! That was why he came home early from fishing that night, and yet Alma Corrigan said he didn't get to bed till three!'

'I think so. And when she realized what had happened she took her lipstick and murdered Marcia's doll with it.'

'Poor Alma.'

'Yes. Well, it's over for her, too. I rather think they've both had a fright, and they realize that they do matter to each other after all. . . .' He paused for a moment, looking down at me under lowered brows. 'And now,' he said, in a totally different voice, 'shall we talk about us?'

I did not reply. My heart was beating lightly and rapidly somewhere up in my throat, and I could not trust my voice. I could feel his eyes on me again, and when he spoke, he did so slowly and deliberately, as if with some difficulty.

He said: 'I'm not going to begin with apologies and self-abasement, though God knows you have plenty to forgive me for, and God knows, too, why you have apparently forgiven me. I'll say all that to you later on. No, don't speak. Let me finish. . . . What I want to say to you now is quite simple, and it's all that matters in the world to me. I want you back, Gianetta. I do most damnably want you back. I suppose I knew I'd been a fool–a criminal, brutal fool–about two days after you'd gone, and then my pride stepped in and stopped me coming after you.'

I remembered how I had told Alma Corrigan that there was no room for pride in marriage. His next words were almost an echo; almost.

He said: 'But pride and love won't go together, Gianetta. I discovered that. And I do love you, my darling; I don't think I ever stopped.' He took me gently by the shoulders, and turned me so that I had to face him. 'Will you have me back, Gianetta? Please?'

'I never did have any pride where you were concerned Nicholas,' I said, and kissed him.

Later—a long time later—he said, rather shakily: 'Are you sure? Are you sure, my darling?'

'Quite sure.' The words were decided enough, but my voice was as uncertain as his. I added, foolishly: 'Darling Nicholas.'

'Gianetta *mia*. . . .'

Later—a rather longer time later—he held me away from him, and laughed. 'At least, this time, there's no doubting the solid worth of my affections!'

'Why not?'

He looked down at me with the old, mocking look. 'If you could see yourself, my Lady Greensleeves, you wouldn't ask me that! And if Hugo were here—'

'Which God forbid—'

'Amen. . . . No, don't try and tidy yourself up: it couldn't be done, and in any case I like you dirty, wet, and semi-ragged. I want to concentrate on your beautiful soul.'

'So I noticed.'

He grinned, and his arm tightened round my shoulders.

'It wasn't just coincidence that I met you here, you know.'

'Wasn't it? But how—'

'Your father,' he said succinctly.

'D'you mean to tell me—'

He nodded, still grinning. 'I got into touch with your people again some time ago. As you know, the divorce upset them very much, and they were only too anxious to help me put things straight.' He smiled down at me. 'Poor Gianetta, you didn't stand much chance. Your father told me flatly that you'd never be happy without me, and your mother—well, I don't think she ever has quite grasped the fact that we were divorced, has she?'

'No. For Mother, divorce just doesn't exist.'

'That's what I understood. Well, I was here at the beginning of May, and I happened to write to your father from this address, to ask him about *The Golden Bough*. A little later I rang him up—I was at Armadale then—and he told me you were due for a holiday, and that he'd contrived—'

'Contrived!' I said dazedly. I began to laugh. 'The—the old Macchiavelli! And Mother said it must have been "meant"!'

'It was meant all right,' said Nicholas grimly. 'I thought that all I needed was a chance to talk to you. . . .' He smiled ruefully. 'And then you ran away from me and I thought that perhaps your father was wrong and it really was finished. I'd been so sure . . . I deserved a set-down, by God I did. And I got it. You came—and I couldn't get near you. . . .'

He gave a bitter little laugh. 'So of course I behaved just about as badly as I could. I said some pretty filthy things to you, didn't I? I've no excuse, except that I thought I'd go crazy, being so near you, and having no—no claim. Somehow the biggest shock to my egoism was when I found you'd even discarded my name, and my ring.'

'I only dropped them when I saw your name in the register. Look.' I held out my left hand. The white circle on the third finger stood out sharp and clear against the tan. Nicholas looked at it for a moment, while a muscle twitched at the corner of his mouth, then he turned again and pulled me into his arms. His voice was rough against my hair. 'So you're going to let me walk straight back into your life? After what I did? After—'

'You said we'd not talk about that.'

'No, I like things made easy, don't I? It would serve me right if you turned on me now, and told me to get back where I belonged, and stop making a mess of your life.'

'No,' I said.

The lark had left his nest again, and was bubbling up through the clear air. I touched Nicholas' hand softly. 'Just don't—don't ever leave me again, Nicholas. I don't think I could bear it.'

His arm tightened. He said, almost with ferocity. 'No, Gianetta, never again.'

The lark rocked, feather-light, snowflake-light, on the crystal bubbles of his song. The great hills drowsed, drifting head under wing in the luminous haze.

I stirred in his arms and drew a little breath of pure happiness.

'What d'you bet,' I said, 'that when we arrive at Tench Abbas, Mother'll meet us just as if nothing had ever happened, and serenely show us both into the spare room?'

'Then we'd better get married again before we get there,' said Nicholas, 'or I won't answer for the consequences.'

And so we were.

Airs
Above the
Ground

MARY
STEWART

Airs Above the Ground

For my father
Frederick A. Rainbow

Chapter One

Nor take her tea without a stratagem.
Edward Young: *Love of Fame*

Carmel Lacy is the silliest woman I know, which is saying a good deal. The only reason that I was having tea with her in Harrods on that wet Thursday afternoon was that when she rang me up she had been so insistent that it had been impossible to get out of; and besides, I was so depressed anyway that even tea with Carmel Lacy was preferable to sitting alone at home in a room that still seemed to be echoing with that last quarrel with Lewis. That I had been entirely in the right, and that Lewis had been insufferably, immovably, furiously in the wrong was no particular satisfaction, since he was now in Stockholm, and I was still here in London, when by rights we should have been lying on a beach together in the Italian sunshine, enjoying the first summer holiday we had been able to plan together since our honeymoon two years ago. The fact that it had rained almost without ceasing ever since he had gone hadn't done anything to mitigate his offence; and, when, on looking up 'Other People's Weather' in The *Guardian* each morning, I found Stockholm enjoying a permanent state of sunshine, and temperatures somewhere in the seventies, I was easily able to ignore the reports of a wet, thundery August in Southern Italy, and concentrate on Lewis's sins and my own grievances.

'What are you scowling about?' asked Carmel Lacy.

'Was I? I'm sorry. I suppose I'm just depressed with the weather and everything. I certainly didn't mean to glower at you! Do go on. Did you decide to buy it in the end?'

'I haven't made up my mind. It's always so terribly difficult to decide . . .' Her voice trailed away uncertainly as she contemplated the plate of cakes, her hand poised between a meringue and an éclair. 'But you know what they're like nowadays, they won't keep things for you. If I wait much longer they'll simply sell it, and when that happens, one realises one's really wanted it like mad all along.'

And if you wait much longer, I thought, as she selected the éclair, it won't fit you any more. But I didn't think it unkindly; plumpness suits Carmel Lacy, who is one of those blonde, pretty women whose looks depend on the fair, soft colouring which seems to go on indestructibly into middle age, and to find a whole new range of charm when the fair hair turns white.

Carmel—whose hair was still a rather determined shade of gold—had been my mother's contemporary at school. Her kind of prettiness had been fashionable then, and her good-tempered softness had made her popular; her nickname, according to my mother, had been Caramel, which seemed appropriate. She had not been a close friend of mother's at school, but the two girls were thrown together in the holidays by the nearness of their

families, and by professional connections between them. Carmel's father
had owned and trained racehorses, while my grandfather, who was a
veterinary surgeon had been, so to speak, surgeon in attendance. Soon after
the girls left school their ways parted: my mother married her father's
young partner, and stayed in Cheshire; but Carmel left home for London,
where she married 'successfully', that is, she acquired a wealthy London
banker whose dark, florid good looks told you exactly the kind of man he
would be in his forties, safely ensconced in the Jaguar belt with three
carefully spaced children away at carefully chosen schools. But the marriage
had not worked out. Carmel, to all appearances the kind of soft maternal
creature who you would have sworn would make the ideal wife and mother,
combined with this a possessiveness so clinging that it had threatened to
drown her family like warm treacle. The eldest girl had gone first, off into
the blue with a casually defiant announcement that she had got a job in
Canada. The second daughter had torn herself loose at nineteen, and
followed her Air Force husband to Malta without a backward look. The
husband had gone next, leaving a positive embarrassment of riches in the
way of evidence for the divorce. Which left the youngest child, Timothy,
whom I vaguely remembered meeting around his grandfather's stables
during school holidays; a slight, darting, quicksilver boy with a habit of
sulky silences, readily forgivable in any child exposed to the full blast of his
mother's devotion.

She was moaning comfortably over him now, having disposed (as far as I
had been able to follow her) of her dressmaker, her doctor, her current
escort, her father, my mother, two more cream cakes and, for some reason
which I cannot now remember, the Postmaster General . . .

'. . . And as a matter of fact, I don't know what to do. He's being so
difficult. He knows just how to get on my nerves. Doctor Schwapp was
saying only yesterday—'

'Timmy's being difficult?'

'Well, of course. Not that his father wasn't just the same, in fact his father
started the whole thing. You'd really think he'd have the decency to keep
out of Timmy's life now, wouldn't you, after what he did?'

'Is he coming back into Timmy's life?'

'My dear, that's the whole point. It's all just come out, and that's why I'm
so upset. He's been writing to Timmy, quite regularly, imagine, and now
apparently he wants him to go and see him.'

I said, feeling my way: 'He's abroad, isn't he, your–Tim's father?'

'Graham? Yes, he's living in Vienna. We don't write,' said Carmel with
what was, for her, remarkable brevity.

'And has he seen anything of Timothy since the divorce?' I added
awkwardly: 'I didn't know what the arrangements were at the time, Aunt
Carmel.'

She said with an irritation momentarily more genuine than any feeling
she had shown up to now: 'For goodness' sake don't call me that, it makes
me feel a hundred! What do you mean, you don't know what the
arrangements were? Everybody knew. You can't tell me your mother didn't
tell you *every single detail* at the time.'

I said, more coldly than I had meant to: 'I wasn't at home, if you remember: I was still in Edinburgh.'

'Well, Graham got access, if that's what you mean by "arrangements". But he went abroad straight away, and Timmy's never seen him since. I never even knew they were writing . . . And now this!' Her voice had risen, her blue eyes stared, but I still thought that she sounded aggrieved rather than distressed.

'I tell you, Timmy just burst it on me the other day, boys are so thoughtless, and after all I've been to him, father and mother both, all the poor boy has . . . And all without a word to me! Would you believe such a thing, Vanessa? *Would* you?'

I hesitated, then said more gently: 'I'm sorry, but it seems quite natural to me. After all, Timothy hasn't quarrelled with his father, and it seems a pity to keep them apart. I mean, they're bound to want to see each other now and again, and you mustn't think you mean any the less to him because he sometimes feels the need of his father. I–it's none of my business, Carmel, and I'm sorry if I sound a bit pompous, but you did ask me.'

'But not to tell me! So underhand! That he should have secrets from me, his mother . . . !' Her voice throbbed. 'I feel it, Vanessa, I feel it *here*.' She groped for where her heart presumably lay, somewhere behind the ample curve of her left breast, failed to locate it, and abandoning the gesture, poured herself another cup of tea. 'You know what it says in the Bible about a thankless child? "Sharper than a something's paw it is," or something like that . . . ? Well, I can tell you as a mother, that's *exactly* how it feels! Sharper than the whatever-it-is . . . But of course, I can't *expect* you to understand!'

The more than conscious drama which was creeping into Carmel's conversation had dispelled any pity which I might have been feeling for her, and centred it firmly on Timothy. And I was wondering more than ever just where I came in. She had surely not telephoned me so urgently just because she needed an audience; she had her own devoted Bridge set with whom, doubtless, all this had already been gone over; moreover, she had managed to make it clear already that she didn't expect either sympathy or understanding from anyone of my generation.

'I'm sorry, I'm not being unsympathetic, I am trying to understand; but I can't help seeing Timothy's side of it too. He's probably just wild to get a holiday abroad, and this is a marvellous chance. Most boys of his age would grab at any chance to go to Austria. Lord, if I'd had relatives abroad when I was that age I'd have been plaguing the life out of them to invite me away! If his father really does want to see him—'

'Graham's even sent him the money, and without a *word* to me. You see? As if it wasn't hard enough to hold them, without him *encouraging* them to leave the nest.'

I managed not to wince at the phrase. 'Well, why not just be sweet about it, and let him go? They always say that's the way to bring them back, don't they? I know how you feel, I do really; but Mummy used to say if you hang on to them too hard, they'll only stay away, once they've managed to get free.'

As soon as the words were out I regretted them; I had been thinking only of Timothy, and of somehow persuading Carmel to do what would in the end hurt herself and her son the least; but now I remembered what my mother had been speaking about, and was afraid I had cut rather near the bone. But I need not have worried. People like Carmel are impervious to criticism simply because they can never admit a fault in themselves. She could see no reference to her own triple domestic tragedy, because nothing would ever persuade her to believe that any part of it was her fault; any more than those people who complain of being unloved and unwanted ever pause to ask if they are in fact lovable.

She said: 'You haven't any children, of course. Doesn't Lewis want them?'

'Have a heart. We've not been married all that long.'

'Two years? Plenty of time to start one. Of course,' said Carmel, 'he's not at home much, is he?'

'What have my affairs and Lewis's got to do with this?' I asked, so sharply that she abandoned whatever tack she had been starting on.

'Only that if you had children of your own you wouldn't be so gay and glib.'

'If I had children I hope I'd have the sense not to put fences round them.' That I still spoke sharply was not entirely due to exasperation with Carmel; the trend of this futile conversation was, minute by minute, reminding me of the fences that only a short while ago I had been trying to put round Lewis. I added: 'Besides, Timothy isn't a child, he's what? Seventeen? I think it's you who don't understand, Carmel. Boys grow up.'

'If they didn't grow *away* so. My baby son, it seems only yesterday—'

'When does his father want him to go?'

'Whenever he likes. And of course he's wild to go.' She added, with a spite that sounded suddenly, shockingly genuine: 'As a matter of fact I don't mind him *going*. I just don't want him to feel he owes it to Graham.'

I counted ten, and then said mildly: 'Then send him off straight away, and let him think he owes it to you.'

'I might if I thought—' She checked herself, with a quick look I couldn't read. She was fiddling rather consciously again with the bosom of her dress, not her heart this time, but what lay more or less directly over it, the very beautiful sapphire and diamond brooch that had been one of Graham Lacy's guilt offerings to her. Then she spoke in quite a different tone: 'As a matter of fact, Vanessa, I'm sure you're right. I *ought* to let him go. One ought to make oneself realise that one's babies grow up, and that one's own feelings hardly matter. After all, they have their lives to live.'

I waited. It was coming now, if I was any judge of the signs.

'Vanessa?'

'Yes?'

She pricked her finger on the brooch, said a word which one never imagines that one's mother's generation ever knew, blotted the bead of blood on her table napkin, and met my eyes again, this time with a steely determination which didn't quite match the suppliant's voice she used. 'I wonder if you could help me?'

'I? But how?'

'I really do agree with all you've said, and as a matter of fact it would suit me quite well to have Timmy away for a little while just now, and I really *would like* to let him go, but you see, Timmy is such a *young* seventeen, and he's never been away from home before, except to a school camp, and that's different, isn't it? And I can't go with him myself, because it would be quite *impossible* . . . meeting Graham . . . I don't mean I wouldn't *willingly* sacrifice myself for him, but he was really quite rude when I suggested it, and if he did go off with Graham then *I'd* be on my own, and I hate foreign countries, they're so uncomfortable, besides not speaking English, and you can say what you like, I'm not going to let that child go alone among foreigners. So then I thought of you.'

I stared at her. 'Now I really don't understand.'

'Well, it's quite simple. I knew you'd been going on holiday with Lewis this month, and then he had to go on business instead . . .' Being Carmel, she couldn't, even when she wanted a favour from me, quite repress that look of malicious curiosity . . . 'But I did think you'd probably be joining him later, and if you were, then if you and Timmy could travel together it would solve everything, don't you see?'

'No, I don't. If Graham's in Vienna, I can't see how I—'

'The thing is, you'd be *there*, and you've no idea what that would mean to me. I mean, just letting him go off like that to meet Graham, with no idea of what their plans were or anything, and Timmy never writes, you know what boys are, and of course I'd sooner not be in touch with Graham myself, at *all*. But if I knew you and Lewis were somewhere around–I mean, Lewis must know his way about in foreign countries by now, and I expect he's fairly reliable on the whole, isn't he?'

She made it sound a rather doubtful quality. Just then Lewis was at rock bottom in my estimation, but I defended him automatically. 'Naturally. But I can't go with Tim, I'm afraid . . . No, Carmel, please listen. It isn't that I wouldn't do it like a shot if I were going to Vienna, but we're going to Italy for our holiday, and besides—'

'But you could join him in Vienna first. It would be more fun, wouldn't it, and salvage a bit of the holiday you've missed?'

I stared at her. 'Join him in Vienna? But–what do you mean? We can hardly ask Lewis—'

'If it's the fare, dear,' said Carmel, 'well, since you'd be sort of convoying Timmy, I'd expect to take care of that.'

I said with some asperity: 'I think I could just about manage it, thank you.'

It was one of Carmel's more irritating characteristics to assume that everyone else was penniless, and that Lewis, who made what seemed to me a very good thing indeed out of his chemical firm, would hardly have been able to afford a car if it hadn't been run on an expense account. But then, my standards were not Carmel's. I added dryly: 'I expect I'd be able to swop the tickets.'

'Then why not, What's to stop you joining him out there, once his business is finished? It would save him having to come back here for you, and you'd get the extra time, and a bit of extra fun, too. I mean, I'd be happy to stand you both the difference in the fares. But you can see that it did seem the most marvellous piece of luck that Lewis was in Austria, and you might be thinking of joining him? As soon as I knew, I rang you up.'

'Carmel. Look, stop these wonderful plans and just listen, will you? I'm

not likely to be going to Vienna, now or later, for the simple reason that
Lewis is not in Austria. He's in Sweden.'

'In Sweden? When did he leave Austria?'

'He didn't. He's been in Sweden all along. In Stockholm, if you want to
know. He went on Sunday, and I heard from him on Monday.'

I didn't add that the only message in four days had been a very brief cable.
Lewis was capable as I was of holding tightly to a quarrel.

'But you must be wrong. I'll swear it was Lewis. And Molly Gregg was
with me, and Angela Thripp, and they both said, "Oh, that's Lewis
March!" And it was.'

I said: 'I don't know what you're talking about.'

'Well, yesterday.' She made it sound as if I was merely being stupid, as I
had been over Timothy. 'We were shopping, and there was an hour to
Angy's train and we wanted somewhere to sit, so we went to the news
cinema, and there was something–a disaster or something, I simply can't
remember what–but it was Austria somewhere definitely, and Lewis was in
it, as plain as plain, and Molly said to me, "Oh, that's Lewis March!" and
Angela said, "Yes, look, I'm sure it is!" And then the camera went closer
and it was, I'm quite certain it was. So of course I thought straight away of
you, and I thought you might be going there too, any day, so when Tim got
too maddening and sulky about it, I rang you up.'

I must have been looking more stupid even than she had been implying.
'You're telling me you saw Lewis, my husband Lewis, in a news-reel of
something happening in Austria? You can't have done, you must be
mistaken.'

'I'm never mistaken,' said Carmel simply.

'Well, but he can't be—' I stopped. My blank protestations had got even
through Carmel's absorption in her own affairs: in her eyes I could see the
little flicker of malicious curiosity flaring up again. In imagination I could
hear Angela and Molly and Carmel and the rest of them twittering over it . . .
'And he's gone off and she didn't know, my dears. Do you suppose they had
a row? Another woman, perhaps? Because she obviously hadn't the *faintest*
idea where he was . . .'

I glanced at my watch. 'Well, I'll have to be going, honestly. I wish I
could help you, I do really, but if Lewis has been in Austria somewhere it
would just be a flying trip down from Stockholm. You wouldn't believe the
way they push him about sometimes. I never quite know where he'll turn up
next . . .' I pushed back my chair. 'Thanks awfully for the tea, it was lovely
seeing you. I must say I'm intrigued about this news-reel . . . Are you
absolutely certain that it was Austria? Whereabouts, do you remember?
And can't you remember what was happening? You said–a disaster . . .'

'I tell you, I can't remember much about it.' She was rather pettishly
fishing in her bag for her purse. 'I wasn't really noticing, I was talking to
Molly, and it was only when Lewis came on . . . Well, that's that, I suppose.
If you're not going, you're not going, and Timmy can't go either. But if you
change your mind, or if you hear from him, you'll let me know, won't you?'

'Of course. If you're right, there may be something waiting for me at
home.' I hesitated, then said, I hoped casually: 'Which cinema was it, did
you say?'

'Leicester Square. And it was him, it really was. We all recognised him straight away. You know the way he has.'

'I know all the ways he has,' I said, more dryly than I had meant to. 'At least, I thought I did. And you really can't remember what was happening?' She was busy applying lipstick. 'Not really. Something about a circus, and a dead man. A fire, that was it, a fire.' She put her head to one side, examining the curve of her rouged lips in the tiny mirror. 'But it wasn't Lewis who was dead.'

I didn't answer. If I had, I'd have said something I'd have been sorry for.

The news theatre was dark and flickering, and smelt of cigarettes and wet coats. I made my way blindly to a seat. At this time of the day the place was half empty, and I was glad of this, as it meant that I could slip into a back row where I could sit alone.

A coloured cartoon was in progress, with animals quacking and swaggering across the screen. Then came some sort of travelogue; Denmark, I think it was, 'Hans Andersen's Country', but I sat through it without seeing it. It seemed a long time before the news came round, and longer still before we had done with the big stuff, the latest from Africa, the Middle East, the Grand Prix, the Test . . .

All at once there it was. 'Circus Fire in Austrian Village . . . Sunday night . . . Province of Styria . . . An elephant loose in the village street . . .' And the pictures. Not of the fire itself, but the black and smoking aftermath in the grey of early morning, with police, and grey-faced men in thick over-coats huddled round whatever had been pulled from the wreck. There was the circus encampment in its field, the caravans, mostly streamlined and modern, the big top in the background, and behind it a glimpse of a pine-covered hill, and the glint of a white-washed church tower with an onion spire. In the foreground was a screen—a sort of temporary hoarding—with advertising matter pasted on it; a photograph I couldn't see, some man's name and something about '*Eine absolute Star-Attraktion*', and then a list of prices. Then something must have shoved against the screen, for it fell flat on the trampled grass.

Yes, it was Lewis. He had been standing in the shelter of the screen, and for a moment, obviously, had no idea that the cameras were now on him. He was standing quite still, on the edge of the crowd that was watching the police, staring, like all of them, at the burnt-out wreck, and at something which lay still hidden from the cameras. Then he moved his head in the way he had—oh yes, I knew that way—and, amazingly, I saw the expression on his face. He was angry. Quite plainly and simply angry. I was all too recently familiar with that anger . . . but there, where every other man wore the same expression either of solemn respect or of shocked horror, the anger was somehow incongruous and disturbing. And this quite apart from the fact that this was certainly Austria and not Sweden, and that on Monday morning I had had a cable from him from Stockholm . . .

There was a girl beside him. As she moved, I saw her beyond him. A blonde, young and rather more than pretty in that small-featured, wide-eyed way that can be so devastating, even in the early morning and dressed in a shiny black raincoat with a high collar. Her hair hung in long, fair curls over the glossy black collar, and she looked fragile and small and lovely. She was pressed close to Lewis's side, as if for protection, and his arm was round her.

She looked up and saw the cameras on them both, and I saw her reach up and touch him, saying something, a quick whispered word that matched the intimate gesture.

Ninety-nine people out of a hundred, in that situation, would glance instinctively at the camera, before either facing it self-consciously, or turning out of its range. My husband didn't even look round. He turned quickly away and vanished into the crowd, the girl with him.

In the same moment the circus field vanished from the screen, and we were inside a sagging canvas tent, where an elephant rocked solemnly at her moorings, apparently muttering to herself.

'. . . the two dead men. The Police continue their investigations,' the commentator was saying, in that indifferent voice, as the picture changed again to a bathing beach on the South Coast of England . . .

The *Mirror* had it—a dozen lines at the bottom corner of page six, under the headline: CIRCUS BLAZE RIDDLE.

Police have been called in to investigate a fire which caused a night of terror in a small Austrian village near Graz. Elephants ran amok when a caravan belonging to a travelling circus caught fire, knocking down and injuring a six-year-old girl, and causing havoc in the village. Two men who had been sleeping in the van were burned to death.

The *Guardian* gave it eight lines just above the Bridge game on page thirteen.

Two men were churned to death on Sunday night when a wagon belonging to a travelling circus caught fire. The circus was performing in the village of Xlhalf?Wfen, in the Styrian province of Austria, near Grabz.

Next morning, Friday, I did hear from Lewis. It was a note in his own handwriting, dated on Monday, and postmarked Stockholm, and it read:

> Have almost finished the job here, and hope to be home in a few days' time. I'll cable when you can expect me. Love, Lewis.

That same morning I rang up Carmel Lacy.

'If you still want a courier for your baby boy,' I told her, 'you've got one. You were quite right about Lewis . . . I've had a letter, and he's in Austria, and he wants me to join him there. I'll go any time, and the sooner the better . . .'

Chapter Two

Not yet old enough for a man, nor young enough for a boy; as a
squash is before 'tis a peascod, or a codling when 'tis almost an
apple: 'tis with him e'en standing water, between boy and man.
He is very well-favoured, and he speaks very shrewishly: one
would think his mother's milk were scarce out of him.

Shakespeare: *Twelfth Night*

Timothy Lacy had changed, in that startling way children have that one
ought to expect but never does.

He had grown into a tall boy, resembling as far as I could see neither
parent, but with a strong look of his grandfather, and a quick-moving,
almost nervous manner which would weather with time into the same wiry,
energetic toughness. He had grey-green eyes, a fair skin tending to freckles,
and a lot of brown hair cut fashionably long in a style which his mother had
deplored loudly, but which I secretly rather liked. The expression he had
worn ever since his mother had officially handed him over in the main
lounge at London Airport—much as she had handed over her spoilt spaniel
in my father's surgery—had been, if one put it kindly, reserved. If one put it
truthfully, he had looked like a small boy in a fit of the sulks.

He was fumbling now with his seat belt, and it was obvious from his
unaccustomed movements that he had never flown before; but I dared not
offer to help. After Carmel's tearful—and very public—handing over of her
baby, it would have seemed like tucking his feeder round his neck.

I said instead: 'It was clever of you to get these seats in front of the wing.
If there's no cloud we'll have a marvellous view.'

He gave me a glance where I could see nothing but dislike. The thick,
silky hair made a wonderful ambush to glower through, and increased the
resemblance to a spoilt but wary dog. He did mutter something, but at that
moment the Austrian Airlines Caravelle began to edge her silky, screaming
way forward over the concrete, and he turned eagerly to the window.

We took off exactly on time. The Caravelle paused, gathered herself, then
surged forward and rushed up into the air in that exciting lift that never fails
to give me the genuine old-fashioned thrill up the marrow of the spine.
London fell away, the coast came up, receded, the hazy silver-blue of the
Channel spread out like wrinkled silk, then the parcelled fields of Belgium
reeled out below us, fainter and fainter with distance as the Caravelle
climbed to her cruising height and levelled off for the two hours' stride to
Vienna. Clouds flecked the view below, thickened, lapped over it like fish-
scales, drew a blanket across it . . . We hung seemingly motionless in the
sunlight in front of our whispering engines, with the marvellous pageant of
clouds spread, at no more than the speed of drifting surf, below.

'Angel's eye view,' I said. 'We get a lot of privileges now that only the
gods got before. Including destroying whole cities at a blow if it comes to
that.'

He said nothing. I sighed to myself, gave up my attempts to take my own
mind off the situation ahead of me, and opened a magazine. Lunch came,

and went, temptingly foreign, with *Apfelsaft* or red wine or champagne, the boy beside me so pointedly refraining from comment on what was obviously a burstingly exciting experience for him that I felt a flicker of irritation pierce my own preoccupations. The Caravelle tilted slightly to starboard; Nürnburg must be somewhere below that cloud, and we were turning south-east for Passau and the Austrian border. The trays were cleared, people stood, stretched, moved about, and the trolley of scent and cigarettes was wheeled up the aisle in nice time to block the passengers' access to the lavatories.

The pretty stewardess in her navy uniform bent over me. 'Would you care for cigarettes, madam? Perfume? Liquor?'

'No, thank you.'

Her eye went doubtfully to Timothy, who had turned back from his window. 'Cigarettes, sir?'

'Of course.' He said it promptly, and rather too loudly, and I caught the edge of a glance at me. 'What kind have you?'

She told him, and he made his choice and fumbled for the money. As she handed him the statutory packet of two hundred, I saw his eyes widen, but he successfully hid dismay, if that was what he was feeling, and paid. The trolley moved on. With some panache, but without another glance at me, Timothy tucked the cigarettes down into his airline holdall, and got out a paperback mystery. Silence hovered again, conscious, ready to strike.

I said: 'You know, I couldn't really care less if you want to smoke all day and all night till you die of six sorts of cancer all at once. Go right ahead. And as a matter of fact, the sooner the better. You have the worst manners of any young man I ever met.'

The paperback dropped to his knees, and he looked at me full for the first time, eyes and mouth startled open. I said: 'I know quite well that you're perfectly capable of travelling alone, and that you'd prefer it. Well, so would I. I've got troubles enough of my own, without bothering about yours, but if I hadn't said I'd go with you, you'd never have got away. I know you're sitting there fulminating because you've had a kind of nursemaid tagged on to you, but for goodness' sake aren't you adult enough to know that there are two sides to everything? You know you'd get on fine on your own, but your mother doesn't and there's no sense in making gestures to reassure oneself, if they're only distressing other people. Surely all that really matters now is that you have got your own way, so why not make the best of it? We're stuck with each other till I get you—or you get me—safely into Vienna, and you meet your father. Then we're both free to go about our own affairs.'

Timothy swallowed. The action seemed to use the muscles of his whole body. When he spoke, his voice cracked infuriatingly back for a moment into falsetto.

'I–I'm sorry,' he said.

'I didn't want to make you talk if you'd rather read or watch the view,' I said, 'but as a matter of fact I always get nervous on take-off, and if one chatters a bit about things it takes one's mind off it.'

'I'm sorry,' said Timothy again. He was scarlet now, but his voice had got back to the norm required of a young man who could comfort a nervous woman on take-off. 'I hadn't realised you were feeling like that. I was so—that is, it's all been so . . . I couldn't think how I was going to . . .' He stopped floundering, bit his lip, then said with devastating simplicity: 'The cigarettes were for Daddy.'

As an *amende honorable* it was superb. It also had the effect of taking the wind right out of my sails. And he knew it. I could see the glint in the grey-green eyes.

I said: 'Timothy Lacy, you have all the makings of a dangerous young man. I'm not in the least surprised your mother's afraid to let you out alone. Now tell me what to call you. I know your mother calls you Timmy, but it sounds a bit babyish to me. Do you prefer Timothy, or Tim?'

'I'll settle for Tim.'

'Well, mine's Vanessa.'

'That's an awfully pretty name. Are you called after Vanessa Redgrave?'

I laughed. 'Have a heart, I'm twenty-four. I don't know where they got the name from, probably just something my mother found in a book. As a matter of fact, it's a butterfly, or rather a family of butterflies, rather pretty ones, peacocks and painted ladies, and so on. Fair and fickle, that's me, born to flit from flower to flower.'

'Well,' said Timothy, 'that's a bond between us, anyway. They used to call me Mothy for short at my prep. school. I say, you can see a bit now through the clouds. There's a river . . . Do you suppose it's the Danube?'

'Could be. We more or less follow it the last part of the way.'

'If you're going to be frightened when we land,' he said kindly, 'I'll hold your hand if you like.'

'Isn't she beautiful?' asked Timothy.

The clouds we drifted across now, a mile above our own shadow, were Austrian. They looked just the same. Timothy, slightly crumpled-looking, and melting minute by minute into relaxation, had got to the stage of showing me photographs. This one was of a girl on a grey pony. It was an oldish print, fading a bit, and the girl, plump and fair and sitting solidly in the saddle, I was a bit startled to recognise Carmel.

'Er, yes.' Nothing that her son had told me up to now—and he had poured out a good deal about the Lacy *ménage* which I was sure Carmel would prefer me not to have heard—nothing had led me to expect the enthusiasm with which Timothy now held out his mother's photograph. I asked rather lamely: 'How old was she then?'

'Pretty old when that was taken. About fifteen. You can tell by the tail.'

'You can tell by the what?'

'The tail. Actually that pony's of the Welsh "Starlight" strain, and they're pretty long-lived; they don't start to look old till they're dying on their feet.' Then he recollected himself. 'Gosh, listen to me telling you! As if you didn't know all that, being practically a vet.'

'Not so much of the "practically", please! I qualified just before I was married.'

'Did you? I hadn't realised.'

'If it comes to that,' I said, 'I was "practically" a vet as you call it, before I even started at the Dick Vet.—that's the Veterinary College in Edinburgh where I went. You can't be brought up all your life in a veterinary surgeon's house and not learn a heck of a lot about the job.'

'I suppose not . . . It'll be like me, getting sort of brought up with the horses at my grandfather's place. Did you ever practise?'

'Officially, only for about six months, but in actual fact you do a lot of practical work as a student, especially in your final year. You travel out to farms, and handle the animals, and you learn to make your own diagnoses, use X-rays, assist operations–the lot. After I got my diploma I started work as Daddy's assistant, but then I met Lewis and got married.'

'What exactly does he do, your husband?'

'He's employed by Pan-European Chemicals. You'll have heard of it; it's not as vast as I.C.I., but it's getting on that way. Lewis is in the Sales Department. He's planning to change over now to another branch, because his job takes him abroad too much–he used not to mind, but we hardly seem to have seen each other since we were married. To begin with I used to go home while he was abroad, and work with my father, but then I started helping out now and then at the P.D.S.A.–that's the People's Dispensary for Sick Animals–near where we live in London, and that keeps my hand in.'

'Gosh, yes: I'm sorry about the "practically", it was a howling insult.' He sat quiet for a moment, riffling through the remaining photographs in his hands. I saw that they were mostly of horses. He seemed completely relaxed now and at ease, his random remarks and silences coming as easily as among his contemporaries. Which, in fact, I now felt myself to be: oddly enough, this was the effect which my school-mistressy outburst had produced in both of us, as if we had quarrelled and now had made it up on equal terms, with a licence to say what we felt.

He said suddenly: 'I hate London. It was all right when grandfather was alive, I was allowed to go there a lot in the hols. Mummy didn't seem to want me around so much then, when the girls were still home. If only she'd kept the place on . . . got somebody in to manage it . . . not just sold it . . .' He snapped the photographs together into a pack, pushed them into their envelope and tucked them decisively down into the holdall. 'And now that I've left school, it just looked as if it was going to be London all summer, and I felt I couldn't stick it. So I had to do something drastic, hadn't I?'

'Like harrying your poor mother into parting with you? I shouldn't worry; she'll survive it.'

He gave me a quick, bright glance, and seemed about to say something, but thought better of it. When he did speak, I felt sure this was not what he had been going to say. 'Have you ever been to Vienna before?'

'No.'

'I wondered if you were interested in the Spanish Riding School. You know, the team of white Lipizzan stallions that give those performances of *haute école* to music. I've wanted to see them all my life.'

I said: 'I know of them, of course, but I can't say I know much about them. I'd certainly love to see them. Are they in Vienna now?'

'They live in Vienna. The performances are put on in a marvellous building like a big eighteenth-century ballroom, in the Hofburg Palace. They perform every Sunday morning; only, I'm afraid, not in August.

They'll begin again in September . . .' He grinned. 'If I know anything about it, I'll still be here. But one can go into the stables any time and see them there, and I believe you can get to the training sessions and see the work actually going on. My father's been in Vienna now for six months, and I'm hoping he'll know a few of the right people by now, and get me in behind the scenes.' He glanced away out of his window. 'I believe we're beginning to lose height.'

I looked thoughtfully at his averted profile. Here was yet another change. Now that he was launched on something that appealed to him, that genuinely mattered, his voice and manner had lost the remaining touches of awkward youth. This was a young man talking about his subject with the air of knowing far more about it than he was bothering to impart. But not quite, yet, with the air of knowing exactly where he was going: there was a lurking trace of defiance still about that.

I asked, to keep him talking: 'Why is it called the "Spanish" Riding School?'

'What? Oh, because the Lipizzan stud was founded originally with Spanish horses. I think it's about the oldest breed of horse we've got–they go right back to the Romans, Roman cavalry horses in Spain being crossed with Arabians and so on, and they were the best war-horses you could get, so they were sold right, left, and centre all over Europe in the Middle Ages, and when the Austrian Stud was founded at Lipizza they bought Spanish stock for it.'

'Hence the name Lipizzan . . . Yes, I see. Didn't Austria give up Lipizza to Italy after the first war, or something?'

He nodded. 'One gathers it was a marvel the horses didn't disappear altogether, when the Austrian Empire broke up. I suppose when the Republic was started nobody was much interested in a relic of, well, high life, but then they started giving public performances–they'd become State property, of course–and now the Austrians are frantically proud of them. The Stud had a pretty ropy time at the end of the last war, too, when Vienna was bombarded; you'll remember how Colonel Podhajsky, the Director, got the stallions safely out of Vienna, then the mares were rescued from Czechoslovakia by the American Army, and the stud was set up in some barracks or other at Wels in the north, before they got re-settled at Piber.'

'Yes, I knew that. Piber, was it? Where's that? Somewhere in the south, isn't it?'

'It's down in Styria, not far from Graz. What's the matter?'

'Nothing. Go on. Tell me about the stallions.'

He looked at me for a moment as if to see whether I was genuinely interested or not, then he went on, his manner a rather touching blend of didacticism and boyish enthusiasm.

'Well, they're bred at Piber, then when they're four, the best of them go to Vienna to be trained. The others are sold. The ones at Vienna take years to train. I suppose one of the things that makes the performance so exciting isn't just that it's beautiful, but that—' He glanced at me again, hesitated, then said almost shyly: 'Well, don't you think there's something a bit thrilling about the–the *oldness* of it all, movements and figures passed down right from the year One, right from Xenophon, you know, the *Art of*

Horsemanship—isn't it rather marvellous to think of the idea of *haute école* going right back to the fifth century B.C.? But with the Lipizzans it isn't even ordinary *haute école*; after all, you can see normal dressage anywhere at shows . . . what's so beautiful is the way they've blended the dressage movements in to make the "figure dances" like the School Quadrille, and then of course the "airs above the ground".'

'The what? Oh, you mean those marvellous leaps the horses do.'

'Yes, they call them the *Schulen uber der Erde*,' said Timothy. 'They're as old as the hills, too. They were the old battle movements all the war-horses had to learn if they were to be any good—I mean, if you were using both hands for shield and sword or whatnot, you had to have a horse that would jump to order in any direction at a moment's notice. Half a minute—if you'd like to look at these . . .'

He bent to fish in his holdall. We were coming down through cloud, steadily losing height, and already here and there people were making small movements of preparation for landing. But even the novelties of flying seemed lost on Timothy now.

He straightened up, slightly flushed, eagerly producing a book heavily illustrated by photographs.

'See, there they are, these are the different figures.' He pushed the hair back out of his eyes and spread the book open on my knee. 'All the stallions can learn to do the ordinary dressage movements—like the *piaffe*, that's a sort of high trot on the spot; and that lovely slow trot they call the Spanish trot—but I believe only the best of them go on to the actual leaps. There, see? They're terribly hard to do, and some of the horses never do manage them. They take years to train, and develop terrific muscles for it . . . Look at that one there . . . he's doing the *levade*, it looks just like rearing, except for the way he bends his hocks, but I believe it's a terrific effort to hold.'

'It look it. That's like the pose you see in all the old statues, and old battle pictures and so on.'

'That's exactly what it is! If somebody took a swipe at you in battle your horse was supposed to get between you and him, poor thing.'

'Well, I hope it had armour, that's all,' I said. 'These are lovely, Tim. Oh, he's a beauty, isn't he? Look at that head, and those wise eyes. He knows a thing or two, that fellow.'

'I'll say,' said Timothy. 'That's Pluto Theodorosta; he was the absolute tops, I believe; he died just recently. He was Colonel Podhajsky's favourite. I don't know which is the top stallion now, I think it's Maestoso Mercurio. There, that's him, and that one's Maestoso Alea—you can see their heads are similar, coming from the same strain . . . That's Conversano Bonavista—he was favourite of the last Director's. Look, isn't this a marvellous photograph? That's Neapolitano Petra doing the *courbette*; I believe it's the most difficult leap of the lot. There was some story, I think it was about him; they were going to present him to some Eastern potentate or something, for a compliment, but his rider killed him, and then shot himself so they shouldn't be parted.'

'Good heavens. Is it true?'

'I don't know. They don't put that sort of thing in any of the books about stallions, but I heard quite a lot about them from an Austrian trainer who was in England for years, and used to visit my grandfather. I've probably got the story wrong, but actually, I wouldn't be surprised. You know how you can get to feel about horses . . . and when you've worked as these men do, every day with a horse for–oh, lord, twenty years, perhaps . . .'

'I believe you. There's a dark one, Tim. I thought they were all white?'

'He's a bay, actually, Neapolitano Ancona. They used to be all colours, but they've gradually bred the colours out, all except the bay, and now there's always one bay in the show by tradition.'

'Where do they get their names? That's two Neapolitanos and two Maestosos.'

'They all come from six original stallions. They take their first name from the stallion, and the second from their dam.'

I said, with genuine respect: 'You seem to know an awful lot about them.'

He hesitated, flushed, and then said flatly: 'I'm going to get a job there if they'll have me. That's why I came.'

'Are there really six sorts of cancer?' asked Tim.

'Are there what?' After his last bombshell, I had not felt called upon to make, or even capable of offering, any comment, and a pause had ensued, during which the flight hostess announced in German and English that we were approaching Vienna, and would we kindly fasten our seat belts and extinguish our cigarettes . . .

We dropped out of cloud, and, it seemed close below us now, flat, cropped stubble fields of Austria unrolled and tilted. Somewhere ahead in a hazy summer's evening was Vienna, with her woods and her grey, girdling river.

And now Timothy appeared to be distracting me with cheerful small talk from the approaching terrors of landing.

'I meant the six sorts of cancer you can get from smoking.'

'Oh, I remember,' I said. 'Well, I expect there are, but don't take it to heart, if you're worrying about your father. I dare say he can take care of himself.'

'I wasn't worrying about him. At least, not in the sense you mean.'

There was something in his voice which told me that this was not, after all, merely a bit of distracting small talk. On the contrary, the carefully casual remark dangled in front of me like bait.

I rose to it. 'Then what are you worrying about?'

'Is your husband meeting you at the airport?'

'No. He–I'm to get in touch with him after I get there. I've booked a room at a hotel. So if I may, I'll beg a lift into town with your father and you. Unless, of course, you want to shake off your nursemaid before you meet him?'

But he didn't smile. 'Actually, he's not meeting me.'

'But your mother said—'

'I know she did. But he's not. I–I told her he was, it made it easier. It was a lie.'

'I see. Well, then—' Something in his expression stopped me. 'Does it matter all that much?' I asked.

'That's not all.' He cleared his throat. 'It's—I thought it would be all right, but now it's come to the point, I'm beginning to wonder. I dare say,' he added with a sudden, fierce bitterness that disturbed me, 'I dare say she's right, and I'm a stupid kid who shouldn't be out loose, but I—' He swallowed. 'Did you say you'd got a hotel?'

'Yes. It's right in the centre. On the Stephansplatz, opposite St Stephen's Cathedral. Why? Would you like to go there first with me?'

'If you don't mind.'

'Fine,' I said briskly, 'we'll do that. Look, have you room in your holdall for these magazines?'

'Yes, here, let me. Mrs March—'

'Vanessa, please. You know, you don't have to tell me anything you don't want to.'

'I think I'd better.'

'Here, Tim, relax, it can't be as bad as that. What have you done? Forgotten to tell him which day you're coming?'

'It's worse than that. He's not even expecting me. He didn't ask me to come at all. I made it all up, to get away. In fact,' said Timothy desperately, 'he hasn't written to me since he left. Not once. Oh'—at something which must have shown in my face— 'I didn't mind, really. I mean, we were never all that close, and if he didn't want to, well, it was up to him, wasn't it? You're not to think I told all those lies to Mummy about him writing because I—because I felt he should have done, or something. I only did it so that I could get away.'

He finished the terrible little confession on a note of apology. I couldn't look at him. It was all I could do not to state loudly and clearly just what I thought of his parents. 'In other words,' I said, 'you're running away?'

'Yes. In a way. Yes.'

'And now that you're stuck with a nursemaid who looks like handing you over personally, you've had to tell her?'

'It wasn't that.' He looked grateful for the calm neutrality of my tone. 'I could have got away from you easily. It just didn't seem fair, when you'd be the one to be left with all the row.'

'I see. Thank you. Well, we'll have to think this out, won't we? How are you off for money?'

'I've got about twenty pounds.'

'If your father didn't send you the money for the fare, where did you get it?'

'Well, I suppose I stole it,' said Timothy.

'My poor Tim, you are breaking out, aren't you? Who from?'

'Oh, nobody. It was my Post Office account. I was supposed to leave it alone till my eighteenth birthday. That,' said Timothy clearly, 'is pretty soon, anyway.'

'Am I to take it you didn't intend to get in touch with your father at all? Did you only use the fact that he lives in Vienna as an excuse to get away?'

'Not really. I've got to live somewhere till I get the job, and twenty pounds won't last for ever. I expect there'll be a bit of a turn-up, but you get over it.'

He spoke without noticeable apprehension, and I was reassured. Perhaps he was tougher than I had thought. It seemed as if he might need to be.

I said: 'Well, we'll go together to my hotel first, shall we, and have a wash and so forth, and ring your father up. I expect he'll come for you . . . That is, if he's home. I suppose you don't know if he's in Vienna now? It's August, after all; he may be away an holiday.'

'That's what the twenty pounds is for,' said Timothy. 'The—well, the interregnum.'

I got it then with a bang. I turned to stare at him, and he, back in ambush behind the heavy lock of hair, eyed me once again warily, but this time—I thought—also with amusement.

'Timothy Lacy! Are you trying to tell me you've lied to your poor mother and gone blinding off into the blue without having the foggiest idea where your father even *is*?'

'Well, he does live in Vienna, I know he does. The money comes from there—the money to pay for school and so on.'

'But you don't actually know his address?'

'No.'

There was a rather loaded silence. He must have misunderstood my half of it, for he said quickly: 'Don't think I'll be a nuisance to you. If it's too late to get hold of Daddy's bank or something, I'll just take a room at the hotel till Monday. You don't need to bother about me at all. I'll be fine, and there's masses of things I want to do. When's your husband joining you?'

'I don't quite know.'

'You'll be telephoning him tonight?'

Another pause. I took a breath to speak but I didn't need to. The grey-green eyes widened. The lock of hair went back.

'Vanessa March!' It was a wickedly perfect imitation of the tone I had used on him, and it crumbled the last barriers of status between us. 'Are you trying to tell me that you've lied to my poor mother and gone blinding off into the blue without having the foggiest idea where your husband even *is*?'

I nodded. We met one another's eyes. Unnoticed, the Caravelle touched down as smoothly as a gull. Outside the windows the flat fields of Schwechat streamed past, lights pricking out in the early dusk. The babel of foreign voices rose round us as people hunted for coats and hand-baggage.

Timothy pulled himself together. 'The orphans of the storm,' he said. 'Never mind, Vanessa, I'll look after you.'

Chapter Three

In all the woes that curse our race
There is a lady in the case.
W. S. Gilbert: *Fallen Fairies*

In the event, Timothy's father proved very easy to locate. He was in the telephone book. It was Tim himself who discovered this, while I, sitting on my bed in the large, pleasant, and rather noisy room of the Hotel Am

Stephansplatz, was telephoning our first tentative inquiries down to the reception desk about banking hours in Vienna.

'It must be him,' said Timothy, pushing the directory page under my nose. 'Look, there it is. Prinz Eugenstrasse 81. The telephone number's 63 42 61.'

'And the banks are shut now, so he may be there, or someone'll be there who knows where he is. He'll have a housekeeper, surely?' I cradled the receiver, and swung my legs down off the bed. 'Well, if only Lewis is as easy to find, all our troubles will be over by dinner-time. At least,' I amended it, 'some of them. Go ahead then, it's all yours . . . and the girl at the switchboard speaks English.'

'It's not that. My German's not bad, I did it for "A" levels; and as a matter of fact I'm panting to try.'

'Well, then?' Then, as he still hesitated: 'Be your age, Tim.'

He made a face at me, then grinned and lifted the receiver. I went into the bathroom and shut the door.

Under the circumstances it seemed a remarkably short conversation. When I went in again he had put back the receiver and was leaning on the window-sill, watching the crowds thronging the pavement outside St Stephen's Cathedral.

He said, without looking round: 'He wasn't annoyed.'

I opened a suitcase and began to lift my things out. 'Oh, he was there, was he? Good. Well, that's one trouble on the way out. I'm very glad. Is he coming for you, or will you get a taxi?'

'He was just going out, as a matter of fact,' said Tim. 'He won't be in till pretty late. He's going to a concert with his fiancée.'

I shook out a dress rather carefully and hung it away. 'I suppose you didn't know about her?'

'No, I told you he never wrote. Her name's Christl. I think it's short for Christian.'

'Oh? Austrian?'

'Yes. Viennese. It's a rather pretty name, isn't it?'

I lifted another frock from my case. 'I don't suppose he'd tell you much about it on the phone.'

'Not much. I told him you were here. He said he couldn't get out of the concert, but would we meet them afterwards for supper at . . . I wrote it down . . . at Sacher's Hotel. It's by the Opera House. Eleven o'clock in the Blue Bar.'

He had turned back now from the window and was watching me. His face gave no clue to what he was thinking. I raised an eyebrow. 'Flying high on your first night out of the nest. "Eleven o'clock in the Blue Bar." It sounds like something out of Ian Fleming. What price the apron strings now?'

'Well,' he said, 'it's what I wanted, isn't it?'

'My dear,' I said, 'do you mind?'

'To be quite honest, I don't know. Should I?'

'It would be very understandable if you did. It's rather a thing to have thrust at one just like that, a parent marrying again.'

'Yes. My mother's going to marry again, too.'

It was one of those things to which there seems to be no reply at all. I couldn't think what to say. I just stood there with my hands full of stockings, and probably looking as stupid as I felt. 'I had no idea,' I said at last.

'Oh, it's not official, and as a matter of fact she said certainly not when I asked her flat out, but I'm pretty sure. In fact I'd take a small bet.'

'Do you like him?'

'He's all right. It's John Linley, the publisher; do you know him?'

'No, but I remember your mother did mention the name.' I hoped I hadn't sounded as relieved as I felt: compared with some of Carmel Lacy's 'men-around-town', a publisher sounded the height of respectability. Not that it mattered to me what happened to Carmel Lacy, but I was beginning to find that I rather cared what happened to Timothy.

He didn't pursue the subject. He said: 'What does this hotel charge for bed and breakfast?'

I told him. 'I suppose your father won't have had time to make arrangements for you? I was wondering whether we'd have to take your case along to Sacher's, or call for it here later.'

'Well,' said Timothy, 'that's rather the point. He didn't say anything about my joining him. In fact, I got the impression that it was the last thing he wanted. Oh, I don't mean my coming to Vienna, he took that in his stride, after he'd got over the surprise; and as a matter of fact he was rather decent about it. He—well, he obviously isn't going to send me back or anything, and I've got the feeling he might even be pretty helpful about the job. There wasn't time to talk about it, because he was in a hurry getting ready to go out, and he just said something about work permits, and thinking it over later on, but why not simply have a holiday to start with, and was I all right for cash.'

'I like the sound of that last bit,' I said. 'Well anyway, I expect you'll get things fixed up when you see him tonight. He'll probably want you to move in there tomorrow.'

'That's just what I wouldn't bet on,' said Timothy. 'I told you he was pretty nice about my suddenly turning up like this, but I think it rather threw him. He wanted to see me, all right, but I'm certain he didn't want me staying with him, and that's one reason why he was so dashed forthcoming about money.' This wasn't cynicism, but merely a matter-of-fact observation of the kind that would paralyse most parents if they could know what their children know about them. 'Actually,' he added, 'I got the impression that he has someone living with him already.'

I looked at him for a moment, was satisfied with what I saw, and said: 'Then let us hope, Tim dear, that it's Christl, or things will begin to get altogether too complicated.'

'Poor father,' said Timothy unexpectedly, and laughed. 'I've put him in a spot, haven't I? I expect he's sweating on the top line now. Well, I'd better see if I can book that room. I hope they've got one; they've probably only got suites, or something with private bathrooms and all that jazz.'

'Well, it's a bit late for you to find anywhere else, and I gather your father's prepared to finance you. I'd go ahead. Dash it, he owes you the night's lodging at least!'

'Dead right he does. And then there's always blackmail. I've a golden future, haven't I?' And Timothy crossed to the telephone.

Well, I thought, as I stowed away the last pair of shoes, this was indeed what he had wanted. But there must be easier ways of growing up than tearing oneself loose from the apron strings, and then being thrown into the cold and foreign winds by a careless male hand, with a few coins flung after you. It was surprising, really, how normal and nice Timothy appeared to be . . .

'That's all right,' said Timothy, putting down the receiver. 'Number 216, one floor up. That's me settled. Now, what about you? Are you going to stay in and do your telephoning now, or go out and get something to eat first? I don't know about you, but I can't wait till eleven. I'm starving.'

I glanced up. 'You're being very tactful. Does it hurt? You must be wondering like mad what I'm playing at.'

He grinned. 'Well, I don't just feel I'm in a position to criticise.'

I shut the wardrobe door and sat down in one of the arm-chairs. 'If you can hold off from food for five minutes, I'll tell you.'

'Only if you want to.'

'Fair's fair. Besides, I'd like to tell somebody. It's very simple and rather depressing and probably a bit sordid, and I dare say it happens every day. Only I thought it wouldn't ever happen to me. We were going away on holiday, Lewis and I, and it was the first really long break since we were married just over two years ago. I told you he works for P.E.C., and they slave-drive him, only they pay pretty well, and he's always enjoyed the travelling. He never knew whether he'd be sent to Hong Kong or to Oslo next, and it suited him. Then we got married. And he said he'd change his job, only it would take time to train his successor, so we decided we'd just take it as it came for a couple of years. It was Lewis who suggested giving it up, not me. I know I've not behaved particularly well, but it was his idea in the first place. You see, we both want a family, and, the way things are now, it wouldn't be fair on them . . . the children.'

He didn't say anything. He was back at the window again, and appeared to be tracing out with his eye, stone by stone, the massive façade of St Stephen's.

'Well' – I tried hard to stop sounding defensive–'he told me finally he was leaving the department in mid-August this year, and we were going to have a holiday, a whole month, and go just where I wanted–he didn't care, he'd seen it all, he said he just wanted to be with me. It was, you know, another honeymoon. The first was only ten days. Then, just before we were due to go, they asked him to take on one more assignment. A week, two weeks, they couldn't be sure how long it would take. Just when we were getting ready to go; we'd got the tickets, I was packing, and everything.'

'What a rotten thing,' said Timothy to St Stephen's.

'That's what I thought. And said. The thing was, they couldn't order him, they made it a request, but he said he couldn't turn it down, he'd have to go himself, there was no one else. So I said what about the man they'd been training, but Lewis said this was something that had come out of his last job, and he'd have to do it himself. And of course I was so disappointed that I went all feminine and unreasonable and threw a scene, one of those classic scenes, "you think more of your rotten job than of me", and that sort of thing. And I've always *despised* women who did that. A man's job is his life, and you've got to take it as it comes and try to be as loyal to it as he is . . . But I wasn't.'

'Well,' said Timothy, 'I don't blame you. Anybody would have been upset.'

'The trouble was, of course, that Lewis was furious, too, with having to change his plans. He said couldn't I see that he didn't want to go at all, and that it wasn't anything to do with not wanting to be with me, but that there was no alternative. So I said well, why couldn't he just take me with him this time for a change, and when he said he couldn't, surely I knew that by this time, I really blew up. Then he got furious, and we had the most dreadful row. I said the most awful things, Tim, I still think about them.'

He looked at me with gravity that somehow seemed enormously youthful. 'And now you're just torturing yourself all the time because you've hurt his feelings?'

'Lewis,' I said, rather too carefully, and forgetting momentarily who I was talking to, 'is selfish, obstinate, and arrogant, and has no feelings of any kind whatsoever.'

'Yes,' said Timothy, 'I mean no. But if you know he doesn't want you to join him, why did you come, especially if you're still so furious with him?'

I looked down at my hands, which were clasped together rather too tightly on my knee. 'That's more sordid still, I'm afraid. I think he's with a woman, and that's something I can't quite laugh off the way we did with your father.'

'Vanessa—'

'I'm sorry, Tim, I'm not behaving well. I'm certainly not a fit and proper person to chaperon you, let alone preach to you, with the damned nerve I had, but I'm so unhappy I've got to do something. That's why I came.'

'Please don't be unhappy.' He was as awkward with his comfort as any man is at any age, but touchingly kind with it. 'I'm sure you must be wrong. Whatever anyone's been telling you, you'll find there's nothing in it.'

'Yes. Yes, I'm sure you're right.' I sat up straighter in the chair, as if by doing so I could shake off my thoughts. 'And it wasn't anything anyone told me, it was just an impression I got, and I'm sure it was wrong; all that's the matter with me is that I do feel guilty about the things I said. It would have been all right if he hadn't had to go straight away. When you get married, Timothy'–I managed a smile at him–'never part on a quarrel. It's hell. When I think about it now . . . He just went storming out of the flat, and then, when he got to the door, he stopped, as if he'd suddenly thought of something, and came back to me. I wasn't even looking at him. He kissed me goodbye, and went.'

I looked up at him sombrely. It was a relief to put it at last into words. 'It only came to me afterwards, but it was the way a man would act if he knew he was going to do something dangerous, and he didn't want to part like that. And now I know that's true. That's why I came.'

He was staring at me. 'What do you mean? "Dangerous"? What sort of danger could he be in? How can you know?'

'I don't know. Let me tell you the rest; I'll be as quick as I can.' And I told him all about the news-reel and the chain of events which had made me decide to come out to Austria and see for myself what was going on.

He listened in silence, perched now on the arm of the other chair.

When I had finished, he was quiet for a minute or two. Then he pushed the hair back from his forehead with a gesture that I was beginning to recognise as a signal of decision.

'Well, as far as locating the circus is concerned, that'll be dead easy. There are hardly any tenting circuses–that's travelling circuses–left these days, and everyone in Austria will probably know where this one was. We can ask the hall porter, and go on from there. Shall we go and do it now?'

I stood up. 'No, we'll eat first. We'll go out and find a real Viennese restaurant, and do ourselves proud, shall we? Then when we feel a bit stronger, I'll tackle the Case of the Vanishing Husband and you can take on the Father and the Fräulein.'

'We'll both tackle them both.' He uncoiled his length from the arm of the chair and stood up. He was half a head taller than I was. He looked down at me, suddenly shy. 'I was an awful ass this morning. I–I'm terribly glad we came together after all.'

'That makes two of us,' I said, reaching in the wardrobe for my coat. 'For heaven's sake, let's go and eat.'

Not only did Tim's German prove more than equal to the occasion, but the hall porter was every bit as helpful as the telephone directory had been. He identified the circus immediately as the Circus Wagner, and the village where the accident had taken place as the village of Oberhausen, situated some way beyond Bruck, in the Gleinalpe, the hilly region that lies to the west of the main road from Vienna to Graz and the Yugoslav border.

'Really, there's nothing to this detective business,' said Timothy relaying this information to me. My own German is of the sketchy variety which allows me to understand public notices, and to follow simple remarks reasonably accurately if they are made slowly enough, and preferably with gestures; but Tim's schoolboy German, though certainly slow and liberally laced with pantomime, seemed fairly fluent, and it got results.

'Ask him about the fire,' I said. 'It may have been a serious one if they know so much about it up here in Vienna.'

But no, this was not the case. The hall porter's very gestures were reassuring. The only reason he knew so much himself was because he himself came from the village near Innsbruck where the Circus Wagner had its winter quarters, and not only did he know the owner and some of the performers, but he seemed to have a fair idea of their summer route through the country. The fire? Ah, that had been a terrible thing; yes, indeed, two men had been killed, a fearful affair it was, a living-wagon burned in the night, and the men with it. Who were they? Why, one of them was the horse-keeper. The hall porter, it appeared, had known him, too, a good man, good with the horses, but he drank, you understand . . . No doubt he had been drunk when the accident happened, knocked over a lamp, been careless with the bottled gas . . . these things were too easy to do in such cramped quarters, and something of the sort had happened once before . . . The only reason they kept him on, poor old Franzl, was because he was some sort of relation of Herr Wagner himself, and then he was such a very good man with the horses . . .

'And the other man?'

But here the hall porter's information ran out abruptly. I didn't need German to understand the lifted shoulders and spread hands. This, he did not know. It was no one belonging to the circus, or the village. Herr Wagner himself had not known him; he had not known, even, that there had been a second man in old Franzl's wagon that night. There were even rumours—he himself had heard them—that it had not been an accident, that Franzl had been involved in some crime, and that he and the other man had been murdered as a result; but then there were always such rumours when the police would not close a case straight away; whereas anyone who had known old Franzl would realise that such an idea was absurd, quite out of the question... As for the other man, he believed that he had been identified, but to tell you the truth, he had not read about this in the papers, or had forgotten it if he had...

He smiled deprecatingly, and shrugged his wide shoulders once again. 'It is over, you understand, *gnädige Frau*, and the newspapers lose interest. Indeed, they would hardly have taken the trouble to report poor old Franzl's death, if it had not been for the elephant . . . A circus is always news, and particularly if there is an elephant . . . You saw some of the stories, perhaps? The truth of the matter was that there was only one elephant, a very old one, kept just for the parades, and she had in fact broken her rope, but had gone only a little way into the village, and had touched no one. The little girl, who was reported to be injured, had fallen down while running away in terror; the elephant had not touched her at all.'

'Ask him,' I said, 'ask him if he's ever heard of a man called Lewis March.'

'Never,' said the hall porter, for once mercifully brief.

I wouldn't have ventured the question but that it was obvious that the man was so delighted to have an audience for his story that it never occurred to him to wonder at our interest. A few more questions, and we had gathered all that we had wanted to know. Two days ago the circus had still been in Oberhausen, detained there by the police; its next stop was to have been Hohenwald, a village some fifty kilometres deeper into the Gleinalpe. There was a train at nine-forty next morning which would get me into Bruck before midday, and it was even possible that the local bus service might operate as far as Oberhausen, or, if necessary, Hohenwald, by the very same night. It was certainly possible to find somewhere to stay in any of these villages; there was an excellent small Gasthof in Oberhausen itself, called (inevitably, one felt) the Edelweiss, and I must, also inevitably, merely mention the hall porter's name to Frau Weber, and I would be more than welcome . . .

'Gosh,' said Timothy, as we let ourselves out of the hotel again into the brilliant noisy square, and turned towards the Kärntnerstrasse, 'I wish I was coming with you. I've always wanted to get inside the works of a circus, if that's what you call them. You'll promise to ring me up tomorrow night, won't you, and tell me how you got on, and what's happened?'

'I promise—that is, if I know where to get hold of you.'

'There's that,' he agreed. 'Well, if father and Christl won't have me, I'll come with you. I really don't feel you ought to be allowed to go all that way on your own! Are you sure you wouldn't like me to come with you and buy the tickets and find out about the buses?'

'I'd love you to. I might even hold you to that. And now, if we're to get to Sacher's in time, we'd better get a move on. Can you really eat another meal? I thought you were a bit rash with that *Hühnerleberisotto* at the Deutsches Haus.'

'Good lord, that was hours ago!' Timothy had quite recovered his buoyancy with the meal; he charged cheerfully along the crowded pavement, examining the contents of every shop window with such interest and enthusiasm that I began to wonder if we would ever reach our rendezvous. 'What is this Sacher's anyway? It sounds a bit dull, a hotel. Will there be music?'

'I've no idea, but it certainly won't be dull. Everyone who comes to Vienna ought to go there at least once. I believe it's terribly glamorous, and it's certainly typical of Old Vienna, you know, baroque and gilt and red plush and the good old days. It was started by a Madame Sacher, ages ago, some time in the nineteenth century, and I believe it's still fairly humming with the ghosts of archdukes and generals and all the Viennese high society at the time of the Hapsburgs. I think I even read something in a guide book about an archduke or something who went there for a bet in absolutely nothing whatever except his sword and maybe a few Orders.'

'Bang on,' said Timothy, 'it sounds terrific. What would my mother say?'

Sacher's Hotel was all that I had imagined, with its brilliantly lit scarlet and gold drawing-rooms, the Turkey carpets, the oils in their heavy frames, the mahogany and flowers and spacious last-century atmosphere of comfortable leisure. The Blue Bar, where we were to meet Graham Lacy and his lady, was a smallish, intimate cave lined with blue brocade, and lit with such discretion that one almost needed a flashlight to find one's drink. The champagne cocktails were about eight and sixpence a glass. Tim's father produced these for the company with very much the air of one who was producing a bribe and trying not to show it. Christl, on the other hand, did her best to pretend that this was a perfectly ordinary occasion, and that she and Graham had champagne cocktails every evening. As, perhaps they did.

Somewhat to my own surprise, I liked Christl. I don't quite know what I had been expecting, a predatory Nordic blonde, perhaps, on the model of the one I had seen with Lewis. She was indeed a blonde, but not in the least predatory, at least to the outward eye. She was plump and pretty, and looked as if she would be more at home in the kitchen putting together an omelette for Graham, than sitting in the Blue Bar at Sacher's, taking him for a champagne cocktail. She wore a blue dress, which exactly matched the colour of her eyes, and there were no rings on her hands. Timothy's father was still recognisably the man I remembered, with the years and the weight added to the florid good looks, and the extra heartiness of manner added by the embarrassment of his son's descent on his Viennese idyll with a presumably virtuous female companion.

That it was an idyll was not long in doubt. He was in love with the girl–she was some twenty years younger than he was–and he made it plain. He also (though to do him justice he tried not to) made it plain that

Timothy's appearance in Vienna at this moment was, to say the least of it, inopportune. By the time he had shepherded us through into the dining-room for supper I saw with misgiving that resentment or insecurity had brought the sullen look back to Timothy's face.

I saw that Christl was watching him, too; and saw the exact moment at which–while Graham was busy with the menu and the head waiter–she set herself deliberately to charm him. It was beautifully done, and was not too difficult, since she was not much older than he was, was very pretty, and had in full measure that warm, easy Viennese charm, which (as Vienna's friends and enemies both agree) 'sings the song you want to hear'. Before the wine was half down in our glasses, Timothy was looking entertained and flattered, and eating as if he had seen no food for a fortnight, while his father, also visibly relaxing, was able to devote himself to me.

He had already thanked me very pleasantly for accompanying Timothy across the Continent, and skated skilfully enough over the reason why he couldn't offer his son his own hospitality that night. He asked now with civil indifference after Carmel's health, and with equal indifference about that of my family, but it was soon obvious that he was curious to know what I was doing in Vienna, and just how Carmel had managed to involve me in her affairs, so I gathered that Timothy had said nothing to him in their brief telephone conversation.

'Oh, I'm just on holiday,' I said. 'My husband was called away to Stockholm just as we were setting off for a holiday together, so I came on here myself, and he'll be joining me soon.'

'In Vienna?'

'No, in Graz. We planned a motoring holiday in South Austria, and I'm going down there tomorrow myself. It was just luck that I happened to be heading this way at the same time as Timothy.'

'Indeed,' said Graham Lacy politely. 'That should be delightful. Where were you planning to go?'

Since I had only that moment so to speak, launched myself and Lewis on a motoring tour of southern Austria, I naturally hadn't the faintest idea. But I had two years' experience of the married woman's way out of any difficulty. I said immediately: 'Oh, I left all that to my husband. He's worked out a route, and to be quite honest I can't really remember exactly where he plans to go. I just sort of relax and go along with him.'

'Ah, yes,' said Graham Lacy, and then, to his son: 'And what are your plans, Tim?' Timothy, caught off guard by the direct question, swallowed, flushed, and said nothing. He had been listening to my string of lies with no betraying gleam of surprise, even, perhaps, with amusement; but now, faced either with confessing that he had come to Vienna naturally expecting his father to take him in, or with himself inventing some spur-of-the-moment story, he was so dumb. There was a painful pause.

I opened my mouth to say something, but Christl rushed into the pause, saying in her pretty, soft voice: 'Well, of course, he has come to see Vienna! What else? Timmy'– she said it charmingly, *Timmee*–'I wish I could show Vienna to you myself! There is so much to see, I should love to take you everywhere–all the places the tourists visit, the Hofburg, Schönbrunn, the Prater, Kahlenberg, and then all the places that the Viennese themselves go to–but I cannot, I am going out of Vienna tomorrow. I am so very disappointed, but you see I have promised; it is so many months since I have seen my parents, and they have been pressing me, and I have promised to go.'

'But—' began Graham Lacy.

She touched his hand, and he stopped obediently, but the look of surprise on his face was a dead give-away, and it was not difficult to interpret the look she gave him. It was quite obvious that she intended to clear herself out of Graham's apartment with the greatest possible speed so that he would be free–indeed, obliged–to do the right thing by his son.

'Well . . .' began Graham Lacy. He cleared his throat. 'Tomorrow's Sunday, so I've a free day. What do you say, old man, shall I come along about eleven or so, and collect you and your stuff? Then after you've settled in we could go out and do some of the sights? I don't have a great deal of time during the week, but you'll soon find your own way about.'

Timothy's glance went from one to the other. I realised that he had seen as much as I had. He was a little flushed, but he said, composedly enough: 'That's terribly nice of you, Daddy, but I won't descend on you just yet. I'd actually planned to go south with Vanessa tomorrow.'

If Graham or Christl felt relief, they neither of them showed it. Graham said: 'Indeed? It's very nice of Mrs March to ask you, but if she and her husband are setting off for their tour, they'll hardly want—'

'We won't be starting for a day or two,' I said quickly 'I'm still not quite sure how soon Lewis will be able to join me, so I'll have a bit of time to fill in before we set off. I'd love to have Tim with me.'

'Don't worry, I shan't land myself on them,' said Timothy cheerfully, and quite without irony. 'In any case I've been planning to get down into Styria somehow and visit Piber, and see the Lipizzan stud there, so if Mrs March wants company, it'll be killing two birds with one stone. If you don't mind being called a bird in public, Vanessa?'

'Delighted,' I said.

'Then,' said young Mr Lacy calmly, 'that's settled. I'll ring you up, Daddy, when I'm coming back to Vienna.' And he turned his attention to the sweet trolley, from which he presently selected a quite enormous portion of *Sachertorte*, a rich and very sweet chocolate cake topped with whipped cream.

I had the strong impression that the company settled down to drink their coffee with a distinct air of relaxation and relief all round. When we finally left the dining-room, Timothy and his father vanished in perfect amity in the direction of the cloakroom, and, when they returned, I thought I could see from their differing expressions of satisfaction that Graham had 'come through' quite handsomely with funds, without his son's having to resort to the blackmail he had threatened.

'Well,' said Graham, as we bade each other goodnight, 'I hope you enjoy yourselves. Take care of Mrs March, won't you, Timmy? And let me know when you're coming back to Vienna. If only you'd thought to let me know this time . . .' He added, awkwardly, 'I'm afraid this has been a rather odd welcome to my long-lost son.'

The cliché, would-be jocular, fell rather sadly among the shadows of

Vienna's midnight pavement.

Timothy said cheerfully: 'I'll remember next time. And thanks for tonight, it's been smashing.'

The Peugeot drove off. Timothy and I turned to walk back to our hotel. 'Do you mind?' he asked.

'You know I don't. I told you I'd be glad to have you. That, at least, wasn't a lie . . . And talking of lies, we brushed through that pretty well, wouldn't you say? She's a nice girl, Tim.'

'I know that. I did mind at first. I couldn't help it. But I don't now, not a bit.' We were passing the lighted windows of Prachner's bookshop: I saw that he had a look I had not seen in him before, buoyant and clear and free. 'After all,' he said, 'he's got a perfect right to his own life, hasn't he? You can't hang on to people for ever. You've got to let them go.'

'Of course,' I said.

Chapter Four

Ay, now I am in Arden; the more fool I. When I was at home I
was in a better place; but travellers must be content.
                                    Shakespeare: *As You Like It*

We drove into the village of Oberhausen at about five o'clock next day.

Now that Timothy was coming with me, I had abandoned my original plan of going by train to Bruck or Graz, and hiring a car from there. Moreover, it was Sunday, and I was not sure if such arrangements could be made on a Sunday afternoon. But in Vienna, it seemed, anything could be arranged at more or less any time, especially with the efficient and willing help of the desk staff of the Hotel Am Stephansplatz.

So it came about that Timothy and I left Vienna in a hired Volkswagen shortly before noon next day, making our way out through the mercifully thin Sunday traffic with me at the wheel and Timothy, map on knee, guiding me with remarkable efficiency out along the Triester Strasse, past the car cemetery, and on to the Wiener Neustadt road.

It was a beautiful day. As we ran south-west from Vienna along the *Autobahn* the countryside, at first dull and scabbed with urban industry, began to lift itself by degrees from the flat monotony of the plain. Beyond Wiener Neustadt we found ourselves in a rolling landscape of forested slopes, green pastures, and romantic crags girdled by silver streams and crowned with castles.

It was a scene from the idylls rather than from romance, pastoral rather than Gothic. The valley bottoms were rich with crops, and the hayfields stretched golden right up to the spurs of the hills. Even when the road—magnificently engineered—began its twisting climb to the Semmering Pass, there was still nothing in the grand manner about the scenery; the great slopes of pine forest were only a shelter and a frame for the peaceful human picture below.

We ate at Semmering–a resort which, at four thousand feet, is sunny all winter and which now, in the height of summer, had air so dizzyingly clear as to make Timothy extra ravenous even by his standards, and to restore to me something of the appetite which had been taken away by the nervous tension that I hadn't yet admitted, but which increased steadily as we neared the end of the journey.

We were on our way again by three, descending through more and more beautiful country till, a few kilometres beyond Bruck, we left the main road and its accompanying river, and turned up the valley of a tributary.

I pulled off the road on to a verge felted with pine needles.

'You've got a licence, haven't you, Tim? Would you like to drive?'

'Love to,' he said promptly. 'Are you tired?'

'A bit. It's a bit over-concentrated, with the left-hand drive, and driving on the wrong side, and all the cars out for the Sunday afternoon stampede. I must say you were marvellous over the road signs. I hope I'll do as well for you, or have you got your eye in by now?

'I think so,' he said as we changed over. 'It doesn't look as if there'll be much traffic up this little road, anyway.'

He took a few moments to examine the controls and play with the gear-box, and then we moved off. Not much to my surprise–I had long since ceased to underrate Timothy–he turned out to be a good driver, so that I was able to relax and think about what lay ahead of me, while I pretended for pride's sake to be admiring the scenery.

This was not difficult. The road ran at first through pine-trees with a widish tumbling stream to the right, then, rounding a green bluff, it began to climb, curling along under cliffs hollowed by quarries and heavily overhung by the forests above, while beside us the stream fell ever more steeply through a series of rapids, and on the far bank the rocks crowded in.

But soon we were out of the narrow defile into a wide placid basin girdled by hills. Here the road ran straighter, bounded to either side only by green meadows knee-deep in white and yellow flowers. Behind the meadows rose the hills; at first softly, furred with grass, their green curves framed by the pines which flowed downhill to fill every fold and crevice of the slopes, as if the high forest were crowding so thickly on the crests that it overflowed down every vein and runnel of the land below, like whipped cream running down the side of a pudding. At the upper limits of this dense crowded forest soared the cliffs again, shining escarpments of silver rock threaded in their turn by the white veins of falling water.

But these were still in no sense overpowering hills. They fell short of majesty, staying, as it were, on the periphery of vision, while the eye was held by the nearer landscape with its rolling, golden greens, and the cheerful domestic charm of the small houses that were clustered here and there round their churches and farms. The hay had been cut, and was drying, woven round its poles like dark gold flax round the spindles, while below it the shorn fields lay as smooth as plush. Here and there were shrines, like tiny churches cut off at the apse, with flowers in front of some painted statue, and martins wheeling in and out under the shingle roof. The village houses, too, were painted, the walls all washed with pink, or pale blue, or white, while every window had its window-box tumbling with petunias, geraniums, marguerites. Every house, it seemed, had its small orchard heavy with apples and peaches, and its apricot tree trained against the bright wall. Everything glittered, was rich, shone. The little village churches, humbly built of paint-washed plaster and roofed with wooden shingles, each thrust up a spire or an onion dome topped with a glittering gold weathercock. The cattle grazing peacefully in the fields were honey-coloured, and bore large, deep-ringing bells. The valley scene was so rich, so sunlit, and so peaceful, that the eye hardly strayed up to the rocks behind. They were only a background to this entrancing pastoral, painted in with the long shadows of late afternoon.

The first thing I saw, as we ran into the village of Oberhausen, was the poster, CIRCUS WAGNER, wrapped round a tree-trunk. The second was the circus itself in a field to the right of the road, a motley collection of tents, wagons, and caravans, grouped in an orderly confusion round the big top.

Timothy slowed to a crawl as we both craned to see.

'Well,' he said, 'they're still here. That's something, anyway. What are we going to do first?'

'Go straight through and try to find the Gasthof. Didn't the hall porter say it was at the far end of the village? Let's find it, and get ourselves settled before we do anything else.'

'O.K.'

The village street closed in. It was narrow, with no pavements, apart from a foot or two of beaten dust which formed a verge to either side and which was separated from the road by trees. Here and there a gabled window, or a flight of steps, thrust out to the edge of the road, forcing the people to abandon the footpaths and walk among the traffic. This they did with the utmost casualness: in fact the road, being smoother walking, was fuller than the footways, as the slow aimless Sunday crowd strolled about it at will, crossing in front of the cars without a glance. Since (as in most Austrian villages) the use of the horn was forbidden, our progress was very slow and circumspect. Timothy's pungent but perfectly cheerful running commentary was mercifully audible only to me.

At length we emerged from the narrows into an open square where an old well stood, and seats were set under the trees that surrounded the cobbled space. Ahead of us a church lifted a pretty onion spire with a gilt arrow for weathercock. The road divided to either side of the church.

I said: 'I think we'd better stop and ask the way. If we go up the wrong street, among these crowds, heaven knows where we'll get to before we can turn.'

He drew carefully in to the side, stopped in the shade of a plane tree, and leaned out of his window. He hadn't far to go for help: a cheerful trio of women was passing the time of day in the middle of the road with half a dozen children skirmishing round their skirts. They all answered him at once, with explicit gestures, while the children, apparently stricken dumb and paralytic at the sound of Timothy's accent, crowded round, staring at us with round blue eyes.

At length he drew his head in. 'Don't tell me,' I said, 'let me guess. It's the road to the right.'

He grinned. 'And we can't miss it. They say it's very nice along there, and quiet, because the other road's the main one. I say, I like this place, don't you? Look at that thing in the middle, the well or whatever it is, with that wrought-iron canopy. It's rather fine. Gosh, do you see that *Konditorei*, the baker's shop with the café tables inside? I could do with some of those cakes, couldn't you? We could come out and buy something as soon as we get settled . . .'

He chattered on, pleasantly excited, hanging out of his window in the hot sun. But I had ceased to listen, or even to see. The pretty village, with its lively, milling crowds, had fallen away, to become a shadowy background only for one person. I had seen Lewis's blonde.

She was pausing beside the well to speak to someone, an old woman in black, who carried an armful of flowers. She was half facing the other way, and was some forty yards off, but I thought I could not be mistaken. Then she turned, and I was sure. This was the girl I had seen in the news-reel. Moreover, in the flesh, and in the bright light of day, she was prettier even than I remembered. She was of small to medium height, with a slender curved young figure, and fair hair tied neatly back in a pony tail. Gone was the 'kinky' look that the black waterproof and dishevelled hair had given her; she was charmingly dressed now in the traditional white blouse, flowered dirndl, and apron. She looked about eighteen.

As I watched her, she bade a laughing goodbye to the old woman, and came straight towards the car.

'Tim,' I said softly, 'pull your head in and shut the window. Quick.'

He obeyed immediately.

'That girl, coming towards the car, the pretty one, the blonde in the blue dirndl—that's the girl I saw in the news-reel. No, don't stare at her, just notice her, so that you'll know her again.'

She came straight towards us, through the banded shadows of the tree-trunks, and passed the car without a glance. I didn't turn, but I saw Tim watching her in the driving mirror.

'She's going straight on down the street. Shall I wait?'

'Yes. Try to see where she goes.'

After a pause he said: 'I can't see her any more, there are too many people milling about, but she was heading straight down the street, the way we came.'

'Towards the circus field?'

'Yes. Would you like me to do a quick "recce" and see just where she goes?'

'Would you?'

'Sure thing.' He was already half out of the car. 'I've always fancied myself in the James Bond line, who hasn't? You stay there and pay the parking fine.'

The door slammed behind him. I tilted the driving mirror so that I could watch his tall young figure striding back down the middle of the street with all the magnificent local disregard for traffic. Then he, in his turn, was lost to view.

I leaned back in my seat, but not to relax. It was no surprise to feel myself trembling a little as my eyes reluctantly, yet feverishly, searched the crowds.

It was true, then, that my eyes had not deceived me: so much of it was true. Now that I had had this confirmation, I found it a profoundly disconcerting experience. The sight of Lewis and the girl in the dark cinema, that flickering brief scene still echoing with ugly tragedy and made more mysterious by its foreign setting, had been like a dream, something distant, unreal, gone as soon as seen, and believed no more than a dream in daylight. And as always, the light of day outside the cinema had set the dream even further apart from the world of reality. My own hasty action in coming out to Austria had seemed even while I did it as unreal as the dream itself; and up to now the enchanting strange prettiness of the country had helped the illusion that I was still far astray from reality.

But now . . . Oberhausen, the circus, the girl herself . . . And next, Lewis . . . ?

'What, no parking ticket?' It was Tim, back at the window.

'No parking ticket. You made me jump, I never heard you.'

'I told you I'd found my vocation.' He folded his length beside me into the driving seat. 'I shadowed your subject with the greatest possible skill, and she did go to the circus. I think she must belong there, because she went straight in through the gate and then round towards the caravans. The village people–quite a lot were there with children–were being allowed in, but they all went to the other side; there's a menagerie or something there, open to the public. There was a man taking the money at the gate, but I didn't ask questions. Was that right?'

'Yes, quite.'

'And I've got news for you. They're leaving tomorrow. There was a sticker across the poster, last performance tonight at eight o'clock.'

'Oh? We're just lucky, then. Thanks a lot, Tim.'

'Think nothing of it. It was fun. I tell you, I've come to the conclusion I'll be wasted on the Spanish Riding School. James Bond isn't in it–though as a matter of fact, Archie Goodwin's my favourite detective; you know, Nero Wolfe's assistant, handsome and efficient and a devil with women.'

'Well, now's your chance,' I said. 'If we don't fall over Lewis pretty soon, I'll send you after the girl.'

'What they call "scraping an acquaintance"? Can do,' said Tim cheerfully. 'Golly, if this road gets much narrower, we'll scrape more than that . . . Wait a moment, though, I believe this is it.'

The Gasthof Edelweiss was charming, and, in spite of its name, without a hint of chichi. It was a long, low, single-storeyed house, with a shingle roof where doves sunned themselves, and window-boxes full of flowers. It lay at the very edge of the village, and in fact the road petered out in front of it to continue on past the house as a country track leading to some farm. Between house and road lay a space of raked gravel where tables stood under chestnut trees. There were a few people sitting there over coffee or drinks. Between their feet the doves strutted and cooed. Swallows, thinking already perhaps of the hotter south, wheeled and twittered overhead. One could smell the pines.

Timothy and I were offered adjacent rooms, giving on the wide veranda at the back of the house. Here the windows faced the fields, and the small spotless rooms were very quiet. Mine had a pinewood floor scrubbed white, with two small bright pseudo-Persian rugs, solid pine furniture, and one reasonably comfortable chair. There was a really beautiful old chest of dark

wood with painted panels, a rather inconvenient wardrobe, and a lot of
heavy wrought-ironwork in the lamp brackets, and on the door, which was
studded and barred like something from a Gothic cathedral. On the walls
were two pictures, bright oily colours painted on wood; one showed an
unidentifiable saint in a blue robe killing a dragon; the other a very similar
saint in a red robe, watering some flowers. It seemed that in Austria there
was a pleasantly wide choice of saintly qualities.

I unpacked quickly, I had thought I would be glad to be alone, just to
think about what was to come, but in fact I found that I was refusing to
think about it. I had, as it were, switched my mind out of gear and was
concentrating only on folding away my clothes, on selecting something
fresh to wear, and on the drink which I would shortly have with Timothy
under the chestnut trees.

But when I was ready to go, I still lingered. I pushed the long windows
wide, and went out on to the veranda.

This was set only two or three feet above ground level, so that immediately beyond the rail, and directly, it seemed, beneath one's feet, the
fields began. These had been recently mown, and the almost forgotten smell
of new-mown hay filled the late afternoon. Beyond the stretches of shorn
velvet the river ran, sunk deep in trees, and behind this feathered girdle of
ash and willow rose the pines, slope after slope to the silver mountain-tops.
One side of the valley was deep in shadow. It was nearly half past six.

A sound made me look round. Timothy had come out of his window on to
his section of veranda. He had put on a clean shirt and looked alert and
excited.

'There you are, I thought I heard you. I wondered if you'd decided what
to do next?'

'Actually, I hadn't. I'm sorry, I'm afraid I'm a bit of a dead loss. I haven't
got over seeing that girl. It was a bit of a facer if you want the truth, like
seeing a ghost.'

'You mean you didn't really believe in her till now? I know exactly what
you mean,' added Timothy surprisingly. 'I felt a bit the same about Christl.
But you know, I don't know why you're worrying, not about *her* . . . I mean,
if there was any connection . . . seeing them together on the news-reel like
that . . . it wouldn't be—' He hesitated, trying to choose his words, then
abruptly abandoned finesse. 'Dash it, she may be pretty and all that, but *you*
don't need to worry about her! You're beautiful! Did no one ever tell
you?'

It was a fact that, now and again, people had; but I had never been so
touched—or so completely deprived of speech.

I said eventually: 'Thank you. But I—it's not just that side of it that's
worrying me, you know. It's just that I've no business to be here at all, and
now I'm not so much wondering how to find him as what in the world to
say to him when I do . . .' I turned my back to the fields, and straightened up
with what might pass for decision. 'Oh, well, it's done now, and the circus is
the obvious lead. Did you say it started at eight? Then we've plenty of time.
We can have a meal and talk to Frau Weber, and then walk down through
the village. If this village is anything like our village at home, the bush
telegraph's faster than the speed of light. In fact, if he's here still, he

probably knew all about us within thirty seconds of my signing the hotel register.'

'If this is the last performance, they'll start the pull-down the minute it's over, and they'll be clear of the place by morning.' He eyed me. 'I thought–shall I just go along there now, and see about getting tickets?'

'But if they've been stuck here a week there'll be no rush, and—' I laughed. 'Oh, I see. Well, why not? If you do track down "the subject", you won't do anything rash, will you?'

'The soul of discretion,' he promised. 'I won't say a word. I'll be back in good time for dinner.'

'I bet you will,' I said, but he had already gone.

Chapter Five

I see, lady, the gentleman is not in your books.
Shakespeare: *Much Ado About Nothing*

The shadows of the chestnuts lay lightly across the café tables, and there was a slight warm breeze which fluttered the red checked cloths. Curled in the roots of one of the trees, an enormous St Bernard dog slept, twitching slightly from time to time in his dream. The place was quiet and very peaceful. I sat sipping my vermouth, telling myself that I must think, must think . . . and all the time my eyes were fixed on the street up which presently, I was sure, Lewis must come.

So strong was my imaginative sense of his presence that when, in fact, Timothy reappeared, coming at high speed up the street, I was almost startled to see him. Next moment I was genuinely startled to see who he had with him. Not Lewis, but–inevitably, it now seemed–Lewis's blonde.

Next moment they were standing beside the table, and Timothy was performing introductions.

'Vanessa, this is Annalisa Wagner. She belongs to the circus . . . You remember we saw a circus in the field the other side of the village? Miss Wagner, this is Mrs—' Too late, he saw the pitfall. He stopped dead.

I said, watching the girl: 'My name is March. Vanessa March.'

'How do you do, Mrs March?' There was no flicker of expression outside the normal non-committal politeness. She had, I noticed sourly, a charming voice, and her English was excellent.

'Won't you join us for a drink, Miss Wagner?'

'Why, thank you. If you would please call me Annalisa?'

Timothy said: 'What will you have?'

'Coffee, please.'

'Only coffee? Not a vermouth or something?'

She shook her head. 'You'll find that we circus people drink very little. It's something that doesn't pay. Just coffee, please.'

Timothy lifted a hand to the passing waitress, who responded immediately–an unusual circumstance in any country, but in Austria (I had already discovered) a miracle. It seemed he was even going to pass the waiter test with honours. He and the girl sat down, Timothy telegraphing 'Over to you' with a subdued air of triumph that had nothing to do with the waitress, Annalisa with a smile and a graceful spread of the blue-flowered skirt.

Seen at close range, she was still very pretty, with an ash blonde Teutonic prettiness quite different from Christl's. One could not picture Fräulein Wagner as altogether at home in a kitchen. She would seem more in place among those slim, tough beauties who win Olympic medals for skating, or who perform impossible feats of skill and balance in the slalom. I wondered if the impression of fragility and helpless appeal that I had got from the news-reel had been assumed for Lewis's benefit, or if it had merely shown up in contrast to his size and air of tough competence. Or perhaps–I realised it now, more charitably–she had just been caught in a moment of shock and distress. It appeared that it was her circus, after all.

I said as much. 'Your name's Wagner? The circus must belong to you, to your family?'

'To my father. Timothy says that you are coming to see it tonight?'

'Yes. We're looking forward to it. We've only just arrived, but I understand that you're leaving tomorrow, so we don't want to miss you.'

She nodded. 'We move on tonight, after the show. We have already been here too long.' I waited, but she didn't pursue this. She asked: 'You are keen on circuses?'

I hesitated, then said truthfully: 'Not altogether. I've never liked performing animals much, but I love the other acts–high wire, trapeze, the clowns, all the acrobats.'

'Not the horses?'

'Oh, I didn't count the horses as "performing animals!" I meant bears and monkeys and tigers. I love the horses. Do you have many?'

'Not many, we are a small circus. But a circus is nothing without its horses. With us they are the most important of all. My father works the liberty horses: we think ourselves they are as good as the circus Schumann, but of course, we have not so many.'

'I'll look forward to seeing them, I always love them, and they're my friend's ruling passion.'

She laughed. 'I know. I found him down in the horse lines. I don't know how he got in.'

Timothy said: 'I took a ticket for the menagerie, but you couldn't expect me to look at parrots and monkeys when I could see the horses just round the corner.'

'No, it is not a good menagerie, I know. It is just a side-show for the children.'

I said: 'What good English you speak.'

'My mother was English. I still get plenty of practice, because a circus is a very mixed place, really international. We have just now all sorts: the clowns are French, and the high-wire act is Hungarian, and the trampoline artistes are Japanese, and there is a comic act with a donkey, which is English, and an American juggler–besides the Germans and Austrians.'

'United Nations,' said Tim.

'Indeed.' She dimpled at him. 'And on the whole really united. We have to be.'

'Have you an act yourself?' I asked.

'Yes. I help my father with the liberty horses . . . and there is a sort of rodeo act near the beginning. But my own act is a riding one. I have a Lipizzan stallion—'

'You have a what?' Timothy's interruption was robbed of rudeness by his obviously excited interest.

'A Lipizzan stallion. This is a breed of horse—'

'Yes, I know about them. I'm hoping to get to Piber to see the stud, and later on to see a performance in Vienna. But do you mean you have a *trained* stallion? I didn't think they ever sold them.'

'He is trained, yes, but not at the School. My grandfather bought him as a four-year-old, and my uncle trained him . . . and me also.'

'In high school work?'

She nodded.

'And you have a riding act of your own? You're a—a what is it?—an *écuyère*?'

She had soared, I could see, in Timothy's estimation, from being 'the subject' or 'Lewis's blonde', to star billing in her own right. I realised that my own estimate of her had been right: a young woman who was capable of the concentrated skill and strength needed to put a high school stallion through his paces was about as fragile as pressed steel. 'Gosh!' said Timothy, glowing with admiration.

She smiled. 'Oh, not what you will see in Vienna, I assure you! None of the "airs above the ground" except the *levade*, and sometimes the *croupade* . . .' She turned to me. 'This is a leap right off the ground where the horse keeps his legs curled up—is that the word?'

'Tucked under him,' supplied Tim.

'His legs tucked under him, and lands again on the same spot. We tried to teach him the *capriole*, where he leaps in a *croupade* and then kicks the back legs straight out, but this is very difficult, and he cannot do it, so now I leave it alone. It is my fault, not his.'

In view of the admiration in Timothy's eyes I half expected him to contradict this, but he didn't. He was, like her, dedicated enough to know that it is never the horse's fault.

She added: 'But in the other exercises he is wonderful. He is one of the Maestoso line, Maestoso Leda, and he is so musical . . . but there is no need for me to tell you. You will see him for yourselves tonight, and if he is good tonight I will try the *croupade*, especially for you.'

We murmured our thanks. Tim's eyes were shining. I was going to have my work cut out to keep Annalisa as Suspect Number One in my Case of the Vanishing Husband.

He was saying: 'I can hardly wait. Was he with the other horses? I didn't see him.'

'You were at the wrong end of the stable.' She dimpled at him again, charmingly. 'You should have trespassed first at the other end. Yes, he is there. Would you like to come round tonight after the show and see the horses? There will be time before we pull down.'

'You bet I would!' Then recollecting himself, with a glance at me, 'Vanessa—'

'I'd like to very much,' I said. 'How many have you?'

'Altogether twenty-seven, and then the ponies. The liberty horses are very good ones, you'll like them, Timothy, they are palominos, and we have twelve, very well matched. There will be only ten of them fit to work tonight, but it is still very beautiful to watch.'

'"Fit to work"?' I asked, wondering if she intended what the phrase implied, or if her English had its blind moments. 'Is there something wrong with the others?'

'Not really, but they're so valuable that one must be extra careful. There was an accident last week, and some of the horses were hurt. One of the wagons caught fire in the night, quite near the stable lines, and some of the horses injured themselves, with fear, you understand.' She added, quietly: 'But it was more serious than a few horses hurt. There were two men in the wagon, and they were killed, burnt to death.'

'How very dreadful. How did that happen?'

'We are still not very sure.' I thought she was going to stop there, but then she lifted her shoulders in a shrug and went on: 'But if you are staying in the village, you will hear all about it, everybody in Oberhausen talks about nothing else for a week. This is why the circus has had to stay here so long, because the police came, and made inquiries.' She made a little face. 'That is what they call it, "making inquiries"—hour after hour they asked questions and raked about and only today they say, "Tomorrow you may go. It is over."'

'I'm sorry. It must have been very distressing.'

'It was a bad time for my father.' The blue eyes lifted to mine. 'The wagon belonged to Franz Wagner, his cousin . . . my Uncle Franzl. I always called him that, though really he was my second cousin . . . I suppose he always seemed old to me. He joined us when I was a little girl.'

I forgot all my preconceived feelings about her in a genuine rush of sympathy. 'My dear Fräulein . . . my dear Annalisa, I'm sorry. I hadn't realised it was a relative . . . that's awful. You must have had a terrible time.'

She shrugged again, not uncaringly, but dismissively. 'It is over.'

'And the other man? There was another, you said?'

'He was nothing to do with the circus. He must have met my Uncle Franzl somewhere, and gone back to his wagon for a drink—a talk, who knows? We did not know there was anyone else there with him. They pulled my Uncle Franzl out . . . He lived for a little, only a few minutes. But it was only when the wagon was nearly all burned that they found the . . . the other one.'

'I see.' I was silent for a moment. Perhaps I ought not to press her, but though she had spoken sombrely, the subject didn't appear to distress her unduly now. She must have repeated all this a hundred times during the past week. 'But they did find out who the second man was?'

She nodded. 'He was an Englishman. His name was Paul Denver, and he belonged to some British firm which has a branch in Vienna . . . I didn't understand what sort of work, but I think it was something to do with farming. My father had not heard of him, and we don't know how Uncle

Franzl met him—we had only arrived that day in Oberhausen, you understand. We don't usually give a performance on a Sunday, so they think that Uncle Franzl went out that evening drinking somewhere, and met this man, and got talking to him, and then they came back together and . . . perhaps they talked late, and drank a little more . . . You can picture to yourself how it might be . . .'

She paused, and I said: 'Yes.' I could picture it only too well. The wagon would burn like a torch. And beside it the stables, the plunging, panic-stricken horses, the screaming from the menagerie, the chaos of shouting.

'It was the lamp that fell,' she said. 'Afterwards they found the hook had broken that held it. It was the noise from the horses that gave the alarm. Then people began shouting that there was someone else in the wagon, but it was burning hard by that time; and then the other Englishman came running out of the dark and helped to pull him out. It turned out that he knew him; he had come to Oberhausen to meet him.'

It was Timothy who said: '"The other Englishman"?'

'Yes. He works for the same firm and he had just arrived in Oberhausen, driving from Vienna, and he saw the fire, and came to help.'

It was Timothy who asked: 'And when did he leave?'

'Leave?' said Annalisa. 'He is still here. He—' Then she stopped and smiled, and with the smile the strained look lifted and the sparkle came back. She was looking beyond me, to where someone had come in from the street. 'Why, here he is,' she said.

A man had just turned in from the street under the dappled shade of the chestnut trees. He paused there, looking towards our table. I believe I was already half out of my chair, regardless of what Annalisa might think. I heard Timothy say something, some question. And then the newcomer moved forward from the patch of shadow into the sunlight, and I met, full on, his indifferent, unrecognising eyes, and slight look of surprise.

I think I said: 'No, no it's not,' to Timothy, as I sank back into my chair.

Across me Annalisa was calling out : 'Lee! Come and join us!'

Then the newcomer was standing over us, and introductions were being made.

'Lee,' said Annalisa, 'this is Vanessa March. Vanessa, Mr Elliott . . . And this is Tim.'

I murmured something, heaven knows what, and the two men greeted one another. Mr Elliott pulled up a chair next to mine.

'I take it you must just have arrived here, or we'd have heard all about you long ago. In a place this size every movement is reported.'

I managed to pull myself out of the turmoil into which the appearance of the 'other Englishman' had plunged me, and answered him civilly, if slightly at random. 'Oh, I can believe that. Yes, we've only been here an hour or so. We came from Vienna today by car.'

'And what brings you to Oberhausen?'

'Oh, just . . . touring around.' I caught Timothy's eye on me, worried and speculative even while he replied to some remark of Annalisa's, and made another effort. 'Actually, we—I was expecting to meet my husband down here . . . that is, in Graz . . . but after we got there we heard that he couldn't make it after all. So we thought we might as well take a run out to see the countryside while we were here . . . It's very lovely, isn't it?'

'Very. You're staying in the village, then?'

'Only for the night. We're here, at the Edelweiss. We'll go back . . . that is, we'll go in the morning. Tim's got plans to visit Piber, you know, the Lipizzaner stud, so we'll probably go back that way. I can put in the time till I get a message from my husband.'

Some fragment of what I was feeling must have shown through the carefully social mask I had put on. He said, in a tone which seemed meant to sound comforting: 'I'm sure that will be soon.'

I managed a creditably bright smile. 'I hope so! But meanwhile Tim and I intend to enjoy ourselves, starting with the circus tonight.'

'Tim is your brother?' This was from Annalisa. 'He didn't tell me his other name. Not March?'

'No, anyway that'd have made me a brother-in-law,' said Timothy. 'My name's Lacy. No relation. Just companion, chauffeur and general dogsbody.'

'Dog's body?' She made two words of it, puzzled. 'Why do you call yourself that? To me, it sounds not at all polite.'

'It isn't,' I said. 'He's trying to make out that he gets all the work to do organising our trip. I must say I wouldn't have got far without his German. All right, dogsbody, organise a drink for Mr Elliott, will you?'

'If you can do that in under twenty minutes,' said Mr Elliott, 'you're worth your weight in platinum. Good God!' This as the waitress, obedient still to Timothy's lightest gesture, paused by our table. The three of them plunged into a discussion, Mr Elliott in what sounded like, and probably was, flawless German.

As she sped away, I turned to him, composed now.

He had taken a pipe out of his pocket and was lighting it. It made him look very English. Apart from this, in his nondescript and rather shabby clothes, he might have been anything, anybody, from anywhere. He was tallish, and toughly built, and when he moved it was with a kind of springy precision that indicated strength and muscular control. But his voice and personality, while pleasant enough, struck me then as being singularly colourless. His hair was brown, his eyes of an indeterminate shade somewhere between blue and grey. His hands were good, but I could see a broken nail, and dirt ingrained in them as if he had been working hard at some dirty job. Since I had gathered from Annalisa that he was here as a representative of his firm, this hardly seemed in character, but perhaps he had been lending a kindly hand around the circus. His clothes bore this out; they looked like cheap holiday clothes which had recently had rough and even dirty wear.

I said: 'And you? I understand from Fräulein Wagner that you're down here on business. I was very sorry to hear about the accident.'

'She told you about that, did she? Yes, one of the men who died was a colleague of mine. He'd come down here on a project investigating farming methods and use of fertilisers, and I was actually on my way to meet him when it happened.'

'I'm sorry.' We exchanged a few commiserating phrases, then I asked: 'What is your firm, Mr Elliott?'

'Our Vienna connection is Kalkenbrunner Fertilisers.'

'Oh? Perhaps you know my husband's firm, Pan-European Chemicals?'

'Of course, though I can't for the moment recall any of their people. Stewart, did he work for them? Craig? I may have met your husband, but I don't remember, I'm afraid. Is he in Vienna often?'

'I haven't the faintest idea,' I said, with perfect truth, though not perhaps with perfect civility. I was feeling the strain of this polite conversation about nothing. 'Here's your drink. Have you been here ever since the accident happened?'

'Yes. The police inquiries went on rather a long time, and since my firm was willing to give me leave till things were cleared up, I stayed and gave a hand where it was needed.' He smiled. 'Not with the police, with the circus. There's your definition of a dogsbody, Annalisa . . . what I've been doing for the past week.'

'You? You have been marvellous!' The look she gave him was almost as glowing as the one Timothy had given her. 'Mrs March, you've no idea . . .I told you we were a small circus, and this means that everybody has to work hard. And after Uncle Franzl's death . . . I think we had not realised how much he did. Perhaps this is always the way when someone dies? He was not a performer, you understand. He was a wonderful rider, but he would do no circus work—I mean, he would not work an act . . . But he was in charge of the horses, and I told you, he trained Maestoso Leda, and taught me my act . . .'

It seemed to be some kind of release to her to talk, and we all listened quietly. Beside me, Mr Elliott sat very still and relaxed, his eyes never leaving the girl.

'I remember it well,' she said, 'when he joined us. It was ten years ago, when I was eight, and my grandfather was still alive. We were near Wels, in Upper Austria, and my grandfather had just bought Maestoso Leda, and the Lipizzans themselves were staying in Wels at that time, and we went to see them. You can imagine'—this to Timothy—'how excited they made me! There was also a big horse fair in Wels, and this was the lucky thing, because my Uncle Franzl happened to be there with a dealer he went with after he left the Czech circus where he had worked. I think before that he was in the Army . . . He had not been close to the family, you understand. But he came to see my grandfather, and when we went north that night, into Bavaria, he went with us.' She smiled. 'Now, I can hardly remember the time when he was not part of our circus. I even forgot that his name was not Wagner . . . My grandfather wished him to change it, and he did. He took charge of all the stable work, and the—what do you call the saddles and the bridles and things? Not harness . . .'

'Tack?' suggested Timothy.

'Thank you, yes, that's it. He was also the vet.—the doctor for the horses. So you can imagine what it has been like, with so many of the animals damaged with the panic on the night of the fire, and my father with so much to attend to. He had no time for the horses, and Rudi, that's the chief groom, broke his arm getting the horses out . . . So I've had to do it, and Lee has helped me. Of course some of the artistes have helped also, but they have to practise for themselves every day . . . It has not been easy.'

'I'll say,' said Mr Elliott with feeling. 'Who was it said that hell was a paradise of horses?'

'Nobody,' I said dryly. 'They said England was a paradise for horses and a hell for women.'

'Is it?' asked Annalisa, interested.

'It has its moments. Go on, Mr Elliott. Are we to understand that you've been grooming twenty-seven horses for a week?' For the life of me I couldn't help glancing at his clothes.

He saw it and grinned. 'I have indeed. I have ministered, you might say, to every detail of their toilet. The grooming's the easiest part, once you've discovered that the hair grows from bow to stern, and you have to brush that way; from the bite to the kick, you might say. The extraordinary thing is, they like it. At least, one gathers they do most of the time. I've only been bitten once.'

'You poor thing,' I said. 'And I believe ponies are worse.'

'A Hungarian gentleman did them. He has the advantage of only being three feet high himself. Oh, it's been a most instructive week, I shall be sorry to leave.'

Annalisa said: 'I wish you would not leave. We shall not know what to do without you.'

'I must say it'll be a bit deadly to go back to the old routine,' said Mr Elliott. He glanced at his watch. 'Annalisa, I hate to break the party up, but I really think we should be going. All those beautiful horses to get ready for the show.'

'Goodness, yes!' She got to her feet. The waitress appeared at Timothy's elbow as we all followed suit, and there was the inevitable polite wrangle between Timothy and Lee Elliott over the bill. Timothy—I would have backed him anywhere by now—won easily.

'Well, thanks very much,' said Mr Elliott.

'It's been lovely to meet you,' said Annalisa, 'and we shall see you later? When the show is finished, just ask anybody, they will tell you where to come.' She laughed unaffectedly. 'I shall feel like a prima donna with visitors coming to ask for me after the show. I hope you enjoy it. *Kommst du, Lee?*'

They went. We sat down. I said: 'I thought you'd have wanted to go and help.'

'I thought I'd better stay with you,' said Timothy. He looked at me. 'Do you feel all right? You look awfully funny.'

'Funny? How d'you mean?'

'Well, when he came, you went as white as a sheet. I suppose you were expecting your husband.'

I nodded.

'So was I. When she said "the other Englishman" was still here, I thought we were home and dry.'

I shook my head. 'No. When she heard my name was March, she never reacted. If a Mr March were here in the village—'

'Dash it, how stupid can one be? I'd forgotten that!' Then he frowned. 'But that was at the very start . . . before the Elliott chap turned up. Why did you still think it could be Mr March, when she said, "Here he is"?'

'I didn't. I thought it *was*. There's a difference . . . Listen, Tim—' I found I was clutching a fold of the tablecloth so tightly that my nails had gone through the thin material. I let it go, and began to smooth out the crushed fabric. 'I–I've made a dreadful mistake. When I saw Mr Elliott first, I thought for a moment that it *was* Lewis. When he came nearer, into the light, I saw I was wrong. Now do you see what I've done?'

He did indeed. He was ahead of me. 'You mean he–this Elliott chap–was the chap you saw with Annalisa on the news-reel, not your husband at all? That he's enough like him for you to–that he's a sort of *double* of your husband? Gosh!' For the life of him he couldn't quite suppress a gleam of pleased excitement, but this faded abruptly as he took in the further implications of what I had said. 'Gosh!' It was a different intonation this time. 'You mean that you've come all this way to Austria, and all the time he *is* in Stockholm, just where he said he was?'

'Just exactly that,' I said.

There was a silence, so full of comment that it sizzled.

'It's . . . a bit complicated, isn't it?' he said.

'That, my dear, is the understatement of the year.'

'What are you going to do?'

I said: 'What would you do, chum?'

'Well, eat, to start with,' said Timothy, unhesitatingly, and looked round for the waitress.

Chapter Six

To see a fine lady upon a white horse.
Nursery Rhyme

Understandably, there was something a little depressed about the Circus Wagner that evening. Normally, as Timothy pointed out, a small travelling circus stays only for one night in a place like Oberhausen, but the Circus Wagner had been obliged to stand for a week. I gathered that there had been no performance on the week-nights following the disaster of the fire, but the normal two Saturday performances had been permitted, and now with the Sunday show the circus was attempting to recoup some of its losses; but since most of the local people and those from the nearby villages had already been to yesterday's performances, attendance was thin, and Timothy had had no difficulty in getting what he called 'starback' seats for us. These, the best seats, were rather comfortable portable chairs upholstered in red plush, right at the ring-side. As we sat down I saw that the place was half full of children, many of them in the ring-side seats. It turned out that Herr Wagner had reduced prices all round for today, and the children from this and the surrounding villages were perfectly happy to fill the places and see the same show over again for the price. It was a good move; it brought in a little money, and saved the performers from the depressing echoes of an empty house.

A dwarf in a scarlet baggy costume sold us our programme and ushered us into our chairs. The tent was filled with music from some vast amplifier:

as always in Austria, the music was pleasant; even in a small village circus we were expected to listen to Offenbach and Suppé and Strauss. The tent was not a big one, but the floodlights on the poles at the four 'corners' of the ring threw so much brilliance down into the ring that above them the top of the tent seemed a vast floating darkness, and very high. Caught by a flicker of light the high wire glittered like a thread. On their platforms near the tops of the poles the electricians crouched behind their lights, waiting. There was the circus smell, which is a mingling of sharp animal sweat and trampled grass, and with this the curiously pungent smell of Continental tobacco.

The big lights moved, the music changed, and a march blared out. The curtains at the back of the ring were pulled open, and the procession began.

For a small circus, the standard of performance was remarkably good. Herr Wagner himself was the ringmaster, a short stocky man, who, even in the frock-coat and top-hat of his calling, looked every inch a horseman. The 'rodeo', which followed the procession, was an exciting stampede of horses—real old-fashioned 'circus' horses, piebald and dun-coloured and spotted—supporting a wild-west act with some clever rope work and voltige riding. Annalisa appeared only briefly, barely recognisable as a cowgirl eclipsed by a ten-gallon hat, and riding a hideous spotted horse with a pink muzzle and pink-rimmed eyes, which looked as clumsy as a hippo, and was as clever on its feet as the Maltese Cat. Then came a comic act with a donkey, and after it Herr Wagner again, with his liberty horses.

These were beautiful, every one a star, ten well-matched palominos with coats the colour of wild silk, and manes and tails of creamy floss. They wheeled in under the lights, plumes tossing, silk manes flying, breaking and reforming their circles, rearing one after the other in line, so that the plumes and the floss-silk manes tossed up like the crest of a breaking wave. Rods and shafts of limelight, falling from above, wove and criss-crossed in patterns of golden light, following the golden horses. Light ran and glittered on them. They were sun horses, bridled and plumed with gold, obedient, you would have sworn, to the pull of those rods of light, as the white horses of the wavecrests are to the pull of the moon.

Then the tossing plumes subsided, the flying hoofs met the ground again, the music stopped, and they were just ten self-satisfied horses, queuing at Herr Wagner's pockets for sugar.

Timothy said in my ear: 'You can't tell me those pampered darlings ever bit anyone.'

I laughed. 'You mean Mr Elliott, our horse expert? He did a good job of grooming on them, anyway. They look wonderful.'

'If he's as green about it as he makes out, he's a hero to take on this lot. Funny sort of chap, didn't you think?'

'In what way, funny?'

'Odd. If he's an executive type you wouldn't expect him to stay on here and get down to a job of hard work like that. Bit of a mystery about it, I thought.'

'Perhaps he's keen on Annalisa.'

'He's too old—' indignantly.

'No man's too old till they hammer down the coffin lid.'

'They screw down coffin lids.'

'Goodness, the things you know. Come to that, he's no older than Lewis. Do you see him anywhere?'

'Who?'

'Mr Elliott.'

'No,' said Timothy. 'He'll be out the back madly brushing Maestoso Leda from bow to stern and combing out his rudder. Did you mind coming tonight?'

'Mind? Why should I?'

'Well, you must be beastly worried. I must say you're taking it marvellously.'

'What else can I do? If you want the truth I feel a bit punch-drunk; it's a right pig's ear, as they'd say at home. In any case, there's nothing I can do till tomorrow, so we may as well enjoy ourselves while we can.'

Timothy said: 'It occurred to me, if you cabled Stockholm—'

But here, with a deafening crash of brass, and a wild cheer, the clowns came tumbling in, and Timothy, clutching his programme and rocking with laughter, took a dive straight back into childhood. And so, to be fair, did I. It was an act which needed no interpreting, predictable to the last laugh, being a version of the old water act, and the wettest one I had ever seen, with a grand finale involving a very old elephant who routed the whole gaggle of clowns with a water-spouting act of her own which–to judge by the gleam in her clever piggy eye–she much enjoyed.

After the clowns a couple of girls dancing on a tight-rope with pink parasols. Then a troupe of performing dogs. And then Timothy took his finger out of his programme, turned and grinned at me and whispered, 'Wait for it.'

The trumpets brayed, the ringmaster made his announcement, the red curtains parted, and a white horse broke from the shadows behind the ring and cantered into the limelight. On his back, looking prettier than ever, serene and competent, and tough as a whiplash in a dark blue version of a hussar's uniform, was Annalisa. This horse was not plumed and harnessed as the liberty horses had been; he was dressed for business, but the bridle was a magnificent affair of scarlet studded with gold, and his saddle-cloth glittered and flashed with colour as if every jewel that had ever been discovered was stitched into its silk.

'Oh, boy,' said Tim reverently.

His eye was on the stallion, not on the girl, and, remembering the picture of Carmel on her pony, I smiled to myself. But here the rider did deserve some of the reverence. I knew that all the steps and figures the stallion was now performing so fluidly and easily, took years of intensive and patient training to teach. Even though she had not herself done all the training, it took great skill to put a horse through these dressage movements as she did, without any of her own guiding movements being visible. She seemed simply to sit there, part of the horse, light and graceful and motionless, as the white stallion went through his lovely ballet.

Prompted by Timothy's whisper, I recognised the movements; the slow, skimming, Spanish Walk; the dancing fire of the standing trot, or *piaffe*; the shouldering-in which takes the horse diagonally forward in an incredibly smooth, swimming movement; and then, as she had promised us, the 'airs above the ground'. The stallion wheeled to the centre of the ring, snorted, laid back his ears, settled his hind hoofs in the sawdust, then lifted himself and his rider into a *levade*, the classic rearing pose of the equestrian statues. For two long bars of music he held it, then touched ground again for a moment, and—you could see the bunch and thrust of the muscles—launched himself clean into the air in a standing leap. For one superb moment he was poised there, high in the air, caught and lit dazzlingly white by the great lights, all four legs tucked neatly under him, all his jewels flashing and glancing with a million colours, but not it seemed more brilliant than the gleam of the muscles under the white skin or the lustre of the steady dark eye. One looked for his wings.

Then he was on the ground again, cantering round the ring, nodding and bowing his head to the applause which filled even that half empty tent. Then, still bowing and pawing the ground, he backed out of the ring and was lost in the darkness behind the curtain.

I let out a long breath. I felt as if I had been holding it for hours. Timothy and I smiled at one another.

'What's the anticlimax?' I asked him.

He looked at his programme. 'Oh, here's your *absolute Star-Attraktion*. . . . Sandor Balog, he's called. It's "Balog and Nagy", the high wire.'

'For goodness' sake, it always terrifies me.'

'Me, too,' said Timothy happily, settling back as the high wire sprang into the light and the two men started their racing climb towards it. The music swung into a waltz, one of the men started out along the wire, and in the carefully wrought tensions of the act all other preoccupations fell away, and tomorrow—Lewis or no Lewis—could take care of itself.

When we came out of the circus tent with the crowd we found it was quite dark.

'This way,' said Timothy, leading me round to the left of the big tent. Here, earlier in the day, there had been an orderly crowd of wagons and tents, but many of these had now gone. Already workmen were attacking the big top, the tent-men unhooking the sides or walls of the tent, rolling the canvas to leave for the trailer-men to pick up. Lights were still on inside the big top, presumably to help the work of the pull-down. I saw the two high-wire artistes now clad in sweaters and jeans and plimsolls, dismantling their gear from the top of the king-poles. The hum of the big generator had stopped, and a small donkey engine had taken over, fussily supplying the remaining lights by which the circus people worked. Men in overalls hurried past us carrying ladders, boxes, crates, baskets of clothes. A tractor pulling some large trailer churned its way slowly and carefully over the uneven ground towards the gate.

'The lions, I think,' said Tim. 'Can you smell them? The stables are round this way. Mind your foot.'

I dodged a bit of rope trailing from some bundle that a couple of girls were carrying. I recognised one of the dainty young dancers from the tight-rope act looking no less graceful but very different in close-fitting black pants and sweater.

Next moment a welcoming shaft of light shone out across the trampled grass in front of us. It spilled out from the door of a caravan where, silhouetted against the light and holding back the rough curtain which had covered the doorway, stood Annalisa, peering out into the night.

'Tim, Mrs March, is that you? I'm sorry I couldn't come to show you the way, but I was busy changing.'

She ran down the steps. Gone was the smart young hussar in blue velvet, and here once more was the slender girl with the blonde pony tail. But she hadn't gone back to the blue dirndl. She was wearing–like the other artistes we had seen–pants and sweater. Hers were dark blue. She had cleaned the circus make-up off her face, and this now looked fresh and scrubbed clean, without even any lipstick. She looked business-like and ready for work, but as feminine as ever.

'I'll take you to see the horses straight away. They will not be moving till they are taken to the morning train, but they'll be being bedded down now. Did you enjoy the show?'

'Very much indeed,' I said, 'and you most of all . . . That's quite honest, Annalisa, you were marvellous. It was a wonderful act, one of the best things I've ever seen . . . And thank you very much for the *croupade*, you both did it beautifully, we were terribly impressed.'

'It was terrific!' Timothy chimed in with enthusiasm, and we both praised her warmly, and as we walked along between the lighted windows of the rows of vans, I could see how she glowed with unaffected pleasure.

'It is too much–you are too good . . .' She sounded almost confused by our praise. 'He did do it well tonight, did he not? It was a good evening . . . I am glad for you . . . One cannot always be sure. I think, if there had been more time to train him, he could have been a very good horse. But in a circus, you see, there is no time; we cannot afford to keep a horse for all the time it takes to train them in the advanced leaps, they have to work, and this spoils them, they are never polished. In the Spanish Riding School they can train for years before they let them perform. Even then, some of the stallions never get to do the leaps. This is kept for the best ones.'

'Well,' I said, 'it still looked pretty good to me . . . and the palominos were magnificent.'

'Oh yes, they are lovely. Well, here they are. I brought some pieces of carrot if you would like to give them . . . ?'

The horses were housed in a long tent, which, on the inside, looked every bit as solid and permanent as a stable. A few lights burned, showing up rows of horses' rumps half hidden by their rugs, tails swishing lazily. There was the sweet ammoniac smell of hay and horses, and the comfortable sound of munching. Farther down the stable a couple of men were working, one forking straw, the other, duster in hand, shining up the metal studding on a piece of tack hanging from a pole. From a corner in the shadows came the whicker of greeting, and I saw the beautiful white head flung up as the stallion looked round at Annalisa.

Shorn of his jewelled trappings and standing at ease, Maestoso Leda was still beautiful, even though not so impressive as he had been on parade. Seeing one of the famous Lipizzans now for the first time at close quarters, I was surprised to realise how small he was; fourteen hands, I supposed, give or take an inch, stockily built with well-set-on shoulders and sturdy legs and feet, big barrelled, big chested, with the thick stallion neck and the power in the haunches that was needed for the spectacular leaps to which these animals could be trained. Something about the shape of his head recalled those old paintings of horses that one had always dismissed as inaccurate—those creatures with massive quarters round and shining as apples, but with swan-curved necks and small heads with tiny ears; now I could see where they came from. His was—if one could use the word—an antique head, narrow, and sculptured like a Greek relief, while the rest of his body was massively muscled. The eye was remarkable, big and dark and liquid, gentle and yet male.

He whickered again at the sight of the carrots and bent his head to receive them. Annalisa and Timothy fed him, and the two of them were soon busy with him, almost crooning over him as they handled him. I watched for a little, then wandered off down the lines to look at some of the others. They were mostly stallions, the palominos looking at this close range a good deal more impressive than the Lipizzaner, but all relaxed and resting comfortably. I noticed one or two bandaged legs among the others, and a nasty graze skinning over on one palomino rump, but on the whole it seemed to me that the Circus Wagner had got off lightly. Nothing terrifies horses so much as fire, and if even one or two, in their panic-stricken plunging, had lashed out or broken loose, they could have caused immense damage to themselves and others.

At the far end of the stable one or two horses were lying down already, so I didn't go past them, since no horse will allow you to pass his stall without his getting up, and I didn't wish to disturb them. But the ponies I talked to, mischievous shaggy little beasts, twice as quick and twice as naughty as their big brothers, and at this moment all twice as wide awake. By the time I had worked my way back to the beginning where Annalisa and Timothy still stood talking softly in the royal box, the two stablemen had gone, and all seemed settled for what remained of the night. In the stall next to the end one—opposite the white stallion—stood another horse of much the same height and build as the Lipizzaner, but very different to look at. He was a piebald, with ugly markings, and he stood with his head drooping and mane and tail hanging limply, like uncombed flax. I thought at first it was the clever ugly beast that Annalisa had ridden in the rodeo, then saw that this was an older horse. His feed was scarcely touched, but his water bucket was empty. As I watched, he lowered his head and blew sadly around the bottom of the dry bucket.

I spoke softly, then laid a hand on him and went in.

Annalisa saw me, and came across.

'Because we spend so much time with the King horse, you talk with the beggar? I am sorry, there is no carrot left.'

'I doubt if he would want it,' I said. 'He hasn't touched his feed. I wasn't just being democratic; I thought he looked ill.'

'He is still not eating? He has been like this all the week.' She looked from the full manger to the empty bucket, and a pucker of worry showed between her brows. 'He was my Uncle Franzl's horse, the poor old Piebald . . . Ever since the fire he has been like this; nobody else looked after him, you see, always my uncle. He is old, too; my uncle used to say they were two old men together.' She bit her lip, watching the horse. 'I think he is—what is the word?—weeping for my uncle.'

'Fretting. That may be true, but I think there's something wrong physically, too. The horse is in pain.' I was examining him as I spoke, running a hand down the neck, turning back the rug to feel the withers. 'See how he's sweating; he's wringing wet over the withers and down the neck, and look at his eye . . . his coat's as rough as a sack, Annalisa. Has anyone seen him?'

'The vet came from Bruck after the fire, and he has been twice more since then. On Thursday, he was here.'

'And he looked at this one?'

'He looked at them all. Not this one, perhaps, after the first time, because there was nothing wrong.' She looked doubtfully at me, then back at the old piebald. 'Yes, I can see he does not look very good, but if there had been anything . . . anything to see . . .' She hesitated.

Tim said: 'Vanessa's a vet.'

Her eyes widened. 'You? Are you? Oh, then—'

'Has the horse been working?' I asked.

She shook her head. 'He doesn't work, he is old, I think more than twenty. My Uncle Franzl had him in Czechoslovakia even before he joined us ten years ago. They tried at first to use him—they had a liberty act then with mixed horses—but he was slow to learn, so he was done very little. He was a pet of my Uncle Franzl's, or perhaps my father would not have kept him. I told you, we cannot afford to keep a horse that does not work, so in the old days, before there was money for all the tractors and motor caravans, he helped to pull a wagon, and Uncle Franzl used to ride him, and give rides to the children. But now . . .' she looked distressed . . . 'if he is ill—we are moving the horses in a few hours, and in three days we leave Austria and cross the frontier. I am afraid of what my father will say.'

'You've found something?' said Timothy to me.

I had indeed found something. Just above the knee on the off foreleg was a nasty swelling. I showed this to them investigating further, while the old horse stood with drooping head, turning once to nuzzle me as my fingers felt and probed the leg.

I said to Tim: 'Hold his head, will you? Gently, there, old man.'

'What is it?' asked Annalisa, peering over my shoulder.

'It's a haematoma, a blood-swelling. He must have hurt himself during the fire, or perhaps had a kick from a loose horse, and he's torn one of the flexor tendons . . . Look, these, here . . . It wouldn't show for a day or two, and if he isn't working nobody would notice. And the rug's been hiding the swelling. But it must be dealt with now. It's a very nasty leg.'

'Yes, I can see, it looks terrible. But how "dealt with?" What will you do?'

I looked up. 'I? I'm not your veterinary surgeon, Annalisa. You'll have to get the man from Bruck. I ought not to interfere.'

'He ought not to have missed it,' said Tim roundly. 'Anybody could see the beast's ill.'

'No,' I said, 'be fair. I'm sure in the normal course of things somebody would have seen it, but the circus's own horse-keeper is dead, and Herr

Wagner's had far too much on his plate this past week. I told you this wouldn't develop straight away, and if no one called the veterinary surgeon's attention to it later, it could easily have been overlooked.'

'What will have to be done?' asked Annalisa.

'It ought to be lanced—cut—and drained, and the leg stitched.'

'Could you do it?'

I straightened up. 'If you mean do I know how, yes, I do. But you have a veterinary surgeon, Annalisa, you should get him.'

'On a Sunday night? At nearly midnight? And we leave for the train at six?'

Tim said: 'Couldn't you, Vanessa?'

'Tim, I shouldn't. I don't know what the etiquette is here, and I've no business to walk in and do the man's work for him. Come to that, it is professional "work". It's probably even illegal, without permits or something. Besides, I've no instruments.'

'There are Uncle Franzl's things,' said Annalisa. 'They were saved. I have them in my wagon. *Please*, Vanessa.'

'It's nothing to do with the chap from Bruck, anyway,' said Tim. 'He'll have been paid, won't he? Now the circus moves on, and that's an end of him.'

'Yes!' She took him up eagerly. Between them the old horse stood motionless, his coat rough under my hand. It felt hot and scurfy. 'You will be our new vet! I appoint you, I myself! And if it is not legal, then nobody need know!'

A new voice spoke from the tent door, startling us all.

'If what is not legal?'

Chapter Seven

Dost think I am a horse-doctor?
Marlowe: *Doctor Faustus*

Herr Wagner himself stood there, a thick-set, powerful-looking man, with a big head and a mane of brown hair going grey. He had a ruddy, weather-beaten complexion, and brown eyes under fierce brows. These now took in the scene with lively curiosity.

Behind him was a taller man, a slim, wiry figure in black whom I recognised as the *Star-Attraktion* of the high wire, the Hungarian Sandor Balog. He had dark hair slicked back above a broad forehead with thin black brows 'winged' above eyes so dark they were almost black. The nose was flattish and the cheek-bones wide, and when he smiled, the lower lids of his eyes lifted, tilting the eyes and giving the face a Mongolian look. The nostrils were prominent and sharply carved, the lips full and well shaped. A disturbing face, perhaps a cruel one. He wasn't smiling now. He was looking, not (as one might have expected) at the two strangers near the horse's head, but with fixed intensity at Annalisa.

'Who are your friends, Liesl?' asked Herr Wagner.

'Father! *Lieber Gott*, but you startled me! I never heard you! Oh, this is Mrs March, she is English, staying in the village, and this is Tim, who travels with her . . .'

She included the Hungarian in her introductions. I noticed that she didn't look directly at him, whereas he never took his eyes off her, except to brush me, momentarily, with an indifferent glance. Herr Wagner greeted us courteously, then his eyes went to the horse.

'But what was this about a vet? Did I hear properly? And what is "not legal"?'

Annalisa hesitated, started to speak, then glanced at me. 'You permit?' Then, turning back to her father, she plunged into a flood of German which, from her gestures, was the story of her acquaintance with us, and the recent discovery of Piebald's injury.

To all this, after the first minute or so, the Hungarian paid little attention. I noticed that as the name of Lee Elliott occurred in the narrative, his gaze sharpened on the girl, so that I wondered if Sandor Balog, like me, had credited Mr Elliott with 'intentions' in that direction. If so, he didn't like it. But after a bit, it appeared, the narrative bored him. He wandered into the next stall–the end one of the row, where harness hung and trestles stood with saddles over them–and stood there, idly fingering the bright jewellery on Maestoso Leda's saddle, but still watching the girl.

She finished her story on a strong note of persuasion, where I caught the word 'Bruck', and a significant glance at her watch.

But–not much to my surprise–Herr Wagner didn't lend his weight to her appeal. He turned to me and in broadly accented but quite fluent English, thanked me for what he called my 'trouble' and 'great kindness', but finally, 'believed he must not trouble me'.

'My daughter is young, and a little'–he shrugged his wide shoulders and smiled charmingly–'a little impulsive . . . She should not be asking you this thing. You are a visitor, a lady, this is not a thing to invite a lady to do.'

I laughed. 'It's not that. I am a veterinary surgeon, and I'm used to worse jobs than this, it was only that–well, it simply isn't my affair. You have your own man. He'd certainly come tonight if you telephoned. If you haven't got the telephone here, I'll do it for you, if you like, from the Gasthof Edelweiss . . . or rather, Tim will. He speaks German.'

Herr Wagner didn't answer for a minute. He had come into the stall and was examining the horse with some care.

'. . . Yes, I see. I see. I am ashamed that this was not seen. I will speak to Hans and Rudi; but you understand, *gnädige Frau*, there has been so much . . . and always my cousin Franzl he sees to this old horse himself. The boys perhaps were doing their own work–their own regular horses, *verstehen Sie?*–and this old one, he is missed. The poor old one, yes . . .'

He ran a caressing hand down the horse's neck, gave it a pat that had something valedictory about it, and straightened up.

'Well, it is late. You will have some coffee before you go, eh? No, no, I mean it. My Liesl always makes the coffee at this hour . . . This is why I come to find her, she is neglecting her old father.'

'Thanks very much,' I said, 'but if I'm to ring this man up for you, I'd better get straight back. It's after midnight.'

Herr Wagner said: 'I shall not trouble you, *gnädige Frau*.'

It was Timothy who understood before I did, who had seen the significance of that farewell caress, and had added to it Annalisa's reiteration that 'no circus can afford to keep a horse which does not work'. One could not blame Herr Wagner for his decision to jettison old Piebald now; he hadn't earned his keep for quite some time, and, according to Annalisa, hadn't even qualified for a pension. A working circus cannot keep pets.

I saw Timothy stiffen, still holding the headstall, his eyes fixed on Herr Wagner. His free hand crept to the horse's nose, cupping round the soft muzzle in a gesture at once protective, and pathetically futile. The horse lipped his fingers. Tim looked at me.

I said: 'Herr Wagner, I'll operate now, if you'll let me. It'll be over in half an hour, and once I've got the leg fixed up you can move him to the train. He'll be as right as rain and fit for work in three or four weeks.'

Herr Wagner stopped in the tent doorway. I thought he was going to brush the matter aside, but Tim said, 'Please,' in a voice as young and unprotected as his face, and I saw the older man hesitate.

'Yes, father, please,' said the girl.

The Hungarian said nothing. You would have thought we were all of us separated from him by a glass screen. He had Annalisa's saddle and cloth over his arm now, and was waiting to follow Herr Wagner out of the stable.

Herr Wagner spread his hands wide in a gesture of deprecation. 'But we cannot ask you—' he began.

'I wish you would,' I said, and smiled. I put everything I had into that smile. 'That's all we need to make it legal.'

Annalisa said suddenly: 'No! It is I who ask! After all this talk, it is I! I had forgotten! This was Uncle Franzl's horse, so now it is mine . . .' She swung round on her father, hands spread in what was almost a parody of his own gesture. 'Is this not so, father? Did not Uncle Franzl leave me all his things . . . all that were saved, the pictures, and his flute, and the parrot . . . and old Piebald, too? So if he is mine, and I ask Vanessa to look after him . . . and if he can go to the train . . . ?'

She finished back on the note of pleading, but her father was already laughing, his square brown face lit up and rayed with wrinkles.

'*So* . . . you see how she rules me, this child of mine? Always a reason she finds to have her way—like her mother she is, very the same as her mother. Oh, yes, it is true that Franzl wished you to have everything . . . it is true perhaps that the horse is yours . . .' He gave his great ringmaster's laugh, so that the sleeping horses stirred in their stalls, and the chains jingled and rang. 'All right, all right, if you wish, if you wish, children all of you. What do you need, *gnädige Frau*?'

'The instruments Annalisa said she had. Hot water. Nylon suturing material. I'll have to give an anti-tetanus injection; have you got the stuff? Good. And more light. I don't want to move him, I'd rather do it in his own stall, it'll upset him less, but I must have some sort of spotlight.'

'I have a good flashlight,' said Annalisa. 'It's in my wagon. And Sandor has one, too. Will you get it, Sandor, please?'

'*Natürlich.*' It was as if a puppet had spoken—or rather, a creature from the ballet stage, so remote from us had that black-clad, graceful figure been in the shadows of the end stall. His voice was curiously light and hard. He spoke pleasantly enough, without emphasis, and had turned to go, when I stopped him.

'No, please . . . Thank you all the same, but it doesn't matter. A flashlight won't be enough. I wondered if someone could rig a light down here off a long flex? You know, a wire.'

'That is easy to do,' said Herr Wagner, adding in German, 'Sandor, would you be good enough to do this for them? You know where to find the flex and all the things you need. Don't lumber yourself with that saddle, just leave it here. Annalisa won't mind if it stays here for the night for once.'

'I was going to take it to my own wagon to mend it. I see some stitching is loose.'

Tim translated in my ear: 'It's all right. He's only taking the saddle to dump in his own wagon, and then he's going to get a flex and rig the light. I say, I'm sure he was going to have the old horse put down.'

'I thought so, too.'

'Is this a bad operation?'

'Not at all. Have you never seen this kind of thing before?'

'No, only the usual minor things, fomentations and so on. I'm afraid I shan't be much help, but I'll do my best if you want.'

'Herr Wagner probably knows all about it, but thanks all the same. I'd a lot sooner have you than the boy friend, anyway.'

'Him? You don't think he is, do you?'

I laughed. 'No, only that he'd like to be. He doesn't look the type to run errands for girls otherwise. And what else did he come here for? Just to carry her saddle away for her? He didn't look too pleased to be co-opted as lighting expert.'

'If it comes to that,' said Tim, 'he offered to stitch it up for her, or something, if I got it right. His German's a lot worse than his English.'

'Well, there you are,' I said, vaguely, then forgot about Sandor Balog. What mattered now was the horse.

Once Herr Wagner had made up his mind to let me operate, he was helpfulness itself. The stablemen had all gone off duty; they had the early start to face, and were getting their sleep. But Herr Wagner and Annalisa stayed, and we had a surprise helper in the shape of the dwarf who was the clowns' butt in the *entrée*. His name was Elemer, and like Sandor Balog he was a Hungarian, being, I supposed, the 'Hungarian gentleman' who 'had the advantage of only being three feet high' and who had been helping Mr Elliott with the stable work in the recent emergency. He certainly seemed to know where everything was, unlike Balog, who did bring flex and tools as requested, but thereafter restricted his help to watching the dwarf and lifting him to reach the light socket—this last with some comment in Hungarian which made the little man flush angrily and compress his lips. And when the light was finally rigged, the *Star-Attraktion* retired gracefully into the shadows of the next stall to watch the performance, while the dwarf bustled to help Annalisa and Timothy.

They had conjured up a Primus stove from somewhere, and on it had managed to bring a large enamel bucket full of water to the boil while the light was being rigged and I, with Herr Wagner watching, checked over the contents of the dead Franzl's instrument case.

It held everything I could want, scalpel, knife, dressing and artery forceps, suturing material, cotton-wool galore. All these went into the bucket to boil, while Annalisa and Timothy went off to her wagon for another pan for me to wash in.

In a quarter of an hour or so all was ready. The light was rigged and steady, the boiling water drained off the sterile instruments, and I had washed up and started work.

I noticed that Herr Wagner was watching closely. Even if he did not value the horse, he was too good a horseman to hand over the animal to someone and then leave him unsupervised. He said nothing, but washed up himself and then stood near me, obviously constituting himself my assistant.

I clipped the horse's leg and cleaned the area with surgical spirit, then reached for the hypodermic. As Herr Wagner put it into my hand, I caught sight of Tim's face, taut and anxious, watching across the horse's neck. There was nothing for him to do, so he stood by the animal's head and spoke to him gently from time to time, but in fact the boy seemed much more disturbed by the operation than the patient, and looked so anxious at the sight of the needle that I gave him a reassuring grin.

'I'm going to give him a local, Tim, don't worry. He won't feel a thing, and twenty minutes from now he'll be doing a *capriole*.'

'What d'you give him?'

'Procaine. It goes by some German trade name here, but that's what it is. That's it between the vaseline and that brown tube labelled "Koloston". I'm going to infiltrate the procaine right round the area. Now watch. You run the needle in under the skin, near the swelling . . . There, he never blinked, and that's the only prick he'll feel. Then you put it in again, at the end of the anaesthetised bit . . . see? He doesn't feel that . . . run it along the second side of your square. This way, you deaden the whole area. Then the third side . . . and the last. Now, give it time, and when I incise the haematoma he won't feel a thing.'

The beam of light shifted, sending the shadows tilting. I glanced up quickly, before I remembered that it was the dwarf Elemer who was holding the wooden batten to which the lamp had been hooked.

'That is better now?' His deep guttural came from elbow height, and I glanced down, self-conscious now and hating myself for showing it. He was in deep shadow behind the bright bulb, and I couldn't see the misshapen body or the tiny arms that clutched the batten, but the light reflected on his upturned face, which was the face made familiar by so many of the old tales that take deformity for granted, *Snow-white*, *Rumpelstiltskin*, and the rest. Only the eyes were unexpected; they were dark, the iris as dark as the pupil, big eyes fringed with thick short lashes; eyes where thoughts could not be read but only guessed at. Not for the first time I reflected that the normal, let alone the privileged, have a burden of guilt laid automatically on them from the cradle.

I said: 'Thank you, it's fine.' In spite of myself, I spoke just a shade too heartily. I saw him smile, but it was a kind smile. I turned quickly back to the job.

'Scalpel, please,' I said, and reached out a wet hand. Herr Wagner put the scalpel into it. The beam of light was steady on the haematoma. I bent forward to cut.

The cut was about four inches long. The swelling cut as cleanly as an orange, and, as cleanly almost as orange juice, the serum flooded out of it and down the horse's leg, followed sluggishly by the blood, which, in a week, had formed a sizeable, stringy clot. You could almost feel the relief as the thing split and the pressure was lifted. Old Piebald's ears moved, and Tim whispered something into one of them.

'Forceps,' I said.

I don't know whether Herr Wagner knew the English words, but he obviously knew the drill; as he handed me the dressing forceps I saw from the corner of my eye that he also had the artery forceps ready in case of any seepage from my cutting. And when I had pulled away the clotted blood with forceps, the cotton-wool was ready to my hand without my having to speak.

In a short time the wound was clean. I dusted it generously with sterile penicillin powder, and reached silently for the suturing needle. It was there. Six blanket sutures, and the thing was done, and Herr Wagner had ready the pad of dry cotton-wool rolled in bandage, to put over the wound for protection.

I smiled up at Timothy, who still watched rather tautly across Piebald's unmoving (and you would have sworn indifferent) head.

I said: 'That's that. He's survived, and he hasn't bitten me—yet. You see this pad Herr Wagner's made for me? We call that a dolly. I stitch it on now—'

'You *stitch* it on? You mean you stitch it to the *horse?*'

'Where else? Only to the skin—and he won't feel it any more than he's felt the rest. Watch.'

I laid the dolly—the size and shape of a generously filled sausage—along the line of the stitched cut, then knotted the nylon suturing thread in the skin to one side of it, carried the thread close across the dolly, and knotted another stitch in. It took four stitches, then the dry pad lay snugly over the wound.

'Won't he worry at it and pull it off?' asked Tim.

'Not unless the wound's infected, and starts to itch or hurt him, but it looked beautifully clean to me. It's my guess he'll never even know the dolly's there. It can come off in three or four days' time. Now, there's just his anti-tetanus shot and penicillin, and that will be that. Pull his mane across, will you, Tim, I'll put this in the neck . . . There you are, old darling, that's you . . .' I smoothed my hand down the drooping neck. 'I think you'll live.'

'Yes,' said Herr Wagner, behind me, 'thanks to you, *gnädige Frau*, he will live.'

There was something in his voice that made it more than just a phrase. Timothy's eyes met mine, and his face broke into a grin. Old Piebald rolled a big dark eye back at me, and said nothing.

'You'll have some coffee now?' said Annalisa.

It was not so much a question as an order, and I didn't protest as she led the way to her wagon. I was suddenly very tired, and longing for the day to be over, but in the pre-dawn chill the thought of coffee was irresistible.

Behind us, in the stable, Elemer and Herr Wagner were settling Piebald for what was left of the night. Sandor Balog came with us. I gathered that it had been kind, even condescending, of an artiste of his calibre to have helped as far.

It seemed that his kindness—or his interest in Annalisa—didn't impel him to anything more domestic. He settled with me on the bench at the table in her wagon, and allowed her to serve the coffee alone. Timothy did offer help, but was refused, and sat down beside Sandor, looking round him with frank pleasure.

The living-wagon was—just at present—very untidy, but still rather attractive. Though it was a newish caravan, the pattern of circus life with its century-old traditions had modified its streamlined modernity to give it the authentic old gypsy wagon flavour. The stove near the door was of white enamel, and burned bottled gas, but the lamp swinging over it looked like an old converted storm lantern, and the little table was covered with a brilliant red cloth with a fringe, for all the world like a gypsy's shawl. A faded striped curtain hung over the forward doorway through which could be glimpsed the corner of a tumbled bunk covered with clothes; the light caught the edge of the blue velvet riding costume, and glittered off the jewelled handle of a whip. On a hook near one window hung the hussar's cap with all its amethysts and diamonds and its osprey plume which wavered and tossed a little in the warm draught from the stove. Between window and stove was the dressing-shelf, with candles stuck to either side of a square mirror with a chipped corner. The candles had guttered down into big blobs of grey wax and the shelf itself was smeared heavily with red and carmine and the white of powder. There was a splash of pink liquid powder across the looking-glass. A wicker cage, swinging from a hook and shrouded with a green kerchief, completed the gypsy picture. Our voices roused the inmate to a sort of sleepy croak, and I remembered Annalisa's saying something about Uncle Franzl's parrot.

'But this is terrific, it really is!' Timothy was enthusiastic, and very wide awake still. 'It's just how I've always imagined it. Aren't you lucky? Gosh, fancy living in a house when you could have a wagon, and move on every day or so!'

She laughed. 'I wonder if you would say the same thing at five o'clock in the morning? Sugar, Vanessa?'

'No, thank you.'

'This is yours, Sandor. Sugar Tim?'

'Yes, please.'

I curved my hands round the hot blue cup. The coffee was delicious, fragrant and strong, and through the coffee-scent came, seductively, another even more delicious—the smell of hot, freshly baked bread. Annalisa put a dish on the table; *croissants*, fresh sweet bread with new butter melting on it.

'*Götterdämmerung*,' said Timothy reverently, if inappropriately. 'Did you make them?'

She laughed. 'No, no! They come from the village bakery. Lee brought them.'

Sandor looked up. 'He is here still?'

'He goes back tomorrow. Oh, you mean is he here, in the circus? No. He came down to the stables while Vanessa was busy with the horse, but only for a minute.'

'Did he?' I said. 'I didn't see him.'

'He didn't stay. He only watched for a minute, then he went to get the bread, but he wouldn't stay for coffee, either.'

'Was he at the show?' asked Sandor.

'I don't think so. I didn't see him. Did you?' This to Tim and me.

'No.'

To my surprise, this didn't please Sandor either, but then it appeared that a Lee Elliott safely anchored in a ring-side seat was preferable to a Lee Elliott at large back stage . . . possibly in Annalisa's wagon.

He said, with a savage intensity that seemed out of place and somehow shocking: 'I don't know what he is doing here still. He did what he came for on Monday, then why did he not go back?'

'Because I asked him to stay.' Annalisa's voice was light and cold. 'More coffee, Vanessa?'

'Thank you. It's lovely.'

'*You* asked him to stay?'

'Yes. Why not? What objection have you got, Sandor Balog?'

It was obvious that, whatever his objection was, it was a violent one. I thought for a moment that he was going to explode into words. The black eyes glittered, the nostrils flared like a horse's, but then the full lips folded sullenly over his anger, and he looked down, stirring his coffee in silence. I found myself hoping for Annalisa's sake that her cool manner hid no warmer feeling for him; he might be playing lapdog now, but it seemed to me a thin disguise for a creature much nearer to the wolf.

'Tim,' said Annalisa, 'have some more. Another *croissant*?'

'I'd love it. Thank you. Personally,' said Timothy, muscling in on his third bun with undiminished zeal, 'I'd say Mr Elliott had real executive sense. This is a terrific idea, raiding a bakery in the middle of the night. I must do it some day. Will you thank him for us if you see him again?'

'We shall be gone before he gets up. You may see him yourself.'

'Where's he staying?'

'He sleeps over the bakery; it's the one in the square, there's a Frau Schindler who lets a room there.'

'Big deal,' said Tim. 'I told you he was smart. I wish we'd thought of that.'

'Gimme a bit, you greedy bastard,' said the parrot suddenly, directly over my head. I jumped, and spilled coffee, and Annalisa and the parrot laughed heartily. The green kerchief, twitched aside by a powerful beak, came down over my head like an extinguisher.

'*Levez, levez*,' said the parrot. 'Shake a leg, Peter, *changez*, hup! Get your mane hogged, you goddam limey, you! *Gib mir was! Gib mir was!*'

'For pete's sake!' said Tim. He tore off a bit of *croissant*. 'All right, old chap, here. No, not like that, you fool, like that. There.'

'Put your comb up,' said the parrot, accepting the bread.

'*I'm* not a flipping cockatoo,' said Tim.

'Don't teach him any more words, please,' said Annalisa, laughing, 'and keep your nose away from the bars, Tim, he's a terrible bird.' She was helping me to emerge from the folds of the green kerchief. 'I am sorry, he is so terrible . . . I do not know who had him before Uncle Franzl, but he's very . . . what is it? . . . he's a real *Weltbürger*, and from all the worst places!'

'A cosmopolitan,' said Tim. 'Dead right, he is! That bird's been around.'

The parrot made a comment, this time in German, that got Annalisa to her feet.

'Please, we must cover him up again before he really starts! I'm sorry, Vanessa, did the scarf go in your coffee? It's quite clean.'

'Let me,' said Sandor Balog. He, too, was laughing, and it transformed him. There was (I saw it sinkingly, because I was getting to like Annalisa) quite a powerful animal attraction there. He and Tim draped the cage once more, while Annalisa tried to get me fresh coffee, but this time I refused.

'We must go. Look at the time, and you people have an early start. No, really, it was nothing, you're very welcome . . .' This as she began once again to thank me for what I had done.

'If you come near us again,' she said eagerly, 'please come to see us. We shall be leaving Austria in two or three days' time, but we go today to Hohenwald, and after that to Zechstein. If you are near us, on your motor tour, you will call, will you not? If you wish to watch the show again, it will be a pleasure, any time; we will keep you the best seats. But in any case, my father and I would be glad to welcome you.'

Sandor Balog rose also. 'I shall see you to the gate.' When we protested that there was no need, he produced a slim flashlight from his pocket. 'Yes, please. The ground is all muddy where the tractors have been, and there is not much light. Please allow me.'

'In that case,' I said, 'thank you. Goodnight, Annalisa, and *auf Wiedersehen*.'

'*Auf Wiedersehen*.'

'*Merde, alors*,' said the parrot, muffled.

Chapter Eight

The statements was interesting, but tough.
Mark Twain: *Huckleberry Finn*

'Probably just seeing us off the premises,' said Timothy later, as we walked through the sleeping village towards the Gasthof Edelweiss. The air was still and cold. A clock in the church tower struck two, with a thin, acid sweetness. A chain jingled, and a dog grumbled in its throat somewhere. 'I say, you don't really think there could be anything between him and Annalisa, do you? I thought he was an absolute wart.'

'Not on her side, I'm sure. Anyway, you can leave our Sandor safely to Herr Wagner and the parrot.'

He chuckled. 'I rather cared for the parrot. I'd like to hear him—That's odd.'

'What's odd?'

'I thought I saw someone over there . . . the other side of the square, by those trees.'

'Well, why not?'

'I'm sure it was Mr Elliott.'

'Well, why not?' I said again. 'He's probably been down for some more buns for himself, and now he's walking off the indigestion. Come along, Tim, I'm just about dropping.'

But tired as I was, when at length I was ready for bed I found sleep far away, and myself restless. I padded across the boards in my bare feet to open the long windows, and went out on to the veranda to look at the night. Next door to mine, Timothy's window was open, too, but his light was out already. In the distance the clock struck the half hour. Nearer at hand a soft chiming echoed it as a cow stirred in her stall.

The night was sweet, cold and clear. The stars seemed close to the mountain-tops, as if they were sharp points of reflection off some high snow struck by the moon, and their light showed the soft slopes of meadow and fir wood in silver monochrome and shadow. You could have traced the countryside by its scents alone. Immediately below the veranda the clover and mown hay; beyond it pines, and the cold scent of running water; faint food-smells from the Gasthof kitchen; somewhere a homely whiff of pig, and the sweet smell of the cows with their bells sleepily ringing in the byre.

It was still and peaceful and very lovely. Anybody should be able to sleep.

I padded back across boards already faintly damp with dew, and got into bed. The only covering was a large eiderdown, or feather puff, light and warm, but apt to expose the feet when one pulled it up under one's chin. I curled up facing the window, tucked the puff round me as best I might, and wondered about Lewis . . .

I don't think I was asleep, but I may have been floating into the edge of it, because the tiny noise from outside brought me fully awake with a start. I didn't move, but strained my ears. Nothing. But I was certain some-thing—or someone—had moved out there.

Then the hand parted the curtains. He didn't make a sound, just slid between them like a ghost. As I sat up in bed, pulling the puff round me, he was already turning to draw the long windows shut. They latched with a tiny click. He stood there just inside the windows, quite still, listening.

'All right, Mr Elliott,' I said, 'I'm awake. What brings you this way? Couldn't you find your way to Annalisa's wagon, or was Sandor Balog standing guard?'

He came forward towards the bed. Even on the bare floors he moved without a sound, incredibly quietly, like a cat. 'I think I'm in the right place.'

'What makes you think that, Mr Lee Elliott? What makes you think that after what's been going on you have the faintest right to come wandering in here like a tomcat on the prowl, and expect a welcome?'

'Oh, well, if we're talking about rights . . .' said Lewis, sitting down on the edge of the bed, and taking off his shoes.

'And now,' I said, 'supposing you start? What in the world are you doing here, and what's your connection with Annalisa?'

'How like a woman to start at the wrong end,' said Lewis. 'I'll ask the questions, please. First of all, what are *you* doing here, and who is that boy?'

'Keep your voice down, he's next door.'

'I know. I looked in when I came along the veranda. He was sound asleep.'

'Efficient, aren't you? You know who he is; I told you, it's Tim Lacy. Don't you remember Carmel? I'm sure you met her once. She gave us that horrible decanter for a wedding present.'

'Ah, yes, that fair fat female, I remember. All soft and sweet, and full of icy draughts at the edges, like this damned feather thing on the bed. Must you have all of it, incidentally? I'm getting cold.'

'Then you'd better get your clothes on again. It would be bad enough if Tim or Frau Weber heard you and came in, let alone finding you like that—'

'I suppose I had. A life of sin is beastly uncomfortable,' said Lewis peacefully, sitting up and reaching for his trousers.

'Well, for pity's sake, can't you tell me why we're having to lead it? When I saw you standing there tonight, I nearly fainted. I'd have yelled out in another second.'

'I know. That's why I gave you the high sign to say nothing. I must say you passed it off very well. Did the boy guess?'

'No, but he told me I looked funny.'

'Well, so you did. You looked as if you'd seen a ghost.'

'Of course I did! It was the most unnerving thing that ever happened to me. As a matter of fact, for one dreadful moment, when you looked straight through me like that, I wondered if I could have been mistaken. Lewis, those clothes, where did you get them? They were absolutely disgusting.'

'Yes, weren't they?' He sounded remarkably complacent about it. 'Do you mean to tell me that you honestly did wonder whether you'd made a mistake or not?'

'Yes, truthfully.'

'Well—damn, I can't find my sock—I hope I've convinced you now.'

'Oh, yes. Same old technique, same old Lewis. It's you all right, I'd know that old routine anywhere.'

He grinned. 'Well, so long as you're sure . . . where the hell is that sock? Do you think I could put the light on for a moment?'

'No, I do not. If I'm not allowed to claim you as my husband with benefit of clergy here and now, I'm not going to let my reputation go straight down the sink by being discovered in bed with you. I've got Tim to think of.'

'Oh, yes, Tim. You still haven't told me why you're here with him. Ah, there's the sock. Go on, your move, I'm listening.'

'It's not in the least important how I got here, or why I'm with Tim,' I said sharply, 'but I should have thought it was perfectly obvious what brought me here. Lewis—'

'I'll tell you my part of it later. No, my darling Van, this matters . . . I must know how you found out I was here in Oberhausen. I'll tell you why all in good time, but you've got to tell me your end of it here and now. Of course it's obvious what brought you here; you knew I was here; now I want you to tell me how you knew.'

'I knew you were with the circus, and when we asked in Vienna where it was, they said the accident had happened in Oberhausen. We came down. We thought the circus might have already left, but that people would know where it had gone.'

He was pulling on his sweater now, a thick dark affair. As he emerged from it he paused for a moment, and turned his head. He said, in a stilled, listening voice:

'The news-reel cameras?'

'Heavens, how on earth did you guess so quickly? Yes, Carmel Lacy saw the news-reel, and thought she recognised you, and she wanted someone to convoy Timothy to Vienna, so she rang me up. She assumed I'd be joining you out here sooner or later.'

'I see. I saw the camera, but I didn't know whether I'd got on to it or not, and of course I was hoping I wasn't recognisable. I suppose you went to see it yourself?' I nodded. 'How recognisable was it?'

'Fairly clear, I'm afraid. Does it matter?'

He didn't answer that. 'Fancy your seeing it. It's one of those things.' He was silent again for a moment. 'It never entered my head it could get as far as you. But as soon as I saw you here in Oberhausen I realised you must have found out somehow, and that was all I could think of. Have you any idea if it got on to television?'

'Not in England, I'm pretty sure. I usually watch the news, and I haven't seen it. And I'm sure if it had been on, and anyone had recognised you, it would have got back to me.' I sat up, hugging my knees, and pulling the feather puff round me. 'Lewis, what *is* all this? I got your cable from Stockholm on the Monday. Did you send it?'

'No.'

'I thought you couldn't have. And then there was the letter; that came on Friday. I suppose that was given to someone to post for you?'

'Yes.'

'But—why Stockholm? Why not just Vienna anyway?'

'I had to have somewhere clear away from where you and I were going. It wouldn't have been easy to stall you off coming if it had been more or less on the way. As it happens,' said Lewis a little bitterly, 'I'd have done better to spare the extra few lies, if I was going to be so bloody careless as to get myself into the news.'

'And you had to stall me off?'

'Yes.'

I said miserably: 'You can see what I thought when I saw the news-reel. I couldn't believe there was anything wrong between us, not really . . . but I–I'd been so unhappy, and after what we'd said to each other that dreadful afternoon—'

'That's over. We'll not talk about that any more.' That it was over, had never even been started, had been agreed between us some half hour earlier.

'No, all right. I love you very much, Lewis.'

He made the kind of noise a husband considers sufficient answer to that remark—a sort of comforting grunt—then reached across to the pocket of his jacket where it hung over the chair, for cigarette and lighter, and lay down again beside me on the single bed.

'There. Decent enough for you? No, keep that beastly puff thing; wrap it round you, sweetie, I'm warm enough now . . . I see. You saw this news-reel thing, worked it out that I was here in Austria when I'd told you I was going to Stockholm; thought, presumably, that I might have been sent from Stockholm to Austria on business; but when you got the note allegedly written from Stockholm on the day you knew I was near Graz, you decided you'd come to see what it was all about. That it?'

'More or less. I think in a silly sort of way it was Carmel Lacy asking me to travel with Tim that really made me decide to come. It seemed to—well, to fit in so. It was as if I was being pushed to Austria, as if I was sort of *meant* to come. Besides, I had to know what you were up to. It was obvious there was something.'

'And what did you think I was up to?'

'I didn't know. When I saw the girl—Annalisa—she was on the film too, you know—'

'Was she? Yes, I see.' He sounded rather pleased than otherwise. He blew a smoke-ring which feathered up, ghostly in the frail light that showed through the gap in the window curtains. 'Don't you trust me, then?'

'No.'

'Fair enough,' he said mildly, and a second smoke-ring went through the first.

I shot up beside him. '*Lewis!*'

'Keep your voice down, for pity's sake!' He reached a lazy arm and pulled me down close to him. 'You can, as a matter of fact. I thought I'd just given you the best reasons why you should.'

'Or why I shouldn't.'

'Depending on the point of view? There's something in that.' He sounded no more than placidly amused. 'Lie still, girl, and don't be unrestful. We haven't much time, and I want to hear the rest.'

I obeyed him. 'All right. And don't forget there's quite a lot that I want to hear as well.' I told him, as quickly as I could, all that had happened. 'After you'd left us this evening with Annalisa, I didn't know whether to tell Timothy the truth or not, but I thought I'd better wait until I'd talked to you, so I pretended I'd made a mistake. You'd given me a hint you'd be seeing me soon, so I half expected you at the circus.'

'I came down later. I watched you operating.'

'I know you did. My spies are everywhere.' I felt him laugh quietly to himself. 'What's the joke?'

'Nothing. I take it you got the buns?'

'Yes, thank you very much. You've a life-long admirer in Timothy; he thinks you show real executive sense. Why didn't you stay? You must have known I was looking round corners for you.'

'I thought I'd keep out of your way till we could talk alone. Anyway, I was afraid of putting you off. You do a nice job, Mrs March.'

'Poor old Piebald, Herr Wagner was going to put him down, I think. He was Franzl's, and he's pretty well useless. However, he'll be all right now, and officially, I gather, he's Annalisa's, and I've a feeling she'll let him end his days in peace for her uncle's sake. Incidentally, I warn you, you're about to lose her to Timothy.'

'Well, I hope he can shoot straight,' said Lewis. 'Half the rodeo act and all the clowns are in love with her, not to mention that Balog character, and the dwarf. And if you say "Are you?" I shall do you a violence.'

'Are you?'

He tightened his arm round me, and I snuggled my cheek close into the crook of his shoulder, against the rough sweater. There was a long, comfortable silence. I heard the tiny hiss of tobacco as he drew on the cigarette, and the fire ate along the tube.

'As a matter of fact,' I said, muffled, 'I don't care any more why you're here. You're here, that's all. Darling Lewis. The only thing is, mayn't I stay with you? Can we have our holiday now, soon, here? Whatever it is you were doing, have you finished it?'

'Almost. Once I've reported back to Vienna, that's probably it.'

'You're going there tomorrow?'

'Today. Yes.'

'I gather you'd rather go alone. Then if I wait for you here—no, not here, somewhere where you can be Lewis March—could you come back when you've made your report, and we could have our holiday together as from then?'

'It's possible. What about the boy?'

'Annalisa can have him,' I said sleepily. 'Fair exchange. Lewis, you're not lying on this clean bed with those ghastly trousers on, are you?'

'Good heavens, no. Those were the ones I wore for mucking out the stables.'

'They looked like it.' I chuckled. 'Did you really groom the horses?'

'I did. Did I tell you one of those damned yellow ones bit me? The things I do for England . . . I should get both danger money and dirt money this time.'

There was a silence.

'Well, I suppose it's my turn now. Listen, Van, my dear, I ought not to tell you even now, but as things are, I think I've got to, and in any case I know by this time I can trust you with anything I've got, and'—I heard the smile—'I'm quitting, anyway. Besides, I've been thinking, and I've a feeling I'll want your help.' He stretched the other arm and stabbed out his cigarette in the ash-tray on the bedside table. Then he put the hand behind his head. 'Now, we haven't much time, because we must both get some sleep. I'll make it fast, and give you only the bare facts. You'll be able to supply the details for yourself, once you know the score. All this tangle about Stockholm, the cable, the letter, the Lee Elliott nonsense, the lies—you'll see why, when I've told you the rest.'

He paused, then went on softly, his eyes on the ceiling, where the dark beams were swimming faintly into the first light of dawn.

'What I told you earlier this evening about my job in Oberhausen was true, as far as it went. Paul Denver and I worked for the same employer, and I was on my way down here to meet him, when the fire happened, and he died. I got into Oberhausen in the small hours of Monday morning. I knew Denver was in touch with the circus, and as soon as I got to the village I saw the fire in the circus field, and went straight in. When I didn't see Paul, and people were shouting about there being a second man in the wagon, I guessed who it was.'

'Annalisa said you just came running out of the dark and helped them.'

'Yes. When we got him out he was dead. Franz Wagner was still alive.'

He was silent for a moment. 'So much was true. Now for the rest. Here it is. My job at P.E.C. is a perfectly genuine one, but I also do other jobs from time to time for another employer, sometimes under other names. This was one of them. Some of my trips abroad are for my—well, call it my secondary job. P.E.C. don't know, of course, and I won't tell how the trips are fixed; nor will I tell you the name of my own Department . . . but take it from me, in the Sales Department of P.E.C. there's so much coming and going that all things seem to be possible.' I heard the even, soft voice alter as he smiled. 'There you have it, in all its sizzling drama. Some of my jobs—the ones I've refused to take you on—have been what you'd call cloak-and-dagger assignments.'

'Cloak-and-dagger? You mean Secret Service? *Lewis!*' I struggled to take it in. 'You mean you're a—an agent? A . . . *spy?*'

He laughed. 'Take your pick of titles. We're not choosey.'

'Lewis, it's—I can't believe—*you?*'

'As ever was. I'm sorry if it's a wild disillusionment.' He turned his head sharply. 'Why, darling, you're shivering! Honey, it's not dangerous . . . We don't all go roaring off in special Aston Martins loaded down with guns and suicide pills—more likely a bowler hat and a brief-case and maybe a roll of notes for bribing some snotty little informer. Good God, you've seen how dangerous this job is—grooming horses.'

'"The things you do for England."'

'Exactly that. And all that's happened is I got bitten by a palomino stallion.'

'And Paul Denver died.'

'And Paul Denver died.' The smile left his voice. 'Yes, I know what you're thinking, but there's no evidence that it's anything but an accident. Heaven knows the police have kept the circus standing long enough, while they went over everything with a fine tooth-comb. Franz Wagner had had a small fire break out in his wagon once before—and he was a drunk. Mind you, that made him the person for Paul to get next to, if there was information to be got: another thing, I couldn't see Paul getting equally so sozzled that a fire could break out round him. But the reason for that wasn't far to seek. He'd had a crack on the head. Which is why, with my nasty suspicious nature, I've spent so long trying to find some shred of evidence that would make it something other than an accident. But I can't. On the other hand, there was evidence that the hook holding the oil lamp had broken, and the lamp had fallen, and it seems it could have knocked Paul silly for long enough to burn him to death, while old Franz, who was merely very drunk, survived long enough–he was farther away from the source of fire–to be pulled out. He was able to speak–just. One imagines that if there'd been "foul play" he'd have tried to say something about it, but he didn't.'

'I hadn't realised he was coherent.'

'He was conscious, but I wouldn't say coherent, poor old chap. The shock had knocked the drink out of him, but he was in pain, and besides, there was a terrible flap going on, with men trying to get the horses out of the stable lines just beside where he was lying, and he could talk about nothing else but the horses and all the gear in the stable . . . There was a bit of a wind, and at one time they were afraid the stables might catch fire. We tried to question him, but all he would do was rave on and on about the horses–the Lipizzaner, mostly–and some precious saddle or other from Naples that he seemed to set store by.'

'That was all?'

'As far as we could make out. We tried to tell him the horses were safe–the white stallion was out first of all, as a matter of fact–but I don't know if it got through to him. He was still talking about him–the Lipizzaner–when he died.' He paused for a moment. 'It was Annalisa he was trying to talk to . . . She was there all the time. It's fairly distressing to watch anyone die of burns, Van. Afterwards, when the police descended on them, and her father had to leave her . . .'

I knew he was trying to explain, without seeming to explain, the apparent swiftness of intimacy between himself and the girl. I said: 'It's all right, I understand. You're a comforting person to have around. Couldn't she make out what Franzl was saying, then?'

'Not really. She says that none of the harness is Italian, it's all Austrian made, and there's nothing of any value, as far as she knows. It all seemed to mean nothing. So there's your mystery. Whatever Franzl had on his mind, it wasn't murder. Paul's death looks like one of those damned accidents that can cut right across the best-laid plans. If I'd got here a couple of hours earlier, I might have located him in time to stop whatever happened, and to hear what he had to tell me.'

'You say you were already on your way to meet him. You'd been sent to get some information from him?'

'Yes. What seems to have happened is this: Denver's been in Czechoslovakia, and he came out a few days ago. He put in his report at Vienna Station–that's what we call our clearing-house for Eastern Europe–and then he went on leave here in Austria. As far as anyone knew, I gather, he was just doing as he said, and taking a holiday. All right. Next thing, the Department got a message–coded cable–asking for me to go out immediately, me and no one else. He had made contact with the Circus Wagner, and I was to pick him up there as Lee Elliott (I'd worked with him under that name before). Well, what Paul asked for he usually got, so I came. The rest you know.'

'And you've no idea why he sent for you?'

'The only clue I have is the contact he'd made with the circus–that, and the fact that he insisted on its being I who joined him. You see, the circus is crossing into Yugoslavia in two days' time, and Paul and I had worked there

together before. I speak pretty good Serbo-Croat. Now, Paul's cover and
Lee Elliott's are quite good enough to get across the border without burying
ourselves in a circus, so I can only imagine that Paul had got himself into the
circus because whatever he had found, and was following up, is centred
there.'

'Something or someone who *hasn't* got good cover, trying to get over the
border?'

'That's the obvious conclusion. A circus is one group of people that tends
to have the freedom of frontiers, even of Iron Curtain ones; but among all
that crowd of men and goods and animals . . . Well, without a lead, it's
hopeless. I've hung around and made myself useful, and fraternised
madly–and I've found nothing.'

'And that's your report? Just negative?'

'A nice useful negative. A splendid last assignment.'

'Will they leave it at that? I mean, is there any chance they'd want you to
stick with it–to cross the border?'

He stirred. 'I don't think they'll send me, no. But . . . well, I can't think
why else Paul insisted on the "Lee Elliott" stuff, if he hadn't expected to go
back there.' His hand moved to ruffle my hair. 'Don't cross bridges, darling,
it may not be necessary. But if it were, the only risk would be another bite
from that perishing yellow stallion.'

I said: 'What you're trying to tell me is, you might go for your own
personal satisfaction?'

He said slowly: 'If you put it like that, yes. I don't see that the
Department will want me to take it further, as things are; but . . .' He
hesitated for the first time. 'My own satisfaction, yes, call it that. It isn't a
hunch: I don't ride hunches. But I knew Denver, and if he had something to
tell me, it's probable that it mattered. You'll have to forgive him. He had no
idea that I was going on leave, or that I was quitting. I'm sorry.'

'Don't. We've had all that. I'm not saying any of those things again. If it
matters, it matters. The only thing is, I'll come too, this time. No, don't
laugh at me, I mean it. If you're going under your own steam, there's no
reason why I shouldn't, and I may even be able to help. I've got as good a
connection with the circus as you have–I'm vet-in-chief, and I've been
invited in any time I like. Besides, I've got a patient I have to see to.'

'*Entendu.* Have you also got a visa?'

'No.'

'Well, then . . . No, I'm not laughing you off; I told you I want your help,
and I do want you to do just what you've said–stick with the circus till it
leaves. Listen to me. I've got to go back to Vienna in the morning, and in
any case my reasons for sticking around the circus are wearing a bit thin,
and will hardly survive the pull-down, let alone the move across the border.
But by the sheerest luck you're here, and you've got this cast-iron–and
totally innocent–connection with them. They've got two more nights in
this country, at Hohenwald, then Zechstein, then the border. Now, if you
and Timothy should just happen to be travelling much the same route as
that . . . and if you happened to take such a keen professional interest in your
old piebald patient that you felt you must look in on them again . . . That's
all, don't ask any specific questions, just look and listen. Get in back stage,

talk to people, move around and keep your eyes open. I told you I don't ride hunches, but I can feel it in my bones, there's something up . . . The point is that whatever's wrong, whoever's wrong, they'll relax once they're rid of Denver's friend and colleague—me. And if they do relax, you may see or hear something.'

'And if we do?'

'Do nothing. Understand? *Do nothing.* Wait for me.'

'You'll come back soon?'

'Yes. Possibly tonight. Certainly by Tuesday night.'

'What sort of thing, Lewis?'

'God knows, I don't. Anything that's out of pattern. There may be nothing; but Denver asked for me, and Denver was heading for the border, and Denver died . . . You've got it clear? I don't want you to do anything, and certainly to take no risks at all. All you have to do is forget I was here, forget this conversation, and stay with the circus until I get in touch with you again. All right?'

'All right. And you needn't keep reassuring me, I'm not a bit nervous, just happy.' I moved my cheek against the sweater. 'You did say "by the sheerest luck", didn't you?'

'That you were here? I did.'

'Hush a minute, I think I heard Tim move.' From next door came the heavy creak of the bed, as Timothy presumably roused and turned over. We lay still, clasped closely. After a while there was silence again.

He said very softly: 'I ought to go. Damn!'

'What about Timothy?'

'Leave it for the moment. What he doesn't know won't hurt him. The trouble is this bloody alias . . . If you know his people, he'll find out who I am in any case, sooner or later, so we'll have to tell him. We can cook up some story for him—a special investigation for P.E.C. involving an insurance claim; something like that. I'll have to think. He may even decide for himself that I've some connection with the police, and that won't matter; it'll help to keep his mouth shut. He's all right, isn't he?'

'I'd trust him further than I can see.'

'Fair enough, as long as we don't trust him with anything we haven't a right to. When I get back I'll talk to him. I'll really have a go.' He sat up. 'Now, final arrangements. Tomorrow, or rather today, you'll be at Hohenwald. You'd better keep in touch. Try to ring some time during the evening. The number's Vienna 32 14 60. I won't write it down, I want you to remember it. Got it?'

'I think so. Vienna 32 14 60. And do I ask for Mr Elliott?'

'Yes, please. If I'm not there someone else will answer. I'll tell them to expect your call. The next night you'll be at Zechstein, that's the take-off point for the border. I'll join you there. There's a hotel a couple of miles north of the village, a new one; it's the old castle, and they've converted it, and I believe it's rather a fascinating place. Try and get rooms there, anyway. It's a fair distance out of the village, so that if I do come and join you there, I won't be seen and identified by half the parish . . . Have you enough money?'

'For the time being, anyway. Will this castle place be very expensive?'

'Probably. Never mind, I'll see if I can get you on the strength! Book double, will you, in case I can join you as Mr March. Now I really must go.'

'I suppose you must. Oh, Lewis, it's beastly cold without you.'

'Is it, sweetie? Tuck that thing round you tighter, then, and go to sleep.'

'I never felt less like sleep. I'll see you out.'

I swung my feet out of bed, reached for my dressing-gown, and folded it round me. He had shrugged himself into his jacket, and was sitting down pulling on his shoes. They were, I noticed, rubber-soled plimsolls.

I dropped a kiss lightly on his hair. 'You're too darned good at this, Casanova. Do you suppose you can get back into your own place without being seen and heard?'

'I'll try. In any case Frau Schindler will only think I've been helping the circus pull-down.'

I unlatched the windows, and pushed them very quietly open. The cold scents of the dawn came in, as the starlight shivered and slackened towards morning. The breeze was rustling the grasses.

Lewis went past me like a shadow, and paused at the veranda rail. When he turned back, I went out.

He said softly: 'The breeze'll help. Nobody'll hear me go.' He kissed me. 'Your reputation's safe a little longer, Mrs Prim.'

I took him by the lapels of his jacket, and held on to them rather tightly. 'Take care of yourself. Please take care of yourself.'

'Why, what's this?'

'I don't know. Just a feeling. Take care.'

'Don't worry, I'll do that. Now get yourself to bed, and go to sleep.'

And suddenly, I was alone. I thought I heard, over the rustling of the grass, a deeper rustling, and then it was gone.

I turned back from the veranda rail, to see Timothy, in his pyjamas, standing at the open window of his room, staring at me.

For a moment, everything stopped; the breeze, the sounds of the night, the blood and breath in my body: for one long pulse of silence I could neither speak nor move.

He made no movement either, but, though I knew that Lewis had made no sound, I knew also that Timothy had seen him.

I suppose we stared at one another for a full half minute. It seemed like a year. He had not to be told yet; I had had my instructions; and at the unthinking level of fear which had prompted my last exchange with Lewis, I knew that they might matter. There was only one thing to do; assume that Timothy had seen nothing, and hope that he wouldn't dare broach the subject without my giving him a lead.

I said: 'Hullo, couldn't you sleep?'

He came slowly out through the long windows until he was only a couple of feet away. In the growing light I could see him clearly. There was nothing in his face that one could put a name to, no curiosity, or embarrassment, or even surprise. His features had been schooled to a most complete indifference. He was going to play it exactly as I could have wished.

I think it was his very lack of expression that decided me. Boys of seventeen ought not to be able to look like that. Whatever Carmel and

Graham Lacy had done between them to Timothy, I wasn't going to be responsible for adding another layer to that forcible sophistication.

And nothing would serve but the truth. It was emphatically not the time to ask, with exasperated affection, what he thought I could possibly have been getting up to with Lee Elliott after half an hour's acquaintance. He had seen the kiss, after all. Besides, as soon as the first impact had worn off, he would certainly put two and two together, and arrive at the truth. He might as well have it now, and from me. Lewis would have to forgive me; but if Timothy could be trusted later, he could be trusted now.

I took in my breath and leaned back against the rail.

'Well, it's a fair cop,' I said, lightly. 'Now I suppose I'll have to confess I lied to you about our Mr Elliott.'

'Lied to me?'

'Afraid so. You remember I told you he was my husband's double?'

'Yes, of course.' His face had changed, emerging somehow from that pre-selected expression of indifference. I suppose his lightning conclusion was the obvious one, but somehow the relief and pleasure on his face made it a compliment. 'You mean it *was* your husband, himself? You mean that chap Elliott—your husband *was* actually here all the time? The news-reel was right?'

'Just that. As soon as I saw him I realised he didn't want to be made known—and then Annalisa said, "This is Lee Elliott", so I just shut up and said nothing.'

'In disguise? Really? Gosh!' The old familiar Timothy was back; even in the cool half light I could see the sparkle of excitement. 'I said he was mysterious, didn't I? No wonder you were punch-drunk tonight and wouldn't make plans about cables to Stockholm!' He took a breath. 'But why? Was there something wrong about the fire, then, after all?'

'Don't ask me why, he didn't explain, only that there's something involved that his firm doesn't want to be made public, so for the moment we'll have to keep his secret.' I gave a little laugh. 'This'll be a great blow to his pride; he was so sure nobody'd heard him.'

'As a matter of fact I didn't hear him. I'd woken up, and couldn't go to sleep again straight away, and I felt a bit hot under that eiderdown affair, so I just came over to open the window wider.' He added, naïvely: 'As a matter of fact I got a bit of a fright. I wondered what in the world he was doing snooping around here. I was just going to tackle him, and see if you were all right, when you came out of the window.'

'And you realised it had been a reasonably friendly visit.' I laughed. 'Well, thanks for looking after me. Now you know all, as they say . . . At any rate you know as much as I do, but keep it dark, there's a dear. I'm not supposed to have told you who he was.'

'O.K. Goodnight.'

'Goodnight.'

And I went back to my cold bed.

Chapter Nine

Sometime he trots, as if he told the steps
With gentle majesty and modest pride:
Anon he rears upright, curvets and leaps,
As who should say 'Lo, thus my strength is tried.'
                    Shakespeare: *Venus and Adonis*

Next morning it was with a sense almost of shock that, as the car approached the other end of the village, I saw in place of the bustle and the big top of the circus, merely an empty field. There was the trampled circle, with the remains of sawdust and tanbark strewn where the ring had stood. Wisps of blowing straw were all that were left of the warm stable where the horses had slept, and where I had operated last night.

Tim stopped the car at the gate of the field.

'It's funny, isn't it? Like a field full of ghosts.'

'I was just thinking that. It looks quite incredibly deserted, as if Aladdin or someone had rubbed a lamp, and the whole thing had been spirited away . . . Like the end of a story.' I looked towards the corner of the field, where the blackened grass and a few charred sticks indicated the scene of the tragedy. 'And a sad story, too. I wonder if they were glad to get away? What did you stop for?' For he was getting out of the car.

'I thought I'd get something to eat on the way. I won't be long–that is, unless you'd like to come back with me, and maybe have a cup of coffee at the *Konditorei?*'

'I'll come.'

The smell of fresh baking from the little bakery-cum-café was enough to snare anybody, and it would have been too much to expect Tim to pass it without a visit. The little window on the shady side of the morning square was filled with fragrant stacks of breads and excitingly foreign confections. Timothy gave them his earnest consideration, while I waited, trying not to look as if all my attention was fixed on the side door, where a notice saying *Zimmer frei* might indicate that the visitor had already left.

'Vanessa, do look at the names of these things! Aren't they marvellous? *Sandgugelhupf* . . . isn't that smashing? How about a nice *Sandgugelhupf* each? Or a *Polsterzipf?* Oh, look, it can't really be called a *Spitzbub*, can it?'

'I don't see why not, anything seems possible in this language. What about *Schokoladegugelhupf*–and I do rather care for the *Schnittbrot.*'

'I think that only means sliced bread,' said Timothy. 'It is a marvellous language, isn't it?'

'I'm going to start learning it, as from today,' I said. 'I wish there was a shop where I could get a book, but there won't be one here, and we're not going through Bruck, either, today. Have you got one?'

'Only a phrase book, but you can borrow it if you like. It's quite a good one, as they go . . . Don't you just adore phrase books? The things they imagine one might want to say . . . they're almost as good as one's Greek grammar at school. I remember one of the first sentences, I had to put into

Greek was, "She carried the bones in the basket." I'm still wondering whose bones, and why.'

'Well, there you are, it's stuck in your memory all this time, which is what I suppose school books are meant to do. I'll bet you remember that bit of Greek better than any other you did.'

'As a matter of fact it's about the only bit I do remember, and just think how useful. The best thing I've come across so far in my German phrase book is in the section for "Air Travel". "Will you please open the windows" seems to me a funny thing to say to anyone on a plane, somehow.'

'Not seriously? You must be kidding. Is it really in the book?'

'Yes, honestly.'

'Well, if all the phrases are as useful as that—'

'Good morning,' said Lewis, just behind us.

He wasn't wearing the plimsolls this morning, but he had still moved very quietly. If it was getting to be a habit, I thought, it was a habit he could just get out of again. I didn't want to die of heart failure.

I said, 'Good morning,' a little breathlessly, wondering as I spoke if I should tell him straight away that Timothy knew, but Timothy was already greeting him with aplomb almost as professional as his own, and then it was somehow too late.

Timothy said: 'Oh, hullo, Mr Elliott, good morning. You haven't gone yet? I wondered if you'd have left when the circus did.'

'Too early for me. The last wagons were due to go at about five, I think. I didn't hear them.'

'You must be a very sound sleeper,' said Timothy cheerfully. 'I imagined there'd be a lot of coming and going in the village during the night, but perhaps it doesn't disturb you?'

'Thank you,' said Lewis, 'no. I had an excellent night; far better than I had expected.'

'Tim,' I said quickly, perhaps even sharply, 'you'd better choose what you want in the way of buns, and go in and buy them. We really ought to be setting off.'

'O.K.,' said Tim amiably, and vanished through the shop doorway.

'Honours about even,' I said, 'but will you please not score your points across my marriage bed? The boy knows, Lewis.'

'Does he?' I was relieved to see that he looked, after the first frowning moment, no more than amused. 'The little so-and-so, does he indeed?'

'I had to tell him. He saw you leaving last night.'

'I must be slipping.'

'No, it was pure accident. But I had to tell him.'

'I suppose so. Don't worry. How much does he know?'

'Only who you are. He thinks it's some mysterious business mission for P.E.C. May I tell him you asked me to keep in touch with the circus?'

'I don't see why not. Tell him the firm may want more details about Denver's death, and I may have to come back, so meantime I've asked you to stick around. That's nothing but the truth, after all. You can refer any other questions to me.'

'I doubt if he'll ask them. Tim's all right.' It was a measure of what had happened in the last two days, that I knew that the phrase—and all it implied–was true. 'When do you go?'

'I'm on my way now. You all right?'

'Fine. We're just setting off for Hohenwald, but Tim was afraid of starving on the way. Have you got a car here?'

He nodded to one which stood under the trees near by, a shabby fawn-coloured Volvo which nevertheless looked powerful. He was decently dressed this morning, I noticed, though still not recognisably Lewis March, my husband. This was still the anonymous and professionally insignificant Lee Elliott. I could see now that his very ability to melt into apparent insignificance was one of the tools of his trade, but nothing, I thought, could take from Lewis the precision and grace of movement which spoke always of strength and self-command, and could sometimes–when he allowed it–give him elegance.

He lifted his head, narrowing his eyes against the morning sun. 'What's the boy stocking up with food for? You haven't a great way to go . . .' And then, very softly: 'Stop looking at me like that, for goodness' sake, my dear girl. You look as if you were bringing me gold and frankincense.'

'And why not? I has my rights too, Mr M.' I added aloud: 'Exactly how far is Hohenwald, anyway? How far does a circus normally go in a day?'

'About thirty or forty miles. It's roughly fifty kilometres to Hohenwald. You should have a lovely run; the gradients aren't bad, and there's some beautiful country. Have lunch at Lindenbaum, and take your time.'

When Timothy emerged from the shop with his arms alarmingly full of packages, Mr Elliott was giving me directions for a pleasant day's drive, with a map drawn on the back of an old envelope. I noticed that the envelope was addressed to 'Lee Elliott, Esq., c/o Kalkenbrunner Fertiliser Company, Meerstrasse, Vienna'.

'Well,' I said, 'we'll go. Have a good journey.'

'And you,' said Lewis. 'Enjoy yourselves . . . *Auf Wiedersehen*, then, and remember me to Annalisa.'

As we drove off, Timothy shot a sideways glance at me. 'Was that just a crack?'

I laughed. 'No. In any case, you're a fine one to talk about making cracks. I may tell you, Lewis knows.'

He looked startled, then grinned. 'Oh, you just told him? You mean he knows I know?'

'Yes, and leave it at that, will you, before I get muddled. All is now in the clear . . . and thank goodness we can talk.'

This was the first chance we had had of private conversation since our daybreak meeting on the veranda. Breakfast had been a more or less public function in the Gasthof, with Timothy's devoted waitress watching our every move, but now, as we left the village behind us, we had not only the road, but the whole countryside, seemingly, to ourselves.

The road was, as Lewis had promised, idyllic. The morning sun cast long, fresh blue shadows, and the hedges were thick, and full of honeysuckle and white convolvulus. A hay cart had been that way, and the wisps of hay were hanging golden from the hedge in the still morning.

I began to explain to Timothy what Lewis had asked me to do, indicating merely that Lewis and his firm were not satisfied with the verdict of

'accident' on Paul Denver, and were still curious to know what connection–if any–the latter had had with the circus people, and if he could
have incurred any enmities which might have led directly to his death.

'All he wants me to do,' I said at length, 'is keep in touch with the circus,
as veterinary surgeon if they need me, or just as a friend. He's very emphatic
that no questions are to be asked, or detective work done . . . there's no room
for your Archie Goodwin act, Timothy. In fact I don't know whether you
want to stay in on this or not? It chimes in exactly with what I'd like to do
myself–I mean, if I can't join Lewis straight away, then I'm quite happy to
stooge around here till he comes back, and maybe be a bit of help to him at
the same time. And I do want to keep an eye on the old horse. But if you'd
rather cut loose here and now, and go to Piber—'

'No, not a bit. Gosh, no, I'd love to stay, if you'd have me . . .'

His protestations were almost violently convincing, and only faded into
silence when we caught up with the hay cart. This was enormous, and top-
heavily laden, creaking along on its wooden wheels behind two plodding
sorrel horses. The road was narrow, overhung with high hedges, and with
ditches to either side.

'. . . If you're sure you could do with me?' finished Timothy, as we
negotiated the hay cart with three centimetres to spare on either side, and
buzzed happily on up the next incline.

'I'm beginning to think I can't do without you,' I said.

'That settles it then. Hohenwald it is.'

The village of Hohenwald was much smaller than Oberhausen. It lay a mile
or so behind the main road, in a pretty hanging valley, and was little more
than a cluster of houses grouped round its church whose tower rose,
crowned with a bell of grey-green shingles, above splayed roofs and gables
of red tile. An arched stone bridge spanned a narrow mountain river, and
led what traffic it could into the cobbled square. To south and west the land
fell away in smiling orchards and fields of corn, some of them cut, golden
among the greens, while to north and east the mountains lifted their stepped
ramparts of pine forests. The verges of the gravel road were white with
dust.

The sense of loss we had felt in leaving Oberhausen was cancelled here,
even before we reached the village, by the sight of the now familiar posters
wrapped round trees and gate-posts, and then by the Circus Wagner itself,
settled in a field beside the river. It seemed odd to see, in this completely
different setting, the same tents and wagons and big top, the whole build-up
of the circus so exactly the same. It was indeed as if some genie's hand had
picked it up complete and set it down again here, some thirty miles away.

It was mid-afternoon when we arrived, and the first performance would
not start till five, but already children were crowding in a noisy and excited
mob round the gate of the field. I saw the dwarf, Elemer, sitting on the gate
and talking to the children, and making them laugh. He looked up and saw
us as the car went by, and smiled and lifted his small hand in a wave of
welcome. So the news would go before us.

There was some coming and going of tourists in the village, but for all
that we got beds easily enough at another small and scrupulously clean

Gasthof beside the church. Shortly after four, we walked back to the circus field.

As we passed the big top, I paused and looked inside.

The grass was fresh, the ring strewn with fresh sawdust, and on the platforms that crowned the enormous king-poles, electricians were busy putting the last touches to the wiring. The top itself, with its floating spaces, looked different, lit now from above with the curious unreal diffused light of sunshine through canvas. The whole space echoed to the sound of hammering and shouting as the tent-men put up the last of the wooden tiers of scaffolding and arranged the benches on them. Someone on a high ladder was hanging the rear curtains in place, the crimson drapes through which the horses would come. A couple of clowns, already in costume but without their make-up, stood talking very seriously in the centre aisle.

In spite of the differences, it was hauntingly the same as last night, and though at the moment this was only a tent enclosing an alien air, I got the strongest feeling that it was full and echoing with the hundreds of past performances, the music of past songs and dances and laughter.

As we emerged again into the sunlight and I saw the strange gate, the strange village, the strange bell-shaped roof of the church tower against its backdrop of pines, I found myself experiencing a sudden sharp sense of loss—which I hadn't felt that morning—to realise that Lewis was not here. He was possibly already in Vienna. Last night's episode might have been a dream, gone to join the flickering unreality of that almost forgotten news-reel.

Annalisa was expecting us, and, to my relief, seemed pleased that we had come, and very eager that I should take another look at the piebald horse.

'But of course you are welcome! I wish I could ask you both in now, but I am dressing, as you see.' All we had in fact seen of her so far was a face peering past the curtain that hung over the doorway of her sleeping-wagon. In spite of her welcoming smile and obviously real pleasure, I thought she looked pale—the gaiety and sparkle had gone. I wondered if she had had any sleep at all last night. 'But you will come afterwards again and have coffee? You'll go to the performance, yes?'

'Timothy's going to see the show again, and if I know him, he'll see your act twice,' I said, 'but I don't think I will, thank you. I'll just go round to the stables. How's the patient?'

'Better, much better. He's a different horse already. He hardly limps at all, just a little, as if he was stiff . . . not a real limp at all.'

'We call it "going short",' I said. 'Is he eating?'

'Not much . . . but he really does look better. I am so grateful to you.'

'Think nothing of it. I take it you'll keep him now?'

I smiled as I spoke, and she responded, but (I thought) with a rather wintry charm, and said merely: 'Then I shall see you later? *Also gut!* If you want to come in here and use my wagon, please do so, it's never shut. Come in and make coffee if you want it, anything. Just what you wish.' The smile again, better this time, and the head vanished.

'She looks tired,' I said. 'I hope she manages her act all right. Well, see you later, Tim.'

The stables, too, were uncannily the same. There was the same smell, the same rows of horses' rumps and idly swishing tails, but the sun was white on the canvas, and the air of sleepy peace was gone. The liberty horses were being prepared for the show. The rugs had been stripped off them, and their skins gleamed in the light. Half a dozen were already wearing their harness. Men hurried to and fro carrying rugs, surcingles, plumed bridles. The Shetland ponies, some of them getting excited, were beginning to fuss, nibbling one another's necks and switching their long tails. The Lipizzan stallion in his stall near the door stood placidly, head down, ears relaxed, taking no notice of the fuss and bustle. It was difficult to realise that in less than an hour's time he would be in the ring, magnificent in the spotlights, clothed with gold and jewels and flying through the air. Here in his dim corner he looked ancient and heavy with wisdom, and as earthbound as a horse of white stone.

Opposite him the piebald stood with drooping head, but as I approached his eye rolled back, and he moved an ear in greeting. What I had taken to be a boy was hunched in the next stall, busy over a piece of harness, but when he spoke, I realised that it was the dwarf Elemer.

'So you are back to see the suffering one.' I don't know where the dwarf had learnt his English; it was guttural and stilted, but the vowels were cultured. His voice was deep and pleasant.

'Yes. He looks a lot better.'

'He has eaten a little. Not enough. But he will mend . . . '

I went into the stall to look at the horse. 'So Annalisa was saying.'

'. . . For what it is worth,' the dwarf said. He lifted the jewelled saddle off its trestle, and began to hump it rather painfully across to the white stallion's stall. It almost hid him from sight, and the girth was trailing, but I thought I knew better than to offer help.

I turned my attention to the horse. The dolly was still in place, the swelling had vanished, and he accepted my hands without wincing. I moved him back a pace in his stall, and saw that he was putting the leg to the ground with more confidence already. The coat still stared, but his eye was brighter, and his general countenance very much better than last night.

I straightened up. '"For what it is worth"?' I wasn't quite sure if I had heard the guttural murmur aright. 'Do you mean they *won't* keep him?'

He shrugged. The effect, with the tiny short arms and the big shoulders, was awful. I had to exert sharp control to stop myself from looking away. 'Who knows?' was all he would say, and set one of those shoulders to the white stallion's hock to make him move over.

Then all of a sudden, it seemed, the show was on us. The horses went streaming out for the first act. I saw the 'cowboys' swing up into their saddles, and the 'Entry of the Gladiators' came thudding from the big top. The groom Rudi hurried into the Lipizzan's stall and, taking the saddle from Elemer, heaved it one-armed on to the stallion's back. I had been wrong about the dwarf's susceptibilities; the groom cracked some joke in German which, from the accompanying gesture, had some reference to Elemer's height, but the latter only laughed and went scuttling under the stallion's belly to fasten the girth. I straightened up from my examination of the piebald's leg, and stood fondling his ears, while I watched the white stallion putting on, jewel by jewel, his royal dress. Then the dwarf came across to me.

'They are starting. Are you going in to see the show again?'

I shook my head. 'I was wondering . . . I suppose this old chap won't have had any exercise at all since the fire? Has he even been out to grass? I thought not. You know, a bit of gentle walking would do him a world of good, and a bit of grazing would do even more. I wondered if there was anywhere I could take him? Do you think the verge of the road? Would it be allowed?'

'Of course,' said the dwarf, 'you must do as you wish, you know what is best. But do not take him to the road, there is too much dust. Go the other way.' The little arm gestured towards the far door of the stable. 'Behind this field there is a wood, but it is not a big wood just a—what do you say?—a belt of trees, perhaps twenty metres wide. There is a gate, and a path up through the trees, and above them is a little alp; it is common land, and there is good grass there. Nobody will stop you.'

'Can I leave him grazing there till the pull-down?'

'Of course. You will not want to hobble him, no? Then if you wait one moment, I will get you the tether and a peg.'

It was easy enough to find the place. At the far side of the field the ground lifted sharply away from the flat land where the tents stood, and the late sun gilded the young fir cones with amber and threw into deep shadow the path that wound upwards through the trees. The wood of the gate was damp, and it creaked a little as I opened it and led the old horse through. We went slowly. He put his off fore to the ground perhaps a little tenderly, but he was by no means lame; at most his gait was stiff, and as we made our way gently up the mossy track between the pines he seemed to go better with every step. He lifted his head, and his ears pricked with the first sign of interest he had shown. Even I, with my poor human senses, could smell the rich scents of that summer's evening.

Above the belt of pines lay the alp the dwarf had told me of, a long terrace of flat green, dotted here and there with bushes, and walled on every side by the dark firs. Someone had scythed down the long meadow grass, and the hay lay drying here and there in little piles; where it had been shorn the new grass was fresh and tender green, and full of flowers. The air smelt of honey.

The horse shouldered his way past me into the sunlight, dropped his head and began to graze. I left him to it, and carrying the slack of the tether took the peg into the middle of the meadow and drove it in, then moved a little way off and sat down.

The ground was warm with the day's sun. Faintly from below the belt of pines came the circus music, muted and made more musical by the distance. I sat listening, enjoying the last of the sunshine, while I contentedly watched the now greedy grazing of the old stallion. The grass was thick with familiar meadow flowers—hare-bells, thyme, eyebright, and, where the scythe had not yet passed, the foaming white and yellow of parsley and buttercups. What was not so familiar was the fluttering, rustling life of the meadow: the whole surface of the field seemed moving with butterflies— meadow browns, blues, sulphurs, fritillaries, and few of my own Vanessas, the red admirals and tortoiseshells. Their colours flickered among the flowers, each vanishing momentarily as it clung and folded, then opening to its own bright colour as it fluttered on. Even the green roots of the grass were alive, as countless grasshoppers hopped and fiddled there. The air droned with bees, all zooming past me, I noticed, on the same purposeful track, as if on some apian *Autobahn* of their own. They were all making for a little hut, the size of a small summer-house, chalet-style and beautifully built of pine, and as full of tiny windows as a dovecot. It was, in fact, a bee-house, a sort of collective hive for several swarms, each one with its own tiny bee-door, behind which it made its honey in candle-shaped combs. Amused and interested, I watched the laden bees aiming like bullets each for its own door, remembering how, even a few years ago, in my own childhood, the English meadows, too, had been alive with wings, and how quiet now was the poisoned countryside.

From beyond the pines, sounding surprisingly remote, the cracked bell of the little church chimed six. There had been an interval of silence from the circus. I supposed it was the clowns' act, or the performing dogs: now, faintly and sweetly, but quite distinctly in the still clear air, the music started again. I heard the fanfare and recognised it; it was the entrance of Annalisa and her white stallion. The trumpets cut through the air, silver, clear and commanding. Old Piebald stopped grazing and lifted his head with his ears cocked, as one imagines a war-horse might at the smell of battle and the trumpets. Then the music changed, sweet, lilting and golden, as the orchestra stole into the waltz from *Der Rosenkavalier*.

There was some enchantment in hearing it at that distance on that lovely evening in the Alpine meadow. I settled my back comfortably against one of the little soft haycocks, and prepared to enjoy the concert; but then something about the old horse caught my attention, and I sat up to watch.

He had not lowered his head again to graze, but was standing with neck arched and ears pricked, in a sort of mimicry of the white stallion's proud posture. Then, like the white stallion's, his head moved, not in an ordinary equine toss, but with a graceful, almost ceremonial movement of conscious beauty. A forefoot lifted, pointed, pawed twice at the soft ground; then slowly, all by himself, bowing his head to his shadow on the turf, he began to dance. He was old and stiff, and he was going short on the off fore, but he moved to the music like a professional.

I sat among the lengthening shadows of the lonely meadow, watching him, somehow infinitely touched. In this way, I supposed, all old circus horses felt when they heard the music of their youth: the bowing, ceremonious dance of the liberty horse was something which, once learned, could never be forgotten.

And then I realised that this was not the movement of a liberty horse. It was not dancing as the palominos had 'danced'; this was a version, stiff but true, of the severely disciplined figures of the high school: first the Spanish Walk, shouldering-in in a smooth skimming diagonal; then the difficult *pirouette*, bringing him round sharply to present him sideways to his audience; then as I watched he broke into a form of the *piaffe*. It was a travesty, a sick old horse's travesty, of the standing trot which the Lipizzaner had performed with such precision and fire, but you could see it was a memory in him, still burning and alive, of the real thing perfectly

executed. In the distance the music changed: the Lipizzaner down in the
ring would be rising into the *levade*, the first of the 'airs above the ground'.
And in the high Alpine meadow, with only me for audience, old Piebald
settled his hind hooves, arched his crest and tail, and, lame forefoot clear of
the ground, lifted into and held the same royal and beautiful *levade*.

And this, it seemed, had been enough. He came down to all four feet,
shook his head, dropped his muzzle to the grass, and all at once was just an
old tired piebald horse pegged out to graze in a green meadow.

Chapter Ten

This is the attitude in which artists depict the horses on which
gods and heroes ride.
                Xenophon: *The Art of Horsemanship*

'Tim,' I said, 'you're not proposing to sit through the whole of the second
house too, are you?'

'No, I wasn't, though I'd have liked to see Annalisa ride again. Why, did
you want me?'

'Yes, and I want you to skip Annalisa too, if you will. I've got something
to show you, and it's something you won't want to miss. No'–in response to
a quick inquiring look from him–'nothing to do with that. Something
purely personal. Will you come with me?'

'Well, of course. Where?'

'Away up the hill behind the field. I'm not going to tell you anything
about it, I want you to see for yourself.'

It was dark now, but the moon was coming up clear of the mountains and
the trees. The air was very still, and the bats were out. The horse had moved
on a little, grazing quietly.

'Oh, you've got old Piebald here,' said Timothy. 'Goodness, he looks a
different creature. He's eating like a horse, as they say.'

'Exactly like a horse. But–*How noble in reason! how infinite in faculty! in
form, in moving, how express and admirable! . . . the beauty of the world! the
paragon of animals!*'

'What on earth's that?'

'*Hamlet*, with a dash of Noël Coward. Look, come over here, the grass is
damp now, but there's a log; we can sit on that.'

'What were you going to show me?'

'You'll have to wait for it. It's something that happened, and I hope it'll
happen again. Here, sit down. Listen how clearly you can hear the music.'

'Mm. That's the liberty act, isn't it? There, that's the end. Now it'll be
the clowns. What is it, Vanessa? You sounded sort of excited.'

'I am a bit. Wait and see. It may not happen, I–I simply don't know, and
I may have been wrong. I can't help feeling now that it was all my
imagination, but if it wasn't, perhaps you'll see it, too.'

It was a beautiful night, the air clear and still. The butterflies had all gone,

and the bees were quiet in their bee-house. In the silence I thought I could
hear the cry of bats high up above the trees. The swish of the horse's hoofs
through the grass, and the tearing sound of his cropping, were very loud in
the still air. The moon rose clear of a low cloud that hugged the hill.

I said softly: 'Listen, those are the trumpets. Don't say a word, now.
Keep still.'

At first I thought it wasn't going to happen. The trumpets shivered the
air, distant, silver, brave: the old horse grazed. An owl flew low across the
field, silent, ghostly white in the moonlight. The horse lifted his head to
watch it. The trumpets called on unheeded.

The waltz from *Der Rosenkavalier* wound its way up through the pines.
Beside me on the log Timothy sat obediently still.

The waltz beat on softly; five bars, six bars—and then it happened. The
old head lifted, the neck arched, the forefoot went out in that arrogant
beautiful movement, and the piebald glided once more into his own private
and ceremonious dance. This way and that he went, his hoofs striking the
turf softly. The moonlight flooded the meadow, blanching all colours to its
own ghostly silver. The pines were very black. As the stallion rose in the last
magnificent rear of the *levade*, the moonlight poured over him bleaching his
hide so that for perhaps five or six long seconds he reared against the black
background, a white horse dappled with shadows, no longer an old broken-
down gypsy's piebald, but a *haute école* stallion, of the oldest line in Europe.

Timothy neither moved nor made a sound until it was over; then we
turned and looked at one another.

'Am I right?' I asked.

He merely nodded, saying nothing. I had a suspicion that he was as
moved as I had been by the sight, and was—boy-like—concerned not to show
it. When he spoke, it was in a normal, even casual voice, but I knew I had
been right. 'The poor old chap,' he said.

'He's been good, in his day,' I said.

'I'll say.' His voice sharpened, as he began to think. 'But, here, I don't
understand! If the horse was trained, why should they talk of getting rid of
him?'

'He's old. I had a good look at him: he's over twenty.'

'But nobody's given his age as a reason for putting him down, it's always
been that "he's no use, he can do nothing, the circus can't afford to keep a
horse who does nothing". You remember Annalisa said they'd tried him in
the liberty routine and he was no use.'

'If he was a highly trained dressage performer when they got him, he'd
take badly to a new routine.'

'Yes, but if he's "highly trained", you'd think they could use him
somehow. Or at any rate sell him. He'd fetch good money, even at twenty.'

'Perhaps,' I said, 'they don't know he's a trained performer.'

He turned to stare at me. In the strong moonlight it was possible to see
one another quite clearly.

'*Don't know?*'

I said: 'Well, they can't know, can they? You've just quoted the things
they've said . . . and tonight, again, I got the impression they thought he was
hardly worth my trouble.' I told him what the dwarf had said.

He sat for a while, frowning down at the grass. 'Well, where does this get us? We'll tell them, of course. They'll hardly—'

'I'm not sure that we should.'

His head jerked up at that. 'What d'you mean?'

'I've been thinking,' I said. 'This was Franz Wagner's horse. You remember what Annalisa told us, that he joined the circus ten years ago when it was somewhere in the north, and he happened to be working there with a dealer in a horse fair, and he brought this horse with him from the other circus, the Czech one. Now, you can't tell me that if he'd owned a horse trained like this one, and with this sort of talent, he'd have said nothing about it, if there hadn't been something wrong. Why, if he brings a performing stallion with him (and goes on riding him in private, apparently), does he say nothing, not even cash in on what could be a big asset? Well, it's certainly quite irrelevant to what Lewis wants to know, but Franz Wagner is part of Lewis's puzzle picture, after all. 'Anything that's out of pattern,' he said, and from all points of view we could bear to know a bit more about old Franzl. If it comes to that, Tim, he changed his name, remember?'

'So he did. And refused to work an act . . . appear in public.'

I said slowly: 'What if the horse was really valuable, and he'd actually *stolen* it from the circus he was in before? I've a feeling that old Mr Wagner—Annalisa's grandfather—must have known about it, making him change his name and all that, but I'm pretty sure the others weren't told . . . Not that it matters now, it all happened a long time ago, and the man's dead; but if he stole one thing, he may have stolen others, and considering he's somewhere in Lewis's "mystery", it might be worth following it up. If he'd done anything bad enough to lie low for, all these years, you might think that Paul Denver's connection with him was—'

'Wels,' said Timothy suddenly. 'She said Wels, didn't she?'

'I beg your pardon?'

'Annalisa said that when he joined the Circus Wagner they were playing at a place called Wels, in the north, near the Bavarian border.'

'That's right, she did. I say, Tim, you remember she said that the circus was actually pulling down when he joined them? At least, she implied it. If he was actually on the run at the time, what better cover could he have? All the muddle and traffic of the horse fair in the town, and then the circus crossing the border that very night . . . One more man and a horse could easily—'

'The Spanish Riding School was in Wels till 1955,' said Timothy.

The interruption was as brief and to the point as his last one, but, as before, I didn't get the implications straight away.

'Yes? She'd been to see them, she said. What would—?'

I stopped short, and I felt my mouth open as I gaped at him. I don't remember either of us getting to our feet, but I found myself standing there, while we stared at one another.

I said, hoarsely, 'It can't be, Tim. It simply can't be. There'd have been a fuss—police—'

'There was.' He sounded as dazed as I was. 'Wait . . . listen . . . it's all coming clear now. You remember that story I told you on the plane, the one about the groom cutting his horse's throat and then killing himself? Well, I got it wrong. That's an old story, I don't even know if it's true, but I told you, it was never published, and of course I never knew the names. But there was another story which *was* published; I'd read it in one of these books I've got, and I'd got it muddled in my mind with the earlier story.' He took a long breath. 'Do you remember my showing you the photograph of Neapolitano Petra, and telling you he was the one who'd been killed? I was wrong. He disappeared, ten years ago this summer, and one of the stablemen disappeared along with him.'

There was a silence. We both turned like puppets pulled by wires, to look at the old piebald grazing at the other side of the field.

'The markings,' said Timothy. 'How would he do it?'

'I don't know, it would be easy enough–hair dye, something of that sort.' I swung back on him suddenly. 'That would account for it!'

'Account for what?'

'The feel of that horse's coat. I noticed today it was still feeling rough and sort of harsh even though the fever had gone, and his coat shouldn't have been staring any more. I'm sure it was one of the black patches I was touching, you know how brittle and hard hair feels when it's dyed often. It bothered me a bit, it didn't feel quite right. We won't see much at this time of night, but I'd like to take a look at those black patches by daylight! Tim—' I checked myself. 'No, look, it's nonsense, all of it! I still don't believe it!'

'Neither do I,' said Timothy, 'but it fits, you know, it really does. Just think, if it was Franz Wagner, how easily he could do it; take the stallion out somehow–I've read that conditions at Wels were sometimes a bit chaotic for the Riding School, and the local horse fair would make it a bit more so–disguise him, and then simply melt into his uncle's circus, which was luckily just on the pull-down. Perhaps he did it just on impulse, because the cover was there handy . . . he may even have been drunk . . . and then, when he realised what he'd done, he didn't dare confess. And he daren't let the horse perform in public, either, or do so himself; but he couldn't resist riding him in private–it's obvious he's kept him in practice of a sort.'

'But why? If he was going to make nothing out of it, why steal the creature?'

He said slowly: 'I can't help thinking it was partly bloody-mindedness, a sort of revenge. That's what comes through the story as I read it: it said "the stableman" had joined the Riding School from some Army company in Styria, and he'd worked his way up to junior *Bereiter*–that's a rider–but he was a bit wild always, and quarrelled with the senior riders, and then got the idea they had a grudge against him and he wasn't being given a chance. Then he did get his chance at a performance, and turned up drunk, and was put right back to stable-hand on the spot. I expect he'd have been sacked, but they were having a job to get people at all in those years, and he was good with the horses when he was sober.'

Another of those silences. '"Turned up drunk",' I said softly. '"An Army company in Styria." I suppose the Czech circus was just a story they made up for cover . . . Merciful heavens, it does fit. Of course, none of the books would mention the man's name?'

'No, but it could be found out.'

'Yes . . . yes. That's the side of it we'll have to think over.'

'You seem sure they don't know.'

I said: 'I can't believe they do. They gave no sign of it over all this business of the haematoma, with the spotlight–literally–on the old stallion . . . Besides, we can't say a word to them one way or the other till we're sure, and I don't know quite how to set about it. The National Stud aren't likely to tell us the name of the groom and if we ask the police they may wonder why we want to know, and we might get Herr Wagner and the circus into trouble. If you look at it the other way, we ought to tell them first, I suppose.'

'I think we can find out fairly easily on our own,' said Timothy.

'No, we mustn't. We can't afford to go round asking all sorts of questions, for Lewis's sake. I told you the Archie Goodwin stuff was out.'

'Not that. It's much simpler. We can find out here and now. The real Lipizzans–the Riding School Lipizzans, that is–are all branded. I've always felt myself that it was rather a pity to disfigure a white horse with a brand, but they each carry three. There's a big "L" on the near-side cheek, that's for Lipizzan, obviously. If he's bred at the National Stud, there'll be a crown and a "P" for Piber on the flank. And on the side they do some sort of hieroglyphic which gives the actual breeding, the sire's line, and the dam. I'm not at all sure that I could decipher that, but I think if we find he's got all three brands, we can be pretty sure we're right.'

'Well,' I said, 'what are we waiting for?'

The moonlight threw our shadows long and black across the turf as we walked over to the grazing horse. He was out of the moonlight now, and in the shadow of the pines, his black patches showing very dark and hiding his real shape so that he looked, not like a horse, but like floating patches of some moving ectoplasm.

I said: 'You may be right, dear heaven, you may be right. You notice what a lot of black there is on his near side? The cheek, the ribs, the flank–all the places where you said the brands would be?' The horse lifted his head as we reached him, and I took hold of the halter. 'They're horrible great ugly marks, too . . . You'd think it would go to his heart to . . .'

My voice trailed off. The horse had pushed his muzzle against my chest and Tim had run his hand gently but quickly down past the forelock, past the eye and over the near cheek. I saw the boy's fingers, pale in the moonlight, moving over the black skin. They felt, hesitated, then slowly traced out the shape of a big 'L'.

He said nothing. Nor did I. In silence as he dropped his hand I put mine on the horse's cheek. The skin was damp where the dewy grass had brushed him. There, ever so slightly ruffling the hair, I could feel the outline of the old brand. It was there, the 'L' for Lipizzan. And so was the crowned 'P' for Piber. And so was some complicated pattern on the ribs, where, faintly, could be traced something that might be an 'N' and a 'P' . . .

Neapolitano Petra blew gustily at the front of my dress, pulled his head away, and took another mouthful of the dew-wet clover.

Still in silence, Timothy and I turned and left him there, and made our way slowly down the path between the pines.

Here the moonlight didn't penetrate and it was very dark. For a time we picked our way in silence. Then Timothy said rather inadequately: 'Well, it is.'

I said: 'I was just remembering the parrot.'

'The parrot? Oh, yes, I remember, those French commands he gave; they were the traditional high school ones. He'd have picked them up from Franzl.'

'Were they? I didn't know that. I was thinking of the "Peter". It could be his name for the horse.'

We had reached the wicket gate leading from the wood to the circus field. As Timothy swung it open for me, excitement broke from him in a little laugh.

'We're getting good and loaded with secrets, aren't we? Do you suppose this one'll be any good to your husband and P.E.C.?'

'Heaven knows, but I can hardly wait to unload it on him! It's no good ringing him up again tonight: I tried earlier, and they said he wouldn't be available. But he's coming south as soon as he can, they said, and when he does, all our troubles will be over.'

'Famous last words,' said Timothy, and in his hand the gate creaked shut with what sounded like a mocking echo.

Chapter Eleven

A castle, precipice-encurled . . .
Browning: *De Gustibus*

Our arrival on the following day at Zechstein had about it the same curious quality of familiarity that we had encountered at Hohenwald: the circus posters, the slow lumbering of the last wagons and caravans into place in the fields on the outskirts of the village, the big top already up against its background of green; and the now familiar faces and vehicles seen everywhere.

The village lay in a wide valley where a river meandered lazily southward. At this point the valley floor was less than a mile wide, the ground rising on each side at first gently, with rounded hills, then more steeply into slopes of mixed forest—oak and chestnut, beech and holly—towards the precipitous fir woods and, finally, towering silver crests of rock. Spurs thrust out here and there from the valley walls, forcing the river to wind in shining detours round their rocky bases. The village, with its pretty church, its bridge, its mill, its wine shop with the bush hanging outside, was cradled in one such curve of the valley, and it was not until the road rounded the bluff beyond the village that we cold see the castle.

On the far side of the river another great buttress of the mountain had thrust out to deflect the course of the river sharply back on itself. At the end of this buttress was a crag, itself rugged and crenellated like a castle, its precipitous outer side dropping sheer to the river which here slid dark and deep round the base of the cliff. This high promontory was connected to the mountainside by a narrow hogs-back ridge crowded to the top with pines, rank on rank of them, dark and beautiful, contrasting vividly with the sweet green of the meadows below and the blazing blue of the afternoon sky. And, perched on the outermost edge of the crag, like something straight out of the fairy books of one's childhood, was the Schloss Zechstein, a miniature castle, but a real romantic castle for all that, a place of pinnacles and turrets and curtain walls, of narrow windows and battlements and coloured shields painted on the stone. There was even a bridge; not a drawbridge, but a narrow stone bridge arching out of the forest to the castle gate, where some small torrent broke the rock-ridge and sent a thin rope of white water smoking down below the walls. The castle was approached by a narrow metalled road which, branching at right angles off the main road in the valley below, led between heraldic pillars and over another graceful bridge, thereafter zigzagging steeply up to disappear in the thick mountain woods. For all its rugged approach and its carefully preserved mediaeval for-tifications the place was not in the least forbidding. It was charming–not a castle for the guide-books, but a castle to be lived in.

When at length our little car had roared its way up the winding road to the ridge we found that the bridge to the castle gate was nothing like so slender as it had appeared from below. It was a stout well-kept structure, wide enough to take one car at a time. We drove over it and in through an archway into a small cobbled courtyard.

There was very little sign in the hall of the castle that the place was now a hotel. It was a biggish square hall with a stone-flagged floor and panelled walls, and a wide staircase leading up to a gallery. All the woodwork was of pine. There was a green porcelain stove in one corner, unlit at this time of the year, and a heavy wooden table on which stood the register and various other bits of hotel paraphernalia. A man in shirt-sleeves and green baize apron carried our luggage in for us and showed us where to register, then picked our bags up and prepared to lead us to our rooms. I started towards the stairs, but he stopped me, saying with an over-casual air that did not conceal his pride:

'This way, *gnädige Frau*. There is a lift.'

I must have shown my surprise. In a place like this, one hardly counted on modern plumbing, let alone such conveniences as lifts. He smiled. 'One would not expect it, no. It has just been put in. This is the first summer that we have had it. It is a great convenience.'

'I'm sure it is. How marvellous.'

'This way. I am afraid there is a little way to go down the passage here, towards the kitchens, but you will understand the Count did not wish such modern things to spoil the centre part of the castle. It would have been a pity to cut the panelling in the hall.'

As he spoke he was leading us down a long dim corridor, its flagged floor covered with rush matting. I said: 'The Count?'

'The Count and Countess still live here,' the man explained. 'You understand this has been their family home for many generations. They have, themselves, their own rooms in that part of the castle, the other side.' He nodded his head back the way we had come, indicating the rooms to the opposite side of the central hall. The kitchen corridors we were traversing were in the north wing; no doubt the Count and Countess had kept the southern wing for themselves, while the main block of the castle, the centre block which faced the entrance and the bridge, was used as a hotel.

I said: 'Do they run the hotel themselves, then?'

'No, madam, there is a manager, but the Countess herself takes a great interest. Here is the lift.'

He had stopped in front of what looked like a massive pine door with the huge iron studs and hinges which I was beginning to expect everywhere in Austria. Hidden in the stone to one side of it, in another tangle of wrought iron, was an electric push button. The lift arrived without a sound, and proved to be one of the most modern possible variety, the self-service kind of which I am always stupidly terrified, and which has a panel of controls and buttons and switches that look every bit as complicated as the business end of a computer. But it took us safely and smoothly and, it seemed, in about three seconds, to the third floor.

My room was impressive and rather beautiful, placed about centrally on the main corridor, in a jut of the eastern wall which allowed its windows a magnificent view of the valley. It also appeared to include one of the charming pepperpot turrets that give the castle its fairy-tale appearance, the main part of the room being square, but with a wide round embrasure in one corner which had been charmingly furnished with a little writing table and two chairs. There was also in the embrasure a narrow door which must give on to some kind of balcony, or more probably—and much more romantically—the battlements.

Just as I had finished my unpacking, a tap on the door heralded Timothy.

'This is a smashing place, isn't it? But I must say it scares me a bit. Do you suppose one dares to ask for some tea?'

'I expect so, though heaven knows how. Perhaps you blow a peal on a slughorn, or beat on your shield with your sword—or, I'll tell you what, if you look around you'll find a long embroidered tassel, and if you pull it you'll hear a bell clanging hollowly in some dark corridor a million miles away, and then some bent old servitor will come shuffling in—'

'There's a telephone by the bed,' said Timothy.

'Good heavens, so there is. How disappointing. Never mind, you go ahead and order tea. Do you want it up here? I want to look outside this little door if I can.'

The turret door was unlocked, and it did indeed lead to the battlements. There was a narrow walk which joined my turret with another about fifty yards away on the south-east corner of the castle. The walk ran along the eastern wall of the castle, between the battlements on one side which crowned the sheer drop to the river, and the steep pitch of the roof, and ended at the south-east turret in a narrow spiral of stone steps which corkscrewed up round the outside wall and led presumably to the tiny battlemented roof at the top. My own turret was charmingly crowned with a spire like a witch's hat, and had as weathercock a flying dragon. The roof slopes and gables were tiled with red, the castle walls were of honey-coloured stone, and every spire was tipped with gold—here a globe, there a flying swan, above my head a dragon. I leaned over the battlements: the stone was hot with the afternoon sun. A cool little breeze stirred the air, and in it I could hear the deep sound of the river below the cliff.

Timothy said behind me: 'Tea's coming. I say, what a terrific view! Can you see the village?'

'No, but those farms down there must be on the very edge of it. Look, can you see that little white chalet affair, up in the pines on the other side? I think the circus field must be somewhere below that. I remember noticing the chalet as we came past.'

'How far away do you suppose it is?'

'As the crow flies, only about a mile, but by that road, heaven knows. Isn't it a heavenly place?'

'Couldn't be better. Your husband's a picker, isn't he?'

'Invariably.'

'All right,' said Tim, grinning, 'I bought that one. Well, I agree. What time do you expect him?'

'I don't know, and they told me nothing when I phoned. I suppose it's even possible he won't be able to come tonight, but he did say he would for sure, and the circus goes tomorrow. I'm just hoping.' I didn't add that I was praying, too. It was also still possible that he would have to follow the circus into Yugoslavia, and the prospect filled me with fears that were probably absurd, but none the less real. 'I'll ring up later,' I added. 'If he's already on his way I suppose they'll tell me.'

'At least I'm supposed to know him now. I'm sure it would have been a bit of a strain.'

'On me, perhaps,' I said dryly. 'You two seem to take deception in your stride; it's horrifying.'

'I got the impression he'd take most things in his stride, as a matter of fact.'

'You could be right.'

'So our next move—after tea that is—is the circus?' He glanced at his watch. 'There's bags of time, it's only three now. We can talk to them before the first house.'

We had discussed the affair of the old piebald at some length that morning on our leisurely drive from Hohenwald in the circus's wake, and had made what was really the only decision, that we would have to tell Herr Wagner and Annalisa what we had discovered, without waiting for Lewis's possible arrival.

('Because after all,' Timothy had said, 'Franz Wagner's dead, and he's the criminal, not them. And the circus crosses into Yugoslavia in the morning, and after that into Hungary, so if there's to be any question of returning the horse it'll have to be decided today.')

'Yes,' I said now, 'we can be down there well before four. Oh, listen, isn't that the tea coming now? Go and let him in, there's a dear.'

It was the same servant with the green baize apron. He carried an enormous tray on which was a beautiful antique silver tea service, and on a Dresden plate some remarkably small and rather dry-looking biscuits.

I had followed Timothy back into the room. 'Oh, thank you very much. Would you mind putting it here, on the writing table? Thanks. Are you doing all the work here today?'

He grinned as he set the tray down. 'It feels like it, madam, but you could say that this was almost a holiday for us. We've had a big party of Americans who left this morning, and now there is nobody but yourselves, so many of our people are taking time off. There's a circus in the village, and most of them want to go to see it.'

'It's a very good circus, too,' said Tim. 'We saw it at Hohenwald.'

'Oh, indeed? I shall go myself at five o'clock, and then come back to let others go. Most of the servants here are from the village, and they go back to sleep at their homes at night.'

An exclamation from Timothy made me turn. He had been standing beside the window embrasure, and now stared out northward. 'What in the wide world's that? Look over there, over the top of the trees, clouds of smoke. Do you suppose it's a forest fire?'

I looked over his shoulder. Farther north, up the valley, in the opposite direction from the village, there were indeed clouds of black smoke apparently pouring out from among the trees, high up on the hillside.

I said: 'Surely there are no houses up there. What on earth can it be? Do you really think it could be a forest fire, er—?' This to the servant.

'My name is Josef, madam. No, that is not a fire, it's just what we call *Die Feuerwehr*, the "fire-engine".'

'The "fire-engine"?'

'It has a lot of names, *Der Flügelzug*, the "flying train", or some people call it *Der Feurige Elias*, "Fiery Elijah", after the other one in the Salzkammergut. It is a little mountain train.'

'You mean a train, a real train?' asked Timothy. 'Right up there? Why, that's hundreds of feet up, maybe thousands.'

'Yes, it is high, but this is one of those mountain railways, I don't know the English word for them—nowadays they build cable cars, and chair lifts, to go up these slopes, that's the modern way, but this old railway was built, oh, many many years ago, nearly a hundred years ago. It runs up on a small wheel that holds it, a cog, is that the word?'

'Rack and pinion,' said Timothy. 'Works on a pinion wheel and a cogged rail. We call it a rack railway.'

Josef nodded. 'That is it. A rack railway, I'll remember that. It's very popular, partly'—he laughed—'because it's so old-fashioned; the Americans like it. It starts, oh, away down the valley, perhaps five or six kilometres from the village here. There's a little lake farther along, and one or two small hotels, a place for tourists. It's called Zweibrunn Am See. In the summer it can be very crowded.'

'Where does the railway go to? Right up the mountain?' I asked.

'Yes, right to the top.' He pointed again. 'You cannot see the summit from here, though you can from the back rooms. From your room, sir, you will see it. The railway goes right up between this hill and the next, to the highest peak, and up there there is a little Gasthaus—a place where you can have refreshments. You can imagine the panorama. You can see right across the mountains into Yugoslavia, and into Hungary. If you are going to be here for a few days, madam, you must make this trip. The best time is early in the morning; the first train goes up at seven.'

I said: 'I should love to go up, but I'm quite sure I shan't manage it at seven. Well, thank you very much, Josef.'

'Is that all, madam?'

'Yes, thank you. Oh, no, just a moment, please. Has there been any word when my husband is expected, Mr Lewis March?'

'I had no message, madam, and there is nothing at the desk.'

'I see. Thank you.'

As the door shut behind him I turned to see Timothy eyeing the tea-tray with dismay. 'Is that what they call tea?'

'For goodness' sake, it's barely three o'clock. Don't tell me you're hungry again after that colossal lunch?'

'That was hours ago. I say, do you suppose he's gone? Do you think I could nip along to my room and get some of the things I bought? Thank goodness I had the sense to lay in some stores. You wouldn't say no to some really nice *Gugelhupf*, would you?'

'As a matter of fact, no, I'd love it. Where is your room, anyway? Next door?'

'No, it's on the other side, about two down the corridor. The single rooms aren't nearly as grand as this, and mine looks out over the courtyard, but it's still lovely. You can see right away up to the mountain-tops. D'you think it's safe to go now?'

The door shut cautiously behind him. I sat down and began to pour tea.

There was nobody in the hall. Somewhat to Timothy's derision, I refused to go down in the lift with him, but the descent of the wide staircase was sufficiently rewarding in itself, giving as it did on every floor a magnificent and slightly different view of the valley. Timothy had already gone out to the car, and I didn't follow him immediately, but went down the dim corridor towards the kitchen.

I got as far as the lift door without catching any glimpse of the man in the baize apron, or anyone else. Ahead of me the corridor stretched blankly with the doors shut and silent. I went along as far as the next corner and there hesitated for a moment, but just as I turned to go back towards the hall I heard a door open, and next moment an old man came into view. He saw me hesitating there, and approached.

'Good afternoon. Is there anything I can do for you?' His English was only very slightly accented, and his voice was gentle. He had a thin face and white hair worn rather long, and he walked stoopingly. His clothes—of some foreign-looking country tweed—were of curiously old-fashioned cut.

I said: 'Oh thank you, but I didn't want to bother anyone. I know you're short-handed today; I just wanted to give a message to Josef—the man who took our luggage up.'

'Ah, yes, he has gone to the other part of the house. If you come this way I will send him to you.' As we went back the way I had come, towards the hall, the old man added: 'My wife sent for him, but I don't think she will keep him long.'

I realised then who he must be. 'Forgive me, but are you—perhaps you are—?' I hesitated, not sure how properly to address an Austrian Count. He bent his head in a courteous gesture, which was at once a nod and a slight bow. 'I am Graf Zechstein, at your service.'

We had reached the hall, and he was leading the way across this towards a heavy carved door on the opposite side with 'Private' engraved on it in Gothic type, but I stopped.

'Then perhaps–if you could spare me a moment, please, it was actually you I was wanting. I was only looking for Josef to ask him to take a message to you.'

'Of course. Is there some way in which I can help you?'

I hesitated. 'It's rather a long story, and of course I'll willingly tell it to you, but what I wanted to ask you was simply this: is there a stable here at the castle, or anywhere a horse could be housed for a night or two–or perhaps, better still, somewhere where it could be put to graze? You might say I've . . . well, sort of come by a horse, and I need somewhere to put it at least for tonight. If it's at all possible?' I finished a little doubtfully.

He showed not the slightest surprise. 'But certainly there are stables, and if you wish to stable your horse, naturally there will be a place. You have only to tell Josef. And if you wish to graze him there is no difficulty about that; anywhere outside on the mountain you will find grazing; we are not so very high here, and there are many spaces in the forest where the grass is good. Josef will see to this for you. When your horse is brought, just ask Josef where everything is. I myself will give him the message now.'

I had opened my mouth to explain a little further when I realised that he neither required nor expected any further explanation. It could be that one simply did not query the eccentricities of one's guests, or perhaps he himself still vividly remembered a past when everyone arrived with horses; or it might simply be that he as Count Zechstein had never had to deal with any such request before in person. This was for Josef–like, it appeared, everything else. The Count was already nodding and smiling to me and turning away, so I contented myself with thanking him, and then went out to where Timothy waited with the car.

'Sorry to keep you waiting, but I was finding out if we could house old Piebald, if the circus does decide to leave him with us. I saw the Count himself, and it's all right; there's a stable still in commission, and he says there's plenty of grazing outside. He never even raised an eyebrow–in fact, I've a strong feeling that he rather expects his guests to roll up in barouches, or coaches and six, or something of that sort. Anyway, poor Josef's got to see to it. I'm wondering if he'll get to the circus after all. Are you going to drive?'

'Driving up that little road is one thing,' said Timothy, 'and driving down is another. I rather think it's your turn. I don't want to be selfish. And I may say if you think a coach and six ever got up to this castle in its whole history you've a stronger imagination than I have.'

'One thing has been occurring to me,' I said. 'If you're really serious about wanting a job at the Spanish Riding School, you could hardly make a better start than by bringing home one of their long-lost stallions.'

He grinned. 'The thought had entered my twisted little mind.'

'Then you are serious? Good for you. Well, in you get, then, let's be on our way. I wonder if they've ever had a Lipizzan stallion stabled here before?'

'"Airs above the ground",' he quoted, as the little car nosed its way across the narrow bridge. 'Well, I'll bet the great Neapolitano Petra's never been stabled higher in his life, that's one thing. Incidentally, how is he going to get up here?'

'You're young and strong,' I said cheerfully, 'you're going to lead him. I'm sorry I can't say ride him, but that's not possible yet.'

'I had a feeling you had something like this laid up for me,' said Timothy, 'when you said you couldn't do without me. There's always a comeback to that one. What a good thing I had that *Gugelhupf* for tea, isn't it?'

Chapter Twelve

When the foeman bares his steel,
Tarantara, tarantara!
We uncomfortable feel,
Tarantara.

W. S. Gilbert: *Pirates of Penzance*

'But what on earth are we going to do?' asked Annalisa.

It was barely half an hour before the first performance was due to start. We were all in her wagon, Timothy, myself and Herr Wagner, rotund and perspiring, already dressed for the ring and looking extremely worried. Annalisa, in her cowgirl's costume for the first act, was hurriedly making up her face in front of the mirror. Timothy and I had told our story, and to our surprise Herr Wagner had accepted it immediately.

'I believe you,' he said, 'I believe you. I do not even need to see the brands . . . No, no, I knew nothing, and I suspected nothing, but you might say I *felt* it . . . here.' A hand gestured perfunctorily towards his brawny chest. 'I do not pretend that I ever thought about Franzl's horse, why should I? I am not a curious man . . . and what a man has done, where he has been, that is his own affair. If my dear wife had been alive, ah, that would have been different. But I, I ask nothing.'

He paused, head bent, apparently studying the table-top, then looked up and nodded at us, slowly, though neither Timothy nor I had spoken.

'My father? Oh, yes, he must have known. But what would you? He was a man who cared all for his family, and nothing for the law. What would you have him do? Franzl was his nephew, his sister's son, and one must look after one's own. The penalty for stealing such a horse would be very heavy; a trained stallion is beyond price, and besides, it is State property . . .' He lifted his wide shoulders. 'Tell you the truth, I did not know until now that Franzl had been in the *Spanische Reitschule* . . . We had heard nothing for many years, you understand: I thought he had learned his dressage with the cavalry at Wiener Neustadt. He used to speak of his service there. I tell you, in a circus we have many people, of many kinds; they come, and they go. If they tell you of themselves, then you listen . . . But you do not ask. No, you do not ask. We are artists, we of the circus, and we have our own affairs which take all our time, our lives, our—what shall I say?—our whole strength. I think you have a saying, "Live and let live." In the circus, we let live.' He mopped his brow with a vast red handkerchief. 'Do you understand me?'

We assured him that we did, which appeared to relieve him enormously. He became practical then, and brisk, with one eye on his watch, and the other on Timothy and myself, and I knew quite well that he was thinking of his circus's schedule (not the performances, but the frontier passage in the morning) and trying to weigh up what our attitude was going to be.

'There is only one thing to do,' he said, 'there is only one thing that is both right and convenient, and that is to return the horse where he belongs.' He rolled a brown knowing eye at me. 'I am a business man, *gnädige Frau*, but I am also honest, when occasion permits. When honesty and business go together, then I am grateful to the good God. To me, to the circus, the horse is useless. It therefore seems'—he checked himself—'it seems to me right, in whatever case, to confess the whole to the Directors, and return the horse. Especially as there cannot well be any trouble for the circus now. Do you not agree?'

'Certainly.'

'Don't stick your neck out,' said the parrot.

Herr Wagner gave a surreptitious glance at his watch.

'But you also see my difficulty? Tomorrow we cross the border, and we do not return to Austria until the winter, when we come back to our permanent home near Innsbruck. So, as you say, with the best will in the world, I do not know how this thing shall be done.'

I had a look at my watch, too; it was twenty minutes to five. Having found out all we needed to know about Herr Wagner's reactions, I decided to cut this short. I said: 'If you would trust Timothy and myself with the horse, and leave him in our care, we would be delighted to do all that was required.'

Herr Wagner's look of astonished delight did him great credit. So did his protestations, which even managed to sound genuine. But we persuaded him, and he allowed himself to be persuaded. If we really meant it . . . if we could really find the time . . . there was no one with whom he would rather leave the animal . . . he was sure that the *Herr Direktor* of the National Stud would be so overwhelmed that he would render us every possible assistance . . .

And finally, amid a torrent of mutual goodwill, it was all arranged. Even the parrot contributed, though not with noticeable helpfulness. The only person who had said nothing was Annalisa.

'There is only one thing,' said Herr Wagner. 'This is after all a valuable horse, and he was stolen, and his value has been much diminished. Though I myself and the circus cannot well be blamed, there will be questions, and there may be a certain unpleasantness . . . There may even be proceedings. If this should happen—'

'Don't worry about that now,' I said. 'Neither Timothy nor I will get into trouble, and I don't see that you can, either. In any case, if they want to see you, you'll be coming back before winter. Be sure we'll make it very clear that neither of you knew a thing about it till we told you.'

'That's right,' said Timothy.

Annalisa, her face bright with paint, but still with that strained look about

her eyes, had been sitting down, listening in silence to the conversation.
Now her eyes lifted, and she said, very quietly:

'I did know about it.'

Her father swung round. '*You knew?* You knew about this?'

She nodded. 'Two days ago I knew.'

'Two days? Then you mean–it was not from Franzl—'

'No, no, indeed not. It was only when Vanessa operated, on Sunday
night. She wanted the instrument case for the operation, and afterwards
when I washed the instruments and put them away, I found . . . these.'

From the bench beside her she lifted the instrument case, opened it, and
pulled out the bottom drawer, where one usually keeps papers–prescription
forms, folders about new drugs, and so on. She lifted some of these out, and
there underneath was a bundle of newspaper clippings. Naturally I couldn't
read them, but I could see the repetition of the name 'Neapolitano Petra'
and the photographs, in different poses, of the great stallion; and Timothy
told me afterwards that they all related to the stallion's disappearance.
These, now, Annalisa spread before us on the table, with the gesture of one
who does in literal fact throw her cards on the table, and herself on the
mercy of her audience.

'And there is this,' she said.

She dropped the last piece of paper on top of the rest. This was a
photograph, yellow and frayed at the edges, of a white horse standing by a
stable door, and beside him a man in the uniform of the Spanish Riding
School.

As Herr Wagner reached for it, she laid her final trophy on the table, the
brown tube labelled 'Koloston', which had fleetingly caught my eye while I
was operating.

I picked it up. 'What's this? I saw it there, and I just thought it must be
the German trade name for some sort of ointment. Don't tell me . . . It's hair
dye?'

She nodded dumbly, then turned to her father. '*Papa*—'

He took no notice. He was shaking his head over the cuttings, looking at
once shocked and deeply touched.

'Franzl,' he said. 'So it is true . . . All this time. Poor Franzl.'

I said gently to Annalisa: 'Why are you worrying so? You could have done
nothing. In any case, we'll say you didn't know till we told you. Even if
you'd wanted to, you couldn't have done much before today.'

'I know. But it is not this'–with a gesture to the clippings–'that troubles
me.' She turned her eyes back to her father, and I saw they had filled with
tears. 'You see, when poor Uncle Franzl was dying, he must have tried to
tell me. Now, when I read these papers, I know what he said. He was trying
to tell me about the horse. He said its name . . . over and over he said its
name, and he spoke of "the Lipizzaner", but of course I thought he meant
Maestoso Leda. I thought he was worrying in case Leda was hurt in the fire.
We could only hear a few snatches of what he said; he spoke of Vienna, and
"the Lipizzaner", and even of his harness . . . and now I know he was telling
us to take Neapolitano Petra back to Vienna, even his saddle and bridle,
which came with him. "*Neapolitano Petra's Sattel*", he said, and we
thought he spoke of a "Neapolitan saddle", and this puzzled us, because

there is no such thing here. But this is what he must have meant. It is the one I use for Maestoso Leda.' A tear ran glassily over the blackened lashes. 'We did not understand, and he was trying to confess, to make . . . to make . . .' She faltered over the word.

'Reparation,' I said.

Her father patted her hand. 'Do not trouble yourself, my Liesl, we shall make it now.' He added some soft phrases in German which made her nod, and dry her eyes, then, with another glance at his watch, he became again his brisk self. 'I shall have to go. If you would prefer to stay, and talk again later . . . ?'

I shook my head. 'There's no need, if you're satisfied. We'll take the horse straight away, if we may, and deal with the next stage of the problem as it comes. The only thing that bothers me is what we're going to do if they don't want him back at the Stud now?'

Timothy said promptly: 'I'll have him.'

'And if you don't get your job, what then? Ship him back to England? What would your mother say?'

He grinned, and made a little grimace which showed all too clearly how far in the last couple of days he had come from those apron strings.

Herr Wagner was on his feet. 'They will take him. You need have no fear of that. Their stallions live for thirty years, and when they die they are remembered. His name will still be on his stall, and fresh straw waiting. And now I must go. It is time. But there is a little matter of recompense; there will be all the trouble to which you will be put, the trouble and expense that we cannot expect you to bear for yourselves. This is ours. There will be the matter of a horsebox on the train from here to Köflach, for Piber, and other things. You will let me know.'

I started to say something, but he waved it aside with sudden, unanswerable simplicity.

'You must allow me to make this reparation at least. My cousin Franzl would rest more easily if he knew.'

'Very well,' I said, 'I'll let you know the cost.'

He fished in some inner pocket and produced a card. 'Here is my address, the most permanent address I have; our winter quarters near Innsbruck. And perhaps you will leave yours with us? Now, there is also the matter of your own professional services towards the horse—'

But this I would not allow, and he made no attempt to override me, but merely thanked me again, and then, with more protestations of goodwill and gratitude, relieved and beaming, he took his leave.

We went with Annalisa down to the stable tent. Elemer was busy with the white stallion, while the ugly pied horse she used for the rodeo was saddled and waiting, with Rudi at its head.

Annalisa plunged into rapid explanations in German, while the other horses, ready for the ring, were already streaming past with tossing manes and tails, and the music sounded loudly from the big top. Old Piebald flung his head up and whickered at the sight of me, and we went into the stall, where presently Annalisa followed us.

'I have told them—not everything, but that you are to take the horse. Elemer will help you—Oh!' Her hand went to her mouth.

'What is it?'

'The saddle! I was forgetting the saddle . . . You must take that, too.' She swung back to the men. 'Elemer, Rudi—'

'Look,' I said quickly, 'if it's on your horse, why not leave it? I'm sure it doesn't matter. We can take another if you insist, but I doubt if they'll bother about a thing like that.'

But she persisted, obviously intent on purging the Circus Wagner of theft as completely as possible. She directed another flood of German to Elemer, and Timothy crossed the stable to help him lift the jewelled saddle off the white stallion. 'In any case,' said Annalisa to me, 'you may need a saddle, and I wish you to take his own. But you see how we have decorated it for the circus . . . all those jewels . . . if I had had time to take them off—'

I laughed. 'I see what you mean. It's not exactly what they're used to at the Spanish Riding School! But don't worry about it, I'll take them off before we send it back. If you want the jewels back, you'll have to tell me how to send them. Would the Innsbruck address be all right, the one your father gave me?'

She shook her head. 'No, they're nothing, they are glass, stage pieces only. Please keep them, and do as you wish with them. Some of them are quite pretty, and I should like you to have—' But there Rudi interrupted with something in German, and she said quickly: 'There is the music. I must go. Goodbye, goodbye and thank you. God be with you both.'

She leaned forward suddenly, light as a dandelion puff, and kissed Timothy on the mouth. Then, with a hand from Rudi, she was up in the saddle, and the pied horse, with a jingle of curb chains and a thudding of hairy hoofs, was gone through the curtains at the back of the big top.

Timothy, laden with the saddle, stood staring after her. Elemer said something to Rudi, who, smiling, went off down the stable. The dwarf came across.

'I have sent him to get a bridle. How will you take the horse?'

'We're staying up at the castle,' I said. 'Tim's going to lead him up there, and I've made arrangements for him to be stabled. I can take the saddle up myself in the car.'

'I'm afraid you will have a lot of work to make it plain again.'

'Think nothing of it, I'll do it tonight. Look, are you sure she won't want the trimmings back? Some of them are awfully pretty . . . Look at this one. You know, that would look lovely on a dress—stage jewellery, of course, but it's really very pretty, with the gold filigree and tremblers, and anyway, it wouldn't matter if it didn't look real: who'd wear a sapphire that size, apart from Grand Duchesses?' I fingered the jewel; it was a big brooch, loosely stitched to the pommel, and flashed in the light as I touched it.

'Why don't you wear it, then? It will suit you. It's loose anyway.' And before I could protest, the dwarf had produced a knife from somewhere, and had cut the "jewel" from the pommel, and handed it to me with a little bow that was unspeakably grotesque, and yet not comic at all.

'Wear it and remember us all, *gnädige Frau*. It is a pretty thing, but your eyes make it look dim. I wish it could be real. Here is your bridle. Let Rudi put the saddle in the car for you. *Auf Wiedersehen, mein Herr,*' this to

Timothy, and then, taking my hand and kissing it: '*Küss die Hand, gnädige Frau.*'

The ungainly little figure shambled out with its comic red costume flapping round the tiny legs.

As far as I could see, from an examination of Piebald's leg, there was nothing to stop Timothy leading the horse the couple of miles uphill to the castle. As I told him cheerfully, the exercise would do them both nothing but good. 'I'll go straight up there myself now, and I'll expect you when I see you. Are you going to stay to see the high school act again?'

'I don't think so. I–I feel this is a good moment to leave on, somehow,' said Timothy, very creditably. For a first kiss it had been a pretty good one, and public, at that.

'For both of us,' I said. 'Then *auf Wiedersehen* yourself, Tim, and take care of our horse.'

I had left the car, unlocked, just outside the field gate. By the time I reached it Rudi had already left the saddle in the back seat, and gone back to his job. I could hear the bursts of applause for the clowns' *entrée*. Soon the trumpets would sound, and the white stallion would be making for the ring–tonight with only half his jewels.

I got into the car, and was reaching for my handbag to get out my key, when I realised that I had left the bag in Annalisa's wagon. Annoyed with myself for the delay–for I was anxious to find out if Lewis had arrived yet–I got out of the car and ran back to the wagon.

The bag was just where I had left it, on the seat under the bird cage. The parrot, which was sulkily eating a tomato, cocked its head to one side, and made some remark in German which sounded extremely rude.

I said: 'Get stuffed, mate,' picked up the bag, and ran down the wagon steps.

I collided with Sandor Balog. Whether he had just been passing, or whether he had been intending to go up into the wagon, I didn't know, but we were both moving fast, and I almost fell. His hands shot out and steadied me. They were remarkably strong, and, startled as he was, he must have gripped me harder than he had meant to; I remember that I cried out, not only with the start he had given me, but with the pain of his grip.

He muttered something, and let me go.

In my turn I had started some sort of breathless apology when his voice broke curtly across mine. 'Where have you been?'

I stared at him in some surprise. 'What do you mean?'

He jerked his head towards the wagon door. 'She's not in there. She's in the ring, or will be in a moment. What were you doing?' His eye had even flicked down to the handbag which I held.

I said, coldly: 'What do you think I was doing? Stealing something?'

'You were talking to someone.'

'Yes, I was. Him.' It was my turn to jerk my head towards the wagon door.

He gave me a queer look from those narrow black eyes, then took a swift step past me, peering up into the lighted doorway. He was dressed ready for his act in the striking black costume that I had seen poised so spectacularly in the lights and shadows of the big top, and he had wrapped a long cloak round himself, in which he looked rather splendid and satanic–and as if he would be the first to think so.

He turned back, looking a little at a loss. I got the impression that he had started something he hadn't meant to–that some other urgent preoccupation had jerked him into speaking as he had done, and that now he was out of his reckoning.

'Do you mean that damned bird?'

'Who else?'

'Get stuffed, mate,' said the parrot, and threw a piece of tomato accurately at the door-jamb. It ran soggily down the wood.

The Hungarian opened his mouth, thought better of what he was going to say, and shut it again. He moved out of the parrot's range, trying to keep it casual. For my part, I was trying not to laugh. If the circus hadn't been crossing the border next morning I would have sent the parrot a crate of tomatoes with my compliments.

'I'm sorry,' said Sandor Balog at length. The apology sat even more badly on him than the aggressive inquiries had done. 'I did not for a moment realise who it was. You . . . are differently dressed. We get many strangers who come round, and . . .' He shrugged his wide shoulders, not finishing the sentence. 'Is the boy here?'

'Yes, he's down in the stable.' I left it at that. I could see no reason why I should offer any further explanation to Sandor Balog. I wondered why, if he had not at first recognised me, he had seen fit to address me in English; but this was another question which I did not particularly wish to explore.

Behind him the music of *Der Rosenkavalier* swayed and swung in the shadows. Fleetingly, I wondered if old Piebald was doing his *pas seul* down in the crowded stable. I rather thought not. It was something kept for solitude.

I said, pleasantly enough: 'There's Annalisa's music now. It'll be you next. I shan't be seeing you again, so I'll say goodnight, and good luck.'

But he didn't move. 'Where did you get that?' He was looking at the jewel on my frock.

'Now, look,' I said, 'I told you I hadn't been stealing. That was a present, a parting gift if you like to call it that, a souvenir. But don't worry, it isn't real, it's off the Lipizzan's saddle. I've had quite a bit of loot tonight, one way and another. Goodnight.'

I turned away abruptly and headed for the gate. I thought for a moment that he was going to say something more, but the applause from the big top warned him and held him back. He turned with a swirl of his black cloak and went rapidly the other way.

The parrot started, in an unpleasant, wavering falsetto, to sing 'O for the wings of a dove'.

Chapter Thirteen

He found a stable for his steed,
And welcome for himself, and dinner.
W. M. Praed: *The Vicar*

It was the Count himself who greeted me on my return to the castle.

It was dusk now, and here and there in the castle light pricked out yellow in the gloom. A lamp over the arched gateway cast a small pool of light on to the bridge: there was another over the main door, and others, here and there in the narrow windows, threw a pattern of light and shadow over the cobbled court. High up in a turret a solitary lighted window made one think of fairy tales again; Curdie's grandmother might sit spinning there, or Rapunzel of the long hair, or Elsa watching for the seven swans.

As I parked the car prosaically at one side of the court, and mounted the steps, the Count came out of the great door.

'Ah, Mrs March,' he greeted me, then stopped, looking past me at the car almost as if he had never seen such a thing before. I remembered our theory that his guests normally came in a coach and six. 'Did I not understand that you proposed to stable a horse for the night?'

'Oh, yes, please, I do, but he'll be brought up later. Timothy–that's the young man I was with–he'll be bringing him.'

'Ah, your man will bring him. I see.' Now his eye fell on the saddle lodged in the back seat of the car. If he noticed the vulgarity of its jewelled and tinselled trappings he made no sign. 'I see you have brought your saddle up yourself. Josef will carry it in for you, but meantime I am sure you will want to see for yourself where we shall house your horse.'

'I think—' I began, but he had already turned away to cross the courtyard towards the west side, the side nearest the mountain, where the entrance archway divided into two what must be the store-rooms and outbuildings of the castle. From the gate to the north-west corner I could see a line of smaller arches; one or two of these were shut by heavy studded doors, but the three nearest the corner were open. I saw something which could have been the bonnet of a car, gleaming in the darkness behind the centre one of these, and in the bay to the left of it the glint of some brightly spoked vehicle which I couldn't see properly, but which from its height I guessed might even be the coach and six.

The Count pushed open one of the doors in an arch which might have belonged to a young cathedral, and took down a lantern from its hook. This, he proceeded to light–not, to my disappointment, with a tinderbox, but with a perfectly ordinary match. Then, with a brief apology for leading the way, he went ahead of me, holding the lantern high.

Not even the brushed and combed tidiness of Tim's grandfather's racing stables had prepared me for such splendour as I now saw. This was a decayed and cobwebbed splendour, it was true, but in the wavering light cast by the lantern held high above the old man's head, the empty magnificence of the stables was impressive in a haunted Gothic way that the comforts of modern living had dispelled from the castle itself. This was the real thing, a sharply evocative glimpse of a whole vanished way of life. Almost the only thing that had survived from this corner of that way of life, I reflected, was the unbreakable rule which still held good; that you attended to your horse's comfort before you saw to your own.

Nothing, it seemed, had been too good for the Zechstein horses. The place was vaulted like a church, the interlaced arches of the ceiling springing from pillars of some dark mottled stone which could have been serpentine. The walls were panelled up to the proper height with what could only be black oak, and the partitions between the boxes—there were no stalls—were of the same wood faced and inlaid. On the wall over each box was carved a large shield surmounted by a crest, and on the shields, dim in the shadows, I could see Gothic lettering. I couldn't read it, but I guessed that these were still the names of the vanished horses, each above his box. It was no surprise to see that the mangers appeared to be made of marble.

The place was, of course, by no means empty. Since the inmates had disappeared the clutter of years had gradually built up in the boxes and the fairway. Through an open door at the far end of the stable I could see—as the Count led me that way—what I had guessed to be the coach and six, standing in the arcaded coach-house beyond. It was indeed a carriage of some kind; the edge of the lantern's glimmer caught the gold picked out on the wheels and doors. Parked beyond it, and looking less incongruous than one would have imagined, was the sleek gleam of the modern car.

The box at the end of the stable was empty, and looked swept and clean. The manger had been scoured out, and beside it was a bale of straw. As the old man held the lantern up I saw the name on the carved shield above the box: 'Grane'. The Count said nothing, and I didn't ask, but I had a strong feeling that the loose-box had not just been swept out and the manger scoured for old Piebald: I thought it was kept that way. The name looked freshly painted, and the metal corn bin against the wall by the coach-house door was comparatively new.

'You will see,' said the Count, 'that there is a peg for your bridle here at the side of the box. Josef will show your man the saddle-room, and the feed.'

I had already decided that the horse would be better out grazing for the night, and I had noticed a pleasant little alp, just nicely sheltered by trees and less than a hundred yards from the bridge, but I certainly hadn't the heart to say so. I thanked the Count, admired the stable, and listened for a while to his gentle reminiscences of past days as he led me back towards the door. Here he stood back for me to pass him, and then reached up to put the lantern, still lit, back where it had hung before.

'Your man will doubtless put it out when he has finished here.' Then, as the light swung high, something about me seemed to catch his attention. I saw that, like Sandor a short time ago, he was looking at the 'jewel' on my lapel.

He was a good deal more civil than Sandor had been.

'Forgive me, I was admiring your jewel. It is a very pretty thing.'

I laughed. 'It's not really a jewel at all, I'm afraid, it's just a trinket. It was given me by someone down at the circus in the village as a souvenir. Perhaps I should have told you before—the horse I'm looking after has been with the circus for a little, and he was hurt, so they're leaving him in my care for a day or two.' I touched the brooch. 'I suppose this is a little token of gratitude for what I did; it's only glass; I admired it and they took it off the horse's saddle for me. It is pretty, isn't it?'

'Very pretty.' He peered more closely, with a little apology. 'Perhaps, yes, perhaps one can see that it is, after all, not real. I suppose that if it were, you would not be wearing it, but it would be safely locked away. A jewel that one can wear without fear is after all the best kind of jewel. No, what drew my attention was that it looked familiar. Come with me, and I will show you.'

He led me at a brisk pace back across the courtyard, up the steps and across the hall through the door marked 'Private'.

The private wing of the castle was in its own way rather like the stables—no dust or cobwebs or clutter, but with the same general air of having stepped back about half a century. The same dim lighting was also still in evidence, for, though the castle's electricity did extend as far as this, it seemed to have been put in by someone with a dislike of modern innovations. The bulbs were small, faint, few and far between. The old Count, walking briskly ahead, led me up a gracefully curved staircase to a wide landing lit by a forty-watt bulb, and stopped in front of a canvas on the wall, so big that—though we could have done with the stable lantern—I could see it fairly well. It seemed to be painted mostly in shades of brown varnish, but, properly cleaned and with better lighting would turn out to be a portrait, a good deal larger than life, of a lady in the frilled and ruffled satins of the era of the Empress Maria Theresia.

'You see,' said the old man, pointing.

And indeed I did. Perhaps originally the brooch had been painted more brightly than the rest, or perhaps some freak of time had left the varnish a little more transparent on this piece of the canvas, but in the dim painting it stood out remarkably clearly; a big brooch pinning the lace at the lady's bosom. And as far as one could make out, almost exactly like the one I was wearing. There was the gold filigree work, the central blue stone, the mass of small brilliants, and the same five dangling 'tremblers'. The only real difference was that about the painted lady's jewellery there could be no possible doubt; no one with that pale hard eye and Hapsburg jaw would have worn anything off a circus saddle.

'Goodness, it is like, isn't it?' I exclaimed. 'Who is she?'

'She was my great-grandmother. This same jewel appears in two of the other portraits, but alas, they are not here, or I could show them to you. They are both in the *Alte Pinakothek* in Munich.'

'And the jewel itself?'

Any wild thoughts I may have had of stolen treasure turning up as circus jewellery and ending up on my shoulder came to a speedy end at his reply. 'Also, alas, in Munich. Most of my family's jewels are there. You may see them some day, perhaps.' He smiled. 'But meantime I hope it will give you pleasure to wear the most famous of them. It was a gift from the Czar, and there are romantic stories about it which are almost certainly not true . . . But romance persists, and the jewel has been much copied.'

'I'll make a special trip some day to Munich to look at it,' I promised, as we turned away. 'Well, that's really rather exciting! Thank you very much for showing me the portrait: I'll treasure my present all the more now because it'll remind me of Zechstein.'

'That's very charming of you, my dear. Now, I won't keep you; you will perhaps want to see your man. But perhaps some time you will give me the pleasure of showing you the rest of the castle? We still have quite a few treasures here and you may find it interesting.'

'I shall be delighted. Thank you.'

With the same air of slightly abstracted gentleness he saw me down the stairs and back into the hall. There was a woman there now, behind the big refectory table which did duty as a hotel desk. She had been writing, and was leafing through a stack of papers which were clipped together with a big metal clip. She was middle-aged, with a squat, dumpy figure and greying hair drawn tightly back. She had pendulous cheeks, and a little beak-mouth pursed between them like an octopus between two stones. I took her to be the receptionist, or perhaps the housekeeper, and wondered why, when she looked up and saw me preceding the Count from the south wing, her face, far from expressing the conventional welcome due to a hotel guest, showed what looked like cold surprise.

The Count's gentle voice spoke from behind me.

'Ah, there you are, my dear.'

'I've been to the kitchens. Were you looking for me?' This, then, must be the Countess. Perhaps the white blouse and flowered dirndl which she wore, suitable perhaps for someone of Annalisa's age, were her concession to her new status as owner of a hotel. She spoke, as her husband had spoken, in English. Her voice in contrast to his was rapid and a little sharp, seeming to hold a perpetual undertone of exasperation.

She turned the exasperation, perhaps tempered a little, on to me. 'Nowadays, it seems, one has to see to everything oneself. How do you do? I hope you'll be comfortable here. I am afraid, just at present, the service is not what it should be. But in these country places things become more and more difficult every day, even with the modern improvements. It's very difficult indeed now to get local help, and we find that the servants we get from the town don't wish to stay in any spot quite so isolated as this . . .'

I listened politely as she went on to tell me of her domestic troubles, murmuring something sympathetic from time to time. I had heard this kind of thing before many times from hotel-keepers in my own country, but never delivered with quite this air of grievance. I began to wonder at what point I should be made to feel that I must offer to make my own bed. When she paused at last, I said soothingly: 'But it's charming, it really is. My room is lovely. And the whole place is so beautiful and really seems admirably kept. I find it so exciting to be able to visit a real castle like this. It must have been wonderful in the old days.'

The tight lines of her face seemed to slacken a little. 'Ah, yes, the old days. I am afraid that now they seem a very long time ago.'

The Count said: 'I was showing Mrs March the portrait of Gräfin Maria.'

'Ah, yes. I am afraid the best of the portraits are no longer here. We have to live as best we can, in ways which we would once have considered impossible.' She lifted her shoulders, solid under the frilly blouse. 'The best of everything is gone, Mrs March.'

I murmured something, uncomfortable and even irritated as one always is in face of a determined grievance. This, it seemed, was one of those angry natures that feeds on grievance; nothing would madden her more than to know that what she complained of had been put right. There are such people, unfortunates who have to be angry before they can feel alive. I had sometimes wondered if it were some old relic of pagan superstition, the fear of risking the jealousy and anger of the gods, that made such people afraid of even small happiness. Or perhaps it was only that tragedy is more self-important than laughter. It is more impressive to be a Lear than a Rosalind.

I said: 'Have you had any word yet from my husband, Countess? He hoped he might get here tonight.'

'From Mr March? Yes . . .' She began again to riffle through the papers in front of her. 'One moment . . . He sent a telegram to us. Ah, here it is.' She handed a telegraph form across to me. It was, of course, in German.

'I wonder if you'd please translate it for me?'

'It only says: "Regret must cancel tonight's reservation",' said the Countess, 'but there is another for you, if I can find it . . . ah, yes, here.'

I took it. This one was in English, and it ran: 'Very sorry unable join you yet will get in touch love Lewis.'

I let it drop to the table. I saw the Countess's hard little grey eyes watching me curiously, and realised that my face must be showing a disappointment quite startlingly intense. I pulled myself together.

'What a pity. He just says he can't join me yet, but that he'll get in touch. I suppose he may telephone me tomorrow, or perhaps even tonight. Thank you very much . . . I think I'll go outside now, and see if my young friend is on his way up with the horse.' I smiled at the Count. 'Thank you again.'

I turned quickly to go. I was in no mood to stay and explain all over again to the Countess about the horse. But if she had been going to query my last statement she got no chance, because her husband was already speaking to her. 'Did you say you were expecting another guest tonight after all, my dear? Who is this?'

'Another Englishman. A Mr Elliott.'

By the mercy of heaven I had my back to them, and was already hurrying across the hall, for nothing could have hidden from them the surprise that must have showed unguarded on my face. In counting the hours to seeing Lewis, I had quite forgotten his alias, and that he had implied he might still have to use it.

The name had brought me up short for a moment, but I managed to pretend I had stumbled over the edge of a rug, and then simply kept going to the door without looking round. But I didn't hurry now. As I reached it, I heard her add:

'He has just telephoned. He can have Room (some number I didn't catch); it is ready. We must tell Josef when he comes back.' She had dropped into German now, but I thought I understood the next bit as well. 'He will not be here for dinner. He couldn't say what time he would get here. He thought it might be late.'

It didn't take as long as I had expected to cut the jewels off the saddle. I carried the lantern into the stable, where I sat down on the bale of straw to do the job, with a small pair of very sharp scissors that I usually carry in my handbag. I'd have taken it upstairs to my room, where the light was better, but it was heavy, and Josef was at the circus, and I hadn't seen anyone else to ask; and besides, it smelled rather too strongly of horse.

So I sat in the lantern light picking at the jewels, while the tiny noises of the stable rustled round me.

The stones were loosely sewn, and came off easily enough. The tinselled braiding at the edge had been half stitched, half glued, and left a mark when at last I managed to pull it away; but nothing, I thought, to matter. The saddle, of soft pale leather with a rolled pommel, had obviously been a good one originally, but it was now very shabby, and both lining and leather showed signs of much mending.

All the same, when I had finished, and dropped the glittering handful of glass into my pocket, I looked round for a peg to hang the old saddle on, safely out of reach of marauders. The rustling in the recesses of that elaborately baroque stable hadn't been imagination; nor had it just been mice. Shabby or no, I wasn't going to leave the *Spanische Reitschule*'s saddle to the mercy of the Zechstein rats.

The only peg that was big enough was broken. It was no use perching the thing astride a partition, and I didn't believe in the old Count's saddle-room—at least, not in working order. In any case I didn't want to wait for Josef, or go looking for it myself in the dark. But the metal corn bin was rat-proof and roomy, and Piebald would not need corn tonight. I lifted the lid and put the saddle carefully down on the corn, then hung the lantern where I had found it, and went out to meet Timothy.

I went out through the archway on to the bridge, and stopped there, leaning over the parapet.

Above me, shadowy, soared the walls and spires and turrets of the castle, pricked here and there with windows full of yellow light. Beyond the bridge, shadow after shadow soared the pine-woods, sharp with their evening scent, and away down below in the dim valley clusters of lights marked the outlying farms. Apart from these the only sources of light in the veiled landscape were the river which still showed as a faintly luminous ribbon sliding along the valley floor, and just below me the pale juts of rock on which the bridge was built. From somewhere beneath came the trickling, splashing sound of the falling stream, but the big river at the foot of the cliff was silent.

The night was so still that if Piebald were already on his way I thought I should have heard the clip-clop of his hoofs, but there was silence, not broken this time by distant music from the circus. Even the faintest echo of this was cut off, I supposed, by the bluff that hid the village from view.

The distant sound of a motor engine broke the silence first, and I saw the lights coming along the valley road from the direction of the village. Then it had passed the road junction at the river bridge, and the lights curled along up the valley, and were lost to sight. Not Mr Lee Elliott. Not yet.

In any case—I had been trying to think it out—he would come from the north. Approaching from Vienna he would not have to pass through the village, but would turn off at the bridge for the castle. If he arrived while the performance was still going on he was unlikely to meet any of the circus people, and if he came after eleven the wagons would be moving south. It was extremely unlikely that anyone who had known Mr Lee Elliott would see the man in the closed car driving rapidly up to the Schloss Zechstein; and indeed, in hoping to arrive as 'Lewis March' he must have reckoned on this.

His use of the disguise, then, could only mean that he planned to make another contact with the circus. And in twelve hours from now, the circus would be out of the country.

At that moment, faint and far away, I heard the sound of hoofs, the slow clip-clop, clip-clop, of a walking horse. They must have started up the steep road. The hoof-beats were steady and quite regular; it seemed that old Piebald was no longer 'going short'. I straightened up and strolled off the bridge and on down the road between the pines to wait for them.

Someone had put a stout wooden seat at the edge of the road, in a gap between the trees, facing outwards over the valley. I felt it cautiously; the wood was still dry, the damps of night had not yet reached it. I sat down to wait. The clip-clopping hoofs grew momentarily fainter as Timothy and the horse rounded some curve of the road, and trees crowded between to deaden the sound. Then, a few minutes later, they emerged nearer and louder.

It was all the scene needed, I thought, looking up where, on my left, the turrets rose dark and faintly lit against the stars . . . the silence, the stars pricking out, the charmed hush of the trees, and now the slow sound of the approaching horse. One almost expected De la Mare's Traveller or some wandering knight in armour to emerge from the pine-woods into the starlight.

The last stretch of the road must have had its verges heavily felted with pine needles, for when Timothy and the horse at last appeared rounding the bend in the road below me, they seemed to be moving as silently as any story-book apparition. It occurred to me then that this—this mundane appearance of mortal boy and horse, treading cautiously up the soft verge to save the lame leg—was every bit as dramatic as any romantic legend . . . the old stallion, deposed, menial, debased by his ugly coat, a sort of Frog Prince who might soon be back in his own royal place. He came now, plodding beside the boy through the moon-thrown shadows, the steely light that slithered across his pied coat making of him just another barred silver shadow. But the black would soon be gone; I had noticed tonight that it was growing out already. As I called out and moved I saw his head jerk up and his ears prick forward sharply, so that for a moment he looked a young horse again. He actually quickened his pace, and then I heard him give that lovely soft whickering through his nostrils. I remembered what Herr Wagner had said: 'His name will still be on his stall, and fresh straw waiting.' I hoped he was right, and, more even than that, I hoped that Timothy and I were right. There would be certain difficulties if the Frog Prince turned out just to be a frog after all.

Then his muzzle had dropped softly into my hand and I was caressing his ears and telling Timothy across him what the arrangements were–including those for Mr Lee Elliott–for the coming night.

I didn't add what was very much in the forefront of my own mind regarding Mr Lee Elliott–which was that, if Timothy and Lewis and I were the only occupants of the central part of the castle, at least tonight Mr Elliott would be able to prowl into my bedroom without any fear of discovery.

Chapter Fourteen

I girdid up my Lions & fled the Seen.
Artemus Ward: *A Visit to Brigham Young*

I must have been asleep when at last he came.

After the usual pattern of Continental hotels, my room had double doors where the bedroom, originally very large, had been reduced in size so that a bathroom could be added between it and the main corridor. I never heard the opening and closing of the outer door, but when the inner door of the room opened I was, it seemed, instantly awake.

The room was dark; the heavy curtains drawn close across the window and the turret embrasure completely shut out the moonlight. I heard the door close swiftly behind him, then he hesitated, presumably getting his bearings. He didn't feel for a light switch, and he must have been able to see something, for I heard the ancient floorboards creak as he approached the bed.

I said sleepily: 'Darling, over here,' and turned, groping for the bedside light.

The sound stopped abruptly.

'Lewis?' I said. My hand had just found the switch.

A thin pencil of light from a small pocket torch shot out to dazzle me. It caught me full in the eyes. A swift whisper came: 'Keep still. Take your hand off that switch.' But even as he spoke, instinctively, I had pressed the switch and the light came on.

It wasn't Lewis. Standing about eight feet away from the foot of my bed was Sandor Balog, with the torch gripped in his hand.

'What are you doing here? Who are you looking for?'

Shock and fright made me speak loudly and shrilly. He had stopped exactly where he was, no doubt sensing that if he had moved a single step, fright would have got the better of me and I would have screamed. Now he thrust the torch back into his pocket. 'Keep quiet, will you? Keep your voice down, and if—'

I said furiously: 'Get out of here! Get out at once! Do you hear me? Get out of my room immediately!' And I rolled quickly over to reach for the bedside telephone.

And now he did move. In two swift strides he was beside the bed, and his left hand shot out to grip my wrist just before I could touch the receiver. It was the second time that evening that I'd felt the strength of those hands, and this time the grip was both violent and cruel.

'Stop that, I tell you!' He wrenched my arm brutally aside, and flung me back bodily against the pillows.

I screamed then, with all my strength. I think I screamed Lewis's name, as I tried to throw myself out the farther side of the bed away from Sandor, but he pounced again, grabbing my flying arm once more with that brutal hand, and wrenched me back on to the pillows, and as I opened my mouth to scream again he hit me hard with his other hand across the mouth.

The blow slammed me hard back against the head of the bed. As my head and body were driven back, he hit me again. I don't think I fought any more; I hardly remember. In any case it would have been futile. The next few moments were a daze of shock, fear and pain, in which, abandoning the attempt to call out or run for help I cowered back against the pillows trying, uselessly enough, to protect my face with my free hand. I'm not even sure if he hit me again. I think he did, but eventually when he saw that I was cowed and quiet he dropped the vicious grip on my arm and moved away from me, back to the foot of the bed.

I put both hands to my bruised face, and tried to stop my body trembling.

'Look at me.'

I didn't move.

He voice altered. 'Look at me.'

Slowly, as if by doing so I would tear away the skin from my cheeks, I pulled away my hands. I looked at him. He was standing now at the foot of the bed, just at the edge of the pool of light cast by the bedside lamp, but I knew that I was still well within reach of that lightning athlete's pounce of his; and even without that I couldn't have hoped to run out of range of the gun which he now held in his right hand.

The gun shifted fractionally. 'You see this?'

I didn't speak. I was biting my lips together to stop them shaking, but he could see that I could see it.

He said: 'You've just seen how much use it is to scream in a place like this. There are two doors to this room, and the walls are half a metre thick, I should think, and in any case there's only that boy here, isn't there, the other side of the corridor, and quite a long way away? He'll be sleeping like a baby . . . but if you did manage to wake him, madame, that would be too bad for him. Do you understand?'

I understood very well. This time I nodded.

'All right . . . and if you try to touch that telephone again it will also be too bad for you.'

'What do you want?' I had meant it to sound furious, but my voice came out in a sort of thin whisper, and I cleared my throat and tried again. It still didn't sound like my own voice at all, and I saw him smile. At the smile, some tiny seed of anger stirred somewhere inside me, sending a flickering thread of warmth through the cold and the fear.

'You were expecting someone, weren't you?' The smile grew. 'Or do you welcome all comers to your room, madame?' He lounged against the foot of the bed, holding the pistol carelessly, his look at once contemptuous and appraising. Deep inside me the little flame caught and began to burn. I said, and was pleased to hear how steady and cold my voice sounded: 'You can see how much I welcomed you.'

'Ah, yes, the virtuous lady. You thought the husband had managed to get here after all, yes?'

So the first remark had been no more than a thug's routine insult. He contrived in some way to make the second sound equally offensive, and I managed to wonder fleetingly why any normal woman hates to be called 'virtuous'. But this was no more than a passing irony; with his mention of my husband, the immediate fears for myself had fled, and I had begun to think.

The thug knew that Lewis had been due. He had discovered that Lewis was delayed. Therefore, apparently, he had broken into my room to tackle me alone . . . Without knowing anything further, I accepted Sandor Balog at this point as the enemy in Lewis's shadowy assignment, as the centre of the circus 'mystery'. No doubt I should know soon enough if he had come to find out from me anything about Lewis . . .

My heart was beating in my throat somewhere. I swallowed, and said, fairly creditably:

'You didn't come here to be offensive. What did you come for? What is it to you when my husband is expected?'

'Nothing, my dear lady, except that perhaps I could not have come . . . like this . . . if he had been here.'

'How did you know he wasn't here? If it comes to that, how did you know he was expected? I didn't tell anyone at the circus.'

A quick shrug of the broad shoulders. He still looked very much the circus athlete. He had, of course, changed from his performer's outfit, but he was still wearing black–tight dark trousers and a black leather jacket which looked as supple and sleek with muscle as the skin of a wild animal. 'You don't imagine I would come up and break into a place like this without finding all about it first, do you? Some of the servants live in the village. They were at the performance, and it was easy to talk to them afterwards and find out who the guests were. In this part of the world it is not customary for hotels to lock their doors at night, and I imagined that, short-handed as they were, there would be no night porter on duty . . . at any rate, not all night. So there was nothing to do but walk in and look at the register to find your room number–and make sure that he had not come after all.' That grin again. 'So don't try to frighten me, will you, madame, by persuading me your husband's going to come in and catch me here. And even if he did'–a brief gesture with the gun–'I could deal with him as easily as with you, no?'

'No, you stupid animal,' I thought, but I didn't say it. I tried not to show the immediate relief I was feeling. Whatever he had come for, it was not Lewis, and it was apparent that he had not identified Lewis with Lee Elliott. He could hardly have found that 'Elliott' was expected, since I knew that Josef had only been told on his return from the circus, when the village contingent of servants had already left. So, though Balog didn't know it, Lewis was on his way, and, in place of the bewildered and frightened tourist he presumably imagined my husband to be, he would find himself tangling with a professional at least twice as tough as himself.

I said: 'All right. You've made your point. You've frightened me and you've hurt me and you've made it very clear that I've got to do what you tell me. Supposing you tell me what it is? What have you come here for? What do you want?'

'The saddle,' he said.

I stared at him. 'The what?'

'The saddle. When I saw that brooch affair on you, I never guessed . . . but then Elemer told me about the horse, and said you'd brought the saddle up here, too. Where is it?'

'I don't understand. What can you possibly want?'

'You're not asked to understand. Just answer me. Where did you put it?'

I kept my eyes on his face. Suddenly, I thought I understood only too well, and it took all my self-control not to let them flicker towards the dressing-table drawer where, wrapped in a handkerchief, lay the little pile of 'jewels' that I had cut off the harness tonight.

'It's in the stable, of course,' I said, in a tone of what I hoped was surprise. 'Where else do you think?'

He made a quick movement of impatience, a slight gesture, but one containing so much suppressed violence that I felt myself flinch back against the pillows. 'That's not true. I went there first, naturally. Do you think I'm a fool? One of the servants told me the old man still kept a place for horses here, so I went straight there to look. I saw you'd put the horse to graze on the hill, and I thought the tack would be in the stable, but there was no sign of it. Did you bring it up here to tamper with it? Where is it?'

'Why should I tamper with it? It is in the stable, it's in the corn bin.'

'The corn bin? What sort of story's that? Don't lie to me, you little fool, or—'

'Why should I lie to you? All I want is to get you out of here as soon as possible. I don't know what you want with the saddle and I don't care, and I'm not stupid enough to fight you over it when it's quite obvious I can't win. It's perfectly true I put the thing in the corn bin. There are rats in that stable–I saw traces of them, and I didn't want the saddle left out and damaged in the night. In case you didn't know, corn bins are usually made of metal, simply to keep the rats away from the grain. You'll find the saddle in the bin beside the door to the coach-house.' I had been holding the bedclothes up above my breast, and now I pulled them closer round me with what I hoped was a gesture of dismissive dignity. 'And now will you please get the hell out of here?'

But he didn't move. There was the now familiar gesture with the pistol. 'Get up and get dressed.'

'*What?*'

'You heard me. Hurry up.'

'Why should I? What are you talking about? What are you going to do?'

'You're coming with me.'

I was still clutching the bedclothes tightly under my chin, but I could feel the dignity slipping from me. I felt myself begin to tremble again. 'But I–I've told you the truth. What reason would I have to lie? I tell you, you'll find the thing in the corn bin. Why can't you just go down there and take it and go away?'

Again that impatient movement that was a threat. 'Do you think I'm going to walk out and leave you here to raise the place? Now come along, don't argue with me. Do as I say and get out of that bed.' He gestured with the gun again towards the side of the bed away from the telephone and away from the door.

There seemed to be nothing for it. Slowly I pushed back the bedclothes and got out on to the floor. My nightdress was double nylon, but I felt naked. I remember that the feeling was not so much one of shame, as of sheer helplessness, the feeling that must have driven the first naked man to fashion weapons for himself. It is possible that if it had been I who held the gun I should have felt fully clothed.

I picked up my clothes. 'I'll dress in the bathroom.'

'You'll dress here.'

'But I wouldn't be able to—'

'Damn you, don't argue. Get dressed. I'm in a hurry.'

Despising myself for the pleading note in my voice, I said: 'All right, if you'll please look the other way—'

'Don't be a fool. I'm not going to rape you. All women are the same, they think you've got nothing else to think about. Now get on with it and hurry up.'

I did the best I could on the principle that what we don't see isn't there. I turned my back on him, so I couldn't see whether he watched me or not, but I knew that he did. If he had moved I'm not sure what I would have done, pistol or no pistol. But he didn't stir. He stood stone still, about three yards from me, and I could feel his eyes all over me as I got clumsily, fumblingly into my clothes, and tried to fasten them with shaking fingers. I didn't put on the dress I had worn for dinner; he let me take slacks and sweater and an anorak from the wardrobe. I dragged the things on and zipped them up. The warm hug of the woollen clothing was marvellously comforting, and as I pulled on my shoes I was brave enough to tackle him again.

'And when you've got the saddle, what then?'

'Then we shall see.'

I stood up. My physical fear of him had been so immediate and overpowering that I had not been able to think clearly about the situation, but now, sharply faced with the prospect of leaving the lighted room that belonged to me, and going out with this brutal thug into the dark, my mind had begun to race, ticking the facts up and adding them as neatly as a cash register.

The stallion's saddle, covered with 'jewels': Sandor's solicitude for that saddle (I had been right in thinking he was not the type to run errands for Annalisa): the talk of 'loose stitching', yes, and the brooch which had hung loosely, and which Elemer had pulled off for me: Sandor's eye on it . . . he had presumably tackled Elemer immediately, only to hear that the whole harness, jewels and all, had gone up to the Schloss Zechstein. And now, Sandor asking me if I had 'tampered with it'. Yes, it all came together, with the other facts which (as yet) he didn't know—the Count's interest in my brooch, and the portrait of the Countess Maria wearing a sapphire that was in the museum at Munich . . .

Or was it? If Sandor Balog had, indeed, managed a theft of this magnitude where better could he hide such jewels than among the tawdry glitter of the normal circus trappings? If—as seemed more likely—he was just a courier for the thieves, how better get them out of the country?

So my innocent interest in the horse had pushed me firmly—and right against Lewis's orders—into the middle of this dangerous affair.

And that it was dangerous there could be no manner of doubt. If Sandor had taken my word for it and gone down again to the stable, I could have made my way to the servants' wing for help before he found that the jewels had gone and came back to get them—and me. But he was taking me with him; I should be in the stable with him—alone with him—when he took the saddle out from the bin and found it stripped of its treasure.

One more thing was certain: for Sandor there was a great deal at stake. Tonight he had shown how ruthless he could be, and I had no doubt that he was prepared to be worse than that. This, I was sure, was a man easily capable of murder.

Murder . . . On the thought, the last of the facts fell into place: the burnt-out wagon and the dying words of Franzl the horse-keeper; the insistent mumble (misinterpreted by Lewis and Annalisa) about 'Neapolitano Petra's saddle'. Franzl might (as Annalisa had imagined) have been trying to confess the theft of the horse; but the insistence on something as trivial as the saddle implied that, in the moment of dying, he had forgotten that the horse's name meant nothing to them, and was trying desperately to pass on the discovery for which he had been murdered, and Paul Denver with him. It seemed that the Piebald story had, after all, held a hotter clue than we had dreamed of, to Lewis's 'mystery'.

And what had been worth two deaths to Sandor Balog then, might be worth another now.

Well, no jewels were worth a death. And every minute of delay brought Lewis closer. I said quickly: 'Just a minute. This saddle you're taking so much trouble for. I know why you want it.'

That stopped him. 'What do you know?'

'I know about the jewels you've stolen. That brooch that Elemer gave me that came off the saddle, that was one of them, wasn't it?' I would have liked to startle him further by telling him that I had recognised the jewels, but I had no wish to endanger the old Count by hinting that he had known the brooch. Nor was I going to risk my own neck by knowing too much about Franzl. I went on rapidly: 'You gave it away when you tackled me tonight outside Annalisa's wagon; why should you care what happens to a piece of glass off a saddle? And now coming up here after it, it's obvious, I'd be a fool if I didn't see. Well, it's nothing to do with me, they're not my jewels, and I'm certainly not going to risk anything for them. If you drag me down to that stable now and I show you the saddle, it won't do you much good. You don't think I wanted to take that saddle all covered with circus stuff, do you? I took the jewels off.'

'Jewels,' he said. 'Jewels. You took the jewels off the saddle?'

'Yes, I did. I offered to put them in a box and send them back to Annalisa at Innsbruck but she said she didn't want them. You can take them; as far as I'm concerned, you can take the lot. Only just get out of this room and leave me alone. You'll be across the frontier in a few hours, so why should you worry? Just go away now and take them with you.'

He was still staring as if I had taken leave of my senses. Then I saw the flicker of calculation behind the narrow dark eyes, and acted quickly, concerned not to let him begin thinking. If I could satisfy him by giving him the jewels, hustle him somehow out of the room, get that massive door locked on him . . . He might imagine himself safe, ready to cross the border within a matter of hours, with only me and Timothy—foreigners, and comparatively helpless—knowing something about him. It wasn't much of a hope, but it was all there was. It surprised me, in the fleeting moment I had to be surprised, that Lewis and the weight of his Service should be after a crime of this nature, but if this was indeed Lewis's quarry I wasn't fool enough to think that I could deal with him. I knew what Lewis himself would want me to do: stay safe, wait for him, and then help him to lock himself on to Sandor's wake.

I swung quickly round to the dressing-table, dragged open a drawer, and lifted out the glittering pile of stones which lay bundled in a clean handkerchief. I hoped he wouldn't notice that the sapphire brooch wasn't there.

For the first time, I approached him of my own will, and, ignoring the pistol, thrust the bundle at him. 'Here you are. This was what was on the saddle. Now get out, and I hope it chokes you.'

He made no move to take them. Then suddenly he laughed. It was the sound of quite spontaneous amusement.

I said, disconcerted: 'What's the matter? Why don't you take them?'

He said contemptuously: 'Jewels? Those are jewels only fit for a horse. Or perhaps a woman. Now, don't waste my time.'

Then, as I stood with the things still cupped in my hands, gaping at him, he reached out one of those narrow calloused hands and scooped three or four of the stones from the bundle. He rolled them in his palm, so that they glittered and shone in the lamplight, green and red and something topaz yellow. He laughed again.

'An emerald, and a ruby, and—what, a yellow diamond? Oh yes, they are very fine, these crown jewels of yours.' Then suddenly the smile was gone, and that white-toothed animal look was back. 'These are glass. Fool. Do you think I would waste my time over such things as these? Even if they were real, what kind of market would there be for these things in my country? People over there don't want jewels, they want dreams, yes, dreams . . . beautiful dreams for the damned . . . You can always sell dreams.' With a flick of the wrist he sent the stones flying. I heard them hit the floor and roll away behind the window curtain.

I said: 'You're crazy.'

'Perhaps. And now we go.'

I backed away as far as I could, and came up against the dressing-table. 'And if I refuse?' My voice was breathless. 'You really think you could get away with shooting me?'

'Oh, this.' His glance down at the gun was almost casual. 'I should not shoot you. That was just to frighten you.' A twist of those strong fingers and the gun was reversed in his hand. 'I should hit you with it, see, knock you out, and then . . .' A gesture towards the window . . . 'It's a long drop, I believe.' He smiled at me. 'The only reason I don't do it now is because I still want that saddle, and I don't trust you, my pretty lady.'

He had moved over to the door while he spoke, and his hand was on the knob, ready to ease it open. He slanted his head, listening. Then the narrow black eyes glinted at me, and he said softly: 'Now, tidy the bed and pick up your nightdress. Don't go near the telephone . . . That's right. And pick up those jewels. We want the room to look as though you'd dressed and gone out of your own free will, don't we?'

I obeyed him; there seemed nothing else to do. After watching me for a moment, he pulled the door open quietly, and now was half through it, listening intently for any sound in the corridor. I could hear nothing. I stooped to pick up the red stone. The other two had rolled beyond the heavy curtains which masked the turret embrasure. For the moment, satisfied with my obedience, he wasn't watching me; all his attention was on the silent spaces of the corridor. My shoes were light and made no sound on the carpet. I reached casually through the curtains as if to pick up the other fallen stones . . .

He didn't turn. As silently as I could I slid between the curtains into the dark embrasure, and then like a flash I was fumbling at the catch of the little door that gave on the battlements.

Chapter Fifteen

. . . Blinkin' in the lift sae hie.
Robert Burns: *Willie Brewed a Peck o' Maut*

It opened without a sound, and I slipped out. I could hardly hope to have more than a few seconds' start–in fact, I think I hardly even hoped to escape this way, but my flight had been purely instinctive. There was nowhere else to go.

If I could get the key silently from the lock, and relock the door again on the outside, I could not imagine that he would risk making the noise necessary in forcing it or shooting it open. I had no idea what the time was, but if he had come up after the second house was over, most of the circus would be already on its way. He might well cut his losses, gamble on my having spoken the truth, go down for the saddle and hurry away with all speed.

But I didn't have time to put this lightning theory to the test. Even as I grasped the key to pull it from the lock, he realised what I was doing. I heard a quick exclamation from the room beyond the curtain, and the creak of the floor as he started after me.

I whipped out, slammed the door behind me and ran along the narrow walk behind the battlements.

The moonlight was hard, brilliant, merciless. It showed me my way clearly, but as clearly it showed my running form to Sandor. I was barely two-thirds of the way along between the battlements and the steep-pitched roof to my right, when I heard the door yanked open behind me and his urgent voice. 'Stand still or I'll shoot!'

I don't know whether I believed the threat or not: I didn't take time to think about it. I could feel terror between my shoulder-blades, but I never paused. Like a bolting hare, I ran headlong for the little door that I had seen in the second tower.

I heard him leap the steps, clear down to the stone walk. He landed lightly as a cat. Three more strides and I was at the tower. The door was the duplicate of the one in my own turret. I stumbled up the steps, seized the handle and pushed with all my strength. The door was locked.

I whirled, momentarily at bay, the palms of my hands pressed hard against the door behind me. He was coming. He was half way over. He had thrust the gun into his pocket and both his hands were free.

For one crazy moment I thought there was nowhere to go but straight up the steep slope of the tiles beside me. I suppose it might have been safe enough; they were dry and I was rubber shod, and if I had slipped I would only have fallen back to the walk. But Sandor was on the walk.

And below the battlements was darkness, and empty space, and the distant deep river . . .

Then I saw the steps, a little curved flight twisting up on the outside of the tower and round behind it; the stairway I had noticed earlier in the day, and had forgotten. It went up, not down, but it was the only way to go. I was flying up it, and round the curved wall of the turret and out of his sight, before he had reached the bottom step.

They talk about people winged by fear. I suppose I was, and it must be remembered that Sandor, athlete though he was, had put in two strenuous performances that night. I know that I gained on him up that dreadful twisting spiral. On the moonlit side it was easy, and even when we twisted back into the black shadow of the side away from the moon, it seemed I couldn't put a foot wrong, though I heard him stumble and waste his breath in an ugly expletive, and once he paused, gasping, and called out another threat or command. And then the little staircase whipped round the last curve of the turret and, it seemed, shot me out on to the open leads of the top of the castle.

I was past thinking. I didn't even dare pause to see where I was or what was ahead of me. I had a vague impression of moonlit leads broken by peaks and slopes of tiles tilted and shining in the moon, like icy steep-sided mountains shouldering their way up at random out of a plain; of gold-crowned pinnacles and turrets, of cowled chimney-pots and carvings like great chessmen set out round the edges of the roof, and here and there the great tubes of open chimneys, like ranked cannon blindly raking the sky. In the hard washed moonlight, it was like some nightmare world without plan or relevance.

I ran for the nearest cover, a great stack of chimney-pots, with beyond them the reassuring scarp of a steep-pitched roof.

The leads were ridged, trip-wire ridges, some two or three inches high, every six feet or so. I jumped one of them safely enough and swerved to avoid a broken chimney-pot which was lying lodged against the next.

He was near the head of the steps now. He'd seen me. He called something else in that furious breathless voice.

I could just see his head and shoulders; his feet must have still been five or six steps down. I don't remember thinking at all; it was pure instinct that made me check, turn, stoop for the piece of chimney-pot, and with both arms and all my strength, heave it over the ridged leads and send it rolling straight for the top of the steps.

It went true. It hit the head of the steps with a clatter, and hurtled straight over them and down. It must have caught his legs and swept his feet from under him, for his head and shoulders vanished with a crash, a slithering, and a flurry of breathless oaths, and I heard the flimsy iron railing creak as his body was thrown against it.

I didn't wait. As I dived for the shelter of the chimney-stack, I heard the pot in its turn hit the iron railing, then, seconds later, crash somewhere on the cliffs below, and later again, the dwindling crash and tinkle of the fragments falling piecemeal to the river.

Then I was past the chimney-stack and dodging quickly among the steep rooftop shadows.

I had gained time, but I certainly couldn't hope to dodge him for long, nor hide from him for any length of time in that exposed confusion. What I had to do, and fast, was to find a way down. He would–equally certainly–make sure I couldn't get down the way I had come, but where there was one outside stair, there might well be two . . .

Running still swiftly, but as softly as I could, I dodged past two enormous stacks, through the covering shadow thrown by a hexagonal roof, and ran for the battlements beyond. If there were any stair, I thought it would be on the outside. I had, in fact, some hazy memory of having seen such a stair, but where it was I couldn't in my confusion and terror remember.

The turret with the stairs up which we had come had been at the south-eastern corner of the castle, at the junction of the central hotel block and the south wing occupied by the Count and Countess. As soon as I had gained the shelter of the chimney I had turned north, for it was in the north wing that the servants slept, and where I might expect to find help. Moreover, I hoped that the other corner turret, at the north-east, would have a stairway the twin of the first by which I might get down into the north wing.

I was now half way back along the centre block, about level with my own turret–I recognised the pointed roof and the winged dragon catching the moon. Deep in a shadowed corner I risked a pause to listen, fighting to control my breathing and hear above my thudding heart if there were still sounds of pursuit.

I heard him straight away. He wasn't coming fast; he was some distance away, at fault, casting about like a hound that has lost the scent. But a hound that knows its quarry's there ahead of it, and that it only has to go on to drive that quarry into a corner, will hardly give up and turn back for lack of scent. He came on.

But he cannot have been sure which way I had first run. Now, just as I tensed to bolt again, I heard him stop. He stood there for what must have been a full minute, listening (I supposed) as I was listening. I could imagine him, lithe and tough and black in his sleek animal's suit, peering among the angular shadows for a sight of me. I kept very still.

He took two slow steps forward, then stopped again. I was pressed back into my corner, my hands digging into a crevice of the stone, almost as if I would have burrowed my way into it, like a worm burrowing into a bank. Under my rigid fingers a piece of mortar broke away. It fell into my hand, silently, harmlessly, but the moment's imaginary sound that it might have made brought a spasm of terror so intense as to bring the sweat out on to my face.

Next second the feel of the rough mortar, a piece about the size of a pigeon's egg scoring my sweating palm, suggested something to me; an old trick, but worth trying—and I had very little to lose by trying it. Cautiously, I eased myself away from the stone, making no sound at all, then, still hidden, lobbed the piece of mortar as far as I could the way we had come, back towards the south wing of the castle.

The sound it made, falling with a crack and a slither a long way off, was satisfactorily loud; even more satisfactorily, it sounded very like a stone dislodged accidentally by someone's foot. I heard the creak of rubber as he whipped round where he stood, and then the sounds, light but distinct, of his feet racing back the way he had come.

For a moment I thought of following quietly in his wake, and taking the chance of slipping down the same turret stair; but there was too much open roof to cross, and he might well be watching it.

I couldn't hear him now. It was to be assumed that he was hunting me along the southern wing. Turning the other way, I dodged along through the sharp lights and shadows, stumbling sometimes, both hands spread out in front of me, for so weird was this lunar landscape that, however brilliant the moonlight, one felt as if one was running blind.

In front of me loomed the turret at the north-east corner, the twin of the one up whose stairway I had come. Here, surely, must be the second stairway which I was so sure that I remembered . . . ?

There was indeed a stairway: the head of it lay in the shadow away from the moon. But as I ran up to it I saw that it was ruinous, its top railed stoutly off with timber, and the first half-dozen steps hanging, crumbling, over vacancy.

But beside it, in the wall of the tower, straight in front of me there was a door.

This was like all the other castle doors, heavy, and lavishly studded and hinged with wrought iron. There was no latch, only a big curved handle, which, as I seized it and pushed, felt under my hands as if it were the shape of some animal, a griffin or a winged lizard. The door was immovable. I pushed and pulled, hardly believing that this, which had loomed up in front of me as a sort of miracle of escape, was not, after all, going to work.

I think it was at this moment that it occurred to me seriously, for the first time, that perhaps I was not going to get away, that the thing which happened to other people might, now, soon, be going to happen to me. Possibly the very fairy-tale atmosphere of the castle—the lonely valley, the turrets, the moonlight, the battlements, this door with the griffin handle—the trappings of childhood's dreams and of romance, once become actual, were seen to be no longer dreams but nightmare. Caught up in one's own private world of fantasy, perhaps one would always trade it for an acre of barren heath under the grey light of day.

There was even, set in the stone beside the door, the familiar bell-push mounted in wrought iron. I pressed it. It seemed the perfectly normal thing to do in this crazy night. I believe it would have seemed perfectly normal if the door had opened silently and a wizard had bowed me in among the cobwebs and the alembics . . .

But nothing happened. The door was immovable, blank in the moon-light.

They say that every end is a beginning. Even as I stood there, with my hand on the silly bell, feeling the courage, and even the driving fear, spill out of me to leave me sprung and spent, I remembered where I had seen the other stair.

For me it couldn't have been better placed. It was a wide stone stairway leading down beside one of the gate towers–the twin turrets which flanked the main gateway at the bridge. Originally these towers had been joined by a stretch of machicolated curtain wall, a narrow catwalk above the gate, but this had fallen into disrepair and was a mere skeleton, simply an arched span of crumbling stone joining the two towers. The southern gate tower, similarly, had fallen into ruin, and had been left in its decay with its stairway fallen away and its roof sticking up like a jagged tooth. But the northerly one, I knew, was whole and perfectly negotiable, and it gave on the courtyard and the steps and the front door of the castle and the bridge and the road up which Lewis would be coming . . .

There was still no sign of Sandor. Chin on shoulder I slithered out of the shadow of the turret, round the curve, and then ran and dodged my crazy way along the rooftop towards the gate tower on the west front.

I was right. The stairway was there. And it was open. The head of it lay full in the moonlight, fifty yards ahead of me. As I burst out of shadow into the full glare of the moon, running, I saw Sandor again. He had done just as I had hoped. He had run right round the other wing of the castle, and was now heading for the opposite side of the gate–the side with the broken turret.

He had seen me. I saw the gun flash threateningly into his hand; but I knew that, here of all places, he wouldn't dare to shoot. In any case I couldn't go back; there was nowhere to go back to; he could reach the turret up which we had come before I could. And I could get down to the courtyard, down my stairway. He couldn't. His was broken, the turret itself just a jut of crumbling fangs. To get to me he would have to go all the way back. I ran forward.

I had run twenty yards, not looking at him, my whole being intent simply on the head of that stone staircase, when I suddenly saw what he was doing. I had forgotten who–or what–Sandor was. To a man who worked daily on the high wire, a nine-inch wall, in whatever state of repair, was as wide as a motorway. He never even hesitated. He went up that broken turret like a leaping cat, and then was on top of the arch and running–not walking, running–across it towards me.

As I stopped dead, I saw something else. Away below, down the hillside, down among the dark trees away to the right, I thought I saw the lights of a moving car.

It was silly, it was futile, but I screamed his name. '*Lewis, Lewis!*' I doubt

if the cry could have been heard from farther than ten yards away; it came
out only as a sort of sobbing gasp, not even as loud as the cry of an owl.
Sandor was three brisk strides from the end of the arch, straight above the
stair head. I turned and ran back the way I had come.

He leapt down to the leads and came after me.

At least now I knew my way, and at least I now knew he didn't intend to
shoot me. With a thirty-yard lead I might yet make the corner turret and the
steps down to my own room. And now there would be someone to run to.
Lewis.

Almost immediately I realised that, even with the lead I had, I couldn't
hope to do it. My very fear had exhausted me, and Sandor's physical
strength and fitness were far greater than my own . . . I didn't have my
hands held in front of me now. Blind or not, I simply ran as hard as I could
back the way I had come along the rooftop maze of the north wing, round
the turret where that nightmare magic door stood in the shadows fast
shut . . .

It was wide open.

I was almost past it when I saw, out of the corner of my eye, the blank,
black oblong of the open door. Sandor was barely ten yards behind me. I
could never reach my own turret now. This, whatever it was, was the only
port in a storm. I jerked round like a doubling hare and almost fell through
the open door.

He overran me. My sudden movement, as I seized the jamb of the door
and swung myself round and back in through the gap, took him completely
by surprise. I must have vanished almost literally from under his hands. I
saw him shoot past me as I swung back into the shadow, and then I found
myself sprawling breathless against a slippery wall on the inside of the
tower.

I had not known what to expect inside the door—some kind of stairway,
perhaps; but there was no such thing. As I swung round the door jamb into
the blackness, I found myself on a level slippery floor, and then, as I
staggered and put my hands out to the wall to save myself, the door through
which I had come slid fast shut behind me, and a light came on.

The floor, the shining steel walls, the light, dropped frighteningly
downwards like a stone, and I went with them. It was the lift.

Chapter Sixteen

O Lewis . . . !
Shakespeare: *King John*

There was barely time even to register this. It was only afterwards that I
knew what had happened. When the lift had been installed they had made a
thorough job of it and extended the shaft to the roof to give access to the
rampart walks, and (I found later) a belvedere on the south side. My half
crazy, wholly thoughtless action in pressing the bell-push had summoned

it, and as I had swung myself into the small metal box one of my hands, outstretched and flailing for balance, must have caught the controls as I fell, and sent the lift earthwards.

I hardly realised when the dropping motion ceased. I was gasping and sobbing for breath, and still just picking myself up shakily from the floor, when the drop finished as smoothly as it had started, and with a click the doors opened. I caught a glimpse of some dimly lit passage outside, empty and silent. Dazedly, my hands slipping on the ribbed metal of the lift wall, I pulled myself to my feet, still barely aware of what was happening, and moved shakily towards the open doors.

They shut in my face. The metal cage moved again–this time, upwards. He had called it from the roof. He must have been standing with his thumb pressed on the button, and now, locked in my small metal trap, I was being hurtled straight back to the roof.

I flew at the controls. I had no idea what they were, and in any case all the labelling was in German. But one knob was red, and at this I shoved with all my strength. With a sickening sensation and a jar, the lift stopped in mid-flight. I jammed hard with my thumb at the lowermost of the rank of buttons, released the red, and after perhaps two seconds of intolerable pause I felt the lift drop once more . . .

This time I was pressed against the doors, waiting, one hand spread against the metal, ready to push, the other clutching the only movable object in the lift, a big oblong trough for cigarette butts, a foot long by nine inches wide, which had been standing in the corner underneath the control panel.

The doors slid open easily on to darkness. Before they were a foot apart I was through them and had turned to ram the metal trough between them as they slid shut. They closed smoothly on the metal, gripped it, held–and stayed open, nine inches apart.

It was enough. The lift didn't move. I turned in the shaft of light from its wedged door to see where I was.

I was standing on stone, rough stone flags, and I could tell somehow from the feel of the air around me that this was no corridor, but a large room or space. It was cold with the dank chill that one associates with cellars: and in a moment I saw that this was in fact where I must be. Back in the dimness, the faint glint from crowded ranks of bottles showed me that this was the wine cellar, neatly situated at the junction of the kitchen wing and the central block of the castle. They had certainly made a comprehensive job of the new lift, roof to dungeon. And, I reckoned, if they used the lift to come down for the wine there must surely be a light switch near it . . . ?

There was. My fingers, slithering and padding over the wall to either side of the lift, found the switch and pressed it, and a light, dim enough, but more than adequate, flicked into life just as the lift light (presumably on a time switch) went out.

If the lift had been an anachronism behind the panelling of the castle corridors, here it seemed like something from another world. I was in a great vaulted space, treed like a forest with squat massive pillars which supported the low ceiling on great branches of stone. Stacked here and there between the pillars were the racks for wine, themselves by no means new, but young compared with this Gothic dungeon, partly hewn, I suspected, out of the living rock of the crag. The shadowed spaces between the pillars seemed to stretch infinitely in every direction. From where I stood I could see neither door nor staircase, though patches of deeper darkness seemed to indicate where passages might lead off underneath the rest of the castle.

I swung back to face the lift and tried, remembering how it was situated on the upper floors, to imagine exactly where under the castle I stood now. Somewhere along to my right would be the main part of the castle with the central staircase. Off to my left the kitchen premises, and beyond them the stables and the gatehouse . . .

I bit my lip, hesitating. It was impossible to guess what Sandor's next move would be. I didn't know whether he had seen the lights of the approaching car; I thought not. But in any case it might be supposed that, with time slipping on, he would cut his losses, abandon the chase, and make straight for the stairway by the gate and the stable. Or he might go back by the way he had come, through my bedroom, in which case he would come down by the main staircase . . .

There was no way of guessing. Only one thing was certain, that I wasn't going to stay down here in this echoing vault. I had to get out somehow to the upper air, to the courtyard. And even if Sandor was there, there also any minute now would be my own safety, Lewis.

Only then did it occur to me that my safety was Lewis's danger. If by chance, as he entered the courtyard or the castle, he were to meet Sandor, then I no longer had any illusions about what the latter would do, and Lewis was unsuspecting, and for all I knew unarmed.

Foolishly or not, I was not going in the lift again. I turned to my left, and running between the pillars, began to search for a way out.

I was back in the world of fantasy, Red Riding Hood lost in the depths of the grey forest . . . on every side, it seemed, the vast stone trunks stretched away, ribbing the floor with shafts of darkness. Soon the dim electric light was lost behind the crowding pillars, and I was groping my way from stone to stone, stumbling on the uneven flags, heading apparently for deeper and ever deeper darkness.

At the very moment when I faltered, ready to turn back towards the light—even, perhaps, to use the lift and risk meeting Sandor in the upper corridors—I saw light ahead of me, and soon recognised this for a shaft of moonlight falling through some slit window in the outside wall. I ran towards this.

It was an old spearhead window deep in a stone embrasure, and it was unglazed. The sweet night air poured through it, and outside I got a glimpse of the moonlit, glinting tiers of pines, and heard faintly the sound of falling water. Inside, just beyond the window, and reasonably well lit by the edge of the moonlight, was a flight of stone steps leading upwards. At its top was the usual heavy door, liberally studded with iron. Praying that it wouldn't be locked, I half ran, half stumbled up the steps, and seizing the big round handle, lifted the massive latch and pushed.

The door opened smoothly and in silence. Cautiously I pushed it open a foot and peered out.

A corridor this time, flagged floor, rush matting, dim lights, probably somewhere near the kitchens. To my left it stretched between closed doors to a right-angled corner; but only twenty yards to my right it ended in another vaulted door. This was locked and bolted on the inside, but the bolts soon yielded, and quietly enough I was through. Outside was darkness and moonlit arches and a confusion of massive shapes. I shut the door softly and leaned back in the shadows, getting my bearings.

In a moment I had it. I had come out into the coach-house. The shape looming in front of me was the ancient closed carriage, its shaft sticking up like a mast and bisecting the moonlit archway that opened on the courtyard beyond. Beside it was the car, a big old-fashioned limousine. I tiptoed forward between the two vehicles, and, pausing at the edge of one of the arches, peered out into the courtyard.

This was empty. I could hear no sound. In the bright moonlight that edged the scene like silverpoint, nothing stirred, but at almost the same moment I heard the purr of a car's engine mount the last hill towards the castle, mount and grow and distort into a hollow echo as the car crossed the bridge. Then the lights speared through the archway, and a big car—a strange one—stole into the courtyard, swung round with its headlights probing the shadowed corners, and came to a quiet stop with its bonnet no more than a yard from the open archway of the coach-house.

The lights went off. The engine died, and Lewis got quietly out of the car and reached into the back seat for his bag.

As he straightened, bag in hand, I breathed: 'Lewis.'

He did not appear to have heard me, but just as I nerved myself, regardless of possible danger, either to call him more loudly, or to go out into the open towards him, he turned, threw his bag into the front of the car, got back into the driver's seat himself, and re-started the engine. As I still hesitated, tense and shaking, I heard the hand-brake lift, and the car, without lights, slid forward and into the open arch of the coach-house.

I remembered, then, his trained reaction to the news-reel cameras. When a whisper came from the dark, he was not likely to give anything away to a possible watcher. The car came to a stop a yard from me; he got out quietly with the engine still running, and said, very softly: 'Vanessa?'

Next moment I was in his arms, holding him tightly enough to strangle him, and able to say nothing but 'Oh love, oh love, oh love,' over and over again.

He took it patiently enough, holding me close against him with one arm, and with his hand patting me, comforting me rather as one does a frightened horse. At last he disengaged himself gently.

'Well, here's a welcome! What's the matter?' Then in a suddenly edged whisper: 'Your face. How did that happen? What's been going on? What's wrong?'

I had forgotten my bruised cheek. Now I realised how sore it was. I put a hand to it. 'That man . . . it's that man from the circus . . . Sandor Balog, the Hungarian, you know who I mean. He's here, somewhere about, and oh, Lewis—'

My whisper cracked shamefully, half aloud, and I gasped and bit my lip and put my head down against him again.

He said: 'Gently, my dear, it's all right. Do you mean the high-wire act

from the circus? He did that to your face? Look, my dear, look, it's all right
now . . . you're all right now. I'm here . . . Don't worry any more. Just tell
me. Can you tell me about it? As quickly as you can?'

He had sounded startled and very angry, but somehow not surprised. I
lifted my head. 'You came back as Lee Elliott because you knew about
him?'

'Not about him, no. But I was expecting the worst–having to get next to
the circus again. Now it may not be necessary. If this is it breaking, pray
heaven it does so this side of the frontier. Now, quickly, my darling. Tell
me.'

'Yes, yes, I'll try, but he's somewhere about, Lewis. He's somewhere
here, and he's got a gun.'

'So have I,' said my husband matter-of-factly, 'and we'll see him before
he sees us. What's behind that door?'

'A back passage, somewhere near the kitchens, I think. I came up that
way from the dungeon.'

'My poor sweet. Come on, then, back here, behind the car . . . If he comes
out that way now, we'll get him. And if he comes in through the arch we'll
see him easily. Keep your voice down. Now, please, Van, if you can . . . ?'

'I'm all right now. Everything's all right now. Well, it started with
Annalisa giving us the old piebald horse that belonged to Uncle Franzl, so
we arranged to bring him up here tonight and his saddle and bridle along
with him . . .'

As briefly and as quickly as I could I told him everything that had
happened, even the business of the jewelled brooch and the portrait. 'And I
think he'll have gone back that way,' I finished, 'to my room. There was still
the brooch, and the stones that were spilt on the floor. He said all that about
their not being valuable, but I think he was only talking stupidly to put me
off. "Dreams for the damned," he said he was selling, "you can always sell
dreams." He was still determined to get the saddle, and I don't see why, but
it means he's bound to see if I was telling the truth about putting it in the
corn bin, so whichever way he comes down, he'll be making for the stable,
and he may have seen you arrive–and if not, he'll have heard you–and now
he'll be waiting for you to go in, before he slips out and away. Lewis, if you
don't go in the main door, he'll wonder why; and if you do, and he sees you,
he'll recognise you, and then—'

But he hardly seemed to be listening. He was still holding me, but half
absently, with his head bent, thinking.

'"Dreams for the damned",' he quoted softly. 'I begin to see . . . And he
still wants the saddle, does he?' He lifted his head, and his whisper sounded
jubilant. 'By God, I think you have broken it, at that, bust it wide open! No,
I'll tell you later. Where are the stables? Next door?'

'Yes, that way. That's the connecting door, beside the carriage. And
there's a door off the courtyard.'

'Right. He won't have gone back to your room: I think you can take it he
was telling the truth, and the "jewels" really are only stage props. Why
bother to lie, and throw them down like that, when he'd already had to give
himself away to you, and was probably going to get rid of you anyway? No,
the only reason he was interested in the brooch was because it meant you'd

been meddling with the saddle . . . And he still wants the saddle, which means he'll be making for the stable. Do you reckon he's had time to get down off the roof, pick up the saddle, and get out over the bridge before I arrived?'

I tried to think back. 'It's hard to judge, it seemed like years, but I suppose it's only been a few minutes . . . No. No, I'm sure he hasn't.'

'Then either he's still above the gate waiting to come down, or he's already in the stable waiting for me to go. In either case he'll have seen or heard the car arrive. Stay there half a minute, while I think.'

He drifted from my side like a shadow, then from the car came clearly audible movements, the creak of upholstery, a grunt, a sharp revving of the engine before he killed it, the sound of his feet on the cobbled floor, and finally the slam of the car door.

Then he was beside me again, with his case in one hand. His free arm went round me, pulling me close. I could feel the calm, unhurried beat of his heart, and his untroubled breathing stirred my hair. As my own body relaxed into this unruffled calm I reflected that it was something to be able to hand over to a professional. It was something that that sleek animal in black leather should find he had tangled, not with a stray English tourist and her bewildered husband, but with Our Man (Temporary) in Vienna.

'I'll have to go in by the front door,' said Lewis. 'He'll be waiting for that. I'll see he doesn't recognise me if he's watching, and he won't know the car. I've brought a Merc this time. Then I'll come straight back here, by that door of yours. The lay-out's simple, I'll find it in two minutes. Will you let me leave you here for two minutes?'

'Yes.'

'That's my girl. Now, just on the off-chance he's inside, you'd better not go back in there. Stay out here. Not in the car . . . what about that old carriage? Yes, the door's open. In you go, then, and keep still. I'll be back.'

'What are you going to do?'

'As far as you're concerned, I suspect he'll cut his losses, and he won't know how fast to get out of it. But I also think he'll get in touch with his bosses straight away, and when he does I want to be there. So I think we'll let him take what he wants.'

'You mean you're just going to let him go? Now? Tonight? Not do anything to him?'

His hand touched my bruised cheek very gently. He said: 'When I do lay hands on him, I promise you he'll never walk a high wire again, or anything else for that matter. But this is a job.'

'I know.'

I couldn't see him smile, but I heard it in his voice. 'We both know a bruise on your cheek is worth more than a cartload of Top Secret papers, but the fact remains, I'm afraid, that I'm still on the pay-roll.'

'All right, Lewis. It's all right.'

'Get in there, then, and stay still. I won't be long.'

'Lewis . . .'

'Yes?'

'Be—careful, won't you? He's dangerous.'

Lewis laughed.

The inside of the old carriage enclosed me like a small safe box, smelling fusty and close, of old mouldering leather and straw. There were curtains at the windows, thick and dampish; they felt like brocade. With fingers fumbling in the dark I found the loop that held them, and loosened it, and the curtains fell across the window, shutting out what little light there was. Then I crouched back on the burst and prickly squabs to wait.

Though I could see nothing, shut safely away in the darkness of my little box, I found that I could hear. The top sections of the carriage doors were of glass, rather like those of a railway compartment, and on the side nearest to the stable either the glass was broken, or the window had been lowered and was standing wide. I could feel a draught of air from it, and almost immediately I heard the sound of stealthy footsteps in the courtyard, and then the quiet click of the stable latch.

Now, the old carriage was parked within two yards of the wall dividing stable and coach-house, beside the connecting door. This was shut, but, peering out avidly between the folds of damp brocade, I saw a wide bar of light at the foot of the door wavering a little, but growing as Sandor, flashlight in hand, approached the end of the stable nearest me, where the corn bin stood.

He was being quiet, but not especially so; he must have watched Lewis, the late-coming guest, go into the house; he would guess it was the delayed husband, but might count himself safe enough for the time it would take for Lewis to reach his room, find his wife gone, and start to look for her. All he wanted now was to get what he had come for, and escape as quickly as possible.

There was a soft metallic clink as the corn bin lid was lifted. A shuffling sound followed, and a falling rustle as the saddle was lifted clear of the corn, then it was dumped on the floor, and the lid closed.

He didn't hurry away as I had expected. I strained my ears to hear what he was doing, but couldn't guess . . . I heard more shuffling sounds, even the noise of his rapid breathing, and presently I could have sworn that I heard the sound of ripping cloth. Since there were no more 'jewels' left for him to tear away, he must be opening the thing up. Lewis was right; the 'jewels' were worthless after all; there must be something else contained in the saddle, and, sooner than carry away the whole clumsy burden, Sandor was taking the time to remove whatever he had so carefully stitched into the padding. I remembered his offer to stitch the thing, and its much-mended look.

Two minutes, Lewis had said. With no light to see the time, there was no judging it at all. It might have been two minutes, or four, or forty, but it was probably not much more than Lewis's two, before, quite suddenly, near me, the sounds ceased.

In the silence that followed, I heard again the click of the stable latch, and steps approaching, quiet but unconcealed.

Unbelievingly, horrified, I heard Timothy's voice.

'Who's that—why, Herr Balog! What are you doing here?' And then, sharply: 'What on earth are you doing with that saddle? Look, just what is going on around here? And where's Vanessa? Ah, you—'

The rush of feet; the brief sound of a scuffle; a cry from Timothy, bitten off. A thud, and then the racing sound of retreating footsteps. They made for the stable door, and out, then I heard them cross the corner of the courtyard, to be lost as he reached the archway and the bridge.

'Timothy!' Somehow I got the carriage door open. I stumbled out, missing the single step and almost falling. The light had gone with Sandor, but my hands found the door handle and the massive key of their own volition, and in a matter of seconds I had the big door open and was in the stable.

Moonlight spilled mistily through the cobwebbed window opposite Grane's box. Beside the corn bin, huddled on the floor near the wreck of the saddle, lay Timothy.

I flew to kneel beside him, and almost choked on a cry of thankfulness as he moved. He put a hand to his head, and struggled strongly enough up on to one elbow.

'Vanessa? What happened?'

'Are you all right, Tim? Where did he hit you?'

'My head . . . no, he missed . . . my neck . . . blast, it's sore, but I think it's all right. It was that swine Sandor, you know, the—'

'Yes, I know. Don't worry about that now. Are you sure you're all right? You went with the most awful crack, I heard you clear through the door, I thought you'd hit your head on the corn bin.'

'I think that must have been my elbow. Hell, yes, it was, the funny bone.' He was sitting up now and rubbing his elbow vigorously. 'I think it's paralysed, probably for life, the stinking swine. I suppose he's made off? I say, he was ripping the saddle open. What in the world—?'

'What in the world—?' The echo came from the shadows just behind us, and we both jumped like guilty things upon a fearful summons. We'd have made very bad agents, Timothy and I. It could easily have been Sandor returning: but it was Lewis, looking for one fantastic second not like Lewis at all, but like something as dangerous as Sandor himself, and straight from Sandor's world.

But almost before we had seen the gun in his hand it had vanished from sight again, and he said: 'Timothy, it's you. I suppose you caught him at it. What the devil brought you down? No, never mind, he's gone and I've got to get after him. Did you see what he took?'

'Packets of some kind, flat packets . . . about the size of those detergent samples they shove through your door.' Timothy abandoned the elbow, and began to scramble to his feet. 'He's left one, anyway. I fell on it.'

Almost before the boy's body had left the ground, Lewis had pounced on the thing. It was an oblong flat package, not much bigger than a manilla envelope, made apparently of polythene. Lewis whipped a knife out and slit a corner of it, gingerly. He sniffed, then shook a few grains of powder into the palm of his hand, and tasted them.

'What is it?' asked Timothy.

Lewis didn't answer. He folded the cut corner down, and thrust the package back into Timothy's hands, saying abruptly: 'Keep that safely for me, don't let anyone see it. Are you all right?'

'Yes, quite.'

'Then stay with Vanessa.'

'But I—'

But Lewis had already gone. I heard the door of his car open and then slam behind him as he got in. The engine raced to life.

As the Mercedes swung backwards out of the coach-house I jumped up and ran out into the courtyard. The car swept back in a tight arc and paused. I jumped at the offside door and dragged at the handle. Lewis leaned across and flicked the lock open and I pulled it wide.

'Yes?'

'I'm coming with you. Don't ask me not to, please. I won't get in your way, I promise. But don't ask me to stay away.'

He hesitated only fractionally. Then he jerked his head. 'All right, get in.' As I scrambled in beside him, Timothy reached in over my shoulder and pulled open the lock of the back door.

'Me, too. Please, Mr March. I could help, I honestly could. I'd like to.'

Lewis laughed suddenly. 'Come one, come all,' he said cheerfully. 'It's just as well I've handed in my cards, isn't it? All right, get in, only for God's sake hurry.'

Before Timothy's door was shut the Mercedes had leapt forward from a standing start, swept round with a whine of tyres, and was shooting for the narrow archway like a bullet from a gun. Her headlights flicked on momentarily, the archway lighted, leapt at us, echoed past us with a slam like the smack of a sail. The bridge boomed for a second beneath us, and then, lights out, engine silken and quiet, we were running downhill under the tunnel of the dark pines.

Chapter Seventeen

If Lewis by your assistance win the day . . .
Shakespeare: *King John*

'I don't suppose he's using lights either,' said Lewis. His voice was rather less excited than if he had been driving to meet a train. 'But take a look and see if either of you can see where he is, will you?'

'Did he have a car?' asked Timothy

'A jeep. At least, I saw a jeep parked to one side among the trees when I was on my way up. I had a look at it. I'll bet it was his. See if you can see anything.'

The Mercedes swung left-handed into the first arm of the zigzag and Timothy and I peered out and down, through the black stems of the trees. At first I could see nothing, but then, just as Lewis swung wide to take the next bend, I saw a flash of bright light, momentarily, it seemed a long way below.

Timothy and I both exclaimed together: 'There! There he is!' I added quickly: 'There was just a flash a fair way down. It's gone again.'

Timothy said: 'Wasn't there a sort of woodman's hut away down there? I seem to remember noticing it before. When his lights flashed on, I thought I saw it in the beam.'

'Yes, there was,' said Lewis. 'Damnation.'

'Why?'

'I think I know why he put his lights on. Just beside that hut there's a forest track going off. I can't imagine why he should flash his lights unless he wanted to see his way into it. He'd manage it easily enough with a jeep, but whether we can with this car's another matter. We'll see. Well, supposing you tell us what happened, Tim. What were you doing down in the stable!'

'Something woke me, I'm not sure what it was. A cry or something. Did you call out, Vanessa?'

'Yes.'

'That must have been it, then . . . But I wasn't sure. You know how you lie awake and wonder what it was that wakened you? Well, I lay and listened for a bit, and I didn't hear anything else, and I thought I must have been mistaken. Then–I don't know . . . I felt sort of uneasy; so after a bit I got up out of bed and went to the door. I thought I heard a door open somewhere, so I opened my own door and looked out into the corridor. But there was nobody there, and then I definitely heard a sound. I thought it was from Vanessa's room.'

'That would be when he had my inner door open,' I said. 'You might have heard something.'

'Yes? Well, anyway . . . It occurred to me then that you might have come, Mr March, and you might have been going to Vanessa's room, so I thought I'd just made a fool of myself, and I went back into my own room and shut the door. I was wide awake by that time, so I went across to the window, and just stood looking out. The moonlight was marvellous, and I just stood looking, and–well, thinking . . . and then I thought I saw someone dodging about among the battlements, over by the gate tower. I couldn't see at all clearly, because of the trees beyond, and the shadows, and at first I thought I was just being imaginative, but after a bit I was certain there was someone there. So I shoved some clothes on and ran along to tell Vanessa. I mean, enough odd things have been happening to make me wonder, if you know what I mean.'

'We know what you mean,' said Lewis.

'I opened the outside door of Vanessa's room to knock on the inner one, but that was wide open, and then I saw the room was empty and the curtains were pulled back all anyhow, and the little door was open. So of course I went out on the roof. I was a bit uneasy now–I mean, you and Vanessa might just have gone for a moonlight walk or something, but I didn't think you'd have left the door open, or the curtain dragged back like that . . . In any case, I kept pretty quiet, and I'd got a fair way round the roof when I saw the car arrive. Everything was dead quiet, so I just stood and waited where I couldn't be seen. Then you went into the castle, and you hadn't been gone two seconds when I saw him move. I couldn't see who it was, but it was Sandor, of course. He was on the roof beside the gate tower. He ran down those steps into the courtyard. I looked over, and saw him go into the stable.'

'So,' said Lewis, rather dryly, 'naturally, you followed him.'

'Yes. Well, naturally.' Timothy sounded faintly surprised. 'I mean, there was the cry I thought I'd heard, and all the mystery and everything. I don't know what I thought about it, I thought it might have something to do with old Piebald. After all, he was a stolen horse, and I suppose he's valuable. But I tell you I didn't think about it at all, I just went in very quietly, and there he was on the floor, ripping the saddle to pieces. I think I asked him what he was up to, and then he went for me. I'm sorry if I've done anything wrong and spoilt things.'

'You jumped the gun a bit, but probably not much. He hadn't much time to spare, and I still hope we're not going to lose him. In any case, I'm grateful to you for your care of my wife.'

'Oh . . .' Timothy swallowed, then managed, negligently enough, and man to man: 'Well, naturally, anything I can do . . .'

'Believe me, you've done plenty. Whether you meant it or not, it was a master-stroke getting that package. Now we know exactly where we are. I really am grateful to you for that.'

'Single-minded swine,' I said, without rancour.

I saw him grin. Timothy cut in again from behind us. 'What was it? Something must be pretty valuable.'

'It is. Hang on to your package, Mr Lacy. It's several hundred pounds' worth of cocaine, unless I'm much mistaken.'

'Cocaine! Drugs? Dope rings, and all that jazz? Gosh!' Timothy sounded neither shocked nor alarmed, but only excited and vastly pleased. 'Gosh! I say, Vanessa, did you get that? Sandor Balog, eh? I knew he was a stinker! And I'm sure there were at least half a dozen packets, maybe more. Big deal.'

'As you say,' said Lewis calmly, 'big deal. And likely to be bigger. It is indeed dope rings and all that jazz. I've a feeling that you two little do-gooders with your long-lost Lipizzaner have got a lead on a ring the police have been trying to break for quite some time, but leave that great thought for later: here's the hut. Hang on.'

The Mercedes rocked to a stop. Just by the offside door was a break in the thick trees, where a rutted woodland ride led off, twisting upwards and out of sight through the forest.

'Wait,' said Lewis, and swung out of the car. I saw him stoop over the verge, examining it closely in the moonlight which struck brightly down the open ride.

A moment later he was back in his seat and the car was moving again.

'Not that way?' I asked.

'No sign of it. He's making for the main road, thank God.'

'I gather you don't think he'll be heading back for the circus?'

'I doubt it. He knows your husband's arrived, and that he—the husband—will certainly raise an alarm as soon as possible. Balog can't possibly go over now with the circus . . . not carrying the stuff, that is . . . He'll reckon that that will be the first call the police will make after we alert them, and obviously the circus will be stopped at the frontier and searched from stem to stern . . . if that's the right idiom for a circus?'

'It does seem to be the only one you know,' I said.

'Are you a Navy type?' asked Timothy.

'I once owned half of a twelve-foot dinghy, and I've fallen in twice on the Norfolk Broads. If you think that qualifies me—hold it, he's throwing out the anchor.'

Below us the red lights blazed suddenly. The Mercedes slowed sharply to a crawl. Beside the road the trees were sparse, and we could see over and down the next slope. We were half way down the hill. The jeep's brake lights vanished, but flashed again as he turned out on to the bridge.

Lewis said: 'We'll wait and see which way he turns. Left, for a bet . . . I don't think he'll risk going back through Zechstein . . . Can you see him?'

'Just,' said Tim, craning. 'There . . . he touched the brakes again. Yes, he's turning left, away from the village. What d'you reckon he'll do?'

The Mercedes surged forward smoothly. 'What would you do, mate?' asked Lewis.

'Telephone the boss,' said Tim promptly. 'You can't tell me that blighter's anything but a second-class citizen. He'll not be able to make his own decisions.'

'That's just what I'm hoping for—that our second-class citizen may give us a lead to higher things; if not to the boss in Vienna, then to the local contact. It could be the best thing that happened, your bolting him like that.' I wondered if he was thinking, as I was, of the trip across the frontier which he might not now have to make. 'He's got the stuff on him now—he may think he's got it all—and he's been startled by you two into running for it. He won't be in a panic hurry yet, because he won't have any idea we're after him so quickly, and he's certainly not worried that the police can have taken him up yet. The evidence is, from the way he blazed his lights, that he thinks he's still on his own. So we follow and watch.'

'If I were him,' said Timothy, 'I'd ditch the stuff, and fast.'

'He well may. If he does, we may see him, with luck.'

'Yes, but we've got him anyway, haven't we? Oh, I see, someone else would have to come and pick it up, and you could have it watched?'

It had occurred to me that Timothy was taking with remarkable ease Lewis's change from P.E.C. salesman to armed investigator. But then, I supposed, it was to be expected. Timothy was not unintelligent, and I had offered no explanation of Lewis's original disguise as Lee Elliott; and now Lee Elliott had turned up once more, armed, remarkably well informed, and fully prepared to launch himself without hesitation or question into the wake of a drug smuggler. Timothy must have made some more or less dramatic guess long since.

I was proved right next moment. He leaned forward between the two front seats as the Mercedes swam down the last arm of the zigzag and turned on to the bridge:

'What sort of gun is it?'

'Beretta ·32,' said Lewis, and I heard Timothy give a long sigh of pure happiness.

The car swept silently across the narrow bridge, and turned north into the main valley road. Lewis said: 'Here we go. We'll move up. Thank God for the moonlight.'

The Mercedes seemed to leap forward. Timothy said: 'If he does telephone his bosses, surely one can't trace calls from an automatic telephone? Or can the police do that kind of thing?'

'No. But there's a good chance we can find some contact. You mayn't realise,' added Lewis, 'that in Austria the public telephones are only for local calls. If Balog wants to get to Vienna—or anyone outside this *Bezirk* or district—he'll have to do so from a private telephone . . . and private calls can still be traced.'

'You mean, if he wants a private phone at this time of night he'll have to ask a friend of his, and so—?'

'Exactly. Any friend of Sandor Balog's who lives so near the border, and who lends his telephone at three in the morning, will bear watching.'

'Especially,' said Timothy, 'if the Hungarian Rhapsody ditches the dope there, too?'

I saw Lewis grin again. 'You have the makings,' he said, and then fell silent, watching the road.

He was driving fast now, and for a time none of us spoke.

The road followed the line of the river, twisting between river and cliff, now and again running under trees whose black shadow would sweep blindingly over the car like clouds across the moon, then out again into the bright glare of moonlight which seemed to expose us, lightless though we were, like a fly crawling up a window. Once, I glanced back. High, pale, glinting in the moonlight, glimmered the Schloss Zechstein, tipped with gold. Then the car snarled under a railway bridge, swept round a badly cambered corner, and the tyres were whirring over a stretch of bumpy *pavé*.

'There!' said Timothy.

'Yes,' said Lewis. In the same moment that Timothy spoke, I had seen it too; a small black fleeing shape, the square shape of the jeep, mounting the long hill ahead of us, barely three hundred yards away. For a moment, as he mounted the crest of the hill, he was exposed against the moonlit sky beyond, and then he vanished.

'As far as I remember there's a stretch of wood a bit farther on,' said Lewis. 'He should be well into that before we have to expose ourselves on the hilltop, even supposing he's watching for us. And I think there's a village some way beyond the wood. Get the map out, will you, Van? There's a torch in there. Tell me how far the village is.'

I obeyed him. 'There's a village called St Johann, just beyond the wood. What's the scale?'

'An inch.'

'About two kilometres from here, then. No more.'

'Good. That may be it. There'll be a phone-box there.'

Next moment we in our turn were sweeping over the crest of the hill, and there in front of us, as Lewis had said, was the sprawled darkness of the wood, an avalanche of thick trees spilled down from the mountainside above, and flooding the valley right to the river bank. Beyond this, clear in the moonlight, shone a cluster of white painted houses, and the spire of a village church with its glinting weathercock. Only a glimpse we had of it, and then the car dropped quietly down the hill with a rush like that of the castle lift, and we were whispering through the dark tunnel of the pines. The road slashed through the forest as straight as a footrule, and at the far end of the wooded tunnel we could see yellow points of light which must be the lamps in the village street.

The end of the tunnel hurtled towards us. I think I half expected that Lewis would leave the car in the shelter of the wood, and reconnoitre the village telephone on foot, but when we were two-thirds of the way through the wood, he suddenly switched on the headlights, slowed, and took the village street at a reasonably decorous speed.

It was very short. I saw a little Gasthof with painted walls; a low-browed house brilliantly white for a fleeting second with a great fruit tree throwing shadows against the wall; a well; a row of cypresses against the church wall; a big barn with wood stacked up along its side, and just near it a little café set back from the road, and the glint of glass from the corner where the telephone box stood . . .

And, in the shadow of the cypresses, the jeep parked.

With a whirl of light and the snarl of our engine we were round the corner, up the hill past the barn, and running over the hollow boards of a wooden bridge.

'He was there,' said Timothy, excitedly, 'he was there. I saw him.'

'I saw the jeep,' I said.

'He was in the phone booth, just as you said,' said Timothy.

Lewis didn't answer. Just beyond the village, the woods began again. As the car ran under their shadow, he switched the lights off, stopped, backed off the road, and turned back the way he had come.

He switched off the engine then, and the big car coasted silently down the gentle slope back towards the village. Any noise we might have made crossing the wooden bridge was drowned effectively by the noise of the tributary stream as it rushed down to meet the river. Then we were off the road, and on to the rough grass in the lee of the barn, where fruit trees crowded to make a thicker shade. The big car drifted round through these in a quiet circle, and was brought to a halt into the lee of the barn, facing the road, but hidden from it.

Lewis spoke softly. 'Keep down, both of you. If he sees this he'll think it's just something parked here for the night. If he's at all worried about the car he saw going at a reasonable speed and with its lights on, he'll think it's lost ahead of him. This way, we can see which way he heads when he's finished, and get after him with no time lost. Now, I'm going out to see what he's up to. Don't make a sound, please.'

He slid out of the car, shut his door very gently behind him, and all in a moment was lost in the shadows of the building.

I wound down my window silently to listen. I could hear nothing but the sounds of the night. Somewhere near by cattle moved in a byre, and I heard the sweet, deep tone of a bell, stirring as it were in sleep. In the distance a dog rattled a chain and barked once, and then was silent. Nearer at hand, suddenly, a cock crew, and I realised that the brightness of the moonlight was fading and blurring towards the dawn.

Neither Timothy nor I spoke, but as he followed my example and wound down the rear window of the car to listen, I glanced back and caught his eye, and he smiled at me, a brilliant smile of pure, uncomplicated excitement.

Then, shockingly loud in the still air, came the sound of the jeep's engine.

It revved up sharply, and we heard the tyres whine forward on gravel and then meet the metal road.

I made a swift gesture to Timothy, but it wasn't necessary. His head had already vanished before I myself ducked down below the dashboard of the Mercedes. I heard the jeep's engine roar up through its gears. For a moment it was impossible to tell, crouched down as I was under the dashboard of the car, which way the jeep was heading. But then the sound burst past the end of the barn, and went by within a few yards of us.

He was still travelling north. As the bridge boomed hollowly under him, I risked a look. The jeep was already invisible in the thick shadow of the trees. He was using no lights.

Next moment the car door was pulled silently open and Lewis slid in beside me. Our engine sprang to life, and we were away on the track of the jeep before he had even shut the door behind him.

'He was going at a terrific lick,' I said.

'Wasn't he?' said Lewis. The speedometer swung to the right and held steady.

Timothy's head came between us again. 'I suppose you didn't see him hide the drugs in the shadow of the old barn?'

'No. Nor did he hand them to a one-eyed Chinaman with a limp. But the negative result's as good. He still has them on him, and he has his orders. So you might say we have ours.'

'Orders?' It was the nearest Tim had come to a direct query about Lewis's activities, and Lewis answered him with a calm assumption of frankness that sounded—at the time—not only convincing but adequate.

'I was speaking figuratively. I'm not a policeman, Tim. I'm a private citizen who's walked into this while engaged in a private—a very private—inquiry for my own firm. The common denominator of the two affairs is Paul Denver, who must have come across some clue to this business in Czechoslovakia (where the circus was recently) and decided to follow it up in his own time. His death could have been an accident, but in the light of what's happened now, I'll take an even bet it wasn't. We can take it that Franz Wagner found out about the stuff in the saddle, and talked in his cups, as they say . . . He must have said just enough in front of Sandor to frighten him, and then Sandor may have found him with Paul, and decided to stop him talking then and there. He may have joined the pair of them, waited till Franzl was pretty well incapable, then tackled Paul, pulled the lamp down, and set the place alight. The fact that Franzl had had a fire before may have suggested ways and means to him. How he caught Paul out, I've no idea . . . but God willing, we'll get it all out of him before the night's out. Sorry.'

This as he swerved, with no diminution of speed, to avoid a fallen bough protruding into the road. 'So don't go thinking we've any official standing; we haven't. We were merely first on the scene, thanks to you and your horse-rescue act. And you might say I've got my own urgent private reasons now for an interview with Herr Balog . . . But I've done my best to legitimate us—I rang up Vienna from the Schloss Zechstein.'

'Vienna?' I said cautiously.

'A man I know,' said Lewis. The easy voice was convincing in its very casualness. 'This is Interpol's territory, the Narcotics Branch. I don't know any of the Narcotics boys themselves, but I do know a couple of men in Interpol. I once'—this was thrown quickly over his shoulder for Tim's benefit—'I once got involved in Vienna over a client I'd come to see who turned out to have a forged import licence. I rang up this chap from the castle. It was a lightning call, and all I could tell him was that I thought we might be on to the edge of the drug ring. Incidentally, I asked just for the record if there'd been a jewel robbery of any size, and there hasn't, in Munich or anywhere else. So there's that red herring disposed of, and you can keep your sapphire, Van . . . But Interpol seemed to think that Sandor and the circus might well be the set-up they're looking for—and Tim's package proves that it is—so I'm to go right ahead. They obviously can't give us any immediate help, since we don't know ourselves where this chase is going to lead us, but there'll be patrol cars out any minute now looking for the jeep, and the circus will be stopped at the frontier, and the Graz police alerted to be ready for a call from me.'

'Then we'd better not lose him, had we?' Tim's voice was a touchingly faithful imitation of Lewis's cool tone, but the excitement came through, and I saw Lewis smile to himself. A sudden affection for them both caught at me irrelevantly, chokingly.

Lewis said: 'Officially or unofficially, God help us if we do. Have you got the map, Vanessa?'

'Yes.'

'I want to get up as close as I dare behind him without frightening him. I think now I know this part of the world fairly well, but keep me posted as we go, will you? When's the next turn-off?'

I crouched over the map, straining my eyes. The light of the pocket torch slid and jerked over it as the Mercedes raced along the winding, badly surfaced road. 'We should be out of the trees in a minute. Then there's a stretch of about half a mile along the river. It's clear there; you might be able to pick him up. Then we turn away from the river, and there's a curly bit, back in trees again, I think . . . Yes. Then a bridge, not across the river, but across another stream coming down. Then the valley takes a turn to the left, the west. That's about three miles ahead. There's nothing going off except tracks.'

'Tracks? How are they marked? Double lines?'

'Just a minute . . . Single dotted lines, most of them. That means they're just country tracks, doesn't it? Half a second, there's one with double lines. It's very short; it leads down, yes, it just leads down to a farm. We must have passed that already, Lewis. It was just the other side of that wood. I'm sorry, I didn't see it in time.'

'Never mind. It's very unlikely that he was making for that.'

'Why?' asked Timothy.

'Because then he wouldn't have stopped to telephone, he'd have gone straight on. It was only another mile. Go on, Vanessa.'

'The next proper turn-off's about four miles ahead, in a village. It's called Zweibrunn Am See, and it looks very small, just a hotel or two and a few houses at the edge of a little lake. This road, the one we're on, goes straight through it along the lake; but there's another branching off to the left in the middle of the village. I can't see clearly enough to see the contours, but the road's terribly twisty, and it must be going uphill. Yes. Yes, it seems to be a dead end, just off up into the mountain. The main road goes straight on, and after the village—'

'Zweibrunn Am See?' said Timothy. 'Josef told us about that, remember? He said it was a little tourist place, where the rack railway started.'

'Oh, yes, I remember that. Then this must be a mountain road. Half a minute, I think I can see the railway marked. Would it be a line like a fish's backbone? It goes up to nowhere, as far as I can see.'

'The rack railway?' said Lewis. 'I know where you mean, then. There's a restaurant place, a Gasthaus, on top of the mountain. It's a fair way up, two or three thousand anyway from the floor of the valley. I expect your road goes up to the same place. Ah, thank God we're off that bit of road. If anything should be marked like a fish's backbone, that should.'

We shot out of the deep shadow of the woods into the open valley. Under the racing wheels the road seemed to smooth itself and straighten, and the Mercedes went forward like a horse suddenly given the spur.

'And there he is,' added Lewis.

And there indeed he was, a tiny, racing shadow, barely a quarter of a mile ahead. To our right the river, smooth here, gleamed like silver, and the road lay in a sort of blurred brightness in the light of the dying moon. Along the water-meadows the faint white haze of early morning was rising from the grass. The cattle stood knee-deep in it. The air pouring through my half open window was pure and cold and sharp with the scent of pines.

'Won't he see us?' Tim's voice was quick with apprehension.

'I doubt it,' said Lewis. 'We're not in his mirror yet, and he'd have to turn right round and take a good look to see us at all, and he's not going to do that, not at that speed. If he's expecting to be chased at all, he's expecting the police, and they'd be after him with all lights blazing, I have no doubt.'

'He must have had a fright when we came after him through the village.'

'I'm sure he did, but if we'd been police we'd have stopped then and there. We couldn't help seeing the jeep, and he knew it. He wasn't expecting them to be after him as quickly as that. No, I don't think he has any reason to be apprehensive. I'll try to close up a little, when we get near the turning. We don't want to overshoot him.'

'What are you going to do?'

'Heaven knows,' said Lewis cheerfully, 'play it as it comes, and keep our powder dry.'

'With a Beretta—' began Timothy.

'There's the village,' I said quickly, 'just beyond that curve. I can see the church spire over the trees.'

Next moment the fleeing jeep had vanished round the curve.

'Then hold on to your hats,' said Lewis. 'This is where we close up.'

Chapter Eighteen

What! will the line stretch out to the crack of doom?
Shakespeare: *Macbeth*

Lewis had been right. It seemed that Sandor was not worried about the possibility of being followed. As the jeep reached the outskirts of the cluster of houses on the edge of the lake, we were barely two hundred yards behind him. But he gave no sign that he was aware of the following car. He slowed down for the village street, and when he reached the turn-off by the big hotel, he swung left without a pause.

A matter of seconds later we took the turn after him.

The road was narrow and very steep, almost immediately beginning its twisting course up the hillside. As we turned into it our quarry was already invisible, but even above the sound of our own engine the roar of the jeep's engine echoed back as it tore its way up the narrow canyon between the houses.

Lewis made a sound of satisfaction. 'This is a push-over. We've only to keep a couple of bends behind him and he hasn't a chance of knowing he's followed . . . though heavens knows it may be a different matter when we get up above the tree line.'

'Can you see?' I asked. To me the road was barely visible, its gravel surface pitted, and streaked with the shadows of the houses, and here and there lost deep in blackness under looming trees.

'Well enough.' And indeed the Mercedes was climbing at a fair speed. He added: 'I suppose, Tim, that the biter isn't being bit. Anything behind us?'

'Good lord.' Timothy sounded thoroughly startled. There was a pause. 'No. No, I'm sure there isn't. Should there be?'

'Not that I'm aware of,' said Lewis tranquilly, 'but it's as well to know. He made a telephone call, after all, and it needn't necessarily have been to warn the people ahead of him. My God, what a road! Van, I suppose it's not the slightest use asking you to look at the map under these conditions?'

'Not the slightest, I'm sorry, I can't see a thing.'

'Well, at least there's no need to look for turnings,' said Lewis. 'There'll be nothing going off this but a chamois track. All we have to avoid is running slap into his rear bumper.'

We were clear of the few houses now, and the road, though not quite so steep, was aiming along the flank of the mountain, and had deteriorated into something little more than a track with a gravel surface here and there badly broken. Below us lay the little cluster of houses and the church and the gleaming waters of the small lake. Above us, to the left of the road, the mountain pines were already crowding. The road ran under a dense and overhanging wall of them, like a river under a breakwater. Then at the next upward bend it twisted back and was into them, burrowing immediately through deep forest, only here and there shaking itself clear of trees so that for a few yards the fading moonlight, coupled with the growing light of dawn, could show us the way. Lewis drove with no noticeable hesitation and certainly with no diminution of speed. But I thought it was not a road I would have cared to drive myself even in broad daylight.

As we raced and lurched upwards, bend after bend, I could hear above us the intermittent splutter of the jeep's engine, the sound coming in sharp echoing gusts as trees and rocks flashed between to cut it off. Above the sound of our own motor it came as little more than a recurrent echo for which one had to listen, and to Sandor in the jeep it was to be hoped that the noise of our climb, less audible by far than his, came merely like a periodic echo of his own.

The trees were thinning. The road twisted again under us, and the Mercedes lurched across ruts and swung round another hairpin, running momentarily clear of forest, so that down to our right we got a sudden dawnlit view of the valley bottom tucked between its dark hills. The lake was polished pewter wisping with silver mist. The stars had gone, and the moon hung in the morning air, rubbed and faded like a thin old coin.

The Mercedes came to a rocking halt, and the engine died. Lewis wound down his window and in with the cold damp air came the mountain silence, broken only by the stuttering roar of the jeep's engine somewhere above us.

'The map, please.'

I handed it over, folded open at the place. He studied it for a moment, peering close in the light of the probing torch.

'As I remembered. This doesn't go the whole way up. There's some building marked . . . I don't know what, it doesn't look much, but there's a halt for the rack railway, and the road doesn't go any farther. That's about two-thirds of the way up. The remaining third is only traversed by the railway. The rocks up there look pretty sheer; there are crags marked. The railway goes right to the restaurant on the summit; I suppose it tunnels some of the way. Thanks.' He dropped the map and torch back on to my knee and started the car again. 'I reckon we're almost there now. Wherever he's making for, he'll have to leave the jeep at the end of the road, and that can't be more than about three bends above us. We'll stop while we're still under cover of his engine. Here's a good place.'

A matter of seconds later the Mercedes was berthed deep in the shadow of the trees with her nose to the road, and Lewis was giving us our orders in an urgent undertone.

'You'd better both come with me, only for God's sake keep quiet and keep under cover. Stay about twenty yards back and don't break cover until I give you the sign. I may need you, even if it's only as messengers. Here's the spare car key. I'm leaving it here.'

At the foot of a tree a clump of toadstools showed sharply in the misty dusk. They had long pallid stems and scarlet caps spotted with white—the traditional toadstools of fairy-tale. A small flat stone lay beside them. As Lewis stooped to lift this and thrust the spare key underneath, Timothy said sharply:

'He's stopped.'

'Then come on,' said Lewis, and swinging himself up the bank, vanished at a run up through the trees towards the next branch of the road.

We followed him. The going was very steep; smooth enough, clay and rock covered with pine needles, but here and there the rock was loose and there were brambles, so we went carefully, glad of the now steadily growing light.

The next arm of the track was some seventy feet above where the Mercedes was parked. Lewis, above us, was edging his way cautiously out among the thinning trees, to stand there motionless for a moment, hardly visible even to us. The light was in that curious shifting phase between the clear brilliance of moonlight and the brightening day; where it fell most strongly it was a pearled and misty grey, but everything lacked definition; the trees, the track, the grey rock, the hanging woods still above us, looked as insubstantial and vague as those in a badly focused and fading film.

It was even difficult to be sure when Lewis gestured us to follow him, but suddenly the place where he had been standing was empty. Panting a little, I laid hold of a sapling and pulled myself, in my turn, up to the edge of the road. This was empty. But a faint movement in the trees to the other side of it showed where he was heading up towards the last curve before the building. As we followed, I was thankful to realise that our progress was covered by the splash and fall of a small rivulet tumbling down from some spring and losing itself in a stone-faced gully by the roadside.

Lewis was pausing above us once more, but this time after he had beckoned us up he stayed where he was, and as we scrambled to his level he reached an arm down, pulled me up and held me.

The first thing I saw was the building. This was not a house, but simply a small square chimneyless block with a pitched roof of corrugated iron, set at a passing place of the railway—one of those short stretches of double track where trains can pass—and acting perhaps as a shelter for railwaymen or a place for storing materials. Whatever it was, it marked the end of the road. Outside it the track petered out in a cleared space of beaten earth and gravel which looked like a disused quarry, overhung with bushes and ragged saplings. Just at present the place was a tangle of misty shadows, but backed well into it under some hanging creeper that dangled from the rock above, I could dimly see what I took to be the jeep.

There was no light or movement anywhere.

Lewis said softly: 'There's the jeep, do you see? But he's not there. I've just seen him a little farther up the hill. He's still alone, and it's pretty clear he has no idea there's anybody after him. I'd bet my last penny he's going up to the restaurant—there's nowhere else to go—and he's going up by the railway. I'm going straight after him. Tim, I want you to take a look at that jeep. Do you think you could immobilise it? Good man. Do so, and have a quick look at the building–I don't suppose for a moment that the stuff's there, he hasn't had time, but you know what to look for. Then come on up after us. You can't get lost if you stick to the railway. Vanessa, you'll stay with me.'

We ran across the open piece of road, dodged past the quarry in the shelter of the overhang, and were soon picking our way round the side of the building. Behind us came the faint metallic noises of Timothy tackling the jeep. As we slid past the door of the shed, Lewis tried it quickly. It was locked. 'Well, that saves a bit of trouble,' he said. 'Not that it'd be there, but no stone unturned is the motto of the P.E.C. Sales Department.'

'You've got yourself quite a job, then, considering the terrain,' I said dryly.

'You're telling me. I'm praying to all the gods at once that he'll double straight up to the restaurant and dump it there. Here's the railway, and it looks as if there's a path of a sort running beside it . . . Just as well, railways are hellish to walk along. Can you manage it?'

He was already leading the way at a good pace. The question, I gathered, had been no more than one of those charming concessions which make a woman's life so much more interesting (I've always thought) than a man's. In actual fact, Lewis invariably took it serenely for granted that I could and would do exactly what he expected of me, but it helps occasionally to be made to feel that it is little short of marvellous for anything so rare, so precious, and so fragile to compete with the tough world of men.

'Whither thou goest, I will go. Excelsior,' I said heroically, going after him up the perfectly easy path beside the track of the railway.

This was a narrow-gauge affair, cutting its way up through rocks and trees in what was, for a railway, a series of frightening slopes. Some of its climbs would, indeed, have been steep even for a motor road. I had not before seen how a rack railway worked. Between the rails, which gleamed like steel ribbons with the constant daily use, was the rack, like nothing more or less than a heavy cog-wheel unrolled and laid flat, a fierce-looking toothed rail standing well above the other two. I supposed that some answering pinion wheel on the engine engaged with the teeth of the rack line and held the train, whether climbing or descending the steepest gradient, at the same controlled and regular speed.

We were still making our way through trees, but these were now more sparsely scattered, and soon gave way to the barer slopes of the higher reaches of the mountain. Visibility was still poor. The only movement I could see was that of the mist which shifted and clung between the scattered pines, and once a big black bird—a jackdaw—which flew clumsily down past us with a startled 'Tchack!'

'Where did you see him?' I asked.

Lewis pointed above and ahead to where the line swooped in a lifting curve round a shoulder of white rock. 'Just a glimpse of him there. He was going at a hell of a speed.'

He himself was setting no mean pace. By the time he had reached the same corner I was beginning to feel a little more genuinely precious and fragile myself, but I was able to get my breath while he left me to reconnoitre the stretch ahead of us. Apparently the line was clear, for he beckoned me up beside him again, and on we toiled. At least, I toiled. Lewis seemed as fresh as a daisy. In fairness to myself I thought that anyone would have been feeling fragile after what I had already been through that night. All Lewis had had to do was to drive two hundred kilometres or so since he had left Vienna . . . .

We got along at a fair speed, prospecting carefully at the bends, and making very little sound. Fortunately my shoes were rubber-soled, and Lewis, though not wearing what I had dubbed to myself his spy kit, seemed able to move as quietly as he had done in my bedroom at Oberhausen. And presently there was no need of cover at all, because the mist came down.

I suppose this would in normal circumstances have made the going much more difficult, but it lifted just then the worst of our responsibilities, that of being seen by our quarry; and there was certainly no danger of our losing the way with visibility varying from ten to twenty-five yards. The railway led us as surely as a pillar of fire into the dim heights of the mountain.

But by no means as straight. If we had to keep to its track we had to go the long way round. It was to be assumed that the permanent way would double back on itself to take the easiest course up the mountain, as a road zigzags its way up the steepest slopes. If we had been able to see, we could have short-circuited the curves; as it was, not knowing the terrain, and afraid of where a false step or a false trail might lead us, we were forced to stay beside the rails. There was only one comfort in this, that, unless he knew the mountainside very well indeed, Sandor Balog would have to do the same thing. With any luck we should be following closely on his exact trail, and in his turn, Timothy would be able to trace us.

Lewis said: 'It'd be interesting to know what time the first train comes up.'

'I do know. The first one's at seven. The porter told us, and there was a sort of time-table in the hall at the hotel, and we checked with that, because we thought that if we were here a few days, we might take the trip.' I added, grimly: 'It seems funny, doesn't it, to think of coming up here for pleasure?'

He grinned. 'You never know your luck.'

Then he put his arm out quickly, barring my path, and we stood still. Ahead of us the mist had thinned, smoking momentarily aside to show us a long empty stretch of the mountain ahead. I saw long reaches of pale rock, strewn with dwarfed bushes and drifts of thick tough grass, and here and there a solitary tree, warped and broken by frost, and reaching long fingers down the wind. What bushes there were were low growing, thin-leaved mountain varieties, that seemed to cling against grey rock where nothing should have been able to survive.

But I hardly took this in, except as a quick impression. I was looking at Lewis. That last response of his had been casual, even ironic, but—it came to me like a blinding light out of the thin mist—he had meant it. I knew every tone of his voice, and he had meant it. For me the night had held terror, relief, joy, and then a sort of keyed-up excitement; and drugged with this and sleeplessness, and buoyed up by the intense relief and pleasure of Lewis's company, I had been floating along in a kind of dream—apprehensive, yes, but no longer scared; nothing could happen to me when he was there. But with him, I now realised, it was more than this; more positive than this. It was not simply that as a man he wasn't prey to my kind of physical weakness and fear, not just that he had the end of an exacting job in sight. He was, quite positively, enjoying himself.

'Lewis,' I said accusingly, 'can you possibly be *wanting* some rough stuff?'

'Good heavens, no!' He said it very lightly, and it was a lie—a lie he didn't even trouble to follow up, but gave it away with the next sentence. 'Is your face still sore?'

'My face? I—yes, I suppose it is.' I put a hand to the swollen cheek,
realising how stiff my bruised mouth was. 'I was too busy to think about it,
but it must look awful, does it?'

'Not from this side, beautiful. Praise be, this blessed mist's clearing just
in time. There's a tunnel ahead.'

'A tunnel?'

'Yes. See? It looks like a cave mouth. Heaven knows how long it is. I wish
to God we could see a little farther, and take a short cut straight up. Too bad
if we had to—ah!'

Even as he spoke there came another of those queer freak currents of
air, lifting the mist away. He pointed straight up the mountainside away
from the rail track. 'There, you can see where the track goes, cutting along
above this again. Come on, we'll take a chance on this. Let's by-pass this
tunnel.'

Luck was still with us. A few minutes' scramble brought us to the place he
had seen, with only a few stray trails of damp mist to blur our way, though
the crest of the mountain remained lodged in cloud, mercifully blinding our
quarry to the pursuit. We had seen no more sign of him and heard no sound,
except here and there the trickle and splash of little springs that threaded
the rock, and once the bells of sheep still tingling in some small agitation
from Sandor's passage ahead of us.

Just before the mist of the upper track swallowed us in our turn, we saw
Timothy away below. He waved, then spread his hands in the time-
honoured gesture which means 'I found nothing'. Lewis lifted a hand in
acknowledgement, then pointed higher up the mountain. The gesture said
as clearly, 'Follow us', and the distant figure, wasting no time, turned aside
from the railway and began the steep scramble after us.

'Are we going to wait for him?' I asked.

'We can't afford to, but he can't get lost. There's always the railway.
That's a good lad, Vanessa. From what you tell me, his father must be a fool.
What's he going to do?'

'He's talking of a job with the Spanish Riding School. I don't know what
Carmel would say, but I think she'll find he's a bit over her fighting weight
now—and of course if she's marrying again she may be too wrapped up in
that to bother. I don't know what the regulations are about getting work
here, Lewis? He's hoping his father can help.'

'I could probably help him there myself. I know a man— Watch that
stone, it's loose.'

'You know, I'm beginning to think you're quite handy to have around.'

'Time alone will tell,' he said, with a glance up ahead through the mist.
'We'll see what Tim says, anyway. But if I'd a son like that . . . Managing all
right?'

'I'm with you, literally all along the line.'

'Meaning we can give it some thought, as soon as this job's over?'

'Why not? I dare say supply can meet demand, as the P.E.C. Sales
Department would put it.'

He reached a hand back and helped me up a steep patch. 'How my other
Department would put this I hate to think; but thank God it's turned out to
be a police job after all.'

'And Tim and I have a perfect right to be here and help as ordinary citizens?'

'Indeed you have. What's more, so have I, in as private a capacity as you like. Mark you, I'm certain there'll turn out to be a Security tie-up, simply because Paul sent for me in the first place; but that's another story, as they say, and by the time we're through with this the Department may well decide to let someone else cope with it. I have a feeling that Lee Elliott has just about exhausted his cover with the Circus Wagner. As for your part in this, even if I weren't quitting, I doubt if my Department could raise much hell over it now.'

'A man'll do anything when he's under notice,' I said.

'How right you are.'

At something in his tone I said quickly: 'What d'you mean?'

'What I have to discuss with Sandor,' said Lewis, 'isn't exactly in the book.'

'You mean your "private reasons" for wanting to catch up with him?'

'Exactly that. Any objections?'

'I can hardly wait.'

'I always did say you weren't a nice girl. Damn this mist, it's a mixed blessing. From what I can see of this blessed mountain, they couldn't be better placed. I seem to remember that the place has what's called a "panorama" . . . that is, it's got a clear signalling-line across at least two borders.'

'What are you going to do?'

'Go straight in, if I can, and pick up Balog, his contact, and the dope. The police might have got more information by just watching the Gasthaus, but Balog knows his cover's been blown, so we might as well muscle straight in and pick up the two of them before they clear out of it. Something'll turn up if they take the place apart—and two birds can be made to sing faster than one.'

'What do you want me to do?'

'When we get there, stay under cover till I give the word. I may need you to do the telephoning, if I have my hands too full . . . Or, if anything goes wrong, you're to get straight downhill with Tim, get to the car, drive down to the hotel and get them to telephone the police at Graz. Then get the local bobby and a few solid citizens and send them up here. Don't come back yourself.' He smiled down at me. 'Don't look like that; that's only if things go wrong, but they won't . . . I'm only doing what they call covering all contingencies. Got it?'

'Yes.'

'Now we'd better stop talking. Sound carries in mist the way it does over water, and I don't think it can be far now.'

'Look,' I said.

Away above us, and slightly to the left, nebulous and faint through the fog, like a strangled star, a light suddenly pricked out and hung steady.

'Journey's end,' said Lewis.

'Or the start of the fun?' I asked.

'As you say,' he agreed, smoothly.

Chapter Nineteen

Heat not a furnace for your foe so hot
That it do singe yourself.

Shakespeare: *King Henry VIII*

The Gasthaus was not a big building. As far as one could see in that misty half-light, it was solid, long, white-washed, with the roof of grey wooden shingles so common in the valleys, and to one side a sheltered veranda made of pine where tables were laid in summer. It lay some twenty yards beyond the final halt of the rack railway. At the other side of the Gasthaus lay a terrace edged with a low wall, a belvedere, beyond which the cliff dropped sheer away for some two or three hundred feet, but on the railway side, from which we approached, it was just an ordinary long low building with shuttered windows and a heavy door, to the side of which were the refuse bins and crates of empty bottles.

It was from one of these windows—the only one unshuttered—that the light came which Lewis and I had followed. Half the outside shutter had been pushed open, and the window with it, back against the wall. It was possible that this had been done deliberately after Sandor's telephone call in order to guide him up the mountain in the mist. There was no other light.

There was a shed at the terminus of the rack railway, a squat oblong building which did duty as a station. We ran forward under cover of this, and dodged through the crush barriers to the misty window at the rear. Between the window and the Gasthaus there was no cover except the stacked boxes and dustbins near the wall. We could see clean in through the open window, and what was going on in the room was as obvious and well lighted as something on a picture stage.

The room was the kitchen. To the left as I looked I could see the gleam of the big cooking stove and above it a row of copper pans and a blue dish hanging. Against the wall opposite the window could be seen the top of a kitchen dresser, shelves of some sort with more of the blue dishes, and some cardboard boxes stacked. The wall to the right, where presumably the door was, I couldn't see. The end of a big scrubbed table jutted out near the window. More important than anything, on the wall beside the dresser, at shoulder height, was an old-fashioned telephone, and near this Sandor Balog stood, talking hard to another man, obviously his host, who stood by the stove with his back to the window. From what I could see of him this was a stocky, heavily built man, with thinnish, greying hair. He had an old overcoat huddled on anyhow, over what I assumed were pyjamas or whatever he wore at night. He was in the act of lifting what looked like a coffee-pot off the top of the stove, and had paused to say something over his shoulder to Sandor.

All this I got in one swift impression, for in that moment Lewis, with a breathed 'Stay here', had left my side and was running lightly across the intervening space between the shed and the kitchen wall.

He ran in a curve, keeping out of the direct line of vision, and in a few seconds, unnoticed, was backed up against the wall to the side of the open window, from where, presumably, he could hear what was being said.

I don't know to this day whether the light in that room was electric or whether it came from a lamp, but in the uncertain dawn it seemed very strong, and lit the scene in the kitchen with startling clarity, in spite of the veils and fingers of mist that still drifted between; whereas Lewis, crouched beyond the direct beam of the light, was less than half visible. All the same, I saw the gun in his hand . . .

But at the same moment a movement within the room caught my eye. The second man carried the coffee-pot across to the table, still talking, and proceeded to pour coffee into a couple of mugs. I saw the steam of it rising, and I still remember—overlaying even the excited apprehension of the moment—the glorious sudden pang of hunger caused by the sight of that coffee. I seem to remember that I could even smell it; but that of course was ridiculous. There were still twenty yards of damp grey air between us.

Next moment I forgot the coffee completely. I saw Lewis drift away from the window, along the wall, to try the door.

It was locked; they must have shut it again after Sandor had been admitted. Lewis drifted, ghost-like, back towards the window. I was surprised that they had left that, but perhaps they hadn't noticed, and Sandor, after all, had shown no suspicions of being followed.

Even as the thought crossed my mind, he did notice it. He said something, pointing, then put his mug down on the table, and turned towards the telephone. His host glanced, shrugged, then stepped towards the window. He was going to shut it. Sandor had lifted the receiver, and was waiting. And Lewis—I could see it now—Lewis, incredibly, had put out a hand to hold the window and shutter tightly back against the outside wall.

The man thrust out an arm and yanked at the window. It jerked, and stuck. He pulled it again, and even from where I stood I could hear his irritable exclamation as it still stayed fast open. Sandor gave a half glance over his shoulder, then turned back to the telephone, and said something brief into it, a number, perhaps. The man at the window leaned right out over the sill and reached to one side to pull it to.

Lewis hit him hard over the head. The heavy body slumped across the sill, then slowly slipped back into the lighted room. It had hardly begun to slide before Lewis had gone with it, and was astride the sill, silhouetted sharply against the light, with the gun in his hand.

At the same moment, an upstairs light came on.

I left my hiding-place, and ran like a hare across the intervening space towards the kitchen window.

All hell had broken loose in the kitchen. Lewis, of course, had had to jump blind for the window and, though he must have heard Sandor at the telephone, he could only guess at the situation inside. Quick though he had been, Sandor had had a moment's warning, for even as Lewis jumped for the sill, Sandor slammed the receiver back and whirled round, reaching for his hip.

But he never got his gun levelled. Lewis shot. He didn't shoot to kill: it seemed he was content with shattering one of the blue dishes on the dresser; but the shot had its effect. It managed to freeze Sandor where he stood, and then at a barked command he sent his gun skidding across the floor to Lewis's feet.

I heard Sandor say incredulously: 'Lee Elliott! What in hell's name?'

Lewis cut across him. 'Who is this man?'

'Why, Johann Becker, but what in the devil's name—?'

I said breathlessly, from the window: 'A light went on upstairs. Someone's awake.'

Sandor's face, as he saw me, changed almost ludicrously. It held amazement, then calculation, then a kind of wary fury. 'You? So it's you who are responsible for this crazy nonsense? What's she been telling you?'

Lewis had neither moved nor turned at the sound of my voice. He said: 'Come on in. Pick up that gun. Don't get between me and Balog.' Then to Sandor, curtly: 'Who else is in the house?'

'Well, Frau Becker, of course. Look, are you crazy, Elliott, or what? If you'll listen to me, I can—'

'Keep back!' snapped Lewis. 'I mean this. It won't be a plate next time.' As Sandor subsided, I slid quickly in through the window and stooped for the gun. 'That's my girl,' said Lewis, still with eyes and gun fixed on Sandor. 'Have you ever handled one of those things before?'

'No,' I said.

'Then just keep it pointing away from me, will you? It doesn't much matter what happens to Balog, but I want you to keep Frau Becker quiet with that, so—'

Sandor said furiously: 'Look, will you tell me what this is about? That girl–the gun–what the hell's she been telling you? You must be crazy! She thinks—'

Lewis said impatiently: 'Cut that out. You know as well as I do why I'm here. I've heard pretty well all I want to know, but you'll save yourself a lot of trouble if you'll tell me just where Becker and his wife come in—'

He got no further. The door of the room was flung open, and in surged one of the most enormous women I have ever seen.

She had on a vast pink flannel nightgown with a blue woollen wrapper over it, and her hair was in tight plaits down her back. She may have been roused by Sandor's arrival, but it was the sounds of the first scuffle that had lit her window, and now the pistol shot had brought her downstairs. It hadn't apparently occurred to her that a pistol shot in the night was anything to be afraid of; what she had apparently come to investigate was the sound of broken crockery. I can only assume that she thought her husband and his visitor were indulging in some kind of drunken orgy, for she swept into that room like Hurricane Chloe, unhesitating and unafraid–and poker in hand.

I jumped to intercept her, thrusting the pistol at her much as David must have waved his little sling at Goliath.

She took no notice of it at all. She lifted an arm the size of a York ham to sweep me aside, and bore down on the men. And I'm sure it wasn't the sight of her unconscious husband, or the raging Sandor, or even Lewis's pistol, that brought her up all standing for one magnificent moment in front of the dresser.

'My dish! My dish!' It was only later that Lewis translated for me, but the source of her emotion was unmistakable. 'My beautiful dish! You destroy my house! Burglar! Assassin!'

And, poker raised high, she bore down on Lewis.

I'm still not particularly clear about what happened next. I jumped for the woman's upraised arm, and caught it, but in her attempt to wrench herself free of me she sent us both staggering across the room, and for a moment we reeled between Lewis and Sandor.

Lewis leaped to one side to keep Sandor within range, but it was too late.

Sandor went for Lewis's gun hand like a tiger to its kill, and the fight was on.

I didn't see the first stages of that fight; I was too busy with Frau Becker. If Lewis was not literally to be weighted clean out of the battle, it was up to me to keep the lady out of it. Even he, I supposed, could hardly shoot the woman.

It was all I could do not to shoot her myself. For two or three sizzling minutes all I could hope for was to hold on madly to the hand which held the poker, and prevent my own gun from going off, as I was shaken about that room like a terrier hanging on to a maddened cow.

Then suddenly she collapsed. She folded up like a leaking grain sack, and went down as if I had indeed shot her. By the mercy of heaven a chair was in the way, and into this we went together, me on her ample lap, still hugging her like an avid nursling. I thought at first that the chair had smashed under our combined weights, but it was a rocking chair, and, tossing like a ship at sea, it shot screeching backwards to fetch up against the door just as Timothy, white-faced and bright-eyed, came hurtling through the window, tripped over the prostrate Becker, swept a mug off the table in falling, and landed on the floor in a pool of coffee.

Whether the sight of a third assassin was too much even for Frau Becker, or whether (as I suspect) the smashing of the mug had finally broken her spirit, she was finished. She opted out of the fight, sitting slumped there in the rocking chair, massive, immobile, wailing in German, while I picked myself up off her and took the poker from her, and Tim rolled off her husband and took the poker from me, and then together we turned to watch the other hurricane that was sweeping that hapless kitchen.

The two men were evenly matched, Sandor's strength and sheer athletic skill against Lewis's toughness and training. Sandor was still hanging on to Lewis's gun hand, while Lewis fought grimly to free himself and regain control with the gun. At the moment when we turned they were both, tightly locked, hurtling back against the hot front of the stove. It was Lewis who was jammed there, for two horrible seconds; I was too distraught to hear what he said, but Timothy told me afterwards with unmixed admiration that he had learned more in that two seconds than he had in six years at public school—which, I gathered, was saying a lot. I know that as Lewis cursed, I screamed, and Tim jumped forward, and then Lewis's wrist was brought with a crack across the edge of the stove and his gun flew wide, to go skittering under the table, and then he kneed Sandor viciously in the groin and the locked bodies reeled aside and came with a back-breaking slam against the table's edge, while Tim's poker, missing them by inches, smashed down on the stove top to send the kettle flying.

'My kettle!' moaned Frau Becker, galvanised afresh.

'*Tim! The other man!*' I shrieked, holding her down.

Becker was moving—was even on his feet. Sandor saw him, gasped something, and the man lurched forward.

But not to help. He was making for the telephone. He was at it.

Lewis said, quite clearly, 'Stop him!' and somehow swung Sandor away from the table. One of Sandor's hands, those terrible steel hands, was at Lewis's throat. I could see the flesh bulge and darken under the fingers. The sweat was pouring off both men, and Sandor breathed as if his lungs were ruptured. Then instead of pulling away I saw Lewis close in. He had Sandor round the body; he heaved him up and across, somehow twisting his own body . . . then suddenly brought him slamming down across his knee in a back-breaker. Before Sandor could roll painfully free, Lewis had dragged him up again, and I heard the sickening sound of bone on flesh as he hit him hard across the throat.

Becker wasn't lifting the receiver. He was yanking at the wires with all his strength.

I yelled: 'Put that down!' and swung the useless gun away from the struggling men, towards Becker. He ignored me. I didn't know if I had a mandate to shoot him, and I doubt anyway if I could have hit him even at that range. I reversed the gun and jumped for him.

I was just too late. Tim had whirled, jumped, and struck, just as the telephone wires came away with a scatter of plaster and a splintering of wood, and poor Becker went down once more, and lay still.

'My dish!' wailed Frau Becker. 'My beautiful cups! Johann!'

'It's all right,' I said feebly, desperately. 'We won't hurt you, we're police. Oh, Tim—'

But there was no more need of Tim and his poker. The fight was over.

Lewis was getting to his feet, and dragging Sandor up with him. The latter's breathing was terrible, and though he still struggled, it seemed to be without much hope of breaking the cruel grip that held him.

I think I started forward, but Tim caught at me and held me back. He had seen before I had what was happening.

Sandor was being forced, step by sweating step, towards the stove.

It was all over in seconds. I still hadn't grasped what Lewis was doing. I heard Sandor say, in a voice I didn't recognise:

'What do you want to know?' And then, quickly, on a sickening note of panic: 'I'll tell you anything! What do you want?'

'It can wait,' said Lewis.

And with the other's wrist in his grip, he dragged the arm forward, and began to force it out towards the stove where the kettle had stood.

Sandor made no sound. It was Timothy who gasped, and I think I said: 'Lewis! No!'

But we might as well not have been there.

It happened in slow motion. Slowly, sweating every inch of the way, Lewis forced the hand downwards. 'It was this hand, I believe?' he said, and held it for a fraction of a second, no more, on the hot plate.

Sandor screamed. Lewis pulled him away, dumped him unresisting into the nearest chair, and reached for the gun I was still holding.

But there was no need for it. The man stayed slumped in the chair, nursing his burned hand.

'Keep your hands to yourself after this,' said my husband, thinly.

He stood there for a moment or two, getting his breath, and surveying the results of the hurricane: the unconscious Becker, the wrecked telephone, the woman snuffling in the rocking chair, Tim with his poker, and myself probably as pale as he, shaken and staring.

Timothy recovered himself first. He went scrambling under the table, and emerged with the gun–the precious Beretta–held carefully in his hand.

'Good man,' said Lewis. He smiled at us both, pushing the hair back out of his eyes, and seeming suddenly quite human again, 'Van, my darling, do you suppose there's any coffee left? Pour it out, will you, while Tim and I get these thugs tied up. Then they can tell us all the other things I want to know.'

Chapter Twenty

Emprison'd in black, purgatorial rails.
Keats: *The Eve of St Agnes*

As Timothy and I emerged from the Gasthaus, it came somehow as a surprise to realise that it was full light. Cloud or mist still hung around the summit of the mountain, so that it was impossible to see into the distance, but the visibility was now two or three hundred yards, and clearing every moment. The air seemed thin, grey and chill, but the coffee had worked wonders for us.

I said: 'Have you the foggiest idea what time it is? I didn't put my watch on.'

'Nor did I, but I noticed the time by the kitchen clock. It's about half past four.'

'It's a mercy that didn't get smashed, too. Poor Frau Becker. Lewis seems pretty sure she knows nothing about it, so the worst she'll suffer is being deprived of her husband's company for a bit.'

'I'd have said the worst was the bust dishes.'

'You've got something there. Oh gosh, and the grass is wet. It's beastly cold, isn't it?'

'What's that to us?' said Timothy buoyantly. 'Intrepid, that's us. Archie Goodwin also ran.'

I said, a little sourly: 'You got some sleep, I didn't.'

'There's that,' he admitted. 'And then you've had a pretty rough time, belting about like that on the roof.'

'I suppose you don't reckon you had it rough, being hit on the head by Sandor in the stable? Or do you take that kind of thing in your stride? Look, for goodness' sake, don't try to go at such a speed. This grass is beastly slippery, and there's a lot of loose rock about. And you're carrying that thing.'

'That thing' was Sandor's automatic, which Timothy handled with what was to me a terrifying and admirable casualness.

'I hope you do know all about those things?'

He grinned. 'Well, yes, it's dead easy. As a matter of fact this is rather a neat little thing. My grandfather had an old Luger left over from the war. The first war. I used to go potting rabbits with it.'

'You loathsome boy. I wouldn't have thought it of you.'

'Oh,' he said cheerfully, 'I never got one. Have you any idea how difficult it is to pot at rabbits with a Luger?'

'I can't say that I have.'

'As a matter of fact, it's impossible. My hands so far are pretty clean of blood, but at this rate whether they'll stay so or not I just have no idea. I say, that was some scrap up there in the kitchen, wasn't it? Why did he burn Sandor's hand? To frighten him and make him talk?'

'I don't think so. It was a private thing.'

'Oh? Yes, I remember, he said so. You mean they got across one another in the circus or something?'

I shook my head. 'Sandor hit me.'

His eyes flew to my bruised face. 'Oh . . . oh, I see.' I could see myself that his admiration for Lewis had soared to the edge of idolatry. I thought with resignation that men seemed in some ways to pass their lives on an unregenerately primitive level. Well, I could hardly cavil. I had had a fairly primitive reaction myself to my husband's eye-for-an-eye violence in the kitchen. That I was coldly ashamed of it now proved nothing.

'Well, whatever it was for,' said Timothy, 'it did the trick. He didn't know how fast to spill the beans. Did you understand any of it?'

'No,' I said. Lewis's quick interrogation–since it included the Beckers–had been in German. 'Suppose you tell me now.'

So, as we hurried down through the damp greyness, he passed the main items across to me. The important thing from our point of view I knew already; that (as Lewis had overheard before he had even entered the room) Sandor had managed to cache the drugs on his way up the mountain, in a tree on a section of railway that Lewis and I had short-circuited. He had in fact got to the Gasthaus only a very few minutes before we did, and had still been telling Becker about his flight with the drugs when Lewis had arrived under the window to listen. This bit of information Lewis could probably have got out of them later: where the luck had come in was in the timing of his own attack through the window. He had managed to delay it just long enough to hear the Vienna number that Sandor had given over the telephone.

So there had not been much difficulty with Sandor. Tim had been right; I had seen for myself that he hadn't known how fast to talk. I supposed that, as well as his immediate fear of Lewis, there was some hope of leniency if he turned State Evidence. And Becker had followed suit. At first he had tried to shout Sandor into silence, but soon changed his tune when he realised how much Lewis knew. And presently the facts–and the names–began to emerge . . .

'Not everything by a long chalk,' said Tim, 'but then they're only messengers. But Lewis says there'll be plenty to find when the police start to take the Gasthaus apart, and he did get the Vienna number just before Sandor had to slam the phone down. Of course, the exchange may have put the call through before they knew he'd rung off, and the Vienna end may have got the wind up; but Lewis says they'll hardly fold their tents like the Arabs when it might just be a wrong number, and even if they tried, they couldn't clean up before Interpol starts moving. In any case there'll be more than enough for Interpol to get a wedge in here and there, and crack the ring open. I suppose if Sandor was passing the stuff along through Yugoslavia into Hungary, Interpol could fix a trap up to catch the people at the other end. Or so Lewis seems to think.'

Something about his voice as he spoke made me shoot a glance at him. Not quite authority, not quite patronage, certainly not self-importance; but just the unmistakable echo of that man-to-woman way that even the nicest men adopt when they are letting a woman catch a glimpse of the edges of the Man's World. Timothy had joined the club.

I said, not quite irrelevantly: 'He thinks a lot of you, too. Now, for heaven's sake, I hope we can find this blighted tree where Sandor said he'd put the stuff.'

'The stretch between the tunnels. A lonely, blasted pine. It's just as good,' he said joyously, 'as a one-eyed Chinaman with a limp. Oh, we'll find it, don't you worry! There's the railway again now.'

We had gone at a fair speed down the first long slope of rock-strewn grass, cutting across one of the arms of the rack railway. This went in a wide sweep for some quarter of a mile to the right but curved back again to pass about two hundred and fifty yards below us. We could just see the pale-coloured cutting in the rock where the line lay, and beyond it, the grey distances of morning with one or two darker shapes of bushes looming like ghosts. The grass was soaking. The thick turfs squelched under our feet like sponges, and the longer fronds swung heavy with drops like dimmed crystals which drenched us to the knee. Everywhere among the grey rocks there were clumps of some large violet gentian, just unfurling, a sight which would have stopped me in my tracks at any time but this. As it was, I don't think I even took particular trouble not to tread on them, but hurried on down the hill, intent only on one thing, speed.

We reached the shallow cutting where the railway ran and I jumped down into it with a thump. Behind me Timothy slithered with a rattle of stones and a sharp lamentable phrase as he slipped on the wet grass and almost lost his balance.

'Watch it. Are you O.K.?'

'Yes. Sorry. I wish I'd my boots here. These shoes are murder on wet grass. Can you see the next bit of line below this?'

'Not from here. The slope's more gradual, but we'll go straight on.' Once again we ran forward and down over the tufted alpine grass. Timothy was ahead of me now. Visibility was getting better, and the colours even seemed to be growing warmer towards sunrise. On this part of the mountain there were more bushes, thick clumps of juniper and mountain rhododendrons, and sometimes we had to make longish detours round hollows where rocks had fallen in long since, and which were treacherously overgrown with thistles and long grass.

In front of me Timothy faltered, seemed to cast round like a hound at fault, and then stopped. I came up to him.

'What is it?'

'There's no sign of the railway. Surely it should be there?' He turned a dismayed face to me. 'Supposing we've lost it? When it went back there to the left it must have been going round the other side of the mountain. We're probably on the wrong bit altogether now . . . It all looks so much alike. I wish to goodness we could see farther . . . If only we could see right down, we'd probably be able to see the lake and the village and everything, then we'd know where we were. D'you think we'd better go back to find the railway and follow it down?'

'Surely not. I don't see how we can have missed it. Wait a minute, Tim, stand still. It's getting clearer every minute . . . Look down there . . . No, farther to the right. That tree, that dead one, with the divided trunk. It's just the way he described it. What d'you bet that's the very one? Straight bang on the target, who'd have thought it? Come on!'

He caught at my arm as I ran past him. 'But where's the railway? Between two tunnels, he said.'

'Don't you see?' I threw it at him over my shoulder. 'That's why we can't see the line . . . We're probably crossing the upper tunnel now. Between the tunnels, the line'll be in a cutting. I'll bet you it's lying down there, just below that little cliff where the pine is. Come on, let's look.'

And sure enough, it was. The dead pine stood, split and hollow, clinging to the face of a low cliff, and there, some fifteen feet below its exposed roots, ran the railway. Seventy yards down the track yawned the black exit of the first tunnel, and about the same distance the other way was the entrance to the second. It was the place.

'Bang on,' I said. 'This is it. How's that for radar?'

'Do you home on to drink as well as drugs?' asked Timothy. 'Vanessa March, dope-hound. This is terrific! Let's have a look!'

When, from the top of the little cliff, we examined the tree, we realised that it was not quite as easy to get at as it looked. A six inch wide track, presumably made by rather athletic goats, twisted its way down towards the permanent way. One had to step off this track, and, hanging tightly to the trunk of the dead tree, reach up to the obvious hiding-place, a hole in the main trunk some five feet from ground level.

'Airs above the flaming ground,' said Timothy. 'I suppose it would be dead easy for Sandor. Well, you'd better let me have a go. You go on down to the bottom, and I'll chuck the packages to you.'

'If they're there.'

'If they're there,' he agreed, and set his foot gingerly on one of the exposed roots of the tree, while equally gingerly I slithered past him and edged my way down the goat track on to the permanent way.

And they were there. As Tim, clinging like a monkey, managed to shove a hand into the hollow of the tree, I heard him give a barely suppressed whoop of triumph. 'I can feel them! I can't get high enough up to see, but there's the corner of one, two . . . yes, three . . .'

'He said there were eight. With the one you've got, that makes seven in the tree.'

'There's another, that makes four. I wish I dared stand up. If I hitch myself a bit higher, I may be able to reach down and feel to the bottom of the hollow. Yes . . . five, six . . . and seven. Gosh, if there's one thing I hate it's putting a hand into a hollow tree. You always feel as if a squirrel's going to latch on with all its teeth.'

'If Lewis is right it's a wonder that stuff isn't biting. Can you just chuck them down to me one by one?'

'Can do,' said Tim, and the first one came flying. It was solidly packed, a nice oblong package with what felt like several smaller packets inside it, flat and neat and wrapped in waterproof and sealed down. A few hundred pounds' worth of dreams and death. I shoved it in my anorak pocket. 'O.K., next, please.' The others came dropping down in turn and I stowed half away and left the others out for Tim.

'There,' he said from above, 'I think that's the lot. Was that seven?'

'Yes, seven, don't bother any more, I'm sure he was telling the truth. Watch yourself.'

'It's all right, I'm hanging on like a Bandar-log. No, I can feel, there's nothing more. Right, I'm coming down.'

It was as he eased his way off the tree roots back on to the goat track that it happened. Either he trod on something loose, or else those treacherous soles slid on the damp rock, for he missed his footing, and came hurtling down to the railway track in a sort of slithering feet-first fall which would have landed him in an unpleasant little drainage gully at the edge of the track which was filled with broken stones, but that in a frantic effort to save himself he managed a wide sprawling leap which carried him clear of it and on to the railway itself.

He landed completely out of control, his feet skidding on the wet gravel, his left foot coming hard up against the metal line, his right just missing this, but being driven against the raised central rail, the rack; and next moment, with a sharp cry of pain, he was sprawling right there at my feet, among the scattered packets which I had laid aside for him.

'Tim, Tim, are you all right? Are you hurt?'

I went down on my knees beside him. He had made no attempt to pick himself up, but seemed to be bunched all anyhow, ungainly over the rails. His head was down. He was making gasping sounds of pain, his body hunched tightly over the right foot.

'I . . . I think it's stuck . . . my foot . . . Oh, God . . . it's broken or something.'

'Here, let me see. Oh, Tim!'

It was the right foot. By the force of his slithering, feet-first fall, it had been driven hard forward into the little space underneath the centre rail where this was lifted clear of the gravel, and the solid sole of his shoe had jammed there, with the foot twisted at a horrible angle.

'Hold on, I'll try to get it out.' But wrestle as I would with the shoe, it was fixed tight, and though Tim had now got control of himself and was making no sound, I was afraid how much I might hurt him if I persisted.

'We'll get the shoe undone, then you can try to slip your foot out of it.'

The laces, of course, were soaked, and knotted tightly. I said: 'We'll have to cut them. Have you a knife?'

'What?' He was very white and there was sweat on his face. He looked as if he might faint. I had once sprained an ankle badly myself, and could distinctly remember the feeling of nausea that came through the pain.

'A knife. Have you a pen-knife?'

He shook his head. 'Sorry.'

I bit my lip, and tackled the laces. I had nothing with me either, not even a nail file, and Tim's foot was swelling rapidly. After minutes, it seemed, of frantic wrestling, and a broken finger-nail, I gave up. In a very short time it would be impossible to get the shoe off at all without cutting the leather. Scrabbling, searching desperately among the gravel, I found a sharp-edged stone, but after only a few moments' experiment with that I had to give up. It wasn't possible to saw downwards on to the swollen foot.

'I'll try and scrape out some of the gravel under your foot. Perhaps we can loosen the shoe that way.' But when I attacked the ground underneath the rail, I found that for this short space, the rail was running over solid rock. There was nothing to be done. And indeed, I dared do no more. For all I knew the foot was broken, and the bitten-down pain in the boy's face terrified me.

All the same it was Timothy who made the only possible suggestion.

'You'll have to leave it. You can't do it yourself. Go and get help. I'll be all right. It's not so bad when we're not hacking at it, and if I turn myself like this . . . yes, that's better. I'll be O.K. Honestly. I–I'll give it time and then try again. And anyway, it's Lewis who matters just now. You'd better do as he said, and send help. Even if you did get me out, you certainly couldn't get me down the hill. Go on, you'll have to leave me.'

'Tim, I hate to, but—'

'It's the only thing to do.' He was, understandably, curt. 'You get down there to the telephone. Take the gun. I dropped it over there.'

I picked the pistol up from where it had skidded, and pushed it into his hand. 'I don't want it. I'd rather leave it with you. Here. All right, I'll go. I'll be as quick as I can.'

'Don't forget the dope. You'd better take the lot. I don't exactly fancy being left stuck here with all that strewn round me, even if I do have a gun.' He managed a smile. 'Good luck.'

'And to you.'

And I turned and ran.

As I reached the first scattered trees at the edge of the wood, the sun came up.

It was almost a surprise to find the shed, the jeep, and the quarry exactly as we had left them, except that now the early sun, streaming between the pines, took away some of the ghostly loneliness of the place and made it a picture of golden lights and sharp blue shadows. Thankful for this at least, I ran on past the quarry and down the road into the wood.

The Mercedes was there. And there, under the little stone beside the red and white elfin toadstools, was the key. I let myself into the car, stripped off my anorak with the clumsily bulging pockets and threw it into the back seat, then started the engine. It lit at a touch. The tyres tore at the gravel as it lurched forward, and I turned it gently on to the rutted surface of the track and headed it downhill.

It was a heavy car, far heavier than I had been used to driving, and the bends were sharp. I had to make a severe effort to suppress in myself the feeling of hurry, to crush any feelings of urgency or danger right out of mind, and just concentrate on getting this powerful car down this very unpleasant and difficult little bit of road. What would happen if we met anything coming up, I couldn't even begin to imagine . . .

But at least it was daylight. Already the sun was brilliant, laying great palisades of light between the pines all the way along the road. I wound my window down and let in the sharp sweet air. Birds were singing wildly, almost as if it were spring. I thought I heard a cock crow not far off, and somewhere, nearer still, a train whistled. In spite of myself, my spirits lifted. It was morning, the sun was up, and soon now all this would be over.

The road rounded a thick knot of pines, and below me, now, were the green rolling foothills, with beyond them the glitter of a spire and the glint of the lake. Smoke was rising from a farm chimney, and a little beyond that, behind a thick belt of pines, another column of smoke, black this time, spoke of some factory or other already at work. Seen in the morning light this peaceful pastoral scene couldn't possibly hold any terrors. All I had to do was to go down into the pretty village and go to the hotel. They would be awake there, and moving, and they would speak English, and there was a telephone . . .

I drove carefully round the last bend and headed the Mercedes down the straight slope, past the railway station and towards the village. I remember that the only thing which made me brake and pause as I passed the station was that the gate was open and a man in blue dungarees was sweeping the little stretch of platform between the miniature ticket office and the siding where the train stood with its curious little tilted engine and its three carriages waiting for the day. There would certainly be a telephone here.

He had seen me. He paused in his sweeping and looked up. I stopped the car, and hung out of the window.

'Excuse me, do you speak English?'

He put a hand up to his ear, and then with a sort of maddening deliberation, turned to lay aside his broom before he approached the car.

Torn between the desire to drive straight away and waste no more time, and the desire to get to the first available telephone as quickly as possible, I shoved open the car door, jumped out, and ran in through the station gate to meet him.

'Excuse me, do you speak English?'

I think he said no, and I think, too, that undaunted he started on a flood of totally unintelligible German, but I was no longer listening.

There were two sidings in the tiny station. In one of them stood the train, with its little down-tilted engine ready to push the three carriages up the long mountain track; the other siding was empty. From it, a long shining section of track led up into the pine woods and vanished. And away up in the same direction beyond the first tree-clad foothill, I saw that towering column of thick black smoke that I had taken to be the smoke from some factory chimney; and I remembered two things. I remembered the column of smoke that Josef had called the 'fire-engine', or 'Fiery Elijah'; and I remembered the engine's whistle I had heard three minutes ago.

I whirled on the man, and pointed up the track.

'There! That! A train? A train?' He was elderly, with a drooping moustache, and watery blue eyes which would normally be rayed with laughter lines, but which now were puckered and puzzled and a little rheumy with the early morning. He stared at me with complete non-comprehension. I waved again frantically at the standing train, at the smoke above the trees, at the track, in a sort of desperate pantomime; and then pointed to my wrist.

'The time . . . the first train . . . seven o'clock . . . *Sieben Uhr* . . . train . . . gone?'

He gestured towards the wall behind him where I now saw a station clock marked half-past five, and then, pointing like me up towards the smoke on the mountain, he poured out another flood of German.

But it wasn't necessary. I had seen that the black smoke was indeed marching slowly, but steadily, inexorably, up through the trees, and now, clear above them, over a lovely rounded slope of sunny green, I saw the engine moving, an engine exactly like the one standing here in the station, but pushing only one carriage. Not even a carriage, something that looked like a truck . . .

Beside me, the old man said: 'Gasthaus . . . Café,' and then proceeded with some pantomime involving the train standing at the platform. If he had been speaking in purest English it couldn't have been more clear. I understood quite well now. The time-table that I had studied had of course only put down the trains scheduled for the tourists, and the first one did indeed run at seven o'clock. No one had seen fit to mention that an engine took supplies up for the restaurant at half-past five.

German or no German, the telephone was not a blind bit of use in this. The old man was still talking, volubly, kindly, and rather pleased to have an audience at this ungodly hour of the day. I believe I said 'Thank you', as I turned and left him still talking to the empty air.

By the mercy of heaven there was room to turn. The Mercedes swept round like a boomerang, and I put her at that ghastly little road again with something of the fine careless rapture that I might have indulged in on the Strada Del Sol.

Chapter Twenty-one

The best of all our actions tend
To the preposterousest end.
Samuel Butler: *Satire upon the Weakness and Misery of Man*

At least going up was a little easier than coming down.

I had been too preoccupied during my recent descent to notice much more than the surface of the road, and of course on our way up in the early hours it had been dark and I had been wrestling with the flashlight and the map. Now as I drove the big car like a bomb up that horrible little road I was trying desperately to recall the relationship between road and railway.

As far as I could remember, there were only two places where they conjoined. A few bends above the station the road met the track, and ran along with it for perhaps a hundred yards before a rough escarpment carried the train away to the left along the edge of the mountain, while the road doubled back to the right on the long sweep below the edge of the forest proper. The second place was at the quarry–the end of the road. And that would be my last chance to catch him.

In cold blood, I doubt if I could have hoped to do it in the time, but I was past thinking, past reckoning what might happen if I miscalculated with this heavy car on these violent hairpin bends. She was so heavy and the road was so bad that I could hardly spare a hand for the gears, so I kept her in second and hauled her round the corners with no regard at all for either tyres or paintwork. Afterwards we found a dented hub cap, and a long scrape in the enamel on the offside, but I have no recollection of how they happened. I just drove the big car on and up as fast as I dared, and tried to remember how soon it was that we came to the railway.

The fifth or sixth bend, slightly easier than the others, brought us round facing a long straightish sweep between trees through which the sunlight blazed, strong now, barring the rutted road across and across, like a railway track barred with sleepers. Away at the end of this a cloud of black smoke hung, puffed, trundled deliberately by.

I put my foot down. The bars of shadow accelerated across us in one long flickering blur. And then suddenly the shining rails swooped in from our left to join the road.

For perhaps a hundred and thirty yards track and road ran side by side. The stretch of rail-track was empty, but there was black smoke still hanging in the boughs of the trees. I steadied the car on the narrow road and leaned as far out of my window as I could, straining to see forward up the railway before it curved away into the darkness of the forest, where the cliffs hid it from the sun.

It was there. I saw the square black tail of the little engine with its hanging lamp, lit for the mountain mists, swinging a small vanishing red eye into the tunnel of trees. Above it the appalling black cloud of smoke puffed furiously.

It was going slowly, the gradient so steep there that I could see the roof of the truck beyond the engine, and beyond that again the fretted curve of the rack up which it was hauling itself, cog by cog and puff by puff. There were two men in the cabin, one leaning out to look forward up the track, the other absorbed in up-tilting what looked like a bottle of beer. I shoved my hand down on the horn and held it there.

I'll say this for the Mercedes; she had a horn like the crack of doom. 'Fiery Elijah' must have been making a fair amount of noise, but the horn positively tore the forest apart.

Both men looked round, startled. I leaned out of my window and waved frantically, shouting—futile though it was—the most appropriate German word I could think of: '*Achtung! Achtung!*' After a couple of seconds' agonising pause I saw one of them—the driver—reach out a hand as if for the brake.

Another few yards and my road would bear me away from the railway again. I trod on my own brake and hung out, waving more frantically than ever.

The driver found what he had been reaching for, and pulled. It was the steam whistle. The engine gave a long, friendly *toot-toot*. The other man lifted his beer-bottle in a happy wave. The engine gave a third and last toot, then the forest closed in behind it and it was gone.

Why I didn't run the Mercedes off the track I shall never know. I just managed to wrench her nose round in time, as the road bore away from the railway, and along under the skirts of the forest. I still had the one chance, and through my exasperated fury I realised that it was a fairly strong one. Even with the extra distance she had to travel the Mercedes would surely be more than capable of reaching the railwaymen's hut in time for me to stop the train . . .

She had certainly better be. All that this last little effort had done was to make the train announce its coming to Timothy, and, however the boy had felt before, he would certainly be sweating it out now, trapped up there with the approaching engine mounting the hill puff by puff towards him.

Mercifully with every yard, with every curve, I was more used to the car, and with every curve the gradient eased and the bends grew wider. I have no idea at what speed we took the last six or seven stretches of that road, but it seemed to me as if the whole hillside was reeling past me and down in a long flickering blur of sun and shadow, and then suddenly we were up round the last bend, and in front of us was the space with the railwaymen's hut, and the shining stretch of track beside it.

I couldn't see the train.

The Mercedes zoomed along the last straight stretch like a homing bee, and fetched up with shrieking tyres and rocking springs within a yard of the railwaymen's hut. I jumped out of her and ran forward on to the line.

I had done it. Below where I stood I saw the smoke, perhaps a quarter of a mile away, where the engine chugged its stolid, unexcited way up the rack. They could not, of course, yet see me; would not see me until the engine broke from the cover of the trees some fifty yards away. I hoped they would, even at that early hour, keep a sharp look out forward. If I sounded the horn again, perhaps, or waved something . . . if I had anything red . . .

But I had seen how they had reacted to that horn before. And to my waving. In my mind's eye I saw it all again, repeated here with horrible finality: the horn, my waving, the cheerful responsive waves of the two men, and then the engine going past me and the red swinging lamp disappearing round the far curve . . .

The red rear lamp. There was at least the Mercedes.

I ran back to the car. As I jumped in and slammed the door, the cloud of black smoke burst above the trees to my left and I saw the blunt nose of the truck. I switched the car's lights full on, shoved her into gear, and drove her as hard as I could for the railway lines.

As her front wheel hit the rail, I thought at first she was going to be deflected, but the tyre bit, clung, climbed, and then lurched over, the rear tyre after it, and the Mercedes stopped once more, her two near wheels over the offside track, her rear lights, brake lights and all blazing what message they could towards the approaching train. For good measure I jammed my hand down hard over the horn as well, while I leaned across and with my free hand shoved open the offside door. I would give them till twenty-five yards, and then I would be out of the car like a bolting rabbit. If they didn't see the car I could do nothing to save her, but I didn't imagine that the train could come to very much harm; locked on its cogs it would probably weather the collision.

Why had I thought the engine slow? It seemed to be roaring up the hill all of a sudden with the speed of a crack express train. The black smoke burst and spread. I could hear the heavy panting of the little engine, great beats of it, above the blare of my horn. Thirty-five yards. Thirty. And I thought I heard a shout. I let go the horn and started my dive towards the open door. There was the clang of a bell, and a shrill furious whistle from the engine. I flung myself out of the door and ran clear.

With a horrible shriek of brakes, another toot and a flurry of angry shouts, 'Fiery Elijah' came to a standstill about seven yards behind the Mercedes.

The two men leaped down out of the cabin, and advanced on me. A third—there had been a guard after all—swung down from the truck. The co-driver was still holding the beer-bottle, but this time as if it were a lethal weapon, which from his face, he looked fully prepared to use. They both started to talk at once, or rather to shout, in furious German—and I can think of no better language to be furious in. For a full half minute, even had I been Austrian myself, I couldn't have got a word in edgeways, but stood there helpless before the storm, my hands out in front of me almost as if to ward off a blow from the beer-bottle.

At last there was a pause, on a fusillade of shouted questions, not one word of which I understood, but of which the gist was naturally very plain.

I said desperately: 'I'm sorry. I'm sorry, but I had to do it. There's a boy on the line higher up, farther along, a boy, a young man . . . A—a *Junge*, on the *Eisenbahn*. I had to stop you. He's hurt. Please, I'm sorry.'

The man with the beer-bottle turned to the one beside him. This was a big man in dark grey shirt, old grey trousers, and a soft peaked cap; the driver. '*Was meint sie?*'

The driver snapped a couple of sentences back at him and then said to me, in a ghastly guttural, which at that moment I wouldn't have exchanged even for a Gielgud rendering of Shakespeare: 'Is that you crazy are? There is no young on the line. There is on the line an auto. And why? I ask why?'

'Oh, you speak English! Thank God! Listen, *mein Herr*, I'm sorry, I regret I had to do this, but I had to stop the train—'

'*Ach* yes, you have the train stopped, but this is a danger. This is what I will to the police tell. My brother, he is the police, he will of this to you speak. For this you must pay. The Herr Direktor—'

'Yes . . . yes . . . I know. Of course I'll pay. But listen, please, listen. It's important, I need help.'

All of a sudden, he was with me. The first reaction of his own shock and anger had ebbed momentarily and let him see what must be showing clearly in my face, not only the swollen bruises, but the strain of the night and my terror for Timothy. Suddenly, in place of an angry beefy bully, I found myself confronted by a large man with kindly blue eyes who regarded me straightly, and then said: 'There is trouble, yes? What trouble? Why do you my train stop? Say.'

'There is a young man, my friend, he fell on the line up there. His leg is hurt.' I pantomimed it as best I could. 'He is on the railway line. He can't move. I was afraid. I had to stop you. Do you understand? Please say you understand!'

'Yes, I understand. This young man, is he wide?'

'Not very. As a matter of fact, he's quite thin.' I caught at myself.'Is he *what?*'

'Wide.' He waved towards the upper track. 'This is not right, no? In German, *weit*. Is he wide from here?'

'Oh, *far* . . . Is he *far*! Not very, only a little farther—more far—beyond the tunnel, the first tunnel.' How the devil did one pantomime a tunnel? Frantically I tried, and somehow he seemed to understand even this—or else perhaps he by-passed the explanation and was content to act on what he certainly had understood.

'You will show us. We shall now the auto off bring.'

It didn't seem to take those three burly men long to shift the Mercedes. I made no attempt to help them. Reaction was hitting me, and I simply sat down on a pile of sleepers and watched without seeing them as they strained and rocked at Lewis's poor car until at last she came clear and was shoved away from the rails. Then between them, almost as if I were a parcel, they heaved me up into the cab of the engine, and with a positively horrifying eruption of vile black smoke and a straining shriek of cog wheels 'Fiery Elijah' resumed his slow ascent.

I suppose there is something in every one of us, boy or girl, which at some level, or at some age, makes us want to drive an engine. Now that my apprehension had lifted, I almost enjoyed the ride, and indeed of all the engines that I have ever seen, this one, though certainly not the most exciting, was the most entertaining, being a nineteenth-century relic and possessing all the almost forgotten charm of the nursery trains of childhood. Its steep tilt, so absurd and pathetic on the flat, meant that on the upward climb the floor of the cabin was level. The tank was squat and black, the smoke stack enormous and funnel-shaped, and every available inch of the engine, it seemed, was festooned with tubes, wires, and gadgets of unimaginable uses. The paint was black, the wheels scarlet, and the whole thing was smelly, dirty, diabolically noisy and entirely charming. If the baroque age had produced a railway engine, this would certainly have been it.

We were soon clear of the trees, and ahead of us in the morning sunlight the line lay like a deeply clawed triple scratch through the white limestone.. We threaded our way along a naked curve of hill clothed with the tufted turf thick with gentians, and then the line ran into a cutting, and rough perpendicular walls of rock crowded us from either side to a height well above the roof of the truck; so closely indeed that I shrank back into the cabin, but not before I had seen, some hundred yards ahead of us, the black mouth of the first tunnel.

I shouted as much, quite unnecessarily, to the driver, who grinned and nodded and made signs that I should keep back in the cabin and under the cover of the roof. He could have spared himself the pains. I had ducked already. The tunnel looked singularly uninviting and not nearly big enough, but through it we went, with what I'll swear was not more than a foot to spare.

It was quite a long tunnel, and if I had been digging it myself I would certainly not have dug it any bigger than need be, but going through it was like being threaded like cotton through a narrow bead. In the tight, heavy blackness the din was horrifying. The enormous beating bursts of smoke from the engine, magnified a thousand times, volleyed and echoed back from the sides of the rocky tube. And there was the steam. Within twenty seconds of our entering the tunnel the place was like a steam bath, and a dirty one at that. It was enough to beat the wits out of anybody, and when the driver put his hand on the throttle and reduced speed I could—Tim or no Tim—almost have screamed at him to go on as fast as he could out of this inferno of heat and blackness and shattering noise. I am certain that no guard—even if his eyes would have adjusted to the sudden light after this utter blackness—could have kept a lookout forward and been in time to see Timothy on the line.

Light was running now through the filthy clouds of smoke that lined the tunnel. One could see the fissures and bulges of the rock. It grew stronger. The air cleared. As I pulled myself up to look, sunlight struck suddenly straight ahead of us, and then our front, the nose of the truck, was out in it, and the sharp edge of black shadow was sliding back over the shining roof towards the engine.

A bell clanged, sharply. Again I heard the sliding screech of brakes, and the scream of steel on steel. The train stopped with a great puffing sigh, then a long hiss of escaping steam which shut off sharply, leaving the engine simmering gently in the still mountain air like a steam kettle.

I put a hand to the rail and vaulted down to the gravel.

'Tim, Tim, it's me! Are you all right?'

He was still there, his foot still wedged under the rack. When I ran up to him he was slowly uncurling himself from what looked like some desperately cramped position, and I realised that, hearing the train, he had tried to cram his long body down between the rack and the rail, hoping that if the worst happened and the train ran over him unseeing he might escape one or other of the wheels. That he could not have done so was quite obvious, and this he must have known. If he had been white before, he now looked like death itself, but he pulled himself back into a sitting position and even managed, lit by relief as he was, some sort of a smile.

I knelt beside him. 'I'm sorry, you must have heard it coming for miles. It was the best I could do.'

'A bit . . . over-dramatic, I'd say.' He was making a magnificent effort to take it undramatically, but his voice was very shaky indeed. 'I felt like Pearl White or somebody. I'll never laugh at a thriller again.' He straightened up. 'Actually, I'd say it was a pretty good best. Transport and reinforcements for Lewis, all at one go. Did they let you drive?'

'I never thought to ask. Maybe they'll let you, on the way down.'

I put an arm round him and helped to prop him up. The men had run up the track with me, and, though I could see Timothy was trying to pull himself together still more and dig out his fund of German for explanations, there was no need. The driver and guard lost no time in starting efficient work on his shoe, and in a matter of seconds had the laces cut from the now badly swollen foot and were beginning, very gingerly and gently, to cut the leather of the shoe. The co-driver was also a man with a fine grasp of situation. As the others started work he vanished back in the direction of the truck, and now appeared with a flat green bottle which he uncorked and presented to Timothy with a phrase in German.

'The flask, she was for the Gasthaus,' explained the driver, 'but Johann Becker he will not speak no.'

'I'm dead sure he won't,' said Tim. 'What is it?'

I said: 'Brandy. Go on, it's what you need, and for pity's sake don't drink it all. I could do with half a pint myself.'

And presently, as the brandy went round—the railwaymen had evidently felt the strain of the recent excitement quite as much as Timothy or I—Tim's foot was drawn gently out of the wreck of his shoe, and willing hands were half carrying, half supporting him back towards the waiting train.

The truck, where they deposited us, was stacked high with stores, but there was just room to sit on the floor, and the doors (I noticed) could be locked.

'We will now,' said the driver to Timothy, 'take you straight up to the Gasthaus. No doubt Frau Becker will attend to your foot, and Johann Becker will give you breakfast.'

'If you have the money,' said the guard sourly.

'That is no matter, I shall pay,' said the driver.

'What are they saying?' I asked, and Tim told me.

'Well, I wouldn't guarantee the breakfast,' I said, 'but actually, we could hardly do better than go straight up with them. I can't think of a better way to bring those thugs down to the village than in this truck. And we've even provided the escort of solid citizens Lewis asked for—the driver's the policeman's brother, and they're none of them great friends of Becker's, from the sound of it. Do you suppose you could explain to them before we start, that when we get up there, they're going to find my husband with the

Beckers and another man at the other end of an automatic pistol, and that they, as solid citizens, must render him every assistance and take the whole boiling down and hang on to them till the police come?'

'Well, I could try. Now?'

'If you don't tell them before we start you'll never make yourself heard. "Fiery Elijah" rather makes his presence felt. Go on, have a bash—that is, if you've got the German to tell them with?'

'O.K., I can but try. I wish I knew the German for cocaine . . . What's the matter?'

'The cocaine,' I said blankly. 'I'd forgotten all about it. I left it in my pockets in the back of the car.'

'*You what?* Well, if the car's locked—'

'It isn't. In fact, the key's still in it,' I said.

We stared at one another for a long moment of horror, then suddenly and with one consent began to laugh, a weak, silly sort of laughter that turned to helpless giggles, while our three friends stood over us looking sympathetic and filling in time on the bottle of brandy.

'Well, I only hope,' said Timothy at length, dabbing his eyes, 'that you've got the English to explain to Lewis in.'

And so it was that Lewis, sitting on the edge of Frau Becker's kitchen table drinking Frau Becker's coffee and holding Frau Becker, her husband, and her husband's friend at the business end of the Beretta, was relieved of his vigil, not by the cold-eyed, tight-jawed professional men he must have been expecting, but by a peculiarly assorted gang of amateurs, two of whom were slightly hilarious, not to say light-headed, and all of whom smelt quite distinctly of Herr Becker's brandy.

It was some four hours later.

The cocaine had been recovered, our prisoners had been delivered to the correctly tight-jawed, cold-eyed professionals, and the battered Mercedes had somehow brought us all home to the Schloss Zechstein where Timothy's foot had been fixed up by a doctor who had talked soothingly about sprains and a day in bed; and I had had a bath and (feeling genuinely fragile now) was floating in a happy dream of relief and reaction towards the bed, while Lewis dragged off his wrecked clothes and fished in his case for a razor.

Then I remembered something, and stopped short.

'Lee Elliott!' I said. 'That's who they'll think you are! Did you register as Lee Elliott?'

'I didn't register as anything. There was a female in the hall who bleated something at me, but I just said "Later" and pressed the lift button.' He threw his sweater into a corner and started on his shirt buttons. 'Come to think of it, the porter did start in the other direction with my case, but I took it from him and came along here.'

'Lewis—no, just a minute, darling . . . *Hadn't* you better go down straight away and get it cleared up?'

'I've done all the clearing up I'm doing for one day. It can wait till morning.'

'It's morning now.'

'Tomorrow morning, then.'

'But—oh, darling, be serious, it's after ten. If anyone came in—'

'They can't. The door's locked.' He grinned at me, and sent the shirt flying after the sweater. 'If we need to reopen communications, we can do so later—by telephone. But for the present, I think it can come off the hook . . . There. First things first, my girl. I want a bath and a shave, and—didn't you hear what the doctor said? A day in bed's what we all need.'

'You could be right,' I said.

Epilogue

His neigh is like the bidding of a monarch, and his countenance
enforces homage.

Shakespeare: *Henry V*

The hall was white and gold, like a ballroom. The huge crystal chandeliers,
fully lit, glowed as ornaments in themselves rather than as light, for the
September sunshine streamed in through the great windows. Where there
should have been a polished dance floor there was a wide space of sawdust and
tanbark. To begin with it had been cleanly raked into a pattern of fine lines,
but the hoofs had beaten it into surfy shapes as the white stallions paced and
danced and performed their grave beautiful patterns to the music.

And now the floor was empty. The five white horses had filed out through
the archway at the far end of the hall and vanished down the corridor
towards their stable. The Boccherini minuet faded into a pause of silence.

The packed alcoves of people craned forward. Every seat was full, and
in the gallery people were standing, trying to see past one another's shoulders,
the movement and the whispering and the crackling of programmes filling
the sunlit pause. Beside me Timothy leaned forward, taut with excitement,
and on my other side sat Lewis, relaxed and sunburned, reading the
programme as if nothing else mattered in the world but the fact that on this
Sunday morning in September the great Neapolitano Petra was back at the
Spanish Riding School, and the Director himself was going to ride him, and
all Vienna had come to see.

Beyond the archway the lights grew to brightness. The half-door opened.
A horse appeared, his rider sitting still as a statue. He paced forward slowly
into the hall, ears alert, nostrils flared, his movements proud and cool and
soberly controlled, and yet somehow filled with delight.

There was no hint of stiffness now. Round he came, the dancing steps
made even more beautiful by their silence: the beat of the music hid even the
muffled thudding in the sand, so the high floating movements of the hoofs
seemed to take the stallion skimming as effortlessly as a swan in full sail. The
light poured and splashed on the white skin where the last shadows of black
had been polished and bleached away, and his mane and tail tossed in thick
fine silk like a flurry of snow.

The music changed: the Director sat still: the old stallion snorted,
mouthed the bit, and lifted himself, rider and all, into the first of the 'airs
above the ground'.

Then it was over, and he came soberly forward to the salute, ears moving
to the applause. The crowd was getting to its feet. The rider took off his hat
in the traditional salute to the Emperor's portrait, but somehow effacing
himself and his skill, and presenting only the horse.

Old Piebald bent his head. He was facing us full on, six feet away, looking
(you would have thought) straight at us; but this time there was no

welcoming whicker, not even a gleam in the big dark eye that one could call recognition. The eyes, like the stallion's whole bearing, were absorbed, concentrated, inward, his entire being caught up again and contained in the old disciplines that fitted him as inevitably as his own skin.

He backed, turned, and went out on the ebb-tide of applause. The grey half-door shut. The lights dimmed, and the white horse dwindled down the corridor beyond the arch, to where his name was still above his stall, and fresh straw waiting.